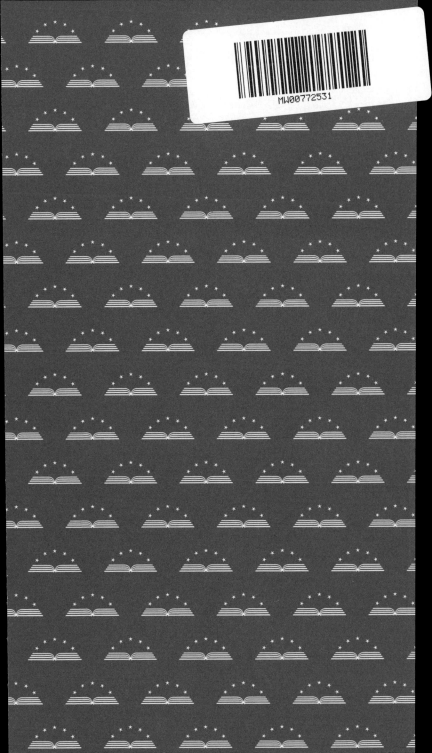

CHARLES PORTIS

# CHARLES PORTIS

## COLLECTED WORKS

---

*Norwood*
*True Grit*
*The Dog of the South*
*Masters of Atlantis*
*Gringos*
Stories & Other Writings

Jay Jennings, *editor*

THE LIBRARY OF AMERICA

# Contents

# NORWOOD

For A.

NORWOOD HAD to get a hardship discharge when Mr. Pratt died because there wasn't anyone else at home to look after Vernell. Vernell was Norwood's sister. She was a heavy, sleepy girl with bad posture. She was old enough to look after herself and quite large enough, but in many ways she was a great big baby. Everybody out on the highway said, "What's going to happen to Vernell now?" Several people out there on the highway put this question to Brother Humphries and his reply was a thoughtful, "I don't know. I'm trying to work something out." He talked to a man in Texarkana who worked something out with the Red Cross man at Camp Pendleton and the Red Cross man in turn worked it out with the major who handled hardship discharges. Norwood had to see the major three times and talk to him about personal and embarrassing things. The major had a 105-millimeter ashtray on his desk. He was not an unkindly man and he expedited the matter as best he could. Norwood took his discharge, which he felt to be shameful, and boarded a bus in Oceanside that was bound for his home town of Ralph, Texas—with, of course, many intermediate stops. The big red-and-yellow cruiser had not gone far when Norwood remembered with a sinking heart that in all the confusion of checking out he had forgotten to go by Tent Camp 1 and pick up the seventy dollars that Joe William Reese owed him. This was a measure of his distress. It was not like Norwood to forget money. Joe William should have come by and paid him. *He* would have if *he* had owed the money. But no, that was not Joe William's way.

Thinking about it, on top of this discharge business, sent Norwood further into depression. He decided he would sit up straight all the way home and not look at the sights and not sleep and not push the Recline-o button and not lean back thirty or forty degrees the way he had planned. Nor would he talk to anyone. Except for short answers to direct and impersonal questions such as "Do you have the time?" or "What town is this?" But he did not sulk long. He slept for 335 miles, leaning back at the maximum Trailways angle, and when he awoke he struck up a conversation with a friendly young couple name of Remley. The Remleys had been picking asparagus in the Imperial Valley and were now on their way home with their asparagus money. Traveling with them was their infant son Hershel. Hershel was a cheerful, bright-eyed little fellow. He was very well behaved and Norwood remarked on this.

Mrs. Remley patted Hershel on his tummy and said, "Say I'm not always this nice." Hershel grinned but said nothing.

"I believe the cat has got that boy's tongue," said Norwood.

"Say no he ain't," said Mrs. Remley. "Say I can talk aplenty when I want to, Mr. Man."

"Tell me what your name is," said Norwood. "What is your name?"

"Say Hershel. Say Hershel Remley is my name."

"How old are you, Hershel? Tell me how old you are."

"Say I'm two years old."

"Hold up this many fingers," said Norwood.

"He don't know about that," said Mrs. Remley. "But he can blow out a match."

Norwood talked to Mr. Remley about bird hunting. Mrs. Remley talked about her mother's people of near Sallisaw. Hershel made certain noises but said no words as such. Mrs. Remley was not bad looking. Norwood wondered why she had married Mr. Remley. One thing, though . . . he knew about bird dogs.

Norwood invited them to stop in Ralph and stay with him for a few days. He would borrow Clyde Rainey's dog and they could go quail hunting. Vernell was in bed sick with grief and beyond comfort when they arrived. She had not even been able to attend the funeral. Norwood put the Remleys in Mr. Pratt's old bedroom and he set up a cot for himself in the kitchen. Brother Humphries did not like the looks of the Remleys and he told Norwood as much. Or rather he told him that with Vernell here in bed and in the shape she was in and all, it might not be the best thing to be bringing in boomers like that off the bus. Norwood said they would only be there for a couple of days. Sometime during the night the Remleys decamped, taking with them a television set and a 16-gauge Ithaca Featherweight and two towels. No one could say how they got out of town with that gear, least of all the night marshal. The day marshal came by and looked at the place where the television set had been. He made notes.

Norwood and Vernell did not live right in Ralph but just the other side of Ralph. Mr. Pratt had always enjoyed living on the edge of places or between places, even when he had a choice. He was an alcoholic auto mechanic. Before his death they had moved a lot, back and forth along U.S. Highway 82 in the oil fields and cotton patches between Stamps, Arkansas, and Hooks, Texas. There was something Mr. Pratt dearly loved about that section of interstate concrete. They clung to its banks like river rats. Once, near Stamps, they lived in a house between a Tastee-Freez stand and a cinder-block holiness church. There had been a colorful poster on one side of the house that said ROYAL AMERICAN SHOWS OCT. 6–12 ARKANSAS LIVESTOCK EXPOSITION LITTLE ROCK. On the other side of the house somebody with a big brush and a can of Sherwin-Williams flat white had painted ACTS 2:38.

They later moved to a tin-roof house that was situated in a gas field under a spectacular flare that burned all the time. Big copper-green beetles the size of mice came from all over the Southland to see it and die in it. At night their little toasted corpses pankled down on the tin roof.

The Pratts did their washing and shaving on the front porch because that was where the pan was, and the mirror. You could see better out there. Little Vernell—when she *was* little—would stand out in the yard in her panties and wave a stick or a carburetor at all the transcontinental motorists. She may well have caught some of them going both ways—the salesmen in black Dodge business coupés with no back seats—so frequently did the Pratts move from one side of the road to the other. Mr. Pratt did not prefer one side of U.S. 82 over the other.

When they moved to Ralph, Norwood quit school and went to work at the Nipper Independent Oil Co. Servicenter, and with his first money he built his mother a bathroom. He did all the carpentering and put in the fixtures himself. Most of the stuff was secondhand—the water heater and the commode and the lumber—but he bought the bathtub new from Sears, and it *was* a delight. It was low and modern and sleek, with a built-in thing for the soap. There was a raised wave design on the bottom. Mrs. Pratt was well pleased and said so.

But she was gone these many years and now the old mechanic too, he who had shaken his head and wiped his hands and told at least a thousand people they were losing oil through the main bearing, had joined her. Norwood missed the funeral but Clyde Rainey had gone and he said it had all been very nice. More people came than reasonably could have been expected. There were a good many flowers too. The funeral home had scrubbed Mr. Pratt down with Boraxo and Clyde said he had never seen him looking so clean and radiant.

Norwood picked up his old job at the Nipper station and Clyde was glad to have him back. Norwood was a good worker and was not known to be a thief. The station featured dishes and cheap gasoline. All credit cards were honored. The rest rooms were locked for the protection of the customers. Inside the station itself there was a tilted mirror along the back wall to deceive the eye and make the place look bigger. Outside, eye-catching banners and pennants and clever mobile signs fluttered and spun and wheeled over the pumps. On top of the station there was a giant billboard showing a great moon face with eyeglasses. It was a face beaming with good will. It was, of course, Nipper himself, the famous Houston oilman. A little cartoon body had been painted on beneath the face, with one hand holding a gas hose and the other extended to the public in a stage gesture, palm outward, something like Porky Pig when he is saying, "That's all, folks." Along the bottom of the sign there was a line of script, in quotation marks, indicating that it was a message direct from the Nipper pen. "*Thank you for riding with Nipper*," it said. "*Won't you call again?*"

Vernell cried and moped around the house for almost two months. Brother Humphries' wife and the other ladies of the church were good about bringing food over. They brought fried chicken and potato salad and coconut cakes and maca-roni and cheese and baked sweet potatoes with marshmallows melted on top. The Home Demonstration agent came by and gave Vernell some housekeeping tips and some printed matter. When the woman left, Vernell went back to bed and forgot all the tips. But in time she came around. One morning she got up and washed her face and cooked Norwood's breakfast. She was still a little sickly though and the doctor told Norwood not to let her work too hard. He continued to do most of the cooking and housekeeping, and he stayed close and busied himself with little personal projects.

Sometimes he sat on the back steps wearing a black hat with a Fort Worth crease and played his guitar—just three or four chords really—and sang "Always Late—With Your Kisses," with his voice breaking like Lefty Frizzell, and "China Doll" like Slim Whitman, whose upper range is hard to match. The guitar wasn't much. It was a cheap West German model with nylon strings he had bought at the PX. He also put in a lot of time on his car. He had bought a 1947 Fleetline Chevrolet with dirt dobber nests in the heater and radio for fifty dollars. He put in some rings and ground the valves and got it in fair running shape. He loosened the tappets and put up with the noise so as to keep Vernell—who *would* race a motor—from burning the valves. She burned a connecting rod instead.

He made home improvements too. He ripped off the imitation brick siding on the house—Mr. Pratt had called it nigger brick—and slapped two coats of white paint on the walls in three days. He cleaned up the front yard and hauled off all the truck differentials and engine blocks and disembodied fenders, and took down the "I Do Not Loan Tools" sign from the persimmon tree. He thinned out the weeds in the big ditch in front of the house with a weed sling and gave the mosquitoes down there fits with twenty gallons of used motor oil. He had two loads of pea gravel dumped and spread over the driveway and he whitewashed some big rocks and laid them out for borders. There was some lime left over so he soaked some more rocks and laid out a globe-eagle-and-anchor emblem on the ditch slope facing the highway. He put his serial number under it.

One night he came home from work and said, "I'm tard of working at that station, Vernell."

"What's wrong, bubba?"

"Every time you grease a truck stuff falls in your eyes and your hair and down your back. You got it pretty easy yourself. You know that?"

"Why don't you get a hat?"

"I got plenty of hats, Vernell. I don't need any more hats. If all I needed was another hat I would be well off."

"What do you want to do?"

"I want to get on the *Louisiana Hayride*."

"Well, why don't you go over there and get on it, then?"

"You can't just go over there and get on it. They have to know something about you. You have to audition. They don't just let anybody on it that wants to. I guess you thought people just showed up at KWKH and said I want to be on the *Hayride*."

"You're as good as some of 'em I've heard on it."

"I know I'm *good* enough to be on it. That's not it."

"Well look, let me have a half a dollar so I can go to the show with Lorene."

"Let you have a half a dollar?"

"I'm going to the show with Lorene."

"I wish I had somebody around to give me half a dollars. I have to work for mine. They don't give me anything down there at the station. I have to work for every dime and then pay taxes on that. I never even see that tax money."

"I know, you told me about that."

"You don't act like it. I'll tell you something else. Maybe I would have some money if people paid me what they owed me. Joe William Reese owes me seventy dollars and has never paid me to this day."

"You told me about that."

"He'll never pay me that money."

"Maybe he will sometime."

"Naw he won't."

"He might. You ought to write him or call him. He might of forgot it his own self."

"You don't even know him, Vernell. If you knew him you wouldn't say that."

After Vernell had gone to the show Norwood went back to the station and used the phone. He called the Reese residence in Old Carthage, Arkansas. An old woman answered who talked very fast. She said Joe William had come, shed his uniform, and gone, and was now believed to be in New York City.

"What is he doing up there?"

"Lord, I don't know. Don't ask me."

"When will he be back?"

"He didn't say. We don't look for him any time soon. *I* don't anyway. Old Carthage is too little for Joe William. Who is this?"

"This is Norwood Pratt over in Ralph, Texas. I wanted to talk to him about some money he owes me."

"Who? Joe William?"

"Yes ma'am."

"What was your name?"

"Pratt. Norwood Pratt."

"I don't believe we know any Pratts in Texas. There's a J. B. Pratt here that sweeps out the courthouse. He used to come around and sharpen scissors. I don't know when I've seen that old man. He always did good work."

"Joe William and me was in the arm service together."

"Say you were?"

"Yes ma'am."

"Well, I don't know what to tell you. I'm his grandmother. But I'm a Whichcoat. That is I married a Whichcoat. My daughter was a Whichcoat before she married Joe William's father. The Reeses all came in here from Tennessee after the war. The sawmill was here then, and the compress too. Well, one compress is still here for that matter, but they tore the big one down, oh Lord, *years* ago. My maiden name is Finch. You've probably heard of old Judge Finch. He was on the Fourth Circuit here for so long? All the papers have written him up."

"Have you got Joe William's address there?"

"I'll have to ask Daughter about that."

Norwood wrote Joe William a card at the New York address and watched the mail with anxiety for three weeks. It was worse than waiting on something from Sears. Nothing came. He wrote another one and put an extra stamp on it this time. There was no answer. Clyde Rainey said, "What's bothering you, Norwood?"

"Nothing."

"You don't seem to have your mind on your business."

"I'm all right."

"Are you feeling all right?"

"I'm fine, Clyde. If there was anything wrong with me I would go to the doctor."

"You don't look right to me."

One warm summer evening, shortly after the Ralph B&PW Club had given up on trying to teach Vernell how to type, Norwood was out in the yard cutting the grass with a push mower he had borrowed from the station. He took his shirt off and then put it on again. The mosquitoes were fierce. Vernell was sitting on the front porch with a dishpan in her lap, shelling peas. She said, "I wonder if Mama and Daddy can look down from heaven tonight and see how nice the yard looks." Norwood stopped mowing. "I don't know, Vernell. Did you go down and talk to that woman at the hotel today like I told you to?"

"Well, I had some things to do. I'll go one day next week."

"Naw you won't. You'll go the first thing in the morning."

She cried and took some aspirins and went to bed, but Norwood hauled her out the next morning and made her dress and shave and he told her that she was going to be working at the New Ralph Hotel Coffee Shop that very day or he would know the reason why.

"I don't feel good, bubba," she pleaded. "I don't know how to do it. I'm liable to get the orders wrong."

"I got you this job and you're going down there. Just get that through your head."

"What if I get the orders wrong?"

"Well, don't get 'em wrong. Get 'em right."

"I don't think I can do it."

"Yes, you can."

"I can't."

"Look, all you do is write on these tickets what they want and take it back to the cook's window. Anybody can do that. Listen. A man will come in and you will give him a glass of water and a menu. Then he will study it and decide what he wants. All right. If he wants number two, you put number two on this side of the ticket and then the price over here. He might want some tea too. All right, put a big T under the number two and the price of the tea over there under the number two price. Then when he's through you add up all the prices and put on the tax and that's his bill. You ask him if there will be anything else and then give him his bill."

"I know all that."

"You are too afraid of people, Vernell. That's your trouble."

The job worked out too well. Money and position went to Vernell's head. She stopped crying. Her health and posture improved. She even became something of a flirt. She grew daily more confident and assertive and at home she would drop the names of prominent Lions and Kiwanians. Norwood listened in cold silence as she brought home choice downtown gossip and made familiar references to undertakers and lawyers and Ford dealers. Norwood had nothing to counter with. No one you could quote traded at the Nipper station. The customers were local Negroes and high school kids, and out-of-state felons in flight from prosecution and other economy-minded transients, most of whom carried their own strange motor oil in their back seats, oil that was stranger and cheaper than anything even in the Nipper inventory. Some weeks, with her tips, Vernell made more money than Norwood. It was a terrible state of affairs and Norwood would not have believed that things were to become worse almost overnight.

Then with absolutely no warning Vernell married a disabled veteran named Bill Bird and brought him home to live in the little house on the highway. Bill Bird was an older man. He had drifted into Ralph for no very clear reason after being discharged from the VA hospital in Dallas. He took a room at the New Ralph Hotel, monthly rate, and passed his time in the coffee shop, at the corner table under the fan, reading *Pageant* and *Grit* and pondering the graphs in *U.S. News & World Report*. Vernell took to Bill Bird at once. She liked his quiet, thoughtful air and his scholarship. She kept his cup filled with coffee and during lulls she would sit at his table and enjoy him. Bill Bird was at the same time attentive to Vernell in many little ways.

One afternoon she said, "I declare, Bill, you just read all the time. It must make your eyes hurt."

Bill Bird shook himself out of a hypnotic reading trance and put his paper down and rose to offer her a chair. "Sit down, Vernell. Relax for a minute. You're working too hard."

"Well, I will for just a minute."

Bill Bird tapped the newspaper with his pipe. "I was reading an interesting little piece there in the *Grit*. A retired high school band director in Fort Lauderdale, Florida, has taught his fox terrier to play 'Springtime in the Rockies' on the mouth harp. He holds it on with a little wire collar device. Like this."

"Well, I'll be," said Vernell. "A dog playing songs. I'd like to see that. I bet that's cute."

"That wasn't what I meant," said Bill Bird. "I mean I suppose it *is* cute, but it's more than that. It goes to show that animals are a lot smarter than people think. I honestly believe that one day we may be able to talk to them. By that I mean *communicate* in some fashion. There's a lot of interesting research going on in that field."

"What else can he sing, that dog?"

"Well, it doesn't say. It just says he is limited to a few simple melodies because of his small lungs. Now he doesn't *sing*, Vernell. He *plays* these songs on a mouth organ. A harmonica. His name is Tommy."

"I'd like to hear that scamp play. They ought to put him on television sometime."

Bill Bird hummed the opening of "Springtime in the Rockies" and thought about it for a minute. "That's not exactly a simple tune, you know. I think it represents a pretty amazing range for a dog."

"You must know something about every subject in the world, Bill. Somebody could sit here and write a book just listening to you."

"Oh I don't know about that, Vernell. I will admit this: I have always been curious about things. The world about me. Like most of your scientists I am interested in the *why* of things, and not just the *what*. Sometimes I think I might have been happier if I didn't have such a searching mind."

"You couldn't be any other way. You know that."

"Some people go through their entire lives and are completely satisfied with the *what*. They don't ask questions."

"They don't know any better."

"They are content to go along in the old patterns, the same old ruts, never realizing how much richer and fuller their lives could be."

"That's all they know."

"How much does your man on the street know of psychology?"

"Nothing. They don't know anything."

"How many of them can even vote intelligently? I was reading in *Parade* the other day that more people can identify Dick Tracy than the Vice President."

"People ought to read more. And not just the funnies either."

Norwood knew Bill Bird on sight and he had heard Vernell speak of him often enough but he had no idea anything was up. And now here he was, this middle-aged stranger, in Norwood's home, at his breakfast table, in his bathroom. It was not clear how or where or even in what war Bill Bird had fallen. Sometimes he spoke of Panama. There seemed to be nothing much wrong with him, apart from irregularity and low metabolism. He had all his limbs, his appetite was good.

Bill Bird received a lot of official brown mail, and, no doubt, a regular check, but he did not offer to pay anything toward the general household expenses. After meals he would excuse himself and go to the bedroom and close the door. He kept a little duffel bag in there filled with supplementary treats for his own exclusive use—Vienna sausages, olives, chocolate chip cookies. He had no problem adjusting from hotel life to home life. He bumped around the house, sockless, in some tan, army-looking dress shoes and an old corduroy VA robe. He was in and out of the bathroom with his magazines. He made an hourly circuit through the kitchen to look in the stove and the refrigerator and all the cabinets and the breadbox and indeed into everything that had a door.

Norwood did not like the sound of Bill Bird's voice. Bill Bird was originally from some place in Michigan and Norwood found his brisk Yankee vowels offensive. They argued about the bathroom. Bill Bird had made himself a little home in that bathroom. He used all the hot water. He filled up the cabinet with dozens of little bottles with typing on them, crowding Norwood's shaving gear out and onto the windowsill. He used Norwood's blades. He left hairs stuck around in the soap—short, gray, unmistakable Bill Bird hairs. Norwood had built the bathroom, it was his, and the thought of Bill Bird's buttocks sliding around on the bottom of the modern Sears tub was disagreeable. They argued about the Marine Corps. Bill Bird said it was vastly overrated. He cited personal experiences and magazine articles. For all the Marines' talk of the Halls of Montezuma, he said, there had actually been only a handful of Marines at the siege of Chapultepec. Regular army troops, as usual, had won the day there.

Norwood said he had been told by people who knew that certain army units in Korea in 1950 had abandoned their weapons and equipment and even their wounded while under Chinese attack. Many of the wounded had been rescued by Marines. Bill Bird said he knew this to be untrue. He also informed Norwood that it was a Federal offense to strike a disabled veteran, not to say ruinous damage-wise in the courts. They argued too about Norwood's plan to leave his job at the Nipper station and strike out blindly for Shreveport and a musical career on the *Louisiana Hayride*, the celebrated Country and Western show presented Saturday nights on KWKH, a 50,000-watt clear channel station serving the ArkLaTex. It was foolish, Bill Bird said, to leave a job before you were sure you had another job. Vernell said that made plenty of sense to her. Bill Bird said that if you had a job you could always get a job. Vernell concurred. He went on to say that it was hard to get a job if you did not already have a job. "Bill is right about that," said Vernell. They argued about the seventy-dollar debt and ways and means of collecting it. Bill Bird said the best approach would be to pay some lawyer ten or fifteen dollars to write that fellow a scare letter. "Then I would be out eighty-five dollars," said Norwood. Well, said Bill Bird, he, for one, was tired of hearing about that confounded seventy dollars.

The compactness of the Pratt house was such that three-way conversations could be and very often were carried on from three different rooms, with none of the parties visible to the others. "You beat anything I ever saw, bubba," said Vernell, who was in the bedroom ironing on this night. "We're both of us making good money now and we got the house fixed up and you've got your car and Bill's here and you just want to throw it all to one side and take off for Shreveport. You don't even know anybody in Shreveport."

Norwood was sitting at the kitchen table eating a warmed-over supper. He'd been late getting home from the station and they had not waited. He kept his hat on while he ate, his pale green Nipper hat with the black bill. It was a model the Miami Police Department had used in 1934. He held his left thumb in a glass of ice water. The thumb, sticky with shaving cream, was swelling and throbbing and purpling. He had fixed flats that day for three big state gravel trucks, one after the other, and when he was breaking down one of the wheels a locking ring had snapped back on his thumb.

"Well, when you get in Shreveport and run out of money," came the Michigan voice of Bill Bird, through a cloud of bathroom steam, "Vernell and I will not be able to send you any."

Norwood speared a sausage patty with his fork and gave it a hard flip through the bathroom doorway.

"Hey!" said Bill Bird. "All right now!" He emerged from the steam in some green VA convalescent pants that were cinched up with a drawstring. Except for his tan shoes, that was all he had on. He was holding the sausage on his open palm, level, like a compass, and he was studying it. "Did you throw this, Norwood?"

"What is it, Bill?"

"You know what it is. It's a sausage."

"I wondered what that was," said Norwood. "I saw a arm come in the back door there and chunk something acrost the room. I thought maybe there was a note on it."

Bill Bird called into the bedroom. "Vernell, come in here a minute. I want you. Norwood's throwing food."

Vernell came in and looked at Bill Bird's naked torso. "Goodness, Bill, put on some clothes. Norwood's trying to eat his supper."

"Look at this," said Bill Bird.

"That's a sausage," she said.

"I know what it is. He threw it at me in the bathroom."

"What for? What would he want to throw a sausage for?"

"I don't know, Vernell. It's beyond me. I *do* know you could very easily put someone's eye out like that."

She gave a little laugh. "I don't think you could put anybody's eye out with a sausage." Then she saw from Bill Bird's face that this was not the ticket. She turned to Norwood. "What made you want to do it, bubba?"

Norwood went on eating. "You two would drive anybody crazy," he said. "Going on all night about a sausage."

"It's something you would expect out of a child," said Bill Bird. "You know I've tried to get along with him, Vernell, but you can't treat him like a responsible adult. He should be made to apologize for this. *Now* would be the time for it."

"Bubba, tell Bill you're sorry. Come on now. It won't hurt you."

"I don't know why I ought to apologize if some stranger comes along and throws a sausage in the house at *him*. All I saw was his sleeve, Bill. I couldn't tell what color it was, it happened so fast."

"I'll tell you what's going to become of your brother, Vernell," said Bill Bird. "He's going to wind up in the penitentiary. They have some people there who will set him straight on a few things. You can count on that. I read an article the other day about the seven danger signs of criminal tendencies in the young. I've marked it in there for you to read. I think you will be a little disturbed, you should be, to learn that your own brother has the same personality profile as Alvin Karpis."

"Bubba was just playing with you, Bill."

"I'll say this: Unless his attitude undergoes a great change he will be in the pen within five years, just as sure as we're standing here. Now. We'll consider this incident closed."

Norwood made himself two biscuit and Br'er Rabbit Syrup sandwiches and went out on the front porch to eat them and wait on the bath water to get hot. Down the highway beyond the Nipper station the lights of the skating rink made a dull yellow glow. Insect bulbs of low wattage. The music came and went in heavy waves. It was a record of a boogie-woogie organist playing "Under the Double Eagle." Norwood threw one of the biscuit sandwiches out to a red dog that was traveling through town, going east, possibly to Texarkana, and watched him eat it in one gulp. Then he went out and started the Fleetline and listened for a minute to the clatter of the burnt rod and the loose tappets—it sounded like a two-cylinder John Deere tractor—and drove down to the skating rink. Sometimes, after the first session, you could pick up a country girl there looking for a ride home.

It was a clear warm Friday night and there was a big crowd. The tent flaps were rolled up all the way around. Some of the bolder girls were wearing short pleated skirts that bounced. The boys were skating fast, working hard at it, as though they were delivering important telegrams. Out front some Future Farmers of America were horsing around beside a billet truck, playing keep-away with a softball. The boy they were keeping

it away from was smoking a cigarette and was also wearing an
FFA jacket. "Here, you want it? I'm really gonna let you have
it this time." The boy would never learn. They were keeping
it away from him because he looked like a baboon. Norwood
wandered around to the back of the tent and stood by himself leaning against a big pecan tree and watching the skaters
through the chicken wire. He was there only a minute or two,
checking out the girls, when he heard someone cracking nuts
on the other side of the tree.

He peered around for a look. A very thin and yet very broad
man was standing there expertly cracking pecans in his hands
and getting the meats out whole. He was as flat and wide as
a gingerbread man. He was wearing a smooth brown saddle-
stitched sport jacket and some blue slacks with hard creases
and a pearl-gray cattleman's hat. He grinned and dusted the
hulls from his huge flat hands and extended one to Norwood.

"Hello there, Norwood."

Norwood shook his hand. "I thought I heard somebody
back there. Do you know me?"

"Well, I feel like I do. I see your name stitched there over
your pocket. Of course you might have someone's else's shirt
on. In that case your name might very well be Earl or Dub for
all I know."

"Naw, it's my shirt all right."

"My name is Fring. I'm glad to know you, Norwood. Tell
me, is everyone at home well?"

"Just getting along fine. How about your folks?"

"They're all dead except for me and my brother Tilmon.
I'm fine and he's doing very well, considering his age. Here,
take this home and read it when you get a minute." He handed
Norwood a pamphlet. It said, *A non-cancellable guaranteed re-
newable for life hospitilization policy, underwritten by one of the
Mid-South's most reliable insurance firms. No age limit. PAYS
up to $5,000.00 for sickness or accident. PAYS up to $400.00 for surgery. PAYS prescription benefits. PAYS home nurse benefits. PAYS
iron lung fees. PAYS . . .* "You don't have to read it now. Take
it home and study it later. Compare it with your present program, in light of your current insurance needs. Talk it over
with those at home. That little policy just sells itself."

Norwood put it in his pocket. "A insurance man."

"Well, among other things, yes. My brother Tilmon and I have a good many business interests. I'm also in mobile homes and coin-operated machines. I am a licensed private investigator in three states. We have a debt collection agency in Texarkana. I know you've heard of our car lots over there. Grady Fring?"

"You're not Grady Fring the Kredit King?"

"I am indeed."

"No reasonable offer refused."

"The very same."

"You can't convince Grady your credit is bad."

"Right again."

Norwood laughed. "Well, this *is* something. I've seen your signs and heard your things on the radio a lot. *Grady has gone crazy* and all that."

"I would certainly be disappointed if you hadn't heard them," said Grady. "If I told you what our advertising budget was last year, you wouldn't believe it. That's where you've got to put your money if you want to move the goods. You know what I believe in?"

"What?"

"Volume."

"What?"

"Volume. Volume. I don't care what I make off anything— six dollars, a quarter, a dime—as long as I can move it. Sell it! Move it! Give it away! But just clear it on out of the way and bring something else in, and then we'll sell it too. Yessir, I do believe in volume. Why aren't you out there skating with all those pretty girls?"

"I'm not too good a skater."

"Do you come out here much?"

"Some. Every now and then."

"I'll bet you know all those girls out there."

"I know some of 'em."

"This is my first visit," said Grady, "to this particular roller drome. I get around a good deal at night, you see. I am also connected with a New Orleans talent agency and that part of my work takes me around to many . . . highway institutions. What our agency does—it's fully licensed—is seek out and recruit lovely young girls over the Mid-South. Girls seeking a career in show business. Girls who want to leave home. You may not realize it but we have some of the sweetest little girls in the country right around in these parts."

"We sure do."

"I'd put them up against girls from anywhere."

"That Cresswell girl is a good skater," said Norwood. "She's about the best one around here. That one there with the lights on her skates."

"Yes, I've had my eye on her. She's a dandy. And sweet too. Do you know her folks? What does her daddy do?"

"I don't know what he does. Her mama works down at the Washateria."

"How old is she?"

"About fifty-six."

"No, I mean the girl."

"Oh. She's about seventeen. I think she gets out of high school this year."

"I'd rather not fool with them if they're under nineteen or twenty. You will understand, Norwood, I am not necessarily looking for skating skills. What about you, do you live here in town?"

"Yeah. I live down there just the other side of that Nipper station."

"Old Nipper! I was looking at your uniform when you first came up. He's an old friend of mine, you know, Nipper is. I used to do some investigating for him down in Houston. I was practicing a little law then too. What a man! Money? Norwood, he's richer than the fabled Croesus. Have you ever met him?"

"I never did. I seen his plane a few times. He used to fly over town dropping out copies of the Constitution."

"Well, he's quite a man. I was on his education committee for three years and I was a judge in the Nipper Junior High Essay Contests that were so big. I was one of the judges. Perhaps you sent one in yourself?"

"What?"

"The Nipper Essay Contest. For junior high kids."

"I didn't hear anything about it."

"You should have got in on that, Norwood. Everybody got a little prize of some kind. And the winners, we gave them some wonderful scholarships. Their theme was 'Communism in the National Council of Churches.' They laid it right on the line. Wrote their hearts out. I was proud to be a part of it."

"Do you still work for Nipper?"

"No, not any more. We had a falling out, I'm sorry to say. I traded him some rent houses for a registered bull and he got mad about it. Subsequently I left Houston."

"Did you beat him on the trade?"

"Yes, I confess that I did. I took him like Stonewall Jackson took Nathaniel P. Banks in the Valley of the Shenandoah. That is to say, decisively."

"He didn't like that."

"He wasn't used to it."

Norwood looked at his watch. "Well, I got to get on back to the house and take a bath. My thumb's hurting."

Grady touched his arm. "Wait a minute. I'd like to talk to you about something. I *might* be able to put you next to something. Have you got a couple of minutes?"

"Yeah, I guess so."

"I tell you what we *could* do. We *could* go over to my car and have a drink and talk about it there."

"All right."

It was a big new Buick Invicta with red leather upholstery. Grady brought out a bottle of Old Forester from under the seat. There was some crushed ice in a milk shake carton. Norwood held the paper cups and Grady poured.

"This is a nice car," said Norwood.

"Yes, I'm doing right well," said Grady. "How many tubes do you think that radio has?"

"I don't know. It looks like a good one."

"Twenty-four. There's not another one like it in this part of the country. Listen to that tone. It's like FM."

Norwood listened. "That tone *is* good."

"What happened to your thumb?"

"Nothing. I mashed it."

"You better put something on it when you get home."

"I already did."

"Unguentine is good for something like that."

"I put some shaving cream on it."

"Unguentine is a lot better. It has special healing ingredients that shaving cream doesn't have. It goes to work on that soreness."

"Was that what you wanted to tell me?"

"No," said Grady, and he took off his hat and arranged himself sideways on the seat in the attitude of a man getting down to business. "No, it's something else. You're a big strong boy, Norwood. I've got a place for you, I think. Here's the deal: We buy these bad debts from stores and filling stations at twelve cents on the dollar. Then we go out and collect what we can. A top-notch, hustling, aggressive agent can make good on forty per cent of that paper. He can make those profligate bastards cough up. And anybody, with my training, can make good on twenty-five per cent of it. I'll train you and buy you a suit and some Florsheim shoes and furnish you with one of my late model demonstrator cars and we split halves on everything above the line. Everything above my twelve per cent investment. What do you think?"

"I don't think I would be much good at that."

"You're not interested in making money."

"Naw, I didn't say that. I said I didn't think I would be much good at it. I got a debt of my own I can't collect. Another thing is, I don't have much education. For that kind of job. Wearing a suit."

"Education requirements are minimal. Let me be the judge of that."

"Well, naw, I don't think so."

"Hmmm," said Grady, and he poured some more of the Forester. "Tell me this, how would you like a trip to California?"

"I been to California."

"That doesn't mean you can't go again."

"It's too far."

"How about a trip to Chicago? . . . New York? . . . Atlanta?"

"New York?"

"That's right, New York City. A wonderful trip, all expenses paid. Plus—and get this—fifty dollars clear for you, found money, right off the top."

"This is not some kind of contest."

"No, no, this is a straightforward job offer. Are you a good driver?"

"Yeah."

"Good enough. You see, Tilmon and I ship off some of our surplus cars, our good ones, to other parts of the country, where we can get a better price for them. It's the drivers who have all the fun. Speeding across the country in a late model car, seeing all the sights."

"I would take one to New York."

"That's it."

"How long would it take?"

"You'll be back in a week after a wonderful paid-for trip. Many of your friends will envy—"

"How would I get back?"

"You drive back. That's part of the deal. You take one up and bring one back."

"I don't get that."

"What is it you don't get?"

"Well, if I take one up and bring another one back, you're right back where you started. I don't see how that would put you ahead much."

"That's because you don't understand the market. Some cars are worth more up there and some are worth more down here because of freight costs and other variables. Take a Mercedes now, it will cost you a good two hundred dollars more down here. It all has to do with the market. You won't be dead-heading back, don't worry about that."

"I hope these are not stolen cars."

Grady looked at Norwood for a long moment. "I don't know whether you meant that seriously or not. We are legitimate businessmen, Norwood. We are in the public eye. We hold a position of trust in the community. We could hardly afford to jeopardize that position by playing around with hot cars. I think you spoke before you thought. No, we welcome legal scrutiny of all our affairs at all times."

"I don't want to get in any trouble."

"Naturally not. One way to avoid it would be not to repeat your highly actionable remark about hot cars."

"I *do* need to see somebody in New York."

Grady put on his glasses and consulted a billfold calendar by the light of his twenty-four-tube radio. "Hmmm. How does a next Sunday morning departure sound to you?"

"That's pretty quick."

Grady shrugged.

"I don't know," said Norwood. "I'd have to think about it. I'd have to talk to my sister about it."

"By all means, talk to your sister. Discuss it with her. What is her name?"

"Vernell."

"What a lovely name," said Grady. He reached in the back seat and fumbled around in a big pasteboard box and brought forth a styrene comb and brush set and a little bottle of perfume with a blue bow on it. "Give this to Vernell with my warmest regards." He nodded toward the back seat. "We had a lot of honorable mention prizes left over in the last Nipper contest."

"This is mighty nice of you."

Grady waved it off. "It's nothing. Now. My phone number's on this card. Feel free to call me at any time, collect. I would appreciate it if you called on this matter by Thursday noon."

The ice in the milk shake carton was now soupy but they had another short drink anyway. When Norwood opened the door to leave, Grady had an afterthought. "Wait a minute," he said. "Let me see your watch." Norwood showed it to him. Grady studied it critically through the reading part of his glasses, under the radio light. He tapped the crystal with a long, dense, yellow fingernail. "With all respect to you, that's a piece of junk." Then he slipped his own watch off, a flat shiny one with a black face and gold pips instead of numbers, and gave it to Norwood. "I don't want you to go home tonight till you have a good timepiece on your wrist. You can just put that other one away in your drawer somewhere. Sell it to a nigger if you can. . . . No, don't say a word. I want you to have it. I get these at well below cost."

"This is mighty nice of you, Mr. Fring."

"Mr. Fring nothing. Call me Grady."

Norwood drove home and thought about how he would put it to Clyde about taking off from the station. Clyde would ask five hundred questions. Vernell and Bill Bird would be a problem too. They would gnaw on it for days like two puppies with a rubber bone. Norwood had a long reflective bath. He put some more shaving cream on his thumb. While he was combing his hair he took up an oblique pose in front of the mirror and gave himself a lazy smile, like some smirking C & W star coming up out of the lower right-hand corner of an 8 by 10 glossy.

He played some records for a while in his sleeping porch bedroom and imagined himself having a smoke backstage with Lefty Frizzell: "*Hey Norwood, you got a light?*" His green pinstripe Nipper trousers were hanging on the back of a chair, with Grady's insurance tract sticking up out of a hip pocket. Norwood got up from bed in his shorts and took the tract into the front bedroom. He turned on the light, giving the sleeping Bill Birds quite a start.

"Get out of here," said Bill Bird.

"What is it, bubba? What do you want?"

"I found the note that was on that sausage, Bill. You didn't look hard enough."

"Turn that light off and get out."

"What does it say, bubba?"

"It says, '*Dear Bill Bird. If you know what's good for you you'll stop talking about things you don't know anything about. Yours truly, the Commandant of the Marine Corps.*'"

"That's very funny. Now get out. I'm not going to tell you again."

"We're trying to sleep, bubba. Bill needs his rest."

Vernell and Bill Bird did not approve of the New York trip. "You don't even know anybody in New York," said Vernell. Norwood was shining his thirty-eight-dollar stovepipe boots. They were coal-black 14-inchers with steel shanks and low walking heels. Red butterflies were inset on the insteps. He was putting a mirror gloss on the toes with lighter fluid and a nylon stocking.

"You can't reason with him, Vernell," said Bill Bird. "It's like talking to a child. I think we have made our position clear. Even to him. I hope so. I hope he's not planning on wiring us for money when he gets up there stranded."

Norwood ignored him. "Vernell, don't be driving my car much while I'm gone. If you have to use it take it easy. That bad rod is liable to go at any time. I'm afraid it's already scored the crankshaft. I'll have to turn that goose when I get back. . . . I don't want *him* driving it at all."

Vernell thought this was unfair. "Bill can drive a car all right."

"Naw he can't."

"He can too. He's just used to an automatic transmission."

"Uh huh."

"Bill can drive as good as I can."

"Well, you can't drive either. The only thing is, you're my sister. I might as well turn my car over to a rabbit."

"You'd have to get special extensions for the pedals," said Bill Bird.

"Now I mean it, Vernell," said Norwood. "I don't want to come back here and have somebody tell me they seen Bill Bird driving around town in that car. Let him walk. It'll do him good."

Norwood rode to Texarkana early Sunday morning in the rain with a boy in a butane truck who had a date over there for church. He wore his black hat, the brim curled up in front to defy wind resistance, and his stovepipe boots. One trouser leg was tucked in and the other hung free, after the fashion. The boots were glorious. He had his sunglasses on too, and his heavy Western belt buckle, which portrayed a branding scene in silver relief.

25

Except for those stylish items, he was not really dressed up. There was a job to be done and a long drive ahead. His good slacks and his tight tailored shirt, with curved arrow pockets and pearl snaps, were packed away in a canvas AWOL bag. He was dressed for the trip in a starchy, freshly ironed Nipper uniform. At the last minute he decided to take along the West Germany guitar. It was zipped up in a soft clear plastic case.

The Kredit King was waiting in his Buick in front of the Tex-arkana post office as per the arrangement. He was deep in conversation with a man who was leaning on his window. The man was holding a cardboard bucket with GRADY'S BAIT RANCH printed on it. Norwood put his gear in the back seat and got in the front. The man outside straightened up to leave and Grady shook his hand through the window. "There's plenty of corn meal in there. They don't eat much. All you want to do is sprinkle a little water in there every two or three days." When the man left, Norwood said, "Who was that?"

"I don't know," said Grady. "Some fellow passing through town. He wanted to know if there were any opportunities here for a taxidermist. I'll talk to anybody. Talk to a *nigger* and you might learn something. I sold him four hundred worms." He looked at his watch. "You're right on the money, Norwood. I like a man who does what he says he'll do."

"I got me a good watch."

"You have for a fact. . . . Here, let me get a look at you. That's all right. You look like the Durango Kid, perhaps better known as Charles Starrett. What's the guitar for?"

"It's mine, I thought I'd take it with me."

"You didn't tell me you were a musician."

"I fool around with it a little, that's all."

"You should have said something about it. I have a few contacts in the music game."

"You do?"

"Well, I know some of those boys. I have some music machines down around Bossier City."

"Do you know anybody on the *Louisiana Hayride?*"

"I know everybody on the *Louisiana Hayride.*"

"That's what I'd like to get a shot at."

"I expect I could pick up the phone and do you some good. We'll talk about that another day. Right now we'd best get to the business at hand. I know you're anxious to get rolling."

Grady unfolded a map of New York City and laid it out on the steering wheel. The delivery point, a garage in Brooklyn, was marked with a circle. Grady explained about the route. It was very complicated. He went over it again, then once more. Norwood lied and said he thought he had it. Grady gave him the map and a stiff fiber envelope holding titles and pink slips and two sets of keys and a Gulf credit card in the name of Tilmon Fring and twenty-five dollars expense money.

Norwood said, "I guess I'll get some more in New York then."

"Some more what?"

"Well. I don't know. Some more money."

"Wasn't that credit card in there?"

"Yeah, there's a credit card here. But I was wondering if this was enough money." He held up the five fives.

Grady was baffled and hurt. "That's the usual. I thought it would be ample. I've never had this come up before. This is embarrassing. You have your credit card. Figure a six-day trip at the very outside, that's more than four dollars a day for your meals and the little contingencies of the road. These warm nights you can pull over and catnap right there in the car if you get tired. Most of the drivers drive straight through. Arnold has a comfortable cot in his garage—"

"When do I get the fifty dollars?"

"When you get back. Cash on delivery."

"I couldn't get it now?"

"Why no. You're not even bonded, Norwood."

"What does that mean?"

"That means you get your money when you get back."

"I'd like to have some of it now."

Grady showed signs of distress. He took a kitchen match from his pocket, one with garlands of blue lint on it, and burrowed earnestly in one ear with it. When he was through he examined the match and buzzed down the automatic window a couple of inches and tossed it out. He brought his billfold from his inside coat pocket. "Here's what I'll do, Norwood. I've never done this before. I'll give you another ten toward expenses. We'll write that off. That's expenses. Then—I'll give you an advance of twenty-five. That's off your fifty. Now I'll hold the balance here—*on my person*—and then, see, you'll have that much more when you get back. To buy things that

you need and want. Go off to New York with a lot of money
and you'll *spend* a lot of money. I've seen it happen too often. . . . You know, some people would be willing to pay *us*
for an opportunity like this."

Norwood counted the money and folded it into a hard
square and stuck it in his watch pocket.

"Okay?" said Grady.

"Okay."

"You won't have to sign a voucher on that advance. And
you needn't bother to make an exact accounting on the expense money. We're informal. We like to give our agents a free
hand. So far as it's consistent with good business practice." He
started the car and turned to Norwood with a grin. "I have a
surprise waiting for you."

They drove half a mile or so through the Arkansas side of
town and pulled into an alley full of puddles, behind an ice
plant. As it turned out there were two surprises. The first was
that there were two cars to be delivered, not one. There they
were, bumper to bumper, a big 98 Oldsmobile in front and a
Pontiac Catalina behind, gleaming and smelling pleasantly of
new paint. "We always give them a coat of Duco," said Grady.
"It's a small enough investment and it can add two hundred
dollars to a car's value. That Olds is like new. Twelve thousand
actual miles. Never used a pint of oil. It's a clean car too. Well
taken care of. It will be a joy to drive. You won't even know
you're pulling anything with that new reflex tow bar. It has a
patented action. We've just started using those and they *are*
dandies."

An old man in khakis and a blue suit coat came up to open
Grady's door. He kept one hand in his pocket and his shoulders were hunched up against the drizzle. He had an orange
folder of RJR cigarette papers up in his hatband to keep them
dry. They were getting wet.

"This is my brother Tilmon," said Grady. Then he raised his
voice and said, "Tilmon, this is Norwood. He's our new driver.
He's a good one too. He's a dandy. He's the man who rode the
mule around the world."

Tilmon snickered and shook hands with Norwood. There
was a frosty glaze on top of his right sleeve where he had been
wiping his nose. He took the other hand out of his pocket and

gave Norwood a flyer. It said, *Need $$$$$—FAST? Get one of Grady's cost-controlled loans—BY MAIL!* There was a picture of Grady at the bottom holding a fistful of money. *Yes, Grady is ready to lend you up to $950.00—IN THE PRIVACY OF YOUR OWN HOME!*

"How are you?" said Tilmon.

"Just fine," said Norwood.

"Grady is a cutter, ain't he?"

"He sure is."

"How do you like him?"

"I like him all right."

"You do what he says now."

"I will."

"Just to look at Tilmon," said Grady, "you wouldn't think he was a very astute businessman, would you?"

Norwood looked him over again. "*I* wouldn't have thought it, naw."

"Volume is his middle name. Isn't that right, Tilmon? *I say volume is your middle name.*"

Tilmon said "Tee-hee-hee." His tongue fell out as if to receive a coin.

The second surprise was Miss Phillips. She was sitting in the rain on her suitcase—a handsome blue air travel model—with a newspaper on her head. She was eating peaches from a can with a wooden ice cream spoon. She was a long tall redbone girl. She was wearing a shiny green party dress with shoulder straps, and some open-toed shoes that were just on the point of exploding with toes. She glowered. She looked formidable.

"You run off with the gotdamn car keys and left the doors locked, Fring," she said. Her voice was a piercing whine.

"So I did. I'm sorry about that, Yvonne."

"I'm not *about* to pay for cleaning this dress. Look at it."

"We'll take care of it. Everything will be wonderful. Just keep your shirt on a minute."

"Don't tell me what to do."

"Norwood," said Grady, "this is the extra added attraction. I want you to meet Miss Yvonne Phillips. She hails from Belzoni, Mississippi, by way of New Orleans, the Crescent City. She *is* a dandy. Our talent agency down there is sending her to New

York. Since it was convenient I arranged for her to ride up with you. I thought you would welcome the company."

"Yeah. Okay. It's fine with me." He tipped his hat and greeted her.

Miss Phillips glared at Grady. "I hope you don't think I'm gonna ride to New York with this country son of a bitch."

Grady laughed. "She'll cool off, Norwood. It's really me she's mad at, not you. She thought she was going up on a Delta jet. Perhaps you can understand her disappointment. I didn't think you would mind her coming along."

"Naw, it's fine with me. If she wants to. I don't think she wants to."

"She'll get over that."

"I wish Sammy Ortega was here," said Miss Phillips. "He'd break your arm."

"I'd like to see him try it," said Norwood.

"I was talking to Fring, I wasn't talking to you," she said. "But he'd get you too if he felt like it, you bigmouth country son of a bitch. He'd kick your ass into the middle of next week."

"I'd like to see him try it."

"You just got through saying that. Don't keep saying the same thing over and over again. Don't you have good sense?"

"You said you was talking to *him* the first time."

"You *peckerwood*."

"That'll be enough," said Grady. "I don't want to hear any more out of you, little lady. Pick up your grip and go over there by the car and wait. I need to have a word with my driver."

"Somebody will get you one of these days, Fring."

"I said hush. Now get your things and move."

She flounced off and yelled at Tilmon and got him to carry her bag.

Grady hitched at his trousers with his wrists and popped his hands together. "Okay, buddy boy, you're gassed up and ready to go. Remember now, the George Washington Bridge, the West Side Drive, the Brooklyn-Battery Tunnel, the Belt Parkway, Exit Twelve, Parsons Street, Arnold's Garage. Follow instructions and watch the signs and you can't miss it. Now listen to this too. You are not authorized to deal with anyone except Arnold. If he's not there then wait on him. The garage is open twenty-four hours and he'll be expecting you late Monday night or early Tuesday morning. He'll take care of everything —up to and including Miss Phillips. She has expense money so she will pay for her own meals. Don't let her pull anything. Of course you may want to work out some personal understanding with her, I don't know. I leave that to your own discretion. In any case remember that we are counting on you to arrive by Tuesday morning at the latest. Got it?"

"I think so."

"Okay. Drive with care now. Watch the other fellow. Stay within the speed limits. Don't get picked up in some little town. Those laws are for our own protection. A car is just like a gun. In the wrong hands it is nothing less than an instrument of death."

The tandem cars splashed down the alley and wheeled around the corner of the ice plant and were gone. A peach can clattered on the street. Grady and Tilmon listened to it until it stopped rolling.

Grady said, "How much did they stick you for those peaches?"

"Thirty-nine cents," said Tilmon.

"They saw you coming, didn't they? That wasn't even a number two can."

"Thirty-nine cents is what they cost."

"I know what they do, they charge you more on Sunday. They jump those prices up on you. They'll all do it. I don't expect we'll run into many grocers in the Kingdom of Heaven, Tilmon."

NORWOOD AND Miss Phillips sped north on U.S. 67. He told her fifteen or twenty jokes and pointed out amusing signs and discussed the various construction projects along the way but she wasn't having any. Except to tell him to slow down, she absolutely refused to talk. She sat rigid and sullen far over against her door. Off and on she pretended to be sleeping. She tried not to move at all but every few minutes she would scratch, or shift about on the seat, her shiny dress squeaking, and each time Norwood would turn to her with a smile.

"You don't have to look over here every time I move," she said. "Keep your eyes on the road." When she opened the vent glass she did it very abruptly, and dropped her hands away like a calf roper in a rodeo, so as to prevent Norwood from seeing and noting and enjoying the act. As it was, he caught only the last part of it.

In Little Rock he asked if she would like to stop for a Coke or go to the ladies' room. 'I'll let you know when I want to stop, Mr. Big Red." She was in her dozing position again.

"I don't know what you're so mad about," he said, "but we got a long ways to go yet. We could make a right nice trip out of it if you wouldn't act that way. I would like to be your good friend, Laverne."

She didn't even open her eyes. "Yeah, I bet you would. My name is not Laverne, it's *Yuh-von*. I don't want *you* calling me anything."

On they rode in hostile silence through the rice fields and the one-stoplight towns of eastern Arkansas. The rain let up some but the trucks were still throwing up muddy slop on the windshield. Grady was right about the reflex tow bar. It was a little wonder. There was no bucking and yawing on the curves, even at high speed. He was right about the Olds too. It was clean and fast and powerful. The tinted glass made it snug inside. Everything worked, the radio, the clock, even the windshield squirters. Norwood could have driven that 98 Oldsmobile through all eternity and never stopped.

They stopped in De Valls Bluff to get some peaches. Miss Phillips paid for them but she wouldn't get out of the car. Norwood had a barbecue sandwich and a Nugrape. They ate in the car and pressed on. Just before they got to Brinkley Norwood broke the silence with a shout and hit the brakes. "Hey look at that!" Miss Phillips bolted and her red knees bumped against the dashboard. Some of the peach juice splashed from the can and ran down her legs. "What is it!" she said. "Where!"

"You missed him," said Norwood. "There was a possum back there crawling through that fence. He looked like a big old slow rat."

Miss Phillips was frantically daubing at her legs with wads of Kleenex. "You son of a bitch!"

Norwood hit the brakes again. "You want to go back and see him?"

More juice erupted from the can, and this time two or three golden Del Monte slivers with it. They stuck on her dress and made dark growing splotches. "What the hell is wrong with you, fellow!" she shrieked. "Look at what you've done! You think I want to see a possum crawling through a fence!"

"He's already through the fence," said Norwood. "He's back there in that field now looking for something. He's probably looking for some chow."

"You're the biggest peckerwood son of a bitch in the world!"

"I don't like that kind of talk out of a girl, Laverne. How would you like your mama to hear you talking like that?"

Miss Phillips had no answer. She quite unexpectedly broke into tears. She did not cry loud but she cried dramatically and long. It went on for miles, the snuffling and the little chirping noises. Norwood considered and dismissed seven or eight things to say. They were on the approaches to the Memphis Bridge when he went back to the first one.

"I didn't aim to make you cry. I'm sorry I brought that up about your mama."

"That's not what I'm crying about, stud."

"I'll just keep my mouth shut from now on. No matter what I see."

Miss Phillips wiped her eyes. Some of her fire was gone. "I wish I was in Calumet City, Illinois. I don't want to go to New

York. Sammy Ortega is a bartender in Calumet City and he could get me a job there easy."

"Is he the one that's gonna whup everybody?"

"Sammy may not look very big in his street clothes," she said, "but he can press two hundred pounds over his head. He can speak four languages too."

"What are they?"

"What?"

"What are the languages?"

"English and Spanish and I don't know what all. Italian."

"What is he, a Mexican?"

"He's Spanish."

"A lot of Mexicans are named Jesus."

"What's wrong with that?"

"Nothing. I thought maybe it was something you didn't know."

The traffic was heavy on the bridge. Norwood was on the inside, fast lane and he was twisting his neck trying to get a look at the three big oil barges that were chugging along downstream in the muddy Mississippi far below. A small wooden sign in the center of the bridge said SHELBY CO., TENN.

"You just crossed the state line," said Miss Phillips. "Now they can send you to the Federal pen." Norwood brought the cars to a skidding stop. Miss Phillips was thrown forward and her head slammed against the windshield. "You can't stop here, you fool!" A white station wagon smashed into the back of the Pontiac. Miss Phillips was thrown backward this time, from the neck up, and her head slammed against the center post. The driver of the station wagon had jumped out and he was running for Norwood and shouting. He had a bloody head. Norwood put the accelerator on the floor and the Oldsmobile sat down hard and shot off again with rubber squealing. Norwood yelled back at the man with the bloody head. "I'll see you in town!" Miss Phillips was crying again. There was a big swelling knot on her forehead. She was holding her head and rocking back and forth on the seat. Norwood said, "I got to get out of here." They were forty miles from Memphis and passing through Covington, Tennessee, before he said another word.

"Grady told me a lie."

"What did you think he would do?" said the red-eyed Miss Phillips. She was holding a wet Kleenex on her forehead. "I feel sorry for anybody like you. You are the peckerwood of all peckerwoods."

"I'm getting tired of that peckerwood business."

"Well, stop calling me Laverne then."

"I don't see how anybody from Belzoni, Mississippi, can call anybody else a peckerwood. How big is Belzoni? . . . It couldn't be too big. You'd hear more about it if it was."

"For your information, I spent a lot of time in New Orleans, *Mr. Red on the Head*. I count that as my home."

"It's *not* your home though."

"If you live someplace a long time you can count it as your home."

"Naw you can't. . . . You could live in Hong Kong for seventy-five years and Belzoni would still be your home."

"Don't sit there and tell *me* what *my* home is."

"I *am* telling you. Somebody needs to tell you."

"I hope a cop stops you. I really do. They'll have you locked up down there in that Atlanta pen so fast it'll make your head swim. You're sitting over there right now just scared to death."

There was some truth in this. It was a tough problem. Norwood would think about it for a while and rest for a while. It was like looking at the sun. He waited on something to come to him, some plan. What road was he on? Where was the gas gauge on this oversize jet plane dashboard? Half a tank? Where had he stopped? Somewhere. The man had checked him out on the revoked credit card list. Like he was somebody who shouldn't have a credit card. Anyway, nothing much could happen as long as they were moving along like this. Darkness fell and the problem lost much of its urgency. Norwood's mind was soon on other things.

They made only one stop in Kentucky, a peach stop in some little place just across the Ohio River, and, lost in their own thoughts, said nothing to each other until they were approaching Evansville, Indiana. The radio had been droning on for hours untended and a gospel hour was in progress when Miss Phillips reached over and turned the dial.

Norwood said, "What are you doing?"

"I'm trying to get WWL in New Orleans," she said. "You

can pick it up a long ways late at night. I want to hear *Moon-glow with Martin*."

Norwood pushed her hand away and regained the gospel program. "I was listening to that."

"We been hearing preachers all night." She changed stations again.

Norwood turned it back. "This one is explaining why they don't have any pianos in the Church of Christ. I want to hear him. Don't put your hand on the radio again."

"Well, I *don't* want to hear him."

"I do though."

"You're not the boss."

"I'm the boss of this car."

Miss Phillips fumed. The preacher went on uninterrupted. In closing he said he was prepared to pay ten thousand dollars cash to anyone who could show him scriptural authority for having a musical instrument in a church.

"I wisht I knew more about the Bible," said Norwood.

He considered and mused on the offer for some little time. "I wonder if he would really pay you? . . . It looks like he'd have to if he said it over the air. . . . Well . . . I'd whup his ass if he didn't."

"I'm tired of this preaching," said Miss Phillips.

"Hank Snow's son is a preacher," said Norwood. "The Reverend Jimmie Rodgers Snow. He's got him a church off over there in Tennessee somewhere."

"I want to hear some music."

"What church do you belong to, Laverne?"

"None of your business."

"The Church of God?"

"I belong to just as good a church as you do. Probably a lot better one."

"Well, maybe you do and maybe you don't. I belong to the Third Baptist Church in Ralph, Texas, and I'm proud of it."

"I figured you would belong to the Fourth Baptist Church."

"They don't have one in Ralph."

"That's why you don't belong to it."

"The Missionary Baptists, they all go over to Hooks. I think the Free Will Baptists just get together at somebody's house. We're gonna have air conditioning in the new annex if they ever get it finished. Do they have air conditioning in the Pentecost Church in Belzoni?"

"My church comes under the head of my business."

"If I was a Holy Roller I wouldn't be ashamed of it. I would be proud of it."

"I would too, if I was a Holy Roller."

"Only half the people that *are* in the church are saved."

"Has that car back there got a radio in it?"

Norwood checked it out in the mirror. "It's got a aerial, yeah."

"Well, stop and let me go get in it. I want to hear *Moonglow with Martin*."

"You can't ride back there. It'll look funny. Some cop is liable to stop us."

"I don't care. If you don't stop I'll holler out at the next cop I see. At the next anybody."

"All right, change the station. Get whatever you want on this radio."

"I want to get back in that other car. I want to hear it on *that* radio now."

Norwood pulled over and stopped. He got the fiber envelope out of the glove compartment and gave her the keys to the Pontiac. "Here. All you're gonna do is run that battery down and probably get us arrested." They rode into Evansville like that, Norwood in his car, Miss Phillips in hers. There was nothing doing in downtown Evansville. Night lights were burning in the stores but the streets were still and deserted. Miss Phillips began blatting her horn. It boomed and rang and echoed, and Norwood's first impulse was to step on it, but he stopped. Miss Phillips got back in the Olds.

"What's wrong with you now?"

"I want some coffee," said Miss Phillips. "I don't like it back there in that car with nobody driving it."

At an all-night diner on the edge of town they sat on stools and had coffee and cold sugary fried pies. Miss Phillips was morose. She had knots on her head fore and aft, and her legs were sticky with dried peach juice. The green party dress looked awful. Norwood snapped at the counter girl for putting cream in his coffee. She said she didn't know where he was from but if you wanted it black you had to say so. He told her he was from a place where they let you put your own cream in your coffee. From little syrup pitchers with spring lids.

Miss Phillips, wistfully eating her fried pie, was not listening to this byplay. "Sammy would get me a job right off," she said. "But I wouldn't want Grady to know where I was. I guess you would tell him."

"I wouldn't tell him what time it was," said Norwood. "After the way he done me."

"He's a disbarred lawyer and he knows a thousand ways to get you in trouble. I'd be afraid you would tell him where I went."

"Naw, I said I wouldn't. I wisht you *would* go on. It would be a load off my mind."

"I'm sorry I talked so ugly to you, Red. Why don't you let me have one of those cars?"

Norwood put the keys on the counter. "I don't want anything more to do with *you* or them cars. Take both of 'em, Laverne, and go on. You can give one to Sammy. Tell him hello for me."

"I can't drive but one. You'll have to unhook 'em."

It was a job getting the reflex tow bar off. All he had was a pair of pliers. Somebody with big shoulders and a four-way lug wrench had jammed those nuts down to stay. It was no use, not with pliers. He kicked it and beat it with a rock. Finally he attacked it with a jack handle and chanted "*This time . . . this time . . . this time . . .*" until it broke loose. Miss Phillips had no goodbye for Norwood. She took the Oldsmobile without a word or a wave and roared off into the Midwestern night flinging driveway gravel. The tow bar, its ingenious patented action now so much junk, was dragging along behind, bouncing on the highway and kicking up sparks.

Norwood drove the Pontiac out past the last lights of town and turned off on a dirt road. He turned off that road onto a two-rut road and then into what looked like a blackberry patch. He gunned it through the thicket and over arm-size saplings, giving the Indiana forest folk a scare, until it hit some bigger trees and stopped. He forced his door open against the bushes and got out and looked around. This was not such a smart idea. What would a car be doing here? Somebody would report it first thing tomorrow. He tried to back it out but the rear wheels were sunk hub deep in sand and wouldn't rock free. Well, he was tired of fooling with it. He took a towel from his bag and gave the door handles and the interior a good wiping down. It had been a proud day when he had given the Marine Corps his fingerprints and now they were up there in some drawer in Washington waiting to do him in. He ran his hand under the seat to see if he had left any clues. Any peanuts or guitar picks or things they could look at through a microscope. It smelled a little of Miss Phillips down there. He burned the fiber envelope and its contents and then he zipped up his bag and slung the guitar across his back and walked a good three miles back toward town to the nearest filling station. He stood on the highway under the station's harsh blue mercury lights and swatted bugs out of his face.

THE SUN was coming up before he got a ride. It was a bread truck. The driver was a round sloping man who was wearing an official bread hat with a sunburst medallion and a T-shirt that was so thin hairs were breaking through it. A bulldozer watch fob lay on his lap. Norwood thought at first he had rubber bands around his wrists. They were fat and dimpled like baby wrists.

"This is against the rules," said the bread man, "but I just can't pass a man up. My wife says I'm too kind for my own good."

"Well, I sure appreciate it," said Norwood. "I was getting pretty tired."

The truck was a delivery model with no passenger seat and Norwood had to sit on a wooden bread box. He laid the guitar across his knees. There was a bad shimmy in the front wheels and this made the guitar bounce and hum.

"I'll have to make a few stops, but a man begging a ride ought to be glad to get whatever he can."

"This is fine. I appreciate it too."

"Have you got a dollar to help on the gas?"

Norwood gave him a dollar. "Do you have to pay for your own gas?"

The man looked straight ahead. "Sometimes I do."

"How much does a job like this pay?" said Norwood. "A bread job?"

"Well, it don't pay as much as heavy construction work but you don't have to work as hard neither. I used to drive a D-8 cat till I hurt my back. Didn't do anything while I was on workmen's compensation. Just went to the show all the time. I like *The Road Runner.*"

"Yeah, I do too."

"I could watch that scutter for an hour."

"I believe I could too."

The bread man began to rumble with quiet laughter. "That coyote or whatever he is, a wolf or something, every time he gets up on a clift or somewhere with a new plan, why the Road Runner comes along on some skates or has him some new

40

invention like a rocket or a big wrecker's ball and just busts that coyote a good one." He laughed some more, then fell into repose. In a minute or two his face clouded with a darker memory. "Noveltoons are not any good at all," he said. "It's usually a shoemaker and a bunch of damn mice singing. When one of them comes on I get up and go get me a sack of corn or something."

They shimmied on down the road. At the first stop, a road-side grocery store, Norwood got a quart of milk and had the grocer make him a couple of baloney and cheese sandwiches with mayonnaise. He leaned on the meat box and ate and watched the bread man do his stuff. The bread man carried old bread out and brought new bread in. He squatted down and arranged it on the rack. Norwood noticed that he was poking finger holes in the competitors' loaves. Their eyes met, just for a second, and the bread man looked away. He tried to recover by doing peculiar things with his hands, as though he had a funny way of arranging bread. Norwood was not de-ceived. The bread man had no gift for pantomime and he did not seem to consider that from a range of eight or nine feet it is easy enough to tell whether someone is or is not punching holes in bread.

He said nothing about it and neither did Norwood. But back on the road the guilty knowledge hung heavy over the conversation. The bread man tried to get something going again. He asked Norwood if that was a Gibson guitar, but be-fore Norwood could answer the man said, "My whole family is musical. Some families are like that. My sister used to play trombone solos in church. Daddy played the accordion and we would all sing. He could really play that thing. And didn't know note one."

"They're hard to beat," said Norwood, agreeably. "I like to hear a good accordion."

"Daddy passed on two days after Labor Day of 1951," said the bread man, forestalling any suggestion that they go hear the old gentleman play.

They picked up another hitchhiker. This one was carrying a sack of garden tomatoes. Norwood made room for him on the box. The man was grateful and deeply apologetic and he insisted on shaking their hands. Norwood had never seen a man so happy to get a ride. "This sure is nice of you," he kept saying.

"I'm not supposed to do it," said the bread man. "I just don't like to pass anybody up. Might need a ride myself sometime. How far are you going?"

"I'm going on in to Indianapolis. My wife is in the hospital there. She doesn't have any sweat glands."

"I never had a cold in my life," said the bread man.

"It was sure nice of you to stop like that. A lot of people are scared of hitchhikers. I guess you can't blame 'em."

"Have you got a dollar to help on the gas?"

The man looked frightened. "No sir, I sure don't. All I got is sixty cents and I was going to get my wife some ice cream with that. That's why I'm thumbing. I'm supposed to get a little check Friday."

The bread man stopped the truck and nodded at Norwood. "Well, it wouldn't be fair to him if I let you ride. He paid his dollar."

"I don't care," said Norwood. "It's all right with me."

But the bread man made no move to get the truck going again. He looked impassively into the distance.

"I tell you what, if you'll let me ride I'll try to do something nice for somebody else on down the road. I'll return the favor that way. I'll do somebody else a good deed and tell them to pass it on. . . . Maybe it'll go all the way around the world. . . ."

It was no use. The man got out with his sack of tomatoes after riding fifty yards. "Well . . . thank you anyway. . . . I'm sorry . . . if it was Friday I would have the money." He was pained at having caused trouble. Everybody was right but him.

The bread man drove away and glanced at Norwood to see how he was taking it. "He wasn't going to do anything for anybody down the road. That was a load of crap."

"I think he would have," said Norwood. "You ought to let him ride."

"You think so, huh? Why didn't you pay his dollar?"

"I didn't think about that. I guess I could have. . . . Let's go back and get him."

"I'm not running a bus service. Anyway, I didn't like his personality."

"You should of let him ride."

"Maybe *you* don't like *my* personality."

"I don't know you very well."

"Maybe you think I have personality trouble."

"I just don't know you."

"That's not any kind of answer. Why don't you say what you think? You think I don't know that some people don't like me because of my personality? I know that. My wife wants me to take a course. They're giving one at the hotel next week that's supposed to help you in sales work. It makes people like you."

"Why don't you take it?"

"What do you know about it? You're just a hitchhiker begging rides."

"Well . . ."

"You saw me back there roughing up that bread, didn't you?"

"Yeah, I did."

"I got nothing to hide. *They* started it. What do you want me to do?"

"It's none of my business."

"You mighty right it's not. The Vita-White guys *step* on my bread. Mash it all in with their feet. No telling what kind of germs is on their shoes. They don't care. A little child's death don't mean anything to them."

"I believe I'll get out along here, just anywhere."

"I'm going on in to town."

"I believe I'll get out anyway."

"That's fine with me. I'll be glad to get rid of you. You're not friendly."

He pulled over on the shoulder and stopped short. Norwood said, "much oblige," and got out.

"You need to do something about your personality, hitchhiker. That's what you need."

"What *you* need is about forty dollars worth of front end work on this truck," said Norwood. "Some new kingpins."

"I hope don't nobody pick you up."

"No use in you hoping that. Somebody will."

At a pool hall in Indianapolis a rack boy with a Junior Tracy haircut and a good opinion of himself told Norwood that if he was going to New York he wouldn't bother with hitchhiking, he would go out to the Pennsylvania yards and catch him a freight train. Norwood shot snooker with him most of the afternoon and lost $2.75, then downed two chili dogs and went out to the rail yards and wandered around in the dark.

He had never done this before. There were tracks and more tracks and empty flatcars and switch engines banging around and trains coming in and trains going out. The thing was to ask somebody. He walked over to the station and talked to a Negro man in coveralls who was pushing a mail buggy. The man pointed out a freight train that was being made up for Philadelphia and said be careful. Norwood circled all the way around to the end of the train—instead of just crawling over a coupling—and came back up the other side where it was darker. He walked along like an inspector giving all the boxcar hatches a shake, and finally found one he liked. It was a faded blue L & N car with a banged-up door that wouldn't close all the way. No one could lock that door on him. He slid it back and struck a match and looked in. Big sacks of flour, hundred-pounders, were stacked high at each end of the car, almost to the roof. There was an open space in the middle of the car. He pushed his bag and guitar in and climbed in after them.

It was pitch-dark inside and hot, close, airless. Well, he would be riding at night. It would be cooler when they started moving. The floor was nothing but splinters. He wished he had a flashlight. It was probably dangerous striking matches with all that flour. He pulled some of the sacks down and fashioned himself a place to sleep. It looked like a nest for some bird that never lived on this earth. He slipped his boots off and settled back into it and tipped his hat over his eyes range style. No. Better be ready for a fast move. Better put the boots back on. Like getting caught by the gooks in one of those sleeping bags that zipped only halfway down. A suicide bag. He ate a dime Payday and then peeled an orange and ate it and lay there quiet and watchful in that ghostly Pillsbury darkness until the train moved.

It started with a clanging jerk. Norwood was half asleep. He turned on his side and adjusted his hat. Drops of sweat ran across his back and tickled. He was sweating like a hog. Did hogs sweat? No. That's why they like mudholes. Mules did, and horses. Out in the sun they had shiny wet skins. He tried to remember what a hog's skin looked like out in the sun. He couldn't remember seeing a hog in the sun. For any length of time. Hogs didn't have to work. Had anybody ever tried to *make* one work? Maybe they tried it a long time ago in history, and just gave up. And told their sons not to bother with it any more. Better not leave the guitar out loose like that. All kinds of folks riding trains. He looped the shoulder cord around his wrist a couple of times. The bag was under his head, safe. Everything was secured. The head is secured. Some boot standing there at the door with a swab at port arms trying to keep you out. Even when it was secured for regimental inspection they had to keep one bowl and one urinal open. Everybody knew that. Why did they keep on trying to pull that swab on you? Norwood dozed and woke and blew flour out of his nose and slept and groaned and dreamed crazy dreams about Miss Phillips. The train stopped and started all night long. It seemed to last about three days.

The train was slowing for the block in Philadelphia when Norwood suddenly awoke. He was asleep one second and wide awake the next. A thin wall of sunlight was coming through the doorway crack, with a lot of stuff dancing around in it. Something was wrong. It was his feet. He felt air on his feet. He sat up and there wasn't anything on them except a pair of J. C. Penney Argyles. Somebody had taken his thirty-eight-dollar stovepipe boots right off his feet. "*Son of a bitch!*" He got up and climbed over the floor and pulled sacks this way and that way but there was no one to be found, and no boots.

Soon it was so thick with flour dust in the car that he had to slam one of the doors back and stick his head out for air. The trouble was, two of the sacks had broken. After he caught his breath he dragged them over and pushed them out. The second one snagged on the bad door and hung there for a moment blowing flour up in his face. Then he began *flinging* sacks out, good ones, till he got a cramp in his neck.

The train entered the yard with long blats from the diesel horn and as it lurched in for a stop Norwood grabbed up his gear and bailed out in his sock feet. It stung. He squatted there and looked long and hard up and down the train, through the wheels, to see if anybody else was jumping off. Nobody. He dusted himself off, whacking his trousers with his hat, and decided to do some backtracking along the roadbed.

He couldn't walk far. The rocks and clinkers hurt his feet and he sat down on a stack of crossties to put on another layer of socks. While he was sitting there smoking a cigarette he saw two men in the distance coming up the tracks. One of them was wearing a luminous orange jacket. It was blinding. He might have had some job that required him to be easily spotted by aircraft. Norwood waited.

The one with the jacket was a tall whiskery man. He was also wearing a St. Louis Cardinals' baseball cap. By his side, stepping smartly along with a knotty walking stick, was a short angry little man with a knapsack on his back. He was covered from head to toe with flour, except right around his eyes and mouth.

"What happened to you, neighbor?" said Norwood.

"You should of seen it," said the man with the Cardinal cap. "Some thug was throwing flour out of a boxcar and Eugene here was walking along not thinking about anything when one of 'em hit him. One of them sacks."

"Was he hurt?"

"Well, it didn't hurt him, but it didn't help him none either."

He wanted to stop and talk about it some more, the sexagenarian Cardinal, but his short chum kept moving. He didn't even glance at Norwood. He looked like a man who was going somewhere to report something. Norwood had to run around in front of him to stop him. "Hey wait a minute. I better have a look in that pack. Somebody got my boots last night." The flour man looked up and fixed Norwood with two evil red eyes, but said nothing. The Cardinal did not like the turn things had taken. Maybe he could explain it again.

"We don't know anything about any boots. Eugene got hit with some flour, that's all. Some thug was throwing it off the train. I got hit with a mail pouch myself once but it wasn't anything like this. This was like a flour bomb went off."

Norwood moved around behind the flour man and reached up to undo the straps on the knapsack. With that, the flour man went into action. He was like lightning. He was a tiger. He spun around and hit Norwood on the arms three or four times with his stick and when it broke he popped Norwood in the mouth with a straight left and then he jumped up on his back and stuck there like a small white bear. The knapsack on *his* back was like a yet smaller bear.

"Look out! Look out!" the Cardinal was saying. He had jumped back well clear of the action. "Turn him loose, Eugene! He's another Hitler!"

Norwood was dancing around jabbing at the man with his elbows trying to shake him off. He backed him up and bumped him against the crossties. The man's ankles were locked together in front and Norwood broke them loose but the man had a hold on his neck that wouldn't quit. "You better get him off before I bust his head open," said Norwood, stopping to rest a minute. He was breathing hard. His upper lip was bloody.

The Cardinal moved in a little closer. Maybe something could be worked out now. "Eugene don't weigh very much, does he?" he said.

"I still don't want him on my back."

"He's light enough to be a jockey. Of course he's way too old."

"How long does he generally hang on?"

"I don't know. I never seen him do that before. . . . They say a snapping turtle won't let go till it thunders. That's what I've heard. I never was bit by a turtle. My oldest sister was bit by a mad fox. They didn't have any screens on their house and it come in a window one night and nipped her on the leg like a little dog will do. They carried that fox's head on in to Birmingham in some ice and said it was mad and she had to take all them shots. She said she hoped she never did get bit by nair another one."

Norwood kicked his feet forward and fell backward on the flour man and they hit the deck in a puff of white. The flour man was squeezed between Norwood and the pack and it knocked the wind out of him. He made a lung noise like *gunh!* He turned loose and sat up and brushed himself off a little, still defiant but not fighting any more. Norwood opened the knapsack and poked around in it. There were rolled-up clothes and a cast-iron skillet and pie pans and a can of Granger and cotton blankets and copies of *True Police Cases* and a mashed store cake and crackers and cans of chili and lima beans and an insulated plastic cup and a bottle of 666 Tonic and a clock and an old five-shot top-breaking .32 revolver with a heavy fluted barrel and taped-on grips. No boots. But in one of the side pouches he did find some shoes.

They were old-timers' high tops with elastic strips on the sides. Norwood tried them on and walked around flexing them and looking at them in profile. They were plenty loose. Eugene didn't have feet, he had flippers. Norwood said, "I'll give you two dollars for these dudes."

"Those are my house shoes," said Eugene, speaking for the first time and the last.

"A man comes along and needs some shoes, you ought to want to help him. You already got some good shoes on."

"Eugene doesn't want to sell his house shoes," said the Cardinal.

"*You* stay out of this," said Norwood.

"You international thug. You're just like Hitler and Tojo wrapped up into one."

Norwood tried Eugene once more. "Look, you can get another pair of these dudes easy for six bits at the Goodwill Store. I'm offering you two dollars. What about me? I don't have any shoes. I lost some thirty-eight-dollar boots last night. They took 'em right off my feet. They didn't give *me* anything."

"You better give Tojo what he wants, Eugene. He'll terrorize you if you don't. That's the way he does business."

"Don't call me Tojo any more."

"This is a free country, *thug*. You can call people anything you want to. Can't you, Eugene?"

Norwood rolled the two dollar bills into a cylinder and pushed it into Eugene's shirt pocket. "I ought not to give you anything. Jumping up on people's backs. They'll put you in a home somewhere if you don't watch out."

NORWOOD PAID his fare and rode a commuter special in to New York. He sat in the smoking section in a green padded seat that faced crossways and took up both armrests with his elbows. He bought some coffee in a paper cup with handles, and a heavy cakelike doughnut that stuck in the throat. It had an unpleasant spicy taste. "You want the rest of this?" he said to the man sitting by him.

"No, thanks."

"I didn't put my hands on it."

"Thanks but no."

Norwood placed it in the chrome ashtray between them. The man glanced down at it. In a minute or two he did it again. "I didn't see any other place to put it," said Norwood. He picked it up and put in his empty cup and held it. His hands were cold. Too much smoking? He flexed his fingers and made the joints pop. A bow-tied man across the aisle, not much himself but maybe some pretty girl's father, was watching him. Norwood stared back. The man looked up at the light fixture on the ceiling to calculate its dimensions and efficiency. There were no girls on the train, no women at all, only these clean men. They bathed every day, every morning. He caught another one looking at him down the way. He *was* a mess, no doubt about it. The sole of one shoe was flopping and he had B.O. pretty bad. His red beard was beginning to bristle and there were patches of flour like dirty snow on his back where Eugene had been. One day Eugene would let somebody have it with that .32. Get a face full of hot powder himself, with that loose cylinder.

He had some more coffee at a stand-up counter in Penn Station and the people there looked at him too, but not for long because they had to get back to their newspapers. He picked up his change and looked at it. "Hey wait a minute," he called to the girl. She had black hair piled up high and dark tiger eyes. She came back and gave the counter a quick wipe with a blue sponge that had one cornflake riding on the stern. She looked at the dime and nickel in his hand. That was right.

People watched furtively over their papers. This guy with the hat was going to start something.

"What is it?" said the girl.

"I guess you didn't hear the radio this morning," he said.

"I don't gitcha."

He pointed at the fifteen cents. "The weatherman said no change today."

"Oh fer Chrissakes."

Somebody on the other side of the plastic orange juice vat said, "What did he say?" and somebody else said, "I couldn't hear it." They all went back to their papers. Whatever it was, it was over.

A friendly airman third class found Joe William's number in the Manhattan directory and Norwood tried to give him a quarter but he wouldn't take it. He brought his bag and guitar into the booth with him and dialed. The phone started to ring, then made an unsatisfactory noise and a recorded voice came through to say the number had been disconnected. He got his dime back and dialed the operator. After a short discussion she passed him on to a supervisor.

"That number has been disconnected, sir," said the supervisor.

"Yeah, that othern told me that. Do you know if he's gone home or what?"

"We don't have that information."

"I thought he might of left word with somebody in case somebody needed to get aholt of him."

"No sir, we don't have that kind of information."

"I guess you can't keep up with everybody, can you?"

"No sir, we can't."

"Uh-huh. Well. Goodbye."

"Goodbye."

He washed up in the men's room but it didn't help much. What he needed was a bath and a shave. His hair was stiff and in places it hurt when he mashed down on it in a certain way. This was no place to shave, worse than a barracks head. Traffic and flushing and people combing their hair behind you and not enough flat surfaces around the bowl to put your stuff on. The faucets had strong springs in them so you couldn't let the water run. A man bumped him and said "Sorry" and

Norwood quickly checked his billfold and made sure the hip pocket was buttoned. This was the kind of place pickpockets liked. Those boogers had quick hands. Be all in your clothes and you wouldn't know it. He dried off under a hot air blower.

Outside, a porter pointed him toward Times Square. As he made his way up Seventh Avenue a man with puffy eyes (dope fiend?) stopped him and tried to sell him a four-color ball-point pen for a dollar. Norwood brushed him off. What did they think, that he was somebody who would buy something like that on the street? No telling what they were thinking, the way he looked. That he would be amazed at a lot of things. Like *Tarzan's New York Adventure*.

He looked at the movie posters on both sides of Forty-second Street and had a glass of beer and some giant corrugated French fries. The windows were full of many good buys in transistor radios and field glasses. Did any one live upstairs over the movie theaters? He saw himself on television at Robert Ripley's Believe It or Not Odditorium, and looked at all the curios downstairs, believing most of them but not believing the one about Marshal W. M. Pitman of Wharton, Texas, shooting a bullet right into a crook's gun in 1932. Still, there was the gun, and why would they make it up? Across the street he watched a man with a beanie at a sewing machine. The man was talking like Donald Duck and sewing names on other beanies. *Stella* and *Fred* and *Ernie*. His workmanship was good. How did he get that job? What did it pay? Being able to sew names and talk like Donald Duck. He walked up as far as Fifty-ninth Street, where things began to peter out, then came back. There was a man in a Mr. Peanut outfit in front of the Planters place but he was not giving out sample nuts, he was just walking back and forth. The Mr. Peanut casing looked hot. It looked thick enough to give protection against small arms fire.

"Do they pay you by the hour or what?" Norwood said to the monocled peanut face.

"Yeah, by the hour," said a wary, muffled voice inside.

"I bet that suit is heavy."

"It's not all that heavy. I just started this morning."

"How much do you get a hour?"

"You ast a lot of questions, don't you?"

"Do you take the suit home with you?"

"No, I put it on down here. At the shop."

"The one in Dallas gives out free nuts."

"I don't know anything about that. They didn't say anything to me about it."

"He don't give you many, just two or three cashews."

"I don't know anything about that. I work at the post office at night."

"Well, I'll see you sometime, Mr. Peanut. You take it easy."

"Okay. You too."

A woman in the Times Square Information Center, about forty but with a smooth powdered neck he wouldn't have minded biting, gave him a subway map and told him that the best way to get to the East Eleventh Street address was to take the BMT to Union Square, then change to the Fourteenth Street–Canarsie line going east and get off at First Avenue. It was impossible to remember. On his way to the subway entrance he stopped at a shoeshine parlor to ask again. Or it was not so much a parlor as a notch in the wall with room for only one chair and the shine man himself, who was small and dark and aproned.

"Say—"

"Beat it, fellow," said the shine man, not looking up from his work. "I don't have time to answer questions."

"I just wanted to know—"

"You wanna know something, ask a cop. They get paid for it. I pay two hundred dollars a month for this rathole and at twenty cents a shine that means I got to shine two thousand individual shoes just to pay the rent."

Norwood forgot his own problem at once. "You're not figuring your tips in on that?"

"I don't have time to talk, fellow. Beat it, okay? If I was on the city payroll it would be different. Everybody thinks I'm on the city payroll."

"You're trying to make it sound like you have to shine more shoes than you really do. Why don't you figure your tips in on it?"

The shine man stood up and put one fist on his hip and did a Mediterranean fast burn. "You can't figure it that way, Mr. Smart Guy. You gotta figure it on your base rate, which is twenty cents. A lotta smart guys think they know more about my business than I do."

The man in the chair put down his magazine. "Look, I'm in kind of a hurry," he said.

"Sure, you're in a hurry," said the shine man. "*I'm* in a hurry, everybody in the *world* is in a hurry except this smart guy that has time to go down the street telling everybody how to run their business. How can I work with a smart guy standing over my shoulder telling me how to run my business? The answer is—*I can't.*"

"Leave him alone, buddy," said the man in the chair.

"Go bother Mayor Wagner," said the shine man. "He needs advice. Tell him how to run the city. He's on the city payroll. Don't bother me, bother somebody on the city payroll."

The subway was cleaner and more brightly lighted than Norwood had expected, and it moved faster. He jostled his way forward to the front car and looked through the glass with his hands cupped around his face. He was disappointed to find the tunnel so roomy. Only a very fat man could be trapped in it with a train coming. The air smelled of electricity and dirt.

In one of the pedestrian tunnels at the Union Square stop a man was stretched out on the concrete having a fit and forcing people to step around him in the narrow passageway. Norwood watched him as he gave a few terminal jerks and a long sigh. He knew he should look to see if the man had swallowed his tongue, the way they used to have to do with that Eubanks boy in the fifth grade, but he didn't want to put his finger in the man's mouth unless he had to. It was all right for doctors. They didn't care where they put their hands. He lifted the man by the armpits and propped him against the wall. The man rolled his eyes. His legs were rubbery and he couldn't stand alone.

"You want some water?" said Norwood.

"Water? Yeah."

"Well . . . I don't have any. How about a cigarette?"

"You can't smoke down here."

"What's wrong with you?"

"I'll be all right in a minute."

A woman with some packages stopped and inquired and Norwood told her to go see if she could find somebody. She said she would tell a transit policeman. Norwood waited. Without the blockage people rushed along now in a steady stream. No policeman came. A foot brushed the guitar and made it ring. The man closed his eyes and took a nap standing there. No policeman. Norwood reached out into the stream and grabbed a man's arm, a dapper man in a neat metallic suit.

"Hold this fellow up a minute."

The man jumped and did as he was told. Then he said, "Hey, what is this, you?"

Norwood was picking up his gear. "Somebody's coming to get him. They're on the way."

"Where are you going? What do you think you're doing? You can't detain me like this. I'm an officer of the court. I've got to get downtown."

"We all got to catch trains. I can't be down here helping folks out all day myself. I don't even live here."

"I won't be put in a false position, you. This is a false position."

"I got to go."

Norwood found the Canarsie line with no trouble but on the train he let his mind wander and the next thing he knew he was under the river, and then in Brooklyn. Arnold. Was he on the phone to Grady? He crossed over the platform and doubled back on another train and this time he stood by the doors all the way. Daylight again. First Avenue and Fourteenth. Tenements and garbage cans. This was where people lived in New York. Leo Gorcey and his pals working up a plan in the candy store. Huntz Hall messing up everything. *Satch*.

It was a short walk to the address on Eleventh Street. On the sidewalk in front of the place some shirtless Puerto Rican boys were roasting marshmallows over a smoldering mattress.

Norwood stopped and looked at the tenement number and rested the guitar on his foot. "You boys having a big time?"

"It's a campfire," said one. He was wearing huge comic sunglasses and had his head tilted back to keep them on. He offered Norwood a blackened marshmallow from the end of a straightened-out coat hanger.

"I believe I'd rather have one right out of the sack. They ain't gonna taste like anything cooked over hair." He reached for the cellophane package but another boy grabbed it off the stoop. Norwood let it pass. "You boys need to get you some wood. You need a wood far for these dudes."

"We don't have any wood."

"Go down at the store and get you a apple box. They'll let you have one. Pine would be better than what you got here."

The boy who grabbed the marshmallows pointed at the guitar. "Can you play that?"

"Yeah and I'm liable to get it out just any minute and sing a song. Do yall know a old boy name Joe William Reese?"

Nobody said anything.

"I know this is where he lives. I got it on a piece of paper."

Nobody said anything.

"When will you play that guitar?" said the grabber.

"It's hard to say. I might not play it all now."

"Marie has a guitar. She knows a hundred songs."

"She don't know that many."

"She does too."

"I don't know but one myself. It's about a squirrel. He lived out in the woods and every time he would get something good his friends would be hungry and they would come around and want some. They'd say, 'Hey, squirrel, let me have a bite of that Clark bar.' And the squirrel, he would say, real mean, 'Naw! I'm on eat it all myself! It's good too!' And pretty soon out there in the woods they were all calling him the stingy squirrel and he didn't have any more friends to play with."

The boys looked at Norwood.

"Well, it's more what you would call a story than a song," he said. "There's a good lesson in it."

He examined a row of mailboxes in the foyer and Joe William's name was there all right, although it had been penciled over # 2. The hall was dark and there were dust balls that the broom had missed. They rolled along like miniature tumbleweeds. Norwood struck a match and found # 2 the first shot. He stood outside the door for a moment. There was movement inside. He unzipped the guitar and without tuning up he hit one loud nylon chord and sang:

> *There'll be smoke on the water*
> *And the land and the sea*
> *When our army and navy*
> *Overtake the enemee . . .*

A dog started barking upstairs, a little scrappy one, and some woman took it up and started yelling down. The stairwell echoed with female Spanish abuse. The door opened a foot or so and Norwood gave his guitar a little trick spin and dropped into a boxing stance. "Whuddaya say, tush hog," he said. But it wasn't Joe William at all. It was a short, bushy-headed young man in a green sweater. He was eating a sandwich. He said, "What is all this?"

Norwood said, "Oh. I thought Joe William Reese lived here."

"Well, he did, but he's gone now. You just missed him."

"Where did he go?"

"Back home. Some place in Arkansas. He left a couple of days ago. You a friend of his?"

"We was in the service together. How Company, Third Batt, Fifth Marines. He owes me some money."

"I take it you're from Arkansas too."

"Naw, I'm from Ralph, Texas. We used to live in Arkansas but when I was in the seventh grade we moved over to Ralph. It's just the other side of Texarkana. Bowie County."

"I see. Well, how is everything in Bowie County?"

"Just fine. What did he go back home for?"

"Well, as I get it, he was following this girl."

"What girl?"

"Some girl from his home town. I forget her name. She was up at Columbia more or less killing time and she wanted to go to Paris or Italy or someplace but her father said she'd have to put in some time at home first. Reese is trying to marry her. It was all very complicated. I can't remember the details. I gather her family has some money."

"Yeah, I know about her. He's been sweet on her for a long time."

"So. That's the story. He left."

"What was he doing here?"

"Working at the post office."

"He could of done that at home."

"That's true enough. But then the girl was up here. Look, you want some coffee or something? You look pretty beat. I was just having lunch."

"I don't care if I do."

"Come on in."

"I wouldn't mind having a sandwich either."

"Sure thing. I'm afraid all I have is potted meat."

"That'll be fine."

"It'll have to be on hamburger buns too, I'm out of bread."

"That'll be fine."

"This stuff is cheap but it's very nutritious." He picked up the can and read from it. "Listen to this: 'beef tripe, beef hearts, beef, pork, salt, vinegar, flavoring, sugar and sodium nitrite.' Do you know what tripe is?"

"It's the gut part."

"That's what I thought. I suspected it was something like that."

"It's all meat. Meat is meat. Have you ever eat any squirrel brains?"

"No, how are they?"

"About like calf brains. They're not bad if you don't think about it. The bad part is cracking them little skulls open. One thing I won't eat is hog's head cheese. My sister Vernell, you can turn her loose with a spoon and she'll eat a pound of it before she gets up. Some people call it souse."

"Why do they call it that?"

"I don't know. You got to have a name for everything."

"Yes, I hadn't thought of that. Well, they're both good names. *Tripe. Souse.*"

It was a railroad apartment with peeling pink walls and a bathtub in the kitchen. There were two open suitcases on the living room couch and a big pasteboard Tide carton in the center of the room which was overflowing with books and wads of newspaper. A middling big roach was trying to climb out of the bathtub on the lower slope. He seemed addled and he kept slipping back. Norwood sat at the kitchen table and cleared away ashtrays and magazines to make an eating space on the tablecloth. He picked up an aerosol insect bomb and gave a couple of test sprays from it.

"This was where Joe William lived?"

"Yes."

"I figured he'd have a nicer place than this."

The bushy-headed young man was putting a pan of water on the stove. "It's not much, is it?" he said. "But it's not as nasty as the one just overhead, if you can believe that. That was mine. I moved down here yesterday afternoon. The rent's the same. This one is a little more convenient too."

"How much is the rent?"

"Sixty a month."

"Damn. You could make payments on a right nice house for that. Everything is high in New York, ain't it?" He made himself a sandwich and started in on it.

"Yes, I suppose it is. By the way, my name is Dave Heineman."

Norwood shook his hand. "Glad to meet you, Dave. Mine is Norwood Pratt. What are you, an Italian?"

"No, I'm a New York Jew."

"Oh."

"Do you know any Jews?"

"I don't know. I don't think so. Well, there's Mr. Haddad at Haddad's store in Ralph. *We Clothe the Entire Family*. That's what he has on his window."

"He sounds Syrian to me."

"He might be. I wouldn't know the difference. I was in boot camp with a Jew from Chicago name Silver. I didn't know he was one till somebody told me. Instead of saying 'Turn out the light' he would say 'Lock the light.' You couldn't break him from it."

"Why did you think 'Heineman' was Italian?"

"You just look kind of Italian."

"This Silver, was he a pretty good soldier?"

"Well, he wasn't a soldier, he was a Marine. Yeah, he was all right. Except for saying lock the light. What do you do, Dave, do you work at the post office too? Everybody I've met so far works there."

"No, I don't really work anywhere. Here at home. I'm a free-lance travel writer. Just from handouts though, I don't travel anywhere, yet. Sunny and gracious old Lima, city of contrasts, where the old meets the new. Old guys making pots and plying similar ancient trades in the shadow of modern skyscrapers. That's what I write."

"Is there any money in it?"

"Not the way I do it. There is if you can grind it out. What I'm after is trips, freebies, some of that big time freeloading. Once you get on that circuit you're in. My problem is I'm lazy.

I've got a Provence piece due at the *Trib* this afternoon and I haven't written a word. I've been sitting here all morning drinking coffee and smoking and reading match covers. Hunt's fabulous tomato sauce recipes. *Draw Me. Finish High School at Home.* Did you finish high school, Tex?"

"Naw."

"I didn't think so. Here, take these, look into that course."

"Thanks. The water's boiling."

Heineman made the instant coffee in two big red striped Woolworth mugs. "How was the trip up?" he said. "Maybe I can do a piece about it. 'See America First.'"

"It was all right," said Norwood. "Some hobo got my boots on the train. He was one more slick customer. He took 'em right off my feet and I didn't see him or hear him. Yeah, and I wisht I could get aholt of that sapsucker. He'd *think* boots. I wouldn't care if it was the hobo king. It may of been the hobo king. He was plenty slick. Well, I'm not being serious there."

"About what, the king?"

"They have got a king. That's right, this is no lie, I read this. They have got them a king just like England and France and he rules over every tramp in America just like a . . . *king.*"

"I noticed your shoes. Your Congress gaiters."

Norwood shifted gears from the hobo realm and looked at his shoes with a puzzled frown, as though he wasn't sure how they got on his feet. "I just picked these things up," he said. "A man give 'em to me. They're not too much really."

"I don't see anything wrong with them. What's wrong with them?"

Norwood twisted one around on his foot. "I do have to say this: They're comfortable dudes."

"Let me get this straight. You're saying that *comfort* and not *style* is the most important feature of that shoe, is that it?"

Norwood was spreading some more meat paste on a bun. He stopped and held the knife upright on the table in his fist and looked around. He looked like an overgrown nursery rhyme character with expectations of a pudding. "Where's the mannaze?" he said.

"There's not any," said Heineman. "You'll have to use that mustard, what's left of it."

"Mannaze is better with potted meat." He scraped the mustard jar with his knife and got the stuff out in little dobs. "How about pickles?"

"No, it seems I'm out of everything, Tex. I didn't know you were coming or I would have laid in some things. Some pearl onions. A relish tray. Perhaps a salad."

"You know, I feel like a fool coming up here all this way and then Joe William is gone back home. I could of stopped off by his house on the way up. I come within just a few miles of it. I didn't even think about that. His folks said he was up here."

"How much does he owe you? If that's not too personal."

"Seventy dollars."

"Yeah, well, I'd call that a fool's errand all right. Even if you had caught him here you probably wouldn't have gotten the money. He's a bigger sponge than I am. He fooled me with that country boy act and got out of here owing me twenty-five."

"How did he go home, with that girl?"

"I don't know if he went *bodily* home with her or not. I think he flew."

"Flew? And here I am riding freight trains and he's the one that owes me money."

"Well, it's not enough to get upset about it, is it?"

"What do you mean?"

"I mean seventy dollars is not really worth all the trouble, is it? Traveling what? Two thousand miles? And losing your boots? Figure it out."

"I was coming up here anyway. He owes me the money. It's not a gambling debt, it's out of my pocket."

"Yeah, but it's only seventy dollars. And what are your chances of getting it back with a guy like Reese? Didn't you ever lose any money before? Hell, forget it. Go on back to—where do you work, Tex?"

"I did work at the Nipper station in Ralph."

"Then forget it and go on back to the Nipper station in Ralph. I think you've got too much anxiety invested in that debt."

"I said I *did* work there. I don't work there any more. I'm a Country and Western singer now."

"All right, the point is, the money's gone."

"I'll get it."

"Okay, have it your way."

"Besides, I'd like to see him."

"Okay."

"It's not just the money."

"Okay, all right. It's none of my business anyway."

Heineman got up and went to the refrigerator and brought back a little carton of cottage cheese. "You want some of this?"

Norwood said, "I don't eat that stuff."

"Good. There's not enough to split anyway." He put salt and pepper on it and ate it from the carton.

"Do you know any beatnik girls?" said Norwood.

Heineman ate and thought about it for a minute. "I know some who *look* like beatniks. I guess it's the same thing. There's one on the third floor. Yes, Marie's a beatnik by any definition. Would you like to meet her?"

"Well, yeah."

"She sings, you know. I think you'll like Marie." He stopped eating and sniffed. He made a face and went to the living room window and leaned out. "Okay, Raimundo, knock off the grabass," he said. "I told you not to burn any more of those stink bombs out there."

Raimundo was the one with the big sunglasses. He and the others kicked up sparks. "It's a campfire!" he said.

"No, it's not a campfire, it's a mattress fire on East Eleventh Street and it stinks. Now put some water on it."

Raimundo went into another defiant spark dance. "We don't want to."

"I said put it out."

"We're having fun."

"That may be, but I don't want you to have any fun. Fire Commissioner Cavanagh doesn't want you to have any fun either. He was on the radio about this very thing. I think I'll call him."

"You don't have a phone."

"Come on now, don't be a pest. It's a neighborhood disgrace. The *Post* will be down here taking squalor pictures."

"I want my fifty cents," said Raimundo.

"Don't start in on that again. You'll get your money."

"When?"

"Soon." He pulled both windows down and came back to

the kitchen and resumed work on the cottage cheese. "Little bastards. I hope they all get respiratory diseases this winter."

"If it was me," said Norwood, "I would be ashamed of myself borrowing money from little boys."

"I don't actually borrow it from them. They don't have any to speak of. Raimundo runs a few errands for me."

"Say, is it okay if I shave here?"

"Yeah, that's it right there, the kitchen sink. The john itself is in the back. When you get through we'll go up and see if Marie is in and take her over to Stanley's. I don't feel like doing that piece anyway."

Marie was agreeable in many ways, if a little odd. Through deafness or inattention she never heard anything the first time. "*What?*" she would say. "*What's that?*" She took Norwood up to The Cloisters and twice for rides on the Staten Island Ferry, always wearing the same loose orange silky blouse. She didn't work anywhere and she didn't seem to have any friends. She didn't do anything. Once on the boat Norwood put his arm around her waist and she removed it and said he took a lot for granted and that she would let him know when she was ready to be "pawed." He tried it again the next day but she still wasn't ready. They played guitar duets in her apartment, with Norwood plunking chords, and they sang folk songs from a book.

"You don't really like folk songs, do you?" she said.

"They're all right," he said. "I like modern love numbers better."

Marie was a speech major from Northwestern and one night she read aloud from her favorite book, which was something called *The Prophet*, and Norwood listened and clipped his fingernails. She fed him and seemed to welcome his company but nothing ever got off the ground in the way of funny business. Every night he traipsed back downstairs and slept on Heineman's couch. It was rough and nubbly and left red waffle marks on his face and hands. It was too short too. On the fourth day he got up and toppled on the floor. His legs were dead from the knees down. When circulation was restored he went upstairs and told Marie he was leaving. She said, "What?" and he said, "I said I got to go."

"Oh. You're leaving."

"Yeah, I got to get on down the road."

"Oh. Well. You'll have to write me a long letter about Shreveport."

"Yeah, I'll have to do that."

"About the program and all."

"Okay."

"Well. All the best, Norwood."

"Yeah, you take it easy, I'll see you sometime."

H E WALKED to Union Square in a light drizzle and stopped at the Automat for a dish of baked beans with a hot dog on top. It was the best thing he had found to eat in New York and by far the cheapest. The place was packed with damp bums who smelled like rancid towels and he had to wait for a seat. One fell vacant and he darted in and got it. Then he saw that he had forgotten his silverware. He left the dish of beans on top of an *Argosy* magazine to stake a table claim and went back to the cutlery stand. While he was gone the girl with the dirty dishes wagon picked up his beans and an Oriental gentleman across the table got the magazine. A man with a bowl of oatmeal got the seat. Norwood came back and thought at first he had the wrong table, then he recognized the Chinese gent. He grabbed the magazine from the foreigner's clever hands and turned to the oatmeal man. "You got my seat." The man's fast reply was "I don't see your name on it." Norwood stood there with his knife and fork and paper napkin.

Just then a big man in a blue suit, not a bum but some sort of manager, appeared in the middle of the room and started clapping his hands. "It's not raining out there now," he said. "Everybody who's not eating—*outside!*" He clapped and bellowed and there was a sullen, shuffling movement toward the door. He spotted an immobile Norwood. "That goes for you too!"

Norwood said, "I had some beans here a minute ago. You can ask anybody at this table. Except this one. He got my seat."

"It's not raining out there now. Let's go!"

"I ain't studying that rain, man. I'm trying to tell you that somebody got my chow that I paid good money for."

"Don't give me a hard time. *Outside!*"

One of the bums who was being stampeded called back from the revolving door, "Hey, it *is* raining out here!"

Norwood put his heavy duty silverware down on the table and left. Within two hours he had said goodbye to the hateful town and was speeding south in a big Trailways cruiser. He was thinking about purple hull peas sprinkled down with pepper sauce.

There was nothing to see along the featureless turnpike to Washington except elbows in the passing cars below. He read his magazine. He dozed awhile. A famous athlete in the seat behind him, now reduced to traveling by motor coach, said, "Niggers have taken over all the sports except swimming. They don't know how to swim."

In Washington there was a layover and a change of buses and a new driver. He was a cheerful fatso with his hat tipped back and although the signs said DO NOT TALK TO OPERATOR he started right in cracking jokes and carrying on with the passengers. Norwood wanted to get in on it and he went up front to scout for a seat but they were all taken. Maybe later. He had two seats to himself at the back. He took off his guitar and put his feet up in the seat, sitting crossways.

Darkness fell and a low white moon was running along with the bus just behind the tops of the scraggly Virginia pines. Norwood had his head wedged in against the seat and the window, using his hat. He watched the moon and made it go up and down by closing one eye and then the other. *Moonlight in the pines . . . and you were so fine . . .* How did people write songs anyway? . . . *Moonlight in the pines . . . and in this heart of mine . . . you were so fine . . . your lips were sweet as wine . . . moonlight on the road . . . moonlight on the bus . . . moonlight on the trail. . . . A Republic Picture. . . . Hey, Gabby, the widder was looking for you. Aw tarnation, Roy. Roy and Dale and the Sons of the Pioneers having a good laugh on Gabby. Roy's real name was Leonard Slye. . . .*

The bus slowed and pulled over and stopped on the shoulder. A girl with a flashlight and a shopping bag full of clothes and a blue and white overnight case got on, talking away and stumbling on the cord from some unseen appliance in the bag. She would have fallen had not the driver, the fat and courteous J. T. Spears, jumped from his seat to catch her.

"You didn't have to run so hard, little lady," he said, "I saw you coming."

She was out of breath. "I thought I had plenty of time. I got to talking there on the porch and then I saw your yellow lights come over the hill and I just took off aflying. They were all laughing and hollering at me, '*Run, Rita Lee, run,*' and then that cord from my hair drier came aloose . . ."

She was a pretty little girl with short black hair and bangs and bejeweled harlequin glasses. A little thin in the leg but not too thin. She was wearing a bright yellow dress with a white daisy on one side of the skirt part.

Norwood stood up in a kind of crouch and tried to indicate that he was friendly and that he had a good place to sit back there. She came down the aisle and stopped and he stowed her gear in the overhead rack and she thanked him and took the seat in front of him, next to a woman with blue hair.

They hit it off fine, the girl Rita Lee and the woman, and began at once to exchange confidences. The woman was a dental assistant from Richmond with a twenty-year pin who had been to Washington to see how laws are made. It was her first visit to Congress. "People who live right around something don't care anything about it," she said. "I bet if I lived at the Grand Canyon I wouldn't go out and look at it much. And other people would be driving thousands of miles to see it." Her husband had disappeared two years before and was subsequently found working as an able seaman on a sulfur boat, through a rude postcard he had foolishly sent her from Algiers, Louisiana. He was now back home, but living in the garage and drinking.

The girl Rita Lee had been visiting her grandmother and certain cousins in Virginia. She was from near Swainsboro, Georgia. She was now on her way to Jacksonville, North Carolina, for a showdown with someone named Wayne at Camp Lejeune. Although she did not have a ring—she had not pressed him on that—they had had an understanding for more than a year now and she wanted to know what was up. There had been no letter for almost two months.

"What is he, a officer?" said the woman.

"Boy, that's a good one," said Rita Lee. "Lord no, he's a Pfc down there in the Second Marines."

Norwood stuck his head up in the notch between the two seats. "Do you mean the Second *Marines* or Second Marine *Division?*" he said.

They looked up at him.

"When you say *Marines* that means regiment. If you mean *division* you have to say *division*. Now he could be in the

Second Marines, Second Marine Division, I'm not saying that. But he might be in the Sixth or Eighth Marines too and still be in the Second Division, that's all I'm saying."

"I don't know what it is right off hand," said Rita Lee. "I'd have to look on a envelope. All I know is he drives a tank down there in the Second Marine something."

"There's nothing wrong with tanks," said Norwood. "Gunny Crankshaw used to be in tanks. That dude had a Silver Star. He shot down the gates of Seoul University. He had all his khakis cut down real tight and he would just strut around like a little banty rooster. Ever once in a while he would stop and take his handkerchief out and knock the dust off his shoes."

There was a heavy silence. The bus swerved to avoid a big tire fragment in the road but bumped across it anyway.

"That's where somebody throwed a recap," said Norwood. "They get hot enough and they'll just peel right off. You can't tell about a recap. But if I'm driving on gravel a lot I'd rather have one. They'll hold up better. It's harder rubber."

"I think we've had about enough out of you," said the dental assistant. "You're butting into a private conversation."

"I was just trying to be friendly."

"Well, you'll have to get back in your own seat. We can't talk with your head up there like that."

At the bus station in Richmond Rita Lee had a Pepsi-Cola and a sack of peanuts. Norwood moved in on the stool beside her and ordered coffee.

"Whuddaya say."

"Oh, you, hi. Say, I like your hat." She poured the peanuts into the bottle and shook it and fizzed a little into her mouth from an inch or two away. The goobers boiled up in carbonated turmoil. "My hair is just a mess."

"It don't look like a mess to me."

"I washed it and rolled it up and had it looking so nice and now look at it. It was running for that bus. What are you doing with that cowboy hat on?"

"I thought you liked it."

"I'll say this, it's a tall one."

Norwood stirred his coffee and talked to her with his head turned just slightly; he knew he wouldn't be able to talk straight if he looked directly into her face. *What a honey!* It might even knock him off the seat. "This ain't a bad looking bus station for Richmond," he said. "You'd be surprised how little that one is in New York."

"I know a girl that went to New York and got a suckruhturrial job right off making ninety-five dollars a week. She was the FHA Charm Queen two years running. *And smart?* She didn't know what a B was."

"They put butter on ham sandwiches up there," he said. He put a dime in the remote jukebox unit and played a Webb Pierce selection.

"I know why you're wearing that hat. You're a singer yourself."

"How did you know?"

"I saw your guitar on the bus."

"I fool around with it some." He looked in all his pockets and then forgot what he was looking for.

"Have you made any records?"

"Well, I'm just getting started. I may cut some platters when I get to Shreveport." *Cut some platters?*

"I bet you'll be a big star one of these days and your folks will be so proud of you."

He wound his watch.

"Is that your home, Shreveport?"

"Naw, my home is Ralph, Texas, down there the other side of Texarkana. It ain't too far from Shreveport."

"Have you got a wife anywhere?"

"Naw."

"I was supposed to been married last March. It was all my fault, I said no we better wait. Wayne, see, he wants to do everything right now and after he thinks about it he don't want to do it any more."

"That's a mighty nice dress you got on."

"Thank you, I made it myself. He may have him some old girl down there. That handsome devil, all the girls wanted him back home but they couldn't get him from me. He would favor Rory Calhoun a lot if his neck was filled out more."

Norwood was doing a pushup from the stool.

"What's wrong with you?" she said.

"Nothing."

"You keep doing things."

Nothing was said about it but there was a tacit understanding that they would sit together when they got back on the bus. Norwood did not try anything right away, although much of his discomfort had passed. There in the half-light of the bus he could not see her face clearly. Her voice alone and presence did not stun and confound his brain.

They talked. He edged closer to her through a series of leg crossings and body adjustments. Soon he had his arm over her shoulder. No resistance. He let it slide down a little and began squeezing the soft flesh of her upper arm. It was wonderful. The way he was doing it, with just a thumb and finger, giving a thick pinch here and there, was like a witch testing a captured child for plumpness. Rita Lee couldn't decide whether she liked it or not. She had been grabbed and wrenched about in many different ways but this was a new one. She stiffened.

"I was afraid of this," she said. "I was afraid the minute I sat down here you would think I was looking for love on a bus."

Norwood didn't stop, nor did he answer, not liking to have attention called to what he was doing when he was at this kind of thing. He nuzzled her. "I mean it now," she said, but not with any firmness, and he cleared his throat and kissed her and she relaxed, Wayne the Marine out of mind. He went back to the arm business, still not saying anything or acknowledging in any way that anything was going on.

After a time she said, "Norwood?"

"What?"

"Tell me something."

"What?"

"What is your all-time Kitty Wells favorite?"

"I'd have to think about it."

"Mine is 'Makin' Believe.'"

"Yeah, that's mine too."

"Listen."

"What?"

"I'd like to hear you sing sometime."

"Okay."

"Why don't you sing something now? I'd like to hear something now."

"Not on the bus."

"You could do it soft."

"Naw, not on the bus."

"What is your singing style like?"

"I don't know."

"Yes you do. Who do you sing like?"

"Have you ever heard Lefty Frizzell sing 'I Love You a Thousand Ways'?"

"No, I never even heard of Lefty Frizzell."

"I don't guess I can explain it then."

"You got a scar back here on your neck. It looks awful. There's not any hair growing on it."

"I fell off a water truck in Korea."

"Did you do any fighting over there?"

"I got in on the tail end of it."

"Did you kill anybody?"

"Just two that I know of."

"How did you do it?"

"I shot 'em."

"I mean but how?"

"Well, with a light machine gun. They were out there in front of the barb war and one of 'em hit a trip flare. It was right in front of my bunker and they just froze. My gun was already laid on 'em, except I had to traverse a little and I cranked off about thirty rounds and dropped 'em right there."

"Did they scream?"

"If they did I didn't hear 'em. A bunch of mortars come in and when that let up me and a old boy from South Carolina name Tims went out there and throwed a plank acrost the war and brought their bodies back."

"I bet you got a medal."

"For that? Naw. The skipper didn't even like it much. He wanted a prisoner. He thought I should of run out there with my .45 and said 'You two gooks are under arrest.'"

"You should of got a medal."

"You don't get medals for things like that. Unless you're a officer. They give 'em to each other."

"If I had killed anybody I don't think I could sleep at night."

"That's what we was there for."

"I know that but still."

"It didn't bother me none. It wasn't no more than shooting

squirrels. Naw, it wasn't as much because squirrels are not trying to kill *you*. With big one-twenty mortars."

"I never even seen anybody dead close up and I don't want to either."

"Them two needed killing anyway. If they had dropped down flat when that flare went off I couldn't of depressed my gun down far enough to hit 'em."

"Come on now, hon, and sit up a minute. I'm about to fall off this seat."

Norwood sat up and moved over to his side and lit a cigarette. Rita Lee didn't exactly want this, a total disengagement, and she snuggled up against him and put his arm, dead weight, across her shoulders.

"You're a lot heftier than Wayne is," she said. "He's tall and stringy. His best friend in the Marines is a nigger. What it is, he likes nigger music and nigger jokes. He can talk like one pretty good. After he got his car him and Otis Webb robbed every Coke machine in the county. People commenced rolling 'em inside at night. Otis had to go to reform school because he was sixteen and a nigger and the judge told Wayne he could either go to the pen or the Marines. Wayne took me out to eat at Otis's house one time and their floor was as clean as any shirt you got in your drawer. You're not even listening to me."

"Yes I am."

"Let me have a drag off that."

"This Wayne don't sound like much to me."

"Well, he's sorry in a lot of ways, I never said he wasn't, but he's got a kind heart. I'll say this, the world would be a better place to live and work in if everybody was as nice to niggers as Wayne."

"I guess you got your mind set on marrying him."

"I don't know if I do or not and that's the gospel truth. I don't know if I'm coming or going, my heart is so mixed up."

"What do you aim to do if he don't want to get married?"

"Well, I thought some about going and stay with my sister in Augusta and get in beautician school. She teaches at Mr. Lonnie's School of Hair Design. But she's so funny about people staying with her. She gets to where she sulls up and won't talk and slams doors. It's pure d. meanness is what is it. She needs somebody to just slap the snot out of her."

"You could go with me."

"Go with you and do what?"

"Just go with me. Go to Shreveport with me."

"You mean get *married*?"

"You don't have to get married to go to Shreveport with somebody."

"Boy, that's a good one."

"Well, you don't."

"Rita Lee Chipman does, hon."

"Maybe we'll get married then. When we get to Shreveport."

"You're just saying that."

"Naw I'm not."

"Yes you are."

"Naw I'm not. Really."

"I can't tell if you're serious or not, Norwood. I don't even know you. You meet somebody on a bus and ask them to marry you right off. You must think I'm just a plaything of love."

"Naw I don't."

"You don't even know me."

"I know you well enough."

"What do you like about me?"

"Well. A lot of things. I like the way you look."

"I'll tell you this, I don't like to have tricks played on me. I read a true story the other day about a girl that fell in love with a good looking novelties salesman and he took her to Louisville, Kentucky, and then run off and left her there at a motel that had a little swimming pool out front. She didn't know a soul in Louisville, Kentucky. She didn't hardly have a change of clothes. She was just walking around the streets there thinking every minute somebody was gonna jump out and get her."

"Did she go in that pool any?"

"Some woman from the courthouse come and got her and put her in a home. That's where she wrote the story from, it said."

"Well. I told you what I would do."

"I'd have to tell Wayne."

"You could write him a card."

"That wouldn't be right. Either way I'll have to go down there and talk to him."

"You want me to go with you?"

"You better just do what you want to do."

"I'll go down there with you then."

"I was wondering if you would say that."

"Right here is where your novelties salesman would back out."

"Norwood, I think I'm falling in love with you. If you were sick I would look after you and bathe you."

"Yeah, but don't talk so loud."

"I wonder if you really love me. Do you?"

"Yeah."

"Do you think you can say it?"

"I will sometime. Not on the bus."

"You don't mind saying it in a song, why can't you say it talking?"

"A song is different. You're just singing a song there."

"It's not hard for people who really mean it to say it."

"It is if somebody's trying to make you say it. When somebody gets your arm around behind you and wants to make you say 'calf rope,' well, you don't want to say it then."

They reached Jacksonville in the very early morning. The sun was not hot yet but it was bright and painful to their grainy eyes. A dozen or so Marines in limp khaki and with ruined shoeshines were hanging about the station waiting for the last liberty bus back. Fatigue and unhappiness were in their faces, as of young men whose shorts are bunching up. A city cop and an MP sat together in a squad car outside, slumped down in the seat, not talking, and too bored or tired even to go to the trouble of looking mean. Inside the station on a bench some mail-order baby chicks were cheeping away in a perforated box. Bargain chicks. No guarantee of sex, breed or color. Did anybody ever get fifty little roosters? Norwood and Rita Lee passed on through to the café and had an unpleasant breakfast.

Rita Lee was out of sorts. Her cheeks were red from all the nuzzling and she had rubbed them down with some powerful Noxzema. Norwood commented on the smell of that popular medicated cream.

"Maybe if you'd ever shave sometime I wouldn't have to use it," she said.

"I don't have all that stiff a beard."

"What happened to my face then?"

"I don't know. I can use a regular thin Gillette five times."

The waitress was at the end of the counter filling sugar dispensers with a scoop. "Hey Red," she called out, "is yall's sugar thing full?"

"Yeah, it's all right," said Norwood. "We already too sweet as it is anyway." This sally brought a chuckle from the waitress.

"I guess you'd like to take *her* to Shreveport with you," said Rita Lee.

"She don't have enough meat on her bones," he said.

Norwood's idea was to go through channels, to call the reception center at the base or the officer of the day and have this Wayne sent to the proper visiting place at the proper time. That was the way to go about it. Rita Lee didn't like the idea in that it alerted Wayne and gave him time to hide or flee. Her plan was simply to go out there and personally track him down and suddenly appear at his side. Norwood could not convince her that this was unrealistic thinking.

Yes, but that was the way she wanted to do it. And furthermore she didn't want him going out there with her now. Three exclamation marks appeared over Norwood's head. No, her mind was made up. He could wait on her here in town if he was of a mind to. She would be back whenever she got back.

"What time?" he said.

"How do I know? Why? You figuring on leaving?"

"Naw. I just wondered. So I could be here."

"I don't know how long I'll be."

"You ought to be back by dinnertime, don't you think?"

"I can't say because I don't know."

"Well, I'll be here looking for you about one."

"I wonder if you will be."

"Yeah, well I know I'll be here. You worry about your own self being here."

When the shuttle bus backed out of the dock Norwood waved bye to her with one finger. She looked at him but she didn't wave. He watched the bus until it was gone. She wouldn't be back and he had lost a day and $4.65 getting his ticket changed. *Take care of him and bathe him!* He would wait until one but no longer. Catch the first bus out.

He walked about town, down the long main street, but nothing much seemed to be open. The penny arcade was buttoned up tight. A long-armed Negro boy was squeegeeing the windows at Woolworth's, where they were having a Harvest of Values sale. The bargains were spilling out of a big gold foil cornucopia, and were artistically mixed in with one short ton of candy corn. Norwood's eye was attracted to the X-tra soft finespun cotton T-shirts with reinforced necks, three for $1.29.

"Will them T-shirts hold up?"

"Says whut?" said the squeegee boy.

"Them T-shirts you got on a special there, will they draw up on you after you wash 'em?"

"Uhruh, they'll all draw up some."

"That ain't a bad price. I might be back and get me a half a dozen of them dudes. I'm always out of T-shirts."

"You know you right? Man can't have too many of 'em."

Down the street a piece Norwood stopped at a hardware store, thinking he would go in and run his hand through the turnip seed and look at the knives and see how much shotgun shells cost in North Carolina. He shook the door but it was locked. So was the furniture store next door. There was a white card behind the door glass here with a phone number on it and it said call R. T. Baker in case of emergency. *Hello, Baker? I hate to bother you at home but I need a chair right now.* There was a tattoo parlor and Norwood looked at the dusty samples in the window. He had a $32.50 black panther rampant on his left shoulder, teeth bared and making little red claw marks on his arm. He had never been happy with it. Not because it was a tattoo and you couldn't get it off—so what?—but because it was not a good panther. Something about the eyes, they were not fully open, and the big jungle cat seemed to be yawning instead of snarling. Norwood complained at the time and the tattoo man in San Diego said it wouldn't look that way after it had scabbed over and healed. Once in Korea he sat down with some matches and a pin and tried to fix the eyes but only made them worse. Many times he wished he had gotten a small globe and anchor with a serpentine banner under it saying *U.S. Marines—First to Fight*. To have more than one tattoo was foolishness.

It got hotter and white town soon ran into nigger town. Norwood heard movement in one of the beer joints and he tried the door and it opened. A Negro woman was standing on a chair in there painting the wall dusty pink with a roller. "We closed, hat man," she said.

"Yeah?"

"It's off limits for you anyhow."

"It ain't nothing off limits for me. I ain't even in the service."

"Let in all civilians, Ernestine," said a funny quacking voice. "All save one."

Norwood was already inside. A big window fan was blowing hot air across the room. The woman got down from the chair grumbling and went to the door and made a fuss getting it latched. "You the last one coming in till I get that wall Kem-Toned, I don't care who it is. You better not be over the hill either."

The man with the funny voice was a midget of inestimable age. He was sitting on the end of the bowling machine runway with his legs crossed. On his face there was a Sydney Green-street look of weary petulance. He was wearing a seersucker suit, an untied black bow tie and some black and white wingtip shoes. "Do go on with your work, Lily," he said. "I'll keep tabs on this young man." He seemed to be drunk, or at least tight.

Norwood got a can of beer from the green cooler, which was an old Dr. Pepper box with a chunk of ice in it and some rusty cold water that made his hand hurt. *Do Not Set On Drink Box* said a handwritten sign that was taped to the side. Another one on the wall behind the counter, a bought one, said, IF YOU CAN GET CREDIT AT THE POST OFFICE YOU CAN GET CREDIT HERE. Norwood leaned on the box and drank his beer. It was good and cold.

"Are you staring at me, you lout?" said the midget.

Norwood turned away from him and watched the paint being rolled on.

"It's very rude, you know. No, you probably don't know. . . . Tell me, what is your I.Q.? It would interest me to know that figure. Do you even know? No, that's a foolish question."

Norwood turned back to him. "My service GCT was a hundred and twenty-five, shorty. All you got to have to get in OCS is a hundred and twenty. I thought it was a right good score myself."

"Ah, a rise. Now I demand to know your name."

"Yeah, well I'd like to know yours first."

"I see. So that's the way it is. I don't suppose you've ever heard of Edmund B. Ratner, the world's smallest perfect man?"

"I can't say I have, naw."

"That's a pity." He shook his can. "Look here, this is quite empty. Be a sport and fetch me one of those tall Buds. My foot is asleep."

Norwood looked at him for a moment, then got a beer out of the cooler and took it to him. "You're too kind," said the little man. "Sit down, sit down. Here's to your wonderful country." He took a long pull from the can. Norwood sat at a table. The man pooched his belly out and slapped it with both hands. It was a sizable paunch. "Disgusting, isn't it," he said. "I told you a lie a minute ago. I am not actually the world's smallest perfect man. Not any more. I *do* have reason to believe I am the world's smallest perfect *fat* man."

"Well, my GCT ain't a hundred and twenty-five either."

"That's very good. You're a better sort than I took you for."

"You not from around here, are you?"

"Good heavens no. I'm in show biz."

"I figured you must be with some circus."

"Yes, funny little chaps cavorting under the big top. Do you think all midgets work for circuses?"

"I figured *you* did."

"It's true enough, I did. I worked for all the best ones too. The Cirque d'Hiver, the Moscow State Circus, Ringling Brothers. All the rest are rubbish. But the truth of the matter is, my friend, I am now on the way down."

"I'm trying to get in show business myself. Hillbilly music. You probably don't like it."

"On the contrary, I do. Some of it. Hank what's his name—?"

"Hank Williams?"

"No."

"Hank Thompson?"

"No."

"Hank Locklin?"

"No."

"Hank Snow?"

"That's it, Hank Snow. . . . *'cause I got a pretty mama in Tennessee and I'm movin' on, I'll soon be gone.* . . . I once lived in a trailer with a geek, a man of heroic depravity, who played that record over and over. He couldn't hear it enough. He was a nasty drunk, a hopeless sort of fellow, always falling asleep with a cigarette and burning his blankets. Well, they wanted burning, I daresay, but I couldn't put up with that. Live with a firebug? It was out of the question. An absolute human wreck."

"Hank Snow's from Canada. The Singing Ranger."

"What, are you booked in some club here?"

"I never even been on a stage yet. I'm trying to get started."

"Oh, you'll make it. Stick with it. A matter of time, that's all."

"I hope so."

"No doubt about it. It's really quite funny in a way, our paths crossing like this. You're on the way up and I'm on the way down. Two curves on a graph intersecting at . . . this place. Well, that's a bit fanciful. I know I've had too much. But I'm not one of your garrulous, sentimental drunks, so you needn't worry on that score. Dramatizing themselves, as if anyone else cared. No, I've been on my own since I was a child. My father sold me when I was just a pup."

"Sold you?"

"Yes."

"I don't believe that."

"It's true, yes. He sold me to a man named Curly Hill. Those were *dreadful* times! My father, Solomon Ratner, was not an uneducated man but he was only a junior railway clerk and there were so many mouths to feed. And imagine, a midget in the house! Well, Curly came to town with his animal show—he toured all the fairs. He saw me at the station and asked me how I would like to wear a cowboy suit and ride an Irish wolfhound. He had a chimp named Bob doing it at the time. I directed him to my father and they came to terms. I never learned the price though I expect it was around twenty pounds, perhaps more. Now understand, I don't brood on it. Curly was like a second father to me, a very decent, humorous man. He came from good people. His mother was the oldest practical nurse in the United Kingdom. I saw her once, she looked like a mummy, poor thing. The pound was worth five dollars at that time."

"Are you with a circus here?"

"No, no, I thought I told you, I left circus work. Now that was a silly business. I let my appetite run away with me. I can't account for it, it came and it went. Pizzas, thick pastramis, chili dogs—nothing was too gross and I simply could *not* get enough. Some gland acting up. I grew four inches and gained almost two stone. Well, the upshot was, they took away my billing as World's Smallest Perfect Man and gave it to a little goon who calls himself Bumblebee Billy. I ask you! Bumblebee Billy! All his fingers are like toes. Needless to say, I was furious and I said some regrettable things to the boss. The long and short is, I was sacked altogether."

"Them are regular little hands you got."

"Of course they are."

"If you were out somewhere without anything else around, like a desert, and I was to start walking towards you I would walk right into you because I would think you were further off than what you were."

"I've never heard it put quite that way. Well, it's a matter of scale. I'm not a dwarf, you know."

"Maybe you don't like to talk about it."

"No, it's all right, I'm not the least bit sensitive. I do dislike the way newspapers throw the word around. 'Governor So-and-so is a moral midget.' That annoys me."

"What are you doing now?"

"What indeed. A good question. I would have to say nothing. I lived in New York for the past two years. Opening supermarkets, you know, with second-rate film cowboys. I was an Easter bunny for Macy's and a leprechaun in the St. Patrick's Day parade. That sort of thing. *Terrible!* I thought I had touched bottom. Then last month my agent persuaded me to join a U.S.O. troupe as stooge for this perfectly impossible comedian. You never heard such embarrassing blue jokes in your life. He has little pig eyes that glitter and burn with malice. Just an impossible man to work for. After last night's performance at the Marine post here we were driving back to town and whenever he would say anything I would answer, 'Yes, Mr. Pig Eyes' or 'No, Mr. Pig Eyes' or 'Is that so, Mr. Pig Eyes?' He slapped my face—he didn't hit me with his fist —he slapped me and I gave notice immediately and wired my agent for train fare to the Coast. I'm hopeful of getting some television work."

"You been here drinking all night?"

"Well, no, not here. In my room at the hotel. I was up there drinking gin and 7up and pacing about and trying to read a paperback book but I was much too upset to keep my mind on it. When the gin was gone I came out for some air and that colored lady there, Lily, God bless her, was kind enough to let me in. I'm still waiting for the money order."

They drank some more beer and ate boiled eggs and pickles. Edmund showed Norwood some clippings, a couple of them in laminated plastic, and some photographs. There was a picture of him and the beloved Curly surrounded by dogs, and one of him and a midget woman, both in fur hats, standing in front of the Kremlin. "I hated Russia," he said. "Such a dreary place! I'm bound to say though, in all fairness, that midgets are exempt from taxes there. Don't ask me why. One of Stalin's whims, I suppose." He also had a deck of miniature cards and he demonstrated a royal shuffle. Norwood told him about his trip and his plans and about waiting for Rita Lee.

"I guess that sounds pretty dumb to you."

"Not at all," said Edmund. "It rather depends on the girl, doesn't it? Do you love her?"

"Well, yeah."

"Then there's nothing more to be said. I take the simple view. You must marry her. Everyone should be married, and particularly in a vast and lonely country like this. I say that because I was once married myself."

"If she shows up."

"We had three lovely years together. She was Lithuanian, a fair girl, a little Baltic pearl. She was mad for sour cream. It all fell apart as things will, but still we had the three years. Such memories! She left me for my good friend, Laszlo the Cyclist. At least I thought he was my friend. It was very shabby treatment they gave me. Laszlo pretended to an interest in dominoes—that's my game—and it gave him access to our quarters, and opportunities. The thin end of the wedge. Perhaps I was to blame, I don't know. I have my moods. Well, afterward he came to me and said, 'I hope you are not angry.' There's cheek for you! I said, 'No, Laszlo, I am not angry, but I *am* hurt. You might have said something, you know. We can no longer be friends.' I was very sharp with him."

There was a barbecue shack across the street and Norwood wanted to get some spareribs but Edmund insisted on going back to the hotel because he was anxious to find out about the money. Also, he said, his "seat" was in the hotel dining room. He retied his bow tie without a mirror, put on a tan porkpie straw hat with colorful band, and they sauntered down the street in the noonday sun, this curious pair, Norwood throttling back on his normal pace.

The money had arrived. The desk clerk at the hotel gave Edmund the notice and said he would have to pick up the money itself at the Western Union office.

"Very good," said Edmund. "But I think Norwood and I shall have our lunch first. Can you recommend anything?"

"The meat loaf is all right."

"Splendid."

Edmund had dietetic pear salad and onion soup with croutons and the meat loaf and fried eggplant and blackberry cobbler with whipped cream. He sat up high on his padded riser. It was the kind of seat used to elevate small boys in barber chairs, except that Edmund's was a customized, collapsible model. Norwood had a DeLuxe Cheeseburger. The food was good and they ate without talking. From time to time there was laughter from an adjoining room where the local Lions were listening to a speech.

Shortly, out of a thoughtful silence, Norwood said, "What's the most you ever made as a midget?"

"Net or take-home?"

"That first."

"Two seventy-five a week."

"*Damn*."

"I thought it would last forever."

"That's a lot of money a week."

"I didn't save a dime."

"How was that meat loaf?"

"Very good. It wasn't jugged hare at Rule's but it was very good. The cobbler was excellent. You're not taking the train, are you?"

"The bus."

"How far west?"

"Well, to Memphis first."

"Do you know if the bus is a Vista-Dome?"

"I imagine it'll just be a regular bus."

"Well, see here, I don't know how to put this, exactly. I'm just a bit apprehensive about traveling cross-country in the States alone. It's silly, I know. Civilized country and all that. But you see, I once had a bad experience in Orange, New Jersey. I was all alone. It could have happened anywhere, of course. Mischievous boys, that's all. One of those things. What I'm driving at is this: Would you and your girl friend mind terribly if I sort of tagged along with you? That is, as far as Memphis?"

"Yeah, be glad to have you. The only thing is, I don't know when we'll be leaving. I might have to go out there to the base after her."

"It's an awful intrusion, I know. Still, I thought, better for you to be inconvenienced than me in a state of terror. I won't get in the way. Trust me on that. I realize three's a crowd."

"Well, not on a bus it ain't, so much."

"This is very good of you. I do carry a tear-gas fountain pen but I can't say it gives me much confidence. I just know it will misfire when I need it. And that's the kind of thing that would make a bully even madder."

The man at the Western Union office gave Edmund some trouble because he guessed wrong on the amount of the money order and because the name was spelled *Bat*ner on the wire. Edmund had asked for two hundred dollars but the agent had seen fit to send only one hundred dollars, along with a message saying NO MORE ADVANCES FAT MIDGET. SEE FARBER COASTWARD. MILT. Edmund went into a theatrical fury and slapped various cards and credentials down on the counter, which is to say up on the counter. The suspicious clerk examined them one by one, affecting to read all the print on them. It was clear that he disapproved of people whose affairs were so mismanaged they had to have money wired to them.

"Look here, sir," said Edmund, "consider the probabilities. Do you think it very likely that there are two fat midgets in this wretched backwater expecting money orders from New York, one named Edmund B. *Rat*ner and the other Edmund B. *Bat*ner? *Really!*"

"We have to be careful, bud. You run into some mighty funny things in this business."

"Nothing quite that funny, surely."

"If I make a mistake it's my ass, not yours."

"You *functionary.*"

The man satisfied himself that he was not being tricked by a cunning gang of midget money-order thieves and he unhappily released the money. Edmund got his bags at the hotel and they started for the bus station. On the way they were diverted into the penny arcade. Norwood looked in some disappointing viewers billed "Cuties on Parade" and "Watch Out! Hot Stuff!" and stamped his name on a metal disc, then threw it away because the metal was too trashy and light to suit him. They shot at an electric bear with an electric rifle and made him growl. No one else was in the place except the woman in the change booth. Just outside the arcade on the sidewalk there was a gaudy, circus-looking cage affair. A Dominique hen was imprisoned in it. She was wearing a tiny scholar's mortarboard on her head with a rubber band holding it in place. The sign said:

JOANN THE WONDER HEN
THE COLLEGE EDUCATED CHICKEN

ASK JOANN ANY YES OR NO QUESTION
DEPOSIT NICKEL AND SEE ANSWER BELOW

Joann moved nervously from side to side in her tight quarters. Her speckled plumage was all ruffled up around her neck and in other places it looked damp and sagged. She was hot. There was a crazed look in her eyes.

"Poor devil," said Edmund. "I know just how she feels. This is *criminal.*"

Norwood was getting a nickel ready. "I guess you have to ask her your question out loud."

"Yes, certainly," said Edmund. "And I would pose it as simply as possible."

Norwood stooped over to face the chicken. "Here's my question," he said, then decided not to ask it aloud after all. He inserted the nickel. A light flashed, something buzzed and Joann reached down in the corner and pulled a lanyard with her beak. More buzzing. A white slip of paper emerged from a slit below. The answer was printed on it in dim purple ink. *Charity Endureth All Things.* Norwood studied it, then showed it to Edmund.

"That's hardly a yes or no," he said. "I don't like this kind of thing. They could at least take her out of the sun."

Norwood ran a fingernail across the wire mesh and made affectionate whistling noises at Joann.

Rita Lee was waiting at the station, her face swollen from crying. "I thought you'd gone without me," she said. Norwood started to kiss her, wanted to kiss her, then thought better of it with so many people around and gave her an Indian brave clasp on the shoulder instead. "Wayne is out in the Mediterranean Sea with the Seventh Fleet," she went on, now crying again. "But I didn't care any more. I wanted to go with you all the time. I should of listened to what my heart was telling me last night." She looked up at Norwood through tear-misted eyes and her hands were trembling in the magic and wonder of the moment.

"I think you must mean the *Sixth* Fleet," said Norwood. "The *Seventh* Fleet is out in the Pacific. They don't have anything to do with the *Second* Marine Division."

Edmund was standing off at a discreet distance looking at the books in a revolving rack. Norwood said, "That midget over there, he's going with us as far as Memphis."

Rita Lee looked at him. "You mean *him?*"

"Yeah."

"What for? Who is he?"

"His name is Edmund and he used to work for a circus. His folks sold him. He's going to California now and he's so little he's afraid somebody is liable to go up side his head on the way. You be nice to him."

He took her over for introductions. "A pleasure, I'm sure," said Edmund. "I've heard so many nice things about you."

Rita Lee was wiping her face with a handkerchief. "I hate for you to see me looking like this."

"Oh pooh, you look very sweet if I may say so."

"That's a nice summer suit," she said. "I like your whole outfit. It's very attractive. You look like a little businessman."

"You're altogether too kind."

There was a wait for the bus. Edmund put on his glasses and got out some thick blue notepaper and shook his fountain pen a couple of times—the regular one—and wrote letters. Rita Lee and Norwood sat next to him in the folding seats and held hands, squeezing now and then, until it became moist and uncomfortable. She got up and wandered around, to the ladies' room and the newsstand. Norwood talked to a man who said water tables were dropping all over the country. Rita Lee came back with a frozen Milky Way and some confession magazines and comic books. She read about a miser duck called Uncle Scrooge, and his young duck nephews, whose adventures took place in a city where all the bystanders, the figures on the street, were anthropoid dogs walking erect. Norwood read about Superman and the double-breasted-suited Metropolis underworld. It was a kryptonite story and not a bad one. He went through the book in no time at all and rolled it up and stuck it in his hip pocket. "Did you ever see that dude on television?" he said.

Rita Lee looked up with annoyance from her duck book. "Who?"

"Superman."

"Yeah and I know what you're going to say, he killed himself, the one that played Superman."

"It looks all right when you're reading it. I didn't believe none of it on television."

"You're not supposed to really believe it."

"You're supposed to believe it a little bit. I didn't believe none of it."

When their bus was called Norwood was looking around for a big paper sack, but he couldn't find one. He borrowed Rita Lee's shopping bag and tamped the clothes down in it hard and tight. "You and Edmund take my stuff and get on the bus and get us a seat. I'll be right back." He didn't wait for an answer. He walked quickly down the street to the penny arcade and opened the trap door behind Joann's cage and took her out and put her in the bag. The woman from the change booth came out and said, "What do you think you're doing?"

"I come to get this chicken," he said.

"Oh yeah? What for?"

He draped a smooth nylon slip over Joann's head. "I got to give her a shot."

"Oh yeah?"

He walked quickly back to the station and boarded the bus. The driver punched his ticket without looking twice at the mystery parcel. Norwood made his way back to where Rita Lee was waving and sat down beside her. He put the bag on the floor between his feet and lifted the slip just enough to expose Joann's head. Rita Lee looked on with incomprehension. "It's a Dominecker chicken on my clothes," she said. From across the aisle Edmund was peering over his glasses. "Norwood, how very plucky!"

"I don't want her on my clothes."

"Don't you like chickens?"

"I hate chickens. They have mites. They're filthy dirty nasty things. All they do is mess up the yard."

"This one has had training," said Edmund.

"I don't care nothing about that."

"I like chickens," said Norwood. "You can go in a chicken house at night and they're all sitting there on them poles facing the front like they was riding an elevator."

"Norwood, I don't want that chicken on my clothes. You hear?"

"There's plenty of room over here," said Edmund.

Norwood lifted Joann from the bag and passed her across. Edmund placed her beside him in a sitting position, her feet splayed out in front and her head upright against the back of the seat. It was an extraordinary position for a chicken but Joann was dazed and limp from all the excitement. Rita Lee began to shake out her clothes.

Norwood soon fell asleep, drowsy from the beer and food and movement. Rita Lee and Edmund talked about horror movies and ate their way steadily through the Great Smoky Mountains. At each rest stop the ravenous little man would get off and bring back new supplies of Cokes and corn chips and Nabs crackers.

Just before dark Norwood was roused from his nap by a small boy in wheat jeans who was causing an offensive disturbance. The nature of the disturbance was this: the boy was running up and down the aisle making the sounds of breaking wind by pumping down on a hand cupped under his armpit. Norwood tripped him and jerked him up and shook him and sent him crying to his grandmother.

Rita Lee said, "That was mean, Norwood."

"Well, that kid was out of line."

"You didn't get your nap out and you're cross."

He stretched and looked over at Edmund and Joann.

"I gave her some water from a paper cup," said Edmund. "I broke up some peanuts for her too but she won't eat. I do think she's coming around though."

"Yall get along pretty good," said Norwood. "You ought to take her out to Hollywood with you. Get her in television."

"I expect I'll have my hands full getting myself into television."

"She's plenty smart for a chicken."

"There's no question about it. I'm sure a good agent could get her something. Perhaps some small role in an Erskine Caldwell film."

"Norwood?" said Rita Lee, who was rubbing a finger over the scar on the back of his neck.

"What?"

"I know what kind of ring I want. It doesn't cost a whole lot either. It's one diamond in the middle and two little ones on the sides with things like vines holding 'em on."

"That's what we'll get then."

"You know what would be nice? Listen to this. What we ought to do is get us some Western outfits that would be just alike except mine would be for a girl. You see, they would match. Then when we have a little boy we'll get him one too. Oh yeah, and if it's a girl I want to name her Bonita. I could probably make hers myself. Anyway we'll all be dressed just alike when we go to church and everything."

"I don't like that idea much."

"Why not?"

"I just don't."

"You didn't get your nap out and you're cross."

That night a suicidal owl flew into the windshield but didn't break it and later they saw a house or a barn burning out in an open field. No one seemed to be around it trying to put it out. Still later, seat trouble developed. A sleepy sailor up front sat down on a milkshake left in his seat by a thoughtless child and was forced to look for a dry seat.

Edmund stirred just in time to keep him from sitting on Joann. "I'm sorry," he said, holding his hand over her, "this seat is occupied."

The sailor was a second class bosun's mate with embroidered dragons on his turned-back cuffs and a lot of wrist hair. He looked closer. "That's a chicken," he declared. "You can't save a seat for a chicken. You'll have to put her on the floor, little boy."

Norwood got hold of the sailor's jumper and turned him around. "That ain't a boy, it's a man. You better get you some glasses. Don't sit on that chicken either."

"You think I'm gonna stand up while a chicken sits down? Well, you got another think coming."

"Go find you another seat."

"There ain't any more."

"What happened to the one you had?"

"There's ice cream in it if it's any of your business."

"I might make it some of my business."

"Yeah, well you'll need some help."

"I don't think so."

Rita Lee was frightened. "Norwood didn't get his nap out," she explained to the sailor.

"We'll see what the driver has to say about this," he said.

"Here, there's no need for that," said Edmund. "I can make room for Joann in my seat. Let's not have any more unpleasantness."

Memphis.

Edmund was standing outside the phone booth protesting. "No, really now, I say, it's too much of an imposition—"

"Hush and be still a minute," said Norwood. He sat down in the booth and closed the glass door. Inside on the pebbled, we-defy-you-to-write-on-this wall someone with an icepick had scratched THE USAF IS CRAP in jerky, angular letters. Under that was WE DIE FOR YOU GUYS—AIRMAN, and under that, YEAH IN CAR WRECKS. Norwood got the operator. She said it would be a quarter for three minutes.

The woman who talked fast answered.

"KWOT is the lucky bucks station," she said.

"Hello," said Norwood.

"Is this KWOT?"

"This is Norwood Pratt over in the Memphis bus station."

"Who are you?"

"I want to talk to Joe William Reese."

"He's outside skinning catfish."

"Can you get him to the phone?"

"I don't know." She left.

Norwood waited. The operator asked for another quarter. Then another. His ear reddened and got hot and stuck to his head. He shifted the phone to the other side.

Presently, a voice. "Hello, hello, anybody there?"

"Joe William Reese?"

"Yes, speaking."

"This is First Sergeant Brown at Headquarters, Marine Corps. We've been looking over our books up here and it looks like we owe you some money."

"Yeah? How much?"

"Our books say two thousand and sixty dollars."

"All right, who is this?"

"I told the Commandant you'd probably want to give it to the Navy Relief since you never did give any on payday."

"*Norwood.* Where in the hell are you?"

"I'm over here at Memphis in the bus station."

"What are you doing in Memphis?"

"Nothing. Just passing through. I thought I'd stop by and see you. I been waiting on this phone all day. Some old woman went to get you."

"Oh. Grandmother. She's not supposed to answer the phone. You're just in time. We're having a family fish fry this evening. Do you like frog legs?"

"Not much, naw."

"Well, there's plenty of catfish. You should have been with us last night. We caught a mess of 'em. Two trot lines."

"Did the turtles get your bait?"

"No, they weren't too active last night. I think they were all attending a meeting somewhere. Look, it'll take me about forty-five minutes to get there. You be over in front of the Peabody Hotel. That's right across from where you are."

"Okay. I got a—"

"We might bust a watermelon later, you can't tell. Spit seeds on the girls and make 'em cry."

"Wait a minute. Hold on a minute. I got a couple of people with me. Is it okay if they come?"

"I don't see why not."

"One of 'em is a girl."

"That's fine. Anybody I know?"

"Naw, it's just a girl. I met her a couple of days ago. We're thinking about getting married when we get home."

"Boy, that was fast work. What did you do, pick her up on a bus?"

"Yeah."

"Well sure, bring her on."

"Is there some special place you're supposed to get a wife?"

"No, I guess they're just wherever you find 'em. Buses, drugstores, VFW huts. Don't be so touchy."

"She's good looking. You never seen me with a girl that looked this good before."

"She sounds like a sweetheart, Norwood. Maybe we can get something in the paper about it: *Mr. Pratt Reveals Plans.*"

"This othern is a midget."

"I didn't get that."

"I say this othern with me, he's a midget."

"I don't follow. You mean a short guy?"

"Yeah, well he's short all right but he's not *just* short, he's a midget. He used to be in a circus. You know, a midget. His folks sold him."

"But not to you?"

"Naw, *hell*, Joe William. They sold him when he was a boy. He's about forty-eight years old."

"Okay. Whatever you say. Is there anybody else? Any Japanese exchange students?"

"Naw, that's all. Have you got my money?"

"Yes, I have, I've got it. I'm working. I've been meaning to send it to you. I'm checking cotton acreage."

"That's that government job?"

"Yeah."

"They pay straight time, don't they?"

"No, it's by the hour."

"How much?"

"Two dollars. Sixteen bucks a day, no overtime."

"That's not bad."

"Yeah, it's okay. You furnish your own car."

"You get mileage?"

"No."

"Do you have to have a education?"

"No, not really. You have to carry a stick. Killer dogs lope out from under houses when you drive up."

"I got a chicken over here too. I forgot about her. Have you got some place to put her over there?"

"Look, maybe I better charter a bus for your group."

"Don't get smart about it. This ain't a regular chicken. I wouldn't be carrying just a plain chicken around."

"No, I'm sure there's a good reason why you're traveling with a chicken. But I can't think what it is."

"Well, it's too long to explain over the phone. She was in a box in North Carolina answering questions and it was hot in there."

"I see."

"How's the girl?"

"She's fine. I think she's decided I'm about as good as she's going to do."

Mr. Reese cooked the fish in two iron skillets on a barbecue furnace, which was under a big black walnut tree. The walnuts were scattered underfoot and looked like rotten baseballs. Mr. Reese was a rangy, worried man in khakis. He knew his business with the meal sack and the grease and the fish, never turning them until it was just the right time. He talked to Edmund at length about a staging area he had passed through in Northern Ireland in 1944 and said he had always admired the English for their bulldog qualities.

The front yard was twenty acres or so of Johnson grass with some polled Herefords grazing on it, two of them standing belly deep in a brown, warm-looking pond, for what comfort was in it. Mr. Reese said Johnson grass had a much higher protein value than people thought and that it played an important role in his feeding program. He was uneasy and defensive, and seemed to be afraid that Edmund was secretly amused at his farming methods. By way of changing the subject he said, "I've got eighty paper-shell pecan trees I'd like to show you before dark."

"I'd very much like to see them," said Edmund.

"Of course they're not all that much to look at. They're just trees."

Edmund had bathed and changed and was now wearing white linen slacks and a navy blue blazer, which he kept thumping lint from.

The house was a sprawling 1928 story-and-a-half nature's-bounty farmhouse, done over with Johns-Manville asbestos shingles ("Not One Has Ever Burned."). The front porch was long and wrapped halfway around one side of the house and there were two swings on it. The rich girl Kay sat in one and made room for Norwood but he said he didn't like to sit in a swing and eat. He had never had any meals in a swing but it was something to say. He sat doubled up in a deck chair, hunched forward and holding the paper plate on the floor between his shoes. He cleaned his bones like a cat and made a neat pile of them. He didn't want this girl to think he made a mess when he ate, whatever else she might think. They watched as Joe William made a howling, dusty departure in her Thunderbird.

"He's ruining my tires," she said.

"It ain't helping your bad universal joint none either," said Norwood.

"What's that?"

"It's a thing on the end of the drive shaft. Yours is shot. Can't you hear that clicking? They don't grease them U-joints like they ought to and them little needle bearings just freeze up in there."

"I better get it fixed."

"You'll have to take that whole shaft out. You know where that brace is right there in the middle that holds that carrier bearing study?"

"No, I don't."

"Well, there's two bolts under there that hold that brace to the frame and if you're not careful you'll twist 'em off trying to get 'em out. And right there's where you got trouble."

"In that case I think I'll have someone else do it. I didn't know you were a mechanic."

"Well, I'm just a shade tree mechanic. I can do things like that. I'd be too slow to make a living at it."

"Have a Fig Newton."

"I don't believe I will, thanks. This fish was aplenty. I never was much to eat a cake."

"Joe William owes you some money, doesn't he?"

"Well, he did. He paid me."

"How much was it?"

"Seventy dollars."

"I hope you won't lend him any more."

"You don't have to worry none about that."

"I keep thinking he'll grow up or whatever he needs to do."

"Are you gonna marry him or what?"

"How did that come up?"

"He's a pretty good old boy when you get right down to it."

"I'm not so sure of that."

"A lot of girls would be proud to get him. He had a really good-looking one out in California. She was crazy about him. She had a car too and she'd always fix me up with somebody and we'd go up to the Compton Barn Dance. We had some good times."

"Yeah, that divorcee with the name. I've seen her picture. She has fat arms. Boots or Tuffy or something."

"Teeny."

"I can just see those two together. The blond bombshell and him with his comic patter."

"She looked pretty good to me."

Mrs. Whichcoat filled Rita Lee in on the judge and told her all about the Butterfields. She told about the one who ran up an eleven-hundred-dollar candy bill in Memphis and forced the family to sell a slave to pay it, and about the one who drained the swamps and how he agitated unsuccessfully for a public statue of himself in the square, like the one of Popeye in the Texas spinach capital.

"They all pulled out and went down to Louisiana later, and just made a world of money doing something," she said. "I forget now what it was. They knew how to make money, you have to give them that. How do you like that fish?"

"Oh, it's so good," said Rita Lee.

"I bet you never had any that good where you're from."

"No ma'am, I sure didn't."

"It's not as good as some we've had. Is this your first trip to Arkansas, Wilma Jean?"

"Yes ma'am, it is," said Rita Lee. "Except to Virginia it's my first real long trip anywhere. I been in seven states now."

"Dick Powell is from Arkansas."

"He is? I didn't know that. Dick Powell."

"You can *see* seven states from Rock City," said Mr. Reese. "At least that's what all those bumper signs say. You couldn't prove it by me."

Mrs. Whichcoat turned on Edmund. "Did you ever run across a Dr. Butterfield in Wales?"

"No, but then I've never been in Wales, madam. Unless you count Monmouthshire. Curly hated Wales."

"He was a leading practitioner in some well-known city there," she said. "I can't remember which one. Cousin Mattie corresponded with him for quite a long time. Lord, he may be dead now. That was about 1912. The preachers nearly drove us all crazy then talking about the tariff. You don't hear anything about that any more. They're all on integration now."

Mr. Reese wiped his hands on his apron and searched the skies. He said he would be surprised if they didn't get a shower sometime in the night. "That low started moving in here about four-thirty."

He knew this because he had a thermometer-barometer on the front porch by the door. It was a big tin affair meant to hang on a storefront. There was an orange rooster on it, smiling, so far as a rooster can be made to smile, and crowing about Marvel cigarettes. The Snopesian tackiness of the thing was painful to Mrs. Reese. Mr. Reese took frequent readings and thought about them.

Mrs. Reese did not come outside until the sun was behind the trees because of her skin. She ate some coleslaw and went about being hospitable in her distant way. There were dark pouches under her eyes which an indoor existence and an uncommon amount of sleep did not help much. Things had not worked out well for her. The young planter she thought she was marrying turned out to be a farmer. Her mother got on her nerves. Instead of the gentle Lew Ayres doctor son she had counted on, the Lord had given her a poolroom clown. She claimed descent from the usurper Cromwell and she read a long paper once on her connections at a gathering of Confederate Daughters, all but emptying the ballroom of the Albert Pike Hotel in Little Rock. This was no small feat considering the tolerance level of a group who had sat unprotesting through two days of odes and diaries and recipes for the favorite dishes of General Pat Cleburne. She often managed to leave the impression that she was in Arkansas through some mistake and it was her belief, perhaps true, that only common people had piles.

Edmund and Joe William had to eat the frog legs. No one else would touch them, tasty morsels, although there was a lot of talk about how they were "considered a delicacy" and about how much you would pay for them in a good restaurant. Mrs. Whichcoat sacked up all the fishbones for burning, to keep them from the dogs, and gathered what was left of the cornbread balls for her laying hens.

Mrs. Reese said, "Do you have any new hens, Mama?"

Mrs. Whichcoat did not answer at once. For some time now people had been closing in on her. She knew how quickly one of these casual openings could land her in a jam. Had she left the gas on again? Was this a new attack on her open range poultry policy? She considered several incriminating possibilities. "No, just the same old ones," she said.

"It's very strange," said Mrs. Reese. "I was looking out the bathroom window while ago and I thought I saw a gray one out there with a hat on."

"That one belongs to Norwood," said Joe William. "It's a wonder chicken he brought in from North Carolina."

"Oh, it belongs to *these* people," she said. "I wondered. I couldn't imagine."

"That's pretty funny," said Mr. Reese. "A chicken wearing a hat. I never heard of anything like that before. I guess there's a first time for everything though."

Later Norwood and Rita Lee went around back to check on the subject of all this fun. There she was, squatting in the dust alone, shunned by the other chickens. Norwood held her beak down in a mossy skillet under a faucet. After a few dunkings she drank a little. He found some translucent worms on a chinaberry tree and held them in his hand and tried to get her to eat. She didn't want any. He talked to her and told her they were good and compared them to Safeway grapes. "All right, I'm on give 'em to Rita Lee then. She likes 'em."

"Get away from me," said Rita Lee.

He took the mortarboard off Joann's head but she still wouldn't eat.

Rita Lee said, "Have you ever hypnotized a chicken?"

"I never have."

"You can do it."

"How?"

"Let me see her."

"Wait a minute."

"It won't hurt her. They come right on out of it."

She held Joann's chinless head down to the ground and slowly traced a line in the dust in front of her eyes. A few seconds of this and the chicken lay in position, transfixed.

Norwood said, "I'll be a son of a bitch."

He tried it himself and soon they had all eleven of Mrs. Whichcoat's Rhode Island Reds lying about stupefied. He looked at them, then arranged four or five in a single rank and stood in front of them. "Congratulations, men," he said. "Yall keep up the good work. The skipper just come through the squad bay and there was little piles of crap all over the deck."

"You're silly, Norwood, you know that?"

"I think I'm on take her on with us."

"You're going back on your word."

"I know but she don't get along here with them red pullets."

That night it rained. The wind came up and billowed the curtains and the birds stopped their noise and there was one lone rumble of thunder and then rain. Norwood heard people putting windows down. He waited. Water was dripping outside his window on a piece of tin. When things got quiet again he got up and put on his pants and his gaiters and took a penny box of matches from his shirt pocket and went out in the hall. Rita Lee's room was down at the end by the bathroom.

There were unaccountable cold spots in the hall, as in a spring-fed lake. He stood outside the door for a moment and started to knock, then decided no and quietly opened the door. There was a headboard bumping noise and a frantic scrambling movement on the bed table.

"Hey," he said in a half whisper, "it's me."

"Who is it?" said Edmund. "Who's there?"

Norwood struck a match. Edmund was crouched back against the headboard with his fountain pen at his side. He was wearing shorty pajamas of a golden hue.

"Oh. I was looking for Rita Lee."

"Did you think she was in here?"

"Ain't this her room?"

"No, she's across the hall."

"Oh."

"You certainly gave me a fright."

"I didn't mean to wake you up."

"Well, no harm done." He scratched his head vigorously, giving it a sixty-second workout. "I've still got soap in my hair. Their water is extremely hard."

"I didn't notice that."

"Yes, you can taste it. Very high mineral content."

"Well, I'll let you get back to sleep."

"Did you get your money?"

"Yeah, he paid me."

"Well, look here, do you think you could lend me fifty dollars? I'll have it back to you in two weeks. That's a solemn promise, Norwood. You see, I'm going to be in rather a bind. I've been lying here figuring."

"I'd have to have it back."

"Yes, yes, of course. I feel like an absolute rat but I had no one else to turn to."

"When could I get it back?"

"Two weeks, I swear it."

"Okay. Two weeks."

Norwood took five tens from his billfold and laid them on the foot of the bed. Edmund put on his glasses and got his memo book, chattering all the time, and made a to-do about entering the correct address in his memo book.

"No street, just Ralph?"

"Yeah, that's all. We get our mail at the post office."

Edmund wrote down another address, one in Los Angeles, and tore that sheet from the memo book and crawled to the foot of the bed and handed it to Norwood. "You can always get in touch with me through this chap." He picked up the money. "You're a jewel, Norwood. A veritable precious stone."

Norwood looked at the little torn page. "What will I need to get in touch with you for?"

"Well, you won't, of course. But if you do, there it is."

"Just so I get it back."

"You can count on it. Please trust me on this."

Norwood left and closed the door, the crawling golden vision still in his brain. He crossed the hall and entered Rita Lee's room. "Hey, it's me," he said. She turned on the bed light and turned it off again. He caught only the briefest glimpse of legs and red slip and arms. He struck a match. Now she was under the sheet and had it pulled up under her chin.

"I thought I'd look in on you."

"What for?"

"Well, it was raining. I thought you might be scared."

"I'm not scared of rain. Nobody is."

"There was some lightning too. In here by yourself and everything. I didn't know."

"All I know is I'm about to burn up in this feather bed. You sink right down in it."

"How's your bed?"

"I just got through saying. It's hot."

He struck another match. Outside some night birds had started up again: *ChipOutOfTheWhiteOak . . . TedFioRito. . . .* Whippoorwills. How did two certain birds get together? And then what?

"Norwood, listen hon, somebody is liable to come along."

"Okay."

"Hear? You go on back now."

"I will in a minute."

"No, right now."

"Okay."

"I haven't even got my ring yet."

"Okay."

"Hear?"

"I was laying there in bed thinking about something, Rita Lee."

"What was it?"

"Well, when we get home and get squared away I'm on take

you out to dinner. I'm twenty-three years old and I never taken a girl out to dinner in my life except drive-ins. What I mean is supper but they always call it dinner."

"That'll sure be nice. Do you like Mexican food with a lot of hot stuff on it?"

"Yeah."

"I do too. Listen, here's what I'd like to do: I'd like to live in a trailer and play records all night. See, we'd be in there together with our little kitchen and everything. You can fix those things up pretty nice inside."

"I don't know about a trailer."

"I don't think they cost a whole lot. We could get a used one."

"We'll see about it."

Mrs. Reese gave Rita Lee some sheets and towels and other odds and ends and a jumbo black suitcase with straps on the outside, not a new one but serviceable enough. She also gave her a little talk. Joe William got up late and came in the kitchen and Norwood was sitting there at the table by himself drinking coffee with his hat on and whistling "My Filipino Baby."

"Good morning."

"I figured you'd be out checking cotton today."

"No, not on Saturdays. Sometimes half a day. I've got to do a quick recheck on a colored guy this afternoon but it won't take long. Where's the incredible shrinking man?"

"He's gone. He got up real early and your daddy took him to catch the bus."

"Flew the coop, huh? Well, he was a nice little guy."

"Yeah."

"You want some toast?"

"I already ate."

Mrs. Whichcoat came in the back door with an empty wire basket. She hung it up in the pantry and took off her brown garden gloves. "All the hens have stopped laying," she said. "I didn't get one egg." There was a note of despair in her voice but no surprise. It was as though she had warned all along that there would be treachery one day in the hen house. She went in the living room and turned on the television set.

Norwood said, "We got to get on down the road our own selves."

"You're not leaving today?"

"Yeah, we got to get on."

"You might as well stay the weekend now. I thought we'd go over to Memphis tonight."

"I been on the road too long as it is."

"You want some more coffee?"

"Yeah. Have you got a box or something around here I can carry that chicken in?"

"I expect we can find something."

"How much longer does your job last?"

"Another couple of weeks. Maybe three."

"Is it very hard?"

"No, not usually. We're checking plow-ups now. We go out and make sure they've destroyed what they overplanted. They all overplant. I've got a headache with this one colored guy. You can't tell what he's plowed up. He doesn't have it planted in rectangular fields like everyone else, he's got it in trapezoids and ovals with tomatoes and pole beans running all through it so there's no way you can measure it unless you're Dr. Vannevar Bush. He knows I'll get tired pretty soon and say, Yeah it's okay. Well, they screw him on the allotment anyway. I don't blame him."

"That sounds too hard."

"It's not really."

"I wisht I was home right now."

"Are you going direct to Shreveport?"

"Naw, Ralph first. I'll have to leave Rita Lee there at home for a while and go scout it out."

They drove out to a slough and shot at snakes and cypress knees for an hour or so. After lunch they looked through some stuff in the garage and found a long narrow cage suitable for Joann to travel in. It had once served as a humane catch-'em-alive mink trap, and in fact no mink had ever entered it, such was its humanity. Kay came by in her powerful Thunderbird which nobody in town really wanted to insure and they loaded up and drove downtown and parked under the bus stop sign in front of Junior's EAT Café. Kay gave Rita Lee a little gift-wrapped box with a ribbon on it.

She opened it. "Hey, a cigarette lighter. This is really nice. Thanks."

"That's just what they needed, Kay, an onyx table lighter."

"How do you know what they need? Besides, it's a good one. It's butane."

They sat in the car with the doors open and ate ice cream sandwiches. A young carpenter in striped overalls and with nails in his mouth was fixing Junior's sagging front porch with some new yellow two-by-fours. He had brought his kids to work with him and they were in the cab of a pickup. A little girl with sandy hair was hanging out the window backwards and shaking her head from side to side. "Boy, it looks like the world is blowing up," she said. Kay said, "Don't do that, sugar, it'll make you sick." Two stores down, at Kroger's, a teen-age meat cutter came outside and looked around and then rolled his apron up and leaned back against the building with one foot up and smoked a cigarette.

The little sandy-haired girl said, "Hey Daddy, come here."

"I'll be there in a minute."

"Come here now."

"What is it?"

"Randolph wants to peepee."

"Well, you can help him."

"Yeah, but I don't want to, Daddy."

"Aw *hell.*"

The bus came and Norwood and Rita Lee got on with their plunder and Norwood came back up front and stood on the step. Joe William said, "Let me know how you make out down there with Roy Acuff and Hank Williams and all those guys."

"Roy Acuff is in Nashville, Tennessee, and Hank Williams is dead. He's been dead."

"Well, whoever it is. Look, champ, I'm sorry I took so long on the dough."

"That's all right. Yall will have to come see us when we get us a place."

"Yeah, I'd like to. We'll see what happens. I don't know. You can see how it is here, touch and go. Come back when you can stay longer."

"I'll see you sometime, tush hog. You take it easy."

"Okay."

THE AIR conditioning felt good. Rita Lee got the window seat. She read stories in her love magazines about a lot of whiny girls who couldn't tell the difference between novelties salesmen and Norwoods. *What dopes!* They could expect no more sympathy from Rita Lee, she who had wept bitter tears with them. Along in the back pages of one magazine she ran across an interesting ad. It offered, by mail and on easy terms, a $79.95 wedding set, complete with solitaire diamond engagement ring of unspecified caratage, and two gold bands. *Rush me free booklet of bargains,* said the coupon, *and tell me how high volume sales can mean BIG SAVINGS for me—instead of BIG PROFITS for the jeweler!* The ad showed a man in a Stetson with a jeweler's glass in his eye. He was holding two six-guns and blasting away over his head at some exploding balloons labeled *High Diamond Prices.* Under the man were the words *Yes, Grady Fring is bringing them DOWN!* Rita Lee tore the ad out and put it away. She would discuss it with Norwood later, at a good time. It was not the kind of thing to interrupt him with.

She also saw an interesting sight. On a curve not far from Little Rock a busload of Elks had turned over. The bus was on its right side in the ditch, the front wheels still slowly turning, and the Elks were surfacing one at a time through the escape hatch on the left side, now topside. One Elk lying on the grass, maybe dead, no ball game for him, and others were limping and hopping about and holding their heads. Another one, in torn shirt-sleeves, was sitting on a suitcase on top of the bus. He was not lifting a finger to help but as each surviving brother Elk stuck his head up through the hatchway, he gave a long salute from his compressed-air horn. The big Trailways cruiser began to slow down. When the man saw this he turned with his noise device and hooted it—there could be no mistake—at the driver. Norwood was talking to a man with bulging eyes across the aisle who had gone broke in Mississippi selling premium beer for $3.95 a case on credit, and they both missed it, that hooting part. They did help load the injured into ambulances. The former tavern keeper found a silver dollar in the grass and kept it.

In Texarkana that night Norwood called the Nipper station in Ralph and asked Clyde Rainey to go down to the house and tell Vernell he was over here at the bus station and to come pick him up in the Fleetline. Clyde expressed fears about the Fleetline. He said he could send a boy over in the service truck to get him. He would be glad to do it. Norwood said no, that was all right, just tell Vernell to take it easy.

Rita Lee said, "How long will it take?"

"A good hour," said Norwood. He gave Joann some water and then assembled all their gear in a pile against the wall. They sat down to wait. Norwood didn't see Tilmon Fring over by the pinball machines. Tilmon was watching the games with his hands in his pockets. He was wearing the same suit coat and he still had the orange pack of cigarette papers in his hat like a jaunty press card.

Rita Lee said, "What kind of present have you got for your sister?"

Norwood said, "Nothing."

"You ought to get her something, hon. Even a little something. Girls love to get presents."

"I guess I ought to."

Norwood didn't want to leave their baggage unattended but Rita Lee said she didn't think anyone would bother it since there was a chicken with it. Norwood couldn't figure that one out. They left it there unwatched anyway and walked a few blocks and found a drugstore open. He bought a box of chocolate-covered cherries that was on sale. It didn't look like much when he got it in a sack, away from the display, so he bought a small pillow to put with it, a blue shiny one with fringe on it and a picture of the post office standing astride two states, and the words "Greetings From Texarkana, U.S.A., Home of the Red River Arsenal." It too was on sale. He didn't get Bill Bird anything.

Rita Lee said, "What does your sister look like? Does she look anything like you?"

Norwood said, "Some." He showed her a snapshot from his billfold.

Rita Lee studied it. "People with fat faces have to be careful how they fix their hair," she said. "What's she doing in this junkyard?"

"That's where we live."

"Where's the house? I don't see air a house."

"It's off out there to the side. You can just see the corner of the back porch there the other side of where that dog is standing. The yard don't look like that now. I cleaned it up a whole lot."

"He looks like he'd be a good little watchdog. What is his name?"

"It *was* Buster. I don't know what it is now. He just showed up at the station one day and I kept him. I got him vaccinated and put a collar on him and he stayed about a year and then left again. I never could find that scamp."

"Some nigger probably got him. They'll pick up a little house dog."

"Might of. Or got run over."

"Norwood, listen, how long does it take to get married in Texas?"

"I don't know. I don't think very long."

"I mean getting the papers and all that. Everything."

"I know what you mean but I don't know how long it takes. Two or three days, I guess. Vernell got married in Arkansas. She's got her license up over her bed."

"I wisht we'd hurry up and get where we're going. My eyes hurt."

"We'll be there pretty soon."

They were not far from the bus station when Norwood heard someone calling his name. He knew who it was and he foolishly tried to pretend that he didn't hear. Rita Lee stopped and said, "Hey, that's somebody wants you over there." Grady Fring's Invicta was parked across the street on the apron of a darkened service station. The engine was idling but making no more noise than a rat peeing on a sack of cotton. Grady was looking across the top of the car at them. "It's me," he said. "I'd like to have a word with you if I may." Rita Lee said, "Who is that?" Norwood said, "It's a man I know. You go on down to the station and keep an eye on our stuff. I'll be there in a minute."

Norwood crossed the street. Grady stood there grinning and waiting outside his car with one arm resting on top of the opened door. Norwood had forgotten how tall he was. "Well, you're back," said Grady. He stuck his hand out and Norwood took it and gave it one shake. "I had a momentary impression there that you were trying to dodge me."

"I figured I'd have to see you sometime."

"Yes, indeed. Who's the chippy?"

"The what?"

"The girl, who's the girl?"

"What was that you called her?"

"A chippy. It doesn't mean anything. It just means a sweet little girl."

"I don't think that's what it means."

"You're in a surly mood, Norwood. *Defensive.* It's the voice of fear. I've heard it before."

"What is it you want?"

"Let's start with what happened to my cars."

"Them was stolen cars, Mr. Fring, and you know it."

"Where are they?"

"I left 'em in Indiana."

"Where in Indiana?"

"I don't know. Someplace. I don't remember."

"Were the police in any way involved?"

"Naw."

"You just abandoned them."

"Yeah."

"What about Yvonne? I see her hand in this. The coarse Miss Phillips."

"What about her?"

"Where is she? Where did she go?"

"I don't know where she went."

"And where have you been all this time?"

"I went to see somebody."

"Who?"

"None of your business."

"Look, son, don't try to match wits with me. I'd appreciate it if you'd change your tone. All I'm interested in right now is finding out a few facts. You've cost me a great deal of money and considerable worry. You may be in very serious trouble. I want to know the extent of the damage. Don't you think I'm entitled to know that? What's more, I don't like it. I don't like the way you've abused my good faith in this matter."

"I don't see where I'm in any trouble."

"That's only because you're stupid. What did you do with the car papers? The pink slips and the credit card and all that?"

"I left 'em in the car. Cars."

"You're a real dandy."

"Look, starting right now I don't have any more to do with *you* or them cars. I don't have to talk to you any more. Here, here's your watch, *crook*."

"Yessir, you are a dandy," said Grady. He took the watch and dropped it on the concrete without looking at it and stepped on it with the heel of his shoe. "I could have you locked up right here tonight if I wanted to, did you know that?"

"Yeah, what for?"

"Just anything that came to mind. Vagrancy, mopery."

"I don't think you could do that."

"No? Do you believe your house could burn some cold wintry night? What a tragedy that would be. I advise you to curb your tongue, Norwood, and think this thing through and then give me some straight answers. *Now.* We got off on the wrong foot. Let's try it again. We're not communicating and I think I know why. You think the situation is much more desperate than it actually is. True, you owe me the money for the cars but that can be worked out. I can put you on temporarily as night man at the worm ranch. Perhaps later we can—"

"Burn my house? Was that what you said?"

"I didn't say *I*, the Kredit King, would burn it, no. You misunderstood me. These things do happen though, you can't deny it. They strike the rich and poor alike. Well, come to that, I believe they strike the poor more often than the rich because of their necessarily inferior heating systems. The coal oil stove is a treacherous device. Of course the rich stand to lose more in a fire. There's a certain rough justice in the world. Many of your great philosophers have remarked on it."

"You must be crazy."

"Watch it now. You're taking liberties. Don't make things any worse than they are. Don't let your mouth write a check that your ass can't cash, son."

Norwood was trembling. "I'm through talking," he said, and he made a move to go.

Grady slammed the car door and held up one hand like a traffic policeman. "Whoa, I'm not," he said.

"Get out of my way, you big skinny sapsucker!"

Grady didn't move fast enough and Norwood swung and hit him on the temple with a looping right. Grady ran or danced a couple of steps sideways and dropped to one hand and one knee. Norwood was on him like a bobcat. They fell together and the back of Grady's head bounced on the oily concrete and Norwood hit him five or six times full in the face and mouth, then pressed his forearm down on Grady's neck as hard as he could. "What you gonna do now! Come on, tell me what you gonna do now! Come on, you a big talker!"

Norwood heard someone shouting and when he realized it wasn't himself he looked up and saw a woman out there on the sidewalk in the light. "It's a *fight*!" she was saying. "It's a *fight* over here at this Amoco station! Lord, they're killing each other!" Norwood jumped up and she squealed and ran. He licked his knuckles and blew on them and shook his hand. Grady sat up and groaned. Then he got up on his feet very slowly, coughing and spitting. He stood there bent over and holding his throat. His lower lip was fat and split like a hot sausage and blood dripped on his wingtip shoes and his hard-creased trousers. He leaned against the car with one hand and made loud raspy noises breathing in and out.

Two drifter-looking young men, one of them in a Japan jacket, were standing on the sidewalk looking on. Norwood said, "Yall go on about your business. It's all over." They lingered. Norwood raised his voice. "I said shove off." They sauntered away, taking their time about it. Norwood watched Grady drip for a minute. "Them cars don't mean anything to me," he said. "You just leave me alone, you hear? Just stay away from me. Don't come messing around me or my house or anybody over there. Next time I'll bust your head open with a tar tool. I'll kill you. That's all I got to say."

Rita Lee was waiting at the bus station door. "What in the world?" she said.

"It wasn't anything," he said.

"Yes it was too. Who was that?" She looked at the grease

marks on his trousers and saw his puffy red hand. "Hey, you been in a fight, Norwood!"

"I used to work for him. He was messing around with me and I told him not to and he just kept on."

"Did you whup him?"

"I guess so. Wasn't much to whup."

"I'll bet you really socked him. I wisht I could of seen it. Did he cuss much?"

"Naw, not much. How about breaking out that Noxzema?"

Tilmon, a quivering crystal strand hanging from one nostril, came over with his hands in his pockets and watched with a demented grin while Rita Lee applied the cream to Norwood's knuckles. "What do you want?" said Norwood. "Wipe your nose."

Rita Lee whispered, "Hon, don't start anything with him, he looks like a molester to me. He may be dangerous. There's one calls my sister on the phone all the time. They can't catch him. They say he has a twisted mind."

Norwood said, "They won't be none of 'em calling you at my house."

At the very last, critical moment Tilmon swooped up and wiped his nose with his sleeve and then wiped his sleeve on his coat. "I saw you when you came in," he said. "I called Grady and told him. Hee-hee. I remembered your hat."

"Your brother is over at that Amoco station," said Norwood. "He wants to see you."

"I saw you with that girl. Grady thought it was that othern and I told him it wasn't. He's a cutter, ain't he?"

"Yeah, he's a cutter and you're a dandy. You go on over there now and see about him."

B ILL BIRD said the place for livestock was in the trunk but Norwood said it was too dusty back there. Bill Bird rode in the back seat with his feet up on Joann's mink cage. Rita Lee fell asleep almost as soon as she got in the car and she slept all the way to Ralph, rod noise and all. Vernell ate her sticky cherry cordials and asked any number of questions about the girl and the chicken. Norwood answered them impatiently. He drove and took it very easy because of the bad rod. Rita Lee was curled up on the front seat with her head in his lap. Everything on the highway passed them, even ratty old pickups with one light. Bill Bird, speaking loudly against the clatter and into a 35 m.p.h. breeze that was pouring through a broken window, said, "I notice he hasn't said anything about the money."

"What about it, bubba?" said Vernell. "Did you get your money?"

"Yeah, I got it."

"Well, I hope he's happy now," said Bill Bird. "All that big to-do."

"What about it, bubba, are you happy that you got your money?"

"You're just like a parrot, Vernell," said Norwood. "Yeah, I'm happy about it. Don't ast silly questions."

"You don't have to bite my head off."

"Well, I'm tard of answering questions tonight. Don't ast me any more until tomorrow."

"When I was in the Canal Zone the Signal Corps boys had a famous parrot," said Bill Bird. "It was their mascot. It was a parrot mascot. They had trained it to speak into a telephone . . ."

Norwood wasn't in the mood for a Panama story and he turned on the radio. It took a while to warm up, what with the dirt dobber nests on the tubes, and Bill Bird was through with his story by the time the volume came up. They listened to XEG, Monterey, Mexico, the rest of the way in, which was the loudest station Norwood could get. "Listen to that, would you," exclaimed Bill Bird. "Now who in the world would want a Lord's Last Supper Vinyl Tablecloth?" Vernell said, "Not me. I think they're tacky." Norwood pulled into the pea gravel

109

driveway with the white rock borders and stopped the car up close to the porch and turned the key off. Home. He stretched. Rita Lee whimpered and complained like a child when he tried to wake her. He carried her inside and put her down on the couch. "She's a cute thing," said Vernell. "I'm surprised you could pick up a girl that cute on the bus." Bill Bird said, "Yes, I wondered about that. I hope there's not anything wrong with her." Norwood said, "Mine your own business, Bill Bird," and he went back out to the car to get the rest of the stuff.

# TRUE GRIT

*For my mother and father*

PEOPLE DO not give it credence that a fourteen-year-old girl could leave home and go off in the wintertime to avenge her father's blood but it did not seem so strange then, although I will say it did not happen every day. I was just fourteen years of age when a coward going by the name of Tom Chaney shot my father down in Fort Smith, Arkansas, and robbed him of his life and his horse and $150 in cash money plus two California gold pieces that he carried in his trouser band.

Here is what happened. We had clear title to 480 acres of good bottom land on the south bank of the Arkansas River not far from Dardanelle in Yell County, Arkansas. Tom Chaney was a tenant but working for hire and not on shares. He turned up one day hungry and riding a gray horse that had a filthy blanket on his back and a rope halter instead of a bridle. Papa took pity on the fellow and gave him a job and a place to live. It was a cotton house made over into a little cabin. It had a good roof.

Tom Chaney said he was from Louisiana. He was a short man with cruel features. I will tell more about his face later. He carried a Henry rifle. He was a bachelor about twenty-five years of age.

In November when the last of the cotton was sold Papa took it in his head to go to Fort Smith and buy some ponies. He had heard that a stock trader there named Colonel Stonehill had bought a large parcel of cow ponies from Texas drovers on their way to Kansas and was now stuck with them. He was getting shed of them at bargain rates as he did not want to feed them over the winter. People in Arkansas did not think much of Texas mustang ponies. They were little and mean. They had never had anything but grass to eat and did not weigh over eight hundred pounds.

Papa had an idea they would make good deer-hunting ponies, being hardy and small and able to keep up with the dogs through the brush. He thought he would buy a small string of them and if things worked out he would breed and sell them for that purpose. His head was full of schemes. Anyway, it would be a cheap enough investment to start with, and we had a patch of winter oats and plenty of hay to see the ponies through till spring when they could graze in our big north pasture and feed on greener and juicier clover than they ever saw in the "Lone Star State." As I recollect, shelled corn was something under fifteen cents a bushel then.

Papa intended for Tom Chaney to stay and look after things on the place while he was gone. But Chaney set up a fuss to go and after a time he got the best of Papa's good nature. If Papa had a failing it was his kindly disposition. People would use him. I did not get my mean streak from him. Frank Ross was the gentlest, most honorable man who ever lived. He had a common-school education. He was a Cumberland Presbyterian and a Mason and he fought with determination at the battle of Elkhorn Tavern but was not wounded in that "scrap" as Lucille Biggers Langford states in her *Yell County Yesterdays*. I think I am in a position to know the facts. He was hurt in the terrible fight at Chickamauga up in the state of Tennessee and came near to dying on the way home from want of proper care.

Before Papa left for Fort Smith he arranged for a colored man named Yarnell Poindexter to feed the stock and look in on Mama and us every day. Yarnell and his family lived just below us on some land he rented from the bank. He was born of free parents in Illinois but a man named Bloodworth kidnaped him in Missouri and brought him down to Arkansas just before the war. Yarnell was a good man, thrifty and industrious, and he later became a prosperous house painter in Memphis, Tennessee. We exchanged letters every Christmas until he passed away in the flu epidemic of 1918. To this day I have never met anybody else named Yarnell, white or black. I attended the funeral and visited in Memphis with my brother, Little Frank, and his family.

Instead of going to Fort Smith by steamboat or train, Papa decided he would go on horseback and walk the ponies back all tied together. Not only would it be cheaper but it would be a pleasant outing for him and a good ride. Nobody loved to gad about on a prancing steed more than Papa. I have never been very fond of horses myself although I believe I was accounted a good enough rider in my youth. I never was afraid of animals. I remember once I rode a mean goat through a plum thicket on a dare.

From our place to Fort Smith was about seventy miles as a bird flies, taking you past beautiful Mount Nebo where we had a little summer house so Mama could get away from the mosquitoes, and also Mount Magazine, the highest point in Arkansas, but it might as well have been seven hundred miles for all I knew of Fort Smith. The boats went up there and some people sold their cotton up there but that was all I knew about it. We sold our cotton down in Little Rock. I had been there two or three times.

Papa left us on his saddle horse, a big chestnut mare with a blazed face called Judy. He took some food and a change of clothes rolled up in some blankets and covered with a slicker. This was tied behind his saddle. He wore his belt gun which was a big long dragoon pistol, the cap-and-ball kind that was old-fashioned even at that time. He had carried it in the war. He was a handsome sight and in my memory's eye I can still see him mounted up there on Judy in his brown woolen coat and black Sunday hat and the both of them, man and beast, blowing little clouds of steam on that frosty morn. He might have been a gallant knight of old. Tom Chaney rode his gray horse that was better suited to pulling a middlebuster than carrying a rider. He had no hand gun but he carried his rifle slung across his back on a piece of cotton plow line. There is trash for you. He could have taken an old piece of harness and made a nice leather strap for it. That would have been too much trouble.

Papa had right around two hundred and fifty dollars in his purse as I had reason to know since I kept his books for him. Mama was never any good at sums and she could hardly spell cat. I do not boast of my own gifts in that direction. Figures and letters are not everything. Like Martha I have always been agitated and troubled by the cares of the day but my mother had a serene and loving heart. She was like Mary and had chosen "that good part." The two gold pieces that Papa carried concealed in his clothes were a marriage gift from my Grandfather Spurling in Monterey, California.

Little did Papa realize that morning that he was never to see us or hold us again, nor would he ever again harken to the meadowlarks of Yell County trilling a joyous anthem to spring.

The news came like a thunderclap. Here is what happened. Papa and Tom Chaney arrived in Fort Smith and took a room at the Monarch boardinghouse. They called on Stonehill at his stock barn and looked over the ponies. It fell out that there was not a mare in the lot, or a stallion for that matter. The Texas cow-boys rode nothing but geldings for some cow-boy reason of their own and you can imagine they are no good for breeding purposes. But Papa was not to be turned back. He was determined to own some of those little brutes and on the second day he bought four of them for one hundred dollars even, bringing Stonehill down from his asking price of one hundred and forty dollars. It was a good enough buy.

They made plans to leave the next morning. That night Tom Chaney went to a barroom and got into a game of cards with some "riffraff" like himself and lost his wages. He did not take the loss like a man but went back to the room at the boardinghouse and sulled up like a possum. He had a bottle of whiskey and he drank that. Papa was sitting in the parlor talking to some drummers. By and by Chaney came out of the bedroom with his rifle. He said he had been cheated and was going back to the barroom and get his money. Papa said if he had been cheated then they had best go talk to the law about it. Chaney would not listen. Papa followed him outside and told him to surrender the rifle as he was in no fit state to start a quarrel with a gun in his hand. My father was not armed at that time.

Tom Chaney raised his rifle and shot him in the forehead, killing him instantly. There was no more provocation than that and I tell it as it was told to me by the high sheriff of Sebastian County. Some people might say, well, what business was it of Frank Ross to meddle? My answer is this: he was trying to do that short devil a good turn. Chaney was a tenant and Papa felt responsibility. He was his brother's keeper. Does that answer your question?

Now the drummers did not rush out to grab Chaney or shoot him but instead scattered like poultry while Chaney took my father's purse from his warm body and ripped open the trouser band and took the gold pieces too. I cannot say how he knew about them. When he finished his thieving he raced to the end of the street and struck the night watchman at the stock barn a fierce blow to the mouth with his rifle stock, knocking him silly. He put a bridle on Papa's horse Judy and rode out bareback. Darkness swallowed him up. He might have taken the time to saddle the horse or hitched up three spans of mules to a Concord stagecoach and smoked a pipe as it seems no one in that city was after him. He had mistaken the drummers for men. "The wicked flee when none pursueth."

LAWYER DAGGETT had gone to Helena to try one of his steamboat suits and so Yarnell and I rode the train to Fort Smith to see about Papa's body. I took around one hundred dollars expense money and wrote myself out a letter of identification and signed Lawyer Daggett's name to it and had Mama sign it as well. She was in bed.

There were no seats to be had on the coaches. The reason for this was that there was to be a triple hanging at the Federal Courthouse in Fort Smith and people from as far away as east Texas and north Louisiana were going up to see it. It was like an excursion trip. We rode in a colored coach and Yarnell got us a trunk to sit on.

When the conductor came through he said, "Get that trunk out of the aisle, nigger!"

I replied to him in this way: "We will move the trunk but there is no reason for you to be so hateful about it."

He did not say anything to that but went on taking tickets. He saw that I had brought to all the darkies' attention how little he was. We stood up all the way but I was young and did not mind. On the way we had a good lunch of spare ribs that Yarnell had brought along in a sack.

I noticed that the houses in Fort Smith were numbered but it was no city at all compared to Little Rock. I thought then and still think that Fort Smith ought to be in Oklahoma instead of Arkansas, though of course it was not Oklahoma across the river then but the Indian Territory. They have that big wide street there called Garrison Avenue like places out in the west. The buildings are made of fieldstone and all the windows need washing. I know many fine people live in Fort Smith and they have one of the nation's most modern waterworks but it does not look like it belongs in Arkansas to me.

There was a jailer at the sheriff's office and he said we would have to talk to the city police or the high sheriff about the particulars of Papa's death. The sheriff had gone to the hanging. The undertaker was not open. He had left a notice on his door saying he would be back after the hanging. We went to the Monarch boardinghouse but there was no one there except a poor old woman with cataracts on her eyes. She said everybody had gone to the hanging but her. She would not let us in to see about Papa's traps. At the city police station we found two officers but they were having a fist fight and were not available for inquiries.

Yarnell wanted to see the hanging but he did not want me to go so he said we should go back to the sheriff's office and wait there until everybody got back. I did not much care to see it but I saw he wanted to so I said no, we would go to the hanging but I would not tell Mama about it. That was what he was worried about.

The Federal Courthouse was up by the river on a little rise and the big gallows was hard beside it. About a thousand or more people and fifty or sixty dogs had gathered there to see the show. I believe a year or two later they put up a wall around the place and you had to have a pass from the marshal's office to get in but at this time it was open to the public. A noisy boy was going through the crowd selling parched peanuts and fudge. Another one was selling "hot tamales" out of a bucket. This is a cornmeal tube filled with spicy meat that they eat in Old Mexico. They are not bad. I had never seen one before.

When we got there the preliminaries were just about over. Two white men and an Indian were standing up there on the platform with their hands tied behind them and the three nooses hanging loose beside their heads. They were all wearing new jeans and flannel shirts buttoned at the neck. The hangman was a thin bearded man named George Maledon. He was wearing two long pistols. He was a Yankee and they say he would not hang a man who had been in the G.A.R. A marshal read the sentences but his voice was low and we could not make out what he was saying. We pushed up closer.

A man with a Bible talked to each of the men for a minute. I took him for a preacher. He led them in singing "Amazing Grace, How Sweet the Sound" and some people in the crowd joined in. Then Maledon put the nooses on their necks and tightened up the knots just the way he wanted them. He went to each man with a black hood and asked him if he had any last words before he put it on him.

The first one was a white man and he looked put out by it all but not upset as you might expect from a man in his desperate situation. He said, "Well, I killed the wrong man and that is why I am here. If I had killed the man I meant to I don't believe I would have been convicted. I see men out there in that crowd that is worse than me."

The Indian was next and he said, "I am ready. I have repented my sins and soon I will be in heaven with Christ my savior. Now I must die like a man." If you are like me you probably think of Indians as heathens. But I will ask you to recall the thief on the cross. He was never baptized and never even heard of a catechism and yet Christ himself promised him a place in heaven.

The last one had a little speech ready. You could tell he had learned it by heart. He had long yellow hair. He was older than the other two, being around thirty years of age. He said, "Ladies and gentlemen, my last thoughts are of my wife and my two dear little boys who are far away out on the Cimarron River. I don't know what is to become of them. I hope and pray that people will not slight them and compel them to go into low company on account of the disgrace I have brought them. You see what I have come to because of drink. I killed my best friend in a trifling quarrel over a pocketknife. I was drunk and it could just as easily have been my brother. If I had received good instruction as a child I would be with my family today and at peace with my neighbors. I hope and pray that all you parents in the sound of my voice will train up your children in the way they should go. Thank you. Goodbye everyone."

He was in tears and I am not ashamed to own that I was too. The man Maledon covered his head with the hood and went to his lever. Yarnell put a hand over my face but I pushed it aside. I would see it all. With no more ado Maledon sprung the trap and the hinged doors fell open in the middle and the three killers dropped to judgment with a bang. A noise went up from the crowd as though they had been struck a blow. The two white men gave no more signs of life. They spun slowly around on the tight creaking ropes. The Indian jerked his legs and arms up and down in spasms. That was the bad part and many in the crowd turned in revulsion and left in some haste, and we were among them.

We were told that the Indian's neck had not been broken, as was the case with the other two, and that he swung there and strangled for more than a half hour before a doctor pronounced him dead and had him lowered. They say the Indian had lost weight in jail and was too light for a proper job. I have since learned that Judge Isaac Parker watched all his hangings from an upper window in the Courthouse. I suppose he did this from a sense of duty. There is no knowing what is in a man's heart.

Perhaps you can imagine how painful it was for us to go directly from that appalling scene to the undertaker's where my father lay dead. Nevertheless it had to be done. I have never been one to flinch or crawfish when faced with an unpleasant task. The undertaker was an Irishman. He took Yarnell and me to a room at the back that was very dark owing to the windows being painted green. The Irishman was courteous and sympathetic but I did not much like the coffin he had placed Papa in. It was resting on three low stools and was made of pine planks that had not been cleanly dressed. Yarnell took off his hat.

The Irishman said, "And is that the man?" He held a candle in his face. The body was wrapped in a white shroud.

I said, "That is my father." I stood there looking at him. What a waste! Tom Chaney would pay for this! I would not rest easy until that Louisiana cur was roasting and screaming in hell!

The Irishman said, "If ye would loike to kiss him it will be all roight."

I said, "No, put the lid on it."

We went to the man's office and I signed some coroner's papers. The charge for the coffin and the embalming was something over sixty dollars. The shipping charge to Dardanelle was $9.50.

Yarnell took me outside the office. He said, "Miss Mattie, that man trying to stick you."

I said, "Well, we will not haggle with him."

He said, "That is what he counting on."

I said, "We will let it go."

I paid the Irishman his money and got a receipt. I told Yarnell to stay with the coffin and see that it was loaded on the train with care and not handled roughly by some thoughtless railroad hand.

I went to the sheriff's office. The high sheriff was friendly and he gave me the full particulars on the shooting, but I was disappointed to learn how little had been done toward the apprehension of Tom Chaney. They had not even got his name right.

The sheriff said, "We do know this much. He was a short man but well set up. He had a black mark on his cheek. His name is Chambers. He is now over in the Territory and we think he was in the party with Lucky Ned Pepper that robbed a mail hack Tuesday down on the Poteau River."

I said, "That is the description of Tom Chaney. There is no Chambers to it. He got that black mark in Louisiana when a man shot a pistol in his face and the powder got under the skin. Anyhow, that is his story. I know him and can identify him. Why are you not out looking for him?"

The sheriff said, "I have no authority in the Indian Nation. He is now the business of the U.S. marshals."

I said, "When will they arrest him?"

He said, "It is hard to say. They will have to catch him first."

I said, "Do you know if they are even after him?"

He said, "Yes, I have asked for a fugitive warrant and I expect there is a Federal John Doe warrant on him now for the mail robbery. I will inform the marshals as to the correct name."

"I will inform them myself," said I. "Who is the best marshal they have?"

The sheriff thought on it for a minute. He said, "I would have to weigh that proposition. There is near about two hundred of them. I reckon William Waters is the best tracker. He is a half-breed Comanche and it is something to see, watching him cut for sign. The meanest one is Rooster Cogburn. He is a pitiless man, double-tough, and fear don't enter into his thinking. He loves to pull a cork. Now L. T. Quinn, he brings his prisoners in alive. He may let one get by now and then but he believes even the worst of men is entitled to a fair shake. Also the court does not pay any fees for dead men. Quinn is a good peace officer and a lay preacher to boot. He will not plant evidence or abuse a prisoner. He is straight as a string. Yes, I will say Quinn is about the best they have."

I said, "Where can I find this Rooster?"

He said, "You will probably find him in Federal Court tomorrow. They will be trying that Wharton boy."

The sheriff had Papa's gun belt there in a drawer and he gave it to me in a sugar sack to carry. The clothes and blankets were at the boardinghouse. The man Stonehill had the ponies and Papa's saddle at his stock barn. The sheriff wrote me out a note for the man Stonehill and the landlady at the boardinghouse, who was a Mrs. Floyd. I thanked him for his help. He said he wished he could do more.

It was around 5:30 P.M. when I got to the depot. The days were growing short and it was already dark. The southbound train was to leave some few minutes after 6 o'clock. I found Yarnell waiting outside the freight car where he had loaded the coffin. He said the express agent had consented to let him ride in the car with the coffin.

He said he would go help me find a seat in a coach but I said, "No, I will stay over a day or two. I must see about those ponies and I want to make sure the law is on the job. Chaney has got clean away and they are not doing much about it."

Yarnell said, "You can't stay in this city by yourself."

I said, "It will be all right. Mama knows I can take care of myself. Tell her I will be stopping at the Monarch boarding-house. If there is no room there I will leave word with the sheriff where I am."

He said, "I reckon I will stay too."

I said, "No, I want you to go with Papa. When you get home tell Mr. Myers I said to put him in a better coffin."

"Your mama will not like this," said he.

"I will be back in a day or two. Tell her I said not to sign anything until I get home. Have you had anything to eat?"

"I had me a cup of hot coffee. I ain't hongry."

"Do they have a stove in that car?"

"I will be all right wrapped in my coat."

"I sure do appreciate this, Yarnell."

"Mr. Frank was always mighty good to me."

Some people will take it wrong and criticize me for not going to my father's funeral. My answer is this: I had my father's busi-ness to attend to. He was buried in his Mason's apron by the Danville lodge.

I got to the Monarch in time to eat. Mrs. Floyd said she had no vacant room because of the big crowd in town but that she would put me up somehow. The daily rate was seventy-five cents a night with two meals and a dollar with three meals. She did not have a rate for one meal so I was obliged to give her seventy-five cents even though I had planned to buy some cheese and crackers the next morning for my daytime eats. I don't know what her weekly rate was.

There were ten or twelve people at the supper table and all men except for me and Mrs. Floyd and the poor old blind woman who was called "Grandma Turner." Mrs. Floyd was a right big talker. She explained to everybody that I was the daughter of the man who had been shot in front of her house. I did not appreciate it. She told about the event in detail and asked me impertinent questions about my family. It was all I could do to reply politely. I did not wish to discuss the thing with idly curious strangers, no matter how well intentioned they might be.

I sat at one corner of the table between her and a tall, long-backed man with a doorknob head and a mouthful of prominent teeth. He and Mrs. Floyd did most of the talking. He traveled about selling pocket calculators. He was the only man there wearing a suit of clothes and a necktie. He told some interesting stories about his experiences but the others paid little attention to him, being occupied with their food like hogs rooting in a bucket.

"Watch out for those chicken and dumplings," he told me.

Some of the men stopped eating.

"They will hurt your eyes," he said.

A dirty man across the table in a smelly deerskin coat said, "How is that?"

With a mischievous twinkle the drummer replied, "They will hurt your eyes looking for the chicken." I thought it a clever joke but the dirty man said angrily, "You squirrelheaded son of a bitch," and went back to eating. The drummer kept quiet after that. The dumplings were all right but I could not see twenty-five cents in a little flour and grease.

After supper some of the men left to go to town, probably to drink whiskey in the barrooms and listen to the hurdy-gurdy. The rest of us went to the parlor. The boarders dozed and read newspapers and talked about the hanging and the drummer told yellow fever jokes. Mrs. Floyd brought out Papa's things that were bundled in the slicker and I went through them and made an inventory.

Everything seemed to be there, even his knife and watch. The watch was of brass and not very expensive but I was surprised to find it because people who will not steal big things will often steal little things like that. I stayed in the parlor and listened to the talk for a while and then asked Mrs. Floyd if she would show me to my bed.

She said, "Go straight down that hall to the last bedroom on the left. There is a bucket of water and a washpan on the back porch. The toilet is out back directly behind the chinaberry tree. You will be sleeping with Grandma Turner."

She must have seen the dismay on my face for she added, "It will be all right. Grandma Turner will not mind. She is used to doubling up. She will not even know you are there, sweet."

Since I was the paying customer I believed my wishes should have been considered before Grandma Turner's, though it seemed neither of us was to have any say.

Mrs. Floyd went on, saying, "Grandma Turner is a sound sleeper. It is certainly a blessing at her age. Do not worry about waking Grandma Turner, a little mite like you."

I did not mind sleeping with Grandma Turner but I thought Mrs. Floyd had taken advantage of me. Still, I saw nothing to be gained from making a fuss at that hour. She already had my money and I was tired and it was too late to look for lodging elsewhere.

The bedroom was cold and dark and smelled like medicine. A wintry blast came up through the cracks in the floor. Grandma Turner turned out to be more active in her slumber than I had been led to expect. When I got into bed I found she had all the quilts on her side. I pulled them over. I said my prayers and was soon asleep. I awoke to find that Grandma Turner had done the trick again. I was bunched up in a knot and trembling with cold from the exposure. I pulled the covers over again. This happened once more later in the night and I got up, my feet freezing, and arranged Papa's blankets and slicker over me as makeshift covers. Then I slept all right.

M RS. FLOYD served me no meat for breakfast, only grits and a fried egg. After eating I put the watch and knife in my pocket and took the gun along in the sugar sack.

At the Federal Courthouse I learned that the head marshal had gone to Detroit, Michigan, to deliver prisoners to the "house of correction," as they called it. A deputy who worked in the office said they would get around to Tom Chaney in good time, but that he would have to wait his turn. He showed me a list of indicted outlaws that were then on the loose in the Indian Territory and it looked like the delinquent tax list that they run in the *Arkansas Gazette* every year in little type. I did not like the looks of that, nor did I care much for the "smarty" manner of the deputy. He was puffed up by his office. You can expect that out of Federal people and to make it worse this was a Republican gang that cared nothing for the opinion of the good people of Arkansas who are Democrats.

In the courtroom itself they were empaneling a jury. The bailiff at the door told me that the man Rooster Cogburn would be around later in the day when the trial began as he was the main witness for the prosecution.

I went to Stonehill's stock barn. He had a nice barn and behind it a big corral and a good many small feeder pens. The bargain cow ponies, around thirty head, all colors, were in the corral. I thought they would be broken-down scrubs but they were frisky things with clear eyes and their coats looked healthy enough, though dusty and matted. They had probably never known a brush. They had burrs in their tails.

I had hated these ponies for the part they played in my father's death but now I realized the notion was fanciful, that it was wrong to charge blame to these pretty beasts who knew neither good nor evil but only innocence. I say that of these ponies. I have known some horses and a good many more pigs who I believe harbored evil intent in their hearts. I will go further and say all cats are wicked, though often useful. Who has not seen Satan in their sly faces? Some preachers will say, well, that is superstitious "claptrap." My answer is this: Preacher, go to your Bible and read Luke 8: 26–33.

Stonehill had an office in one corner of the barn. On the door glass it said, "Col. G. Stonehill. Licensed Auctioneer. Cotton Factor." He was in there behind his desk and he had a red-hot stove going. He was a prissy bald-headed man with eyeglasses.

I said, "How much are you paying for cotton?"

He looked up at me and said, "Nine and a half for low middling and ten for ordinary."

I said, "We got most of ours out early and sold it to Woodson Brothers in Little Rock for eleven cents."

He said, "Then I suggest you take the balance of it to the Woodson Brothers."

"We have sold it all," said I. "We only got ten and a half on the last sale."

"Why did you come here to tell me this?"

"I thought we might shop around up here next year, but I guess we are doing all right in Little Rock." I showed him the note from the sheriff. After he had read it he was not disposed to be so short with me.

He took off his eyeglasses and said, "It was a tragic thing. May I say your father impressed me with his manly qualities. He was a close trader but he acted the gentleman. My watchman had his teeth knocked out and can take only soup."

I said, "I am sorry to hear it."

He said, "The killer has flown to the Territory and is now on the scout there."

"This is what I heard."

"He will find plenty of his own stamp there," said he. "Birds of a feather. It is a sink of crime. Not a day goes by but there comes some new report of a farmer bludgeoned, a wife outraged, or a blameless traveler set upon and cut down in a sanguinary ambuscade. The civilizing arts of commerce do not flourish there."

I said, "I have hopes that the marshals will get him soon. His name is Tom Chaney. He worked for us. I am trying to get action. I aim to see him shot or hanged."

"Yes, yes, well might you labor to that end," said Stonehill. "At the same time I will counsel patience. The brave marshals do their best but they are few in number. The lawbreakers are legion and they range over a vast country that offers many natural hiding places. The marshal travels about friendless and alone in that criminal nation. Every man's hand is against him there save in large part for that of the Indian who has been cruelly imposed upon by felonious intruders from the States."

I said, "I would like to sell those ponies back to you that my father bought."

He said, "I fear that is out of the question. I will see that they are shipped to you at my earliest convenience."

I said, "We don't want the ponies now. We don't need them."

"That hardly concerns me," said he. "Your father bought these ponies and paid for them and there is an end of it. I have the bill of sale. If I had any earthly use for them I might consider an offer but I have already lost money on them and, be assured, I do not intend to lose more. I will be happy to accommodate you in shipping them. The popular steamer *Alice Waddell* leaves tomorrow for Little Rock. I will do what I can to find space on it for you and the stock."

I said, "I want three hundred dollars for Papa's saddle horse that was stolen."

He said, "You will have to take that up with the man who has the horse."

"Tom Chaney stole it while it was in your care," said I. "You are responsible."

Stonehill laughed at that. He said, "I admire your sand but I believe you will find I am not liable for such claims. Let me say too that your valuation of the horse is high by about two hundred dollars."

I said, "If anything, my price is low. Judy is a fine racing mare. She has won purses of twenty-five dollars at the fair. I have seen her jump an eight-rail fence with a heavy rider."

"All very interesting, I'm sure," said he.

"Then you will offer nothing?"

"Nothing except what is yours. The ponies are yours, take them. Your father's horse was stolen by a murderous criminal. This is regrettable but I had provided reasonable protection for the animal as per the implicit agreement with the client. We must each of us bear our own misfortunes. Mine is that I have temporarily lost the services of my watchman."

"I will take it to law," said I.

"You must do as you think best," said he.

"We will see if a widow and her three small children can get fair treatment in the courts of this city."

"You have no case."

"Lawyer J. Noble Daggett of Dardanelle, Arkansas, may think otherwise. Also a jury."

"Where is your mother?"

"She is at home in Yell County looking after my sister Victoria and my brother Little Frank."

"You must fetch her then. I do not like to deal with children."

"You will not like it any better when Lawyer Daggett gets hold of you. He is a grown man."

"You are impudent."

"I do not wish to be, sir, but I will not be pushed about when I am in the right."

"I will take it up with my attorney."

"And I will take it up with mine. I will send him a message by telegraph and he will be here on the evening train. He will make money and I will make money and your lawyer will make money and you, Mr. Licensed Auctioneer, will foot the bill."

"I cannot make an agreement with a child. You are not accountable. You cannot be bound to a contract."

"Lawyer Daggett will back up any decision I make. You may rest easy on that score. You can confirm any agreement by telegraph."

"This is a damned nuisance!" he exclaimed. "How am I to get my work done? I have a sale tomorrow."

"There can be no settlement after I leave this office," said I. "It will go to law."

He worried with his eyeglasses for a minute and then said, "I will pay two hundred dollars to your father's estate when I have in my hand a letter from your lawyer absolving me of all liability from the beginning of the world to date. It must be signed by your lawyer and your mother and it must be notarized. The offer is more than liberal and I only make it to avoid the possibility of troublesome litigation. I should never have come here. They told me this town was to be the Pittsburgh of the Southwest."

I said, "I will take two hundred dollars for Judy, plus one hundred dollars for the ponies and twenty-five dollars for the gray horse that Tom Chaney left. He is easily worth forty dollars. That is three hundred and twenty-five dollars total."

"The ponies have no part in this," said he. "I will not buy them."

"Then I will keep the ponies and the price for Judy will be three hundred and twenty-five dollars."

Stonehill snorted. "I would not pay three hundred and twenty-five dollars for winged Pegasus, and that splayfooted gray does not even belong to you."

I said, "Yes, he does. Papa only let Tom Chaney have the use of him."

"My patience is wearing thin. You are an unnatural child. I will pay two hundred and twenty-five dollars and keep the gray horse. I don't want the ponies."

"I cannot settle for that."

"This is my last offer. Two hundred and fifty dollars. For that I get a release and I keep your father's saddle. I am also writing off a feed and stabling charge. The gray horse is not yours to sell."

"The saddle is not for sale. I will keep it. Lawyer Daggett can prove the ownership of the gray horse. He will come after you with a writ of replevin."

"All right, now listen very carefully as I will not bargain further. I will take the ponies back and keep the gray horse and settle for three hundred dollars. Now you must take that or leave it and I do not much care which it is."

I said, "I am sure Lawyer Daggett would not wish me to consider anything under three hundred and twenty-five dollars. What you get for that is everything except the saddle and you get out of a costly lawsuit as well. It will go harder if Lawyer Daggett makes the terms as he will include a generous fee for himself."

"Lawyer Daggett! Lawyer Daggett! Who is this famous pleader of whose name I was happily ignorant ten minutes ago?"

I said, "Have you ever heard of the Great Arkansas River, Vicksburg & Gulf Steamship Company?"

"I have done business with the G.A.V.&G.," said he.

"Lawyer Daggett is the man who forced them into receivership," said I. "They tried to 'mess' with him. It was a feather in his cap. He is on familiar terms with important men in Little Rock. The talk is he will be governor one day."

"Then he is a man of little ambition," said Stonehill, "incommensurate with his capacity for making mischief. I would rather be a country road overseer in Tennessee than governor of this benighted state. There is more honor in it."

"If you don't like it here you should pack your traps and go back where you came from."

"Would that I could get out from under!" said he. "I would be aboard the Friday morning packet with a song of thanksgiving on my lips."

"People who don't like Arkansas can go to the devil!" said I. "What did you come here for?"

"I was sold a bill of goods."

"Three hundred and twenty-five dollars is my figure."

"I would like to have that in writing for what it is worth." He wrote out a short agreement. I read it over and made a change or two and he initialed the changes. He said, "Tell your lawyer to send the letter to me here at Stonehill's Livery Stable. When I have it in my hand I will remit the extortion money. Sign this."

I said, "I will have him send the letter to me at the Monarch boardinghouse. When you give me the money I will give you the letter. I will sign this instrument when you have given me twenty-five dollars as a token of your good faith." Stonehill gave me ten dollars and I signed the paper.

I went to the telegraph office. I tried to keep the message down but it took up almost a full blank setting forth the situation and what was needed. I told Lawyer Daggett to let Mama know I was well and would be home soon. I forget what it cost.

I bought some crackers and a piece of hoop cheese and an apple at a grocery store and sat on a nail keg by the stove and had a cheap yet nourishing lunch. You know what they say, "Enough is as good as a feast." When I had finished eating I returned to Stonehill's place and tried to give the apple core to one of the ponies. They all shied away and would have nothing to do with me or my gift. The poor things had probably never tasted an apple. I went inside the stock barn out of the wind and lay down on some oat sacks. Nature tells us to rest after meals and people who are too busy to heed that inner voice are often dead at the age of fifty years.

Stonehill came by on his way out wearing a little foolish Tennessee hat. He stopped and looked at me.

I said, "I am taking a short nap."

He said, "Are you quite comfortable?"

I said, "I wanted to get out of the wind. I figured you would not mind."

"I don't want you smoking cigarettes in here."

"I don't use tobacco."

"I don't want you punching holes in those sacks with your boots."

"I will be careful. Shut that door good when you go out."

I had not realized how tired I was. It was well up in the afternoon when I awoke. I was stiff and my nose had begun to drip, sure sign of a cold coming on. You should always be covered while sleeping. I dusted myself off and washed my face under a pump and picked up my gun sack and made haste to the Federal Courthouse.

When I got there I saw that another crowd had gathered, although not as big as the one the day before. My thought was: *What? Surely they are not having another hanging!* They were not. What had attracted the people this time was the arrival of two prisoner wagons from the Territory.

The marshals were unloading the prisoners and poking them sharply along with their Winchester repeating rifles. The men were all chained together like fish on a string. They were mostly white men but there were also some Indians and half-breeds and Negroes. It was awful to see but you must remember that these chained beasts were murderers and robbers and train wreckers and bigamists and counterfeiters, some of the most wicked men in the world. They had ridden the "hoot-owl trail" and tasted the fruits of evil and now justice had caught up with them to demand payment. You must pay for everything in this world one way and another. There is nothing free except the Grace of God. You cannot earn that or deserve it.

The prisoners who were already in the jail, which was in the basement of the Courthouse, commenced to shout and cat-call through little barred windows at the new prisoners, saying, "Fresh fish!" and such like. Some of them used ugly expressions so that the women in the crowd turned their heads. I put my fingers in my ears and walked through the people up to the steps of the Courthouse and inside.

The bailiff at the door did not want to let me in the court-room as I was a child but I told him I had business with Marshal Cogburn and held my ground. He saw I had spunk and he folded right up, not wanting me to cause a stir. He made me stand beside him just inside the door but that was all right because there were no empty seats anyway. People were even sitting on windowsills.

You will think it strange but I had scarcely heard of Judge Isaac Parker at that time, famous man that he was. I knew pretty well what was going on in my part of the world and I must have heard mention of him and his court but it made little impression on me. Of course we lived in his district but we had our own circuit courts to deal with killers and thieves. About the only outlaws in our country who ever went to Federal Court were "moonshiners" like old man Jerry Vick and his boys. Most of Judge Parker's customers came from the Indian Territory which was a refuge for desperadoes from all over the map.

Now I will tell you an interesting thing. For a long time there was no appeal from his court except to the President of the United States. They later changed that and when the Supreme Court started reversing him, Judge Parker was annoyed. He said those people up in Washington city did not understand the bloody conditions in the Territory. He called Solicitor-General Whitney, who was supposed to be on the judge's side, a "pardon broker" and said he knew no more of criminal law than he did of the hieroglyphics of the Great Pyramid. Well, for their part, those people up there said the judge was too hard and highhanded and too longwinded in his jury charges and they called his court "the Parker slaughterhouse." I don't know who was right. I know sixty-five of his marshals got killed. They had some mighty tough folks to deal with.

The judge was a tall big man with blue eyes and a brown billy-goat beard and he seemed to me to be old, though he was only around forty years of age at that time. His manner was grave. On his deathbed he asked for a priest and became

a Catholic. That was his wife's religion. It was his own business and none of mine. If you had sentenced one hundred
and sixty men to death and seen around eighty of them swing,
then maybe at the last minute you would feel the need of some
stronger medicine than the Methodists could make. It is something to think about. Toward the last, he said he didn't hang all
those men, that the law had done it. When he died of dropsy
in 1896 all the prisoners down there in that dark jail had a "jubilee" and the jailers had to put it down.

I have a newspaper record of a part of that Wharton trial
and it is not an official transcript but it is faithful enough. I
have used it and my memories to write a good historical article
that I titled, *You will now listen to the sentence of the law, Odus
Wharton, which is that you be hanged by the neck until you are
dead, dead dead! May God, whose laws you have broken and before whose dread tribunal you must appear, have mercy on your
soul. Being a personal recollection of Isaac C. Parker, the famous
Border Judge.*

But the magazines of today do not know a good story when
they see one. They would rather print trash. They say my article is too long and "discursive." Nothing is too long or too
short either if you have a true and interesting tale and what I
call a "graphic" writing style combined with educational aims.
I do not fool around with newspapers. They are always after
me for historical write-ups but when the talk gets around to
money the paper editors are most of them "cheap skates." They
think because I have a little money I will be happy to fill up
their Sunday columns just to see my name in print like Lucille
Biggers Langford and Florence Mabry Whiteside. As the little
colored boy says, "*Not none of me!*" Lucille and Florence can
do as they please. The paper editors are great ones for reaping
where they have not sown. Another game they have is to send
reporters out to talk to you and get your stories free. I know
the young reporters are not paid well and I would not mind
helping those boys out with their "scoops" if they could ever
get anything straight.

When I got in the courtroom there was a Creek Indian boy
on the witness stand and he was speaking in his own tongue
and another Indian was interpreting for him. It was slow going.
I stood there through almost an hour of it before they called
Rooster Cogburn to the stand.

I had guessed wrong as to which one he was, picking out a younger and slighter man with a badge on his shirt, and I was surprised when an old one-eyed jasper that was built along the lines of Grover Cleveland went up and was sworn. I say "old." He was about forty years of age. The floor boards squeaked under his weight. He was wearing a dusty black suit of clothes and when he sat down I saw that his badge was on his vest. It was a little silver circle with a star in it. He had a mustache like Cleveland too.

Some people will say, well there were more men in the country at that time who looked like Cleveland than did not. Still, that is how he looked. Cleveland was once a sheriff himself. He brought a good deal of misery to the land in the Panic of '93 but I am not ashamed to own that my family supported him and has stayed with the Democrats right on through, up to and including Governor Alfred Smith, and not only because of Joe Robinson. Papa used to say that the only friends we had down here right after the war were the Irish Democrats in New York. Thad Stevens and the Republican gang would have starved us all out if they could. It is all in the history books. Now I will introduce Rooster by way of the transcript and get my story "back on the rails."

MR. BARLOW: State your name and occupation please.
MR. COGBURN: Reuben J. Cogburn. I am a deputy marshal for the U.S. District Court for the Western District of Arkansas having criminal jurisdiction over the Indian Territory.
MR. BARLOW: How long have you occupied such office?
MR. COGBURN: Be four years in March.
MR. BARLOW: On November second were you carrying out your official duties?
MR. COGBURN: I was, yes sir.
MR. BARLOW: Did something occur on that day out of the ordinary?
MR. COGBURN: Yes sir.
MR. BARLOW: Please describe in your own words what that occurrence was.
MR. COGBURN: Yes sir. Well, not long after dinner on that day we was headed back for Fort Smith from the Creek Nation and was about four miles west of Webbers Falls.

MR. BARLOW: One moment. Who was with you?

MR. COGBURN: There was four other deputy marshals and me. We had a wagonload of prisoners and was headed back for Fort Smith. Seven prisoners. About four mile west of Webbers Falls that Creek boy named Will come riding up in a lather. He had news. He said that morning he was taking some eggs over to Tom Spotted-Gourd and his wife at their place on the Canadian River. When he got there he found the woman out in the yard with the back of her head shot off and the old man inside on the floor with a shotgun wound in his breast.

MR. GOUDY: An objection.

JUDGE PARKER: Confine your testimony to what you saw, Mr. Cogburn.

MR. COGBURN: Yes sir. Well, Deputy Marshal Potter and me rode on down to Spotted-Gourd's place, with the wagon to come on behind us. Deputy Marshal Schmidt stayed with the wagon. When we got to the place we found everything as the boy Will had represented. The woman was out in the yard dead with blowflies on her head and the old man was inside with his breast blowed open by a scatter-gun and his feet burned. He was still alive but he just was. Wind was whistling in and out of the bloody hole. He said about four o'clock that morning them two Wharton boys had rode up there drunk—

MR. GOUDY: An objection.

MR. BARLOW: This is a dying declaration, your honor.

JUDGE PARKER: Overruled. Proceed, Mr. Cogburn.

MR. COGBURN: He said them two Wharton boys, Odus and C. C. by name, had rode up there drunk and throwed down on him with a double barrel shotgun and said, "Tell us where your money is, old man." He would not tell them and they lit some pine knots and held them to his feet and he told them it was in a fruit jar under a gray rock at one corner of the smokehouse. Said he had over four hundred dollars in banknotes in it. Said his wife was crying and taking on all this time and begging for mercy. Said she took off out the door and Odus run to the door and shot her. Said when he raised up off the floor where he was laying Odus turned and shot him. Then they left.

MR. BARLOW: What happened next?

MR. COGBURN: He died on us. Passed away in considerable pain.

MR. BARLOW: Mr. Spotted-Gourd, that is.

MR. COGBURN: Yes sir.

MR. BARLOW: What did you and Marshal Potter do then?

MR. COGBURN: We went out to the smokehouse and that rock had been moved and that jar was gone.

MR. GOUDY: An objection.

JUDGE PARKER: The witness will keep his speculations to himself.

MR. BARLOW: You found a flat gray rock at the corner of the smokehouse with a hollowed-out space under it?

MR. GOUDY: If the prosecutor is going to give evidence I suggest that he be sworn.

JUDGE PARKER: Mr. Barlow, that is not proper examination.

MR. BARLOW: I am sorry, your honor. Marshal Cogburn, what did you find, if anything, at the corner of the smokehouse?

MR. COGBURN: We found a gray rock with a hole right by it.

MR. BARLOW: What was in the hole?

MR. COGBURN: Nothing. No jar or nothing.

MR. BARLOW: What did you do next?

MR. COGBURN: We waited on the wagon to come. When it got there we had a talk amongst ourselves as to who would ride after the Whartons. Potter and me had had dealings with them boys before so we went. It was about a two-hour ride up near where the North Fork strikes the Canadian, on a branch that turns into the Canadian. We got there not long before sundown.

MR. BARLOW: And what did you find?

MR. COGBURN: I had my glass and we spotted the two boys and their old daddy, Aaron Wharton by name, standing down there on the creek bank with some hogs, five or six hogs. They had killed a shoat and was butchering it. It was swinging from a limb and they had built a fire under a wash pot for scalding water. We tied up our horses about a quarter of a mile down the creek and slipped along on foot through the brush so we could get the drop on them. When we showed I told the old man, Aaron Wharton, that we was U.S. marshals and we needed to talk to his boys. He picked up a ax and commenced to cussing us and blackguarding this court.

MR. BARLOW: What did you do?

MR. COGBURN: I started backing away from the ax and tried to talk some sense to him. While this was going on C. C. Wharton edged over by the wash pot behind that steam and picked up a shotgun that was laying up against a saw-log. Potter seen him but it was too late. Before he could get off a shot C. C. Wharton pulled down on him with one barrel and then turned to do the same for me with the other barrel. I shot him and when the old man swung the ax I shot him. Odus lit out for the creek and I shot him. Aaron Wharton and C. C. Wharton was dead when they hit the ground. Odus Wharton was just winged.

MR. BARLOW: Then what happened?

MR. COGBURN: Well, it was all over. I dragged Odus Wharton over to a blackjack tree and cuffed his arms and legs around it with him setting down. I tended to Potter's wound with my handkerchief as best I could. He was in a bad way. I went up to the shack and Aaron Wharton's squaw was there but she would not talk. I searched the premises and found a quart jar under some stove wood that had banknotes in it to the tune of four hundred and twenty dollars.

MR. BARLOW: What happened to Marshal Potter?

MR. COGBURN: He died in this city six days later of septic fever. Leaves a wife and six babies.

MR. GOUDY: An objection.

JUDGE PARKER: Strike the comment.

MR. BARLOW: What became of Odus Wharton?

MR. COGBURN: There he sets.

MR. BARLOW: You may ask, Mr. Goudy.

MR. GOUDY: Thank you, Mr. Barlow. How long did you say you have been a deputy marshal, Mr. Cogburn?

MR. COGBURN: Going on four years.

MR. GOUDY: How many men have you shot in that time?

MR. BARLOW: An objection.

MR. GOUDY: There is more to this shooting than meets the eye, your honor. I am trying to establish the bias of the witness.

JUDGE PARKER: The objection is overruled.

MR. GOUDY: How many, Mr. Cogburn?

MR. COGBURN: I never shot nobody I didn't have to.

MR. GOUDY: That was not the question. How many?

MR. COGBURN: Shot or killed?

MR. GOUDY: Let us restrict it to "killed" so that we may have a manageable figure. How many people have you killed since you became a marshal for this court?

MR. COGBURN: Around twelve or fifteen, stopping men in flight and defending myself.

MR. GOUDY: Around twelve or fifteen. So many that you cannot keep a precise count. Remember that you are under oath. I have examined the records and a more accurate figure is readily available. Come now, how many?

MR. COGBURN: I believe them two Whartons made twenty-three.

MR. GOUDY: I felt sure it would come to you with a little effort. Now let us see. Twenty-three dead men in four years. That comes to about six men a year.

MR. COGBURN: It is dangerous work.

MR. GOUDY: So it would seem. And yet how much more dangerous for those luckless individuals who find themselves being arrested by you. How many members of this one family, the Wharton family, have you killed?

MR. BARLOW: Your honor, I think counsel should be advised that the marshal is not the defendant in this action.

MR. GOUDY: Your honor, my client and his deceased father and brother were provoked into a gun battle by this man Cogburn. Last spring he shot and killed Aaron Wharton's oldest son and on November second he fairly leaped at the chance to massacre the rest of the family. I will prove that. This assassin Cogburn has too long been clothed with the authority of an honorable court. The only way I can prove my client's innocence is by bringing out the facts of these two related shootings, together with a searching review of Cogburn's methods. All the other principals, including Marshal Potter, are conveniently dead—

JUDGE PARKER: That will do, Mr. Goudy. Restrain yourself. We shall hear your argument later. The defense will be given every latitude. I do not think the indiscriminate use of such words as "massacre" and "assassin" will bring us any nearer the truth. Pray continue with your cross-examination.

MR. GOUDY: Thank you, your honor. Mr. Cogburn, did you know the late Dub Wharton, brother to the defendant, Odus Wharton?

MR. COGBURN: I had to shoot him in self-defense last April in the Going Snake District of the Cherokee Nation.

MR. GOUDY: How did that come about?

MR. COGBURN: I was trying to serve a warrant on him for selling ardent spirits to the Cherokees. It was not the first one. He come at me with a kingbolt and said, "Rooster, I am going to punch that other eye out." I defended myself.

MR. GOUDY: He was armed with nothing more than a king-bolt from a wagon tongue?

MR. COGBURN: I didn't know what else he had. I saw he had that. I have seen men badly tore up with things no bigger than a kingbolt.

MR. GOUDY: Were you yourself armed?

MR. COGBURN: Yes sir. I had a hand gun.

MR. GOUDY: What kind of hand gun?

MR. COGBURN: A forty-four forty Colt's revolver.

MR. GOUDY: Is it not true that you walked in upon him in the dead of night with that revolver in your hand and gave him no warning?

MR. COGBURN: I had pulled it, yes sir.

MR. GOUDY: Was the weapon loaded and cocked?

MR. COGBURN: Yes sir.

MR. GOUDY: Were you holding it behind you or in any way concealing it?

MR. COGBURN: No sir.

MR. GOUDY: Are you saying that Dub Wharton advanced into the muzzle of that cocked revolver with nothing more than a small piece of iron in his hand?

MR. COGBURN: That was the way of it.

MR. GOUDY: It is passing strange. Now, is it not true that on November second you appeared before Aaron Wharton and his two sons in a similar menacing manner, which is to say, you sprang upon them from cover with that same deadly six-shot revolver in your hand?

MR. COGBURN: I always try to be ready.

MR. GOUDY: The gun was pulled and ready in your hand?

MR. COGBURN: Yes sir.

MR. GOUDY: Loaded and cocked?

MR. COGBURN: If it ain't loaded and cocked it will not shoot.

MR. GOUDY: Just answer my questions if you please.

MR. COGBURN: That one does not make any sense.

JUDGE PARKER: Do not bandy words with counsel, Mr. Cogburn.

MR. COGBURN: Yes sir.

MR. GOUDY: Mr. Cogburn, I now direct your attention back to that scene on the creek bank. It is near dusk. Mr. Aaron Wharton and his two surviving sons are going about their lawful business, secure on their own property. They are butchering a hog so that they might have a little meat for their table—

MR. COGBURN: Them was stolen hogs. That farm belongs to the Wharton squaw, Minnie Wharton.

MR. GOUDY: Your honor, will you instruct this witness to keep silent until he is asked a question?

JUDGE PARKER: Yes, and I will instruct you to start asking questions so that he may respond with answers.

MR. GOUDY: I am sorry, your honor. All right. Mr. Wharton and his sons are on the creek bank. Suddenly, out of the brake, spring two men with revolvers at the ready—

MR. BARLOW: An objection.

JUDGE PARKER: The objection has merit. Mr. Goudy, I have been extremely indulgent. I am going to permit you to continue this line of questioning but I must insist that the cross-examination take the form of questions and answers instead of dramatic soliloquies. And I will caution you that this had best lead to something substantial and fairly soon.

MR. GOUDY: Thank you, your honor. If the court will bear with me for a time. My client has expressed fears about the severity of this court but I have reassured him that no man in this noble Republic loves truth and justice and mercy more than Judge Isaac Parker—

JUDGE PARKER: You are out of order, Mr. Goudy.

MR. GOUDY: Yes sir. All right. Now. Mr. Cogburn, when you and Marshal Potter sprang from the brush, what was Aaron Wharton's reaction on seeing you?

MR. COGBURN: He picked up a ax and commenced to cussing us.

MR. GOUDY: An instinctive reflex against a sudden danger. Was that the nature of the move?

MR. COGBURN: I don't know what that means.

MR. GOUDY: You would not have made such a move yourself?

MR. COGBURN: If it was me and Potter with the drop I would have done what I was told.

MR. GOUDY: Yes, exactly, you and Potter. We can agree that the Whartons were in peril of their lives. All right. Let us go back to yet an earlier scene, at the Spotted-Gourd home, around the wagon. Who was in charge of that wagon?

MR. COGBURN: Deputy Marshal Schmidt.

MR. GOUDY: He did not want you to go to the Wharton place, did he?

MR. COGBURN: We talked about it some and he agreed Potter and me should go.

MR. GOUDY: But at first he did not want you to go, did he, knowing there was bad blood between you and the Whartons?

MR. COGBURN: He must have wanted me to go or he would not have sent me.

MR. GOUDY: You had to persuade him, did you not?

MR. COGBURN: I knowed the Whartons and I was afraid somebody would get killed going up against them.

MR. GOUDY: As it turned out, how many were killed?

MR. COGBURN: Three. But the Whartons did not get away. It could have been worse.

MR. GOUDY: Yes, you might have been killed yourself.

MR. COGBURN: You mistake my meaning. Three murdering thieves might have got loose and gone to kill somebody else. But you are right that I might have been killed myself. It was mighty close at that and it is no light matter to me.

MR. GOUDY: Nor to me. You are truly one of nature's survivors, Mr. Cogburn, and I do not make light of your gift. I believe you testified that you backed away from Aaron Wharton.

MR. COGBURN: That is right.

MR. GOUDY: You were backing away?

MR. COGBURN: Yes sir. He had that ax raised.

MR. GOUDY: Which direction were you going?

MR. COGBURN: I always go backwards when I am backing up.

MR. GOUDY: I appreciate the humor of that remark. Aaron Wharton was standing by the wash pot when you arrived?

MR. COGBURN: It was more like squatting. He was stoking up the fire under the pot.

MR. GOUDY: And where was the ax?

MR. COGBURN: Right there at his hand.

MR. GOUDY: Now you say you had a cocked revolver clearly visible in your hand and yet he picked up that ax and advanced upon you, somewhat in the manner of Dub Wharton with that nail or rolled-up paper or whatever it was in his hand?

MR. COGBURN: Yes sir. Commenced to cussing and laying about with threats.

MR. GOUDY: And you were backing away? You were moving away from the direction of the wash pot?

MR. COGBURN: Yes sir.

MR. GOUDY: How far did you back up before the shooting started?

MR. COGBURN: About seven or eight steps.

MR. GOUDY: Meaning Aaron Wharton advanced on you about the same distance, some seven or eight steps?

MR. COGBURN: Something like that.

MR. GOUDY: What would that be? About sixteen feet?

MR. COGBURN: Something like that.

MR. GOUDY: Will you explain to the jury why his body was found immediately by the wash pot with one arm in the fire, his sleeve and hand smoldering?

MR. COGBURN: I don't think that is where he was.

MR. GOUDY: Did you move the body after you had shot him?

MR. COGBURN: No sir.

MR. GOUDY: You did not drag his body back to the fire?

MR. COGBURN: No sir. I don't think that is where he was.

MR. GOUDY: Two witnesses who arrived on the scene moments after the shooting will testify to the location of the body. You don't remember moving the body?

MR. COGBURN: If that is where he was I might have moved him. I don't remember it.

MR. GOUDY: Why did you place the upper part of his body in the fire?

MR. COGBURN: Well, I didn't do it.

MR. GOUDY: Then you did not move him and he was not advancing upon you at all. Or you did move him and throw his body in the flames. Which? Make up your mind.

MR. COGBURN: Them hogs that was rooting around there might have moved him.

MR. GOUDY: Hogs indeed.

JUDGE PARKER: Mr. Goudy, darkness is upon us. Do you think you can finish with this witness in the next few minutes?

MR. GOUDY: I will need more time, your honor.

JUDGE PARKER: Very well. You may resume at eight-thirty o'clock tomorrow morning. Mr. Cogburn, you will return to the witness stand at that time. The jury will not talk to others or converse amongst themselves about this case. The defendant is remanded to custody.

The judge rapped his gavel and I jumped, not looking for that noise. The crowd broke up to leave. I had not been able to get a good look at that Odus Wharton but now I did when he stood up with an officer on each side of him. Even though he had one arm in a sling they kept his wrists cuffed in court. That was how dangerous he was. If there ever was a man with black murder in his countenance it was Odus Wharton. He was a half-breed with eyes that were mean and close-set and that stayed open all the time like snake eyes. It was a face hardened in sin. Creeks are good Indians, they say, but a Creek-white like him or a Creek-Negro is something else again.

When the officers were taking Wharton out he passed by Rooster Cogburn and said something to him, some ugly insult or threat, you could tell. Rooster just looked at him. The people pushed me on through the door and outside. I waited on the porch.

Rooster was one of the last ones out. He had a paper in one hand and a sack of tobacco in the other and he was trying to roll a cigarette. His hands were shaking and he was spilling tobacco.

I approached him and said, "Mr. Rooster Cogburn?"

He said, "What is it?" His mind was on something else.

I said, "I would like to talk with you a minute."

He looked me over. "What is it?" he said.

I said, "They tell me you are a man with true grit."

He said, "What do you want, girl? Speak up. It is suppertime."

I said, "Let me show you how to do that." I took the half-made cigarette and shaped it up and licked it and sealed it and twisted the ends and gave it back to him. It was pretty loose because he had already wrinkled the paper. He lit it and it flamed up and burned about halfway down.

I said, "Your makings are too dry."

He studied it and said, "Something."

I said, "I am looking for the man who shot and killed my father, Frank Ross, in front of the Monarch boardinghouse. The man's name is Tom Chaney. They say he is over in the Indian Territory and I need somebody to go after him."

He said, "What is your name, girl? Where do you live?"

"My name is Mattie Ross," I replied. "We are located in Yell County near Dardanelle. My mother is at home looking after my sister Victoria and my brother Little Frank."

"You had best go home to them," said he. "They will need some help with the churning."

I said, "The high sheriff and a man in the marshal's office have given me the full particulars. You can get a fugitive warrant for Tom Chaney and go after him. The Government will pay you two dollars for bringing him in plus ten cents a mile for each of you. On top of that I will pay you a fifty-dollar reward."

"You have looked into this a right smart," said he.

"Yes, I have," said I. "I mean business."

He said, "What have you got there in your poke?"

I opened the sugar sack and showed him.

"By God!" said he. "A Colt's dragoon! Why, you are no bigger than a corn nubbin! What are you doing with that pistol?"

I said, "It belonged to my father. I intend to kill Tom Chaney with it if the law fails to do so."

"Well, that piece will do the job. If you can find a high stump to rest it on while you take aim and shoot."

"Nobody here knew my father and I am afraid nothing much is going to be done about Chaney except I do it myself. My brother is a child and my mother's people are in Monterey, California. My Grandfather Ross is not able to ride."

"I don't believe you have fifty dollars."

"I will have it in a day or two. Have you heard of a robber called Lucky Ned Pepper?"

"I know him well. I shot him in the lip last August down in the Winding Stair Mountains. He was plenty lucky that day."

"They think Tom Chaney has tied up with him."

"I don't believe you have fifty dollars, baby sister, but if you are hungry I will give you supper and we will talk it over and make medicine. How does that suit you?"

I said it suited me right down to ground. I figured he would live in a house with his family and was not prepared to discover that he had only a small room in the back of a Chinese grocery store on a dark street. He did not have a wife. The Chinaman was called Lee. He had a supper ready of boiled potatoes and stew meat. The three of us ate at a low table with a coal-oil lamp in the middle of it. There was a blanket for a tablecloth. A little bell rang once and Lee went up front through a curtain to wait on a customer.

Rooster said he had heard about the shooting of my father but did not know the details. I told him. I noticed by the lamplight that his bad left eye was not completely shut. A little crescent of white showed at the bottom and glistened in the light. He ate with a spoon in one hand and a wadded-up piece of white bread in the other, with considerable sopping. What a contrast to the Chinaman with his delicate chopsticks! I had never seen them in use before. Such nimble fingers! When the coffee had boiled Lee got the pot off the stove and started to pour. I put my hand over my cup.

"I do not drink coffee, thank you."

Rooster said, "What do you drink?"

"I am partial to cold buttermilk when I can get it."

"Well, we don't have none," said he. "Nor lemonade either."

"Do you have any sweet milk?"

Lee went up front to his icebox and brought back a jar of milk. The cream had been skimmed from it.

I said, "This tastes like blue-john to me."

Rooster took my cup and put it on the floor and a fat brindle cat appeared out of the darkness where the bunks were and came over to lap up the milk. Rooster said, "The General is not so hard to please." The cat's name was General Sterling Price. Lee served some honey cakes for dessert and Rooster spread butter and preserves all over his like a small child. He had a "sweet tooth."

I offered to clean things up and they took me at my word. The pump and the washstand were outside. The cat followed me out for the scraps. I did the best I could on the enamel-ware plates with a rag and yellow soap and cold water. When I got back inside Rooster and Lee were playing cards on the table.

Rooster said, "Let me have my cup." I gave it to him and he poured some whiskey in it from a demijohn. Lee smoked a long pipe.

I said, "What about my proposition?"

Rooster said, "I am thinking on it."

"What is that you are playing?"

"Seven-up. Do you want a hand?"

"I don't know how to play it. I know how to play bid whist."

"We don't play bid whist."

I said, "It sounds like a mighty easy way to make fifty dollars to me. You would just be doing your job anyway, and getting extra pay besides."

"Don't crowd me," said he. "I am thinking about expenses."

I watched them and kept quiet except for blowing my nose now and again. After a time I said, "I don't see how you can play cards and drink whiskey and think about this detective business all at the same time."

He said, "If I'm going up against Ned Pepper I will need a hundred dollars. I have figured out that much. I will want fifty dollars in advance."

"You are trying to take advantage of me."

"I am giving you my children's rate," he said. "It will not be a easy job of work, smoking Ned out. He will be holed up down there in the hills in the Choctaw Nation. There will be expenses."

"I hope you don't think I am going to keep you in whiskey."

"I don't have to buy that, I confiscate it. You might try a little touch of it for your cold."

"No, thank you."

"This is the real article. It is double-rectified busthead from Madison County, aged in the keg. A little spoonful would do you a power of good."

"I would not put a thief in my mouth to steal my brains."

"Oh, you wouldn't, would you?"

"No, I wouldn't."

"Well, a hundred dollars is my price, sis. There it is."

"For that kind of money I would want a guarantee. I would want to be pretty sure of what I was getting."

"I have not yet seen the color of your money."

"I will have the money in a day or two. I will think about your proposition and talk to you again. Now I want to go to the Monarch boardinghouse. You had better walk over there with me."

"Are you scared of the dark?"

"I never was scared of the dark."

"If I had a big horse pistol like yours I would not be scared of any booger-man."

"I am not scared of the booger-man. I don't know the way over there."

"You are a lot of trouble. Wait until I finish this hand. You cannot tell what a Chinaman is thinking. That is how they beat you at cards."

They were betting money on the play and Rooster was not winning. I kept after him but he would only say, "One more hand," and pretty soon I was asleep with my head on the table. Some time later he began to shake me.

"Wake up," he was saying. "Wake up, baby sister."

"What is it?" said I.

He was drunk and he was fooling around with Papa's pistol. He pointed out something on the floor over by the curtain that opened into the store. I looked and it was a big long barn rat. He sat there hunkered on the floor, his tail flat, and he was eating meal that was spilling out of a hole in the sack. I gave a start but Rooster put his tobacco-smelling hand over my mouth and gripped my cheeks and held me down.

He said, "Be right still." I looked around for Lee and figured he must have gone to bed. Rooster said, "I will try this the new way. Now watch." He leaned forward and spoke at the rat in a low voice, saying, "I have a writ here that says for you to stop eating Chen Lee's corn meal forthwith. It is a rat writ. It is a writ for a rat and this is lawful service of said writ." Then he looked over at me and said, "Has he stopped?" I gave no reply. I have never wasted any time encouraging drunkards or show-offs. He said, "It don't look like to me he has stopped." He was holding Papa's revolver down at his left side and he fired twice without aiming. The noise filled up that little room and made the curtains jump. My ears rang. There was a good deal of smoke.

Lee sat up in his bunk and said, "Outside is place for shooting."

"I was serving some papers," said Rooster.

The rat was a mess. I went over and picked him up by the tail and pitched him out the back door for Sterling, who should have smelled him out and dispatched him in the first place.

I said to Rooster, "Don't be shooting that pistol again. I don't have any more loads for it."

He said, "You would not know how to load it if you did have."

"I know how to load it."

He went to his bunk and pulled out a tin box that was underneath and brought it to the table. The box was full of oily rags and loose cartridges and odd bits of leather and string. He brought out some lead balls and little copper percussion caps and a tin of powder.

He said, "All right, let me see you do it. There is powder, caps and bullets."

"I don't want to right now. I am sleepy and I want to go to my quarters at the Monarch boardinghouse."

"Well, I didn't think you could," said he.

He commenced to reload the two chambers. He dropped things and got them all askew and did not do a good job. When he had finished he said, "This piece is too big and clumsy for you. You are better off with something that uses cartridges."

He poked around in the bottom of the box and came up
with a funny little pistol with several barrels. "Now this is what
you need," he said. "It is a twenty-two pepper-box that shoots
five times, and sometimes all at once. It is called 'The Ladies'
Companion.' There is a sporting lady called Big Faye in this
city who was shot twice with it by her stepsister. Big Faye
dresses out at about two hundred and ninety pounds. The bullets could not make it through to any vitals. That was unusual.
It will give you good service against ordinary people. It is like
new. I will trade you even for this old piece."

I said, "No, that was Papa's gun. I am ready to go. Do you
hear me?" I took my revolver from him and put it back in the
sack. He poured some more whiskey in his cup.

"You can't serve papers on a rat, baby sister."

"I never said you could."

"These shitepoke lawyers think you can but you can't. All
you can do with a rat is kill him or let him be. They don't care
nothing about papers. What is your thinking on it?"

"Are you going to drink all that?"

"Judge Parker knows. He is a old carpetbagger but he knows
his rats. We had a good court here till the pettifogging lawyers
moved in on it. You might think Polk Goudy is a fine gentleman to look at his clothes, but he is the sorriest son of a bitch
that God ever let breathe. I know him well. Now they have got
the judge down on me, and the marshal too. The rat-catcher
is too hard on the rats. That is what they say. *Let up on them
rats! Give them rats a fair show!* What kind of show did they
give Columbus Potter? Tell me that. A finer man never lived."

I got up and walked out thinking I would shame him into
coming along and seeing that I got home all right but he did
not follow. He was still talking when I left. The town was quite
dark at that end and I walked fast and saw not a soul although
I heard music and voices and saw lights up toward the river
where the barrooms were.

When I reached Garrison Avenue I stopped and got my
bearings. I have always had a good head for directions. It did
not take me long to reach the Monarch. The house was dark.
I went around to the back door with the idea that it would
be unlocked because of the toilet traffic. I was right. Since I
had not yet paid for another day it occurred to me that Mrs.

Floyd might have installed a new guest in Grandma Turner's bed, perhaps some teamster or railroad detective. I was much relieved to find my side of the bed vacant. I got the extra blankets and arranged them as I had done the night before. I said my prayers and it was some time before I got any sleep. I had a cough.

I WAS sick the next day. I got up and went to breakfast but I could not eat much and my eyes and nose were running so I went back to bed. I felt very low. Mrs. Floyd wrapped a rag around my neck that was soaked in turpentine and smeared with lard. She dosed me with something called Dr. Underwood's Bile Activator. "You will pass blue water for a day or two but do not be alarmed as that is only the medicine working," she said. "It will relax you wonderfully. Grandma Turner and I bless the day we discovered it." The label on the bottle said it did not contain mercury and was commended by physicians and clergymen.

Along with the startling color effect the potion also caused me to be giddy and lightheaded. I suspect now that it made use of some such ingredient as codeine or laudanum. I can remember when half the old ladies in the country were "dopeheads."

Thank God for the Harrison Narcotics Law. Also the Volstead Act. I know Governor Smith is "wet" but that is because of his race and religion and he is not personally accountable for that. I think his first loyalty is to his country and not to "the infallible Pope of Rome." I am not afraid of Al Smith for a minute. He is a good Democrat and when he is elected I believe he will do the right thing if he is not hamstrung by the Republican gang and bullied into an early grave as was done to Woodrow Wilson, the greatest Presbyterian gentleman of the age.

I stayed in bed for two days. Mrs. Floyd was kind and brought my meals to me. The room was so cold that she did not linger to ask many questions. She inquired twice daily at the post office for my letter.

Grandma Turner got in the bed each afternoon for her rest and I would read to her. She loved her medicine and would drink it from a water glass. I read her about the Wharton trial in the *New Era* and the *Elevator*. I also read a little book someone had left on the table called *Bess Calloway's Disappointment*. It was about a girl in England who could not make up her mind whether to marry a rich man with a pack of dogs named Alec or a preacher. She was a pretty girl in easy circumstances who did not have to cook or work at anything and she could

have either one she wanted. She made trouble for herself because she would never say what she meant but only blush and
talk around it. She kept everybody in a stir wondering what
she was driving at. That was what held your interest. Grandma
Turner and I both enjoyed it. I had to read the humorous parts
twice. Bess married one of the two beaus and he turned out to
be mean and thoughtless. I forget which one it was.

On the evening of the second day I felt a little better and I
got up and went to supper. The drummer was gone with his
midget calculators and there were four or five other vacancies
at the table as well.

Toward the end of the meal a stranger came in wearing
two revolvers and made known that he was seeking room and
board. He was a nice-looking man around thirty years of age
with a "cowlick" at the crown of his head. He needed a bath
and a shave but you could tell that was not his usual condition.
He looked to be a man of good family. He had pale-blue eyes
and auburn hair. He was wearing a long corduroy coat. His
manner was stuck-up and he had a smug grin that made you
nervous when he turned it on you.

He forgot to take off his spurs before sitting down at the
table and Mrs. Floyd chided him, saying she did not want her
chair legs scratched up any more than they were, which was
considerable. He apologized and complied with her wish. The
spurs were the Mexican kind with big rowels. He put them up
on the table by his plate. Then he remembered his revolvers
and he unbuckled the gun belt and hung it on the back of his
chair. This was a fancy rig. The belt was thick and wide and
bedecked with cartridges and the handles on his pistols were
white. It was like something you might see today in a "Wild
West" show.

His grin and his confident manner cowed everybody at the
table but me and they stopped talking and made a to-do about
passing him things, like he was somebody. I must own too that
he made me worry a little about my straggly hair and red nose.

While he was helping himself to the food he grinned at me
across the table and said, "Hidy."

I nodded and said nothing.

"What is your name?" said he.

"Pudding and tame," said I.

He said, "I will take a guess and say it is Mattie Ross."

"How do you know that?"

"My name is LaBoeuf," he said. He called it LaBeef but spelled it something like LaBoeuf. "I saw your mother just two days ago. She is worried about you."

"What was your business with her, Mr. LaBoeuf?"

"I will disclose that after I eat. I would like to have a confidential conversation with you."

"Is she all right? Is anything wrong?"

"No, she is fine. There is nothing wrong. I am looking for someone. We will talk about it after supper. I am very hungry."

Mrs. Floyd said, "If it is something touching on her father's death we know all about that. He was murdered in front of this very house. There is still blood on my porch where they carried his body."

The man LaBoeuf said, "It is about something else."

Mrs. Floyd described the shooting again and tried to draw him out on his business but he only smiled and went on eating and would not be drawn.

After supper we went to the parlor, to a corner away from the other boarders, and LaBoeuf set up two chairs there facing the wall. When we were seated in this curious arrangement he took a small photograph from his corduroy coat and showed it to me. The picture was wrinkled and dim. I studied it. The face of the man was younger and there was no black mark but there was no question but it was the likeness of Tom Chaney. I told LaBoeuf as much.

He said, "Your mother has also identified him. Now I will give you some news. His real name is Theron Chelmsford. He shot and killed a state senator named Bibbs down in Waco, Texas, and I have been on his trail the best part of four months. He dallied in Monroe, Louisiana, and Pine Bluff, Arkansas, before turning up at your father's place."

I said, "Why did you not catch him in Monroe, Louisiana, or Pine Bluff, Arkansas?"

"He is a crafty one."

"I thought him slow-witted myself."

"That was his act."

"It was a good one. Are you some kind of law?"

LaBoeuf showed me a letter that identified him as a Sergeant of Texas Rangers, working out of a place called Ysleta near El

Paso. He said, "I am on detached service just now. I am working for the family of Senator Bibbs in Waco."

"How came Chaney to shoot a senator?"

"It was about a dog. Chelmsford shot the senator's bird dog. Bibbs threatened to whip him over it and Chelmsford shot the old gentleman while he was sitting in a porch swing."

"Why did he shoot the dog?"

"I don't know that. Just meanness. Chelmsford is a hard case. He claims the dog barked at him. I don't know if he did or not."

"I am looking for him too," said I, "this man you call Chelmsford."

"Yes, that is my understanding. I had a conversation with the sheriff today. He informed me that you were staying here and looking for a special detective to go after Chelmsford in the Indian Territory."

"I have found a man for the job."

"Who is the man?"

"His name is Cogburn. He is a deputy marshal for the Federal Court. He is the toughest one they have and he is familiar with a band of robbers led by Lucky Ned Pepper. They believe Chaney has tied up with that crowd."

"Yes, that is the thing to do," said LaBoeuf. "You need a Federal man. I am thinking along those lines myself. I need someone who knows the ground and can make an arrest out there that will stand up. You cannot tell what the courts will do these days. I might get Chelmsford all the way down to McLennan County, Texas, only to have some corrupt judge say he was kidnaped and turn him loose. Wouldn't that be something?"

"It would be a letdown."

"Maybe I will throw in with you and your marshal."

"You will have to talk to Rooster Cogburn about that."

"It will be to our mutual advantage. He knows the land and I know Chelmsford. It is at least a two-man job to take him alive."

"Well, it is nothing to me one way or the other except that when we do get Chaney he is not going to Texas, he is coming back to Fort Smith and hang."

"Haw haw," said LaBoeuf. "It is not important where he hangs, is it?"

"It is to me. Is it to you?"

"It means a good deal of money to me. Would not a hanging in Texas serve as well as a hanging in Arkansas?"

"No. You said yourself they might turn him loose down there. This judge will do his duty."

"If they don't hang him we will shoot him. I can give you my word as a Ranger on that."

"I want Chaney to pay for killing my father and not some Texas bird dog."

"It will not be for the dog, it will be for the senator, and your father too. He will be just as dead that way, you see, and pay for all his crimes at once."

"No, I do not see. That is not the way I look at it."

"I will have a conversation with the marshal."

"It's no use talking to him. He is working for me. He must do as I say."

"I believe I will have a conversation with him all the same."

I realized I had made a mistake by opening up to this stranger. I would have been more on my guard had he been ugly instead of nice-looking. Also my mind was soft and not right from being doped by the bile activator.

I said, "You will not have a conversation with him for a few days at any rate."

"How is that?"

"He has gone to Little Rock."

"On what business?"

"Marshal business."

"Then I will have a conversation with him when he returns."

"You will be wiser to get yourself another marshal. They have aplenty of them. I have already made an arrangement with Rooster Cogburn."

"I will look into it," said he. "I think your mother would not approve of your getting mixed up in this kind of enterprise. She thinks you are seeing about a horse. Criminal investigation is sordid and dangerous and is best left in the hands of men who know the work."

"I suppose that is you. Well, if in four months I could not find Tom Chaney with a mark on his face like banished Cain I would not undertake to advise others how to do it."

"A saucy manner does not go down with me."

"I will not be bullied."

He stood up and said, "Earlier tonight I gave some thought to stealing a kiss from you, though you are very young, and sick and unattractive to boot, but now I am of a mind to give you five or six good licks with my belt."

"One would be as unpleasant as the other," I replied. "Put a hand on me and you will answer for it. You are from Texas and ignorant of our ways but the good people of Arkansas do not go easy on men who abuse women and children."

"The youth of Texas are brought up to be polite and to show respect for their elders."

"I notice people of that state also gouge their horses with great brutal spurs."

"You will push that saucy line too far."

"I have no regard for you."

He was angered and thus he left me, clanking away in all his Texas trappings.

I ROSE early the next morning, somewhat improved though still wobbly on my feet. I dressed quickly and made haste to the post office without waiting for breakfast. The mail had come in but it was still being sorted and the delivery window was not yet open.

I gave a shout through the slot where you post letters and brought a clerk to the window. I identified myself and told him I was expecting a letter of an important legal nature. He knew of it through Mrs. Floyd's inquiries and he was good enough to interrupt his regular duties to search it out. He found it in a matter of minutes.

I tore it open with impatient fingers. There it was, the notarized release (money in my pocket!), and a letter from Lawyer Daggett as well.

The letter ran thus:

My Dear Mattie:

I trust you will find the enclosed document satisfactory. I wish you would leave these matters entirely to me or, at the very least, do me the courtesy of consulting me before making such agreements. I am not scolding you but I am saying that your headstrong ways will lead you into a tight corner one day.

That said, I shall concede that you seem to have driven a fair bargain with the good colonel. I know nothing of the man, of his probity or lack of same, but I should not give him this release until I had the money in hand. I feel sure you have taken his measure.

Your mother is bearing up well but is much concerned for you and anxious for your speedy return. I join her in that. Fort Smith is no place for a young girl alone, not even a "Mattie." Little Frank is down with an earache but of course that is no serious matter. Victoria is in fine fettle. It was thought best that she not attend the funeral.

Mr. MacDonald is still away on his deer hunt and Mr. Hardy was pressed into service to preach Frank's funeral, taking his text from the 16th chapter of John, "I have overcome the world." I know Mr. Hardy is not much esteemed for his social qualities but he is a good man in his way and no one can say he is not a diligent student of the Scriptures. The Danville lodge had charge of the graveside service. Needless to say, the whole community is shocked and grieved. Frank was a rich man in friends.

Your mother and I shall expect you to take the first train home when you have concluded your business with the colonel. You will wire me immediately with regard to that and we shall look for you in a day or two. I should like to get Frank's estate through probate without delay and there are important matters to be discussed with you. Your mother will make no decision without you, nor will she sign anything, not even common receipts; hence nothing can move forward until you are here. You are her strong right arm now, Mattie, and you are a pearl of great price to me, but there are times when you are an almighty trial to those who love you. Hurry home! I am

*Thine Truly,*
Jno. Daggett

If you want anything done right you will have to see to it yourself every time. I do not know to this day why they let a wool-hatted crank like Owen Hardy preach the service. Knowing the Gospel and preaching it are two different things. A Baptist or even a Campbellite would have been better than him. If I had been home I would never have permitted it but I could not be in two places at once.

Stonehill was not in a quarrelsome mood that morning, indeed he was not snorting or blowing at all but rather in a sad, baffled state like that of some elderly lunatics I have known. Let me say quickly that the man was not crazy. My comparison is not a kind one and I would not use it except to emphasize his changed manner.

He wanted to write me a check and I know that it would have been all right but I did not wish to take the affair this far and risk being rooked, so I insisted on cash money. He said he would have it as soon as his bank opened.

I said, "You do not look well."

He said, "My malaria is making its annual visitation."

"I have been a little under the weather myself. Have you taken any quinine?"

"Yes, I am stuffed to the gills with the Peruvian bark. My ears are fairly ringing from it. It does not take hold as it once did."

"I hope you will be feeling better."

"Thank you. It will pass."

I returned to the Monarch to get the breakfast I had paid for. LaBoeuf the Texan was at the table, shaved and clean. I supposed he could do nothing with the "cowlick." It is likely that he cultivated it. He was a vain and cocky devil. Mrs. Floyd asked me if the letter had come.

I said, "Yes, I have the letter. It came this morning."

"Then I know you are relieved," said she. Then to the others, "She has been awaiting that letter for days." Then back to me, "Have you seen the colonel yet?"

"I have just now come from that place," I replied.

LaBoeuf said, "What colonel is that?"

"Why, Colonel Stockhill the stone trader," said Mrs. Floyd.

I broke in to say, "It is a personal matter."

"Did you get your settlement?" said Mrs. Floyd, who could no more keep her mouth closed than can a yellow catfish.

"What kind of stones?" said LaBoeuf.

"It is Stonehill the stock trader," said I. "He does not deal in stones but livestock. I sold him some half-starved ponies that came up from Texas. There is nothing more to it."

"You are powerful young for a horsetrader," said LaBoeuf. "Not to mention your sex."

"Yes, and you are powerful free for a stranger," said I.

"Her father bought the ponies from the colonel just before he was killed," said Mrs. Floyd. "Little Mattie here stood him down and made him take them back at a good price."

Right around 9 o'clock I went to the stock barn and exchanged my release for three hundred and twenty-five dollars in greenbacks. I had held longer amounts in my hand but this money, I fancied, would be pleasing out of proportion to its face value. But no, it was only three hundred and twenty-five dollars in paper and the moment fell short of my expectations. I noted the mild disappointment and made no more of it than that. Perhaps I was affected by Stonehill's downcast state.

I said, "Well, you have kept your end of the agreement and I have kept mine."

"That is so," said he. "I have paid you for a horse I do not possess and I have bought back a string of useless ponies I cannot sell again."

"You are forgetting the gray horse."

"Crow bait."

"You are looking at the thing in the wrong light."

"I am looking at it in the light of God's eternal truth."

"I hope you do not think I have wronged you in any way."

"No, not at all," said he. "My fortunes have been remarkably consistent since I came to the 'Bear State.' This is but another episode, and a relatively happy one. I was told this city was to be the Chicago of the Southwest. Well, my little friend, it is not the Chicago of the Southwest. I cannot rightly say what it is. I would gladly take pen in hand and write a thick book on my misadventures here, but dare not for fear of being called a lying romancer."

"The malaria is making you feel bad. You will soon find a buyer for the ponies."

"I have a tentative offer of ten dollars per head from the Pfitzer Soap Works of Little Rock."

"It would be a shame to destroy such spirited horseflesh and render it into soap."

"So it would. I am confident the deal will fall through."

"I will return later for my saddle."

"Very good."

I went to the Chinaman's store and bought an apple and asked Lee if Rooster was in. He said he was still in bed. I had never seen anyone in bed at 10 o'clock in the morning who was not sick but that was where he was.

He stirred as I came through the curtain. His weight was such that the bunk was bowed in the middle almost to the floor. It looked like he was in a hammock. He was fully clothed under the covers. The brindle cat Sterling Price was curled up on the foot of the bed. Rooster coughed and spit on the floor and rolled a cigarette and lit it and coughed some more. He asked me to bring him some coffee and I got a cup and took the eureka pot from the stove and did this. As he drank, little brown drops of coffee clung to his mustache like dew. Men will live like billy goats if they are let alone. He seemed in no way surprised to see me so I took the same line and stood with my back to the stove and ate my apple.

I said, "You need some more slats in that bed."

"I know," said he. "That is the trouble, there is no slats in it at all. It is some kind of a damned Chinese rope bed. I would love to burn it up."

"It is not good for your back sleeping like that."

"You are right about that too. A man my age ought to have a good bed if he has nothing else. How does the weather stand out there?"

"The wind is right sharp," said I. "It is clouding up some in the east."

"We are in for snow or I miss my guess. Did you see the moon last night?"

"I do not look for snow today."

"Where have you been, baby sister? I looked for you to come back, then give up on you. I figured you went on home."

"No, I have been at the Monarch boardinghouse right along. I have been down with something very nearly like the croup."

"Have you now? The General and me will thank you not to pass it on."

"I have about got it whipped. I thought you might inquire about me or look in on me while I was laid up."

"What made you think that?"

"I had no reason except I did not know anybody else in town."

"Maybe you thought I was a preacher that goes around paying calls on all the sick people."

"No, I did not think that."

"Preachers don't have nothing better to do. I had my work to see to. Your Government marshals don't have time to be paying a lot of social calls. They are too busy trying to follow all the regulations laid down by Uncle Sam. That gentleman will have his fee sheets just and correct or he does not pay."

"Yes, I see they are keeping you busy."

"What you see is a honest man who has worked half the night on his fee sheets. It is the devil's own work and Potter is not here to help me. If you don't have no schooling you are up against it in this country, sis. That is the way of it. No sir, that man has no chance any more. No matter if he has got sand in his craw, others will push him aside, little thin fellows that have won spelling bees back home."

I said, "I read in the paper where they are going to hang the Wharton man."

"There was nothing else they could do," said he. "It is too bad they cannot hang him three or four times."

"When will they do the job?"

"It is set for January but Lawyer Goudy is going to Washington city to see if President Hayes will not commute the sentence. The boy's mother, Minnie Wharton, has got some property and Goudy will not let up till he has got it all."

"Will the President let him off, do you think?"

"It is hard to say. What does the President know about it? I will tell you. Nothing. Goudy will claim the boy was provoked and he will tell a bushel of lies about me. I should have put a ball in that boy's head instead of his collarbone. I was thinking about my fee. You will sometimes let money interfere with your notion of what is right."

I took the folded currency from my pocket and held it up, showing it to him.

Rooster said, "By God! Look at it! How much have you got there? If I had your hand I would throw mine in."

"You did not believe I would come back, did you?"

"Well, I didn't know. You are a hard one to figure."

"Are you still game?"

"Game? I was born game, sis, and hope to die in that condition."

"How long will it take you to get ready to go?"

"Ready to go where?"

"To the Territory. To the Indian Territory to get Tom Chaney, the man who shot my father, Frank Ross, in front of the Monarch boardinghouse."

"I forget just what our agreement was."

"I offered to pay you fifty dollars for the job."

"Yes, I remember that now. What did I say to that?"

"You said your price was a hundred dollars."

"That's right, I remember now. Well, that's what it still is. It will take a hundred dollars."

"All right."

"Count it out there on the table."

"First I will have an understanding. Can we leave for the Territory this afternoon?"

He sat up in the bed. "Wait," he said. "Hold up. You are not going."

"That is part of it," said I.

"It cannot be done."

"And why not? You have misjudged me if you think I am silly enough to give you a hundred dollars and watch you ride away. No, I will see the thing done myself."

"I am a bonded U.S. marshal."

"That weighs but little with me. R. B. Hayes is the U. S. President and they say he stole Tilden out."

"You never said anything about this. I cannot go up against Ned Pepper's band and try to look after a baby at one and the same time."

"I am not a baby. You will not have to worry about me."

"You will slow me down and get in my way. If you want this job done and done fast you will let me do it my own way. Credit me for knowing my business. What if you get sick again? I can do nothing for you. First you thought I was a preacher and now you think I am a doctor with a flat stick who will look at your tongue every few minutes."

"I will not slow you down. I am a good enough rider."

"I will not be stopping at boardinghouses with warm beds and plates of hot grub on the table. It will be traveling fast and eating light. What little sleeping is done will take place on the ground."

"I have slept out at night. Papa took me and Little Frank coon hunting last summer on the Petit Jean."

"Coon hunting?"

"We were out in the woods all night. We sat around a big fire and Yarnell told ghost stories. We had a good time."

"Blast coon hunting! This ain't no coon hunt, it don't come in forty miles of being a coon hunt!"

"It is the same idea as a coon hunt. You are just trying to make your work sound harder than it is."

"Forget coon hunting. I am telling you that where I am going is no place for a shirttail kid."

"That is what they said about coon hunting. Also Fort Smith. Yet here I am."

"The first night out you will be taking on and crying for your mama."

I said, "I have left off crying, and giggling as well. Now make up your mind. I don't care anything for all this talk. You told me what your price for the job was and I have come up with it. Here is the money. I aim to get Tom Chaney and if you are not game I will find somebody who *is* game. All I have heard out of you so far is talk. I know you can drink whiskey and I have seen you kill a gray rat. All the rest has been talk. They told me you had grit and that is why I came to you. I am not paying for talk. I can get all the talk I need and more at the Monarch boardinghouse."

"I ought to slap your face."

"How do you propose to do it from that hog wallow you are sunk in? I would be ashamed of myself living in this filth. If I smelled as bad as you I would not live in a city, I would go live on top of Magazine Mountain where I would offend no one but rabbits and salamanders."

He came up out of the bunk and spilt his coffee and sent the cat squalling. He reached for me but I moved quickly out of his grasp and got behind the stove. I picked up a handful of expense sheets from the table and jerked up a stove lid with a lifter. I held them over the flames. "You had best stand back if these papers have any value to you," said I.

He said, "Put them sheets back on the table."

I said, "Not until you stand back."

He moved back a step or two. "That is not far enough," said I. "Go back to the bed."

Lee looked in through the curtain. Rooster sat down on the edge of the bed. I put the lid back on the stove and returned the papers to the table.

"Get back to your store," said Rooster, turning his anger on Lee. "Everything is all right. Sis and me is making medicine."

I said, "All right, what have you to say? I am in a hurry."

He said, "I cannot leave town until them fee sheets is done. Done and accepted."

I sat down at the table and worked over the sheets for better than an hour. There was nothing hard about it, only I had to rub out most of what he had already done. The forms were ruled with places for the entries and figures but Rooster's handwriting was so large and misguided that it covered the lines and wandered up and down into places where it should not have gone. As a consequence the written entries did not always match up with the money figures.

What he called his "vouchers" were scribbled notes, mostly undated. They ran such as this: "Rations for Cecil $1.25," and "Important words with Red .65 cts."

"Red who?" I inquired. "They are not going to pay for this kind of thing."

"That is Society Red," said he. "He used to cut crossties for the Katy. Put it down anyway. They might pay a little something on it."

"When was it? What was it for? How could you pay sixty-five cents for important words?"

"It must have been back in the summer. He ain't been seen since August when he tipped us on Ned that time."

"Was that what you paid him for?"

"No, Schmidt paid him off on that. I reckon it was cartridges I give him. I give a lot of cartridges away. I cannot recollect every little transaction."

"I will date it August fifteenth."

"We can't do that. Make it the seventeenth of October. Everything on this bunch has to come after the first of October. They won't pay behind that. We will date all the old ones ahead a little bit."

"You said you haven't seen the man since August."

"Let us change the name to Pig Satterfield and make the date the seventeenth of October. Pig helps us on timber cases and them clerks is used to seeing his name."

"His Christian name is Pig?"

"I never heard him called anything else."

I pressed him for approximate dates and bits of fact that would lend substance to the claims. He was very happy with my work. When I was finished he admired the sheets and said, "Look how neat they are. Potter never done a job like this. They will go straight through or I miss my bet."

I wrote out a short agreement regarding the business between us and had him sign it. I gave him twenty-five dollars and told him I would give him another twenty-five when we made our departure. The fifty dollars balance would be paid on the successful completion of the job.

I said, "That advance money will cover the expenses for the both of us. I expect you to provide the food for us and the grain for our horses."

"You will have to bring your own bedding," said he.

"I have blankets and a good oilskin slicker. I will be ready to go this afternoon as soon as I have got me a horse."

"No," said he, "I will be tied up at the courthouse. There are things I must attend to. We can get off at first light tomorrow. We will cross the ferry for I must pay a call on an informer in the Cherokee Nation."

"I will see you later today and make final plans."

I took dinner at the Monarch. The man LaBoeuf did not appear and I hopefully assumed he had moved on for some distant point. After a brief nap I went to the stock barn and looked over the ponies in the corral. There did not seem to be a great deal of difference in them, apart from color, and at length I decided on a black one with white forelegs.

He was a pretty thing. Papa would not own a horse with more than one white leg. There is a foolish verse quoted by horsemen to the effect that such a mount is no good, and particularly one with four white legs. I forget just how the verse goes but you will see later that there is nothing in it.

I found Stonehill in his office. He was wrapped in a shawl and sitting very close to his stove and holding his hands up before it. No doubt he was suffering from a malaria chill. I pulled up a box and sat down beside him and warmed myself.

He said, "I just received word that a young girl fell head first into a fifty-foot well on the Towson Road. I thought perhaps it was you."

"No, it was not I."

"She was drowned, they say."

"I am not surprised."

"Drowned like the fair Ophelia. Of course with her it was doubly tragic. She was distracted from a broken heart and would do nothing to save herself. I am amazed that people can bear up and carry on under these repeated blows. There is no end to them."

"She must have been silly. What do you hear from the Little Rock soap man?"

"Nothing. The matter is still hanging fire. Why do you ask?"

"I will take one of those ponies off your hands. The black one with the white stockings in front. I will call him 'Little Blackie.' I want him shod this afternoon."

"What is your offer?"

"I will pay the market price. I believe you said the soap man offered ten dollars a head."

"That is a lot price. You will recall that I paid you twenty dollars a head only this morning."

"That was the market price at that time."

"I see. Tell me this, do you entertain plans of ever leaving this city?"

"I am off early tomorrow for the Choctaw Nation. Marshal Rooster Cogburn and I are going after the murderer Chaney."

"Cogburn?" said he. "How did you light on that greasy vagabond?"

"They say he has grit," said I. "I wanted a man with grit."

"Yes, I suppose he has that. He is a notorious thumper. He is not a man I should care to share a bed with."

"No more would I."

"Report has it that he rode by the light of the moon with Quantrill and Bloody Bill Anderson. I would not trust him too much. I have heard too that he was *particeps criminis* in some road-agent work before he came here and attached himself to the courthouse."

"He is to be paid when the job is done," said I. "I have given him a token payment for expenses and he is to receive the balance when we have taken our man. I am paying a good fee of one hundred dollars."

"Yes, a splendid inducement. Well, perhaps it will all work out to your satisfaction. I shall pray that you return safely, your efforts crowned with success. It may prove to be a hard journey."

"The good Christian does not flinch from difficulties."

"Neither does he rashly court them. The good Christian is not willful or presumptuous."

"You think I am wrong."

"I think you are wrongheaded."

"We will see."

"Yes, I am afraid so."

Stonehill sold me the pony for eighteen dollars. The Negro smith caught him and brought him inside on a halter and filed his hoofs and nailed shoes on him. I brushed the burrs away and rubbed him down. He was frisky and spirited but not hysterical and he submitted to the treatment without biting or kicking us.

I put a bridle on him but I could not lift Papa's saddle easily and I had the smith saddle him. He offered to ride the pony first. I said I thought I could handle him. I climbed gingerly aboard. Little Blackie did nothing for a minute or so and then he took me by surprise and pitched twice, coming down hard with his forelegs stiff, giving severe jolts to my "tailbone" and neck. I would have been tossed to the ground had I not grabbed the saddle horn and a handful of mane. I could get a purchase on nothing else, the stirrups being far below my feet. The smith laughed but I was little concerned with good form or appearance. I rubbed Blackie's neck and talked softly to him. He did not pitch again but neither would he move forward.

"He don't know what to make of a rider so light as you," said the smith. "He thinks they is a horsefly on his back."

He took hold of the reins near the pony's mouth and coaxed him to walk. He led him around inside the big barn for a few minutes, then opened one of the doors and took him outside. I feared the daylight and cold wind would set Blackie off anew, but no, I had made me a "pal."

The smith let go of the reins and I rode the pony down the muddy street at a walk. He was not very responsive to the reins and he worried his head around over the bit. It took me a while to get him turned around. He had been ridden before but not, I gathered, in a good long time. He soon fell into it. I rode him about town until he was lightly sweating.

When I got back to the barn the smith said, "He ain't so mean, is he?"

I said, "No, he is a fine pony."

I adjusted the stirrups up as high as they would go and the smith unsaddled Little Blackie and put him in a stall. I fed him some corn but only a small measured amount as I was afraid he might founder himself on the rich grain. Stonehill had been feeding the ponies largely on hay.

It was growing late in the day. I hurried over to Lee's store, very proud of my horse and full of excitement at the prospect of tomorrow's adventure. My neck was sore from being snapped but that was a small enough bother, considering the enterprise that was afoot.

I went in the back door without knocking and found Rooster sitting at the table with the man LaBoeuf. I had forgotten about him.

"What are you doing here?" said I.

"Hidy," said LaBoeuf. "I am having a conversation with the marshal. He did not go to Little Rock after all. It is a business conversation."

Rooster was eating candy. He said, "Set down, sis, and have a piece of taffy. This jaybird calls himself LaBoeuf. He claims he is a State Ranger in Texas. He come up here to tell us how the cow eat the cabbage."

I said, "I know who he is."

"He says he is on the track of our man. He wants to throw in with us."

"I know what he wants and I have already told him we are not interested in his help. He has gone behind my back."

"What is it?" said Rooster. "What is the trouble?"

"There is no trouble, except of his own making," said I. "He made a proposition and I turned it down. That is all. We don't need him."

"Well now, he might come in handy," said Rooster. "It will not cost us anything. He has a big-bore Sharps carbine if we are jumped by buffaloes or elephants. He says he knows how to use it. I say let him go. We might run into some lively work."

"No, we don't need him," said I. "I have already told him that. I have got my horse and everything is ready. Have you seen to all your business?"

Rooster said, "Everything is ready but the grub and it is working. The chief deputy wanted to know who had done them sheets. He said he would put you on down there at good wages if you want a job. Potter's wife is fixing the eats. She is not what I call a good cook but she is good enough and she needs the money."

LaBoeuf said, "I reckon I must have the wrong man. Do you let little girls hooraw you, Cogburn?"

Rooster turned his cold right eye on the Texan. "Did you say hooraw?"

"Hooraw," said LaBoeuf. "That was the word."

"Maybe you would like to see some real hoorawing."

"There is no hoorawing in it," said I. "The marshal is working for me. I am paying him."

"How much are you paying him?" asked LaBoeuf.

"That is none of your affair."

"How much is she paying you, Cogburn?"

"She is paying enough," said Rooster.

"Is she paying five hundred dollars?"

"No."

"That is what the Governor of Texas has put up for Chelmsford."

"You don't say so," said Rooster. He thought it over. Then he said, "Well, it sounds good but I have tried to collect bounties from states and railroads too. They will lie to you quicker than a man will. You do good to get half what they say they will pay. Sometimes you get nothing. Anyhow, it sounds queer. Five hundred dollars is mighty little for a man that killed a senator."

"Bibbs was a little senator," said LaBoeuf. "They would not have put up anything except it would look bad."

"What is the terms?" said Rooster.

"Payment on conviction."

Rooster thought that one over. He said, "We might have to kill him."

"Not if we are careful."

"Even if we don't they might not convict him," said Rooster. "And even if they do, by the time they do there will be a half dozen claims for the money from little top-water peace officers down there. I believe I will stick with sis."

"You have not heard the best part," said LaBoeuf. "The Bibbs family has put up fifteen hundred dollars for Chelmsford."

"Have they now?" said Rooster. "The same terms?"

"No, the terms are these: just deliver Chelmsford up to the sheriff of McLennan County, Texas. They don't care if he is alive or dead. They pay off as soon as he is identified."

"That is more to my liking," said Rooster. "How do you figure on sharing the money?"

LaBoeuf said, "If we take him alive I will split that fifteen hundred dollars down the middle with you and claim the state reward for myself. If we have to kill him I will give you a third of the Bibbs money. That is five hundred dollars."

"You mean to keep all the state money yourself?"

"I have put in almost four months on this job. I think it is owing to me."

"Will the family pay off?"

LaBoeuf replied, "I will be frank to say the Bibbses are not loose with their money. It holds to them like the cholera to a nigger. But I guess they will have to pay. They have made public statements and run notices in the paper. There is a son, Fatty Bibbs, who wants to run for the man's seat in Austin. He will be obliged to pay."

He took the reward notices and newspaper cuttings out of his corduroy coat and spread them out on the table. Rooster looked them over for some little time. He said, "Tell me what your objection is, sis. Do you wish to cut me out of some extra money?"

I said, "This man wants to take Chaney back to Texas. That is not what I want. That was not our agreement."

Rooster said, "We will be getting him all the same. What you want is to have him caught and punished. We still mean to do that."

"I want him to know he is being punished for killing my father. It is nothing to me how many dogs and fat men he killed in Texas."

"You can let him know that," said Rooster. "You can tell him to his face. You can spit on him and make him eat sand out of the road. You can put a ball in his foot and I will hold him while you do it. But we must catch him first. We will need some help. You are being stiff-necked about this. You are young. It is time you learned that you cannot have your way in every little particular. Other people have got their interests too."

"When I have bought and paid for something I will have my way. Why do you think I am paying you if not to have my way?"

LaBoeuf said, "She is not going anyhow. I don't understand this conversation. It is not sensible. I am not used to consulting children in my business. Run along home, little britches, your mama wants you."

"Run home yourself," said I. "Nobody asked you to come up here wearing your big spurs."

"I told her she could go," said Rooster. "I will see after her."

"No," said LaBoeuf. "She will be in the way."

Rooster said, "You are taking a lot on yourself."

LaBoeuf said, "She will spell nothing but trouble and confusion. You know that as well as I do. Stop and think. She has got you buffaloed with her saucy ways."

Rooster said, "Maybe I will just catch this Chaney myself and take all the money."

LaBoeuf considered it. "You might deliver him," he said. "I would see you did not collect anything for it."

"How would you do that, jaybird?"

"I would dispute your claim. I would muddy the waters. They will not want much to back down. When it is all over they might shake your hand and thank you for your trouble and they might not."

"If you did that I would kill you," said Rooster. "Where is your profit?"

"Where is yours?" said LaBoeuf. "And I would not count too much on being able to shade somebody I didn't know."

"I can shade you all right," said Rooster. "I never seen anybody from Texas I couldn't shade. Get crossways of me, LaBoeuf, and you will think a thousand of brick has fell on you. You will wisht you had been at the Alamo with Travis."

"Knock him down, Rooster," said I.

LaBoeuf laughed. He said, "I believe she is trying to hooraw you again. Look here, I have had enough quarreling. Let us get on with our business. You have done your best to accommodate this little lady, more than most people would do, and yet she will still be contrary. Send her on her way. We will get her man. That is what you agreed to do. What if something happens to her? Have you thought about that? Her people will blame you and maybe the law will have something to say too. Why don't you think about yourself? Do you think she is concerned with your interest? She is using you. You have got to be firm."

Rooster said, "I would hate to see anything happen to her."

"You are thinking about that reward money," said I. "It is a pig in a poke. All you have heard from LaBoeuf is talk and

I have paid you cash money. If you believe anything he says I do not credit you with much sense. Look at him grin. He will cheat you."

Rooster said, "I must think about myself some too, sis."

I said, "Well, what are you going to do? You cannot carry water on both shoulders."

"We will get your man," said he. "That is the main thing."

"Let me have my twenty-five dollars. Hand it over."

"I have spent it all."

"You sorry piece of trash!"

"I will try and get it back to you. I will send it to you."

"That's a big story! If you think you are going to cheat me like this you are mistaken! You have not seen the last of Mattie Ross, not by a good deal!"

I was so mad I could have bitten my tongue off. Sterling Price the cat sensed my mood and he tucked his ears back and scampered from my path, giving me a wide berth.

I suppose I must have cried a little but it was a cold night and by the time I reached the Monarch my anger had cooled to the point where I could think straight and lay plans. There was not time enough to get another detective. Lawyer Daggett would be up here soon looking for me, probably no later than tomorrow. I thought about making a complaint to the head marshal. No, there was time for that later. I would have Lawyer Daggett skin Rooster Cogburn and nail his verminous hide to the wall. The important thing was not to lose sight of my object and that was to get Tom Chaney.

I took supper and then set about getting my things together. I had Mrs. Floyd prepare some bacon and biscuits and make little sandwiches of them. But not so little as all that, as one of her biscuits would have made two of Mama's. Very flat though, she skimped on baking powder. I also bought a small wedge of cheese from her and some dried peaches. These things I secured in a sack.

Mrs. Floyd was alive with curiosity and I told her I was going over into the Territory with some marshals to look at a man they had arrested. This did not satisfy her by any means but I pleaded ignorance of details. I told her I would likely be gone for several days and if my mother or Lawyer Daggett made inquiries (a certainty) she was to reassure them as to my safety.

I rolled up the blankets with the sack of food inside and then wrapped the slicker around the roll and made it fast with some twine. I put Papa's heavy coat on over my own coat. I had to turn the cuffs back. My little hat was not as thick and warm as his so I traded. Of course it was too big and I had to fold up some pages from the *New Era* and stick them inside the band to make for a snug fit. I took my bundle and my gun sack and left for the stock barn.

Stonehill was just leaving when I got there. He was singing the hymn *Beulah Land* to himself in a low bass voice. It is one of my favorites. He stopped singing when he saw me.

"It is you again," said he. "Is there some complaint about the pony?"

"No, I am very happy with him," said I. "Little Blackie is my 'chum.'"

"A satisfied customer gladdens the heart."

"I believe you have picked up some since last I saw you."

"Yes, I am a little better. Richard's himself again. Or will be ere the week is out. Are you leaving us?"

"I am getting an early start tomorrow and I thought I would stay the balance of the night in your barn. I don't see why I should pay Mrs. Floyd a full rate for only a few hours sleep."

"Why indeed."

He took me inside the barn and told the watchman it would be all right for me to stay the night on the office bunk. The watchman was an old man. He helped me to shake out the dusty quilt that was on the bunk. I looked in on Little Blackie at his stall and made sure everything was in readiness. The watchman followed me around.

I said to him, "Are you the one that had his teeth knocked out?"

"No, that was Tim. Mine was drawn by a dentist. He called himself a dentist."

"Who are you?"

"Toby."

"I want you to do something."

"What are you up to?"

"I am not free to discuss it. Here is a dime for you. At two hours before sunup I want you to feed this pony. Give him a double handful of oats and about the same amount of corn, but no more, along with a little hay. See that he has sufficient water. At one hour before sunup I want you to wake me up. When you have done that, put this saddle and this bridle on the pony. Have you got it all straight?"

"I am not simple, I am just old. I have handled horses for fifty years."

"Then you should do a good job. Do you have any business in the office tonight?"

"I cannot think of any."

"If you do have, take care of it now."

"There is nothing I need in there."

"That's fine. I will close the door and I do not want a lot of coming and going while I am trying to sleep."

I slept well enough wrapped in the quilt. The fire in the office stove had been banked but the little room was not so cold as to be very uncomfortable. The watchman Toby was true to his word and he woke me in the chill darkness before dawn. I was up and buttoning my boots in a moment. While Toby saddled the horse I washed myself, using some of his hot coffee water to take the sting out of a bucket of cold water.

It came to me that I should have left one of the bacon sandwiches out of the bundle for breakfast, but you can never think of everything. I did not want to open it up now. Toby gave me a portion of his grits that he had warmed up.

"Do you not have any butter to put on it?" I asked him.

"No," said he, and I had to eat it plain. I tied my roll behind the saddle as I had seen Papa do and I made doubly sure it was secure.

I could see no good place to carry the pistol. I wanted the piece ready at hand but the belt was too big around for my waist and the pistol itself was far too big and heavy to stick in the waist of my jeans. I finally tied the neck of the gun sack to the saddle horn with a good knot about the size of a turkey egg.

I led Little Blackie from his stall and mounted him. He was a little nervous and jumpy but he did not pitch. Toby tightened the girth again after I was aboard.

He said, "Have you got everything?"

"Yes, I believe I am ready. Open the door, Toby, and wish me luck. I am off for the Choctaw Nation."

It was still dark outside and bitter cold although mercifully there was little wind. Why is it calm in the early morning? You will notice that lakes are usually still and smooth before daybreak. The frozen, rutted mud of the streets made uncertain going for Little Blackie in his new shoes. He snorted and snapped his head from time to time as though to look at me. I talked to him, saying silly things.

Only four or five people were to be seen as I rode down Garrison Avenue, and they scurrying from one warm place to another. I could see lamps coming on through windows as the good people of Fort Smith began to stir for the new day.

When I reached the ferry slip on the river I dismounted and waited. I had to move and dance about to keep from getting stiff. I removed the paper wadding from inside the hatband and pulled the hat down over my ears. I had no gloves and I rolled Papa's coat sleeves down so that my hands might be covered.

There were two men running the ferry. When it reached my side and discharged a horseman, one of the ferrymen hailed me.

"Air you going acrost?" said he.

"I am waiting for someone," said I. "What is the fare?"

"Ten cents for a horse and rider."

"Have you seen Marshal Cogburn this morning?"

"Is that Rooster Cogburn?"

"That is the man."

"We have not seen him."

There were few passengers at that hour but as soon as one or two turned up the ferry would depart. It seemed to have no schedule except as business demanded, but then the crossing was not a long one. As gray dawn came I could make out chunks of ice bobbing along out in the current of the river.

The boat made at least two circuits before Rooster and LaBoeuf appeared and came riding down the incline to the slip. I had begun to worry that I might have missed them. Rooster was mounted on a big bay stallion that stood at about sixteen hands, and LaBoeuf on a shaggy cow pony not much bigger than mine.

Well, they were a sight to see with all their arms. They were both wearing their belt guns around their outside coats and

LaBoeuf cut a splendid figure with his white-handled pistols and Mexican spurs. Rooster was wearing a deerskin jacket over his black suit coat. He carried only one revolver on his belt, an ordinary-looking piece with grips of cedar or some reddish wood. On the other side, the right side, he wore a dirk knife. His gun belt was not fancy like LaBoeuf's but only a plain and narrow belt with no cartridge loops. He carried his cartridges in a sack in his pocket. But he also had two more revolvers in saddle scabbards at his thighs. They were big pistols like mine. The two officers also packed saddle guns, Rooster a Winchester repeating rifle and LaBoeuf a gun called a Sharps rifle, a kind I had never seen. My thought was this: *Chaney, look out!*

They dismounted and led their horses aboard the ferry in a clatter and I followed at a short distance. I said nothing. I was not trying to hide but neither did I do anything to call attention to myself. It was a minute or so before Rooster recognized me.

"Sure enough, we have got company," said he.

LaBoeuf was very angry. "Can you not get anything through your head?" he said to me. "Get off this boat. Did you suppose you were going with us?"

I replied, "This ferry is open to the public. I have paid my fare."

LaBoeuf reached in his pocket and brought out a gold dollar. He handed it to one of the ferrymen and said, "Slim, take this girl to town and present her to the sheriff. She is a runaway. Her people are worried nearly to death about her. There is a fifty-dollar reward for her return."

"That is a story," said I.

"Let us ask the marshal," said LaBoeuf. "What about it, Marshal?"

Rooster said, "Yes, you had best take her away. She is a runaway all right. Her name is Ross and she came up from Yell County. The sheriff has a notice on her."

"They are in this story together," said I. "I have business across the river and if you interfere with me, Slim, you may find yourself in court where you don't want to be. I have a good lawyer."

But the tall river rat would pay no heed to my protests. He

led my pony back on to the slip and the boat pulled away without me. I said, "I am not going to walk up the hill." I mounted
Little Blackie and the river rat led us up the hill. When we
reached the top I said, "Wait, stop a minute." He said, "What
is it?" I said, "There is something wrong with my hat." He
stopped and turned around. "Your hat?" said he. I took it off
and slapped him in the face with it two or three times and
made him drop the reins. I recovered them and wheeled Little Blackie about and rode him down the bank for all he was
worth. I had no spurs or switch but I used my hat on his flank
to good effect.

About fifty yards below the ferry slip the river narrowed
and I aimed for the place, going like blazes across a sandbar. I
popped Blackie all the way with my hat as I was afraid he might
shy at the water and I did not want to give him a chance to
think about it. We hit the river running and Blackie snorted
and arched his back against the icy water, but once he was in he
swam as though he was raised to it. I drew up my legs behind
me and held to the saddle horn and gave Blackie his head with
loose reins. I was considerably splashed.

The crossing was badly chosen because the narrow place of
a river is the deepest and it is there that the current is swiftest
and the banks steepest, but these things did not occur to me at
the time; shortest looked best. We came out some little ways
down the river and, as I say, the bank was steep and Blackie had
some trouble climbing it.

When we were up and free I reined in and Little Blackie
gave himself a good shaking. Rooster and LaBoeuf and the
ferryman were looking at us from the boat. We had beaten
them across. I stayed where I was. When they got off the boat
LaBoeuf hailed me, saying, "Go back, I say!" I made no reply.
He and Rooster had a parley.

Their game soon became clear. They mounted quickly and
rode off at a gallop with the idea of leaving me. What a foolish
plan, pitting horses so heavily loaded with men and hardware
against a pony so lightly burdened as Blackie!

Our course was northwesterly on the Fort Gibson Road, if
you could call it a road. This was the Cherokee Nation. Little
Blackie had a hard gait, a painful trot, and I made him speed
up and slow down until he had achieved a pace, a kind of lope,

that was not so jarring. He was a fine, spirited pony. He enjoyed this outing, you could tell.

We rode that way for two miles or more, Blackie and I hanging back from the officers at about a hundred yards. Rooster and LaBoeuf at last saw that they were making no gain and they slowed their horses to a walk. I did the same. After a mile or so of this they stopped and dismounted. I stopped too, keeping my distance, and remained in the saddle.

LaBoeuf shouted, "Come here! We will have a conversation with you!"

"You can talk from there!" I replied. "What is it you have to say?"

The two officers had another parley.

Then LaBoeuf shouted to me again, saying, "If you do not go back now I am going to whip you!"

I made no reply.

LaBoeuf picked up a rock and threw it in my direction. It fell short by about fifty yards.

I said, "That is the most foolish thing that ever I saw!"

LaBoeuf said, "Is that what you will have, a whipping?"

I said, "You are not going to whip anybody!"

They talked some more between themselves but could not seem to settle on anything and after a time they rode off again, this time at a comfortable lope.

Few travelers were on the road, only an Indian now and then on a horse or a mule, or a family in a spring wagon. I will own I was somewhat afraid of them although they were not, as you may imagine, wild Comanches with painted faces and outlandish garb but rather civilized Creeks and Cherokees and Choctaws from Mississippi and Alabama who had owned slaves and fought for the Confederacy and wore store clothes. Neither were they sullen and grave. I thought them on the cheerful side as they nodded and spoke greetings.

From time to time I would lose sight of Rooster and LaBoeuf as they went over a rise or around a bend of trees, but only briefly. I had no fears that they could escape me.

Now I will say something about the land. Some people think the present state of Oklahoma is all treeless plains. They are wrong. The eastern part (where we were traveling) is hilly and fairly well timbered with post oak and blackjack and similar hard scrub. A little farther south there is a good deal of pine as well, but right along in here at this time of year the only touches of green to be seen were cedar brakes and solitary holly trees and a few big cypresses down in the bottoms. Still, there were open places, little meadows and prairies, and from the tops of those low hills you could usually see a good long distance.

Then this happened. I was riding along woolgathering instead of keeping alert and as I came over a rise I discovered the road below me deserted. I nudged the willing Blackie with my heels. The two officers could not be far ahead. I knew they were up to some "stunt."

At the bottom of the hill there was a stand of trees and a shallow creek. I was not looking for them there at all. I thought they had raced on ahead. Just as Blackie was splashing across the creek Rooster and LaBoeuf sprang from the brush on their horses. They were right in my path. Little Blackie reared and I was almost thrown.

LaBoeuf was off his horse before you could say "Jack Robinson," and at my side. He pulled me from the saddle and threw me to the ground, face down. He twisted one of my arms behind me and put his knee in my back. I kicked and struggled but the big Texan was too much for me.

"Now we will see what tune you sing," said he. He snapped a limb off a willow bush and commenced to push one of my trouser legs above my boot. I kicked violently so that he could not manage the trouser leg.

Rooster remained on his horse. He sat up there in the saddle and rolled a cigarette and watched. The more I kicked the harder LaBoeuf pressed down with his knee and I soon saw the game was up. I left off struggling. LaBoeuf gave me a couple of sharp licks with the switch. He said, "I am going to stripe your leg good."

"See what good it does you!" said I. I began to cry, I could not help it, but more from anger and embarrassment than pain. I said to Rooster, "Are you going to let him do this?"

He dropped his cigarette to the ground and said, "No, I don't believe I will. Put your switch away, LaBoeuf. She has got the best of us."

"She has not got the best of me," replied the Ranger.

Rooster said, "That will do, I said."

LaBoeuf paid him no heed.

Rooster raised his voice and said, "Put that switch down, LaBoeuf! Do you hear me talking to you?"

LaBoeuf stopped and looked at him. Then he said, "I am going ahead with what I started."

Rooster pulled his cedar-handled revolver and cocked it with his thumb and threw down on LaBoeuf. He said, "It will be the biggest mistake you ever made, you Texas brush-popper."

LaBoeuf flung the switch away in disgust and stood up. He said, "You have taken her part in this all along, Cogburn. Well, you are not doing her any kindness here. Do you think you are doing the right thing? I can tell you you are doing the wrong thing."

Rooster said, "That will do. Get on your horse."

I brushed the dirt from my clothes and washed my hands and face in the cold creek water. Little Blackie was getting himself a drink from the stream. I said, "Listen here, I have thought of something. This 'stunt' that you two pulled has given me an idea. When we locate Chaney a good plan will be for us to jump him from the brush and hit him on the head with sticks and knock him insensible. Then we can bind his hands and feet with rope and take him back alive. What do you think?"

But Rooster was angry and he only said, "Get on your horse."

We resumed our journey in thoughtful silence, the three of us now riding together and pushing deeper into the Territory to I knew not what.

DINNERTIME CAME and went and on we rode. I was hungry and aching but I kept my peace for I knew the both of them were waiting for me to complain or say something that would make me out a "tenderfoot." I was determined not to give them anything to chaff me about. Some large wet flakes of snow began to fall, then changed to soft drizzling rain, then stopped altogether, and the sun came out. We turned left off the Fort Gibson Road and headed south, back down toward the Arkansas River. I say "down." South is not "down" any more than north is "up." I have seen maps carried by emigrants going to California that showed west at the top and east at the bottom.

Our stopping place was a store on the riverbank. Behind it there was a small ferry boat.

We dismounted and tied up our horses. My legs were tingling and weak and I tottered a little as I walked. Nothing can take the starch out of you like a long ride on horseback.

A black mule was tied up to the porch of the store. He had a cotton rope around his neck right under his jaw. The sun had caused the wet rope to draw up tight and the mule was gasping and choking for breath. The more he tugged the worse he made it. Two wicked boys were sitting on the edge of the porch laughing at the mule's discomfort. One was white and the other was an Indian. They were about seventeen years of age.

Rooster cut the rope with his dirk knife and the mule breathed easy again. The grateful beast wandered off shaking his head about. A cypress stump served for a step up to the porch. Rooster went up first and walked over to the two boys and kicked them off into the mud with the flat of his boot. "Call that sport, do you?" said he. They were two mighty surprised boys.

The storekeeper was a man named Bagby with an Indian wife. They had already had dinner but the woman warmed up some catfish for us that she had left over. LaBoeuf and I sat at a table near the stove and ate while Rooster had a conference with the man Bagby at the back of the store.

The Indian woman spoke good English and I learned to my surprise that she too was a Presbyterian. She had been schooled by a missionary. What preachers we had in those days! Truly they took the word into "the highways and hedges." Mrs. Bagby was not a Cumberland Presbyterian but a member of the U.S. or Southern Presbyterian Church. I too am now a member of the Southern Church. I say nothing against the Cumberlands. They broke with the Presbyterian Church because they did not believe a preacher needed a lot of formal education. That is all right but they are not sound on Election. They do not fully accept it. I confess it is a hard doctrine, running contrary to our earthly ideas of fair play, but I can see no way around it. Read I Corinthians 6: 13 and II Timothy 1: 9, 10. Also I Peter 1: 2, 19, 20 and Romans 11: 7. There you have it. It was good for Paul and Silas and it is good enough for me. It is good enough for you too.

Rooster finished his parley and joined us in our fish dinner. Mrs. Bagby wrapped up some gingerbread for me to take along. When we went back out on the porch Rooster kicked the two boys into the mud again.

He said, "Where is Virgil?"

The white boy said, "He and Mr. Simmons is off down in the bottoms looking for strays."

"Who is running the ferry?"

"Me and Johnny."

"You don't look like you have sense enough to run a boat. Either one of you."

"We know how to run it."

"Then let us get to it."

"Mr. Simmons will want to know who cut his mule loose," said the boy.

"Tell him it was Mr. James, a bank examiner of Clay County, Missouri," said Rooster. "Can you remember the name?"

"Yes sir."

We led our horses down to the water's edge. The boat or raft was a rickety, waterlogged affair and the horses nickered and balked when we tried to make them go aboard. I did not much blame them. LaBoeuf had to blindfold his shaggy pony. There just was room for all of us.

Before casting off, the white boy said, "You said James?"

"That is the name," said Rooster.

"The James boys are said to be slight men."

"One of them has grown fat," said Rooster.

"I don't believe you are Jesse or Frank James either one."

"The mule will not range far," said Rooster. "See that you mend your ways, boy, or I will come back some dark night and cut off your head and let the crows peck your eyeballs out. Now you and Admiral Semmes get us across this river and be damned quick about it."

A ghostly fog lay on top of the water and it enveloped us, about to the waist of a man, as we pushed off. Mean and backward though they were, the two boys handled the boat with considerable art. They pulled and guided us along on a heavy rope that was tied fast to trees on either bank. We swung across in a looping downstream curve with the current doing most of the work. We got our feet wet and I was happy to get off the thing.

The road we picked up on the south bank was little more than a pig trail. The brush arched over and closed in on us at the top and we were slapped and stung with limbs. I was riding last and I believe I got the worst of it.

Here is what Rooster learned from the man Bagby: Lucky Ned Pepper had been seen three days earlier at McAlester's store on the M. K. & T. Railroad tracks. His intentions were not known. He went there from time to time to pay attention to a lewd woman. A robber called Haze and a Mexican had been seen in his company. And that was all the man knew.

Rooster said we would be better off if we could catch the robber band before they left the neighborhood of McAlester's and returned to their hiding place in the fastness of the Winding Stair Mountains.

LaBoeuf said, "How far is it to McAlester's?"

"A good sixty miles," said Rooster. "We will make another fifteen miles today and get an early start tomorrow."

I groaned and made a face at the thought of riding another fifteen miles that day and Rooster turned and caught me. "How do you like this coon hunt?" said he.

"Do not be looking around for me," said I. "I will be right here."

LaBoeuf said, "But Chelmsford was not with him?"

Rooster said, "He was not seen at McAlester's with him. It is certain he was with him on the mail hack job. He will be around somewhere near or I miss my guess. The way Ned cuts his winnings I know the boy did not realize enough on that job to travel far."

We made a camp that night on the crest of a hill where the ground was not so soggy. It was a very dark night. The clouds were low and heavy and neither the moon or stars could be seen. Rooster gave me a canvas bucket and sent me down the hill about two hundred yards for water. I carried my gun along. I had no lantern and I stumbled and fell with the first bucket before I got far and had to retrace my steps and get another. LaBoeuf unsaddled the horses and fed them from nosebags. On the second trip I had to stop and rest about three times coming up the hill. I was stiff and tired and sore. I had the gun in one hand but it was not enough to balance the weight of the heavy bucket which pulled me sideways as I walked.

Rooster was squatting down building a fire and he watched me. He said, "You look like a hog on ice."

I said, "I am not going down there again. If you want any more water you will have to fetch it yourself."

"Everyone in my party must do his job."

"Anyhow, it tastes like iron."

LaBoeuf was rubbing down his shaggy pony. He said, "You are lucky to be traveling in a place where a spring is so handy. In my country you can ride for days and see no ground water. I have lapped filthy water from a hoofprint and was glad to have it. You don't know what discomfort is until you have nearly perished for water."

Rooster said, "If I ever meet one of you Texas waddies that says he never drank from a horse track I think I will shake his hand and give him a Daniel Webster cigar."

"Then you don't believe it?" asked LaBoeuf.

"I believed it the first twenty-five times I heard it."

"Maybe he did drink from one," said I. "He is a Texas Ranger."

"Is that what he is?" said Rooster. "Well now, I can believe that."

LaBoeuf said, "You are getting ready to show your ignorance now, Cogburn. I don't mind a little personal chaffing but

I won't hear anything against the Ranger troop from a man like you."

"The Ranger troop!" said Rooster, with some contempt. "I tell you what you do. You go tell John Wesley Hardin about the Ranger troop. Don't tell me and sis."

"Anyhow, we know what we are about. That is more than I can say for you political marshals."

Rooster said, "How long have you boys been mounted on sheep down there?"

LaBoeuf stopped rubbing his shaggy pony. He said, "This horse will be galloping when that big American stud of yours is winded and collapsed. You cannot judge by looks. The most villainous-looking pony is often your gamest performer. What would you guess this pony cost me?"

Rooster said, "If there is anything in what you say I would guess about a thousand dollars."

"You will have your joke, but he cost me a hundred and ten dollars," said LaBoeuf. "I would not sell him for that. It is hard to get in the Rangers if you do not own a hundred-dollar horse."

Rooster set about preparing our supper. Here is what he brought along for "grub": A sack of salt and a sack of red pepper and a sack of taffy—all this in his jacket pockets—and then some ground coffee beans and a big slab of salt pork and one hundred and seventy corn dodgers. I could scarcely credit it. The "corn dodgers" were balls of what I would call hot-water cornbread. Rooster said the woman who prepared them thought the order was for a wagon party of marshals.

"Well," said he, "when they get too hard to eat plain we can make mush from them and what we have left we can give to the stock."

He made some coffee in a can and fried some pork. Then he sliced up some of the dodgers and fried the pieces in grease. Fried bread! That was a new dish to me. He and LaBoeuf made fast work of about a pound of pork and a dozen dodgers. I ate some of my bacon sandwiches and a piece of gingerbread and drank the rusty-tasting water. We had a blazing fire and the wet wood crackled fiercely and sent off showers of sparks. It was cheerful and heartening against the gloomy night.

LaBoeuf said he was not accustomed to such a big fire, that

in Texas they frequently had little more than a fire of twigs or buffalo chips with which to warm up their beans. He asked Rooster if it was wise to make our presence known in unsettled country with a big fire. He said it was Ranger policy not to sleep in the same place as where they had cooked their supper. Rooster said nothing and threw more limbs on the fire.

I said, "Would you two like to hear the story of 'The Midnight Caller'? One of you will have to be 'The Caller.' I will tell you what to say. I will do all the other parts myself."

But they were not interested in hearing ghost stories and I put my slicker on the ground as close to the fire as I dared and proceeded to make my bed with the blankets. My feet were so swollen from the ride that my boots were hard to pull off. Rooster and LaBoeuf drank some whiskey but it did not make them sociable and they sat there without talking. Soon they got out their bedrolls.

Rooster had a nice buffalo robe for a ground sheet. It looked warm and comfortable and I envied him for it. He took a horsehair lariat from his saddle and arranged it in a loop around his bed.

LaBoeuf watched him and grinned. He said, "That is a piece of foolishness. All the snakes are asleep this time of year."

"They have been known to wake up," said Rooster.

I said, "Let me have a rope too. I am not fond of snakes."

"A snake would not bother with you," said Rooster. "You are too little and bony."

He put an oak log in the fire and banked coals and ashes against it and turned in for the night. Both the officers snored and one of them made a wet mouth noise along with it. It was disgusting. Exhausted as I was, I had trouble falling asleep. I was warm enough but there were roots and rocks under me and I moved this way and that trying to improve my situation. I was sore and the movement was painful. I finally despaired of ever getting fixed right. I said my prayers but did not mention my discomfort. This trip was my own doing.

When I awoke there were snowflakes on my eyes. Big moist flakes were sifting down through the trees. There was a light covering of white on the ground. It was not quite daylight but Rooster was already up, boiling coffee and frying meat. LaBoeuf was attending to the horses and he had them saddled.

I wanted some hot food so I passed up the biscuits and ate some of the salt meat and fried bread. I shared my cheese with the officers. My hands and face smelled of smoke.

Rooster hurried us along in breaking camp. He was concerned about the snow. "If this keeps up we will want shelter tonight," he said. LaBoeuf had already fed the stock but I took one of the corn dodgers and gave it to Little Blackie to see if he would eat it. He relished it and I gave him another. Rooster said horses particularly liked the salt that was in them. He directed me to wear my slicker.

Sunrise was only a pale yellow glow through the overcast but such as it was it found us mounted and moving once again. The snow came thicker and the flakes grew bigger, as big as goose feathers, and they were not falling down like rain but rather flying dead level into our faces. In the space of four hours it collected on the ground to a depth of six or seven inches.

Out in the open places the trail was hard to follow and we stopped often so that Rooster could get his bearings. This was a hard job because the ground told him nothing and he could not see distant landmarks. Indeed at times we could see only a few feet in any direction. His spyglass was useless. We came across no people and no houses. Our progress was very slow.

There was no great question of getting lost because Rooster had a compass and as long as we kept a southwesterly course we would sooner or later strike the Texas Road and the M. K. & T. Railroad tracks. But it was inconvenient not being able to keep the regular trail, and with the snow the horses ran the danger of stepping into holes.

Along about noon we stopped at a stream on the lee side of a mountain to water the horses. There we found some small relief from the wind and snow. I believe these were the San Bois Mountains. I passed the balance of my cheese around and Rooster shared his candy. With that we made our dinner. While we were stretching our legs at that place we heard some flapping noises down the stream and LaBoeuf went into the woods to investigate. He found a flock of turkeys roosting in a tree and shot one of them with his Sharps rifle. The bird was considerably ripped up. It was a hen weighing about seven pounds. LaBoeuf gutted it and cut its head off and tied it to his saddle.

Rooster allowed that we could not now reach McAlester's store before dark and that our best course was to bear west for a "dugout" that some squatter had built not far from the Texas Road. No one occupied the place, he said, and we could find shelter there for the night. Tomorrow we could make our way south on the Texas Road which was broad and packed clear and hard from cattle herds and freighter wagons. There would be little risk of crippling a horse on that highway.

After our rest we departed in single file with Rooster's big horse breaking the trail. Little Blackie had no need for my guidance and I looped the ends of the reins around the saddle horn and withdrew my cold hands into the sleeves of my many coats. We surprised a herd of deer feeding off the bark of saplings and LaBoeuf went for his rifle again but they had flown before he could get it unlimbered.

By and by the snow let up and yet our progress was still limited to a walk. It was good dark when we came to the "dugout." We had a little light from a moon that was in and out of the clouds.

The dugout stood at the narrow end of a V-shaped hollow or valley. I had never before seen such a dwelling. It was small, only about ten feet by twenty feet, and half of it was sunk back into a clay bank, like a cave. The part that was sticking out was made of poles and sod and the roof was also of sod, supported by a ridge pole in the center. A brush-arbor shed and cave adjoined it for livestock. There was a sufficiency of timber here for a log cabin, although mostly hardwood. I suppose too that the man who built the thing was in a hurry and wanted for proper tools. A "cockeyed" chimney of sticks and mud stuck up through the bank at the rear of the house. It put me in mind of something made by a water bird, some cliff martin or a swift, although the work of those little feathered masons (who know not the use of a spirit level) is a sight more artful.

We were surprised to see smoke and sparks coming from the chimney. Light showed through the cracks around the door, which was a low, crude thing hung to the sill by leather hinges. There was no window.

We had halted in a cedar brake. Rooster dismounted and told us to wait. He took his Winchester repeating rifle and approached the door. He made a lot of noise as his boots broke through the crust that had now formed on top of the snow.

When he was about twenty feet from the dugout the door opened just a few inches. A man's face appeared in the light and a hand came out holding a revolver. Rooster stopped. The face said, "Who is it out there?" Rooster said, "We are looking for shelter. There is three of us." The face in the door said, "There is no room for you here." The door closed and in a moment the light inside went out.

Rooster turned to us and made a beckoning signal. LaBoeuf dismounted and went to join him. I made a move to go but LaBoeuf told me to stay in the cover of the brake and hold the horses.

Rooster took off his deerskin jacket and gave it to LaBoeuf and sent him up on the clay bank to cover the chimney. Then Rooster moved about ten feet to the side and got down on one knee with his rifle at the ready. The jacket made a good damper and soon smoke could be seen curling out around the door. There were raised voices inside and then a hissing noise as of water being thrown on fire and coals.

The door was flung open and there came two fiery blasts from a shotgun. It scared me nearly to death. I heard the shot falling through tree branches. Rooster returned the volley with several shots from his rifle. There was a yelp of pain from inside and the door was slammed to again.

"I am a Federal officer!" said Rooster. "Who all is in there? Speak up and be quick about it!"

"A Methodist and a son of a bitch!" was the insolent reply. "Keep riding!"

"Is that Emmett Quincy?" said Rooster.

"We don't know any Emmett Quincy!"

"Quincy, I know it is you! Listen to me! This is Rooster Cogburn! Columbus Potter and five more marshals is out here with me! We have got a bucket of coal oil! In one minute we will burn you out from both ends! Chuck your arms out clear and come out with your hands locked on your head and you will not be harmed! Oncet that coal oil goes down the chimney we are killing everything that comes out the door!"

"There is only three of you!"

"You go ahead and bet your life on it! How many is in there?"

"Moon can't walk! He is hit!"

"Drag him out! Light that lamp!"

"What kind of papers have you got on me?"

"I don't have no papers on you! You better move, boy! How many is in there?"

"Just me and Moon! Tell them other officers to be careful with their guns! We are coming out!"

A light showed again from inside. The door was pulled back and a shotgun and two revolvers were pitched out. The two men came out with one limping and holding to the other. Rooster and LaBoeuf made them lie down on their bellies in the snow while they were searched for more weapons. The one called Quincy had a bowie knife in one boot and a little two-shot gambler's pistol in the other. He said he had forgotten they were there but this did not keep Rooster from giving him a kick.

I came up with the horses and LaBoeuf took them into the stock shelter. Rooster poked the two men into the dugout with his rifle. They were young men in their twenties. The one called Moon was pale and frightened and looked no more dangerous than a fat puppy. He had been shot in the thigh and his trouser leg was bloody. The man Quincy had a long, thin face with eyes that were narrow and foreign-looking. He reminded me of some of those Slovak people that came in here a few years ago to cut barrel staves. The ones that stayed have made good citizens. People from those countries are usually Catholics if they are anything. They love candles and beads.

Rooster gave Moon a blue handkerchief to tie around his leg and then he bound the two men together with steel handcuffs and had them sit side by side on a bench. The only furniture in the place was a low table of adzed logs standing on pegs, and a bench on either side of it. I flapped a tow sack in the open door in an effort to clear the smoke out. A pot of coffee had been thrown into the fireplace but there were still some live coals and sticks around the edges and I stirred them up into a blaze again.

There was another pot in the fireplace too, a big one, a two-gallon pot, and it was filled with a mess that looked like hominy.

Rooster tasted it with a spoon and said it was an Indian dish called sofky. He offered me some and said it was good. But it had trash in it and I declined.

"Was you boys looking for company?" he said.

"That is our supper and breakfast both," said Quincy. "I like a big breakfast."

"I would love to watch you eat breakfast."

"Sofky always cooks up bigger than you think."

"What are you boys up to outside of stealing stock and peddling spirits? You are way too jumpy."

"You said you didn't have no papers on us," replied Quincy.

"I don't have none on you by name," said Rooster. "I got some John Doe warrants on a few jobs I could tailor up for you. Resisting a Federal officer too. That's a year right there."

"We didn't know it was you. It might have been some crazy man out there."

Moon said, "My leg hurts."

Rooster said, "I bet it does. Set right still and it won't bleed so bad."

Quincy said, "We didn't know who it was out there. A night like this. We was drinking some and the weather spooked us. Anybody can say he is a marshal. Where is all the other officers?"

"I misled you there, Quincy. When was the last time you seen your old pard Ned Pepper?"

"Ned Pepper?" said the stock thief. "I don't know him. Who is he?"

"I think you know him," said Rooster. "I know you have heard of him. Everybody has heard of him."

"I never heard of him."

"He used to work for Mr. Burlingame. Didn't you work for him a while?"

"Yes, and I quit him like everybody else has done. He runs off all his good help, he is so close. The old skinflint. I wish he was in hell with his back broke. I don't remember any Ned Pepper."

Rooster said, "They say Ned was a mighty good drover. I am surprised you don't remember him. He is a little feisty fellow, nervous and quick. His lip is all messed up."

"That don't bring anybody to mind. A funny lip."

"He didn't always have it. I think you know him. Now here

is something else. There is a new boy running with Ned. He is
short himself and he has got a powder mark on his face, a black
place. He calls himself Chaney or Chelmsford sometimes. He
carries a Henry rifle."

"That don't bring anybody to mind," said Quincy. "A black
mark. I would remember something like that."

"You don't know anything I want to know, do you?"

"No, and if I did I would not blow."

"Well, you think on it some, Quincy. You too, Moon."

Moon said, "I always try to help out the law if it won't harm
my friends. I don't know them boys. I would like to help you
if I could."

"If you don't help me I will take you both back to Judge
Parker," said Rooster. "By the time we get to Fort Smith that
leg will be swelled up as tight as Dick's hatband. It will be mor-
tified and they will cut it off. Then if you live I will get you two
or three years in the Federal House up in Detroit."

"You are trying to get at me," said Moon.

"They will teach you how to read and write up there but the
rest of it is not so good," said Rooster. "You don't have to go
if you don't want to. If you give me some good information
on Ned I will take you to McAlester's tomorrow and you can
get that ball out of your leg. Then I will give you three days
to clear the Territory. They have a lot of fat stock in Texas and
you boys can do well there."

Moon said, "We can't go to Texas."

Quincy said, "Now don't go to flapping your mouth, Moon.
It is best to let me do the talking."

"I can't set still. My leg is giving me fits."

Rooster got his bottle of whiskey and poured some in a cup
for the young stock thief. "If you listen to Quincy, son, you
will die or lose your leg," said he. "Quincy ain't hurting."

Quincy said, "Don't let him spook you, Moon. You must be
a soldier. We will get clear of this."

LaBoeuf came in lugging our bedrolls and other traps. He
said, "There are six horses out there in that cave, Cogburn."

"What kind of horses?" said Rooster.

"They look like right good mounts to me. I think they are
all shod."

Rooster questioned the thieves about the horses and Quincy claimed they had bought them at Fort Gibson and were taking them down to sell to the Indian police called the Choctaw Light Horse. But he could show no bill of sale or otherwise prove the property and Rooster did not believe the story. Quincy grew sullen and would answer no further questions.

I was sent out to gather firewood and I took the lamp, or rather the bull's-eye lantern, for that was what it was, and kicked about in the snow and turned up some sticks and fallen saplings. I had no ax or hatchet and I dragged the pieces in whole, making several trips.

Rooster made another pot of coffee. He put me to slicing up the salt meat and corn dodgers, now frozen hard, and he directed Quincy to pick the feathers from the turkey and cut it up for frying. LaBoeuf wanted to roast the bird over the open fire but Rooster said it was not fat enough for that and would come out tough and dry.

I sat on a bench on one side of the table and the thieves sat on the other side, their manacled hands resting between them up on the table. The thieves had made pallets on the dirt floor by the fireplace and now Rooster and LaBoeuf sat on these blankets with their rifles in their laps, taking their ease. There were holes in the walls where the sod had fallen away and the wind came whistling through these places, making the lantern flicker a little, but the room was small and the fire gave off more than enough heat. Take it all around, we were rather cozily fixed.

I poured a can of scalding water over the stiff turkey but it was not enough to loosen all the feathers. Quincy picked them with his free hand and held the bird steady with the other. He grumbled over the awkwardness of the task. When the picking was done he cut the bird up into frying pieces with his big bowie knife and he showed his spite by doing a poor job of it. He made rough and careless chops instead of clean cuts.

Moon drank whiskey and whimpered from the pain in his leg. I felt sorry for him. Once he caught me stealing glances at him and he said, "What are you looking at?" It was a foolish question and I made no reply. He said, "Who are you? What are you doing here? What is this girl doing here?"

I said, "I am Mattie Ross of near Dardanelle, Arkansas. Now I will ask you a question. What made you become a stock thief?"

He said again, "What is this girl doing here?"

Rooster said, "She is with me."

"She is with both of us," said LaBoeuf.

Moon said, "It don't look right to me. I don't understand it."

I said, "The man Chaney, the man with the marked face, killed my father. He was a whiskey drinker like you. It led to killing in the end. If you will answer the marshal's questions he will help you. I have a good lawyer at home and he will help you too."

"I am puzzled by this."

Quincy said, "Don't get to jawing with these people, Moon."

I said, "I don't like the way you look."

Quincy stopped his work. He said, "Are you talking to me, runt?"

I said, "Yes, and I will say it again. I don't like the way you look and I don't like the way you are cutting up that turkey. I hope you go to jail. My lawyer will not help you."

Quincy grinned and made a gesture with the knife as though to cut me. He said, "You are a fine one to talk about looks. You look like somebody has worked you over with the ugly stick."

I said, "Rooster, this Quincy is making a mess out of the turkey. He has got the bones all splintered up with the marrow showing."

Rooster said, "Do the job right, Quincy. I will have you eating feathers."

"I don't know nothing about this kind of work," said Quincy.

"A man that can skin a beef at night as fast as you can ought to be able to butcher a turkey," said Rooster.

Moon said, "I got to have me a doctor."

Quincy said, "Let up on that drinking. It is making you silly."

LaBoeuf said, "If we don't separate those two we are not going to get anything. The one has got a hold on the other."

Rooster said, "Moon is coming around. A young fellow like him don't want to lose his leg. He is too young to be getting about on a willow peg. He loves dancing and sport."

"You are trying to get at me," said Moon.

"I am getting at you with the truth," said Rooster.

In a few minutes Moon leaned over to whisper a confidence into Quincy's ear. "None of that," said Rooster, raising his rifle. "If you have anything on your mind we will all hear it."

Moon said, "We seen Ned and Haze just two days ago."

"Don't act the fool!" said Quincy. "If you blow I will kill you."

But Moon went on. "I am played out," said he. "I must have a doctor. I will tell what I know."

With that, Quincy brought the bowie knife down on Moon's cuffed hand and chopped off four fingers which flew up before my eyes like chips from a log. Moon screamed and a rifle ball shattered the lantern in front of me and struck Quincy in the neck, causing hot blood to spurt on my face. My thought was: *I am better out of this.* I tumbled backward from the bench and sought a place of safety on the dirt floor.

Rooster and LaBoeuf sprang to where I lay and when they ascertained that I was not hurt they went to the fallen thieves. Quincy was insensible and dead or dying and Moon was bleeding terribly from his hand and from a mortal puncture in the breast that Quincy gave him before they fell.

"Oh Lord, I am dying!" said he.

Rooster struck a match for light and told me to fetch a pine knot from the fireplace. I found a good long piece and lit it and brought it back, a smoky torch to illuminate a dreadful scene. Rooster removed the handcuff from the poor young man's wrist.

"Do something! Help me!" were his cries.

"I can do nothing for you, son," said Rooster. "Your pard has killed you and I have done for him."

"Don't leave me laying here. Don't let the wolves make an end of me."

"I will see you are buried right, though the ground is hard," said Rooster. "You must tell me about Ned. Where did you see him?"

"We seen him two days ago at McAlester's, him and Haze. They are coming here tonight to get remounts and supper. They are robbing the Katy Flyer at Wagoner's Switch if the snow don't stop them."

"There is four of them?"

"They wanted four horses, that is all I know. Ned was Quincy's friend, not mine. I would not blow on a friend. I was afraid there would be shooting and I would not have a chance bound up like I was. I am bold in a fight."

Rooster said, "Did you see a man with a black mark on his face?"

"I didn't see nobody but Ned and Haze. When it comes to a fight I am right there where it is warmest but if I have time to think on it I am not true. Quincy hated all the laws but he was true to his friends."

"What time did they say they would be here?"

"I looked for them before now. My brother is George Garrett. He is a Methodist circuit rider in south Texas. I want you to sell my traps, Rooster, and send the money to him in care of the district superintendent in Austin. The dun horse is mine, I paid for him. We got them others last night at Mr. Burlingame's."

I said, "Do you want us to tell your brother what happened to you?"

He said, "It don't matter about that. He knows I am on the scout. I will meet him later walking the streets of Glory."

Rooster said, "Don't be looking for Quincy."

"Quincy was always square with me," said Moon. "He never played me false until he killed me. Let me have a drink of cold water."

LaBoeuf brought him some water in a cup. Moon reached for it with the bloody stump and then took it with the other hand. He said, "It feels like I still have fingers there but I don't." He drank deep and it caused him pain. He talked a little more but in a rambling manner and to no sensible purpose. He did not respond to questions. Here is what was in his eyes: *confusion*. Soon it was all up with him and he joined his friend in death. He looked about thirty pounds lighter.

LaBoeuf said, "I told you we should have separated them."

Rooster said nothing to that, not wishing to own he had made a mistake. He went through the pockets of the dead thieves and put such oddments as he found upon the table. The lantern was beyond repair and LaBoeuf brought out a candle from his saddle wallet and lit it and fixed it on the table. Rooster turned up a few coins and cartridges and notes of

paper money and a picture of a pretty girl torn from an illustrated paper and pocket knives and a plug of tobacco. He also
found a California gold piece in Quincy's vest pocket.

I fairly shouted when I saw it. "That is my father's gold
piece!" said I. "Let me have it!"

It was not a round coin but a rectangular slug of gold that
was minted in "The Golden State" and was worth thirty-
six dollars and some few cents. Rooster said, "I never seen a
piece like this before. Are you sure it is the one?" I said, "Yes,
Grandfather Spurling gave Papa two of these when he married
Mama. That scoundrel Chaney has still got the other one. We
are on his trail for certain!"

"We are on Ned's trail anyhow," said Rooster. "I expect it is
the same thing. I wonder how Quincy got aholt of this. Is this
Chaney a gambler?"

LaBoeuf said, "He likes a game of cards. I reckon Ned has
called off the robbery if he is not here by now."

"Well, we won't count on that," said Rooster. "Saddle the
horses and I will lug these boys out."

"Do you aim to run?" said LaBoeuf.

Rooster turned a glittering eye on him. "I aim to do what I
come out here to do," said he. "Saddle the horses."

Rooster directed me to straighten up the inside of the
dugout. He carried the bodies out and concealed them in
the woods. I sacked up the turkey fragments and pitched the
wrecked lantern into the fireplace and stirred around on the
dirt floor with a stick to cover the blood. Rooster was planning
an ambush.

When he came back from his second trip to the woods he
brought a load of limbs for the fireplace. He built up a big fire
so there would be light and smoke and indicate that the cabin
was occupied. Then we went out and joined LaBoeuf and the
horses in the brush arbor. This dwelling, as I have said, was set
back in a hollow where two slopes pinched together in a kind
of V. It was a good place for what Rooster had in mind.

He directed LaBoeuf to take his horse and find a position up
on the north slope about midway along one stroke of the V,
and explained that he would take up a corresponding position
on the south slope. Nothing was said about me with regard to
the plan and I elected to stay with Rooster.

He said to LaBoeuf, "Find you a good place up yonder and then don't move about. Don't shoot unless you hear me shoot. What we want is to get them all in the dugout. I will kill the last one to go in and then we will have them in a barrel."

"You will shoot him in the back?" asked LaBoeuf.

"It will give them to know our intentions is serious. These ain't chicken thieves. I don't want you to start shooting unless they break. After my first shot I will call down and see if they will be taken alive. If they won't we will shoot them as they come out."

"There is nothing in this plan but a lot of killing," said LaBoeuf. "We want Chelmsford alive, don't we? You are not giving them any show."

"It is no use giving Ned and Haze a show. If they are taken they will hang and they know it. They will go for a fight every time. The others may be chicken-hearted and give up, I don't know. Another thing, we don't know how many there is. I do know there is just two of us."

"Why don't I try to wing Chelmsford before he gets inside?"

"I don't like that," said Rooster. "If there is any shooting before they get in that dugout we are likely to come up with a empty sack. I want Ned too. I want all of them."

"All right," said LaBoeuf. "But if they do break I am going for Chelmsford."

"You are liable to kill him with that big Sharps no matter where you hit him. You go for Ned and I will try to nick this Chaney in the legs."

"What does Ned look like?"

"He is a little fellow. I don't know what he will be riding. He will be doing a lot of talking. Just go for the littlest one."

"What if they hole up in there for a siege? They may figure on staying till dark and then breaking."

"I don't think they will," said Rooster. "Now don't keep on with this. Get on up there. If something queer turns up you will just have to use your head."

"How long will we wait?"

"Till daylight anyhow."

"I don't think they are coming now."

"Well, you may be right. Now move. Keep your eyes open

and your horse quiet. Don't go to sleep and don't get the 'jimjams.'"

Rooster took a cedar bough and brushed around over all our tracks in front of the dugout. Then we took our horses and led them up the hill in a roundabout route along a rocky stream bed. We went over the crest and Rooster posted me there with the horses. He told me to talk to them or give them some oats or put my hand over their nostrils if they started blowing or neighing. He put some corn dodgers in his pocket and left to go for his ambush position.

I said, "I cannot see anything from here."

He said, "This is where I want you to stay."

"I am going with you where I can see something."

"You will do like I tell you."

"The horses will be all right."

"You have not seen enough killing tonight?"

"I am not staying here by myself."

We started back over the ridge together. I said, "Wait, I will go back and get my revolver," but he grabbed me roughly and pulled me along after him and I left the pistol behind. He found us a place behind a big log that offered a good view of the hollow and the dugout. We kicked the snow back so that we could rest on the leaves underneath. Rooster loaded his rifle from a sack of cartridges and placed the sack on the log where he would have it ready at hand. He got out his revolver and put a cartridge into the one chamber that he kept empty under the hammer. The same shells fit his pistol and rifle alike. I thought you had to have different kinds. I bunched myself up inside the slicker and rested my head against the log. Rooster ate a corn dodger and offered me one.

I said, "Strike a match and let me look at it first."

"What for?" said he.

"There was blood on some of them."

"We ain't striking no matches."

"I don't want it then. Let me have some taffy."

"It is all gone."

I tried to sleep but it was too cold. I cannot sleep when my feet are cold. I asked Rooster what he had done before he became a Federal marshal.

"I done everything but keep school," said he.

"What was one thing that you did?" said I.

"I skinned buffalo and killed wolves for bounty out on the Yellow House Creek in Texas. I seen wolves out there that weighed a hundred and fifty pounds."

"Did you like it?"

"It paid well enough but I didn't like that open country. Too much wind to suit me. There ain't but about six trees between there and Canada. Some people like it fine. Everything that grows out there has got stickers on it."

"Have you ever been to California?"

"I never got out there."

"My Grandfather Spurling lives in Monterey, California. He owns a store there and he can look out his window any time he wants to and see the blue ocean. He sends me five dollars every Christmas. He has buried two wives and is now married to one called Jenny who is thirty-one years of age. That is one year younger than Mama. Mama will not even say her name."

"I fooled around in Colorado for a spell but I never got out to California. I freighted supplies for a man named Cook out of Denver."

"Did you fight in the war?"

"Yes, I did."

"Papa did too. He was a good soldier."

"I expect he was."

"Did you know him?"

"No, where was he?"

"He fought at Elkhorn Tavern in Arkansas and was badly wounded at Chickamauga up in the state of Tennessee. He came home after that and nearly died on the way. He served in General Churchill's brigade."

"I was mostly in Missouri."

"Did you lose your eye in the war?"

"I lost it in the fight at Lone Jack out of Kansas City. My horse was down too and I was all but blind. Cole Younger crawled out under a hail of fire and pulled me back. Poor Cole, he and Bob and Jim are now doing life in the Minnesota pen. You watch, when the truth is known, they will find it was Jesse W. James that shot that cashier in Northfield."

"Do you know Jesse James?"

"I don't remember him. Potter tells me he was with us at Centralia and killed a Yankee major there. Potter said he was a mean little viper then, though he was only a boy. Said he was meaner than Frank. That is going some, if it be so. I remember Frank well. We called him Buck then. I don't remember Jesse."

"Now you are working for the Yankees."

"Well, the times has changed since Betsy died. I would have never thought it back then. The Red Legs from Kansas burned my folks out and took their stock. They didn't have nothing to eat but clabber and roasting ears. You can eat a peck of roasting ears and go to bed hungry."

"What did you do when the war was over?"

"Well, I will tell you what I done. When we heard they had all give up in Virginia, Potter and me rode into Independence and turned over our arms. They asked us was we ready to re-spect the Government in Washington city and take a oath to the Stars and Stripes. We said yes, we was about ready. We done it, we swallowed the puppy, but they wouldn't let us go right then. They give us a one-day parole and told us to report back in the morning. We heard there was a Kansas major coming in that night to look over everybody for bushwhackers."

"What are bushwhackers?"

"I don't know. That is what they called us. Anyhow, we was not easy about that Kansas major. We didn't know but what he would lock us up or worse, us having rode with Bill Anderson and Captain Quantrill. Potter lifted a revolver from a office and we lit out that night on two government mules. I am still traveling on the one-day parole and I reckon that jayhawker is waiting yet. Now our clothes was rags and we didn't have the price of a plug of tobacco between us. About eight mile out of town we run into a Federal captain and three soldiers. They wanted to know if they was on the right road for Kansas City. That captain was a paymaster, and we relieved them gents of over four thousand in coin. They squealed like it was their own. It didn't belong to nobody but the Government and we needed a road stake."

"Four thousand dollars?"

"Yes, and all in gold. We got their horses too. Potter taken his half of the money and went down to Arkansas. I went to Cairo, Illinois, with mine and started calling myself Burroughs and bought a eating place called *The Green Frog* and married a grass widow. It had one billiard table. We served ladies and men both, but mostly men."

"I didn't know you had a wife."

"Well, I don't now. She taken a notion she wanted me to be a lawyer. Running a eating place was too low-down for her. She bought a heavy book called *Daniels on Negotiable Instruments* and set me to reading it. I never could get a grip on it. Old Daniels pinned me every time. My drinking picked up and I commenced staying away two and three days at a time with my friends. My wife did not crave the society of my river friends. She got a bellyful of it and decided she would go back to her first husband who was clerking in a hardware store over in Paducah. She said, 'Goodbye, Reuben, a love for decency does not abide in you.' There is your divorced woman talking about decency. I told her, I said, 'Goodbye, Nola, I hope that little nail-selling bastard will make you happy this time.' She took my boy with her too. He never did like me anyhow. I guess I did speak awful rough to him but I didn't mean nothing by it. You would not want to see a clumsier child than Horace. I bet he broke forty cups."

"What happened to *The Green Frog*?"

"I tried to run it myself for a while but I couldn't keep good help and I never did learn how to buy meat. I didn't know what I was doing. I was like a man fighting bees. Finally I just give up and sold it for nine hundred dollars and went out to see the country. That was when I went out to the staked plains of Texas and shot buffalo with Vernon Shaftoe and a Flathead Indian called Olly. The Mormons had run Shaftoe out of Great Salt Lake City but don't ask me about what it was for. Call it a misunderstanding and let it go at that. There is no use in you asking me questions about it, for I will not answer them. Olly and me both taken a solemn oath to keep silent. Well, sir, the big shaggies is about all gone. It is a damned shame. I would give three dollars right now for a pickled buffalo tongue."

"They never did get you for stealing that money?"

"I didn't look on it as stealing."

"That was what it was. It didn't belong to you."

"It never troubled me in that way. I sleep like a baby. Have for years."

"Colonel Stonehill said you were a road agent before you got to be a marshal."

"I wondered who was spreading that talk. That old gentleman would do better minding his own business."

"Then it is just talk."

"It is very little more than that. I found myself one pretty spring day in Las Vegas, New Mexico, in need of a road stake and I robbed one of them little high-interest banks there. Thought I was doing a good service. You can't rob a thief, can you? I never robbed no citizens. I never taken a man's watch."

"It is all stealing," said I.

"That was the position they taken in New Mexico," said he. "I had to fly for my life. Three fights in one day. Bo was a strong colt then and there was not a horse in that territory could run him in the ground. But I did not appreciate being chased and shot at like a thief. When the posse had thinned down to about seven men I turned Bo around and taken the reins in my teeth and rode right at them boys firing them two navy sixes I carry on my saddle. I guess they was all married men who loved their families as they scattered and run for home."

"That is hard to believe."

"What is?"

"One man riding at seven men like that."

"It is true enough. We done it in the war. I seen a dozen bold riders stampede a full troop of regular cavalry. You go for a man hard enough and fast enough and he don't have time to think about how many is with him, he thinks about himself and how he may get clear out of the wrath that is about to set down on him."

"I think you are 'stretching the blanket.'"

"Well, that was the way of it. Me and Bo walked into Texas, we didn't run. I might not do it today. I am older and stouter and so is Bo. I lost my money to some quarter-mile horse racers out there in Texas and followed them highbinders across Red River up in the Chickasaw Nation and lost their trail. That was when I tied up with a man named Fogelson who was taking a herd of beef to Kansas. We had a pretty time with them steers. It rained every night and the grass was spongy and rank. It was cloudy by day and the mosquitoes eat us up. Fogelson abused us like a stepfather. We didn't know what sleep was. When we got to the South Canadian it was all out of the banks but Fogelson had a time contract and he wouldn't wait. He said, 'Boys, we are going across.' We lost near about seventy head getting across and counted ourselves lucky. Lost our wagon too; we done without bread and coffee after that. It was the same story all over again at the North Canadian. 'Boys, we are going across.' Some of them steers got bogged in the mud on the other side and I was pulling them free. Bo was about played out and I hollered up for that Hutchens to come help me. He was sitting up there on his horse smoking a pipe. Now, he wasn't a regular drover. He was from Philadelphia, Pennsylvania, and he had some interest in the herd. He said, 'Do it yourself. That's what you are paid for.' I pulled down on him right there. It was not the thing to do but I was wore out and hadn't had no coffee. It didn't hurt him bad, the ball just skinned his head and he bit his pipe in two, yet nothing would do but he would have the law. There wasn't no law out there and Fogelson told him as much, so Hutchens had me disarmed and him and two drovers taken me over to Fort Reno. Now the army didn't care nothing about his private quarrels but there happened to be two Federal marshals there picking up some whiskey peddlers. One of them marshals was Potter."

I was just about asleep. Rooster nudged me and said, "I say one of them marshals was Potter."

"What?"

"One of them two marshals at Fort Reno was Potter."

"It was your friend from the war? The same one?"

"Yes, it was Columbus Potter in the flesh. I was glad to see him. He didn't let on he knowed me. He told Hutchens he would take me in charge and see I was prosecuted. Hutchens said he would come back by Fort Smith when his business was done in Kansas and appear against me. Potter told him his statement right there was good enough to convict me of assault. Hutchens said he never heard of a court where they didn't need witnesses. Potter said they had found it saved time. We come on over to Fort Smith and Potter got me commissioned as deputy marshal. Jo Shelby had vouched for him to the chief marshal and got him the job. General Shelby is in the railroad business up in Missouri now and he knows all these

Republicans. He wrote a handsome letter for me too. Well, there is no beat of a good friend. Potter was a trump."

"Do you like being a marshal?"

"I believe I like it better than anything I done since the war. Anything beats droving. Nothing I like to do pays well."

"I don't think Chaney is going to show up."

"We will get him."

"I hope we get him tonight."

"You told me you loved coon hunting."

"I didn't expect it would be easy. I still hope we get him tonight and have it done with."

Rooster talked all night. I would doze off and wake up and he would still be talking. Some of his stories had too many people in them and were hard to follow but they helped to pass the hours and took my mind off the cold. I did not give credence to everything he said. He said he knew a woman in Sedalia, Missouri, who had stepped on a needle as a girl and nine years later the needle worked out of the thigh of her third child. He said it puzzled the doctors.

I was asleep when the bandits arrived. Rooster shook me awake and said, "Here they come." I gave a start and turned over on my stomach so I could peer over the log. It was false dawn and you could see broad shapes and outlines but you could not make out details. The riders were strung out and they were laughing and talking amongst themselves. I counted them. *Six!* Six armed men against two! They exercised no caution at all and my thought was: *Rooster's plan is working fine.* But when they were about fifty yards from the dugout they stopped. The fire inside the dugout had gone down but there was still a little string of smoke coming from the mud chimney.

Rooster whispered to me, "Do you see your man?"

I said, "I cannot see their faces."

He said, "That little one without the hat is Ned Pepper. He has lost his hat. He is riding foremost."

"What are they doing?"

"Looking about. Keep your head down."

Lucky Ned Pepper appeared to be wearing white trousers but I learned later that these were sheepskin "chaps." One of the bandits made a sound like a turkey gobbling. He waited and gobbled again and then another time, but of course there was no reply from the vacant dugout. Two of the bandits then rode up to the dugout and dismounted. One of them called out several times for Quincy. Rooster said, "That is Haze." The two men then entered the cabin with their arms ready. In a minute or so they came out and searched around outside. The man Haze called out repeatedly for Quincy and once he whooped like a man calling hogs. Then he called back to the bandits who had remained mounted, saying, "The horses are here. It looks like Moon and Quincy have stepped out."

"Stepped out where?" inquired the bandit chieftain, Lucky Ned Pepper.

"I can make nothing from the sign," said the man Haze. "There is six horses in there. There is a pot of sofky in the fireplace but the fire is down. It beats me. Maybe they are out tracking game in the snow."

Lucky Ned Pepper said, "Quincy would not leave a warm fire to go track a rabbit at night. That is no answer at all."

Haze said, "The snow is all stirred up out here in front. Come and see what you make of it, Ned."

The man that was with Haze said, "What difference does it make? Let us change horses and get on out of here. We can get something to eat at Ma's place."

Lucky Ned Pepper said, "Let me think a minute."

The man that was with Haze said, "We are wasting time that is better spent riding. We have lost enough time in this snow and left a broad track as well."

When the man spoke the second time Rooster identified him as a Mexican gambler from Fort Worth, Texas, who called himself The Original Greaser Bob. He did not talk the Mexican language, though I suppose he knew it. I looked hard at the mounted bandits but mere effort was not enough to pierce the shadows and make out faces. Nor could I tell much from their physical attitudes as they were wearing heavy coats and big hats and their horses were ever milling about. I did not recognize Papa's horse, Judy.

Lucky Ned Pepper pulled one of his revolvers and fired it rapidly three times in the air. The noise rumbled in the hollow and there followed an expectant silence.

In a moment there came a loud report from the opposite ridge and Lucky Ned Pepper's horse was felled as though from a poleax. Then more shots from the ridge and the bandits were seized with panic and confusion. It was LaBoeuf over there firing his heavy rifle as fast as he could load it.

Rooster cursed and rose to his feet and commenced firing and pumping his Winchester repeating rifle. He shot Haze and The Original Greaser before they could mount their horses. Haze was killed where he stood. The hot cartridge cases from Rooster's rifle fell on my hand and I jerked it away. When he turned to direct his fire on the other bandits, The Original Greaser, who was only wounded, got to his feet and caught his horse and rode out behind the others. He was clinging to the far side of his horse with one leg thrown over for support. If you had not followed the entire "stunt" from start to finish as I had done, you would have thought the horse was riderless. That is how he escaped Rooster's attention. I was "mesmerized" and proved to be of no help.

Now I will back up and tell of the others. Lucky Ned Pepper was bowled over with his horse but he quickly crawled from under the dead beast and cut his saddle wallets free with a knife. The other three bandits had already spurred their horses away from the deadly cockpit, as I may call it, and they were firing their rifles and revolvers at LaBoeuf on the run. Rooster and I were behind them and a good deal farther away from them than LaBoeuf. As far as I know, not a shot was fired at us.

Lucky Ned Pepper shouted after the riders and pursued them on foot in a zigzag manner. He carried the saddle wallets over one arm and a revolver in the other hand. Rooster could not hit him. The bandit was well named "Lucky," and his luck was not through running yet. In all the booming and smoke and confusion, one of his men chanced to hear his cries and he wheeled his horse about and made a dash back to pick up his boss. Just as the man reached Lucky Ned Pepper and leaned over to extend a hand to help him aboard he was knocked clean from the saddle by a well-placed shot from LaBoeuf's powerful rifle. Lucky Ned Pepper expertly swung aboard in the man's place without so much as a word or a parting glance at the fallen friend who had dared to come back and save him. He rode low and the trick-riding Mexican gambler followed him out and they were gone. The scrap did not last as long as it has taken me to describe it.

Rooster told me to get the horses. He ran down the hill on foot.

The bandits had left two of their number behind and we had forced the others to continue their flight on jaded ponies, but I thought we had little reason to congratulate ourselves. The bandits in the snow were dead men and could "tell no tales." We had not identified Chaney among those who escaped. Was he with them? Were we really on his trail? Also, we found that Lucky Ned Pepper had made off with the greater part of the loot from the train robbery.

The thing might have fallen out more to our advantage had LaBoeuf not started the fight prematurely. But I cannot be sure. I think Lucky Ned Pepper had no intention of entering that dugout, or indeed of approaching it any closer, when he discovered the two stock thieves unaccountably missing. So our plan had miscarried in any case. Rooster was disposed to place all the blame on LaBoeuf.

When I reached the bottom of the hill with the horses he was cursing the Texan to his face. I am certain the two must have come to blows if LaBoeuf had not been distracted from a painful wound. A ball had struck his rifle stock and splinters of wood and lead had torn the soft flesh of his upper arm. He said he had not been able to see well from his position and was moving to a better place when he heard the three signal shots fired by Lucky Ned Pepper. He thought the fight was joined and he stood up from a crouch and threw a quick shot down at the man he had rightly sized up as the bandit chieftain.

Rooster called it a likely story and charged that LaBoeuf had fallen asleep and had started shooting from panic when the signal shots awakened him. I thought it was in LaBoeuf's favor that his first shot had struck and killed Lucky Ned Pepper's horse. If he had been shooting from panic would he have come so near to hitting the bandit chieftain with his first shot? On the other hand, he claimed to be an experienced officer and rifleman, and if he had been alert and had taken a deliberate shot would he not have hit his mark? Only LaBoeuf knew the truth of the matter. I grew impatient with their wrangling over the point. I think Rooster was angry because the play had been taken away from him and because Lucky Ned Pepper had beaten him once again.

The two officers made no move to give pursuit to the robber band and I suggested that we had better make such a move. Rooster said he knew where they were going to earth and he did not wish to risk riding into an ambush along the way. LaBoeuf made the point that our horses were fresh and theirs jaded. He said we could track them easily and overtake them in short order. But Rooster wanted to take the stolen horses and the dead bandits down to McAlester's and establish a prior claim to any reward the M. K. & T. Railroad might offer. Scores of marshals and railroad detectives and informers would soon be in on the game, said he.

LaBoeuf was rubbing snow on the torn places of his arm to check the bleeding. He took off his neck cloth for use as a bandage but he could not manage it with one hand and I helped him.

Rooster watched me minister to the Texan's arm and he said, "That is nothing to do with you. Go inside and make some coffee."

I said, "This will not take long."

He said, "Let it go and make the coffee."

I said, "Why are you being so silly?"

He walked away and I finished binding up the arm. I heated up the sofky and picked the trash from it and boiled some coffee in the fireplace. LaBoeuf joined Rooster in the stock cave and they strung the six horses together with halters and a long manila rope and lashed the four dead bodies across their backs like sacks of corn. The dun horse belonging to Moon bolted and bared his teeth and would not permit his dead master to be placed on his back. A less sensitive horse was found to serve.

Rooster could not identify the man who had returned to rescue Lucky Ned Pepper. I say "man." He was really only a boy, not much older than I. His mouth was open and I could not bear to look at him. The man Haze was old with a sallow wrinkled face. They had a hard time breaking the revolver free from his "death grip."

The two officers found Haze's horse in the woods nearby. He was not injured. Right behind the saddle the horse was carrying two tow-sacks, and in these sacks were about thirty-five watches, some ladies' rings, some pistols and around six hundred dollars in notes and coin. Loot from the passengers of the Katy Flyer! While searching over the ground where the bandits had made their fight, LaBoeuf turned up some copper cartridge cases. He showed them to Rooster.

I said, "What are they?"

Rooster said, "This one is a forty-four rim-fire from a Henry rifle."

Thus we had another clue. But we did not have Chaney. We had not even set eyes on him to know it. We took a hasty breakfast of the Indian hominy dish and departed the place.

It was only an hour's ride to the Texas Road. We made quite a caravan. If you had chanced to be riding up the Texas Road on that bright December morning you would have met two red-eyed peace officers and a sleepy youth from near Dardanelle, Arkansas, riding south at a walk and leading seven horses. Had you looked closely you would have seen that four of those horses were draped over with the corpses of armed robbers and stock thieves. We did in fact meet several travelers and they marveled and wondered at our grisly cargo.

Some of them had already heard news of the train robbery. One man, an Indian, told us that the robbers had realized $17,000 in cash from the express car. Two men in a buggy told us their information put the figure at $70,000. A great difference!

The accounts did agree roughly on the circumstances of the robbery. Here is what happened. The bandits broke the switch lock at Wagoner's Switch and forced the train onto a cattle siding. There they took the engineer and the fireman as hostages and threatened to kill them if the express clerk did not open the doors of his car. The clerk had spunk and refused to open the doors. The robbers killed the fireman. But the clerk still held fast. The robbers then blasted the door open with dynamite and the clerk was killed in the explosion. More dynamite was used to open the safe. While this was going on two bandits were walking through the coaches with cocked revolvers gathering up "booty" from the passengers. One man in a sleeping car protested the outrage and was assaulted and cut on the head with a pistol barrel. He was the only one they bothered except for the fireman and the express clerk. The bandits wore their hats low and had handkerchiefs tied over their faces but Lucky Ned Pepper was recognized by way of his small size and commanding manner. None of the others was identified. And that is how they robbed the Katy Flyer at Wagoner's Switch.

The riding was easy on the Texas Road. It was broad and had a good packed surface as Rooster had described it. The sun was out and the snow melted fast under the warm and welcome rays of "Old Sol."

As we rode along LaBoeuf commenced whistling tunes, perhaps to take his mind off his sore arm. Rooster said, "God damn a man that whistles!" It was the wrong thing to say if he wished it to stop. LaBoeuf then had to keep it up to show that he cared little for Rooster's opinion. After a while he took a Jew's harp from his pocket. He began to thump and twang upon it. He played fiddle tunes. He would announce, "Soldier's Joy," and play that. Then, "Johnny in the Low Ground," and play that. Then, "The Eighth of January," and play that. They all sounded pretty much like the same song. LaBoeuf said, "Is there anything you would particularly like to hear, Cogburn?" He was trying to get his "goat." Rooster gave no answer. LaBoeuf then played a few minstrel tunes and put the peculiar instrument away.

In a few minutes he asked Rooster this question, indicating the big revolvers in the saddle scabbards: "Did you carry those in the war?"

Rooster said, "I have had them a good long time."

LaBoeuf said, "I suppose you were with the cavalry."

Rooster said, "I forget just what they called it."

"I wanted to be a cavalryman," said LaBoeuf, "but I was too young and didn't own a horse. I have always regretted it. I went in the army on my fifteenth birthday and saw the last six months of the war. My mother cried because my brothers had not been home in three years. They were off at the first tap of a drum. The army put me in the supply department and I counted beeves and sacked oats for General Kirby-Smith at Shreveport. It was no work for a soldier. I wanted to get out of the Trans-Mississippi Department and go east. I wanted to see some real fighting. Right toward the last I got an opportunity to travel up there with a commissary officer, Major Burks, who was being transferred to the Department of Virginia. There were twenty-five in our party and we got there in time for Five

Forks and Petersburg and then it was all over. I have always regretted that I did not get to ride with Stuart or Forrest or some of the others. Shelby and Early."

Rooster said nothing.

I said, "It looks like six months would be enough for you."

LaBoeuf said, "No, it sounds boastful and foolish but it was not. I was almost sick when I heard of the surrender."

I said, "My father said he sure was glad to get home. He nearly died on the way."

LaBoeuf then said to Rooster, "It is hard to believe a man cannot remember where he served in the war. Do you not even remember your regiment?"

Rooster said, "I think they called it the bullet department. I was in it four years."

"You do not think much of me, do you, Cogburn?"

"I don't think about you at all when your mouth is closed."

"You are making a mistake about me."

"I don't like this kind of talk. It is like women talking."

"I was told in Fort Smith that you rode with Quantrill and that border gang."

Rooster made no reply.

LaBoeuf said, "I have heard they were not soldiers at all but murdering thieves."

Rooster said, "I have heard the same thing."

"I heard they murdered women and children at Lawrence, Kansas."

"I have heard that too. It is a damned lie."

"Were you there?"

"Where?"

"The Lawrence raid."

"There has been a lot of lies told about that."

"Do you deny they shot down soldiers and civilians alike and burned the town?"

"We missed Jim Lane. What army was you in, mister?"

"I was at Shreveport first with Kirby-Smith—"

"Yes, I heard about all them departments. What *side* was you on?"

"I was in the Army of Northern Virginia, Cogburn, and I don't have to hang my head when I say it. Now make another joke about it. You are only trying to put on a show for this girl Mattie with what you must think is a keen tongue."

"This is like women talking."

"Yes, that is the way. Make me out foolish in this girl's eyes."

"I think she has got you pretty well figured."

"You are making a mistake about me, Cogburn, and I do not appreciate the way you make conversation."

"That is nothing for you to worry about. That nor Captain Quantrill either."

"*Captain* Quantrill!"

"You had best let this go, LaBoeuf."

"Captain of what?"

"If you are looking for a fight I will accommodate you. If you are not you will let this alone."

"*Captain* Quantrill indeed!"

I rode up between them and said, "I have been thinking about something. Listen to this. There were six bandits and two stock thieves and yet only six horses at the dugout. What is the answer to that?"

Rooster said, "Six horses was all they needed."

I said, "Yes, but that six includes the horses belonging to Moon and Quincy. There were only four stolen horses."

Rooster said, "They would have taken them other two as well and exchanged them later. They have done it before."

"Then what would Moon and Quincy do for mounts?"

"They would have the six tired horses."

"Oh. I had forgotten about them."

"It was only a swap for a few days."

"I was thinking that Lucky Ned Pepper might have been planning to murder the two stock thieves. It would have been a treacherous scheme but then they could not inform against him. What do you think?"

"No, Ned would not do that."

"Why not? He and his desperate band killed a fireman and an express clerk on the Katy Flyer last night."

"Ned does not go around killing people if he has no good reason. If he has a good reason he kills them."

"You can think what you want to," said I. "I think betrayal was part of his scheme."

We reached J. J. McAlester's store about 10 o'clock that morning. The people of the settlement turned out to see the dead bodies and there were gasps and murmurs over the spectacle of horror, made the worse by way of the winter morning being so sunny and cheerful. It must have been a trading day for there were several wagons and horses tied up about the store. The railroad tracks ran behind it. There was little more to the place than the store building and a few smaller frame and log structures of poor description, and yet if I am not mistaken this was at that time one of the best towns in the Choctaw Nation. The store is now part of the modern little city of McAlester, Oklahoma, where for a long time "coal was king." McAlester is also the international headquarters of the Order of the Rainbow for Girls.

There was no real doctor there at that time but there was a young Indian who had some medical training and was competent to set broken bones and dress gunshot wounds. LaBoeuf sought him out for treatment.

I went with Rooster, who searched out an Indian policeman of his acquaintance, a Captain Boots Finch of the Choctaw Light Horse. These police handled Indian crimes only, and where white men were involved the Light Horse had no authority. We found the captain in a small log house. He was sitting on a box by a stove getting his hair cut. He was a slender man about of an age with Rooster. He and the Indian barber were ignorant of the stir our arrival had caused.

Rooster came up behind the captain and goosed him in the ribs with both hands and said, "How is the people's health, Boots?"

The captain gave a start and reached for his pistol, and then he saw who it was. He said, "Well, I declare, Rooster. What brings you to town so early?"

"Is this town? I was thinking I was out of town."

Captain Finch laughed at the gibe. He said, "You must have traveled fast if you are here on that Wagoner's Switch business."

"That is the business right enough."

"It was little Ned Pepper and five others. I suppose you know that."

"Yes. How much did they get?"

"Mr. Smallwood says they got $17,000 cash and a packet of registered mail from the safe. He has not got a total on the passenger claims. I am afraid you are on a cold trail here."

"When did you last see Ned?"

"I am told he passed through here two days ago. He and Haze and a Mexican on a round-bellied calico pony. I didn't see them myself. They won't be coming back this way."

Rooster said, "That Mexican was Greaser Bob."

"Is that the young one?"

"No, it's the old one, the Original Bob from Fort Worth."

"I heard he was badly shot in Denison and had given up his reckless ways."

"Bob is hard to kill. He won't stay shot. I am looking for another man. I think he is with Ned. He is short and has a black mark on his face and he carries a Henry rifle."

Captain Finch thought about it. He said, "No, the way I got it, there was only the three here. Haze and the Mexican and Ned. We are watching his woman's house. It is a waste of time and none of my business but I have sent a man out there."

Rooster said, "It is a waste of time all right. I know about where Ned is."

"Yes, I know too but it will take a hundred marshals to smoke him out of there."

"It won't take that many."

"It wouldn't take that many Choctaws. How many were in that marshals' party in August? Forty?"

"It was closer to fifty," said Rooster. "Joe Schmidt was running that game, or misrunning it. I am running this one."

"I am surprised the chief marshal would turn you loose on a hunt like this without supervision."

"He can't help himself this time."

Captain Finch said, "I could take you in there, Rooster, and show you how to bring Ned out."

"Could you now? Well, a Indian makes too much noise to suit me. Don't you find it so, Gaspargoo?"

That was the barber's name. He laughed and put his hand over his mouth. Gaspargoo is also the name of a fish that makes fair eating.

I said to the captain, "Perhaps you are wondering who I am."

"Yes, I *was* wondering that," said he. "I thought you were a walking hat."

"My name is Mattie Ross," said I. "The man with the black mark goes by the name of Tom Chaney. He shot my father to death in Fort Smith and robbed him. Chaney was drunk and my father was not armed at the time."

"That is a shame," said the captain.

"When we find him we are going to club him with sticks and put him under arrest and take him back to Fort Smith," said I.

"I wish you luck. We don't want him down here."

Rooster said, "Boots, I need a little help. I have got Haze and some youngster out there, along with Emmett Quincy and Moon Garrett. I am after being in a hurry and I wanted to see if you would not bury them boys for me."

"They are dead?"

"All dead," said Rooster. "What is it the judge says? Their depredations is now come to a fitting end."

Captain Finch pulled the barber's cloth from his neck. He and the barber went with us back to where the horses were tied. Rooster told them about our scrap at the dugout.

The captain grasped each dead man by the hair of the head and when he recognized a face he grunted and spoke the name. The man Haze had no hair to speak of and Captain Finch lifted his head by the ears. We learned that the boy was called Billy. His father ran a steam sawmill on the South Canadian River, the captain told us, and there was a large family at home. Billy was one of the eldest children and he had helped his father cut timber. The boy was not known to have been in any devilment before this. As for the other three, the captain did not know if they had any people who would want to claim the bodies.

Rooster said, "All right, you hold Billy for the family and bury these others. I will post their names in Fort Smith and if anybody wants them they can come dig them up." Then he went along behind the horses slapping their rumps. He said, "These four horses was taken from Mr. Burlingame. These three right here belong to Haze and Quincy and Moon. You get what you can for them, Boots, and sell the saddles and guns and coats and I will split it with you. Is that fair enough?"

I said, "You told Moon you would send his brother the money owing to him from his traps."

Rooster said, "I forgot where he said to send it."

I said, "It is the district superintendent of the Methodist Church in Austin, Texas. His brother is a preacher named George Garrett."

"Was it Austin or Dallas?"

"Austin."

"Let's get it straight."

"It was Austin."

"All right then, write it down for the captain. Send this man ten dollars, Boots, and tell him his brother got cut and is buried here."

Captain Finch said, "Are you going out by way of Mr. Burlingame's?"

"I don't have the time," said Rooster. "I would like for you to send word out if you will. Just so Mr. Burlingame knows it was deputy marshal Rooster Cogburn that recovered them horses."

"Do you want this girl with the hat to write it down?"

"I believe you can remember it if you try."

Captain Finch called out to some Indian youths who were standing nearby looking at us. I gathered he was telling them in the Choctaw tongue to see to the horses and the burial of the bodies. He had to speak to them a second time and very sharply before they would approach the bodies.

The railroad agent was an older man named Smallwood. He praised us for our pluck and he was very much pleased to see the sacks of cash and valuables we had recovered. You may think Rooster was hard in appropriating the traps of the dead men but I will tell you that he did not touch one cent of the money that was stolen at gunpoint from the passengers of the Katy Flyer. Smallwood looked over the "booty" and said it would certainly help to cover the loss, though it was his experience that some of the victims would make exaggerated claims.

He had known the martyred clerk personally and he said the man had been a loyal employee of the M. K. & T. for some years. In his youth the clerk had been a well-known foot racer in Kansas. He showed his spunk right to the end. Smallwood did not know the fireman personally. In both cases, said he, the M. K. & T. would try to do something for the bereaved families, though times were hard and revenue down. They say Jay Gould had no heart! Smallwood also assured Rooster that the railroad would do right by him, providing he "clean up" Lucky Ned Pepper's robber band and recover the stolen express funds.

I advised Rooster to get a written statement from Smallwood to that effect, along with an itemized, timed and dated receipt for the two sacks of "booty." Smallwood was wary about committing his company too far but we got a receipt out of him and a statement saying that Rooster had produced on that day the lifeless bodies of two men "whom he alleges took part in said robbery." I think Smallwood was a gentleman but gentlemen are only human and their memories can sometimes fail them. Business is business.

Mr. McAlester, who kept the store, was a good Arkansas man. He too commended us for our actions and he gave us towels and pans of hot water and some sweet-smelling olive soap. His wife served us a good country dinner with fresh buttermilk. LaBoeuf joined us for the hearty meal. The medical-trained Indian had been able to remove all the big splinters and lead fragments and he had bound the arm tightly. Naturally the limb remained stiff and sore, yet the Texan enjoyed a limited use of it.

When we had eaten our fill, Mr. McAlester's wife asked me if I did not wish to lie down on her bed for a nap. I was sorely tempted but I saw through the scheme. I had noticed Rooster talking to her on the sly at the table. I concluded he was trying to get shed of me once again. "Thank you, mam, I am not tired," said I. It was the biggest story I have ever told!

We did not leave right away because Rooster found that his horse Bo had dropped a front shoe. We went to a little shed kept by a blacksmith. While waiting there, LaBoeuf repaired the broken stock of his Sharps rifle by wrapping copper wire around it. Rooster hurried the smith along with the shoeing, as he was not disposed to linger in the settlement. He wished to stay ahead of the posse of marshals that he knew was even then scouring the brush for Lucky Ned Pepper and his band.

He said to me, "Sis, the time has come when I must move fast. It is a hard day's ride to where I am going. You will wait here and Mrs. McAlester will see to your comfort. I will be back tomorrow or the next day with our man."

"No, I am going along," said I.

LaBoeuf said, "She has come this far."

Rooster said, "It is far enough."

I said, "Do you think I am ready to quit when we are so close?"

LaBoeuf said, "There is something in what she says, Cogburn. I think she has done fine myself. She has won her spurs, so to speak. That is just my personal opinion."

Rooster held up his hand and said, "All right, let it go. I have said my piece. We won't have a lot of talk about winning spurs."

We departed the place around noon, traveling east and slightly south. Rooster called the turn when he said "hard riding." That big long-legged Bo just walked away from the two ponies, but the weight began to tell on him after a few miles and Little Blackie and the shaggy pony closed the distance on him ere long. We rode like the very "dickens" for about forty minutes and then stopped and dismounted and walked for a spell, giving the horses a rest. It was while we were walking that a rider came up hallooing and overtook us. We were out on a prairie and we saw him coming for some little distance.

It was Captain Finch, and he brought exciting news. He told us that shortly after we had left McAlester's, he received word that Odus Wharton had broken from the basement jail in Fort Smith. The escape had taken place early that morning.

Here is what happened. Not long after breakfast two trusty prisoners brought in a barrel of clean sawdust for use in the spittoons of that foul dungeon. It was fairly dark down there and in a moment when the guards were not looking the trusties concealed Wharton and another doomed murderer inside the barrel. Both men were of slight stature and inconsiderable weight. The trusties then carried the two outside and away to freedom. A bold daylight escape in a fat barrel! Some clever "stunt"! The trusties ran off along with the convicted killers and very likely drew good wages for their audacity.

On hearing the news Rooster did not appear angry or in any way perturbed, but only amused. You may wonder why.

He had his reasons and among them were these, that Wharton now stood no chance of winning a commutation from President R. B. Hayes, and also that the escape would cause Lawyer Goudy a certain amount of chagrin in Washington city and would no doubt result in a big expense loss for him, as clients who resolve their own problems are apt to be slow in paying due bills from a lawyer.

Captain Finch said, "I thought you had better know about this."

Rooster said, "I appreciate it, Boots. I appreciate you riding out here."

"Wharton will be looking for you."

"If he is not careful he will find me."

Captain Finch looked LaBoeuf over, then said to Rooster, "Is this the man who shot Ned's horse from under him?"

Rooster said, "Yes, this is the famous horse killer from El Paso, Texas. His idea is to put everybody on foot. He says it will limit their mischief."

LaBoeuf's fair-complected face became congested with angry blood. He said, "There was very little light and I was firing off-hand. I did not have the time to find a rest."

Captain Finch said, "There is no need to apologize for that shot. A good many more people have missed Ned than have hit him."

"I was not apologizing," said LaBoeuf. "I was only explaining the circumstances."

"Rooster here has missed Ned a few times himself, horse and all," said the captain. "I reckon he is on his way now to missing him again."

Rooster was holding a bottle with a little whiskey in it. He said, "You keep on thinking that." He drained off the whiskey in about three swallows and tapped the cork back in and tossed the bottle up in the air. He pulled his revolver and fired at it twice and missed. The bottle fell and rolled and Rooster shot at it two or three more times and broke it on the ground. He got out his sack of cartridges and reloaded the pistol. He said, "The Chinaman is running them cheap shells in on me again."

LaBoeuf said, "I thought maybe the sun was in your eyes. That is to say, your eye."

Rooster swung the cylinder back in his revolver and said, "Eyes, is it? I'll show you eyes!" He jerked the sack of corn dodgers free from his saddle baggage. He got one of the dodgers out and flung it in the air and fired at it and missed. Then he flung another one up and he hit it. The corn dodger exploded. He was pleased with himself and he got a fresh bottle of whiskey from his baggage and treated himself to a drink.

LaBoeuf pulled one of his revolvers and got two dodgers out of the sack and tossed them both up. He fired very rapidly but he only hit one. Captain Finch tried it with two and missed both of them. Then he tried with one and made a successful shot. Rooster shot at two and hit one. They drank whiskey and used up about sixty corn dodgers like that. None of them ever hit two at one throw with a revolver but Captain Finch finally did it with his Winchester repeating rifle, with somebody else throwing. It was entertaining for a while but there was nothing educational about it. I grew more and more impatient with them.

I said, "Come on, I have had my bait of this. I am ready to go. Shooting cornbread out here on this prairie is not taking us anywhere."

By then Rooster was using his rifle and the captain was throwing for him. "Chunk high and not so far out this time," said he.

At length, Captain Finch took his leave and went back the way he came. We continued our journey eastward, with the Winding Stair Mountains as our destination. We lost a good half-hour with that shooting foolishness, but, worse than that, it started Rooster to drinking.

He drank even as he rode, which looked difficult. I cannot say it slowed him down any but it did make him silly. Why do people *wish* to be silly? We kept up our fast pace, riding hard for forty or fifty minutes and then going on foot for a piece. I believe those walks were a more welcome rest for me than for the horses. I have never claimed to be a cow-boy! Little Blackie did not falter. He had good wind and his spirit was such that he would not let LaBoeuf's shaggy mount get ahead of him on an open run. Yes, you bet he was a game pony!

We loped across open prairies and climbed wooded limestone hills and made our way through brushy bottoms and icy streams. Much of the snow melted under the sun but as the long shadows of dusk descended in all their purple loveliness, the temperature did likewise. We were very warm from our exertions and the chill night air felt good at first, but then it became uncomfortable as we slowed our pace. We did not ride fast after dark as it would have been dangerous for the horses. LaBoeuf said the Rangers often rode at night to avoid the terrible Texas sun and this was like nothing at all to him. I did not care for it myself.

Nor did I enjoy the slipping and sliding when we were climbing the steep grades of the Winding Stair Mountains. There is a lot of thick pine timber in those hills and we wandered up and down in the double-darkness of the forest. Rooster stopped us twice while he dismounted and looked around for sign. He was well along to being drunk. Later on he got to talking to himself and one thing I heard him say was this: "Well, we done the best we could with what we had. We was in a war. All we had was revolvers and horses." I supposed he was brooding about the hard words LaBoeuf had spoken to him on the subject of his war service. He got louder and louder but it was hard to tell whether he was still talking to himself or addressing himself to us. I think it was a little of both. On one long climb he fell off his horse, but he quickly gained his feet and mounted again.

"That was nothing, nothing," said he. "Bo put a foot wrong, that was all. He is tired. This is no grade. I have freighted iron stoves up harder grades than this, and pork as well. I lost fourteen barrels of pork on a shelf road not much steeper than this and old Cook never batted a eye. I was a pretty fair jerk-line teamster, could always talk to mules, but oxen was something else. You don't get that quick play with cattle that you get with mules. They are slow to start and slow to turn and slow to stop. It taken me a while to learn it. Pork brought a thundering great price out there then but old Cook was a square dealer and he let me work it out at his lot price. Yes sir, he paid liberal wages too. He made money and he didn't mind his help making money. I will tell you how much he made. He made fifty thousand dollars in one year with them wagons but he did not enjoy good health. Always down with something. He was all bowed over and his neck was stiff from drinking Jamaica ginger. He had to look up at you through his hair, like this, unless he was laying down, and as I say, that rich jaybird was down a lot. He had a good head of brown hair, had every lock until he died. Of course he was a right young man when he died. He only looked old. He was carrying a twenty-one-foot tape-worm along with his business responsibilities and that aged him. Killed him in the end. They didn't even know he had it till he was dead, though he ate like a field hand, ate five or six good dinners every day. If he was alive today I believe I would still be out there. Yes, I know I would, and I would likely have money in the bank. I had to make tracks when his wife commenced to running things. She said, 'You can't leave me like this, Rooster. All my drivers is leaving me.' I told her, I said, 'You watch me.' No sir, I was not ready to work for her and I told her so. There is no generosity in women. They want everything coming in and nothing going out. They show no trust. Lord God, how they hate to pay you! They will get the work of two men out of you and I guess they would beat you with whips if they was able to. No sir, not me. Never. A man will not work for a woman, not unless he has clabber for brains."

LaBoeuf said, "I told you that in Fort Smith."

I do not know if the Texan intended the remark to tell against me, but if he did, it was "water off a duck's back." You cannot give any weight to the words of a drunkard, and even so, I knew Rooster could not be talking about me in his drunken criticism of women, the kind of money I was pay-ing him. I could have confounded him and his silliness right there by saying, "What about me? What about that twenty-five dollars I have given you?" But I had not the strength nor the inclination to bandy words with a drunkard. What have you done when you have bested a fool?

I thought we would never stop, and must be nearing Mont-gomery, Alabama. From time to time LaBoeuf and I would interrupt Rooster and ask him how much farther and he would reply, "It is not far now," and then he would pick up again on a chapter in the long and adventurous account of his life. He had seen a good deal of strife in his travels.

When at last we did stop, Rooster said only, "I reckon this will do." It was well after midnight. We were on a more or less level place in a pine forest up in the hills and that was all I could determine. I was so tired and stiff I could not think straight.

Rooster said he calculated we had come about fifty miles—
*fifty miles!*—from McAlester's store and were now positioned
some four miles from Lucky Ned Pepper's bandit stronghold.
Then he wrapped himself up in his buffalo robe and retired
without ceremony, leaving LaBoeuf to see to the horses.

The Texan watered them from the canteens and fed them
and tied them out. He left the saddles on them for warmth,
but with the girths loosened. Those poor horses were worn
out.

We made no fire. I took a hasty supper of bacon and biscuit
sandwiches. The biscuits were pretty hard. There was a layer
of pine straw under the patchy snow and I raked up a thick
pile with my hands for a woodland mattress. The straw was
dirty and brittle and somewhat damp but at that it made for a
better bed than any I had seen on this journey. I rolled up in
my blankets and slicker and burrowed down into the straw. It
was a clear winter night and I made out the Big Dipper and the
North Star through the pine branches. The moon was already
down. My back hurt and my feet were swollen and I was so
exhausted that my hands quivered. The quivering passed and I
was soon in the "land of Nod."

ROOSTER WAS stirring about the next morning before the sun had cleared the higher mountains to the east. He seemed little worse for the wear despite the hard riding and the drinking excesses and the short sleep. He did insist on having coffee and he made a little fire of oak sticks to boil his water. The fire gave off hardly any smoke, white wisps that were quickly gone, but LaBoeuf called it a foolish indulgence, seeing we were so close to our quarry.

I felt as though I had only just closed my eyes. The water in the canteens was low and they would not let me have any for washing. I got the canvas bucket and put my revolver in it and set off down the hill looking for a spring or a runoff stream.

The slope was gentle at first and then it fell off rather sharply. The brush grew thicker and I checked my descent by grabbing bushes. Down and down I went. As I neared the bottom, dreading the return climb, I heard splashing and blowing noises. My thought was: *What on earth!* Then I came into the open on a creek bank. On the other side there was a man watering some horses.

*The man was none other than Tom Chaney!*

You may readily imagine that I registered shock at the sight of that squat assassin. He had not yet seen me, nor heard me either because of the noise made by the horses. His rifle was slung across his back on the cotton plow line. I thought to turn and run but I could not move. I stood there fixed.

Then he saw me. He gave a start and brought the rifle quickly into play. He held the rifle on me and peered across the little stream and studied me.

He said, "Well, now, I know you. Your name is Mattie. You are little Mattie the bookkeeper. Isn't this something." He grinned and took the rifle from play and slung it carelessly over a shoulder.

I said, "Yes, and I know you, Tom Chaney."

He said, "What are you doing here?"

I said, "I came to fetch water."

"What are you doing here in these mountains?"

I reached into the bucket and brought out my dragoon revolver. I dropped the bucket and held the revolver in both hands. I said, "I am here to take you back to Fort Smith."

Chaney laughed and said, "Well, I will not go. How do you like that?"

I said, "There is a posse of officers up on the hill who will force you to go."

"That is interesting news," said he. "How many is up there?"

"Right around fifty. They are all well armed and they mean business. What I want you to do now is leave those horses and come across the creek and walk in front of me up the hill."

He said, "I think I will oblige the officers to come after me." He began to gather the horses together. There were five of them but Papa's horse Judy was not among them.

I said, "If you refuse to go I will have to shoot you."

He went on with his work and said, "Oh? Then you had better cock your piece."

I had forgotten about that. I pulled the hammer back with both thumbs.

"All the way back till it locks," said Chaney.

"I know how to do it," said I. When it was ready I said, "You will not go with me?"

"I think not," said he. "It is just the other way around. You are going with me."

I pointed the revolver at his belly and shot him down. The explosion kicked me backwards and caused me to lose my footing and the pistol jumped from my hand. I lost no time in recovering it and getting to my feet. The ball had struck Chaney's side and knocked him into a sitting position against a tree. I heard Rooster or LaBoeuf call out for me. "I am down here!" I replied. There was another shout from the hill above Chaney.

He was holding both hands down on his side. He said, "I did not think you would do it."

I said, "What do you think now?"

He said, "One of my short ribs is broken. It hurts every breath I take."

I said, "You killed my father when he was trying to help you. I have one of the gold pieces you took from him. Now give me the other."

"I regret that shooting," said he. "Mr. Ross was decent to me but he ought not to have meddled in my business. I was drinking and I was mad through and through. Nothing has gone right for me."

There was more yelling from the hills.

I said, "No, you are just a piece of trash, that is all. They say you shot a senator in the state of Texas."

"That man threatened my life. I was justified. Everything is against me. Now I am shot by a child."

"Get up on your feet and come across that creek before I shoot you again. My father took you in when you were hungry."

"You will have to help me up."

"No, I will not help you. Get up yourself."

He made a quick move for a chunk of wood and I pulled the trigger and the hammer snapped on a bad percussion cap. I made haste to try another chamber but the hammer snapped dead again. I had not time for a third try. Chaney flung the heavy piece of wood and it caught me in the chest and laid me out backwards.

He came splashing across the creek and he jerked me up by my coat and commenced slapping me and cursing me and my father. That was his cur nature, to change from a whining baby to a vicious bully as circumstances permitted. He stuck my revolver in his belt and pulled me stumbling through the water. The horses were milling about and he managed to catch two of them by their halters while holding me with the other hand.

I heard Rooster and LaBoeuf crashing down through the brush behind us and calling out for me. "Down here! Hurry up!" I shouted, and Chaney let go of my coat just long enough to give me another stinging slap.

I must tell you that the slopes rose steeply on either side of the creek. Just as the two peace officers were running down on one side, so were Chaney's bandit friends running down the other, so that both parties were converging on the hollow and the little mountain stream.

The bandits won the foot race. There were two of them and one was a little man in "woolly chaps" whom I rightly took to be Lucky Ned Pepper. He was still hatless. The other was taller and a quite well-dressed man in a linen suit and a bearskin coat, and his hat tied fast by a slip-string under his chin. This man was the Mexican gambler who called himself The Original Greaser Bob. They broke upon us suddenly and poured a terrible volley of fire across the creek with their Winchester repeating rifles. Lucky Ned Pepper said to Chaney, "Take them horses you got and move!"

Chaney did as he was told and we started up with the horses. It was hard climbing. Lucky Ned Pepper and the Mexican remained behind and exchanged shots with Rooster and LaBoeuf while trying to catch the other horses. I heard running splashes as one of the officers reached the creek, then a flurry of shots as he was made to retreat.

Chaney had to stop and catch his breath after thirty or forty yards of pulling me and the two horses behind him. Blood showed through on his shirt. Lucky Ned Pepper and Greaser Bob overtook us there. They were pulling two horses. I supposed the fifth horse had run away or been killed. The leads of these two horses were turned over to Chaney and Lucky Ned Pepper said to him, "Get on up that hill and don't be stopping again!"

The bandit chieftain took me roughly by the arm. He said, "Who all is down there?"

"Marshal Cogburn and fifty more officers," said I.

He shook me like a terrier shaking a rat. "Tell me another lie and I will stove in your head!" Part of his upper lip was missing, a sort of gap on one side that caused him to make a whistling noise as he spoke. Three or four teeth were broken off there as well, yet he made himself clearly understood.

Thinking it best, I said, "It is Marshal Cogburn and another man."

He flung me to the ground and put a boot on my neck to hold me while he reloaded his rifle from a cartridge belt. He shouted out, "Rooster, can you hear me?" There was no reply. The Original Greaser was standing there with us and he broke the silence by firing down the hill. Lucky Ned Pepper shouted, "You answer me, Rooster! I will kill this girl! You know I will do it!"

Rooster called up from below, "The girl is nothing to me! She is a runaway from Arkansas!"

"That's very well!" said Lucky Ned Pepper. "Do you advise me to kill her?"

"Do what you think is best, Ned!" replied Rooster. "She is nothing to me but a lost child! Think it over first."

"I have already thought it over! You and Potter get mounted double fast! If I see you riding over that bald ridge to the northwest I will spare the girl! You have five minutes!"

"We will need more time!"

"I will not give you any more!"

"There will be a party of marshals in here soon, Ned! Let me have Chaney and the girl and I will mislead them for six hours!"

"Too thin, Rooster! Too thin! I won't trust you!"

"I will cover you till dark!"

"Your five minutes is running! No more talk!"

Lucky Ned Pepper pulled me to my feet. Rooster called up again, saying, "We are leaving but you must give us time!"

The bandit chieftain made no reply. He brushed the snow and dirt from my face and said, "Your life depends upon their actions. I have never busted a cap on a woman or anybody much under sixteen years but I will do what I have to do."

I said, "There is some mix-up here. I am Mattie Ross of near Dardanelle, Arkansas. My family has property and I don't know why I am being treated like this."

Lucky Ned Pepper said, "It is enough that you know I will do what I have to do."

We made our way up the hill. A little farther along we came across a bandit armed with a shotgun and squatting behind a big slab of limestone. This man's name was Harold Permalee. I believe he was simpleminded. He gobbled at me like a turkey until Lucky Ned Pepper made him hush. Greaser Bob was told to stay there with him behind the rock and keep a watch below. I had seen this Mexican gambler fall from Rooster's shots at the dugout but he appeared now to be in perfect health and there was no outward evidence of a wound. When we left them there Harold Permalee made a noise like "*Whooooo-haaaaaaa!*" and this time it was The Greaser who made him hush.

Lucky Ned Pepper pushed me along in front of him through the brush. There was no trail. His woolly chaps sang as they swished back and forth, something like corduroy trousers. He was little and wiry and no doubt a hard customer, but still his wind was not good and he was blowing like a man with asthma by the time we had ascended to the bandits' lair.

They had made their camp on a bare rock shelf some seventy yards or so below the crest of the mountain. Pine timber grew in abundance below and above and on all sides. No apparent trails led to the place.

The ledge was mostly level but broken here and there by deep pits and fissures. A shallow cave provided sleeping quarters, as I saw bedding and saddles strewn about inside. A wagon sheet, now pulled back, served for a door and windbreak. The horses were tied in the cover of trees. It was quite windy up there and the little cooking fire in front of the cave was protected by a circle of rocks. The site overlooked a wide expanse of ground to the west and north.

Tom Chaney was sitting by the fire with his shirt pulled up and another man was ministering to him, tying a pad of cloth to his wounded side with a cotton rope. The man laughed as he cinched the rope up tight and caused Chaney to whimper with pain. "Waw, waw, waw," said the man, making sounds like a bawling calf in mockery of Chaney.

This man was Farrell Permalee, a younger brother to Harold Permalee. He wore a long blue army overcoat with officers' boards on the shoulders. Harold Permalee had participated in the robbery of the Katy Flyer and Farrell joined the bandits later that night when they swapped horses at Ma Permalee's place.

The Permalee woman was a notorious receiver of stolen livestock but was never brought to law. Her husband, Henry Joe Permalee, killed himself with a dynamite cap in the ugly act of wrecking a passenger train. A family of criminal trash! Of her youngest boys, Carroll Permalee lived long enough to be put to death in the Electric Chair, and not long afterward Darryl Permalee was shot to death at the wheel of a motorcar by a bank "dick" and a constable in Mena, Arkansas. No, do not compare them to Henry Starr or the Dalton brothers. Certainly Starr and the Daltons were robbers and reckless characters but they were not simple and they were not altogether rotten. You will remember that Bob and Grat Dalton served as marshals for Judge Parker, and Bob was a fine one, they say. Upright men gone bad! What makes them take the wrong road? Bill Doolin too. A cow-boy gone wrong.

When Lucky Ned Pepper and I gained the rock ledge Chaney jumped up and made for me. "I will wring your scrawny neck!" he exclaimed. Lucky Ned Pepper pushed him aside and said, "No, I won't have it. Let that doctoring go and get the horses saddled. Lend him a hand, Farrell."

He pushed me down by the fire and said, "Sit there and be still." When he had caught his breath he took a spyglass from his coat and searched the rocky dome to the west. He saw nothing and took a seat by the fire and drank coffee from a can and ate some bacon from a skillet with his hands. There was plenty of meat and several cans of water in the fire, some with plain water and some with coffee already brewed. I concluded the bandits had been at their breakfast when they were alarmed by the gunshot down below.

I said, "Can I have some of that bacon?"

Lucky Ned Pepper said, "Help yourself. Have some coffee."

"I don't drink coffee. Where is the bread?"

"We lost it. Tell me what you are doing here."

I took a piece of bacon and chewed on it. "I will be glad to tell you," said I. "You will see I am in the right. Tom Chaney there shot my father to death in Fort Smith and robbed him of two gold pieces and stole his mare. Her name is Judy but I do not see her here. I was informed Rooster Cogburn had grit and I hired him out to find the murderer. A few minutes ago I came upon Chaney down there watering horses. He would not be taken in charge and I shot him. If I had killed him I would not now be in this fix. My revolver misfired twice."

"They will do it," said Lucky Ned Pepper. "It will embarrass you every time." Then he laughed. He said, "Most girls like play pretties, but you like guns, don't you?"

"I don't care a thing in the world about guns. If I did I would have one that worked."

Chaney was carrying a load of bedding from the cave. He said, "I was shot from ambush, Ned. The horses was blowing and making noise. It was one of them officers that got me."

I said, "How can you stand there and tell such a big story?"

Chaney picked up a stick and pitched it into a big crack in

the ledge. He said, "There is a ball of rattlesnakes down there in that pit and I am going to throw you in it. How do you like that?"

"No, you won't," said I. "This man will not let you have your way. He is your boss and you must do as he tells you."

Lucky Ned Pepper again took his glass and looked across at the ridge.

Chaney said, "Five minutes is well up."

"I will give them a little more time," said the bandit chieftain.

"How much more?" said Chaney.

"Till I think they have had enough."

Greaser Bob called up from below saying, "They are gone, Ned! I can hear nothing! We had best make a move!"

Lucky Ned Pepper replied, "Hold fast for a while!"

Then he returned to his breakfast. He said, "Was that Rooster and Potter that waylaid us last night?"

I said, "The man's name is not Potter, it is LaBoeuf. He is an officer from Texas. He is looking for Chaney too, though he calls him by another name."

"Is he the one with the buffalo gun?"

"He calls it a Sharps rifle. His arm was hurt in the fight."

"He shot my horse. A man from Texas has no authority to fire at me."

"I know nothing about that. I have a good lawyer at home."

"Did they take Quincy and Moon?"

"They are both dead. It was a terrible thing to see. I was in the very middle of it. Do you need a good lawyer?"

"I need a good judge. What about Haze? An old fellow."

"Yes, he and the young man were both killed."

"I saw Billy was dead when he was struck. I thought Haze might have made it. He was tough as boot leather. I am sorry for him."

"Are you not sorry for the boy Billy?"

"He should never have been there. There was nothing I could do for him."

"How did you know he was dead?"

"I could tell. I advised him against coming, and then give in to him against what I knowed was best. Where did you take them?"

"To McAlester's store."

"I will tell you what he did at Wagoner's Switch."

"My lawyer has political influence."

"This will amuse you. I posted him with the horses out of danger and told him to fire a string of shots with his rifle now and then. You must have shooting for the way it keeps the passengers in their seats. Well, he started out all right and then as the job went along I noticed the shots had stopped. I figured Billy Boy had run for home and a plate of mother's soup. Bob went to see about him and he found the boy standing out there in the dark shucking good shells out of his guns. He thought he was shooting but he was so scared he could not remember to pull the trigger. That was how green he was, green as a July persimmon."

I said, "You do not show much kindly feeling for a young man who saved your life."

"I am happy he done it," said Lucky Ned Pepper. "I don't say he wan't game, I say he was green. All kids is game, but a man will keep his head and look out for his own self. Look at old Haze. Well, he is dead now but he should have been dead ten times afore now. Yes, and your good friend Rooster. That goes for him as well."

"He is not my friend."

Farrell Permalee made a whooping noise like that of his brother and said, "There they be!"

I looked over to the northwest and saw two riders approaching the top of the ridge. Little Blackie, riderless, was tied behind them. Lucky Ned Pepper brought his glass into play but I could see them well enough without such aid. When they reached the crest they paused and turned our way and Rooster fired a pistol in the air. I saw the smoke before the noise reached us. Lucky Ned Pepper pulled his revolver and fired an answering shot. Then Rooster and LaBoeuf disappeared over the hill. The last thing I saw was Little Blackie.

I think it did not come home to me until that moment what my situation was. I had not thought Rooster or LaBoeuf would give in to the bandits so easily. It was in my mind that they would slip up through the brush and attack the bandits while they were disorganized, or employ some clever ruse known only by detectives to bring the bandits to heel. Now they were gone! The officers had left me! I was utterly cast down and for the first time I feared for my life. My mind was filled with anxiety.

Who was to blame? *Deputy Marshal Rooster Cogburn!* The gabbing drunken fool had made a mistake of four miles and led us directly into the robbers' lair. A keen detective! Yes, and in an earlier state of drunkenness he had placed faulty caps in my revolver, causing it to fail me in a time of need. That was not enough; now he had abandoned me in this howling wilderness to a gang of cutthroats who cared not a rap for the blood of their own companions, and how much less for that of a helpless and unwanted youngster! Was this what they called grit in Fort Smith? We called it something else in Yell County!

Lucky Ned Pepper shouted out for The Original Greaser and Harold Permalee to leave their watch post and come to the camp. The four horses were saddled and in readiness. Lucky Ned Pepper looked over the mounts, then at the spare saddle that lay on the ground. It was an old saddle but a handsome one, decorated with fixtures of beaten silver.

He said, "That is Bob's saddle."

Tom Chaney said, "It was Bob's horse we lost."

"That you lost," said the bandit chieftain. "Unsaddle that gray and put Bob's saddle up."

"I am riding the gray," said Chaney.

"I have other plans for you."

Chaney set about unsaddling the gray horse. He said, "I will be riding behind Bob?"

"No, it will be too chancy with two men up if it comes to a race. When we reach Ma's house I will send Carroll back to fetch you with a fresh mount. I want you to wait here with the girl. You will be out by dark. We are going to 'The Old Place' and you can meet us there."

"Well, I don't like that," said Chaney. "Let me ride with you, Ned, just out of here anyway."

"No."

"Them marshals will be up here."

"They will guess we are all gone."

I said, "I am not staying here by myself with Tom Chaney."

Lucky Ned Pepper said, "That is the way I will have it."

"He will kill me," said I. "You have heard him say it. He has killed my father and now you will let him kill me."

"He will do no such thing," said the bandit chieftain. "Tom, do you know the crossing at Cypress Forks, near the log meetinghouse?"

"I know the place."

"You will take the girl there and leave her." Then to me, "You can stay the night in the meetinghouse. There is a dummy called Flanagan lives about two miles up the creek. He has a mule and he will see you to McAlester's. He cannot speak or hear but he can read. Can you write?"

"Yes," said I. "Let me go now on foot. I will find my way out."

"No, I won't have it. Tom will not harm you. Do you understand that, Tom? If any harm comes to this child you do not get paid."

Chaney said, "Farrell, let me ride up with you."

Farrell Permalee laughed and made noises like an owl, saying, "*Hoo, hoo, hoo.*" Harold Permalee and The Original Greaser Bob came up and Chaney commenced to plead with them to share their mounts. Greaser Bob said no. The Permalee brothers now teamed together like silly boys, and would give Chaney no sensible answer. Harold Permalee would interrupt Chaney's question each time with mockery, making animal sounds such as are made by pigs and goats and sheep, and Farrell would laugh at the sport and say, "Do it again, Harold. Do a goat."

Chaney said, "Everything is against me."

Lucky Ned Pepper made sure the buckles were fastened good on his saddle wallets.

Greaser Bob said, "Ned, let us cut up the winnings now."

"There will be time for that at 'The Old Place,'" replied the bandit chieftain.

"We have been in two scraps already," said The Greaser. "We have lost two men. I would feel easier if I was carrying my own winnings."

Lucky Ned Pepper said, "Well, Bob, I thought your interest was in saving time."

"It will not take long. I will feel easier."

"Very well then. It suits me. I want you to feel easy."

He reached inside one of the saddle wallets and pulled out four packets of greenbacks and pitched them to Greaser Bob. "How is that?"

Greaser Bob said, "You will not count it?"

"We won't quarrel over a dollar or two." Then he gave one packet to Harold Permalee and a single $50 note to Farrell Permalee. The brothers said, "*Whooooo-haaaaa! Whooooo-haaaaa!*" I wondered that they did not press for more, in light of the total amount realized in the robbery, but I supposed they had agreed to a fixed wage for their services. I judged too that they were somewhat ignorant of the value of money.

Lucky Ned Pepper went to buckle up the wallet again. He said, "I will keep your winnings with mine, Tom. You will be paid tonight at 'The Old Place.'"

Chaney said, "Nothing is going right for me."

Greaser Bob said, "What about the registered pouch?"

"Well, and what about it?" said Lucky Ned Pepper. "Are you expecting a letter, Bob?"

"If there is any money in it we may as well have it now. It makes no sense to carry the pouch about for evidence."

"You still don't feel easy?"

"You are making too much of my words, Ned."

Lucky Ned Pepper thought about it. He said, "Well, maybe so." Once more he unbuckled the straps. He took out a locked canvas bag and cut it open with a Barlow knife and dumped the contents on the ground. He grinned and said, "Christmas gift!" Of course that is what children shout to one another early on Christmas morning, the game being to shout it first. I had not thought before of this disfigured robber having had a childhood. I expect he was mean to cats and made rude noises in church when he was not asleep. When he needed a firm restraining hand, it was not there. An old story!

There were only six or seven pieces of mail in the bag. There were some personal letters, one with twenty dollars in it, and some documents that appeared to be of a legal description, such as contracts. Lucky Ned Pepper glanced at them and flung them away. A bulky gray envelope tied with ribbon held a packet of one-hundred twenty-dollar notes on the Whelper Commercial Bank of Denison, Texas. Another envelope held a check.

Lucky Ned Pepper studied it, then said to me, "Do you read well?"

"I read very well," said I.

He passed over the check. "Is this any good to me?"

It was a cashier's check for $2,750 drawn on the Grangers Trust Co. of Topeka, Kansas, to a man named Marshall Purvis. I said, "This is a cashier's check for $2,750 drawn on the Grangers Trust Co. of Topeka, Kansas, to a man named Marshall Purvis."

"I can see what it is worth," said the bandit. "Is it any good?"

"It is good if the bank is good," said I. "But it must be endorsed by this Purvis. The bank guarantees the check account is good."

"What about these notes?"

I looked over the banknotes. They were brand-new. I said, "They are not signed. They are no good unless they are signed."

"Can you not sign them?"

"They must be signed by Mr. Whelper, the president of the bank."

"Is it such a hard name to spell?"

"It is an unusual name but it is not hard to spell. The name is printed right here. That is his signature, the printed signature of Monroe G. B. Whelper, the president of the Whelper Commercial Bank of Denison, Texas. That signature must be matched over here."

"I want you to sign them. And this check too."

Naturally I did not wish to use my education in this robber's service and I hesitated.

He said, "I will box your ears until your head rings."

I said, "I have nothing to write with."

He drew a cartridge from his belt and opened his Barlow knife again. "This will answer. I will shave the lead down."

"They must be signed in ink."

Greaser Bob said, "We can attend to it later, Ned. This matter will keep."

"We will attend to it now," replied the bandit chieftain. "You are the one who wanted to look at the mail. This paper is worth over four thousand dollars with a little writing. The girl can write. Harold, go to the trash pile and fetch me a good stout turkey feather, a dry one, a big tail feather." Then he pulled the bullet out of the cartridge case with his snag teeth and poured the black powder in the palm of his hand. He spit on it through the gap and stirred the glutinous mess about with a finger.

Harold Permalee brought back a handful of feathers and Lucky Ned Pepper chose one and cut the tip off with his knife and reamed out the hole a little. He dipped the quill into the "ink" and printed *NED* on his wrist in childish characters. He said, "There. You see. That is my name. Is it not?"

I said, "Yes, that is *Ned*."

He handed me the feather. "Now go to it."

A flat rock with one of the contracts laid on it was made to serve for a desk. It is not in me to do poor work where writing is concerned and I toiled earnestly at making faithful copies of Mr. Whelper's signature. However, the makeshift pen and ink were not satisfactory. The writing jumped and spread wide and pinched thin. It looked as though it had been done with a stick. My thought was: *Who will believe that Mr. Whelper signs his banknotes with a stick?*

But the unlettered bandit chieftain knew little of the world of banking except for such glimpses as he got over a gun sight, and he was pleased with the work. I signed and signed, using his palm for an inkwell. It was very tiring. As soon as I had finished one note he would snatch it up and pass me another.

He said, "They are as good as gold, Bob. I will trade them at Colbert's."

Greaser Bob said, "Nothing on paper is as good as gold. That is my belief."

"Well, that is how much a damned Mexican knows."

"It is every man to his own principles. Tell her to hurry along."

When the criminal task was completed Lucky Ned Pepper put the notes and the check in the gray envelope and secured it in his saddle wallet. He said, "Tom, we will see you tonight. Make yourself agreeable to this child. Little Carroll will be here before you know it."

Then they departed the place, not riding their horses but leading them, as the hill was so steep and brushy.

*I was alone with Tom Chaney!*

He sat across the fire from me, my pistol in his waistband and the Henry rifle in his lap. His face was a "brown study."

I stirred up the fire a little and arranged some glowing coals around one of the cans of hot water.

Chaney watched me. He said, "What are you doing?"

I said, "I am heating some water so that I may wash this black off my hands."

"A little smut will not harm you."

"Yes, that is true, or else you and your 'chums' would surely be dead. I know it will not harm me but I would rather have it off."

"Don't provoke me. You will find yourself in that pit."

"Lucky Ned Pepper has warned you that if you molest me in any way he will not pay you. He means business too."

"I fear he has no idea of paying me. I believe he has left me, knowing I am sure to be caught when I leave on foot."

"He promised he would meet you at 'The Old Place.'"

"Keep still. I must now think over my position and how I may improve it."

"What about my position? At least you have not been abandoned by a man who was paid and pledged to protect you."

"You little busybody! What does your kind know of hardship and affliction? Now keep still while I think."

"Are you thinking about 'The Old Place'?"

"No, I am not thinking about 'The Old Place.' Carroll Permalee or nobody else is coming up here with any horse. They are not going to 'The Old Place.' I am not so easily fooled as some people might think."

I thought to ask him about the other gold piece, then checked myself, afraid that he might force me to give over the one I had recovered. I said, "What have you done with Papa's mare?"

He gave no answer.

I said, "If you will let me go now I will keep silent as to your whereabouts for two days."

"I tell you I can do better than that," said he. "I can have your silence forever. I will not tell you again to hold your tongue."

The water was not boiling but it had begun to steam a little and I picked up the can with a rag and flung it at him, then took to my feet in frantic flight. Though caught by surprise, he managed to shield his face with his arms. He yelped and gave immediate pursuit. My desperate plan was to reach the trees.

Once there, I thought to evade him and finally lose him by darting this way and that in the brush.

It was not to be! Just as I came to the edge of the rock shelf, Chaney grabbed my coat from behind and pulled me up short. My thought was: *I am certainly done for!* Chaney was cursing me and he struck me on the head with the pistol barrel. The blow made me see stars and I concluded I was shot, not knowing the sensation caused by a bullet striking your head. My thoughts turned to my peaceful home in Arkansas, and my poor mother who would be laid low by the news. First her husband and now her oldest child, both gone in the space of two weeks and dispatched by the same bloody hand! That was the direction of my thoughts.

Suddenly I heard a familiar voice, and the words were hard with authority. "Hands up, Chelmsford! Move quickly! It is all up with you! Have a care with that pistol!"

It was LaBoeuf the Texan! He had come up the back way, on foot I supposed, as he was panting for breath. He was standing not thirty feet away with his wired-together rifle trained on Chaney.

Chaney let go of my coat and dropped the pistol. "Everything is against me," he said. I recovered the pistol.

LaBoeuf said, "Are you hurt, Mattie?"

"I have a painful knot on my head," said I.

He said to Chaney, "I see you are bleeding."

"It was this girl done it," said he. "I am shot in the ribs and bleeding again. It hurts when I cough."

I said, "Where is Rooster?"

LaBoeuf said, "He is down below watching the front door. Let us find a place where we can see. Move with care, Chelmsford!"

We proceeded to the northwest corner of the rock shelf, skirting around the pit which had figured in Chaney's ugly threats. "Watch your step there," I cautioned the Texan. "Tom Chaney says there are deadly snakes at the bottom having their winter sleep."

From the far corner of the ledge we had a clear prospect. The timbered slope dropped off sharply below us and led to a meadow. This meadow, level and open, was quite high itself and at the other end there was a further descent leading down out of the Winding Stair Mountains.

No sooner had we taken up our vigil than we were rewarded with the sight of Lucky Ned Pepper and the other three bandits emerging from the trees into the meadow. There they mounted their horses and headed them west, away from us. They had hardly started their ride when a lone horseman came out of the brush at the western end of the field. The horse was walking and the rider took him out to the middle of the open space and stopped, so as to block the passage of the four desperadoes.

Yes, it was Rooster Cogburn! The bandits checked up and faced him from some seventy or eighty yards' distance. Rooster had one of the navy revolvers in his left hand and he held the reins in his right hand. He said, "Where is the girl, Ned?"

Lucky Ned Pepper said, "She was in wonderful health when last I saw her! I cannot answer for her now!"

"You will answer for her now!" said Rooster. "Where is she?"

LaBoeuf stood up and cupped his hands and shouted down, "She is all right, Cogburn! I have Chelmsford as well! Make a run for it!" I confirmed the news by shouting, "I am fine, Rooster! We have Chaney! You must get away!"

The bandits turned to look up at us and no doubt they were surprised and not a little disconcerted by the interesting development. Rooster made no reply to us and gave no sign of leaving the place.

Lucky Ned Pepper said, "Well, Rooster, will you give us the road? We have business elsewhere!"

Rooster said, "Harold, I want you and your brother to stand clear! I have no interest in you today! Stand clear now and you will not be hurt!"

Harold Permalee's answer was to crow like a rooster, and the "*Cock-a-doodle-doo!*" brought a hearty laugh from his brother Farrell.

Lucky Ned Pepper said, "What is your intention? Do you think one on four is a dogfall?"

Rooster said, "I mean to kill you in one minute, Ned, or see you hanged in Fort Smith at Judge Parker's convenience! Which will you have?"

Lucky Ned Pepper laughed. He said, "I call that bold talk for a one-eyed fat man!"

Rooster said, "Fill your hand, you son of a bitch!" and he took the reins in his teeth and pulled the other saddle revolver and drove his spurs into the flanks of his strong horse Bo and charged directly at the bandits. It was a sight to see. He held the revolvers wide on either side of the head of his plunging steed. The four bandits accepted the challenge and they likewise pulled their arms and charged their ponies ahead.

It was some daring move on the part of the deputy marshal whose manliness and grit I had doubted. No grit? Rooster Cogburn? *Not much!*

LaBoeuf instinctively brought his rifle up, but then he relaxed it and did not fire. I pulled at his coat, saying, "Shoot them!" The Texan said, "They are too far and they are moving too fast."

I believe the bandits began firing their weapons first, although the din and smoke was of such a sudden, general nature that I cannot be sure. I do know that the marshal rode for them in so determined and unwavering a course that the bandits broke their "line" ere he reached them and raced through them, his revolvers blazing, and he not aiming with the sights but only pointing the barrels and snapping his head from side to side to bring his good eye into play.

Harold Permalee was the first to go down. He flung his shotgun in the air and clutched at his neck and was thrown backward over the rump of his horse. The Original Greaser Bob rode wider than the others and he lay flat on his horse and escaped clear with his winnings. Farrell Permalee was hit and a moment later his horse went down with a broken leg and Farrell was dashed violently forward to his death.

We thought that Rooster had come through the ordeal with no injury, but in fact he had caught several shotgun pellets in his face and shoulders, and his horse Bo was mortally struck. When Rooster attempted to rein up with his teeth and turn to resume the attack, the big horse fell to the side and Rooster under him.

The field now remained to one rider and that was Lucky Ned Pepper. He wheeled his horse about. His left arm hung limp and useless, but he yet held a revolver in his right hand.

He said, "Well, Rooster, I am shot to pieces!" Rooster had lost his big revolvers in the fall and he was struggling to pull his belt gun which was trapped to the ground under the weight of horse and rider.

Lucky Ned Pepper nudged his pony forward in a trot and he bore down on the helpless officer.

LaBoeuf quickly stirred beside me and assumed a sitting position with the Sharps rifle, his elbows locked against his knees. He took only a second to draw a bead and fire the powerful gun. The ball flew to its mark like a martin to his gourd and Lucky Ned Pepper fell dead in the saddle. The horse reared and the body of the bandit was thrown clear and the horse fled in panic. The distance covered by LaBoeuf's wonderful shot at the moving rider was over six hundred yards. I am prepared to swear an affidavit to it.

"Hurrah!" I joyfully exclaimed. "Hurrah for the man from Texas! Some bully shot!" LaBoeuf was pleased with himself and he reloaded his rifle.

Now the prisoner has an advantage over his keeper in this respect, that he is always thinking of escape and watching for opportunities, while the keeper does not constantly think of keeping him. Once his man is subdued, so the guard believes, little else is needed but the presence and threat of superior force. He thinks of happy things and allows his mind to wander. It is only natural. Were it otherwise, the keeper would be a prisoner of the prisoner.

So it was that LaBoeuf (and I too) was distracted for a dangerous moment in appreciation of the timely rifle shot that saved Rooster Cogburn's life. Tom Chaney, seizing the occasion, picked up a rock about the size of a new cooking pumpkin and broke LaBoeuf's head with it.

The Texan fell over with a groan of agony. I screamed and hastened to my feet and backed away, bringing my pistol to bear once again on Tom Chaney, who was scrambling after the Sharps rifle. Would the old dragoon revolver fail me this time? I hoped it would not.

I hurriedly cocked the hammer and pulled the trigger. The charge exploded and sent a lead ball of justice, too long delayed, into the criminal head of Tom Chaney.

Yet I was not to taste the victory. The kick of the big pistol

sent me reeling backward. I had forgotten about the *pit* behind me! Over the edge I went, then tumbling and bouncing
against the irregular sides, and all the while I was grabbing
wildly for something and finding nothing. I struck the bottom with a thump that fairly dazed me. The wind was knocked
from my lungs and I lay still for a moment until I had regained
my breath. I was addled and I had the fanciful notion that my
spirit was floating out of my body, escaping through my mouth
and nostrils.

I had thought myself to be lying down, but when I made to
get up I found I was stuck upright in a small hole, the lower
part of my body wedged in tight between mossy rocks. I was
caught like a cork in a bottle!

My right arm was pinned against my side and I could not
pull it free. When I tried to use my left hand to push myself out
of the hole I saw with a shock that the forearm was bent in an
unnatural attitude. The arm was broken! There was little pain
in the arm, only a kind of "pins and needles" numbness. The
movement in my fingers was weak and I had but little grasping
power. I was reluctant to use the arm for leverage, fearing the
pressure would worsen the fracture and bring on pain.

It was cold and dark down there, though not totally dark. A
slender column of sunshine came down from above and ended
in a small pool of light some three or four feet away on the
stone floor of the cavern. I looked up at the column and could
see floating particles of dust stirred up by my fall.

I saw on the rocks about me a few sticks and bits of paper
and an old tobacco sack and splotches of grease where skillets
had been emptied. I also saw the corner of a man's blue cotton
shirt, the rest of it being obscured by shadow. There were no
snakes about. Thank goodness for that!

I summoned my strength and cried out, "Help! LaBoeuf!
Can you hear me!" No word of reply came. I did not know if
the Texan were alive or dead. All I heard was a low roaring of
the wind above and dripping noises behind me and some faint
"cheeps" and "squeaks." I could not identify the nature of the
squeaks or locate their origin.

I renewed my effort to break free but the vigorous movement made me slip a bit farther down in the mossy hole. My
thought was: *This will not do.* I stopped maneuvering lest I

drop right through the hole to what depths of blackness I could only imagine. My legs swung free below and my jeans were bunched up so that portions of bare leg were exposed. I felt something brush against one of my legs and I thought, *Spider!* I kicked and flailed my feet and then I stopped when my body settled downward another inch or so.

Now more squeaks, and it came to me that there were *bats* in the cavern below. *Bats* were making the noise and it had been a *bat* that attached himself to my leg. Yes, I had disturbed them. Their roosting place was below. This hole I now so effectively plugged was their opening to the outside.

I had no unreasonable fear of bats, knowing them for timid little creatures, yet I knew them too for carriers of the dread "Hydrophobia," for which there was no specific. What would the bats do, come night and their time to fly, and they found their opening to the outer world closed off? Would they bite? If I struggled and kicked against them I would surely shake myself through the hole. But I knew I had not the will to remain motionless and let them bite.

*Night!* Was I to be here then till night? I must keep my head and guard against such thoughts. What of LaBoeuf? And what had become of Rooster Cogburn? He had not appeared to be badly hurt in the fall of his horse. But how would he know I was down here? I did not like my situation.

I thought to set fire to bits of cloth for a signal of smoke but the idea was useless because I had no matches. Surely someone would come. Perhaps Captain Finch. The news of the gun fight must get out and bring a party to investigate. Yes, the posse of marshals. The thing was to hold tight. Help was sure to come. At least there were no snakes. I settled on this course: I would give cries for help every five minutes or as near on that interval as I could guess it to be.

I called out at once and was again mocked by the echo of my own voice and by the wind and the dripping of the cave water and the squeaking of the bats. I told numbers to measure the time. It occupied my mind and gave me a sense of purpose and method.

I had not counted far when my body slipped down appreciably and with panic in my breast I realized that the moss which gripped me in a tight seal was tearing loose. I looked about for something to hold to, broken arm or not, but my hand found only slick and featureless planes of rock. I was going through. It was a matter now of time.

Another lurch down, to the level of my right elbow. That bony knob served as a momentary check but I could feel the moss giving way against it. A wedge! That was what I needed. Something to stuff in the hole with me to make the cork fit more snugly. Or a long stick to pass under my arm.

I cast my eyes about for something suitable. The few sticks lying about were none of them long enough or stout enough for my purpose. If only I could reach the blue shirt! It would be just the thing for packing. I broke one stick scratching and pulling at the shirttail. With the second one I managed to bring it within reach of my fingertips. Weakened as my hand was, I got a purchase on the cloth with thumb and finger and pulled it out of the dark. It was unexpectedly heavy. Something was attached to it.

Suddenly I jerked my hand away as though from a hot stove. The *something* was the corpse of a man! Or more properly, a skeleton. He was wearing the shirt. I did nothing for a min-ute, so frightful and astonishing was the discovery. I could see a good part of the remains, the head with patches of bright orange hair showing under a piece of rotted black hat, one shirtsleeved arm and that portion of the trunk from about the waist upwards. The shirt was buttoned in two or three places near the neck.

I soon recovered my wits. *I am falling. I need that shirt.* These thoughts bore upon me with urgency. I had no stomach for the task ahead but there was nothing else to be done in my desperate circumstances. My plan was to give the shirt a smart jerk in hopes of tearing it free from the skeleton. *I will have that shirt!*

Thus I took hold of the garment again and snatched it toward me with such sharp force as I could muster. My arm seized up with a stab of pain and I let go. After a little tingling the pain subsided and gave way to a dull and tolerable ache. I examined the result of my effort. The buttons had torn free and now the body was within reach. The shirt itself remained clothed about the shoulders and arm bones in a careless fashion. I saw too that the maneuver had exposed the poor man's rib cage.

One more pull and I would have the body close enough so that I could work the shirt free. As I made ready for the job my eyes were attracted to something—movement?—within the cavity formed by the curving gray ribs. I leaned over for a closer look. *Snakes! A ball of snakes!* I flung myself back but of course there was no real retreat for me, imprisoned as I was in the mossy trap.

I cannot accurately guess the number of rattlesnakes in the ball, as some were big, bigger than my arm, and others small, ranging down to the size of lead pencils, but I believe there were not fewer than forty. With trembling heart I looked on as they writhed sluggishly about in the man's chest. I had disturbed their sleep in their curious winter quarters and now, more or less conscious, they had begun to move and detach themselves from the tangle, falling this way and that.

This, thought I, is a pretty fix. I desperately needed the shirt but I did not wish to "mess" further with the snakes in order to have it. Even while I considered these things I was settling and being drawn down to . . . *what?* Perhaps a black and bottomless pool of water where the fish were white and had no eyes to see.

I wondered if the snakes could bite in their present lethargic state. I thought they could not see well, if at all, but I observed too that the light and warmth of the sun had an invigorating effect on them. We kept two speckled king snakes in our corn crib to eat rats and I was not afraid of them, Saul and Little David, but I really knew nothing about snakes. Moccasins and rattlers were to be avoided if possible and killed if there was a chopping hoe handy. That was all I knew about poisonous snakes.

The ache in my broken arm grew worse. I felt some more of the binding moss give way against my right arm and at the same time I saw that some of the snakes were crawling out through the man's ribs. *Lord help me!*

I set my teeth and took hold of the bony hand that struck forth from the blue shirtsleeve. I gave a yank and pulled the man's arm clean away from the shoulder. A terrible thing to

do, you say, but you will see that I now had something to work
with.

I studied the arm. Bits of cartilage held it together at the elbow joint. With some twisting I managed to separate it at that
place. I took the long bone of the upper arm and secured it
under my armpit to serve as a cross-member. This would keep
me from plunging through the hole should I reach that point
in my descent. It was quite a long bone and, I hoped, a strong
one. I was grateful to the poor man for being tall.

What I had left now was the lower part, the two bones of the
forearm, and the hand and wrist, all of a piece. I grasped it at
the elbow and proceeded to use it as a flail to keep the snakes at
bay. "Here, get away!" said I, slapping at them with the bony
hand. "Get back, you!" This was well enough except that I
perceived the agitation only caused them to be more active. In
trying to keep them away, I was at the same time stirring them
up! They moved very slowly but there were so many I could
not keep track of them all.

Each blow I struck brought burning pain to my arm and
you can imagine these blows were not hard enough to kill the
snakes. That was not my idea. My idea was to keep them back
and prevent them from getting behind me. My striking range
from left to right was something short of 180 degrees and I
knew if the rattlers got behind me I would be in a fine "pickle."

I heard noises above. A shower of sand and pebbles came
cascading down. "Help!" I cried out. "I am down here! I need
help!" My thought was: *Thank God. Someone has come. Soon I
will be out of this hellish place.* I saw drops of something spat-
tering on a rock in front of me. It was blood. "Hurry up!" I
yelled. "There are snakes and skeletons down here!"

A man's voice called down, saying, "I warrant there will be
another one before spring! A little spindly one!"

It was the voice of Tom Chaney! I had not yet made a good
job of killing him! I supposed he was leaning over the edge and
the blood was falling from his wounded head.

"How do you like it?" he taunted.

"Throw me a rope, Tom! You cannot be mean enough to
leave me!"

"You say you don't like it?"

Then I heard a shout and the sounds of a scuffle and a dreadful crunch, which was Rooster Cogburn's rifle stock smashing the wounded head of Tom Chaney. There followed a furious rush of rocks and dust. The light was blocked off and I made out a large object hurtling down toward me. It was the body of Tom Chaney. I leaned back as far as I could to avoid being struck, and at that it was a near thing.

He fell directly upon the skeleton, crushing the bones and filling my face and eyes with dirt and scattering the puzzled rattlesnakes every which way. They were all about me and I commenced striking at them with such abandon that my body dropped free through the hole. *Gone!*

*No! Checked short!* I was shakily suspended in space by the bone under my armpit. Bats flew up past my face and the ones below were carrying on like a tree full of sparrows at sundown. Only my head and my left arm and shoulder now remained above the hole. I hung at an uncomfortable angle. The bone was bowed under my weight and I prayed it would hold. My left arm was cramped and fully occupied in holding to it and I had not the use of the hand in fending off the snakes.

"Help!" I called. "I need help!"

Rooster's voice came booming down, saying, "Are you all right?"

"No! I am in a bad way! Hurry up!"

"I am pitching down a rope! Fasten it under your arms and tie it with a good knot!"

"I cannot manage a rope! You will have to come down and help me! Hurry up, I am falling! There are snakes all about my head!"

"Hold on! Hold on!" came another voice. It was LaBoeuf. The Texan had survived the blow. The officers were both safe.

I watched as two rattlers struck and sunk their sharp teeth into Tom Chaney's face and neck. The body was lifeless and made no protest. My thought was: *Those scoundrels can bite in December and right there is the proof of it!* One of the smaller snakes approached my hand and rubbed his nose against it. I moved my hand a little and the snake moved to it and touched his nose to the flesh again. He moved a bit more and commenced to rub the underside of his jaw on top of my hand.

From the corner of my eye I saw another snake on my left shoulder. He was motionless and limp. I could not tell if he was dead or merely asleep. Whatever the case, I did not want him there and I began to swing my body gently from side to side on the bone axle. The movement caused the serpent to roll over with his white belly up and I gave my shoulder a shake and he fell into the darkness below.

I felt a sting and I saw the little snake pulling his head away from my hand, an amber drop of venom on his mouth. He had bitten me. The hand was already well along to being dead numb from the cramped position and I hardly felt it. It was on the order of a horsefly bite. I counted myself lucky the snake was small. That was how much I knew of natural history. People who know tell me the younger snakes carry the more potent poison, and that it weakens with age. I believe what they say.

Now here came Rooster with a rope looped around his waist and his feet against the sides of the pit, descending in great violent leaps and sending another shower of rocks and dust down on me. He landed with a heavy bump and then it seemed he was doing everything at once. He grasped the collar of my coat and shirt behind my neck and heaved me up from the hole with one hand, at the same time kicking at snakes and shooting them with his belt revolver. The noise was deafening and made my head ache.

My legs were wobbly. I could hardly stand.

Rooster said, "Can you hold to my neck?"

I said, "Yes, I will try." There were two dark red holes in his face with dried rivulets of blood under them where shotgun pellets had struck him.

He stooped down and I wrapped my right arm around his neck and lay against his back. He tried to climb the rope hand over hand with his feet against the sides of the pit but he made only about three pulls and had to drop back down. Our combined weight was too much for him. His right shoulder was torn from a bullet too, although I did not know it at the time.

"Stay behind me!" he said, kicking and stomping the snakes while he reloaded his pistol. A big grandfather snake coiled himself around Rooster's boot and got his head shot off for his boldness.

Rooster said, "Do you think you can climb the rope?"

"My arm is broken," said I. "And I am bit on the hand."

He looked at the hand and pulled his dirk knife and cut the place to scarify it. He squeezed blood from it and took some smoking tobacco and hurriedly chewed it into a cud and rubbed it over the wound to draw the poison.

Then he harnessed the rope tightly under my arms. He shouted up to the Texan, saying, "Take the rope, LaBoeuf! Mattie is hurt! I want you to pull her up in easy stages! Can you hear me?"

LaBoeuf replied, "I will do what I can!"

The rope grew taut and lifted me to my toes. "Pull!" shouted Rooster. "The girl is snake-bit, man! Pull!" But LaBoeuf could not do it, weakened as he was by his bad arm and broken head. "It's no use!" he said. "I will try the horse!"

In a matter of minutes he had fastened the rope to a pony. "I am ready!" the Texan called down to us. "Take a good hold!"

"Go!" said Rooster.

He had looped the rope about his hips and once around his waist. He held me with the other arm. We were jerked from our feet. Now there was power at the other end! We went up in bounds. Rooster worked to keep us clear of the rough sides with his feet. We were skinned up a little.

Sunlight and blue sky! I was so weak that I lay upon the ground and could not speak. I blinked my eyes to accommodate them to the brightness and I saw that LaBoeuf was sitting with his bloody head in his hands and gasping from his labors in driving the horse. Then I saw the horse. It was Little Blackie! The scrub pony had saved us! My thought was: *The stone which the builders rejected, the same is become the head of the corner.*

Rooster tied the cud of tobacco on top of my hand with a rag. He said, "Can you walk?"

"Yes, I think so," said I. He led me toward the horse and when I had walked a few steps I was overcome with nausea and I dropped to my knees. When the sickness had passed, Rooster helped me along and placed me in the saddle astride Little Blackie. He bound my feet to the stirrups and with another length of rope he tied my waist to the saddle, front and back. Then he mounted behind me.

He said to LaBoeuf, "I will send help as soon as I can. Don't wander off."

I said, "We are not leaving him?"

Rooster said, "I must get you to a doctor, sis, or you are not going to make it." He said to LaBoeuf as an afterthought, "I am in your debt for that shot, pard."

The Texan said nothing and we left him there holding his head. I expect he was feeling pretty bad. Rooster spurred Blackie away and the faithful pony stumbled and skidded down the steep and brushy hill where prudent horsemen led their mounts. The descent was dangerous and particularly so with such a heavy burden as Blackie was carrying. There was no way to dodge all the limbs. Rooster lost his hat and never looked back.

We galloped across the meadow where the smoky duel had lately occurred. My eyes were congested from nausea and through a tearful haze I saw the dead horses and the bodies of the bandits. The pain in my arm became intense and I commenced to cry and the tears were blown back in streams around my cheeks. Once down from the mountains we headed north, and I guessed we were aiming for Fort Smith. Despite the load, Blackie held his head high and ran like the wind, perhaps sensing the urgency of the mission. Rooster spurred and whipped him without let. I soon passed away in a faint.

When I regained my senses, I realized we had slowed. Heaving and choking for breath, Blackie was yet giving us all he had. I cannot say how many miles we had ridden full out. Poor lathered beast! Rooster whipped and whipped.

"Stop!" I said. "We must stop! He is played out!" Rooster paid me no heed. Blackie was all in and as he stumbled and made to stop, Rooster took his dirk knife and cut a brutal slash on the pony's withers. "Stop it! Stop it!" I cried. Little Blackie squealed and burst forth in a run under the stimulation of the pain. I wrestled for the reins but Rooster slapped my hands away. I was crying and yelling. When Blackie slowed again, Rooster took salt from his pocket and rubbed the wound with it and the pony leaped forward as before. In a very few minutes this torture was mercifully ended. Blackie fell to the ground and died, his brave heart burst and mine broken. There never lived a nobler pony.

No sooner were we down than Rooster was cutting me free. He ordered me to climb upon his back. I held fast around his neck with my right arm and he supported my legs with his arms. Now Rooster himself began to run, or jog as it were under the load, and his breath came hard. Once more I lost my senses and the next I knew I was being carried in his arms and sweat drops from his brow and mustache were falling on my neck.

I have no recollection of the stop at the Poteau River where Rooster commandeered a wagon and a team of mules from a party of hunters at gunpoint. I do not mean to suggest the hunters were reluctant to lend their team in such an emergency but Rooster was impatient of explanation and he simply took the rig. Farther along the river we called at the home of a wealthy Indian farmer named Cullen. He provided us with a buggy and a fast span of matched horses, and he also sent one of his sons along mounted on a white pony to lead the way.

Night had fallen when we reached Fort Smith. We rode into town in a drizzle of cold rain. I remember being carried into the home of Dr. J. R. Medill, with Dr. Medill holding his hat over a coal oil lamp to keep the rain off the mantle.

I was in a stupor for days. The broken bone was set and an open splint was fixed along my forearm. My hand swelled and turned black, and then my wrist. On the third day Dr. Medill gave me a sizable dose of morphine and amputated the arm just above the elbow with a little surgical saw. My mother and Lawyer Daggett sat at my side while this work was done. I very much admired my mother for sitting there and not flinching, as she was of a delicate temperament. She held my right hand and wept.

I remained in the doctor's home for something over a week after the operation. Rooster called on me twice but I was so sick and "dopey" that I made poor company. He had patches on his face where Dr. Medill had removed the shotgun balls. He told me the posse of marshals had found LaBoeuf, and that the officer had refused to leave the place until he had recovered the body of Tom Chaney. None of the marshals was anxious to go down in the pit, so LaBoeuf had them lower him on a rope. He did the job, though his vision was somewhat confounded from the blow on his head. At McAlester's he was given such treatment as was available for the depression on his head, and from there he left for Texas with the corpse of the man on whose trail he had camped for so long.

I went home on a varnish train, lying flat on my back on a stretcher that was placed in the aisle of a coach. As I say, I was quite sick and it was not until I had been home for a few days that I fully recovered my faculties. It came to me that I had not paid Rooster the balance of his money. I wrote a check for seventy-five dollars and put it in an envelope and asked Lawyer Daggett to mail it to Rooster in care of the marshal's office.

Lawyer Daggett interviewed me about it and in the course of our conversation I learned something disturbing. It was this. The lawyer had blamed Rooster for taking me on the search for Tom Chaney and had roundly cursed him and threatened to prosecute him in a court action. I was upset on hearing it. I told Lawyer Daggett that Rooster was in no way to blame, and was rather to be praised and commended for his grit. He had certainly saved my life.

Whatever his adversaries, the railroads and steamboat companies, may have thought, Lawyer Daggett was a gentleman, and on hearing the straight of the matter he was embarrassed by his actions. He said he still considered the deputy marshal had acted with poor judgment, but in the circumstances was deserving an apology. He went to Fort Smith and personally delivered the seventy-five dollars owing to him, and then presented him with a two-hundred-dollar check of his own and asked him to accept his apology for the hard and unfair words he had spoken.

I wrote Rooster a letter and invited him to visit us. He replied with a short note that looked like one of his "vouchers," saying he would try to stop by when next he took prisoners to Little Rock. I concluded he would not come and I made plans to go there when I had the use of my legs. I was very curious to know how much he had realized, if anything, in the way of rewards for his destruction of Lucky Ned Pepper's robber band, and whether he had received news of LaBoeuf. I will say here that Judy was never recovered, nor was the second California gold piece. I kept the other one for years, until our house burned. We found no trace of it in the ashes.

But I never got the chance to visit him. Not three weeks after we had returned from the Winding Stair Mountains, Rooster found himself in trouble over a gun duel he fought in Fort Gibson, Cherokee Nation. He shot and killed Odus Wharton in the duel. Of course Wharton was a convicted murderer and a fugitive from the gallows but there was a stir about the manner of the shooting. Rooster shot two other men that were with Wharton and killed one of them. They must have been trash or they would not have been in the company of the "thug," but they were not wanted by the law at that time and Rooster was criticized. He had many enemies. Pressure was brought and Rooster made to surrender his Federal badge. We knew nothing of it until it was over and Rooster gone.

He took his cat General Price and the widow Potter and her six children and went to San Antonio, Texas, where he found work as a range detective for a stockmen's association. He did not marry the woman in Fort Smith and I supposed they waited until they reached "the Alamo City."

From time to time I got bits of news about him from Chen Lee, who did not hear directly but only by rumor. Twice I wrote the stockmen's association in San Antonio. The letters were not returned but neither were they answered. When next I heard, Rooster had gone into the cattle business himself in a small way. Then in the early 1890s I learned he had abandoned the Potter woman and her brood and had gone north to Wyoming with a reckless character named Tom Smith where they were hired by stock owners to terrorize thieves and people called nesters and grangers. It was a sorry business, I am told, and I fear Rooster did himself no credit there in what they called the "Johnson County War."

In late May of 1903 Little Frank sent me a cutting from *The Commercial Appeal* in Memphis. It was an advertisement for the Cole Younger and Frank James "Wild West" show that was coming to play in the Memphis Chicks' baseball park. Down in the smaller type at the bottom of the notice Little Frank had circled the following:

HE RODE WITH QUANTRILL! HE RODE FOR PARKER!

Scourge of Territorial outlaws and Texas cattle thieves for 25 years!
"Rooster" Cogburn will amaze you with his skill and dash with the six-shooter and repeating rifle! Don't leave the ladies and little ones behind! Spectators can watch this unique exhibition in perfect safety!

So he was coming to Memphis. Little Frank had teased me and chaffed me over the years about Rooster, making out that he was my secret "sweetheart." By sending this notice he was having sport with me, as he thought. He had penciled a note on the cutting that said, "Skill and dash! It's not too late, Mattie!" Little Frank loves fun at the other fellow's expense and the more he thinks it tells on you the better he loves it. We have always liked jokes in our family and I think they are all right in their place. Victoria likes a good joke herself, so far as she can understand one. I have never held it against either one of them for leaving me at home to look after Mama, and they know it, for I have told them.

I rode the train to Memphis by way of Little Rock and had no trouble getting the conductors to honor my Rock Island pass. It belonged to a freight agent and I was holding it against a small loan. I had thought to put up at a hotel instead of paying an immediate call on Little Frank as I did not wish to hear his chaff before I had seen Rooster. I speculated on whether the marshal would recognize me. My thought was: *A quarter of a century is a long time!*

As things turned out, I did not go to a hotel. When my train reached "the Bluff City" I saw that the show train was on a siding there at the depot. I left my bag in the station and set off walking beside the circus coaches through crowds of horses and Indians and men dressed as cow-boys and soldiers.

I found Cole Younger and Frank James sitting in a Pullman car in their shirtsleeves. They were drinking Coca-Colas and fanning themselves. They were old men. I supposed Rooster must have aged a good deal too. These old-timers had all fought together in the border strife under Quantrill's black standard, and afterward led dangerous lives, and now this was all they were fit for, to show themselves to the public like strange wild beasts of the jungle.

They claim Younger carried fourteen bullets about in various portions of his flesh. He was a stout, florid man with a pleasant manner and he rose to greet me. The waxy James remained in his seat and did not speak or remove his hat. Younger told me that Rooster had passed away a few days before while the show was at Jonesboro, Arkansas. He had been in failing health for some months, suffering from a disorder he called "night hoss," and the heat of the early summer had been too much for him. Younger reckoned his age at sixty-eight years. There was no one to claim him and they had buried him in the Confederate cemetery in Memphis, though his home was out of Osceola, Missouri.

Younger spoke fondly of him. "We had some lively times," was one thing he said. I thanked the courteous old outlaw for his help and said to James, "Keep your seat, trash!" and took my leave. They think now it was Frank James who shot the bank officer in Northfield. As far as I know that scoundrel never spent a night in jail, and there was Cole Younger locked away twenty-five years in the Minnesota pen.

I did not stay for the show as I guessed it would be dusty and silly like all circuses. People grumbled about it when it was over, saying James did nothing more than wave his hat to the crowd, and that Younger did even less, it being a condition of his parole that he not exhibit himself. Little Frank took his two boys to see it and they enjoyed the horses.

I had Rooster's body removed to Dardanelle on the train. The railroads do not like to carry disinterred bodies in the summertime but I got around paying the premium rate by having my correspondent bank in Memphis work the deed from that end through a grocery wholesaler that did a volume freight business. He was reburied in our family plot. Rooster had a little C.S.A. headstone coming to him but it was so small that I put up another one beside it, a sixty-five-dollar slab of Batesville marble inscribed

REUBEN COGBURN
1835–1903
A RESOLUTE OFFICER
OF PARKER'S COURT

People here in Dardanelle and Russellville said, well, she hardly knew the man but it is just like a cranky old maid to do a "stunt" like that. I know what they said even if they would not say it to my face. People love to talk. They love to slander you if you have any substance. They say I love nothing but money and the Presbyterian Church and that is why I never married. They think everybody is dying to get married. It is true that I love my church and my bank. What is wrong with that? I will tell you a secret. Those same people talk mighty nice when they come in to get a crop loan or beg a mortgage extension! I never had the time to get married but it is nobody's business if I am married or not married. I care nothing for what they say. I would marry an ugly baboon if I wanted to and make him cashier. I never had the time to fool with it. A woman with brains and a frank tongue and one sleeve pinned up and an invalid mother to care for is at some disadvantage, although I will say I could have had two or three old untidy men around here who had their eyes fastened on my bank. *No, thank you!* It might surprise you to know their names.

I heard nothing more of the Texas officer, LaBoeuf. If he is yet alive and should happen to read these pages, I will be pleased to hear from him. I judge he is in his seventies now, and nearer eighty than seventy. I expect some of the starch has gone out of that "cowlick." Time just gets away from us. This ends my true account of how I avenged Frank Ross's blood over in the Choctaw Nation when snow was on the ground.

# THE DOG OF THE SOUTH

. . . *Even Animals near the Classis of plants seem to have the most restlesse motions. The Summer-worm of Ponds and plashes makes a long waving motion; the hair-worm seldome lies still. He that would behold a very anomalous motion, may observe it in the Tortile and tiring stroaks of Gnatworms.*

—SIR THOMAS BROWNE

# *One*

---

MY WIFE Norma had run off with Guy Dupree and I was
waiting around for the credit card billings to come in so
I could see where they had gone. I was biding my time. This
was October. They had taken my car and my Texaco card and
my American Express card. Dupree had also taken from the
bedroom closet my good raincoat and a shotgun and perhaps
some other articles. It was just like him to pick the .410—
a boy's first gun. I suppose he thought it wouldn't kick much,
that it would kill or at least rip up the flesh in a satisfying way
without making a lot of noise or giving much of a jolt to his
sloping monkey shoulder.

When the receipts arrived, they were in lumpy envelopes and
the sums owed were such that American Express gave way to
panic and urged me to call B. Tucker in New York at once and
work out terms of payment. It was my guess that this "Tucker"
was only a house name, or maybe a hard woman who sat by a
telephone all day with a Kool in her mouth. I got out my road
maps and plotted the journey by following the sequence of
dates and locations on the receipts. I love nothing better than a
job like that and I had to laugh a little as the route took shape.

What a trip. What a pair of lovebirds! Pure Dupree! The
line started in Little Rock and showed purpose as it plunged
straight down into Texas. Then it became wobbly and dis-
orderly. There was one grand loop that went as far west as
Moffit's Texaco station in San Angelo, where sheep graze, and
there were tiny epicycles along the way that made no sense at
all.

I was reminded of the dotted line in history books that represents the aimless trek of Hernando De Soto, a brave soldier
who found no gold but only hardship and a wide muddy river
to which his body was at last committed—at night, they say.
What a man! I was at that time fascinated by the great captains
of history and I sometimes became so excited when reading
about such men as Lee or Hannibal (both defeated, it occurs
to me) that I would have to get up and walk around the room
to catch my breath.

Not that there was space for any real strolling in our apartment on Gum Street. Norma wanted to move to a bigger place and so did I—to a bigger and *quieter* place—but I resisted going to the houses and apartments she had scouted out because I knew from experience that they would not be suitable.

The last one had been a little chocolate-brown cottage, with a shed of the same rich color in the back yard. The real-estate fellow showed us around and he talked about the rent-like payments. In the shed we came across an old man lying on a cot. He was eating nuts from a can and watching a daytime television show. His pearly shins were exposed above his socks. A piece of cotton covered one eye.

"That's Mr. Proctor," said the real-estate bird. "He pays fifty a month for the shed and you can apply that, see, on your note." I didn't want an old man living in my back yard and the real-estate bird said, "Well, tell him to hit the road then," but I didn't want to do that either, to Mr. Proctor. The truth was, we couldn't afford a house, not even this cottage, living on my father's charity as we were, and Norma either could not or would not find an apartment with thick walls made of honest plaster. I had specified this as against the modern dry-wall material, which not only conducts sound readily but in many cases seems to amplify it.

I should have paid more attention to Norma. I should have talked to her and listened to her but I didn't do it. A timely word here and there might have worked wonders. I knew she was restless, and anxious to play a more active part in life. She spoke in just those terms, and there were other signals as well.

She announced one day that she wanted to give a party in our apartment with the theme of "Around the World in 80 Days." I couldn't believe my ears. A party! She talked about applying for a job as stewardess with Braniff Airlines. She bought a bicycle, an expensive multi-geared model, and joined a cycling club against my wishes. The idea was that she and her chums would pedal along leafy country lanes, shouting and singing like a bunch of Germans, but from all I could see they just had meetings in the damp basement of a church.

I could go on and on. She wanted to dye her hair. She wanted to change her name to Staci or Pam or April. She wanted to open a shop selling Indian jewelry. It wouldn't have hurt me to discuss this shop idea with her—big profits are made every day in that silver and turquoise stuff—but I couldn't be bothered. I had to get on with my reading!

Now she was gone. She had gone to Mexico with Guy Dupree, for that was where my dotted line led. The last position was the Hotel Mogador in San Miguel de Allende, where I drew a terminal cross on the map with my draftsman's pencil and shaded it to give an effect of depth.

The last receipt was just twelve days old. Our Mexican friends have a reputation for putting things off until another day and for taking long naps but there had been no snoozing over this bill. I looked at Dupree's contemptuous approximation of my signature on the receipt. On some of the others he had signed "Mr. Smart Shopper" and "Wallace Fard."

Here he was then, cruising the deserts of Mexico in my Ford Torino with my wife and my credit cards and his black-tongued dog. He had a chow dog that went everywhere with him, to the post office and ball games, and now that red beast was making free with his lion feet on my Torino seats.

In exchange for my car he had left me his 1963 Buick Special. I had found it in my slot at the Rhino Apartments parking lot, standing astride a red puddle of transmission fluid. It was a compact car, a rusty little piece of basic transportation with a V-6 engine. The thing ran well enough and it seemed eager to please but I couldn't believe the Buick engineers ever had their hearts in a people's car. Dupree had shamefully neglected it. There was about a quarter-turn of slack in the steering wheel and I had to swing it wildly back and forth in a childlike burlesque of motoring. After a day or two I got the hang of it but the violent arm movements made me look like a lunatic. I had to stay alert every second, every instant, to make small corrections. That car had 74,000 miles on it and the speedometer cable was broken. There was a hole in the floor on the driver's side and when I drove over something white the flash between my feet made me jump. That's enough on the car for now.

This business came at a bad time. Just a month earlier—right after my twenty-sixth birthday—I had quit my job on the copy desk at the newspaper to return to school. My father had agreed to support me again until I had received a degree of some sort or at least a teaching certificate. He had also presented me with the American Express card, he having had a good business year sprucing up old houses with Midgestone. As I say, the birthday was my twenty-sixth, but for some reason I had been thinking throughout the previous year that I was already twenty-six. A free year! The question was: would I piddle it away like the others?

My new plan was to become a high-school teacher. I had accumulated enough college hours over the years for at least two bachelor's degrees but I had never actually taken one. I had never stayed long enough in any one course of study. I had no education hours at all but I did have some pre-law at Southwestern and some engineering at Arkansas. I had been at Ole Miss too, where I studied the Western campaigns of the Civil War under Dr. Buddy Casey. Don't talk about Virginia to Dr. Bud; talk about Forrest!

For a long time I had a tape recording of his famous lecture on the Siege of Vicksburg and I liked to play it in the morning while I was shaving. I also played it sometimes in the car when Norma and I went for drives. It was one of those performances —"bravura" is the word for it—that never become stale. Dr. Bud made the thing come alive. With nothing more than his knuckles and the resonating sideboards of his desk he could give you caissons crossing a plank bridge, and with his dentures and inflated cheeks and moist thick lips he could give you a mortar barrage in the distance and rattling anchor chains and lapping water and hissing fuses and neighing horses. I had heard the tape hundreds of times and yet each time I would be surprised and delighted anew by some bit of Casey genius, some description or insight or narrative passage or sound effect. The bird peals, for instance. Dr. Bud gives a couple of unexpected bird calls in the tense scene where Grant and Pemberton are discussing surrender terms under the oak tree. The call is a stylized one—*tu-whit, tu-whee*—and is not meant to represent that of any particular bird. It has never failed to catch me by surprise. But no one could hope to keep the whole of that lecture in his head at once, such are its riches.

I say I "had" the tape. It disappeared suddenly and Norma denied that she had thrown it away. After making a few inquiries and turning the apartment upside down I let the matter drop. That was my way. I once read about a man who would

not let his wife know how he liked for things to be done, so
that she could offend him. That was never my way. Norma and
I had our squabbles, certainly, but never any scenes of rage like
those on television with actors and actresses screaming at one
another. It was give and take in our house. Two of my rules did
cause a certain amount of continuing friction—my rule against
smoking at the table and my rule against record-playing after 9
P.M., by which time I had settled in for a night of reading—but
I didn't see how I could compromise in either of those areas.

Norma was married to Dupree when I met her. She had
golden down on her forearms and a little blue vein or artery
that ran across her forehead and became distended and pulsed
noticeably when she was upset or expressing some strong opinion. You hardly ever see the wives of people who work for
newspapers and I'm embarrassed to say I can't remember the
occasion of our first meeting. I had sat next to Dupree on the
rim of the copy desk. In fact, I had gotten him the job. He was
not well liked in the newsroom. He radiated dense waves of
hatred and he never joined in the friendly banter around the
desk, he who had once been so lively. He hardly spoke at all
except to mutter "Crap" or "What crap" as he processed news
matter, affecting a contempt for all events on earth and for the
written accounts of those events.

As for his height, I would put it at no more than five feet
nine inches—he being fully erect, out of his monkey crouch
—and yet he brazenly put down five eleven on all forms and
applications. His dress was sloppy even by newspaper standards
—thousands of wrinkles! It was a studied effect rather than
carelessness. I know he had to work at it, because his clothes
were of the permanent-press type and you can't make that
stuff wrinkle unless you bake it in a dryer and then crumple
it up. He had a nervous habit of rubbing his hands back and
forth on his trousers when he was seated and this made for an
unsightly condition called "pilling," where the surface fibers
form hard little balls or pills from being scuffed about. Pilling
is more often seen on cheap blankets than on clothing but all
of Dupree's trousers were badly pilled in front. His shirts were
downright dirty. He wore glasses, the lenses thick and greasy,
which distorted the things of the world into unnatural shapes.
I myself have never needed glasses. I can read road signs a

half-mile away and I can see individual stars and planets down to the seventh magnitude with no optical aids whatever. I can see Uranus.

For eleven miserable months Norma was married to Dupree and after some of the things she told me I was amazed that she could go back to him. His kissing frenzies! His carbide cannon! Still, there it was. I had no idea that anything was going on. How had he made his new approaches? What were his disgusting courtship techniques? Had the cycling club been a ruse? There had been some night meetings. But Dupree already had a sweetheart! A friend at the paper told me that Dupree had been seeing this person for several months—a mystery woman who lived upstairs in a gray house behind the Game and Fish Building. What about her?

Norma and I were getting along well enough, or so I thought. I have mentioned her restlessness. The only other thing I could put my finger on was a slight change in her manner. She had begun to treat me with a hearty but impersonal courtesy, something like a nurse dealing with an old-timer. "I'll be right with you," she would say, or, when presenting me with something, "Here we are, Midge." She had always called me by my last name.

I think now this coolness must have started with our algebra course. She had agreed to let me practice my teaching methods on her and so I had worked out a lecture plan in elementary algebra. I had a little blackboard, green actually, that I set up in the kitchen every Thursday at 7 P.M. for my demonstrations. It was not the kind of thing you like to ask a person to do but Norma was a good sport about it and I thought if I could teach her ninth-grade algebra I could teach just about anything to anybody. A good sport, I say, but that was only at the beginning of the course. Later on she began to fake the answers on her weekly tests. That is, she would look up the answers to the problems in the back of the textbook and copy them without showing me her step-by-step proofs. But wasn't this a part of teaching too? Wouldn't I have to deal with widespread cheating in the raucous classrooms of our public schools? I handled it this way with Norma. I said nothing about her dishonesty and simply gave her a score of zero on each test. Still she continued to look up the answers, whether I was watching her or not. She would complete the test in two or three minutes and sign her name to it and hand it to me, saying, "There you go, Midge. Will there be anything else?"

Of course I knew she felt sorry for Dupree in his recent troubles and I suppose she must have come to see him as a romantic outlaw. I didn't feel sorry for him at all. The troubles were entirely of his own making. You can't go around bothering people and not expect some inconvenience yourself. The trouble was politics. He had lately become interested in politics and this had brought his nastiness into bloom.

That is, it was "lately" to me. I didn't see Dupree much for seven or eight years, when he was away at all those different schools, and the change was probably more gradual than it appeared to me. He had once been a funny fellow. I don't often laugh out loud, even when I can recognize a joke as being a good one, but Dupree could always make me laugh when he did a thing called The Electric Man. As The Electric Man or The Mud Man he could make anyone laugh. And sometimes he would go out one door and come in at another one, as though he had just arrived, having moved very quickly in concealment between the two points. It wasn't so funny the first time—but he would keep doing it!

To the best of my knowledge he had never even voted, and then someone must have told him something about politics, some convincing lie, or he read something—it's usually one or the other—and he stopped being funny and turned mean and silent. That wasn't so bad, but then he stopped being silent.

He wrote abusive letters to the President, calling him a coward and a mangy rat with scabs on his ears, and he even challenged him to a fistfight on Pennsylvania Avenue. This was pretty good coming from a person who had been kayoed in every beer joint in Little Rock, often within the first ten minutes of his arrival. I don't believe we've ever had a President, unless it was tiny James Madison with his short arms, who couldn't have handled Dupree in a fair fight. Any provocation at all would do. One of his favorite ploys was to take a seat at a bar and repeat overheard fatuous remarks in a quacking voice like Donald Duck. Or he would spit BB's at people. He could fire BB's from between his teeth at high velocity and he would sit there and sting the tender chins and noses of the drinkers with these little bullets until he was discovered and, as was usually the consequence, knocked cold as a wedge.

I will have to admit that Dupree took his medicine without whining, unlike so many troublemakers. I will have to admit that he was not afraid of physical blows. On the other hand he did whine when the law came down on him. He couldn't see the legal distinction between verbal abuse and death threats, and he thought the government was persecuting him. The threats were not real, in the sense that they were likely to be carried out, but the Secret Service had no way of knowing that.

And he had certainly made the threats. I saw the letters myself. He had written such things to the President of the United States as "This time it's curtains for you and your rat family. I know your movements and I have access to your pets too."

A man from the Secret Service came by to talk to me and he showed me some of the letters. Dupree had signed them "Night Rider" and "Jo Jo the Dog-Faced Boy" and "Hoecake Scarfer" and "Old Nigger Man" and "Don Winslow of the Navy" and "Think Again" and "Home Room Teacher" and "Smirking Punk" and "Dirt Bike Punk" and "Yard Man."

He was arrested and he called me. I called his father—they didn't speak—and Mr. Dupree said, "Leavenworth will be a good place for him." The U.S. Commissioner had set bond at three thousand dollars—not a great deal, it seemed to me, for such a charge—but Mr. Dupree refused to post it.

"Well, I didn't know whether you could afford it or not," I said, knowing he would be stung by any suggestion that he might not be rich. He didn't say anything for a long moment and then he said, "Don't call me again about this." Dupree's mother might have done something but I didn't like to talk to her because she was usually in an alcoholic fog. She had a sharp tongue too, drunk or sober.

It certainly wasn't a question of the money, because Mr. Dupree was a prosperous soybean farmer who had operations not only in Arkansas but in Louisiana and Central America as well. The newspaper was already embarrassed and didn't want to get further involved. Norma put it to me that I ought to lend Dupree a hand since he was so absolutely friendless. Against my better judgment I got three hundred dollars together and arranged for a bondsman named Jack Wilkie to bail him out.

Not a word of thanks did I get. As soon as he was released from the county jail, Dupree complained to me that he had been fed only twice a day, oatmeal and pancakes and other such bloodless fare. A cellmate embezzler had told him that federal prisoners were entitled to three meals. Then he asked me to get him a lawyer. He didn't want Jack Wilkie to represent him.

I said, "The court will appoint you a lawyer."

He said, "They already have but he's no good. He doesn't even know the federal procedure. He'll start talking to this guy when he's supposed to be talking to that other guy. He waives everything. He's going to stipulate my ass right into a federal pen. A first offender."

"You'll have to get your own lawyer, Dupree."

"Where am I supposed to get him? I've called every son of a bitch in the yellow pages."

A good lawyer, he thought, would be able to forestall the psychiatric examination at the prison hospital in Springfield, Missouri. That examination was what he feared most, and with good reason, even though the finding would no doubt have provided a solid defense. In any case, he didn't really need a lawyer, good or bad, because on the following Friday night he jumped bail and ran off with my wife in my Ford Torino.

Since that night I had been biding my time but now that I knew where they were, more or less, I was ready to make my move. I had very little cash money for the trip and no credit cards. My father was floating somewhere on a lake near Eufaula, Alabama, in his green plastic boat, taking part in a bass tournament. Of course I had had many opportunities to explain the thing to him but I had been ashamed to do so. I was no longer an employee of the paper and I couldn't go to the credit union. My friend Burke never had any money. I could have sold some of my guns but I was reluctant to do so, saving that as a last resort. Gun fanciers are quick to sniff out a distress sale and I would have taken a beating from those heartless traders.

Then on the very day of my departure I remembered the savings bonds. My mother had left them to me when she died. I kept them hidden behind the encyclopedias where Norma never tarried and I had all but forgotten about them. Norma was a great one to nose around in my things. I never bothered her stuff. I had a drawer full of pistols in my desk and I kept that drawer locked but she got it open somehow and handled those pistols. Little rust spots from her moist fingertips told the story. Not even my food was safe. She ate very little, in fact, but if some attractive morsel on my plate happened to catch her eye she would spear it and eat it in a flash without acknowledging that she had done anything out of the way. She knew I didn't like that. I didn't tamper with her plate and she knew I didn't like her tampering with my plate. If the individual place setting means no more than that, then it is all a poor joke and you might as well have a trough and be done with it. She wouldn't keep her hands off my telescope either. But the Hope Diamond would have been safe behind those *Britannicas.*

I retrieved the bonds and sat down at the kitchen table to count them. I hadn't seen them in a long time and I decided to line them up shoulder to shoulder and see if I could cover every square inch of table surface with bonds. When I had done this, I stood back and looked at them. These were twenty-five-dollar E bonds.

Just then I heard someone at the door and I thought it was the children. Some sort of youth congress had been in session at the capitol for two or three days and children were milling about all over town. A few had even wandered into Gum Street where they had no conceivable business. I had been packing my clothes and watching these youngsters off and on all day through the curtain and now—the very thing I feared—they were at my door. What could they want? A glass of water? The phone? My signature on a petition? I made no sound and no move.

"Ray!"

It was Jack Wilkie and not the kids. What a pest! Day and night! I went to the door and unchained it and let him in but I kept him standing in the living room because I didn't want him to see my savings-bond table.

He said, "Why don't you turn on some lights in here or raise a shade or something?"

"I like it this way."

"What do you do, just stay in here all the time?"

He went through this same business at the beginning of each visit, the implication being that my way of life was strange and unwholesome. Jack was not only a bondsman and a lawyer of sorts but a businessman too. He owned a doughnut shop and some taxicabs. When I said he was a lawyer, I didn't mean he wore a soft gray suit and stayed home at night in his study reading Blackstone's *Commentaries*. If you had hired him unseen and were expecting that kind of lawyer, you would be knocked for a loop when you got to court and saw Jack standing there in his orange leisure suit, inspecting the green stuff under his fingernails. You would say, Well, there are a thousand lawyers in Pulaski County and it looks like I've got this one!

But Jack was a good-natured fellow and I admired him for being a man of action. I was uneasy when I first met him. He struck me as one of these country birds who, one second after meeting you, will start telling of some bestial escapade involving violence or sex or both, or who might in the same chatty way want to talk about Christ's Kingdom on Earth. It can go either way with those fellows and you need to be ready.

He had some big news for me this time, or so he thought. It was a postcard that Norma had sent to her mother from Wormington, Texas. "Gateway to the Hill Country," it said under the photograph of a low, dim structure that was the Wormington Motel. Gateway claims have always struck me as thin stuff because they can only mean that you're not there yet, that you're still in transit, that you're not in any very well defined place. I knew about the card already because Mrs. Edge, Norma's mother, had called me about it the day before. I had met her in front of the Federal Building and looked it over. Norma said she was all right and would be in touch later. That was all, but Jack wanted to stand there and talk about the card.

I studied the motel picture again. Next to the office door of the place there was another door opening into what must have been a utility room. I knew that Norma with her instinct for the wrong turn had opened it and stood there a long time looking at the pipes and buckets and tools, trying to figure out how the office had changed so much. I would have seen in a split second that I was in the wrong room.

I said, "They're not in Wormington now, Jack. It was just a stopover. Those lovebirds didn't run off to Wormington, Texas."

"I know that but it's a place to start."

"They'll turn up here in a few days."

"Let me tell you something. That old boy is long gone. He got a taste of jail and didn't like it."

"They'll turn up."

"You should have told me he was a nut. I don't appreciate the way you brought me into this thing."

"You knew what the charge was. You saw those letters."

"I thought his daddy would be good for it. A slow-pay rich guy maybe. I thought he just meant to let the boy stew for a while."

"Guy has given Mr. Dupree a lot of headaches."

"I'm going to report your car stolen. It's the only way."

"No, I can't go along with that."

"Let the police do our work for us. It's the only way to get a quick line on those lovebirds."

"I don't want to embarrass Norma."

"You don't want to embarrass yourself. You're afraid it'll get in the paper. Let me tell you something. The minute that bail is forfeited, it'll be in the paper anyway and by that time you may not even get your car back."

There was something to this. Jack was no dope. The paper didn't run cuckold stories as such but I thought it best to keep my name out of any public record. That way I could not be tied into Dupree's flight. Tongues were already wagging, to be sure. Everyone at the paper knew what had happened but what they knew and what they could print—without the protection of public records—were two different things. All I wanted to do now was to get my car back. I was already cuckolded but I wouldn't appear so foolish, I thought, if I could just get my car back without any help.

Jack stood there and reviewed the whole case again. He did this every time, as though I might be confused on certain points. When his eyes became adjusted to the murky light, he saw my suitcase on the couch and I saw him taking this in, a suitcase fact. He said, "I don't forfeit many bonds, Ray." I had heard him say that before too.

He left and I quickly gathered my E bonds and stowed them in the suitcase. I selected a .38 Colt Cobra from the pistol drawer and sprayed it with a silicone lubricant and sealed it in a plastic bag and packed it next to the bonds. What else now? The lower-back capsules! Norma never went anywhere without her lower-back medicine and yet she had forgotten it this time, such was her haste in dusting out of town, away from my weekly embraces. I got it from the bathroom and packed it too. She would thank me for that. Those capsules cost four dollars apiece.

I made sure all the windows were locked and I found a country-music station on my big Hallicrafters radio and left it playing at high volume against the kitchen wall. There was a rock-and-roll twerp with a stereo set in the next apartment and his jungle rhythms penetrated my wall. Noise was his joy. He had a motorcycle too. The Rhino management had a rule prohibiting the repair of motorcycles in the parking lot but the twerp paid no attention to it. One night I called him. I was reading a biography of Raphael Semmes and I put it down and rang up the twerp and asked him if he knew who Admiral Semmes was. He said, "What!" and I said, "He was captain of the *Alabama*, twerp!" and hung up.

Everything was in readiness. My checklist was complete. I called a cab and typed a note and tacked it to the door.

*I will be out of town for a few days.*
*Raymond E. Midge*

The cabdriver honked and picked his way slowly down Broadway through the little delegates to that endless convention of Junior Bankers or Young Teamsters. Their numbers seemed to be growing. I had left the Buick Special with a mechanic on Asher Avenue to get the solenoid switch replaced on the starter. The cabdriver let me out in front of a filthy café called Nub's or Dub's that was next door to the garage. Nub —or anyway some man in an apron—was standing behind the screen door and he looked at me. I was wearing a coat and tie and carrying a suitcase and I suppose he thought I had just flown in from some distant city and then dashed across town in a cab to get one of his plate lunches. A meal wasn't a bad idea at that but it was getting late and I wanted to be off.

The mechanic told me I needed a new motor mount and he wanted to sell me a manifold gasket too, for an oil leak. I

wasn't having any of that. I wasn't repairing anything on that
car that wasn't absolutely necessary. This was a strange attitude
for me because I hate to see a car abused. Maintenance! I never
went along with that new policy of the six-thousand-mile oil
change. It was always fifteen hundred for me and a new filter
every time.

And yet here I was starting off for Mexico in this junker
without so much as a new fan belt. There were Heath bar
wrappers, at least forty of them, all over the floor and seats
and I hadn't even bothered to clean them out. It wasn't my
car and I despised it. I had done some thinking too. The
shock of clean oil or the stiffer tension of a new belt might
have been just enough to upset the fragile equilibrium of the
system. And I had worked it out that the high mileage was
not really a disadvantage, reasoning in this specious way: that
a man who has made it to the age of seventy-four has a very
good chance of making it to seventy-six—a better chance, in
fact, than a young man would have.

Before I could get out of town, I remembered the silver
service that Mrs. Edge had passed along to Norma. What
if it were stolen? I wasn't worried much about my guns or
my books or my telescope or my stamps but if some burglar
nabbed the Edge forks I knew I would never hear the end of it.
My note would invite a break-in! I returned to the apartment
and got the silver chest. On my note saying that I would be out
of town for a few days a smart-ass had written, "Who cares?"
I ripped it off the door and drove downtown to the Federal
Building where Mrs. Edge worked. She wore a chain on her
glasses and she had a good job with a lot of seniority at the
Cotton Compliance Board.

She wasn't in the office and no one could tell me where she
was. What a sweet job! Just drift out for the afternoon! I called
her house and there was no answer. I wondered if she might
have found a place where she could dance in the afternoon.
She was crazy about dancing and she went out almost every
night with big red-faced men who could stay on the floor with
her for three or four hours. I mean smoking soles! She called
me a "pill" because I would never take Norma dancing. I say
"never" and yet we had scuttled stiffly across the floor on certain special occasions, although our total dancing time could

be readily computed in seconds, the way pilots measure their flying time in hours. I believe Mrs. Edge did prefer me over Dupree, for my civil manner and my neat attire if nothing else, but that's not to say she liked me. She had also called me "furtive" and "a selfish little fox."

I decided that she was probably out for an afternoon of city obstruction and I went to the west side of town and cruised the parking lots of the big shopping centers looking for her car. On certain days of the week she and several hundred other biddies would meet at these places and get their assignments, first having taken care to park their Larks and Volvos and Cadillacs across the painted lines and thus taking up two parking spaces, sometimes three. Then they would spread out over town. Some would go to supermarkets and stall the checkout lines with purse-fumbling and check-writing. Others would wait for the noon rush at cafeterias and there bring the serving lines to a crawl with long deliberative stops at the pie station. The rest were on motor patrol and they would poke along on the inside lanes of busy streets and stop cold for left turns whenever they saw a good chance to stack up traffic. Another trick was to stick the nose of a car about halfway into a thoroughfare from a side street, thereby blocking all traffic in that lane. Mrs. Edge was a leader of this gang. Turn her loose and she would have a dancing academy in the post office!

It was dark when I gave up the search. This silver wasn't old or rare or particularly valuable and I was furious with myself at having wasted so much time over it. I didn't feel like going all the way back to the apartment, so I just left the chest in the car trunk.

I was off at last and I was excited about the trip. The radio didn't work and I hummed a little. When I reached Benton, I was already tired of driving that car. Twenty-five miles! I couldn't believe it. I had a thousand miles to go and I was sleepy and my arms were tired and I didn't see how I was going to make it to Texarkana.

I pulled in at a rest stop and lay down on the seat, which had a strong dog odor. My nose was right against the plastic weave. This rest stop was a bad place to rest. Big diesel rigs roared in and the drivers left their engines running and made everybody miserable, and then some turd from Ohio parked a horse trailer next to me. The horses made the trailer springs squeak when they shifted their weight. That squeaking went on all night and it nearly drove me crazy. I slept for about four hours. It was a hard sleep and my eyes were swollen. A lot of people, the same ones who lie about their gas mileage, would have said they got no sleep at all.

It was breaking day when I reached Texarkana. I stopped and added some transmission fluid and put through a call to Little Rock from a pay station and woke up Mrs. Edge. I asked her to call my father on his return and tell him that I had gone to San Miguel de Allende in Mexico and would be back in a few days. The silverware was safe. What? Mexico? Silver? She was usually pretty quick but I had given it to her in a jumble and she couldn't take it in. It was just as well, because I didn't want to discuss my private business with her.

The drive to Laredo took all day. Gasoline was cheap—22.9 cents a gallon at some Shamrock stations—and the Texas police didn't care how fast you drove, but I had to keep the Buick speed below what I took to be about sixty because at that point the wind came up through the floor hole in such a way that the Heath wrappers were suspended behind my head in a noisy brown vortex. It was late October. The weather was fine but the leaves weren't pretty; they had just gone suddenly from green to dead.

I bought a quart of transmission fluid in Dallas and I stopped twice to cash bonds. The girl teller in the bank at Waco stared at me and I thought I must be giving off a dog smell. I got a roll of quarters from her and hefted it in my fist as I drove along.

Just south of Waco I looked about for some sign of the big gas line, the Scott-Eastern Line, but I could never determine where it crossed under the highway. My father and Mr. Dupree had helped build it, first as swabbers and then as boy welders. The Sons of the Pioneers! They had once been fairly close friends but had drifted apart over the years, Mr. Dupree having made a lot more money. My father resented his great success, although he tried not to, always giving Mr. Dupree credit for his energy. The hammer and the cutting torch, he said, were Mr. Dupree's favorite tools. My father's touch was much finer, his welding bead smoother and stronger and more pleasing to the eye, or so I am told. Of course he no longer made his living at it but people still called him on occasion when there was a tricky job to be done, such as welding airtight pressure seams on thin metal, or welding aluminum. Thin metal? Give him two beer cans and he'll weld them together for you!

In South Texas I saw three interesting things. The first was a tiny girl, maybe ten years old, driving a 1965 Cadillac. She wasn't going very fast, because I passed her, but still she was cruising right along, with her head tilted back and her mouth open and her little hands gripping the wheel.

Then I saw an old man walking up the median strip pulling a wooden cross behind him. It was mounted on something like a golf cart with two spoked wheels. I slowed down to read the hand-lettered sign on his chest.

JACKSONVILLE
FLA OR BUST

I had never been to Jacksonville but I knew it was the home of the Gator Bowl and I had heard it was a boom town, taking in an entire county or some such thing. It seemed an odd destination for a religious pilgrim. Penance maybe for some terrible sin, or some bargain he had worked out with God, or maybe just a crazed hiker. I waved and called out to him, wishing him luck, but he was intent on his marching and had no time for idle greetings. His step was brisk and I was convinced he wouldn't bust.

The third interesting thing was a convoy of stake-bed trucks all piled high with loose watermelons and cantaloupes. I was amazed. I couldn't believe that the bottom ones weren't being crushed under all that weight, exploding and spraying hazardous melon juice onto the highway. One of nature's tricks with curved surfaces. Topology! I had never made it that far in my mathematics and engineering studies, and I knew now that I never would, just as I knew that I would never be a navy pilot or a Treasury agent. I made a B in Statics but I was failing in Dynamics when I withdrew from the field. The course I liked best was one called Strength of Materials. Everybody else hated it because of all the tables we had to memorize but I loved it, the sheared beam. I had once tried to explain to Dupree how things fell apart from being pulled and compressed and twisted and bent and sheared but he wouldn't listen. Whenever that kind of thing came up, he would always say—*boast*, the way those people do—that he had no head for figures and couldn't do things with his hands, slyly suggesting the presence of finer qualities.

# *Two*

---

IN LAREDO I got a six-dollar motel room that had a lot of
posted rules on the door and one rubber pillow on the bed
and an oil-burning heater in the wall that had left many a salesman groggy. It was the kind of place I knew well. I always try
to get a room in a cheap motel with no restaurant that is near a
better motel where I can eat and drink. Norma never liked this
practice. She was afraid we would be caught out in the better
place and humiliated before some socialites we might have just
met. The socialites would spot our room key, with a chunk of
wood dangling from it like a carrot, or catch us in some gaffe,
and stop talking to us. This Laredo room also had a tin shower
stall and one paper bath mat.

I went to a discount store and bought three quarts of transmission fluid and some food for the road and a Styrofoam ice
chest and a frozen pie. I didn't want the pie but I did want the
carton it came in. Back in the shadows of my room I replaced
the pie with the Colt Cobra and sealed the box with tape. The
cylinder of the revolver made a bulge in the carton and I regretted that I had not brought a flat automatic. Then I put
the innocent-looking carton at the bottom of the ice chest and
covered it with little crescents of ice from the motel dispenser.
This was against motel policy, the crescents being intended for
solitary drinks in the room instead of bulk use.

But I filled the chest anyway and on top of the ice I arranged
cans of beer and packets of baloney and cheese in a festive
display. The pie itself, lemon, I carried about in the room for
a while, putting it down here and there. I couldn't find a good
place for it. Finally I took it outside and left it by the dumpster
for a passing rat, who would squeak with delight when he saw
those white billows of meringue.

The better motel was across the wide street. I went over
and scouted the place out, the magazine rack and the lounge
and the restaurant. No salad bar but that was all right. I noted
too that a person would have to pass through the steaming
nastiness of the kitchen in order to reach the toilet. The people
who were running the motel seemed to be from some place

like North Dakota instead of Texas, and they all seemed to be worried about something, distracted. I could hear carpentry work going on in the kitchen and occasional shouts.

You can usually count on a pretty good chicken-fried steak in Texas, if not a chicken-fried chicken, but I didn't like this setup. All afternoon I had been thinking about one of those steaks, with white gravy and a lot of black pepper, and now I was afraid these people from Fargo would bring me a prefabricated vealette pattie instead of fresh meat. I ordered roast beef and I told the waitress I wanted plenty of gristle and would like for the meat to be gray with an iridescent rainbow sheen. She was not in the mood for teasing, being preoccupied with some private distress like the others. She brought me a plate of fish sticks and the smallest portion of coleslaw I've ever seen. It was in a paper nut cup. I didn't say anything because they have a rough job. Those waitresses are on their feet all day and they never get a raise and they never get a vacation until they quit. The menu was complete fiction. She was serving the fish sticks to everybody, and not a uniform count either.

After supper I went into the darkened lounge. It was still "happy hour" and the place was packed with local people. I saw no socialites. I had trouble getting a stool at the bar because when one fell vacant I would wait for a minute or two to let it cool off, to let the body heat dissipate from the plastic cushion, and then someone else would get it. The crowd cleared out when the prices went up and then I had the bar pretty much to myself. I could see a man standing at the far end writing a letter with a pencil. He was laughing at his work, a lone bandit writing cruel taunts to the chief of police.

I ordered a glass of beer and arranged my coins before me on the bar in columns according to value. When the beer came, I dipped a finger in it and wet down each corner of the paper napkin to anchor it, so it would not come up with the mug each time and make me appear ridiculous. I drank from the side of the mug that a left-handed person would use, in the belief that fewer mouths had been on that side. That is also my policy with cups, any vessel with a handle, although you can usually count on cups getting a more thorough washing than bar glasses. A quick slosh here and there and those babies are right back on the shelf!

Across from me there was a dark mirror and above that a mounted deer's head with a cigarette in his mouth. Back in the table area a woman was playing an electric organ. No one was shouting requests to her. I was the only person in the place who applauded her music—a piece of traveler's bravado. And after a while I didn't clap either. I had no character at all. If the other customers had suddenly decided to club the poor woman with bottles, with those square gin bottles, I suppose I would have joined in. Here was something new. We all know about the gentry going to seed but here was something Jefferson had not foreseen: an effete yeoman.

An old man wearing clown shoes came through the door and began to play a kind of tune on a toy trombone. He hummed into the tiny instrument, as with a comb and tissue paper. The Mexican bartender chased him out. Then another man came in and sat down beside me. I was annoyed, because there were plenty of empty stools. I stiffened and waited for him to start talking. I avoided eye contact. Any minute now, I said to myself, this fellow is going to order an Old Charter and 7-Up and tell me he had gone to boot camp with Tyrone Power. I couldn't see his face but I watched his hairy paw as it reached across me and grabbed a handful of matchbooks from the courtesy bowl. Greenish fingernails and a heavy silver ring with a black stone.

He punched me on the shoulder and laughed. It was Jack Wilkie. I couldn't believe it.

He said, "How's the little car holding up?"

"It's doing all right."

"Little car drives out good, does it?"

"What are you doing here, Jack?"

"It's all in the day's work." He was windblown and his knit shirt was sagging and damp with sweat but he was pleased with the effect he had achieved and he kept punching me and laughing.

Mrs. Edge had told him about the Texarkana call and he had immediately divined my plan. He had made up the lost time easily enough in his Chrysler Imperial. Tomorrow morning he would drive to San Miguel and pick up Dupree and take him back to Little Rock. It was as simple as that. He seemed to think San Miguel was right across the border.

"You should have told me where he was, Ray."

"I was going to tell you as soon as I got my car back. I wanted to get my car without your help."

"You should have told me about this Mexico thing. We could have worked something out. This is business to me."

"I know that."

"What difference does it make as long as you get your car?"

"It's not the same thing."

I gave him what information I had and he wrote down "Hotel Mogador" on a paper napkin. He said I might as well ride along with him to San Miguel in the comfort of the big Chrysler. I halfway agreed. It seemed the only thing to do, except maybe forget the whole business and go back to Little Rock like a whipped dog. There was no way I could beat him to San Miguel in the little Buick.

I said, "How are you going to get Dupree out of Mexico? Your warrant won't be any good down there."

Jack was scornful. "*Warrant*. That's a good one. Warrant's ass. I don't need a warrant. All I need is a certified copy of the bond. I'm a party to the action. That's better than a warrant any day. I can take custody anywhere. The dumbest person in this motel knows that."

The woman at the organ was singing. She had been singing for some time but this was no background stuff; this song was a showstopper and we had to take notice: "And then they nursed it, rehearsed it, . . . And gave out the news . . ."

The old man with the big shoes came back and this time he was wearing a bellboy's cap with a strap under his chin. He ran through the place waving a scrap of paper and shouting, "Phone call! Phone call for the Sheriff of Cochise! Emergency phone call! Code ten!" The bartender ducked under the bar flap and popped a rag at him and chased him out again and I could hear the old man's shoes flopping down the hall.

Jack said, "Who was that old guy?"

I said, "I don't know."

"They ought to lock that son of a bitch up."

"I think it's Halloween."

"No, it's not. A guy like that wouldn't know what day it was anyway. This place smells like a kennel. Did you eat here?"

"Yes."

"Can you recommend anything?"

"I can't recommend what I had."

"Some hot-tamale crap?"

"I had fish."

"That's a mistake. A place like this. Let's go to some nice steakhouse. I'm hungry."

"I've already eaten."

"How about the track? Why don't we take a run out to the dog track and make some quick money? Let them dogs pay for our trip."

"They don't have dog races here, Jack."

"I think they do."

"They don't have legal gambling in Texas."

"I think they have dog races."

"I don't think so. Out in the streets maybe. Among themselves."

"Across the border then. I know they have some kind of racing in Juárez."

"That's way up there at El Paso."

I still didn't see how Jack could take Dupree out of Mexico without going through some sort of legal formality. He kept telling me he was "the surety" and "a party to the action" and that such a person could go anywhere in the world and do just as he pleased. He said, "I don't care where they are. I've taken these old boys out of Venezuela and the Dominican Republic."

We sat there and drank for a long time. Jack showed me his handcuffs, which he carried in a leather pouch on his belt. He also had a blackjack, or rather a "Big John" flat sap. He didn't carry a gun. He said he loved the bail-bond business. His wife thought it was sleazy and she wanted him to give it up and devote all his time to the practice of law, which he found dull.

"I was in the army and nobody wanted to see me," he said. "Then I was a salesman and nobody wanted to see me. Now they're glad to see me. Let me tell you something. You're doing that old boy a real service when you get him out of jail. Sure, everybody has to go to jail sometime, but that don't mean you have to stay there."

I asked Jack if he could help me get a job as an insurance adjuster. I had often thought of becoming an investigator of some kind and I asked him if he could put me on to something, perhaps a small shadowing job. The paper had once given me a trial as a police reporter, although hardly a fair one. Two days!

Jack wasn't interested in this subject and he wouldn't discuss it with me.

He wanted to talk about his family. He had a jug-eared stepson named Gary who smoked marijuana and made D's in school and spent his money on trashy phonograph records. The boy also spent a lot of his time and money at an amusement arcade downtown and Jack said he had ugly sores in his right eyebrow from many hours of pressing his eye against the periscope of the submarine game. The thought of this boy and his smart mouth and his teen mustache made Jack angry. But he didn't hold it against his wife that she had given birth to the unsatisfactory kid and brought him to live in the Wilkie home.

He poked me with a finger and said, "My wife is just as sweet as pie. Get that straight." And a little later he said, "I'm glad my wife is not a porker." He told me she had "firm muscles" and he told me about all the birthday presents and Christmas presents he had given her in recent years. He said she had never locked him out of the house.

I didn't see how Jack Wilkie could have a very nice wife and I was tired of hearing about her. He left to get a cheeseburger and I thought about his remarks. The insinuation seemed to be that Norma was not as sweet as pie. When he got back, I asked him if that was his meaning and he said it wasn't.

He had spilled food on his knit shirt. I told him that I thought an investigator going on a trip should wear a coat and tie. He didn't hear me. He was looking at the mounted deer head. He jumped up on the bar and straddled the walkway behind the bar and took the cigarette from the deer's mouth and flung it down on the duckboards. Then he turned on the bartender. "That's not right and you know it's not right," he said. "That's not the thing to do. Don't put another cigarette in that deer's mouth."

The Mexican bartender was slicing limes. With his hooded eyes and his little mustache he looked like a hard customer to me. He was fed up with these antics in his bar, I could tell, and I thought he was going to do something. But he just said, "I didn't put that one in there."

Jack climbed down and started telling me about all the different people who had attacked him while he was just doing his job. Everybody who attacked him was crazy. He pulled up a trouser leg and showed me a pitted place on his calf where a crazy woman in Mississippi had stabbed him with a Phillips screwdriver. Then he raised his knit shirt and showed me a purple scar on his broad white back where he had been shot by a crazy man in Memphis. One of his lungs had filled up with blood and when he came around in the emergency room of Methodist Hospital he heard the doctor ask a nurse if she had the key to the morgue. A close call for Jack! Not everybody was glad to see him!

Nothing more was said about our business. I left him there drunk on the stool. He said he would see me at breakfast.

I returned to my room across the street and went to bed and lay with my head under the rubber pillow to keep out highway noise. I couldn't sleep. After a time I could hear knocking and bumping and voices outside. Someone seemed to be going from door to door. Maybe trick or treat, or the Lions Club selling brooms. Or the dumbest person in the motel looking for his room. My turn came and I went to the door. It was the old man in the big shoes. He was also wearing a white cotton jacket or smock. With his purple face up close to mine, I saw his bad eye and I had the momentary impression that I was looking at Mr. Proctor. But how could that be? Mr. Proctor was snug in his brown shed in Little Rock, eating canned peanuts and watching some hard-hitting documentary on television. The man gave me a card. Scriptural quotations, I thought, or the deaf-and-dumb signs.

"What is this? What are you doing?"

"I'm just fooling around," he said.

It was my guess that he had been a veteran handyman here on motel row, known all up and down the street as Dad or Pete. Then one day he was falsely accused of something, stealing sheets maybe, and fired summarily with no pension. He was now getting back at people. This was his way of getting back at the motel bosses. But when I asked about this, he said, "No, I'm just fooling around. It's something to do. My wife is an old shopping-cart lady. That's Mrs. Meigs I'm speaking of. She picks up bottles all day and I do this all night."

"You weren't wearing that jacket thing before."

"This is my traffic coat. Mrs. Meigs made it for me so the cars and trucks could see me at night and not run over me. It's just got this one button in the middle and these two pockets here at the bottom. How do you like it?"

"I like it all right. It looks like a pharmacist's coat."

"It don't have near enough pockets to suit me but you can't have everything."

"What else do you do? What else are you going to do to-night?"

"First let me tell you what I'm not going to do. I'm not going to stand here any longer and talk to you. If I gave this much time to everybody, I'd never get through my rounds, would I?"

He produced a harmonica, not a trombone this time, and rapped it against his palm in a professional way to dislodge any spittle or crumbs. He stuck it in his mouth and inhaled and exhaled, making those two different sounds, in and out, and then he rapped it again to clear the passages and put it away. I had nothing to say to that, to those two chords, and he bolted and was gone.

I took the card to bed and studied it. Tiny things take on significance when I'm away from home. I'm on the alert for omens. Odd things happen when you get out of town. At the top of the card there were two crossed American flags printed in color. Under that was the ever-popular "Kwitcherbellyachin" and at the bottom was "Mr. and Mrs. Meigs/ Laredo, Texas." On the back of the card Meigs or his wife had added a penciled postscript: "adios AMIGO and watch out for the FLORR."

I couldn't make anything out of this and I turned off the light. I could hear a Mexican shouting angrily at Meigs down the way. I still couldn't sleep. I got up again and drank one of the beers from the ice chest. I looked at the card again. "Kwitcherbellyachin"! I thought, Well, all right, I will. I decided to leave at once. I would get the jump on Jack. It was worth a try. I dressed quickly and loaded the suitcase and the ice chest in the trunk of the car.

Nothing at all was stirring in downtown Laredo. I didn't bother with the Mexican car insurance. I drove across the Rio Grande and on the other side of the bridge a Mexican officer flagged me into a parking compound that was enclosed by a high wire fence.

I was the only person entering Nuevo Laredo at that dead hour but it still took a long time to get my tourist card and car papers. The Mexican officer at the typewriter didn't believe that my Arkansas driver's license was really a driver's license. At that time it was just a flimsy piece of paper torn from a pad and it looked like a fishing license. I gave him the registration slip for my Torino and he didn't bother to look outside to see if that was in fact what I was driving. The big problem was the typing. When you run up against a policeman at a typewriter, you might as well get a Coke and relax.

While I was waiting, an idea drifted into my head that made me laugh a little. The idea was to get this Mexican fellow and Nub or Dub on a television show for a type-off. You would have them on a stage glaring at each other from behind their big Underwoods and Nub would try to peck out "Choice of 3 Veg." on his menu while this Mexican was trying to get "Raymond Earl Midge" down on his form. People would be howling from coast to coast at those two slowpokes. I slipped the man a dollar bill folded to the size of a stick of gum. I did the same with the porters and customs men outside.

This was the thing to do, I had been told, but it bothered me a little. You could look on a dollar as a tip and you could also look on it as a small bribe. I was afraid one of these fellows might turn out to be a zealot like Bruce Wayne, whose parents were murdered by crooks and who had dedicated his entire life to the fight against crime. An attempted bribe, followed by the discovery of a pistol concealed in a pie carton, and I would really be in the soup. But nothing happened. They palmed those dollars like carnival guys and nobody looked into anything. The customs man marked my suitcase with a piece of chalk and a porter stuck the decals on my windows and I was gone. I was free and clear in Mexico with my Colt Cobra.

Those boys were sleepy and not much interested in their work, it's true enough, but I was still pleased at the way I had brought it off. I couldn't get over how composed I had been, looking prison right in the face. Now I was surprised and lightheaded, like a domestic fowl that finds itself able to fly over a low fence in a moment of terror. Vestigial Midge powers were rising in the blood. I was pleased too that I was in Mexico and not at home, but that works both ways because after sunrise I met Americans driving out of Mexico and they all appeared to be singing happy songs.

I waved at children carrying buckets of water and at old women with shawls on their heads. It was a chilly morning. *I'm a gringo of good will in a small Buick! I'll try to observe your customs!* That was what I put into my waves.

The poor people of Mexico were the ones without sunglasses. I could see that right off the bat. The others, descendants of the great Cortez, he who had burned his ships at Veracruz, were stealing small advantages in traffic. They would speed up and hog the center line when you tried to pass them. They hated to be passed. I say Cortez "burned" his ships because everyone else does, but I know perfectly well that he only had them dismantled there on the beach—not that it takes away from his courage.

A few miles from the border there was a checkpoint and an officer there examined my papers. Nothing matched! I was driving a completely different car from the one described on the form. He couldn't deal with such a big lie so early in the morning and he gave the papers back to me and waved me on.

The desert road was straight and the guidebook said it was boring but I didn't find it so. I was interested in everything, the gray-green bushes, the cactus, a low brown hill, a spider crossing the road. Later in the morning a dark cloud came up that had a green rim and then rain fell in such torrents that cars and buses pulled over to wait it out. A desert rainstorm! You couldn't see three feet! I turned on the headlights and slowed down but I kept going until the brake linings got wet and wouldn't hold.

I don't like to piddle around when I'm on the road and this stop made me impatient. If you stop for ten minutes, you lose more than ten minutes' driving time. I don't know why, but I do know why slow ships can cross the Atlantic Ocean in just a few days. Because they never stop! My ankles and my new cordovan shoes were soaked from water sloshing up through the hole in the floor. I sat out the storm there on the shoulder of the road reading *The Life and Glorious Times of Zach Taylor*, by Binder. It was not the kind of title I liked but it was a pretty good book.

After the sun came out, I drove slow and rode the brakes for a while until they were dry. I was still on the straight part of the highway north of Monterrey when a big yellow car came racing up behind me and stayed right on my bumper. More Mexican stuff, I thought, and then I saw that it was Jack Wilkie in his Chrysler Imperial. I could see him in my mirror, laughing and tapping a finger on the steering wheel, in time, I supposed, to some radio music. I could see his big silver ring and some frosty flecks of doughnut sugar around his mouth. That was how close he was.

I tapped the brake pedal just enough to flash the brake light but I kept the accelerator depressed. Jack thought I was going to stop suddenly and he braked and skidded. His right-hand wheels dropped off the ledge of the pavement onto the dirt shoulder and dust was boiling up behind him. Then he recovered and got on my bumper again, still laughing. I didn't like that laughing. The brake-light trick was the only one I knew so I just started going faster and faster. Jack stayed right with me, inches away. He was playing with me. He could have passed me easily enough but he was going to run the Buick into the ground or make me give up, one or the other. I drove the little car as fast as it would go, which I guessed to be around ninety or so. That was nothing at all for the Imperial but I had a six-cylinder engine and a little air-cooled, two-speed transmission that was squealing like a pig.

We went roaring along like this for four or five miles, bumper to bumper, two hell drivers, and I was beginning to lose my stomach for it. I didn't even know what the point of it was. The sheet metal was vibrating and resonating and it appeared fuzzy to the eye. Particles of rust and dirt were dancing on the floor. Candy wrappers were flying everywhere.

I've had enough of this, I said to myself, and I was just about ready to quit when the exhaust system or the drive shaft dropped to the highway beneath the Chrysler and began to kick up sparks. Jack was done for the day. I shot over a rise and left him with a couple of honks. *Harvest yellow Imperial. Like new. Loaded. One owner. See to appreciate. Extra sharp. Good rubber. A real nice car. Needs some work. Call Cherokee Bail Bonds and ask for Jack. Work odd hours. Keep calling.*

# Three

I LOST some more time in and about the adobe city of Saltillo looking for the Buena Vista battlefield. I couldn't find it. Binder's maps were useless and the Mexicans pretended they had never heard of Zachary Taylor and Archibald Yell. At the height of the battle, when it might have gone either way, the cool Taylor turned to his artillery officer and said, "A little more grape, Captain Bragg." Remarks like that were embedded in my head and took up precious space that should have been occupied with other things but wasn't.

I gave up the search and pressed on south atop a desolate plateau. It was cool up there and the landscape was not like the friendly earth I knew. This was the cool dry place that we hear so much about, the place where we are supposed to store things. The car ran well and I glowed in the joy of solitary flight. It was almost a blessed state. Was I now a ramblin' man, like in the country songs? *Sorry, lady, but I got to be ramblin' on!* Or was this just a trip? Whenever I saw a person or a domestic animal, I would shout some greeting, or perhaps a question—"How do you like living here in Mexico?"—just the first thing that came into my head. I stopped for the night at a camper park in Matehuala. A young Canadian couple in a van shared their supper with me.

I slept in the car again, although I didn't much like it, being exposed that way to people walking by and peering in the windows, watching me sleep. It was like lying supine on the beach with your eyes closed and fearing that some terrible person in heavy shoes will come along and be seized by an impulse to stomp on your vulnerable belly. I rose early and shaved with cold water in the washhouse. The Canadians were up too, and they gave me a slice of pound cake and a cup of coffee. I was in San Miguel de Allende by noon.

The Hotel Mogador was only a block or so from the main square, or *jardín*, as they called it, which is to say "garden." There wasn't one guest in the place. Dupree and Norma had been gone for a little over three weeks. I was not greatly surprised at this, and not much concerned. From this point, I thought, tracing two foreigners and a chow dog in a blue Ford Torino could be no very hard task. I had not realized there were so many other Americans in Mexico.

The owner of the hotel was an accommodating man and he showed me their room, the blocky wooden bed, the short bathtub faced with little blue tiles. I had no particular feeling about the room but I certainly didn't want to stay in it, as the man suggested. I questioned him closely. Did they say where they were going? No. Had they perhaps moved to another hotel here? Possibly, but he had not seen them around town. Was there a trailer park in San Miguel? Yes, behind the Siesta Motel on the edge of town.

It had been in my mind all along that I would find them in a trailer park. I suppose I thought it would be a suitable place for their meretricious relationship. I had a plan for that trailer. I would jerk open the flimsy door with such force that the stop-chain would snap. Dupree would be sitting down eating a bowl of cereal, holding a big spoon in his monkey hand. I would throw an armlock on his neck from behind. While he sputtered and milk drops flew from his mouth, I would remove my car keys and my credit cards from his pockets. Norma would say, "Let him have some air!" and I would shove him away and leave them there in their sty without a word.

I drove out to the place on the edge of town but it wasn't a mobile-home community of the kind I had visualized. It was literally a trailer park, a dusty field where Mom and Dad could park their Airstream for a day or two and let their big Olds 98 cool off. The place was all but deserted. At one end of the field there was a square lump of a motor home and at the other end was an old school bus that had been painted white and rigged as a camper. The bus had been given a name, "The Dog of the South," which was painted in black on one side, but not by a sign painter with a straight-edge and a steady hand. The big childish letters sprawled at different angles and dribbled at the bottom. The white paint had also been applied in a slapdash manner, and it had drawn up in places, presenting a crinkled finish like that seen on old adding machines and cash registers. This thing was a hippie wagon.

I went to the Mogador and had lunch in the courtyard with the owner. I had to take two meals there with my room. There were flowers and cats all around us. I could see the pale blue sky above. We had onion soup and then some veal cutlets and rice. The hotel man fed table scraps to the cats and so I did the same. What a life!

He said he had been a bit mixed up before and had shown me the wrong room. The Norma-Dupree room was actually one floor above the first room he had shown me, and was in fact the very room he had given me. Did I wish to be moved? I said no, it made no difference. Then there was a disturbance in the kitchen and he went to investigate. When he came back, he said, "It was nothing, the mop caught fire. All my employees are fools."

This Mexican lunch was a long affair and before it was over we were joined by a tall bird wearing metallic-silver coveralls. He was a Canadian artist who made paper rabbits. He showed me one and it was a pretty well done bunny except for the big eyelashes. The price was ten dollars. I remarked that there seemed to be quite a few Canadians in Mexico.

He bristled. "Why shouldn't there be?"

"Out of proportion to your numbers, I mean. It was just a neutral observation."

"We're quite free to travel, you know. We can even go to Cuba if we wish."

"I'm not making myself clear."

"Do please make yourself clear."

"Well, there are two hundred million Americans and twenty million Canadians, and my country is closer to Mexico than yours, but I get the impression that there are just about as many Canadians here as Americans. At this table, for instance."

"You're not the only Americans. You people just stole that name."

"Look here, why don't you kiss my ass?"

"So bright of you. So typical."

It was my guess that this queer was having big trouble selling his overpriced rabbits. That was the only way I could account for his manner. The hotel man became jolly and tried to patch things up. But this too annoyed the artist and he got up and flounced out, stopping for a moment under the archway as he thought of something pretty good to call me, which was "rat face."

He thought it was pretty good but it was old stuff to me, being compared to a rat. In fact, I look more like a predatory bird than a rat but any person with small sharp features that are bunched in the center of his face can expect to be called a rat about three times a year.

We finished our meal in peace and then I went downtown to trade bonds for pesos. The bank was closed for lunch until 4 P.M. Some lunch! I wandered about town on foot looking for my Torino.

There was a bandstand in the central square, and some wrought-iron benches and some noisy flocking birds with long tail feathers. I took them to be members of the grackle family. There were elegant trees too, of the kind that architects like to sketch in front of their buildings. A few gringos were scattered around on the benches, dozing and reading newspapers and working crossword puzzles. I approached them one by one and made inquiries. I got nowhere until I mentioned the dog. They remembered the dog. Still, they could give nothing more than bare sighting reports. I could get no leads and no firm dates.

Hippies interfered with my work by stopping me and asking me the time. Why did they care? And if so, why didn't they have watches? The watch factories were humming day and night in Tokyo and Geneva and Little Rock so that everyone might have a cheap watch, but not one of these hippies had a watch. Maybe the winding put them off. Or maybe it was all mockery of me and my coat and tie. The same hippies seemed to be stopping me again and again, though I couldn't be sure.

A retired army sergeant told me that he had chatted for a bit with Dupree. He said they had discussed the curious drinking laws of the different states, and the curious alcoholic beverages of the world, such as ouzo and pulque, and he made me glad I wasn't there. In all his travels over the world, he said, he had found only one thing he couldn't drink and that was some first-run brandy in Parral, Chihuahua.

"Where did you talk to him?"

"That Southern boy?"

"Yes."

"Right here. I don't sit in the same place every day. It's not like I have my own bench but I *was* here that day. The boy sat over there and bought a Popsicle for his dog."

I wondered if the man might be confused. The Popsicle business sounded all right but I couldn't see Dupree sitting here being civil and swapping yarns with Sarge.

"Did he say where he was going from here?"

"I don't believe he did. He didn't have a whole lot to say."

"And the girl wasn't with him?"

"I didn't see any girl, just the dog. A big shaggy chow. The boy said he was going to trim his coat. He was worried about the tropical heat and humidity and he said he was going to give him a close trim with some scissors. He wanted to know where he could buy some flea powder and some heavy scissors."

"When was this?"

"It's been a while. I don't know. They come and go. Did he steal your dog?"

"No. Did you see him after that?"

"I saw him once in a car with some other people."

"Was it a Ford Torino?"

"No, it was a small foreign car. All beat up. It was some odd little car like a Simca. They were just cruising around the *jardín* here. I didn't pay much attention."

Other people? Foreign car? Dupree was not one to take up with strangers. What was this all about? But Sarge could tell me nothing more, except that the people were "scruffy" and appeared to be Americans. He pointed out the drugstore on the corner where he had sent Dupree for the flea powder. Then he took a ball-point pen and some glasses from his shirt pocket and I jumped up from the bench in alarm, fearing he was about to diagram something for me, but he was only rearranging his pocket stuff.

I thanked him and went to the drugstore and learned that an American wearing glasses had indeed bought some flea powder in the place. The woman pharmacist could tell me nothing else. I was tired. All this chasing around to prove something that I already knew, that Dupree had been in San Miguel. I couldn't get beyond that point. What I needed was a new investigative approach, a new plan, and I couldn't think of one. I looked over the aspirin display.

"*¿Dolor?*" said the woman, and I said *Sí*, and pointed to my head. Aspirins were too weak, she said, and she sold me some orange pills wrapped in a piece of brown paper. I took the pills to a café and crushed one on the table and tasted a bit of it. For all I knew, they were dangerous Mexican drugs, but I took a couple of them anyway. They were bitter.

On the way to the bank for a second try I got sidetracked into a small museum. The man who ran the place was standing on the sidewalk and he coaxed me inside. The admission fee was only two pesos. He had some good stuff to show. There were rough chunks of silver ore and clay figurines and two rotting mummies and colonial artifacts and delicate bird skulls and utensils of hammered copper. The man let me handle the silver. I wrote my name in the guest book and I saw that Norma and Dupree had been there. In the space for remarks Dupree had written, "A big gyp. Most boring exhibition in North America." Norma had written, "I like the opals best. They are very striking." She had signed herself Norma Midge. She was still using my name. I stood there and looked at her signature, at the little teacup handles on her capital N and capital M.

The book was on a high table like a lectern and behind it, tacked to the wall, was a map of Mexico. I drew closer to admire the map. It dated from around 1880 and it was a fine piece of English cartography. Your newer map is not always your better map! The relief was shown by hachuring, with every tiny line perfectly spaced. The engraver was a master and the printer had done wonders with only two shades of ink, black and brown. It was hand-lettered. I located myself at about 21 degrees north and 101 degrees west. This was as far south as I had ever been, about two degrees below the Tropic of Cancer.

Then after a few minutes it came to me. I knew where Dupree had gone and I should have known all along. He had gone to his father's farm in Central America. San Miguel was technically within the tropics but at an elevation of over six thousand feet the heat here would not be such as to cause dog suffering. And there was no humidity to speak of. They were on that farm in British Honduras. That monkey had taken my wife to British Honduras and he had planned it all in the Wormington Motel!

I was excited, my *dolor* suddenly gone, and I wanted to share the good news with someone. *¡Misión cumplida!* That is, it was not exactly accomplished, but the rest would be easy. I looked about for a place to gloat and soon hit on a bar called the Cucaracha.

It was a dark square room with a high ceiling. Some padded wooden benches were arranged in a maze-like pattern. They faced this way and that way and they were so close together that it was hard to move about. I drank bourbon until I figured out what it cost and then I switched to gin and tonic, which was much cheaper.

The customers were mostly gringos and they were a curious mix of retired veterans and hippies and alimony dodgers and artists. They were friendly people and I liked the place immediately. *We've all run off to Mexico*—that was the thing that hung in the air, and it made for a kind of sad bonhomie. I was surprised to find myself speaking so freely of my private affairs. The Cucaracha people offered tips on the drive south to British Honduras. I basked in their attention as a figure of international drama. My headache returned and I took some more pills.

One of the hippies turned out to be from Little Rock. I never thought I would be glad to see a hippie but I was glad to see this fellow. He had a hippie sweetheart with him who was wearing white nurse stockings. She was a pretty little thing but I didn't realize it for a while because her electrified hair was so ugly. It was dark in there too. I asked the hippie what he did and he said he drank a liter of Madero brandy every day and took six Benzedrine tablets. He asked me what I did and I had to say I did nothing much at all. Then we talked about Little Rock, or at least I did. I thought we might have some mutual friends, or if not, we could always talk about the different streets and their names. The hippie wasn't interested in this. He said, "Little Rock is a pain in the ass," and his sweetheart said, "North Little Rock too."

But it didn't matter, I was having a good time. Everything was funny. An American woman wearing a white tennis hat stuck her head in the doorway and then withdrew it in one second when she saw what kind of place it was. The Cucaracha gang got a good laugh out of this, each one accusing the other of being the frightful person who had scared her away. I talked to a crippled man, a gringo with gray hair, who was being shunned by the other drinkers. He said he had shot down two Nip planes when he was in the Flying Tigers. He now owned a Chiclets factory in Guadalajara. People hated him, he said, because his principles didn't permit him to lend money, or to buy drinks for anyone but himself. He described for me the first six plays of an important Stanford football game of 1935, or I should say the first six plays from scrimmage, since he didn't count the kickoff as a play.

There were two Australian girls across the room and the Flying Tiger said they wanted to see me. He told me they had been trying to get my attention for quite a while. I went over at once and sat with them. These girls were slender cuties who were hitchhiking around the world with their shoulder bags. But it was all a hoax, the invitation, and they didn't want to see me at all. I sat down by another girl, this one a teacher from Chicago, and then I had to get up again because the seat was saved, or so she said. I watched that empty seat for a long time and it wasn't really saved for anyone. A hippie wearing striped bib overalls came in from the bar and sat beside her. She advised him that the seat was saved but that bird didn't get up. "You can't save seats," he said. What a statement! You can't save seats! I would never have thought of that in a thousand years!

I forgot about the bank business and I sat there and drank gin and tonic until the quinine in the tonic water made my ears hum. Someone that night told me about having seen Dupree with a fellow wearing a neck brace but I was too drunk to pursue it and the thing went completely out of my mind. I began to babble. I told everybody about my father's Midgestone business, how the stone veneer was cut with special band saws, and how it was shaped and sanded. I told them about my great-grandfather building the first greenhouse in Arkansas and how he had developed a hard little peach called the Lydia that was bird-resistant and well suited for shipping, although tasteless. I couldn't stop talking. I was a raving bore and I knew it too, but I couldn't stop. It was important to me that they know these things and who would tell them if I didn't?

They fled my presence, the hippies and vets and cuties alike, and left me sitting alone in the corner. I kept drinking, I refused to leave. They had all turned on me but I wasn't going to let them run me off. There was a lot of old stuff on the jukebox

and I who had never played a jukebox in my life had the waiter
take my change after each drink and play "It's Magic" by Doris
Day. She was singing that song, a new one to me, when I first
entered the place. I had heard of Doris Day but no one had
ever told me what a good singer she was.

Sometime around midnight the hippie couple from Little
Rock got into a squabble. I couldn't hear what he was saying
because his voice was low but I heard her say, "My *daddy* don't
even talk to me like that and you *damn* sure ain't!" The little
girl was blazing. He put his hand out to touch her or to make
some new point and she pushed it away and got up and left,
stepping smartly in her white stockings and brushing past an
old man who had appeared in the doorway.

He was a fat man, older than the Flying Tiger, and he was
looking from left to right like an animal questing for food. He
wore a white hat and a white shirt and white trousers and a
black bow tie. This old-timer, I said to myself, looks very much
like a boxing referee, except for the big floppy hat and the army
flashlight clipped to his belt.

He looked around and said, "Where's the boy who's going
to British Honduras?"

I said nothing.

He raised his voice. "I'm looking for the boy who's going to
British Honduras! Is he here?"

If I had kept my mouth shut for five more seconds, he
would have gone his way and I would have gone mine. I said,
"Here I am! In the corner! I'm not supposed to talk!" I hadn't
spoken for a long time and my voice croaked and had no authority in it.

"Where?"

"Over here!"

"I can't see you!"

"In the corner!"

He bumped his way across the room and took off his hat and
joined me on the bench. His white pants were too long and
even when he was seated there was excess cloth piled up on top
of his shoes. "I couldn't see you over all those heads," he said.

I was still fuming, a resentful drunk, and I took my anger
out on him. "You couldn't see any normal human being over
here from where you were standing. I'm not a giraffe. For your

information, sir, a lot of navy pilots are five seven. Why don't you try calling Audie Murphy a runt? You do and you'll wake up in St. Vincent's Infirmary."

He paid no attention to this rant. "My bus broke down and I need to get back on the road," he said. "When are you leaving?"

"They won't let me talk in here."

"Who won't?"

"All these juiceheads. You'd think they owned the place. I have just as much right to be here as they do and if they don't want to hear about the greenhouse they can all kiss my ass! These juiceheads never grew anything in their lives!"

Neither had I for that matter but it wasn't the same thing. The old man introduced himself as Dr. Reo Symes. He looked to be in bad health. His belt was about eight inches too long, with the end curling out limp from the buckle. There were dark bags under his eyes and he had long meaty ears. One eye was badly inflamed and this was the thing that made me feel I was talking to Mr. Proctor or Mr. Meigs.

He said he was from Louisiana and had been making his way to British Honduras when his school-bus camper broke down. He was the owner of The Dog of the South. He asked if he might ride along with me and share the expenses. Overdoing everything like the disgusting drunk that I was, I told him that he would be more than welcome and that there would be absolutely no charge. His company would be payment enough. He questioned me about my driving skills and I assured him that I was a good driver. He said he was afraid to take a Mexican bus because the drivers here had a reputation for trying to beat out locomotives at grade crossings. He offered me some money in advance and I waved it aside. I told him I would pick him up in the morning.

I had planned on searching the sky that night for the Southern Cross and the Coalsack but when I left the bar it was overcast and drizzling rain. I bought two hot dogs from a man pushing a cart around the square. One block away the town was totally dark. I staggered down the middle of the cobbled street and tried to make it appear that I was sauntering. In the darkened doorways there were people smoking cigarettes and thinking their Mexican thoughts.

A hotel cat, a white one, followed me up the stairs to my room and I gave him one of the hot dogs. I didn't let him in the room. That would be a misplaced kindness. He would take up with me and then I would have to leave. Just inside the door there was a full-length mirror and the image it gave back was wavy and yellowish. I knew that Norma must have stood before it and adjusted her clothes. What would she be wearing? I liked her best in her winter clothes and I couldn't remember much about her summer things. What a knockout she was in her white coat and her red knit cap! With Jack Frost nipping her cheeks and her wavy nose!

# *Four*

---

Rain was still falling when I got up in the morning. After I had paid the hotel bill, I had seven or eight dollars and around sixty pesos left. There was a terrible metallic clatter when I tried to start the car. A bad water pump or a bad universal joint will give you notice before it goes but this was some sudden and major failure, or so I thought. A broken connecting rod or a broken timing chain. Strength of materials! Well, I said to myself, the little Buick is done.

I got out and opened the hood. There was the white cat, decapitated by the fan blades. I couldn't believe it. He had crawled up into the engine compartment of this car, not another car, and there was my bloody handiwork. I couldn't handle anything. I couldn't even manage the minor decencies of life. I could hardly get my breath and I walked around and around the car.

A boy with some schoolbooks stopped to watch me and I gave him ten pesos to remove the carcass. I tried to get a grip on myself. Idleness and solitude led to these dramatics: an ordinary turd indulging himself as the chief of sinners. I drove down to the square and waited for the bank to open. My hands were shaking. I had read somewhere that white cats were very often deaf, like Dalmatian dogs. I had dry mouth and tunnel vision.

The bank manager said he could not cash the bonds but he could accept them as a deposit if I wished to open a checking account. They should clear in about a month. A month! Why had I not cashed them all in the States? What a piddler! Norma would have enjoyed this and I couldn't have blamed her for it. I was always impatient with this kind of childish improvidence in other people.

The Siesta trailer park was now a field of mud. Dr. Symes was having coffee in his white Ford bus. The passenger seats had been removed from the thing and replaced by a clutter of household furnishings that had not been anchored or scaled down or customized in any way. There was a dirty mattress on the floor and a jumble of boxes and chairs and tables. It was an old man's mess on top of a hippie mess. I accepted a roll and passed up the coffee. I loved those Mexican rolls but I didn't like the looks of the doctor's cup and I've never cared for instant coffee because it has no smell.

I was frank with him. I explained the bonds problem and I showed him exactly how much money I had. It was a bad moment. I was already embarrassed by my behavior in the bar and now, after all the expansive talk of a free ride, I was making myself look like a cheap liar. I made him a proposition. I would drive him to British Honduras if he would pay for the gasoline and other expenses. When we reached Belize, I would wire home for money and repay him half of his outlay. In the meantime I would give him five of my savings bonds to hold.

He was suspicious and I could understand that, although the deal seemed fair enough to me. The bonds were not negotiable, he said, and they were of no use to him. I pointed out that they did have a certain hostage value. It would be in my interest to redeem them. He looked at me and he looked outside at the car. It sat funny because the tires were of different sizes. He said, "All right then, let's go," and he flung his coffee through a window.

There was a staple-and-hasp affair on the bus door and he locked it with a brass padlock. He brought along his grip and a gallon of drinking water in a plastic jug and a sack of marshmallows. We left The Dog of the South parked there in the mud.

He was wary. He had little to say. He tried the radio, longer than I would have, and then gave it up. He said, "If a man wanted to get the news in this car, he would be out of luck, wouldn't he?"

"This is not my car. Everything works in my car."

The skies were clearing and the morning sun was blinding. He reached up for the right-hand sun visor that had never been there. His hand fell away and he grunted.

"It runs okay," I said.

"What's all that vibration?"

"The motor mounts are shot."

"The what?"

"The motor mounts. They look like black jelly down there. A V-6 shakes a lot anyway. It'll be all right after we get up some speed."

"Do you think it'll make it?"

"Yes, I do. It's a good car." I had said that just to be saying something but I thought it over and decided it was true.

"I hope a wheel doesn't fly off this thing," he said.

"I do too."

He worried a lot about that, a wheel flying off, and I gathered it had happened to him once and made an impression on him.

When we reached Celaya, which was only thirty miles or so from San Miguel, I left the highway and went downtown. I drove slowly up one street and down another. I thought I might see some shell-pocked buildings or at least a statue or a plaque of some kind.

Dr. Symes said, "What are you doing now?"

"This is Celaya."

"What about it?"

"There was a big battle here in 1915."

"I never heard of this place."

"I figure it was the third bloodiest battle ever fought in this hemisphere."

"So what?"

"Some sources say the fourth bloodiest. Obregón lost his arm here. Pancho Villa's army was routed. Do you know what he said?"

"No."

"He said, 'I would rather have been beaten by a Chinaman than by that *perfumado*, Obregón.'"

"Who were they fighting?"

"It was a civil war. They were fighting each other."

"I never heard of it."

"Well, it wasn't that long ago, and it was all right here, in this very town. I'll bet there are plenty of old-timers walking around here who were in that fight. If my Spanish was better, I would try to find one and talk to him."

"Let's don't do that."

The doctor made a show of counting his money. He said he had only about fifty dollars. His scuffed leather wallet was about a foot long and it was chained to his clothing in some way. It was like the big wallets carried by route men, by milkmen and potato-chip men.

There were three grades of gasoline in Mexico at that time and I had been buying the top grade, the Pemex 100. Now, to save money, the doctor's money, I began using the middle grade, which was supposed to be around 90 octane. I don't believe it was that high, because on the long mountain pulls the pistons rattled like empty bottles in a sack.

This noise bothered the doctor. He said, "The old Model A had a spark advance you could manipulate. I don't know why they got rid of it. Well, that's your Detroit smarties. The hand choke too. That's gone. *Been* gone."

"What's wrong with your bus?"

"I think it's a burnt wheel bearing. My right front wheel. The wheel was shaking and there was a grinding racket coming out of that hub. I had a man look at it in a garage in Ciudad Victoria."

"What did he say?"

"I don't know what he said. He greased it. I went on and it did all right for a while. Then that wheel commenced shaking again and I was afraid that booger might fly off on me."

But the doctor didn't talk much, except to make complaints, and I thought it was going to be a long silent trip. I made some travel observations. I said that Mexican parents seemed to be kinder and more affectionate to their children than American parents. He said nothing. I remarked on the new buildings, on the flamboyant Mexican architecture. He said, "There's not much going on inside those buildings."

My abrupt steering movements bothered him too. He sat rigid in the seat and watched and listened. He complained about the dog smell on the seat and the dust that came up from the floor. He drank from a bottle of B and B liqueur. He said he had the chronic bronchitis of a singer and had used this liqueur for his throat ever since the government had barred the use of codeine in cough syrup.

"Pure baloney," he said. "I've seen every kind of addict there is and I've never known one person who was addicted to codeine. I've taken fifty gallons of the stuff myself. Wine will drive you crazy faster than anything I know and you can buy all the wine you want. Well, that's your Washington smarties. They know everything."

"Are you a medical doctor?"

"I'm not in active practice at this time."

"I once looked into medicine myself. I sent off for some university catalogues."

"I'm retired from active practice."

"These doctors make plenty of money."

"That's generally true, yes. I would be well fixed today if I had paid more attention to my screening methods. Screening is your big worry. I was always more concerned with healing. That was a serious mistake on my part. My entire life was ruined by a man named Brimlett. I didn't screen him."

After a time he seemed to realize that I wasn't going to rob him and I wasn't going to wreck the car. He relaxed and took off his big hat. There was a pointed crest of hair at the back of his head like that of a jaybird. He couldn't remember my name and he kept calling me "Speed."

I learned that he had been dwelling in the shadows for several years. He had sold hi-lo shag carpet remnants and velvet paintings from the back of a truck in California. He had sold wide shoes by mail, shoes that must have been almost round, at widths up to EEEEEE. He had sold gladiola bulbs and vitamins for men and fat-melting pills and all-purpose hooks and hail-damaged pears. He had picked up small fees counseling veterans on how to fake chest pains so as to gain immediate admission to V.A. hospitals and a free week in bed. He had sold ranchettes in Colorado and unregistered securities in Arkansas.

He said he had had very little trouble with the law in recent years, although he had been arrested twice in California: once for disturbing divine service, and again for impersonating a naval officer. They were trifling matters. He was collared in San Diego on the last charge; the uniform was a poor fit and he was too old for the modest rank he had assumed. He said he was only trying to establish a short line of credit at a bank. A friend from Tijuana named Rod Garza bailed him out and the thing never even came to trial. The church arrest had grown out of a squabble with some choir members who had pinched him and bitten him and goosed him. They were trying to force him out of the choir, he said, because they claimed he sang at an odd tempo and threw them off the beat. One Sunday he turned on them and whipped at them with a short piece of grass rope. Some of the women cried.

I asked him if he had ever visited Yosemite National Park when he was in California.

"No, I never did."

"What about Muir Woods?"

"What?"

"Muir Woods. Near San Francisco."

"I never heard of it."

"I'd like to see some of that country. I've been to New Mexico and Arizona but I never made it all the way to California. I'd like to go out there sometime."

"You'll love it if you like to see big buck niggers strutting around town kissing white women on the mouth and fondling their titties in public. They're running wild out there, Speed. They're water-skiing out there now. If I was a nigger, that's where I would go. It was a nigger policeman that arrested me outside that little church in Riverside. Can you beat it? He put the cuffs on me too, like I was Billy Cook. You don't expect a California nigger to defer to a white man but I thought he might have shown some consideration for my age."

"Did you go to jail?"

"Just overnight, till Monday morning. The municipal judge fined me thirty-five dollars and told me to find myself another church to sing in."

I asked him if he was going to British Honduras on vacation and he said, "Vacation! Do you think I'm the kind of man who takes vacations?"

"What are you going down there for?"

"My mother's there. I need to see her."

His mother! I couldn't believe it. "Is she sick?" I said.

"I don't know. I need to see her on some business."

"How old is she?"

"She's so old she's walking sideways. I hate to see it too. That's a bad sign. When these old folks start creeping around and shuffling their feet, church is about out."

He wanted to see her about some land she owned in Louisiana near the town of Ferriday. It was an island in the Mississippi River called Jean's Island.

"It's not doing her any good," he said. "She's just turned it over to the birds and snakes. She pays taxes on it every year and there's not one penny of income. There's no gain at all except for the appreciated value. She won't give it to me and she won't let me use it. She's my mother and I think the world of her but she's hard to do business with."

"It's not cultivated land?"

"No, it's just rough timber. The potential is enormous. The black-walnut trees alone are worth fifty thousand dollars for furniture veneer. The stumps could then be cut up and made into pistol grips. How does fifty thousand dollars sound to you?"

"It sounds pretty good."

"Some of those trees are whoppers. Double trunks."

"Maybe you could get a timber lease."

"I'd take a lease if I could get it. What I want is a deed. I don't mean a quitclaim either, I mean a warranty deed with a seal on it. So you understand what I'm telling you?"

"Yes."

"Did you say *timber* lease?"

"Yes."

"That's what I thought you said. Why would you want to cut the timber?"

"That was your idea. The walnut trees."

"I was only trying to suggest to you the value of the place. I'm not going to cut those trees. Are you crazy? Cut the trees and the whole thing would wash away and then where would you be? Do you want my opinion? I say leave the trees and make a private hunting preserve out of the place. I'm not talking about squirrels and ducks either. I mean stock the place with some real brutes. Wart hogs and Cape buffalo. I don't say it would be cheap but these hunters have plenty of money and they don't mind spending it."

"That's not a bad idea."

"I've got a hundred ideas better than that but Mama won't answer my letters. What about a Christian boys' ranch? It's an ideal setting. You'd think that would appeal to her, wouldn't you? Well, you'd be wrong. How about a theme park? Jefferson Davis Land. It's not far from the old Davis plantation. Listen to this. I would dress up like Davis in a frock coat and greet the tourists as they stepped off the ferry. I would glower at them like old Davis with his cloudy eye and the children would cry and clutch their mothers' hands and then—here's the payoff —they would see the twinkle in my clear eye. I'd have Lee too, and Jackson and Albert Sidney Johnston, walking around the midway. Hire some people with beards, you know, to do that. I wouldn't have Braxton Bragg or Joseph E. Johnston. Every afternoon at three Lee would take off his gray coat and wrestle an alligator in a mud hole. Prize drawings. A lot of T-shirts and maybe a few black-and-white portables. If you don't like that, how about a stock-car track? Year-round racing with hardly any rules. Deadly curves right on the water. The Symes 500 on Christmas Day. Get a promotional tie-in with the Sugar Bowl. How about an industrial park? How about a high-rise condominium with a roof garden? How about a baseball clinic? How about a monkey island? I don't say it would be cheap. Nobody's going to pay to see one or two monkeys these days. People want to see a lot of monkeys. I've got plenty of ideas but first I have to get my hands on the island. Can you see what I'm driving at? It's the hottest piece of real estate in Louisiana, bar none."

"Are you a student of the Civil War, Dr. Symes?"

"No, but my father was."

"What was that about Bragg? You said you wouldn't have Bragg walking around in your park."

"My father had no time for Bragg or Joseph E. Johnston. He always said Bragg lost the war. What do you know about these revolving restaurants, Speed?"

"I don't know anything about them but I can tell you that Braxton Bragg didn't lose the war by himself."

"I'm talking about these restaurants up on top of buildings that turn around and around while the people are in there eating."

"I know what you're talking about but I've never been in one. Look here, you can't just go around saying Braxton Bragg lost the war."

"My father said he lost it at Chickamauga."

"I know what Bragg did at Chickamauga, or rather what he didn't do. I can't accept Joseph E. Johnston's excuses either for not going to help Pemberton but I don't go around saying he lost the war."

"Well, my father believed it. Pollard was his man. A fellow named Pollard, he said, wrote the only fair account of the thing."

"I've read Pollard. He calls Lincoln the Illinois ape."

"Pollard was his man. I don't read that old-timey stuff myself. That's water over the dam. I've never wasted my time with that trash. What's your personal opinion of these revolving restaurants?"

"I think they're all right."

"Leon Vurro's wife said I should have a fifty-story tower right in the middle of the park with a revolving restaurant on top. What do you think?"

"I think it would be all right."

"That's your opinion. I happen to have my own. Let's cost it out. Let's look a little closer. All right, your sap tourists and honeymooners are up there eating and they say, 'Let's see, are we looking into Louisiana now or Mississippi, which?' I say what the hell difference would it make? One side of the river looks just like the other. You think it would be cheap? All that machinery? Gears and chains breaking every day? You'd have to hire two or three union bastards full time just to keep it working. What about your light bill? A thousand dollars a month? Two thousand? You'd have to charge eighteen dollars for a steak to come out on a deal like that. And just so some sap and his family can see three hundred and sixty degrees of the same damned cotton fields. I don't like it myself. Do you have the faintest notion of what it would cost to erect a fifty-story tower? No, you don't, and neither does Bella Vurro. And you probably don't care. I'm the poor son of a bitch who will have to shoulder the debt."

"Look here. Dr. Symes, I know that Bragg should have been relieved earlier. Everybody knows that today. Joe Johnston too, but that's a long way from saying they lost the war."

"What line of work are you in, Speed?"

"I'm back in college now. I'm trying to pick up some education hours so I can get a teaching certificate."

"What you are then is a thirty-year-old schoolboy."

"I'm twenty-six."

"Well, I don't guess you're bothering anybody."

"The Civil War used to be my field."

"A big waste of time."

"I didn't think so. I studied for two years at Ole Miss under Dr. Buddy Casey. He's a fine man and a fine scholar."

"You might as well loiter for two years. You might as well play Parcheesi for two years."

"That's a foolish remark."

"You think so?"

"It's dumb."

"All right, listen to me. Are you a reader? Do you read a lot of books?"

"I read quite a bit."

"And you come from a family of readers, right?"

"No, that's not right. That's completely wrong. My father doesn't own six books. He reads the paper about twice a week. He reads fishing magazines and he reads the construction bids. He works. He doesn't have time to read."

"But you're a big reader yourself."

"I have more than four hundred volumes of military history in my apartment. All told, I have sixty-six lineal feet of books."

"All right, now listen to me. Throw that trash out the window. Every bit of it."

He reached into his grip and brought out a little book with yellow paper covers. The cellophane that had once been bonded to the covers was cracked and peeling. He flourished the book. "Throw all that dead stuff out the window and put this on your shelf. Put it by your bed."

What a statement! Books, heavy ones, flying out the windows of the Rhino apartment! I couldn't take my eyes from the road for very long but I glanced at the cover. The title was *With Wings as Eagles* and the author was John Selmer Dix, M.A.

Dr. Symes turned through the pages. "Dix wrote this book forty years ago and it's still just as fresh as the morning dew. Well, why shouldn't it be? The truth never dies. Now this is a first edition. That's important. This is the one you want. Remember the yellow cover. They've changed up things in these later editions. Just a word here and there but it adds up. I don't know who's behind it. They'll have Marvin watching television instead of listening to dance music on the radio. Stuff like that. This is the one you want. This is straight Dix. This is the book you want on your night table right beside your glass of water, *With Wings as Eagles* in the yellow cover. Dix was the greatest man of our time. He was truly a master of the arts, and of some of the sciences too. He was the greatest writer who ever lived."

"They say Shakespeare was the greatest writer who ever lived."

"Dix puts William Shakespeare in the shithouse."

"I've never heard of him. Where is he from?"

"He was from all over. He's dead now. He's buried in Ardmore, Oklahoma. He got his mail in Fort Worth, Texas."

"Did he live in Fort Worth?"

"He lived all over. Do you know the old Elks Club in Shreveport?"

"No."

"Not the new one. I'm not talking about the new lodge."

"I don't know anything about Shreveport."

"Well, it doesn't matter. It's one of my great regrets that I never got to meet Dix. He died broke in a railroad hotel in Tulsa. The last thing he saw from his window is anyone's guess. They never found his trunk, you know. He had a big tin trunk that was all tied up with wire and ropes and belts and straps, and he took it with him everywhere. They never found it. Nobody knows what happened to it. Nobody even knows what was in the trunk."

"Well, his clothes, don't you think?"

"No, he didn't have any clothes to speak of. No *change* of clothes. His famous slippers of course."

"His correspondence maybe."

"He burned all letters unread. I don't want to hear any more of your guesses. Do you think you're going to hit on the answer right off? Smarter people than you have been studying this problem for years."

"Books then."

"No, no, no. Dix never read anything but the daily papers. He *wrote* books, he didn't have to read them. No, he traveled light except for the trunk. He did his clearest thinking while moving. He did all his best work on a bus. Do you know that express bus that leaves Dallas every day at noon for Los Angeles? That's the one he liked. He rode back and forth on it for an entire year when he was working on *Wings*. He saw the seasons change on that bus. He knew all the drivers. He had a board that he put on his lap so he could spread his stuff out, you see, and work right there in his seat by the window."

"I don't see how you could ride a bus for a year."

"He was completely exhausted at the end of that year and he never fully recovered his health. His tin trunk had a thousand dents in it by that time and the hinges and latches were little better than a joke. That's when he began tying it up with ropes and belts. His mouth was bleeding from scurvy, from mucosal lesions and suppurating ulcers, his gums gone all spongy. He was a broken man all right but by God the work got done. He wrecked his health so that we might have *Wings as Eagles*."

The doctor went on and on. He said that all other writing, compared to Dix's work, was just "foul grunting." I could understand how a man might say such things about the Bible or the Koran, some holy book, but this Dix book, from what I could see of it, was nothing more than an inspirational work for salesmen. Still, I didn't want to judge it too quickly. There might be some useful tips in those pages, some Dix thoughts that would throw a new light on things. I was still on the alert for chance messages.

I asked the doctor what his mother was doing in British Honduras.

"Preaching," he said. "Teaching hygiene to pickaninnies."

"She's not retired?"

"She'll never retire."

"How does she happen to be in British Honduras?"

"She first went down there with some church folks to take clothes to hurricane victims. After my father died in 1950, she went back to help run a mission. Then she just stayed on. The church bosses tried to run her off two or three times but they couldn't get her out because she owned the building. She just started her own church. She says God told her to stay on the job down there. She's deathly afraid of hurricanes but she stays on anyway."

"Do you think God really told her to do that?"

"Well, I don't know. That's the only thing that would keep me down there. Mama claims she likes it. She and Melba both. She lives in the church with her pal Melba. There's a pair for you."

"Have you ever been down there?"

"Just once."

"What's it like?"

"Hot. A bunch of niggers."

"It seems a long way off from everything."

"After you get there it doesn't. It's the same old stuff."

"What does your mother do, go back and forth to Louisiana?"

"No, she doesn't go back at all."

"And you haven't seen her but once since she's been there?"

"It's a hard trip. You see the trouble I'm having. This is my last shot."

"You could fly down in a few hours."

"I've never been interested in aviation."

"I'm going down there after a stolen car."

"Say you are."

He kept twisting about in the seat to look at the cars approaching us from behind. He examined them all as they passed us and once he said to me, "Can you see that man's arms?"

"What man?"

"Driving that station wagon."

"I can see his hands."

"No, his arms. Ski has tattoos on his forearms. Flowers and stars and spiders."

"I can't see his arms. Who is Ski?"

He wouldn't answer me and he had no curiosity at all about my business. I told him about Norma and Dupree. He said nothing, but I could sense his contempt. I was not only a schoolboy but a cuckold too. And broke to boot.

He nodded and dozed whenever I was doing the talking. His heavy crested head would droop over and topple him forward and the angle-head flashlight on his belt would poke him in the belly and wake him. Then he would sit up and do it over again. I could see a tangle of gray hair in his long left ear. I wondered at what age that business started, the hair-in-the-ear business. I was getting on myself. The doctor had taken me for thirty. I felt in my ears and found nothing, but I knew the stuff would be sprouting there soon, perhaps in a matter of hours. I was gaining weight too. In the last few months I had begun to see my own cheeks, little pink horizons.

I was hypnotized by the road. I was leaning forward and I let the speed gradually creep up and I bypassed Mexico City with hardly a thought for Winfield Scott and the heights of Chapultepec. To pass it like that! Mexico City! On the long empty stretches I tried to imagine that I was stationary and that the brown earth was being rolled beneath me by the Buick tires. It was a shaky illusion at best and it broke down entirely when I met another car.

A front tire went flat in a suburb of Puebla and I drove on it for about half a mile. The spare was flat too, and it took the rest of the afternoon to get everything fixed. The casing I had driven on had two breaks in the sidewall. I didn't see how it could be repaired but the Mexican tire man put two boots and an inner tube in the thing and it stood up fine. He was quite a man, doing all this filthy work in the street in front of his mud house without a mechanical tire breaker or an impact wrench or any other kind of special tool.

We found a bakery and bought some rolls and left Puebla in the night. Dr. Symes took a blood-pressure cuff from his grip. He put it on his arm and pumped it up and I had to drive with one hand and hold the flashlight with the other so he could take the reading. He grunted but he didn't say whether it pleased him or not. He crawled over into the back seat and cleared things out of his way and said he was going to take a nap. He threw something out the window and I realized later it must have been my Zachary Taylor book.

"You might keep your eye peeled for a tan station wagon," he said. "I don't know what kind it is but it's a nice car. Texas plates. Dealer plates. Ski will be driving. He's a pale man with no chin. Tattoos on his forearms. He wears a little straw hat with one of those things in the hatband. I can't think of the word."

"Feather."

"No, I can think of feather. This is harder to think of. A brass thing."

"Who is this Ski?"

"Ted Brunowski. He's an old friend of mine. They call him Ski. You know how they call people Ski and Chief and Tex in the army."

"I've never been in the service."

"Did you have asthma?"

"No."

"What are you taking for it?"

"I don't have asthma."

"Have you tried the Chihuahua dogs in your bedroom at night? They say it works. I'm an orthodox physician but I'm also for whatever works. You might try it anyway."

"I have never had asthma."

"The slacker's friend. That's what they called it during the war. I certified many a one at a hundred and fifty bucks a throw."

"What do you want to see this fellow for?"

"It's a tan station wagon. He's a pale man in a straw hat and he has no more chin than a bird. Look for dealer plates. Ski has never been a car dealer but he always has dealer plates. He's not a Mason either but when he shakes your hand he does something with his thumb. He knows how to give the Masonic sign of distress too. He would never show me how to do it. Do you understand what I'm telling you?"

"I understand what you've said so far. Do you want to talk to him or what?"

"Just let me know if you see him."

"Is there some possibility of trouble?"

"There's every possibility."

"You didn't say anything about this."

"Get Ski out of sorts and he'll crack your bones. He'll smack you right in the snout, the foremost part of the body. He'll knock you white-eyed on the least provocation. He'll teach you a lesson you won't soon forget."

"You should have said something about this."

"He kicked a merchant seaman to death down on the ship channel. He was trying to get a line on the Blackie Steadman mob, just trying to do his job, you see, and the chap didn't want to help him."

"You should have told me about all this."

"Blackie was hiring these merchant seamen to do his killings for him. He would hire one of those boys to do the job on the night before he shipped out and by the time the body was found the killer would be in some place like Poland. But Ski got wise to their game."

"What does he want you for?"

"He made short work of that sailor. Ski's all business. He's tough. He's stout. I'm not talking about these puffy muscles from the gymnasium either, I'm talking about hard thick arms like bodark posts. You'd do better to leave him alone."

All this time the doctor was squirming around in the back trying to arrange himself comfortably on the seat. He made the car rock. I was afraid he would bump the door latch and fall out of the car. He hummed and snuffled. He sang one verse of "My Happiness" over and over again, and then, with a church quaver, "He's the Lily of the Valley, the bright and morning star."

I tuned him out. After a while he slept. I roared through the dark mountains, descending mostly, and I thought I would never reach the bottom. I checked the mirror over and over again and I examined every vehicle that passed us. There weren't many. The doctor had given me a tough job and now he was sleeping.

The guidebook advised against driving at night in Mexico but I figured that stuff was written for fools. I was leaning forward again and going at a headlong pace like an ant running home with something. The guidebook was right. It was a nightmare. Trucks with no taillights! Cows and donkeys and bicyclists in the middle of the road! A stalled bus on the crest of a hill! A pile of rocks coming up fast! An overturned truck and ten thousand oranges rolling down the road! I was trying to deal with all this and watch for Ski at the same time and I was furious at Dr. Symes for sleeping through it. I no longer cared whether he fell out or not.

Finally I woke him, although the worst was over by that time.

"What is it?" he said.

"I'm not looking for that station wagon anymore. I've got my hands full up here."

"What?"

"It's driving me crazy. I can't tell what color these cars are."

"What are you talking about?"

"I'm talking about Ski!"

"I wouldn't worry about Ski. Leon Vurro is the man he's looking for. Where did you know Ski?"

"I don't know Ski."

"Do you want me to drive for a while?"

"No, I don't."

"Where are we?"

"I don't know exactly. Out of the mountains anyway. We're near Veracruz somewhere."

I kept thinking I would pull over at some point and sleep until daylight but I couldn't find a place that looked just right. The Pemex stations were too noisy and busy. The doctor had me stop once on the highway so he could put some drops in his red eye. This was a slow and messy business. He flung his elbows out like a skeet shooter. I held the army flashlight for him. He said the drops were cold. While I was at it, I checked the transmission fluid and there were a lot of little blue flashes playing around the engine where the spark-plug cables were cracked and arcing.

He napped again and then he started talking to me about Houston, which he pronounced "Yooston." I like to keep things straight and his movements had me confused. I had thought at first that he came to Mexico direct from Louisiana. Then it was California. Now it was Houston. Ski was from Houston and it was from that same city that the doctor had departed in haste for Mexico, or "Old Mexico" as he called it.

"Who is this Ski anyway?"

"He's an old friend of mine. I thought I told you that."

"Is he a crook?"

"He's a real-estate smarty. He makes money while he's sleeping. He used to be a policeman. He says he made more un-assisted arrests than any other officer in the colorful history of Harris County. I can't vouch for that but I know he made plenty. I've known him for years. I used to play poker with him at the Rice Hotel. I gave distemper shots to his puppies. I removed a benign wart from his shoulder that was as big as a Stuart pecan. It looked like a little man's head, or a baby's head, like it might talk, or cry. I never charged him a dime. Ski has forgotten all that."

"Why did you tell me he was looking for you?"

"He almost caught me at Alvin. It was nip and tuck. Do you know the County Line Lounge between Arcadia and Alvin?"

"No."

"The Uncle Sam Muffler Shop?"

"No."

"Shoe City?"

"No."

"Well, it was right in there where I lost him. That traffic circle is where he tore his britches. I never saw him after that. He has no chin, you know."

"You told me that."

"Captain Hughes of the Rangers used to say that if they ever hanged old Ski they would have to put the rope under his nose."

"Why was he after you?"

"Leon Vurro is the man he really wants."

The highways of Mexico, I thought, must be teeming with American investigators. The doctor and I, neither of us very sinister, had met by chance and we were both being more or less pursued. What about all the others? I had seen some strange birds down here from the States. Creeps! Nuts! Crooks! Fruits! Liars! California dopers!

I tried not to show much interest in his story after the way he had dozed while I was telling mine. It didn't matter, because he paid no attention to other people anyway. He spoke conversational English to all the Mexicans along the way and never seemed to notice that they couldn't understand a word he said.

The story was hard to follow. He and a man named Leon Vurro had put out a tip sheet in Houston called the *Bayou Blue Sheet*. They booked a few bets too, and they handled a few lay-off bets from smaller bookies, with Ski as a silent partner. They worked the national time zones to their advantage in some way that I couldn't understand. Ski had many other interests. He had political connections. No deal was too big or too small for him. He managed to get a contract to publish a directory called *Stouthearted Men*, which was to be a collection of photographs and capsule biographies of all the county supervisors in Texas. Or maybe it was the county clerks. Anyway, Ski and the county officers put up an initial sum of $6,500 for operating expenses. Dr. Symes and Leon Vurro gathered the materials for the book and did some work on the dummy makeup. They also sold advertisements for it. Then Leon Vurro disappeared with the money. That, at any rate, was the doctor's account.

"Leon's an ordinary son of a bitch," he said, "but I didn't think he was an out-and-out crook. He said he was tired. Tired! He was sleeping sixteen hours a day and going to the picture show every afternoon. I was the one who was tired, and hot too, but we could have finished that thing in another two weeks. Sooner than that if Leon had kept his wife out of it. She had to stick her nose into everything. She got the pictures all mixed up. She claimed she had been a trapeze artist with Sells-Floto. Told fortunes is more like it. Reader and Advisor is more like it. A bullwhip act is more like it. She looked like a gypsy to me. With that fat ass she would have broke the trapeze ropes. Gone through the net like a shot. We had to work fast, you see, because the pictures were turning green and curling up. I don't know how they got wet. There's a lot of mildew in Houston. You can bet I got tired of looking at those things. I wish you could have seen those faces, Speed. Prune Face and BB Eyes are not in it with those boys."

"You must think I'm a dope," I said. "You never intended to publish that book."

"No, it was a straight deal. Do you know the Moon Publishing Company?"

"No."

"They have offices in Palestine, Texas, and Muldrow, Oklahoma."

"I've never heard of it."

"It's a well-known outfit. They do job printing and they put out calendars and cookbooks and flying-saucer books and children's books, books on boating safety, all kinds of stuff. *A Boy's Life of Lyndon B. Johnson.* That's a Moon book. It was a straight enough deal."

"How much money did Leon Vurro get?"

"I don't know. Whatever was there, he cleaned it out. It's a shame too. We could have finished that thing in two weeks. We were already through the M's and that was halfway. More, really, because there wouldn't be many X's and Z's. You never know. Maybe Leon was right. You have to know when to lay 'em down. It was a weekend deal, you see. There's a lot of mischief on weekends and not just check-kiting either. Leon cleared out the account on Friday afternoon. I was in San Antonio trying to sell ads for that fool book. The word got out fast on Leon but it didn't get to me. It didn't reach the Alamo City. I got back in my room in Houston on Sunday night. I was staying at Jim's Modern Cabins out on Galveston Road. My cabin was dark and the window was open. You had to leave your windows open. Jim doesn't have air conditioning except in his own office. He's got a big window unit in his office that will rattle the walls. I walked by my front window and I could smell Ski's fruity breath. He has diabetes, you see. These young doctors tell everybody they have diabetes but Ski really has it. I knew he was waiting inside that cabin in the dark and I didn't know why. I left with hardly any delay and then it was nip and tuck in south Houston. I made it on down to Corpus and traded my car for that hippie bus at the first car lot that opened up. I knew I didn't have any business driving a car forty feet long but that was the only unit on the lot the fellow would trade even for. I thought it might make a nice little home on the road. Your top gospel singers all have private buses."

"Why would Ski be after you if Leon Vurro got the money?"

"Leon's wife was behind all that. Bella set that up. I never said she was dumb."

"How do you know all that stuff if you left town so fast? That part is not clear to me."

"You get a feel for these things."

"I don't see how you could get a feel for all the circumstances."

"I should never have tied up with Leon. People like that can do nothing but drag you down. He didn't know the first thing about meeting the public and he was never dressed properly. They'll bury that son of a bitch in his zipper jacket."

"How did you know, for instance, that Leon had cleaned out the bank account?"

"I always tried to help Leon and you see the thanks I got. I hired him to drive for me right after his rat died. He was with Murrell Brothers Shows at that time, exhibiting a fifty-pound rat from the sewers of Paris, France. Of course it didn't really weigh fifty pounds and it wasn't your true rat and it wasn't from Paris, France, either. It was some kind of animal from South America. Anyway, the thing died and I hired Leon to drive for me. I was selling birthstone rings and vibrating jowl straps from door to door and he would let me out at one end of the block and wait on me at the other end. He could handle that all right. That was just about his speed. I made a serious mistake when I promoted Leon to a higher level of responsibility."

I pressed the doctor with searching questions about the Houston blowout but I couldn't get any straight answers and so I gave it up.

# Five

---

THE SUN came up out of the sea, or I should say the Bay of Campeche. The warm air seemed heavy and I had the fanciful notion that it was pressing against us and holding us back. I say "seemed" because I know as well as any professional pilot that warm air is less dense than cool air. I had forgotten about the baloney and cheese in the ice chest. We ate the marshmallows and rolls, and after the rolls got hard I threw them out to goats along the way.

In the town of Coatzacoalcos I double-parked on a narrow street in front of an auto supply store and bought two quarts of transmission fluid and a small can of solvent. This solvent was a patent medicine from the States that was supposed to cure sticking valves and noisy valve lifters. Dr. Symes was worried about the clicking noise. He wouldn't shut up about it.

Down the way I found a shady grove of palm trees just off the road. I got out my plastic funnel and red fluid and topped up the transmission. Then I read all the print on the solvent can. There were warnings about breathing the stuff and lengthy instructions as to its use. At the very bottom there was a hedging note in red that had caught my eye too late: "May take two cans." I poured half of it through the carburetor at a fast idle and emptied the rest into the crankcase. The clicking went on as before.

Dr. Symes said, "I can still hear it. I think you've made it worse. I think it's louder than it was."

"It hasn't had time to work yet."

"How long does it take?"

"It says about five minutes. It says it may take two cans."

"How many cans did you get?"

"One."

"Why didn't you get two?"

"I didn't know that at the time."

He took the empty can from me and studied it. He found the red note and pointed it out to me. "It says, 'May take two cans.'"

"I know what it says now."

"You should have known a car like this would need two cans."

"How was I to know that? I didn't have time to read all that stuff."

"We'll never get there!"

"Yes, we will."

"Never! We'll never make it! Look how little it is!" The size of the can was funny to him. He went into a laughing fit and then a coughing fit, which in turn triggered a sneezing fit.

"Half of the cars on the road are making this noise," I said. "It's not serious. The engine's not going to stop."

"One can! One can of this shit wouldn't fix a lawn mower and you expect it to fix a Buick! Fifty cans would be more like it! You chump! You said you'd take me to Mama and you don't even know where we are! You don't know your ass from first base! I never can get where I want to go because I'm always stuck with chumps like you! Rolling along! Oh, yes! Rolling along! Rolling on home to Mama!"

He sang these last words to a little tune.

I knew where we were all right. It was the doctor himself who had funny notions about geography. He thought we were driving along the Pacific Ocean, and he had the idea that a momentary lapse at the wheel, one wrong turn, would always lead to monstrous circular error, taking us back where we started. Maybe it had happened to him a lot.

We drove straight through without stopping anywhere to sleep. The road was closed on the direct route across southern Campeche and so we had to take the longer coastal road, which meant waiting for ferries and crossing on them in the night. It also meant that we had to go north up into Yucatán and then south again through Quintana Roo to the border town of Chetumal.

What these ferries crossed were the mouths of rivers along the Gulf, two rivers and a lagoon, I believe, or maybe the other way around, a long stretch of delta at any rate. Dr. Symes remained in the car and I strode the decks and took the air, although there was nothing to see in the darkness, nothing but the bow waves, curling and glassy. There was fog too, and once again I was denied the spectacle of the southern heavens.

I had told the doctor that the engine wasn't going to stop and then in the midday heat of Yucatán it did stop. He might have thrown one of his fits if we had not been in a village with people standing around watching us. He sulked instead. I thought the fuel filter was clogged, the little sintered bronze device in the side of the carburetor. I borrowed two pairs of pliers and got it out and rapped it and blew through it. That didn't help. A Mexican truck driver diagnosed the trouble as vapor lock. He draped a wet rag over the fuel pump to cool it down, to condense the vapor in the gas line. I had never seen that trick before but it worked and we were soon off again.

The road was flat and straight in this country and there was very little traffic. Visibility was good too. I decided to let the doctor drive for a bit while I took a short nap. We swapped seats. He was a better driver than I had any reason to expect. I've seen many worse. The steering slack didn't throw him at all. Still he had his own style and there was to be no sleeping with him at the wheel. He would hold the accelerator down for about four seconds and then let up on it. Then he would press it down again and let up on it again. That was the way he drove. I was rocking back and forth like one of those toy birds that drinks water from a glass.

I tried to read the Dix book. I couldn't seem to penetrate the man's message. The pages were brittle and the type was heavy and black and hard to read. There were tips on how to turn disadvantages into advantages and how to take insults and rebuffs in stride. The good salesman must make *one more call*, Dix said, before stopping for the day. That might be the big one! He said you must save your money but you must not be afraid to spend it either, and at the same time you must give no thought to money. A lot of his stuff was formulated in this way. You must do this and that, two contrary things, and you must also be careful to do neither. Dynamic tension! Avoid excessive blinking and wild eye movement, Dix said, when talking to prospects. Restrain your hands. Watch for openings, for the tiniest breaches. These were good enough tips in their way but I had been led to expect balls of fire. I became impatient with the thing. The doctor had deposited bits of gray snot on every page and these boogers were dried and crystallized.

"This car seems to be going sideways," he said to me.

The car wasn't going sideways and I didn't bother to answer him.

A little later he said, "This engine seems to be sucking air."

I let that go too. He began to talk about his youth, about his days as a medical student at Wooten Institute in New Orleans. I couldn't follow all that stuff and I tuned him out as best I could. He ended the long account by saying that Dr. Wooten "invented clamps."

"Medical clamps?" I idly inquired.

"No, just clamps. He invented the clamp."

"I don't understand that. What kind of clamp are you talking about?"

"Clamps! Clamps! That you hold two things together with! Can't you understand plain English?"

"Are you saying this man made the first clamp?"

"He got a patent on it. He invented the clamp."

"No, he didn't."

"Then who did?"

"I don't know."

"You don't know. And you don't know Smitty Wooten either but you want to tell me he didn't invent the clamp."

"He may have invented some special kind of clamp but he didn't invent *the clamp*. The principle of the clamp was probably known to the Sumerians. You can't go around saying this fellow from Louisiana invented the clamp."

"He was the finest diagnostician of our time. I suppose you deny that too."

"That's something else."

"No, go ahead. Attack him all you please. He's dead now and can't defend himself. Call him a liar and a bum. It's great sport for people who sit on the sidelines of life. They do the same thing with Dix. People who aren't fit to utter his name."

I didn't want to provoke another frenzy while he was driving, so I let the matter drop. There was very little traffic, as I say, in that desolate green scrubland, and no rivers and creeks at all, but he managed to find a narrow bridge and meet a cattle truck on it. As soon as the truck hove into view, a good half-mile away, the doctor began to make delicate speed adjustments so as to assure an encounter in the exact center of the bridge. We clipped a mirror off the truck and when we were well clear of the scene I took the wheel again.

Then one of the motor mounts snapped. The decayed rubber finally gave way. Strength of materials! With this support gone the least acceleration would throw the engine over to the right from the torque, and the fan blades would clatter against the shroud. I straightened out two coat hangers and fastened one end of the stiff wires to the exhaust manifold on the left side, and anchored the other ends to the frame member. This steadied the engine somewhat and kept it from jumping over so far. I thought it was a clever piece of work, even though I had burned my fingers on the manifold.

For a little car it had a lot of secrets. Another tire went flat near Chetumal, the left rear, and I almost twisted the lug bolts off before I figured out that they had left-hand threads. Far from being clever, I was slow and stupid! Of all the odd-sized tires on the car this one was the smallest, and when I got it off I saw molded in the rubber these words: "Property of U-Haul Co. Not to be sold." A trailer tire!

Dr. Symes waited in the shade of some bushes. My blistered fingers hurt and I was angry at myself and I was hot and dirty and thirsty. I asked him to bring me the water jug. He didn't answer and I spoke to him again, sharply. He just stared at me with his mouth open. His face was gray and he was breathing hard. One eye was closed, the red one. The old man was sick! No laughing fits here!

I took the grip and the water jug to him. He drank some chalky-looking medicine and almost gagged on it. He said he was dizzy. He didn't want to move for a few minutes. I drank the last of the tepid water in the jug and lay back in the shade. The sand was coarse and warm. I said I would take him to a doctor in Chetumal. He said, "No, it's just a spell. It'll pass. I'll be all right in a minute. It's not far to Mama's place, is it?"

"No, it's not far now."

He took off his long belt and this seemed to give him some relief. Then he took off his bow tie. He unchained the giant wallet from his clothes and handed it to me, along with his flashlight, and told me to see that his mother got these things, a Mrs. Nell Symes. I didn't like the sound of that. We sat there for a long time and said nothing.

The booted tire thumped all the way in to Chetumal, and then to the border crossing, which was a river just outside of town. The officer there on the Mexican end of the bridge paid no attention to my faulty papers but he didn't like the doctor, didn't want to touch him or brush up against him, this hollow-eyed old gringo with his mouth open, and he was determined not to let him leave Mexico without his bus. Dr. Symes's tourist card was clearly stamped "*Entro con Automóvil*," as was mine, and if one enters Mexico with an *automóvil* then one must also leave with it.

I explained that the doctor's bus had broken down through no fault of his own and that he intended to return for it after a brief visit with his ailing mother in Belize. The officer said that anyone might tell such a story, which was true enough. The law was the law. Produce the bus. Dr. Symes offered the man a hundred pesos and the man studied the brown note for an instant and then shook his head; this was a serious matter and money could not settle it, certainly not a hundred pesos.

I took the doctor aside and suggested that he give the man five hundred pesos. He said, "No, that's too much."

"What are you going to do then?"

"I don't know, but I'm not giving that son of a bitch forty dollars."

I saw a red bus cross the bridge with only a brief inspection at each end. I told the doctor I would take him back to Chetumal. He could wait there until dark and catch a red bus to Belize. Then, very likely, there would be a different officer here at this post. The doctor would probably not be noticed and the bus ride would not be a long one. It was only another eighty miles or so to Belize.

He was wobbly and vague. He had heat staggers. I couldn't get any sense out of him. He had diarrhea too, and he was drinking paregoric from a little bottle. We drove back to Chetumal, the tire bumping.

He said, "Are you going to dump me, Speed?"

"You won't let me take you to a doctor."

"I never thought you would just throw me out."

"I'm not throwing you out. Listen to what I'm saying. You can take a bus across the border tonight. I'll see that you get on it. I'll follow the bus."

"I thought we had a deal."

"I don't know what you expect me to do. I can't force these people to let you out of the country."

"You said you'd take me to Belize. I thought it was a straight deal."

"I'm doing the best I can. You forget I have my own business to see to."

"That's hard, Speed. That's strong. I don't know you but I know that's not worthy of you."

"What you need is a doctor."

"I'll be all right if I can just get something cool to drink."

I parked on the waterfront in Chetumal and got him out of the car and walked him over to a dockside refreshment stand. We sat on folding metal chairs under a palm-thatched cabaña rig. He looked like a dead man. When the waitress came over, he rallied a little and tried to smile. He said, "Little lady, I want the biggest Co'-Cola you are permitted to serve." She was a pretty Indian girl with sharp black eyes. He tried to wink, and said, "They're getting these little girls out of Hollywood now." A man at the next table was eating a whole fresh pineapple with a knife. I ordered a pineapple for myself and a Coca *grande* for the doctor.

There was a rising wind. Small boats were chugging about in the bay. Vultures walked boldly along the dock like domestic turkeys. The doctor drank three Cokes and asked for his wallet back. I gave it to him.

"What happened to my flashlight?"

"It's in the car."

He saw something shiny and leaned over and scratched at it, trying to pick it up.

I said, "That's a nailhead."

"I knew it wasn't a dime. I just wanted to see what it was."

"I've got to get the spare fixed and I need to see about the bus. I want you to wait right here and don't go wandering off."

"I'm not riding any bus."

"What are you going to do then?"

"I'm not going off a cliff in a Mexican bus."

His old carcass was very dear to him.

We sat in silence for a while. I went to the car and got my Esso map of British Honduras. It was a beautiful blue map with hardly any roads to clutter it up. Just down the bay from here was a coastal village in British Honduras called Corozal. Why couldn't the border be bypassed by water? There were plenty of boats available. It wouldn't be much of a trip—a matter of a few miles.

I proposed this plan to the doctor and showed him how things lay on the map. To keep it from blowing away, I had to anchor the corners with bottles. Over and over again I explained the scheme to him but he couldn't take it in. "Do what, Speed?" he would say. He was fading again.

Most of the boats were now coming in. I walked along the dock and talked to the owners, trying to explain and sell the plan to them in my feeble Spanish. I got nowhere. They wanted no part of it. There was too much wind and the water was too rough and it would soon be dark. Maybe tomorrow, they said, or the next day. I put the map back in the car and returned to the table. Dr. Symes was drinking yet another Coke. The girl wanted her money and he was trying to match her for it, double or nothing. He had a ready line of patter for all cashiers, the idea being to confuse them so that they might make an error in his favor.

"It's no use," I said. "The wind is too high. It's too dangerous. It was a bad plan anyway. You'll have to ride the red bus and that's all there is to it."

"The wind?" he said.

Newspapers were being whipped against our legs and the tablecloth was snapping and donkeys were leaning against buildings and the heavy traffic light that hung over the intersection was standing about thirty degrees off vertical, and into the teeth of this gale he asked me that question.

"A bus. I'm going to put you on a bus. It's the only way."

"Not a bus, no."

"Do you want to see your mother or do you want to stay here?"

"Mama?"

"She's waiting for you just down the road. You can be there in no time. The bus is safe, I tell you. This is flat country. There are no mountains between here and Belize, not one. It's a coastal plain. I'll see that you get there. I'll drive right along behind the bus."

"Send me over the mountains in a bus, is that it? That's your answer for everything. Did you make sure it has no brakes? I don't even know the name of this town. I wanted to go to Belize and you land us in this place instead. Why do we keep hanging around here anyway?"

"You can be in Belize in just a few hours if you'll listen to me and do what I say. Do you understand what I'm telling you?"

In my desperation I had fallen into the doctor's habits of speech. He must have spent half his life shouting that hopeless question. I thought of hiring an ambulance. Surely the border guards would not interfere with a mercy dash. But wouldn't it be very expensive?

Someone pinched me on the fleshy part of my upper arm and I jumped. An Indian boy about seventeen years old was standing behind me. "Corozal?" he said. He took me over to the slip where his wooden boat was tied up, a slender homemade craft with an old-fashioned four-cycle outboard engine on the stern. It was about a six-horse engine, with a high profile. I asked about life preservers. *No hay*, he said. I indicated that the water was rough and getting rougher all the time. He shrugged it off as inconsequential. We quickly reached an agreement.

The doctor was too weak and confused to resist. I took his wallet again for safekeeping and we loaded him into the boat. I gave the boy a ten-dollar bill and promised him a twenty— a balloon payment to encourage compliance—upon delivery of the old man in Corozal. The boy jerked the rope many times before the engine started. Then he pushed off and I, with great misgivings, watched them leave, the little boat battering sluggishly through the whitecaps. The sun was going down. The doctor had lied to me about his funds. That wallet was packed with twenties and fifties.

I drove back to the border crossing and had no trouble getting out of Mexico. At the other end of the bridge I had to deal with a British Honduras officer. He was a dapper Negro in shorts and high stockings and Sam Browne belt. I had shed my coat long ago but I was still wearing my tie. I was filthy and I needed a shave.

He asked my occupation. I said I was a businessman. He pointed out that my spare tire was flat. I thanked him. Was I a doctor? What was I doing with a doctor's bag? What was the silverware for? I had no very good answers for him. He poked into everything, even the ice chest. The ice had melted days ago and the cheese and baloney were spoiled. The water was brown from the rusting rims of the beer cans. At the bottom of this mess my Colt Cobra was washing about in the plastic bag. I had forgotten all about it. The old man had made me neglect my business! The officer wiped the pistol dry with a handkerchief and stuck it in his hip pocket. He shook his finger at me but said nothing. He was keeping it for himself.

He asked if I planned to sell the Buick and I said no. He wrote his name and address for me on the back of a card advertising the Fair Play Hotel in Belize and said he would be happy to handle the sale. I took the card and told him I would keep it in mind. He said I didn't look like much of a businessman to him. I described my Torino and asked about Norma and Dupree and the dog—and was I knocked for a loop when this bird said he remembered them. He remembered the car and the pretty girl and yes, the red dog, and the fellow with the glasses who was driving; he remembered him very well.

"Played that 'Sweet Lorraine' on the mouth harp."

"No, that wouldn't be him. That wouldn't be Dupree."

"Yes, and 'Twilight Time' too."

I couldn't believe my ears. Was it possible that some identical people had passed through here with a chow dog in a blue Torino? An antimatter Dupree playing tunes on a mouth organ! A young Meigs! The doctor had told me that I could expect the same old stuff down here but this didn't sound like the same old stuff to me.

I asked about the road to Belize. Was it paved? Should I chance it with no spare tire? He said it was an excellent road, much better than anything I had seen in Mexico. And not only that, but I would now be able to get some good gasoline for a change. The Mexican petrol was inferior stuff, he said, and it smelled funny. Here it had the proper smell.

There was a T-head pier in Corozal and I stood at the end of it and waited anxiously in the dark. The wind had dropped off somewhat. Now it was cool. I supposed there was some colorful local name for it, for this particular kind of wind. I was just fifteen degrees or so above the equator and I was at sea level and yet I was chilly. A cool snap like this on the Louisiana island and the doctor would have a thousand coughing chimps on his hands. I could make out a few stars through the drifting clouds but not the Southern Cross.

I began to worry more and more about that little boat in open water at night. It wasn't the open sea but it was a big bay, big enough for trouble. Why had I suggested this? It would all be my fault, the sea disaster. Criminal folly! The boat would be swamped and the doctor, a nuisance to the end, would flail away in the water and take the Indian boy down with him.

A Spanish-looking man joined me at the edge of the pier. He was barefooted, his trouser legs rolled up, and he was pushing a bicycle. He parked the bike and looked out at the water, his hands in his pockets, a brooding figure. I didn't want to intrude on his thoughts but when the wind blew his bike over I thought it would then be all right to speak, the clatter having broken his reverie. I said, "*Mucho viento.*" He nodded and picked up his bike and left. Much wind. What a remark! No wonder everybody took foreigners for dopes.

I heard the engine popping and then I saw the boat low in the water. Choppy waves were breaking against it. The boy was angry because the doctor had vomited marshmallows and Coke in his boat. The old man was wet and only semiconscious. We laid him out on the pier and let him drain for a minute. It was like trying to lug a wet mattress. I gave the boy an extra ten dollars for his trouble. He helped me get the doctor into the car and then he fearlessly took to the dark water again.

Part of the road to Belize was broken pavement and the rest was washboard gravel. Great flat slabs of concrete had been wrenched out of place as though from an earthquake. What a road! Time after time the Buick's weak coil springs bottomed out, and I mean dead bottom. When we came bounding back up on the return phase, I feared that something would tear loose, some suspension component. I worried about the tires too. The gravel part was only a little better. I tried to find a speed at which we could skim along on the crests of the corrugations but with no luck. We skittered all over the roadbed. The doctor groaned in the back seat. I too was beginning to fade. My head throbbed and I took some more of the bitter orange pills.

# *Six*

---

IT WAS late when we reached Belize and I didn't feel like asking directions and floundering around in a strange place. It wasn't a big town but the streets were narrow and dark and irregular. I found a taxicab at a Shell station and I asked the Negro driver if he knew a Mrs. Nell Symes, who had a church here. It took him a while to puzzle it out. Did I mean "Meemaw"? Well, I didn't know, but I hired him to go to Meemaw's anyway and I trailed along behind in the Buick.

The church was a converted dwelling house, a white frame structure of two stories. Some of the windows had fixed wooden louvers and some had shutters that folded back. The roof was galvanized sheet iron. It was just the kind of old house that needed the Midgestone treatment.

A wooden sign beside the door said:

*Unity Tabernacle*
*"Whosoever will"*

The house was dark and I rapped on the door for a long time before I roused anyone. I heard them coming down the stairs very slowly. The door opened and two old ladies looked out at me. One was in a flannel bathrobe and the other one was wearing a red sweater. The one in the sweater had wisps of pink hair on her scalp. It was a bright chemical pink like that of a dyed Easter chick. I could see at once that the other one was Dr. Symes's mother. She had the same raccoon eyes. She used an aluminum walking stick but she didn't appear to be much more decrepit than the doctor himself.

"Mrs. Symes?"

"Yes?"

"I have your son out here in the car."

"What's that you say?"

"Dr. Symes. He's out here in the car."

"Reo. My word."

"He's sick."

"Who are you?"

"My name is Ray Midge. He rode down from Mexico with me."

"Are you with the postal authorities?"

"No, ma'am."

"We weren't even thinking about Reo, were we, Melba?"

The other lady said, "*I* sure wasn't. I was thinking about a snack."

Mrs. Symes turned back to me. "Has he got some old floozie with him?"

"No, ma'am, he's by himself."

"You say he's in the car?"

"Yes."

"Why is he staying in the car? Why doesn't he get out of the car?"

"He's sick."

"Go see if it's really him, Melba."

Melba came out to the car. I opened a door so the dome light would come on. She studied the rumpled figure in the back seat. "It's Reo all right," she said. "He's asleep. He's lost weight. His clothes are smoking. He's wearing those same old white pants he had on last time. I didn't know pants lasted that long."

Mrs. Symes said, "He may have several pair, all identical. Some men do that with socks."

"I think these are the same pants."

"What about his flashlight?"

"I don't see it."

"It's in there somewhere," I said.

Neither of the ladies was able to help me unload the doctor. I couldn't carry him but I managed to drag him inside, where I laid him out on a church pew. He was limp and his flesh was cool and his clothes were indeed steaming. Then I went back and got his grip. Mrs. Symes was not much concerned about his condition. She seemed to think he was drunk.

"That poison has to be metabolized," she said. "You can't hurry it along."

I said, "He's not drunk, ma'am, he's sick. I believe he needs a doctor."

Melba said, "We don't use doctors."

"You're lucky to have good health."

"Our health is not particularly good. We just don't go to doctors."

The downstairs part was a chapel and they lived upstairs. Mrs. Symes asked if I would like some supper. I don't like to eat or sleep or go to the bathroom in other people's homes but this was an emergency. I needed food and I kept hanging about in hopes of just such an invitation. I followed them up the stairs.

The electric lights flickered on and off and then failed altogether. I sat at the kitchen table in the soft yellow glow of a kerosene lamp. Mrs. Symes gave me some cold chicken and some warmed-over rice and gravy and biscuits. There was a bowl of stewed tomatoes too. What a meal! I was so hungry I was trembling and I made a pig of myself. Melba joined me and fell to on a second supper. She ate heartily for a crone, sighing and cooing between bites and jiggling one leg up and down, making the floor shake. She ate fast and her eyes bulged from inner pressures and delight. This remarkable lady had psychic gifts and she had not slept for three years, or so they told me. She sat up in a chair every night in the dark drinking coffee.

Mrs. Symes asked me a lot of personal questions. She and Melba, unlike the doctor, found my mission romantic, and they pressed for details. I was dizzy and tired and not at all in the mood for a truth session but I didn't see how I could leave abruptly after eating their food. Melba asked to see a picture of Norma. I didn't have one. Some detective! Some husband! They could tell me nothing about Mr. Dupree's farm. They had never heard the name. Their church work was concerned entirely with Negro children, they said, and I gathered that they had little to do with the other white people in the country. They did know some Mennonite farmers, from whom they bought milk, and they seemed to have an uneasy professional acquaintance with an Episcopal missionary whom they called "Father Jackie." Mrs. Symes was suspicious of the doctor's unexpected arrival.

She said, "Do you know the purpose of his visit?"

"He said he was worried about your health."

"What else did he say?"

"He said you had a church here."

"What else?"

"That's about all."

"How would you characterize his mood? Generally speaking."

"I would say it varied according to circumstances. He was not in one mood the whole time."

"I mean his feeling about coming here. Was it one of apprehension? Resignation?"

"I can't say it was either one of those. I don't really know him well enough to answer your question, Mrs. Symes. To say whether his mood departed from normal in any way."

"Is that his automobile out there?"

"No, ma'am. He has a bus but it broke down on him in Mexico."

"A bus?"

"It's an old school bus. It's fixed up so you can sleep in it and cook in it."

"Did you hear that, Melba? Reo has been living in a school bus."

"A school bus?"

"That's what Mr. Midge here says."

"I didn't know you could do that."

"I didn't either. I wonder how he gets his mail."

"He doesn't live in the bus all the time," I said. "It's the kind of thing you take trips in, like a trailer."

"I'll bet Reo talked your head off."

"Well, he didn't talk so much tonight. He's been feeling bad."

"He didn't talk at all until he was six years old. He was a strange child. Otho thought he was simple. What did he tell you about Jean's Island?"

"He said he had some plans for developing it."

"Did he say he owned it?"

"No, he didn't say that. He said you owned it."

"That island was dedicated as a bird sanctuary years ago."

"I see."

"How can you *develop* a place, as you put it, if it's already been dedicated?"

"Well, I don't know. I guess you can't."

"If I turned it over to Reo, the bulldozers would be there tomorrow morning. It would be the biggest mess you ever saw. Some people just love to cut trees and the poor whites are the worst about it. I don't know where Reo gets that streak. Man is the most destructive creature there is, Mr. Midge."

Melba said, "Except for goats. Look at Greece."

"I wouldn't mind letting Reo have the place if he would live on it and farm it and behave himself, but he won't do that. I know him too well. The first thing you know, Marvel Clark or some other floozie would get her hands on it. I know Marvel too well and she's got enough of my stuff as it is. But she will never get her hands on that land as long as I have anything to say about it."

I said, "Do you think I should go downstairs and check on him?"

"He'll be all right. That poison has to be worked out through the breath. What did he tell you about his arthritis clinic in Ferriday?"

"I don't believe he mentioned that."

"Did he tell you about his Gifts for Grads?"

"Gifts for Dads?"

"Gifts for *Grads*. It was a mail-order scheme. He was advertising expensive watches at bargain prices in all kinds of sleazy magazines. People would send him money but he wouldn't send them any watches. A postal inspector came all the way down here from Washington, D.C., looking for him. He said Reo was going all over the country making fraudulent representations and calling himself Ralph Moore and Newton Wilcox."

"Dr. Symes didn't say anything about Gifts for Grads."

"Is that woman Sybil still living with him?"

"I just don't know about that. He was by himself when I met him in Mexico."

"Good riddance then. He brought an old hussy named Sybil with him the last time. She had great big bushy eyebrows like a man. She and Reo were trying to open up a restaurant somewhere in California and they wanted me to put up the money for it. As if I had any money. Reo tells everybody I have money."

Melba said, "No, it was a singing school. Reo wanted to open a singing school."

"The singing school was an entirely different thing, Melba. This was a restaurant they were talking about. Little Bit of

Austria. Sybil was going to sing some kind of foreign songs to the customers while they were eating. She said she was a night-club singer, and a dancer too. She planned to dance all around people's tables while they were trying to eat. I thought these night clubs had beautiful young girls to do that kind of thing but Sybil was almost as old as Reo."

"Older," said Melba. "Don't you remember her arms?"

"They left in the middle of the night. I remember that. Just picked up and left without a word."

"Sybil didn't know one end of a piano keyboard from the other."

"She wore white shiny boots and backless dresses."

"But she didn't wear a girdle."

"She wore hardly anything when she was sunning herself back there in the yard."

"Her shameful parts were covered."

"That goes without saying, Melba. It wasn't necessary for you to say that and make us all think about it."

"Dr. Symes didn't say anything about Sybil to me."

"No, I don't suppose he did. Did he tell you about the hearing-aid frauds of 1949?"

"No, ma'am."

"No, I don't suppose he did. The shame and scandal killed Otho just as sure as we're sitting here. Reo lost his medical license and he's been a sharper and a tramp ever since. My own son, who took an oath to do no harm."

I didn't know who Otho was but it was hard to believe that any person in Louisiana had ever keeled over from fraud shock. I tried to think about that dramatic scene and then Melba put her face in mine and started talking to me. Both ladies were talking to me at the same time.

Melba said that her first husband had abandoned her in Fer-riday and that her second husband, a handsome barber who didn't believe in life insurance, had dropped dead in New Or-leans at the age of forty-four. After that, she made her own way, giving piano lessons and selling foundation garments. She now received a tiny green Social Security check and that was her entire income. Five dollars of it went each month to Gamma chapter of some music teachers' sorority. She didn't remember much about the first husband but she thought often of the opinionated barber husband, idle in his shop in the quiet 1940 New Orleans sunlight, watching the door for customers and searching through the *Times-Picayune* over and over again for unread morsels.

Mrs. Symes raised her voice. "I wish you would hush for a minute, Melba. I've heard all that stuff a thousand times. I'm trying to ask a question. It looks like I could ask one question in my own home."

Melba didn't stop talking but I turned my head a bit toward Mrs. Symes.

She said, "What I'm trying to find out is this. When you are at your home in Arkansas, Mr. Midge, do you get much mail?"

"I don't follow."

"Cards, letters. First-class matter."

"Not much, no, ma'am."

"Same here. I'm not counting all those absurd letters from Reo. Are you a witnessing Christian?"

"I attend church when I can."

"Do you pray every night for all the little babies in Little Rock?"

"No, ma'am, I don't."

"What kind of Christian do you call yourself?"

"I attend church when I can."

"Cards on the table, Mr. Midge."

"Well, I think I have a religious nature. I sometimes find it hard to determine God's will."

"Inconvenient, you mean."

"That too, yes."

"What does it take to keep you from attending church?"

"I go when I can."

"A light rain?"

"I go when I can."

"This 'religious nature' business reminds me of Reo, your man of science. He'll try to tell you that God is out there in the trees and grass somewhere. Some kind of *force*. That's pretty thin stuff if you ask me. And Father Jackie is not much better. He says God is a perfect sphere. A ball, if you will."

"There are many different opinions on the subject."

"Did you suppose I didn't know that?"

"No, ma'am."

"What about Heaven and Hell. Do you believe those places exist?"

"That's a hard one."

"Not for me. How about you, Melba?"

"I would call it an easy one."

"Well, I don't know. I wouldn't be surprised either way. I try not to think about it. It's just so odd to think that people are walking around in Heaven and Hell."

"Yes, but it's odd to find ourselves walking around here too, isn't it?"

"That's true, Mrs. Symes."

"All the children call me Meemaw. Why don't you do like they do and call me Meemaw?"

"Well. All right."

"Have you read the Bible?"

"I've read some of it."

"Do you go through your Bible looking for discrepancies?"

"No, ma'am."

"That's not the way to read it. I have a little test I like to give to people like you who claim to be Bible scholars. Do you mind taking a little test for me?"

"Is it a written test?"

"No, it's just one question."

"I don't mind taking your test, Meemaw, but there is a mis-understanding here. You asked me if I had read the Bible and I said I had read some of it. I did not say I was a Bible scholar."

"We'll soon know, one way or the other. All right, the wedding feast at Cana. John 2. Jesus turned six pots of water into six pots of so-called wine. His first miracle. His mother was there. Now do you believe that was alcoholic wine in those pots or unfermented grape juice?"

"What does the Bible say?"

Melba said, "The Bible just says wine. It says good wine."

"Then that's what I say. I say wine."

Mrs. Symes said, "It's your notion then that Jesus was a bootlegger?"

"No, it's not."

"He was no more a bootlegger than I am. That so-called wine was nothing more than fresh and wholesome grape juice. The word is translated wrong."

"I didn't know that."

"Do you claim to know the meaning of every word in the Greek language?"

"No, I don't. I don't know one word of the Greek language."

"Then why should your opinion be worth anything in a matter like this? Father Jackie is bad enough and you don't even know as much as he does."

Melba said, "Let's see what he knows about Swedenborg."

"He won't know anything about Swedenborg."

"It won't hurt to see, will it?"

"Go ahead and ask him then."

"What do you know about a man named Emanuel Swedenborg, Mr. Midge?"

"I don't know anything about him."

"He personally *visited* Heaven and Hell and returned to write an astonishing book about his experiences. Now what do you think of that?"

"I don't know what to think."

Mrs. Symes said, "Have you read Mrs. Eddy's books?"

"No, ma'am."

"What is your work in this world?"

"I don't know what it is yet. I'm back in school now."

"It's getting pretty late in the day for you to have so few interests and convictions. How old are you, Mr. Midge?"

"I'm twenty-six."

"Later than I thought. Think about this. All the little animals of your youth are long dead."

Melba said, "Except for turtles."

Something small and hard, possibly a nut, dropped on the tin roof and we waited in silence for another one but it didn't come. I asked directions to the Fair Play Hotel, and Meemaw, as I now addressed her, told me I would be more comfortable at the Fort George or the Bellevue. I was agreeable and didn't pursue the matter, but the man at the border had given me a card for the Fair Play and it was there I meant to stay. The lights came back on and in a very few minutes Melba's electric coffeepot began to bubble and make respiratory noises like some infernal hospital machine. Mrs. Symes looked me over closely in the light.

"I know you'll excuse a personal reference, Mr. Midge. Are you handicapped?"

"I don't follow."

She lifted one of my trouser legs an inch or so with the tip of her aluminum cane. "Your feet, I mean. They look odd the way you have them splayed out. They look like artificial feet."

"My feet are all right. These are new shoes. Perhaps that accounts for their unnatural fullness."

"No, it's not that, it's the way you have them turned out. Now there, that's better. You remind me a whole lot of Otho. He never could get the hang of things."

"I've heard you mention Otho two or three times but I don't know who he is."

"Otho Symes, of course. He was my husband. He never could get the hang of things but he was just as good as gold."

Melba said, "He was a nervous little man. I was afraid to say boo to him."

"He wasn't nervous until he had his operation."

"He was nervous before his operation and after his operation both."

"He wasn't nervous until they put that thing in his neck, Melba. I ought to know."

"You ought to but you don't. This boy doesn't want to hear any more about Otho and I don't either. I want to find out something about his wife and why she left him. He hasn't told us that."

"I don't know why she left."

"You must have some idea."

"No, I was very much surprised."

Mrs. Symes said, "Are you trying to tell us that you and your wife were on cordial terms?"

"We got along all right."

"Never a harsh word?"

"She called me a pill sometimes."

"A pill, eh."

"That was her mother's word but Norma took it up."

"They were both calling you a pill to your face?"

"Yes. Not, you know, day and night."

"Did she open your mail and read it?"

"No, ma'am. That is, I don't think she did."

Melba put her rouged face in mine again and said, "One moment, Mr. Midge. You told us just a while ago that you didn't get any mail. Now you're talking about people intercepting your mail. Which is it? Do you get any mail or not?"

"I said I didn't get much mail. I get some."

Mrs. Symes said, "I'll bet the little girl's kitchen was just filthy all the time."

"No, it wasn't either."

"Can she cook anything that's fit to eat?"

"She's a pretty good cook."

"Can she make her own little skirts and jumpers?"

"I don't think so. I've never seen her sewing anything."

"What about raisins? Does she like raisins?"

"I've never seen her eating any raisins."

"I'll bet she likes yellow cake with hot lemon sauce poured over it."

"I believe she does, yes. I do too."

"What about chocolate cake?"

"She likes all kinds of cake."

"All right then, tell me this. When she's eating chocolate cake late at night, does she also drink sweet milk from a quart bottle till it runs from the corners of her mouth?"

"I've never seen her do that."

"That's a picture I have of gluttony."

"I don't know how you got the idea that Norma is a glutton, Meemaw. The fact is, she eats very little. She's very particular about what she eats and how she eats it."

"A clean feeder then, according to you."

"Very clean."

"Melba used to do that very thing late at night. That cake thing with the milk."

"No, I didn't."

"Yes, you did."

"There never was a bigger lie. I don't know why you keep telling people that."

"I know what I know, Melba."

The lights went off again. I thanked them for the supper and the hospitality and got up to leave. Melba asked me to wait a minute. She had the burning lamp in her hand and she had turned the wick up a notch or two for a bright flame. Then she went to a dark corner and struck a pose there with the lamp, holding it above her head. She said, "Now I just wonder if you two can guess who I am."

Mrs. Symes said, "I know. The Statue of Liberty. That's easy."

"No."

"Florence Nightingale then."

"No."

"You're changing it every time I guess it."

"I'm the Light of the World."

"No, you're not, you're just silly. You're so silly, Melba, it's pitiful. It's downright embarrassing to me when we have guests."

This time I did leave but before I got all the way down the stairs Mrs. Symes called after me. She asked if I thought there was any chance that Reo was going about doing good by stealth. It wouldn't have hurt me to say yes, there was an excellent chance of that, but I said I just didn't know. She asked if I had any Lipton's dried soups in the car, or a fall and winter Sears catalogue. Of course I didn't and I felt bad because I had nothing like that to give them, even though they had roughed me up a little with their hard questions.

# *Seven*

I LEFT Dr. Symes steaming in the dark chapel and made my way back to the arched bridge over the little river that ran through Belize. I had guessed, correctly, that this bridge was the center of town. Two or three blocks upstream I found the Fair Play Hotel, which was a white frame house like the tabernacle. I parked the car in front and again went through the unpleasant business of waking people up.

A thin Negro woman was the manager of the place. She was surly, as anyone might have been in the circumstances, but I could sense too a general ill-feeling for me and my kind. She woke a small Negro boy named Webster Spooner, who slept in a box in the foyer. It was a pretty good wooden box with bedding in it. I knew his name because he had written it on a piece of paper and taped it to his box. At the foot of his make-shift bed there was a tomato plant growing in an old Texaco grease bucket.

I wrote and addressed a brief message to my father asking him to wire me $250. The woman said she would have Webster Spooner attend to it when the cable office opened in the morning. I gave her a five-dollar bill and a few ten-peso notes —all the money in my pocket—and she pinned it to the message and put it away in a shoe box.

Would my car be safe on the street? It might be or it might not be, she said, but in any case there was no enclosed parking. I thought of removing the cable from the coil to the distributor so as to foil thieves but I was too weary to fool with that car anymore. The woman, whose name was Ruth, went back to bed. Webster Spooner carried my bag upstairs and showed me to my room. He said he would keep an eye on the car. I didn't see how he was going to do that from his box. I knew he was a sound sleeper. The woman Ruth had almost had to kill him to get him awake.

My room overlooked the black water of the little river or creek. I opened a window and I could smell it. One drop of that stinking water would mean instant death! As soon as I arrive at any destination, my first thoughts are always of departure and how it may be most quickly arranged, but it was not so in this case. Fatigue perhaps. I settled in. I went to bed and stayed there for two days.

Twice a day Webster Spooner came by and took my order for a bowl of sliced bananas and a small can of Pet milk. I had the same thing each time and he carefully wrote it down each time in his notebook.

Webster said he had other jobs. He washed police cars and he sold newspapers and greeting cards. The tomato plant was one of his projects. He sometimes referred to the woman Ruth as his "ahntee," which is to say his aunt, but I got the impression that they were not actually related. He said she took half his earnings.

He always had a fresh question for me when he caught me awake. Could a Dodge Coronet outrun a Mercury Montego? How did you keep score in the game of bowling? They got very few American guests here at the Fair Play, he said, and the ones they did get drove sorry-looking cars like mine or else they were hippies with dirty feet and no cars at all. Ruth didn't like the Americans but he, Webster, rather liked them, even if they did keep him hopping with their endless demands for ice and light bulbs and towels and flyswatters. Even the wretched hippies expected service. It was in the blood.

I discovered later that Ruth called me "Turco" and "the Turk" because of my small pointed teeth and my small owl beak and my small gray eyes, mere slits but prodigies of light-gathering and resolving power. What put it into her head that these were distinctive Turkish features, I had no way of knowing, nor did I know why she should be down on the Turks too, but there it was. "See what the Turk wants now," she would say to Webster, and, "Is Turco still in bed?"

I had him get me some envelopes and an assortment of colorful stamps and I addressed some British Honduras covers to myself in Little Rock. I slept off and on and I had a recurring dream. I read the Dix book, or tried to. My mind wandered, even on the strong passages that the doctor had underlined. I read a guidebook. The writer said the people of this country were "proud," which usually means "barely human" in the special lingo of those things. But wasn't Ruth proud? The very word for her. I calculated the trip expenses. In the bathroom down the hall I found a paperback book with no covers and took it back to bed with me. I read almost two pages before I realized it was fiction, and worse, a story set in the future. Some bird was calling up for a "helicab." I dropped it on the floor, which is to say I didn't fling it across the room, although I could tell it had been flung many times. I listened to the radio that was always playing in the next room. That is, I listened to the English portions. There were alternate hours of broadcasting in English and Spanish.

I paid particular attention to a California evangelist who came on each morning at nine. I looked forward to this program. Was the man a fraud? He was very persuasive and yet there was a Satanic note in his cleverness. I couldn't work it out.

The headboard of the bed was covered with some cheap white synthetic material—in this land of mahogany—and the name KARL was carved into it in block letters. Each time I woke up, I was confused and then I would see that KARL and get my bearings. I would think about Karl for a few minutes. He had thought it a good thing to leave his name here but, ever wary, not his full name. I wondered if he might be in the next room. With his knife and radio he might be on the move constantly, like J. S. Dix.

The recurring dream made me sweat and writhe in the damp bedclothes. I couldn't trace it back to any event in my waking life, so to speak. I relate this dream, knowing it is ill-mannered to do so, because of its anomalous character. Most of my dreams were paltry, lifeless things. They had to do with geometric figures or levitation. My body would seem to float up from the bed, but not far, a foot or so. There was no question of flying. In this Belize dream there were other people. I was sitting at a low coffee table across from an intelligent, well-dressed woman who wanted to "have it out." She had a fat son named Travis who was about seven years old. This boy was encouraged by his mom to have opinions and make pert remarks. The three of us were always seated around the coffee table on the stylish woman's pneumatic furniture. She drove home telling points in some dim quarrel while the boy Travis chirped out show-business quips.

"Be my guest!" he would chirp, and, "Oh boy, that's the story of my life!" and, "Yeah, but what do you do for an encore!" and, "Hey, don't knock it if you ain't tried it!" and,

"How's that for openers?" and, "You bragging or complain-
ing!" and, "Welcome to the club, Ray! Ha ha ha ha ha ha ha
ha." I had to sit there and take it on the chin from both the
woman and Travis.

Ruth sent for me early on the third day. I took a bath and
shaved and put on some clean clothes. My legs were shaky as
I went down the stairs. Ruth wanted her room money and her
Pet milk money. I had heard nothing from Little Rock. Norma
had abandoned me, and now, it seemed, my father as well. I
tried to figure out how many days I had been gone. It was
just possible that he had not yet returned from the Alabama
bass rodeo. Flinging his plastic worm all over the lake! His
Lucky 13! His long-tailed jigs! He caught fish that weighed
three pounds and he talked about them "fighting." Killer bass!
It was possible too that he was tired of fooling with me, as with
Mr. Dupree and Guy. Weaned at twenty-six! Places like Idaho
had governors my age. The great Humboldt was exploring the
Orinoco at my age instead of sniveling about a money order.

Ruth was hard to deal with. Her Creole speech was hard to
understand. She wouldn't look at me when I spoke to her and
she wouldn't answer me or give any sign of acknowledgment.
I was thus forced to repeat myself and then she would say, "I
heard you the first time." But if I didn't repeat myself we would
just stand there in a silent and uneasy impasse.

I offered to let her hold some bonds until my money arrived.
She wanted cash and she wanted it at that moment. I didn't
know what to say to her, how to keep talking in the assertive
Dix manner. She glowered and looked past me. A crackpot like
Karl had the run of the place but my E bonds were no good.
That was her idea of fair play. Webster Spooner was listening
to all this. He was reclining in his box and working in his note-
book but he was listening too.

"He have money in that long notecase," he said. "Big
money."

It was true. I still had the doctor's wallet and I had forgotten
about it. I went back to the room and got it from the suitcase.
I paid Ruth twenty American dollars and I thought this would
put me on a new footing with her, but it seemed to make her
even more disagreeable. I asked her where the government agriculture office was and she ignored me. I asked her where the
police station was and she turned her back to me and went

through the curtain to her living quarters. I rang the bell but she wouldn't come back.

I was annoyed with Webster for poking around my room while I was asleep but I didn't mention it. I asked if he could run an errand for me. He said nothing and kept working in his notebook. He and Ruth both had decided that I was the sort of person they didn't have to listen to. There were certain white people that they might have to listen to but I was not one of them. I spoke to him again.

"I'm busy," he said.

"What are you doing?"

"I'm drawing the car of tomorrow."

"Yes, I see now. It looks fast. That's nice work. Everything will have to wait until you're finished with it."

I went out into the soft tropic morning. Roosters were crowing all over Belize. My two-day torpor was gone and I was ready for business. Webster had put his tomato plant out on the sidewalk for the sunlight hours. There were two green tomatoes on it.

The little Buick was filthy but it appeared to be intact. There was a leaflet under the windshield wiper. The letters at the top of the sheet were so big and they were marching across the paper in such a way that I had to move my head back a little from normal reading range to make out the words.

LEET WANTS THIS CAR

Hullo, my name is Leet and I pay cash for select motor cars such as yours. I pay promptly in American ($) Dollars. I pay the duty too so as to spare you bother on that Score. Please see me at once on the Franklin Road just beyond the abandoned Ink factory and get an immediate price quotation. Before you deal with a nother person ask yourself these important questions. Who is this Person? Where was he yesterday and where will he be tomorrow? Leet has been in business at the same location for Six Years and he is not going any where. Here's hoping we may get together soon. I am a White Man from Great Yarmouth, England, with previous service in the Royal Navy. With every good wish, I am, yours for Mutual Satisfaction,

Wm. Leet
Leet's Motor Ranch
Franklin Road
Belize, B.H.

I threw it away and got my Esso map from the glove compartment and retrieved the doctor's flashlight from under the seat.

Where were the government buildings? I set out toward the arched bridge to find them. No one was about on the streets. I stopped to read signs and posters. A band called the Blues Busters was appearing at an all-night dance. The movie house was featuring a film of a Muhammad Ali fight. I made a plan for breakfast. I would stop at the second restaurant that I came to on my left.

It was a Chinese place and not a restaurant as such but rather a grocery store with a coffee machine and an ice-cream machine and a few tables. An old Chinese man was wiping off the stainless-steel ice-cream machine. Maintenance! The firemen of Belize were gathered there at two tables for coffee and rolls. A piece of luck, I thought, my hitting on the very place that the firemen liked. They looked at me and lowered their voices. I didn't want to interfere with their morning chat so I bought a cone of soft ice cream and left.

Across the way on the bank of the river there was a public market, a long open shed with a low tin roof, where bananas and pigs and melons were sold, though not this early in the morning. Outside the shed on the dock there were three men skinning a giant brown snake that hung from a hook. There, I said to myself, is something worth watching. I went over and took up a close viewing position and ate my ice cream. The job was soon done, but not with any great skill. The long belly cut was ragged and uncertain. It might have been their first snake. They kept the skin with its reticulated pattern and dropped the heavy carcass into the river where it hung for a moment just beneath the surface, white and sinuous, and then sank.

As I thought over what I had seen, very much puzzled as to how the specific gravity of snake flesh could be greater than that of water, someone came up behind me and pinched my upper arm and made me jump, as before, in Chetumal. I had come to fear this salute. It was Webster Spooner this time. He had his newspapers and greeting cards. He seemed to be embarrassed.

"Are you vexed with me, sor, for going through your things?"

"I am a little, yes."

"I was looking for a President Kennedy dollar."

"I don't have one."

"I know you don't."

"You missed the big snake. There was a monster snake hanging up there just a minute ago. Some sort of constrictor."

"I see him last night."

"How would you like to tangle with that big fellow?"

Webster twisted about and gasped as though in the clutches of the snake. "He be badder than any shark."

"I saw your tomatoes. They looked pretty good."

"A bug done eat one of 'em up."

One bug! A whole tomato! I asked again about the government offices and this time Webster was helpful and agreeable. But it was Sunday, I was surprised to learn, and the offices wouldn't be open. I unfolded the blue map and spread it out on one of the market tables.

"All right, Webster, look here. You will recognize this as a map of your country. An American named Dupree owns a farm here somewhere. I need to find that farm. I want you to go to your police connections and get them to mark the location of that farm on this map. I'm going to give you five dollars now and that's for the policeman. When you bring the map back to me, I'll have five dollars for you. How do you like that?"

He took pains to get Dupree spelled right in his notebook and he didn't whine or raise difficulties, as might have been expected from the corrupt Travis. I described my Torino and told him to be on the lookout for it. He asked me if I could get him a Kennedy dollar. He had that coin on the brain. Every time he got his hands on one, he said, Ruth took it away from him.

"I'll see if I can find you one," I said. "It's a half dollar and I should tell you that it probably won't be silver. All our coins now are cupronickel tokens of no real value. I want that Dupree information just as soon as you can get it. I'll be walking around town for a while and then I'll be at the Unity Tabernacle. I'll wait for you there. Do you know that church?"

Webster not only knew it, he was a sort of lapsed member. The tomato plant in the Texaco bucket had started as a church project. He didn't go much anymore, he said, because he had seen all the movies. He liked the singing and the Christmas

program and the Easter egg hunt and he didn't mind seeing
the Heckle and Jeckle cartoons over and over again. But the
rest of it was too hard. And Mrs. Symes, no fool, had rear-
ranged the schedule so that the Bible quiz was now held *before*
the movie—and no one was admitted late.

He showed me his selection of greeting cards. I bought one,
and a newspaper too, the first one I had ever seen that was
actually called the *Daily Bugle*. It was made up entirely of political abuse, mean little paragraphs, and I threw it away.

For the next two hours or so I made figure-eight walking
circuits of all the downtown blocks. I saw a good many Ford
Galaxies, the big favorite here, but no sleek Torino of any
model. Some of the dwelling houses had cozy English names
. . . Rose Lodge, The Haven. I stopped at the Fort George
Hotel for coffee. Some British soldiers were there, still a little
drunk from the Blues Busters dance, and they were talking to
an American woman who was at the next table with a small
boy. They asked her why Americans said "budder" and "wad-
der" instead of "butter" and "water" and she said she didn't
know. I asked them about their regiment and they said it was
the Coldstream Guards. Were they lying? I couldn't tell. The
Coldstream Guards! The hotel desk clerk was a woman and
she said she vaguely remembered a Mr. Dupree, remembered
his renting a car, and she thought his farm was south of town
somewhere but she wasn't sure.

The door of Unity Tabernacle was bolted against quiz-
dodgers. I hammered away on it until I was admitted by a boy
monitor wearing a safety-patrol belt. The chapel was dark. Mrs.
Symes was showing a George Sanders movie to a dozen or so
Negro children who were scuffling on the pews. She herself
was running the projector and I stood beside her and watched
the show for a while. It was a Falcon picture. A wild-eyed man
with a tiny mustache was trying desperately to buy a ticket in an
enormous marble train station. Mrs. Symes said to me, "He's
not going anywhere. The Falcon is laying a trap for that joker."
Then she gave me a pledge card, a card promising an annual gift
of $5 ( ), $10 ( ), or $25 ( ) toward the support of the Unity
mission. I filled it out under the hot inner light of the projector.
The name and address spaces were much too short, unless you
wrote a very fine hand or unless your name was Ed Poe and

you lived at 1 Elm St., and I had to put this information on the back. I pledged ten dollars. It was just a pledge and I didn't have to pay the money at that moment.

The doctor had been removed to a bed upstairs. I found him awake but he was still gray in the face and his eye looked bad. He was sitting up, shapeless as a manatee in a woman's pink gown. He was going through a big pasteboard box that was filled with letters and photographs and other odds and ends. His hair had been cut, the jaybird crest was gone. He needed a shave. Melba gave me some coffee and a piece of cinnamon toast. She said that the three of us presented an interesting tableau, what with one person in bed, one in a chair, and one standing. Dr. Symes was fretful. He wouldn't talk until Melba had left us.

"What happened to your hair?" I said.

"Mama cut it with some shears."

"Do you need anything?"

"Yes, I do. They won't let me have any medication, Speed. They've put my bag away. They don't even keep a thermometer. I've lost my money and I've lost my book. I can't find my grooming aids. Some Mexican has got my flashlight."

I gave him his wallet and his flashlight and told him that the Dix book was safe in my room. This brought him around a little. He fingered through the money but he didn't count it.

"I appreciate this, Speed. You could have put the blocks to me but you didn't do it."

"I forgot all about it."

"Where in the world have you been?"

"Asleep."

"Is that asthma acting up on you?"

"No."

"Where are you staying?"

"At a hotel down there on the creek."

"A nice place?"

"It's all right."

"Do they have roof-garden dancing and a nice orchestra?"

"It's not that kind of hotel. How's your diarrhea?"

"I've got that gentleman turned all the way around. I'm excreting rocks now when I can do my job at all. Did you get your sweetie back?"

"I'm not trying to get her back. I'm trying to get my car back."

"Well, did you get it?"

"Not yet. I'm working on it."

"Taking to your bed won't get it. You need to get after it."

"I know that."

"You need to read Dix. You need to read Dix on how to close."

"I didn't get very far in that book."

"He tells you how to close a sale. Of course it has a wider application. The art of closing, of consummation. Master that and you have the key to the golden door of success. You need to let Dix take you by the hand."

"I read the part about not imposing on people but I never did that anyway."

"You read it wrong. It is *necessary* to impose on them. How else can you help a sap? Did you read the chapter on generating enthusiasm?"

"I read part of it."

"Read it all. Then read it again. It's pure nitro. The Three T's. The Five Don'ts. The Seven Elements. Stoking the fires of the U.S.S. *Reality*. Making the Pep Squad and staying on it."

"I read the part about the fellow named Floyd who wouldn't work."

"Marvin, not Floyd. Where do you get Floyd? There's no Floyd in any book Dix ever wrote. No, this was Marvin. It's a beautiful story and so true to life too. Old sorry Marvin! Pouting in his hotel room and listening to dance music on the radio and smoking one cigarette after the other and reading detective magazines and racing sheets. Sitting on the bed trying to dope out his six-dollar combinations. That guy! Wheeling his sap bets for the daily double! Dix knew Marv so well. Do you recall how he summed him up—'Hawking and spitting, we lay waste our powers.' I was once a Marvin myself if you can believe that. I had the blues so bad I was paralyzed. Then I read Dix and got off my ass."

"My money hasn't come in from Little Rock yet."

"What's the holdup?"

"I don't know."

"How long do you expect me to carry you?"

"It should come in today. I'm looking for it today. Anyway, you've still got my bonds."

"I don't want any more of your bonds. I'm caught up on bonds."

"It should come in today. I figure I owe you about thirty dollars."

"How do you figure that?"

"It's about fourteen hundred miles from San Miguel. I figure sixty dollars for the gas and oil and other stuff."

"How much for the motorized canoe ride?"

"Do you think I'm going to pay half of that?"

"People are careless when they're spending other people's money. That stuff is hard to come by."

"It wasn't a canoe. It was a boat."

"I have to work for my money. I'm not like you."

He had sorted the memorabilia from the box into three piles on the bed and took a long brown envelope from one of the piles and waved it at me. "Come here a minute, Speed. I want to show you something."

It was a new plan for Jean's Island. On the back of the envelope he had sketched an outline of the island, which was shaped like a tadpole. On the bulbous end he had drawn a dock and some rectangles that represented barracks. This was to be a nursing-home complex for old people called The City of Life. He and his mother would live on the island in a long yellow house, he at one end and she at the other, her bathtub fitted with a grab-bar. Together they would run the nursing home. He would supervise the medical care and she would minister to the spiritual needs. He anticipated a licensing problem because of his record but he thought he could get around that by registering the thing in his mother's name. And in Louisiana there was always some official you could pay to expedite such matters. He had also drawn in a nine-hole golf course. I didn't get the connection between the nursing home and the golf links and I asked him about this but he wasn't listening.

"A lot of bedpans and bitching, you think, but I'm talking about a seventeen-percent bottom-line profit," he said. "I don't mind fooling with these old people. Never have. Put a half-grain of phenobarbital in their soup every night and they won't give you much trouble. They've all got money these days. They all get regular checks from the government."

"You've got quite a few buildings there. What about your construction money?"

"No problem at all. Tap the Feds for some Hill-Burton funds. Maybe float some Act 9 industrial bonds. Hell, mortgage the island. Roll over some short notes. I figure about eight thousand five hundred square feet under roof for the long house, with about six thousand feet of that heated and cooled. The rest in storage rooms and breezeways. Put your cooling tower down at this end, with about forty-five tons of air conditioning. I don't say it's a sure thing. If it was a sure thing, everybody would be in it. But you have to go with the odds and you have two high cards right off in me and Mama."

"Your mother said that island was dedicated as a wildlife refuge."

"Have you been discussing my business with her?"

"She was the one who brought it up."

"Jean's Island has never been dedicated in any legal sense."

"I'm just telling you what she said."

"She meant it was posted, that's all. No hunters and no trespassers. She doesn't know the difference. Why would she be paying taxes on it if it was dedicated?"

"I don't know."

"You're mighty right you don't. Did you get the impression that she might be willing to come to terms on the island?"

"I didn't get that impression."

"Not favorably disposed then."

"She's afraid some woman will get her hands on the property."

"Some woman?"

"She talked about a woman named Sybil."

"What has Sybil got to do with it?"

"I don't know."

"Sybil's all right."

"Your mother doesn't approve of her."

"Sybil's all right but she came down here and showed her ass is what she did. She ran her mouth all the time. I was disappointed. It was a misplaced confidence on my part. I should never have brought her down here, but it was Sybil's car, you see."

"There was another woman. Your mother mentioned another woman named Marvel Clark."

"Marvel!"

"Marvel Clark. Do you know her?"

"Do I know Marvel. My old valentine. Mama must be losing her mind. What has Marvel got to do with anything?"

"Is she one of your sweethearts?"

"She's a rattlesnake. I didn't see it at first. Mama told me not to marry her. She knew those Clarks. I didn't see it until we were married and then I saw it with great clarity. Even so, I miss her sometimes. Some little thing will remind me of her. Can you imagine that? Missing a coiled rattler."

"I didn't realize you had a wife."

"I don't have a wife. Marvel gave me the gate thirty-five years ago, Speed. She said she'd had enough. She said she would shave her head and become a nun in the Catholic church before she would ever get married again. She cleaned me out good. She got my house and she got a lot of Mama's furniture and she even had my medical equipment attached."

"Well, there you are. Your mother is afraid she will get the island too."

"Get it how? Not through me."

He searched through the box and brought out an old photograph showing a thin girl in a dotted dress. She was sitting in a playground swing and she was holding a squinting child on her knees. This was the doctor's former wife, Marvel Clark Symes, and their infant son Ivo. Dr. Symes with a wife! I couldn't believe it. She was a pretty girl too, and not a floozie at all. And baby Ivo! Of course the boy was grown now; that picture must have been forty years old.

Ivo was a roofing contractor in Alexandria, Louisiana, the doctor told me, where Marvel Clark now made her home as well. He said he had not communicated in any way with her for more than twenty years. I gathered that he was also estranged from his son, calling him as he did, "a roofing thug," and saying that he hoped God would let him, the doctor, live long enough to see Ivo in the penitentiary at Angola.

"I don't know what Mama can be thinking about," he said. "There is no possible way Marvel could get the land through me. She has no more legal claim on me than does any strange woman passing by on the street."

"I'm just telling you what she said."

"The divorce was final. That bond has been severed and forever set at naught. Those are the very words on the decree. That's as final as you can get. How much more do you want?"

"I don't know anything about it."

"You're mighty right you don't. Go look it up at the courthouse in Vidalia and then you might know something about it."

I went to the window and watched the street below for Webster Spooner. I looked across the rusty tin roofs of Belize. I couldn't see the ocean but I knew it was out there where the roofs stopped. Dr. Symes asked if I would get him some medicine and some shaving gear. I said I would and he began to write prescriptions on scraps of paper. Downstairs I could hear some bouncy 1937 clarinet tootling.

"What is that?"

"What?"

"That music."

"That's Felix the Cat. Mama loves a picture show. I brought her some cartoons and shorts when I was down here with Sybil. Felix the Cat and Edgar Kennedy and Ted Fiorito with his dance band. I brought Melba a thousand-piece puzzle. Mama loves a picture show better than anybody I know except for Leon Vurro. Listen to this, Speed. Here's what I had to put up with. I would be in that hot cabin in south Houston trying to flatten out those photographs with brickbats and Leon would be off downtown in some cool picture show watching *Honky-Tonk Women* or *Women in Prison*. A grown man. Can you beat it? I've never wasted my time on shows. Don't you know they've got those stories all figured out before you even get to the show? Leon would sit there in the dark like a sap for two or three hours watching those stories and then he would come out on the street just as wild as a crib rat, blinking his eyes and looking around for women to squeeze. Not Bella but strange women. Oh, yes, I used to do it myself. There is very little folly I have missed out on in my life. I never wasted my time on shows but I was a bigger hog for women than Leon ever was. Talk about your prisoners of love. Talk about your boar minks. There was a time when I was out almost every night squeezing women but I stopped that foolishness years ago. A big waste of time and money if you want my opinion, not to mention the toll on your health."

Melba was sitting in her chair in the next room, the central room, and when the cartoon was over she went downstairs to play the piano. The children sang, their devotions passing up through this bedroom and on through the tin roof to the skies. Dr. Symes hummed along with them and sang bits of the hymn.

"This is not a feasible program," he said, indicating the business downstairs. "I think the world of Mama but this is just not a feasible setup. Fooling around with a handful of kids. Don't take my word for it. Check it out with your top educators and your top communicators. What you want is a broad base. This is a narrow base. What you want is a healing service under a tent, and then when things go slack you can knock the poles down and fold that booger up and move on. Or a radio ministry. A telephone ministry would beat this. You'll never prosper on a deal like this. It doesn't make any sense. This is like old man Becker in Ferriday. Let me tell you what he would do. He would be in the back of his hardware store weighing out turnip seed at eight cents a pound, just busting his ass with that little metal scoop, the sweat just rolling off him, while people were standing in line up front trying to buy five-thousand-dollar tractors."

He gave me some money and I left to get the medicine. There were amber nose deposits on the prescriptions. The old man left a mucous track behind him like a snail. I bought a razor at Mr. Wu's grocery but I couldn't find a drugstore that was open so I walked across town to the hospital, another white building. The nurse who ran the dispensary was an Englishwoman. She didn't believe those prescriptions for a minute but she sold me the stuff anyway, some heart medicine called Lanoxin, and some Demerol, which I knew to be dope, and some other things in evil little bottles that I suspected of being dope. It was all for a "Mr. Ralph Moore" and the doctor had signed his own name as the prescribing physician. I explained that he was the son of Mrs. Symes at the Unity church. He had also asked me to get him a dozen syringes but the woman wouldn't sell me any. I didn't press the matter. Babies were crying and I wanted to get out of that place.

Near the hospital there was a city park, a long green field with a statue at one end that looked new and not very important. There was a steel flagpole with no flag. The brass swivel snaps on the rope were jingling against the pole. A woman was sitting tailor-fashion on the grass with a sketch pad. I recognized her as the American girl who had been in the Fort George dining room. The small boy was asleep on a beach towel beside her. I waved. She didn't want to raise her busy hand from the pad but she did nod.

The service was over when I got back to the tabernacle. Mrs. Symes and Melba and a chubby Negro girl in a green dress were in the doctor's room drinking iced tea. The girl was helping Mrs. Symes stick paper stars in an attendance ledger. There was a Scrabble board on the bed and the doctor and Melba were playing this word game. He said, "The millionaires in Palm Beach, Florida, are not having any more fun than we are, Melba." I gave him the sack of drugs and shaving supplies and he left at once for the bathroom. Mrs. Symes asked where I had attended church.

"Actually I haven't been yet."

"Did you sleep late?"

"I've been pretty busy."

"Our lesson here today was on effectual calling."

"I see."

"Do you indeed? Do you even know what effectual calling is?"

"I can't say I do, no, ma'am. I suppose it must be some special religious term. I'm not familiar with it."

"Elizabeth, can you tell Mr. Midge about effectual calling?"

The plump girl said, "Effectual calling. Effectual calling is the work of God's spirit, whereby, convincing us of our sin and misery, enlightening our minds in the knowledge of Christ, and renewing our wills, He doth persuade and enable us to embrace Jesus Christ freely offered to us in the gospel."

"That's very good, but what about the benefits? That's what we want to know. What benefits do they that are effectually called partake of in this life?"

The girl had a ready answer for that too. "They that are effectually called," she said, "do in this life partake of justification, adoption, sanctification, and the several benefits which, in this life, do either accompany or flow from them. We gain assurance of God's love, peace of conscience, joy in the Holy Ghost, increase of Grace, and perseverance therein to the end."

"That's very good, Elizabeth. There are not twenty-five Americans who could answer that question, and we call ourselves a Christian people. Or don't you agree, Mr. Midge?"

"It was a hard question."

"Mr. Midge here goes to college and he has a good opinion of himself but he may not be quite as clever as he thinks. It may even be, Elizabeth, that we can teach him a thing or two."

The girl was pleased with her performance. She had finished her tea and now had her hands arranged in a prim manner on her knees, her small pink fingernails glowing against the green dress.

There was no sign of Webster Spooner. Mrs. Symes had not seen him. She said Webster was a good reader and a good speller and a good singer but he wouldn't stay in his seat. The girl Elizabeth said he was a bad boy who always answered "*Yo*" instead of "Present" when the roll was called.

"I don't think we can call Webster a bad boy, can we?" said Mrs. Symes. "He's not a bad boy like Dwight."

The girl said, "No, but Dwight is a very bad boy."

Mrs. Symes asked me what the doctor had been talking about and I said very honestly that we had been discussing her missionary work. I felt like a spy or a talebearer, reporting back and forth on these conversations. She said she knew what Reo thought of her program but what did I think? I said I thought it was a good program.

She said one couldn't judge these things by the conventional standards of worldly success. Noah preached for six hundred years and converted no one outside his immediate household. And Jeremiah, the weeping prophet, he too was widely regarded as a failure. All you could do was your best, according to your lights. She told me that there was no one named Raymond in the Bible and that drunkenness was the big social problem in this country.

Then she talked to me at length about Father Jackie, the Episcopal missionary. He had the only Tarzan film in the country, she said, and he had finally agreed to let her have it for one showing. Father Jackie had a prankish nature that was very tiresome, and the negotiations for the film had been maddening and exhausting—but well worth the effort. The word on Tarzan would spread fast! Father Jackie was busy these days drafting a new catechism for the modern world, and he was composing some new Christmas carols too, and so he had decided to cut back on his movies and his preaching and teaching duties in order to complete these tasks. He was an odd bird, she said, but he had a good heart. His mother was now visiting him here in Belize.

Melba said, "His mother? I didn't know that. His mother is here?"

"I told you about meeting her in the swap shop."

"No, you didn't."

"Yes, I did."

"You didn't tell me any such thing."

"You never listen to me when I have some piece of news like that."

"What does she look like?"

"I don't know what she looks like, Melba. She just looks like all the rest of us."

"The reason I ask is that I had a vision of an older woman with a white parasol. She was holding it on her shoulder and buying something at the market. Eggs, I think. I saw her just as clearly as I see you now."

"This woman didn't have a parasol. She wasn't even wearing a hat."

"Was she a kind of yellowish woman?"

"She *was yellow*, yes."

"Yellow eyes?"

"I didn't notice her eyes so much but her face was certainly yellow."

"A yellow face."

"That's what I said."

"That's what I said too."

"You said yellow eyes."

"At first I just said yellow."

That ended that. I played Scrabble with Melba. Mrs. Symes hugged and kissed the girl Elizabeth, calling her "baby," or rather, "bebby," and the girl went away. I could hear Dr. Symes in the bathroom singing a song called "My Carolina Sunshine Girl." He was shaving too, among other things, and he looked much better when he came back. He stood beside his mother for a moment and put his arm around her shoulder.

"How are you feeling this morning, Mama?"

"I never felt better in my life, Reo. Stop asking me that."

A small framed picture on the wall caught his attention and he went over to examine it. It was a picture of something brown.

"What is this?" he said. "Is this the Mount of Olives?"

"I don't know what that is," she said. "It's been up there for years. We never use this room any more since Melba has been staying in her chair."

"Who painted this picture? Where did you get it, Mama? I'd like to know how I could get a copy of it."

"You can have that one if you want it."

He crawled back into bed and resumed the Scrabble game. "Where is your puzzle, Melba?" he said. "Where is that jumbo puzzle I brought you the last time? Did you ever finish it?"

"No, I never did start it, Reo. It looked so hard. I gave it to one of the children."

"It was a funny picture of dogs wearing suits."

"Yes, dogs of different breeds smoking pipes and playing some card game."

"Mama, why don't you show Speed here your hurricane poem. He's a college professor and he knows all about poetry."

"No, I don't want to get that stuff out right now. I've got it all locked up."

"What about your stories, Melba? Why don't you show Speed some of your stories?"

"He doesn't want to see those things."

"Yes, he does too. Don't you, Speed?"

I explained that I was very far from being a college professor and that I never read poems or fictional stories and knew nothing about them. But the doctor kept on with this and Melba brought me her stories. They were in airmail tablets, written in a round script on both sides of the thin paper.

One was about a red-haired beauty from New Orleans who went to New York and got a job as a secretary on the second floor of the Empire State Building. There were mysterious petty thefts in the office and the red-haired girl solved the mystery with her psychic powers. The thief turned out to be the boss himself and the girl lost her job and went back to New Orleans where she got another job that she liked better, although it didn't pay as well.

Melba had broken the transition problem wide open by starting almost every paragraph with "Moreover." She freely used "the former" and "the latter" and every time I ran into one of them I had to backtrack to see whom she was talking about. She was also fond of "inasmuch" and "crestfallen."

I read another story, an unfinished shocker about a father-and-son rape team who prowled the Laundromats of New Orleans. The leading character was a widow, a mature red-haired woman with nice skin. She had visions of the particular alleys and parts where the rapes were to occur but the police detectives wouldn't listen to her. "Bunk!" they said. She called them "the local gendarmes," and they in turn called all the girls "tomatoes."

A pretty good story, I thought, and I told Melba I would like to see the psychic widow show up the detectives and get them all fired or at least reduced in rank. The doctor was going back and forth to the bathroom, taking dope, I knew, and talking all the time. He wouldn't read the stories but he wanted to discuss them with us. He advised Melba to get them copyrighted at once.

"What if some sapsucker broke in here and snatched one of your stories, Melba, and then put his own name on it and sold it to some story magazine for ten thousand dollars? Where would you be then?"

Melba was upset. She asked me how one went about this copyright business and I couldn't tell her because I didn't know. Dr. Symes said she would be wiser to keep the stories locked in her drawer instead of showing them to every strange person who came in off the street. He gave no thought to the distress he had caused the old lady and he went on to something else, telling of the many red-haired people he had known in his life. Mrs. Symes had known some of the ruddy folk herself and she spoke of their hot tempers and their sensitive skin, but the doctor wasn't interested in her experiences.

"You'll never find a red-headed person in a nuthouse," he said to me. "Did you know that?"

"I've never heard that."

"Go to the biggest nuthouse you want to and if you can find a red-headed nut I'll give you fifty dollars. Wooten told me that years ago and he was right. Wooten was a doctor's doctor. He was the greatest diagnostician of our time, bar none. Surgery was only his hobby. Diagnosis, that's the high art of medicine. It's a genetic thing, you see, with these redheads. They never go crazy. You and I may go crazy tomorrow morning, Speed, but Melba here will never go crazy."

Melba had been stirring her iced tea violently for about four minutes. She put her face in mine and winked and said, "I'll bet I know what you like." From her leering expression I thought she was going to say, "Nooky," but she said, "I'll bet you like cowboy stories."

The morning wore on and still there was no Webster. I thought of calling the hotel and the cable office but Mrs. Symes had no telephone. I kept hanging around, thinking she would surely ask me to stay for lunch. I was weak from my dairy diet. The doctor said he would like some jello and I wondered at his craving for gelatinous food. Mrs. Symes said jello was a good idea. I could smell the sea and what I wanted was a plate of fried shrimp and fried potatoes.

But jello it was and by that time the doctor was so full of dope and so addled from the heat that I had to help him to the table. His eyelids were going up and down independently of one another and his red eye was glowing and pulsing. He talked about Louisiana, certain childhood scenes, and how he longed to go back. He said, "Mama, you're just going to fall in love all over again with Ferriday." Mrs. Symes didn't argue with him, this return to the homeland being clearly out of the question. Then he wanted to move the dining table over by the window where there was more light. She said, "This table is right where I want it to be, Reo."

Melba and I filled up on lime jello—transparent, no bits of fruit in suspension—and peanut-butter cookies with corrugations on top where a fork had been lightly pressed into them. That was our lunch. The doctor talked on and on. He held a spoonful of jello above his bowl but thoughts kept racing into his head and he could never quite get it to his mouth.

"Speed, I want you to do me a favor."

"All right."

"I want you to tell Mama and Melba about my bus. They'll get a big kick out of that. Can you describe it for them?"

"It's an old Ford school bus painted white."

"All white?"

"Totally white."

"Are you sure about that?"

"Everything was painted white. The windows and the bumpers and the wheels. The grille and all the brightwork too. The propane bottle. It looked like house paint and it was brushed on instead of sprayed."

"Wasn't there something painted in black on the sides?"

"I forgot about that. 'The Dog of the South.'"

"The Dog of the South? Do you mean to say that was the name of the bus?"

"Yes."

"All right then, ladies, there you are. Very fitting, wouldn't you say? No, I take that back. A dog, any dog with a responsible master, is well off compared to me."

Melba said, "You shouldn't call yourself a dog, Reo."

"It's time for plain speaking, Melba. Let's face it, I'm a beggar. I'm old and sick. I have no friends, not one. Rod Garza was the last friend I had on this earth. I have no home. I own no real property. That bus you have just heard described is my entire estate. I haven't been sued in four years—look it up: City of Los Angeles versus Symes, it's still pending for all I know—but if anyone was foolish enough to sue me today, that old bus would be the only thing he could levy against."

Mrs. Symes said, "Whose fault is it, Reo? Tell me that."

"It's all mine, Mama, and nobody knows it better than I do. Listen. If I did have a home and in that home one room was set aside as a trophy room—listen to this—the walls of that room would be completely barren of citations and awards and scrolls and citizenship plaques. Can you imagine that? Can you imagine the terrible reproach of those blank walls to a professional man like me? You could hardly blame me if I kept that shameful room closed off and locked. That's what a lifetime of cutting corners has done for me."

"You had some good friends in Ferriday," Mrs. Symes said. "Don't tell me you didn't."

"Not real friends."

"You went to their barbecues all the time."

"The kind of people I know now don't have barbecues, Mama. They stand up alone at nights in small rooms and eat cold weenies. My so-called friends are bums. Many of them are nothing but rats. They spread T.B. and use dirty language. Some of them can even move their ears. They're wife-beaters and window peepers and night crawlers and dope fiends. They have running sores on the backs of their hands that never heal. They peer up from cracks in the floor with their small red eyes and watch for chances."

Melba said, "That was the road of life you chose, Reo. It was you who sought out those low companions."

"You're absolutely right, Melba. You've done it again. You've put your finger on it. A fondness for low company. I wasn't born a rat or raised a rat. I don't even have that excuse. I wasn't raised a heathern. My mother and father gave me a loving home. They provided me with a fine medical education at Wooten Institute. I wore good clothes, clean clothes, nice suits from Benny's. I had a massive executive head and million-dollar personality. I was wide awake. I was just as keen as a brier. Mama can tell you how frisky I was."

She said, "I was always afraid you would be burned up in a night-club fire, baby."

The doctor turned on me. "Listen to me, Speed. A young man should start out in life trying to do the right thing. It's better for your health. It's better in every way. There'll be plenty of time later for you to cut these corners, and better occasions. I wish I had had some older man to grab my shoulder and talk turkey to me when I was your age. I needed a good shaking when my foot slipped that first time, and I didn't get it. Oh, yes. My face is now turned toward that better land, but much too late."

Mrs. Symes said, "You had a good friend in Natchez named Eddie Carlotti. He had such good manners. He never forgot himself in the presence of ladies like so many of your friends would do. He drove a Packard automobile. It was an open car."

"A human rat," said the doctor. "The world's largest rodent. He's four times the size of that rat Leon used to show. That wop is probably in the Black Hand Society now, shaking down grocery stores. I could tell you a few things about Mr. Eddie Carlotti but I won't. It would turn your stomach."

"What about the Estes boy who was so funny? He always had some new joke or some comical story to tell."

"Chemical story?" said Melba.

"*Comical* story! He and Reo were inseparable chums at one time."

"Another rat," said the doctor. "And I'm not talking now about brown *norvegicus*, your common rat, I'm talking about *Rattus rattus* himself, all black and spitting. Walker Estes would trip a blind man. The last time I saw him he was stealing Christmas presents out of people's cars and trucks. Working people too. I can tell you who didn't think he was funny. It was that sharecropper's little daughter who cried on Christmas morning because there was no baby doll for her, and no candy or sparklers either."

Melba said, "It's amazing what people will do."

"Listen, Melba. Listen to this. I'd like to share this with you. There used to be a wonderful singer on the radio called T. Texas Tyler. Did you ever hear him?"

"When was he on the radio?"

"He was on late at night and he was just a fine fellow, a tremendous entertainer. He had a wonderful way with a song. He sang some lovely Western ballads. They always introduced him as 'T. Texas Tyler, the man with a million friends.' I used to envy that man, and not just for his beautiful voice. I would think, Now how in the world would they introduce me if I had a singing program on the radio? They couldn't say, 'The singing doctor,' because I was no longer a licensed physician. They wouldn't want to say, 'The man with a few rat friends,' and yet anything else would have been a lie. They wouldn't know what to do. They would just have to point to me and let me start singing when that red light came on. Don't ask me what happened to Tyler, because I don't know. I don't have that information. He may be living in a single-wide trailer somewhere, a forgotten old man. Where are those million friends now? It's a shame how we neglect our poets. It's the shame of our nation. Tyler could sing like a bird and you see what it got him in the end. John Selmer Dix died broke in a railroad hotel in Tulsa. It wasn't a mattress fire either. I don't know who started that talk. Dix had his enemies like anybody else. The lies that have been told about that man! They said his eyes were real close together. A woman in Fort Worth claims she saw him flick cigarette ashes on a sleeping baby in a stroller cart. And Dix didn't even smoke! He published two thin books in forty years and they called him a chatterbox. He had the heart of a lion and yet there are people who believe, even to this day, that he was found cowering in the toilet when they had that big Christmas fight at the Legion hut in Del Rio. Anything to smear his memory! Well, it doesn't matter, his work was done. The New York jumping rats have already begun to tamper with it."

Mrs. Symes said, "Reo, you were speaking of rats and that made me think of the river rat named Cornell something who used to take you duck hunting. A famous duck-caller. Cornell something-or-other. His last name escapes me."

"Cornell Tubb, but it's no use going on with this, Mama."

"I remember his full name now. It was Cornell Tubb. Am I wrong, Melba, in thinking that you have some Tubb connections?"

"My mother was a Tubb."

"It's no use going on with this, Mama. I tell you I have no friends. Cornell Tubb was never my friend by any stretch of the imagination. The last friend I had on this earth was Rod Garza, and he was completely dismembered in his Pontiac. They put a bum in his car and blew him up."

"You're not eating. You asked for this jello and now you're just playing with it."

"I wonder if you would do me a favor, Mama."

"I will if I can, Reo."

"I want you to tell Speed here the name of my favorite hymn. He would never guess it in a hundred years."

"I don't remember what it was."

"Yes, you do too."

"No, I don't remember."

"'Just as I am, without one plea.' How I love that old song. And I'll tell you a secret. It means more to me now than it ever did. The theme of that hymn, Speed, is redemption. 'Just as I am, though tossed about, with many a conflict, many a doubt.' Can you understand the appeal it has for me? Can you see why I always request it, no matter where I am in my travels? I never go to these churches where all their hymns were written in 1956, where they write their own songs, you know. Don't look for me there. I'm not interested in hearing any nine-year-old preachers either."

Mrs. Symes said, "I'll tell you what I do remember, Reo. I remember you standing up there in the choir in Ferriday in your robe, just baying out, 'I'd rather have Jesus than silver or gold!' and all the time you were taking advantage of the deaf people of Concordia Parish. You were taking their money and putting those enormous Filipino hearing aids in their ears that squealed and buzzed when they worked at all, and in some cases, I believe, caused painful electric shock."

Melba said, "It's amazing what people will do. Look at the ancient Egyptians. They were the smartest people the world has ever known—we still don't know all their secrets—and yet they worshiped a tumblebug."

The doctor was still holding the green jello in his spoon, quivering and undelivered. This annoyed Mrs. Symes and she took the spoon from him and began to feed him, thus shutting him up.

She and Melba conferred on their plans for the Tarzan showing. Folding chairs would have to be borrowed to accommodate the crowd. Perhaps Father Jackie would lend them his self-threading and noiseless and yet powerful new projector, in which case standby fuses would be needed.

I asked questions about this Father Jackie and learned that he had been a maverick priest in New Orleans. There he had ministered to the waifs who gather about Jackson Square. One night these young drifters surrounded his small Japanese car, shook it for a while, and then turned it over. They dragged him out into the street and beat him and left him bleeding and unconscious. When he had recovered from the assault, his bishop pondered over the problem and then decided that Belize would be a good place for Father Jackie. Mrs. Symes objected to his breezy manner and his preposterous doctrines and his theatrical attire, but, deep down, she said, he was a genuine Christian. She was well pleased with her Tarzan deal.

I said, "Wait a minute. I've heard of this fellow. I've handled news accounts about this man. This is the well-known 'Vicar of Basin Street.'"

"No, no," she said. "This is another one. Father Jackie has a steel plate in his head. He plays the cornet. He's an amateur magician. He claims he has no fear of the Judgment. I don't know anything about the other fellow."

Dense heat was building up in the house. I helped the doctor back to his bed. Mrs. Symes went to her own room to nap. There was a box fan in the central room, where we had eaten, and I lay down on the floor in front of it to rest for a minute or two. I was heavy and sodden with jello.

Watch out for the florr! When I woke up, it was almost 3:30 in the afternoon. What a piddler! Melba was in her chair looking at me. No slumber for Melba. That is, I thought she was looking at me but when I stood up, her dreamy gaze did not move from some point in the void where it was fixed. The temperature was about 97 degrees in that room and she was still wearing her red sweater. It wasn't for me to instruct Melba in her Christian duties but surely she was wrong to be trafficking with these spirits.

# Eight

THE POST office itself wasn't open but there was a man on duty in the cable office. He leafed through the incoming messages and found nothing for me. I walked back to the hotel. The young men of Belize were shadowboxing on the streets and throwing mock punches at one another. Webster Spooner was in front of the hotel dancing around the tomato plant and jabbing the air with his tiny fists. He too had attended the matinée showing of the Muhammad Ali fight.

"I'm one bad-ass nigger," he said to me.

"No, you're not."

"I'm one bad-ass nigger."

"No, you're not."

He was laughing and laying about with his fists. Biff Spooner! Scipio Africanus! I had to wait until his comic frenzy was spent. He had taken care of the map business all right, but instead of bringing the map to me he had fooled around town all morning and then gone to the movie.

I saw that I could count on Webster to do one thing but not two things in immediate succession. On the other hand I didn't have his five dollars, or his Kennedy coin. I did have a little money that I had diverted into my own pocket from the doctor's wad, though not as much as five dollars. Webster shrugged and made no fuss, being accustomed to small daily betrayals.

In the white margin at the top of the map the policeman had written, "Dupree & Co. Ltd. Bishop Lane. Mile 16.4." This Bishop Lane was not printed on the map and the policeman had sketched it in, running west and slightly south from Belize. He had marked the Dupree place with a box. Nearby was a Mayan ruin, as I could see from the pyramid symbol. He had marked another place in the south—"Dupere Livestock"—but the spelling was different and this was clearly an afterthought. In the bottom margin he had signed his name: Sgt. Melchoir Wattli.

So at long last I had found them and now I was ready to

make my move. Leet had left another leaflet on the windshield of the Buick and I threw it away. I inspected the hood for cat tracks and I had a look underneath. Then I remembered the roll of quarters and I got it from the glove compartment and gave it to Webster, showing him how to conceal it in his fist. It stuck out from one end and made his fingers bulge in a dead giveaway.

The quarter was not a very interesting coin, I conceded, and I said it was true that Washington, whose stern profile was stamped on it, had a frosty manner, and that he was not a glamorous person. But, I went on, warming to this theme, he was a much greater man than Kennedy. ¡Gravitas! The stuffed shirt, the pill—this sort of person had not always been regarded as a comic figure. I had enormous respect for General Washington, as who doesn't, but I also liked the man, believing as I did that we shared many of the same qualities. Perhaps I should say "some of the same qualities" because in many ways we were not at all alike. He, after all, had read only two books on warfare, Bland's *Exercises* and Sim's *Military Guide*, and I had read a thousand. And of course he was a big man while I am compact of build.

Webster pointed out that Sergeant Wattli had used a pencil instead of a pen so as not to permanently mar the beautiful blue map. I decided that I would make a gift of the map to the officer when I was done with it, though I said nothing to Webster at the time. That was my way. These flashy people who make a show of snatching off a new necktie and presenting it to someone on the spot, to someone who has admired it—that was never my way.

The filthy Buick started on the first shot. Detroit iron! You can't beat it! Bishop Lane began as a city street and then at the edge of town it changed abruptly into two sandy ruts, which comfortably absorbed the tire thump. There were no suburbs, not even a string of shanties. I drove across pine flats and I was much surprised at finding this conifer in the tropics. I had heard or read somewhere that the taproot of a pine tree plunges as deep into the earth as the tree grows tall, the identical length, and I didn't see how this was possible. I thought about the happy and decent life of a forest ranger. A fresh tan uniform every morning and a hearty breakfast and a goodbye peck from Norma at the door of our brown cottage in the woods. It was a field well worth looking into.

The sand changed to black dirt and mud. I drove through shallow creeks and the water splashed up on my feet. I was entering a different kind of forest, dark woods that pressed in and made a leafy tunnel of the road. There were scrub trees and giant trees, nothing in between. The big ones had smooth gray trunks and few branches except at the very top where they spread into canopies. Roots flared out at the base for buttressing support. I watched for parrots and saw none.

I met no traffic and saw no people either until I came to the Mayan ruin. Two Indian men were there working with machetes. They were hacking away at brush and swatting at mosquitoes. Here and there on the ground they had placed buckets of smoldering woody husks that gave off white smoke —homemade mosquito bombs.

It wasn't a spectacular ruin, nothing to gape at, just a small clearing and two grassy mounds that were the eroded remains of pyramids. They were about twenty feet high. On one of them a stone stairway had been exposed, which led up to a small square temple on the top. Farther back in the woods I could see another mound, a higher one, with trees still growing from it. I stopped to inquire about the Dupree place.

The Indians spoke no English and they couldn't seem to understand my scraps of Spanish either but they were delighted to see me. They welcomed the break from their hopeless task. They seemed to think I had come to tour the ruin and so I followed them about. I tried to stand in the white smoke and it kept shifting around, away from me. The Indians laughed at this perverse joke of nature, so often on them but this time on me. We looked into a dark stone chamber. There were shiny crystals on the walls where water had been dripping for centuries. The chamber next to it had a canvas curtain across the doorway and there were bedrolls and a radio inside. These birds lived here!

We climbed the stone steps and looked into the temple. I ran my hand over the carvings. The stone was coarse-grained and badly weathered and I couldn't make out the design but I knew it must be a representation of some toothy demon or some vile lizard god. I had read about these Mayans and their impenetrable glyphs and their corbeled arches and their madness for calculating the passage of time. But no wheel! I won't discuss their permutation calendar, though I could. I gave the Indians a dollar apiece. They asked me for cigarettes and I had none. But that was all right too, I was still a good fellow. They laughed and laughed over their hard luck.

I left with no information about the Dupree place. About two miles farther along I came to a pasture airstrip with a limp windsock, and then a house, an unpainted structure made of broad reddish planks. It stood well off the wet ground so that Webster or Travis might have walked upright beneath it. I would have had to crouch. There was a sorry fence around the house, a sagging wire affair, and a sign, "KEEP OUT THIS MEANS YOU," on the makeshift gate. There was a porch with a rope hammock hanging at one end. In a shed next to the house there was a green tractor.

I parked in a turnout across the road from the house. It was a turning-around place and a garbage dump too, with bottles and cans and eggshells and swollen magazines scattered about. I had no way of measuring 16.4 miles but I thought I must be getting close. These people here would surely know something about the Dupree farm, unless Sergeant Wattli had put me altogether wrong. There was a terrible stink in the air and I thought at first it came from the garbage. Then I saw two dead and bloated cows with their legs flung out stiff.

I got out of the car and started across the road and then stopped when a red dog came from beneath the house. Was this Dupree's chow dog? He yawned and stretched one front leg and then the other one. He looked deformed with his coat trimmed, his big square head now out of proportion to his diminished body. A clear plastic bag was tied around each of his feet.

He walked to the gate and looked at me without recognition. After a while he registered me in his dog brain as a negligible presence and then he sat back on his haunches and snapped at mosquitoes. I couldn't believe this was the same dog I had known in Little Rock, the same red beast I had seen springing from cover to nip the ankles of motorcyclists and to send small children into screaming flight down the sidewalk.

He had been unmanned perhaps by the long journey and the shearing and the plastic bags on his paws.

The screen door opened and Dupree came out on the porch. He was shirtless, his skin glistening with oil, and he was wearing a tall gray cowboy hat. He had grown a beard. His cowboy boots had pointed toes that curled up like elf shoes. This was a new, Western Dupree. He had a new walk too, a rolling, tough-guy walk. He wasn't wearing his glasses and he squinted at me with one eye. The other one was black and almost closed. His lips were broken and swollen. They had already been at him with their fists here. People's justice! He was holding my .410 shotgun by the barrel in the position that is called "trail arms" in the drill manuals.

"Popo?" he said.

The weak-eyed monkey couldn't even make out who I was. He didn't even recognize his own car.

I said, "Well, Dupree, I see you have some little boots on the dog."

"He doesn't like to get his feet wet. Is that you, Waymon?"

He sometimes called me by this countrified version of "Raymond," not in an affectionate way but with malice.

"You have a lot to answer for, Dupree."

"You'll get your money back. Don't worry about it. Who's with you?"

"Nobody."

"Who told you where I was?"

"Tell Norma to come on out."

"She's not here."

"Then where is she?"

"Gone. Sick. How did you get here anyway?"

"I don't see my Torino."

"I sold it."

"Where?"

"Everybody will get their money as soon as I can get a crop out. Don't push me. The best thing you can do is leave me alone."

"I'm coming into that house."

"No, you better hold it right there." He raised the shotgun. I didn't think he would shoot but you never know. Here was an unstable person who had threatened the President. It was a pump gun, an old Model 42, and I wasn't sure he even knew how to work it but I certainly didn't want to be killed with a .410.

"This is not much of a place," I said. "I was expecting a big plantation. Where are the people who do the work?"

"They're gone too. The head bozo quit and they all went with him. They tore up the generator and the water pump before they left. They shot some of the cows and ran the others off. About what you could expect. I'm through with those creeps."

"Tell Norma to come out on the porch for a minute."

"She's not here."

"Is she afraid to face me?"

"She's gone, vamoosed."

"I think she's in there looking out at me from somewhere."

"There's no one here but me."

"Does your father know you're here?"

"I'm through with him. His day is over. I'm through with you too. You don't have a clue to what's going on. You never did. Are you driving my Buick Special?"

"Yes."

"How did it do?"

"It did all right but I'm not here to discuss that."

"I thought clods like you were always ready to discuss cars."

"Not this time."

He went over to the hammock and sat down in it with the gun across his knees. I was standing in the road trying to think of what to do and say. I had started with a great moral advantage but it seemed to be slipping away. Was Norma in that house? I couldn't tell. Dupree was a liar but you couldn't even count on him to lie.

I said, "What about the woman who lives behind the Game and Fish Building?"

"What about her?"

"Why didn't you bring her with you?"

"Because I didn't want to."

"Did Norma rub that oil on you?"

"These are my natural body oils. We're short of water. Now leave me alone. Everybody will be paid."

"I'm not leaving until I talk to Norma."

"She doesn't want to talk to you. She said she was tired of living with a little old man."

"She never said that."

"She said she was tired of looking at your freckled shoulders and your dead hair."

"Norma never told you that. She doesn't talk that way."

"She doesn't like your name either."

I knew this was a lie too. From Edge to Midge was at worst a lateral move—no hybrid vigor to be expected from our union —and Norma was never one to make hateful remarks. Leave him alone! Next to me he was the least importuned person in Little Rock—people fled from rooms at the sound of his voice —and he kept saying leave him alone. I took a couple of steps toward the gate. He raised the shotgun.

"Better hold it right there."

"Why can't I come in if Norma is not there?"

"Because all my papers and my graphics are on the table. Does that answer your question?"

"What kind of papers? I didn't know you had any papers."

"There's a lot you don't know."

"Where did you sell my car? How much did you get for it?"

"Everybody will be paid in time. That's if they stop bothering me."

"Did you think I would come all the way down here just to listen to a few of your lies and then go home?"

"You'll get your money. And then you'll be happy. It doesn't take much for people like you."

"What will you do, mail it to me? Should I go home and watch the mail?"

"You'll get it."

"When?"

"As soon as I can get a crop out."

"Get a crop out. I'd like to see that. What kind of crop? You don't know the first thing about farming, Dupree. You don't know how to do anything. Look at that fence."

"You don't have to know much. What you have to know is how to make niggers work. That's the hard part."

"You say that from your hammock. Do you know Webster Spooner?"

"No."

"He's the bellboy at my hotel. He has three jobs, if not four. I'll bet you haven't made one friend in this country."

"You goofball."

"Put that shotgun down, you coward, and meet me out here in this road like a man and we'll see who the goofball is."

Instead of making his blood boil, my straightforward challenge only made him toss his head.

"I'm coming into that house, Dupree."

"Better not try it."

"Then I'll have to come back."

"Better not come at night."

"I have a .44 magnum out here in the glove compartment. It's as big as a flare pistol. You can fire just four more rounds from it and the next day the arch of your hand is so sore and numb you can't pick up a dime. That may give you some idea of its power and range. I'd rather not have to use it."

"What crap."

"I'm going now but I'll be back. Tell Norma I'm staying at the Fair Play Hotel in Belize."

"She's not interested in your accommodations. And I'm through passing along information from lower-middle-class creeps like you. I never did like doing it. Your time is coming, pal, soon. You better just leave me alone. If you people would leave me alone, maybe I could get some work done on my book."

"Your book?"

"My book on horde control."

"I didn't know about this."

"Shaping up the skraelings. Getting them organized. I'll tell them about rights and grievances they haven't even thought of yet in New York City. It's a breakthrough. Nobody has ever been able to get their attention and hold it for any appreciable length of time. I've hit on a way to do it with low-voltage strobe lights and certain audio-visual techniques that I'm not going into at this time. I couldn't expect you to understand it. My outline is almost complete but now I've lost another day's work, thanks to you."

Letters weren't enough for him. This monkey was writing a book! I said, "We are weaker than our fathers, Dupree."

"What did you say?"

"We don't even look like them. Here we are, almost thirty years old, and neither one of us even has a job. We're worse than the hippies."

"Leave it to you to come up with some heavy thinking like that. You find me trapped here in this land of niggers with your water-waster wife and you say we are weaker than our fathers. That's just the kind of crap I'm through passing along."

"I'll be back, Dupree."

"Why do you keep calling me by my name?"

"How do you wish to be addressed now?"

"You're saying my name too much."

"I'll be back."

"Better not come at night."

"I'm leaving this bottle right here in the road. It's Norma's lower-back medicine. Make sure she gets it before a car runs over it."

He went into the house. After a moment I saw the weak glow of a candle or an oil lamp from an inner room. I called out for Norma. There was no answer. I knew it was my duty to walk into that yard and up those steps and into that house but I was afraid to do it. I thought of ramming the two front pilings of the house with the Buick, thereby causing the house to topple forward and spilling forth Dupree through a door or window. Nothing to disconcert a proud man like a sudden tumble from his home. But might not Norma be injured too, flung perhaps from a bathtub? The hammock was still moving and I stood there and counted the diminishing oscillations until the thing came to rest at bottom dead center. I would lay Dupree out in that hammock when I had killed him. I would take a stick and pry his teeth apart—they would be clenched in a rictus—and I would place the candle between them. I would leave him in the hammock with the candle burning in his mouth and let the Belize detectives make of it what they would. I poked idly about in the garbage dump with my foot and turned up nothing of any real interest except for a one-gallon pickle jar. I put it in the car and left.

When I drove by the Mayan ruin, the two brush-cutters were taking another break and this time they had cigarettes. They were talking to a third man who was sitting astride a three-wheel motorcycle rig. Little crosses were painted all over the wooden cargo box and the name "Popo" was spelled out in red plastic reflectors on the back. There were brown-paper sacks in the cargo box. I waved. Then it came to me. Those were probably Dupree's supplies. I turned around and went back.

The Indians thought I wanted to tour the ruin again and so I did. Popo joined us. He was Spanish. We looked into the stone chambers again. Mosquitoes swarmed in our faces. Popo sat on a scooped-out block of stone that must have been a kind of altar. He smirked and crossed his arms and legs and asked me to take his picture. I didn't think he should behave that way on someone's altar but the Indians themselves found his antics funny and in any case I had no camera. Some gringo. No smokes and no camera and no money!

Popo spoke a little English. He said he had seen no woman at the Dupree place, no other person at all since the workers had left, but he had made only one previous delivery and he had not been inside the house. Dupree would not let him go past the gate. I looked through the paper sacks. I found no Pall Mall cigarettes, Norma's brand, or any other kind, and no single item that might have been for her exclusive use, except possibly for a bottle of hand lotion. But maybe Dupree had now taken up the use of Jergen's lotion. It was hard to say what he might or might not be doing in that house, in his strange new life.

I gave Popo a savings bond and told him that Dupree was flying back to the States in a few hours. An emergency at home. He would no longer need this service. Popo was to keep the food and the beer and the kerosene and the change too, if any. Dupree wanted Popo and his family to have these things.

Popo was baffled. What about his glasses? What about the *remedios*, the *drogas*? He showed me Dupree's eyeglasses, wrapped in a repair order, and a big bottle of St. Joseph aspirins and a smaller bottle of yellow Valium tablets. I hadn't known that Dupree was a pillhead on top of everything else but I can't say I was surprised.

I said yes, Dupree did want the glasses and the drugs and I would see that he got them. Popo was reluctant to go along with all this and I gave him another E bond. The Indians pressed me again for cigarettes and I gave them each a bond too. I asked Popo about these birds. He said they were brothers. They worked for the government and they had been here for years fighting the brush. They could make the clearing no bigger because the stuff grew up behind them so fast. There was a third brother somewhere around, Popo told me, but he was always hiding in the woods and was seldom seen by outsiders.

I made sure that Popo followed me back to town and I drove slow on the sandy part so as not to dust him up.

# Nine

THE CHINAMAN'S store was still open and I bought some crackers and a thick oval can of Mexican sardines and took them to my room. Karl's radio was playing at moderate volume. I don't think I had even noticed it until I heard the announcer say, "No more calls, please, we have a winner." Then Karl switched it off for the first time since my arrival.

Or maybe tube collapse or power failure or a political coup at the station itself. They always went for the radio station in these places. I wondered if they had ever had a really first-class slaughter of students here. Better watch my step. Dupree had better watch his smart mouth too. Name your cat or dog after the Prime Minister in a place like this and you would be in the jug but pronto.

And there would be no fool here to go his bail, if they had bail. His papers! His book! His social program! It was some sort of nasty Communist claptrap, no doubt, with people who sounded a lot like Dupree as the bosses. He would tell us what to do and when to do it. The chairman! He would reward us and punish us. What a fate! Give me Mr. Dupree any day. The book would never be finished of course. The great outline of history! His slide shows! His skraelings! Pinch their arms and he could get their attention. But was Norma in that house or not? That was the important thing.

I ate my sardine supper and took a bath. I washed the big pickle jar, along with the top, and put them on the window-sill to dry. Then I called down the stairs for Webster Spooner. He appeared with his notebook, ready for any assignment. I showed him the jar.

"A little surprise for you, Webster."

"Sor?"

"I thought you might have some use for it. It's clean. You can save pennies in it. Keep a pet fish maybe. You would have to change the water. If you decide on the fish."

He looked it over but I could see he wasn't interested in it and I suggested he give it to Ruth, who could make some household use of it. He took the jar away and a few minutes later I heard Ruth slam it against something and break it.

I went to bed and reviewed the day's events, a depressing exercise. I had not handled myself so badly, I thought, and yet there were no results. I must do better. Tomorrow I would enter the Dupree house, come what may. I would watch for an opening and then make a dash across the road. What I needed was a timetable of things to do. An orderly schedule. I sat up in bed and ruled off a sheet of paper with evenly spaced lines and corresponding numbers down to sixteen. It was a neat piece of work, the form itself.

But I suddenly despaired of trying to think of that many things to do and of getting them in the proper order. I didn't want to leave any blank spaces and I didn't want to pad it out with dishonest filler items either, like "tie shoes." What was wrong with me? I had once been very good at this kind of thing. I crumpled the paper and dropped it on the floor.

The sardine stink filled the room and overwhelmed the river stink. Outside on the street I heard the slow grinding whine of a Mopar starter—a Plymouth or a Dodge or a Chrysler. The engine caught and idled smoothly and after a minute or so the car drove away.

Jack Wilkie, perhaps, in his Imperial. He had finally arrived. He had been outside watching my window. But no, Jack would never lurk. He might break down the door but he wouldn't lurk. That was more in my line. I felt queasy. I took two of the orange pills. I can't say I was really sick, unless you count narcolepsy and mild xenophobia, but I was a little queasy. If there had been a gang of reporters outside clamoring to know my condition, Webster would have had to announce to them that it was satisfactory.

I slept and dreamed fitfully. In one dream I was looking through a Sears catalogue and I came across Mrs. Symes and Melba and the doctor modeling lawn furniture. They were wearing their ordinary clothes, unlike the other models, who were in bright summer togs. The other dream took place in a dark bar. The boy Travis was sitting on a stool with his legs dangling. That is, he looked like Travis, only his name seemed to be Chet this time. He was drinking from a tall frosted glass and he was waiting for five o'clock and victims to chirp at. I took a seat at the other end of the bar. He didn't see me for a while and then when he did see me he shifted around and said, "So how you been, Ray? You never come around anymore." I said I was all right and I asked about his mother. Chet said she was fine. He offered to buy me a drink and I said I had to go to Texarkana.

I woke early and saw that I had been drooling on the pillow. The ear hair couldn't be far behind now. I washed and dressed and ate the rest of the sardines and drove back to the Dupree place.

The hairy monkey was up early too. I had no sooner parked in the turnout than he came to the door with the .410. He said nothing. I opened all the car doors to catch any breeze that might come up and sat in the driver's seat with my feet outside on the garbage. Dupree went back inside. The medicine bottle full of four-dollar capsules was still standing in the road where I had left it.

Now and then I would get out as though to start across the road and he would instantly appear at the door. He must have been sitting just behind it in the shadow. I called out for Norma. I told her that I had her medicine and her silver and that if she would just come to the fence for a minute I would give it to her. There was no answer.

After the engine had cooled off, I sat on the hood with my heels hooked on the bumper. At the end of each hour, just as the second hand hit twelve, I called out for her. Late in the morning Dupree came out and sat in the hammock with the gun on his lap. He read a magazine, holding it about five inches from his eyes.

He wouldn't answer me when I spoke. His plan, I could see, was to keep silent and not acknowledge my presence, except for the countering moves with the shotgun. When he looked about, he pretended not to see me, in the way of a movie actor whose eyes go professionally blank when tracking across the gaze of the camera. The dog picked up on his mood and he too ignored me. Dupree sat there with his magazine, feigning solitude and peace. He fondled his belly and chest with his fingertips the way some people do when they find themselves in swimming trunks. I got one of the rusty cans of warm beer from the trunk and made a show of opening it and drinking it.

Around noon he stood up and stretched. He strolled out into the yard and peered down the road with his watery eyes. I had been waiting for some such move.

"Popo is not coming today," I said. "He's not coming tomorrow either." I held up his eyeglasses but he wouldn't look at me. "I have your glasses here, Dupree. They're right here. I have your aspirins and your dope too. Look. Here's what I think of your dope." I poured the yellow pills out and crushed them into the garbage with my foot. He couldn't see what I was doing and the effect was thus lost.

He made no reply and went over to the green tractor and climbed up on it and tried to start it. It was a diesel and by nature hard to start. Dupree lacked patience. His contempt for machinery was unpleasant to watch. He slammed and wrenched things about. A gentler touch and maybe a shot of ether into the breather and it probably would have cranked right up, but Dupree, the farmer's son, knew little of these matters. When he might have been learning how to start a tractor, he was away at various schools, demonstrating in the streets and acquiring his curious manners and his curious notions. The student prince! He even had a place to run to when things got hot.

He went back to the porch and sat on the hammock. I drank another can of warm beer. He suddenly made up his mind to speak, saying, "I suppose you've told everybody where I am, Burke."

"Not yet, no."

He was calling me Burke! There followed a silent interval of about an hour before he spoke again. He said, "Those aspirins are for my dog." I had been quietly thinking over the Burke business and now I had to think about the aspirins and the dog. I should explain that Burke worked on the copy desk with us. It is true that Burke and I were only dimly perceived by the world and that a new acquaintance might have easily gotten us confused, might have hailed Burke on the street as "Midge," or introduced me to another person as "Burke," but Dupree knew us well from long association, knew the thousand differences between us, and I could only conclude that he was now so far advanced in his political thinking that he could no longer tell one person from another. I should say too that Burke was by far the best copy editor on the desk. Even Dupree was better at the work than I, who have never had a firm grasp of English grammar, as may be seen. The flow of civic events that made up the news in our paper was incomprehensible to me too, but Burke shone in both these areas. He was always fretting over improper usage, over people saying "hopefully" and "finalized," and he talked knowledgeably about things that went on in the world. That's enough on Burke.

I got the St. Joseph bottle from my pocket and threw it across to the porch. Dupree picked it up and took it back to the hammock and ate four or five aspirins, making a show of relishing them, as I had done with the beer. He said, "My dog never took an aspirin in his life." You couldn't believe a word he said.

That afternoon he tried the tractor again. He got it to chug a few times but the black smoke and the noise of the cold idle knock startled him and he shut it down at once. I stayed there all day. It was a blockade. I was ready to intercept any delivery or visitor, but no one came. There was nothing, it seemed, beyond this place. I watched the windows for Norma, for flitting shadows. I was always good at catching roach movement or mouse movement from the corner of my eye. Small or large, any object in my presence had only to change its position slightly, by no more than a centimeter, and my head would snap about and the thing would be instantly trapped by my gaze. But I saw no sign of life in that house. All this time, of course, I was also watching and waiting for the chance to dash across the road. The circumstances were never quite right and, to put it plainly, I funked it again.

It was still daylight when I got back to Belize and I drove aimlessly about town. Sweat stung my eyes. The heat was such that I couldn't focus my mind. The doctor and Webster Spooner and I had all contrived to get ourselves into the power of women and I could see no clear move for any one of us. It was hard to order my thoughts.

I stopped at the Fort George Hotel for something to drink. The bar was on the second floor and it overlooked a kind of estuary. The water was still and brown and not at all inviting. Out there somewhere, I knew, was a coral reef with clear water and fish of strange shapes and dazzling colors. The bar itself was nice enough. I was up to my old trick of rooming in a cheap place and drinking in a better place. I saw the American woman and the boy sitting on a couch by the windows.

Low tumbling clouds approached from the Caribbean. I drank a bottle of Falcon beer. It had a plain label. There were no boasts about choice hops and the stuff had won no medals at any international exposition but it was cold and tasted like every other beer. Exercise, that was what I needed. That always cleared the brain. I could jog around the entire city and look for my car at the same time. But wouldn't children jeer at me all along such a circuit? Pelting me, perhaps, with bits of filth. And what about the town dogs, all at my heels? It would be much more sensible to install some muscle-building spring devices in the privacy of my room. A stationary bicycle. But Webster would have the devil of a time getting that stuff up the stairs. No, a brisk swim. That would be just the thing. An isolated beach and some vigorous strokes in foamy salt water.

The clouds drew closer and gusts of wind ruffled the surface of the brown water. Drops of rain struck the windows. I left my stool and moved across the room for a better look at things, taking a table next to the American woman. Four pelicans in a column were gliding over the water, almost touching it. Behind them came two more. These two were flapping their heavy wings and they were climbing up to the misty edges of the cloud. A shaft of lightning struck the second bird and he contracted into a ball and fell like a rock. The other one took no notice, missing not a beat with his wings.

I was astonished. I knew I would tell this pelican story over and over again and that it would be met with widespread disbelief but I thought I might as well get started and so I turned to the woman and the boy and told them what I had seen. I pointed out the floating brown lump.

She said, "It looks like a piece of wood."

"That's a dead pelican."

"I heard the thunder but I didn't see anything."

"I saw the whole thing."

"I love storms."

"I think this is just a convective shower. Afternoon heat."

This woman or girl was about thirty years old and she was wearing blue jeans and one of those grain-sack shirts from Mexico with the faded printing on it. Her sunglasses were parked high on her head. I asked if I might join her. She was indifferent. She had a hoarse voice and both she and the boy had sunburned faces. Her name, I learned, was Christine Walls. She was an artist from Arizona. She had a load of Arizona art in her van and she and the boy had been wandering about in Mexico and Central America. She extended an index finger across the table, for shaking, it finally dawned on me, and I took it and gave it a tentative shake.

I told her that I had recently dreamed of just such a tableau as this—a woman and a small boy and I seated before a low table. She didn't know what to make of me. First the pelican and now this. The details, I should say, didn't correspond exactly. Christine didn't have nice clothes like those of the woman in the dream and Victor didn't appear to be a little smart-ass like Travis, although he was clunking his heels against the seat in a rhythmic way that I found irritating. Still, the overall picture was close enough. Too close!

She asked my date of birth. We exchanged views on the heat. I remarked on her many sparkling rings and said that my wife Norma was also fond of silver and turquoise. She asked me what the prevailing colors were in Little Rock and I couldn't remember, I who am so good on colors. She said her former husband was a Mama's boy. His name was Dean Walls and he wouldn't make a move without first consulting his mother. He was a creepy spider, she said, who repaired watches in a well-lighted cubicle on the first floor of a large department store. We talked about the many different vocations in life and I had to confess that I had none. The boy Victor was being left out of our conversation and so I asked him if he was enjoying his travels. He didn't answer. I asked him how many states he had been in and he said, "More than you." Christine said she planned to return to college one day and study psychology, and that she would eventually make her home in Colorado or San Francisco or maybe Vermont. An earlier plan to marry again had collapsed when her fiancé was killed in a motorcycle accident. His name was Don and he had taught oriental methods of self-defense in a martial arts academy.

"They called it an accident," she said, "but I think the government had him killed because he knew too much about flying saucers."

"What did he know?"

"He knew a lot. He had seen several landings. He was a witness to those landings outside Flagstaff when they were kidnapping dogs."

"What kind of dogs?"

"What kind of dogs were they, Victor?"

"Collies and other work dogs. The aliens stunned them first with electric sticks."

"Yes, and Don had seen all that and so the government had to silence him."

I asked if she and the boy would like to join me in a swim before dark.

"In the pool?"

"No, I'm not a guest here. I was thinking about the beach."

"I love to walk the beach but I can't swim."

"How does it happen that you can't swim, Christine?"

"I don't know. Have you been here long?"

"Just a few days."

"How was your trip down?"

"It was a nightmare."

"A nightmare. I love that. Have you had much trouble with the money?"

"No, I haven't exchanged any yet."

The boy Victor clapped one hand to his forehead and fell back against the seat and said, "Oh brother, is he in for it!"

Christine said, "You're not just a-woofin', buddy boy. This money is really something else. They call it a dollar but it's not the same value as ours. It's worth some odd fraction like sixty-eight cents. Even Victor can't get it straight. Hey, Ray, I want to ask you a question before I forget it. Why are there so darned many hardware stores in Belize?"

"Are there a lot? I hadn't noticed that."

"I've seen two already." She touched my arm and lowered her voice. "Don't stare but wait a second and then look at that fantastic girl."

"Where?"

"That black waitress. The way she holds her head. See. Her regal bearing."

Two hardware stores didn't seem like a lot to me. This was Staci talk. Nerve gas. I would have to stay on my toes to follow this stuff. She suddenly went into a contortion, trying to scratch a place on her back that was hard to reach. She laughed and twisted and said, "What I need is a back scratcher."

I thought she meant just that, a long bronze rod with little claws at one end, and maybe she did, but then I saw what a good chance I had missed for an initial intimacy, always so awkward. The moment had passed, needless to say, the itching abated, by the time I had worked it all out.

Christine wasn't a guest at the Fort George either. She was looking for a place to take a bath. She had tried to rent a room with bath for an hour or so instead of an entire day but the Fort George didn't offer that plan and neither did it accept works of art in payment. I volunteered the use of the communal bath at the Fair Play. She quickly accepted and began to get her things together.

Then I thought about trying to get her past Ruth without paying. I wasn't in the mood for any hotel comedy. I had spoken too soon. The towels were never quite dry at the Fair Play. The bathroom was a foul chamber too, and the door wouldn't lock, the knobs and the brass mechanism being completely gone, the wood all splintered around the hole, where some raging guest had forced an entry or an exit. I knew what would happen. This boy Vic would say, "P.U., Mom!" and make me look bad. So I took them instead to the Unity Tabernacle. They followed me in the van. It was a Volkswagen and it made a four-cylinder micro-clatter. There were decals of leaping green fish and bounding brown deer on both sides of the vehicle, a sporting touch I would not have associated with Christine and Victor—or with Dean, for that matter.

# *Ten*

M RS. SYMES was in front of the church. She was wearing a man's felt hat and she was talking to a gang of boys who were milling about, waiting to see Tarzan. She was upset because Father Jackie had not yet delivered the film for the big showing.

This Christine distraction annoyed her further but she told me to take the girl in and show her the bath. I expected no less, even though I knew that Mrs. Symes's tangled creed must be based more or less on faith rather than works. The doctor himself had told me that she had fed more tramps during the Depression than any other person in Louisiana.

Christine decided to do her laundry too, and I helped her carry it up the stairs, sacks of the stuff. There is always more to these pickup deals than first meets the eye. She proceeded to steam up the place. First she scrubbed Victor down and then she washed her Arizona clothes in the bathtub and hung them about inside on tables and lamps and other fixtures.

Melba didn't like this intrusion. She sat in her chair sulking and chewing on something brittle, or munching rather. Dr. Symes, hearing the stir, peered out from his bedroom. He saw me and he waved a sheet of paper and he came over to join me on the couch.

"Good news, Speed," he said. "Hold on to your hat. Mama has agreed to write a letter for me."

"What kind of letter has she agreed to write?"

"A wonderful letter of authorization. It's a new day."

She still refused to lease him the island but he had persuaded her to let him use the island in some ill-defined way. Or so he said. In fact, Mrs. Symes had written nothing. The doctor had written a legal-sounding statement on a sheet of Melba's crinkly airmail paper that gave him the right "to dig holes and erect fences and make such other improvements on Jean's Island as he may deem necessary or desirable." It only remained, he said, to get the old lady's signature, and a notary public to witness it and to squeeze the paper with his pliers-like seal.

Notarized or not, the letter didn't impress me much. "What about your financing?" I said. "The banks will want more than this."

"What do you know about it?"

"My father is in the construction business."

He read through the statement. "This would be enough for me. What more could they want?"

"They want to see a lease or a land contract. They want something that will hold up. Your letter doesn't even describe the property."

"It says Jean's Island plain enough."

"Maybe there's another Jean's Island. They want metes and bounds."

"I don't believe you know what you're talking about."

"Maybe not."

"I've never believed it. I don't believe you know your ass from first base. I was closing deals before you were born. Mama owns the land outright and that makes her the principal. This letter makes me her agent. Will you sit there and tell me that the law of agency has been repealed?"

What he was groping for, I thought, was a letter giving him power of attorney but I didn't want to go on with this and antagonize him further. For all my big talk of finance, it was I who needed a loan, and a quick one. The doctor went to his bedroom and brought back the big pasteboard box. He pawed angrily through the stuff. "I'll give you metes and bounds," he said. "I'll give you section, township, and range."

The plan I had hatched while reclining on the couch was to take Christine to the Fort George for a seafood supper, leaving Victor here at the movie. It was an improper sort of business for a married man who was not legally separated but the idea wouldn't go away. An alternative plan was to get supper here at the church and then take Christine out for drinks alone, which would be much cheaper, unless she went in for expensive novelty drinks. I couldn't tell from the feel of things whether they had eaten supper here yet or not.

I asked the doctor cold if he could let me have another twenty dollars.

Instead of answering my question, he showed me a photograph of his father, the squeamish Otho. It was a brown print on crumbling cardboard. Then he showed me a picture of an intense yokel with a thick shock of hair parted in the middle. The boy was wearing a white medical smock and he was sitting behind a microscope, one hand holding a glass slide and the other poised to make a focal adjustment. It was Dr. Symes himself as a student at Wooten Institute. Young microbe hunter! The microscope had no solid look of machined steel about it, no heaviness, and my guess was that it was a dummy, a photographer's prop.

There were more photographs, of Marvel Clark with Ivo and without Ivo, of an adult Ivo standing by his roofing truck and his hot-tar trailer, of houses, cars, fish, of people on porches, in uniform, of a grim blockhouse medical clinic, of people at a restaurant table, their eyes dazzled by a flash bulb like movie stars caught at play. He showed me a picture of the Wooten Panthers, a scraggly six-man football team. A medical school with a football team! Who did they play? The coach was Dr. Wooten himself, and Dr. Symes, with his bulk, played center. But there seemed to be no picture of the island, the only thing I was curious about.

Suddenly the doctor gave a start and a little yelp of discovery. "Another one! I missed this booger!" It was a window envelope that had not been opened. He wasted no time in ripping the end off and shaking out a check. It was a monthly insurance check for $215 made out to Mrs. Symes. It was almost a year old. "Some of them go back eight and nine years," he said, folding it and sticking it in his shirt pocket. "This makes thirty some-odd I've found so far."

"Why doesn't she cash them?"

"She cashes some and she forgets some. People like Mama, they don't care whether an insurance company can balance its books or not. They never think about things like that. The Aetna books mean less than nothing to her."

"What will you do with them?"

"What do you think?"

"Your mother will have to endorse them."

"They'll be well endorsed, don't worry about it. That's no step for a stepper. And Mama will get it all back a thousand-fold. This is just seed money for the first drilling rig. This is just peanuts. I'm talking big bucks." He looked about for eavesdroppers and then lowered his voice. "There's a billion cubic feet of natural gas under that island, Speed. I plan to have two producing wells down by the first of the year. Do you think that's an unrealistic goal?"

"I don't know. What about The City of Life?"

"The what?"

"The nursing home. The long yellow house."

Waves of confusion passed across his face. "Nursing home?"

"On Jean's Island. The City of Life."

Then he was able to remember, but just barely, and he dismissed it out of hand as though it had been an idea of mine. He resumed his search through the big box and he sang softly the words of "Mockingbird Hill." He passed along odd items of interest to me. I looked at an old diary that Mrs. Symes had kept. It wasn't a very satisfactory one, in that there were only a dozen or so brief entries in it covering a period of five years. The last one had been made on a September day in 1958. "Dry summer," she had written. "Mangoes bitter this year. God's plan unfolding very slowly." I repeated my request to the doctor for a loan and got no answer.

He was studying a brittle newspaper clipping. "I wish you would look at this," he said. "I don't know why in the world Mama keeps all this stuff."

It was an editorial cartoon of a fat man with buttons popping from his shirt. With one hand the chubby figure was clutching a wedge of pie and with the other he was holding out a Band-Aid and saying, "Here, apply this!" to an injured man with his tongue lolling and tire tracks across his head and x's for eyes. The caption underneath said, "Our own Doc Symes."

"What's that about the pie?"

"Newspaper humor. Those boys love to dish it out but did you ever see one who could take it like a man? I weighed about two hundred and ninety-five then. I had to special-order all my suits from Benny's in New Orleans. Fifty-four shorts. I'm just a shadow of that man. The Shreveport *Times* put dark glasses and a fez on me and called me Farouk. This was the original frame-up. I was suspended for six months. They accused me of practicing homeopathy, of all things. Can you imagine that?"

"I've heard of homeopathy but I don't know what it is."

"The hair of the dog. There's a little something to it but not much. There's a little truth in everything. I never practiced it but any stick was good enough to beat a dog like me. Can you see what I'm driving at?"

"Was this the hearing-aid deal?"

"No connection whatsoever. This was my arthritis clinic. The Brewster Method. Massive doses of gold salts and nuxated zinc followed by thirty push-ups and a twelve-minute nap. None of your thermo tubs or hydro baloney. You don't hear much about it anymore but for my money it's never been discredited. I saw marked improvement in those who could actually raise themselves from the floor. The older people found it painful, naturally, but that was the humidity as much as anything. I was to blame for the atmospheric conditions too, you see. Granted, the humidity is around a hundred percent in Ferriday, but everybody can't go to Tucson, can they?

"I worked day and night trying to help those people, trying to give them some relief. I never made so much money in my life and the doctors' gang couldn't stand it. My prosperity just stuck in their craw. 'Get Symes!' they cried, and 'Bust Symes!' and 'Kick him where it hurts!' That was all they could think about for two years. Well, here I am. You will judge of their success. I haven't been a newsmaker for years."

"I don't see how the homeopathy ties in."

"It doesn't tie in. Brewster had once been a homeopath, that's all. He later became a naturopath. So what? He had one or two good ideas. I'll look you square in the eye, Speed, and tell you that I have never practiced anything but orthodox medicine. This was a setup, pure and simple. They were lying in wait. It wasn't my medicine that stirred those boys up, it was my accounts receivable. You can bank on it, that's the only reason any doctor ever turns another one in."

Christine was bustling about in white shorts and a pale blue work shirt that was knotted in front so as to expose her red abdomen. I could tell she was older than Norma from the fatty dimpling on the backs of her thighs. It was like the patterns you sometimes see in blown sand. She had washed her hair, and her ears stuck through the wet brown strands. I found her very attractive with her sunburn and her hoarse voice and her brisk manner. She was making friends with Melba and I liked that too, a young person deferring and giving her time to an older person. She was showing Melba something, a book or a purse or a stamp album. The old lady had been out of sorts and now she was jiggling her leg up and down, making the floor shake again. Christine was charming Melba!

"A patient named J. D. Brimlett developed osteomyelitis," said the doctor. "That was the claim anyway. I'm convinced he already had it. He had everything else. Emphysema, glaucoma, no adrenal function, you name it. Two little hard dark lungs like a pair of desiccated prunes. He belonged in a carnival instead of an arthritis clinic. The world's sickest living man. No blood pressure to speak of and you couldn't find a vein to save your ass. Renal failure on top of everything else. The Mayo brothers couldn't have pulled that chump through, but no, it was my zinc that killed him. A Class B irritant poison, they said. I should have screened him out. I should have closed my eyes and ears to his suffering and sent him on his way. I didn't do it and I've been paying for that mistake ever since. There's always a son of a bitch like Brimlett hanging around, doing anything to get attention, dying even, and just ruining things for everybody else. Do you want it in a nutshell? I was weak. I was soft."

He raised a hand to repel shouts of protest and then went on, "It wasn't the zinc and they knew it. I took a five-pound bag of the stuff to my hearing and offered to eat it all right there with a spoon but they wouldn't let me do it. Brewster himself admitted that it would give the skin a greenish tint. There was never any secret about that. You get a trivial cosmetic problem in exchange for relief from agonizing pain. Many people considered it a bargain. Talcum powder is cheap enough. It's true, in a very few cases the eyebrows fell out but I've seen cortisone do far worse things. Can you see it now? Do you see what I'm driving at? It was all a smoke screen. The point is, you can't cross the doctors' union. Cross those boys and they'll hand you your lunch. Forget the merits of your case. They kicked Pasteur in the ass. Lister too, and Smitty Wooten. They know everything and Symes is an old clap doctor."

Outside it was dark. I excused myself and went downstairs to get the chest of silverware from the car. When I opened the church door, the milling boys fell back and looked at me in silent terror, fearing another announcement about the movie being delayed. I made my way through them and I saw that Leet or one of his tireless runners had put another leaflet under a windshield wiper.

The silver chest had been knocked around in the trunk. It was greasy and scuffed and the leatheroid skin was peeling and bubbling up in places from glue breakdown. I put the chest under my arm and slammed the trunk lid. I thought I heard someone call my name. I couldn't place the voice, though it was familiar in some way.

I said, "What?"

"This way."

"Where?"

"Over here, Ray."

"Where? Who wants to see me?"

One of the older boys with a cigar said, "Nobody want to see you, mon. The peoples want to see Tarzan." A good laugh all around at my expense.

The forks and spoons and knives were jumbled about in the chest and I stopped on the stairs to sort them out and stack them in their proper notches and hollows before making my presentation to the doctor. He said nothing when I set it on his lap and opened it, Mrs. Edge's shining array of cutlery under his red eye. I told him that I needed some more money at once and that if I had not settled the entire debt by noon tomorrow the silver service was his to keep. It was all too fast for him, my proposition and the heavy thing on his knees. I said nothing more and waited for him to take it in.

Victor had settled in at my old spot in front of the fan. His mother had spread out the beach towel for him. One side of the towel was a Confederate flag and on the other side there was a kneeling cowgirl in a bikini. Her body was sectioned off and labeled "Round," "Chuck," "Rump," and so on, like a side of beef, and the Western cutie was winking and saying, "What's your cut?" Victor was belly down on the towel reading a Little Lulu comic book. The book was in Spanish but he was still getting a few chuckles from it. "Hoo," he would say, and, "Hoo hoo." There might have been a dove in the room. Dr. Symes looked about for the source of these murmurs.

I said, "That's sterling silver. It's a complete set. All I want is fifty dollars on it until tomorrow."

"Certainly not. Why would I want to tie up my money in spoons? You'd do better to take this to a pawnbroker or a chili joint."

"It's just until noon tomorrow."

"Bill me later. That's your answer for everything. It's no good, Speed. You'll never get anywhere living on short-term credit like this. It's a bad game and I just can't keep carrying you. Who is that little chap on the floor?"

"He's the son of that girl in the bathroom."

"The one who's washing all the clothes?"

"Yes."

"Now who is she?"

I tried to tell him but as he was swinging his big head around Melba swam into his ken and he forgot Christine. He called out, "Melba, can you hear me?"

"I heard that," she said. "I haven't been listening to you, if that's what you mean."

"I want you to get up out of that chair this very minute."

"What for?"

"I want you to get up out of that chair and start walking two miles every day."

"No, Reo."

"Now isn't this a fine thing. She says no to her doctor."

He closed the chest and moved it to one side, away from me, in a proprietary way. I didn't think we had made a deal and I knew I had no money. Mrs. Symes had just made the painful trip up the stairs and she was standing at the top gasping for breath, trying to remember something, what the trip was for. She gave it up as a bad job and went back down the stairs.

The doctor handed me another envelope from the box. "Take a gander at that one, will you? Never opened. I wrote that letter to Mama from San Diego almost three years ago. How in the world can you do business with someone like that?"

"This letter was postmarked in Mexico."

"Old Mexico? Let me see. Yes, it sure was. Tijuana. I was going back and forth to the Caliente track. Notice the thick enclosure. Rod Garza had drawn up a prospectus for me. I wanted Mama to look it over and see if she wouldn't co-sign a note. I wrote this very letter in Rod's law office."

I pointed out that my previous loans were already secured by the bonds, that I had returned his wallet when he thought it was lost, and that this silver set was worth several hundred dollars. He appeared to consider the points and I thought he might even be wavering, but his thoughts were many miles to the northwest.

"Rod had been reprimanded twice by the Ethics Committee of the Tijuana Bar Association," he said, "but he could always work himself out of a corner. All except for that last one. You can't talk your way out of an exploding car, there's not enough time. And they knew he was no leaper. Oh, they had cased him, all right. They knew just how quick he was off the mark. He's gone now and I miss him more every day. Strawberries! Can you imagine that? We were trying to raise strawberries on government land. Rod got some boys out of prison to do the work, if you could call it work. As fast as you got one of those pickpockets on his feet, the one behind you would be squatting down again. And hot? You think this is hot? Those pimps were dropping in their tracks. Rodrigo would park his black Pontiac out there in the desert and then roll the windows up to keep the dust out. When we got back to it, the seat covers would be melting. Open the door and the heat blast would make you faint. An inferno. You could have roasted a duck in the trunk. Precious memories, how they linger. Listen to me, Speed. If your time is worth more than twenty cents an hour, don't ever fool with strawberries. I helped Rod every way I knew how. We were just like David and Jonathan. When he was trying to get his patent, I took him up to Long Beach and introduced him to a good lawyer name of Welch. Rod had an interest in a denture factory in Tijuana and he was trying to get a U.S. patent on their El Tigre model. They were wonderful teeth. They had two extra canines and two extra incisors of tungsten steel. Slap a set of those Tiger plates in your mouth and you can throw your oatmeal out the window. You could shred an elk steak with those boogers. Did I say Everett Welch? I meant Billy. Billy is the lawyer. He's the young one. I had known his father, Everett, you see, back in Texas when he was a scout there for the Cubs or the White Sox, one of the Chicago teams. He was a great big fine-looking man. He later went to Nevada and became minister of music at the Las Vegas Church of God, introduced tight harmony to those saps out there. He sold water to Jews. Jews are smart but you can put water in a bottle and they'll buy it. He had a high clear voice and when he sang ''Tis so sweet to be remembered on a bright or cloudy day,' you could close your eyes and swear you were listening to Bill Monroe himself. And get this. He's the only man I ever knew who saw Dix in the flesh. He met him once in the public library in Odessa, Texas. Listen to this. Dix was sitting at a table reading a newspaper on a stick and Welch recognized him from a magazine picture. It was right after that big article on Dix, right around the time of that famous June 1952 issue of *Motel Life* with the big spread on Dix, pictures of his trunk and his slippers and his mechanical pencil and some of his favorite motel rooms. The whole issue was devoted to Dix. There was a wide red band across the cover that said, 'John Selmer Dix: Genius or Madman?' I didn't have enough sense to stash away a copy of that magazine. I could name my own price for it today. That's the only place where Dix's Fort Worth address was ever published in full."

This was not, as I first thought, a speech or a proclamation that Dix had made in Fort Worth, but rather a post office box number and a zip code.

Dr. Symes continued, "This was during the period, you may remember, when Dix was on strike. He had repudiated all his early stuff, said *Wings* was nothing but trash, and didn't write another line, they say, for twelve years. Nobody really knows why. Oh, there were plenty of theories—that he was drunk, that he was crazy, that he was sick, that he was struck dumb before the immensity of his task, that he was just pissed off about something—but nobody really knows. Do you want my thinking on it? I believe he was actually writing all that time, that he was filling up thousands of sheets of paper with his thoughts and then just squirreling the stuff away in his tin trunk. But for some reason that we can't understand yet he wanted to hold it all back from the reading public, let them squeal how they may. Here's my opinion. Find the missing trunk and you've found the key to his so-called silent years. You've found a gold mine is what you've found.

"Anyway, Welch tried to talk to him there in the Odessa library, whisper to him, you know, across the table, but Dix wouldn't say anything. He wouldn't even admit he was Dix. He wanted to read his paper and every time Welch asked him a question Dix would just drum his feet under the table real fast, to show he was annoyed. Welch handled it all wrong. He got mad and grabbed the man by the throat and made him confess he was John Selmer Dix. Then Welch cooled off and apologized and Dix said that was all right but not to ever disturb him again while he was reading the *Star-Telegram*, that his private life was his own and all that. Now the question is, was that stranger really Dix? If it *was* Dix, answer me this. *Where were all his keys?* Everett Welch admitted to me that he saw no jumbo key ring on the man's belt and that he heard no clinking of keys when he was shaking him. Even so, Welch swears it was Dix he talked to that day. Welch is an honest man but I wasn't there and I can't say. I just don't know. The man may have been a very clever faker. There were plenty of fakers going around then, and they're still going around. You've probably heard of the fellow out in Barstow who claims to this day that he is Dix. I've never believed it. He lives out there in the desert in a caboose with his daughter and sells rocks. Can you beat it? Dix in the desert with his delicate skin. Selling ornamental quartz out of an old Southern Pacific caboose. If you believe that, you'll believe anything. Do you know what he says? He says the man who died in Tulsa was just some old retired fart from the oil fields who was trading off a similar name. He makes a lot of the closed coffin and the hasty funeral in Ardmore. He makes a lot of the missing trunk. Good points, you might think, but I've got a trump for him. *Dix never had a daughter!* There's another faker, in Florida, who claims he is Dix's half brother. Go see him out there on the edge of Jacksonville and he'll let you look at the trunk for a fee. A trunk is more like it. He won't dare to open it and you have to stand back about four or five feet behind a rope to even look at it. That little room is dark too, they say. Let me save you a trip to Florida, Speed. I've seen that crook's picture. They ran a picture of him and his little Dix museum in *Trailer Review* and I can tell you he bears no resemblance whatsoever to Dix and is in no way related to him. You can look at a man's ears and tell."

Here the doctor paused, having found the title abstract. He thumbed quickly through the pages until he came to the legal description of the island property. He showed me the authoritative figures, taking delight in the fractions and the "SW" and "NE," and then he left for his room to draft another letter.

I was desperate and shameless and I asked Melba if she could lend me ten dollars. She was willing enough but she couldn't help me because she had cashed a check for Christine and had only a dollar or two left in her purse. She showed me the yellow check. It had been folded so long the creases were fuzzy. It was a two-party check on a bank in Mesa, Arizona. There was nothing left to do but go and see Leet.

# *Eleven*

ALL THAT was left of the old ink factory was a tall brick chimney, round and tapering, of the kind that often marks the site of a small college or government hospital. Leet's Motor Ranch, a lesser dream, was a field of weeds that adjoined the factory grounds. It appeared to be more of a salvage yard than a used-car lot, more of a cemetery than a ranch. Two old industrial boilers from the ink factory were standing upright at the entrance to Leet's drive, forming a kind of grand portal. I say "from the ink factory" but that is only a guess because I know next to nothing about the manufacture of ink, whether it is ever boiled or subjected to bursts of steam at any stage, and these boilers may have had an entirely different origin.

I passed between them and drove down the lane and parked in front of Leet's headquarters shed, which was also his dwelling place. It was lighted in front by a yellow bulb. Behind the shed there were three columns of derelict cars, their hoods and trunk lids raised as though for a military inspection. I could hear the steady hum of insects or of advancing rust in the damp field. The only operable vehicle I could see, the only one on wheels, was a Dodge Power Wagon with a winch and a wrecker boom on the back.

Leet was sitting under the yellow light on a disembodied car seat. He had put his picture book aside and he was listening to organ music that came from two disembodied car speakers. They were connected to a disembodied cassette player which was in turn hooked up to a disembodied car battery with two alligator clips. He was pink instead of white and he had the fat pink hands of a child, little star-shaped hands, remarkably clean for his trade. They were clasped across his belly and he was stretched out with his ankles crossed.

I knew he had just polished off a big bowl of porridge or parsnips or some such dish, I having spotted him at once for a house pig like me who cherished his room and his kitchen treats and other solo and in-house indulgences. Beside him on top of a wooden ammunition box I saw a giant English chocolate bar, about ten inches by four inches by one inch, a stack of car magazines, and a three-gallon water cooler with a tin cup chained to it. Everything was within easy reach of the pink hands.

He didn't rise to greet me. He put on a pair of round glasses and said, "That looks like an old V-6 Buick."

"That's what it is."

"Dual-path transmission?"

"It's air-cooled. I don't know the name of it."

"Noisy timing chain?"

"It's a good car."

"No doubt, but it has a very rum transmission. Once it goes, that's it. You can't find spares."

"That should make it all the more valuable."

"In what way?"

"This car could be a ready source of those hard-to-get spares, as you call them."

"There's no market, my friend. The demand is zero. Do please give me credit for knowing my own business."

"I may sell the car if I can get my price."

"Not to me you won't."

I confronted him with one of his leaflets. "You said you wanted this car."

"No, I don't want that one. What's the true mileage?"

"I don't know. It's a good car. I made it down here all right. That's something, isn't it?"

"Yes, I'll give you that."

He took a flashlight and raised the hood. "What's all that wire around the manifold?"

"Coat-hanger wire. Engine restraint. Broken motor mount."

"Roadside repair?"

"Yes."

"That's interesting." He pulled the dipstick from the transmission and smelled the end of it. Then he started the engine and listened to it through a wooden yardstick, his ear at one end of the stick and the engine block at the other. Then he took a rubber mallet and went around tapping on the body panels. I drank a cup of his cold water.

"Mind the bees," he said. "They can smell fear."

There were white beehives in the shadows beside the shed. Striped bees that looked heavy were going about their deliberate business. I had never known they worked at night. Behind the hives I saw a Ford hulk. It was a long-hooded Torino covered with dried gray mud. The wheels were gone and it was resting flat on the ground amid some coarse flowers.

Leet completed the inspection and returned to his seat, slapping his palm with the yardstick. "You've got bad rust, my friend. I happen to know something about oxidation and what you've got is out of control."

"Where did you get that Torino? That's the first one I've seen down here."

"You don't see many. These niggers like the full-size models. Galaxies and Impalas."

"I have one like that, only mine is blue."

"That one's blue. Fellow burnt up the engine idling it. I hauled it in for a hundred dollars American and sold the air conditioner the same day for two hundred. I got another hundred for the radio and tape deck, and I got eighty for the tires and the baby moon hubcaps. Everything went but the sheet metal, and went fast too. I wish I had another one."

"How did he burn it up idling it?"

"He was idling it at about fifty-two hundred rpm's. Fell asleep with his foot on the accelerator. Drunk, I suppose, or a nut case. Just sat there dozing away with the engine screaming until the pistons seized. Beautiful 351 Windsor engine. Clean carburetor, clean battery terminals. Clean valve covers until the paint was cooked. No mess or oil seepage. No corrosion. The car had been well cared for."

"That's a shame."

"Yes, it's a great pity. Nice windfall for me, of course."

I already knew the truth but I moved in for a closer look and I saw my Arkansas inspection sticker in the corner of the windshield. This muddy shell was my Torino. I wiped off some of the mud with my hand.

Leet said, "I can give you two hundred for the little Buick. I pay the duty. It's an orphan, as I say, and you won't do any better than that."

"You've already bought my car, Leet. This Torino is my car. I have the title to it."

"Really?"

"Yes."

"It's a bit late to be speaking up."

"Dupree had no right to sell it."

"He had the car."

"Are you going to make it good?"

"Say again?"

"I say, are you going to make it good?"

"Do you mean am I going to reconstruct that car for you? Nothing of the kind. What a hope."

"I mean compensation."

"It's not on, my friend. I bought it in good faith."

"I don't believe you did. You said yourself it was a windfall. You spoke of Dupree as a nut case."

Leet flexed his shrimplike fingers. "I would hardly make those admissions again, would I? To a third party."

"Dupree had no papers. You bought it without a title."

"Listen to our little lawyer."

"I'll have to see about this in town."

"See about it all you please. Your word against his. It's nothing to do with me."

"It's more than my word. I have the papers."

"All right, here's some law for you, chum. The car was licensed in Arkansas and the boy had an Arkansas driving license. He had possession of the car. It was not for me to assume he was a thief. I would have been wrong to do so. That's nothing more nor less than good English law."

"Is it English equity?"

"Say again?"

"Equity. Fair play, like the hotel."

"Equity's grandmother. You can't put it all on me. You have a duty to look after your own stuff."

"That's just what I'm doing. I'll have to see about this."

"I thought the car was his to sell. I bought it. That's it. Bob's your uncle. Now you come along and say it's your car. Very well, I pay you too. Now tomorrow a third man comes to the Motor Ranch and makes a similar claim. Do I pay him, and the fourth and fifth man as well? How long could I stay in business, paying for the same car day after day? Not six years."

"Your third man wouldn't have the papers."

"You and your bleeding papers."

As a sign that our business was concluded, he picked up his book, *Flags of the World*, and found his place, Morocco and Mozambique, and fell into a deep study of these banners. It was an English or European book from the looks of the murky colors, or maybe it was the yellow light that made them appear so. I had a fellow-pig feeling for him, and I had the feeling too that he was the last of the Leets, that the House of Leet was winding up here in this tropical junkyard.

I said, "To tell the truth, Leet, I don't care about that car. It's not even mine. My father paid for it like everything else I have. I hate to find it here like this but my quarrel is not with you. I see that now."

These friendly words dispelled the chill somewhat.

He said, "The boy was odd and I suspected something. I'll give you that."

"He has a lot to answer for."

"I knew it was a funny business, I can't say I didn't. But then you get a lot of funny business in this place."

"It wasn't the car at all. I see that now."

"I knew he was a lunatic when I played this. Give a listen. I found this tape under the seat. You'll think it's a comedy recording like I did. I don't know what it is, a dramatic reading or some loony recitation."

He put the cassette into the tape player and the voice of Dr. Buddy Casey rang out across the dark field.

"'*Can you help us, Captain Donahue?*' *he cried. '*Yes, Major,*' *came the stout reply, '*my men are fresh and they are just the fellows for that work!*'"

Leet laughed. I snatched the tape from the machine. "That's mine too, Leet." The sudden noise had made the insects stop their racket for a moment but they were soon at it again.

I drove away in the Buick, not deigning to sell it, and I put the whole thing out of my mind, as though Leet had never been cast upon this shore with his fat fingers. I thought instead of Christine and her wet hair. I speculated on squeezing her, and more, being married to her, our life together in Vermont. She was a very good-natured girl. Resourceful too. Would she have to go to the doctor a lot? They all seemed to collapse right after the vows, even the robust ones like Christine. Female disorders. There are one or two points on female plumbing that I have never been clear on. And yet there was Mrs. Symes, in the pink for her age, and Otho in his grave these many years. But what would Christine and I talk about on long drives, or even on short ones? And what about Victor? Turn him over to Dean maybe. Pack all his little shirts and trousers and socks —doll socks!—in a box and send him to Dean. Tag him for Phoenix and put him on an express bus. Then Christine and I could have our own son, little Terry, a polite child, very nimble and fast on his feet.

I passed a sandy turnoff with a sign that said "TO THE BEACH" or something like that, and I fixed the location in my mind. I would take Christine there, to that very spot, for a night swim. It was just the kind of thing that would appeal to her, a moonlight swim. Perhaps Melba would make us some sandwiches. We would go in the van. If that van could talk! I would teach her how to swim in the luminous sea. She probably thought she would die if she put her face under water.

When I drove up to the church, a jeep was pulling away and Christine was in it. She shouted something back to me. The driver was a bearded man in a monk's robe and a planter's straw hat. One of his sandaled feet was cocked up on the floor sill of the jeep in swaggering G.I. Joe fashion. I waved and called after them but they didn't stop, my voice never having arrested anything in flight.

The movie had started. The chapel was packed with excited boys and I could hardly get in the door. I had always liked Tarzan well enough but I didn't see why this white lord of the jungle should be such a favorite with Negroes. Their own people were shown in these films as jabbering and rolling their eyes and dropping their packages and running away at the first sign of trouble. For solid action give me a submarine picture or a picture that opens with a DC-3 having engine trouble over a desert. I pushed my way through to the projector table where Mrs. Symes was leaning on her aluminum cane. The boy Victor was sitting there on her stool, hunched forward and looking like Jack Dempsey. He had been into Mrs. Symes's paper stars and he had stuck one on each of his fingernails.

Sweat was trickling down the poor old lady's powdered cheeks. She was trembling from the heat and intensity in the room. She was wearing a long black dress for the occasion and some pearl devices on her earlobes. The old projector clattered away, Father Jackie not having seen fit to bring along his deluxe machine. The lip movements on the screen were just a beat or so behind the voices.

I told Victor to get up and let Mrs. Symes have the seat. He made a move but she said no, she would rather stand. There was a bright green fly on her veined hand and she didn't seem to feel it. The fly was so still and so cleanly articulated that it didn't look quite real; it looked like something from a jewelry shop or a joke shop.

"Christine wants you to look after Victor," she said to me.

"Look after Victor?"

"She's gone with Father Jackie."

"I don't follow."

"Father Jackie wanted to show her the coconut dolls at the folk art center."

"At night? How long will that take?"

"She wants you to look after Victor till she gets back."

"I can't look after Victor."

"I'm busy, Mr. Midge. It's too hot to talk. I'm trying to watch this, if you don't mind."

"What about Father Jackie's mother? You said she was here. Why can't she look after him?"

"I'm trying to watch this."

It was an old Tarzan picture I had somehow missed on television. He seemed to be in the Coast Guard this time. He was patrolling the bayous of Louisiana in his cutter and he was having trouble with Buster Crabbe, who was some sort of Cajun poacher or crook. They were squabbling over the same sweetheart too, and the girl didn't know what to do. She had the foolish notion that she might be able to reform Buster Crabbe. Everyone was addressing Johnny Weissmuller as "Dave" or "Skipper" instead of Tarzan. A clever wrinkle, this undercover business, but we were all impatient for him to shed his uniform and go into some Tarzan action with vines and big cats and crocodiles. It seemed to me they were putting it off too long.

The boys had settled down by the time Mrs. Symes changed the reel. Some were asleep. I saw Webster Spooner standing against the wall, rocking slowly like a small bank guard, his hands behind his back. It was hot and close in that room and I had no place to sit. I was hungry too. I wanted to flee but I was stuck with Victor. Look after Victor! If the kid broke his arm or got sick or run over by a truck, it would all be my fault! Maybe I could get Webster to act as a companion and relieve me of some of the burden.

The show droned on and the boys began to stir and mutter. Before the second reel was done, one of them stood up in the life-giving radiance from the projector and said, "This don't be Tarzan, Meemaw."

"It is too," she said. "Sit down."

But it wasn't. It was just Johnny Weissmuller in the Coast Guard and not even at war. We could watch this thing all night and he wasn't going to stop being Dave. Father Jackie had a full bag of tricks!

The boys began to drift out in twos and threes and the door monitor made no effort to stop them. I asked Victor if he didn't want to leave too. He seemed to be drugged, stupefied. I caught Webster as he was making his way to the door.

"How are you tonight, Webster?"

"Meemaw is vexed."

"I know. Here, I want you to meet Victor Walls. Victor, give me your attention for a minute. This is Webster Spooner, a friend of mine. He's the bell captain at my hotel. I have a job to do and I want you boys to help me."

"What kind of job?"

"An important job. We're going for a drive."

Both of them rode in the front seat. I stopped at the Fair Play and told them to wait in the car while I went to my room and put on my boots. Ruth was gone. I went behind the desk and poked around to see if anything had come in for me. I opened the shoebox and found the message to my father, with the money still pinned to it. Ruth had never sent it to the cable office. All my letters were there too, the British Honduras covers I had addressed to myself in Little Rock. What a hotel!

I unpinned the money and took it with me upstairs and searched my room for boots. They were not in the suitcase and they were not under the bed. Where could they be? There was no other place in this bare cube of a room where black engineer's boots might be concealed. A dog, I said to myself.

Some town dog has nosed open the door here and carried off my boots in his mouth. But both boots? Could a dog manage that? Two trips maybe. Or two dogs. But had I in fact ever seen a dog in the hotel? No. Not counting the foyer where they sometimes gamboled and fought around Webster's box. I had never seen a dog on the stairs or in the hallway. Then it came to me with a swelling rush that I didn't own a pair of black engineer's boots either, or any other kind of boots.

Next door I could hear a heavy person walking back and forth on the creaking boards. Karl, perhaps, pondering his next move, whetting his knife and pacing, trying to decide whether to buy a new radio or get the old one repaired, the old tube set that had served him so well in so many different rooms. I felt a visceral twinge of pain, lungs maybe, and I sat down on the bed to wait for it to pass. The pain was concentrated in one burning spot about the size of a dime. I wondered if I might have been hit by a small stray bullet sometime during the afternoon. I had handled news accounts of men who had been shot and then walked about for hours, days, a lifetime, unaware of such wounds. Maybe the heart itself. I took the last of the orange pills, first blowing off the pocket lint. Downstairs the boys were honking the horn.

# Twelve

I DROVE with care on Bishop Lane. The shadows were deceptive under the headlights and it was hard to tell the big holes from the little holes. I soon became fatigued from making so many judgments, half of them wrong, and so I gave up making them, or rather, acting on them, and I hit the holes as they came, without regard to width or depth.

Victor had shaken off his grogginess in the night air. After each violent jolt he would shout, "Good deal, Lucille!" and Webster would laugh. Victor fiddled with all the knobs too, and he wanted to know why things didn't work, the dash lights and the radio.

He said, "How much will this thing do, hey? What kind of old car is this anyway? I hate it. You need to get you a Volkswagen where you can sit up high. My mom says Volkswagens are the most powerful cars in the world." There was a sharp edge to his voice. The little Yankee had never been taught to say "sir."

"It'll do plenty," I said, and I stepped on the gas and we hit the creeks at high speed. Water shot up through the floor and the boys began to squeal and jump about. Now I was driving recklessly.

A catlike animal sprang into the road and then stopped. I saw his face in the glare and it looked almost human in that brief moment of indecision. He decided against chancing it, the full crossing, and scrambled back to his starting place.

"A fox!" said Victor.

"No," I said. "That was a coati, or coatimundi. He's related to another animal that we know well. A very clever fellow who washes his food. He has a ringed tail and a black burglar's mask. Can anyone tell me the name of that animal?"

They weren't listening to me. We came up out of a creek bottom and topped a low rise and there in the middle of the road was a dead cow. I swung the car to the left, catching the bloated corpse with the right headlights. It was only a glancing blow and I didn't stop. Both headlights on the right side were smashed and the steering was further affected so that there was now almost a half-turn of slack in the steering wheel. The position of the crossbar on the wheel was altered too, from horizontal to vertical, and with this new alignment I couldn't seem to get my hands placed right.

"Webster?"

"Sor?"

"Who is responsible for removing dead animals from your roads?"

"I don't know."

"One of those rib bones could go right through a tire at today's high speeds."

It was more than I could do to keep the car in the narrow lane, what with the steering and the lighting problems. We swung from one side to the other, our progress describing a sine curve. Bushes slapped against the undercarriage each time we left the road. It didn't occur to me to slow down. On one of these swoops we hurtled through the Mayan clearing where the Indian brothers had retired for the night to their stone chamber. That is, I could see the glow of a candle behind the doorway curtain as we passed within inches of it, but we were in and out of the place before they could do much more than exchange apprehensive glances.

The end came a few minutes later. Webster and Victor were wrestling and crawling back and forth over the seat and one of them kicked the shift lever down into reverse, which, on this singular car, was on the far right side of the shifting arc. The transmission shuddered and screeched and quit before I could make a move, my hands being occupied with the wheel. The car coasted to a stop in a marshy place.

"Now see what you've done!"

We got out and stood around in the mud. The boys were quiet for a change. I would have cut a limb and gladly beaten them both but you always have to weigh one thing against another and I didn't want to listen to their bawling. They might have run too, the second one anyway. I could hear transmission fluid dripping and I could smell the odor of burnt sugar. There was another sound that I couldn't place immediately. Something unpleasant was disturbing the air. Then I figured out that it was rock-and-roll music and that it must be coming from the Indians' transistor radio.

I said, "All right then, we'll walk. It's not far now. There better not be any more monkeyshines, I can tell you that."

"Where are we going?"

"We're going to see Guy Dupree."

"You don't have no electric torch?"

"We don't need one. I can see at night. I can see stars down to the seventh magnitude. Just stay behind me and step where I step."

Above the trees in the narrow cut of the road there was a dazzling band of stars. My eye went directly to the Clouds of Magellan, although I had never seen them before. I knew then that I would not be able to see the Southern Cross, not at this time of year. I had only a rough picture in my mind of the southern celestial sphere but I did know that the Southern Cross was very far away from those clouds, perhaps as much as 180 degrees. I pointed out the two galaxies to Webster and Victor, or tried to. They found the large cloud easily enough but I couldn't make them see the pattern, the luminous smudge of the small cloud, low in the south.

I said, "Can anyone tell me what a galaxy is? A little knowledge about these things can greatly increase our enjoyment of them."

There was no answer, as before, with the much easier raccoon question. Webster asked me about a red star, not Betelgeuse or Antares, directly overhead. I couldn't identify it. "These are poor horizons," I said, "and I'm not really familiar with these skies. Now here's something interesting. Victor and I can't see all those stars where we live. We have different stars, you see, depending on how far north or south we live."

Victor spoke up. "My mom says this is the age of Aquarius."

I set off down the road at a brisk marching pace. Victor continually disobeyed my orders. He ran ahead and stirred up some small hopping birds, shooing them before him with his hands.

"Stop chasing those birds, Victor. You can't catch a bird. I want you both to stay behind me. I'm supposed to be in front at all times."

"What kind of birds are they?"

"They're just road birds."

"Can they talk?"

"No."

"Do they lay their tiny eggs in the road?"

"I don't know. Get behind me and stay there. I won't tell you again."

"I hate this road and I hate all these trees."

"You boys must do just as I say. I want us to stay together. If you mind me and don't give me any more trouble, I'm going to buy you each a nice gift when we get back to town. But you must do just what I say."

Webster said, "I already know what I want. I want a tack hammer and a rubber stamp with my name on it and a walkie-talkie radio."

"The tack hammer and the rubber stamp are all right. I'm not buying any walkie-talkie."

Victor said, "I don't get this. What are we doing out here anyway?"

"I told you we're going to see Guy Dupree. He has my wife in his house out here and I mean to go in there after her. I'm through fooling around with him. It's a long story and I don't want to go into it any further than that."

"What was his name again?"

"Guy Dupree."

"You mean you're going to fight this Guy Dupree?"

"Yes."

"Oh boy, this will be good. I'm glad I came now. Will you have to kill him?"

"No more chatter."

"Oh boy, this will really be good. What we ought to do is cut off Guy Dupree's head with a knife and see what his eyes look like then."

"What I want you to do is hush."

"If somebody got my mom, I'd cut off his head and see if it could talk and then I would watch his eyes to see if they moved any."

"Webster is minding me and you're not. Do you know what that means, Victor? That means he'll get a nice gift and you'll get nothing."

No sooner had I commended Webster for his silence and put him forward as an example than he pinched my arm and asked a question. "Does Guy Dupree be in the hands of the devil?"

"Guy Dupree is sorry. We'll leave it at that. I can't answer any of your questions about the devil. That's out of my field."

"Meemaw say the devil he have a scaly body and a long tongue that run in and out of his mouf like a snake."

"That's a traditional representation, yes. And goat feet."

"She say he have a gold pocket watch a million years old that don't never run down."

"I've never heard anything about the watch."

"He always know what time it is."

"My mom says there's no such thing as the devil."

"Your mom is misinformed about many things, Victor. She may well be wrong about that too."

"How do the devil be everywhere at one time?"

"I don't know, Webster. I tell you I can't answer questions like that. You see me as a can-do guy from the States, but I don't have all the answers. I'm white and I don't dance but that doesn't mean I have all the answers. Now I want you both to listen up. From here on in we're playing the quiet game. I don't want to hear another peep out of anybody until I give the all-clear signal, which will be my open hand rotating rapidly above my head, like this."

Victor said, "I want a pellet gun for my present. I want one you can pump up about thirty times."

"I'm not buying any pellet gun. Forget it. That's out."

"Why can't we have what we want?"

"I'm not buying any expensive junk. The pellet gun and the walkie-talkie are both out."

"I hate these mosquitoes."

As for the gifts, I had already given some thought to setting Webster up in the snow-cone business. No one seemed to be selling snow cones in this steaming land. A small cart and an ice scraper and some flavored syrups and conical paper cups and he would be ready to roll. Mr. Wu knew a good thing when he saw it. He was making a fortune off soft ice cream and spending it on God knows what Oriental cravings, or more likely, stashing it away in a white Chinese sock with a toe pouch. Webster would have the advantage of being mobile. He could take his refreshing ices directly to the chicken fights and harvest festivals. One thousand grape snow cones at the summer corn dance! I had not yet mentioned the idea because I didn't want it to get out. Something cheap would do for Victor. I had seen a little book called *Fun with Magnets* in the window of a variety store in Belize. The book was faded and shopworn and I could probably get it for less than a dollar.

He was walking along behind me chanting, "Guy Dupree, Guy Dupree, Guy Dupree," and Webster picked it up, this chant. I made them stop it. Victor asked me if they could walk backward.

"You can walk any way you please as long as you keep up and don't make a lot of noise."

"Can we hold our knees together and just take little short steps?"

"No, I don't want you to do that."

"You said—"

"I don't want you to walk like that. And if you don't shut up I'm going to put a rubber stopper in your mouth."

"A stopper? I don't get that."

"One of those things that babies suck on. With a flange and a ring on the outside. If you behave like a baby, I'll have to treat you like a baby."

He was quiet for a while and then he began to pester me with questions about the Buick. How would we get back to town? What if a crook stole it? What would I do if it was full of animals when we got back?

"I may just leave it there," I said. "A man told me today that there are no spare parts here for that particular transmission. I'm no longer interested in that car and I'm not answering any more questions about it. Do you hear me?"

"You can't just leave your car out in the woods."

"The subject is closed. I don't want to hear another word. I haven't had anything to eat since this morning and I can't answer any more questions."

"If you leave it there, how will you get back to Texas?"

"I'm not *from* Texas."

"You can't ride in our van."

"Have you heard me say at any time that I wanted to ride in your van?"

"We just have two bucket seats. One is mine and one is my mom's."

"For your information, Victor, I plan to fly home with my wife."

"Yeah, but what if the plane goes into a tailspin and you don't have a parachute to bail out in?"

"The plane is not going into a tailspin for the very simple reason that these commercial pilots know what they're doing. All those planes get regular maintenance too. So many flying hours and that's it, they're back in the shop."

There was no light in the Dupree house and I wondered if he had heard us coming. All this chatter. He was very likely posted at one of the darkened windows and cooking up a plan. I felt sure he couldn't see us in any detail with his feeble eyes. He wouldn't be able to make out that Webster and Victor were children. For all he knew, they could be short hired thugs or two boy detectives. I had a plan of my own. I didn't intend to expose the boys to any real danger but I thought they could serve well enough and safely enough as a base of fire. I knew that the attacking force should always be at least three times the size of the defending force.

I marked off a place beside the garbage dump and told the boys, whispering, to gather rocks and place them in a pile there.

"What kind of rocks?"

"Rocks like this, for throwing. Not too big and not too little."

We set about our task without speaking. The quality of the rocks was poor, running mostly to thin limestone shards, and even these were hard to find. Victor appeared to be doing a fine job. He scurried about and made two and sometimes three trips to the pile for every one that Webster and I made. Then I saw that he was just picking up whatever came to hand, sticks and cans and clods of dirt, and was making the rock pile ridiculous with these things. He soon stopped work altogether and said he was tired.

"All right," I said. "We'll rest for a minute."

Webster said, "What do these rocks be for?"

"We're going to throw them at that house."

"At Guy Dupree's house?"

"Yes."

"I don't like to do that, sor."

"Dupree has my wife in that house and she may be sick. People get sick down here."

Webster was shamed into silence.

"How would you like it if a gang of howling raiders came over here from Guatemala and stole your women? You would strike back, wouldn't you? And very properly so. We'll make Dupree keep his head down with these rocks and then I'll dash across the road. I'll be in the house before he knows it."

We lined up three abreast and flung a volley across the road. I was disappointed by the puny effect, by the soft thunks of the rocks striking wood. I had the boys lie down, against the possibility of a shotgun blast, but there was no answer of any kind, not even a bark.

I stepped up the attack. With each salvo our aim improved and before long we were breaking windows. Webster and Victor quickly got into the spirit of the thing, so much so that I had to restrain them. Still there was no response. I mixed things up so that Dupree could not count on a recurring pattern. One volley might follow another instantly, or there might be an interval of several minutes. Once, instead of loosing the expected flurry of small rocks, I heaved one big rock the size of a cantaloupe onto the porch. Watch out for the florr! Dupree would soon be whimpering for his pills.

But he was clever and after a while I could see that his plan was to sit out the barrage. He hoped to discourage us and wear us down. Two could play that game. I stopped all activity.

"We'll wait one hour exactly," I said. "If we keep perfectly quiet, he'll think we've left and then we'll let him have it again harder than ever. That's the thing that will break him."

"When will you make your dash, sor?"

"I'll make my dash when I'm ready. Put that in your notebook."

The minutes dragged. I anticipated a problem keeping the boys still and I wished I had brought something with which they could pass the time, perhaps a little ball they could roll back and forth. But they were exhausted and they fell asleep at once despite the mosquitoes.

I lay down too, behind a low rock parapet. It was very quiet out there for a jungle, or more accurately, a marginal rain forest with a few deciduous trees. I strained to see and hear things, always a mistake, the reconnaissance manuals say, leading one to see animated bushes. Once I thought I could make out two small, dim, ratlike figures walking upright, holding hands and prancing in the road. I even imagined I could hear rat coughs. Curious illusion. I checked the time again and again. My watch crystal was fogged on the inside. I lost interest in the wheeling stars. It occurred to me that if I had brought along the doctor's flashlight I could move about giving fake signals.

I crawled forward a few feet and fashioned myself a new watching place, recalling that Pancho Villa had been a great night mover. The troops would be sitting around the campfire and he would yawn and say, "Well, boys, I think I'll turn in," or something to that effect in Spanish, and then he would lie down and roll up in a blanket in full view of everyone. But he wouldn't stay in that place! He would move three or four times during the night and not even the most trusted of his Dorados could say where General Villa might finally turn up the next morning. I crawled forward again. And perhaps once more.

I dozed and woke. I thought I could see the Southern Cross, the broken cross pattern of stars, just brushing the southeast horizon. But was that possible? I dozed and woke again. Baby frogs with a golden sheen were capering about at my feet. They were identical in size and appearance, brothers and sisters hatched from the same jellied mass, and they all moved as one like a school of fish when I wiggled a foot. I looked at them and they looked at me and I wondered how it was that I could see them so clearly, their placid frog faces. Then I realized it was dawn. The frogs only looked golden. I was lying in the middle of the road and I had slept for hours. The world's number one piddler had taken to his bed again.

Webster and Victor slept on. There was an odd stillness as though some familiar background machinery had stopped. I could see on the porch scattered evidence of the rock storm. I got up and entered the yard through the flimsy gate. The dog was nowhere about.

At the foot of the steps I called out for Norma, although I knew there was no one in the place. I could sense this was an empty house. I went about inside from room to squalid room. There were containers of water everywhere, buckets and cans and jugs. On the back porch there was a washtub filled with water. A drowned gray bat was floating in it, his fine wet fur slightly darker than the galvanized tub. There were no Dupree papers to be seen on the kitchen table, only some orange peelings and a slender bottle of red sauce and a small photograph. It was a picture of Dupree and his dog that had been taken in one of those coin-operated photo booths. There they were, their heads together, Gog and Magog, looking dully at me. I came across nothing of Norma's, no golden hair on a pillow, but I didn't look closely at things and I didn't stay long.

# *Thirteen*

THE BUICK was sunk to the bumpers in black mud. A D-9 Caterpillar couldn't have pulled it out of that muck, von Guericke's vacuum principle being what it is, implacable, and in another day or so the car would be swallowed whole by the earth. Leet's scouts had not yet found it and the windshield was clear of leaflets. I could see inside that a disgusting mound of living mud had forced its way up through the floor hole.

We walked on to the Mayan ruin, our trouser legs wet with dew and picking up grass seeds along the way. We were sore from sleeping on the ground and our faces and hands were blotchy with mosquito bites. I led the way. We kept our early-morning thoughts to ourselves. Victor carried a rock that was coated with dark green moss on one side. He wouldn't answer any questions about it, wouldn't say what his plans were for the rock. He just kept shifting it from hand to hand as his clenching fingers grew tired.

Our approach to the ruin was in no way noisy or alarming but neither was it stealthy enough to permit us a glimpse of the third brother. He had already flown to his hiding place. The other two were as merry as ever at the prospect of another full day in the brush. They greeted us with shouts of laughter and they gave us some coffee and tortillas and canned white lard from their meager stores. We spread the lard on the tortillas.

After breakfast we toured the ruin. They pulled a stone from the pyramid and showed me their hidden cache of figurines and other artifacts, but they wouldn't let me handle the objects. Then they pointed to the tire ruts in the soft earth and they acted out a car blasting through the clearing, each in his own way, in a kind of motor dance. A drunken Popo, I suggested, but they indicated that Popo's rig was much smaller and slower than the phantom machine. They asked me for cigarettes again and I gave them some of the money I had taken from Ruth's shoe box. They got out their E bonds and I thought at first they were trying to give them back to me. They went to the cache and brought back an incised monkey skull to add to the bonds. Finally I got the drift. They wanted to exchange these things for a little nine-volt radio battery. Of course I had no battery and I gave them the rest of my money and accepted the skull. We shook hands all around.

Victor and Webster were dozing in the grass. I got them on their feet and we walked another two miles or so before we caught a ride in a pickup truck. The driver was an American, a hippie-looking fellow but rugged too at the same time, a pioneer. We rode in the back with the milk cans, our rigid limbs splayed out in all directions to provide support.

We got out at the market in Belize. The air was moist and very still. Webster treated us to some Pepsi-Colas at the Chinaman's store and I was a little surprised at this because most children are close with their money. Mr. Wu himself was indisposed, or maybe around the corner making a deposit at Barclays Bank, under that heraldic black eagle sign, or maybe he was just sleeping in. His mother or wife or sister was running the store. The firemen were at their table and I said to myself, Things are happening all over and they go on drinking their coffee. As long as it isn't a fire, they don't care.

Webster left for his hotel duties. Victor and I walked on to the tabernacle. Christine's van was parked in front of the place and so was Father Jackie's jeep. I knew Christine would have some sharp words for me when she saw her son's swollen face.

The door was open but no one seemed to be about. The chapel was in disarray. Some of the borrowed chairs were overturned and the floor was littered with flat scraps of paper that would be hard to sweep up. The movie projector was still on the table uncased, the lenses unprotected from drifting bits of lint that would take on a hairy, jerky life when magnified and illuminated.

We went upstairs. Christine had moved her bags in and there by the door to the doctor's room was his pebbly grip, all packed. More suitcase facts. The breakfast or supper dishes were still on the table. I couldn't understand the sudden housekeeping decline. I stood there and thoughtfully ate some cold black beans from a bowl. I was eating at every opportunity. Victor curled up in Melba's chair. His chin glistened with lard. Christine probably wasn't much of a cook. The lard tortillas had been perfectly acceptable to him.

I roused him and we went back downstairs and then we

heard voices from behind the movie screen. There was a door in the rear wall that opened into a yard and it was there we found them—Dr. Symes and Melba and Christine and Father Jackie. But where was Mrs. Symes?

This back yard was a nook I had not known about, a small fenced area with crushed white shells on the ground. Roses grew along the board fence and there were chairs made from rough sticks and leather straps, although there was none for me. Under the roof drain there was a rain barrel, to catch soft water for hair-washing. The place was no doubt intended as a meditation spot, a private retreat, but on this occasion everyone was eating watermelon. Dr. Symes used salt. He couldn't see the fine white grains as they dribbled from the shaker and he bounced them off the back of his hand so as to gain some idea of the rate of flow. The flesh of the watermelon was orange instead of red.

Victor went at once to Christine's lap. The rock was a gift for her. She said, "Hey, a super mossy!" and she looked it over and then put it aside and began to pick bits of dirt and gravel from Victor's hair. She had no words at all for me and no one was curious about our adventures because of a grave development that overshadowed such things. Far from being a luau, this was a wake!

Mrs. Symes had suffered a stroke and, I gathered, had died during the night. Dr. Symes and Christine had taken her to the hospital in the van, and had stayed there with her until they were told there was no hope. I couldn't believe it. A person I knew. Here one day and gone the next. An old enough story but it never fails to knock me for a loop. Then I get over it about as fast as anyone else and very soon I am able to carry on again. Melba cut me a section of watermelon and I sat on the rough shells and ate it with my fingers.

Father Jackie, who had a strong nasal voice, was doing most of the talking. He said, "She drank far too much ice water but you couldn't tell her anything."

Dr. Symes shifted his weight about on the sagging leather straps. He was fully dressed, even to the hat and bow tie and flashlight. On the ground beside his chair there was an old-fashioned steel lockbox, of a dark green color. He wiped his sticky hands on his white trousers. I could see he was impatient

with Father Jackie's lay opinion, with the notion that cold
water could cause death or even serious illness. He had been
holding his mother's aluminum cane between his knees and
now he began to rotate it rapidly back and forth between his
open hands, like a scout trying to make fire. All this in preparation for an important statement.

Before he could get it out, Father Jackie said, "I know one
thing. There was nothing on this earth that Meemaw was
afraid of."

"She was afraid of hurricanes," said Melba. "Waterspouts.
Any strong wind or black rain from the south. That little cloud
right up there would make her uneasy. She was afraid that bits
of flying glass would cut her neck."

Father Jackie told a story about a trip he had taken with
Mrs. Symes to a place called Orange Walk. They had gone in
his jeep to attend a sale or an auction of some kind at a bankrupt ranch. Throughout that day he had played various good-
natured tricks on her, some of which she turned back on him
to good effect. It was an interesting story, if a little long, full
of lively incident illustrating different aspects of the old lady's
character.

What part of the U.S.A. did Father Jackie hail from? I wrestled with this problem and couldn't work it out. He talked on
and on. A theory formed in my head on the origin of his nasal
tones. It was this. When he was a small child, his prankster
father—a bitter man, jealous of the boy's promise—had taught
him to speak in this fashion, taught him to honk, to recite,
"The three lintle kintons they lost their mintons and they began to cry," thus fixing the habit early and assuring his failure
in the world, the boot from every job, even street attacks. But
was that really probable? Wasn't it more likely that this was
just a kind of pulpit whine that was taught in his particular
seminary?

The Orange Walk story was a pretty good one, as I say, and
when it was over, Christine laughed and squeezed his knee in
an intimate way and said, "You stinker you!" One of his knees
showed through the parting of the brown robe. He reached
over and plucked a shiny coin from Victor's ear and said, "My
goonness, what's this?" But the boy was in a stupor again, his
mouth ajar, and the illusion did not delight him.

Dr. Symes saw his chance and got his statement out. He said, "I don't know what the poets of Belize are doing this morning but I can tell you what they should be doing. They should all be in their little rooms composing memorials to that grand lady."

A large speckled insect flew slowly about before our faces, going in turn from one speaker to the next as though listening. Melba slapped at it ineffectually. She asked me if I had a camera. I said no and then she asked Dr. Symes. "I sure don't," he said. "Marvel used to have a little box camera but I myself have never owned one. I have never personally photographed anything in my life. Why do you ask such a question?"

"I thought it would be nice to have our picture taken out here with the roses and then later we could look at it and say, Yes, I remember that day."

Dr. Symes said the last time he had his picture made was in California. It was for his driver's license and they wouldn't let him wear his hat. "Don't ask me why. It's just some rule they have. No hats and no caps. They've got a million rules in California and that just happens to be one of them." He shook his head and laughed at the memory of the bizarre place.

Melba said, "If it's your own hat, I don't see why you couldn't wear it if you wanted to."

"I don't either, Melba, but you can't. I've seen plenty of good pictures of people wearing hats. Some of the finest pictures I've ever seen have been of people with their hats on. All I'm saying is that it's forbidden in California."

Father Jackie said he had a 35-millimeter camera at his cottage. But this was just by way of information and he made no move to go and get it. Christine said that her former husband, Dean, had a number of expensive cameras and that his favorite subject was his watch-repair tools. He would arrange the tiny instruments on a green cloth and photograph them from atop a stepladder, the challenge being to capture all the tools with a minimum of distortion. She was not allowed in the room while he was doing this but afterward he would show her the finished prints and ask her which one she liked best. After she had left Dean and moved to Mesa, she said, he annoyed her by prowling outside her apartment at night and shining different kinds of lights through her windows. I don't know whether she meant lights of different intensities or lights of different colors because all she said was "different kinds of lights."

Father Jackie asked Melba if she wanted him to arrange for death notices in the local papers and the New Orleans papers.

"Let's hold up on that," said the doctor. "We don't want to rush into this thing."

"I'll be glad to type up a full obituary if you'll give me the information. I'll tell you right now, these newspapers will just throw your stuff in the wastebasket if it's not written up on a typewriter. I found that out from writing letters to the editor."

The doctor said, "Just hold up on that, if you will, my friend. You can do what you please at this end, but I have already told Melba that I will handle the Louisiana end. I will make all the notifications that need to be made. Do you understand what I'm telling you?"

"It's no trouble, I assure you."

"I appreciate that and I appreciate your concern but I want you to leave that part of it alone."

"Whatever you say."

"Fine, fine. That's what I say."

Dr. Symes then told Melba that he didn't like the idea of his mother being buried here in this Honduras mud, so far from her real home in Louisiana where Otho lay. Melba said it was a question of a person's wishes. Mrs. Symes had insisted on burial in the Belize cemetery with the pirates and drowned children and nameless wanderers, and a person's last wishes, when reasonable, had to be respected. She had not insisted on one of those simple funerals that cause everybody so much trouble, but there were one or two special requests. Her age, for instance. She was sensitive about her age and didn't want a date of birth inscribed on her tombstone. So be it. Melba intended to see that all of Nell's reasonable wishes were carried out.

The doctor made no strong protest. "Very well," he said. "I leave it in your hands, Melba. I know you'll do the right thing. Whatever you decide to do will just tickle me to death."

"I don't see why you can't stay for the funeral."

"You know I would if I could. We can't always do what we'd like to do, Melba. I'm needed in Ferriday now and it's a trip

I can't put off. It's imperative that I be on the ground there personally. I won't be missed here anyway. There'll be so many mourners at the service that you'll have to put up loudspeakers outside the chapel. And all around the altar, just beaucooz of beautiful flowers. I'd give anything if I could see that lovely floral display, or just one glistening tear in the eye of some small child whose heart Mama had touched."

They had already been over this ground, I could tell. Melba sent me to the market for a second watermelon and when I came back they were discussing very frankly the disposal of Mrs. Symes's property. Melba had been a witness to the will and she knew the terms. It was clear that she and the doctor had already chewed over this matter too, and were returning to it now for mere secondary comment. Even so, I was able to get the picture and it was a bleak one for Dr. Symes. His mother had left him nothing. Nothing, that is, except for the green lockbox, which contained a poem she had written about a hurricane, of some three hundred-odd verses. The tabernacle went to Melba, and certain sums of money to the girl Elizabeth and to a cabdriver and handyman named Rex. The rest of the estate went to Mrs. Symes's great-granddaughter, Rae Lynn Symes, who was Ivo's daughter. It was a handsome settlement and was to be used to further the girl's music education.

Wasn't this a sensational disclosure? A bombshell? The doctor's hopes all dashed? And yet he showed little concern. He was subdued, all right, but there was also a kind of monstrous jauntiness in his manner.

I said, "What about Jean's Island?"

"She gets the island too," he said. "There's not a thin dime for me but there's hundreds of thousands of dollars for Rae Lynn and her piano lessons. You can see where that puts Marvel. Right in the driver's seat. Mama has now brought about the very situation she so hoped to avoid."

"Then there's nothing to be done."

"I wouldn't say nothing."

"What then?"

"Let me tell you how it is, Speed. I need to be on the ground in Louisiana. All right? Nuff said?"

It wasn't quite enough but it was all I was ever going to get. Victor was asleep. Christine held him with one arm and she was sketching something with her free hand. She said, "How old was Meemaw anyhow?"

I said, "Melba just got through saying that her age was a secret, Christine. Didn't you hear that about the tombstone?"

"I didn't hear that. What was it?"

It wasn't that Christine's question was improper in itself but I thought she should have been paying closer attention to what people were saying. I had been thinking about the tombstone business all along, even during the more important will discussion, wondering at this posthumous vanity. What were Mrs. Symes's fears? That cemetery strollers would pause before her stone and compute the age? *Here, look at this one. No wonder she's dead.*

Christine tore the sketch from her pad and passed it around. It was a portrait of Melba with her hands clasped together on her lap in resignation. Christine may have been an artist, who can say, but she was no draftsman. The only thing she got right was Melba's hair, the wisps. The face was misshapen and dead, a flat, identikit likeness with one Mongoloid eye lower than the other. But Melba herself was pleased, if not with the portrait, at least with the attention. She said, "You're a fine girl, Christine."

Dr. Symes came to his feet and stretched. He asked Melba if he could keep the aluminum cane and she said he could take what he pleased from his mother's personal things.

"No, no, the stick is all. I have my lockbox and I'll just take this stick along for support and protection. It will also serve as a memento, what is it, mori."

"We ought to be ashamed of ourselves, talking like this, and poor Nell down there in the hospital struggling for her life."

"She's beyond the struggle, Melba. You can take my word for it as a physician."

"I don't know, Reo. You remember way back there when she had the incurable bone disease. The doctors just gave up on her. You remember they said she had to die. They said she would never rise from her bed. Five doctors said she had to die in three days. They wanted to give her a shot and just put her to sleep like an animal. And that was thirty-six years ago. I expect every one of those doctors is dead today."

"Pneumonia, Melba. Aspiration. Pulmonary fluids. The infection is setting in at this moment and she'll never be able to throw it off. I've seen way too much of it with these old people. You can take my word for it, church is out this time."

He gathered up his lockbox and said, "And now if you good people will excuse me I'm going to the hospital and kiss my old mother goodbye." He tapped my shoe with the cane and said, "Speed, behave yourself," and he went away.

I had rebuked Christine for not listening and all the time it was I who had been asleep at the switch. Mrs. Symes had not yet expired!

A few drops of rain fell on us, big ones. Melba said the big drops meant that we could expect a downpour, along with violent electrical discharges from the sky. She caught a silver drop in her hand and closed her fingers on it and said it reminded her of something we might find interesting. It was a recent vision. She had seen Dr. Symes being struck down by a big truck on a busy American highway. It was night and sleet was falling on the expressway and she could only see him off and on by the headlights of the giant trucks as they hit him over and over again, tossing him about like a bullfighter.

As she spoke, the speckled insect hovered in front of her eyes in an annoying way. She slapped at it again and said, "Get out of here, you naughty bug!" She asked us not to divulge the grim vision to Dr. Symes if we saw him again, and she went inside.

There followed an awkward silence, as with strangers being suddenly thrown together. Then Father Jackie leaned toward me and said that Mrs. Symes was a good woman but she had no business baptizing little children, or anyone else. She had no authority. And she had no business filling their heads with a lot of Calvinist nonsense. As for Melba, he said, tapping one finger to the steel plate in his own reconstructed skull, she was a little cracked. She laughed at inappropriate times. She had once given a little girl a toasted mouse for her cat. I didn't say anything because I didn't want to invite further confidences from this fellow.

Christine asked me who John Selmer Dix was and I told her he was a famous writer. Father Jackie said he had read a number of Dix's books and had found them excellent. He said he had always been fond of English detective stories, though he objected to the English practice of naming all the American characters Hiram or Phineas or Homer, and of making them talk in an odd way. I couldn't follow that, and then I saw that he must have Dix mixed up with some other bird, with the vain grunts of some other writer. He asked Christine if she would like to join him for lunch at his cottage.

"Some of the guys and chicks from the Peace Corps are dropping in for a rap session," he said. "I know you'll like them. They're really neat dudes. It's a regular thing we have. Nothing fancy, I assure you. We just have red wine and cheese and crackers and other munchies and we kick around a few ideas. But don't say I didn't warn you! It can get pretty heated at times!"

Christine said she thought she would stay at the tabernacle and relax and visit with Melba and listen to the rain on the tin roof.

He said, "How about you, Brad?"

He thought my name was Brad! I recognized the polite afterthought for what it was and I suspected too that those Peace Corps people might have guitars and so I too declined.

# Fourteen

M ELBA WAS right about the downpour. There wasn't a great deal of lightning but the rain fell and the wind blew. Wooden shutters were battened down all across town. Broken palm fronds and power lines had fallen to the streets. The electricity was knocked out early and all the stores were dark inside, though it wasn't yet noon. I sloshed through the foyer of the Fair Play Hotel where an inch or so of water had already accumulated. Ruth was gone. Webster's sleeping box had begun to float and I put it up on the counter.

I ran up the stairs and found a skinny stranger sitting on my bed. He was wearing heavy boots of a European design, with laces running from one end to the other. He was sitting there in the gloom writing in a spiral notebook. He jumped when I opened the door and he closed the notebook and shoved it under a pillow. This bird has been composing something! I had caught him in the very act of putting pen to paper and his shame was painful to see.

"What do you want?" he said.

"This is my room."

"This is the one they gave me."

"Where's my suitcase?"

"I don't know. This is the room they showed me. There was nothing in here. Are you checking out?"

"I didn't think so, no."

He was tall and yellow and fleshy around the middle, an ectomorph with a paunch. He looked to be an intelligent person. His stuff was packed in a rubberized cloth bag that was choked off tight at the top with a drawstring. He pulled it closer to him and rested one hand on it in a protective way. He saw me as a threat not only to his notebook but to his bag too.

I questioned him. He said he was booked on a Nicaraguan Airlines flight to New Orleans but it had been canceled because of the weather. For the past few months he had been back in the hills prospecting for immaculite and jade and tail feathers from the rare quetzal bird. He was now going home to see his brother ride in a prison rodeo, and, if it could be worked out, he also wanted to attend the state fair. Then he would return here to his immaculite diggings and to certain jade-bearing stream beds.

"What is immaculite?" I said. "And why is it mined?"

"It's a fine crystal that is used in precision optical instruments."

"Is that it?"

"That's it. That's the story of immaculite."

"It's funny I've never heard of it. I wouldn't mind seeing some of that stuff."

"I don't have any with me. I don't have any jadeite or quetzal feathers either."

The way he said it made me think he was lying. My clothes were soaked and I was dripping water on the floor. We had to speak with raised voices because of the rain drumming on the tin roof. The din was terrible and I thought of Christine, who was not often treated to a tattoo like this in Phoenix.

"I'm wondering about my things," I said. "Did the boy or the woman take my suitcase out of here?"

"I don't know anything about it. This is the room they gave me. I've already paid for it but if there's been a mistake I'll be glad to move to another room."

"Look here, why should there be a problem about going to the state fair?"

"There's not any problem that I know of."

"I got the idea that there was some problem. It's no great trick to go to the fair, is it?"

"The rodeo is in Huntsville and the fair is in Dallas."

"Two widely separated towns then. That's all you meant to say."

"Yes."

He was still uncomfortable from having been caught red-handed at his vice—writing songs or what?—and I could see too that our loud, expository conversation was distasteful to him, he just having come in from the solitude of the bush. The wind peeled back a sheet of tin above his head. The thing flapped up and down a few times and then blew away. It will be understood when I say "tin" that I am using the popular term for galvanized and corrugated sheet iron. A cascade of water came down on the bed and we pushed it to an inside corner of the room. Now we had to talk even louder because of the wind shrieking through the hole in the roof. But that hole, I told myself, will act as a safety vent and will keep the house from exploding or imploding under a sudden pressure differential. The floor heaved and the walls creaked. The frame structure was ill-suited for withstanding these violent stresses.

"I think this is a hurricane," he said. "What do you think?"

"It's certainly a severe depression of some kind."

"Maybe we should go to another place."

"All the other houses are just like this one."

"The Fort George Hotel is fairly solid."

"But don't they stay inside? Where you are?"

"I think we should try for the Fort George."

"You may be right."

He took his own sweet time in opening the bag and packing the notebook and tying it up again, in a special way. It was all something of an act, this cool manner we were at such pains to display to one another, but in fairness I must say that I was not unnerved by this convulsion of nature. The storm made a change from the enervating heat and it is not going too far to say I found it bracing—or much too far. I should say too that it provided a welcome distraction from my personal problems.

The Texas fellow carried his bag under one arm. His running gait was badly coordinated and funny, mine deliberate. He ran like a duck. Water was running in the streets, which made it hard to lift our feet. We moved in a darting fashion from the lee of one house to that of another. The black creek was backed up and out of its banks, whether from the heavy rains upstream or from the driven sea blocking its discharge, I couldn't say, perhaps both. There seemed to be no pattern in the way the wind was blowing. It came from all points of the compass. The velocity was irregular too, and it was the gusts that did most of the damage. My concern was for the twisted sheets of tin that were banging about. One of those things could take your head off. Some of the roofs had been completely stripped, leaving only exposed beams and stringers. I saw a gum tree with its limbs more or less intact but every leaf blown away. It had a wintry look.

We didn't make it to the Fort George. A policeman hustled us off the street into a fenced compound and put us to work in a sandbag brigade. The wire fence enclosed a motor-pool area behind the police station, and this was a scene of wild activity. Men were running about and Bedford trucks and Land-Rovers were coming and going through the gate. Most of the workers seemed to be prisoners. They had been turned out of jail to fill small sisal bags with sand and broken oyster shells. The stuff was piled up in mounds at a construction site near the garage bays.

There weren't nearly enough shovels. The Texas fellow and I were assigned to the loading detail. We carried sandbags, one in each hand, and slung them up into the truck beds. They were then hauled away to build dikes and to weigh down the flimsy roofs—much too late, it seemed. A big black officer with a riding crop and a bullhorn was directing things. I couldn't understand a word he said. They called him Captain Grace. He had a Webley revolver in a canvas holster on his hip. As befitted his rank, he was the calmest man in the yard.

Everyone had his job. Webster was there and he and some other boys held the bags open while the prisoners filled them. A third gang tied the tops with string and the rest of us were loaders. The rain swept across us in blinding sheets, and the sand, wet though it was, swirled about in eddies, stinging our arms and faces. We were working in the open but the chainlike fence provided some protection from flying objects. I had no opportunity to ask Webster about my things.

There were two white Americans among the jailbirds— a young doper and an older, heavier man. He was barefooted, this older fellow, as were all the prisoners, and he wore a knit shirt that was split on both sides from his exertions. He appeared to be the boss of the shovelers. They were hard put to keep up, there being so few of them, and he was trying to prod them on to heroic efforts with a lot of infield chatter. His team! He was digging like a madman and yelling at the boys for being slow and for not holding the bags fully open. I had noticed him early but he was little more than a noisy wet blur to me.

I soon made a pickup at his station and he said, "Wrong way! Wrong way! Get your bags on this side and go out the other way!" I had been holding my head down to protect my eyes against all the blowing stuff and when I raised it to get a look at this loud person I was knocked for a loop. It was Jack Wilkie! I spoke to him. He recognized me and waved me off. We were meeting under strange circumstances in a faraway place and there were many questions to be answered—but this was no time for a visit! That was what I understood him to be saying with his urgent gestures. He hadn't shaved for several days and there were clumps of sand stuck to his copper-wire whiskers. He had to keep hitching up his trousers because he had no belt.

I went back to work and considered the new development. Someone called out to me. It was the skinny fellow from Texas, hanging on the back of a truck and holding to one end of a long wooden ladder. He had been shanghaied into a new gang, a ladder gang. His bag was stowed in one of the garage bays and he wanted me to keep an eye on it while he was gone. I nodded and waved, indicating that I would do so, message understood. The truck pulled away and that was the last time I saw that mysterious bird alive. His name was Spann or Spang, more likely Spann.

Three army trucks came through the gate and wheeled about together in a nice maneuver. British soldiers jumped to the ground with new shovels at the ready. Now we had plenty of shovels but there was no more sand. The army officer and Captain Grace conferred. A decision was quickly reached. All the small boys were left behind and the rest of us were herded into the trucks and taken to some grassy beach dunes north of town. The captain led the convoy in his blue Land-Rover. Jack and I were together and there were about twenty other men in the back of our truck. We had to stand. The tarpaulin top was gone and we clung to the bentwood frame members. I could see that I was taller than at least one of these Coldstream Guards, if indeed that's who they were. We were flung from side to side. Jack punched out angrily at people when they stepped on his bare toes.

Captain Grace had made an excellent choice. This new place was the Comstock Lode of sand and I could hardly wait to get at it. The dunes were thirty feet high in places and were situated about three hundred yards from the normal shoreline, so we were fairly well protected from the sea. Even so, an occasional monster wave swept all the way across the beach and broke over the top of the dunes, spraying us and leaving behind long green garlands of aquatic vegetation. The sand had drifted up here between an outcropping of rock and a grove of palm trees. The slender trunks of the palms were all bent in picturesque curves and the fronds at the top stood hysterically on end like sprung umbrellas. None of the trees, however, had been uprooted, and I decided then that this blow, already falling off somewhat, was probably not a major hurricane.

It was a good place for sand, as I say. The only catch was that the trucks had to cross a strip of backwater on the inland side of the dunes. The water wasn't very deep but the ground underneath was soft and the trucks wallowed and strained to get through it with a full load of sandbags. We were now filling them and loading them at a much faster rate. Jack took charge once again and whipped us up into frenzies of production. No one seemed to mind. The prisoners and the soldiers thought he was funny and the officers stood back and let him do his stuff.

The truck drivers followed one another, taking the same route across the water each time, such was their training or their instincts or their orders, and they soon churned the fording place into a quagmire. As might have been foreseen, one of the trucks bogged down and we, the loaders, had to stand in the water and remove every last bag from the bed. Thus lightened, the truck moved forward about eight inches before settling down again.

The officious Jack stepped in and began to direct this operation too. He took the wheel from a soldier. It was a matter of feel, he said. The trick was to go to a higher gear and start off gently and then shift down one notch and pour on the steam at the precise moment you felt the tires take hold. Jack did this. The truck made a lurch, and then another one, and things looked good for a moment, before all ten wheels burrowed down another foot or so, beyond hope. Jack said the gear ratios were too widely spaced in that truck. The young British officer, none too sure of himself before, pulled Jack bodily from the cab and told him to stay away from his vehicles "in future" —rather than "in *the* future."

The second truck went down trying to pull the first one out and the third one made a run to town and never came back, for a reason that was not made known to us. We had a mountain of undelivered bags and no more empties to fill. Shovels were

downed and we lay back against the bags, our first rest break
in four or five hours. By that time there was very little fury
left in the storm, though the rain still came. An army sergeant
walked back and forth in front of us to show that he himself
wasn't tired.

"Good way to get piles," he said to us. "Best way I know.
Sitting on wet earth like that." But no one got up, just as no
one heeded him when he warned us against drinking a lot of
water in our exhausted state.

Jack was breathing noisily through his mouth. He was the
oldest and he had worked the hardest. The palms of his hands
were a ragged mess of broken blisters. I watched my own fingers, curled in repose, as they gave little involuntary twitches.

It was our first chance for a talk. Jack said he had had his
Chrysler towed into Monterrey, where he arranged to have the
drive shaft straightened and two new universal joints installed.
There had been no difficulty in tracking me from San Miguel.
The juiceheads at the Cucaracha bar had put him on to the
farm in British Honduras. He couldn't locate me immediately
in Belize. He went to the American consul and learned of the
two Dupree farms in the country. I had missed a bet there,
going to the consul, but Jack missed one too. He went to the
wrong place, the Dupere farm, the one south of town.

The ranch manager there was an old man, he said, a Dutchman, who claimed he knew nothing of any Guy Dupree from
Arkansas. Jack wasn't satisfied with his answers and he insisted
on searching the premises. The old man reluctantly allowed
him to do so and before it was over they had an altercation,
something about an ape. It must have been a pet monkey, only
Jack called it an ape.

"That nasty ape followed me around everywhere I went," he
said. "He stayed about two steps behind me. The old man told
him to do that. I had seen him talking to the ape. Whenever
I opened a door or looked into a building, that nasty beast
would stick his head in and look around too. Then he would
bare his nasty teeth at me, the way they do. The old man had
told him to follow me around and mock me and spit on me. I
told that old Dutchman he better call him off but he wouldn't
do it. I said all right then, I'll have to shoot him, and then he
called him off. That was all. It didn't amount to anything. I

wouldn't have shot the ape even if I had had a gun. But when I got back to town they arrested me. That old guy had radioed ahead to the police and said I pulled a gun on him. I didn't even have a gun but they took my belt and shoes and locked me up."

The black prisoners had begun to stir. They had come to their feet and were muttering angrily among themselves. The young American doper said they wanted cigarettes. Their tobacco and their papers were wet and they wanted something to smoke. It was a cigarette mutiny! Captain Grace whacked the ringleader across the neck with his leather crop and that broke it up. He ordered everyone to be seated and he addressed us through his bullhorn.

I couldn't make out what he was saying. Jack couldn't make it out. I asked a red-faced corporal and I couldn't understand him either. The young doper had acquired an ear for this speech and he explained it all to us. The emergency was now over. The prisoners and the soldiers were to wait here for transport. Those of us who had been roped in off the streets were free to go, to walk back to town if we liked, or we too could wait for the trucks.

Captain Grace got into his Land-Rover and signaled the driver to be off. Then he countermanded the order with a raised hand and the driver stopped so short that the tires made a little chirp in the wet sand. The captain got out and came over to Jack and said, "You. You can go too."

"Thanks," said Jack. "Are you going to town now in that jeep?"

"Yes, I am."

"How about a lift?"

"Lift?"

"A ride. I need a ride to town."

"With me? Certainly not."

"You've got my shoes at the station. I can't walk all the way in like this."

Captain Grace was caught up short for a moment by Jack's impudence. He said, "Then you can wait for the lorries like everyone else."

We walked all the way back to Belize, my second long hike of the day. Since Jack was handicapped, I let him set the pace.

We soon pulled ahead of the others. Jack was barefooted but he was not one to dawdle or step gingerly on that account. He stopped once to rest, hands on knees, head low, in the dramatic posture of the exhausted athlete. The sun came out. We rounded a bend in the road and a cloud of pale blue butterflies appeared before us, blown in perhaps from another part of the world. I say that because they hovered in one place as though confused. We walked through them.

Jack talked about how good the fried eggs were in Mexico and how he couldn't get enough of them. They were always fresh, with stand-up yolks, unlike the watery cold-storage eggs in our own country. He talked about eggs and he talked about life. There was altogether too much meanness in the world, he said, and the source of it all was negative thinking. He said I must avoid negative thoughts and all negative things if I wanted my brief stay on earth to be a happy one. Guy Dupree's head was full of negative things, and so to a lesser extent was mine. That was our central problem. We must purge our heads, and our rancorous hearts too.

For all I knew he was right, about Dupree anyway, but this stuff didn't sound like Jack. This didn't sound like the Jack Wilkie I knew in Little Rock who had a prism-shaped thing on his desk that said, "Money Talks and Bullshit Walks." It was my guess that he had been reading something in his cell. Two or three days in jail and he was a big thinker! The ideas that are hatched in those places! I told him that Dupree's malaise, whatever it might be, was his own, and that to lump the two of us together was to do me a disservice.

"Food for thought," he said. "That's all. I won't say any more."

The waters had receded from town. We were greeted by a spectacular rainbow that arched from one end of the estuary to the other. I watched for it to shift about or partially disappear as our angle of approach changed but it remained fixed. The color bands were bright and distinct—blue, yellow, and pink—with no fuzzy shimmering. It was the most substantial rainbow I've ever seen. There were mud deposits in the streets and a jumble of grounded boats along the creek banks. They lay awkwardly on their sides. Their white hulls had fouled bottoms of a corrupt brown hue not meant to be seen. Everyone seemed to be outside. Women and children were salvaging soggy objects from the debris. The men were drunk.

Jack went into the police station to claim his things. I stayed outside in the motor pool and looked around for Spann's bag. It was gone. I had told him I would keep an eye on his bag and then I didn't do it. Someone had made off with it. Someone was at this very moment pawing over his songs and his jade and his feathers, which, I suppose, Spann himself must have stolen, in a manner of speaking. I found out later about his death. He was hanging sandbags over the crest of a tin roof—one bag tied to each end of a length of rope—when he slipped and fell and was impaled on a rusty pipe that was waiting for him below in the grass.

Jack came out on the porch fully shod in his U.S. Navy surplus black oxfords. His socks, I guessed, had been mislaid by the property clerk, or perhaps burned. He stood there chatting in a friendly way with a black officer, Sergeant Wattli maybe, two comrades now in law enforcement. All was forgiven. Jack saw me and waved his car keys.

The yellow Chrysler was parked in one of the garage bays. We looked it over and Jack pointed to some blood spatters on the license plate and the rear bumper. He laughed over the success of his trap, which was a razor blade taped to the top of the gas-filler cap. An unauthorized person had grabbed it and sliced his fingers. For a person whose own hands were bloody, Jack showed amazing lack of sympathy. No such security measures had been taken at the front of the car. The battery was gone. The two cable heads hung stiffly in space above the empty battery pan. Jack was angry. He said he was going to demand restitution. He was going to demand of Captain Grace that the city of Belize buy him a new battery.

"I'll be right back and then we'll go get us some bacon and eggs."

He went into the station again but this time he didn't come out. I grew tired of waiting and left a note in the car saying I would be at the Fair Play Hotel taking a nap.

# Fifteen

I MADE my way through a sea of boisterous drunks. It was
sundown. There would be no twilight at this latitude. The
air was sultry and vapors were rising from the ground. The
drunks were good-natured for the most part but I didn't like
being jostled, and there was this too, the ancient fear of being
overwhelmed and devoured by a tide of dark people. Their
ancient dream! Floating trees and steel drums were piled up
beneath the arched bridge. Through a tangle of branches I saw
a dead mule.

A man pinched my arm and offered me a drink from a bottle
—clear rum, I think. A few translucent fish scales were stuck
to the bottle. He watched me closely for signs of gratitude.
I took a drink and sighed and thanked him and wiped my
mouth with the back of my hand in an exaggerated gesture. At
the edge of the stream some children were taunting a coiled
black snake with an inflated inner tube. They were trying to
make him strike at it. He would bump it with his snout but
he had already sensed that the fat red thing wasn't living flesh,
only a simulacrum, and he refused to bring his hinged fangs
into play.

I asked about Webster. The children hadn't seen him. I wondered how he and other people had fared during the storm,
thinking of them one by one, even to Father Jackie's mother,
on whose yellow flesh I had never laid eyes. Had Dr. Symes
made it safely out of town? And if so, how? He wouldn't ride
a bus and he wouldn't fly and he was certainly no sailor. What
did that leave?

Cars and trucks were moving once again in the streets. There
was a lot of honking, at drunks who blocked the way, and in
celebration too of life spared for another day. I picked out the
distinctive beep of a Volkswagen and almost at the same instant
I saw Christine in her van. She was caught in the traffic jam.
She was beeping away and slapping her left hand against the
door. Victor was in his seat blowing a plastic whistle.

I went to her and said, "You shouldn't be out in this."

"I'm all right. It's Melba."

The glass louvers on the driver's side were open and I saw Melba lying down in the back, nestled in amid all the art and green coconuts.

"What's wrong with her?"

"I don't know. I'm trying to get her to the hospital."

"This is an emergency then."

"You bet your boots it is."

I walked point, flapping my arms in front of the van and clearing the way like a locomotive fireman shooing cattle from the tracks. "Gangway!" I shouted. "Make a hole! *¡Andale!* Coming through! *¡Cuidado!* Stand back, please! Hospital run!" I can put up a fairly bold show when representing some larger cause than myself.

All the rolling tables were in use at the hospital and I had to carry Melba inside the place and down a long corridor jammed with beds. She weighed hardly anything. She was all clothes. Her eyes were open but she wasn't speaking. There was standing room only in the emergency room and not much of that. Victor found a folded wheelchair in a closet and Christine pulled it open and I set Melba down into it. We couldn't find anything in the way of restraining straps and so I put a big Clorox carton on her lap to keep her from pitching forward.

Christine waylaid a nurse or a female doctor and this person looked into Melba's eyes with the aid of a penlight and then went away, doctor-fashion, without telling us anything. I rested Melba's chin on top of the empty brown box to make her more comfortable. A male doctor, an older man, began to shout. He brandished a stainless-steel vessel and ordered everyone out of the room who wasn't a bona-fide patient. He had to repeat the order several times before anyone made a move. Others took up the cry, various underlings. Christine told me that proper identification was very important in a hospital. We looked about for admittance forms and name tags. But now the crazed physician was shouting directly at us. He wouldn't allow us to explain things and we had to go. I wrote "MELBA" on top of the box in front of her chin and we left her there. I couldn't remember her last name, if I had ever known it.

Scarcely was I out of the room when I was pressed into service again. This time it was helping orderlies push bedridden patients back to their rooms. These people, beds and all, had been moved into the central hallways during the storm, away from the windows.

Christine went off on her own to look for Mrs. Symes and to buck up sick people. She made a cheery progress from bed to bed, in the confident manner of a draft-dodger athlete signing autographs for mutilated soldiers. Some were noticeably brightened by her visits. Others responded not at all and still others were baffled. Those capable of craning their necks stole second and third glances as she and Victor passed along.

I worked with a fellow named Cecil, who knew little more about the layout of the hospital than I did. He was out of sorts because it was his supper hour. He looked sick himself and I took him at first for an ambulatory patient, but he said he had worked there almost two years. Once he led us blundering into a room where seven or eight dead people were laid out on the floor, the tops of their heads all lined up flush as though by a string. Spann must have been among them but I didn't see him that time, having quickly averted my gaze from their faces.

Our job was not as easy as it might seem. The displaced beds were not always immediately outside the rooms whence they came, and there were complicated crossovers to be worked out. The patients were a nuisance too. They clamored for fruit juice and dope and they wanted their dressings seen to and they complained when we left them in the wrong rooms or when we failed to position their beds in precisely the same spots as before. Cecil, old hand at this, feigned deafness to their pleas.

I was dead on my feet, a zombie, and not at all prepared for the second great surprise of that day. I found Norma. It was there in that place of concentrated misery that I found her at last, and my senses were so dull that I took it as a matter of course. Cecil and I were pushing her into an empty room, a thin girl, half asleep and very pale, when I recognized her from the pulsing vein on her forehead. Her hair was cut short and there was a red scarf or handkerchief tied around her neck, just long enough to tie and leave two little pointed ends. Some thoughtful nurse has provided this spot of color, I said to myself, though it was no part of her job to do so. My heart went out to those dedicated ladies in white.

I spoke to Norma and she looked at me. There were dainty globules of sweat on her upper lip. She had trouble focusing. I had a weak impulse to take her in my arms, and then I caught myself, realizing how unseemly that would be, with Cecil standing there. I drew closer but not rudely close. I didn't want to thrust my bird face directly into hers as Melba had done so often to me.

"Midge?" she said.

"Yes, it's me. I'm right here. Did you think it was a dream?"

"No."

She couldn't believe her eyes! I explained things to Cecil, babbling a little, and I searched my pockets for money or some valuable object to give him, to mark the occasion, but I had nothing and I just kept patting him on the back, longer than is usually done. I told him that I would now take charge of her and that he could go on about his business. Cecil was turning all this over in his brain and I could see he didn't believe she was my wife, even though she had called my name. I could see in his eyes that he thought I was a perverted swine who would bear watching. And it is to his credit, I suppose, that he refused to leave me alone with her. He stood in the doorway and watched for his supper and kept an eye on me.

I questioned Norma at some length. Her answers were slow in coming and not always to the point. I was patient with her and made every allowance for her condition. She said she had been in the hospital about a week or ten days. Her appendix had been removed. A week ago? Yes, or maybe longer. Then why was she not yet on her feet? She didn't know. How had she happened to get appendicitis? She couldn't say. Had she been in a private room all along, or a ward? She couldn't remember. Couldn't remember whether there was anyone else in her room or not? No. Did she not know there was a great difference in the cost of the two arrangements? No.

She turned away from me to face the wall. The maneuver made her wince. She stopped answering my questions. I had been careful to avoid mention of Dupree and other indelicate matters but I had somehow managed to give offense. I smoothed out her sheet and pulled it tight here and there. She didn't shrink from my touch. She had turned away from me but my touch wasn't loathsome to her.

"I have a little surprise for you," I said. "I brought your back pills all the way from Little Rock."

She extended a cupped hand behind her.

"I don't have them now but I did have them. What is your doctor's name?"

No reply.

"I want to have a talk with that bird. What is he giving you? Do you know?"

No reply.

"Do you realize you're just skin and bones?"

"I don't feel like talking, Midge. I'm trying to be polite but I don't feel good."

"Do you want to go home?"

"Yes."

"With me?"

"I guess so."

"What's wrong with me?"

"You just want to stay in the house all the time."

"I'm not in the house now. I could hardly be further out of the house."

"You don't want me back."

"Yes, I do. I'm hard to please too. You know that."

"I don't feel like talking right now."

"We don't have to talk. I'll get a chair and just sit here."

"Yes, but I'll know you're there."

I found a folding chair and settled in for a vigil. An elderly fat woman passed by in the hall and Cecil grunted and directed her into the room. It was his mother. She had his supper in a plastic bucket. He glared at her for being late, a hurricane was no excuse, and he picked over the food and rejected outright some of the things in the bucket. I was surprised she didn't know what he liked after all these years. Maybe it was impossible to anticipate his whims. They exchanged not a word. Cecil had no thanks for her and she was content to stand there and hold the bucket in silence and watch him eat, a slow, grinding business.

An unconscious old man was wheeled into the room and then a girl came by with trays of food on a cart. Norma drank some tea but I couldn't get her to eat anything. The sick man in the other bed was snoring. I ate his supper. A nurse stopped in to take temperatures. She ordered Cecil to the nursery, where he was needed to clean up a mess. He said he was off duty now and was going home, addressing the nurse as "Sister," though she wasn't a nun. He and his mother left.

The nurse told me that Norma was slow in recovering because she would eat nothing but ice. She was dehydrated too, from a long siege of diarrhea. But there was no fever to speak of and no other signs of peritonitis. Weren't intravenous fluids indicated, I asked, in cases of dehydration? At this implied reproach the nurse became snippy. As for the current plan of treatment, she said, I would have to take that up "with doctor" —not "with *the* doctor."

I crumbled some bread into a glass of milk and every half-hour I woke Norma and forced her to swallow a spoonful or two. Later, another nurse came around with some candles and asked that the lights and the fan be turned off so as to allow more electricity for areas of greater need. It didn't matter to me about the light because the emergency generator was producing just enough wattage to heat the bulb filament a dull red. I missed the fan for its companionable hum. After the first candle burned out, I didn't light another one. A small gray coil of anti-mosquito incense smoldered on the windowsill. The smoke curled about the room in a long tendril that kept its integrity for quite some time. I fanned Norma with a magazine when I thought about it. She asked me to stop waking her. I told her it wouldn't be necessary if she would only finish eating the bread and milk and the little cup of yellow custard with the nutmeg on top. She grudgingly did so and then we both slept, I in my chair.

She woke me before daylight and asked for a glass of crushed ice. Ice at five in the morning! I got some ice cubes at the nursing station and chopped them up with a pair of scissors. Now she was fully awake and ready to talk. I suppose it came more easily to her in the dark. She crunched on the ice and told me about her travels with Dupree. I was fascinated. Her voice was little more than a whisper but I hung on every word. She could have been one of Melba's psychic heroines, with eyes "preternaturally bright."

What a story! What a trip! They had first gone to Dallas, where Dupree was to meet with the well-known radical photographers, Hilda Monod and Jay Bomarr. I say "well known," although Norma had never heard of these people. Dupree had been in touch with them through a third party in Massachusetts, a fellow who had vouched for him, telling Hilda and Jay that Dupree had threatened to kill the President and was okay. He also told them, or maybe it was Dupree himself, that Dupree owned a shopping center in Memphis which produced a vast income that was now available to the radical movement. Hilda and Jay were eager to confer with him, or so they said.

But they didn't show in Dallas, telephoning instead from Florida to say they would be delayed, that they were conducting a workshop at a home for old radicals in Coral Gables. Dupree was to continue on to San Angelo and wait. There was another hitch and he was told to proceed to Wormington and see a fellow named Bates. Bates was to put them up in his house. But Bates had not been informed about the arrangement and he refused to talk to Dupree. Bates owned a cave near Wormington in which the temperature remained constant at 59 degrees Fahrenheit. How this grotto figured in the overall plans of the radicals, or if it figured at all, Norma couldn't say, and it must remain a matter for speculation. She and Dupree checked in at the motel. He paced the room and became impatient and called Hilda and Jay with an ultimatum. Either they stopped giving him the runaround or he would take his money and ideas elsewhere.

A meeting in Mexico was agreed upon, at San Miguel de Allende. Hilda and Jay were to take part in a seminar there with a visiting radical from Denmark. It would be a safe and quiet place to talk business. But they needed a car. Could Dupree furnish them with a car? Not at that time, he said, but once in San Miguel, on completion of a satisfactory personal interview, he would give them the keys to a Ford Torino.

So off they went to Mexico. Norma drove most of the way because Dupree wanted to polish up the presentation he was preparing for the two infamous radicals. He shuffled his papers and muttered to himself and ate candy bars and drank pink Pepto-Bismol from a bottle. He was very excited, she said, but he wouldn't discuss his ideas on the new social order with her, saying she was too dumb to understand his work.

Why, at that point, did she not slap his face and come home?
"I don't know," she said.

She didn't know! She knew he had threatened the President
of the United States and that he was now involved in some
other devilish political enterprise and on top of that he was
making rude personal remarks, and still she hung around for
more! Then I saw the answer. I'm slow but sure. I had read
things and heard many songs about people being poleaxed
by love and brought quivering to their knees and I thought
it was just something people said. And now here it was, true
love. She was in love with that monkey! I was amazed but I
couldn't really hold it against her. I knew she was puzzled by
life and marriage, thinking the entire range of men ran only
from Dupree to me and back again, and I couldn't really be
angry with her, in her pitiable condition. She told me later that
Dupree had promised her they would be remarried "in a forest," where they would exchange heart-shaped rings and some
sort of on-the-spot vows. He had no shame.

Jay and Hilda limped into San Miguel a week late. They
had been held up for a few days in Beaumont, Texas, after a
tailgater had rammed their Saab sedan from behind, and there
had been many subsequent breakdowns along the way. Neither of them drove, of course, and they traveled with three
flunkies who handled all such chores. Five stinking radicals in
a three-cylinder Saab! Norma couldn't remember the names of
the flunkies. She said they wore small caps and moved about
quickly like squirrels and smiled in a knowing way when they
looked a person in the face. Jay and Hilda were polite to her
but the flunkies made fun of her accent.

The conference was a failure. Jay and Hilda were upset to
learn that Dupree owned no shopping center and had no
money of his own and no intention whatever of giving them
a car. Not only that, but he talked to them in a familiar way,
as an equal or a superior, as one having authority, saying he
wanted them to revise their entire program from top to bottom, incorporating, among other things, a new racial doctrine.
He showed them some provocative slogans he had written,
for shouting. He even lectured them on photography. They
couldn't believe their ears! Norma said Jay Bomarr was particularly indignant. Since the Beaumont crash he had been wearing

a rigid and uncomfortable plastic collar around his neck and he couldn't easily turn aside as Dupree ticked off important points on his fingertips.

The meeting ended with recriminations and with Dupree's papers scattered on the floor of the Bugambilia Café. There followed several empty days. Dupree walked about town with his dog. Norma had already begun to suffer from internal disorders and she didn't range far from the hotel. I forced her to describe every bite she had eaten since leaving Little Rock, so far as she could remember. She became peeved and irritable as I hammered away at her but it was worth it in the end because in this way I was able to put my finger on the rancid peanuts that had started her trouble. Once the point was cleared up, I permitted her to go on with her story.

She said the radicals passed most of their time in a snack bar just off the square. Long-distance calls could be made there and Jay was a great one for the telephone. There they sat at a table all day, holding court before young admirers and taking their skimpy meals and conspiring lazily and placing and receiving numerous phone calls. One flunky was posted in the crumpled Saab at all times to watch the camera gear. The other two called themselves the Ground Observer Corps, and they moved around town and eavesdropped on conversations and then reported back to Hilda and Jay on what people were saying, the topics of the day in that particular place. Hilda, who had little to say, appeared to be the real boss of the gang.

Dupree stopped in once and tried to stare them down from the doorway of the snack bar. They turned their chairs around. He came back the next day and walked slowly through the place with his dog. He went out the back door and reappeared almost instantly at the front door again. The chow dog was now in on the trick! If the radicals were knocked for a loop, they didn't let on and they continued to regard Dupree with a contemptuous silence.

The Dane never showed up but they had the "seminar" anyway, under some shade trees in a place called the French Park. Jay Bomarr opened it with his famous speech, "Come Dream Along with Me." I had heard it myself, at Ole Miss of all places, back in the days when Jay was drawing big crowds. It was a dream of blood and smashed faces, with a lot of talk about "the people," whose historic duty it was to become a nameless herd and submit their lives to the absolute control of a small pack of wily and vicious intellectuals. Norma said it went over fairly well with the young Americans and Canadians, judging from the applause. No Mexicans came except for the professor who was chairman of the thing. Dupree was there, standing at the front, and he heckled Jay for a while. He had a New Year's Eve noisemaker, a ratchet device that he swung around. The flunkies took it away from him and carried him off in the woods and beat him up.

Hilda followed Jay at the speaker's stand, to discuss her prize-winning photographs of "hermits." That is the word Norma understood Hilda to say, though it may have been something else. Varmints? Linnets? Spinets? Harlots? Norma couldn't be sure because Hilda was interrupted early by Jay, who had a disturbing announcement. Their thermos jug had been stolen. He said no questions would be asked if the person who had taken the jug would return same without delay. The appeal failed. Hilda tried threats. She said she was going to stop talking if the jug was not returned at once. There were groans of consternation from the crowd of young shutterbugs. The three flunkies made a lightning search through the park and turned up various objects but nothing in the way of a thermos jug. Someone offered Hilda a replacement jug of comparable size and quality. She said that wouldn't do at all and she put away her lecture materials and declared the seminar suspended until further notice. Jay and the professor tried to persuade her to continue, promising a full investigation. She said it was out of the question. The radicals packed their visual aids and returned to the snack bar, there to await the collapse of the conscience-stricken thief.

All that is fairly clear. Norma told it to me in a straightforward way and I have made it even clearer in my summary. But she could give me no satisfactory account of the rest of the journey, nothing but tantalizing scraps. She couldn't even remember when the idea first came up of going on to British Honduras. Dupree had told her it was an idyllic spot. She looked forward to her forest wedding there.

Then, she said, he began to behave "strangely," and for her to make such an acknowledgment I expected to hear next that Dupree had been seized by nothing short of barking fits. But it wasn't quite that. After leaving San Miguel he spoke to her through a small megaphone. She had asked him to repeat some remark—on just one occasion—and after that he pretended to believe she was deaf. He rolled a piece of cardboard into a cone and taped the ends, and he pretended to believe she couldn't hear him unless he spoke through it, directly into her ear from a foot or so away. The memory of the farmhouse made her shudder. She was there for about four days and sick the whole time. Terrible things went on outside. The workers shot the cows and beat up Dupree and destroyed the water pump. From that point on he was impossible. He went into a rage when he caught her bathing in the washtub, using scarce water. He accused her, through the megaphone, of malingering, and he accused her of introducing worm pills into his food. He had some deworming medicine for his dog and he couldn't find it. By that time the pain in Norma's side was hardly bearable and even Dupree could see that she was seriously ill. He drove her into town at night and left her at the hospital, and that must have been the night he got drunk and burned up my Torino.

What a story! Denmark! Coral Gables! But I was beginning to fade and I could no longer follow the details. Norma asked me to get her some more ice and I told her what we both needed now was not ice but a little more shut-eye.

The old man in the other bed woke at dawn. He woke suddenly and raised his head about an inch, gravity overtaking him there, and said, "What the devil is going on anyway?"

"I don't know," I truthfully replied.

He had one boggling, red-rimmed eye like Mr. Proctor. He wanted coffee and I went to see if I could find some.

# Sixteen

RUTH HAD bounced me from the Fair Play without a hearing and Webster had taken my bag to a cheaper hotel called the Delgado, and told the manager there, another woman, that I was a model roomer in every way except for that of payment. She took a chance on me. There was no difficulty. I went personally to the cable office and wired my father for money and got it the next morning. The Delgado wasn't as conveniently located as the Fair Play and had fewer amenities. The rates, however, were very reasonable.

I took Norma from the hospital in a taxicab and put her to bed in my room. The woman boss at the Delgado made a kind of fish soup or stew that was pretty good and I fed this to Norma, along with boiled rice. The English doctor had told me she could eat whatever she liked but I thought it best to be on the safe side and I allowed her no fried foods. I had to turn down her request for fresh pineapple too, it being so coarse and fibrous. After two days of forcing soup down her gullet I had her on her feet again, taking little compulsory hikes about the room. She tottered and complained. I bought her a shark's-tooth bracelet. I read to her from old magazines until she asked me to stop doing it.

Mrs. Symes had slept through the hurricane. She herself was released from the hospital that same week, though she continued to be more or less bedridden. Christine and the girl Elizabeth attended to her. The stroke had left a slight paralysis in her left arm and a slight speech impediment. Still, she didn't appear to be severely disabled.

"Another blast from Almighty God," she said to me. I nodded, not knowing whether she meant the storm or the stroke. Christine was flexing the old lady's arm and fingers so that the muscles would not become atrophied.

"Do you know why these things are sent?"

I said, "No, ma'am, I don't."

"They are sent to try us. Tell me this. Are the doors sticking too?"

"Yes, they are."

"I thought as much. It makes it hard for us when the doors stick."

"I was wondering if you would do me a favor, Meemaw."

"I will if I can, hon. You see the sorry shape I'm in."

"I was wondering if you would write a note to Captain Grace on behalf of a friend of mine. He's in jail and needs some help."

She had forgotten my first name and she asked me what it was. I told her and she told me once again that there was no one named Ray in the Bible. But that was all right, she said, Ray would do as well as any other name here on earth. Only God knew our true names.

Everyone was either sick or in jail. Melba was laid up in the bedroom with the brown picture on the wall. There had been nothing really wrong with her at the hospital but when she came out of her trance in the emergency room she got up and walked home and it was this unaccustomed trek across town that had put her under. So she was in bed too, for the first time in years, and Christine had her hands full, what with all the cooking and nursing. Brave Christine! The girl Elizabeth was a good worker too, and Victor was a useless whiner. I asked him why he didn't go outside and play and get out of Christine's hair and he said a chicken had pecked him on the street.

I did what I could, at the urging of Mrs. Symes, to find out what had happened to the doctor. I inquired at the bus station and the airport and the consular office. I took another look at the dead bodies in the hospital, where I saw poor Spann, his busy pen stilled forever. I inquired at the Shell station and the Texaco station. I talked to fishermen. When I visited Jack in jail, I looked over all the prisoners. Of course I had my eye out for Dupree too. I thought there was an excellent chance he might have been arrested again, for one thing or another. I found no trace of either of them. Mrs. Symes said she had a strong feeling that Reo was dead, cut off abruptly in his sins. Melba said no, he was still very much alive and she knew it in her bones. I found Melba's hunch the more convincing of the two.

I had dropped in at the tabernacle to report my investigation a failure, and to pick up the silver set, having in mind a nice surprise. I was going to take one of those round spoons from the silver chest and feed Norma her soup with it, and then, with a flourish and a roguish smile, reveal to her the familiar floral pattern on the handle. This, I thought, an unexpected touch of home, would trigger happy domestic memories, by way of the well-known principle of association.

But first I had to go by the newspaper office. Mrs. Symes wanted me to call there and have the doctor's name added to the published list of missing persons. Webster and some other boys were in front of the place dividing up a stack of *Bugles*. On an impulse, and this was very unlike me, I gave him Mrs. Edge's silver. I called him over and said, "Here, do you want this? I'm tired of fooling with it." The chest was wrapped in an old towel and he was suspicious. "It's not a jar this time," I said. "That's sterling silver." I advised him to take it to Father Jackie or some other trustworthy adult for safekeeping or for sale.

"My point is this. I don't want you to let Ruth take it away from you." I told him to cultivate good study habits and I left him there holding the heavy chest and went to the Delgado and told Norma what I had done, apologizing for my rash action. She said she didn't care. She wanted to go home.

Finally I was able to get Jack released from jail, no thanks to the American consul. That bird said it was none of his business and he wouldn't interfere even if he could. The testimonial note from Mrs. Symes did the trick, combined with an irregular payment and a promise that Jack would leave the country immediately. He was glad to be free again. We got a used battery at the Texaco station and I suggested a quick run out on Bishop Lane. I would show him the Dupree place and he could look around and maybe pick up some leads, see some things that had escaped my untrained eye. But Jack was no longer concerned with Dupree. He said, "You can do what you want to, Ray. I'm going home."

Norma and I rode home with him in the Chrysler. He drove all the way with his sore hands, not trusting other people at the wheel. What a trip! What a glum crew! Norma snapped at me, and Jack, who had been reading things in his cell again, talked about economic cycles and the fall of the Roman Empire and the many striking parallels that might be drawn between that society and our own. Norma called me "Guy" a couple of times. My own wife couldn't even remember my name.

I told them about the pelican that was struck by lightning. They didn't believe it. I tried to tell them about Dr. Symes and Webster and Spann and Karl and their attention wandered. I saw then that I would have to write it down, present it all in an orderly fashion, and this I have done. But I can see that I have given far too much preliminary matter and that I have considerably overshot the mark. So be it. It's done now. I have left out a few things, not least my own laundry problems, but I haven't left out much, and in the further interests of truth I have spared no one, not even myself.

Our journey home was a leisurely one. Jack drove only during daylight hours. We stayed in nice motels. Norma perked up a little after I began to let her order her own meals. We stopped at a beach south of Tampico for a swim in the Gulf. Norma wore her dress in the water like an old woman because she didn't want Jack to see the raw scar on her abdomen. A man came along with a brazier made from a bucket and he broiled some shrimp for us right there on the beach. The food and beer made us sleepy and we stayed the night. Jack slept in the car.

Norma and I lay on the warm sand all night under a piece of stiff canvas that Jack carried in his trunk. We listened to the surf and watched the incandescent streaks of meteors. I pointed out to her the very faint earthshine on the darker, gibbous part of the new moon. She admitted that her escapade with Dupree had been very foolish and I said we must now consider the matter closed. We reaffirmed our affection for one another.

The next day we were all in good spirits and we sang "Goodnight, Irene" and other old songs as we approached the border at Matamoros. The euphoria in turn passed as we drew closer to home and when we reached Texarkana we were pretty much ourselves again. Jack became solemn and he began to pose rhetorical questions. "What is everybody looking for?" he said. Norma didn't hesitate; she said everybody was looking for love. I gave the question some thought and then declared that everybody was looking for a good job of work to do. Jack said no, that many people were looking for those things, but that everybody was looking for a place where he could get food cheap—on a regular basis. The qualification was important because when I mentioned the cheap and tasty shrimps we had eaten on the beach, Jack said yes, but you couldn't count on that Mexican bird coming by every afternoon with his cooking can and his bulging wet sack.

Much later we learned that Dupree had gone overland—walked! in cowboy boots! bumping into trees!—down into Honduras, the genuine Honduras. He went first to a place on the coast called La Ceiba and then caught a ride on an oil-survey plane to the capital city of Tegucigalpa. I looked for him to come dragging in after a few months. A lot of people leave Arkansas and most of them come back sooner or later. They can't quite achieve escape velocity. I expect it's much the same everywhere. But that monkey is still down there, as far as I know.

I never said anything to Mr. Dupree about my Torino. I do know he paid off the bail forfeiture and I suspect he used his political influence to have the charge against Guy shelved, if not dropped altogether. Dupree's whereabouts are certainly no secret but nothing has been done toward having him picked up and extradited.

His mother has flown down there twice to see him, the second time to take him a pit bulldog. That was the kind of dog he wanted and he couldn't find one in Honduras. She must have had no end of trouble introducing that dog into another country by air, particularly a grotesque animal like the pit bull, but she managed to do it. I don't know what happened to the chow dog. She tells everyone Guy is "thinking and writing" and is doing fine. I have heard from other people that he walks around Tegucigalpa all day in a narcotic haze, nodding at Hondurans and taking long strides in his runover boots. He keeps his left hand in his pocket, they say, with the right hand swinging free in an enormous military arc. I assume she sends him money. You can cadge drinks but I think you have to have money for dope.

At Christmas I mailed Mrs. Symes a Sears catalogue and I enclosed my own copy of Southey's *Life of Nelson* for Webster. I heard nothing from Belize and I suspect the parcel was lost or stolen.

Norma regained her health and we got on better than ever before. We went to football games and parties. We had a fine Christmas. We went to the Cancer Ball with Mrs. Edge and

one of her florid escorts and I even danced a little, which isn't
to say I became overheated. In January I got my B.A. degree
and I decided to stay in school and try engineering again, with
an eye toward graduate work in geology and eventual entry
into the very exciting and challenging field of plate tectonics.
Then in April, after the last frost, Norma became restless again.
She went to Memphis to visit a friend named Marge. "Goodbye, goodbye," she said to me, and the next thing I knew she
had her own apartment over there, and a job doing something
at a television station. She said she might come back but she
didn't do it and I let her go that time. It's only about 130 miles
to Memphis but I didn't go after her again.

# MASTERS OF ATLANTIS

# I

YOUNG LAMAR JIMMERSON went to France in 1917 with the American Expeditionary Forces, serving first with the Balloon Section, stumbling about in open fields holding one end of a long rope, and then later as a telephone switchboard operator at AEF headquarters in Chaumont. It was there on the banks of the Marne River that he first came to hear of the Gnomon Society.

He was walking about Chaumont one night with his hands in his pockets when he was approached by a dark bowlegged man who offered to trade a small book for two packages of Old Gold cigarettes. The book had to do with the interpretation of dreams. Corporal Jimmerson did not smoke, nor did he have much interest in such a book, but he felt sorry for the ragged fellow and so treated him to a good supper at the Hotel Davos.

The man wept, overcome with gratitude. He said his name was Nick and that he was an Albanian refugee from Turkey. After supper he revealed that his real name was Mike and that he was actually a Greek from Alexandria, in Egypt. The dream book was worthless, he said, full of extravagant lies, and he apologized for imposing in such a way on the young soldier. He apologized too for his body odor, saying that nerve sweat or fear sweat made for a stronger stink than mere work sweat or heat sweat, or at least that had been his experience, and that he was always nervous when he spoke of delicate matters.

Perhaps he could repay the kindness in another way. He had another book. This one, the *Codex Pappus*, contained the secret wisdom of Atlantis. He could not let the book out of his hands but, as an Adept in the Gnomon Society, he was permitted to show it to outsiders, or "Perfect Strangers," who gave some promise of becoming Gnomons. Lamar, who was himself an Entered Apprentice in the Blue Lodge of the Freemasons, expressed keen interest.

It was a little gray book, or booklet, hand lettered in Greek. There were several pages given over to curious diagrams and geometric figures, mostly cones and triangles. Mike explained that this was not, of course, the original script. The original

book had been sealed in an ivory casket in Atlantis many
thousands of years ago, and committed to the waves on that
terrible day when the rumbling began. After floating about
for nine hundred years the casket had finally fetched up on a
beach in Egypt, where it was found by Hermes Trismegistus.
Another nine years passed before Hermes, with his great powers, was able to read the book, and then another nine before
he was able to fully understand it, and thus become the first
modern Master of the Gnomon Society.

Since those days the secret brotherhood had seen many
great Masters, including Pythagoras and Cornelius Agrippa
and Cagliostro, but none greater than the current one, Pletho
Pappus, whose translation this little book was. Pletho lived and
taught in the Gnomon Temple on the island of Malta, with his
two Adepts, Robert and a man named Rosenberg.

Lamar was embarrassed to say that he had not heard of this
Society, nor was he aware that flotsam of any description, literary or otherwise, had ever been recovered from Atlantis. What
was the book about? Mike apologized again, saying he was
bone tired. Could they continue their discussion another time?
He could hardly keep his eyes open and must now find himself
a dark doorway where he might curl up and try to get a little
rest. But Lamar would not hear of this and he arranged for
Mike to be put up in the Hotel Davos.

Their friendship flourished. They had many meals together
and many long talks. Lamar paid for Mike's food and shelter
and cigarettes, and even bought him a cheap suit of clothes. Bit
by bit the truth came out. Mike confessed that his real name
was Jack and that he was an Armenian from Damascus. He was
here on a mission. Pletho, with an eye to expanding the activities of the secret order to the New World, had sent him here to
Chaumont, disguised as a beggar, to look over the Americans
and determine if any were worthy of the great work. So far he
had found only one.

Lamar was embarrassed again. But Jack insisted that yes,
Lamar was indeed worthy and must now prepare himself for
acceptance into the brotherhood. Lamar did so. First came the
Night of Figs, then the Dark Night of Utter Silence. On the
third night, a wintry night, in Room 8 of the Hotel Davos,
Lamar Jimmerson folded his arms across his chest and spoke to

Jack the ancient words from Atlantis—*Tell me, my friend, how is bread made?*—and with much trembling became an Initiate in the Gnomon Society.

This work done, Jack said that he was at last free to divulge his true Gnomon identity; he was Robert, a French Gypsy, and he must now hasten back to Malta to report his success to the Master, the success of the American mission. He would leave the *Codex Pappus* in Lamar's care, for further study, and as a kind of token of good faith, or surety, and he would return in a month or so with more secret books, with Lamar's ceremonial robe and with sealed instructions from Pletho himself. There was a $200 charge for the robe, payable in advance. This was merely a bookkeeping technicality, one of Rosenberg's foolish quirks, and all rather pointless, seeing that Lamar would begin drawing $1,000 a month expense money as soon as his name was formally entered on the rolls. Still, Robert said, he had always found it better to humor Rosenberg in these matters.

Lamar saw no more of Robert and heard nothing from Malta. He wrote letters to the Gnomon Temple in Valletta but got no answers. He wondered if Robert's ship might have been torpedoed or lost in a storm. There was no question of his having run off with the robe money because he, Lamar, still had the *Codex*, along with Robert's "Poma," a goatskin cap he had left behind in his room. This Poma was a conical cap, signifying high office, or so Robert had told him.

The Armistice came and many of the doughboys set up a clamor to be sent home at once, though not Corporal Jimmerson, who remained loyally at his switchboard. He even volunteered to stay behind and help with all the administrative mopping-up tasks, so as to replenish his savings. In May 1919, he received his discharge in Paris, and went immediately to Marseilles and got deck passage on a mail boat to the island of Malta.

On arrival in Valletta he took a room at a cheap waterfront hotel called the Gregale. He then set out in search of the Gnomon Temple and his Gnomon brothers. He walked the streets looking at faces, looking for Robert, and clambered about on the rocky slopes surrounding the gray city that sometimes looked brown. He talked to taxicab drivers. They professed to know nothing. No one at the post office could help. He managed to get an appointment with the secretary to the island's most famous resident, the Grand Master of the Knights of St. John of Jerusalem, but the fellow said he had never heard of Gnomons or Gnomonry and that the Grand Master could not be bothered with casual inquiries.

Lamar found three Rosenbergs and one Pappus in Valletta, none of whom would admit to being Master of Gnomons or Perfect Adept of Hermetical Science. He tried each of them a second time, appearing before them silently on this occasion, wearing his Poma and flashing the *Codex*. He greeted them with various Gnomon salutes—with his arms crossed, with his right hand grasping his left wrist, with his hands at his sides and the heel of his right foot forming a T against the instep of his left foot. At last in desperation he removed his Poma and clasped both hands atop his head, his arms making a kind of triangle. This was the sign for "Need assistance" and was not to be used lightly, Robert had told him. But Pappus and the Rosenbergs only turned away in fright or disgust.

Was he being too direct? A man who wishes to become a Freemason must himself take the initiative; his membership cannot be solicited. With Gnomonry, as Robert had explained, it was just the reverse. A man must be *invited* into the order; he must be *bidden* to approach the Master. Perhaps he was being too pushy. He must be patient. He must wait.

Just at that time, at the sidewalk café outside the Gregale, with the cries of sea birds all about him, Lamar met a young Englishman named Sydney Hen. Sydney was Keeper of the Botanical Gardens in Valletta, and as such had been exempted from war service. He too was curious about things. Not only was he a student of plant life but he also collected African artifacts—spears and leather shields and such—and he read strange books as well, and speculated on what he had read, hoping to piece together the hidden knowledge of the ancients.

The two young men hit it off fairly well, particularly after Lamar had let slip the fact that he had in his possession a book of secret lore from Atlantis. They walked along the quay together, sometimes arm in arm, though Lamar found this European custom distasteful. They talked far into the night about the enigmas of the universe.

Sydney kept after Lamar to show him the *Codex Pappus*, and Lamar kept putting him off in a polite way, saying he was not sure under what conditions he could properly show the book to a Perfect Stranger. Lacking immediate guidance from his superiors, Robert and Pletho, he was not sure just what he could and could not do. He would have to think it over.

"And quite right too," said Sydney, who did most of the talking on these dockside rambles. He had strong opinions. The Freemasons had gone wrong, he said, through their policy of admitting every Tom, Dick and Harry into the Lodge, and the modern, so-called Rosicrucians were *not* the true Brethren of the Rosy Cross, far from it. And this stuff from India, this Eastern so-called wisdom, was a complete washout. He had looked into it and found it to be a quagmire of negation. It looked sound enough and then you thumped it and it gave off a hollow ring.

On Sunday afternoons Sydney presided over a kind of literary salon at his hillside villa, which was ablaze with flowers the year round. Lamar, told that he would not feel comfortable with such people, was never invited. Then one Sunday he was invited. Sydney said, "Come on up and meet the gang, Lamar!" Lamar was not favorably impressed by all the slim, chattering young men at the gathering, nor they with him, but the food was good and Sydney's sister, Fanny Hen, a crippled girl, was kind to him, very attentive.

When he returned to the Hotel Gregale that night he found that his room had been ransacked. Nothing, as far as he could tell, had been stolen. His Poma and *Codex* were still safe behind the loose board in the linen closet. Probably children looking for war souvenirs, he thought, and he was careful to stuff his puttees and some other things behind another loose board. The next morning, just as he stepped out into the street, something came whipping past his ear like a boomerang. Careless kids, throwing a marlinspike around. Later that same day, at dusk, he was assaulted on the street. He was walking around a corner when a man struck him full in the mouth with a long wooden oar and knocked him flat. As he lay there in a daze

two or three men were suddenly all over him, handling him
roughly and ripping his clothes in search of something. Waterfront thugs, he later decided, who had taken him for a rich
American. The laugh was on them.

The sunny days passed, and the warm nights, and Lamar ran
out of money. No word came from Robert or Pletho. Time to
take stock. He was a Gnomon Initiate with a hidden Master,
a book he couldn't read, some thirty-odd stitches in his lips
and no robe. He did have his Poma. But when to wear it? He
looked about town for work. Sydney said he might be in a position to make a personal loan against the *Codex Pappus*. Lamar
said it would hardly be fitting to mortgage the Codex.

The only job he could find was one cleaning boots and emptying chamber pots at the Gregale. There was no pay but he did
get his meals and the use of a cot in the basement. The Gregale
guests, mostly English poets and Greek honeymooners, were
poor tippers. Now and then a poet would fling him a three-
penny bit. The Greeks, when they left anything at all, left tiny
brass coins in their broad shoes that could not be exchanged.
But these Greeks—brides, grooms, chubby merchants—were
quite generous in another way. They translated the *Codex Pappus* for Lamar, a page or two at a time. He allowed no single
Greek to see much more of the book than that, being fearful
lest the entire text be exposed to a Perfect Stranger.

The pages of handwritten English accumulated. At length
the work was finished. Lamar bound the leaves together with
a shoelace and began his study. He sat on the cot at night,
wearing his Poma, and labored over the hard passages, reading a sentence over and over again in an effort to wrest some
meaning from it, as he brushed away on the high-top yellow
boots of the poets. In later years, in his introductory remarks
to Gnomon aspirants, he was fond of saying, "Euclid told the
first Ptolemy that there was no royal road to geometry, and I
must tell you now, gentlemen, that the road to Gnomonism is
plenty tough too."

He committed the entire work to memory, all eighty-eight
pages of Atlantean puzzles, Egyptian riddles and extended alchemical metaphors. He knew every cone and every triangle by
heart, just as he knew the 13 Hermetical Precepts, and how to
recognize the Three Secret Teachers, Nandor, Principato and

the Lame One, should they make one of their rare appearances before him in disguise. Soon he began to wonder if he might not be an Adept. He became sure of it one afternoon when he overheard a remark in the street—"Don't worry about Rosenberg." That is, he did not become sure of it at that moment, but only a little later, as the words continued to ring in his head and swell in volume. This, surely, was what he was waiting for. The sense of the message was obscure but there could be no doubt that the signal was genuine. This was Pletho's oblique way of communication.

As an Adept he now felt free to put the whole business before Sydney, with a view to bringing him into the brotherhood. Sydney had come to doubt the existence of the book from Atlantis and he could no longer receive Lamar, a bootblack, socially at Villa Hen, but the two young men still managed to see one another on occasion, behind the giant ferns at the Botanical Gardens or at one of the low waterfront cafés. So it was, at a sidewalk table of the Café Gregale, that Lamar told Sydney the full story of Robert, the *Codex*, Hermes, the Poma, the translation, the voice in the street.

Sydney heard him out, his skepticism giving way to excitement. He looked through the two booklets, one Greek, one English. He read Greek, though with difficulty, forming each word slowly with his mouth and on the bilabials blowing little transparent bubbles that quivered and popped. Then he turned in impatience to the English version and read hungrily. "This is marvelous stuff!" he said, in a fairly loud voice. "I can't make head or tail of it!" He had to speak up over the shouting and scuffling that was taking place in the street. It was some political disturbance that did not concern them. Sydney wanted to take the books home and study them at leisure, but Lamar said he could not, at this time, let them out of his hands. Trying to soften the refusal, he pointed out that the *Codex* was largely incomprehensible without the keys that Robert had revealed to him. These keys were never to be written. They could only be spoken, from one Gnomon to another.

Sydney became agitated and demanded to be given the keys and taken into the Society at once. Then he sighed and asked Lamar's pardon. He took Lamar's hand between his two hands and begged that allowance be made for his short temper. He had been a very naughty boy. The only thing now was for Lamar to move into Villa Hen, where he could live in that comfort and peace so necessary to the scholar, and give instructions in this great work in the proper way.

Lamar accepted the invitation and the next day he carried his bag up the hill to the villa. Fanny Hen, the crippled girl, was not around. He asked about her and Sydney said he had moved her into a boardinghouse down the way so that Lamar might have her room. But Lamar would not hear of this and the girl was soon restored to her room. Lamar slept in the library.

Fanny had made no very distinct impression on him before, apart from her kindness and her game leg. Now he began to notice other things about her. She was small and dark like her brother, but there the resemblance ended. Where Sydney was moody Fanny was sprightly, and where Fanny was open Sydney was sly. She had been an army nurse and her right knee was stiff from shrapnel wounds received in the final Flanders offensive of September 1918. She wore billowy shirts with striped neckties.

Sydney was an apt pupil, much quicker than himself, Lamar had to admit. He cut short his work at the Botanical Gardens and came home early each evening, flinging his black cape carelessly from his shoulders and quickly slipping into his red silk dressing gown, eager for another long session with Lamar in the locked library. He smoked black Turkish cigarettes and sipped Madeira. From time to time he rubbed his hands together. When he had grasped a Gnomonic point he would say, "Quite!" or "Quite so!" or "Just so!" or "Even so!" and urge Lamar to get on with it. The progress slowed somewhat when they came to the symbolic figures. Sydney found himself in a tangle with these cones and triangles. He often confused one with another and got the words slightly wrong.

During the day Lamar enjoyed the company of Fanny Hen. They discussed their war experiences. He expressed regret that he was not free to tell her, a woman, about Gnomonism, except in very general terms, but there it was, he was under certain vows. She said she understood and that, after all, women had their little secrets too. He told her about Gary, Indiana, carefully pointing out that his people had nothing to do with the steel mills. She talked about girlhood escapades at The Grange,

Little-Fen-on-Sea, which was her home. They sat at the piano and sang "Beautiful Dreamer." They went to the harbor and watched the boats and ate Italian sausages. She made light of her "silly knee" and apologized for being such a slow walker. Slow or fast, he said, he counted it a privilege to be at her side and would consider it a great honor if she would take his arm.

In little more than a month of intense study Sydney became an Initiate in the Gnomon Society. Within another month he was an Adept, and then, as a peer of Lamar's, he began to speak out on things. He suggested how the course of study might be organized along more efficient lines. The ritual of investiture could be improved too. A processional was needed, a long solemn one, and more figs and more candles, and some smoldering aromatic gums. Lamar agreed that such touches were appealing. The innovations seemed harmless enough and might even be useful, but how could two Adepts presume to do such things without direct authorization from Pletho Pappus or some other Master?

Then Sydney Hen uttered the thought that had been troubling Lamar for some weeks. It was a wild thought that he had often suppressed. "Can't you see it, man? You're already a Master! We're both Masters! You still don't see it? Robert was Pletho himself! Your Poma is the Cone of Fate! You and I are beginning the New Cycle of Gnomonism!"

So saying, Hen produced a Poma of his own, one he had had run up in red kid, and then like Napoleon crowned himself with it.

Thus boldly expressed and exposed to the blazing light of day, the thing could be seen clearly, and Lamar knew in his heart that it was true. He was Master of Gnomons and had been Master of Gnomons for perhaps as long as six weeks. He had not, however, suspected for one moment that Sydney might be a Master too, and this news took his breath away. What was more, Sydney said he believed himself to be a "Hierophant of Atlantis." Lamar was puzzled by the claim, there being no such title or degree in Gnomonism, to the best of his knowledge.

Over the next few days Sydney outlined an Alexandrian scheme whereby he and Lamar would take Gnomonism to the world. He, Sydney, would be responsible for Europe and Asia, and Lamar would establish the ancient order in the Americas, in accordance with Pletho-Robert's plan. There was no time to lose. He all but pushed Lamar out of the house, saying he was terribly sorry but an unsecured personal loan was out of the question. He must make his way back home as best he could.

Lamar, as a veteran in distress, was able to get a hardship loan from the American consul, upon surrender of his passport, just enough to pay steerage fare to New York in the sweltering hold of a Portuguese steamer. Fanny kissed him goodbye at the dock and so the rough accommodations bothered him hardly at all.

# 2

L AMAR WAS hardly noticed as he passed through New York with his *Codex* and continued on his journey home by rail. In Gary he picked up his old job as clerk in his uncle's dry goods store. He took his meals and his baths at the YMCA down the street, and slept in the back of the store. Here, in the shadowy storage room, with the drop light and the cardboard boxes, he established Pillar No. 1 of the Gnomon Society, North America.

He was unable to recruit his uncle, who said he didn't have time to read a lot of stuff like that, much less memorize it. Nor did Lamar have any luck with his old school chums. His first success came with a traveling salesman named Bates, who set up Pillar No. 2 in Chicago. Bates was followed by Mapes, and Pillar No. 3, in Valparaiso, Indiana. Mapes was a football coach, ready to try anything. He hoped that Gnomonic thought might show him the way to put some life into his timorous and lethargic team. Mapes was followed by—nobody, for quite a long time. Three Pillars then, and three members, all told, and that was what Lamar had to show for almost two years of work.

By this time he had made a typewritten copy of the *Codex*. The string-bound manuscript version was getting dog-eared and did not make a good impression. The typewritten copy did not make a much better impression but it was easier to read. Lamar could see that many men did not accept this as a real book either, judging from their hard faces as they flipped through it, pausing over the triangles and recoiling, and then giving it back to him.

What was needed was a properly printed book. Bates told him about a Latvian newspaper in Chicago, where, in the back shop, English could be set in type and printed without anyone there understanding a word of it. Lamar went there and ordered fifty copies of the book and asked the Letts not to break the plates but to keep them readily available for reorders. The books had blue paper covers and were bound with staples.

Some years were to pass before the first printing was exhausted. The 1920s were later to be celebrated as a joyous decade but to Lamar it was a time of the grossest materialism and of hollow and nasty skepticism. No one had time to listen. Fanny Hen's letters kept him going. Her monthly letter, lightly scented, was the one bright spot in his gloomy round. She was now in London with Sydney, or Sir Sydney, he having become the fourth baronet on the death of his father, Sir Billy Hen, the sportsman. Sydney was disappointed in his patrimony, which amounted to little more than a pile of Sir Billy's gambling debts, but he had pushed on with that energy characteristic of the Hens to set up his Gnomon Temple on Vay Street, and, according to Fanny, was doing quite well with it. Lamar kept Fanny's current letter in his inside coat pocket, where he could get a whiff of it with a slight dip of his head, and where it was handy for rereading over his solitary meals. In his replies to her he always enclosed a money order for fifteen dollars and said he hoped she would use the small sum for some little personal luxury she might otherwise deny herself.

In the spring of 1925 Lamar went on the road as a salesman, working out of Chicago under Bates with a line of quality haberdashery. It was a good job and at first he did well with it, so well that he was able to make a down payment on a small house in Skokie and a transatlantic proposal of marriage. Fanny accepted, against the wishes of her mother, who was worried about Chicago gangsters, and of brother Sydney, who stood to lose an unsalaried secretary. She arrived at New York on the *Mauretania*. Lamar took her to Atlantic City, where they were married in a Methodist chapel. The honeymoon was delightful. From their hotel room high above the beach they could watch the battering waves. They took rides together on the Boardwalk in the ridiculous rolling chairs and had late suppers at Madame Yee's with tiny white cups of tea. It was the last carefree time the young Jimmersons were to know for several years.

Fanny Jimmerson was fond of her brick bungalow in Skokie, which she fancied to be in the exact center of the continent, and she might have kept it had she not unwittingly stirred up the embers of Gnomonism. Lamar no longer talked much about the Gnomon Society. Repeated failure to interest others in the secret order had worn him down. He no longer bothered his fellow drummers in hotel lobbies with confidential talk about the Cone of Fate. Now here was Fanny telling him of Sydney's great successes in London. He had brought hundreds of men into the brotherhood, including some very famous members of the Golden Order of the Hermetic Dawn and the Theosophical Society. His building fund for the Temple was already oversubscribed.

Lamar, stung, turned on her one night and spoke sharply. The two situations were hardly comparable, he said. Sydney was dealing with a class of men who had a sense of the past and a tradition of scholarship. How well, he asked, would Master Sydney fare with the 13 Precepts on a smoking car of the Illinois Central? How far would he get with his fine words on the streets of Cicero, above the din of careening beer trucks and blazing machine guns?

Fanny said she was sorry, that she had not meant to goad him. She just thought he might be interested in Sydney's work. After all, they were, were they not, brothers in this secret order? Lamar said she was absolutely right. He asked her to forgive him for raising his voice. It would not happen again. He was, of course, pleased to hear that Sydney was doing well and she was right to remind him of his duty.

Once again he set about in earnest to find recruits, to the neglect of his clothing sales. He told his buyers that he had something in his sample case more beautiful than painted silk neckties and more lasting than Harris tweed, and the best part was that this thing would cost them nothing more than a little hard study at night.

Bates too pitched in anew. Through a friend at the big Chicago marketing firm of Targeted Sales, Inc., he got his hands on a mailing list titled "Odd Birds of Illinois and Indiana," which, by no means exhaustive, contained the names of some seven hundred men who ordered strange merchandise through the mail, went to court often, wrote letters to the editor, wore unusual headgear, kept rooms that were filled with rocks or old newspapers. In short, independent thinkers, who might be more receptive to the Atlantean lore than the general run of men. Lamar was a little surprised to find his own name on the list. It was given as "Mr. Jimmerson." His gossiping neighbors in Skokie, it seemed, had put him down for an odd bird. They had observed him going into his garage late at night in a pointed cap and had speculated that he was building a small flying machine behind those locked doors, or pottering around with a toy railroad or a giant ball of twine.

He and Bates wrote letters to the seven hundred cranks, with questionnaires enclosed that had been run off at the Latvian printshop. They waited. They sorted out the replies. Those men who seemed to have the stuff of Gnomons in them got second questionnaires, and such of these as came back went through a further winnowing. The process culminated with Bates or Lamar appearing on the doorsteps of the worthy few, *Codex Pappus* in hand.

"Good morning," Lamar would say to the householder at the door. "I am—*Mr. Jimmerson.*"

It was during this period that Lamar, still a young man, became known to all and sundry, young and old alike, as "Mr. Jimmerson." He and Bates, with Gnomon gravity, had always addressed one another as "Mr. Bates" and "Mr. Jimmerson," and this form now took hold in the wider world. Fanny continued to call him "Lamar," as did Sydney Hen, and much later, Morehead Moaler, but few others took that liberty, not even Austin Popper.

Mr. Bates and Mr. Jimmerson worked long hours for the Society and even bagged a member now and then. When they were fired from their sales jobs they hardly noticed, and they used their final commission checks to pay for a new line of printed study materials. The loss of the little brick house through foreclosure was more troubling. Mr. Jimmerson could see that Fanny was upset and he promised to make it up to her one day. Good soldier that she was, she made no fuss. They packed their goods and left Skokie, and when they were gone, the neighbors, peering from behind curtains, spilled out of their houses and went for the garage at a trot to see what they could see, with any luck a small airship.

The Jimmersons moved into a rented room in Gary, where Fanny prepared budget meals on an electric hot plate. It was a cheerless winter. Mr. Bates often shared their dinner of baked beans and white bread spread with white oleomargarine. Neither of the two Gnomons paid much heed to the Pythagorean stricture against eating beans and the flesh of animals, although they did feel guilt in the act until Austin Popper came along and explained that this rule was never laid down by Pythagoras, but was rather an interpolation by some medieval busybody, and that in fact there was nothing Pythagoras liked better than a pot of Great Northern beans simmered with a bit of ham hock.

The new members of the order, to be sure, paid certain fees, and the Society's bank balance at this time stood at around $2,000, but Mr. Jimmerson was careful to keep that money separated from his personal funds, lest there be any breath of scandal. Fanny thought he should pay himself a small salary as Master of all the Gnomons in America, or at least take some expense money. Sydney didn't stint himself at his London Temple. He even had a full staff of servants. Mr. Jimmerson said that Sir Sydney could do as he pleased, but as far as he, Lamar Jimmerson, was concerned, the great work was not for sale. She must understand that his position was a fiduciary one, one of trust.

Fanny saw there was nothing for it but for her to take a job. She found work as a nurse's aide at Hope Hospital, in the physical therapy ward, where she soon became a great favorite with patients and staff alike. After completing a brief refresher course she took the state examination and received her license as registered nurse, along with a supervisory position in the therapy ward that paid $150 a month.

Mr. Jimmerson knew nothing of this. He had noticed that they were eating better, pork chops and such, and living better. They seemed to be living in a different place, in a clean new apartment just down the street from Hope Hospital, but he was so preoccupied that he had not bothered to inquire into these new domestic arrangements. Fanny was reluctant to tell him about the job. With all his quirky principles he was sure to have objections to working wives. He would put his foot down. As it turned out, he didn't mind at all, and as he became swamped with paperwork he even encouraged her to take courses in accounting and hectograph operation, and lend him a hand. She did so, and, with an hour snatched here and there from her busy day, she also prepared the typescripts of his first three books, *101 Gnomon Facts*, *Why I Am a Gnomon* and *Tracking the Telluric Currents*. These works, written for the general public, contained no secret matter, nor were they indexed or annotated.

Things began to pick up toward the end of the decade, and then in 1929, with the economic collapse of the nation, the Gnomon Society fairly flourished. Traders and lawyers and bricklayers and salesmen and farmers now had time on their hands. They had time to listen and some were so desperate as to seek answers in books. By the summer of 1931 there were more than forty Pillars in six states, and in January of the next year Mr. Jimmerson went to his Latvian printers and placed an order for 5,000 copies of the *Codex Pappus*.

The Letts were in serious financial trouble. Their newspaper had already gone under and the printshop was just barely afloat. But Mr. Jimmerson was not one to forget his friends. True, they had garbled important passages in his books and left pages uncut and bound entire chapters upside down, but they had also extended credit to him in those dark days when it could not have been justified in a business way. He was now in a position to return the favor. The firm was to be reorganized as the Gnomon Press. No one would be fired. The production of Gnomon tracts and books would have priority but the shop would be free to take in outside jobs as well. When this announcement was made, and translated, amid heavy Baltic gloom in the back shop, the printers at first were stunned, and then they cheered Mr. Jimmerson and threw their paper hats in the air.

With success came the inevitable attacks. There was the usual sour grapes disparagement and mockery of outsiders looking in. Pagan nonsense, said the bishops. At best a false science, said the academic rationalists. An ornate casket with no pearl inside, said the Masonic chiefs. A foolish distraction from the real business of life, said the political engineers. A nest of cuckoos who like to dress up and give themselves titles, said the newspaper writers.

None of these gentlemen could say just what Gnomonism was—the Archbishop of Chicago had it confused with Gnosticism—but they all agreed it was something to stay clear of. *Why the secrecy? Who are these people? Whatever it is they are concealing must be evil. What are their long-range plans? Do they claim magical powers? What are they up to with all their triangles?*

Lies were spread about the Gnomons. They were said to carouse in their meeting halls, which had painted windows like mortuaries, dancing the night away with much chanting and tambourine shaking, following their ritual meal of bulls' blood, lentils and smoked cat meat. There was at least one physical attack. A young man from Northwestern University tracked Mr. Jimmerson down and demanded a refund of the dollar he had paid for a copy of *Why I Am a Gnomon* and an apology for foisting it off on the public. He said the book was "not any good at all" and "just awful stuff," and when Mr. Jimmerson hesitated in his reply the young man ripped the little book into two pieces and flung them away and then punched the Master in the face. Fanny did not know about the fracas until the next morning, when she noticed that her husband's lips and nose were stuck fast to his pillow with dried blood. He told her it was nothing, that he believed the young bruiser had assaulted him as a writer rather than as a Gnomon, and that in any case all this abuse was contemptible, not to say futile. Their enemies were much too late. The Gnomon Society had taken root in the New World and was here to stay.

This became clear for all to see on April 10, 1936, when the Gnomon Temple was dedicated in Burnette, Indiana, the most fashionable suburb of Gary. It was a mansion of Bedford limestone, which, with grounds and outbuildings, occupied a good part of the 1400 block of Bulmer Avenue, the most fashionable street of Burnette. An iron-and-steel tycoon, lately deceased, had built it, with little regard for expense, and his widow, eager to be off to Palm Beach, sold it to the Gnomon Society for $180,000. Mr. Jimmerson was uneasy over the prospect of moving into so grand a house and he had to be persuaded by the Council of Three, Bates, Mapes and Epps, that it was necessary for the Master to live in the Temple, at the center of the web, just as it was necessary for the Temple to be monumental, have great mass, be gray and oppressive to every eye that gazed upon it.

# 3

S IR SYDNEY HEN cabled fraternal congratulations from London. It was another wonderful day for the Society, he said. He regretted that he could not attend the dedication but his health was such that he was no longer able to travel. He was suffering greatly from fevers, fluxes and the dry gripes and could hardly get away from the bathroom for an hour at a time. He suspected that he was being given a debilitating poison by Rosicrucian agents from France. The cable was dated "Anno, XVII, New Gnomon Cycle," and was signed "Hen, Theos Soter, Master and Hierophant, C.H., F.S.A.," with the letters standing for "Companion of Hermes" and "Far-Seeing Arbiter." Thus had the advanced degrees of Gnomonry begun to proliferate.

Mr. Jimmerson quickly became adjusted to the comforts of Temple life. The Council had been wise to insist on his living here. He particularly liked the Red Room, with its big fireplace, the bookshelves that rose to the ceiling, the wine-colored carpet and the wall coverings of wine-colored silk. Here he settled in. In the Red Room a man could study and think. Here he could get down to business on his new book, *The Jimmerson Spiral*.

Fanny liked the oversize bathtubs and the canopied beds and the rose bower and the splashing fountain. She had a number of servants at her disposal, these including a cook, a gardener, two maids and a butler-chauffeur named Maceo, a quiet Negro man who had the additional duty of sweeping out the Inner Hall of the Black Throne, into which neither Fanny nor the maids, as females, were allowed to penetrate.

Mr. Jimmerson's office was fully staffed too, and overseen by one Huggins, whose title was editorial advisor. Huggins was a journalist, an irritable, alcoholic bird of passage who brought certain professional skills to bear on the production of Gnomon printed matter. Austin Popper was the mail boy. That was the job description but he was not really very boyish at the age of nineteen—or maybe it was twenty-four, or even thirty. Even at that time Popper was coy about his age, and his origins, and no one could pin him down on these things.

Popper was quick in every sense of the word. His physical movements were quick and sure, and he could learn a new task in short order and execute it with confidence. He had a ready fund of information gleaned from newspapers and popular magazines. He kept his eyes open. He remembered names. His charm was effective on both men and women, and even the misanthropic Huggins became fond of him. Mapes and Epps thought him just a shade ambitious but they too found his company pleasant, against their will.

When Huggins was drunk, Popper covered for him, and when Huggins had editorial disputes with the Master, or printing disputes with the Letts, it was young Popper who stepped in to smooth the ruffled feathers and suggest a sensible accommodation. Huggins soon found himself working for Popper, and still they remained friends.

But Huggins was bound to be left behind anyway since he refused to become a Gnomon. Out of a natural perversity and a newspaperman's terror of being duped, he refused to join anything, and so remained a P.S., or Perfect Stranger, while Popper answered the summons with alacrity and went on to become a power in the great brotherhood. Soon he was writing speeches for the Master and helping him with his books. He talked and wrote with facility, seldom at a loss for a word, or an opinion. He was never Master of Gnomons, nor even a member of the Council of Three, but the common perception that he directed the organization was not far off the mark.

What Popper did was transform the Gnomon Society. Having gained the confidence of the Master, he was able to persuade him that they must broaden their appeal. The way to do this was to relax the standards. The *Codex Pappus*, for instance, was much too difficult for most beginners and should be revised. There was too much memory work for the ordinary man; the staggering volume of this stuff must be reduced. Only in this way could the Society expect to grow and become a force in the world.

Mr. Jimmerson said, "And how would you go about all this, Austin?"

Popper was turning through the pages of the *Codex*. "The first thing we must do, sir, is get rid of some of these triangles."

"You would do away with the symbolic forms?"

"Oh no, not all of them. I would keep the Cone of Fate. Under no circumstances would I tamper with the Jimmerson Spiral."

"But you think there are too many triangles? The simplest of polygons?"

"Far too many, sir, for the people I have in mind. Do you remember in school how hard it was to get anyone to join the Geometry Club?"

"I don't believe we had a Geometry Club in our school."

"Neither did we but you see what I mean."

"The ordinary man, you say. Why should we concern ourselves with ordinary men? Pletho tells us that most of them are pigs or children."

"Some of them are pigs, certainly, but I need not remind you, sir, that it is our ancient business to transmute base matter into noble matter."

"The great work."

"As you say. All I want to do, sir, is prepare a simplified version of the *Codex* for use at a new and elementary level of our craft. Then, step by step, we can lead these men on to the *Codex Pappus* itself and pure Gnomonism."

Popper spoke of thousands of new members and at last the Master came around. He took the proposal to the Council of Three, or T.W.K.—Those Who Know. Mr. Bates liked the idea. Mapes and Epps conceded that it might have some merit —but was Austin Popper the right person to direct such a program? He was willful, erratic. He was vain in his personal appearance. He was sometimes facetious in a most unbecoming way. In his writing he had a vulgar inclination to make everything clear. He had not yet learned to appreciate the beauties of allusion and Gnomonic obfuscation—that fog was there for a purpose. He couldn't see that to grasp a delicate thing outright was often to crush it.

But in the end, under pressure from the Master, they gave way and Popper was authorized to proceed. An abridged *Codex* was prepared, and a new teaching syllabus. A new probationary degree called "Neophyte" was created.

Popper went on the road with his mission, due east, to To-
ledo and Cleveland, where he placed small, mystifying notices
in the newspapers, and then met in hotel rooms with those
men of Ohio who responded. It was a period of trial and error. There was no shortage of idle men on Lake Erie but the
wisdom of Atlantis, clarified though it now was, still did not
hold their attention. Popper had to grope about for ideas they
could hearken to. Little by little he worked things out. Most of
the triangles and a good many of the oracular ambiguities had
already been pruned from the *Codex*, and Popper went further
yet. The Cone of Fate was not exactly abandoned but he no
longer talked about it except in response to direct inquiry. The
Gnomonic content of his lectures diminished daily as the Popper content swelled. Soon he had a coherent system, one with
wide appeal, and he had to book ever larger rooms and halls to
accommodate the growing number of men who came to hear
his words of hope.

For this was what he gave them. Through Gnomonic
thought and practices they could become happy, and very
likely rich, and not later but sooner. They could learn how to
harness secret powers, tap hidden reserves, plug in to the Telluric Currents. It was all true enough. Popper plugged them
in to something of an electrical nature and he bucked them
up with the example of his own dynamic personality and they
went away thinking better of themselves.

The Gnomon wave was cresting, and it was at this high
point that Morehead Moaler of Brownsville, Texas, became
a Gnomon, perhaps the most steadfast of them all. But little
notice was taken of him at the time, or of his remote Texas
Pillar, what with all the national excitement. There were articles in the press about "the mysterious Mr. Jimmerson" who
remained concealed in his "Egyptian Temple" in Burnette, Indiana, while his spokesman, Austin Popper, went about teaching "a lost Egyptian science." *Look*, the magazine, published
an account of a Popper rally in Philadelphia, with a striking
photograph of a roomful of solemn men standing with their
hands clasped atop their heads. Popper appeared on a network
radio show in Chicago, a breakfast show, and was received
with whistles and sustained applause from the friendly oldsters
in the audience. He marched around the breakfast table with

them, and one jolly old man, whose name he failed to catch in the hubbub, presented him with a talking blue jay. He caught the bird's name, Squanto, but just missed catching the name of the old gentleman, whose smiling red face he was to see often in his dreams, the face saying its name, but just out of earshot, never with quite enough force.

Mr. Jimmerson, at the urging of the Council, called Popper in off the road and said, "This has gone too far, Austin. I want you to stop playing the fool. I want you to show some dignity. They tell me you have a Victrola now and a talking bird."

Popper was contrite. He promised to conduct himself with restraint in the future. Then he went back on the road and resumed his old ways. He led his followers in cheers and he played bouncy tunes on a windup phonograph, marking the beat with wildly swooping arms. He engaged in comic dialogues with Squanto. He continued to court the press and he even had his picture taken with politicians. These were two of the Four P's that all Gnomons were under orders to shun, the other two being the Pope and the police. He continued to weaken the membership requirements until admittance to the order became almost effortless. The two nights of initiation were reduced to a token twenty minutes, with no insistence on figs, and the Pledge was no longer eight densely printed pages of Hermetical mystery lore and bloody vows of faith to the Ten Pillars of Atlantis—all to be recited without stumbling once—but rather one short paragraph that was little more than a bland affirmation of humility before the unseen powers of the universe.

Still, there was something to be said for Popper. He *did* bring in thousands of new members, a few of whom turned out to be good Gnomons, and all of whom paid monthly dues and bought books and study materials from the Gnomon Press.

Mr. Jimmerson was of two minds. He wavered. One day he was resolved that Austin must go and the next day he would defend him in a heated session of the Council. More than once he had to raise his little bronze rod, the Rod of Correction, to calm tempers. Mapes and Epps demanded that Popper be silenced. If not, they warned, he would soon be their Master. Already he had changed the Society into an ungainly beast that Pletho Pappus would hardly recognize, to say nothing of Pythagoras and Hermes Triplex, and if they, the Master and Council, stood by and allowed this headstrong young man to further corrupt the brotherhood, then the judgment of history would indeed be hard on them, and rightly so.

The argument was telling and in his heart Mr. Jimmerson knew that something would have to be done. In February 1940 the painful decision was made. Austin Popper was to be formally "humbled," and assigned to a menial administrative job in the Temple. The axe was poised, and then, just before it fell, something happened that changed the picture.

A few months before, in September 1939, with the outbreak of war in Europe, Sir Sydney Hen had fled England with his robes billowing behind him and come to Toronto, Canada. Mr. Jimmerson invited him to make his home in the Temple in Burnette. Hen declined with thanks. Every courtesy was extended to him by the Canadian Gnomons, who found him a suite of rooms in a lakefront residential hotel that was filled with chattering widows.

Fanny Jimmerson went to Toronto for a Christmas reunion with her brother and she was very much upset at what she found. He was bent and had lost his teeth. His neck was prematurely wattled. The elf locks were gone and indeed all his hair except for a semicircular fringe in back that hung straight down, dead and gray like Spanish moss. The poisoning report, the henbane story, which Fanny had dismissed as one of Sydney's hysterical flights, turned out to have been all too true, though the French Rosicrucians had been unjustly blamed. The poisoner was a young man named Evans who had been lightly dusting Sir Sydney's muffins with arsenic on and off over the years. Hen described him as a "paid companion." The boy's motive was not clear, with the police suggesting that Welsh peevishness was somehow behind it all, and in any case there was not enough evidence to prosecute. "All I could do was pull his ears and sack him," said Hen.

Fanny extended her visit so as to nurse Sydney and prepare restorative meals for him. She brightened up the place with bits of song and decorative touches and small pots of vegetation, including some of Sydney's favorite ferns and spiky desert succulents. His appetite gradually returned. She bundled him up and took him for walks along the lake. The icy winds made his cheeks glow. His eyes cleared. She bought him a puppy and Hen taught the little dog to shake hands and how to untie simple knots that had been loosely tied in one of his older sashes.

Some of the ladies in the hotel approached Fanny to ask if it was true that her brother was a baronet. Physical wreck that he was, Sir Sydney still had a certain air, and the ladies were curious about him, this titled mystery figure on the sixth floor. Fanny responded in a friendly way and the ladies proposed a tea party, with Sir Sydney as guest of honor. He agreed to attend, to allow the ladies to honor him and look him over for a half hour or so, if certain conditions were observed. There must be no receiving line, no cameras and, above all, no handshaking. He would not stand or even sit. Arrangements must be made for him to recline. The conditions were met. Hen wore a white cassock and gold chain and embroidered slippers. He thoroughly enjoyed the affair. The cakes were good and the ladies hovered about his recumbent form and listened attentively to his far-ranging opinions.

Toward the end of January, Fanny left him in fairly good health and in the hands of a rich widow named Babette. A few weeks later, in February, a Toronto newspaper published a long letter from Hen that rocked the Gnomon Society.

He began his remarks with an attack on Popper, calling him "Austin Rotter" and "a low American farceur" and "a confidence trickster of the very lowest type," and went on to bring a full and stinging indictment against American Gnomonism. No doubt, he said, the leadership in Indiana, U.S.A., meant well, but it was very weak. Substantial changes could be expected now that he, Hen, was on the scene. As Grand Prior of World Gnomonry he was seriously considering revocation of the charter of the American Temple in Burnette, and would certainly do so if that Temple did not act soon to purge itself of Popper and Popperism.

All this, out of the blue. It was quite a spirited blast from such a frail figure. Mr. Jimmerson's reply was strong stuff too. He gave an interview to a Chicago newspaper, saying it was shameful that a Master, albeit a junior one, of the Gnomon

Society, a secret brotherhood based on principles of Hermetical and Pythagorean harmony, had seen fit not only to make such false and scandalous charges, but to make them publicly. As for any "charter," there was none to be revoked, just as there was no such title in Gnomonry as "Grand Prior," but if there was ever any revoking to be done, then he, Lamar Jimmerson, First Master of the New Cycle, successor to Pletho Pappus and tutor to Sydney Hen, would do it.

Hen came back with another letter to the editor, a short one this time, to the Chicago newspaper. He wrote:

> Please be advised that the Gnomon Society can no longer recognize degrees awarded by the gang of Indiana ruffians led by the impostor Lamar Jimmerson, who styles himself First Master of the New Cycle. Lamar Jimmerson is Master of Nothing. He is a grey nullity whose teaching is worthless and whose conversation is tiresome beyond belief and whose book, *The Jimmerson Spiral*, purporting to contain some later writings of Pletho Pappus, is the most brazen forgery since the Donation of Constantine.

Trailing after Hen's signature there were many titles and capital letters.

So it was that the break came and the Society divided into the Jimmerson school and the Hen school, and thus did Popper escape the axe. To discipline him now, the Council saw, would give the appearance of acknowledging Hen's authority and yielding to it.

The bitter exchanges went on and on. Hen's favorite weapon was the letter of ridicule. Mr. Jimmerson fought back with a barrage of pamphlets that kept the Latvian printers hopping. Then Hen stepped up the campaign, initiating the battle of the books, by having his people remove Mr. Jimmerson's books from libraries and bookstores and destroy them. Popper countered with a program of defacement, ordering the Jimmerson men to fill in all the closed loops of letters in Hen's books with green ink, to underline passages at random in that same green ink and to scrawl such comments in the margins as "Huh??!!" and "Is this guy serious?" and "I don't get it!" in red ink, the aim being to break the reader's concentration and so subvert the message. He also commissioned a drawing of

a pop-eyed, moronic human face, that of a collegiate-looking
fellow with spiky hair and big bow tie, and had rubber stamps
made of it. The face had a strange power to annoy, even to
sicken the spirit—one had to turn away from it—and Popper
directed that it be stamped on every page of Hen's books, in
a different place on each page so that the reader could not
prepare himself.

# 4

THE PRESS grew tired of Gnomons and moved on to other things. The public likewise lost interest, almost overnight. War was coming, the country was preparing for a mighty crusade and the Popper rallies suddenly had a shabby, dated air of selfishness about them. The crowds dwindled away to nothing. Popper had run out his string, or so it appeared.

He went back to the Temple to think. Once the life of the luncheon table, he now took a sandwich outside to the fountain and ate alone, or rather with Squanto, the two of them resting on the rim of the circular stone basin. There were goldfish in the pool, and at the center of it, atop a cone of granite, there was fixed the gnomon, or upright part of a sundial, a flat bronze object resembling a carpenter's square. From a window in the Red Room, Mr. Jimmerson could look out on the scene, at the sparkling plumes of water, at the little shifting rainbows, at the simple bronze symbol of his order, at a chastened Austin Popper. He found it pleasing. This was the proper state of things at the Temple, the right pitch, this drowsy afternoon air of not much going on, a state very close to that of sleep.

But with the Japanese attack on Pearl Harbor, Popper was off and running again. Here was an opportunity. Once more he was alive with ideas. First came the Gnomon blood drive, with the brothers laid out in rows, rubber tubes coming out of their left arms and their right arms raised in military salutes for the news photographers. Then on to the army. The Society's first duty in this crisis, Popper said, was to set an example, and how better to do it than for the entire male staff of the Temple —excluding the Master, who, in a manner of speaking, had already borne arms for his country—to enlist in the army as a body. It was their duty and it was just the kind of thing to catch the eye of President Roosevelt and the national press.

The Council agreed and even the cynical Huggins acquiesced. They rallied to the colors *en bloc*. Popper arranged for full press coverage of the swearing-in ceremony at the Federal Building in Chicago. Bates, Mapes and Epps wore their robes.

Maceo and Huggins stood slightly to one side with the rest of the staff in fuzzy 1941 business suits. All were solemn and held their right hands up in a rigid way, fingers tightly closed. Popper himself did not take the oath, explaining to the others that the Secretary of the Navy had placed him on "strategic standby." Just what this was and how he came to be placed on it, he was not free to disclose, other than to say that he was working for the Secretary in an undercover capacity. From high official sources, he said, he had learned that he was number eight on Herr Hitler's American execution list, to be shot on sight as a public nuisance.

Whatever Popper's naval duties may have been, they did not require him to range far from Burnette, Indiana. He stayed close to the Temple, where he alone now had the ear of the Master, and where he worked long hours developing new schemes for gaining the patriotic spotlight.

Their next move, he advised Mr. Jimmerson, should be to go to Washington with a carefully prepared plan for winning the war through the use of compressed air and the military application of Gnomonic science. He had already worked out a schedule. First they would pay a courtesy call at the White House and then go to the War Department for a working session with General Marshall. There the full plan would be presented. Afterwards they would hold a press conference and give a report, a kind of broad outline of the plan, cleared of secret matter but including a few tantalizing details. For the newsreel photographers there would be a demonstration of *boktos*, or Pythagorean butting, the old Greek art of self-defense, which was to be incorporated into the army's physical training program. That same night, having arranged for five minutes of radio time on the Blue Network, Mr. Jimmerson would sit before the microphone and again discuss the Gnomon victory plan in a general way, closing with some brief inspirational remarks for the nation.

"Air?" said Mr. Jimmerson.

"*Compressed* air," said Popper. "What you're thinking of, sir, is ordinary air, the air we breathe, which is so soft and gentle we hardly notice it. Compressed air is something else again. It packs a real punch."

He explained, Mr. Jimmerson listened and became thoughtful. He had no qualms over releasing sharp blasts of air against such vicious enemies as the Jap and the Hun and sending them tumbling across the battlefield, but surely it would be wrong to allow the Hermetical Secrets to be used in the bloody business of warfare. He expressed his misgivings.

Popper said, "Remember, sir, we're talking about barbarians here. One of our early Masters wasn't so squeamish in dealing with them. One of the very greatest of Masters."

"Who was that?"

"Archimedes. Don't you recall how he jumped into the battle with all his scientific tricks to help defend Syracuse against, who was it, Tamerlane, I believe, yes, and won the day? Or no, wait, they surrendered, and when it was all over Tamerlane found our man drawing triangles in the dust with his finger."

"Didn't he ask Tamerlane to get out of his light?"

"How right you are, sir. So he could finish working out his geometry problem."

"He couldn't see to work for the shadow."

"No, sir."

"The fellow was blocking off his light."

"Yes, sir."

"Standing in the doorway, don't you see, with the sun behind him so that his shadow made it hard for Archimedes to see what he was doing down there in the dust."

"With his figures, yes, sir."

"Down there on some kind of dusty floor."

"Yes, sir, I understand."

Mr. Jimmerson fell into another thoughtful silence. Presently he said, "We talk of light. Pletho Pappus tells us we must labor in darkness in order to bring light. I'm sure you know the passage, Austin, and yet you seem to think it is our business to attract attention and make a public spectacle of ourselves. How do you reconcile the two positions?"

Popper finessed the question by not answering it. By way of reply he said that a news photograph of Lamar Jimmerson wearing his Poma and his Master's gown and having a chat with President Roosevelt in the White House would cut the ground from under Sydney Hen. Such a picture would be of more value than a million pamphlets in showing to the world just who the true leader of Gnomonry was. Hen would seethe with rage and stamp his little feet like Rumpelstiltskin when he saw that picture in *Life* magazine.

"A wonderful scene, don't you agree, sir? Hen furioso. What I wouldn't give to see that little dance."

Mr. Jimmerson agreed that Sydney's fit would make an amusing show, and he had to agree too that in these dark days the President certainly had a call on his best advice. "I suppose you're right, Austin. We must do what we can."

The ten-point victory plan was prepared and in early June of 1942 the two Gnomons took it to Washington in a locked briefcase. Some thought was given to having Maceo drive them in the black Buick, but then there was the problem with gasoline ration stamps—and Mr. Jimmerson would countenance no dealings with the black market—and so in the end they went by rail. They traveled by day coach, no Pullman space being available, and had to stand part of the way. Fanny had wanted to go but she was five months along in a surprise, mid-life pregnancy and her husband would not allow it. Hotel rooms were all but impossible to get. At the last minute their congressman was able to secure them one small room at an older downtown hotel called the Borger. It was a threadbare place near the bus station. The trip was hot and tiring. At the Borger a midget bellboy called Mr. Jimmerson a "guy."

"Is that guy with you?" he said, in his quacking midget voice, as Mr. Jimmerson, a little dizzy from his long train ride, veered off course in crossing the lobby.

"Yes, he is," said Popper.

"Hey! Hey! Hey! Yeah, you! Where do you think you're going? The elevator's over here!"

Their room was just wide enough for the two single beds and a little leg space between them. Popper sat on one bed and began at once to make telephone calls. He seemed to be trying to make appointments. It struck Mr. Jimmerson that he had left all this until very late. Mr. Jimmerson lay on the other bed and looked over his speaking notes. Tomorrow was the big day.

Popper winked at him and said he had just arranged a double date with two hostesses named Bobbie and Edna who worked at a nearby night spot that had a good rumba band. "I think you'll like Edna, sir. She's a fine, strapping girl. A real armful, Bobbie tells me."

Mr. Jimmerson was astonished. Popper said, "My little joke, sir, nothing more. When people are hot and weary I've often found that a light note is just what the doctor ordered."

That night three Gnomons from the local Pillar came to call on the Master. One was a chubby young man named Pharris White. He was a part-time postal clerk who attended law school at night and who wrote long letters to the Temple on the subject of certain prime numbers and their Pythagorean significance, or lack thereof. Sometimes he sent telegrams. In the hollow place under his lower lip there was a tuft of seven or eight yellow bristles. He carried a satchel. Though he was only a Neophyte, he spoke very freely to the Master, even offensively, demanding to know why he, White, as an ordinary Gnomon, was denied access to the truly secret books by Those Who Know, and kept in dismal ignorance of the truly secret rituals and the truly secret numbers.

Mr. Jimmerson politely told him that he could hardly be expected to discuss such matters on a social occasion like this. White took notes. The other two Gnomons were older men, a municipal judge and a retired streetcar motorman, who simply wanted to meet Mr. Jimmerson and bask in his radiance and have him sign their copies of *Why I Am a Gnomon*.

Popper, still on the telephone, became annoyed with them as they chattered and shuffled about in the tiny room, adding their body heat and cigar smoke to the stifling air, and when he saw Pharris White stealthily rooting around in Mr. Jimmerson's bag he jumped up from the bed and ordered them all to leave. The Master had given them quite enough of his time. He was here on an important government mission and had papers to study.

As they trooped out, Popper caught White by the sleeve. "One moment, White. Let's have a look at your Gnomon card. I want to check the watermark."

"My card is in order."

"Then you won't mind."

White produced his membership card. Popper glanced at it and then whipped out a rubber stamp and stamped VOID across it in purple block letters. "There. You are now a P.S. Get out."

"You can't do this."

"On your way. We don't know you."

"You're making a big mistake."

"And don't write us any more letters. Understand? You savvy?"

"You think you can treat me this way because I'm poor and have to go to night law school."

"All law schools should be conducted at night. Late at night, in rooms like this. No, I'm turning you out of the Society, White, because there's something wrong with your mind. I can see it in your eyes. They don't look right to me. Your eyes and your pallor tell me all I need to know. Maybe you can get some help elsewhere. We just don't have the time to fool around with people like you. Why aren't you in the army, anyway?"

Pharris White left with his satchel.

Mr. Jimmerson slept badly. He couldn't get his limbs distributed comfortably on the narrow bed. The scene with the young man had been disturbing and he was homesick and concerned about his wife—a middle-aged woman expecting a child—and he had forebodings about what the next day would bring. Popper continued to ring up people far into the night. His telephone manner was unctuous. Mr. Jimmerson turned away from the wheedling voice and the glow of the table lamp and tried to rest. When at last he did sleep his exhalations were moist and troubled.

The next morning, as he inspected himself in a mirror, he told Popper that it had been a mistake to leave Fanny at home. She would have remembered to unpack his gown and hang it up. It was now all wrinkled and puckered. The garment was made of unbleached linen, with a few golden threads interwoven in the cloth to catch the light. Just below the right shoulder, in gold leaf, there was the figure of a gnomon, enclosing a staring all-seeing eyeball.

Popper assured him that the wrinkles would go away after he had walked about some; gravity and the steamy Washington air would do the trick.

"But where is my Rod? My Rod is not here, Austin."

"You can't find your Rod of Correction?"

"I know I packed it. I saw it yesterday."

"That slug Pharris White. He must have taken it."

"Surely not."

"Yes, I saw him pawing over your things with his nimble, mail-sorting fingers. He probably thought it was gold. I should have searched him."

"Do you know, he pulled my necktie."

"I wish you had spoken up, sir."

A hasty inventory showed that White had made off not only with the Rod, in its rosewood box with silver fittings, but also with Mr. Jimmerson's knotted rope, for escape from burning hotels, and some miscellaneous papers and a complete suit of the Master's cambric underwear. The strange clerk had apparently stuffed away in his satchel whatever fell to hand.

The missing Rod of Correction was a bronze bar about as long as a new pencil and just a bit thicker. Better suited perhaps for poking than for administering any sort of serious beating, it had nonetheless great symbolic power, the power of the Magisterium, and Mr. Jimmerson had only to raise it a fraction of an inch to silence even a roaring speaker like Austin Popper.

"Well, if it's gone, it's gone," said Popper. "Anyway, good riddance to Pharris the white rat and much good may it do him. We need to shake a leg, sir. Here, let me help you with your Poma."

He pulled the cap down snugly against the ears and fastened the chin strap. The strap was a recent innovation, strictly for street wear, a protective measure against the Poma's being blown away or snatched in broad daylight by one of Hen's men. He walked around the listless figure, tugging here and there at the gown, then stepped back to appraise the effect. "Behold! The Master of Gnomons! Ready to go forth! Come on, sir, chin up. Take it from me, things will look much brighter after some coffee and scrambled eggs."

But Mr. Jimmerson did not feel much better after breakfast. The sidewalk was already hot at nine o'clock and the soles of his ceremonial sandals were very thin. People looked at him. Children stopped to stare openly at his feet, great spreading white organs that were coated with hair like the feet of some arctic bird. He danced about on the hot concrete, alternately placing one foot atop the other, as Popper tried to hail a cab.

It was a long day, full of disappointments, and in later years Mr. Jimmerson's memory mercifully failed him as to the sequence of events. His congressman was kind enough to pose with him on the Capitol steps for a photograph but after that he met with nothing but indignities.

For all his telephoning, Popper had come up with nothing more than a brief note from the congressman, which asked in guarded language that courtesy be shown to his two constituents, Mr. Jimmerson and Mr. Popper. There were no appointments. The note availed them nothing at the White House gates. There they were stopped by guards, suspicious of the Master's unusual attire, and were not even permitted to enter the grounds with the tourists, much less see the President. One guard said, "Is the circus in town? I didn't know the circus was in town." Another kept saying, "So solly, no can do," as Popper protested the treatment.

Next they were turned away from the State Department. Then on to the War Department, where the note did get them past the duty officer in the lobby. They wandered about in that labyrinth for hours. The Battle of Midway was taking place at this time and anxious military men were racing up and down the corridors shouting bulletins at one another. The two Gnomons were bounced from office to office. No one had time to hear them out or look at the victory plan or even allow them to sit down for a moment. Mr. Jimmerson's gown became soaked with sweat. The peak of his Poma wilted and toppled over. Popper finally cornered a young army captain who agreed to give them a few minutes of his time. But he seemed to think they were astrologers and that their plan had to do with the stars and he sent them on to the Naval Observatory.

It was there, on Observatory Hill, that the two became separated. Mr. Jimmerson found a bench under a big tree and stopped there to rest while Popper went inside the main building to reconnoiter and to confer with such pipe-smoking men of science as he might find there. They would be receptive to new ideas, unlike the military blockheads downtown.

Mr. Jimmerson dozed off. When he woke, with a start, he was hungry and thirsty. There was no sign of Popper, no sign of life at the Observatory. He heard a bell. It was the bell that had wakened him. He looked about and saw a man pedaling along on an ice-cream cart down on the broad avenue. He called out to the man and stumbled down the hill after him, only to realize on arrival that he had no money. His gown was pocketless. He asked the man where the nearest water fountain and public toilet might be. Probably at the zoo, said the ice-cream man, over that way. Over yonder. Out over in there.

At the zoo a bum called Mr. Jimmerson a "schmo." The bum was reclining on the grass with a friend and said, "I wonder who that schmo is." The other bum ventured no guess. Mr. Jimmerson passed the rest of the day there admiring the great cats and looking into the queer dark eyes of the higher apes. There was reckoning behind those eyes but the elegance of the triangle would forever escape them. In the lion house he found a dime. His corset would not allow him to bend over far enough to pick it up. He pushed it along with his foot while trying to form a recovery plan, and then a boy came along and grabbed it.

By the most direct route it was about three miles from the zoo to the Borger Hotel, but Mr. Jimmerson, confused by the radial street pattern, hiked the better part of five miles before he reached his room that evening, gasping and barefooted, his golden sandals having disintegrated along the way.

"Here he is now," said Popper, jumping up from the bed. There was another man in the room. "Come in, sir, you're just in time. Were your ears burning? We were just talking about you. I was telling Cezar all about you. Here, I want you to meet Cezar. I want you to meet the most interesting man in Washington, D.C."

He made no reference to the aborted mission. He said nothing about compressed air or the victory plan or the bedraggled appearance of the Master, whose bloody feet, if nothing else, certainly invited comment. The stranger was a neat little package of a man, well finished, in belted European suit. He had a spade beard and curly black hair. Popper introduced him as Professor Cezar Golescu, assistant custodian of almanacs and star catalogues at the Naval Observatory.

"Cezar is like you, sir, a great seeker of truth. I've been telling him a bit about Pletho Pappus. He wants very much to

read the *Codex* and have a look at our archives. And let me tell
you something. This fellow has some very exciting ideas about
the reclamation of gold. Some ideas that have made me sit up."

Mr. Jimmerson said, "I think I'd like something to eat, Austin, if you don't mind. And some cold tomato juice."

"Of course you do. I should have thought of that. Any civilized person would have thought of it, but no, not me. I was
too busy talking. Me and my big mouth!"

He called room service and had some food sent up on a rolling table. The professor wasn't hungry, and in any case, he said,
he always dined alone. He spoke with sleepy-eyed hauteur.

It came out that Golescu was a Scottish Rite Freemason,
which is to say, oddly enough, a Mason of the French school.
He was also a Rosicrucian, an Illuminate, a Brother of Luxor,
a Cabalist, a Theosophist, a Knight of Corfu and many other
things too, some of them seemingly incompatible. He showed
his membership cards with some pride. It came out too that
he was a student of alchemy, and not the symbolic kind with
its concern for the redemption of man's corrupt nature, but
the real thing, the bubbling, smoking alchemy of the crucible
that transforms base metal into dense yellow gold. He had academic credentials. He held degrees from the Institute of Oil
and Gases and the Institute of Nonferrous Metals in Bucharest, had taught "science" at the Female Normal College in
Dobro and had been librarian at the Royal Wallachian Observatory, with its three-inch reflecting telescope, limited mostly
to moon studies, atop Mount Grobny. But his abiding interests
were alchemy and a lost continent called Mu, a once great land
6,000 miles long and 3,000 miles wide that was now at the
bottom of the Pacific Ocean.

The food came, Mr. Jimmerson dug in. Popper and Golescu resumed their discussion of alchemy, with Popper stating
forcefully that while the Gnomon Society was in fact privy to
this ancient secret (though the practice was under ban in the
New Cycle), the Rosicrucians, otherwise very decent fellows,
had been running a stupendous bluff in the matter, ever since
their first shadowy appearance in Europe some three hundred
years ago. They knew nothing. Golescu put questions to him.
Popper's answers were ready if equivocal. Mr. Jimmerson ate
his supper and said little.

Out of courtesy rather than any real curiosity, he asked the professor how he had happened to leave his homeland—was it not called the breadbasket of Europe?—and come to America.

Golescu considered the question. "Romanian peoples are restless peoples," he said. "Our first thought is to fly, to get away from other Romanians. Here, there, Australia, Washington, Patagonia. Impatient peoples, you see. Always the jumping around. Very nervous. In all Romanian literature there is not a single novel with a coherent plot."

Mr. Jimmerson had difficulty following this kind of thing but Popper encouraged the little man and drew him out.

Golescu became louder and more assertive, revealing himself as an independent thinker. Charles Darwin, he said, had bungled his research and gotten everything wrong. Organisms were changing, it was true enough, but instead of becoming more complex and, as it were, ascending, they were steadily degenerating into lower and lower forms, ultimately back to mud. In support of this he cited the poetic testimony of Hesiod, and gave the example of savages with complex languages, a vestige of better days. He had dubbed the process "bio-entropy" and said that it could clearly be seen at work in everyday life. One's father was invariably a better man than one's self, and one's grandfather better still. And what a falling off there had been since the Golden Days of Mu, when man was indeed a noble creature.

He was an authority on history and literature and boasted of having solved mysteries in these fields that had baffled the greatest scholars of Europe. Through Golescuvian analysis he had been able to make positive identification of the Third Murderer in *Macbeth* and of the Fourth Man in Nebuchadnezzar's fiery furnace. He had found the Lost Word of Freemasonry and had uttered it more than once, into the air, the Incommunicable Word of the Cabalists, the *Verbum Ineffabile*. The enigmatic quatrains of Nostradamus were an open book to him. He had a pretty good idea of what the Oracle of Ammon had told Alexander.

"So, where is your mysteries now?" he said. "Gone. Poof. For me, child's play."

His favorite books, the ones he never tired of dipping into, were Colonel James Churchward's *The Lost Continent of Mu*,

*The Children of Mu* and *The Sacred Symbols of Mu*, along
with Ignatius Donnelly's *Atlantis: The Antediluvian World*—
though he could only agree with Donnelly's theories up to a
certain point. He was proud of having introduced these works
to southeastern Europe. He had presented many papers on
them to learned societies, and had given many popular lectures, illustrated with lantern slides.

"Go to Bucharest or Budapest and say 'Mu' to any educated
man and he will reply to you, 'Mu? Ah yes, Golescu.' In Vienna
the same. In Zagreb the same. In Sofia you shouldn't waste
your valuable time. The stinking Bulgars they don't know
nothing about Mu and don't want to know nothing."

With a sudden flourish he brought a small copper cylinder
from his vest pocket. "How old do you think this is, my friends?
A thousand years? Five thousand? Do you think it came from
Egypt? From some filthy mummy? Then I am sorry for your
ignorance. This is a royal cylinder seal from Mu, the Empire
of the Sun. See? The cross and solar device? It is unmistakable. Golescu can even tell you the name of the artisan who
made it. Here, use my glass and be good enough to examine
these tiny marks. You see? Those strange characters spell the
name Kikku, or perhaps Kakko. I admit to you freely that in
the state of our present knowledge Muvian vowels are largely
guesswork. But yes, I also tell you that a living, breathing man
with the sun shining on his face and with a name something
like Kikku fashioned this beautiful object in the land of Mu
—hold on to your caps—*fifty thousand years ago*! I would like
it back now. And please, no questions about how it came into
my hands. Questions about Kikku the coppersmith of Mu?
Fine. I am at your service. Only too pleased. Questions about
how did Golescu get his hands on this wonderful seal? I am
too sorry, no, not at this time. You will only be wasting your
valuable breath."

Mr. Jimmerson knew a thing or two about sunken conti-
nents himself and he was amazed that a college professor such
as Golescu could be taken in by Churchward's nonsense. For
he too had read *The Lost Continent of Mu*, a book in which he
had found almost every statement to be demonstrably false.
No small literary achievement, that, in its way, he supposed,

but then there were people like Golescu, and innocent people as well, perhaps even children, who were gulled by Churchward's fantastic theories. Donnelly was sound enough, a genuine scholar, but Churchward would have it that Mu—"the Motherland of Man"—was the original civilization on earth, that it was a going concern 25,000 years before Atlantis crowned its first king! What a hoax! Three hundred pages of sustained lying! How was it that the American government couldn't put a stop to these misrepresentations and this vicious slander of Atlantis? Or at least put a stop to these cocksure foreigners coming into the country with their irresponsible chatter about Mu?

But Mr. Jimmerson, his temples pounding with blood, saw that it would be improper for him to engage in a quarrel with such a man and he said nothing.

It was getting late. Golescu, egged on by Popper, seemed to be just reaching his stride. He called for two pencils and "two shits of pepper." Popper found pencils and sheets of paper. The professor proceeded to give a demonstration of his ambidexterity.

"See, not only is Golescu writing with both hands but he is also looking at you and conversing with you at the same time in a most natural way. Hello, good morning, how are you? Good morning, Captain, how are you today, very fine, thank you. And here is Golescu still writing and at the same time having his joke on the telephone. Hello, yes, good morning, this is the Naval Observatory but no, I am very sorry, I do not know the time. Nine-thirty, ten, who knows? Good morning, that is a beautiful dog, sir, can I know his name, please? Good morning to you, madam, the capital of Delaware is Dover. In America the seat of government is not always the first city. I give you Washington for another. And now if you would like to speak to me a sequence of random numbers, numbers of two digits, I will not only continue to look at you and converse with you in this easy way but I will write the numbers as given with one hand and reversed with the other hand while I am at the same time adding the numbers and giving you running totals of both columns, how do you like that? Faster, please, more numbers, for Golescu this is nothing. . . ."

Popper said, "Oh boy, is he cooking now! How about this fellow?" Mr. Jimmerson tried to cut the performance short by calling room service and asking for another pot of coffee and some more cherry pie. Despite the interruptions, the professor went on and on, and again declined the offer of food, his policy of solitary dining extending to cover even such small fare as this.

His last show of the night had to do with some small pinnate leaves taken from a vine or herb that he refused to identify. "Not at this time, no, I am too sorry. That is for me alone to know." He had taken five or six of the leaves from his coat pocket and was holding them up for examination. They were still faintly green and glossy on the upper side, though dry and curling.

"Isn't he something?" said Popper, pointing with a toothpick. "Look at that, sir, *leaves*. He had *leaves* in his pocket. I wonder what kind of leaves they are. In what way are they special, do you think? Well, you can just bet there's a story behind them, and a good one too. What in the world will this fellow come up with next?"

Mr. Jimmerson didn't care to guess. He was ready for bed.

Popper said, "Wait. I think I've got it. I do believe Cezar is going to brew us a pot of tea. Yes, some sort of Romanian health beverage or Rosicrucian Pluto Water."

"Not tea, no," said Golescu. He had cleared a space on the table, pushing back the crockery and napkins and bones and rinds and crusts and other rejected edges of things, and placed there a candle stub and two glass vials of chemicals and a little hand-cranked grinder, with which he began to macerate the leaves. "A demitasse, eh, ha ha, such a funny joke. Perhaps you like this cyanide in your tea. What, you take one gram or two? For me, no, thank you very much. Ha ha. Tea."

Mr. Jimmerson retired. He slept through the crushed leaves experiment, waking now and then to note with irritation that the lights were still on and that Austin and the professor were still talking. On his next trip, and God grant it would not be soon, he must remember to bring along his plywood board for a bed stiffener. And tomorrow he must not forget to pick up a box of dark chocolates for Fanny. A mingling of darkness and light. He would have used that, Pletho's favorite phrase for the world, to good effect in his radio speech. He had never had much confidence in the victory plan, or even fully understood all its many points, but why had the radio address been canceled? Politics? He had never thought much of Roosevelt anyway, or of his party. Rum, Romanism and Rebellion wasn't the half of it these days.

# 5

HE WENT back to Indiana and took little further interest in the war. He slept through much of it. Let someone else deal with the Central Powers this time. And the Japs. According to the newspapers, the little monkeys couldn't see very well. They were clever, and quick on their feet too, remarkable jumpers, but their jiujitsu would prove useless against the rapid and sustained fire of our Lewis guns.

Still, as with many others, Mr. Jimmerson was to suffer loss and misfortune. Even the birth of his son turned out to be a mixed blessing. Coming to motherhood so late, Fanny was much taken with the child, and she lavished all her attention on this tardy arrival, baby Jerome, to the neglect of her husband. "Look, Lamar!" she said. "What a little pig he is for his milk!" Sometimes Mr. Jimmerson held Jerome on his knee and patted his back and said jip jip jip in his face in the way he had seen others do, but he really didn't know what to make of the drooling little fellow and his curling pink feet, almost prehensile. And he was at a loss to understand the change that had come over his wife. People seemed to be pulling away from him, receding.

He passed more and more of his time alone, in his wing-back chair before the fireplace in the Red Room, a copy of the *Codex Pappus* in his lap. At the age of forty-six he had become chair-bound. Pharris White's remarks had set him wondering if there weren't perhaps some higher secrets he had missed, something implicit, some deeply hidden pattern in the fine tapestry of Pletho's thought that had escaped him, and so he read and pondered and drifted in and out of sleep while the baby crawled about on the Temple carpets and great armies clashed around the world. At the age of forty-six Mr. Jimmerson was already looking forward to his senescence.

Meanwhile, Sir Sydney Hen, Bart., had become mobile. Now radiant with health and joined in a kind of marriage to the rich widow Babette, he began to stir. His new book, *Approach to Knowing*, had just been published, and it was his claim that he had written the entire work, excepting only bits of connective

506

matter, while in a three-day Gnomonic trance, this being an exalted state of consciousness not to be confused with an ordinary hypnotic stupor or any sort of Eastern rapture. It was revealed to him in the trance that he had "completed the triangle" and "scaled the cone" and been granted "the gift of ecstatic utterance," all of which meant that he had gone beyond Mastery and was no longer bound by law or custom.

Deep waters, as Hen himself admitted. There was more. Other men—other Gnomons, that is—could aspire to this singular state, and might even achieve it by undergoing a rigorous program of instruction in Cuernavaca, Mexico. Babette owned a house in Cuernavaca, a sprawling, enclosed place with swimming pool and blazing gardens, and it was here that Hen established his New Croton Institute for Advanced Gnomonic Study.

Candidates for the school were carefully selected. They had to have clear eyes and all their limbs. There was a fee of $1,200, payable in advance, nonrefundable. There was one week of forgetting followed by three weeks of learning. There was a rule of silence. They slept on a cold tile floor and fed on alfalfa sprouts and morning glory seeds. Their reading was restricted to Hen's books. Hen stood behind a screen as he taught them, in the morning and again in the afternoon, to lute music, or rather to lute strumming. Noel Kinlow could not actually play the lute; he simply trailed his fingers across the strings from time to time, on a signal from Hen, to point up some significant recurring word or phrase. The candidates were bled weekly, by Kinlow, and not of the customary pint but of an imperial quart at each draining. On successful completion of the program, with thin new blood coursing through their emaciated bodies, they were at last permitted to look Hen in the face. He embraced them and presented them with signed copies of *Approach to Knowing* and with some black gloves of the kind worn by the Templar Masons, and sent them on their way, staggering across Babette's courtyard. Any lingering, as of graduation day fellowship, was discouraged. Kinlow herded them to the door, saw them clear of it and closed it sharply behind them.

This Noel Kinlow was Hen's current male companion, a young Englishman who had been an elevator boy at the apartment house in Toronto when Hen picked him up. Babette did not approve of the arrangement but was comfortably resigned to it. As a woman of the world she knew this was the price she must pay for being Lady Hen, consort to the Master of Gnomons (Amended Order), and she found the price acceptable.

They made a striking group. Hen, of course, was always distinctive in his black cape and red Poma. Babette, who was buxom to say the least of it, wore bright yellow caftans and other loose garments that trailed the floor, so that one could only guess at the contours of her body, though one could make a pretty good guess. She was also fond of pendulous ear ornaments. The reedy Kinlow, in contrast to Babette, liked tight clothes, the tighter the better, and he usually came forth in a pinch-waist lounge suit made of some mottled, speckled, yellowish-green material. It was a hue not met with in nature and not often seen outside the British Isles, where it has always been a great favorite with tailors. The little yapping terrier, when traveling, sported a starched white ruff.

All through the war years this colorful family—Sir Sydney, Lady Hen, the little dog and the light-stepping Kinlow—could be found bowling up and down the continent between Toronto and Cuernavaca, sometimes in a Pullman compartment and sometimes in a white Bentley sports saloon, chatting merrily, sipping Madeira and snacking on pâté and Stilton cheese, there being no rule of silence or forbidden food at Hen's antinomian level.

Mr. Jimmerson was saddened to see his old friend now so completely estranged and sinking ever deeper into the murk of self.

He said, "I don't understand what he means by going beyond Mastery. What's next, do you think, Austin?"

"It's hard to say with Hen, sir. Nothing would surprise me. Astral traveling. Tarot cards. At this moment he may be prancing through the woods playing a flute. The man's an enigma to me."

They were sitting in the Red Room before a fire. Mr. Jimmerson was turning over the pages of Hen's latest book, *Approach to Growing*, a sequel to *Knowing*. Popper was reading an encyclopedia article about California. On the table between them, under the fruitcake and coffee cups, there was a mudstained letter from Sergeant Mapes in Italy, which neither of them had gotten around to opening. Above the fireplace there was a color portrait of the Master in full regalia, and from the mantel there hung Jerome's Christmas stocking, lumpy with tangerines and Brazil nuts, though he had no teeth. Jerome was asleep. Fanny was out with church friends distributing Christmas baskets to the poor.

Popper fed a glazed cherry to Squanto. The jaybird was getting old. One wing drooped and he no longer talked much in an outright way. During the night he muttered. Mr. Jimmerson leaned forward and jostled the burning logs about.

"But why should Sydney be so bitter?" he said. "All these ugly personal remarks about you and me."

"Ah now, that's something else. That's quickly explained. First there's his nasty disposition. Then there's his envy of your precedence in the Society. Then there's this. Hen is English. We, happily, are Americans. In the brief space of his lifetime he has seen his country eclipsed by ours as a great power. Hen very naturally resents it."

"I never thought of Sydney in that way, as a patriot."

"Listen to this, sir. The motto of California is 'Eureka!' Isn't that interesting? *Eureka. I have found it.* What is our motto here in Indiana? Do you happen to know?"

"Let's see. No. Our state bird—"

"Surely we have a motto."

"Yes, but I can't remember what it is. I've been doing some thinking, Austin, and I have an idea that Sydney must be under the influence of some malignant magnetic force. This fat lady he has taken up with. I wonder if—"

"Look, sir, a picture of Mount Whitney. Isn't that a magnificent sight? It gladdens the heart."

"Yes. The snow. On top."

"Correct me if I'm wrong but I don't believe we have any eminence in Indiana much higher than a thousand feet."

"Yes, I think you can say that nature presents a more formidable face in California. But you know, Austin, I sometimes think if I could just talk to Sydney man to man for a few—"

Popper took the book from Mr. Jimmerson's hands and flung it into the fire. "Excuse me, sir, that was very rude, I know, but I can't sit here and let you torment yourself with that poison."

"You might at least have—"

"Listen to me, sir. Hen and his ravings and his Mexican concentration camp—this is just a piddling episode in the vast time scale of Gnomonism. The man's a mayfly, the fluttering creature of an hour. Why should we take any notice of him? He works in sun-dried bricks. We are building in marble with Pletho. Now I want you to put Hen out of your mind. Will you do that for me?"

They looked into the blaze and waited silently for the flash point. The book covers writhed and then burst into yellow flames. "There. A fitting end for trash."

It was not Popper's way to interrupt the Master or snatch objects from his hand but on this night he was tense. He was leaving the Temple the next day, leaving Burnette, pulling stakes, in circumstances that did not allow him to say goodbye. Over the past few months he had conferred often with Golescu in Washington via telephone. Their plans had been carefully laid and on this very night the professor was approaching Chicago by rail. Popper was to join him the next morning at Union Station and from there they would travel west together.

The trip had been delayed over and over again because of Golescu's difficulty in settling on an auspicious date for leaving his job and making a journey and undertaking a new enterprise. Popper himself was not so particular as to the alignment of the planets. He had a problem with the U.S. Selective Service, and it was one of growing urgency. He had never registered for the draft and had been lying low, in the Temple, since the Washington trip. Then, an informer, one of Hen's men, turned his name in to the local draft board. A series of notices and summonses were sent to Popper, with little result, and his secretary, a dull girl, unwittingly aggravated the situation.

Popper had instructed her to answer all unknown correspondents with a Gnomon leaflet and a photograph of himself on which he had written: THANKS A MILLION, AUSTIN POPPER. This was faithfully done. The draft board, in response to its letters and telegrams, had received five or six of these autographed pictures before turning the matter over to the G-men.

But when these officers finally arrived at the Temple with a warrant, Popper had been gone for almost a week, leaving behind him an enormous telephone bill and a note to Mr.

Jimmerson saying that Laura had taken a turn for the worse and that he was racing to her bedside in San Francisco.

Mr. Jimmerson was bewildered. He read the note several times and turned it over to look for help on the blank side. Who was Laura? He had never heard Austin speak of a sweetheart or sister or any other dear one of that name, sick or well.

He showed the note to one of the federal agents, a hefty young man who seemed familiar but whom he could not place. He did not recognize Pharris White, still neckless but trimmed down a bit and wearing a tan fedora. White was now in the FBI, which had become something of a haven for lawyers seeking to avoid military service. He shook the warrant in Mr. Jimmerson's face. "I mean to serve this personally," he said. "If you're holding out on me, Jimmerson, I'll put you away in a cell with Popper. Nothing would please me more. This Master of Gnomons business doesn't cut any ice with me. Did you ever hear of misprision of a felony? Accessory after the fact? Here, I want to see that cap." He examined the Poma with rough disdain and even placed it clownishly atop his own head. The agent in charge of the raid spoke sharply to him about these unprofessional antics and made him return it.

Mr. Jimmerson said he was confident that he would hear from Austin in the next few days. The draft evasion matter could only be a misunderstanding. A telephone call to the Navy Department would clear it up at once. From Popper's secretary the agents learned that Popper had been singing and humming snatches of California songs in recent weeks.

Thus there were signs in abundance pointing to the Golden State, Popper believing that one could not lay it on too thickly, and it was there that the search for him was foolishly pressed.

# 6

POPPER AND Golescu stepped off the Burlington Zephyr in Denver, well short of San Francisco, and then took a bus to the old mining town of Hogandale, Colorado, high in the mountains, at the headwaters of the Rio Puerco, known locally as the Pig River or Nasty River. Popper carried one suitcase and a perforated box with Squanto in it. Golescu had a good deal of luggage, including two sacks of dried mud. Wasting no time, they rented a derelict house at the foot of the sloping main street of Hogandale and went to work.

It was a hard winter for the two city men, neither of whom had ever handled an axe or shovel. At night they tramped through the snow to the abandoned gold mines and collected buckets of dirt. The frozen ground was utterly lifeless, a mineral waste, but Golescu had the European notion that the back country of America was alive with snakes and scorpions and so took great care where he placed his feet. Popper assured him that these vermin were asleep. The real menace to the hikers of America, he said, was the rusty nail. Boards bearing these upright nails were lying about everywhere. Puncture your foot on one and within an hour your jaw would be locked firmly shut, never again to open, and you would be raving with brain fever. Golescu minced his steps with even greater care. By day the two men chopped wood and stoked the iron stoves and tended their potted plants.

The professor had brought with him a plentiful supply of seeds and cuttings. Soon every windowsill in the old two-story frame house was crowded with pots and makeshift receptacles, from each of which sprouted a spiky green shaft. The pots were tagged by number. A log was kept for each one. There was detailed information as to the different potting soils—the fertilizer content, the acid-alkali balance and, most important of all, the origin of the soil, the mine it came from, whether the Perkins Drift, the Old Woman No. 2 or the Black Dog. In addition, there were control pots, some containing pure sand and others gold-free mud from the banks of the Potomac in Washington.

This plant that was the focus of all their attention was creeping bagweed, or *Blovius reptans*, a mat-forming vine found growing rank in England and Europe along roadsides and in ditches and untended lots. The pinnate leaves of bagweed were alternately evergreen and deciduous, so that while some leaves were shed over the year, the vine was never barren of greenery. In this respect it was like the magnolia tree and the live oak. Bagweed, which had a way of choking out other vegetation, was universally despised by gardeners. Livestock refused to eat it. Even goats turned away from it. Bugs and worms gave it a wide berth. Bagweed had little decorative value, and despite the strong camphor smell given off by the bags or pods, it had never found a place in folk medicine. Apparently unremarkable, then, except for its hardiness and seeming uselessness, creeping bagweed did have one redeeming quality, and this was nothing less than the power to deposit gold in its leaf cells. To be sure, the gold appeared in only microscopic traces, but it was gold nonetheless, and gold that was easily recovered and of an elemental purity.

Professor Golescu had hit on the bagweed discovery, or rediscovery, after piecing together clues found here and there in hundreds of books on alchemy, most notably in the works of Theophilus the Monk and Dr. John Dee. The revelation came in stages. For years he had prowled the library stacks and bookstalls of Bucharest, avid from his youth to lift the veil and know all. As early as 1934 he had broken through certain allusive writings to learn that gold might be taken from the leaves of a common flowering plant.

Identifying the leaves, however, was another matter, and to this problem he finally had to apply the tedious method of systematic exhaustion. He planted at least one specimen of every genus offered in the colorful seed catalogues of England and Holland. He crushed and processed thousands of leaves, using cyanide and zinc shavings as extractives, and in the end he always came up with the same mess of black sludge, but never any gold.

Then in the summer of 1940, while he was in London waiting for his American visa to be forged, it struck him suddenly that the plant might be one not cultivated by man, some nuisance growth, and he went out into the countryside and gathered seeds from a variety of nettles, thistles, dandelions, nipplewort, chickweed, bagweed and other coarse vegetation. He resumed his experiments at his boardinghouse in Washington, and two years later, in the spring of 1942, he first saw the tiny points of gold precipitating on the zinc flakes. He drew his head back from the spectacle with a start. The jeweler's loupe dropped from his eye. "So. And I am not expecting you from this stinkweed."

Golescu regarded other men with contempt. They were so many dim background figures in the central drama of the world, which was the life of Cezar Golescu, and he took no interest in them except as they might be able to alter the course of the drama, whether to aid him or thwart him. He enjoyed dazzling them with a show of learning now and then, but there were so many things they were unworthy of knowing or incapable of understanding, and these things he kept locked away in his head. Of his gold research he spoke not a word to any person in Europe or America until the chance meeting with Popper.

Popper's presence had something to do with it; men naturally confided in him and sought his approval. Even Golescu was not immune. He found himself boasting to this stranger and blurting out things. But there was more to it than that. He was concerned as to how he might best exploit his discovery and had decided that what he needed was an American business partner who knew the ground. Popper's intelligence was, of course, of a lower order than his own—so much the better for control purposes—but Popper was clearly a man of affairs, with that lupine glint in his eye that suggested he would usually be at the forefront of any scramble for a prize.

The thing that tipped the scales was Gnomonism. One of the few secret orders that Golescu had not been able to penetrate was the Gnomon Society, his difficulty being that he had never found a Gnomon until Popper came along. Did the organization even exist? Was there anything in it? He took pride in his Masonic degree, for he knew that his white linen apron was more ancient than the Golden Fleece or Roman Eagle, and more honorable than the Star or Garter, but so many of these brotherhoods had let him down with their grandiose claims and paltry secrets. Still, one could not give up the quest. Much

ancient wisdom lay hidden, even from Golescu—the arts of
Mu, the Alkahest formula, the *elixir vitae*—and it was his mission to search it out.

Perhaps the Gnomons did know something. In any case, the
hand of fate was evident in that first encounter with Popper at
the Observatory. It was a day on which the moon was in crescent, signifying increase. Popper had loomed up before him
quite suddenly, like some figure in an oriental tale, identifying
himself not only as a Gnomon but as Cupbearer Royal to the
Master himself. He had spoken well, saying, "I don't know
your name, sir, or what your work is, but I can see that you are
a man of exceptional powers. I saw it from thirty yards away."

And Popper had quickly proven himself worthy of the professor's confidence, seizing on the bagweed discovery to show
how it might be turned to account. If the weed produced a
little gold out of indifferent soil, he reasoned, then why should
it not produce a great deal of gold when planted in soil known
to be auriferous? The idea had somehow not occurred to Golescu and he was stunned by what he saw as a brilliant leap.
Two heads were indeed better than one, if the other one was
Popper's.

Their plan took form. Popper called it Banco Plan. They
would go to abandoned gold mines in the West and surrepti-
tiously test the soil. When they had located the most produc-
tive property they would lease it as cheap grazing land and
plant it in bagweed. Entire mountain ranges would be covered
with a carpet of creeping bagweed. Nature would do most of
their work and no stamping mills or monstrous smelters would
be needed—only a leaf chopper, a few vats and some cheap
chemicals. Within a year or two they would be sitting atop tons
of gold, which they would sell off in measured driblets, in the
way of the South African diamond kings, so as not to swamp
the market.

By way of a cover story, Popper introduced himself to the
citizens of Hogandale as Commander DeWitt Farnsworth of
Naval Intelligence, lately wounded in the Philippines. He affected a limp and wore a soft black hat and Lincolnesque shawl.
He had come to the mountains to convalesce in the sparkling
air, as well as to help his refugee friend, Dr. Omar Baroody,
with his sticky experiments in weed saps, from which he hoped

to develop a new kind of rubber, so desperately needed in the war effort. Herr Hitler and General Tojo would give a good deal to know Dr. Baroody's location.

As it turned out, no one in Hogandale cared. The fifty or so inhabitants were a dispirited lot of nesters and stragglers who had been beaten down by life. Brooding as they were, constantly, over their own humiliations, defeats, wrecked hopes, withered crops, thoughtless children and lost opportunities, they had no curiosity at all about the two strange men who had rented the old Taggert house at the bottom of the hill.

After a few weeks Popper no longer bothered with the false names or the limp, though he did continue to use the walking stick. He felt safe. They were not likely to be found out here, marooned in pelagic America, far from any shipping lanes and with no smudge of smoke on the horizon.

For security reasons Golescu would allow no strangers in the house, not even a cleaning lady. Most of the housekeeping chores fell to Popper. He found the work and the reclusive life disagreeable and often had to remind himself of the great reward that lay at the end of the ordeal. Eating as they were on one ration card, Golescu's, they had to stint on coffee, sugar and fresh meat. Their food ran largely to canned soup, potted meat, boiled eggs, crackers, white bread and dark molasses.

The house was cold. The only insulation was newspaper sheets pasted to the rough plank walls, and the paper was now in tatters, with the long black columns of Colorado news crumbling away. The one warm room downstairs was the kitchen, where Popper set up his cot, next to the cast-iron range. There he cooked and washed and read magazines and talked to Squanto. Golescu made his nest in an upstairs room, which he kept locked and where he maintained a potbellied stove and a small brick furnace and a hand-cranked blacksmith's forge. Late into the night he could be heard clumping around up there tending his vessels.

From the very beginning he had pestered Popper about the Gnomon secrets, pressing for admittance into the brotherhood. But Popper, usually so accommodating, made excuses and put him off, until one night he bluntly told him that he must give up all hope of ever becoming a Gnomon.

"No Moslems, I'm sorry," he said. "No Mussulmen. It's a

different culture. Alien thought patterns. I don't say it's fair but there it is. Furthermore, I should tell you that all these personal appeals are embarrassing to me and demeaning to you. My hands are tied, you understand. Our laws are written in blood on the dried guts of a serpent. But look here, Cezar, don't take it so hard. You people have your rich oral tradition. Your songs of the desert. Why can't you be satisfied with that?"

Golescu knew nothing about the desert, and the truth was that Moslems *were* eligible for membership in the Society—the candidate had only to profess belief in the Living God, much as a Mason must acknowledge the Great Architect of the Universe, with no further religious test—and for that matter Golescu was not a Moslem but a communicant of the Romanian Orthodox Church. He could not get this simple fact across to Popper. What was more irritating, Popper affected a solicitous curiosity about the professor's supposed faith. Suddenly and unexpectedly in the middle of a conversation he would raise some Islamic point.

"Are you permitted to eat sardines?" he said. "Please don't hesitate to speak up if I offend." And "Tell me honestly, Cezar, is it true that Mahomet's body is suspended in midair in his tomb? Have you seen that with your own eyes?"

After a while Golescu stopped protesting and made no response of any kind to these queries. He turned sullen and abandoned all efforts to become a Gnomon. Then in an amazing turnabout, Popper announced one morning that the observation period was over and that Cezar must now prepare himself for instruction.

"A time of testing," he said. "Nothing personal, I assure you. Everyone is turned down at first. Those who come to us unbidden must undergo special scrutiny. We like to put them under stress and observe the squirming pattern. Sometimes we slap their faces and see if they cry. Some do. You would think they had been beaten within an inch of their lives. But all that is behind us now. On behalf of the Gnomon Society I bid you welcome. You are that one man in a hundred thousand who is ever chosen."

The professor was so moved as to express gratitude, a rare lapse, and he was further shaken to learn that "the passing over" into Gnomonism was the work of a single afternoon.

The instruction was scanty. Golescu had not seen so short a creed since he had attended that Knights of Corfu school in Vienna. The pledges and oaths were of a familiar kind and gave him no problem, but he was troubled by Popper's warning about the Dark Laws. These were nine arbitrary rules that Neophytes and Initiates were not allowed to know. Should they violate one, however, they would be cast out of the Society. The induction ceremony lasted only about an hour and concluded with Golescu's running around the Taggert house seven times with his mouth open.

Popper stood on the front porch in overcoat and shawl and urged him on. "Pace yourself!" he shouted. When the circuits were completed he went down the steps to congratulate the professor, who was gasping and whose whiskers were coated with frost. He took Golescu's hand in a firm and prolonged Gnomon grasp and formally proclaimed him a Neophyte and Brother in Good Standing.

Brothers or not, the two men were already drifting apart. The hard work, the deadly cold, the dull diet, the isolation—all these things made for short tempers. They began to find fault and snap at one another. The fog was depressing and added to their feeling of confinement. From morning till night the lower end of Hogandale was enveloped in a white mist, and living in this cloud made them irritable and affected their sense of balance and depth perception. They glided into doorframes, as on shipboard, and stubbed their toes on the stairs.

Golescu made the better adjustment, but he had his bagweed. The plants flourished in their pots despite the cold and the weak light. He became attached to them, stopping at each one on his morning round to jot a note or poke about in the dirt or playfully thump the little gray bags that dangled beneath the gray blossoms.

Popper, who had no interest in horticulture as such, drew closer to Squanto. He and the jay took their meals together at the kitchen table while Golescu ate his soup and crackers alone in his upstairs room. It was at this time that Popper began to drink heavily.

Hogandale had two business establishments. At the top of the hill on the highway there was a Sinclair gasoline station, where the bus stopped, and down the way, past a dozen empty store buildings, there was a combination saloon-grocery-post office called Dad's Place. Every afternoon at about four o'clock Popper could be seen emerging from the mist below, a black apparition with a stick, not so much the boulevardier as the hiker with his staff, leaning forward against the slope and marching steadily upward toward the first drink of the day at Dad's Place.

The saloon was dark and drafty and smelled of kerosene. There was no music, not even a radio, and no popcorn or other gratis snacks. Dad and the few customers, grizzled coots to a man, were sunk in a torpor so profound as to choke off all attempts at conversation. Displays of robust ignorance Popper was prepared for, but not this morbid hush. At first he brought Squanto along to perform. He would put seeds, crumbs or bits of cheese in one ear. Squanto would peck at the stuff and all the while Popper would nod and make quiet replies as though the bird were whispering things to him. Squanto delivered cigarettes up and down the bar. He told fortunes from a deck of playing cards, plucking one card from a spread fan. Popper had lately taught him to say "cock-a-doodle-doo," the words, but none of this amused the barflies and so he gave it up and left Squanto at home.

There was a whiskey shortage too and in order to get one shot of bourbon Popper first had to buy three shots of nasty brown rum. Getting drunk at Dad's Place was little better than staying sober at home and so one afternoon he passed it by and went to the top of the hill and caught a bus for Rollo.

Rollo was the county seat and had life more or less as Popper remembered it. There were theaters, churches, banks, bars, streetlights. There was a schoolhouse made of fieldstone, with paper flowers pasted to the windows, and a playground where the children joined hands and danced about in a circle at recess. There was a courthouse, also of fieldstone, and Popper used this as a pretext for his frequent trips, telling Golescu that he was looking up land titles at the clerk's office.

Actually he was scouting out the bars. The best one was in the Hotel Rollo. The drinks there were good, the toilet was clean and just off the lobby there was a small writing room, with desk and free stationery, where Popper sometimes wrote letters to the editor of the local newspaper, commenting on current affairs and signing himself "Harmless Elderly Man" and "Today's Woman." But the hotel drinks were expensive and Popper finally settled on a place across the street called the Blue Hole, where they were cheaper. This bar was congenial without being boisterous and the management there insisted on only one shot of rum to one of bourbon.

Popper soon became a favorite with the Blue Hole regulars, he having put it about that he was a wounded airman, the pilot of a "pursuit ship" who had been obliged on more than one occasion to "hit the silk." He could not, however, be drawn much further on the subject of aerial combat. He waved off questions, shaking his head modestly and offering to buy a round of drinks.

In a short time he came to like the rum, to prefer it, to demand it. The cheaper and rawer it was, the better he liked it. He reflected on this quirk of human nature and told June Mack, the barmaid, that it was one of God's most merciful blessings that people grew to love the things that necessity compelled them to eat and drink. The Hindoos, for example, ate nothing but rice, and you would have to use bayonets to make them eat chicken and dumplings. It was the same with the Eskimos and their blubber. Don't, whatever you do, try to snatch blubber away from an Eskimo and force on him a thirty-two-ounce T-bone steak, medium well, with grilled onions and roasted potatoes.

June Mack took a shine to Popper. He was an excellent tipper and by far the most romantic figure she had ever had the pleasure to serve. She hung on his words and learned that in college he had been a star athlete, captain of both the varsity eleven and the varsity nine. He had gone on to become a New York playboy in top hat, living a life of ease and frivolity, carousing nightly with his lighthearted pals and their madcap sweethearts along "old Broadway." Then with the war came responsibility. He disliked talking about these experiences but she could see that he had suffered and that for all his bright manner there was some secret sorrow in his life.

Popper became fond of June too, and each time she brought his drink, always a generous measure, he would catch her withdrawing hand in flight and give her fingers a little lingering squeeze. One thing led to another. He treated her to dinners and walked her home after work to her wee house on Bantry Street. Their problem, the ancient predicament of lovers, was one of finding a place where they might be alone. Neither of them owned a car and it was much too cold for any sort of outdoor dalliance. June lived with her mother in a house that had only three small rooms, so there was nothing doing at Mack house.

One day Popper proposed a visit to his "ranch" in Hogandale. June was not nearly so coy as he supposed her to be and she accepted at once. Indeed, she could hardly believe her luck, Austin Popper being easily the best catch in the Blue Hole if not in all of Rollo. She was curious about the ranch. Popper was vague as to its size, speaking of it as "my little spread in the clouds," or dismissing it as one of his many hobbies. She knew he had a shadowy partner, a sick old man, and that they grew experimental plants in their house, some kind of high-protein weed that would revolutionize the cattle business, but it was not always easy to follow the things Austin said and she had no very clear picture of the arrangement.

Sunday was June's free day. Popper came to call before noon and made complimentary remarks about her auburn hair, set in rigid waves by some heat process, and her harmonizing green dress. He suggested that they take a turn around the courthouse square, so he could show her off, and then go on to the Hotel Rollo for an elegant Sunday feed before catching the bus to Hogandale.

But June had two surprises for him. It was time to show her stuff in the kitchen and she would treat him for a change. She had collected some things in a sack and would prepare him a home-cooked meal at the ranch. Popper was pleased. He rummaged about in the sack and saw that she had picked up some of his favorite tidbits, including chicken livers, fudge, deviled eggs and a can of sweetened condensed milk, very hard to find these days. With that they would make some snow ice cream.

The second and greater surprise was that Mother Mack was to accompany them. She, a plump squab like her daughter, hastened to say that she hoped Mr. Popper would not take it amiss, as suggesting in any way that June needed a chaperone, or that she, Mrs. Mack, was pushing herself forward. It was just that she had been housebound all winter and would like to join them in their outing, in their excursion through the countryside and a day at the ranch. Would it be inconvenient? She knew that three made a crowd. Would she be excess baggage?

"Certainly not," said Popper. "The more, the merrier. Three, you know, is the perfect number. Unity plus two. It's just the thing. I should have thought of it myself."

He was already a little drunk and on the bus ride to Hogandale he got worse. He drank openly from half-pint bottles of rum that he kept stowed in the major pockets of his overcoat and suit coat. There was a certain amount of gurgling and spillage that June found embarrassing. Here was a loutish side of Austin she had not seen before. At the Blue Hole he was always the gentleman, always removing his hat and never spitting or blowing his nose on the floor or using foul language. She wondered if he might be nervous. Men were so odd in their dealings with women.

What had escaped June's notice in recent weeks was that Popper had become a drunk. The decline had been rapid, and she, blinded by affection, had failed to recognize the signs— the rheumy eye, the splotchy face, the trembling hand, the loss of appetite, the repetitive monologue, the misbuttoned shirt and, perhaps most conclusive, the use of ever smaller bottles, this being the pathetic buying pattern of many alcoholics. She knew nothing of his solitary drinking, at all hours, in bed, on the street, in moving vehicles and public toilets. Huggins at his worst had never been so completely bedeviled.

He became loud and jolly on the bus, talking to the passengers at large about his dream of the night before, in which a rat had raced up his trouser leg. June and her mother looked away. An old woman at the back said, "A rat dream means your enemies are stirring. That's what the dream book says."

On arrival in Hogandale, June was annoyed to find that she and her mom would have to walk down a steep hill. Their short legs and platform shoes were ill suited for such a rough descent.

Popper said, "This tramp in the snow will get our blood going. It will make us crave our dinner all the more."

As they stumbled along, June suddenly remembered Austin's partner. She expressed concern that there might not be enough food for four people, and further, that the food was rich and perhaps unsuitable for an old man in poor health.

"Oh no, he won't be joining us," said Popper. "Cezar is not a sociable man. He lies up all winter and lives off his hump. He'll be upstairs mashing his weeds. I'll leave a little pot of something outside his door that he can eat with his ivory chopsticks. If we're lucky we won't even catch a glimpse of him."

They had reached the desolate edge of town.

"Careful now, ladies, watch your step."

On a rocky lot there loomed up out of the mist an old house made of gray boards. It was frankly a house, angular and upright: There were no cows about and no pens, barns, troughs or other signs of pastoral industry. No collie dog named Shep ran to greet them. The woodpile was just that, a low sprawl of sticks minimally organized, like something beavers might have thrown together. Under a window toward the rear of the house there was a snow-capped mound of cans and garbage. It was a ranch unlike any the two Macks had ever seen before.

"A little haze today," said Popper, assisting the ladies up the icy front steps. "It's nonsense, of course, keeping our doors locked like this, but Cezar insists on it. All these chains. I have to humor him in such things. He was once a very distinguished man in his field but is now just as crazy as a betsy bug."

Inside the house there was a greenish gloom. June was almost overcome by the camphor smell. She was no stranger to the fetid rooms of bachelors but this place had a sharper odor, like that of the sickroom. Bagweed covered the floor. The house was ankle deep in foliage, the thick green mat broken only by narrow trails which Popper and Golescu had beaten down in their passage across the rooms. The runners had ramified and intertwined so that it was no longer possible to identify a particular leaf with a particular plant, except at or near the base of that plant. Chairs and tables were frozen in position by the strangling coils of bagweed. Along the windows some of the sill boards had been split by the driving force of the weed.

June said, "Look, Austin, there's a bird in the house!"

"What, a bird? Impossible."

"There. On the back of that chair. See? I mean, jeepers, a bird in the house!"

"I believe you're right. Yes, it is a bird, June, and it looks to me like a blue jay, a very impudent corvine bird. I wonder how he got in. Don't worry, I'll handle this. Maybe you'd better stand back, Mrs. Mack, until we know where we are with this animal. I mean to get to the bottom of this 'bird in the house' business."

He whacked the cane against his palm and advanced on Squanto. "Well now, what's your game? Speak up, sir, how did you get in? Did you think this was a bird sanctuary? Are you looking for bright objects to steal? Or is it food? Did you think you were going to nip in here and then just nip out again with some of my toasted nuts? Nothing to say? Not talking today, are we? You might at least have the courtesy to greet my guests."

Squanto cocked his head from one side to the other and then gave his speech. *"Welcome June. To Mystery Ranch. Welcome June. To Mystery Ranch."*

The words were fairly clear and the Macks were delighted. Popper extended his forearm. The bird hopped onto it and sat there with the gravity of a falcon.

"Oh yes, they thought you were a bad boy, Squanto."

"Squatto, is it?" said June.

"Squanto."

"A talking bird," said Mrs. Mack. "I've heard of people keeping canary birds but not jaybirds. I didn't know they could talk."

"He's quite old now and new words are difficult for him. It gets harder and harder to drive anything into his little crested head. Anyway, Squanto and I are glad you enjoyed our little joke. I happen to think a light note is important. It sets a friendly tone. It breaks the ice. Speaking of which, let us move on to the kitchen, ladies. I'll stoke up the fire and we'll be much warmer in there. The vines are not so thick on the floor there and I've moved the cot and the table back against the wall. We may want to dance later. The important thing now, as I see it, is for June to get into her apron toot sweet. We've had our bit of fun, and now, I don't mind telling you, I'm ready to get down to serious business and tackle some of those chicken livers on toast points."

In the kitchen there were black windrows of soot on the floor but little bagweed, except around the base of the walls. The table and chairs were spackled with white-capped bird drop-pings. Burlap bags were stuffed around the window frames. Overhead there was a long stovepipe and from the rusty elbow joint there came a steady fall of fine soot.

"Here, ladies, drape these towels over your heads, if you will, please. Don we now our gay apparel. That black stuff will get in your hair and it's the very devil to get out, not to mention your nose and ears."

Popper and Mrs. Mack sat at the table while June bustled about. Mrs. Mack would have liked to rest her arms on the table but the oilcloth was sticky with molasses. It pulled fibers from her sweater. The kitchen was poorly furnished. The few cooking vessels had deposits of carbonized grease at their bottoms. There were no measuring, beating or sifting instruments. The only condiments were salt and pepper, all mixed together in a glass jar with ice-pick holes in the lid.

"Saves a step or two," said Popper. "Takes the guesswork out of seasoning."

June and her mother drank hot chocolate topped off with floating marshmallows. Popper stayed with his rum, mixing it with hot water and molasses. He talked on and on in an extravagant way that confused Mrs. Mack. All she could think to say was, "Well, aren't you smart!" to the bird, who had lapsed into muttering and squawking. Popper drank and chattered away and tried to pick out a tune by dinging a spoon against the glassware. June was a plain cook, no bay leaves or underdone chicken breasts for her, but she was a good cook and she became more and more exasperated with Austin. All this loving effort for a babbling drunk.

When at last the dinner was served his head fell. The Macks likewise bowed, and then after a time they saw that he was not, as they had thought, lost in a prayer of thanksgiving, but asleep. They left him to his nap and spoke in whispers as they ate. His head sank in jerks and his face was not far from the livers and congealing gravy on his plate when there came a voice from the doorway.

"What do these women want? Get this gang of women out of here."

It was Professor Golescu. He was wearing bib overalls with a black buzzard feather stuck in the breast pocket. With his worker's cap and pointed beard and glittering eyes he looked like V. I. Lenin. June was astonished. Austin had spoken of his associate as "demented" and "badly stooped" and as having "abnormal brain rhythms," and yet here was no such pitiful figure but rather a well-formed and dynamic little man who set her pulse racing.

The cold draft from the open door brought Popper around. He shuddered and sat up. "Ho. Cezar. Come in and warm yourself. Ladies, my partner, Cezar Golescu. He comes to us from the Caspian Sea and his name means 'not many camels.'"

Golescu said, "Who are these women? Our agreement was no women and no drink."

"Don't mind him, ladies. You must make allowances. He has no manners. I had always thought that the laws of hospitality were universal but it seems Cezar and his people, the Shittite people of central Asia, have their own ideas about these things. Look at those eyes. We are entering a new age of reptiles."

"Where is my soup?"

"He wants his soup. Well, we can't talk soup until you take off your cap. These ladies are my guests."

"You are drunk again, Popper."

"Not at all. We are simply having a civilized evening of good food and good conversation. Where is the harm in that? It makes for a change. This is my good friend from Rollo, Miss June Mack. And over here, though you would never guess it, is her mother, the very charming Mrs. Mack. Now if you think you can be polite, Cezar, you are welcome to join us. Or you can go back to your weeds. Suit yourself but we can't have you standing there in the doorway scowling at us like that."

Golescu was wearing brown knit gloves with the finger ends cut off, gardener style, the better to feel things and take their measure. His exposed fingertips were a larval white. He tapped them together and stared at June. Her pug nose did not come up to his leptorhine ideal of female beauty but in other ways she pleased him. A long woodpecker nose and heavy legs— "the big hocks," as he put it—these were the qualities that Golescu first looked for in a woman. June met his appraising gaze with her own.

"I want these women out of here," he said, and wheeled about and left.

Popper turned up his hands. "My apologies. What more can I say? You see how it is. The man is loco. I know we must appear ridiculous to you, living here like this, like wild beasts in this Mato Grosso, but you get deeper and deeper into a hole and you don't know quite how to get out. Anyway, our party pooper is gone and let's say no more about him."

June said, "What about his soup?"

"Don't worry about him. He keeps coconut cookies in his room. I've seen them. You'll never believe me when I tell you what he has on his wall up there. Diplomas? A favorite poem in a frame? Some bathing beauty? Not on your life. Give up? It's a picture of his king."

"You haven't eaten anything, Austin."

"Nothing? Are you sure?"

"You look gray. I'll heat up those livers. It won't take a minute."

"No, no. To tell you the truth I'm a little queasy. Just a spoon or two of ice cream maybe."

He ate a bowl of snow ice cream and then pulled some blankets about his shoulders and curled up on the cot and fell asleep again, facing the wall.

Twilight came early to Hogandale, when the sun dropped below the peak of Puerco Mountain. June lighted the kerosene lamp. Mrs. Mack announced that she had had quite enough of ranch life and was ready to go. June was about ready too, but outside it was growing dark and sleet was rattling against the windows. She knew nothing about the bus schedule and she had no intention of walking back up the hill unescorted. She tried to rouse Popper. The more she shook him, the more he contracted into a ball-like form, presenting a smaller and smaller surface to the attack.

June took the lamp and boldly made her way through the bagweed and up the stairs. The banister glistened with hoarfrost. She found Golescu's room and spoke to him through the locked door. He said nothing. She explained the situation, that Austin was in a deep sleep, out for the night apparently, and that she and her mother wished to return home. Could he not help them? There was a scrabbling movement within the room but there came no reply. Sobs and hysterics, she decided, would avail her nothing with this man, a tough foreigner of some kind, not likely to be moved by female tears. She stood there and considered how best to flush him. Cajolery? Money? Warm food?

The door opened and the professor appeared before her with one hand casually at rest in a coat pocket. The cap was gone and in its place there sat an alpine hat. He had changed his work clothes too and was now wearing a belted woolen suit and dotted bow tie. The buzzard feather was in the breast pocket. He wore glasses with perfectly round black frames. General Tojo himself had no glasses that were any rounder.

"How would you like to go to the pictures with Golescu?" he said.

Surprisingly enough, he knew when the buses ran, and he escorted the Macks all the way back to Rollo. They arrived in time to catch the last show at the Majestic. He knew his way about town and had in fact been to this theater two or three times before.

Popper had told June that nothing would get the professor out of the house, but there was one thing and that was a Jeanette MacDonald movie. He seldom missed one. Cut off as he was from the world, he still managed to stay current on the coming attractions in Rollo by way of movie calendars that were delivered by hand each month over the entire county, even to the old Taggert house. When a new calendar came, he circled any notice of a film starring Miss MacDonald and laid his travel plans accordingly.

On this night, of course, any picture would do. He had not had such a soft armful as June Mack at his side in a very long time, and the show itself and its featured players were a matter of indifference to him.

As luck would have it, there was a musical cartoon of the kind he liked, with some toys coming to life in a toy shop after the toy maker had gone to bed. He hummed along with the singing dolls. The feature was good too, a murder mystery with a circus setting, in which an escaped gorilla figured as a red herring. It was not June's kind of picture. She liked the ones with big city nightclub scenes, with perky cigarette girls in their cute outfits, and dark sleek men who whispered orders to henchmen, and pale ladies in white satin gowns who drank highballs and took calls on white telephones. The selected short subject was puzzling to Golescu. It was all about a luxurious rest home in California for retired movie stars, a beautiful estate set in rolling hills, with cottages and swimming pools and all the latest medical equipment. Nothing was too good for the Hollywood old-timers who had worn themselves out with their antics before the camera. When it was over the lights came up and ushers appeared at a quick march to collect money for the home in cardboard buckets. Each of the Macks gave a dime. Golescu dropped in a penny. America, so far from the Danube, was a strange land and he was still not clear as to the nature and extent of his duties here. Among other things, it seemed, he was expected to help Errol Flynn with his retirement plans.

At the close of the program the moviegoers shuffled out and paused in the lobby to put on their heavy coats and think over some of the things they had seen. Golescu looked into their faces. "Where are the Red Indians?" he said. "For months I am living in the West and I am seeing no Amerinds."

June said, "I think they live in Arizona, don't they, Mom?"

"You got me."

"Arizona or New Mexico, one. Wait a minute. I forgot about Thomas. He's some kind of Indian."

"I am anxious to see the solemn old chiefs in their round hats," said Golescu. "Their squaws and papooses. Those noble faces are from Mu. I am most anxious to measure their heads."

At Mack house, after Mrs. Mack had said good night and gone to her room, the professor sat on the sofa with June and showed her his membership cards from various secret brotherhoods. Then some tricks. He wrote with both hands. He balanced a glass of water on his forehead, tossed three nickels into the air and caught them on the back of one hand. He drove two nails with a hammer in each hand. June offered him some squares of fudge. He declined. He brought out his cylinder seal and told her a little about Kikku and the burial customs of Mu. But he went through all this in a mechanical way, with none of the old Golescu brio, and after a time fell silent.

June ventured a thought. "Do you want to know what I think, Cezar? I think you must have some secret sorrow in your life."

He admitted that his work was not going well and that life

in the old Taggert house was grim. Hogandale was worse than Mount Grobny. He didn't know how much longer he could tolerate Popper's drinking and his insults. The man was a lunatic. He had once been at the very top of the Gnomon Society, a trusted keeper of the secret knowledge of Atlantis, and was now a raving drunk. You never knew what was going on in his head, what he might say next, or even what his raucous bird might say.

"But you and Austin are alike in some ways," said June. "No, it's true. Do you want to know what I've noticed? I've noticed that neither one of you ever laughs. Austin has a wonderful smile but that's as far as it goes. And you never even smile."

"So, you expect me to cackle, do you? My dear girl, Romanians are known all over the world for their hilarity. I love nothing better than to laugh but my life it is not a joke. Or it is a joke if you like but not a good one. I am engaged in serious work and how can I do it properly when I am living in an icehouse with a crazy man and eating garbage? Such conditions. Yes, and I am half crazy myself from inhaling mercury fumes. How can I laugh? Much better I was living in Mu fifty thousand years ago."

Following these remarks there was a lull, a highly charged calm, and then with no warning the professor sprang. He threw his arms around June and buried his face in her stiff and tawny wavelets and called her his "little mole" and his "tulip."

June was taken by surprise. From cultivated men she expected more chat, a longer stalking period, as with Austin, who had sat on this same sofa and pawed her a little in an absent-minded way, and pecked her on the cheek, but never making a decisive move. Perhaps he had held back out of wariness, sensing the steady gaze of Mother Mack on the back of his neck, she with one inflamed eyeball pressed to a door crack and her teeth bared in a rictus from the painful effort to see and hear everything. Or from a failure of nerve, or concern about the difference in their ages. Or from a simple lack of ardor. Whatever his reasons, Popper had been much too slow off the mark to suit June and had thereby forfeited his chance.

# 7

O N MONDAY morning Popper awoke in a tangle of blankets. He lay there and turned matters over in his head. Why could not their production of gold be further facilitated by nature? Get some bugs to eat the bagweed. Then feed the bugs to frogs and the frogs in turn to snakes. At each step of the pyramid there would be a greater accretion of gold, and at the apex, serpents of gold, their scales glittering with the stuff. He must present the idea to Cezar.

He also resolved to stop drinking and to ask June Mack to marry him.

"Today's the day, Squanto."

He got up and for the first time in months went through his Gnomonic breathing exercises. One could fall off the Jimmerson Spiral but one could also swing back aboard. He boiled some eggs, a long business at this altitude, and made coffee with the same water. He ate two eggs and left two for Cezar. On one he idly scrawled, *Help. Captive. Gypsy caravan.* Cezar wasn't such a bad fellow. A pouting little pedant and much too full of himself but a man of some substance for all that. What was their production of gold anyway? He must ask Cezar.

"Watch this," he said to the bird, and went about collecting bottles and pouring rum down the sink. Renunciation was not only exhilarating, it was easy.

Squanto was resting in the sunken crown of an old felt hat. His head was pulled down into his shoulders and his neck feathers were fluffed out against the cold drafts. He had the crazed look of a setting hen. Popper spoke words of assurance to him. Spring was just around the corner. June would suffuse their dreary lives with sunshine. Her very name gave promise of it.

There was a lot to be said for the ladies, he told the unblinking bird, apart from their physical charms. They were loyal. Hard workers. They were on the whole a civilizing force and had made good fathers and useful citizens out of many a slavering brute. Women were brave too and not the least bit squeamish about the corruptions of the flesh. If anything they were attracted to that muck. All those nurses. At the same time

you must keep them in check or they would drive you crazy.
They would presume and push. They were contentious, unreasonable, expensive, randomly vicious and would demand far
too much of your attention. There was nothing meaner than a
mean woman. With their gabble and nagging they could give
you a preview of Hell. But that was the worst of it and there
was much to be said for them.

As he was leaving, Popper paused in the doorway and said,
"Just a little longer, Squanto. Hogandale is not such a bad
place. We'll look back on all this later and have a good laugh
together."

He took the noon bus to Rollo and went directly to the barbershop in the basement of the Hotel Rollo. There in a back
room he had a shower bath, a long steamy pounding, while his
suit was being pressed and his shoes shined. Then a shave with
hot towels. On the way out, with his burnished cheeks glowing
like apples, he stopped in the bar for a short beer, which hardly
counted as a drink. The bartender said a man had been looking
for him.

"Who was it?"

"I don't know. There was something of the bill collector
about him. I told him nothing."

"Good work."

Popper had the bar to himself. He ordered another beer and
took it to the table by the big bay window. He looked out
on the town of Rollo with goodwill. Seeing the post office,
he was tempted again to send a postcard to Mr. Jimmerson.
How thrilled the Master would be to get a Poppergram out
of the blue. But the time for that had not come. Outside the
courthouse he saw a deputy sheriff in Sam Browne belt reading something. No doubt a writ of some kind. A short man
stood beside him, waiting. He wore a fedora and long brown
overcoat that brushed the tops of his shoes. No doubt a lawyer,
about to swoop.

It was true, the man was a lawyer, but he was also Special
Agent Pharris White, and the deputy was reading, not a writ
of attachment, but an FBI sitrep, or situation report, which
ran: *Popper, Austin. Age unknown. Origins obscure. Position
and momentum uncertain. Disguise impenetrable. Tracks dim.*

*Sightings nil. Early apprehension doubtful.* The reading done, the deputy and the short man got into a green Ford sedan and drove away. Popper did not recognize White and made nothing much of the scene, now so neatly concluded.

He moved on to the Blue Hole, greeting the regulars with his usual "Keep 'em flying!" They cringed on their stools from the sunlight that came streaming through the open doorway, and they too reported that a man had been looking for him. The fellow's manner had put them off. He seemed to think he was the cock of the walk, if not the bull of the woods, and the barflies had told him nothing. "Good work," said Popper, and he bought a round and took a short rum himself so as not to put a damper on the occasion. June Mack had not yet come on duty.

Just as he settled in at the bar, Popper heard a familiar voice. He turned and saw Cezar Golescu, not where he should have been, at the old Taggert house wolfing down eggs, but here in the Blue Hole, back there in a dark booth having a glass of wine against the teachings of the Koran and talking to some crew-cut Indio.

"Cezar!"

"Yes, I saw you come in, Popper, but I can't talk to you now. I am engaged in private business."

"What in the world are you doing here? In your belted suit?"

"A private matter. I will be with you shortly."

Popper went back to the booth. "This won't wait, I have something that will make you sit up. Have you thought of using bugs to help process our stuff?"

"Yes, I have. No bug known to science will eat B.W. Bugs are not on my agenda today. If you don't mind, this is private business."

"Then I will leave you to it."

"Please do."

Popper returned to the bar and Golescu resumed his lecture to Thomas, the Ute Indian. Thomas drove a coal delivery truck. He was a man about sixty years old with close-cropped gray hair. No consumptive oriental type with flat face and thin limbs, he was a big strapping Plains Indian with fierce Armenoid features. He had just finished eating fifteen dollars worth of fried oysters, the house specialty, and was now smoking a cigar and drinking a mixture of beer and tomato juice. Golescu was paying.

On the table between them the professor had spread out his many membership cards for Thomas to see. He had already taken measurements of Thomas's skull and was now going through the epic tale of Mu once again, of how, after the cataclysm, a handful of survivors had been left perched on rocks in the middle of the Pacific Ocean, the water lapping at their feet, and how from that remnant Thomas and all his red brothers had sprung.

Thomas had understood most of this the first time around. He found it only a little less convincing than the story of how his people had hopped from rock to rock across the Bering Strait, at low tide, but he still couldn't see how it affected him personally, or his coal route, and had said little in response.

"Yes, I am sitting here face to face with a living, breathing fossil," said the professor. "I have dreamed of this moment. You, Thomas, are nothing less than a degraded Muvian."

Thomas said nothing. Golescu tried another approach. "Just for the moment let us forget the rest and look at the two languages and how they so nicely correspond." He spread his fingers and pushed them together in an interlocking way to give an example of correspondence. "Like that. See? It is amazing how the language of Mu and your own tongue, the Uto-Aztecan tongue—not your physical tongue, of course—" Here Golescu pointed to his own tongue with jabbing motions, and shook his head no.

"Did I hear you right? Did you call me degraded?"

"Please, no, a scientific term. There is no offense. 'Devolved,' if you like. I myself am a degraded Roman. I boast of it. Does that surprise you? I know you have heard of the great Roman Empire. Those were my people, Thomas. Did you think I was a Slav or a Goth? What a funny joke. My people came to Dacia under Trajan's Roman Eagle. I am more Roman than Mussolini, who pretends he is restoring the Empire. Is my name not Cezar? What the hell kind of name is Benito? Mexican? Names are important. I will tell you that if Remus had killed Romulus then the Roman Empire would have been the Reman Empire and the Catholic peoples would go on their pilgrimages to the eternal city of Reme and I myself would be a degraded Reman. But all that is by the way and my point is simply this, that each of us has a noble heritage. And yet what is mine compared to yours? Nothing. Agriculture, metallurgy, bathrooms, celestial navigation, radios, typewriters—all these things your people of Mu invented many years ago. And your calendar! So accurate! Like a fine watch of seventeen jewels!"

June arrived, wearing loose, pajamalike trousers that were gathered in at the ankles. Popper moved to meet her at the door. He took her hand but before he could speak she said, "Austin! You look so nice! You've heard the news, then? It sure gets around fast in Rollo these days."

"What news is that?"

"Cezar and I have an understanding."

"A what?"

"We are seeing each other now. You were so silly last night. Cezar took me home and we fell in love right there on Bantry Street."

"Cezar Golescu took you home?"

"Yes, and shame on me, I let him get fresh. It was like lightning hit us, Austin."

Popper dropped her hand and leaned forward on his stick for support. He had a vision of June sitting on Cezar's lap. He saw little beardless Golescus crawling around on the floor of Mack house and peeping out at the guests from behind the furniture. How bold she was. Nothing of the stammering maiden twisting a handkerchief in her hands.

"This is hard to believe, June."

"We can still be friends, can't we?"

"Why yes, certainly."

She turned about in a modeling move to show her red Scheherazade pants. "How do you like my new outfit?"

"Very nice."

"Cezar doesn't want other men looking at my legs."

"I see."

"There was something else I wanted to tell you but I can't remember what it was."

"This will do for now."

Rising voices came from the Golescu booth.

Thomas said, "It sounds to me like you're leaving God out of this."

Golescu said, "I have not mentioned God."

"Wasn't that what I said?"

"But this is about Mu."

"I don't see how you can leave God out of this unless you're cut off from God yourself. He is right here at this table."

"In a sense, yes. I fully agree."

"God made the sun. I don't worship the sun and never did."

"Not you personally, no, but in Mu they saw the sun as the central manifestation of God's glory, as did so many early peoples. In Colonel Churchward's book you will find it all clearly explained."

"I wouldn't have that book in my house. I wouldn't have it in my truck."

"Please—"

"Where are you from anyway, you Nazi devil? You dog eater. You call me a fossil and you say I'm degraded but I'll tell you something, mister, you're the one who is cut off from God and not me. I have felt His burning breath on my face."

"I am hearing it, the poetry of Mu!"

Thomas left in anger, pausing at the bar to turn and point his finger at Golescu and say, "There's no way in the world I can walk with that man and walk with God at the same time."

Popper went to the booth and slid into Thomas's seat. "Who's your pal?"

"His name is Thomas. A private matter."

"He left his cap."

"He will come back for it."

It was a railroad man's cap, made of some striped material like mattress ticking. The high bloused crown was blackened with coal dust and hardened from repeated soakings of sweat.

"I'm not so sure," said Popper. "This cap has seen plenty of hard service. He may well write it off and buy a new one. Something with earflaps this time."

"Thomas will come back and apologize to me. I know these people better than they know themselves."

"No, Thomas can't walk with you and neither can I. We're finished, Cezar. Where are you keeping our stuff? I want an accounting. I want my gold and I want it now."

"Very well."

Golescu took the buzzard feather from his coat pocket and removed a tiny plug from the end of the shaft. He tapped out a little powdery heap of gold on the table. "There. Banco. Half is yours. Take it and go."

"There's not enough gold there to crown a tooth."

"About six dollars' worth."

"Where's the rest of it? This is one of your desert tricks."

"There is no more. That is our winter's work. That is our golden harvest from eleven hundred pounds of leaves."

"You've gone wrong somewhere in your recovery methods."

"No, I have not gone wrong. I have tried everything—zinc, cyanide, caustic soda, chlorine, distillation, sublimation, calcination, fulmination. Let us not forget high-temperature incineration. Always the result is the same. This dirt, that dirt, always the same result. The production of gold is constant but small. It is not a function of the soil. Your idea was no good. Very stupid. Gold from the earth, you said, and you bring us out here to the headwaters of the Puerco River to get rich. I listen to a foolish American who never in his life taught science. Bagweed does not take up bits of gold from the earth, you stupid man. No, it *makes* gold. It *synthesizes* gold. All you have done is waste my valuable time."

"What you're saying is that creeping bagweed is a hoax. In Washington you told me you could work wonders. You had me worrying about swamping the market with gold. Now you tell me we have broken our backs for six dollars."

"Bagweed is bagweed. You cannot question the integrity of the plant."

"My big mistake was to trust you."

"I snap my fingers at you."

"You were never a team player, Cezar."

"May I say you look like an eel, Popper?"

"You and your planet of Mu. I should have known better."

"Mu is not a planet, you ignorant man. Please, take your gold and go. It is good that we go our different ways. I am on the way up and you are on the way down. Me to big things, you to the gutter."

"I won't soon forget your slights and snubs of Squanto. Not once have you ever spoken to him, or even nodded to him in passing."

"It is true what you say there. I don't talk to birds."

"I was right to keep you out of the Society. Oh, yes, you're still a P.S. and don't you forget it. Did you think a Neophyte was a true Gnomon? You made a fool of yourself, Cezar, running around the house out there with those two windblown runnels of frozen snot curling across your cheeks."

Golescu was shaken. He sipped at the red wine to cover his confusion, then tossed his head and said, "Ha. I laugh at your Cone of Fate. To me it was all such a funny joke."

"I'll tell you something else. I have watched you eating."

"What?"

"Through my spyhole. I watched you in your room."

"You spy on my privacy?"

"A bit of quiet fun."

"This is a shameful thing you confess to."

"I watched you eating your macaroons. Not the straight-forward bites of an honest man, just ratlike nibbling around the edges. A kind of savoring, I suppose. Making it last too. I watched you leaning over your table lost in thought. The Führer at his map table. I saw you writing drivel in your diary. The bagweed of journals—one part gold per trillion. And late at night—often I waited up for this show—I watched you punching up your pillow for minutes on end, and then lining up your little shoes beside the bed, always in the same place, ready to be jumped into like firemen's boots. I've seen that picture of your king on the wall too."

"My king?"

"Over your bed. King Zog."

"Zog? Are you mad? What do I care for Zog of Albania? That picture is a hand-tinted photograph of my mother."

"Yes, no doubt that's what you told our immigration people. You had your story ready. You knew you were on thin ice, bringing a picture of your king into our republic, where we bend the knee to no man. When they found it and confronted you with it, you went into a Babylonian flutter and said, "No, no, it's just Mom Golescu!""

June brought a bowl of peanuts to the table. "My two hand-some beaus," she said. "Listen, Austin, I remembered what it was I wanted to tell you. A man came by the house this morning looking for you. It was an FBI man named Pharris White in a real long overcoat. He said he knew you."

"FBI" registered clearly enough but for a moment Popper could not place the name. Then he remembered. But Pharris White a federal dick? Could it be the same person? P. White of the long telegrams? What next? The winter was frittered away, his sweetheart beguiled by a Turk and now jail.

"Yes, an old lodge brother. Overcoat White. Thank you, June."

Golescu caught her hand and kissed her fingers as she was leaving. He smirked at Popper.

But Popper was thinking about Letter Plan. This was an escape maneuver prepared in anticipation of such news. He would thread his way west on a series of local buses to San Francisco and there take refuge in Chinatown with an old Gnomon friend, James Wing. The plan was named for Poe's tale "The Purloined Letter," whose point Popper had misunderstood to be this, that the best hiding place is that place where a search has already been made. Poe was only one of many well-known authors with whom Popper professed familiarity, and of whose works he had read not a single word. He came by his information on such matters indirectly, through magazines, radio programs and hearsay.

For an instant, in his panic, he thought of leaving Squanto behind.

"What are you doing?" said Golescu.

Popper was pushing the table away from him. He pushed it against Golescu's midriff and pinned him to the back of the booth. With a puff of breath he blew away the heap of gold. Golescu struggled but could not raise his arms. Popper took a rubber stamp from an inside pocket and stamped VOID across each of the professor's membership cards, still spread on the table, eight or nine of them, Rosicrucian, Brothers of Luxor, every last one of them. Golescu kicked and threw his head about and squealed and snarled but there was nothing he could do. Popper tipped the table over and left the Blue Hole at a run.

He circled about through alleys for a time and then ducked into a pool hall with painted windows. He drank bottled beer and waited there in the smoky room. When night came he hired a taxicab to take him to Hogandale. It was an old car, high and square, with oval rear window, just an evolutionary step or two beyond the kind with bicycle wheels and tiller. The going was slow. The driver was an old man who said he hoped to keep the car running until 1950. By that time, according to the newspapers, the war would be over and everyone would be flying around in autogyros.

He was a sporting old man and gave no difficulty when Popper asked him to stop at the top of the hill in Hogandale and turn off his lights. Popper went forward on foot to see how things lay. He saw a Ford sedan parked in front of Dad's Place. He made the connection. Yes, it was the one with the twin spotlights he had seen in front of the courthouse. The man with the deputy must have been Pharris White. They were in Dad's Place now, trying to get some sense out of Dad and the coots, a hopeless business.

Popper thought at first to wait them out, then wondered if audacity might not be the better card. A lightning sortie. Quickly in and out to get Squanto.

He went back to the cab and asked the old man to coast down the hill with no lights and glide to a stop at the old Taggert house. "A child custody case," he explained. "I'm picking up Baby Bill for his mother." Even so, the descent was noisy. The unpowered car made more racket than Popper would have believed possible. The old man stood on the brakes, worn-out mechanical brakes, and the car slewed about in a great screech of metal on metal. But no one emerged from the saloon.

The ground fog had lifted from lower Hogandale. The old Taggert house stood clearly revealed in the moonlight. Popper wondered if the time would ever come when he would miss the place and its white vapors, as he missed the Temple. Probably not, he decided.

"Honk your horn if anyone comes along."

"It don't work."

"I won't be a minute."

He was a little drunk. He fumbled with the keys and the ice-cold locks and chains. His feet became tangled in the bagweed and he kicked at the stuff. He had trouble finding a lamp and getting it lighted. "I'm back," he called out to Squanto. "It's me. We're going bye-bye. We're off again but not on the choo-choo this time. It's Letter Plan and James Wing. We'll have our own little upstairs room on Grant Avenue."

When he entered the kitchen he found Squanto dead in the crown of the old hat. His toes were curled and his beak agape. Popper dropped the lamp. The burning kerosene spread across the floor. He reached for the stiff little body, the plumage all purple, blue, black, gray and white. Would it never end, this evil day that had begun with such promise? Now here was Squanto dead and the house afire. He wrapped the bird in a handkerchief. "You were a good friend, Squanto," he said. "You couldn't sing and you weren't much of a flier but I know in your heart you soared." He put the shrouded body in a coat pocket and stamped ineffectually at the fire.

Headlights raked across the window. There came the sound of car doors slamming. Popper went to the window and wiped at the frost with his coat sleeve.

There in the yard was the Ford, lights ablaze, and Pharris White standing beside the taxicab. He was holding a flashlight on the old man. But could that be White? The fellow must have shed a hundred pounds. The Justice Department had certainly trimmed him down. At his former weight he would not have had the agility expected of a special agent, and there would be the risk too of his getting stuck in doorways and bathtubs, further cramping his efficiency, not to mention Mr. Hoover's chagrin at having to call out the fire department repeatedly to dislodge one of his men with hacksaws, wrecking bars, acetylene torches and grease.

Would the old man talk? He could hardly be expected to perjure himself for a stranger. Did it matter? It would be no feat for a man like Pharris White, with his legal training, to see a taxicab parked at a house and from it deduce or infer a passenger. Now the deputy sheriff was moving away from the Ford. No doubt he had been chosen for his knowledge of the terrain and for the blinding speed with which he could pinion a man's arms behind him. He was pointing and shouting. He had seen the fire, and Popper's face in the window. More shouts. White sprinted for the front porch, moving well, Popper noted, at the new weight. The deputy was circling around to the back.

The fire, still more or less local, was gathering itself for a general eruption. When the officers opened the two doors, front and rear, a draft of air swept through the house and the flames swirled up as in a turbine. Popper protected his face with the crook of one arm while using the other to flail away at the crumbling floor with his stick. He cleared a sizable hole, grabbed his bag and dropped through to the ground. In the ensuing confusion he crawled away from Hogandale, frantically brushing coals off his high-pile overcoat.

He made his way across the frozen surface of the Nasty River, here little more than a creek, its corruption locked up for the winter, and then up the slope of Puerco Mountain, the talus giving way under his feet. When he rested he lay spread-eagled on the earth like a man holding on for dear life to a flying ball. He could feel no Telluric Currents flowing into his body. The mountain was dead. Near the peak was the main shaft of the mine called Old Woman No. 2. Inside he found a cranny he liked. He scooped out a little grave for Squanto with a sharp rock. One day they would put him away like this, with dirt in his mouth. He ended the day on his knees, gasping for breath and smelling of burnt wool.

# 8

HUGGINS AND Epps did not return from the war. Bates, Mapes and Maceo came back to the Temple to find the Master in his chair in the Red Room, much as they had left him. He looked much the same, except for his Poma. Corrosive fumes from the steel mills had eaten small holes in it and left it all but hairless.

Mr. Jimmerson had settled deeper into a life of contemplation. In the morning he read a page or two of Pletho and attended to the administrative duties of the Gnomon Society, a half hour's work at most, there being only four active Pillars left in the country. During the afternoon he dozed and dipped into old books. At night he revised his list of pallbearers again and again, and, with his love for fine print, reviewed his many insurance policies with the aid of a magnifying glass.

The Temple itself was in disarray. Maceo was shocked by the mess. The problem was that Mr. Jimmerson was now living alone in the big stone house.

Fanny had left him and taken little Jerome with her to Chicago. She was now following a career of her own in door-to-door sales of cosmetics. That is, she had started at that level, but in just two years had risen to become an executive vice-president of the company, and as such, commander of all the salesladies in the Great Lakes District. There was no divorce. Indeed, she was still fond of Lamar and she paid his property taxes and his utility bills, but she had her own work now and no longer wished to share his sessile life by the fireside.

Mr. Jimmerson looked on the separation as a temporary one, he having read in a newspaper article that women in mid-life often pulled such stunts as this. They became unbalanced from some female condition called "menopause" and took up such things as painting, spelling reform and politics. The condition soon passed and they came around. But Fanny didn't come around and she didn't come back, except for brief visits. In a short time the household staff was gone too. Mr. Jimmerson couldn't remember to pay them and they drifted off one by one.

Mapes and Maceo set about to put things right again. Mr. Bates, who was ailing, was not of much help. Maceo cleaned up the Temple and the grounds. He soon had the house back in efficient working order, with regular changes of towels and bed linen, and regular meals. His specialty was gravy. The four bachelors grew fat on it. They ate gravy on potatoes, gravy on rice, gravy on toast, gravy on biscuits, until their foreheads shone with grease. The big biscuits were broken into steaming halves with the fingers, then laid flat and slathered with gravy, then further divided into quadrants with a furious clacking of cutlery on the Temple china. And there was always plenty of dessert, for Maceo had been a cook on a submarine, where the men were plied with pies and ice cream as a bit of extra compensation for their hazardous duty.

Mapes had the harder task of reviving the Society. It seemed shameful that he and the Master should be as fat as pigs while the brotherhood languished. But what to do? Some strong restorative was needed. Was he the man for the job? He had doubts. Wasn't he more the faithful custodian of the flame than the great captain? Much as he disliked Popper, he knew that Popper would not hesitate to act—no, he would be pounding on the victim's chest with his fists and shouting to the nurses for more voltage and ever more powerful injections.

But that was Popper's way. His, Mapes's, way would be more in keeping with the dignity of the order. Slow, perhaps, and not very dramatic, but leading in the end to a healthy growth, as opposed to the pathological growth of the Popper years.

After long consultations with the Master, and by telephone with the remaining Pillars, Mapes prepared a recovery plan. There were two major recommendations.

The first was that an effort be made to attract young men to the Society—specifically young war veterans. Along with them, perhaps, would come some federal money. That was what everyone looked to now. It would be no easy job. Today's young men were dazzled by the claims and presumptions of science. They had been taught to jeer at other systems of thought. Yes, the scientists were riding high these days, preening themselves over their latest triumph, the A-bomb. They were boastful men of insufferable pride, these materialists in white smocks who held the preposterous belief that nothing could be known but through the five senses. But the great wheel was turning and Mapes suspected that these fellows had had their day.

The second recommendation was that peace be made between the Gnomon Society and the Gnomon Society (Amended Order). A reconciliation would have to be worked out at the very top, between Mr. Jimmerson and Sydney Hen, and then in orderly stages the divided brotherhood could come together in Pythagorean harmony. Here again there would be difficulty —a fine touch would be needed in any approach to the prickly Hen. All the same, Popper would not be around to interfere and to antagonize Hen, and what better time than now for a truce, with the entire world turning to peaceful pursuits?

H EN HAD also been lying fallow in recent years. Since the battle of the books there had been hardly a peep out of him. Rumors floated up from Cuernavaca but nothing in the way of direct and reliable reports.

Some of the rumors were scandalous, such as the one that he was keeping two Mexican women on the side, in addition to his lawful wife, Babette. A diet of pine nuts and tiny yellow peppers was said to have made a new man of him, and a wild man at that. There was a story that he was dosing himself daily with enough laudanum to stupefy three strong men. Another one had him dead, stabbed by Mexican monks, or drowned in his onyx bathtub by Babette and Kinlow, who had grabbed his ankles and held them high while he glubbed in the soapy water. There were whispers that he was making pots, ashtrays, wallets and sandals, and composing discordant music in a peculiar scale and notation of his own devising.

All lies. The truth was that Sir Sydney, except for an unwonted silence, was pretty much the same old Hen. He had closed his advanced study program—the cow-eyed acolytes got on his nerves—and what with the disruptions of war and his own negligence his Amended Order of Gnomons had collapsed. At this time he had fewer than a dozen active followers left, among them Mr. Morehead Moaler of La Coma, Texas, who also belonged to Mr. Jimmerson's order. Mr. Moaler somehow managed to keep a foot in both camps. Hen had heard nothing from his London Temple in almost two years. But then neither had the world heard anything from Hen. He published nothing and said nothing ex officio. Even within the walls of the New Croton Institute his speech was less a matter of words than of long, plaintive sighs.

TO HEAR MUCH AND SPEAK LITTLE

These words of Pletho Pappus he had carved across the archway at the entrance of the Institute.

The silence was a calculated one and came about in the following way. Hen fell sick. After a day or two in bed he had

Kinlow hire some public mourners. Kinlow rounded up some old women in shawls and had them stand outside the villa and wail, their arms raised in quivering supplication. He then hired some newspaper editors to publish accounts and photographs of the demonstration, all going to show what a beloved figure the Master of Gnomons (Amended Order) had become in Mexico. A news service picked up the story and spread it about. The response was good. There came letters and telegrams expressing sympathy, a few visitors and even some applications for membership in the Society.

Hen's illness was not serious, no arsenical muffins this time, but it did keep him laid up for a while and he put off answering the mail and receiving visitors until he should feel a bit stronger. Kinlow noticed that the volume of mail grew. More visitors came. Some stood outside on tiptoe and tried to catch a glimpse of the Master through the barred windows. Kinlow pointed out to Hen that his retreat from view had enhanced his stature. There were benefits to be gained from preserving a grand silence. Myths grew in the dark. Hen was thus persuaded to adopt his new role of "the Sphinx of Cuernavaca."

He was not to emerge from his shell, or what Kinlow called "the Pyramid of Silence," until the summer of 1945, when the All Clear was sounded across Europe. In July of that year Hen announced that he was returning home to England. The joys of quiescence, while real enough, were pale indeed when compared to those of center stage.

He chose New York for his first public appearance. There in a dockside press conference he said that he felt called upon to help rebuild his country, from which he had been away far too long. The cloistered life was important, and not to be despised, but the great dreamers and thinkers must never forget that they were also citizens, or in his case a subject, but in any case, members of the larger community with certain obligations.

He had prepared a White Paper for the government, having to do with the restructuring of English society along Gnomonic lines. He saw a special counseling role for Gnomons in the postwar world, particularly in London, "the epicenter of Gnomonism," and could only hope that His Majesty's ministers would prove receptive to his scheme for "a new order of reality and England happy again." These ministers must, however, get it through their heads that under no circumstances would he, Sir Sydney Hen, be available as a candidate for public office. Likewise, whilst he could hardly disobey a direct command from his king, he believed the House of Lords to be altogether too puny an arena for a man of spirit.

"And now, goodbye and God bless you," he said in closing. "We'll see you again in about three years. There is much work to be done."

The New York reporters took all this down and put it in their papers in strings of stiff little paragraphs of equal size and diminishing importance.

But in Southampton, England, the ship reporters were not so kind to him. They came aboard in a pack with photographers and were turned loose on the celebrity passengers, who had been assembled in the first-class dining saloon. The journalists looked over the field, then moved in quickly on a tennis star in white, a surly poet in rags, assumed for the occasion, and a movie actress of the second or third rank. Hen was ignored, written off as a bishop in some church or other.

He, Babette and Kinlow were in full feather too, a photographer's delight if nothing else, but Hen could get no attention. One reporter, an older man, vaguely remembered him and paused for a moment to listen. Hen launched into his prepared remarks, then stopped to ask the man why he wasn't taking notes.

"Rubbish" was the reporter's brutal reply. "You flatter yourself. This is not an interview. You're a back number, Hen. I should have bet you were long dead, mortally beaned by a falling coconut in some brown place like Morocco. Or from squatting out in the sun too long and eating too many dates. You'll be lucky to get a bare mention in the arrivals column."

It was a bitter homecoming. In London he found that his Temple had been seized in default of taxes and turned into a government home for unwed mothers. The big bronze doors had been taken away to be melted down for munitions. There was no room to be had at the Savoy, where he had once kept a suite, or at any other hotel. His club, the November Club, grudgingly agreed to put him up for a night or two on a camp bed, but refused to accept Babette or Kinlow, or even let them through the door. They were left to spend their first night in London walking the streets and resting in a Leicester Square movie theater. Hen's old friends were not forthcoming. His few remaining Gnomon brothers were dead or widely dispersed. His female cousin at Little-Fen-on-Sea would not return his calls. People on the street looked straight through him, as though they could not see his aura, or the odic fire streaming from his fingertips.

He appealed to the Botanical Roundtable and the Association of Distressed Gentlemen, and through these groups was at last able to get a room. It was an attic bedroom across the river in a Lambeth rooming house, which seemed to be filled with Egyptians. The room was small, with scarcely enough space for the three travelers and their nine trunks. All three had to sleep in one bed, Hen, his wife and male secretary, with Babette placed in the sunken middle for balance. Lying there against her broad back, listening to the whining of Kinlow on the other side of the mound, Sir Sydney could not believe that things had come to such a pass. Could this be England, treating her distinguished men so?

It was certain that some monstrous campaign had been mounted to humiliate him, or worse still, to efface his name. He wondered if the French Rosicrucians might not be behind it. Or Madame Blavatsky's people. Or some of Aleister Crowley's grisly gang. Or the Druids. Or the crafty Popper, who very likely had some of his agents here among all these Yank soldiers. Or the Freemasons, whom he had once suspected of setting up an X-ray machine in the house across from the Temple, and directing the beams into his bathroom at head level. It was never proven but how else explain the bathroom buzz in his ears? They had covered their tracks well, these sons of Hiram, and had squared the police with a Masonic wink. They were all in the Craft together.

Some sinister body was at work to bring him down, of that there could be no doubt. The method employed was obvious. It was the old story—these people were deflecting his Gnomonic waves and scattering them so that they were lost into the air, adding somewhat to the reddish glow of London. But wasn't there something wrong here too on a different scale? With the war over, he had expected to come home to a jubilee, and yet everything was so dreadful. The place was in tatters.

Where was the festival? The emanations were all wrong and there was no energy release. There was no egg for his breakfast either, no butter for his toast, no melon slice, no hot water for his bath. Even clothing was rationed, though Kinlow did manage, through the black market, to lay in a supply of the peculiar green suiting material he so loved.

Their stay was cut short, from three years to four days. Babette, fingering the golden topaz that lay on her bosom, complained that she had not yet seen any shows, heard any concerts, attended any parties or met any important people. She had so hoped to be presented at court. What about Stratford? What about their tour of Kew Gardens? What did it mean, all this marching and countermarching?

Hen did not often cross Babette—*La Mujerona*, the Big Woman, as she was known to the servants in Mexico—but this time he took a firm stand, so angered and shaken was he.

"Enough," he said to her. "Have done, woman. We're leaving. It is my will."

The timing was all wrong, he explained. It was a terrible mistake, this journey, and they were returning at once to the flowers, the sunshine and the fresh tomatoes of Cuernavaca. The Hen convoy, borne here on a wicked tide, was wheeling about.

He ordered Babette to pack and he sent Kinlow along to the British Museum with the white marble bust, warning him to take care with it, not to dally, to stay out of the pubs and leave the soldiers alone. Hen had commissioned a Mexican artist to fashion this heroic bust of himself, a startling object, a sort of Aztec Hen, with jade eyeballs and coral teeth. He had intended to make a ceremonial presentation of it to the nation, but now, fearful of another rebuff, thought it best to handle the matter quietly.

Kinlow grumbled about having to lug the statuary across town.

"The thing must weigh fifty pounds, sir."

"Not another word. Go."

Kinlow could not find a taxi. He set out walking. In the middle of Lambeth Bridge he stopped to rest and watch the boats. Then, in a swelling fit of anger, he lifted the bust over the railing and dropped it into the river. On his return he was still pouting.

"Do you mind?" he said, in his sharp way, to an old man who was blocking the doorway of the rooming house. The man had a bulging forehead. He wore thick glasses and a black bowler hat with curling brim, a size nine at the very least, and a black suit with trouser legs that were too short. At his heels there were arching holes in his socks, providing a glimpse of ankle flesh that was none too clean. His rattail mustaches were so void of color as to be barely visible. He made no apology and did not give way.

"One minute, please, of your time, sir. Is this number 23 Grimalkin Crescent?"

"It is."

"Sir Sydney Hen is putting up here?"

"Yes, if it's any of your business."

"Ah. Then there's no mistake. I'm sure the Master must have his reasons for dossing down here with all these Gyppos. Do you have a cigarette?"

"I don't smoke."

"And quite right too. What so many people fail to consider is the damned insidious expense of tobacco. You are not by any chance Sir Sydney yourself?"

"Of course not."

"You would be a younger man?"

"Much younger."

"I don't see well at close range, no matter what you may have heard about my extraordinary spectacles, but I should have known from your step that you were a younger man. Yes, from an older man you expect a stumbling, festinating gait like mine. You do know Sir Sydney, I take it."

"I am his private secretary."

"What luck. I saw his name in the arrivals columns and they sent me along here from his club. I thought there must be some mistake with the address. Too bad about the Temple, eh? Hard lines. All those stinking nappies in the hallways. But we mustn't weep over a pile of bricks. When can you arrange an appointment for me?"

"What do you want? Who are you?"

"My name is Pletho Pappus. I come to speak of clotted bulls' blood and of a white heifer that has never known the yoke."

"How very interesting."

"My card."

"Pletho Pappus is long dead."

"Presumed dead. It suited me to lie low for a season."

"How very interesting."

"It is near the time when I shall make many things clear. Would you like to know why our Gnomon Society is not prospering? Let me tell you, sir. It's because there are too many backbiters, cankerworms and cheesehoppers in positions of authority. These people must go."

"I think you're talking absolute bloody nonsense."

"My card."

Kinlow took the card and read it. There was an address in a lower corner, and in the center these words:

T. Pappas
*Eastern Knick Knacks*
*Honourable Dealing*

"This says T. Pappas. It's not even spelled the same way."

"A ruse. Theodore."

"So? A printed card. Your name is Pappas. London is full of Greeks and I daresay many of them are named Pappas. If you truly are from Greece. I rather suspect Dublin. By way of Hyde Park."

"Will you be good enough to present my card to Sir Sydney?"

"Sir Sydney is out. He's engaged elsewhere. He's not buying any rugs just now."

"When will he be free?"

"I don't know. His calendar is quite full."

"Do you have a cigarette?"

"No."

"Perhaps I should wait here."

"No, that won't do."

"No trouble at all, I assure you."

"It's not on, my friend."

"Quite all right, I don't mind waiting."

"Very well. Look here. Sir Sydney is lunching at his club tomorrow. Be there on the pavement at one sharp and he will give you three minutes to state your business."

"Wonderful. One, you say? That will suit my convenience too. Now as to the etiquette. Even as a child I was a stickler for form. What's the drill? Are there some things I should know? May one, for example, contradict Sir Sydney on small matters?"

"No, one may not. You may not dispute his lightest remark. Remove your hat as you approach him and keep your eyes well cast down. No handshaking and no sudden movements in his presence. Speak only when spoken to and then briefly and to the point. And no need to bring along any of your Eastern titbits. Now off you go, chop-chop, there's a good fellow."

But the old man stood his ground and placed his hand over the doorknob when Kinlow reached for it. His mustaches began to undulate with what seemed to be a life of their own. Neither dark nor bushy, there was nothing of the Aegean about them. The two growths were set far apart and twisted into thin strands, so that the effect was of insect feelers or catfish barbels. He took off his glasses and wiped his eyes with his woolen necktie. "Here, would you care to look through my spectacles while I do out my eyes? Would you like to see how the world appears to Pletho Pappus?"

"No."

"It's not the phantasmagoria you might expect. It's not at all what you might expect. Won't you have a go?"

"No."

"The offer is not an idle one. I think you will be pleased."

"Get out of my way, you brute."

"Well, I mustn't keep you. Until tomorrow then, at one. Yes, the November Club, an excellent idea." He rubbed his belly with the flat of his hand and rotated his jaw about in ponderous chewing movements. "A bite of lunch and then some talk. Nothing fancy for me, thanks, a cold bird will do, with a bit of cabbage and some green onions. I can't remember when I last had green onions. With a drop of something along the way." He threw his head back and raised his fist to his mouth in a drinking arc, with thumb and little finger extended. "Then some serious talk. Blazing words, in such combinations as Sydney Hen has not heard before. Until tomorrow, then. A very good day to you, sir."

The next day at one Sir Sydney was a long way from his club. He was at sea having his lunch on board a Mexican sugar boat called *La Gitana*, the only transatlantic vessel on which passage for three could be found at such short notice. It was a comfortable ship. The weather was good. Babette, like most wives, handled adversity better than her husband, and she was determined to make a pleasant voyage of it, despite the lack of such amenities as a swimming pool, deck chairs and midmorning bouillon. The *Gitana* had a jolly master, Captain Goma y Goma, and a jolly crew. Each night after supper the off-watch gathered in the lounge under the bridge to hear Babette perform at the upright piano. Her milk-white fingers flashed over the yellow keys, true ivory, and she sang famous arias, after which there was a less formal session, a sing-along, with free beer, courtesy of the Señora. The party went on far into the night, with the men singing the ballads and dancing the dances of their native lands.

Hen took no part in it. He sulked and took to sighing again. He kept mostly to his cabin, but now and again appeared on deck, making his way forward to the prow, where he would strike a pose with his cape streaming behind him. He stood there at the very apex with his hands braced against the converging sides and his head thrust forward and cleaving the wind like a figurehead. He mused on the throne of Atlantis, and the crowned skulls of the ten princes, utterly lost in the mud many fathoms beneath his feet. He felt his isolation. He felt the great weight of being a living monument of Atlantis, indeed its only monument. Jimmerson and his crowd hardly counted.

The ship was three or four days out when Kinlow remembered to tell Hen about the old man with thick glasses. Hen, who was not very attentive to the spoken word, didn't take in the account the first time around. Listening closely to other people, he found, and particularly to Kinlow, hardly ever repaid the effort. The name Pletho did, however, register with him at some level, and later in the day he asked to hear again about the old man.

Kinlow made an amusing anecdote of it, only slightly distorting the facts. He told how he had been accosted by this false Pletho with a dwarf's wedgelike head and holes in his socks, and of how the man had been impertinent in seeking an audience. The old fellow made outrageous claims and obscure remarks, whereupon Kinlow cut short the blather and sent him packing, end of story.

Hen thought it over. He had a sleepless night. At breakfast in the morning he demanded a more detailed report. He
wanted a full description of the man and he wanted to know
his exact words. After this was given, he questioned Kinlow
closely.

"I want to see that man's business card. Where is it?"

"I threw it away."

"What was the address on it?"

"I don't remember."

"What amulet or ring did he wear?"

"None, that I could see."

"Did he have—great personal charm?"

"He had no charm."

"What did you make of his eyes? What impression did you
get from his eyes?"

"An impression of pinkness and of welling moisture."

"What evidence did he give in support of his charge that the
Gnomon Society was infested with cheesehoppers?"

"He gave no evidence at all."

"Just the bald accusation?"

"Nothing more."

"Did you inspect his boots?"

"I inspected his socks."

"Was he wearing a surgical boot on one foot? A heavily
built-up shoe on either of his feet?"

"I didn't inspect his boots. I can only say that they must have
been dark and shabby, in keeping with the rest of his togs."

"It did not occur to you that the man may very well have
been who he said he was? Pletho, in his sly mode?"

"Frankly it did not, no, sir."

"Or very possibly the Lame One?"

"No, sir."

"He may well have a younger brother, Teddy Pappus, for all
we know."

"Yes, sir."

"And you refused, repeatedly, to look through his glasses?"

"Yes, sir."

Hen dismissed Kinlow. All day long he paced the forward
deck in thought. He walked back and forth in the rain, with
a point of light, a bit of St. Elmo's fire, playing about on the

brass button atop his Poma. That night he summoned Kinlow to his cabin and had him relate yet again the account of the old man in the doorway. Kinlow appeared in his dancing pumps. He had grown tired of this grilling and was annoyed at being called away from the party in the lounge. Babette's opera selections were so much yowling to him, but that business was over now and the real fun had started. He put his hands on his hips and rolled his eyes in exasperation and rattled off the story again in a singsong manner. Then he whirled about to go.

Hen stopped him with a clap of his hands. "None of your pirouettes in here, sir! Don't turn your back on me! Be seated! This instant!"

Kinlow did as he was told.

Hen said, "You take far too much on yourself, Noel. Do you have any idea of what you've done to me? No, of course not. Thanks to you, I am a forgotten man. I am all but ruined, thanks to your Pyramid of Silence. And now in your brash ignorance you have turned away from my door the one man who—"

"Really, sir."

"Don't interrupt me. The one out of all others—"

"That sod? You can't be serious. I mean to say, really now."

"Not another word. Listen to me. Did the bulls' blood mean nothing to you? Think, man. The burnt bullocks of Poseidon. That was the sign. A child would have seen it. Pletho Pappus, I tell you, was at my very doorstep and you send him away like a beggar."

"You didn't see this man, sir. You didn't see his ears. You didn't smell him."

"What then, do you expect Pletho to appear before us in a cloud of fragrance? We know nothing of his current situation, what access he may have, if any, to a lavatory. His standards of personal hygiene may not be ours. He's an extraordinary man, I grant you, but he's only a man and this is just the sort of playful approach he would take. His little effects. The genuine Pletho touch. His pungent mode. He would hardly feel obliged to sponge down for the likes of you. I should have known him at once, fresh or foul. Oh, you make me sick. I can't bear the sight of you. Get out. Go to your cabin and remain there. No more fandangos for you, sir. Hand over those castanets!"

Kinlow brazenly defied the order and continued to move freely about the ship and to carouse nightly in the lounge. Hen went to Captain Goma y Goma and demanded that Kinlow be shut away under guard for the rest of the voyage. The captain temporized, not being clear on just what the offense was, and in the end he had Kinlow take his meals in the galley with the cook so that Hen would not have to look at him across the table.

Hen set off another stir late one night. He woke suddenly from a vivid dream and sounded the fire alarm, turning out the crew. It had come to him in the dream that Pletho, who could lower his respiration rate to that of a toad, had stowed away in the baggage. Nothing would do but an immediate search. All nine trunks had to be brought to his room and emptied, the clothing heaped on the floor. When this was done, with no result, Hen went about rapping on the panels, in the way of a conscientious volunteer examining a magician's trunk. But no hidden compartment was found and no dormant Pletho.

By the time the *Gitana* docked at Veracruz neither Kinlow nor Babette was speaking to Hen. Babette had made the mistake of trying to cheer up her husband. She went to him one afternoon, at the bow, with a surprise gift she had been holding back until the proper moment. It was an English rose cutting in a can of English earth—just the thing, she thought, to lift his spirits. But he saw the gesture as a taunt and he took the can and flung it into the ocean. Babette slapped his face and got rouge on her hand. He pushed her away.

Such bitter feeling led to a separation, with Babette stopping over in Veracruz for an indefinite stay. The accommodating Captain Goma y Goma made the necessary arrangements and personally saw to her comfort. Kinlow stayed too, in a small room adjoining Babette's refrigerated suite atop the Hotel Fénix. In the early morning he could hear the scrape of her coat hangers on a pipe as she selected her outfit for the day. They shared a balcony, where they took their breakfast together, with the harbor panorama all before them, and the marching naval cadets, and from which height Kinlow dropped orange peelings and worthless coins onto the heads of the sidewalk people some eighty feet below.

"Please yourself," said Hen to his two bedfellows, and he traveled on by train and bus to Cuernavaca, alone with his thoughts. He wondered if the gardener had cut back the oleander and the bougainvillea. He wondered if the maids had strangled his little dog. Of all the mysteries of Gnomonism, and there were many, none was so baffling to him as the mystery of how Pletho Pappus had gone about choosing Lamar Jimmerson and Noel Kinlow as the two men on the planet to whom he would show himself.

# IO

MAPES HAD made no measurable gains for the Society. The Veterans Administration, having looked over his prospectus and the *Codex Pappus* and the various works of Mr. Jimmerson, rejected without comment the Society's application to have Gnomonism accredited as a course of study for veterans—which meant no government money by way of the GI Bill. Diplomacy too proved to be a blind alley. Mapes's delicately composed letters to Sir Sydney Hen went unanswered, thereby stalling the Jimmerson-Hen understanding.

It all came to nothing, then, three years of hard work, or rather less than nothing, as the Society in Mapes's hands had actually lost ground. At the close of his stewardship there remained only two dues-paying Pillars left in the country, outside Burnette. One was in Naples, Florida, under the direction of a baker named Scales, and the other was Mr. Morehead Moaler's group in La Coma, Texas, just outside Brownsville.

Six big reclining chairs stood empty in the Red Room as a daily reminder to Mapes of his failure. He had bought these matching leather recliners and arranged them before the fireplace in a semicircle for the summit meeting that, it appeared, would not now take place. Mr. Jimmerson and Sir Sydney, with their aides, all of flag rank, were to have sat in them at varying angles, the ones they found most comfortable, feet well forward, this pride of recumbent lions hammering out the truce terms, popping up and falling back as the moment demanded, in the give-and-take of negotiation.

Mr. Jimmerson kept to his old wingback chair. Nearby was Austin Popper's chair, in which no one else was permitted to sit, not even Mapes, who had to provide his own, a stool, drawn up close to the Master, the better to get and hold his attention. This made for a clutter of chairs and tables in a fairly small area, seven of the chairs never used.

Mapes often felt that his words were lost in all the furniture. He could keep the Master's attention for no longer than two or three minutes at a time. There was no one else in the big stone house he could talk to. Mr. Bates was in and out of the hospital and Maceo never had much to say.

Mr. Jimmerson had lately taken to walking about in the Temple with his face in a big book of one kind or another. He moved at a slow glide through the rooms, reading silently. Now and then he stopped and broke into a low, appreciative murmur over some happy turn of phrase or some interesting fact come to light. "Just looking something up," he would say, with an apologetic grin, when encountered on one of these strolls.

Mapes came to the unhappy conclusion that the Master had lost his sense of mission and had abandoned himself to the study of antiquarian lore for its own sake. The old man simply would not bestir himself. He was content to pad around the Temple in his molting Poma, looking things up in books. He offered no guidance, no word of praise or blame. Mapes felt unappreciated and just barely visible in the long shadow cast by Austin Popper. He decided there was nothing more he could do. It was time to begin his new life in radio.

He remained at the Temple until the following spring, when he applied for admission to a school for radio announcers in Greenville, South Carolina. The school was owned and operated by an old army friend. A prompt reply came, offering him the position of dean of the school. He accepted, but put off telling the Master of his decision for a day or two, shrinking from what he believed would be a painful scene.

But the Master took the news in stride. He said, "You're much too hard on yourself, Mapes. We'll talk about that another time. Here, I want to show you something."

They were in the Red Room. Mr. Jimmerson held a world atlas on his knees opened to a map of North America. He had been tracing straight lines on it with pencil and ruler. The lines joined Burnette, Indiana, with Naples, Florida, and La Coma, Texas. "Take a look at this."

Mapes looked and said nothing.

"Well? Don't you see? How our Temple and the two Pillars form the points of an equilateral triangle?"

"Yes, I see that."

"It could hardly be chance."

"No, I suppose not."

"I was just looking something up in the atlas when it jumped out at me."

"Yes. I wonder, though."

"What?"

"This Burnette–La Coma line seems to be a little longer than the other two."

"A bit perhaps."

Mr. Jimmerson was peeved with Mapes, who, for all his dedication, had never shown warm feeling for the symbolic forms. He had a good mechanical understanding of them but the music escaped him. Neither was he quick, like Austin, to grasp the significance of a thing.

"Perhaps just a bit. Or a simple illusion. There is a certain distortion, as you well know, in all map projections."

"That's true."

"Doesn't this suggest something to you?"

"I'm not sure I see what you're getting at, sir."

"Gnomon solutions for Gnomon problems. No shadow without light. Pletho's Twenty-seventh Proposition."

"The Twenty-seventh?"

"'Look not to the meridian of the land of the seven rivers but look rather to the delta and know that the way in is likewise the way out.'"

"You see some application?"

"Certainly I do. What are we looking at here if not the Greek letter delta? You worry too much, Mapes, about trivial things, and you miss the important event right under your nose."

"I do worry about our slippage in membership. You don't think that's an important problem, sir?"

Mr. Jimmerson didn't think so. His reading of the situation was that no such problem existed. Gnomonism was self-correcting. The brotherhood had contracted, true enough, in terms of crude numbers, but that need not be regarded as a real decline. It might even be argued that the Society was now standing at flood tide, what with the perfect triangular balance of Burnette, Naples and La Coma. What they must do now was clear enough. This particular triangle with one side perhaps a bit forced, must be enclosed in a circle, a curving line that would ever so gently touch the vertices and then continue on its endless flight. Within that figure would be allegorical values to be carefully worked out, using Pletho's sliding segmentation scale and the compass of Hermes. Then, and not before then, the Jimmerson Spiral might be introduced into the calculations, with what amazing results time would show. The way in was the way out.

Mapes took his leave for South Carolina. Mr. Jimmerson and Mr. Bates and Maceo wished him well in his radio career. They said they would miss him but did not go so far as to ask him to stay on.

# II

I T WAS another spring four years later when Popper turned up at the Temple. Rumors about him had drifted in to Burnette but nothing in the way of direct and reliable reports. There was one story that he had been found dead of multiple gunshot wounds in a Joplin tourist court. Another one had him walking the streets of Los Angeles in an alcoholic daze, wearing brick-red rayon trousers, feigning deafness and living on charity. In yet another one he was said to be locked away in a state institution, where he was hopping, barking, twitching and kept under close restraint.

Mr. Jimmerson dismissed these rumors as nothing more than Sydney Hen's poisonous gossip. Austin had his own good Gnomonic reasons for whatever it was he was doing. He would return to the Temple in his own good time.

A light drizzle was falling on the day he came back. Maceo was outside, standing in the shelter of the gazebo. He was watching the big cement trucks with their tilted ovoid vats turning slowly about. Popper appeared on foot, picking his way through the construction litter. Maceo followed his approach but didn't recognize him in his horn-rimmed glasses, tan raincoat, black wig and soft plaid hat. There was nothing deceptive about the wig. It was ill-fitting and too black, and the hair was matted in ropes and whipped up into whorls and peaks and frozen in place with wax.

"Here, have a pen on me," he said to Maceo. "One of the new ballpoints. Say, what's going on here, my man? New highway? Elevated expressway?"

Maceo looked away and fell into the minstrel-show performance that he used with white strangers. "Sho is," he said.

"Right over the old stables. And look, the big oaks are gone too, and the rose arbor and the garage. There's the old Buick exposed to the weather. I don't like this. I call this a dirty shame. This was once such a showplace. That house was the architectural glory of Burnette."

"Sho was."

"I used to live here, you know."

"Sho nuff?"

"Is the Master in?"

"He at his books. Busy with his thoughts."

"I tried to call. What happened to the phone?"

"Mr. J. taken it out. He say nobody ever call 'less they want something."

"That's the Master for you. But what's going on? All the curtains drawn. The place is like a tomb."

"Mr. J. say some things easier to see in the dark."

"What a brain. That's the Master all over. You still don't know me, Maceo?"

Maceo raised his eyes and looked him over. "Well, I declare. Mr. Austin Popper."

"Sho is. Put 'er there, compadre. I'm back."

They went inside to the Red Room. Mr. Jimmerson was in his chair with a book. "Yes?" he said, peering up at the stranger with the grotesque hair. "Can I do something for you?"

Popper took up a position before the fireplace. He crossed his arms and arranged his feet in a Gnomonic stance and uttered the first words of the ancient Atlantean exchange.

"*Tell me, my friend, how is bread made?*"

"*From wheat,*" said Mr. Jimmerson, now roused.

"*And wine?*"

"*From the grape.*"

"*But gold?*"

"*You come to inquire of me?*"

"*I come in all humility.*"

"*It is well that you do so.*"

"*What is it then that you propose?*"

"*Whatever it is, you may be sure I shall perform.* Austin? Is that you?"

"It's me, all right. How in the world are you, sir? What are you doing here in this red twilight? You've put on some weight, I see. You and Maceo both. Here, sir, I brought you a little necktie organizer. I don't know what I would do without mine."

Popper gave no very good reasons for his long absence or for his failure to communicate with the Temple. He waved off questions about the recent past, explaining that he was still not free to discuss his intelligence work for the government. "It'll all come out in thirty years, that secret stuff," he said. He went on to say that he was now living in "a western city," where he was happily married to an attractive older woman named Meg. Meg not only had money of her own but was a trained dietician into the bargain. All their meals were scientifically planned and prepared. She bought him a new red Oldsmobile every year. They had a town house, a cabin on the lake, and kept registered spaniels. For two years running they had been voted the cutest couple at their country club. On alternate weekends, when they were not entertaining guests at home, they distributed baskets of food, representing a nice balance of the four food groups, to poor people.

"You'd love Meg, sir. She's just a great gal. But hey, I'm talking too much about Meg and myself. I want to get filled in on you. How I've missed the old gang. You and me and Mr. Bates. Huggins, Maceo, Mapes, Epps. What would be the odds on putting together another team like that? You couldn't do it these days. Tell me, sir, what's new with you? Can you put me current? Who's cutting your hair, by the way?"

"Maceo."

"I know you used to like your temples left full but they do say the close crop is more sanitary. Tell me, how is Mr. Bates?"

"He's in a nursing home."

"You're not serious."

"His back was hurting and so they pulled all his teeth."

"Doing fairly well now?"

"His back still hurts. He can't eat anything."

"But coming around nicely? Getting proper care?"

"They don't turn him over often enough."

"He's bedfast?"

"Not exactly."

"Gets up every day and puts on his clothes?"

"Not altogether, no. Not every day."

"Off his feed, you say."

"No, he stays hungry. He just can't chew anything."

"But his color's good?"

"Not real good."

"But otherwise fit? Has all his faculties? Takes an interest in community affairs?"

"Not much, no."

"How I've missed the old Red Room. But you know, I don't remember these recliners at all. What are all these big chairs for?"

"They've been here for years, Austin. Mapes brought them in here and lined them all up for some kind of meeting."

"Good old Mapes. Such a useful fellow to have around. I hear he's more or less running the show these days."

"Oh no, he's gone. Mapes left us some time ago. He went off somewhere to go into radio work."

"Radio repair?"

"I don't think so."

"Not commentary."

"Yes, I believe it was his plan to talk on the radio. I can't say I've ever heard him talking on the radio."

"What, Mapes at the mike? The big broadcast of 1952? I'm sorry, sir, I don't see it. I see Mapes at middle-level retail management. I don't see Mapes at the console with a bright line of patter."

"I may have it wrong. Do you still have your cockatoo, Austin?"

"Blue jay. No, sir, he caught the flu and died, poor little fellow. Back during the war."

"You didn't get another one."

"No, sir, I couldn't very well get another Squanto. Besides, Meg won't have anything around but blooded dogs."

"Look, Austin, your chair. I saved it for you. It hasn't been moved. Your room is waiting for you too."

It soon came out that Popper's visit was more than a social call. He had a plan. Life had been good to him, he said. His country had been good to him and Indiana had been good to him. Any number of people had been kind to him along the way, most memorably Mr. Jimmerson, who had taken him in when jobs were hard to come by, and who had launched him on the Jimmerson Spiral. Lately, in his prosperity, he had been reflecting on all this, and considering various ways of repaying the debt of honor. Direct handouts of money were not the answer. A shower of rupees in the street was always good fun but the gesture had no lasting effect. The solution he had hit on was political. Public service was the answer. His contribution would be to the cause of better government, whereby all would benefit. What he wanted to do was to help Mr. Jimmerson become governor of Indiana.

It was a breathtaking proposal. "Governor?" said Mr. Jimmerson.

"Yes, and I've already done a little spadework in preparation. You know Dub Polton, don't you, sir?"

Mr. Jimmerson made an effort of memory. "No, I don't think so."

"The writer? Surely you've heard me speak of him. My old friend Dub? W. W. Polton, our Indiana author?"

"No, I can't place him."

"I'm surprised. Well, you can take it from me, we're lucky to get him."

"Get him for what?"

"You've probably read his Western novels without making the connection. *Abilene Showdown? 'Neath Pecos Skies?* Dub wrote those under the name of Jack Fargo."

"I don't read many new books."

"Dub goes way back. He's an old newspaper reporter. His first book was a WPA project called *The Story of the Fort Wayne Post Office, 1840–1940.* It seems to me there used to be a copy of that lying around here in the Temple."

"I don't remember it."

"His first and, some people say, his best. My personal favorite is *Here Comes Gramps!* A humorous family memoir. You know how I like a light touch. Dub's a real pro, and not a bad egg once you get to know him. He's done it all. Humor, suspense, poetry, romance, history, travel—there's nothing he can't handle. He wrote *So This Is Omaha!* in a single afternoon. Did you ever read a detective story called *Too Many Gats* by a man named Vince Beaudine?"

"No."

"That was Dub. Does Dr. Klaus Ehrhart ring a bell? *Slimming Secrets of the Stars?*

"No."

"Dub puts that name on all his health books. How about Ethel Decatur Cathcart? I know you must have heard about her very popular juvenile series. All those Billy books—*Billy on the Farm, Billy and His Magic Socks.* The kids are crazy about them. Well, Ethel is Dub."

"I don't know any of these people and I don't understand what you're talking about, Austin."

"I'm sorry, sir. I can see now that I've only confused you by throwing all these names at you. I just wanted to give you some idea of Dub's background to show how fortunate we were in signing him up. He's a very busy man and he doesn't come cheap."

"Signing him up for what?"

"For your biography. The campaign biography."

"Oh come now, Austin, I can't run for governor."

"Why not?"

"You know very well that as the Master of Gnomons I can in no way involve myself in politics. Pletho strictly forbids it."

"*Partisan* politics. Surely that's the meaning of the rule. And a darn good rule too, if you ask me. But don't you see, that's what we're out to change. The demagoguery and deal-cutting. People are tired of these professional politicians who hog all the elective offices. Everyone trying to get his snout in the trough. I believe the people are ready for a scholar, who, at the same time, has proven executive ability. A man who won't be in there just to feather his own nest. The administrator of a great if little known empire. Why not Lamar Jimmerson for a change?"

"No, no, it's out of the question."

"Our problem is that you've been submerged here in the Red Room for so long. Our first job will be to put you on view in some way. Get you talked about. That's where the biography comes in. Then we'll line up some speaking engagements for you up and down the state. I'm telling you, sir, it can work. There's a time to lie back and a time to strike. I know how these things are done. Our time to strike is now. What is it they say? The man and the hour are met."

Mr. Jimmerson became agitated. It was such an incredible business and yet he had to admit that he liked the idea of the biography, and, come to that, of being governor. Why not indeed? Governors had to come from somewhere and it was his impression that more of them were elected by default, grudgingly, as the best of a poor lot, than by any roar of general approval. Who was the current one? Biggs? Baggs? Boggs? Bugg? Megg? No, Meg was Austin's wife and a fine woman too from all accounts. But *were* the people ready for a scholar? He thought not. They certainly weren't ready for Gnomonism. But then it was not as though you had to meet some absolute standard of fitness; you just had to get a few more votes than the fellows who happened to be running against you at the time, each one defective in his own way. The country had been off the gold standard for years. You wouldn't be running against George Washington, but only Baggs or Bugg. And Austin knew something about these matters. The swearing-in —that would be a grand moment. One hand on the Bible, the other raised, Fanny at his side. A solemn moment. Altogether a serious undertaking. Would he be a good and wise ruler?

He said, "I just don't know about all this, Austin. It's all so sudden and new to me. I have so much unfinished work to do here in the Temple."

"You bet your boots you do and I'm not going to take up any more of your time today. May I offer a thought? Sometimes it helps to put our ideas down on paper. Why don't you prepare a list of questions and we'll get together on it soon. I want you to meet Dub and we'll have to get the phone put back in. A candidate for governor will need a telephone."

Later in the week Fanny Jimmerson came to call. She too had a plan.

"Where's the boy?" said Mr. Jimmerson, who always put this question. It was not his practice to say the boy's name.

"He has his archery lesson on Friday," she said.

This was true enough, though any excuse would serve— a flute lesson, a head cold, his tummy hurt or he was having a tea party for his dolls and his baby owl. Jerome usually managed to beg off from these little day trips to Burnette. The gloom of the Temple frightened him. Maceo the black man frightened him. The fountain no longer gushed, no wading to be done there, and there were no children to play with, and no kittens, puppies or piglets to pet. His father, who, unaccountably, gave off wafts of a sweetish, tropical odor, something like that of a cantaloupe, frightened him too. When Mr. Jimmerson made an awkward attempt to embrace Jerome, the boy went stiff and arched his body so as to avoid touching the human tooth that hung from a chain across his father's belly. A gift from Sydney Hen in happier days, this relic was a huge yellow molar that was said to have been extracted posthumously from the jaw of Robert Fludd, the great Rosicrucian.

Fanny limped about the Red Room spraying disinfectant into the air. She spoke to her husband about his weight and about the dilapidated state of the Temple. There were stagnant pools of water in the yard, she said, and clumps of weeds that looked like cabbages. Things were falling into decay all around. Property values were plummeting in the shadow of the big elevated expressway that was cutting across the heart of Burnette.

She complained about the rats, who could be heard pattering and scuffling in the walls, and about Maceo, who continued to turn her friends away from the Temple. She had sent some people along—an Episcopal bishop, some bridge players, a Miss Hine, a retired physician, a troop of Brownies—to look in on Mr. Jimmerson and Maceo had turned them away at the door one and all.

"I don't understand it. I should think you would enjoy a bit of company now and then. It's not healthy, locking yourself away in here so you can eat pies and read all these monstrous books with *f*'s for *s*'s. Not a wholesome life, Lamar. I want to talk to you about Miss Hine and a new arrangement."

She took him out for a drive, then treated him to supper at a downtown cafeteria. He told her about Austin's return.

"Austin Popper? I thought he was killed in the war."

"He's been living out West with his wife, Meg. She buys him a new car every year."

"Austin Popper! With that purplish bird on his shoulder! I haven't thought of him in years!"

"The bird passed away."

He explained about the biography and the race for governor.

"Yes, that sounds like something Austin would cook up," she said. "I must say I always rather liked him, but you couldn't believe a word he said. Of course you're not going to do it."

"I haven't decided."

"You know your own business best, Lamar, but I believe you will be making a great mistake if you go ahead with this."

"Nothing is settled. I do want to talk to that Polton fellow about the book. Austin is meeting with him now. He's a well-known writer."

"Don't misunderstand me. I think you would make an excellent governor. President, even. Well, perhaps not President. I'm just saying that grubbing for votes is not your work. The hurly-burly of it all. Indiana is not Atlantis."

Shinn's cafeteria, their favorite eating place for years, offered good plain food and organ music. Quite a few unshaven bums were here tonight, Fanny noticed, more than last time, lingering over coffee and cigarettes and putting off the next move. Attracted, no doubt, by the blood plasma center next door, where they could always pick up a few dollars. The town was changing.

The dessert trolley creaked to a stop at the Jimmerson table. Mr. Jimmerson looked over the colorful display. He reached for a cup of yellow custard and Fanny gently slapped his hand away. "No, Lamar, you're quite mistaken if you think you're going to have a sweet."

The elderly lady at the organ finished her recital. She rose from her bench, acknowledged the thin applause with a smile that was greatly out of proportion to it, then made her way across the room to the Jimmerson table. Fanny greeted her warmly.

"Do sit down, Naomi, and have some coffee with us. How well you play. And look at you, always so well turned out. It's not fair, you with your musical gift and your eye for clothes too. You make the rest of us look like frumps. Lamar, you remember Miss Naomi Hine, don't you? She worked for me selling door to door until her legs gave way. Isn't she the daintiest thing you ever saw? A perfect Dresden doll. But don't be deceived, Naomi could put her little foot in the door with the best of them."

Mr. Jimmerson had seen this woman's pale head smiling and dipping and swaying above the elevated bulk of Shinn's organ but he did not remember having met her. "How do you do," he said.

"I've heard so much about you, Lamar," said Miss Hine.

Then Fanny got down to business and talked about the new arrangement.

# 13

For all his jaunty prose, W. W. Polton was a glum little man. Everything he saw seemed to let him down in some way. He was so small that he wore boys' clothes, little suits of a skimpy juvenile cut, the coats chopped off very short. He had the wizened walnut face of a jockey. He was rude. Time after time he cut Mr. Jimmerson short in his reminiscence. He had bad table manners and he scratched the parquet floors with the metal taps on his zippered, high-heel ankle bootlets. He drank one Pepsi-Cola after another, leaving behind him a trail of wet bottles atop fine pieces of furniture.

Mr. Jimmerson, informed by Popper that the artist could not be held to ordinary standards of civility, tried to make every allowance for the fellow. He talked openly to Polton about the Gnomon Society, revealing all that he could reveal to a Perfect Stranger, except on the subject of membership figures. In that area he was evasive. He described the workings of the Jimmerson Spiral and he talked of the high points in his life, of his dramatic meeting with Pletho Pappus in France, of the winning of Fanny Hen, of the flowering of the Society in the 1930s, of the Sydney Hen scandal and subsequent schism.

Polton, however, had his own ideas about the shape and content of the book. He had his own vision to impose and he arrived at the Temple with his own title for the biography—*His Word Is Law!*—before he had even met Mr. Jimmerson. He proceeded to fashion the work accordingly.

His methods of inquiry were odd, or so they seemed to Mr. Jimmerson. He rejected all suggestions from the subject of the biography and he refused to read any of the Gnomonic texts. Whenever Mr. Jimmerson ventured onto that ground, Polton cut him short. "Nobody wants to hear about those triangles, Jimmerson. Do I have to keep saying it?" Such structural matter as he needed in the way of names, dates and places, he gleaned from old scrapbooks and from direct interrogation of the Master.

Mr. Jimmerson felt that the questions were all wrong. For one thing, Polton seemed to have the idea that Gnomonism had come out of the Andes. He kept asking about "your curious beacons and landing strips in Peru" and "the pre-Incan race of giants" and "the sacred plaza of Cuzco." He pressed the Master about his "prophecies" and his "harsh discipline" and his "uncanny power to pick up signals from outer space," a power which Mr. Jimmerson had never claimed to possess. At the same time Mr. Jimmerson had to admire the man's virtuosity as a reporter, for in all these hours of grilling Polton took not a single note.

Popper, meanwhile, as chairman of the Citizens Committee to Elect Mr. Jimmerson, had prepared a long statement for the press, announcing the candidacy. The statement ran to six sheets. WHY NOT MR. JIMMERSON FOR A CHANGE? was the heading. Directly beneath, in slightly smaller type, were two more questions: WHO IS MR. JIMMERSON? and WHERE DOES MR. JIMMERSON STAND? Below that there came thirty-six thick paragraphs of very fine type, with a check mark by each one, introducing Mr. Jimmerson to the public and purporting to give his position on this and that. It appeared to be the usual campaign stuff—leadership, the future, education, highways, no new taxes at this time—nothing that anyone could be expected to quarrel with or read through to the end. Not even Mr. Jimmerson, with his hearty appetite for black lumps of print, could finish it.

Nor could the Indiana editors, who gave the announcement only a brief mention in their newspapers, those who gave it a mention at all.

"Don't worry," said Popper. "They'll have to take notice when the book comes out. They'll have to provide full coverage when you start making your speeches around the state."

Within a week the writing of the book was done, Polton's manuscript delivered. Popper changed the title to *Hoosier Wizard*, with the subtitle of *Conversations with Mr. Jimmerson*, and whisked the pages away to a job printer before the Master could look them over. His work finished and the balance of his $1,200 fee in hand—paid by Fanny Jimmerson—W. W. Polton moved on, this elfin artist in elevated bootees, anxious to begin work on a new Vince Beaudine thriller he had sketched out in his head while listening to Mr. Jimmerson, or pretending to do so.

"It was all so fast," said Mr. Jimmerson.

"Time is short," said Popper.

He spoke of "seeing the book through the press," and with the Gnomon Press no longer in existence, the Letts scattered, he had the printing and binding contracted out on a low-bid basis.

He did not speak of paying for it. Popper claimed to have a rich wife and, as Mr. Jimmerson remembered it, had suggested that he would underwrite both the book and the campaign, and yet now when the matter of financing came up, he went vague, saying only that his affairs out West were "unsettled." He seemed to be short even of pocket money. Again Fanny Jimmerson had to foot the bill—$7,000 for 21,000 copies of *Hoosier Wizard*. But that was the end of it, she said. They could expect nothing more from her in the way of subsidies for these Gnomon projects.

Popper told Mr. Jimmerson not to worry. "Funds will be rolling in soon from book sales and campaign contributions. You're going to love this biography, sir. I read it at a sitting. Dub has done a beautiful job. When you consider how little time he had."

They were in the Red Room. Mr. Jimmerson received his freshly minted copy of the book with trembling eagerness. His life in print for all the world to study! He turned through the pages, stopping here and there to read a bit. His conversation, he saw, had been rendered very freely. He could not, in fact, recall having made any of these preposterous statements, nor could he recognize himself in Polton's portrait of the Master of Gnomons.

"Corpulent genius" was fair enough. "Viselike grip" was good. It was pleasing to see his oyster eyes described as "two live coals." The fellow had a touch, all right, but how had he come up with such things as "the absolute powers of a Sultan" and "the sacred macaws of Tamputocco" and "Peruvian metals unknown to science" and "the Master awash in his oversize bathtub" and "likes to work with young people" and "a spray of spittle"? Why was he, Lamar Jimmerson, who never raised his voice, shown to be expressing opinions he had never held in such an exclamatory way that droplets of saliva flew from his lips?

And why was there no mention, that he could find, of Hermes Trismegistus or the Jimmerson Spiral? Why was his name repeatedly misspelled? What was all this about the big bathtubs? Why was so little space devoted to the exposition of his thought and so much space given over to Maceo—"the brooding darky"—who was presented falsely as that popular figure of melodrama, the sinister servant? Where did Polton get the idea that there was a gong in the Temple?

Popper said, "Why don't you read it later, sir? It's probably not fair to the book, just dipping into it at random like that."

"He keeps going on about Peru, Austin. I know nothing whatever about Peru, its major cities, its principal exports, let alone its secrets. I was expecting something—"

"Something quite different, I know. Don't worry, sir, yours is a perfectly normal reaction. The blanching, the starting eyes, the rapid breathing, the hand groping about for support. You should see your face. It's alarming, I know, like hearing your voice on a machine for the first time, but you'll get used to it. This is the way these things are done now. Some of that stuff you mustn't take too much to heart. We have to allow the writer his little fillips. He has to keep the readers moving along. Lazy bums, most of them, as you well know, and fainthearted to boot. A little diversion before nodding off is all those bozos are looking for. You must try to see it as a whole."

"Then you think it's a good book?"

"I'm not going to sit here and tell you that I approve of every single word. Frankly speaking, and just between us, there is more than one passage in there that I don't understand. I know for a fact that Dub has worked in some odds and ends he had left over from a book he did on South America, but that's a common practice now, I'm told, widely accepted, and really, when you get right down to it, where's the harm? I will say this. That work has its own Polton integrity. Give it some time. Believe me, *Hoosier Wizard* will grow on you. I'll tell you something else. It's going to make some people sit up."

But the thing that made them sit up was not *Hoosier Wizard*; it was a paragraph toward the end of the campaign statement that had gone unread until now. This was the dread Paragraph 34, which declared that Governor Jimmerson, upon taking office, would move quickly to sponsor legislation that would close all the nursing homes and old folks homes in the state, and further, would force all householders in Indiana, rich and poor alike, to take in their aged parents and care for them at home "until death should supervene and they be carried away in the course of nature."

The first person to see the threat, and perhaps the only one ever to read the entire document, was the editor of a labor union bulletin in nearby Gary, a man with a keen eye for the sleeper clause in a contract. He sounded the alert by way of a front-page editorial in his paper, with the headline A NUT FOR GOVERNOR? The editorial began with these words: "Who does this guy Jimmerson think he is anyway?" and closed with these: "Let's show this bum where he gets off!"

Others took up the cry. A tide of fear rolled across the state. The householders had visions of their old mothers and fathers suddenly appearing on their doorsteps in cracked shoes, sheaves of medical prescriptions in hand, their goods tied up in bulging pasteboard boxes at their feet.

The daily newspapers were unanimous in denouncing the proposal, calling it "hasty" and "zany" and "ultimately, when all is said and done, not in the best interests of our elder citizens." The chairmen of the Republican and Democratic parties called it "a gross imposition" and "just a terrible idea." In Indianapolis the Kleagle of the Wabash Klavern of the Ku Klux Klan told reporters he was looking over bus schedules in preparation for dispatching a small flogging squad to Burnette "to give this Mr. Jimmerson the whipping of his life." *The Thunderbolt*, monthly organ of the Communist Party, said, "L. Jimmerson is perhaps the least progressive of all the candidates and there is really nothing to be done with such a hyena except string him up by the heels like B. Mussolini." In country club bars there was angry murmuring and threats of taking to the streets in gangs to protest the Jimmerson family relocation scheme.

Popper said nothing. He was in and out of the Temple. Inside, Mr. Jimmerson glided about as usual with a big book in his hand, looking things up. He seldom read the political news in his paper and so was unaware of the furor, until the afternoon the man came to put in the new telephone. The first call to come through to the Temple was a death threat, taken by the telephone installer, who passed on the gist of the message. Wrong number, Mr. Jimmerson assumed, for why should anyone want to "rip his belly open." But then there were more calls, all from strangers and all abusive, and at the end of the day he knew he had done something to annoy a good many people out there.

But what? What were they talking about? Was this another of Sydney Hen's terror campaigns? Had Sydney broken out of Mexico? Perhaps these people were just disappointed buyers of *Hoosier Wizard*. If so, sales must have been brisk indeed, to judge from the number of infuriated callers.

"It'll blow over in a few days," said Popper. "A tempest in a teapot. I wouldn't worry about it. I've already sent out corrections to the papers."

"Some of those people sounded serious."

"All bluster. People who make threats never actually do anything."

They were in the Red Room. Mr. Jimmerson was looking over some of his old lecture material. He got a whiff of something off Popper's breath that he couldn't identify. It was rum. Popper's face was flushed. He hurriedly explained about the offending paragraph in the position paper.

"Then it's not *Hoosier Wizard*?"

"Not at all. It hasn't really taken off yet. I doubt if we have sold four copies. This is something else altogether. But it's old news and fading fast. Let me tell you what I have lined up for us."

"Fanny didn't think it was a very good book."

"Did she just skim through it?"

"I don't know. She said she couldn't see where all the money went."

"*Hoosier Wizard* is not a woman's book, sir. But that's not what this fuss is all about. It's about this Paragraph 34 that would close all the nursing homes. You told me how slack they were in rotating Mr. Bates on his bed. I simply expressed your concern and suggested a remedy. No real harm done. I've already repudiated it. I explained that it was just a trial balloon. That's yesterday's news and we must put it behind us. Here, let me tell you about my coup. I've lined up a major speaking engagement for us. On the twenty-fourth—mark your calendar

—we kick off the campaign with a speech at Rainbow Falls State Park. You'll be addressing the Busy Bees."

"Is that the lawyers' club?"

"The very exclusive lawyers' club. Their annual retreat. It wasn't an easy booking, I can tell you, and we must make the best of it."

"I've never been to Rainbow Falls. They say you have to watch your step down there on those slick rocks."

"Right here, see, two-thirty P.M., which was to have been free time, they've penciled you in on their program, between these seminars on 'Making the Worse Cause Appear the Better' and 'Systematic Estate Looting and No One the Wiser.' This is the break I've been looking for. It's a wonderful opportunity."

"Will it be safe? Fanny thinks I should stay in the Temple for a while."

"Perfectly safe. A woodland setting, a secluded lodge, a select audience. Oh, they may be put off a bit at losing their free time. I suppose some of them would prefer to be out on the links knocking a ball around and telling off-color stories, but remember, these men are senior attorneys and distinguished members of the bench. We don't have to fear catcalls or gunplay. They won't be hurling buns at you. They won't try to hoot you down and drive you from the podium. These Busy Bees have clout and money and we're going to need some of those people in our camp."

"All the newspaper articles about Rainbow Falls mention that slippery footing. It seems there's some kind of green stuff growing on those wet rocks down there."

"Yes, but you understand, sir, we're not going down there for a dip. We won't have time to wade the shallows with our trousers rolled up and our shoes in our hands. We're going down there to cultivate some of the most important men in the state. We need to stake out some key ground early. Wasn't it Bismarck who said, 'He who holds the—something or other —controls the—something else'? Controls the whole thing, you see. It was Bismarck or one of those boys with a spike on his hat."

"Kaiser Bill had a spike on his helmet. One of his arms was withered, you know, but I forget which one."

"We'll need a good strong speech. But not too strong. We don't want to overwhelm our audience the first shake out of the box. A light note won't be amiss, not in your opening remarks. An open, friendly tone. There's no telling what weird notions they have about us out there."

"Did you say two-thirty?"

"At two-thirty on the twenty-fourth, yes, sir. But I think we should leave early and allow some time for a little 'Let's get acquainted' session when we get there."

"That's when I have my nap. What about my nap?"

"You can sleep in the car. Maceo will drive us down in the Buick. Will it run, by the way? I've noticed weeds and flowers growing around the tires."

"We don't use it much."

Mr. Jimmerson had begun to move his papers about and hold them up to his eyes. "I've been looking over some of my old talks here, Austin. It's surprising how well they have stood the test of time, if I do say so myself. What do you think about giving them 'Gold, the Celestial Fire Congealed'? That was always well received."

"It would go right over their heads, sir. Something with broad appeal is what we want for the Busy Bees. Not too much about Atlantis. These men are clever but they are not attuned to higher thought."

"How about 'A Stroll Through History'?"

"Your survey of eleven civilizations? There won't be enough time. They're only giving us about twenty-three minutes and we'll want to leave a little cushion at the end for a question period. But not too much of a cushion."

"'Gnomonism Today'?"

"I don't think so. *Hoosier Wizard* gives us Mr. Jimmerson the Master of Gnomons. Out there on the stump we want to present Mr. Jimmerson the man. Our theme is change. 'Why not Mr. Jimmerson for a change?' That's our pitch. Let's try to work up something along those lines."

# 14

OVER THE following weekend Miss Naomi Hine made five trips across town in her little green Crosley car. She was moving her things into the Gnomon Temple. This was the beginning of the new arrangement, whereby the Temple, or part of it, was to become a rooming house, or "guest lodge," as Fanny Jimmerson put it. With some paying guests, she had determined, the big place could pay its own way and thus relieve her of a financial burden. The Gnomon Society, now little more than a corporate ghost, remained the nominal owner, but Fanny felt free to make these dispositions since it was she who had paid the bills for so many years.

Miss Hine, in exchange for a suite of rooms and a small salary, would act as manager. The guests were to be chosen with care. They were to be clean, quiet, nonsmoking, nondrinking Christian gentlemen of the kind that downtown landladies are forever seeking through the classified ads, and perhaps sometimes even finding.

Mr. Jimmerson was to be inconvenienced no more than was necessary. He, Popper and Maceo would keep their bedrooms and bathrooms, along with the Red Room, the screened porch and the inviolable Inner Hall. They would share the kitchen with Miss Hine. The roomers would room upstairs and enter through a back door so that Mr. Jimmerson would not have to see them and nod to them in their comings and goings.

No one had advised Maceo of the new arrangement and at first he refused to let Miss Hine into the Temple. His doorkeeping duties had become confusing. Mapes had instructed him to keep everyone out, by way of protecting the Master from insurance salesmen. Then Fanny Jimmerson had sent word down to let everyone in. Then Popper had come along and countermanded that order, ending the open-door policy. With all these threats in the air, Maceo was to screen out obvious thugs and yeggs, all newspaper reporters, which was to say all prowlers wearing shabby suits, and anyone else who looked the least bit odd. For Maceo this would be most white people. The Temple callers all looked more or less moonstruck to him and he could not be bothered trying to sort them out. A little wren like Miss Hine or a maniac with a machete, it was all the same to him.

But Miss Hine's entry was not delayed long and she was soon moving freely about inside the Temple, opening windows, pulling down old calendars and offering decorator tips. She even talked of "knocking out" interior walls.

Mr. Jimmerson had reservations about the new arrangement. He was concerned about careless roomers who might let bathtubs overflow above his head or doze off with burning cigarettes in their yellow fingers. He was suspicious of Miss Hine, the organ player, and her background in public entertainment. The woman was getting on in years but she was clearly a coquette, a flapper, with those scarlet fingernails and blue eyelids. Such women were blazing inside and he feared that at the earliest opportunity she would try to back him up against the kitchen table and press her paps against him and try to nuzzle him and kiss him, married man or not. Would she be parading around the house in her step-ins? Hardly a fit sight for Maceo to see. What could Fanny be thinking of, to put him in such an awkward position? It could only lead to the tawdry spectacle of two women, and old friends at that, fighting over him.

Several days passed and Miss Hine made no improper advances. At no time did she attempt to pin Mr. Jimmerson's ample hams against a tabletop, or touch him in a suggestive manner. But he remained wary and took care to stay just beyond her grasp, sometimes moving crabwise in a quick little shuffle that startled her.

Miss Hine had her own fears, and of course her own little ways. She wrote her name on bits of paper and strips of adhesive tape and tagged all her food. This, from long experience with female roommates, who, without permission, had guzzled her milk and gobbled her cherry tomatoes and pineapple rings and cottage cheese. Here in the Temple it was a needless precaution. Just as she had no designs on Mr. Jimmerson's person, neither did he have designs on her food, all very light fare.

Largely a leaf eater, she could make a meal out of a salad of sickly white shoots. She ate her supper at the cafeteria and such cooking as she did at home ran to cold soup, jellied soup, underdone fish and canned vegetables warmed up in a pan of tap water. Her bread was dry toast. Nothing there to tempt Mr. Jimmerson, no likely medium into which a love potion might be introduced.

On the morning of the twenty-fourth he was ready with his speech, despite the domestic upheaval. He was waiting on the screened porch. He looked at his watch. Austin was sleeping late again. He looked out over the grounds. Maceo was tinkering with the Buick. "The Burick," he called it. The builders of the elevated highway were standing about chatting and smoking. It was hard to catch them in the act of working, of actually joining one structural member to another, but somehow their work got done. The big concrete pilings had now risen to such a height as to block out the Chicago skyline, the higher crags of which had once been just visible through the industrial haze. The loss of the vista meant nothing to Mr. Jimmerson. The soaring handiwork of Chicago Man was less substantial to him than the orichalcum spires of Atlantis.

His glance fell on Miss Hine's sewing machine. She had established a sewing nook at one end of the long porch, and her stuff was there to stay from the settled looks of it. Natural light, she said, was just the thing for fine sewing, and she had proceeded to set up her tailor shop here, where, strictly speaking, she had no right to be. "The solarium," she called it.

The woman was popping up everywhere. Only last night she had proposed a game of cards in the Red Room, another area where she had no business. "How about a hand of canasta, Lamar?" she had said. "You're not doing anything, are you?" Not doing anything! Couldn't the woman see all those books and papers in his lap? Did she think he had time to waste on parlor games? She had her own sitting room, why couldn't she sit in it? She had also presumed on a very brief acquaintance to call him Lamar. There were just three people left on earth who addressed him so—his wife, Sydney Hen and Mr. Bates—and he saw no reason why this little woman should be the fourth. Not even W. W. Polton had taken such a liberty.

All this, with the best yet to come, the roomers. Soon there would be a pack of coughing drifters bumping around upstairs, alcoholic house painters and clarinet players, tramping to the bathroom at all hours of the night. Still, to give the woman her due, she had been very decent in offering to mend his clothes and in putting her tiny car at his disposal. She had brought no cats along with her and no miniature dogs. She did not whinny or titter and had not, so far, tried to embrace him. And, in any case, someone would have to stay behind as caretaker of the Temple when he went to Indianapolis. He would need Maceo at his side in the governor's mansion.

One term, at his age, would probably suffice. Was it two years or four? He read through the closing words of his speech and shook his fingers outward in a remembered gesture from the lectern. It was good to be active again. It was all coming back to him now and he was eager to face his old adversaries, the ignorance and indifference of men, row upon row of blank faces and fallen jaws. It was a good speech with an interesting theme, change, although, to be honest, he had never really seen himself as an agent of political change.

What could he, Governor Lamar Jimmerson, Master of Gnomons, do for his fellow citizens? One service came immediately to mind. As his first official act he would order the Parks Department to install a guardrail all around the base of Rainbow Falls, with plenty of warning signs. Such an inviting place and yet so treacherous. At this very moment white-haired judges and rumpled old family attorneys were down there losing their footing and crying out as they fell and bruised their buttocks on those cruel green rocks, first slick and now hard. But then downstream a bit, below the cascade, all violence spent, wouldn't there be a limpid pool where older men in prickly blue wool bathing briefs could paddle about unobserved with swim bladders under their arms?

Outside there was a roar and an expanding plume of white smoke. The construction workers had pushed the Buick off to get it started. It was a 1940 Buick Century, black, with four doors, a straight-eight engine, the starter button under the accelerator pedal. Maceo, behind the wheel, waved off the pushers with thanks, then turned to look at Mr. Jimmerson on the porch. Mr. Jimmerson nodded once in response, to acknowledge that the Buick was living and breathing again. They looked at each other across the way for quite some time.

It was almost ten o'clock when Popper emerged from his room, smelling of rum. He was nervous. His smile was tight. The black wig was riding low on his forehead. He made no apology for being late.

"Are we ready? Is everything in hand? Pawing the dirt, are you, sir? We need to shake a leg. Has Maceo loaded the books? Here, sir, let me help you with your Poma. There we go, snug does it. Say, what happened to the hair on this thing?"

"It's been falling out for years."

"The dapple effect is lost."

"Yes."

"It needs something to set it off."

"No, it's all right."

"But your Poma no longer has focus, sir. It needs something —right here at the peak, some culminating event. A big yellow jewel would do it, or no, a blue Christmas tree bulb powered by a hidden battery. A soft blue radiance atop the Cone of Fate."

"No, it's all right the way it is, Austin. I don't want my cap wired up. It's Sydney who likes trinkets. He has a brass ball or a marble on top of his Poma. That's not for me. You know how I feel about trinkets."

"Your scorn for ornament. I did know but had completely forgotten."

They joined Maceo beside the rumbling, smoking Buick and there engaged in a discussion over which car to take. Mr. Jimmerson was for the Crosley, he having no confidence in the rotted tires on the Buick. Popper argued that the Crosley was too small for three men and several hundred pounds of books. Maceo agreed, and said that he did not care to wear his chauffeur's cap if they took the Crosley. Mr. Jimmerson pointed out that the Crosley was a later model than the Buick, with sound little tires, offering less risk of breakdown.

"But the Crosley is not a touring car, sir," said Popper. "What about your rest? Have you thought of that? I know a little something about sleeping in cars and, believe me, no one has ever taken a nap in a moving Crosley. And what will those lawyers think when we come driving up in such a clownish little car, with the back bumper dragging from all the weight?

'Look, here are three fellows coming up in a pale green Crosley. I wonder who they are. I wonder what their visit means. Pranksters, you think?' Now is that the kind of reception we want? No, sir, the Crosley won't do."

Mr. Jimmerson tapped a sandal against one of the Buick tires. He now wore thin white socks to protect his feet against the chafing straps. "But look at those cracks," he said. "You can see the cords. We could have a blowout and turn over. We might find ourselves stumbling around in a pasture holding our bloody heads."

"They'll hold up if Maceo takes it slow. Heat is the great enemy of tires."

Maceo loaded the Buick trunk with boxes of *Hoosier Wizards*. Popper and Mr. Jimmerson sat in the back on seats of dirty brown plush.

They were off. Out on the highway the white exhaust smoke increased in volume. The cars behind them had to drop back from a normal interval or be caught in a choking, blinding whiteout. The drivers of these cars were hesitant to pass, to move into the dense cloud, the unknown, and, with Maceo taking it slow, there soon developed a long, creeping, serpentine motorcade behind the black Buick.

"Let them honk," said Popper. "A very low form of expression. If they knew who they were honking at they would blush."

Inside the car the sweet smell of rum was strong. Mr. Jimmerson rolled down a window to get relief and asked Popper if he had taken to drinking in the morning now. Popper did not answer the question. Instead, he reached over to Mr. Jimmerson's wattles and took a fold of flesh between thumb and finger. "Patches of gray bristles," he said. "Here and here. You missed a spot or two with your razor. It doesn't look good at all."

Mr. Jimmerson recoiled, and said, "I don't believe I would talk about anyone's looks, Austin, if I was wearing a Halloween wig like you."

Popper raked the clotted black locks out of his eyes. "I'm sorry, sir, I don't know what got into me. I'm on edge, I'm not myself today. Don't pay any attention to me. It's not a pleasant subject, which of us looks the worse, and I should never have introduced it. I doubt if the point could ever really be settled. The truth is that all three of us, Maceo not excepted, could do with a facial tone-up. What am I talking about? I'm sorry, sir, it's my nerves. I had a bad dream last night. I was out in a desert and a rat crossed my path. He was not scurrying, with abrupt starts and stops, none of your rat sprints, but loping like a cheetah. His ears were laid back. This rat had no local business to see to. He was on a cross-country mission. A rat of doom. When I woke I was soaked in sweat and my heart was thumping, and so I had a couple of rum-and-tonics on an empty stomach. I'll be all right when I get a bite to eat. Once we get this maiden speech out of the way everything will come right. Did you have a good breakfast, by the way?"

"Yes."

"Meg calls it the most important meal of the day."

"I had a good enough breakfast but what are we going to do about my lunch?"

"No need to worry on that score, sir. They'll have a lavish buffet down there if I know my lawyers. Great red haunches of meat and crystal tureens piled high with chilled shrimp. Expense no object. These are not abstemious men. It won't be a soup kitchen."

The tires held all the way to Rainbow Falls State Park. The streamer of smoke gave an illusion of speed and as the Buick rolled down the woodland lane it was like the passing of a comet. But the arrival caused no stir. There was no one on the veranda to greet the Master, no receiving line, no photographers, no reception of any kind. Rain was pattering on the leaves. Maceo began unloading the books. Popper led Mr. Jimmerson up the steps and into the great timbered hall.

The lawyers were drowsy. They had been feeding and drinking for more than an hour and many of them were sunk in leather chairs and couches, dozing, the older ones blowing like seals. A few were still on their feet, standing about in pairs, at the bar, around the snooker table, before the cold fireplace, laughing quietly as they exchanged stories of daring raids on public funds, strife fomented, judgments consumed, snares successfully laid.

At the rear of the big room a boy in a short red jacket was sliding a wooden beam across the doors to the dining room. He was locking up. Luncheon was done.

Popper said, "It looks like a fellowship hour."

"Where is the waterfall, Austin? Did we pass it?"

"It's down there in the woods somewhere. This is just what I was counting on, sir. We can meet with these fellows on an informal basis before you give your address."

"Is that the falls I hear? I expected a different kind of noise. I never dreamed that Rainbow Falls would whir."

"That's just some mixing machine at the bar, sir, a little cocktail engine of some kind. Here, let's make the most of our opportunity. Let's wake some of these old bozos up."

Popper took the Master in tow and they went forth to mingle and ingratiate themselves. The first man they disturbed said, "Go back where you came from, fatty." The next two were a bit more friendly, mistaking Mr. Jimmerson for the stage magician who was to perform at the banquet that night. Another one asked to know the name and address of his hatter.

Soon, however, his identity became known. This was the mystical old bird from Burnette who, not even a member of the bar, dared to run for public office. This was the turbulent old fellow from the north who wanted to shut down all the nursing homes and quarter all the old folks with their sons and daughters. The word spread and the lawyers began to mutter.

"What is he doing here?"

"Who invited him anyway?"

"I like his nerve!"

"The gall of some people!"

"What a crust!"

"What a getup!"

"He comes here in his nightgown and tarboosh!"

"The very idea!"

"Of all the nerve!"

"Take a look at the other guy!"

"I thought I had seen everything!"

"This is the limit!"

"This takes the ever-loving cake!"

They began to close in on Mr. Jimmerson and put questions to him in a legal tautolog that he could not follow. The questions became accusations and before long the courtroom gobblers were baiting him from all sides, with no one to gavel them down. The Busy Bees were swarming. Young ones darted in to poke the Master's belly and tug at his gown. Popper tried to answer them and fend them off. Mr. Jimmerson's head swam. He stood there scratching the backs of his hands and saying nothing.

The cross-flow of words became a torrent. It was a talking frenzy. The lawyers were seized, possessed, with a kind of glossolalia. Their speech was no longer voluntary or even addressed to anyone. They jabbered mindlessly into the air, their eyes half closed in a transport, and one man was so driven that he had stopped uttering words altogether and had taken to mooing and lowing and moving his feet up and down in the slow clog dance of a zombie.

Then there came the peal of a little silver bell from above and the hubbub subsided, trailing off through a low ululation to, finally, silence. The strange delirium was broken. A man in a dark suit and with receding waves of gray hair was standing at the rail of the mezzanine gallery. He struck his little bell again with a silver mallet. The lawyers looked up at him, their chief.

"Order," he said. "Pray silence. Busy Bees, your attention, please. Thank you. Tipstaff? Will you wake those delegates on the couches? Will you clear the couches and make a thorough room check? Thank you. A clean sweep-down fore and aft, if you please. Turn them out, Tipstaff, prod their bottoms with your staff, and don't forget to check the canteen and the steam room for skulkers. While you're at it you might check the windows for peepers and sneaks who would learn our tricks. I hate to break up your naps, gentlemen, and your romp, but we have a full docket this afternoon and we really must turn to. It's time to put our brandies and panatelas aside and proceed to business. First, an announcement. A little surprise, or rather a big one. An unexpected guest. I have here at my side a distinguished U.S. Attorney. It is my privilege to know him personally. All of you know him by reputation. So, without further cackle, I give you, gentlemen, the prosecutor's prosecutor, that celebrated pit bull of the Justice Department—"

A pudgy little man stepped forward to the rail. He wore a seersucker suit. His hair was cut in a flat brush.

The lawyers gasped.

"White!"

"Those full cheeks! It's Bulldog White!"

"He's got White!"

"Order," said the chief. "Yes, I have indeed got Pharris 'Bulldog' White, and what is more, my brave advocates, I have persuaded him to read us his full trial notes and citations from *United States* v. *Omega Gypsum Co.*"

White held a fat book aloft and the lawyers cheered.

"And that's not all," said the chief. "Bulldog has also very kindly consented to give us a report on loophole closing. Every year we are closing more and more, but, as we all know, there are still far too many human activities that can be carried on without the intercession of lawyers. Bulldog will give us the current rundown on that from Washington. Ludlow? Is Ludlow on the floor? Ah, Ludlow. It's short notice, I know, Ludlow, but I wonder if you would form up our glee club and give Bulldog a proper welcome."

The man called Ludlow began to shout commands. Thirty or so of the lawyers scrambled about and arranged themselves into three curving ranks. Ludlow stood before them. He rotated a fist high above his head and the men burst forth with a greeting. "Glad to have you, Bulldog! So pleased that you could come!" Then Ludlow sounded a note on his pitchpipe and the men hummed, some of them leaning well into the note. Ludlow raised his arms and the men sang.

> Go, go, go, go,
> Go where e'er you please,
> We're the bow'tied boys of the bar O!
> And aren't we busy bees!
>
> Hail then the

On they sang. Mr. Jimmerson was hungry, not to say weary, and things were moving too fast for him. His strength was failing. Where was the roast beef? Since breakfast at the break of day he had not seen so much as a celery stick. And how explain the behavior of these men? First they rail at him and now they seemed to be serenading him. This was what it was to leave home. These were the shocks to be met with outside the Temple. Would this music never cease?

The song had a good many stanzas. Pharris White stood at the rail, taking the tribute with a frozen smile. His gaze ranged over the scene below, then stopped and lingered on the fat man in the gown. *The Master of Gnomons!* That black man carrying boxes was his servant! And that fellow going for the door was—*Popper!*

"You there! Popper!"

Popper glanced back over his shoulder in the way of one who has heard a great rushing of wings, and for an instant the two men looked each other in the face. Even across that gulf and through the hairy clutter of disguise Pharris White knew his man.

"Stop him!"

"My file is no longer active, White!" shouted Popper.

"Your file will be active as long as I can draw a breath! Stop that man! That's not his natural hair! That's Austin Popper! I have a warrant for his arrest!"

But Popper was already through the doorway before anyone responded. He made for the woods and was crashing through the wet underbrush when the lawyers came storming out onto the veranda. There they stopped short, drawing back from the rain, and milled about, uncertain, awaiting guidance, while precious seconds were lost.

Pharris White appeared and they gathered about him expectantly, with most of them giving ready assent to the authority of this cherubic figure in seersucker.

The fleeing man, White explained to them, was one Austin Popper, a federal fugitive of many years' standing, once thought to be dead. He was an elusive fellow. He was not believed to be armed nor was he considered dangerous in the usual sense of that word. At the same time he was desperate and might well resist arrest with his fists, or, if one lay handy, a stick, or even by butting with his head. But they could be assured he was no bruiser. He was out there somewhere in a crouch but they need not fear his spring. As a runner he was probably no better than average for his age and weight. There was nothing in his record to suggest that either his speed or his endurance was in any way remarkable, and yet here again as a desperate man he might draw on hitherto untapped reserves. This man, the aforesaid Popper, affected an air of boldness. He was clever, though not a man of genuine learning. He lived by his wits. He sometimes traveled with a bird. For many years now he had been using writing paper taken from the Hotel Rollo in Rollo, Colorado. No one could say how much of that paper he had carried off. Of his women and his hobbies nothing was known. He held, or did hold at one time, a high position in the Gnomon Society, an ancient and secret order of global reach, with all that that implied, namely, unstinting aid from his brothers, curious winks and hand signs, a code of blood vengeance, access to great wealth, access to dark knowledge, knowledge that was not always fairly shared with deserving Neophytes of the order. These were a few things to keep in mind.

So much for the man himself. Now to the pursuit plan. It seemed to him, Pharris White, that a long line of beaters sweeping across the park would best meet the situation. They would drive Popper. Feints and stalking maneuvers and circling ploys all had their place, of course, but there came a time when you must engage your enemy directly and whip him in the field, and this, or so it seemed to him, was just such a time. He only regretted that they could not hunt him down with torches and dogs. Their sweep would converge on the rock dome known as the Devil's Pincushion, and there Popper would be taken. Then at last this man could be put away and given plenty of time in solitary confinement to gnaw on his knuckles, to think over his crimes and expiate them in cold darkness. Were there any questions? Suggestions? Had they understood his presentation and could he take it that they were in substantial agreement on all the main points?

It was a fairly long speech, given the urgent nature of the occasion, and there was further delay as the lawyers bustled about looking for sticks. Some of the men, a sizable minority, refused to take part in the manhunt, giving as their reasons advanced age, bad weather, compromised dignity, allergies, dependent children, obesity, fear of biting insects, potential mental anguish, pain and suffering and loss of consortium, unsuitable shoes, low-back pain, weak eyes, hammer toes and religious scruples, but there remained many willing hands and Pharris White soon had them deployed in a long skirmish line.

He stood at the center and a bit forward, facing them, the captain of a kickoff team. "Guide on me!" he shouted, to the left and then to the right. "Guide on my baton! Keep your dress and watch your interval! Now! Let's beat! Let's drive!"

He lowered his stick and the men moved out, flailing away at the spring greenery. Their blood was up again.

But there are many holes in the earth, not all of them scrabbled out with claws or tools of iron, and Popper had found himself a burrow long before that drive began. He sat dripping and panting in the dark hollow place behind Rainbow Falls. Far into the night he sat there in that spherical chamber behind a curtain of falling water. He considered leaving his hat floating suggestively in the pool below, then decided that Pharris White would not be so easily taken in. From time to time he dabbed at his hands with a handkerchief. Wet mud wasn't so bad, but dried mud, cracking with the flex of his hand, and tiny clods dangling from his finger hairs, that was not to be endured.

THERE FOLLOWED another long Gnomonic stasis. Twelve years passed before Mr. Jimmerson made another excursion. He was a pallbearer at the graveside service for Mr. Bates and he went to the doctor now and then but it was a rare day when he set foot outside his limestone sanctuary on Bulmer Avenue. He shunned the light of day and did not leave town again for some twelve years.

No other private residence was left on the street, now cast in cold shadow by the expressway that ran overhead. Standing forsaken, the Gnomon Temple rose up between two parts of the divided highway, within the acute angle of an important interchange, and it sometimes happened that a startled motorist made eye contact with Maceo as he stood before one of the broken windows upstairs, just a few feet away from the streaming traffic.

Directly behind the Temple there was now located a maintenance yard for the city's dump trucks and garbage trucks. This was not the nuisance it might have been because the hammering and clanging that went on inside the yard could not be heard over the traffic roar on the freeway, which was constant, except during the period between 3 and 4 A.M., when there was a slight falling off. Still, in the summer, there was a problem with dust from the yard.

Things had changed out front too. Bulmer Avenue lay in eternal gloom amid a colonnade of pilings, and had become a loitering place for vagrants, petty criminals and youth gangs. When the boys burned tires in the street, the smoke rolled down the corridors of the Temple and stung Mr. Jimmerson's eyes and blackened his nostrils. Tramps came to the door and asked about supper, taking the big house for a rescue mission. There were younger, daring tramps who in winter would lay a plank from one of the freeway pillars to an upstairs dormer window of the Temple, then crawl across it and bed down inside with the pigeons. They left behind them their names written on the walls, their poems, curses and drawings. On the floor they left a mess of wine bottles and newspaper bedding and foul droppings for Maceo and Ed to clean up.

At that, they were less trouble than the paying guests, now long gone, to Mr. Jimmerson's great delight, along with Miss Hine, her innovations and her endless complaints about the sour air in the house. What a time that had been. The vexations! The interruptions! The questions! His answers! *Yes. Yes. What? No.* What a trial for a man engaged in the fine labor of speculative thought. Ed was still here but all the others were gone now, and, with two or three haunting exceptions, their faces forgotten.

The upper part of the Temple had been practically abandoned. Everything upstairs was either broken or stopped up and that area was no longer in use. Winds played about freely through the rooms. There were leaks in the roof. Outside, the old Buick sat earthbound, a rusty black hulk with no wheels. Down in the basement rats nested in the cold boiler.

There was no heat in the house except for that given off by the fireplace in the Red Room, and it was here in the reclining chairs that Mr. Jimmerson, Maceo, Babcock and Ed slept through the long winter nights, the four of them laid out in a row with their hats and coats on, and their blankets tucked up under their arms, like so many first-class passengers on the Promenade deck of a Cunard liner.

Only here and there had the decay been held back. The kitchen still functioned, as did one bathroom. The purple curtains in the Inner Hall had faded and there were bits of plaster on the floor but on the whole this room had retained its static purity, similar to that of the innermost vault of a pyramid.

When the weather was pleasant, Mr. Jimmerson shuffled about from room to room with a big book in his hand, much as ever. "Just looking something up," he would say, in the same apologetic way, but with a grin grown dreadful over the years, so that the person encountered quickly turned away.

Fanny Jimmerson was no longer nearby to keep an eye on things, she having been promoted yet again and rewarded with an assignment to New Jersey, where she now sat on the board of directors of the cosmetics company and lived in semi-retirement. She lived alone in a modest white house about an hour's drive from the scene of her honeymoon, though she did not often make that drive. The boy, Jerome Jimmerson, who was trying to make his way on the New York stage, sometimes came down to spend a weekend with her, but he had his own life now in Japanese puppet theater, and of course his own chums in the close-knit puppeteer community in Greenwich Village, and he did not come down as often as she would have liked. At the beginning of each month, Fanny wrote three letters and mailed them out with checks attached; one went to brother Sydney in Mexico, one to her husband Lamar and one to her son Jerome. Such response as she got was spotty.

As for Miss Hine, she had been called away suddenly to assume another housekeeping burden. One day she packed a few things and drove down to Lafayette to care for her older but smaller brother, Arnold "Tiny" Hine, recently widowed and ailing. It was to be a temporary leave. She was to see Tiny through his convalescence, then return to the Temple. But Tiny's recovery was slow, much slower than the doctor had predicted, and then just when it was thought to be complete he was stricken anew with something the doctor could not quite put his finger on, for all his testing of Tiny's fluids. Tiny complained of a fire in his groin and of a kink in his neck. At times he was in pain—"Don't touch the bed!"—and at other times he was able to go out at night and attend the wrestling matches with his pals. Miss Hine was obliged to extend her stay indefinitely and see to her brother's needs. She fetched things for him, handled his extensive correspondence with coin clubs and coin magazines, served him three meals a day on a tray and turned his television antenna on demand.

This left the Bulmer Avenue rooming house in Burnette without a manager. Neither Mr. Jimmerson nor Maceo was willing to take on the job and attrition soon set in. The roomers got a free ride for a while, as Mr. Jimmerson did not bother to collect the rent, but in the course of things they moved on, fell dead or were arrested, one by one, and no new roomers were taken in to replace them.

The last one was Ed, a young sandy-haired army veteran who wore cowboy clothes and Wellington boots. Ed found a home in the Temple and refused to leave. The food, the pace, the air, the company—everything suited him. He stayed on and was given his meals and a little pocket money in return for helping Maceo around the house. Not that he was of much real help. There was hardly anything Ed could do, even under the strictest supervision. He carried a note in his wallet from a doctor, often brandished, saying that he did not have to work. Neither he nor Mr. Jimmerson could cook and they had a hard time of it, feeding mostly on day-old doughnuts, during that period when Maceo got mixed up with the Black Muslims. This was at about the same time that Popper got mixed up with the left-wing women far away, in an eastern city.

The Black Muslim episode was a curious one. Maceo left in the night and came back in the night without a word. He went to Chicago and stood on a street corner for a month or so wearing a fez, calling himself Fahad Murad, selling Muslim newspapers and trying to scowl at the passing white devils. But it didn't work out, he was no good as a public menace and he didn't find street life in the city fulfilling. He was perhaps too old to become a burning sword of Black Islam and late one night he came back to the Temple wearing his old hat with the Christian brim. He resumed his duties and his old name with no word of explanation.

Then there came bad news from Florida. Scales, the Gnomon baker in Naples, on the Gulf coast, had died, blown up in his garage during the course of an alchemical experiment. There would be no more newspaper clippings from Scales, with photographs showing big sinkholes in Alabama and Florida, giving support to his theory of continental subsidence. What had happened to Atlantis, Scales believed, was now happening to America, though at a less dramatic rate of collapse. Scales, as Scales, was not much missed, even by his family, but with his passing the Gnomon Pillar in Naples was lost, another one down with all hands, and with that loss went the southeastern anchor of the Continental Gnomonic Triangle. So it was that Mr. Jimmerson no longer had an enormous, skewed triangle to work with, but only a bare line from the Temple in Burnette to the last remaining Pillar in the country, that of Mr. Morehead Moaler in La Coma, Texas.

In many ways this simplified his calculations. Working out Gnomonic readings from a line, long or short, vertical or canted, was child's play. But a line had extension only and no depth to speak of. Was this fit work for the Master of Gnomons? Weren't these line readings with their tiresome recurring decimals very feeble stuff? The garage blast in Florida had, overnight, left the Continental Triangle a vast dead zone, and Mr. Jimmerson became despondent when he thought of spending the rest of his life at this paltry business of line analysis.

For a time he all but abandoned his studies, as he had once done years ago. Then one night when he was stretched out on his recliner, with snores and visible puffs of breath all about him, there came a flash of understanding, accompanied by a bodily spasm. The apparent impasse was, he saw, a new opening. A leap at his age! Who would have thought it? For all his accomplishments of the past, he was truly just now hitting his stride. How foolish he had been to think that his best work was behind him.

The leap resolved itself into something called the Jimmerson Lag, which was to complement and shore up the Jimmerson Spiral. The Lag would account for all those troublesome loose ends and recalcitrant phenomena left unaddressed or evaded by the Spiral, or nearly all of them. That which was confused was now made clear, or fairly clear. Briefly put, the Jimmerson Lag postulated a certain amount of slack in the universe. The numerical value of that slippage or lag came to .6002, as best Mr. Jimmerson could reckon it, taking into account the ragged value of *pi*, the odd tilt of the earth, the lopsided nature of the Continental Triangle and many other such anomalies. How Sydney Hen would fume when he learned of this advance! He had been so maliciously eager to belittle the Spiral, only to come around later in his grudging way, first calling it a lucky hit, then trying to claim it as his own idea! So it would be with the Lag. But how to reach Sydney? Was he still alive? He had been silent for a very long time.

With the principle of the Jimmerson Lag conceived and stated, there now remained the elucidation, or rather the obfuscation. The idea had now to be properly clothed in Gnomonic riddles and allegories at generous Gnomonic length. It was no easy task, forming these long sentences in one's head and dictating them against the roar of the freeway traffic, and

Mr. Jimmerson knew that he could never have done the job alone. Maurice was a godsend.

Maurice Babcock came late to the Temple. He was a dark-ish man about fifty years old, of retiring disposition, a court stenographer from Chicago, a Rosicrucian, not fat but with the soft look of a middle-aged bachelor who has a good job, money in the bank, no debts and no family responsibilities. Babcock did his job well. He minded his own business. He did not speak of his aspirations. He ordered his shoes from England, his shirts from Baltimore and his small hats from a hat shop in Salt Lake City that catered to the needs of young Mormon missionaries. He wore these hats in a seasonal color sequence, from opalescent gray through black, high on his head and dead level with the horizon. He took pills and time-release capsules throughout the day, avoided all foods prepared in aluminum cookware and ate a bowl of bran at bedtime to scour the pipes. His fellow workers regarded him as a hypochondriac but then it was not they who suffered from those dull headaches induced by chronic constipation. He remained a bachelor because there was no woman in all Chicago refined enough for him—Dolores herself did not really measure up—and out of a fear of female extravagance, and an even deeper one of getting tangled up in someone else's family. When he found himself alone in an elevator with a pretty girl he would smile at her with the heavy-lidded smile of an Argentine playboy, but saying nothing and meaning no harm. The girls turned away. In his spare time he read. He kept up with medical developments and indulged a taste for esoteric lore.

His introduction to Gnomonism came one Saturday morning when he was poking about in an old bookstore and ran across a cast-off trove of Gnomon pamphlets and books, including a copy of *101 Gnomon Facts*, one of the rare, unsigned copies. He bought the lot for a five-dollar bill, took it home and read it through with wonder, lost in triangles for the weekend. *This is the stuff for me.* He knew it at once. *This is what I've been looking for. My search for certitudes is over.* He hastened to Burnette and called on Mr. Jimmerson, hopeful of getting an autograph, a word or two from the Master's lips, more and thicker books, with footnotes longer than the text proper, perhaps even a signed photograph.

The shabbiness of the Temple put him off. The odor reminded him of the holding cells at the courthouse. He was a little disappointed in Mr. Jimmerson's conversation and badly shaken by his grin. The Master was not the white-maned old gentleman with gaunt face and long fingers he had visualized. The big tuber nose came as a surprise.

But for all that, Babcock came back again and again. He knew he was on to something this time. The Rosicrucians had finer robes and the Brothers of Luxor had eerier ceremonies, but in the way of ideas that could not quite be grasped, neither of them had anything to touch the Cone of Fate or the Jimmerson Spiral. Gnomonism was the first really sound synthesis he had found of Atlantean, Hermetic and Pythagorean knowledge. The only one he had found, come to that. In his head he could feel magnetic forces gathering. He knew of some people who would be surprised when the discharge came. And all for a five-dollar bill! What did the bookseller buy with it one-half so precious?

He was initiated into the Society on a day which he had reckoned to be the cusp of a new Gnomonic cycle. The Master had wanted him to revive the Pillar in Chicago but Babcock begged off, saying he preferred to work here at the Temple, at the heart of things, the big things soon to come. Here under the Master's gaze he could hone himself to a fine edge. The wheel was turning, a time of increase was near and Maurice Babcock's proper place was right here at the center of it all. He saw a map take fire and blaze up, as in the movies when they wish to show the spread of something, usually pernicious.

The workload was overwhelming, for Babcock tried at first to keep his court dates and see Dolores and his doctors now and again, as well as take down Mr. Jimmerson's halting words on his stenotype machine. On the commuter train he studied for his advanced degrees. Back and forth he went between Chicago and Burnette, at all hours. Some nights he slept over in the Temple, collapsing on the reclining chair that had been assigned to him. It was not next to the Master, or at the other end, but, to his annoyance, between Maceo and Ed. Ed said he had "dubs" on the end chair.

Babcock's health, never good, declined. His head throbbed under the overload. His ears rang. Once he lay on his recliner for two days without moving or speaking. He lay there with his mouth open and his hands clenched at his sides, unable to speak or raise his head. Birds might have lighted on his face and walked around. No one disturbed him, a long lie-in was hardly an occasion for comment in the Red Room, but when he came around and regained muscular control he was frightened. Then and there he decided to quit his stenography job, at least until such time as he could come to grips with the situation here at the Temple. First things first. He gave up his Chicago apartment, cut his professional moorings and came to live in the Temple.

Three major projects were in hand. In the morning Babcock worked with the Master for an hour or so on the Jimmerson Lag, and then, for a brief period before lunch, on reconstructing the original text of *Gnomonism Today*. Through some mishap at the Latvian printshop, every other page had been left out. Many years had passed since publication but no one had noticed the error until Babcock caught it with his eagle eye. It was not so much that the flow of the work was disturbed or that the broken sentences from one page to the next did not connect—Gnomon literature was not, after all, that tired old business of a thread to be followed, but more a bubbling spring of words—it was the page numbers. What caught Babcock's eye and escaped all others was that the page numbers were not consecutive.

The third project was the new autobiography. After the long midday rest, Babcock took notes for the new version of Mr. Jimmerson's memoirs, for he, the Master, was still not satisfied with *Hoosier Wizard*. There were good things in it, the book had grown on him, as Austin had predicted, and yet at the same time there was something—*wrong* with it. W. W. Polton had gone wrong somewhere. The book had made little impact on the world. There had been only one review and that a very brief one by some ignorant woman on the local newspaper. "Of limited interest," she had written, and "Pays no compliment to the reader's intelligence." These phrases had stuck in Mr. Jimmerson's head, as two of the more favorable ones, such as might have been extracted for use in promotion of the book. But it was not the words themselves that stung—how could a woman, and a journalist at that, ever hope to understand

Gnomonism? No, the insult lay in the notion that the life and work of Lamar Jimmerson could be dismissed in a single paragraph no longer than a weather bulletin. But the way in was the way out. This new, genuine memoir would put things right. It would be a true autobiography, every word his own, as taken down by the scrupulous Maurice, and this time the world would be forced to take notice. Sydney Hen would have to take notice. A treat for Gnomons and the lay public alike.

Babcock, unlike Polton, did not try to impose his own ideas on the work. He said nothing but he did think the Master dwelled too much on this man Popper, last seen years ago, in flight at Rainbow Falls State Park. It was Austin this and Austin that and please don't sit in Austin's chair. Popper was none too honest, from what Babcock could piece together, a shady customer who had taken to his heels at least twice, just a step or two ahead of the police. Hardly the stuff of high Gnomonism. But the Master would hear nothing against him. He said that Austin was currently moving in some orbit known only to himself, and that he would return to the Temple in his own good Gnomonic time, to take his place in his chair again, to make known the true reasons for his disappearance, together with all the facts about the woman Meg.

Babcock resented Popper, or his shadow, and he was uneasy around Ed, who was all too palpable. He took Ed for a Southerner and tried to stay clear of him. He seldom spoke to him and then only in the imperative mood, master to servant. Babcock knew no Southerners personally but he had seen them in court often enough—Boyce and Broadus and Buford and Othal, and queried the spelling of their names—and Ed's manner and appearance said Dixie to him. He imagined Ed at home with his family, a big one, from old geezers through toddlers. He saw them eating their yams and pralines and playing their fiddles and dancing their jigs and guffawing over coarse jokes and beating one another to death with agricultural implements. Later, through a quiet investigation, using his court connections, Babcock found that Ed was actually from Nebraska, so it wasn't as bad as it might have been, though Nebraska was bad enough.

The confidential records showed that Ed had been discharged from the army for attempting to chloroform women

on a government reservation. The police in several cities suspected him of stealing car batteries and of vinyl slitting. His
mother kept a costume jewelry stall at a flea market in Omaha
and Ed had once tried to run her down with her own car, while
she was in the stall. He had destroyed the fixtures in a North
Platte bus station after losing some money in a vending machine, and had twice set fire to his hospital ward. The medical
report stated that the mahogany tint of Ed's skin was the result
of excessive use of coffee and tobacco, and that while working
as a hospital orderly he had a recurring daydream in which he
was a green-smocked physician with flashing scalpel. It went
on to speak of his "rabbit dentition," to describe him simply
as "odd," and to say that he was "disgusted by people crazier
than he is." Ed's trade was vinyl repair, learned in a government
hospital, though it was indicated in the records that Ed had
opened many more breaches with his razor blade than he had
ever closed with his invisible patches, so called, which leaped to
the eye and never held for long anyway.

Babcock went to Mr. Jimmerson with the reports. He said
he didn't mind so much an occasional outbreak of upholstery
slitting, but were they wise to sleep in the same room with
a pyromaniac who had surgical fantasies? Would they not be
wiser to ease Ed out of the Temple, to find him a room and
a job in Chicago or, better yet, Omaha? It was either that or
chain him to a bed in the attic.

But Mr. Jimmerson wouldn't hear of it. "No no," he said,
"Ed's a good boy. You'll see. He gives no trouble and he's a
big help to Maceo in opening jar lids and keeping the tramps
shooed away. Have you ever looked closely into Ed's eyes,
Maurice?"

"No, sir, I have not."

"The whites have a yellowish cast. But it's more than just
his eyes. There are certain other things too that I can't discuss.
You don't think Ed came here and took a room by chance, do
you?"

"I'm not sure I see what you're getting at, sir."

"It's an idea of mine. You see, I believe that Ed may be
Nandor."

"Ed? One of the Three Secret Teachers?" He smiled at Mr.
Jimmerson with his Latin gigolo smile.

Mr. Jimmerson turned away from it. "I can't say for sure but there are many little things that point that way. There's something in the wind. I can sense it. Something coming to fruition. It may or may not have anything to do with Ed. Time will tell. Besides, we need Ed. Ed's a good soldier. I'm an old soldier myself, you know."

He grinned. Babcock turned away. So that was that. The Master had spoken.

Nor did Babcock have much success in persuading Dolores that this great change in his life was for the best. He went over it again and again, telling her what he could, trying to make her understand the significance of the move.

Dolores was a little younger than Babcock. She was a druggist who lived over a drugstore in the Edison Park section of Chicago with her elderly father, who was also a druggist. She was devoted to her father and to the red-brick drugstore building, valuable corner property, to which one day she would fall heir. Her father's name and the date of construction were spelled out in little hexagonal tiles in the foyer. Dolores was no longer devoted to pharmacy; it was no longer a calling. The great days of pharmacy were over and she had seen the tail end of them, when one weighed powders on delicate balance scales, pounded crystalline substances in a mortar, bound wounds, gave injections and freely prescribed for the neighborhood. Now it was only a matter of counting out pills and typing up labels for the little bottles. Babcock, whom she kept well supplied with samples of all the latest potions from the drug companies, came a distant third in her affections, but still she liked to have him around. She too was reluctant to marry, lest she jeopardize her clear claim to the drugstore, and put her married brothers back in the running for it, but there would come a time, she thought, when she and Maurice would make their home together over that same drugstore.

She said, "You know what I'd like to do, Maurice? I'd like to go over there and look at their towels. Check out the bathroom and the refrigerator. I'd like to size these people up."

"Not today, Dolores. Don't start in again."

"But a tower in Burnette, Indiana. At your age. A professional man like you. I just don't get it, Maurice. I just can't believe there's much to it. You tell me you're sleeping in a chair. You admit you can't get your apricots stewed the way you like them and you say you can't get your brown eggs or your three-bean salad at all. Can't you see you're living in a house of—cards? I almost said a house of pancakes."

"You keep calling it a tower, as though that made it ridiculous. You know very well that it's a Temple and I don't know why you pretend to misunderstand these things. It's not very becoming to you."

"But I never see you anymore, honey. Who's cutting your hair, by the way? It's so short and ragged."

"A man named Maceo. He works at the Temple."

"Your Temple has a barbershop?"

"No, of course not."

"Is that part of it? Short hair?"

"Part of what?"

"Your ritual."

"No, it's just that I'm very busy these days and Maceo is something of an amateur barber. He has these squeeze clippers. He cuts the Master's hair too."

"It makes your head look so small."

Babcock had not thought of his haircut in that way but now he wondered. This pinhead effect—would it slow his advancement? Ruffled, but feigning an icy calm, he said, "My hairstyle and my apricots are not of the slightest importance. What is important is my work. All I ask, Dolores, is that you make an honest effort to understand this decision I have made. So far you have made no effort at all."

Dolores said she would try. But what she continued to see in her head was an old man cackling in a tower.

Fᴀʀ ꜰʀᴏᴍ keeping the tramps shooed away, Ed visited with them every afternoon at the dry fountain. There they napped against the retaining wall and there they perched on the rim of the dry basin, undisturbed, except now and then when the street boys, a shrieking mouse pack, attacked and scattered them with volleys of rocks and chicken bones. Ed went out daily to chat with the tramps and to collect his cigarettes, two or three from each man, filtered or unfiltered, ready-rolls only, no butts or "snipes" accepted, and no menthols. The tramps came to understand that this was the price of resting at the Gnomon fountain, and of Ed's company.

Ed was there on that afternoon in early winter when the blue van pulled up before the Temple. It was a camper van with a roof extension, a white plastic carapace. A constellation of seven white stars was painted on the side of the van and under the stars there were white words.

BIGG DIPPER ENERGY SYSTEMS
CORPUS CHRISTI, TEXAS

This was an event, a vehicle stopping at the Temple, and Ed watched closely. The tramps were burning a sofa in the fountain. Ed was standing there with them in their hand-warming circle. A passenger got down from the van, an older man, and Ed broke for the front steps to intercept him.

"Hold it! You can't go in there!"

"Oh no?"

Two cowboys in a standoff. The older man was wearing a cowboy hat and eyeglasses—not a good combination—and a pale blue suit of western cut with bolo tie. His cowboy boots were made of the pebbly hide of some caramel-colored reptile. He carried a briefcase. On a little finger, deeply embedded in the flesh, there was the plain gold ring of a nightclub singer.

"Who says?"

"No visitors without an appointment. Mr. Babcock's orders."

"Look at this place. It's the House of Usher. Is the Master in?"

"He's always in."

"Who are you?"

"Ed. I'm security."

"Head? Your name is Head?"

"Ed!"

"Well, speak up, Ed. Speak from the chest. Say it with confidence. 'My name is Ed, sir, and how may I be of service to you?' You'll never get anywhere in life mumbling your name like that. Here's a dollar for you and a little perpetual calendar. That's the last calendar you'll ever need. I want you to help Esteban with my bags and then you can get back to your campfire and keep an eye on my motor home."

Ed was dazzled by the stranger's boots. He took the dollar and the little plastic calendar and gave way.

It was an older and thicker Austin Popper, never doubtful of his welcome, come home again to the Gnomon Temple. He started for the door, then had a further thought. "No, the bags can wait." He called out to Esteban, his driver, and told him to collect the tramps at the fountain and take them downtown to Shinn's cafeteria and stand them to a good meal, then to a matinee if there was a picture playing that he and all the tramps could agree on. "But no beer and no cash handouts. You too, Ed. Go on, round up your pals. It's a treat on Esteban and me."

Popper seemed to be puzzled by the objection. He said, "Hot? Brownsville?"

Mr. Jimmerson said, "Well, as you know, Austin, I've never been there. I've just always thought of Texas as a burning land. With scorpions and those desert frogs that spit blood from their eyes. I associate that country with citrus fruit. Don't they call that part of Texas the Panhandle?"

"No, sir, they call it the Valley, but you're right about the fruit. Everywhere you turn in Brownsville and La Coma there are Ruby Reds for the plucking. The sweetest grapefruit in the world. Did I not mention Mr. Morehead Moaler's grove? As for the heat, well, yes, there are some sultry days in July and August, but nothing we can't handle with loose clothing and plenty of liquids. Mr. Moaler's place is, of course, fully air-conditioned. On those hot days we can estivate."

It was late at night and once again Popper was sitting before the fireplace in the Red Room with a proposal for Mr. Jimmerson. Three fifty-pound bags of grapefruit, a gift, lay at his feet. He showed photographs of La Coma with its palm trees and little oxbow ponds. There was a dim picture of Mr. Morehead Moaler in his wheelchair, holding what appeared to be a basketball in his lap. Babcock was tending the fire and listening intently, as in court, without looking at either party, his face impassive. So this was Popper. These were his words. Trucks were blatting on the freeway and at intervals Ed could be heard laughing in the kitchen. He, Maceo and Esteban were back there watching television.

Mr. Jimmerson said, "Pletho tells us we should all sleep in our own beds."

"Beds, yes," said Popper. "He says nothing about reclino chairs."

"I just don't see how it can be done, Austin. I don't see how the Master can leave the Temple."

"By simple decree."

"But isn't travel largely nonsense?"

"Travel is total nonsense. It's a great fraud. Our old friend Zeno tells us that motion is impossible—and proves it, the Greek scoundrel! Well, I can't go that far. I can't go along with Zeno all the way on that, but I do know that travel is one of the greatest hoaxes of our time. But look here, sir, what I'm talking about is not travel as such. We're not going on a sightseeing tour. What I'm talking about is a new life in the sun."

"No, I'm afraid it's too late for me, Austin. I don't see how I could ever leave the Temple. There's too much work left here to do."

"Excuse me, but I don't see a Temple. I see a shell. I see red silk peeling from the walls. You're buried alive here, sir, in the world's noisiest tomb. How can you talk of work with those trucks out there going like the hammers of Hell? Look, our eyes are watering from the fumes. The very air is evil. I don't think you realize what's happened. The Telluric Currents have shifted away from Burnette and nothing can prosper here. Look at Bulmer Avenue. Do you remember how it used to be? Now it's a street of bums and juvenile bullies. On every block you can see a twelve-year-old boy holding a six-year-old boy in a headlock. No, sir, I respectfully beg to differ. I can't see a Gnomon Temple."

Popper's homecoming celebration had been subdued, at his own request. He told Mr. Jimmerson and Maceo that he would take it as a favor if they would not press him closely with questions about the recent past, his memory being faulty and a source of continuing embarrassment. But Mr. Jimmerson did ask him about Meg. Popper said he had never known a woman of that name and was pretty sure he had not been married. Would he not recall such an experience? Nor could he remember any trip to Rainbow Falls. Had he actually been here in the Temple since the war, the big war? Incredible! Not just some astral projection? Amazing! He couldn't recall any such visit.

Mr. Jimmerson brought him up to date on *Hoosier Wizard* and the Jimmerson Lag. Popper made a great fuss over the Lag, praising the grandeur of it, and at the same time expressing surprise that the numerical value of this cosmic slack should be so small—only six-tenths of one percent, and a little more.

They talked of bygone days. Popper fell into a confessional mood. "I haven't had a drink in five years," he said. He spoke of his shame and his wasted years as a drunken bum. Since the war he had drifted aimlessly about the country, a burden on society, guzzling rum when he could get it. He had been in and out of jails and hospitals. He had been on the road living a life of stupor, filth, irregular meals and no certainty of shelter from one night to the next. Pedestrians in many cities had been obliged to step over him as he lay curled up on the sidewalk wearing four shirts, three sweaters and multiple layers of verminous trousers, the cuffs bound tight at the ankles with rubber bands, so that he was sometimes taken for a downed cyclist. Five years ago he had found himself in a charity hospital in Corpus Christi, Texas. The doctors told him he had collapsed in a city park with a heart attack and had been brought gasping to the emergency room by a kind policeman.

"I think it was really more of a head attack," he said. "I wasn't exactly off my rocker, but my memory, feeble enough before, was now shattered altogether. They said I wasn't getting enough oxygen to my brain. Just the odd bubble now and then, as I understand it. Well, not shattered altogether, because I knew my name and there were certain dim but familiar figures that kept appearing in my dreams—not least yours, sir, though I couldn't place you nor understand the significance of your conical cap. But on the whole all was a merciful blank. They were very good to me there in that hospital, pauper that I was. The doctors got me back on my feet with blood-thinner pills. My blood was like tar and I thought I was down for the count. They told me to lay off the Crisco and stay away from salt. Did you ever try to eat mashed potatoes and gravy with no salt? A mule wouldn't eat it. But those doctors got me on my feet, God bless them, and then the nurses put me on to a group of recovered alcoholics. More good people. They took me in and introduced me to their methods. The doctors grudgingly admit that those methods work, where their medico methods fail, but the spiritual aspect bothers them. They don't like any system that doesn't involve pills and injections. But credit where credit's due. First the doctors saved my life and then those people saved it again. I haven't had a drink in five years. They restored my self-esteem. In six months I was a new man, wearing a clean shirt and holding down a good job selling bonds over the telephone from a boiler room. I discovered I had a knack for selling things, a gift for hopeful statement combined with short-term tenacity of purpose. But I wouldn't stay hitched. I had a comfortable life and yet something was lacking. I jumped around a good deal. I tried my hand at real estate, selling beachfront lots out of an A-frame office in a patch of weeds. I sold used cars. 'Strong motor.' 'Cold air.' 'Good rubber.' Those were some of the claims I made for my cars, or 'units,' as we call them in the business. I bought fifty-weight motor oil by the case. Then for a time there I had a costume shop downtown. It was seven feet wide and a hundred and twenty feet deep and poorly lighted. My stock was army surplus stuff and little bellboy suits and Santa Claus suits and animal heads and rubber ears and such. I had more uniforms than Hermann Göring and sometimes for a bit of fun I would wear one myself out on the sidewalk to attract attention. Go through a few drill steps. 'Jackets, bells and Luftwaffe shells!' I cried. 'While they last!' Then I saw another opportunity and sold out to an Assyrian. They like to be on Main Street. The lighting is not a big thing with them. He beat me down on the price but I left a few surprises for Hassan in the inventory. That's when I set up Bigg Dipper, a little operation dealing in oil and gas leases. Small potatoes, you understand, but my own show. That's when I bought my motor home, which is not a luxury but an important business tool. All this time things were coming back to me. No flood of light now, don't get me wrong. I couldn't arrange these events in a consecutive way, and still can't, but I was getting back bits of my past. Little vignettes. Here's an example. The worst block was the 1950s. I had lost that entire decade. Ten years of murk. President Eisenhower? You might as well ask me about John Quincy Adams. Then one morning there at sunrise in Corpus I had a vivid 1950s memory. It was another ocean sunrise in Miami. It was the summer of 1956 and I was in a car with another bum named Dorsey LaRue. Some bums have cars. We had nothing better to do and we were on our way to Detroit to see about getting an advance peek at the 1957 De Sotos but we never made it. We never got out of Miami. Dorsey took his eyes off the road to get a better station on the radio, or maybe to tune in the one he had more clearly, or even to shut it off altogether, I don't know, but he lost control of the car and we smashed into a twenty-four-hour laundromat, scattering night workers and early risers. I remembered that brief motor trip and I remembered James Wing in San Francisco and how kind he was to me. What a gentleman! A hard worker too but he was never really able to get oriental Gnomonism off the ground. I remembered playing fan-tan with James Wing and Dan Soo and Ernie Zworkin. Ernie was the last man in the phone book until Victor Zym hit town out of the blue and nudged him back a space. I remembered riding across the desert stretched out on that long seat at the back of a bus. That was before they put a toilet back there in the corner. There was a newspaper over my face with a headline—I can still see it—that said PREGNANT MOM WITH BAT SENDS 4 PUNKS PACKING. I remembered stealing a banana and getting mixed up with some left-wing women, and then later with a three-hundred-pound doctor named Symes who was trying to put a book together called *Slimming Secrets of the Stars* with a writer named Polton and two promoters named Constantine Anos, unfortunate name, though apt enough, and Dean Ray Stuart. Dean, I should say, was his given name, and he was never, to the best of my knowledge, the chief officer of a college or cathedral, and neither was he connected, as far as I know, to the royal house of Scotland. I doubt if Dean Ray got through the sixth grade. With that bony ridge over his eyes and his mouth ajar he looked like Java Man. He was a publisher but he confided to me once that the only book he had ever read through to the end was Polton's *Billy on the Farm*, as a special favor to Dub, and even there he skipped around some. And his breath. How could I forget that? It would have killed a small bird, I give you my word of honor. You had to fall back a step or two when Dean Ray was confiding. The usual rotten air but with a fishlike tang I've never run into before. What a crew! And the Ivy twins, Floyd and Lloyd, with their matching outfits, always laughing, at the least little thing, and breaking into laughter at the same instant, a dead heat. They looked at each other when they laughed and they opened so wide you could see those little pink flappers at the back of their throats. They were inseparable, I'm telling you, Chang and Eng, and great laughers. Those simultaneous peals haunt my dreams. What a gang! The past, you see, was coming back to me. Now this brings us up to last September when the brain circuits really began to crackle. I was at my luncheon club in Corpus. We meet on Thursdays at the Barling Hotel. Before we sat down to eat I was introduced to the speaker for that day, a state legislator. It was Senator Morehead Moaler, Jr., or 'Junior' Moaler or 'Big Boy' Moaler. Some call him one thing and some the other. Buys all his clothes at the big man's shop. Well, that name rang a bell, or no, it was more like a detonator went off in my head. Suddenly I remembered you, sir, and Maceo. I saw you here in the Red Room. Squanto was up there on the mantel listening to us in his customary attitude, one of perplexity. Bits of my Gnomon past came to me and I saw Gnomon words swarming visibly before my eyes like bees. I remembered that Morehead Moaler had led our strongest Pillar in Texas and I said to myself, Texas is a big state but how many Morehead Moalers can there be here? Well, at least two as it turned out, for Big Boy was the son of our own Morehead Moaler of La Coma, Texas. I was in contact again! I saw what was lacking in my life. I had been cut off all those years from Gnomonism and the Jimmerson Spiral. I sounded Big Boy out and found he didn't know the first thing about the Gnomon

Society, and had no wish to know. He was not a friendly man. When I told him I was in oil he said his first guess would have been grease. But he did arrange for me to meet with his father and I went down to La Coma to pay my respects. What a grand old man! Such pep! So full of fun! He was in his wheelchair and he was wearing his Gnomon sash when he received me there at his beautiful estate. It's right next to the La Coma Country Club, just off the eighth green. Oh, he spoke highly of you, sir, and he was kind enough to remember my work for the Society in the 1930s, which was more than I could do. Do you know what he said to me? He said, 'My life is an open book, Popper,' which was more than I could say. So many chapters better left sealed. We recited the Gnomon Preamble together. I faltered badly but that wonderful old fellow was letter perfect. Do you know what Mr. Moaler thought, sir? He thought he was the last Gnomon. Can you believe it? He thought we were extinct fauna, you and I. His own Pillar had dwindled down to just himself and he feared that you had either passed on or become unhinged. He said he had heard nothing from the Temple in recent years. None of his letters had been answered."

Mr. Jimmerson said, "Well, I don't know what to say to that, Austin. Maceo tells me that the boys sometimes steal mail from our box. But I can't say. I may have his letters back there somewhere. Maurice is helping me catch up on my correspondence. I always wanted to meet Morehead. If only we had had a hundred Morehead Moalers."

"You can and will meet him, sir. Wait till you spring the Lag on him. I want to be ringside for that. Let me tell you about him. So gracious! His gentle humor! His keen glance! We had lunch on the patio, just the two of us, outside the big house. There's a big house and then all around in back there are guest houses. We ate our shrimp salad and strawberry shortcake and listened to sweet little voices raised in song. There were small children out on the grounds having a picnic and when they saw Mr. Moaler they came to their feet and sang to him. After lunch I rolled him around over the estate. It's like a resort, with palm trees and tropical flowers. Did I tell you he made his fortune in sand and gravel? We fed his ducks. I've never seen happier fowls. We had a long talk. We began to confide in one another. He asked me if his son, Senator Junior Moaler, had not struck me as a swaggering moron. Well, what was I to say? After some hesitation I agreed that he had struck me so. A test, you see. Mr. Moaler was testing my honesty. My answer pleased him and he chuckled there in his delicate way beneath the rustling fronds. It was a light note, but not, to my way of thinking, out of place. You see what terms we were on."

Mr. Jimmerson said, "Yes, but you say you don't remember anything about Meg and the registered dogs?"

"No, sir."

"Then tell me this, Austin. Here's something I'm curious about. In all your travels did you never run across Sydney? Did you ever hear anything from him?"

"Who?"

"Sydney Hen."

"Hear from him! I haven't thought of him in ten years! Sir Sydney! Don't tell me he's still creeping around somewhere!"

"Well, I don't know."

"Still clucking, you say?"

"Well, I'm not sure."

"The little prince? Still at large? You're not serious!"

"Well, I don't know for sure."

"But say, we can catch up on Hen later. Plenty of time for that. Make a note, will you, Babcock? Just jot down 'Catch up on Hen' so we don't forget. We were talking about Mr. Moaler. More Moalers and fewer Hens. Let that be our new goal. Right now, sir, I want you to get the picture at La Coma. What we have there is a soft climate, a beautiful estate and a generous patron. We have a rich man who shares our interest in reviving the Society. Listen to this. I sounded Mr. Moaler out about the idea of establishing a Gnomon retreat there and he went me one better. Do you know what he said? He said, 'Why not a new Temple, Popper, right here in the Moaler latitudes?' Now what do you think of that? But wait."

Popper took a small memorandum book from a coat pocket and flipped through the pages in search of something, suggesting that the next point to be made would require precise language. Mr. Jimmerson and Babcock waited in silence and speculated, each in his own way, on what was to come. An important date? Certain dimensions? An extended quotation from Mr. Moaler? A list of names? A poem?

Popper found the page he wanted and jabbed at it with a finger. "There. 'The Great Moaler *Hall* of Gnomons.' That's the name he would like to give to the new Temple. For some reason I keep wanting to call it the Great Moaler *Dome* of Gnomons. I don't know why. That's what comes of not getting enough air to your brain, or the wrong kind of air. A new Temple in Texas, you see, with a library, a laboratory, an observatory, a computer room with humming machines, a carillon, a reflecting pool, a curving palisade of flagpoles to indicate our international character and some shady walkways on which our Adepts can stroll in pairs with their hands clasped behind them, while chatting of philosophical matters and kicking idly at coconut husks. Those are just a few of the things we came up with. The computer room was Mr. Moaler's idea. I would never have thought of it and yet what is Gnomonism if not harmony of numbers? It's amazing what those machines can do. They can reduce everything you know, sir, to a dot. But let's hear what you think of all this, this Great Moaler Dome, or rather Hall. Here I am rattling on and nobody else gets a chance to say anything."

"Well, Austin, it's interesting that you should mention the shifting of the Telluric Currents."

"Wait, I forgot something. I haven't explained the conditions. Let's get that out of the way first, sir, if you don't mind. Plenty of time later for the Telluric Currents. The last thing I want to do is misrepresent Mr. Moaler's position. He is well known for his good works and he is also known for the conditions he lays down. Here's one example. The small children of La Coma are welcome to frolic on his grounds, but whenever they see him they must stop in their tracks and sing to him or dance for him until he gives a 'Cease singing' signal, which is a sharp clap of those cymbals he has welded to his wheelchair. That's his policy. A little song or some little improvised dance. Quid pro quo. It's the same with the Temple. Mr. Moaler thought at one time of bequeathing his estate to his son, Big Boy, and then later to the Sholto Business College of San Antonio, of which he is a graduate. Then still later he thought he might divide it between the two of them. But where did his real interests lie? More important, where did his duty lie? Men of great wealth have great responsibilities.

Had Big Boy or the Sholto people been as attentive to him as they might have been, seeing what was at stake? We went into those questions and others that came up along the way, and I pointed out to him that there were any number of business colleges in this country, probably two or three in San Antonio alone, and all doing a wonderful job too, but that this Great Hall would be a unique institution that would bear his name down through the ages. Mr. Moaler is just as quick as a cat. He saw the cogency of the argument and he is nothing if not decisive. You can't be a quibbler and make that kind of money. He decided right there on the spot to cut Big Boy off and to endow Sholto with a bookkeeping chair, and let it go at that, and to dedicate the remainder of his sand and gravel fortune to this Great Moaler Hall plan—*if*—certain conditions were met. Now we come to his terms and I think you'll agree they're very generous. Here they are in a nutshell. The Master of Gnomons, Mr. Lamar Jimmerson, must go to La Coma and make his home there in the Great Hall, or in one of the guest bungalows, just as he pleases, and he must bring with him the *Codex Pappus* for final repository in the Great Hall, and he must award Mr. Moaler the following degrees—" Here again Popper consulted his notebook. "First Gnomon Knower, Far-Seeing Arbiter, Most High Steward, Grand Almoner, Intimate Counselor, Guardian of the Stone, Judge of the East and Companion of Pythagoras, which is to say, F.G.K., F.S.A., M.H.S., G.A., I.C., G.S., J.E. and C.P., the C.P. entitling him to wear the Poma. These few things, in exchange for which we live on Mr. Moaler's bounty, free from care, like those ducks, while we restore the Gnomon Society to its former eminence. What could be fairer than that? Call me a dreamer if you want to but I believe this is the beginning of a new cycle."

Mr. Jimmerson said, "Am I wearing my Poma now?"

"No, sir, you're not. Your head is as bare as I've ever seen it. Please listen to me. In La Coma you'll be able to work in comfortable surroundings for a change. Once more you'll hold an honored position in the community. Do you realize the police in this town don't even know who you are? They make it their business to know things and they don't even know your name."

"That explains it, then."

"But the Moaler Plan, you see, was no good without you. Were you alive? Able to travel? I was frantic. I tried to call. No phone. There were no replies to my letters and telegrams. I called the Burnette Police Department. The desk sergeant thought the Temple was abandoned, having been condemned by the Health Department or the Fire Department, or both, but he sent a patrolman out to investigate. The patrolman called me back collect and said he found an old man living here downstairs with two or three other people, and a pack of tramps upstairs. He said the place was a mess, he had seen nothing like it in his nineteen years on the force. I said, 'Cluttered but not nasty?' and he said, 'Nasty too. Filthy beyond description.' So here was a cop near retirement, never promoted, been out on the street the whole time, and he had never seen anything like it in all his years on the force. It was a strange report. I told Esteban to gas up the motor home and prepare for a journey north. We came blazing up the Interstate. Esteban has no sense of road courtesy at any time and when he learned that our mission was urgent he blew little foreign cars to one side and cut in ahead of emergency vehicles. Between noon and one he got up to ninety and ninety-five. He says all cops are off the road at that time. They insist on having their lunch at noon on the dot and taking a full hour. I didn't really worry too much about that because I have a deputy coroner's badge and I can usually count on professional courtesy from my fellow officers. All the way up I was wondering what I might find, and here I am and this is what I find. I find the Master here in the Red Room with the walls peeling and the floor carpeted with moldy newspapers and the trucks out there beating his brains to jelly. Over my head I hear the thumps of hoboes turning over in their fitful sleep."

Mr. Jimmerson said, "Then that explains the draft on my head. I put my Poma on and take it off three times a day. I don't wear it all the time because hot vapors rise from my head and collect in it. Usually I have it on at this time of night but I've been feeling a draft up there and it made me wonder. Now I realize that I must have forgotten to put it on that last time, at around six o'clock."

"Unless you put it on and took it off again."

"What?"

"Unless you did put it on again at six and took it off a fourth time."

"Why would I do that?"

"I don't know. A whim. Another steam buildup. I admit it sounds unlikely."

"But on and off four times a day? I would hardly have time to do anything else."

"Yes, but you see, that's another thing, your health. When you get to La Coma you can say goodbye to drafts and head colds, cap or no cap. The first thing I'm going to do is take you out to the beach for a course of sea baths in the Gulf of Mexico. No pounding surf, don't worry, just little brown rollers a foot high. We'll have you tossing a beach ball. We'll put you on a new diet and get those eyes cleared up. You'll have your glossy coat back in no time. There on the border we can get fresh eggs and Mexican range beef and yard chickens that feed on natural substances. No more of this American meat that's been pumped full of female hormones. It's a scandal how they're contaminating our food with these devilish chemicals. All over this country men are developing breasts. You haven't noticed it yourself?"

"I don't get out much these days, Austin."

"You don't have to go out. Jiggle your own and see. Just take a look at Babcock there when he bends over. I'm telling you, sir, it's a national scandal. Our soldier boys are wearing earrings and dancing with one another and drinking pink cocktails festooned with little paper parasols. A wave of foppery is sweeping over our country and it's all the work of those hormones. But let's hear what you think about all this. I know you must have some questions about Mr. Moaler. There are so many things I haven't touched on yet—his fine head of hair, his famous domino games, his deep-pouch coin purse with the snap top, his manner of eating—the way he sniffs his food just before forking it in, and the great care he takes to get a bit of cake and a bit of strawberry and a bit of cream in each spoonful. But please, don't let me give you the idea that Mr. Moaler toys with his food or lingers over it—nothing could be further from the truth. But look here, I think it's time I took some questions from the floor. High time. You'll just have to stop me with your questions or I'll rattle on here all night."

Babcock said, "Am I included in that offer?"

Popper looked at his watch. "Certainly. Fire away."

"Thank you. I have no questions but I do have a comment or two. First, the matter of the Poma. What seems to be uncertain is when the Master last took it off."

"Or why he did not put it back on at six. I understood that to be his concern."

"Yes, but it's all part of the same puzzle. There's a simple explanation. I can tell you that he took his Poma off at around three o'clock in the excitement of your arrival and simply forgot to put it on again. It was a curious lapse and I noticed it at the time."

"You may be right."

"I am right, and I have another point to make. It may interest you to know, Mr. Popper, that the new cycle has already begun. We are well into the new cycle and it has nothing whatever to do with you or Mr. Morehead Moaler or his red grapefruit. I plotted the curve myself and the Master has confirmed it."

Mr. Jimmerson said, "It's true, Austin. Those figures are sound. It's a sharply rising curve, even allowing for the Lag. Maurice worked it out on his slide rule."

Babcock was emboldened by this support. "Let me say further, Mr. Popper, how surprised I am that this Mr. Moaler would attempt to dictate terms to the Master of Gnomons. People come to the Master, he doesn't go to them. The Moaler millions count for nothing here. The Poma is not for sale and Mr. Moaler will just have to make do with his sombrero for a bit longer. We are perfectly content here in the Temple. This is and shall remain the seat of Gnomon authority. Under no circumstances can the *Codex Pappus* be removed from our archives. There is no need for any research institute, such as you mention, and certainly not in Texas. The climate and the southern folkways down there would not suit us at all."

Popper crossed his arms and looked Babcock over anew. "Suit you? Who are you? You have no standing here that I recognize."

"For one thing I am Keeper of the Plumes. I take my duties seriously. Now, you like Texas, Mr. Popper. That's fine. It's just the place for you, a big place, offering plenty of scope for your life of sly maneuver and sudden departure. I think your work is there and I think you should leave us to our work here."

Popper turned to Mr. Jimmerson. "You allow this secretary of yours a good deal of liberty."

"Maurice is a good boy."

"Maurice is a middle-aged boy. Is a boy going to lead us into a new cycle? I can't believe you would put yourself in the hands of this rabbit secretary."

Mr. Jimmerson grinned. "Maurice has a lady friend in Chicago. I think he wants to stay close to her."

"Now we get down to it."

"He's sweet on Dolores. I believe they have marriage plans."

"I might have known there was a woman in it. I never get over it, the power of this mating business. Out there on the woodland floor there are white worms living under rotten logs, blind, deaf, barely able to move, and yet they never fail to find one another, the male and the female. Now Babcock here, he wants to get in on it too. I should have seen through this fellow and all his high-minded talk about the Temple. One minute he's Keeper of the Plumes and the next minute he's Maurice, the ace of hearts. What is she, Babcock, a plump widow with a little money put by?"

"No."

"Some hysterical old maid in a shawl? Some old loudmouth red-headed barroom gal in tight britches?"

"I'm not going to discuss her with you. The subject is closed."

"How old is this woman anyway?"

"I don't see that it's any of your business but Dolores is about forty."

"About forty." Popper's eyes rolled upward. "Around the waist maybe. Did you demand to see a birth certificate?"

"Of course not."

"You couldn't sneak a look at her driver's license?"

"I'm not a sneak."

"They might prove to be interesting documents. Let me tell you something, Shuttlecock. I know the world and you don't. You'd do better to stay away from these crazy and desperate women who hang around barrooms half the night."

"Dolores doesn't even drink."

"As far as you know. How far is that, I wonder."

"I've known her for years."

"And you see nothing odd in that? The delayed consumma-tion? You don't see what's happening? One thing I can still do is grasp a situation and I've seen this one too many times. This old sister has got you on a tether while she waits around for something better to turn up. She's got you staked out as the Last Chance Liquor Store and you can't even see it. Why don't you wake up? Why don't you think of someone besides yourself for a change? You would deny the Master his historic oppor-tunity just so you can continue to carry on with this roly-poly woman in some Cicero motel room whenever you feel like it. What if it gets in the papers? It means nothing to you to see the Society's good name dragged through the mud?"

"I have better things to do than listen to this. We'll see who has the standing around here."

"Go on. Go to the kitchen where you belong. You're a pan-tryman if I ever saw one."

# 17

IT WAS Popper who prevailed, and the appeal of the ocean bathing that swung the Master around, that and the promise that he could ride with Mr. Morehead Moaler atop the lead float in the Charro Days parade, the pair of them wearing oversize sombreros and waving to the crowd along with the dusky beauties of Brownsville. On Sunday morning they left for Texas in the camper van—Popper, Mr. Jimmerson, Maceo and Esteban—with Mr. Jimmerson lightly sedated and strapped to a bunk, and the *Codex Pappus* stowed safely in the icebox.

There was no known ceremony for this unprecedented event, the Master's withdrawal from his Temple, and so Popper, feeling the need for a formal gesture, had Ed go to the roof of the Temple and fire a small bottle rocket over the expressway. Popper watched the ascent and the dying fall from his seat in the van. He waited for the thread of smoke to break up, then said, "So be it. Let's go, Esteban." Mr. Jimmerson was under way.

Babcock and Ed were to follow later. They were to pack whatever seemed worth packing and bring it along to La Coma in a rented truck. All was haste and confusion. Things were unraveling. Babcock was being swept along. His instructions were vague. Popper had given him some money for the truck and a Skelly credit card for gasoline, and said, "You wind up things here, Babcock, and come on when you can. Make sure you get all the books. The Master will very likely want to look something up as soon as he comes around. And don't forget his army stuff. He'll be asking about his puttees and his musette bag. No need to worry, we'll get him there in fine shape. He'll think he's in a Pullman. You come on when you can and we'll look for you when we see you."

He spoke as though there had been a reconciliation. Babcock found himself listening in the same way, nodding and giving assent. But Popper was gone now and what was he, Babcock, to do about the Temple itself? How did one decommission the Temple? Who owned it? He consulted a real estate agent, who advised him to remove the walnut paneling, the giant bathtubs, the fireplace mantels, the oak doors and a few other pieces, and then burn the place for the insurance. There was adequate coverage? Babcock knew that the Master had several shoe boxes packed with insurance policies, all golden scrollwork and gray printed matter, hedges against every mishap that life might bring, but surely they were all expired, and anyway, arson was out of the question. That he had even considered it for a moment was due, he believed, to the corrupting influence of Austin Popper and to the presence of the firebug Ed. He sent the agent on his way.

All this activity had not escaped the tramps, alert to any vacuum in the making. They sensed that authority had fled. Winter was at hand. From their upstairs base they began to probe the downstairs area and to settle in those rooms where they met no resistance. They staked out claims with their dropped bags, mostly green plastic garbage bags.

Ed was no help in driving the squatters out, nor was he of any use in loading the rental truck. He did not mind driving the truck, he said, but the U.S. government had forbidden him to lift anything heavy or otherwise exert himself. He showed the note from the government doctor. Neither could the tramps be induced to work, and Babcock had to hire some boys off the street. He enticed them with signs in the yard that read: "Attention, Boys! Something New! Register Here for Free Toys!"

"Many hands make light work," he said to them, as he organized them into a kind of bucket brigade. Their hands were small but willing. With a certain amount of horseplay and breakage, they moved the goods steadily along into the high-cube bay of the truck—housewares and books and strange Gnomon objects. Ed ate a candy bar and watched.

Down below in the boiler the rats were stirring. The busy patter upstairs had made them curious. The footfalls of the children, light and quick, made them pause and look at one another. They began to quiver and gibber. Then on a signal from their captain they poured forth from the boiler and came slithering up the cellar stairs in a column to see what was going on. In the kitchen they met a horde of cockroaches who had emerged from their dark runs, led by a big bull roach. They too had been disturbed by the new vibrations. Soon the floor was alive.

The boys threw grapefruit and books at these vermin and, caught up in the game, turned on the tramps and gave them a good pelting as well. Some of the tramps had found their way to the Red Room, where they were resting in the recliners and reading magazines before the fire when the attack came. The boys tipped them over. They went berserk. They dashed about screaming. They slid down the banisters and broke windows.

One ran into the street weeping. "That place full of rats and bums," he sobbed out to a knot of loitering young men. They were whites and Negroes about equally mixed, members of a motorcycle gang who had no motorcycles but who foraged about on foot in a shambling troop, led by the oldest male. Their regalia was made of shiny black plastic instead of black leather. They had no bike chains, but only belts as weapons. The leader, a wiry Negro, glowered. He doubled up his plastic belt and whacked it against his leg. "These old stinking winos be making our sweet little chirrens cry," he said. "I know me some bums need a good lesson."

The gang charged up the Temple steps. Babcock, seeing the two-blade propeller emblem on their caps, thought at first they were members of an aero club, young pilots who rushed serum cross-country and who searched for downed chums on week-ends, but he did not think that for long. They swept past him and laid into the tramps with their belts, while kicking at the rats with their black plastic boots.

"Watch out, they hiding!"

"Here's another one!"

"A day at the zoo!"

"They going out the windows!"

One tramp, an old man in an army fatigue cap and a long army overcoat, turned in his flight at the top of the stairs and said, "Two on one is nigger fun!"

"Listen to his old GI jive!"

"Burn his ass!"

Babcock saw that all was up with the Gnomon Temple. This was the end of the line. Some of the invaders were now running through the house gathering armloads of goods. Babcock grabbed the inert Ed, who was enjoying the show, and shook him. "Go start the truck. Roll up the windows and lock the doors and wait for me." Then he went to the Inner Hall for one last check. The roaches crunched underfoot. It was like walking on the peanut hulls at Wrigley Field. A big gray tomcat was pacing about in the Hall with his tail high, giving the place yet one more Egyptian touch. The sight of so many rats appeared to make him uneasy. Babcock retrieved a yellow silk cloth and a silver bowl, whose ceremonial uses he did not know, and made his way back to the front door.

There he was intercepted by one of the gang members, who had left off bashing and seemed to be rehearsing a song. He was doing some intermediate thing between walking and dancing, to the beat of some intermediate thing between talking and singing.

"Can't do without," he said, taking a measured step.

"Can't do without." Another step.

"Can't do without." One more. "Yo' precious love."

Babcock said, "Excuse me."

"Hey, my man, who stay in this old jive house anyhow?"

"Nobody. Excuse me. I must go now."

"Naw, Slick, you got my bowl."

He snatched at the silver bowl and Babcock broke away and ran for the truck. He jumped on the running board, yelling at Ed through the glass. Ed pulled away with a jerk. They were off. The two cargo doors at the rear of the truck were swinging open and books dribbled out all down Bulmer Avenue. Babcock, holding to the mirror bracket, looked back and saw people running into the street to claim the falling prizes. When they saw that the free stuff was only books and that they had been taken in and made to look like fools, they kicked at the copies of *Hoosier Wizard* and *Why I Am a Gnomon* and shouted angry words at the receding white truck with the flapping doors.

## 18

O N THE long ride to La Coma, Babcock came more and more to doubt that Ed was really Nandor. Did they work in concert, these Three Secret Teachers, or independently? Did they even know one another? In what circumstances did they declare themselves? The answers to these and many more questions were not to be found in Ed's face.

Ed drove and Babcock sat beside him, hatless, with the Gnomon bowl in his lap. He missed his hat. His hat was his banner. He had left his pills behind too and his stomach was a blazing pool. Cold rain fell. The windshield wipers juddered back and forth. The road was a straight corridor between bleak fields of corn stubble. Babcock told Ed that if he drove carefully and obeyed orders, then Mr. Jimmerson would buy him the biggest, blackest, most earsplitting Harley-Davidson ever made.

Ed honked at female drivers. He said "woo woo" to them and made kissing noises at them. He said he enjoyed doing security work for Mr. Jimmerson, keeping nuts and gangsters out of grenade range of the Master, but that one day he hoped to marry a woman who owned a Jeep with raised white letters on the tires. He would take her home and ride around town some. "Look," the people would say, "there goes Ed in four-wheel drive, with his pretty little wife at his side." The way to get women, he said, was with a camera. Chloroform was no good, at best a makeshift. But all the girls liked to pose for the camera and became immediately submissive to anyone carrying a great tangle of photographic equipment from his shoulders. You didn't even need film. He said he had once killed a man when he was in the Great Berets by ramming a pencil up his nose and into his brain.

Babcock said, "It's the Green Berets."

"What did I say?"

"You said the Great Berets. But you weren't in the Great Berets or the Green Berets either one, Ed. I don't know why you want to say things like that. I've seen your records."

"I was in a ward with a guy named Danny who was a Green Beret."

"Yes, but that's not the same thing."

"Danny always had his nose in a book. He had a lot of books about this guy called the Undertaker who goes all over the world rubbing out hamsters and kidnappers."

"Hamsters?"

"Gangsters, I mean, and kidnappers and dope bosses. Big crooks. Danny read those books over and over again and he wouldn't loan them out to anyone else in the ward."

"I suppose you called Danny the Professor."

"We just called him Danny. You didn't want to bother him when he was off his medication. Or even when he was on it. Or when he was reading or eating or sleeping or watching TV. He didn't like for you to rap on the door when he was in the bathroom either. Are we in Texas yet?"

"No, we're still in Illinois."

"We're not even in Texas yet and I already miss the Red Room."

"I do too."

"Do you know what's going on?"

"Where?"

"Anywhere."

"No."

"Will our heads clear when we get to Texas?"

"It's hard to say, Ed. We probably shouldn't count on it."

"The road—to honor."

"What?"

"I heard somebody say that once. 'The road—to honor.' Or maybe it was the name of a TV show I saw somewhere. 'The road—to honor.' Did you ever see it?"

"I don't think so."

The truck had a governor on the engine and there was a power fade at about sixty. Babcock kept putting off the call to Dolores. Would she trip over things in her dash to the telephone? No. He felt himself caught in the Jimmerson Bog, or rather Lag. Now and then out of a silence Ed would utter in a defiant way some paradoxical truth he had once heard, or arrived at himself, one that he seemed to think was too little known or appreciated. "Fat guys are strong," he said, and "You can brush your teeth too much." He said his mother was living with a retired gangster who had some stolen red rubies hidden behind a wall socket.

The clouds were low and heavy. Ghostly white hogs rooted in the fields. The farmers of America, Babcock noticed, had stopped wearing straw hats, overalls and high-top shoes, and had gone over to the trucker's uniform of baseball cap, tight jeans and cowboy boots, this outfit having the raffish air of the pool hall. Ed said he had weighed 112 pounds in the third grade, and then in the fourth grade 130 pounds. "I was a little pink pig in grade school." He said Danny had written more than three hundred songs in several three-ring notebooks that he kept under lock and key with his Undertaker books.

At Ed's insistence they stopped at motels with marquees boasting the dreaded Live Entertainment, with howling young demons up on the bandstand playing the amplified music of Hell. Ed showed his doctor's note to waitresses and bartenders. He slapped his fingers to the rhythm of the music on the plastic pad at the edge of the bar. He fondled the pad too but Babcock had already made him surrender his razor blades. Late on Saturday night in the room he watched the long string of football scores on television and cried out, "God almighty!" and "Did you see that!" and fell back on the bed in amazement over such unexceptional scores as 13 to 7 and 10 to 0, from games involving obscure college teams he could have known nothing about. Over breakfast, which had very likely been prepared in aluminum cookware, Babcock had to listen to Ed read aloud from the two features he always sought out in a newspaper, "TV Mailbag" and "On This Day in History."

They passed through Texarkana at night. Babcock said, "Now we're in Texas."

"Which lane do I get in, Skipper?"

"I'll let you know in plenty of time, Ed. We still have about six hundred miles to go."

From the radio there came music and news. Ed talked steadily against this flow. He said he had been a Golden Gloves champion of Nebraska and that plain old Coca-Cola was the best thing to use in wiping bugs off a windshield. He said he had rather have a man coming at him with a gun than a knife.

Vinyl repair had never really interested him but nursing school took too long, not to mention medical school, which went on for years. He wouldn't mind going to that school for circus clowns down in Florida or running the pony ride at a kiddie-land zoo or working in a crime lab. He enjoyed his work as an investigator for Mr. Jimmerson, protecting him from creeps who would disturb his naps and waste his time, and from gang-sters who wanted to kidnap him or rub him out, but what he really liked was the screech of the machine shop. What he really wanted to do was wear goggles and stand over a grind-ing wheel, grinding metal objects down to nearly nothing in a fountain of sparks. If he ever got his hands on any red rubies or won a big lump of money in a lottery he would use it to help poor people instead of throwing it away on women and Jeeps the way so many people did. The last time he had gone home his mother had chased him out of the yard with a Weed-Eater. Texas looked okay so far. It looked better than Chicago. He had never liked Chicago. "Downtown there at night," he said, "I was afraid every minute that some headhunter with a sock over his head was going to jump out at me with a knife and say, 'Boola magoola!'"

Babcock lay in a crouch against the door, limp, feigning sleep, numb under the pounding of Ed's conversation and the strain of looking for Skelly stations. It was another TKO for the golden gloves of Ed. But now at last the sun was out and the weather become mild. Now they could have the windows down. The skies of Texas opened up before them with glori-ous pink streamers that converged to a point over the horizon. Small birds were diving on a big soaring bird, harrying him.

The trip was tiring and a plunge into the unknown but Bab-cock found it pleasant to speculate on how future chroniclers of the Gnomon Society would deal with him and his role in this historic flight south. Then not so pleasant. What if they saw no reason to deal with him at all? It was Popper who was travel-ing with the Master and the *Codex Pappus*, while he, Maurice Babcock, Keeper of the Plumes, straggled along behind in the baggage cart with Ed, who at this moment was eating with hoggish noises a giant peanut log. Nandor dissembling again?

Babcock felt no lift. He felt no access of vigor or courage or understanding. If the Telluric Currents were now rising in

Texas then they must be rising still farther south. He felt if anything a slight drain. His socks had collapsed too, in a lifeless heap around his ankles, and his clothes seemed to be falling apart.

They made one more overnight stop, at a small motel with a children's wading pool, which Ed soon cleared with his rubber snake and his violent splashing. He called out repeatedly for Babcock to watch this antic or that one. By midafternoon of the following day they were passing through the onion farms of the Rio Grande Valley, this place of winter crops, although to Babcock's eye it was less a valley, in the sense of a riverine depression, than a broad coastal plain. Here, Popper claimed, the Society would bloom anew. It would take hold in this warm soil and swell in the sun like a melon.

The expressway came to an end in downtown Brownsville, near the river, which was the border. Ed was preoccupied. He was comparing a government hospital he had just seen with the ones he had known up North.

Babcock said, "Don't get on that bridge, Ed."

Ed drove onto the international bridge and went past the toll booth into Mexico. Learning of his mistake, he made a U-turn in Matamoros and was back in the United States within a minute or so. Still, technically, they had been in Mexico with their truck, and a customs agent ordered them to unload everything for contraband inspection. Every article must be turned out, down to the last wad of newspaper in the last teacup. The job fell to Babcock, Ed being unable to help. Night came. It was under the floodlights that Babcock finally got everything back in the truck, minus the Master's badger-hair shaving brush, this having been seized as a suspected source of some foreign hair disease. Twice in a matter of hours Babcock had moved more than a ton of *Hoosier Wizards*.

He had never known such fatigue. He was concerned too about the late arrival. It was almost midnight before they found La Coma and the Moaler estate, long past the bedtime of elderly Gnomons. There it was at last, the Moaler mailbox, next to the golf course. On that point, at least, Popper had told the truth. But Babcock need not have worried about the late hour. Lights were still burning in the Great Moaler Hall of Gnomons.

## 19

"B UT *ROBBED*?" said Popper. "No, I don't think so. A bank is robbed, Babcock. A temple is plundered or looted. Just as a resignation is tendered, a complaint lodged, charges preferred. Verbs are our action words. You, a secretary of all people, should see to it that your verb always matches up nicely with your—the other thing. You should also try to learn a new word every day and then use it in conversation to fix it in your head."

"Looted then. Or pillaged or sacked, if you like."

Babcock could not understand why his arrival and his dramatic account of the last hours of the Temple should meet with such indifference. Indiana, it seemed, had been shaken off and the new life in Texas begun in earnest. They listened hardly at all—Popper, Mr. Jimmerson and Mr. Moaler, he a little man with brick-red face and a full head of fluffy white hair that looked highly flammable. He sat in a wheelchair. He was not yet wearing his Poma. On his dangling feet he wore what appeared to be Buster Brown scout shoes, size five, with bits of string molded into the rubber soles. The Master himself was even less attentive than usual. He had received the silver bowl and the yellow sash, recovered from the Inner Hall at such risk, with no sign of recognition. From time to time he sneaked a look at Babcock, as though having trouble placing him.

Popper said, "But what happened to your clothes, Babcock? You come here in your rags to make your report. It doesn't show much respect for the Master or Mr. Moaler. Have you and Ed been drinking on the road?"

"No. I don't know what happened."

Popper raised a hand. "Later, please. We can't take up any more time with that now. A political problem has come up and we can't sit around here all night discussing the failure of your buttons and zippers."

They sat in a long, low room of plastic couches and Mexican blankets and dull hues, a room less grand than the Red Room but cleaner and more fragrant, and more comfortable too in its snug way. The Great Moaler Hall was in fact a mobile home. It was a big one, some seventy feet long, with three bedrooms, but it was still a trailer with a flimsy aircraft door and not at all the great manor house that Babcock had been led to expect.

The place was cluttered with Mexican curios made of shells, stones, bones, feathers and corn shucks. There was an inflated plastic globe of the earth, which Mr. Moaler sometimes held in his lap. Atop a bookcase there was a stuffed bobcat. On the floor by Mr. Moaler's wheelchair there sat what Babcock took at first to be a stuffed dog, a small white terrier sitting in the sphinx position, head erect, paws forward, not blinking or moving. A beloved pet preserved? Texas humor? What? Then the dog turned his head. He was alive, a little dog grown unnaturally fat from some sex operation, which had also softened his nature. His name was Sweet Boy.

The guest house was compatible with the Great Hall in both form and scale. It was another, older, smaller trailer, with its own rectangular charm, set back in a thicket of thorny shrubs. Ed was there now having a late supper in the company of Maceo, Esteban and Lázaro. Lázaro was Mr. Moaler's cook and driver. Babcock did not know it yet but he too was to eat there and bunk there with the domestic staff. Farther back in that same thicket there was a third trailer, older and smaller still, where Teresita lived. She was Mr. Moaler's housekeeper, now largely retired.

There were formal expressions of regret all around about the death of the Temple, as though for some distant historical calamity, but nothing in the way of heartfelt sorrow. Popper dismissed the subject. "Well, we can't take up any more time with that tonight." He held up the registered letter. "This is the thing we must deal with now."

There was some confusion over the letter. The Master had taken it into his head that it was an invitation for him to address a session of the Texas legislature. He wished to honor that invitation. But this was a gross misreading of the letter, Popper explained to him again, watching his face all the while for some flicker of understanding, and in any case it would be demeaning for the Master of Gnomons to jump, as it were, whenever these politicos snapped their fingers.

The letter was not quite a subpoena but it was a very firm request, all but commanding "Lamar or James Lee 'Jimbo' Jimmerson and Austin Popper alias Wally Wilson of the Gnolon Society" to appear at a hearing of the Churton Committee on the following Friday in Austin. Senator Churton sought their help as he and his committee members looked into the recent infestation of the state by various cults, sects, communes, cells, covens, nature tribes and secret societies, their aim being to identify the more pernicious ones, those disruptive of public order, those who fleeced the elderly and those who made extravagant claims to truth and authority, preying on the senile, the college students and other credulous and weak-headed elements of society.

Mr. Moaler urged defiance. "Big Boy is behind this," he said. "This is his way of getting back at me for taking you in. He wants those two parking lots of mine downtown. He thinks I don't have enough sense to run my own business. If it was me I would just wad that letter up and throw it in a trash can."

Popper said, "Does Big Boy know anything that might embarrass us?"

"He knows nothing. He doesn't even know that the new cycle has begun. Big Boy knows no more about Gnomonism than"—Mr. Moaler looked around for a good example of Hermetic ignorance—"than Sweet Boy here does."

Mr. Jimmerson said, "But I don't mind answering their questions. I don't see why you and Morehead are making such a fuss, Austin. You know I have nothing in my personal life to hide. I think they are showing great consideration in allowing me to air my views there in the capital."

"They don't want to hear your views, sir, they want your hide. These people are not friendly, they're hostile. I'm thinking about your dignity. I just don't think there's any place for the Master of Gnomons in a vulgar political scrap."

Mr. Moaler said, "If it was me, Lamar, I would tell Churton and Big Boy and that whole gang up there to mind their own beeswax."

Popper thought he saw a third way. They could comply with the summons and at the same time spare the Master from an ugly political confrontation. Following the example of Ed, with his light-duty medical certificate, they could get a note from some medico excusing Mr. Jimmerson on the grounds of ill health. He, Popper, could go alone to the hearing and testify. To capture their hearts? No, that would be asking too much. But he might fend them off. He knew enough to string the senators along, and if they began to probe in delicate areas, then he, as a mere spokesman, could plead ignorance of details. It seemed much the best way to go.

# 20

IT WAS late on Friday night when Popper was called to come forward and be sworn. The big hearing room with its dark wood and high windows had a desolate air. This was the tattered end of the Churton investigation. The television people had left with their blazing lights, but still the room was too warm. Only a handful of spectators remained. The panel of a dozen senators had dwindled down to just three—Churton, Rey and Gammage—all in shirt sleeves. From their raised platform they looked down on Popper with fatigue and dull disapproval.

Senator Churton, the chairman, was a thin, haggard man who smoked cigarettes and made impatient gestures with his gavel. Behind him on a stool sat Senator Junior Moaler, a big man, whose face, like his father's, was congested with blood. There was little further resemblance. Junior was a much bigger man. Here the pygmoid strain in the Moaler blood had skipped a generation. It was Junior, untroubled heir to the Moaler property until this Gnolon band had come along and settled in on his father, who had persuaded the committee to pencil in Jimmerson and Popper as last-minute additions to the witness list, to summon them and show them up for sponges and charlatans. Junior sat anxious on his campstool with a box of papers on his knees, ready to prompt the examiners with questions and feed them damaging material.

Popper was the last witness. He swore to tell the truth, then kissed the Bible, not strictly required, and took his seat with Esteban at the long table. He wore his blue western suit, with a yellow neckerchief this time, tied cowboy style, the knot to one side and the two pointed ends laid out just so.

Senator Churton said, "Thank you for coming, Mr.—is it Popper or Wilson?"

"Popper."

"Mr. Popper then. Thank you for coming and bearing with us. We're running very late. Your boss, I understand, has taken to his bed with the sniffles, or should I say, Mr. Moaler's bed. Is he feeling any better?"

"He was able to eat a little solid food last night."

"Always a good sign. Senator Moaler tells it a little differently. He tells me that this crafty old man, Mr. Jimmerson, is down there in his daddy's trailer lounging around in his shorty pajamas and eating like a hog, with a broad sheen of grease around his mouth, just smacking his big lips and looking around for more."

"I'm not surprised he called in sick," said Senator Gammage. "Eating like that at his age."

"Not true," said Popper. "And I was not aware that Senator Junior Moaler was a member of this committee."

"Big Boy is here at my request. He is acting as an advisor. All perfectly proper. His father's homestead is overrun by a swarm of mystical squatters and you wonder that he takes a personal interest? Perhaps your attorney would like to introduce himself."

"I am not represented by counsel, Mr. Chairman. This man beside me is Esteban, my security chief and director for press hospitality."

"Well and good. But let Esteban keep silent and let him keep absolutely still. All week long we've had these strange people sitting down there, a parade of stargazers, soothsayers and cranks, whispering and grimacing and blinking and suddenly shifting their feet about to some new position. These leg seizures are particularly distracting. One more thing. It's late, we're all tired and we need to wind this session up, so, above all, keep your answers brief. Now you're the representative of this—group. What's it all about, Mr. Popper? What are you Gnolons up to? We don't have to know your passwords or your secret winks and nods but we would like to get some general idea of your mission."

"It's the Gnomon Society, not the Gnolon Society, and I believe I have anticipated all your questions, sir, in my opening statement, if I may be permitted to read it. I have prepared a timely and interesting—"

"No, you may not read it. No statements and no charts. You may present any written materials you have to the bill clerk. Just short answers to our questions, please. That's all we want here."

"Then allow me to say, before we get into those questions, Mr. Chairman, how much I admire the way you have handled this inquiry—the patience you showed with that last witness, Dr. John, and the fairness with which you—"

"Thank you, Mr. Popper. We need to move along. It was your mission I was asking about. Your movement."

"Well, our mission, sir, as you put it, is simply this—to preserve the ancient wisdom of Atlantis and to pass it on, uncorrupted, to those few men of each new generation worthy of receiving it."

"Fair enough. More power to you. You have chapters elsewhere?"

"Yes, sir. We call them Pillars. We have Pillars in all the fifty states and Guam."

"What about your leader? This mysterious Mr. Jimmerson? Who is he and just what is he doing here in Texas?"

"Mr. Jimmerson is the Master of Gnomons. He is in La Coma, Texas, as the invited guest of Mr. Morehead Moaler, himself a Gnomon of very high degree."

"How long will he be here?"

"It's hard to say. At least until we can get our hospital project off the ground."

"What hospital is that?"

"A hospital for poor children we are planning to build in La Coma. These things take time."

"They sure do. What it really comes down to is this, isn't it, Mr. Popper? This sly old man, Mr. Jimmerson, wearing a very peculiar electromagnetic cap, has moved in, bag and baggage, with poor old Mr. Moaler for an indefinite stay, bringing with him his family, a butler, a hairdresser, four or five musicians and various sacred birds and monkeys. Is that not a fair summary of the situation?"

"No, sir, most unfair. The Master, I repeat, is an invited guest. That can be confirmed easily enough. His cap has no magnetic properties. His family did not accompany him on this trip. He does, very naturally, travel with his executive staff."

"He comes off to me as a very sinister figure. Can you tell us a little more about him?"

"I'll be glad to. Lamar Jimmerson is a decorated veteran of the Argonne campaign. He is a man of military bearing and twinkling good humor. He is clean and strong. He suffers from an occasional head cold but is otherwise a fine specimen. He runs six miles a day and maintains the physique of a thirty-year-old man. He is a gentleman. Children and animals take to him instinctively and rub up against him. He is a philosopher. He is a teacher in the great tradition of Hermes Trismegistus and Pletho Pappus. Mr. Jimmerson is the American Pythagoras."

"Quite a man. How come I never heard of him until two weeks ago?"

"Like all the truly wise men in this world, Senator, Mr. Jimmerson is unknown to the world."

"He's not some naked and scrawny sage from India, is he?"

"No, sir."

"What can you tell us about his economic theories?"

"He has none that I know of."

Senator Gammage put in a question. "Is he the one who claims that the Chinese discovered America?"

Senator Churton rapped his gavel. "Later, Senator. Your turn will come. Now tell me this, Mr. Popper. How much does this old man charge for these fraudulent academic degrees that he sells through the mail?"

"Mr. Jimmerson sells no degrees. He sells nothing."

"Are his financial records intact?"

"I believe so."

"You're not going to tell me that they were all blown away in a tornado like those records of Dr. John's, are you?"

"Our records are intact as far as I know."

Senator Moaler leaned forward for a whispered consultation with the chairman. Papers were passed. Senator Churton looked them over and then resumed his examination.

"What can you tell us, Mr. Popper, about Mr. Jimmerson's police record?"

"He has no police record."

"So you say. According to my information he was released from a maximum security prison in Arizona in June of 19 and 58 after serving seven years of a ten-year sentence for armed robbery and aggravated assault. He was going by the name of James Lee 'Jimbo' Jimmerson at the time. It says here that he played various percussion instruments in the prison band."

"That would be another Jimmerson."

"Perhaps. We do know this. You cult people are great ones for altering your names or taking new names."

"Altogether a different person."

"Perhaps. Even so, you can't deny that your man springs from that same Jimmerson family of thugs in Stitt, Arizona, can you?"

"I can and do deny it."

"I understand he practices herbal medicine. A lot of sprouts and berries in his program."

"He doesn't practice any kind of medicine."

"Hypnotism?"

"No, sir."

"Does he conduct pottery classes?"

"No, sir."

Senator Churton took a closer look at his paper and placed his finger on a word. "Or is it poetry classes?"

"He teaches neither of those arts."

"Does he claim to be in contact with spaceships that are circling the earth, communicating on a daily basis with humanoid pilots one meter tall wearing golden coveralls?"

"He makes no such claim."

"I have been told that he is a man with several rather unpleasant personal habits. I won't specify further."

"I don't know what you're talking about."

Senator Gammage broke in. "These unpleasant habits. Around the house? Out in the streets? Where?"

"Around the house," said Senator Churton. "But I would rather not specify further. You will be recognized in due course, Senator Gammage. You can put your questions then, on your own time. We'll leave that and go on to this. Now, Mr. Popper, how do you answer the charge that this cunning old man, Mr. Jimmerson, has come to Texas to work out his imperial destiny?"

"I don't understand the question."

"No? You can tell us nothing about his plans to conquer the earth and divide it up into triangular districts?"

"Mr. Jimmerson has no such plans."

"So you say. But he does maintain a chemical laboratory?"

"We have our little experiments in metallurgy."

"And in magnetism as well?"

"I believe so, yes."

"Experiments that are carried on behind locked doors, I am

told, with vicious dogs patrolling the corridors. What safeguards do you have in place, Mr. Popper? What precautions have you taken to ensure that these experiments do not get out of hand and set the air afire and perhaps melt the polar ice caps?"

"None."

"Very well, then. Let's move on to this dancing school that Mr. Jimmerson runs. How is that connected to your organization? Just what goes on in those classes?"

"Mr. Jimmerson has never run a dancing school."

"It's all right here in this report, with an eyewitness account of the old man himself dancing. It says here that he appeared to be hopped up on some kind of dope."

"That report is completely false."

"Oh? And yet strong narcotic drugs do play an important part in your ceremonies, do they not? In your revels?"

"They do not."

"And lewd dances led by this man Jimmerson? Although you tell us he has never run a dancing school. I have it all right here in black and white, Mr. Popper."

"Not true. I'm afraid you have confused us with another organization calling itself the Gnomon Society. That pathetic little band is led by a man named Sydney Hen, and yes, I believe they do jig about some by the light of the moon. But we have nothing to do with them and they have nothing to do with true Gnomonism."

"Hen, Hen, Hen. Don't we have something here on Hen?" He huddled again with Senator Moaler. There was another flutter of papers. "Oh yes, here we are. Hen the co-founder. Hen in Malta. Hen in Canada. Hen in Mexico. He pops up with frequency in this sleazy tale. A fine fellow too. Both he and your man Jimmerson, it appears, have been living off the earnings of women now for many years. A pretty pair."

"A pretty unsavory pair," said Senator Rey.

"Two rival gangs," said Senator Gammage.

"More a matter for the vice squad, it seems to me, than a legislative body," said Senator Rey.

Senator Churton rapped his gavel. "Order. And when may we expect Hen's arrival in Texas, Mr. Popper? On the next bus? Don't tell me he's already here, pawing our women in Lufkin or Amarillo."

"Your guess is as good as mine, Senator. Personally, I have never clapped eyes on the man."

"You have no knowledge of his whereabouts?"

"No direct knowledge, no, sir. There are several stories going around. I have heard that he was living on a barge in Mexico, wearing a yachting cap and selling fish bait and taking in a Saturday *corrida* now and then and quoting Virgil at the drop of a hat. Another story has him dead, with his remains, a half pint of gray ashes, in the custody of his former wife, the former Lady Hen, who is now Señora Goma y Goma of Veracruz. Another one has it that his acolytes in Cuernavaca have preserved his body in a crock of Maltese honey."

"His entire body?"

"Yes, sir."

"That must be some jug."

"His entire body, intact, except for the lapis lazuli eyeballs in his eye sockets, forever staring but seeing nothing in that golden haze. I have also heard that he is in Cuernavaca in a deep trance of some two or three years' standing, and I have heard that he is not in a trance but is living alone in a small downtown hotel in Monterrey, wearing a beret, calling himself Principato and claiming to be five hundred years old. They say he looks six hundred, with his body all dried up from the desert air. They say he's all head now like a catfish and just tapers away to nothing. These are some of the rumors I have heard."

"Somewhere in Mexico quoting Virgil, if alive. Not much to go on."

"No, sir."

"Still, as long as he stays there. Does he intend to remain there in his Mexican lair, Mr. Popper?"

"As far as I know. If we can speak of the lair of a Hen."

"You mention rumors. Tell me this, if you can. What perverse joy does this man Jimmerson get from starting rumors? Rumors or hoaxes that raise hopes, so soon to be cruelly dashed. What are we to think of such a man?"

"I don't understand the question."

"Let me be specific then. The fifty-dollar jeep. The army surplus jeep, brand-new, crated and packed in Cosmoline, to be bought for only fifty dollars if you could just find the right government agency. Didn't that story originate with Jimbo Jimmerson in late 19 and 45 in Oakland, California?"

"It didn't originate with Lamar Jimmerson."

"And the kidney dialysis machine, to be given away to any community or church group that could collect some great number of old crumpled-up cigarette packs—wasn't that another of Jimbo's lies, first set on wing in a Seattle bar?"

"Mr. Lamar Jimmerson has never been to Seattle."

"Perhaps. I have nothing more at this time. Senator Rey?"

Big Boy Moaler gathered his stuff and moved down the way at a crouch to take up a new whispering position behind Senator Rey, who was sleek and thoughtful. The senator tapped his microphone with a pencil in an exploratory way, then said, "Thank you, Mr. Chairman. Yes, I do have a question or two for this witness. As you can see, Mr. Popper, I have here before me a number of Gnolon or Gnomon books. You prefer Gnomon?"

"I do."

"Why the two names? Don't you find that confusing?"

"We don't have two names."

"A number of Gnomon books, then. There are works here by Sir Sydney Hen—*Approach to Knowing, Approach to Growing, Atlantis a Fable?, Teatime at Teddy's, November Thoughts, Boyhood Rambles* and *The Universe a Congeries of Flying Balls?*, every page of them, I'm sorry to say, badly defaced by vandals with green ink. I have also collected some books and booklets that were presumably written by you, Mr. Jimmerson and this man Pappus. It's hard, really, to say. There's not much information in the front of these books, where we might normally expect to find the names of the author and publisher, the date of copyright and so on. I have here *Gnomonism Today, The Codex Pappus, 101 Gnomon Facts, Hoosier Wizard, The Jimmerson Spiral, Dungeon of Ignorance*—"

Popper broke in. "*Hoosier Wizard* is the work of an outsider. I don't know *Dungeon of Ignorance*. I don't believe that's a Gnomon book."

"It's one of Dr. John's books," said the chairman.

"So it is," said Senator Rey. "I stand corrected."

"And please don't tap the mike again with your pencil.

There's no need for that. The audio system is in perfect working order."

"I stand corrected and rebuked. Anyway, I have looked into these books—I won't say read them through—and I find some puzzling and disturbing things. Maybe you can help me, Mr. Popper. It could be that I just need some guidance. This man Hen, for instance. Hen and his busy pen. I don't understand him. Why all the question marks? Why all these approaches to this, that and the other thing? Why can't he ever tell us of his arrival somewhere? And why must he sink our spirits with his November thoughts when he might lift them with his April reflections?"

"Those are good questions, sir, and I only wish you could get the little trifler up here under a two-hundred watt bulb and beat some answers out of him. His books make me gag."

"You don't defend him?"

"Certainly not. No decent person could defend that trash."

"All right then, let's leave Hen and turn our attention to some of your own stuff. Here. This flat earth business. Now, do you think it would be a good thing for me at this particular point in time to go around telling people that the earth is flat in this day and age? To instruct small children in that belief discredited so many years ago by Christopher Columbus? Would that be the proper way for me to prepare our boys and girls to play constructive roles in this our modern world and to take their places in society and meet all the future challenges of the space age in whatever chosen fields of endeavor they might choose to—endeavor?"

"Well, if you sincerely believed the earth to be flat, then yes, Senator, I suppose it would be your duty to say so."

"Which is how you justify your position. You alone in your great pride are right and everyone else is wrong. The plea of every nut in history."

"I don't know what position you're talking about, sir. The Gnomon Society has never questioned the rotundity of the earth. Mr. Jimmerson is himself a skilled topographer."

"Excuse me, Mr. Popper, but I have it right here in Mr. Jimmerson's own words on page twenty-nine of *101 Gnomon Facts*."

"No, sir, excuse me, but you don't. Please look again. Read that passage carefully and you'll see that what we actually say is that the earth *looks* flat. We still say that. It's so flat down around Brownsville as to be striking to the eye."

"But isn't that just a weasel way of saying that you really do believe it to be flat?"

"Not at all. What we're saying there is that the curvature of the earth is so gentle, relative to our human scale of things, that we need not bother our heads about it or take it into account when going for a stroll, say, or laying out our gardens."

Senator Rey, now tapping his pencil against his teeth, conferred for a time with Senator Moaler, took some papers from him and went on.

"What is this Jimmerson Spiral, or Hen-Jimmerson Spiral, that we hear so much about? Early on it's the Cone of Fate and then that symbol seems to give way to this spiral. What is this helical obsession you people have?"

"There is no such thing as the Hen-Jimmerson Spiral, Senator. You have been taken in, along with so many others, by Sydney Hen, one of the slickest operators of the twentieth century. There is only the Jimmerson Spiral. Mr. Jimmerson is the only begetter. Let me give you the background on that. When the Master first made his discovery known, Hen, an envious little man, jumped in to claim equal credit, citing the historical parallel with Newton and, who was the other one, Darwin, I believe, yes, the pair of them working independently in their own tiny cottages, and then one day, miles apart, clapping their foreheads in unison as they both hit on the idea of phlogiston at the same time. But there was a big difference. Hen, unlike Darwin, would never show his work sheets to anyone, and do you know why? Because they didn't exist."

"Yes, but regardless of whose brain the thing was first cooked up in, just exactly what is it?"

"Now there we're getting into deep waters, sir. I have never known quite how to handle that question when put to me so bluntly by a Perfect Stranger. Years ago, when I was on the lecture platform, I would handle it with a cute little story. I find that a light note sometimes helps. Very often the only way to approach these very difficult concepts is by way of allegory. We have to slip up on the truth. We are obliged to amuse our audience while at the same time we instruct them. You gentlemen will understand. All four of us have stood at the podium, may God forgive us, and addressed the public, and all of us have heard those scampering noises, the tramp of many feet making for the doors, and so we have our own little devices for holding our audience. Now this particular story is a story about three brothers. Let me tell you that story, Senator. Once there were three brothers. The first brother—"

The chairman's gavel came down in a single sharp crack of walnut. "Ask him about something else, Senator Rey, if you don't mind. He's leading you around the mulberry bush. We'll be here all night at this rate. And don't get him started on Hen again."

"Very well. We have annoyed the Chair again, Mr. Popper, so let us move on. Let us have a look at this *Codex Pappus*. I open the book at random here—or farther along—here. Yes, this will do. We have made our way through all the numbers and triangles and here, coming upon a block of text, we think we're in for a bit of plain sailing for a change. Not so. This is what we run into. I quote:

> . . . *and thus the course of the Initiate is made clear. He must emulate Pletho, the son of Phaleres, first Hierophant of Atlantis, pride of Jamsheed, the White Goat of Mendes, who, at the River Loke, on the day of the full moon, of the month Boedromion, when the moon is full at the end of the sign Aries, near the Pleiades and the place of her exaltation in Taurus, with majestic chants and with banners bearing the images of the Bull, the Lion, the Man and the Eagle, the Constellations answering to the Equinoctical and Solstitial points, to which belong four stars, Aldebaran, Regulus, Fomalhaut and Antares, at once marking the commencement of the Sabaean year and the cycle of the Chaldean Saros, conjunctive with the colure of the full moon, bearing in his left hand the four signs or cardinal points, and forsaking the northern regions and the empire of night, and taking his leave of the Three Secret Teachers, Nandor, Principato and the Lame One, goes to slake his thirst at the sign of the Ninth Letter, or Hierogram of Nomu, in the Circle of the Twelve Stones at the base of the Third Wall. . . .*

"And on and on. Now, that Initiate's course is far from being clear to me. Can you give us some idea of what all that means, Mr. Popper?"

"It doesn't mean much of anything in a surface reading like that."

"That's what I would have said too. So much sawdust. I'm surprised to hear you admit it."

"I acknowledge it freely enough. A lot of that is just filler material in the oracular mode to put P.S. off the scent."

"P.S.?"

"Perfect Strangers. Those who are not Gnomons. Others, outsiders. P.S. or A.M. Perfect Strangers or the Ape Men."

"But to what purpose? Apes we may be, but why throw dust in our eyes? Can you explain?"

"Sure can. I thought it would be obvious. We do it to protect our secret knowledge. We don't know whose hands those books might fall into, Senator, and so we are obliged to put a lot of matter in there to weary and disgust the reader. The casual reader is put off at once. A page or two of that and the ordinary man is a limp rag. Even great scholars, men who are trained and well paid to read dull books, are soon beaten down by it. The wisdom is there but in order to recognize it and comprehend it you must have the key. That key is transmitted by word of mouth and only by word of mouth from one Gnomon to another in a closed circuit."

"So if I had the key I could understand this Choctaw."

"If you had the key, Senator, you could read that book with profit. You couldn't fully understand it unless you had the key to that key."

"What, another key?"

"These are our methods. In this way we have kept our mysteries inviolate for sixty thousand years."

"More like sixty years," said Senator Gammage, in that bass organ note that had caused so many cheap radio speakers in west Texas to shudder and bottom out. "Will the senator yield?"

"For the moment."

"Thank you. This won't take long."

Big Boy moved his campstool again, to a new prompting position behind this third and final examiner.

Senator Gammage squared up the stack of papers before him in a bit of stage business. Then he looked over his glasses at Popper for a silent, challenging minute or so, but in the end it was the senator who broke off and looked away, from Popper's unwavering smile.

"Let me say first that what struck me about those books is how slow they start. Maybe it's just me but I thought they started awfully slow."

"It's not just you," said Senator Churton.

"No, I noticed the same thing," said Senator Rey. "You get hardly any sense of movement or destination."

"Well, I wasn't sure. I thought it might be just me."

"No," said Senator Churton.

"I'll tell you something else about those books," said Senator Rey. "I was a happier man before I read them."

"What?" said Senator Churton.

"He said those books made him uneasy," said Senator Gammage.

"They didn't have that effect on me."

"Me neither. Your sensitive Latino, I guess."

"That's not quite what I said."

"Close enough. May I continue, please, with this witness? Now, Mr. Popper, we have heard about Hen and we have heard about Mr. Nickerson, this cunning, grinning old man with feathers around his mouth, and we have heard—"

"It's Mr. Jimmerson."

"Jimmerson, yes, we have heard about him too, and we have heard about your Society and your literature, but we haven't heard much about you personally. I have some odds and ends here that need clarification. Perhaps you could help me."

"I'll do what I can."

"Thank you. Do you present yourself to the public as a petroleum engineer?"

"Petroleum consultant."

"I see. Are you an American citizen?"

"I am indeed. First and last."

"I ask that question because there seems to be some mystery surrounding your origins and your early years. Suddenly you just appear on the scene, a grown man."

"I am an orphan, Senator. I had to make my own way as a child, but I am no less a good citizen for that. I am also an outspoken patriot. My friends tell me I go too far at times but I can't help it, it's always been Fifty-four forty or Fight with me. I'm too old to change now."

"According to my information you sat out the war in a small upstairs room on Grant Avenue in San Francisco, playing fantan with one James Wing, and emerging only for the Victory Ball."

"My military work was confidential and, much against my wishes, remains so to this day. It will all come out in thirty years."

"Is Austin Popper your true name?"

"Yes, sir. It's not one I would have chosen."

"You say that man Esteban is your security chief. Is he armed?"

"He's well armed."

"You fear some attack in this chamber?"

"We have our enemies."

"But you did not always travel in such style, did you? With attendants and a briefcase. I'm thinking now of your years on the road as a bum."

"I was a tramp, yes, sir. I was down and out. I've never tried to conceal that."

"A drunken bum?"

"Yes, sir."

"Calling yourself Wally Wilson?"

"I believe I did use that name at one time."

"Sleeping in haystacks? Stealing laundry off clotheslines and hot pies from the windowsills of isolated farmhouses? Leaving cryptic hobo marks scrawled on fence posts and the trunks of trees?"

"No, sir, I was very much an urban tramp. No haystacks or barns for me. Mostly I walked the city streets wearing cast-off clothes, with overcoat sleeves hanging down to my knuckles. I did live in a box once for about a week. I went from a Temple to a box, so steep was my fall."

"A big crate? A packing case of some kind?"

"A pasteboard box."

"Under a viaduct in the warehouse district of Chicago?"

"No, sir, it was in a downtown park in one of our eastern cities."

"A long box you could stretch out in?"

"A short one. Mr. Moaler lives in what I would call a long box. Mine was very compact. When it snowed I had to squat in it all night with my head between my knees like a yogi or a magician's assistant. Then when morning came I had to hail a policeman or some other early riser to help get my numb legs straightened out again."

"More a stiff garment than a house."

"Yes, sir."

"Hunkered down there in your box, slapping at imaginary insects on your body. Your only comfort a bottle of cheap wine in a paper sack. Supporting yourself with petty thievery, always on the run, with Dobermans snapping at your buttocks. Not a pretty picture."

"It was cheap rum."

"The clear kind?"

"The dark kind."

"As an urban bum, Mr. Popper, did you often stagger into the middle of busy intersections with your gummy eyes and make comical, drunken attempts to direct traffic?"

"No, sir. In my worst delirium I never interfered with the flow of traffic. I never drank any hair tonic either."

"Senator Moaler informs me that you once got mixed up with some left-wing women."

"The senator is correct. But I was a passive figure in that affair."

"You blame it on the rum?"

"They dragged me in off the street. I was too weak to resist. I was a stretcher case."

"What street was this?"

"A side street in one of our great eastern cities."

"How many left-wing women?"

"Three. I didn't know what it was all about. I thought at first they felt sorry for me. I thought they were just three jolly bachelor gals with short hair, bowlers or rock hounds, who went on motor trips together to our national parks and our regional festivals, and on pilgrimages to the boyhood homes of popular singers."

"This was not the case?"

"No, sir, very different. A very different kettle of fish. Let me tell you what happened. They took me in and hosed me down and disinfected me. Then they powdered me all over and dressed me in a loose white shirt and loose white trousers, held up with a piece of twine. It was a kind of Devil's Island outfit and could have done with some touch-up ironing. Then they locked me in a windowless room that had a mattress on the floor."

"What was the purpose of all this?"

"At first I thought it was merely to instruct me in their doctrines. They explained to me why it was necessary to transform this country into the likeness of one of those countries where they can arrest you for laughing in bed. Padlock the churches, bludgeon the dogs, gas the poets—they outlined the entire program for me. They also tried to do something called 'raising my consciousness.' This was a fairly humorous business, their fumbling efforts to break down my natural human resistance to nonsense and falsehood. But it was a soft berth, I was in out of the wet and so I said nothing. I went mute. I fell into a long silence."

"A long silence, Mr. Popper?"

"Long for me, sir. Then they seemed to lose interest in that part of it and they left off lecturing me. No more political workshops. Except now and then they would pop their heads into my room at night and shout one of their beliefs at me. 'It's all blind chance!' they would shriek, and 'We're animals and we perish utterly!' and 'No more private gardens!' But mostly they just let me feed and sleep. I ate well. I had whatever I wanted whenever I wanted it—big T-bone steaks with onions and potatoes, oyster stew, deviled eggs, the end cut of prime rib with horseradish, doughnuts by the dozen, double-X whipping cream on my corn flakes, five or six meals a day."

"New potatoes?"

"No, sir, big Idaho bakers split lengthways and filled with pats of butter. No baloney or chicken franks or other jailhouse grub. It was like a dining car on a train—I wrote out my own orders. Just before turning in at night I had the girls bring me a short stack of buckwheats with sausage links and a glass of cold milk with ice spicules just beginning to form in it. They provided me with a certain amount of rum too."

"What did you make of all this?"

"I didn't know what to make of it but I suspected it would end badly."

"How long did it go on?"

"I don't know. I lost track of time. I had no radio and they wouldn't let me see any newspapers."

"You could have scratched off the passing days on the wall with a nail or a pin—six vertical strokes and then a long diagonal stroke to close out the week."

"I had no pointed instruments. They took my pencil stub away after each meal order. But it was long enough to fatten me up. I grew fatter and sleeker. At night those women would come with their brushes and soft rags and baby oil to curry me and buff me. They ran their hands over my expanding belly. They poked my hams with their fingers. Then they would stand back and look at me and whisper among themselves with their arms folded. Finally it dawned on me. I saw what their game was, from a dropped word or two. I'm slow but I get there, usually around dusk. I saw in their eyes that they meant to cook me. My room was a fattening pen. They were preparing me for a sacrificial barbecue. They meant to eviscerate me and stuff me with celery and roast me, sir, as a symbol of something they hated—men, tramps in their freedom, people of cheerful mien, white Anglo-Saxon Protestants from the heartland, I never knew. Perhaps all four, or even something else. On that point they were never clear."

"No one would miss you. A bum with no connections. No one to inquire. The few people who knew you wouldn't greatly care. These women could spit you and baste you at their leisure. A symbolical porker. Not a bad plan."

"It was a good enough plan."

"A sweet plan. And yet you managed to escape."

"Yes, but there again my role was a passive one. Late one night, perhaps as late as midnight, they came to me with burning candles, very solemn, their faces painted white, and led me into their living room and had me sit in the middle of the floor. They sprinkled meal and blood on my head while muttering something, some kind of Communist maledictions. They began to sway their heads and hum or sing. Then they snuffed out the candles on top of my head and joined hands and began to dance around my obese form."

"Dancing in their bowling shoes?"

"Barefooted."

"But singing? I thought those old Red gals were all business."

"Singing or keening. It wasn't what you and I would call a song. It wasn't an expression of joy. These weren't the Andrews Sisters. It was some kind of Marxist sabbat and I knew my hour had come. Then suddenly, in my despair, I found my voice again. I began to talk, through a nasal obstruction I had at the time. I started talking and before I knew it the afflatus was on me and I couldn't stop talking. I gave those women amusing anecdotes and bits of Gnomon lore. I recalled vivid scenes from childhood. For some reason this annoyed them. It put them in a rage and all at once these Amazons broke off their dance and tied me up in a bedsheet, bagged me if you will, and proceeded to beat me with brooms for what seemed like twenty minutes before rolling me down the stairs and out into the street, where I got pavement burns on my knees. They just sent me sprawling out there on the concrete, which is a good name for that stuff."

"Then what?"

"They left me there. Right there on the street where they had found me."

"That was it?"

"Yes, sir."

"So instead of slitting your throat and broiling you over a bed of coals they just put this sheet job on you. I don't get it."

"Neither do I, Senator. I can only surmise that I did something or said something inadvertently to queer their spell, to contaminate the rite, somehow rendering myself unfit for immolation. That's just my guess."

"Or it could be that they simply turned squeamish when it got down to the nut-cutting. The squeals and gouts of blood. They shrank from it."

"Those three? No, sir, I don't think so. Certainly not Camilla."

"If you ask me he was pretty darn lucky to get away with just those strawberries on his knees," said Senator Rey.

"They got fed up with all his chatter," said Senator Churton. "Can't we go a little faster here?"

"One more question and I'm done," said Senator Gammage.

"You have testified here under oath, Mr. Popper, that this old Indiana buzzard, Mr. Chickering, or Mr. Jimmerson, whatever you want to call him, this old Grand Dragon of yours, has never set foot in Seattle, Washington. We have you on the record there. But Senator Moaler has provided me with incontrovertible evidence that your man was in fact living there in 1959 and 1960. Chuck Jimmerson was the name he was using then. He was working as the host on a local television program called *Your Pet Parade*, as if you didn't know. Thousands upon thousands of people saw Chuck cavorting with small animals and playing the fool on that show and you have the gall to come here and state under oath that Jimmerson never set foot in that city. Would you now like to change your testimony?"

"No, sir. That would be another Jimmerson."

"All those thousands of people are mistaken?"

"It's not the same person."

"So you keep telling us whenever we manage to throw a bit of light into some dark corner of this man's life. It's always somebody else. Well, I give up. We're not getting anywhere with this fellow. You can have this witness back, Senator Rey, and welcome to him."

Senator Rey had no chance to speak. The chairman moved quickly into the opening, switching off all the microphones except his own, and hammering the proceedings to a close *sine die*.

Big Boy Moaler had done his worst and he wondered if it had been quite enough. He thought not. It might have been a different story if his two witnesses had shown up. Where were they? This Popper or Wally Wilson fellow had lost a few tail feathers but no blood to speak of. These Gnolons were well dug in. He supposed he must count himself lucky that the other faction, that Hen force, had not settled in on his father as well.

Popper himself, while thinking he might have done better, was in general agreement with Big Boy, that the attack had largely failed, leaving the Gnomon Society in no immediate danger of eviction. He knew nothing about Texas trailer law but he suspected that there was no really effective way of removing a person from a trailer in the Rio Grande Valley without the use of firearms or tear gas.

## 21

PROFESSOR GOLESCU and Judge Pharris White arrived in Austin on Sunday, too late to testify at the Churton hearing. Notified late, they arrived late. The two men, who were unknown to one another, had flown to Texas at Senator Moaler's urging and at their own expense, both eager to bear witness against Popper. Golescu came from his Auric Laboratories in Sacramento, and Pharris White, a retired hearing commissioner, called Judge by courtesy, from his home in Baltimore.

No one met them at the airport and there were no messages for them at their hotels. Big Boy Moaler, their sponsor, could not be located. They walked the dead Sunday streets of Austin, actually brushing against one another at a downtown newsstand, and then went back to their rooms to wait for Monday morning.

On Monday they had no better luck. They learned, working separately, that Senator Moaler had left the state on a duck-hunting trip. Senator Churton was tracked down to his home in Lufkin but he refused to come to the telephone. His wife advised them that the senator was taking no more calls concerning the recent hearing, and that he was particularly taking no calls from people who identified themselves as professors, judges, scribes, swamis, commanders or masters of this and that. She had never heard of Austin Popper. The hearing was over. Send letters if they must but don't call again.

This was enough for Golescu. He packed his bag in haste and returned at once to Sacramento and his greenhouse, explaining to his wife, June, and their often divorced daughter, Ronelle, back home again herself, that it had all been a trick, a ruse to make him show his head, a scheme engineered by Popper and the Gnomon Society to humiliate him once again, so late in life, to frighten him and show that he, Cezar Golescu, was still under their eye. They wanted to silence him. They wanted him to shut up about Mu and stop showing the seal. Their tentacles were everywhere. Moaler was one of them and no doubt Churton too. They never slept. Nothing was hidden from the

Gnomon host. They were capable of anything—fraud, slander, vandalism, murder, a criminal assault on Ronelle, anything at all. They would rip your tongue out. They knew no law but their Master's decrees and his mad whims.

Bulldog White did not give up so easily. He called the state capitol again and again but could raise no one beyond the switchboard operator. It was the holiday season, she told him, and the office workers were sometimes away from their desks on these festive days. The telephone approach, he decided, was unsatisfactory. Moaler was in his Arkansas duck blind and Churton was incommunicado, hiding behind his wife. All the secretaries at the capitol seemed to be caroling. He gathered his papers and put on his down-filled vest, his blue parka, his blue muffler, his blue knit cap and his rubber overshoes and went out into the springlike weather.

First to a newspaper office, where he thought he might get some straight answers. What he did not know, for all his years in public life, was that newspapers do not welcome direct, un-solicited communication from the public, that they hide their street addresses and telephone numbers in dark corners of in-side pages, when indeed the information is printed at all, that they make onerous demands of letter writers so as to discour-age the traffic and that they treat as pests those citizens who walk in off the streets with inquiries, or even with news.

The newspaper people took White quickly in tow and put him in a small holding room for troublesome callers and told him to wait. He waited. They checked on him at long inter-vals through a peephole, until it became clear that he was not going to leave without a poke or two from the cattle prod. An adolescent sports reporter was sent in to deal with him. The boy knew nothing about Popper or the Churton hearing. He had no idea who Lamar Jimmerson was or where he might be located. The newspaper files were not open to the public; he did know that. "Look," he said, taking White's elbow and guiding him to the door. "Why don't you take this up with your preacher? Here's a complimentary copy of today's paper for you."

"Are you trying to tell me that Popper is still not in custody?"

"I don't know."

"He's taken a powder again?"

"I just don't know, sir."

"You don't know much, if I may say so."

"No, sir. Right this way."

Pharris White found himself out on the street again. He wandered about town in a thoughtful mood, turning over in his head the major allegations he had brought against the Gnomon Society in his brief. It was a solid piece of work. It was watertight. A passerby, taking him for an old bundled-up street vendor, asked to buy a paper. White accepted the man's coin and allowed him to take the paper without understanding the transaction.

After lunch he went to the capitol grounds. He walked the corridors and tunnels of the state buildings, a round blue figure on the prowl. He looked in on jolly office parties. Slabs of fruitcake were thrust at him and he was directed here and there. Late in the afternoon he managed to corner a woman who worked on the Senate clerical staff. She agreed to listen to him.

"I can give you a few minutes," she said. "Let's go to Room 61-B, where we won't be bothered."

She took him to another isolation cell, barren but for a wooden table and two molded plastic chairs. She ushered him quickly to his seat and said he need not take off his big coat or his mukluks.

This time he was determined to establish his credentials early and fully. He showed the woman his certificate of merit from the postal union, awarded for three years of perfect attendance at union meetings. He showed her his Gnomon card, laminated in plastic, the ghostly VOID still just visible, and his FBI ring and a letter of guarded praise from the Attorney General and some newspaper clippings in which his name appeared. He presented her with a photograph of himself in his magistrate's robe, a chubby monk in black, standing before a wall of law books all of identical size and binding, and extending, the viewer could only guess how far, beyond the borders of the photograph in every direction. He signed it: "Best wishes to a fine woman from Judge Pharris White."

Then down to business. He laid out before her on the bare table the brief he had drawn up against the Gnomon Society,

Jimmerson, Popper *et al.*, along with the yellowing warrant for Popper's arrest he had carried about for so long.

"It's all here," he said. "Chapter and verse, going back to 1942. Jimmerson's misfeasance and Popper's crimes against the people. Get Popper and you've got Jimmerson. Bag one and you bag the other. You may object that Popper is only the front man, and up to a point I can agree with you, but I think you may underestimate how much the old man has always relied on Popper. I also have here Jimmerson's ceremonial baton. His so-called Rod of Correction. Look at it. A little rod you couldn't correct a dwarf with. It will make an interesting exhibit."

The woman informed him that these names meant nothing to her and that in any event the Churton hearing was concluded.

"What you must do is separate them," White went on. "First put Popper away and then get Jimmerson on the stand and sweat him. Drag him out of his palace, impound his bank accounts, seize all his secret books and then sweat him good. Trip him up and catch him out. Ask him about his women and his financial intrigues. Ask him about those perforated white shoes he had on in Washington in June of 1942, the kind barbers used to wear. He's an old man and can be easily confused and made to weep and blubber by a good lawyer. Nobody knows how old he really is. You see me as an old man but Jimmerson was already an old man when I was a young man. Even then he was high-handed and arbitrary. It's Master Lamar Jimmerson, you see, who has ultimate control over the Gnomon secrets and I can tell you from personal experience, madam, that there is nothing fair about the way he exercises that control. The lower and middle ranks of the Society get nothing but crumbs. All the real stuff is held back for a privileged few at the top. This is not well understood by the public."

The woman informed him that no more testimony was being taken by the Churton Committee. No more appointments were being made for meetings with committee members. No transcript of the hearing was available and she was unable to give him the addresses of Mr. Jimmerson and Mr. Popper. She herself was not empowered to take depositions. She would, however, be pleased to pass these documents along to the senators for their consideration.

"Turn it all over to you? Here? The Rod too?"

"I will see that they get it, sir."

"I was given to understand that I might serve this warrant personally."

"I will see that it gets in the proper hands."

"I'm not sure you appreciate how strong this material is. How comprehensive."

"I will bring it to the chairman's personal attention."

"Do you question my integrity?"

"No, sir."

"It doesn't disturb you to know that these two men are continuing to make improper use of their secret knowledge?"

"We would have to get back to you on that, sir."

He had not foreseen this, that his vengeance would be wreaked at an administrative level in Room 61-B, in chambers as it were, with the judge on the wrong side of the table, appearing as humble petitioner with cap in hand. He knew he could not expect from the law a hasty determination. He knew, none better, that the law was largely a matter of papers drifting leisurely about on top of heavy tables in dismal rooms like this, but still the proposal had caught him off guard. Could the woman be trusted? She seemed to be efficient. She was clean. They had not been bothered here in this room. She had been truthful about that.

He pushed himself back into the plastic chair. This chair, the guest chair, was tilted slightly forward and waxed, so that the sitter could maintain his seat in it only through a constant bracing effort of the legs. The weaker the legs, the shorter the visit.

"I won't be here tomorrow," the woman said. "Or the rest of the week. Of course, you can always mail it to us if you like. It's up to you."

But it wasn't up to him. His knees were quivering and he was sliding forward again. He felt the papers slipping from beneath his fingertips. The woman was pulling them across the table ever so slowly, her eyes elsewhere. She was disarming him. Pharris White surrendered them without another word, so forceful was the woman's will in this special room of hers. She thanked him on behalf of Senator Churton for his "valuable input." When he was gone she took an express elevator to the basement and went to a closet and dropped the brief and the crumbling warrant into a deep box where letters, telegrams, books, tracts, poems, manifestos and other supplementary reading matter were stored, soon to go up the flue. She kept the brass rod, to be placed with the other little loose treasures in her desk drawer, and went back to her party.

Mr. JIMMERSON and Sir Sydney Hen sat on the beach looking out at the Gulf of Mexico. They sat in deck chairs, not talking much, with their toes burrowing idly in the sand. They looked at the water but they did not plunge into it. There were woolly clouds overhead. A breeze came off the whitecaps, fresh but not sharp, nothing at all to the December blast off Lake Michigan. Many years ago the two Masters of Gnomonry had gazed thus in dumb wonder at another enclosed sea, with the cries of sea birds all around them.

Mr. Jimmerson said, "I am a swimmer but I am not a strong swimmer."

Hen said, "I don't fear the water but I do respect the water."

Hen had lost some of his fire. With his floppy hat and his chalky white face and his sunken eyes and his lipstick he looked like an old villain from a cowboy movie of the 1920s. There was froth in one corner of his mouth. Laughing now made him foam a little.

Once again Mr. Jimmerson said, "You're looking well, Sydney."

"Thank you, Lamar, I quite agree. I feel good too. I seem to expand when Christmas comes round. I bloom at this time of year like the poinsettia."

"With the solstice."

"Yes."

"So many of them. The years have flown."

"I quite agree. Night is gathering."

"But I would have known you in a vast crowd of old men."

"You were always alert, Lamar. It's true enough, though, I haven't let myself go. Laughing keeps me young and fit. Oh, one says that, but no, my real secret is eating things in season. Grapes, melons, exquisite plums that drop to the touch. Vine-ripened tomatoes, blood red, right at their peak, and avocados just as they come in. When nuts come in I eat nuts, and a lot of nuts, and when nuts are out of season I never touch them."

"A regiment of old men."

"My dear fellow, you were always on the qui vive."

"It was all so long ago, Sydney. The World War was just—"

"Ages. Who would have guessed then that our old bones would one day be cast up on this Texas littoral? Not I."

"But you know, it doesn't seem so long ago."

"My dear boy, yesterday."

This was the same Sydney Hen who had once called Mr. Jimmerson "a toad with no jewel in his head" and his followers "a cabal of ribbon clerks," and yet not the same. It was a new, agreeable Hen. He had come to La Coma for a visit from Saltillo, Mexico, his current home, traveling by second-class bus with his current companions, the Gluters, Whit and Adele. He used his Christmas money from sister Fanny to pay for the trip.

So it had come at last, the reunion of the two Masters, and it had all been arranged so simply, through the good offices of the Gluters and Mr. Morehead Moaler, and brought off with so little fuss, given the historic nature of the event and Hen's love for ceremony.

The Gluters, whose present job it was to make a flutter around Sir Sydney, had been in the counseling profession in California before retiring to Mexico. They were not culture-bound, they said, but rather citizens of the world. They were people oriented. They preened themselves over their handling of this Hen-Jimmerson affair, to Babcock's annoyance.

Whit Gluter, with his operatic laugh, hearty and unconvincing, said, "It was all so easy!" and Adele Gluter, striking a pose in her long peasant skirt, fists on hips, said, "Why didn't somebody think of this before, for crying out loud!"

Babcock explained to them that the pace of these things could not be forced. There was no occasion for boasting. The Gnomonic Cycle came around in its own good time, Gluters or no Gluters. As it happened, a new cycle was beginning, and consequently here were the two Masters, face to face again. It was not an occasion for crowing.

The formal meeting, with its promise of drama, took place in Mr. Moaler's trailer. The silver bowl was the centerpiece. Resting on a tripod, it was filled with alcohol, which was set afire. Hen wore a white gown with a red rose embroidered on one sleeve and a strange red animal on the other. It was some fierce heraldic beast clawing its way upward. Mr. Jimmerson's gown was unadorned and a bit tight. Each man wore his Poma, as did Mr. Moaler, newly proclaimed Judge of the East and Companion of Pythagoras. There was no embrace, only a fraternal handshake across the blazing bowl, and the two Masters found little to say to one another at first, but neither was there any unpleasantness.

The solemn Babcock, the indifferent Maceo, the beaming and nodding Mr. Moaler and the grinning Gluters, Adele and Whit, all stood back a little way in respect, and the better to behold the scene, and would have stood farther back had the trailer walls allowed. They applauded the handshake. Whit Gluter took photographs.

Popper knew nothing of these events. He lay in a hospital bed in San Antonio with a plastic tube in his nose. Esteban had dozed off at the wheel on the long drive back from Austin and the van had smashed into a guardrail. Popper, troubled by a dream about dancing white rats, woke for an instant in midair as he was flung from his bunk, only to be knocked cold in the fall. He cracked some ribs. Esteban walked away with cuts on his knees and a little blood running down into his socks.

The days passed. Hen extended his visit. He and Mr. Jimmerson got on better and better. Here on the beach they had even enjoyed a laugh together. They were waiting for the cloud cover to break and night to come. Mr. Jimmerson wanted to show Hen the stars. You couldn't see them from Burnette, only the moon, and the morning star now and then, because of the overpowering glow of Chicago, but here each night the whole staggering business was arrayed overhead in icy clarity. He was pleased with the thought of starlight from deep space striking his bare head after so long a journey, of his skull as the apex of countless triangles of stellar rays. In his moist brain, at the point of decussation, where the rays crossed, who could say what seething processes were going on. The starry spectacle was a common enough sight in the highlands of Mexico, and even more glorious, but Hen, now so agreeable, made no mention of it as he joined in the spirit of the outing. They would sit here together and ponder the two immensities of sea and sky.

More fishermen passed by them, tramping across the sand with rods and buckets, heading in for the day. Hen nudged

Mr. Jimmerson and again they laughed. The laugh was on the fishermen. Earlier in the afternoon a noisy party of these surf casters had walked heedlessly by, passing within inches of the magisterial feet, but taking no notice. Hen said, "The silly billies don't even know who we are. They think we're just two old turtles out here sunning ourselves." Then he and Mr. Jimmerson could not help but laugh at the innocence of those men who would never know of their close brush with the two world Masters.

The two Masters did not go to the beach every night to look at the stars and strain to hear the Pythagorean music, so very hard to pick up over the sloshing noises of the Gulf, and all but impossible if the wind was up—if the wind was up you could pack it in for the night, as far as listening to the music of the crystalline spheres went—and Mr. Moaler did not go to the beach at all. The sand sticking to his wheelchair tires, the salt spray smearing his eyeglasses—this was not for him. What Mr. Moaler enjoyed was a good long game of dominoes, a series of games, with a little chat along the way about Atlantis or the Three Secret Teachers or how ancient peoples might have moved their big blocks of stone around, though not so much chat as to interfere with the flow of play. He liked steady play, with a short break at 10:15 P.M. to catch the weather report on television, and a longer one at around 1 A.M. for coffee and banana pudding. Mr. Moaler did not have cymbals on his wheelchair but he did have a bicycle bell, a thumb bell, and when he rang it three times play was ended for the night.

Hen and Mr. Jimmerson regarded all such games as a waste of time and of one's vital powers but Mr. Moaler was, after all, their host, and so they agreed to humor him and sit in on a few of these sessions. As their play improved, as they became quicker at adding up the little white spots and more adept at sliding the bones around, their resistance gave way and they came to look forward to these games. They too became keen on dominoes, on the variation called Fives or Sniff. Mr. Jimmerson said he didn't know what he had been missing. Hen said, "I think Pythagoras would approve. He tells us that everything is numbers and this is certainly true of Sniff!" Soon they stopped going to the beach. Almost every night the three elderly men could be found in the trailer, playing dominoes and talking until the early hours, with Babcock or Whit Gluter or one of Mr. Moaler's local friends making a fourth at the table.

Babcock welcomed these invitations to the big trailer, as he welcomed every opportunity to escape his own dormitory trailer. Life in the Red Room had been odd but trailer life was odd too. The built-in furniture was fixed in place for all time, welded or nailed into place, so that no woman without an acetylene torch or a crowbar could ever rearrange it. Just going in and out was odd. One moment you were altogether outside the trailer and the next moment you were altogether inside the trailer, with no landing or foyer to soften the passage. Once inside there was the smoke to contend with, from Maceo's cigar and from the cigarettes of Ed and Esteban and Lázaro, who lay about like Chinamen in an opium den, puffing away, watching game shows on television and listening to droning Mexican polkas on the radio. Ed, if that was who he truly was, was still lying low, as Ed. He did no work, he slapped on things to the beat of Mexican accordion music and he laughed and egged them on when Esteban and Lázaro shouted curses at one another. There was a running quarrel between the two that sometimes flared up in an ugly way. At other times they could be great pals, very playful, as when they teased Babcock and locked him out of the trailer and made grotesque faces at him with their noses and lips pressed against the windows.

Such conditions made it hard for Babcock to concentrate on his studies. Work on the new autobiography had bogged down. He had trouble finding essential papers and books. These materials were now all jumbled up outside in a big pile with the Temple furnishings. There was no place to store the stuff and it remained on the ground where it had been dumped, and heaped up into a mound about eight feet high, and covered, after a fashion, with clear plastic sheets. The sheets were anchored all around with rocks and books but they had a way of blowing loose in the night and flapping feebly over the summit of the Temple goods. It was a pyre awaiting the torch.

Teresita's trailer, the smallest of the Moaler fleet, was dark and quiet and would have been ideal for Gnomonic study but for the Gluters, who had been assigned sleeping quarters there. The old lady, Teresita, kept to herself, licking her

trading stamps and sticking them into booklets. She went out
in the morning to feed her two geese and to sweep the ground
outside her door, this last business being almost involuntary.
Something in her Mexican blood drove her, sick or well, to
make those choppy broom strokes against the hard bare earth.
In the evening she fed her geese again and tended her two
flower beds, enclosed within two car tires. She glowered at
Babcock but asked no questions. He found he could work in
her trailer tolerably well, until the Gluters moved in. After that
there was no peace.

A guest bed was available but the Gluters chose to sleep on
the floor of Teresita's little sitting room, on straw mats that
they carried about with them, rolling them out at night and
rolling them up again in the morning and stowing them away
in their ancient suitcase. The Gluters were drawn to the floor.
All their counseling sessions, they said, were conducted with
everyone sitting cross-legged on the floor. In the afternoon
there was more of this tatami rolling, when they had their naps,
followed by sitting-up exercises. Adele directed the calisthenics. All through the day they were in and out of the trailer, with
Adele's pigtail bouncing, and in and out of their big suitcase,
forever buckling and unbuckling, with Whit, in a snarl of belts,
trying hard to please but often getting things wrong.

It was an old black leather suitcase of crinkled finish, on each
side of which was painted, with little skill, their name, thus:
"THE GLUTERS," in a green enamel that did not quite match
the fine patina on the hinges and fittings. Babcock wondered
about the quotation marks. Decorative strokes? Mere flour-
ishes? Perhaps theirs was a stage name. Wasn't Whit an actor?
The bag did have a kind of backstage look to it. Or a pen name.
Or perhaps this was just a handy way of setting themselves apart
from ordinary Gluters, a way of saying that in all of Gluterdom
they were *the* Gluters, or perhaps the enclosure was to emphasize the team aspect, to indicate that "THE GLUTERS" were not
quite the same thing as the Gluters, that together they were
an entity different from, and greater than the raw sum of Whit
and Adele, or it might be that the name was a professional
tag expressive of their work, a new word they had coined, a
new infinitive, *to gluter*, or *to glute*, descriptive of some new
social malady they had defined or some new clinical technique

they had pioneered, as in their mass Glutering sessions or their breakthrough treatment of Glutered wives or their controversial Glute therapy. The Gluters were only too ready to discuss their personal affairs and no doubt would have been happy to explain the significance of the quotation marks, had they been asked, but Babcock said nothing. He was not one to pry.

The Gluters annoyed him in many ways, not least with their insinuations that Hen stood just a bit higher in rank than Mr. Jimmerson. They dared to speak to the Master in a familiar way. They presumed to comment freely on the Telluric Currents, or on anything else. A nuisance, then, these Gluters, but Babcock could not in fairness blame them for the present state of things here at the new Temple, where nothing was going forward.

The Master never looked anything up these days and he kept putting off work on the new book. He seldom spoke of the Lag. There was little mention of Pletho. His only interests seemed to be dominoes and his afternoon cone of soft ice cream and the nightly weather news on television—the actual weather did not interest him, just the news. Each day more papers blew away from the Gnomon pile, lost forever, so many papers that the blizzard was remarked on by golfers out on the links who found strange pages stuck to their legs, and by other residents of La Coma, a town notable for its blowing paper.

No, the blame lay with Hen. It was Hen who had put a chill on things with his shrugs and smiles. Gnomon talk bored him. He professed not to understand the Jimmerson Lag. He treated these matters in a jocular, dismissive way and could not be engaged in serious discussion of any subject other than that of fresh fruit and goat's milk. He said over and over again that he no longer bothered to write books or, a much greater release, read them. "So very tiresome," he said. "Such rubbish. Even the best of them are not very good. Far too many people expelling gas in public these days. Don't you agree, Morehead?" He seemed to suggest that Lamar Jimmerson and others would do well to follow his example.

With so little to do, Babcock took to lingering in bed under heavy medication, sunk in waves of smoke and accordion music that never died. And even there, in his own bed, he could not get away from Whit Gluter and his lank wife, Adele. There was an intercom system that connected all the trailers in the Moaler compound, and Adele used it frequently. She came on at all hours in a hissing blast of static, calling for Whit, telling Whit to report in, asking if anyone had seen Whit, passing on urgent messages for Whit. And, likely as not, Whit would be there, in the bunkhouse trailer, though he did not always respond to the calls. He would be talking to Ed or Lázaro or, at bedside, to Babcock, telling of the Gluter travels in Mexico—so many miles by bus, so many by train, exact figures, the bargain meals, the bargain rooms, the colorful villages, their names.

Whit's delivery was clear, for he had once been a movie actor before he married Adele and became a counselor, specializing in portrayals of informers, touts, pickpockets, eavesdroppers, treacherous clerks and the like, city sneaks of one stripe or another. He was a friendly fellow with a ready laugh, as became a counselor, but with his dark moods too. One morning, in a lull between bus stories, he began to squirm and dart his eyes about as he lapsed for a moment into one of his weasel screen roles. He said, "Uh, look here, have you been making eyes at Adele?"

Babcock could not have been more surprised had Whit suddenly burst into song. "No, of course not. What gave you that idea?"

"This, uh, note. Adele found it in her tatami."

Babcock read the note, which ran:

*Adell*
*I could go for you baby in a big way. How about it? Burn this.*
                                                      *Maurice*

"I didn't write this note, Whit. You can see that's not my handwriting."

"Well, I didn't know. I couldn't be sure. I wouldn't want you to think you could break our marriage up."

Later that same day Adele herself came by. She came to take Whit away for his nap. It was time to roll out the mats again. She stared at Babcock, already at rest. She stood over him, gathering her thoughts, then said, "You have no business looking down your nose at us. Oh, I know what you've been thinking. I'm not dumb. I know what you've been saying. The Gluters are silly. The Gluters are not refined people. I know what you've been saying behind our backs. You think I haven't heard it all before? From people like you? The Gluter woman is a hussy. Adele walks with too confident a stride. Even my gait is found offensive. Adele this and Adele that. Her hair. Her clothes. Whit is foolish. The Gluters are vulgar. Whit is henpecked. The Gluters could do with a bath. Well, what do you know about it? You know nothing whatever about our professional standing. How many radio talk shows have you been on, Mr. Know-it-all? You know nothing about the hundreds of interesting articles we have written or the thousands of successful encounter sessions we have conducted, helping people to expand and grow in many different directions and live their lives to the fullest, or even what personal goals we may have set for ourselves this year. Yes, and I've caught you ogling me, and let me tell you something, mister, you can just put those ideas right out of your head. I've told Whit about it and I've also complained to Sir Sydney. You think Whit is henpecked? It might surprise you to know that Whit sometimes spanks me with one of his sandals. How do you like that, Mr. Babcock? So you can just keep your love letters to yourself, thank you. No, we will not have an affair. You will never hold me in your arms. You and I, Mr. Babcock, will never go stepping out together and I want you to get that through your head once and for all. If you think you're going to break our marriage up you've got another think coming."

This was Adele, roused. Babcock said nothing.

# 23

WHIT'S PHOTOGRAPHS of the reunion turned out to be dark splotches. There was to be a reenactment of the Masters' handshake, to be captured this time on fresh film, before the big dinner on Christmas day.

Popper came rolling in the day before Christmas, in a wheelchair. The chair was a windfall. His roommate at the hospital, an old man, had died, and Popper had bought the man's chair from the distraught widow. He gave her five dollars and said he would take it off her hands. There was nothing wrong with his legs, he could walk well enough, but he liked the idea of making an entrance on high spoked wheels. He would come home wounded in action. Esteban would push him up the ramp and into the trailer, and there he would sit hub to hub with Mr. Moaler, with a knitted shawl over his knees and his hands formally composed in his lap.

So he arrived, to warm greetings from Mr. Jimmerson and Mr. Moaler. They plied him with questions about his injuries but showed only mild interest in his account of the Senate hearing, now such a remote event. Popper, sensitive to his audience, cut short the account, saying that the senators, after hearing the truth of the matter, had given him a unanimous vote of thanks for bringing Mr. Jimmerson to Texas.

"Junior had scared the fool out of everybody with a lot of wild tales about us. People were fainting. Women passing out and children crying. Well, Big Boy had to eat those words. You can bet I set the record straight, and pretty fast too. On the day I left Austin the Christmas shoppers on the streets were talking of nothing else but Lamar Jimmerson and how he had been misunderstood."

"And what did Junior say?"

"Junior didn't know what to say, Mr. Moaler."

Mr. Moaler smiled at the picture in his head of his son, the big fellow, checked and sputtering. "And what repercussions may we expect?"

"None. We're clear. All is well."

The two wheelchairs in such narrow quarters made for a traffic problem. Popper maneuvered his chair about in a clumsy manner. "Watch out for Sweet Boy's tail," said Mr. Moaler. "And his paws. Watch out for my curios. Watch out for the tree." This was the Christmas tree. All the lights on it were blue.

Hen and Babcock were not so pleased to see Popper, nor was Popper pleased to find that Hen had taken his bed. He had been informed of Hen's descent on La Coma but not fully informed, it being his understanding that the visit was to be a flying one of only two or three days. He was greatly surprised to find Hen still here, and, to cap it off, wallowing in his, Popper's, sheets.

"He hasn't left? Sydney Hen is here now? You're not serious!"

"He's back there having his lunch."

Popper rolled himself down the corridor to the end bedroom. Hen was in bed eating greedily from a tray, not fruits of the season but meat loaf and fried potatoes. Adele was seated beside him with pad and pencil. She was there to jot down the words that came to him in his poetic flights, these to be picked over later for gems, such as were suitable for inclusion in the new book he was putting together on the sly. Adele also had a moist towel at the ready for dabbing the tomato sauce off his fingers and chin.

Popper looked at Hen, taking him in. The two men had never met and now they took each other in, shadows become at last sagging flesh. Hen was wearing his Caesar wig with the curly bangs, and Popper his Texas promoter wig, which was a swelling silver pompadour.

"Hen? I'm Austin Popper."

"Popper. Well, well. Lo the bat with leathern wing."

"What do you think you're doing here?"

"Austin ruddy Popper. Augustine writ small. Yes, I daresay you are Popper. You look like Popper. That narrow eye."

"You look like some devilish old diseased monkey."

"Charming. But we shall just have to bear with one another's infirmities, Popper. I with yours and you with mine."

"You've made yourself at home, I see."

"Oh yes, I've become quite fond of my room here. My little nest. A poky little room but oh so comfy. Like a snug cabin on ship or a luxury train. Morehead is very kind. I grow tired of travel."

Adele said, "Should I turn to a fresh page and get this down, Sir Sydney?"

"No, my dear, I think not."

"If I may dab. A red drop there."

"Too kind."

"About to fall."

"Most considerate."

Popper said, "It's time for you to move on, Hen. Back to your hole in Mexico. You're not welcome here. There's no place for you here in our program. You're in my bed. This is not your room. This is my room and I mean to have it back."

"Oh pooh. Do you hear that, my sweet? He makes threats from a wheelchair."

"What have you done with my things?"

"I had your man take them away."

Popper wheeled about and went back to Mr. Jimmerson and Mr. Moaler to present his case. Mr. Jimmerson, who was thinking of turtle riding in the open sea, did not follow the complaint in all its detail but he did say that this squabbling on Christmas Eve was unseemly and that surely some sleeping arrangement satisfactory to all parties could be worked out.

"Lamar is right," said Mr. Moaler. "There's plenty of room for everyone. Plenty of trailers and plenty of warm beds for everyone to lie down in. And if not, we'll *make* room. Let's not spoil our Christmas with a quarrel."

That night they saw Christmas come in at the dominoes table. Popper sat in on the game. He and Hen observed a wary truce. At midnight Mr. Moaler rang the thumb bell on his chair and they broke off play. There were Christmas greetings all around, followed by coffee and banana pudding and some friendly chat.

Mr. Moaler, taking care to get a bit of banana and a bit of yellow pudding and a bit of vanilla wafer in each spoonful, said it was interesting that cattle were mentioned upwards of 140 times in the Bible, but that the domestic hen, a most useful fowl, was mentioned only twice, and the domestic cat not at all. Mr. Jimmerson said that Sydney's recent mention of the turtle had made him think of something he had seen many years ago, and that had been much on his mind lately. It was an old newsreel showing a young man astride a swimming sea turtle. A giant turtle, with his flippers, such odd limbs, flapping smoothly away in the water. The young rider was laughing and waving at the camera. He would be quite old now and Mr. Jimmerson wondered if he retained his good humor and his gleaming teeth and his love for water sports. He wondered where the fellow might be today. Probably gumming his food well inland, said Hen. He went on to say that the domestic dog came in for a good deal of unfavorable mention in the Bible. Popper said that so far tonight no mention at all had been made of the deer, and yet his antlers, shed and regenerated once a year, were thought to be the fastest-growing of all animal substances.

They stayed up for the late weather report—"Winds light and variable"—and exchanged another round of good wishes. "Let's all look our best tomorrow," said Mr. Moaler, with a curious smile. "That is, later today. I have a little something in mind. An interesting announcement to make. Let's all look our best."

With that they turned in. Popper slept on the plastic couch, in the blue glow of the Christmas tree.

Adele, who had a way of getting wind of things, came on the intercom early in the morning to say that everyone was to wear his good clothes to the dinner today. She repeated the message at intervals, sometimes adding, "Let's keep to schedule."

Lázaro was up early too, basting the turkeys, as was Maceo, who had charge of cakes and pies. Teresita prepared the gumbo. This dish, a soup dense with shrimps and hairy and mucilaginous pods of okra, was a Moaler tradition on Christmas morning. Whit loaded his camera, in a darkened bathroom this time.

Popper had Esteban take him out for a drive in the van. He wanted to get away from Adele's voice and all the bustle. On sharp turns the right front tire rubbed against the crumpled fender. They cruised the residential streets and watched with delight the little children wobbling along on their new Christmas bikes and skates. They went to Brownsville and looked over Mr. Moaler's downtown parking lots. No revenue today, no cars, but still the recorded message played endlessly over a loudspeaker, warning those who would park there without paying that their cars would most certainly be towed away, at any hour of the day or night, Sundays and holidays not excepted, at great expense to the trespassers.

Popper said, "This is the greatest business in the world, Esteban. You do absolutely nothing but collect money."

But he wondered if these two weed lots could continue to support Mr. Moaler's expanded household. Would he be announcing sharp cutbacks at the dinner today? Or what? Something to do with the Society? Would he proclaim himself Master?

Esteban said, "Why don't we go back to Corpus, boss?"

"No, I'm just not up to it. I'm tired of all that chasing around. I'm tired of jabbering. I haven't had a drink in five years. Your brewers, your vintners, your distillers, they don't even exist for me anymore, and I try to put a good face on things, but the fact is, Esteban, that I'm still not getting enough air to my brain. The truth is that my powers are failing and I can't cut it any longer. You saw how they worked me over up there at Austin."

Babcock had no Christmas morning duties to perform either. He poked at the pile of Gnomon goods with a stick, looking for his stenotype machine, as a survivor pokes the rubble after a tornado in search of a favorite shoe. The light winds had disturbed the covering sheets again, leaving the mound exposed. The rain and sun had been at work. Alternately soaked and baked, the mass was dissolving, blending and settling into a lumpy conglomerate, something like fruitcake. Around the base there lay exfoliating copies of *Hoosier Wizard*.

Babcock's eye ranged over the big trailer. This was the new Temple, or rather Great Hall. It seemed an unlikely place for one to await apocalyptic events, but then what would be a likely place? He noted that the Hall was growing on him. The stark lines had become pleasing, the horizontal values, the very human scale. It was a Temple that could be hauled away in the night by anyone with a two-inch ball on his car bumper, but then Temples of marble and granite did not last either, as he had reason to know.

"Hey, what do you think Mr. Moaler's announcement will be?"

This from Ed, who had slipped up behind him. Ed was apprehensive.

"I don't know."

"Lázaro thinks he may kick some of us out. Or all of us."

"I don't know anything about it, Ed. We'll just have to wait and see."

Babcock thought he did know what the announcement would be but it was not the kind of thing you could discuss with Ed, who, he knew now, was not Nandor. He had seen it coming. He had felt it coming, this climacteric, this revelation that Mr. Moaler was himself the Lame One, and that Mr. Jimmerson and Sir Sydney were Nandor and Principato, or Principato and Nandor. It was all falling together. He could see now the necessity for the flight south. It was nothing less than the coming together of the Three Secret Teachers.

Adele served Hen his cup of gumbo and his cup of cocoa in bed, and advised him to wear his green silk gown for the reenactment of the Masters' handshake. The gown was of oriental design, with ample sleeves that covered the hands when joined in front, Chinese fashion. There were white four-pointed stars scattered about over it, representing Ptolemy's fifteen fixed stars of the first magnitude.

Adele said, "The green makes a stronger statement and will help to offset Mr. Jimmerson's thicker presence. Your super-tall green Poma will help to diminish him somewhat too."

Hen nodded. He was brooding over Mr. Moaler's interesting announcement. When would it come? Before dinner? After? During? With ding of spoon on glass? What could it be? Interesting to whom? Something to do with the Lag? A recent dream? A vision? A program of compulsory physical exercise? A day trip on a motor launch?

He waved off the gown chatter. "Yes, but what news, Adele? What do you hear about this announcement or proclamation?"

"Ed told Whit that Mr. Moaler thinks there are too many people living here and that he's going to turn some of us out."

"On Christmas day?"

"Ed didn't know when. He got it from Lázaro."

"And who was Lázaro's source?"

"I have Whit working on that now."

"Babcock, you think?"

"I wouldn't think so. He never knows anything."

"Popper?"

"That would be my guess. Through Esteban to Lázaro to Ed."

"Or Popper directly to Lázaro to Ed."

"Or through Maceo to Lázaro."

"They confide?"

"They confer. Over their pots."

"Nothing about a boat ride?"

"No, sir."

"But who is to go? Who is to be given the black spot?"

"Whit is working on that now. Shall I lay out the green silk?"

"Yes, my dear, and then you can draw my tub."

## 24

ADELE TOO chose to make a green statement, with her sea-green terry-cloth coveralls, cinched in at the middle with a pirate's black belt, for the occasion of this extraordinary conclave at Rancho Moaler. Mr. Jimmerson called her Juanita. Never good at sorting women out, he had thought Adele and Teresita to be the same person, though they were nothing at all alike, and he addressed them both as Juanita. Now he saw them together for the first time and was confused. Teresita wore different hues of black.

All were crowded into the big trailer or Great Moaler Hall, and all were spruced up, faces scrubbed, Ed with clean boots, Babcock in borrowed necktie, Maceo in his old tan suit and long pointed tan shoes, Esteban in his frilly white guayabera shirt, Hen resplendent under a green spire, a Merlin hat. Mr. Jimmerson's original Poma looked squat and crude in comparison. Still the eye was drawn to it.

Again the two Masters clasped hands across the burning bowl, before rapt faces. Popper did not lead the applause but he did join in. Whit took shots from different angles. He said, "Hold it, please. That flame is so faint and I want to make sure I get it in." He wanted to catch a blue wisp, seemingly unsupported, on his color film.

Sir Sydney was on edge, unnaturally animated, talking too much and laughing too readily under the tension of waiting for Mr. Moaler's announcement. He said, "Do you know, Lamar, there really is something to this stuff. There were times when I thought I might be deluded. There were moments when I wondered if my condition might not be a pathological one, but now I'm convinced that old Papa Pletho was really on to something."

Mr. Jimmerson said, "It's too bad that Fanny and Jerome can't be here to share in this."

"Yes."

"I don't believe you have any children, do you, Sydney?"

"Oh no, it wouldn't have done for me. I spared the world

the late-life spawn of an aesthete and a socialite. I didn't want to foist off some rotten, helpless, exotic kid on the world. It would never have done. Out of the question. It must all end with me. The Hen line must die with me in what I had hoped would be a Wagnerian finish."

A whiff of sage came from the corn-bread dressing and there were other pleasant smells from the long buffet table. Mr. Moaler struck a green note himself, with a Gnomon sash across his body, which was like that of an Eagle Scout or a South American president. When the ceremony was done and the congratulations had trailed off, he rang his thumb bell. The guests looked at one another and became very still, like Sweet Boy. They steeled themselves. Breathing was suspended. *Here it comes.* Mr. Moaler offered a long prayer of thanksgiving for their many blessings, but made no announcement.

"Amen," said Popper. "After all, we still have our—I started to say our health. But we do still have our wits about us and we still hold our ancient secrets inviolate and we have our Society intact, lean and strong, under the generous patronage of Mr. Morehead Moaler."

There was applause for Mr. Moaler. He stopped it with a raised hand. "Time to eat," he said. Plates were prepared and served to the two Masters, and to Mr. Moaler and Popper in their wheelchairs, the four of them sitting *en banc*. Then the others formed a line and served themselves.

Adele said, "No need to overload your plate like that, Ed. There's plenty of food. You can come back."

Hen helped Mr. Moaler tuck his napkin, showing that he was not too proud to perform such small offices. "A lovely dinner, Morehead. Do you know, I believe I'm recovering some of my old form, thanks to you and your kindness."

"Good food," said Mr. Jimmerson. "Give me the dark meat every time and you can have your white meat."

Popper said, "Did you hear that, Maceo? Lázaro? Teresita? The Master's compliments. Mine too. A real dining experience. How about it, everyone? Can't we show a little appreciation for our cooks?"

More applause.

Outside there was a rustling noise, which, to Babcock,

reminded of that last terrible day in the Temple, sounded like many thousands of cockroaches on the march. Again the guests looked at each other with alarm, in the way of the Atlanteans, when they first heard the rumbling on their single day and night of misfortune. What now? There was a rush for the windows, such that the Great Hall tilted a bit. Outside they saw a magnificent new mobile home, yellow, with pitched roof, being towed in under the palm trees and brushing against the dead fronds. This was Mr. Moaler's surprise. He had bought a new trailer.

His red face was glowing under his Poma. "How do you like it?" he said. "That's your eighty-foot Cape Codder with cathedral roof and shingles of incorruptible polystyrene. It's the top of the line. The Cape Codder is built with sixteen-inch centers and will never sag in the middle like those cheaper models with twenty-inch centers. The furniture is done in indestructible Herculon and there are two master bedrooms for our two Masters. Plenty of room for everybody. By day we'll study or do whatever we please and every night we'll play Sniff."

There were more cheers for Mr. Moaler, on this day of cheers and goodwill. Even Popper, who never laughed, was moved to laugh a little. Another trailer! And the suggestion that there were still more where that one came from! A Gnomon panzer formation in the Moaler grove! It wasn't the Temple of the old days but it was better than being breathed on by Dean Ray Stuart!

Hen, exultant, foaming, almost weeping, said, "I think I'll grow tomatoes by day, Lamar. The Better Boy variety for preference, in this sand. Yes, a little garden for me. How about you?"

"It's study for me, Sydney."

Babcock remained standing at a window but he was not looking at the long yellow flanks of the new Temple. He could feel the Telluric Currents. The pulsing made him a little dizzy. The surge and ebb. He saw what must be done. The flame was faint indeed and he had much work to do. He need no longer take account of the thoughtless multitude in the cities of men or of the three elderly gamesters at their table in their conical caps. He had often suppressed the thought but now he knew in his heart that he himself was a Master and that Maurice Babcock was to be Master of the New Cycle.

Whit said, "What a wonderful Christmas!"

Ed, who no longer missed the Red Room, said, "This is the best party I've ever been to!"

# GRINGOS

# I

CHRISTMAS AGAIN in Yucatán. Another year gone and I was still scratching around on this limestone peninsula. I woke at eight, late for me, wondering where I might find something to eat. Once again there had been no scramble among the hostesses of Mérida to see who could get me for Christmas dinner. Would the Astro Café be open? The Cocina Económica? The Express? I couldn't remember from one holiday to the next about these things. A wasp, I saw, was building a nest under my window sill. It was a gray blossom on a stem. Go off for a few days and nature starts creeping back into your little clearing.

I bathed and dressed and went downstairs to the lobby. Frau Kobold hadn't opened her door yet. She had a room on the ground floor and by this time she was usually sitting in her doorway. She parked there in her high-back wickerwork wheelchair and read paperback mysteries and watched the comings and goings. Fausto himself was at the desk. Beatriz, poor girl, finally had a day off. Fausto saw me but kept his head down, pretending to be absorbed in some billing calculation.

"Well, Fausto, I'm back. *Feliz Navidad.*"

". . . *días,*" he muttered. He was annoyed with me because I had paid him two months rent some weeks back. Now he had spent the money, and I was staying free in his hotel, or so he viewed it. He disliked these *anticipo* payments. Much better that I should get behind in the rent, like everybody else, and be beholden to him. I had arrived in the night, too late to check my mail, and he handed me a letter and a long note, in a flash of fingernails. Not otherwise odd in appearance, Fausto made a show of his high-gloss nails. They were painted with clear lacquer, to indicate, I think, that he was of that class of men who did not have to grub in the earth with their hands.

"*Gracias.*"

"Joor welcome."

The letter was from my unknown enemy who signed himself "Ah Kin" this time. He also called himself "Mr. Rose" and "Alvarado." Or was it a woman? The letter was postmarked here in Mérida, and it read, without date or salutation, "Well, Mr. Jimmy Burns, I saw your foolish red face in the market again today. Why don't you go back where you belong and stay there?" Ah Kin (He of the Sun) used a Spanish typewriter, with all the tildes and accent marks, but I had the feeling he was a gringo. The note was a long telephone message, taken down by Beatriz. A hauling job in Chiapas.

I went outside and smoked a cigarette, looking this way and that, the very picture of an American idler in Mexico, right down to the grass-green golfing trousers. They had looked all right on the old man from Dallas but they made me feel like a clown. They were hot and sticky, too, made of some petroleum-based fiber, with hardly any cotton content. The town was quiet, no street cries, very little traffic. Christmas is subdued in Mérida. Easter is the big festival. Holy Week, when all the fasting and penitence is coming to an end, I could sense nothing in the air. Art and Mike had told me that something was stirring. What? Just something—coming. They couldn't say what. We would see. It was old President Díaz who said that nothing ever happens in Mexico until it happens. Things rock along from day to day, and then all at once you are caught up in a rush of unforeseen events.

The street frontage of the Posada Fausto was not very wide. There was a single doorway at sidewalk level, and beside it a small display window, like a jeweler's window, backed by a velvet curtain. A blue placard behind the glass read SE VENDE. Strangers paused to look but found nothing on display other than dead beetles. What was for sale? The nearsighted drew closer. Finally they realized it was the hotel itself that was being offered. Fausto's hope was that one day some strolling investor or whimsical rich man would stop dead in his tracks there and throw up his hands and cry out, "Just the thing! A narrow hotel on Calle 55! Between El Globo Shoe Repairs and a dark little bodega!" The sign had been there for years, along with the same bugs.

My truck was parked across the street in an enclosed lot. The watchman, old Paco, was asleep in his sentry box, and the wooden gates were secured in exaggerated fashion, like some Houdini contraption, with great looping chains and huge flat padlocks shaped like hearts, and long-loop bicycle locks. It was all a bluff, and if you knew where to look there was a snap link that undid the whole business. There it was in the corner, my white Chevrolet with a camper shell. The old truck was sagging a bit, getting a bit nose-heavy with age. A film of red dust had settled over it. The engine fired up first shot.

I had decided to drive over to one of the tourist hotels on the Paseo Montejo. Their dining rooms would be open. A big gringo breakfast there would be expensive but would hold me for the rest of the day, what with a few supplementary rolls stuffed in my pockets. Then I would go out to the zoo for a few minutes and look over the fine new jaguar.

Paco jumped up in his box and waved me on through, as though he had been on top of things all along. As I was going around the *zócalo*, the central plaza, a girl flagged me down and jumped in beside me without invitation. It was Louise Kurle, the ninety-pound woman, in her tennis cap with the long visor, with her mesh bag and her tape recorder.

She said, "Say, where have you been anyway?"

"Dallas."

"I've been looking for you. I need a ride. Can you take me out to Emmett's place? You need some white shoes and a white belt to go with those pants."

"Where's your car? Where's your strange husband?"

"He's out of town."

"Where?"

"I'm not supposed to say."

"Ah."

"You know how Rudy is."

"I do, yes."

"But first I want to go to church. Come and go with me."

"All right."

"Look what I've got."

She had a package of Fud bacon, a good brand, already limp from the heat, and a small bottle of imitation maple flavoring. She and Emmett were to have a bacon and pancake feed. I was invited.

She wanted to go to the cathedral, but I thought that was too grand for us and I drove instead to a lesser church beside a small park. Everyone was moving inside at that Indio quick-step, the men doffing their straw hats and the women pulling

up their rebozos over their heads. Louise and I composed
ourselves for public worship and entered the dark vault. Not
being a Roman Catholic, I took up the position of respectful
observer, at the very back, from which point I could just make
out flickering candles and the movement of a young priest in
white. I sat alone in a pew and recited the Lord's Prayer, the
King James version from Matthew, asking forgiveness of debts
instead of trespasses. I carried on my business largely in Spanish but I still prayed in English. Louise had to be in the thick of
things. She wasn't a *católica* either but she went all the way up
front to get in on the ceremony and the wafers. I could see her
white cap bobbing up and down, all bill. What was she doing
now? Recording people at prayer?

Children stopped to stare at my green trousers, better suited
for the links. Off to my left in an alcove there was a gray marble figure, a barefooted man, some medieval figure in short
belted coat and flat Columbus hat, shedding two marble tears.
He was about three-quarters life size, standing on a pedestal,
the whole thing fenced off with a low wooden rail. There was
a gate and a contribution box, with people standing in line,
each waiting his turn to approach the statue and give thanks
or ask for something. Surely that was a graven image. It always
took me by surprise to find these secondary activities going on
during a mass. I knew the woman at the end of the line. Lucia
something. She worked at a juice bar, cashier now, up from
squeezer. Then I saw Doc Flandin holding the marble feet. He
had a fierce grip on them with both hands and he appeared to
be demanding something, not begging, though it's hard to tell
with that kind of anguish. I hadn't seen him since his wife died.

The people behind him had begun to stir. Doc was taking
more than his allotted time. Or maybe they didn't like his
belligerent manner in the face of this mystery. Suddenly he
dropped his hands. He was done. He had finished his pleading
and was off like a shot, scuffling along, head down, for the
door. A strange scene. I had never known Doc to take more
than a scholar's formal interest in the church.

Louise had two more stops to make. She took a jar of something that looked like pickled beets to some Indian friends
who lived north of town off the Progreso highway. It was a
Christmas present. The Mayan family gathered in puzzlement

around the jar of red matter. Then she delivered another gift, a Spanish songbook, to an older woman who lived nearby. I watched her standing in the doorway of the hut, trying to explain to the old woman what it was, singing a little. Louise was a good girl. Some days she went out into the countryside plucking bits of blowing plastic from bushes so the goats could get at the leaves. She truly wished everyone well, reminding me of my grandfather, a Methodist preacher, who included the Dionne quintuplets and the Postmaster General in his long, itemized prayers. Louise and Rudy were graduates of some college in Pennsylvania and had come down here to investigate flying saucer landings. Her degree was in Human Dynamics. Rudy had one, a dual degree, he said, in City Planning and Mass Communications. First he would build the city and then he would tell everybody about it in the approved way.

Emmett lived in a trailer park out by the airport. I took a back road and ran over a dead snake on the way. Louise turned on me. "You just drove right over that snake."

"That was an old broken fan belt."

"It was white on the bottom. Do you think I don't know a snake when I see one?"

I told her he was already dead and that women were easily taken in by serpents. Yes, she said, but even running over a dead one in that heedless way showed a lack of delicacy. I had to concede the point. Little Louise was pitching in to help with my program of moral improvement if no one else was.

Three hippies were trudging along the back street in single file. One wore a comic Veracruz hat, a big straw sombrero with a high conical crown that came to a point. Louise waved to them. "A lot of New Age people passing through town." That was her term for hippies.

"What's the occasion?"

"I don't know. They all seem to be going to Progreso."

We had difficulty raising Emmett. He lived in a sturdy trailer, the Mobile Star by name, all burnished aluminum, very sleek, but no longer mobile, at the rear of the park. The wheels were gone, and it rested on concrete blocks. He had bought it here, *in situ*, some years ago, from another American. This was his home now. He didn't like hotel rooms and he didn't like the feudal bother of maintaining a house in Mexico, with servants running underfoot and a parade of vendors coming to the door. This way he could live in an exotic land and at the same time withdraw into his own little American box.

We knocked and called his name. No answer. I knew he must be on the grounds because his air conditioner was humming, or rather his evaporative cooler, which didn't pull as many amps as a real air conditioner, with a compressor. It didn't cool as well either if the air was at all humid.

We set off to look for him, and then he opened the door. "All right. I'm here. I heard you. You have to give people time to get to the door. I can't be at the door one second after you knock." You would think we had caught him upstairs in the tub. He was touchy about his poor hearing. He had heart problems, too, and the worst kind of diabetes, where they cut your legs off and you go blind. His sixth or seventh wife, a local woman, had recently left him.

I said, "How's the single life, Emmett?"

"It's killing me."

Louise presented him with his Christmas gift, a clip-on bow tie, and then apologized several times because she had nothing for me. She and Emmett prepared the food. He liked his bacon burnt. I stirred the maple flavoring into a can of corn syrup. It turned out well enough though I believe I could have gotten a more uniform blend if I had first heated the syrup. The dinner was good—salty and sweet and puffy and greasy all at once. A few pancakes were left over, but nobody ever leaves strips of crisp bacon lying around, nobody I know.

We sat back and Emmett poured us each a *copita* of brandy. He talked about his new medicine and how effective it was. Soon, to my alarm, our chat drifted into a confessional.

Louise said, "I've really found myself here. I could be happy here keeping a herd of milk goats. Rudy hasn't quite found himself yet."

Emmett said, "My life is over, for all practical purposes. I no longer have enough money to keep a woman." He looked back on his long bright empty days in Mexico and said he had lost his honor over the years. He hadn't noticed it going. Small rodents had come in the night and carried it away bit by bit on tiny padded feet. The best I could do in this line, the most I

was willing to do, was to say that I hoped to be more considerate of other people in the coming year. Louise gave me a cold
look. Being a facetious person I got no credit for any depth of
feeling.

She kissed Emmett on top of his bald head and popped his
suspenders and went out for a swim in the pool. This trailer
park had all the amenities. There was a lull. She had a way of
leaving people speechless in her wake. We had already gone
over my trip to Texas. A retired couple had come down here
to spend the winter touring the ruins in their motor home, a
huge thing, of the *Yamato* class, with about ten feet of overhang behind the rear wheels. After a week or two of it, they
longed for home but had no stomach for driving the thing
back. I was hired for the job. They insisted on taking the
coastal route, which they thought would be a straight and
simple shot, but the road was all broken up from the pounding of oil rigs and sugar cane trucks and farm combines. At
Tampico there was a storm, and we had to wait five hours for
the Pánuco ferry. Water was running a foot deep in the city
streets. The *Yamato* plowed right through it. We had to stop
every few hours and let the fat spaniel do his business on the
roadside. Or not do it, as the whim took him. He wouldn't be
coaxed or hurried.

But they were nice people and paid me well and even gave
me some clothes, this green resort attire. In Dallas I bought
an old Chevrolet Impala and drove it down to Belize and sold
it. You can always unload a big four-door Chevrolet or Ford
there, for service as a taxicab. They know what they want. You
can't force a sale. Then I came back to Mérida by bus.

Emmett pulled the curtains and began moving about in
a stealthy way. I knew more or less what was coming. He
brought out a shoebox, inside of which, wrapped in a towel,
was a Jaina figurine.

"What do you think?"

I looked it over. "It's a nice piece."

"Nice? It's mint. What do you think it would bring in New
Orleans?"

"I couldn't even make a guess, Emmett. I'm out of touch.
You know I'm out of the business now."

He smiled. I was riding the bus these days and living at the Posada Fausto and wearing castoff clothing and still no one believed me.

"You might ask Eli."

"I bought it from Eli."

"Well, whatever you do, I don't want to know about it. I really am out of the game. You might pass that word around."

"I was just curious about the current value. I wanted you to see it. You're not the only one around here with an eye for these things. I don't plan to sell it right away. It's a wonderful investment."

It was an investment worth about $35 and there was no telling what he had paid Eli Withering for it. The piece was six or seven inches high, a terra cotta figure of a haughty Maya woman, seated tailor-fashion, with earlobe plugs, bead necklace and upswept hairdo. She held a fan or rattle across her body. There was a piece just like this under glass in a Mexico City museum, dated 800 A.D., and it too was a fake, or a fine copy, as we say.

This one was in mint condition all right. An old gravelooter named Pastor had minted it very recently in his shop at Campeche. It wasn't worth much, unless you could find another gullible buyer, but in a sense it wasn't altogether a fake. Pastor had come by a genuine Maya mold from the island of Jaina and he used it to press out and bake a few of these things now and then. Maybe more than a few. He was getting careless. He had left a sharp ridge on this one, untrimmed, where the base of the mold had pressed against the excess clay. The ridge was much too sharp and fresh. Along the back he had beveled off the clay with his thumb, the way you do with putty on a window pane.

Things had turned around, and now it was the palefaces who were being taken in with beads and trinkets. Emmett carefully wrapped it again and put it away in a drawer. I dozed. I had work to do, bills to pay, an overdue delivery job in Chiapas, but not today. Emmett read a detective novel. He and Frau Kobold read them day in and day out, preferably English ones and none written after about 1960. He said the later ones were no good. The books started going wrong about that time, along with other things. I put the watershed at 1964, the last year of silver coinage. For McNeese it was when they took the lead out of house paint and ruined the paint. I forget the year, when they debased the paint.

Poor Emmett. He had been here more than thirty years, perhaps the only person ever to come to Mexico seeking relief from intestinal cramps, and still he thought he could beat a *zopilote* like Eli Withering, a hard-trading buzzard, at his own game. Emmett came from Denver and went first to Tehuacán for the mineral water treatment, then drifted on to Mazatlán, San Cristóbal, Oaxaca, Guanajuato, Cuernavaca, Mérida, in that order. It wasn't a natural progression or one easy to understand. Along the way he had been married and divorced many times. He could still call all the wives by name. Now his money was gone, from the family-owned chain of movie theaters in Colorado, or almost gone.

I said nothing about the anonymous letter. It was unlikely that Emmett would write such things, but then sometimes he was out of his head, from all that medication.

Later that evening Louise came by the hotel and gave me some green figs and a handmade card for Christmas. She had tried to give Frau Kobold a little knitted belt of some kind, only to be turned away at the door.

"What's wrong with that old woman?"

"She won't accept charity from strangers. I've told you that, Louise."

"A Christmas gift is not charity."

"No, but that's her way. I wouldn't worry about it. Just leave her alone."

She walked around inspecting my room. She pulled the curtain and looked into the closet, which was so shallow that the coat hangers hung at a slant. She asked if she could use my bathroom. When she came out she said, "I didn't really have to go but I wanted to see how you had organized your bathroom. I wanted to check out your shaving things and your medicine cabinet."

"Well? What did you think?"

"I knew you wouldn't have much stuff. I knew it would be neat and noncommittal. Where are all your Mayan things?"

"I don't have any."

"You must have one or two things. Some keepsakes."

"No, I'm not a collector."

"You just dig things up and sell them."

"I used to. A little recovery work, that's all. People make too much of it."

"Rudy says you're not really a college-trained archaeologist."

"Well, he's right about that. All I know is that the older stuff is usually at the bottom."

"You know, I was looking at you today in the truck and you look better at a distance than you do up close. I mean most people do but in your case the difference is striking."

"I'm sorry to let you down."

"That's all right. Can you see anything out of this window?"

"Not much. Just a wall back there and a little courtyard below. A pile of sand and a broken wheelbarrow."

"If I lived here I would have a room with some kind of view."

"I did have one, up front, but I had to move out. I couldn't get any sleep. The women wouldn't leave me alone. They were out there at all hours of the night throwing pebbles against my window."

"Uh huh. Don't you wish."

"You say that but here you are."

"Not for long. I'm way behind on Rudy's tapes. I've still got a lot of typing to do tonight."

# II

YOU PUT things off and then one morning you wake up and say—today I will change the oil in my truck. On the way out I looked in on Frau Kobold. I threaded a needle for her. She was no seamstress but she did do a little mending. "You forgot my cakes," she said. I told her, once again, that when I was out of town she should get Agustín, the boy, to fetch her cakes. "Agustín doesn't show the proper respect," she said. We had been through this before. It was true, she and her husband had once been in Fox Movietone News, but how was the boy to know that? He was polite. What did she expect of him?

I stopped at the desk and gave Beatriz some money, and she promised to see that these confounded cakes were picked up and delivered. She and Fausto were listening to a soap opera on the radio. Fausto said they should put the story of his life on one of those shows and call it "Domestic Vexations" (*Vejaciones de la Casa*). He was suffering from a heaviness of spirit, an *opresión*, he said, because of troubles at home with his wife, all caused by her wicked sister, a *chismosa*, who had nothing better to do than spread poisonous tales.

I was feeling fine myself, back now in my honest khakis, all cotton, stiffly creased and starched hard as boards. I sent them out to a woman who knew just the way I liked them finished. West of town there was a clearing or series of clearings in the dense scrub thicket that covers Yucatán. It was a garbage dump where I changed my oil, adding my bit to the mess. Wisps of greasy smoke rose here and there from smoldering trash. Fumaroles from Hell. The air was so foul here that the rats couldn't take it. A city dump and not a rat to be seen. I parked on a sandy slope and while the oil was draining I shot grease into the fittings. Then I let the truck roll back, away from the oil puddle, so I could lie on my back in a relatively clean place and replace the drain plug and the filter. I poured oil into the filter before screwing it on, to prevent dry scuffing on start-up. It was a little trick I had picked up from a cab driver.

A car drove up. Doors slammed. I saw legs and heard American voices.

693

"What is this guy doing out here?"

"All by himself."

"Long-bed pickup with Louisiana plate. Some kind of sharecropper."

"With a stupid accent. Like Red."

"I've seen that truck before."

"Wait, don't tell me. I believe this guy is—*working on his car*!"

"That's all those cotton-choppers do. Day and night."

"They listen to car races on the radio."

I slid out from beneath the truck. A gang of hippies had piled out of an old Ford station wagon. They called themselves The Jumping Jacks, which name was stuck across the rear window, in letters made from strips of silver tape. The letters had an angular, runic look. The number of these clowns varied. I made them out to be seven this time, three males and four females, though they were hard to count, like the *chaneques* (chanekkies) in the woods. Anyway, a full load for the old Ford Country Squire.

Back in October at Tuxpan they had stolen three ignition wires from my truck. I saw them there on the waterfront as I was going into a café. When I came out they were gone and my wires were gone and a newsboy told me the gringo *tóxicos* in the Ford *guayín*, the station wagon, had been under my hood. I hadn't seen them since, but the car was unmistakable —cracked glass, no wheel covers, a red sock stuffed in the gas filler spout. Once black, the wagon was now streaked and blotched. They had painted it white with brushes, using some kind of water-based paint. A lot of it had peeled off in long curls. It was the only paint job I had ever seen blow away.

The leader was a big fellow with dirt necklaces in the fleshy creases of his neck, a fat man in his forties, with curly black beard, silver earrings, a fringed black vest with no shirt underneath, a rotting blue bandana on his head, and loose white *campesino* trousers. They were cinched up with a rope like pajamas, and the bottoms were stuffed into green canvas jungle boots. Big Dan looked like a wrestling act, beef gone to fat, but with his costume not quite worked out. It wasn't all of a piece yet. Maybe an old biker. Almost certainly an ex-convict. I could see the letters AB—for Aryan Brotherhood—tattooed under his left breast. It was a rough, homemade job done with a pin and spit and burnt match-heads.

He grinned at me, coming forward with a knobby walking stick, taking golf chops at cans and clods. The others hung back. The two boys were much younger than Dan. A pair of cueballs, these fellows, with shaved heads and vacant eyes. Much better than long hair. No hair at all meant you were at a more advanced stage of revolt. One of the girls, or a tall woman rather with lank brown hair, squatted where she stood and lifted her skirt and took a long noisy leak right there on the ground in front of everybody.

Dan called me Curtis. He said, "Merry Christmas to you, Curtis."

"You too."

"And *mucho* happiness for the new year."

The girls laughed. I had seen one of them before, and not, I thought, in connection with this crew. She was a little rabbit they called Red, standing about barefooted on the hot sand. She looked like a Dust Bowl child, a bony waif in a thin cotton dress that hung straight down to her knees. I had seen that face before but couldn't place it.

Dan said, "Well, did you get it fixed?"

"Just about."

"Curtis says he's just about got his truck fixed. What a relief that must be."

The girls laughed again.

"Hey, pal, just having a little fun. My name is Dan. These are my friends. We're The Jumping Jacks and we come from the Gulf of Molo."

"Where is that?"

"It's beyond your understanding, I'm afraid."

"Then why tell me at all?"

"Hey, don't come back at me so fast. We're getting off on the wrong foot here. I was hoping you might be able to help us. We lost all our things. We rely on charity, you see, for our daily needs."

"You came to a poor country to do your begging."

"Not just to beg."

The others chimed in.

"We came down here to clarify our thoughts."

"We have found the correct path."

"Big Dan, he is a lot of man. He is one set apart."

"We have fled the madness and found the gladness."

"People call us trash and throw turnips at us."

"Dan is more than our father."

"We're on our way to the Inaccessible City of Dawn."

"But *El Mago* didn't show up."

Dan spoke sharply to them. "Hey, none of that now. Didn't I tell you about that? Not another word on that." He turned back to me. "I can see you are not a person of wide sympathy, Curtis. Nothing escapes me. I can see right into your soul. Would you believe we have now made twenty-four enemies in the north and twenty-four enemies in the south? No lie. You are exactly the twenty-fourth person in Mexico to find us loathsome and undesirable."

"I would believe fifty-four, Dan."

"Hey! Would you listen to this guy! He keeps coming right back at me!"

He jabbered away, and I went on with my work, opening cans of oil. There was a rustling in the thicket. It was a brows-ing goat, a billy goat, shouldering his way through the brush. His coat was the color of wet sand.

Dan became agitated. "A goat! After him! An unblemished ram! Get the goat!"

The two boys went crashing into the thicket.

"You too, Red! Go, go! I want that animal! Get him! His name is Azazel! He's carrying off all the sins of the people! I must lay my hands on him and say some words!"

"And cut his throat!" said the tall woman.

Red dashed off to help. The other two girls took up the cry, facing each other and going into a hand-slapping game. "Get that goat and cut his throat! Get that goat and cut his throat! What does Dan say? Dan says get the goat. What does Beany say? Beany says cut his throat. . . ."

I finished with the oil and slammed the hood down. I had lost sight of Dan. He had wandered around to the back of the truck and was poking about inside with his stick. When I got there he was pulling the top off a can of my vienna sausages.

He raised the can to me and said, "Your good health," and drank off the juice. "Soup of the day. Do you have any bread?"

"No."

"I can eat these things plain but let me tell you—say, you didn't take us for vegetarians, did you? Wandering herbivores?"

"I hadn't thought about it."

"People get us all wrong. We gladly eat the flesh of animals. When we can get it. Why would God give us sharp teeth if not to rend and tear things with? Let me tell you how I usually go about this. There are seven of these little men to a can. I take three slices of bread and make three foldover sandwiches, with two sausages to each piece of bread, don't you see. Then I take the seventh one, the odd man, and just pop it into my mouth naked, like a grape. I've done it that way for years, and now you tell me you don't have no bread."

I said nothing. He shrugged and ate the sausages. "Do you have anything else to spare? I mean like sardines or beer or shoes or Mexicano rum? Just anything in that line. I like your sleeping bag, all rolled up nice and tight like that. Your plastic lantern, too. I'll bet that thing comes in handy. Does it float or blink or have some special features I should know about? We could use a good light. The nights are long and we stumble in darkness. Maybe we could look through your stuff and just pick out what we want. I know you must set great store by all these material possessions but look here, my friend, it's the season for giving and you have so much."

More laughter from the girls. The tall woman said, "Or maybe he could just lend us a million pesos till payday."

"That's not a bad idea, Beany Girl. It works out well for him too. We get *mucho dinero* for our pressing needs, and he gets to keep all his much-prized possessions. But I don't know about this guy. You might think he would say, '*See see, Seenyore,* your house is my house and my house is your house,' but no, not this guy. Ask Curtis for bread and he don't even give you a stone."

His jocular manner had a dark edge to it that was meant to be unsettling, but it was a transparent act, a bit of old movie business, not well done. The two boys and little Red came back with no goat. A child can hem up a goat, but these three couldn't catch a goat. They talked about it. Beany Girl said that they hadn't really tried. There was a silence. Then, on what must have been a signal from Dan, all of them picked up rocks and looked at me. They stood perfectly still with their mouths gaping. They were a clan of early hunters in a museum diorama. And the rocks were big, not missiles but clubs.

I was wiping my hands on a rag and moving to the cab. I said, "Well, I guess I can spare a few beers. I keep some cans of Modelo in a cooler behind the seat here." I had rigged up a shallow storage compartment back there, really just a raised and squared-off cover made of sheet metal. It ran the width of the cab and appeared to be a structural part of the floor. I kept my double-barrel shotgun there, an ancient L. C. Smith 12-gauge with exposed hammers and double triggers. I had bought it from a hunting guide called Chombo. It was about sixty years old, and long too. I had sawed two inches off the barrels and the thing still looked like a goose gun.

I pulled it out and cocked both hammers and walked over to Dan and touched the muzzle lightly to his belly at the parting of his vest. His flesh jumped in a little spasm from the hot metal.

"No, I guess not. No beer today, Dan. This was all I could find."

"No need to get heavy, man. Have we offended you in some way?"

"*Heavee*," said Beany Girl.

I asked for some identification. Dan said he had none, that he never carried anything on his person.

"Maybe you ought to start. Where are your tourist papers?"

"Gone. Stolen. We got ripped off bad at the beach last night. We were supposed to meet someone at Progreso but he didn't show up. We had all our stuff in plastic bags. That's what we're doing here, man. I thought we could find some useful things here at the dump but this is the worst looking trash I ever saw."

I took his stick and pointed to a spot. "I want all of you to drop the rocks and sit on the ground, right there, back to back. No, better not say anything. Just do it."

Beany Girl had more spirit than Dan and she held back. She was just a little slow to comply, and I had to whack her across the neck with the knobby stick. The blow came as a surprise. It stung and was effective. She was lucky I didn't knock her brains out. A grown woman, squatting down like that in front of everybody. There was no *mingitorio* out here, naturally, but any decent woman would have gone behind a bush. Dan was picking and pulling at his beard. I had to pop him one, too, on the arm. "Get your hand down and keep it down. Nobody talks and nobody moves a finger unless I say so. You got that?"

When I had them all seated and arranged to suit me, I searched the car. There were no papers. I walked around the car breaking glass, punching at the cracked places with the stick. I smashed the headlights too. Then I propped one end of the stick against a wheel and broke it with my foot and flung the pieces away. Dan took that hardest of all. "My staff," he said. I raised the hood and ripped out all the spark plug wires.

Something moved in the brush. I thought one of the hippies had slipped away. Even at rest these Jumping Jacks were hard to count. I wouldn't let them talk but I think they must have set up a high frequency hum to interfere with my head. When I reached the fourth or fifth one in my tally I became confused and had to start over again. But no, it was only the goat. He had come back, a curious fellow, bearing the load of sins well. He munched on a mouthful of briars and watched us with sleepy eyes.

I climbed into the truck with my shotgun and my handful of cables. Three of them were Packard-Delco wires that didn't belong on a Ford. I started the engine and almost at once the oil pressure needle moved. The pump had picked up the oil.

Dan said, "You got us wrong, man. No need for all this. You're not following the correct path."

Blood was roaring in my ears. I had to get away from these people before I did something. I could hardly trust myself to speak. "Don't let me catch you around this truck again," I said.

I still wasn't thinking straight. You let people annoy you and you forget your own best interests. It wasn't until late afternoon that I thought about checking to see if Dan were listed on one of Gilbert's Blue Sheets. I had missed a bet there. Gilbert ran a location service, nominally in El Paso but really out of an office in Mexico City, where these Blue Sheets come from, giving a rundown on Americans thought to be hiding in Mexico. I did a little work for him now and then, when I felt like it, just enough these days to get the monthly bulletins, blue paper stamped all over in red, CONFIDENTIAL, and AGENCY USE ONLY, and NOT FOR CIRCULATION IN U.S., and ALL RIGHTS

RESERVED, GILBERT MOSS. Locate one of these fugitives for
Gilbert and you were paid 40 percent of the posted fee. Bring
the bird in yourself and you got 75 percent. Mostly they were
runaway kids, alimony dodgers and the like, bond jumpers
with a few tax evaders and swindlers and embezzlers, victims of
surprise audits, and a very few violent criminals, but only those
with substantial rewards on their heads. Gilbert was running
a business and not a justice agency. The violent ones gave too
much trouble.

I got my stack of Blue Sheets out of the closet and sat on
the bed and went through them, starting with the latest ones.
Dan may have been in there somewhere, but I lost interest in
him when I came across a photograph of Little Red. I knew I
had seen that face. Her name was LaJoye Mishell Teeter and
she was from Perry, Florida. A runaway. The picture was a poor
one, poorly Xeroxed from a poor reproduction of the missing
persons column in *The War Cry*, the Salvation Army magazine.
But there was no mistaking that rabbit face. The offered fee
was $2,000, which meant $1,500 for me if and when I delivered her.

No time to lose. Back to the dump. I would bring Dan in
and get the Judicial Police here, the federal police, to hold him
on a turpitude charge, if not for kidnapping, while I checked
him out with Gilbert by telephone. The girl was clearly under
age.

I was too late. The Jumping Jacks were gone in their Country Squire wagon, shattered windshield and all. They were resourceful, I had to admit that. The two cueballs must have
stolen some more plug wires, eight of them this time, plus a
coil wire, and maybe a couple of headlights too, or they would
truly be stumbling in darkness tonight. Dan had mentioned
the beach. I drove to Progreso and cruised up and down the
beachfront. Nothing doing. I should have burned that car up
while I was at it.

# III

ONE NIGHT in Shreveport I overheard a man trying to pick up a waitress in a bar. She asked him what he did for a living. He hesitated, then said, "I work out of my car." I thought he would have done better to lie, or even to confess to whatever it was he did out of his car, however awful, rather than to say that. I smiled over my drink in my superior way.

Now here I was years later, working out of my car, not smiling so much, and at a loss to say just what it was I did, out of my car. My truck rather. Light hauling, odd jobs. No more digging runs. I missed them too and I didn't think I would.

Two days after Christmas I was off for Chiapas with a load of mixed cargo. The long telephone message had come from the Bonar College people, who were camped out down there on a river bank, mapping a Mayan ruin called Ektún. Dr. Ritchie or one of his people had called my hotel from the Palenque bus station, the nearest telephone, and given Beatriz a shopping list of things they needed.

I had everything but the *embrague por la* Toyota—a Toyota clutch. That was the Spanish word for it all right, but in Mexico, where so many automotive terms had become Americanized, it was generally called a *cloche*. What kind of Toyota? Car? Truck? What year model? Did they want an entire clutch assembly? They didn't say or Beatriz didn't bother to take it down. Refugio and I had helped them carry their stuff in, and I couldn't remember seeing a Toyota.

Probably they had fried the disc pulling down trees and dragging blocks of stone around. But I wasn't going to buy one and then go through the agony of trying to return it. As a rule you get value for your money in Mexico, but it's hard to get any of it back, to get a deposit returned or any sort of refund. In their financial dealings with gringos, the Mexicans employ a ball-check valve that permits money to flow in only one direction. It can't back up. Buy the wrong one and I would have to eat that clutch, throwout bearing and all.

No *embrague* then, but I had everything else. Peanut butter they craved, and Ocosingo cheese and a sack of potatoes and flashlight batteries and two small hydraulic jacks and canned milk and pick handles and 35-millimeter color slides and bread and twenty-five gallons of gasoline and so on. I also had an old Servel gas refrigerator for Refugio. He had asked me to be on the lookout for one. It was too tall to transport upright—my camper shell was only cab high—so I stowed it sideways and hoped for the best.

Mérida, for all its associations with the Maya empire, is not really very close to any of the major ruins, except for Uxmal and Kabah. Mayapán and Dzibilchaltún are nearby but they don't count for much, not as spectacles. I had a good 300-mile run ahead of me, south to Palenque on paved road, then another seventy miles or so of rough track through the woods. At Champotón on the coast I bought two buckets of fresh shrimp, one for Refugio and one for the college diggers. Refugio was crazy about shrimp.

I reached Palenque in the afternoon and worked the ruins there for an hour or so with my Polaroid camera, taking pictures of tourists at five dollars a shot. Hardly any business. The hippies, sunburnt and dazed, had no money, and the older gringos had their own cameras. I left the Mexican tourists alone, lest I be reported. As a foreigner I wasn't legally permitted to do this sort of thing.

Louise kept telling me the term "hippie" was out of date. She couldn't tell me why. These words come and go, but why had that one been pulled? The hippies hadn't gone away. There were even some beatniks still hanging around here and there in Mexico, men my age, still thumping away on bongos with their eyes closed, still lying around in their pads, waiting for poems to come into their heads, and sometimes not waiting long enough. I did perhaps use "hippie" too loosely, to cover all shaggy young Americano vagabonds. Refugio called the real hippies *aves sin nidos*, birds without nests, and *los tóxicos*, the dopers. These were the real hippies, the *viciosos*, the hardened bums, kids gone feral. I knew the difference between them and the ordinary youngsters knocking around on the cheap with their backpacks.

They came now the year 'round to Palenque, which is everyone's idea of a lost city in the jungle—real hippies, false hippies, pyramid power people, various cranks and mystics, hollow

earth people, flower children and the von Däniken people—
such as Rudy Kurle, with his space invader theories. At night
they sat on top of the pyramids in the moonlight. They were
right to come here, too, to see these amazing temples on a dark
green jungle hillside. The scholars say that Uxmal has the finest
architecture, and of course there is nothing to touch Tikal,
for monumental ruins on the grand, Egyptian scale, but the
hippies got it right instinctively. They knew Palenque was the
jewel of Mayaland.

Between the ruins and the little town of Santo Domingo del
Palenque there was a pasture where they camped out, these
young travelers, with their vans and tents and ponchos. The
rock music never let up. I stopped with my Blue Sheets to walk
around the place and look them over. I took my flashlight and
peered in tents and car windows. I put my light in their faces.
What drove them to herd up like this in open fields? Even as
a kid, and a foolish one, too, all too eager to please my pals, I
couldn't see myself doing this.

It was getting dark. There was no one here I wanted. I
gassed up at the intersection in town and headed inland, up
the valley of the Usumacinta River. The road was paved for a
mile or two then became washboard gravel. It was so rough
that you could drive for miles on a flat tire and not know it.
This was the dry season, so called, and the archaeologists were
stirring again. In my experience it just rained a little less at this
time. Damp season would be more like it. There was no moon.
It wasn't a night for pyramid roosting.

When you see steel drums you're getting close to Refugio's
trading post and salvage yard. He counted his wealth in fifty-
five-gallon drums. They lay scattered along the road and in
the woods all around his place, rusting away and more or less
empty, but still holding the residue of various acids, solvents,
herbicides, pesticides, explosives, corrosives, all manner of
petrochemical goo.

His people had heard me coming and were assembled outside to see who it was. The floodlight was on; dogs were barking. Small children jumped on my bumpers, front and back. A
teenaged boy named Manolo was waving his arms. This was
Refugio's son. He wigwagged me in around the old tires and
plastic pipes to an aircraft carrier landing. The crowd parted

to make way for Refugio—relatives, cronies, employees. He had the paunch of a *patrón* now but still he moved like a bow-legged and cocky little third baseman. The sleeves of his short-sleeve shirt hung well below his elbows. Around his thick neck he wore a Mayan necklace of tubular jade beads, with a heavy silver cross at the bottom.

"Jaime!"

"Refugio!"

We went into an *abrazo* there under the floodlight, with bugs swirling around us.

First I got the gifts out of the way. Some *futbol*, or soccer, magazines for Manolo, and a three-speed hair dryer for Refugio's wife, Sula, and a box of iodized salt. She was afraid of getting a goiter, like her mother. Refugio dredged up half the shrimp from the bucket with his hands and began shouting orders to Sula and the kitchen staff. This many *camarones* were to be boiled at once. Then peeled and chilled and served to him and him alone in a *coctel grande*, with *mayonesa* and green sauce. The rest could be fried with garlic and served up with a lot of rice. That would do for the rest of us.

He shooed everyone away, and we went to his office. It was like the waiting room of a cut-rate muffler shop, with an old brown plastic couch and some odd bits of automotive seating. Refugio sat at his desk, with Ramos at his feet, son of the late Chino, bravest dog in all Mexico. Refugio never would admit that old Chino tucked his tail when he heard thunder. I stretched out on the couch. Manolo brought me a cold bottle of Sidral, an apple-flavored drink, and a wet towel and a dry towel to refresh myself with. He showed me his Christmas present, which was a thirty-three-piece wrench set, all nicely chromed. Manolo had turned out to be a fine boy, from a brat. He was an only child, and Sula couldn't bear to wean him until he was four years old. He was a biter. He bit his playmates and threw rocks at strangers until he was twelve. Now here he was, a fine young man of sixteen.

Refugio turned on the air conditioner in my honor, though it wasn't very hot. The lights dimmed, as for an electrocution. It was only a small window unit but it put a strain on his generator.

"How is the bennee?" he asked me.

"Business is bad, Refugio. Life is hard for a gringo in the Republic these days. I'm selling hammocks on the street now."

"*¡No! Qué desgracia!*" He laughed and drummed his hands on the desk. "And the Doctor?"

This was Doc Flandin.

"I don't see him much anymore. He stays in his big house."

"His tobacco pipe is drawing well?"

"Oh yes."

Mexicans don't smoke pipes and they find them amusing.

"Still he throws his head back? So?"

"Not so much. He's not tossing his old white locks about these days."

"He works hard on his book, no?"

"So he says."

"It will be a hundred pages?"

"More like a thousand."

"No! This is one of your jokes!"

"I speak the truth. *Las mil y una.*"

He laughed and pounded the desk again. "No! What a miracle! So many leaves! Who could ever read them all?"

Not me. I went along with Refugio on that. Short was good in a book.

Then he became solemn and said, "My name is in this book, you know. Refugio Bautista Osorio. On many leaves."

"I know. Mine too. You and me and Chino. The Doctor will make us all famous."

I told him about the Servel refrigerator and how the jet had been changed to use propane gas. I had found it in the port town of Sisal and cleaned it up. He summoned Manolo and another boy and told them to unload it and connect it to his gas bottle and light the burner.

"*¿Cuántos?*" he asked me.

I wrote "$150" on the palm of my hand and showed it to him.

"*Ni modo.*" No way. He made a quick slicing move on one index finger across the other. Too much. Cut your price in half. But he was only playing around. When a price really upset him, he called on St. James and the Virgin both in a whisper.

My pricing policy was simple. I doubled my money and then rounded that figure off in my favor. This refrigerator had cost me around $70, so my price was $150. My terms were cash on delivery, payment in full, *no acepto cheques.*

Refugio took a thermometer from the drawer and held it up. "I will place this in the box, and if the red line gets down to fifty in one hour, then we will talk about the value."

"There was no talk of fifty degrees before."

"Two hours. What can I do? You are my friend."

"All right. If you put that thing in the *congelador.*" The freezing compartment, that is.

"Gringos are so hard."

He wanted to barter and first he offered me an old hospital bed that cranked up and down. Then he dragged a wooden box across the floor, a hand grenade box with a rope loop at each end. It was there that he kept his *antigüedades.* He brought out a mirror, slightly concave, made of a wooden disk and shiny bits of hematite. Some Mayan queen had seen her face grow old in it.

"Worth more than two hundred."

"Yes, but not to me. I'm finished with that. No more relics. *Término.*"

"That is what you say. Look. Fine orange ware." It was a ceramic cup.

"No, I'm serious."

Next a baroque pearl shaped something like a fish. Eyes and mouth and fins had been incised on it.

"No."

"And what do you say to this?"

At first I thought it was a piece of green obsidian and then I saw it was a carved lump of beautiful blue-green Olmec jade. The figure was a hunchbacked man with baby face and snarling jaguar mouth. Very old, even for Olmec. The nostril holes were conical. They had been drilled with wet sand and pointed stick, rather than with the later, bird-bone, tubular drill. I had no feel for Olmec art—more pathology than art—but I knew this weird little man was valuable. I knew a collector in St. Louis who would pay $7,500 for this thing, maybe $10,000. If a man wants something and you're any kind of salesman, you'll make him pay for it.

I knew that Refugio knew it, too, and would never trade it for an old icebox.

He said, "Green, see, the color of life. Dead rocks are brown."

"Where did you get this?"

"Who knows?"

"Tres Zapotes?"

"Who can say?"

"They make these things up at Taxco now, out of chrysolite and serpentine. On bench grinders."

"They don't make that one at Taxco. Look it over. *Impecable*. If you can scratch it with your knife, I give it to you."

"No, it's not bad. As a favor to a friend then. I'll trade you even."

"Ha! That is what you hope and pray to God for!"

What he wanted me to do was take a photograph of it and show the picture around in Mérida and New Orleans, put out some feelers. I had no intention of being a broker in the deal but I humored him and took a couple of shots with my 35-millimeter camera. He posed it beside the Sidral bottle to show the scale. The camera flash made him jump and laugh, as always.

Manolo reported that he couldn't get the Servel to do anything. I advised patience. The cooling to be gotten from a small flame and no moving parts was magical but slow. I reminded Refugio of his old kerosene refrigerator, which took three days to make mushy ice, if you didn't open the door. It was one of the earliest frost-free models.

"Turn it upside down for a bit, Manolo," I said. "Then try it again. Make sure it's level." I had heard somewhere that this headstand treatment did wonders for a balky gas refrigerator, though it seemed that any clots in the system would have been dislodged on the ride down.

Sula brought in the giant shrimp cocktail. The *camarones* were piled high in a soup bowl. Refugio squeezed limes over them and spooned mayonnaise and *salsa verde* on them. I asked him about the Ektún dig. What was all this about a Toyota clutch?

He threw up his hands. The subject disgusted him. He could no longer do business with those people. Dr. Ritchie was a good man, very amiable, but he was down with fever, and this new man, Skinner, who was running things now, was a person of no dignity, a monkey-head, a queer, and a rude animal, *una bestia brusca*. On and on he went. The woman who gave birth to Skinner was no woman at all but an old sow monkey, and his brother, if he had one, was worse than he was, certainly not a man of honor.

What Skinner had done, I gathered, was to insist that Refugio provide detailed price breakdowns on his goods and services, in such an offensive way as to suggest that Refugio was a crook. Nor would the man buy any steel drums or plastic pipe. And he had brought his own rope from the States! To Mexico, the home of rope!

"I can get his *cloche* in Villahermosa. One day and it's there. I can find anything he wants and Manolo can repair anything he can break but how can I do business with a monkey? No, I will never go back while that monkey-head is there."

And a good thing, said Sula, because Ektún was no place for people to linger around at night. For her part she was glad that he and Manolo had stopped going there. So many demons were lurking around those old *templos*, not to mention the *chaneques*, a race of evil dwarfs who lived in the deep *selva*. When you came upon these horrible little men in a clearing, they would point at you and jeer, making indecent noises, and they danced about all the time so you couldn't count them. They hated above all things to be counted. Sometimes they stole chickens.

Refugio was squeezing limes with both hands. "*¡Tu que sabes!*" he said to her. "What do you know? The *chaneques* don't really bother people very much, and as for the demons, all the world knows that they never show themselves in the light of day! At night, well, their powers are stronger, yes, in the hours of darkness they have certain powers, but not strong enough to interfere with a Christian! Not even with one of God's poorest servants! You know nothing of these things!"

All the same, she said, and be that as it may, Ektún was a place of evil gloom, and so was Yaxchilán, and Piedras Negras too, come to that, all those old abandoned cities of the *antiguos* along the river banks, and you couldn't pay her enough money to sleep for one night around those old stones.

Sula was Mayan herself, of the Chontal group, with heavy-lidded eyes and hook nose and receding chin. I had seen her face on a mossy stela at the Copán ruin, carved in stone a thousand years ago. She was one of the few Indians I had ever heard express strong feelings about such matters. The ones I knew—uprooted city dwellers for the most part, admittedly —showed little interest in the monuments of their ancestors. They neither feared nor venerated the *templos* of the old ones.

The Servel didn't make it to fifty at the given time, or even to fifty-five, but the door gasket was bad, I pointed out, and once Manolo had replaced it, the box would surely do the job. It would last for years too. Refugio wrote "$75" on his palm and showed it to me.

"That wouldn't even pay for my gasoline."

But I gave in and settled for a hundred. He agreed it was a good buy.

We stayed up late in the office talking about the old days, and one thing and another. Refugio fed tidbits to Ramos. He asked me to be on the lookout for a Tecumseh gasoline engine with a horizontal shaft, of about eight horsepower, and some of those little German cigarette-rolling machines that you used to be able to find in Veracruz. He asked me if I thought he needed one of those new water beds. "No." Motorized golf cart? "No." Food blender? "Yes, to make *licuados*. Milkshakes." Trash compactor? "No." It would take one the size of a house to compact his trash. He showed me an advertisement for elevator shoes in an American magazine. Could I get him a pair? One of the shoes was pictured, a brown loafer, which promised to give you an invisible three-inch lift above your fellow men.

"Three inches," he said. "How much?"

I showed him with thumb and finger. "Like that. About eight centimeters."

He studied the deceptive shoe with a dreamy smile. Three inches was a little more than he had thought.

# IV

I SLEPT on the couch and was off early. I had breakfast as I drove. Sula had left me a sack of hard-boiled eggs, already peeled, and four buttered slices of Bimbo bread, some salt in a twist of paper, and a single *habanero* pepper pod, the world's hottest. Bimbo is like Wonder bread, or light bread, as we called it in Caddo Parish. I had told her many times that I preferred corn tortillas, but she took that to be a polite gesture or an affectation. She knew the *yanquis* liked their bread finely spun from bleached wheat flour. Sula felt sorry for me because I had no wife to look after me.

The washboard gravel ended just beyond Refugio's place. No more maintenance. From here on the road was just a rough slash across the hilly Chiapas rain forest. The drive had once been a shady one all the way, under the jungle canopy. Now there were cleared pastures with stumps where cattle ranchers had moved in. I met a log truck and saw a Pemex crew at work with their seismic gear, sounding the earth for pockets of oil. Here and there I passed a hut made of sticks and thatch, where a solitary farmer had squatted. This was his *finca*. It was more like camping out than farming.

The road, at this time, ended at the ruins of Bonampák, of the famous wall paintings, but I wasn't going that far. To reach Ektún and the Tabí River, you turned off to the left, or east, on a still more primitive track. I did so, and the trees closed in on me. Limbs whacked against my windows. I moved forward at a creep, but even so my poor truck was twisted and jolted about by rocks and bony roots. The glove compartment door flew open. Screws were backing out of their holes and nuts off their bolts. I had to hold my hand on the gearstick to keep it from popping out of gear. I saw a wild pig, a black squirrel as big as a house cat, darting green parrots. You don't expect parrots to be accomplished fliers, but they go like bullets.

I saw nothing human until I reached the fording place on the Tabí. There was a flash of yellow through the foliage. As I turned the bend, I made out a car stranded in midstream. It was a bright yellow Checker Marathon, towing a pop-top tent trailer. The trailer had been knocked sideways by the current.

Rudy Kurle. What was he doing out here? No use asking. How did he get this far in that rig? I honked my horn.

He was in the back seat, where he must have been asleep. He stuck his head out the window and shouted. "Hey, Burns! Great! This is great! Did you copy my Mayday?"

"What? No!" I could barely hear him over the rush of water.

"I need a jump start!"

He needed more than that.

He had been sitting there all night, dead in the water, trying to start the thing and calling for help on his CB radio, on one channel after another, until he had run his battery down. His DieHard had done died. I seldom turned on my own CB, and in any case there were no signals to pick up out here. The water was about knee deep, but with deeper potholes. He had dropped his right front wheel into one of these. I drove around him and positioned my truck on the hard ground of the opposite bank. I pieced together a chain, a nylon rope, and a nylon tow-strap.

Rudy wouldn't get out of the car to help. The water was too rough, or he didn't want to get his lace-up explorer boots wet, or something. Useless to ask why. Usually he wasn't such a delicate traveler. How long would he have sat there? The river was a tributary of the Usumacinta, tea-colored from dead leaves, only moderately swift at this time of year, and only about sixty feet wide at this ford. A bit more maybe. I'm a poor judge of distance over water.

I went out into the stream with my tow-line, jumping from rock to rock. Another of man's farcical attempts at flight. We keep trying but none of us, not even the high-jumper slithering backwards over his crossbar, ever gets very far off the earth. And yet we come down hard. My bad knee gave way on one of these landings, and I went head-first into the water and tumbled a ways downstream. It didn't matter, getting soaked, as I had to bob all the way under anyway to hook the strap to a frame member.

All the while Rudy was making suggestions. "No, no," I said. "Listen to me. Put it in neutral and just keep the wheels straight. Don't do anything else. Stay off the brakes. Stop talking."

First the chain came loose from my trailer ball, and then the nylon rope, twanging like a banjo string, snapped. The line parted, as the sailors say. Pound for pound stronger than steel! Such is the claim made for these wonder fibers, but I'll take steel. Third time lucky. I removed some rocks in front of his tires and then, in low-range four-wheel drive, in *doble tracción*, I yanked him loose and got him up on the bank, trailer and all, without stopping.

Rudy didn't thank me but he did offer me some food. He had brown cans of meat and crackers he had taken from his National Guard unit in Pennsylvania. All I wanted was a long pull on my water jug. I checked my tires for rock cuts. Wet rubber is easily sliced. Rudy showed me a nick in his bumper. "That's what your strap did." The bumper was decorated in the style of big Mexican trucks, with his road name, "The Special K," painted on it. That was his CB handle.

He said, "Wait a minute. Who told you I was going to Tumbalá anyway?"

"It was all over town when I left. There must have been something in the papers."

"Louise told you. Everybody wants to stick his nose into my business."

"Nobody told me. I'm not going to Tumbalá."

He thought that over as he spread meat paste on a survival cracker with his commando knife. "Well, it's funny, you coming along like this, right behind me."

"Yes, except I'm going to Ektún. This is not the road to Tumbalá."

"Your map says it is."

My map! He showed me. Yes, I remembered now. A month or so ago I had told him about this Tumbalá, a minor ruin on the Usumacinta, with curious miniature temples. They were small stone houses, built as though for people two or three feet high. Rudy was excited. This was his meat, tiny houses. Little rooms! An old logging road, no longer passable, even in four-wheel drive, led to the place, but you could follow it on foot easily enough. Quite a long hike, however. I had explained all this to him and sketched out a rough map.

"No, you came too far, Rudy. You didn't turn soon enough."

"Your map is not drawn to scale."

"Of course not. It's just a simple diagram. But it's easy enough to see where to turn off. You can't drive to Tumbalá anyway. I told you that."

"I was going as far as I could and then set up base camp."

He wore a bush hat with the brim turned up on one side, Australian fashion, and a belted safari jacket with epaulets, rings and pleated pockets, and he wanted to be known as "Rudy Kurle, author and lecturer." He and Louise were in Mexico to gather material for a book about some space dwarfs or "manikins" who came here many years ago from a faraway planet. There was no connection with the *chaneques*, as far as I knew. Their little men were benign, with superior skills and knowledge, and they had transformed a tribe of savages into the Mayan civilization. Not very flattering to the Indians, and it wasn't of course a new theory, except perhaps for the dwarf element. There had been recent landings as well.

As a geocentric I didn't find this stuff convincing. I knew the argument—all those galaxies!—a statistical argument, but in my cosmology men were here on earth and nowhere else, go as far as you like. There was us and the spirit world and that was it. It was a visceral belief or feeling so unshakable that I didn't even bother to defend it. When others laughed at me, I laughed with them. Still, the flying saucer books were fun to read and there weren't nearly enough of them to suit me. I liked the belligerent ones best, that took no crap off the science establishment.

Rudy was often gone on these mysterious field trips, to check out reports of ancient television receivers, pre-Columbian Oldsmobiles, stone carvings of barefooted astronauts strapped into their space ships. The ships were driven by "photon propulsion," although here in the jungle the manikins went about their errands in other, smaller, "slow aircraft." Rudy wouldn't describe the machines for me. He and Louise tried to draw people out without giving anything away themselves. There were thieves around who would steal your ideas and jump into print ahead of you. So much uncertainty in their work.

And so little fellowship among the writers. They shared a beleaguered faith and they stole freely from one another— the recycling of material was such that their books were all pretty much the same one now—but in private they seldom had a good word for their colleagues. There were usually a few of these people in temporary residence in Mérida. They exchanged stiff nods on the street. Rudy even expressed contempt for Erich von Däniken, his master, who had started the whole business, and for lesser writers too, for anyone whose level of credulity did not exactly match his own. A millimeter off, either way, and you were a fool. It was the scorn of one crank for another crank.

We dried off the contact points and the distributor cap and with a jump from my battery we got the Checker running again. The engine was a Chevrolet straight six, the old stove-bolt six, very reliable but looking skinny and forlorn in that big engine bay. To help control this beast on the road, Rudy wore soft leather driving gloves perforated with many tiny holes. Inside the car there was a clutter of boxes, jugs, blankets, gourds, magazines, rocks, books—and a big scrapbook of newspaper clippings, telling of saucer landings in Russia and Brazil, near towns that could not be found in any atlas. The gas pedal was in the shape of a spreading human foot, with the toes all fanned out. It must have been on the car when Rudy bought it because he didn't go in for comic accessories. There was a press sticker on the windshield—PRENSA, in big red letters, courtesy of Professor Camacho Puut.

He followed me on to Ektún. Exploration by taxicab. He took that old Checker into places where few others would have ventured. Rudy was serious about his work. In the bars and cafés of Mérida I had heard anthropologists laughing at him, young hot shots who never left town themselves or who went out for a night or two and then scurried back.

We left the river for a bit and then came back to it downstream to the ruin site. Three pyramids of middling size, partly cleared, and a camp of red and blue tents. A canvas water bag hanging from a limb. A sagging grid of strings lay across the plaza. The Bonar College people stopped work and looked at us. No word of greeting. We came from the outer world bringing good things, and this was our welcome. No more joy here. The dig was falling apart. I had seen it all before.

Sula was right about the demons. The place was infested with them, many thousands of whom had taken the form of mosquitoes. They swarmed in my face as I got down from the truck and walked shin-deep in ground fog. It was cemetery fog from a vampire movie. A mockingbird perched on my bumper and pecked at the smashed bugs. Up high in the trees the howler monkeys were screaming. Our clattering arrival had set them off. It was like cries of agony from cats. You couldn't see them.

I took a bar of yellow laundry soap and went back into the river in my wet clothes. This was a little trick I had picked up years ago in Korea with the First Marine Division. You immerse yourself fully clad and have a bath and wash your clothes at the same time. Then you change into your dry dungarees, all rolled up and resting in your pack. Let dirty clothes rest for a while and they are almost as fresh as clean clothes. A bit stiffer, and the black glaze is still on the collar. There are tigers in Korea, but I never saw one. Nor had I ever caught a glimpse of a jaguar here in the Petén forest. Pumas, ocelots, margays, but not one *tigre*.

I went along to Dr. Henry Ritchie's tent and found him half asleep on a cot, behind a mosquito bar. His clothes were soaked with sweat. His breath came hard. A real gentleman, a good man, as Refugio said, and I always felt a little shame in his presence. Few *arqueos* had that effect on me. He knew my background but was always friendly. After all, as Doc Flandin said, permit or no permit, we all lived and worked by the same words, namely, *there is nothing hid but it shall be opened.*

In a minute or so he saw me sitting there on the stool. He gave me his trembling hand. It was cold. "Jimmy. You're here."

"Just now. I was out of town when your message came or I would have been here sooner. I hear you've been ailing."

"Oh, I've been through this before. Not quite so bad maybe. I can't keep anything down. Did you have a nice Christmas?"

"Very nice, thank you. I brought you some long cigars and a bucket of shrimp."

"Wonderful."

"Why don't I run you in to Villahermosa? I can have you there in the clinic tonight. That's where you belong. No use in punishing yourself."

"I don't know. Maybe tomorrow, if I'm no better. Can you stay over?"

"Sure. We can be off first thing in the morning. You can lie down in the back."

A man came barging through the flap and took off his dust mask.

"You're Burns?"

"Right."

"I'm Eugene Skinner. You should have reported to me first."

This was Skinner, the ape in a shirt. He was a nervous man, about my age, with kinky auburn hair, nappy hair, which must have suggested the monkey to Refugio. It reminded me more of a Duroc hog.

Then Rudy came in and wanted to know if he was at Tumbalá.

Skinner said, "No, my boy, this is Ektún. Which is to say, Dark Stone, or Black Stone. Who are you?"

I introduced him as a friend and a reporter.

Dr. Ritchie said, "Jimmy brought us some fresh shrimp, Gene."

"That's fine. How about the clutch?"

"I didn't bring one."

"They didn't have one in Mérida?"

"I don't know. You didn't tell me what model it was for."

"He doesn't know. We need a clutch, and he brings shrimp."

"What's it doing? Why don't we take a look at it?"

"It won't do any good to look at it."

He barged out again. I followed him and grabbed his arm. "Why haven't you taken Dr. Ritchie out of here? He's in bad shape."

"How? On a motorbike? If you and your pal Bautista had done your job, I would have some transportation here."

The expedition had begun with a respectable little motor pool, now reduced to a single motorcycle, owned by a young graduate student named Burt. The International Travelall was down with a broken axle. The Nissan pickup was in a Villahermosa garage with a blown head gasket. Becker had returned to Chicago in his new Jeep Wagoneer, with a female student who had fallen ill. I was surprised to hear that Becker had bailed out. He who was so eager to get at it. He was a young rich man, a graduate of Bonar College (as was my friend Nardo, the Mérida lawyer) and a dabbler in archaeology. Becker was financing the dig. I think he must have seen himself as Schlie-mann at Hissarlik, or Lord Carnarvon at King Tut's tomb. Camp life didn't suit him, however, and when no treasures were turned up in a week's time, he went home, back to the trading pit of the Chicago commodities market, where things moved faster.

It might have been the digging itself. A man who has never dug a ditch or a well or a deep grave, as distinguished from the shallow grave of crime news, has no notion of the work required to move even a moderate amount of rocks and dirt about in an orderly way with hand tools. At this remote site there were no cheap labor gangs, only a few Lacondón Indians, and the professors and students had to do most of the work themselves. Becker must have looked at his little pile of dirt, his spoil, then saw how much remained to be removed before he could get down to work with the dental pick and the tweezers and the camel's hair brush. He despaired. It may have come to him in the night: *I am only Becker at Ektún.*

The Toyota pickup belonged to Skinner. He had driven down alone from Illinois, arriving a few days after the main party. The problem was that you couldn't disengage the clutch. Pressing the pedal did nothing. The flywheel of the engine was locked up to the driveline. I did what I called taking a look at it. Burt and I lay on our backs and examined the linkage and pooled our ignorance. It was alien to me. Some sort of Nipponese hydraulic booster up there, a slave cylinder. The only clutches I knew had a straight mechanical linkage. What I needed here was Manolo and his thirty-three wrenches. I was only a shade-tree mechanic, and an impatient one at that. Get a bigger hammer or put a bigger fuse in and see if anything smokes. That was my approach.

I decided on a show of violence. Burt and I got the truck going in the lowest forward gear, and I drove around and around the clearing, poking the gas pedal for a lurch effect, and pumping on the clutch pedal, hoping to pop something loose. It worked, to everyone's surprise. The clutch disc had stuck to the flywheel with rust or some fungoid rot and was now free again.

Skinner had been chasing after us, shouting and waving his arms. We were abusing his truck. Now he was doubly annoyed.

All the to-do had ended with a quick fix, and he had made a spectacle of himself before his crew. He was a fat lady running after a bus.

Then he tried to beat me down on my prices. He went over the list, muttering, going into little fake body collapses. As the hated, profiteering middleman, I had seen this show before.

"You must think you've got a gold mine here, Burns."

"If it's such a gold mine then why can't you find anyone else to do it? What about the wear and tear on my truck? My prices are not out of line. I'm not even charging you for the clutch repair."

"Am I supposed to be grateful? It's not as though you actually did anything. I'm not even sure it's fixed. You and Bautista may be able to take advantage of Henry, but you're dealing with me now."

"You called me, I didn't call you."

"And this famous bucket of shrimp. I can't find the price listed. Where have you hidden it?"

"I was throwing it in free, as lagniappe, but now I want thirty dollars for it, and I want it now. I'm not going to stand here and haggle with you, Skinner. Pay me now or everything goes back. Nothing comes off that truck until I get my money."

A bearded engineer named Lund interceded. He took Skinner away to calm him down. In the end they paid. Lund paid me. It was all Becker's money anyway.

Some truckers refuse to lift things, but I wasn't proud in that way. We unloaded the goods and stowed them in the "secure room," which was a stone chamber in Structure II-A. Wonderful dead names these *arqueos* have for their pyramids. The entrance could be closed off with a ramshackle door made of poles and locked with a chain. Here the food was stored, and the more valuable pieces of equipment, and the finds, running largely to fragments of monochrome pottery. There were beads and other knickknacks sealed in clear plastic bags, and some chunks of organic matter—wood and charcoal— wrapped in aluminum foil, for carbon-14 dating. I saw nothing worth locking up. Pots put me to sleep. The romance of broken crockery was lost on me.

Great care would be taken here, every last pebble tagged. Then the loot would be sacked up and hauled away and dumped in the basement of some museum, where tons of the stuff already lay moldering. Buried again, so to speak, uncatalogued, soon forgotten, never again to see the light of day. But the great object would have been achieved, which was to keep these artworks out of the hands of people. Don't let them touch a thing! A sin! A crime against "the people"! By which they meant the state, or really, just themselves. At least Refugio and I had put these things back into the hands of people who took delight in them, if not "the people." We gave these pieces life again. Sometimes I thought there weren't enough of us doing this work. That was the way I put it to myself. I stole nothing. It was treasure trove, lost property, abandoned property, the true owners long dead, and the law out here was finders keepers. That was the best face I could put on it.

Rudy set up his tent camper, not bothering to ask permission. He sat on the black boulder, for which the place was named, and spoke into his tape recorder. "An extremely short astroport oriented from northeast to southwest," I heard him say. He stopped speaking as I approached but was in no way embarrassed.

"A word to the wise, Rudy."

"What?"

"Make yourself useful around camp and they may let you stay. They're short-handed. But don't make a lot of suggestions. Stay out of their hair."

"I know how to behave myself. How far is it to the big river?"

"Not far. Just remember, you're a guest here."

I walked out into the woods about a hundred yards, where there was an oblong structure standing alone, a *temescal*, a Mayan steam bath. Refugio and Flaco Peralta and I had punched a hole in the floor of this house years ago. We found nothing. Actually I lost something, my Zippo lighter, smoothest of artifacts, which rode a little heavy in the pocket. Some *arqueo* might turn it up in a hundred years, and with acid and a strong light bring up the inscription—CHAMPION SPARK PLUGS. I noticed that the carved panel above the door had been cut away with a chain saw. You could see the tooth marks in the stone. As soon as I got out of the business, people started buying everything. Slabs of stone.

There was a beating of wings. A flight of bats came pouring out of the doorway in panic, right into my face. No, they were birds. Swifts. Well named. They nested here but their life was in the air. They ate, drank, bathed, and even mated on the wing, if that can be believed. This aerial life was what the hippies were after. I had tried for it, too, perhaps, in my own way, but with me it was all a bust. I never got off the ground. I peered inside and saw that our pitiful hole was almost filled again with debris and guano. We had dug for treasure in a steam room, fools that we were. It took Doc Flandin and Eli to show us the ropes.

Back at the clearing Skinner was in another rage. "Who keeps moving this?" he said. It was a drafting table. No one confessed. I watched the excavation work at the base of Structure I. Burt was in charge of the job. His people had cut a ragged opening in the thing, such as I had never seen made by professionals. It was a bomb crater. They had broken through the limestone facing and were now into the rubble filler. They were going for the heart.

Mapping then, fine, and a certain amount of poking about and collecting of surface finds, nobody could object to that, certainly not me, but were they really authorized to make such a breach? I suspected them of exceeding the terms of their permit.

"Just a probe," Burt said. "We're going to put it back the way it was."

Some probe. I wondered if Dr. Ritchie knew about this. Well, it was no business of mine. I was in no position to object. Refugio and I would have used a backhoe if we could have gotten one into the woods. And they weren't going to find anything, just more rubble, perhaps the wall of a smaller, earlier pyramid. They had started too high above the base and they didn't have the labor or the equipment to do the job right.

The crew, a bedraggled lot, weren't even screening the spoil. They were two gringo boys, and two Lacondón Indians in long white cotton gowns, with bulging eyes and long black hair. These Lacondones were the last of the unassimilated lowland Maya. You didn't often find them working for hire. For what little cash they needed they sold souvenir bow-and-arrow sets for children that broke on the first pull, or the second. Only a handful of them were left, straggling about in the jungle, living in small clans. They burned copal gum as an aromatic offering to the old gods and kept to the old ways as best they could.

The younger one had some Spanish, and I asked if he knew a hunter named Acuatli who used to roam these parts with a 20-gauge shotgun slung across his back. He wore short rubber boots. Some years back this Acuatli had guided me and two Dutch photographers to Lake Perdido, over in Guatemala, where the Dutchmen took pictures of ducks and white egrets. We had no papers for Guatemala and no mule to carry our goods. We went up the San Pedro River and then followed an old *chiclero* trail overland. I made some money out of it but I wouldn't want to take that hike again. I learned, too, that slipping up on birds requires the patience of a saint.

The Lacondón said that Acuatli sounded like a Mexican name to him. By that he meant Nahuatl. He said in all his life he had never known a person named Acuatli. A few minutes later he told me that Acuatli was dead. It came to much the same thing. Sula had once told me that on the day the last Lacondón died, there would come a great earthquake, and a great wind that would blow all the monkeys out of the trees.

I bought a small bag of cacao beans from these two. Lund came by and wanted to know about Rudy. "Who is that guy? Can you vouch for him?" Lund was a surveyor who was plotting the site with his alidade and rod. He seemed to come third in command, after Skinner. A white towel was draped around his head and fashioned into a burnoose.

"Rudy's all right as long as you don't cross him," I said.

That night there was shrimp again, with onions and peppers and potatoes in a makeshift paella. It was good and there was plenty of it. The mess tent was a blue nylon canopy with mosquito netting hanging down on all sides. We sat on folding chairs and ate off card tables, or rather Carta Blanca beer tables made of sheet metal. There were two hanging lights, powered by a generator. A little cedar bush had been decorated as a Christmas tree. An electric bug killer hung on a pole outside. Bugs flew to the blue light and were sizzled on a grid.

A bath in the river and a good meal had perked up the diggers. Even Skinner was in a good mood. He held up a floppy tortilla and said that corn didn't have enough gluten in it to make a dough that would rise. Still, heavy or not, the flat bread it made was good, and yet nobody seemed to know it outside Latin America and the Southern United States. Corn, potatoes, tomatoes, yams, chocolate, vanilla—all these wonderful things the Indians had given us. Whereas we Europeans had been over here for 500 years and had yet to domesticate a single food plant from wild stock.

The two females left in camp were Gail and Denise, both a little plump, with their brown hair cut short, so that you could see the backs of their necks, all the way up to where the mowed stubble began. Gail was the quiet one. I took her for a mouse and I was wrong about that. She prepared a tray of food to take to Dr. Ritchie.

"No, no," said Skinner. "He's coming. He's up on his feet now. I just went over the work log with him. He'll be along."

Rudy asked if they used a caesium magnetometer in their work. I was uneasy. This had an extraterrestrial ring to me. But no, there was such a device, something like a mine detector, I gathered, for sensing underground anomalies, buried stelae and the like, and they did have one here, though it was down. High tech or low, almost everything here was down. I was proud of Rudy for knowing about the thing.

Dr. Ritchie came stumbling in, and Gail got up to help him along.

Skinner said, "Here's our warlike Harry now. Look, there's a leaf on his shoe."

"Greetings, greetings. Anything left?"

Gail seated him across from me and took off his hat and served him. He was trying hard to be chipper. "Sure smells good. We're in your debt, Jimmy, for this fresh seafood."

"We can pull out tonight if you want to, sir. I can have you in the hospital by midnight. No use putting it off."

"Well, maybe tomorrow. I'm certainly no good to anybody like this. What do you think, Gene?"

Skinner shrugged. "Whatever you say. What's your fee on a deal like that, Burns? Double rate on a hospital run?"

"For you it would be double."

Dr. Ritchie jiggled his soup spoon. "Boys, boys."

Lund picked up on the theme of Indian superiority. He talked about their natural ways, how they were attuned to the natural rhythms of life, their natural acceptance of things, natural religion, natural food, natural childbirth, natural sense of place in the world, natural this, and natural that. All true enough, perhaps, but there was something a little bogus and second-hand about his enthusiasm. It was like some poet or intellectual going on and on about the beauties of baseball.

I lit a cigar and tuned out. We had the Indians to thank for tobacco too. They had given us these long green *puros* for solace. I watched the flashes of bugs being electrocuted. You couldn't hear the crackling sounds, or even the chugging of the generator, for the rushing noise of the river.

Skinner was soon at it again. ". . . an old and honored tradition, I know, this robbing of travelers in out of the way places of the world, but I broke your pal Bautista from sucking eggs and I'm going to break you too."

"You've already broken me, Skinner. I'm cured. I won't be back."

"No, you don't get off that easy. You can't just turn this away. You'll be back. Guys like you are always hanging around where there's a quick buck to be made. You'll be back, but on my terms. No more grand larceny. Next time there'll be a clear understanding."

"We'll see."

I noticed that Dr. Ritchie's jaw had dropped. Flies were walking around on his lips and teeth. The flies know right away. The man was dead. He had just quietly stopped living. As a child I thought you had to go through something called a death agony, certain pangs and throes. They were not incidental but a positive visitation. Death came as a force in itself. We laid him on the ground, and Gail gave him mouth to mouth resuscitation. Burt pounded on his chest. I turned him over and pitched in with my method, long out of date, of pumping up and down on his back. Lund said, "All right. That's enough."

We carried the body to his tent and zipped it up in his sleeping bag. Skinner was shaken. "I thought he just had the flu." He said we would sit up with the body through the night, turn and turn about. He took the first watch. I slept in my truck, after moving it beyond the glow of the electric bug killer. My suspicion was that those things attracted more bugs than they killed. The trick was to lie low. Later it rained a little and that shut up the monkeys. No one called me for my watch. Skinner sat up alone with the body all night.

At breakfast he announced that he and Lund—the Mexicans might want a second witness—would take it out in the Toyota. I was to follow behind in my big truck to see that they made it across the ford. The river was up a bit. They would take the body to Villahermosa, the nearest town of any size, there to make the necessary calls home and to see to the legal formalities and the shipping arrangements. They would return in a day or two. The rest of the crew would carry on here under Burt's direction. He had his trail bike, if any emergency came up. Dr. Ritchie's achievements were well known, his brilliant work on the Tajín horizon, his reconstruction of the Olmec merchant routes. The Bonar expedition could best serve his memory by finishing the job here.

Gail said, "Denise and I are going out, too."

"No need for that."

"I mean we're leaving the dig. We're going home."

"Why?"

"We have our reasons. One reason is that we agreed to work for Dr. Ritchie and no one else."

Skinner looked at them and brushed crumbs around on the tin table. It was a bad moment for Denise. She was almost in tears. Gail turned to me. "Can we ride back to Mérida with you?"

"Sure."

"Can you fly out of there to the States?"

"Yes, of course. Daily flights to New Orleans and Houston."

Skinner said, "Well, I see it was a mistake to bring you along. You've wasted a lot of my time. I thought you were serious students. You realize how this is going to look in my report?"

Gail was calm. "We may have some things to report ourselves."

He thought that over and then came quickly to his feet. "All right, suit yourself. Anyone else. No? Then let's get on about our business."

At this rate Rudy would soon be in charge. The girls went to pack their things. We lashed the body down in the bed of the Toyota so it wouldn't roll about. Skinner said, "I really thought he just had the flu." I drained my two tanks and left the gasoline for Burt, or almost drained them. I kept just enough to make the run back to Palenque.

Rudy gave me a manila envelope to take back to Louise. It was all sealed up with tape. Today he was dressed in camouflage fatigues and black beret with a brass badge on it. I couldn't believe the National Guard had ever issued that cap. From his web belt there hung canteens and other objects in canvas pouches.

"Rudy, I wouldn't wear that military stuff around here. Just down the way there, through all that greenery, is the Usumacinta River, and on the other side of the river is Guatemala."

"So?"

"You might get shot. They're shooting at each other over there, guerillas and government troops. Sometimes there are skirmishes on this side of the river. A lone straggler in that outfit—you're just asking for it."

"With my blond hair they can see I'm a gringo."

"And maybe shoot you all the quicker for that."

"I can take care of myself. I've been out in the field before. You never give me credit for knowing how to do anything."

He was right. I liked Rudy but something about him aroused the bully and the scold in me.

"Look, Burns, don't worry, okay? I always have this stuff right here in my shirt pocket where I can get at it. I have my tourist visa and my car papers and my letter of introduction from Professor Camacho Puut. I know how to get along with people. Nobody's going to bother me when they find out who I am. I have my press card taped to my chest."

"Who you are?"

"That I'm a writer. Down here they respect artists."

"Well, I wouldn't go wandering far in that rig. The Mexicans don't like it either."

"There's a ninety-minute cassette in that envelope. Keep it out of the heat. I've sealed it up in such a way that Louise will know if it's been tampered with."

"Okay."

"And don't tell anybody where I am. Just say I'm at— Chichén Itzá."

"Right. The sacred well."

We stopped at the fording place on the Tabí and loosened the fan belt on the little truck, to keep the fan from turning and throwing water back on the distributor. A family of rusty brown iguanas watched us from an overhanging limb, then plopped into the water on their lizard bellies, a family dive. Skinner dithered and stalled around. Finally he took the plunge in his truck and made it across without mishap.

I was busy dodging roots and hanging onto the gearstick. The girls talked between themselves, about some certificate they probably wouldn't get now. Denise asked me if there were any drugstores in Mérida.

"There's one on every street corner."

Once out on the wider road I dropped back and let Skinner and Lund pull ahead, out of sight. There was no dust, but I disliked being part of a convoy. Denise said she and Gail had not been sick a single day and had washed more potsherds than any four of the others. She wanted me to know that their departure had nothing to do with female hysteria but was rather a carefully considered and justifiable move.

I agreed. "You stayed longer than I would have."

We picked up a hitchhiker, an old man, who piled into the cab with us and sat by the door, silent, with his stick between his knees. He rolled up the window, as I knew he would, to keep the *aires*—evil winds—from swirling about his head, seeking entry. These dark spirits penetrate the body by way of the ears and nose and mouth, and cause internal mischief. He would suffocate on a bus before he would crack a window.

At Refugio's place we had some coffee with hot milk. He was sitting under a shade tree, bolt upright on a wooden chair, with his hands placed stiffly on his knees. He was a pharaoh. Sula was trimming his hair. Manolo was polishing the new red truck.

"No!" said Refugio. "But this is terrible news! Dr. Ritchie! Such an amiable man! There was a light in his eyes! So quiet! Always dedicated to bennee! He leaves small children?"

"I don't know. I wouldn't think so."

He said he had seen the *pagano* Skinner go by in his truck and had wondered. Now Skinner was a pagan monkey. Was his stupid *cloche* then fixed? Yes, I said, but they were going to the wrong town, to Villahermosa. The death had occurred in

Chiapas, and the proper place to deliver the body and make the report was Tuxtla Gutiérrez, the state capital. They didn't know that Villahermosa was across the state line in Tabasco, or didn't think it important. There would be bureaucratic delays, various Mexican hitches. Skinner's temper would flare. He would insult the officials and his problems would be compounded tenfold. He and Lund would be gone for days. The fellow with the motorcycle, Burt, was now the boss at Ektún. He was an agreeable young man. Refugio could now resume his deliveries to the site and perhaps even sell the boy some odd lengths of plastic pipe.

"Yes, this is good thinking, Jaime. But my little green man? You won't forget him?"

It took me a moment to make the connection. His Olmec jade piece, my photograph of same. "No, I won't forget."

The fuel gauge needle had long been resting on E when we reached Palenque. The old man got out at the town plaza. He took off his straw hat and said, "You have my thanks, sir, until you are better paid."

If the girls offered to help pay for the gasoline I would accept. We would split the cost three ways. But I would let it be their own idea to give me money. As they say in New York, I should live so long. They drank Cokes and ate potato chips at the Pemex station while the boy pumped 160-odd liters of leaded Nova into my two tanks. They watched with mild interest and said not a word as I stood there for some little time peeling off fifty-peso notes. Gasoline was fairly cheap then, but they didn't give it away.

On the drive to Mérida the girls played around with the CB radio and scratched at tick bites on their ankles. Denise was a laugher. Her Spanish was excellent and she made jokes with the Mexican truck drivers. She kept asking me what people were doing along the way. "Now what is he doing?" A man lashing milk cans to a motorbike. A man selling bags of soft cheese. A woman bathing a child. If it was some activity I didn't understand, I said it was a local custom, a ritual, just a little thing they did around here to insure a good crop. This was a line I had picked up from the anthropologists.

North of Champotón where the road runs along the Gulf there is a rocky promontory and a small sandy crescent of beach. I stopped to see if anything of value had washed up.

Sure enough, there were two mahogany planks bobbing about in the eddy. They were fine wide planks, newly cut, unplaned, about twelve feet long, soaked and heavy. Gail and Denise helped me drag them up the bank and manhandle them into the truck. When I was going with Beth, she said it was awkward introducing me to her friends as a scavenger. I called this foraging. We had other differences.

How were they fixed, these two girls? Poor graduate students? Was there family money? Neither of them had ever seen a CB radio before. Did that place them socially? Or just regionally? Assuming them to be at least temporarily short, I recommended the Posada Fausto. It was cheap but clean, I told them, certainly no flophouse, and handy to everything. Calle 55 was dark when we arrived. There was a feeble yellow light in the hotel doorway. Fausto's twenty-watt bulb put them off a little. They were expecting a place that offered two complimentary margaritas on check-in.

Denise said, "This is where you live?"

"I keep a room here for when I'm in town, yes. It's all right after you get inside. The rooms are okay. They have high ceilings and ten-speed ceiling fans. You don't need air-conditioning. The doorknobs are porcelain with many hairline cracks. The towels are rough-dried in the sun. Very stiff and invigorating after a bath." I caught myself overselling the place, making it out to be a charming little hotel. It wasn't that but it was all right.

Gail said, "Is that it, next to the shoe place? It doesn't even look like it's open." That was the first peep I had heard out of her for many miles.

What they wanted to do was ride around town some more, make a hotel inspection tour, find a properly lighted one that accepted credit cards but was at the same time reasonably priced, with maybe a swimming pool and a newsstand. This was why I no longer worked with other people—Refugio, Eli, Doc, whoever. The great nuisance of having a debate every hour or so and taking a vote on the next move.

I took them out to the Holiday Inn and dropped them. Then I made a jog over the Calle 61 to deliver Rudy's package. He and Louise had rooms at a place called Casitas Lola. I found her working away, typing up taped dictation from Rudy.

What a job. The machine ran a little fast, and he sounded like a castrato. "Just five more to do and I'm caught up," she said. My gift of cacao beans delighted her. It was Christmas again.

"Did you see Rudy at Tumbalá?"

"I'm not supposed to say. You'll have to read his letter. It's written in lemon juice."

"You think you're oh so funny. Well, there's nothing funny about our security methods. There are people who would pay thousands of dollars just to get a peek at this material. You never have grasped the importance of our work and you never will. Did you know I was a late child?"

"No, I didn't."

"My mother was forty-three years old when I was born. There are so many interesting things you don't know about me. I may tell you some of those things later. I may not. It all depends. I haven't decided yet. Whether to confide in a vandal."

It was a shadowy room with a raftered ceiling, very low, and a single old-fashioned floor lamp with a parchment shade, a good room in which to carry on some quiet mad enterprise. Louise worked at a long table in the pool of light. She sat erect before her typewriter, the perfect secretary, in fashion eyewear, white blouse, and floppy red bow tie. She had blue eyes set far back in her head, so that they appeared to be dark eyes. Her blond ringlets were trimmed short and sort of tossed about. Next door I could hear a child singing, in English. The new people in the next casita, a family from New Jersey. They had moved down here to escape the blast from the coming nuclear war.

"Do you mind very much being called a vandal?"

"No, go ahead."

"I mean after all that's what you are. I've never known one before. I mean who worked at it full time. You'll never guess what I dreamed last night. I dreamed I had a baby and gave it away to Beth. Can you imagine that? Just gave it away. The same day. I said, 'Here's a little baby for you, Beth.'"

"Maybe it was a mutation. A rejected sport."

"I hadn't thought of that. A space baby. Genetically altered. You're joking, but it happens, you know, all the time. The hospitals aren't permitted to report it. But even so, why would I give it away? I would never give my baby away, even if it was a mutant. With his tiny knowing eyes following me around the room."

"I've got to go, Short Stuff. It's late. I've been on the road all day."

"Don't call me that. Wait. I was just going to make some hot chocolate."

"Thanks anyway, no, I'm beat."

"Is it very far away? Where Rudy is? I worry about him traveling all alone in that old car."

"Rudy's okay. He's down in Chiapas with some college people. He'll be back in a few days. The mosquitoes will soon run him off."

"Thanks for bringing the tape. Watch your step. There was a lot of slick stuff out there today."

She meant outside Dr. Estevez's House of Complete Modern Dentistry, where the sidewalk was spattered daily with gobbets of bloody spit.

# V

THE MAYAS had a ceremonial year of 260 days called a *tzolkin*, and then they had one of 360 days called a *tun*, and finally there was the *haab* of 365 days, the least important one, not used in their long calculation. This was simply a *tun*, plus five nameless days of dread and suspended activity, the *uayeb*, corresponding somewhat to our dead week between Christmas and New Year's Day.

Here in Mérida the sky was blue and the air soft, no driving sleet, no dense waves of northern guilt, but there was a seasonal lethargy all the same. The year had run down and nobody was quite ready to start the grind again. These were our nameless days.

Beatriz was moping at the desk the next morning. She said Doc Flandin had called three times asking for me. There was no letter from Ah Kin, only a sharp note from Frau Kobold. Her cakes again! I picked them up for her weekly when I was in town, a big plastic sack of stale muffins and *pastelitos* and broken cookies, which she got from the Hoolywood Panaderia for next to nothing. It was a long-standing arrangement, and this was all she ate, as far as anyone knew. It seems you can live for years on *pan dulce* and Nescafé and cigarettes, and even thrive. She appeared to be none the worse for having smoked 900,000 Faros cigarettes.

I walked over to the Hoolywood and waited for the rejects to be bagged. Someone clapped a hand on my shoulder from behind. It was a man named Beavers and he wanted to borrow ten dollars. I barely knew him but he was on me so fast I couldn't think of a way to say no. He said Flandin was looking for me.

On the way back I paused at the *zócalo* to watch the Mexican flag being raised. There was a color guard and a drum and bugle platoon from the army barracks. I had seen it all many times but I could no more pass up a display like that than I could a car wreck with personal injuries. They were smart looking troops, with one or two corny touches—chromed bayonets and white laces in their black boots, all back-laced and looped about. The rifles were real, though the M-16 makes a poor ceremonial piece—ugly, too short, too black, too much plastic. More a weapon to be brandished defiantly above the head by irregular forces. There it went, the big tricolor, as big and soft as a bedsheet, creeping up inch by deliberate inch. I was trained to run the colors up briskly and bring them down gravely, but this way was all right, too, I suppose.

I saw Beth across the plaza. She was smiling and must have been watching me. Had she caught me muttering to myself? With that bag of crumbs slung across my back I was a cartoon burglar making off with his swag in a pillowcase. She looked good, in her washed-out, pioneer woman way, with little or no makeup, with her hair parted in the middle and pulled back into a knob. She wore a peach-colored dress with shoulder straps. Bollard was with her, sitting lumpily on a bench with a newspaper. What did she see in that cinnamon bear? There's always some jerk who won't rise for the national anthem, his own or anyone else's. No wait, now he was getting up, but grudgingly, humoring Beth, and the natives, in their absurd ritual.

Bollard lived on the top floor of the Napoles Apartments and wrote novels. Of the grim modern kind, if I can read faces. I hadn't read his books. My fear was that they might not be quite as bad as I wanted them to be. Art and Mike said they were no worse than other books. He had a certain following. He called me The Great Excavator, and also, Our Mathematical Friend, after I had once corrected him on a compound interest calculation. He thought he was going to make a fortune off his Mexican telephone bonds. Bollard wasn't always lost in his art, up there in the penthouse. It was a nice place. I had once lived in the Napoles myself, when I was selling those long leather coats.

Beth gave me a mock curtsy. I nodded. Our flickering little romance had just about flickered out. She had taken me at first for a colorful Cajun, sucker of crawdad heads, wild dancer to swamp tunes, then lost interest when she found I was from the Anglo, Arkansas-Texas part of Louisiana. Of our Arklatex folkways she knew nothing. She suspected them to be dark ways, a good deal of sweaty cruel laughter, but of a darkness that wasn't particularly interesting. Then she began to cultivate me again when someone told her I was a pretty fair hand at sorting out genuine Mayan pieces from the modern forgeries. Then someone else told her how I came by my knowledge and she got frosty again.

Frau Kobold was waiting for me in her wicker wheelchair. She wasn't exactly lame, just old. Her bones were dry sticks. I went carefully over the explanation again, how other cake arrangements were going to have to be made when I was gone.

"I don't like people knowing my business," she said.

Her pride, yes, I understood that, but Fausto and Beatriz and Agustín already knew her business, her situation. Louise was right, there was too much stuff in this room. There were bulging pasteboard boxes, packed with clothing and dishes, as for an immediate move. They had been sitting here for years. Mayan relics were jumbled about on tables and chairs. On the walls there were framed photographs of temples and carved stelae taken by her husband, Oskar Kobold, long dead. Some of these prints were fifty years old but they were still the best I had ever seen of low-relief carvings. With all their fierce lighting and fine lenses and fast film, the modern photographers still couldn't capture those shadowy lines the way Oskar Kobold did, which is why the inscription scholars have to rely on drawings.

He died a poor and bitter man, having been cheated of both recognition and money by museums, universities, governments, publishers, all manner of high-minded institutions. They had used his work freely, were still using it, and had paid him trifling fees when they paid at all. Mostly they sent him remaindered books. But then he had a reputation for being prickly and hard to deal with, too, something of a nut. Frau Kobold, the former Miss Alma Dunbar of Memphis, had traipsed about in the bush with him in jodhpurs and pith helmet. She carried his tripod and mixed his chemicals and prepared his wet plates and kept his notes. None of it seemed to mean much to her now. She seldom talked about the old days, except for the time she and Oskar had appeared in a Fox Movietone Newsreel—*Bringing an Ancient Civilization to Light!* Doc said it was a segment lasting two or three minutes. Nothing much pleased her anymore or engaged her interest. She said her sleep was dreamless.

I sat on the bed and had coffee with her. Stale cake is not bad. The shaggy balls of the chenille bedspread were worn down to nubs from countless washings. The mystery novels were within easy reach of the insomniac, all lined up on improvised shelving of pine boards and bricks. She had some new reading material, too, a newsletter called *Gamma Bulletin*, which came once a month from the States, and which I took to be some archaeological journal. She boiled the water with an electric immersion coil in plastic cups.

I said, "Alma, you were rude to a friend of mine the other night."

"Oh? Who?"

"A girl named Louise Kurle. She took the trouble to come by here and wish you a merry Christmas."

"Oh yes. She had been here before. I didn't want to encourage her. I thought she might become a pest. I don't care to make new friends at my time of life."

"You might make an exception. Stretch a point."

"No, I don't think so. I didn't like her manner. She doesn't appreciate who I am."

"She'd be glad to do things for you."

"No, she doesn't fit in around here. Do you think because I'm poor I should have to tolerate fools?"

She showed me her coins, knotted up in a handkerchief, schoolgirl style, and said I had also forgotten about her appointment at the beauty shop. Once a month I rolled her down to the *sala de belleza* to get her hair done, and air her out a bit. She still paid the girls at the *sala* five pesos, having no idea of what the peso was worth these days. Fausto and Doc and I made up the difference behind her back, as we did with her other creditors. Coffee was cheap enough, and postage stamps. She ran through a lot of stamps. But the expenses didn't amount to much, except for the medicine. Terry Teremoto, the crank sculptor, had helped too, with a regular check, until his recent death in Veracruz.

"Well, make another appointment and let me know. I should be in town for awhile. Here, let me see your glasses." They were smeared. I breathed on them and wiped them on the bedspread.

Now it was time for a real breakfast, and I went along to the Express, a sidewalk café where the gringos gathered. Here I was greeted by Vick, Crouch, Cribbs, Bolus, and Nelms, who feigned surprise.

"I wish you would look."

"Not him again."

"You still hanging around?"

I had announced recently, as I did once or twice a year, that I was leaving Mexico for good, going back to Shreveport to join my brother in the construction business. "Yes, but not for long," I said. "You better make the best of me while you can." I chose to sit at another table, one offering a better view of street events, with Simcoe, Pleat, McNeese, Coney, Minim, and Mott. Already there was something to see, a car fire in the cab rank across the street. The cabbies were throwing clods of dirt at it and slapping at it with rags.

Pleat, great favorite with the ladies, said he had owned thirty-odd cars in his lifetime and never once had an engine fire. Coney, the English painter, whose tuneless humming drove people away, said he once had a car fire so hot that the aluminum carburetor melted and ran down over the block. Minim was in the Bowling Hall of Fame. He was a retired bowler and sports poet, and he maintained that bowling was held in even lower esteem than poetry, though it was a close call. He had made more money with his short sports poems, he said, than he had ever made on the bowling circuit, though not much more. Mott always looked sprightly and pleased with himself, like Harry Truman at the piano, with his rimless glasses and neatly combed hair. He had gone crazy in the army and now received a check each month, having been declared fifty percent psychologically disabled. Had they determined him to be half crazy all the time or full crazy half the time? Mott said the VA doctors never would spell it out for him. He had whatever the opposite of paranoia is called. He thought everybody liked him and took a deep personal interest in his welfare. But then everybody did like him.

"Don Ricardo is looking for you," he said.

"So I heard."

Let him look. He knew where to find me. "Don Ricardo" was another of Flandin's self-bestowed titles. This one had never caught on outside his own household. His wife, Nan, had pushed it, and of course the servants had to call him that. The rest of us refused to do so, out of pettiness no doubt. All except for the guileless Mott.

Simcoe said he had seen an interesting thing in the *zócalo* that morning. He had spied a rat high up in the topmost branches of a laurel tree. Minim said rats didn't climb trees and that it must have been a squirrel or a gray bird. Simcoe didn't like having his eyesight or his honesty questioned. He said, "A gray bird eating a Baby Ruth from the wrapper? What speeshees of gray bird might that be?" In the end we agreed that city rats could climb trees but did not often choose to climb trees and that Simcoe was right to report his sighting.

A portly hippie with a two-stranded beard went ambling past our table. McNeese said, "Look at that morphadite creep. On his way to shoot some dope into his old flabby white ass, I'll bet."

Mott said, "Is that the way they do it? Wouldn't he need an assistant? An accomplice?"

Coney said, "I wouldn't touch him with a barge pole."

"What are they up to? Is there some hippie convention?"

"I don't understand how they get across the border."

I had a boy polish my shoes. Coney sketched and hummed. Simcoe read a book. It was all right to do that here. In the States it was acceptable to read newspapers and magazines in public, but not books, unless you wanted to be taken for a student or a bum or a lunatic or all three. Here you could read books in cafés without giving much offense, and even write them. I had seen Bollard doing it, scratching many life-destroying things on a legal pad. McNeese said, "Speaking of hippies, I heard they picked up your man in the station wagon."

"What, here?" I said.

"I don't know."

"Did they get the little girl back?"

"I don't know the details. I just heard something at Shep's about it."

Just then Doc Flandin came up in his slippers. When I first met him he wore a seersucker suit and a spotless Panama, day in and day out. Now he looked like a wino. He was unshaven, and his shirttail was out, and he had an odd little brimless cap pushed down on his ears, of the kind James Cagney used to wear in prison. He beamed down on us with one fist on his hip. We amused him.

"Well, boys, what is it this morning? Pork Chop Hill? Leyte Gulf? Chesty Puller? Service-connected disabilities? Fort Benning?"

Supposedly we sat here all day drinking coffee and telling grotesque military anecdotes, impatiently waiting our turn in a round-robin. Bollard called us the Private Slovik Post of the American Legion.

Minim said, "No sir, our topic today is the sinking peso. We were hoping you might come along and shed some light on the matter."

"What? Economics? Good God. No, not my line, gentlemen."

Coney said, "Do join us, sir, in our banter. Your presence alone would raise the tone of things."

"Oh, I'm not so sure of that. Jimmy, I'd like a word with you."

I followed him across the street to the little park. The old man was in bad shape. His plum face had gone off to the color of lead.

"Where in the world have you been?" he said. "I need to talk to you. Big news. You never come by to see me anymore."

"I've been to your house three times since Nan died."

"What, I was out?"

"Mrs. Blaney said you couldn't be interrupted. I finally got the message."

"Lucille told you that? Well, things have been all balled up lately. Look here, I want you to come by Izamál for lunch at two. Can you do that? It's important."

"Have you cleared this with Mrs. Blaney?"

"I believe you're sulking. A fancied slight? Let me tell you frankly, it's not very becoming. The poor woman made a mistake, that's all."

"Did you hear about Dr. Ritchie?"

"Yes, I did. Too bad."

"It was his heart, I think. I was there. A bad business. He was quite a man in his field, wasn't he?"

"Ritchie was adequate. Undistinguished."

He left me abruptly, and I went back to the Express to use the telephone. I called a man named Lozano, with the Judicial Police, to whom I had made my report about Dan and the runaway girl, LaJoye Mishell Teeter. But no, McNeese had gotten it wrong, Big Dan had not been arrested. Or rather the Municipal Police in Valladolid had picked him up, then let him go. Lozano said the patrolmen had not seen the bulletin on him. Three of them had gone to answer a call about a big gringo who was trying to entice a small boy into his spotted car. They came and handcuffed him, but it was at the end of a shift and they didn't want to bother taking him back to the station, going through all the paperwork, with a foreigner. So they hammered him to his knees with their sticks, gave him a good bloody beating, and turned him loose with a warning.

Lozano said, "We'll have him in a day or two. A car like that."

Hard to say. I wasn't so sure. The Jumping Jacks might well have another car by now. They might be in Belize or Guatemala. Off to their City of Dawn, beyond the range of my understanding.

As for Doc's big news, I could make a pretty good guess at that. His book was finished at long last. Well, it *was* big news. He had been working on the thing for almost forty years, his masterful survey of Meso-American civilization, from Olmec dawn through the fall of the Aztecs. It was a grand synthesis, he said, proving that the several cultures were essentially all the same, or closely related. Along the way he would clear up all the old mysteries. He would show that Quetzalcoatl or Kukulcán was a historical figure and not just some mythical "culture hero," and he would explain the basis for the 260-day year (the human gestation period, with the odd days lopped off) and the twenty-day "month," which seemed to have no astronomical significance. He would set forth in detail the real reasons for the collapse of the Mayan high culture in the ninth century. He would tell us who the Olmecs really were, appearing suddenly out of darkness, and why they carved those colossal heads that look like Fernando Valenzuela of the Los Angeles Dodgers. He would give the location of Aztlán, the original home of the Aztecs, and he would end speculation once and for all on transoceanic contacts, by revealing the simple truth of the matter. He would identify "the dancing men" at Monte Alban, and he would settle the question of the "elephant" carving at Copán. For good measure he would decipher the Mayan hieroglyphics.

Some of it would be nonsense and perhaps a lot of it but not all of it. Flandin was formidable in his way. I was eager to read the part about the glyph translation, hoping it wouldn't be silly. For some time now he had told me he could read the inscriptions. When I pressed him he was evasive. "I can tell you this much and no more, for the present. These writings are not just calendric piffle." Some other kind of piffle then. Thousand-year-old weather reports. *Champion Spark Plugs.* I knew he hadn't actually broken the code, but it was possible that he had hit on some useful new approach to the problem.

Beth was waiting for me in front of the Posada Fausto. She wanted me to haul some chairs for her. They wouldn't fit in Bollard's Peugeot. If you have a truck your friends will drive you crazy. We drove out to a carpentry shop on Colón, where a man named Chelo made tables and things out of withes and sticks and swatches of rawhide leather. He made baby furniture, too, strange rough cradles with a lot of bark showing and little Goldilocks chairs. I tried to sell him my big planks. Chelo said he never worked in mahogany, seeming to suggest there was something vulgar about it. Another artist.

Beth had bought a round table and four chairs, bulky pieces but not heavy, and I transported them and set them up in her courtyard. She had a nice roomy place all to herself behind the museum. There was a flowery patio with bees and paper lanterns and wind chimes and two prowling cats. These people on grants did all right for themselves. She had a grant from some foundation to manage this children's museum, which was a very good one, no expense spared, the idea being to march the local *niños* through in troops and give them some appreciation of their Mayan heritage.

Beth wiped her hands on a fresh towel and tossed it into the hamper. It was one use and out for her. She didn't have to wash them. She made a pitcher of limeade, and we sat in the new chairs. The rawhide was smelly. Bits of flesh still adhered to the skin. I knew a little about the leather business and even

I knew that rawhide must be scraped and dried and stretched properly. Beth denied that there was any smell and then denied that the smell was unpleasant. To her it was agreeable and even bracing. She defended all things Mexican.

"I haven't seen you around. What have you been doing with yourself?"

"Nothing much," I said. "Trying to save some money."

"Out at night drinking with your buddies, I suppose. Ike and Mutt, are they? Those two you're always quoting?"

She meant Art and Mike, the inseparable Munn brothers.

"No, I haven't been drinking at all."

"Will you read something if I give it to you?"

"Sure. What is it?"

"I don't mean now. I'm still working on it. Just some observations. A kind of list. It's about the kind of person you've become."

"A list of my shortcomings then."

"Not exactly that. More about personal growth. Our repetitive acts. How our growth can be arrested and we may not even be aware of it."

"Growth? That sounds like one of Bollard's words."

"Do you think I can't have my own ideas?"

"I think you'd do better to stay away from people like that."

"Like what? Look who's talking. Carleton had nothing whatever to do with this and you know it."

"Well, no, I don't know it. I see you all over town with him."

"Will you read it?"

"I'll read it if you can put it on one sheet of paper."

"Now what is that, some military thing?"

"No, I read about it in a business book. The need for keeping memos and reports short. How it concentrates your thinking and saves time for everybody along the line."

"You're afraid of smart women, aren't you?"

She had used this ploy before, having heard via the female bush telegraph that it was unanswerable. She was right though. I was leery of them. Art and Mike said taking an intellectual woman into your home was like taking in a baby raccoon. They were both amusing for awhile but soon became randomly vicious and learned how to open the refrigerator. Beth asked if I remembered her green sofa that the cats had scratched up. I said I did but I had no memory for particular pieces of furniture, having hauled so much of it. She told a long story about how she had given the sofa to an ungrateful person who had in turn given it away to someone else.

"You're not even listening to me."

"Yes, I am. The green sofa. I tell you what. I've got some things to do. Let me know when you've finished the paper and I'll read it and think it over."

"You're too kind. How much do I owe you for the delivery job?"

"No charge."

"I saw that mud on your truck and all those branches caught up underneath. You've been out ransacking temples again, haven't you? You never did really stop. On top of everything else you're a liar."

On top of all my other defects, too many to be recorded on a single page. I had meant to ask her if Bollard brought cat treats when he came calling, as I had done, but I let it go.

# VI

MEXICAN HOMES as a rule are closed off to the world by high blank walls of yellowish masonry, topped with broken glass to discourage *escaladores*, or climbing burglars. The gardens and fountains and other delights are hidden, as in an Arab city. Each city block is a fortress. But on the Paseo Montejo in Mérida there are two-story houses standing detached with their own lawns and tropical shrubbery. The Paseo is a shady boulevard where the sisal millionaires once lived, a short version of St. Charles Avenue in New Orleans, and a very un-Mexican street.

Doc Flandin lived on the near end of it in a fine white house with a wraparound porch and a little round tower on top, a cupola. Izamál, it was called, or place of the lizard. Doc had come late in life to this luxury, when he married Nan. She had the money.

Mrs. Blaney admitted me this time, making a show of checking her watch. This was to let me know that formal luncheon appointments are one thing and drop-in calls quite another.

"Don Ricardo will see you in his bedroom. Can you find your way? Just follow the music."

"I think I can find it."

I was wandering around in this house before Lucille Blaney had ever set foot in Mexico. I had met Eric Thompson, the great Mayanist, in this very room, with its cold tile floor and grand piano. No one played the piano, but the lid was always propped up on its slender stick. Sir Eric, I should say. He called Flandin Dicky. It was Eric this and Dicky that. I still cringe when I remember how I talked so much that day, trying to show off my piddling scraps of knowledge.

The music came from an old wind-up phonograph. Doc was listening once again to Al Jolson singing "April Showers." I found the old lizard upstairs in his bed, a big canopied affair made of dark oak. The posts and beams were carved with a running fretwork design in the Uxmal style. The room was long and sunny. There were casement windows and a fireplace and a balcony. He allowed Al to finish, then lifted the arm from the thick black record.

"Do you mind if we eat here?"

"No, of course not."

"It would be nicer by the pool, but this way we can have some privacy. Lucille has the ears of a jackrabbit."

"You're no match for that woman, Doc. Nan could handle her, but you can't. She's got your number."

"Well, I can't kick her out now."

"No, it's too late in the day for that."

The maid, Lorena, served crabmeat salad in avocado halves. I told Doc about my run to Ektún, the death of Dr. Ritchie and how that Refugio had asked about his book and his tobacco pipe. He found that funny. He and Refugio had some running joke about the pipe that I wasn't privy to. A little reminder that they had worked together before I came along.

"Was Ritchie one of these trotters or joggers?" he asked me. "Some exercise nut?"

"I don't know. You couldn't do much jogging at Ektún."

"He was not really a good field man, you know."

"No? He had a good reputation."

"Look at all the staff support he had. If I had been set up like that in my sixties, I would have accomplished great things. I would have shown them a thing or two."

"You've done all right. You found the Seibal scepter. That should be enough for one man. Nobody can do very much. Then there's your book."

"They won't acknowledge that I've done anything."

"I saw you in church on Christmas day."

"Well, why not? I'm an old sinner."

"No, I approve. It's just that I hadn't seen you in church before."

"But I was never a public and obstinate sinner. No one can say that."

"No."

"A love for truth too. I've always had a love for truth and that in itself is a sign of grace. Did you never hear that?"

"I don't think so."

"I'm dying, Jimmy. You're talking to a corpse."

"What?"

"It's prostate cancer. I'm waiting for the biopsy report from Dr. Solís, but that's only a formality. I wanted you to know. We won't talk about it. I've arranged for Father Mateo to say some masses for me."

"Have you seen Soledad Bravo about this?"

"No, I haven't consulted any witch doctors, thank you."

"When do you get the report?"

"I don't want to talk about it."

"We don't have to talk about it for three hours, but you can't say something like that and then just drop it."

"There's nothing to be said or done. You can't beat the slow-worm. Sometimes he's not so slow."

"L. C. Bowers beat it. He went up to the Ochsner Clinic in New Orleans, and they cut it out. That was what, three years ago, and he's still walking around."

"Bowers had some lesser form of the thing."

Doc's diseases had to be grand, too. He had never shown much sympathy for the sick, not even for Nan when she was dying, believing as he did that illness was largely voluntary. Giving way. Then whining. He took no medicine himself and he seemed to think that Nan had killed herself through a foolish addiction to laxatives and nasal sprays.

And Soledad Bravo was no witch doctor. She was a modest lady who practiced folk medicine in her home on Calle 55, just down the street from me. She was a *curandera*, who could deliver babies, remove warts, and pull single-rooted teeth, no molars, and she could put her ear to your chest and look at your tongue and your eyes and feel around under your jaw, then tell you what was wrong and give you a remedy. It might be something old-fashioned like arnica or camphorated oil, or it might be some very modern drug, or some simple dietary tip. She kept up with things. Soledad had a gift. She got results. What more can you ask than to be healed? I wouldn't go to anyone else.

"That little round cap you're wearing," I said. "Does that have something to do with your condition?"

"No, but it keeps the vapors in. Vapors were escaping from my head."

"Why not let them escape?"

"I don't care to discuss the cap. My death is imminent and I have some important instructions for you."

"This is not the razor blade deal again, is it?"

"The what?"

I had to remind him. Some years back, fearing a stroke, he had given me a package of single-edge razor blades. Should he be struck down and incapacitated, unable to move, I was to sneak into his room at night and slit his wrists with one of those blades. Others would string him along, he said, but he knew I would do it. This, I think, was intended as flattery. I still carried those Gem blades around in my shaving kit.

"Oh no, there's no question of paralysis with this thing," he said. "I have some morphine tablets that will do the job when the time comes."

"I came over here thinking I would hear that your book was finished. Now you tell me this."

"The book is coming along, don't worry. I'm still at it. Answering a lot of questions that nobody has asked. If I had had any decent staff support, the thing would have been finished long ago. But you know, I make a late discovery. Working fast suits me. It reads better. I learn to write on my deathbed, you see. The schoolboys won't like it but by God they'll have to take notice this time. Oh yes, I know what they say. 'What can you expect? He's French! Brilliant but unsound! I can't keep up with him! This old flaneur has too many ideas! Too many theories!' It's my brio, Jimmy, that they can't stomach. My verve. It sets their teeth on edge. I know how these drab people think and I know exactly what they say about me."

It was worse than that. They didn't say anything. The academics, or schoolboys, as he called them, didn't even take the trouble to dispute his theories. The papers he submitted to scholarly journals were returned without comment. He was never invited to the professional conclaves, other than local ones that the Mexicans sponsored. Mexicans weren't quite as rigid as the Americans and the English and the Germans in these matters of caste.

It seemed to me that he deserved better treatment. Perhaps not complete acceptance, or the centerfold spread in *National Geographic* that he so longed for, but something, a nod in the footnotes even. His great find, the manikin scepter at Seibal, was widely published but never attributed to him. And it was Flandin, with two or three Mexicans, who had argued years ago that it was the Olmecs and not the Mayas who had invented glyph writing and the bar-and-dot numeral system and the Long Count calendar, when American and English scholars—Thompson himself—refused to hear of such a thing. Being prematurely right, and worse, intuitively right, he got no credit for it. Rather, it was held against him. His field work was good and his site reports were, in my lay opinion, well up to professional standards. No brio here; they were just as tiresome to read as the approved ones. His crank claims and speculations made up only about twenty percent of his work but it was a fatal sufficiency. Or say thirty percent to be absolutely fair.

"When do I get to see the glyph chapter?"

"In good time. Camacho Puut is looking it over now. But we're not going to talk about the book."

I wondered what we were going to talk about. Lorena brought us a pot of coffee and some strawberries in heavy yellow cream. Doc asked her if she would go to his office and bring back his—*pistola*—I thought he said. Lorena was puzzled, too, and then seemed to work it out. Doc spoke fluent Spanish, but it was incorrect and badly pronounced.

"I'm worried about Camacho Puut," he said. "I do believe the old fellow is taking some dangerous narcotic drug."

"Oh come on. The Professor?"

"You weren't here. He was sitting right there. I was reading my revised prologue to him and his head was lolling and he could hardly keep his eyes open. It's none of my business if he wants to kill himself with dope but I do think he might consider his family and his own dignity. What about Alma? Have you seen her?"

"I saw her this morning."

"Is she doing any better?"

"About the same."

"Don't say anything but I'm leaving her a small annuity. A little something to help with the rent."

"She won't accept it."

"I'm rigging it up so she'll think it came from Oskar's work. But keep it under your hat."

"Did you ever work with Oskar Kobold?"

"No, never. We hardly spoke. He was an artist of the first rank, I grant him that, but he couldn't get along with anybody. An awful man. He treated Alma like a mule."

"I can't imagine her putting up with that."

"Well, she did. She wasn't hard then. Just a little pale Southern lily with a love for those travel books of John Stephens."

Lorena came back and yes, it was the *pistola* he had asked for. Gun, holster, belt, the whole business coiled up on a wooden tray. She held it forward, not wanting to touch it. Doc said, "*Por mi amigo Jaime*," and so she served it up to me, a .45 automatic on a platter.

Until very recently he had worn this big-bore pistol openly around town, and he always carried it in the bush. At our campsite, just before turning in at night, he would fire it twice into the air. This was an announcement to anyone who might be in the woods nearby. *Here we are. We're armed and we're not taking any crap.* Or sometimes I fired my shotgun, or Refugio his army rifle, an old Argentine Mauser with a bolt handle that stuck straight out.

I slipped the pistol out of the holster. Most of the blueing was gone, and there was a lot of play in the slide. It still looked good. The 1911 aeroplanes and the 1911 typewriters were now comic exhibits in museums, but this 1911 Colt still looked just right. It hadn't aged a day. The clip was crammed from top to bottom with short fat cartridges. I shucked a couple of them out.

"You'll weaken the spring," I said. "Leaving it fully loaded like that."

"Damn the spring. Put them back. I like it full."

So, he was disposing of his things.

"This is for me?"

"No, no, not the gun. That's for Refugio. I want you to see that he gets it. My binoculars too, if I can ever find them, and all my field gear. I'm putting some stuff together in boxes for him, but the pistol is the main thing. You know how he admires it."

*Not the gun.* So. I was to get something else. He was clearing the small bequests out of the way first. I saw where this was leading. I was staggered. Flandin is going to leave me this big white house. There was no one else. Nan was gone, as was his first wife, and the blind sister in Los Angeles. Mrs. Blaney, an old friend of Nan's, was here on sufferance. I didn't see Doc as much of a public benefactor. It was unlikely that he would endow an orphanage or set up a trust to provide free band concerts for the people of Mérida. All his old cronies were gone except for Professor Camacho Puut, who, properly, would get the library and the relic collection. That left me. I had served him well. My reward was to be Izamál.

Mrs. Blaney poked her head into the room. Always looming and hovering, this woman. "Oh. I thought you had gone, Mr. Burns. Don Ricardo usually has his nap at this time."

"No, I'm still here."

Doc said, "It's all right, Lucille. We're talking business."

"Oh. Well, then. I'll just—leave you two."

She left and I asked him if she knew about the cancer.

"Not yet but she suspects something."

That meant she probably did know. Nothing was said about the house. We got down to my instructions. Dr. Solís was to send for me the moment that he, Flandin, died. There would be no lingering decline in a hospital. He would die in this room. I would come at once and stand guard by his bed, allowing no one to move his body for thirty-six hours.

"Are you willing to do that? Without asking a lot of questions? Don't humor me along now. I want an honest answer."

"Yes, I can do that. Do you mean exactly thirty-six hours?"

"No less than that. I want your solemn word."

"You have it. What else? What about the funeral?"

"I've already gone over that with Huerta. You just do your job. You just make sure I'm dead."

He was afraid of being buried alive. A childhood nightmare of screaming and clawing and tossing about in a dark box. It wasn't an unreasonable fear. Any doctor can make a mistake. Funerals were carried out promptly here, and usually there was no embalming. Some morticians offered same-day service. Harlan Shrader died one morning in his hotel room, and we buried him before the sun went down, in a coffin too narrow for his shoulders, and they weren't broad. The box was made of thin pine boards and six-penny nails. Huerta charged us $40 for everything, including the grave plot, and he even put some cowboy boots on Harlan's limp feet. I don't know how he did it, slit them perhaps. We found them in Harlan's closet, but I think they must have belonged to some former occupant. In life Harlan tramped around town in threadbare canvas shoes with his toes poking out, and in death he became a member of the equestrian class. Mott and I paid Huerta. Shep applied to the Veterans Administration for the $250 burial allowance but said he never got it.

"Not a word about this to anyone," said Doc. "I know I can count on you, Jimmy. Now I want you to go up to the attic. The black steamer trunk. It's not locked. Open it up and you'll see a pasteboard box tied up with rope. It's marked NOTES. I want you to bring it down here."

I went up to the attic, an oven, just below the round cupola, and made haste to find the thing. It must have been 150 degrees Fahrenheit in that room. While poking around in the trunk, I came across a blue case with gold lettering. It held a Carnegie Medal for heroism and a citation on thick paper telling how young Richard Flandin, a grocer's delivery boy, had rescued an old lady and her dog, both unconscious, from a burning house in Los Angeles. Quite a little man. Doc in knickers. Sweat dripped from my nose and made splotches on the soft paper. Great boaster that he was, he had never told me about this. Had he forgotten? It served to remind me, too, that he was an old Angeleno, American to the bone, for all his French posturing. In a rare moment of weakness, he confessed to me one night that he was only five years old when his widowed mother made the move from Paris to California with him and his sister. He saved coins. I found a cigar box filled with silver pesos, and I bounced one, nice and heavy, on my hand. It was once one of the world's standard currencies, like the Spanish dollar, or piece of eight, and now a single peso was all but worthless. It was worth less than a single cacao bean, which the Mayans had used for money.

My first improvement to this house would be some roof turbines. Clear out all of this hot air. Would I allow Mrs. Blaney to stay on? Perhaps, but with much reduced authority and visibility.

The pasteboard box was packed with Doc's old notebooks. They were engineers' field notebooks, with yellow waterproof covers and water-resistant pages, each sheet scored off with a grid pattern. On the inner sides of the covers there were printed formulas for solving curves and triangles. I lugged it down to the bedroom and began untying the ropes. I thought he wanted the notes for reference. I thought this had something to do with his book.

"No, bind it back up," he said. "They're yours, Jimmy, to do with as you please. All my early field notes. I want you to have them."

His notes? Not the house then. I was to receive instead this dusty parcel of data. Unreadable scribbling and baffling diagrams with numbers, and here and there the multi-legged silhouette of a bug smashed between the pages. Did the stuff have any value at all? It was like being told that you had just inherited a zircon mine, unless zircons are quarried, I don't know. I was caught up short. I was at a loss.

"This is very good of you, Doc. I wonder though. Shouldn't valuable material like this go to some library or museum?"

"They had their chances. You're not pleased?"

"Yes, of course I am, a great honor, but you know how I live. Right now I'm camping out in a room at Fausto's place. You know how I move around. These notebooks should be catalogued and stored somewhere. I'm no scholar."

"It doesn't matter. You're my good friend. You've been a loyal friend. They're yours. Enough said."

Lorena came back to collect the dishes. Doc told her to go to the bureau and bring out all his—handkerchiefs—I thought he said. *Pañuelos?* She got one, and he said no, all of them, *todos.* They were plain white handkerchiefs, and she made stacks of them on a tray. He indicated that they were for me.

"I want you to have my handkerchiefs, too, Jimmy. All my old friends are dead now, and most of my new acquaintances are ill-bred people of below-average intelligence. Mental defectives for the most part. They don't use handkerchiefs."

Lorena served them to me. Doc waved off my thanks. "You do carry one, don't you?"

"Sometimes."

"I want you to feel free to use them. They're not to be put away now. They're for everyday use. There's plenty of service left in them."

"Well. They're nice handkerchiefs."

"Nothing fancy, but you can't beat long-staple cotton for absorbency and a smooth finish. How many are there?"

Now I had to count them. He wanted to draw this out.

"Twenty-two."

"So many? Well, there you are. Twenty-two flags of truce. You never know when you might need one. Take them, enjoy them. Properly cared for, they will give you years of good service."

"You mean I'm to take them now?"

"Absolutely. They're yours, enjoy them. The notebooks, the handkerchiefs. A lot of good reading in that box. I never could understand these selfish old people who hang onto everything till their very last gasp."

A little later he dozed off. I left through the back door, through the kitchen, by way of all the copper pots, thinking to avoid another encounter with Mrs. Blaney. But there she was, poolside, with her English class. She taught English conversation and ballroom dancing to young Mexican matrons. They were sitting in a half-circle, six or seven of them, holding cups and saucers. Mrs. Blaney was drilling them in garden party remarks.

I made a detour around the swimming pool. Purple blossoms were floating in the water, and a blue air mattress, deflated, swamped and becalmed. Mrs. Blaney called out to me. "Mr. Burns? One moment please. What is that you are carrying away?" The young matrons looked at each other. This must be what you said in English to a person who was leaving your grounds at a smart clip with a box on his shoulder and a gun belt draped around his neck. I kept moving. I was thinking about the cancer demon and other things and I had no time for Lucille Blaney's nonsense. Sometimes I thought she was the one who was sending me the Mr. Rose letters.

# VII

Huerta's funeral parlor was out by the old city wall, with a white glass sign in front, lighted from within. *Inhumaciones Huerta*. I drove around to the workshop and got Huerta out to look at the mahogany planks. Was that enough wood to make a coffin for Dr. Flandin? Or perhaps other plans had been made. I didn't want to interfere. Huerta ran his fingers along the grain. Oh no, this was a wonderful idea. This was more than enough. The mahogany would take a nice finish and would make a much more suitable *ataud* for the Doctor than the ugly metal casket he had chosen. He would dry the wood and stain it and buff it with wax and fashion a fine work of mortuary art. He would use bright copper hinges and fittings. Ulises could do some carving on the lid.

"Not too narrow now," I said.

"Oh no. *Amplio*." He spread his hands to show just how wide. "*Asi de amplio*." But how much time did he have? The Doctor had not been clear about when death would come. I said he had been vague with me, too, but I thought there would be time enough.

On a wooden table nearby a boy was washing down a corpse with a water hose. I stopped to look at the face. Huerta said, "Did you know Enrique? He had a short fit and then dropped dead in his box. Just the way he would have wanted it." The name meant nothing to me, but I recognized him as a man who had kept a newsstand downtown. He had sat half-hidden in a wooden box behind drooping curtains of newspapers and comic books, deaf, addled, smothered in news. It was a shock to see him outside his nest and laid out dead and cold on a wet table into the bargain.

That night I went to Shep's bar for the first time in weeks. There was a going-away party for Crouch and his wife. Shep's In-Between Club was the proper name, and from the outside it looked like a *pulque* joint in central Mexico, a hole in the wall with slatted, swinging saloon doors. No *pulque* was served here, however, and women were allowed to enter. It was bigger inside than you expected it to be and not as dark as you expected. Shep had a Mexican wife, and the place was registered in her name.

Nelms was intercepting people at the swinging doors. He was eating a curled hunk of fried pork skin that had been dipped in red sauce. He started eating street food at mid-afternoon and ate steadily along until about 11 at night. There was a whine in his voice.

"How long have I been coming in here, Burns?"

"I don't know. A long time."

"Shep won't cash my check."

"Why not?"

"I've bought 50,000 drinks in this place and he won't take my check. Can you believe that guy?"

It was hard to get a straight answer out of Nelms. The drinkers were standing two deep at the bar. A good turnout. Crouch and his jolly wife were popular and would be missed. She said, "I like Mérida all right but there's nothing to do here." They were seated at a table amid well-wishers. There was a pink cake. I hoped she would find some interesting activities in Cuernavaca. It would be cooler there anyway, and the gringo drunks would be richer and drunker.

I stopped to wish them luck and then went to the bar, which was a long flat slab of cypress. A man in a baseball cap made room for me. I knew his name, Nordstrom, and he knew mine, and that was about it. He was looking at the ice-skating scene behind the bar, perhaps longing for Milwaukee. The two skaters were dolls on a round mirror. There was some fluffed-up cotton to represent snow. This was Shep's annual Christmas display.

Shep hopped about on a twisted foot. The crowd was such that he himself was serving drinks and washing glasses tonight, along with the regular bartenders, Cosme and Luisito. Cosme gave me a look as he made change. He had an unspoken agreement with a few old customers. We paid only for every other drink and then tipped him the difference, or a little less. Everybody won but Shep, and with his prices he didn't really lose. But tonight, with the boss hovering, the deal was off. I gave Cosme a tiny nod of perfect understanding.

Mr. Nordstrom showed me a piece of engraved amber in the shape of a crescent. He wanted to know how much it was worth and where he could sell it. He said he had paid $50 for it.

It was an ornamental nose clip of a reddish cast, finely worked, probably from Monte Albán or thereabouts, certainly not Mayan, but rare in any case. I had never seen a piece quite like it and I wouldn't have hesitated to ask $750 for it, though there really wasn't enough amber on the market to establish a price range.

He had made a great buy, beginners luck, but I didn't want to encourage him. Still, it was a bit early in my conversion for me to be lecturing others on the evils of the trade. A decent silence was indicated, and I was no good at that either.

"You don't want to get mixed up in this business, Mr. Nordstrom. When you buy this stuff you'll be cheated, and when you go to sell it you may end up in big trouble. It's not worth it. Leave it at the museum. Drop it in the church box."

"I got stung?"

"It's not a bad piece but I really can't advise you."

"Shep said you would know."

"That tall fellow back there in the T-shirt and cowboy hat. He might be able to help you. His name is Eli. But don't go showing it around to just anyone."

Along the bar various claims to personal distinction were being made.

"I have a stainless-steel plate in my head."

"I am one-sixteenth Cherokee."

"I have never voted in my life."

"My mother ate speckled butterbeans every day of her life."

"I don't even take aspirins."

Suarez, the Spaniard, the old *gachupín*, was standing at my right with his newspaper and his glass of Ron Castillo. The chest-high bar was a bit high for his chest. He was a little man who drank alone in public places. He lived and drank alone and unapproached. Once in a while you would catch him shaking with private laughter. He hissed at me and nudged me and pointed to an item in the paper. "*Señor Mostaza*. Read that if you please." He called me that, Mr. Mustard, having once observed me spreading what he thought was far too much mustard on a ham sandwich. I read it, a single paragraph in *Diario*

*Del Sureste*, about an exchange of gunfire between some squatters and a landowner near Mazatlán.

He said, "The straw is beginning to burn, no?"

"No, I don't think so. Too early. This means nothing."

Suarez was always looking for signs of revolution and finding them. It couldn't come soon enough to suit him, this great wind that would blow all the monkeys out of the trees. He was an old communist who had fled Spain in 1939, only to become a fascist here in Mexico, a Gold Shirt. But then he left that banner too and now he had some sort of *pan-hispano-anarcho-rojo-swino-nihilo* program of his own devising. There would be a good many summary executions, with Jews, Masons, Chinamen, Jesuits, and Moros heading the list, and with no parliamentary nonsense—no republican *tontería*. He would close the borders for a period of national cleansing. He would change the marriage laws for some eugenic purpose. It nettled him a little when I called him a *comunista*. He said it made him sound like a pansy (*hermanita*). Back in the days when he was eviscerating priests and burning down churches in Barcelona (Barthalona), he told me, the communists were the squeamish moderates. He had contempt for Mexicans, even though they had given him refuge, or perhaps because of it. It showed their weakness. The French and the Italians were soft too. Spaniards were the only hard Latinos. Julius Caesar would have none but Spaniards as bodyguards —for all the good it did him. Nor did he think much of Americans. We were not a tribe he admired. We were the *Alemanni*, the hairy and dull-witted barbarians from across the Rhine, or in this case the Rio Grande, jabbering away in a Low German dialect called English.

He placed his finger on the Mazatlán dateline. "There. This time the rising will come from the Pacific. The *Alzamiento*."

"You once told me Veracruz."

"*Habladores*," he said, showing me with thumb and fingers how the *Cruzanos* chattered away to no purpose. "No, I am looking to Sinaloa now. I am watching the west."

A hippie with his hair pulled back in a ponytail came traipsing along behind us. Shep reached across the bar and gave him a flick with his fly swatter.

"Just where do you think you're going, pal?"

"To the head."

"No, you're not. You people come in here and never buy anything and what, I'm supposed to provide facilities for you?"

"Hey, what is this? I just walked in. I may get a beer or a Coke or something. I don't know yet. First I got to go to the head."

"Okay, but in and out. Number one and that's all. I don't want you taking a bath back there."

It was too crowded at the bar. I went to the Crouch table and had a piece of cake. Minim recited some verses he had composed for the occasion, a long poem for him, which ended with these words: "And so we say goodbye for now to Peg and Vernon Crouch." Beth was sitting there with Bollard. He wore a white turtleneck sweater. She couldn't stay away from these literary fellows, poets for preference, and they invariably let her down. Last spring there had been Frank, the uninspired poet. She listened to his complaints. She lent him money. It was Minim who told me he was uninspired, though I don't see how he could know. Frank didn't write anything, or at least he didn't publish anything. Beth claimed he burned with a non-luminous flame, and all the hotter for that. Perhaps. A non-flowering plant. He soon drifted away. The Olmecs didn't like to show their art around either. They buried it twenty-five feet deep in the earth and came back with spades to check up on it every ten years or so, to make sure it was still there, unviolated. Then they covered it up again.

Bollard talked about his investments. I had to get away from these poems and telephone bonds, and I moved on to another table, with Art and Mike and a young man named Jerry, who called himself an "ethnomusicologist." He was supposed to be out in the villages spying on people and recording Mayan songs, but he preferred to spend his time and his grant money here at Shep's. We sat there drinking and talking foolishly under the huge fresco map of the Yucatán peninsula. There are many fine wall paintings in Mexico but this wasn't one of them. As a map it was so distorted as to be useless, and it didn't please as art either, or it didn't please me. I know nothing about art, but in my business we gave ourselves these airs. Even Eli had opinions.

The hippie came out of the toilet, having bathed and washed his hair and generally freshened up. He stopped at the bar to bum a cigarette. Vick gave him one and he also gave him some Scripture to think over. "'If a man have long hair, it is a shame unto him,'" he said. "First Corinthians, eleven, fourteen."

Shep swatted the hippie again. "You. Stop hustling the customers. Out."

"Hey, man, you never been down and needed a smoke?"

"Yeah, I have, and you know what I did? The first thing I did was quit smoking and the next thing I did was get a job."

"You can't get a job in Mexico. A gringo can't."

"The hell you can't. You want a job? I'm calling your bluff, pal. I got a job right here for you."

It was a dilemma for the hippie. He knew the job would be something like cleaning out a grease trap and that he would probably be paid not in cash but with some old clothes and broken-down shoes. But then he was shown up if he didn't accept.

"All right, but first I need to see this guy. I'll be back."

"No, don't bother."

Art and Mike didn't believe the story of how Shep, finding himself up against it, had given up his Chesterfields and knuckled down in earnest to a life of hard work. I was inclined to believe it. Jerry sat on the fence. Judgments came hard to him. It was true that Shep didn't exert himself much these days, but I was thinking of a younger Shep, hopping from door to door selling term life insurance, and later, peddling badly worn furniture and carpeting from bankrupt motels. I wondered who bought those rugs. People make fun of salesmen, people with salaries or remittances, who don't have to produce. They have no idea of what a tough game it is. Art and Mike said Shep had a dog's name. Jerry said he had no manners. Art and Mike went further and said he had no soul, or at most the soul of a bug, an ant-size portion of the divine element. I thought they went too far.

Nelms was going from table to table seeking sympathy. "How long have I been coming here? . . . This is how he repays me . . ." He had a drink in one hand and a boiled pig's foot in the other. His lips were frosted with coarse grains of margarita salt. Nardo Cepeda had announced his presence at the bar, crying out every few minutes, "*Beebah Mehico!*" and "We want Nardo!"

Louise and Emmett and a young man in a blue suit joined us. They had been to a movie. The young fellow was introduced to us as Wade Watson, a government clerk from Jefferson City, Missouri, who wrote science-fiction tales in his spare time. "I just flew in this afternoon," he said. "I had seat 28F at the back behind the emergency door. You get more leg room that way. I still can't believe I'm actually in Mérida. The ancient name, you know, was Tiho, or more correctly, T'ho. I won't have time to inspect all the great pyramids and monuments because I have an appointment at the City of Dawn. After I see *El Mago*. First I have to meet with him in the town of Progreso."

Wade's fingernails were bitten down to the quick. Louise had found him wandering the streets and she took him in tow. Art and Mike cautioned him that the Mayaland picture books made things appear bigger than they were, and that the colors were touched up, as with picture postcards. Even so, the ruins were magnificent, and he wouldn't be disappointed. Wade asked where he could catch a bus to Progreso.

Louise had little to say about the movie, something called *Amor sin Palabras*, only that it was "thought-provoking." That was her lowest rating.

Jerry said, "But 'Love without Words'? How did they manage that?"

"Well, of course they didn't," said Emmett. "You never heard so much gabble and twittering in your life."

He bought a round of drinks and said that Louise had been right, this night on the town was just what he needed. He had been cooped up in the trailer too long. He was feeling much better. The new medicine worked better than the old medicine, and the only side effects so far were blurred vision, hair loss, vertigo, burning feet, nightmares, thickened tongue, nosebleed, feelings of dread, skin eruptions, and cloudy urine. Art and Mike said it was a scandal the way she went gadding about town with this old man. She said she was only trying to protect him from fortune-hunting women. Emmett said she was much too late for that. Nelms came by and appealed to her, and she went off with him to see why Shep wouldn't accept his check.

The City of Dawn. That was where Dan and his people were going. I asked Wade about it. "Is it a place or what?"

"Yes, a place, of course, but much more than that. Much more!"

"Where is it?"

"Where indeed."

"You don't know?"

"I see what you're trying to do. You're trying to trap me into an indiscretion."

"Hardly a trap. I simply asked you where it was."

"Aren't we curious!"

No use to press him. Smirking and coy, he was like all the others of his breed. I would have to grab him by the throat to get any sense out of him and I couldn't do that here.

A strolling mariachi band came in and added to the din. We had to raise our voices. Over at the Crouch table they were laughing and shouting in each other's faces, taking feverish delight in their powers of speech. They appeared to be practicing words and phrases on one another, drunken delegates at an Esperanto congress. Mott led the applause for the band and gave the cornet player a handful of money. Louise was at the bar demanding answers from Shep. I caught sight of Eli up there, waving me over. Mr. Nordstrom had gone, and Eli was drinking with Nardo, the lawyer.

They were both drunk or close to it. Nardo clapped me on the back. "What is this, Boornez, you're not in jail?" *Boornez* was his rendering of Burns.

"I'm out on work release."

"No, you're a shadow and they can't see you. They can't see a ghost. You have don Ricardo looking after you too."

"Speaking of that, why aren't you locked up?"

"Me! Nardo in prison! What an idea! But look. Eli here is a real criminal. The question is, how does he stay out?"

"I mind my own business," said Eli.

"And what business is that? Let me tell you something, my *zopilote* friend. The days are over when you gringos can come down here and use my country for a playground."

"I don't think them days are quite over yet, Nardo."

"We'll see! Luisito! Give these two *coyotes* whatever they're drinking and bring me the telephone!"

There was no telephone at the bar and never had been. He and Luisito argued the point once again.

Eli was a solemn drunk with a slightly curved spine and a drooping head. The Mexicans called him The Vulture, *El Zopilote*. He had a pointed beard and long ropy arms with Disney bluebirds tattooed on them. There was a black leather strap on his left wrist, which had no function that I could see, other than to be vaguely menacing.

"What was wrong with that amber piece?" he said.

"Nothing. You didn't buy it?"

He stared at me and went back to his drink. I could see his difficulty. Why would I be sending him such a sweet deal? He couldn't believe that I was really out of the business. Tiny blood vessels were breaking inside his head as he tried to think it out.

"Where was it from, Tepíc?"

"I thought Oaxaca. Zápotec."

"How did he come by it? I mean a guy like that."

"I didn't ask him."

"There's nothing funny about it?"

"Not that I know of."

"Damn. Now he's gone. He only wanted a hundred for it. The amber itself is worth more than that. Where does the old man live?"

"I don't know. You mean where he stay?"

"I mean where he be staying."

"You must mean where he be staying when he at home."

Eli was from Mississippi, and we sometimes fell into this black man patter. "What time it is?" and such stuff as that. We had a lot in common. One difference between us was this: He said shevel and I said shovel. Trust me to go with the crowd. Luisito pushed more glasses at us. "Señor Mott," he said. Mott was treating and circulating about like a host, with a word of welcome for everyone.

"Come on, come on," he said, urging us to clap for the band. "Let's show some appreciation. Isn't that trumpet player great?"

Nardo said Mexicans were the only people in the world who could play the trumpet. Nobody else had the heart for it. Mott said all his life he had envied Harry James, who would go out at night to some ballroom and knock everybody dead playing "Ciribiribin," and then when he got home Betty Grable was there. Nardo said Harry James was a Mexican and that Mexican trumpet players and athletes were the envy of the world.

Mott moved on to greet the others. Eli said that he, too, would go around grinning at the world and buying drinks for everybody if the government sent him a disability check every month. I told him I didn't think he would. He went off to search for Mr. Nordstrom.

Shep was trying to explain things to Louise. "But I'm not running a bank, little lady." She hated those diminutives. "I'll take his check for the amount of his drinks but I'm through handing out cash. With the peso changing from day to day, I can't sit on the paper. I can't afford it no more and I can't make no exceptions."

Nardo had gone into his football chant. He was slapping the bar with his hands. "Nar-do! Nar-do! We want Nar-do!" That was from the stadium fans at Bonar College. They wanted to see Nardo on the field, running back a punt or a kickoff, or knocking some pass receiver cold. He had played both ways, and he was a real player, too, no mere place kicker, as the rumor went. I had seen the newspaper clippings.

He held up a fist to his mouth, a microphone. "Oh yes, that's Nardo Cepeda, and let me tell you something, this little guy never calls for a fair catch! Oh brother, can he scoot! He's a little man, only five-six and a hundred and forty pounds soaking wet, but can he fly! Will you look at that! The little guy can turn on a dime! You can't coach those moves! He's gone! Cepeda is gone! See you later! No way that kicker will catch him now . . ."

It was one of his weaker performances, and suddenly he just stopped. "They think I'm a clown. These people don't know anything. We went twenty-eight and two in three years. I was pretty good for my size, Boornez."

"I know that."

"No, you don't. You think I was just a Division II player. Let me tell you something. If I weighed another ten kilograms I could play for anybody."

"Fausto says you're a good lawyer."

"Not only Fausto. I could get you out of jail in five minutes. Like that." He tried to snap his fingers but they were wet and wouldn't snap. "I know the law, Boornez. Would you like to know how many laws we have in Mexico? We have more than 72,000 laws and regulations. What do you say to that, gringo?"

"I say that's pathetic. That's pitiful for a progressive nation. In my country we have 459,000 laws and regulations. You'll never catch us."

"I know the law. I know how things are done. I could get you out of jail in five minutes. Your friend Eli? No. I wouldn't bother with him. He's looking at Article 33 right now. Did you know that?"

"Well, it's better than jail."

"He may get both. Why don't they let you use the phone up here anymore?"

"I don't know."

"Luisito!"

Article 33 hung over all our heads. This was a catch-all provision in the Mexican constitution whereby any foreigner could be kicked out of the country at any time for any reason at all, or for no stated reason. That was my understanding of it. Not that reasons would be lacking in Eli's case, or in mine. But I had worked with a certain amount of protection, being associated with Doc Flandin, who had friends in Mexico City. He knew all the old-timers at the Instituto Nacional de Antropología, and they allowed him a good many liberties. Nardo, as an active party man, had political influence. He had arranged the dig at Ektún for his small and obscure college in Illinois, which was quite a feat, seeing how few permits were given to foreigners these days. Most of them had to settle for secondary sites in Belize or Guatemala. Just how great a feat it was, I don't think Nardo ever appreciated, or he would have made more of it.

I told him about the Bonar College troubles at Ektún. It came as news to him and not very interesting news. He thought too much fuss was made over all this ancient masonry. What was the appeal of these old *Indios* (the *naturales*, he called them) and their ruined *templos*? It was all a great bore to him, the Maya business, except for the tourist aspect. It gave people the wrong idea about Mexico. Departed glory. Blinking lizards on broken walls. He wanted his country to be thought of as Euro-America or Ibero-America and not Indo-America.

The hippie came back, to my surprise, and with a friend, an older and thinner hippie, who had long brown hair breaking over both sides of his shoulders. They went directly to Vick at the bar. The new hippie said, "You never heard of Samson in the Bible? Samson's strength was in his long hair."

Vick said, "I've heard of Absalom. He was in rebellion against his father. His pride and vanity were in his long hair and it got him hanged from the thick bough of a great oak."

"What about Samuel? Samuel found favor with both God and man and a razor never touched his head. You never heard of Samuel?"

"Nebuchadnezzar had long filthy hair and long green nasty fingernails. He ate grass with the beasts of the field. That was where his pride and vanity got him. He was swollen with pride just like a dog tick all bloated up with blood."

"You're way behind the times, old man. You've got a lot of unresolved anger there too. You belong in an old man's home."

The other hippie corrected him. "Old folks home. Nursing home."

Vick said, "You two belong in the hall of shame."

They laughed at him and went away, the two hippie pals, off to wherever they were bedding down for the night. They had their campgrounds, and their fleeting friendships, too, I suppose.

Nardo challenged me to a 100-meter footrace out in the street. The time had come for barroom displays of strength. I told him I was gone in the knee but would be glad to arm-wrestle him for a drink. He didn't want to do that. I had the reach on him and the leverage. He went off into a dream, brooding and muttering.

One of my quirks too. I didn't do it in the street like *El Obispo*, not yet, but in my room, in the woods, on long drives, I spoke softly but audibly to myself, in the second person, as was only proper. I spoke to a child or a half-wit. *Why can't you put that bottle-opener back in the same place each time and then you'll know where it is.* Doc had called my attention to it. I was trying to get a job with a crew of Mormon *arqueos* in Belize and I gave him as a reference. At the bottom of their letter of inquiry he scribbled, "Jimmy Burns is a pretty good sort of fellow with a mean streak. Hard worker. Solitary as a snake. Punctual. Mutters and mumbles. Trustworthy. Facetious." Doc gave with one hand and took away with the other. The Mormons must have scratched their heads over those last two things. How could he be both trustworthy and facetious? They hired me anyway, and soon I was doing all their hauling. The trick is to make yourself first useful and then necessary. Punctual! Yes, the puniest of virtues, nothing to brag about, but Doc was right, I was always on time. Unheard of here in Mexico.

Now here came Harold Bolus on his two canes, taking his stiff and well-planned steps. "Great news, Jimmy. The Crouches have decided to stay on after all. It was this wonderful party that did it. This is a Who's Who of Mérida and they were touched. They're not leaving." Bolus had lost his legs, the lower parts below the knees, in the Chosin retreat. "My heart's in Oklahoma," he would sing, "but my feet are in Korea." That was his song. He sat on park benches and showed his willowwood shins to children. This was what came of too much dancing, he told them. As a foolish boy he had danced his feet off. Let this be a warning to them. Go easy on the dancing and particularly the spinning about, or when the music was over they would end up like him with nothing left to stand on but two bloody stumps.

I was exhausted. All this talking and listening, a six-months quota for me in one night. My neighbors, Chuck and Diane, stopped to speak. That wasn't quite their names but some names you can't take in. They could have spelled out their names for me every day for six days running and on Sunday morning I would have drawn a blank again. It was embarrassing. They were a nice young couple with a room down the hall from me at the Posada. They were my neighbors and it would be my duty to denounce them after the Suarez revolution, but first I would have to get their names straight. Something like Chick and Diane but not quite that. I wouldn't be permitted to sit it out. Suarez had warned me that anyone who sat back and tried to mind his own business would be arrested and charged with "vexatious passivity."

Back at my room I found a note under my door from Beatriz. Refugio had called from the bus station in Palenque. "He says he is bringing the car back to Mérida tomorrow." What car? I didn't understand the message. Then Nardo and Sloat, drunk, came by my room and woke me up. Shep had closed his place, and the gang was moving on to the Tiburón Club. I told them I was too tired. Besides, I didn't go to disco joints, with all that noise, and I didn't like bars that were upstairs. I ran them off.

A few minutes later there was more rapping at the door. It was Nardo again. He had to brace himself with both hands against the door jambs. "I forgot to tell you something," he said. "Did you notice I was feeling low tonight?"

"No, I thought you were in good form."

"It was off just a little, my natural charm, you know, that everybody talks about. You must have noticed. A touch of *opresión*. I wanted to explain."

"I didn't notice anything."

"But you already know, don't you?"

"Know what?"

"Is there any need to explain? I think you can guess why I'm feeling low."

"No, I can't."

"The *yanquis* took half my country in 1848."

"They took all of mine in 1865. We can't keep moping over it."

"Why not?"

"I don't know. That's what they tell us. We just have to make the best of it. They say we should just go on about our business and leave all that to them."

"Is that all you have to say?"

"That's all I have to say tonight."

"The *coche* is waiting. Come on. Everybody's going to the Tiburón."

"Another time maybe."

"Sloat wants to talk to you downstairs."

"No, you go on. I'll be over later to help mop up the cripples."

"Half my country."

"A few border corrections, that's all."

I had to take him down and put him in the taxicab with the others and give it two hard slaps on the fender, which meant, *go!* Maybe he would manage to forget the old grievance out there on the dance floor. If I knew Nardo he would still be leading the conga line when the sun came up. He spoke good English but his "*yanquis*" came out something like "junkies."

# VIII

A T MID-MORNING Refugio came rolling in with Rudy's bulbous yellow car. The first thing he wanted was a red
snapper, broiled with tomatoes and onions, and a stuffed
pepper on the side. We ate at the Express, where you could
get anything you liked. There were forty-odd entrees on the
menu, and if you wanted something else, an artichoke or a
piece of baby shark liver, they would send out to the *mer-
cado* for it and cook it to your taste. Refugio said he had also
brought the camping trailer out of the jungle, but then a hub
bearing had burned out on the highway and he had left the
rig with a friend. He had the bearing with him, and he had the
little Olmec jade man, too, in a jar of water. It looked like an
evil fetus. He thought jade would crack, as opals sometimes
do, unless you kept it soaked. He planned to sell it while he
was in town.

Yes, yes, yes, but what was he doing with the car? What
was all this? Where was Rudy? The young man who owned
the car?

As to that he couldn't say. He and Manolo had gone to Ektún with some gasoline and odds and ends to sell. All was confusion there. Skinner was still tangled up in Villahermosa, but
Lund had come back to find that this Rudy had disappeared.
He had strolled off into the woods and vanished. They had
searched for him all around the site and as far downstream as
the Usumacinta River. Lund, the bearded *ingeniero*, was unnerved, and furious too, calling me terrible names. He had
directed Refugio to deliver the car and trailer to me, along
with this note.

Mr. Burns
Your friend Kurle has disappeared. I am in no way liable. He
was on his own here as you well know. He walked off down the
river alone. He was not invited here and he was not authorized
to be here and neither I nor Bonar College can be held responsible. You brought him here uninvited. There are witnesses to
that fact. Therefore I am sending his car and his things to you

by way of Señor Bautista. I have notified the police in Palenque and I disclaim any further responsibility.

Sincerely yours,

C. A. Lund
Chief Surveyor

I could see that Lund, having come so recently from the States, was living in terror of lawyers and courts and insurance companies. He feared legal reprisals but he need not have worried. It wasn't so bad down here yet, where extortion was still largely a private matter, arranged quietly and informally between the parties, and cheaper all around for everyone. But he was right, I was in some sense responsible. I had, in a manner of speaking, taken Rudy in to Ektún.

Refugio wanted money. He wrote "$100" in the hollow of his hand and showed it to me. Lund had told him I would pay him a lot of money for delivering the car.

"And look," he said. "I make that long drive with no company."

Solitude was agony to him. A few hours alone with your thoughts could drive you crazy.

"We'll see. The car is just part of it. You'll have to help me find him too. These people don't have much money."

"They have a nice car. They have a nice sleeping trailer and a nice CB radio."

"We'll talk about that after we find him."

He showed me the wheel bearing and told me how it had screeched and smoked. It looked okay to me. The rollers were unscored and they still turned freely in the race. There was too much talk about this bearing. Then it came to me. There had been no breakdown. He was holding the trailer as security against his fee. He was hiding it somewhere. A bird in Refugio's hand was worth thirty or forty in the bush.

He thought the boy would turn up in a day or so, if he was merely lost, and if he was prudent enough to keep going downstream. Once on the big river he was bound to encounter a boat or someone along the banks. And even if he was wandering around in the *selva* he would soon run across a trail and, eventually, a Lacondón village. The Lacondones would bring him out. It was all a big fuss over nothing, a gringo *bulla*, a *bagatela*.

Possibly, but he went too far in assuming that Rudy would do the sensible thing. I suspected that Rudy had gone down the Usumacinta, walking the banks, in search of Tumbalá, the place of the little temples. He was there or he was lost or he was drowned or he was dead of snakebite or he was shot or captured in the guerilla war across the river.

We lingered over coffee. The ragged old man called *El Obispo* passed by on the sidewalk, and we all turned our heads away so as not to meet his evil eye. The danger was small, he never looked up from the ground, but one day he might raise those red eyes. Pedestrians gave way. They peeled off left and right about six paces ahead of him. The effective range of his gaze was not thought to be great. He jabbered away as he walked, saying the same thing over and over again, and today he was moving right along. Some days he took it slow, placing one foot directly in front of the other with the care of a tightrope walker. He was called The Bishop because he slept in a shed behind the cathedral.

Refugio spit between his legs to neutralize the evil. What he hawked up, this heavy smoker, was a viscous ball of speckled matter resembling frog spawn. I had put off telling him about Doc. Now I told him. His hands flew up in alarm. Cancer is cancer in Spanish, too, and the word is avoided in polite company.

"No! Not the Doctor! This is too cruel! I must go to him!"

"Yes, but let me call first. They have a new set-up at that house."

I called Mrs. Blaney and simply told her that we were coming by, and then I dropped Refugio off at Izamál, he carrying his gift .45 in a paper sack. Doc was waiting for him outside. They embraced on the lawn, with Doc calling him by an old nickname, Cuco.

There was another unpleasant duty to perform. I tracked Louise down to the museum, where she was helping Beth take some school children through on a tour. The kids were in blue and white uniforms, and of that age, twelve or so, when the girls are a head taller than the boys. Andean flute music came over the speaker system. A bit of stagecraft, suggestive of eerie rites, but nothing to do with the Maya. Beth also liked to run the lights up and down with the rheostat.

I took Louise aside and told her that Rudy was missing. She didn't collapse in tears but was only fretful. A blank stare, a delicate cough, some floating thought, a quotation from L. Ron Hubbard—I never knew what to expect from her. Maybe she saw this as a merciful release, free at last, from Rudy and his tapes.

"I knew something like this was coming," she said. "I could feel it. It's all my fault because I'm such a coward."

Louise was far from being a coward. She was largely indifferent to the ordinary hazards of life, and yet she had a fear of stinging insects, something to do with an allergy, and she seldom ventured into the deep woods. She seemed to think she was to blame because she had stayed behind.

"It's not as bad as it sounds," I said. "He's just out of touch. We'll find him. I have a friend who knows that country well."

"Do the police know about this?"

"They know in Chiapas."

"Should we notify the vice-consul?"

"It won't hurt."

"I wonder if he can do anything. That man has the pink eyes of a rabbit."

"He'll do what he can."

"What about an air search? Beth would lend me the money to charter an airplane."

"You couldn't see anything but treetops. There's really no such thing as searching the Petén jungle. Miles and miles of unbroken greenery. He hasn't gone far. We'll turn him up along the river somewhere. Tumbalá, probably."

"He may have lost his memory. Rudy may be wandering around down there with no idea of who he is or where he is."

"Has that happened before?"

"No."

I waited for an explanation. None came.

"I'm just turning things over in my mind. Various possibilities. Someone could have murdered him for his tapes."

"You have his latest tape. I brought it to you."

"Not the very latest one. He would have made others by now."

She thought he might have fallen into the hands of hostile Indians. He was lying on the ground, bound hand and foot, with the village elders squatting in a circle around him. They were chewing bitter narcotic leaves as they passed judgment on him, and took their time over it. I assured her that the Lacondón were a peaceable enough folk. They might tease Rudy or sell him a defective souvenir but they weren't likely to knock him in the head. I asked her what he was really up to down there.

"I don't know."

"I think you do know and you better tell me if you want to see him again."

"You're the one who gave him the map to that place. It's all your fault. That place with the little houses you told him about."

"What was on the tape he sent back?"

"Nothing much."

"I want to hear it."

"Rudy has strict rules—"

"I don't care about his rules. Either I hear that tape or I'm not lifting a finger."

"All right, but there's nothing useful on it. I didn't want to mention this—not to you—but it has to be considered. He may very well have been carried away in a spacecraft."

"I don't think that's likely, Louise."

"No, you wouldn't, would you? You don't want us to make a quality contact. Rudy finally makes a quality contact and you resent it. You're jealous of him. You've always been envious of his field equipment and his City Planning degree, and for some reason I don't understand you're trying to stop him from becoming a distinguished author and lecturer. It's small-minded people like you who make it so hard for the rest of us. You're jealous of anybody and everybody who's working on the frontiers of knowledge."

"Yes, but when these visitors do snatch someone, don't they always bring him back? To pass on their warnings about pollution and atom bombs and such?"

"A simple peasant, yes, or some dumbbell off the street, sure, they would bring him back after a quick body scan, but with someone like Rudy they would want to take him onto the mother ship. They would want to go over his notes and listen to his tapes and study his brain. They must have known he was on to something down there. It was a golden opportunity for them."

"Well, no need to borrow trouble. My guess is he hasn't gone far. There's a good chance he's already walked out somewhere."

"Not if they took him back to their own planet."

"No, in that case he's sunk, but there have been no reports of any landings. Someone would have seen the lights. The nights are very dark in Chiapas."

"They don't always use lights in the visible part of the spectrum. They're so far ahead of us in lasers and fiber optics that it isn't funny."

The children trooped out with their teacher, and Beth came over to see what was up. She and Louise badgered me with suggestions, relishing the drama. Beth thought I should use my "underworld connections" to help in the hunt. I went dead silent. Usually I brighten up a bit in the company of women and am not so much the lugubrious bore, my natural and most comfortable role, but my thoughts were far away. I was thinking not of Rudy but of Dan and his tribe and the little runaway girl they called Red. Yes, that was me to a T, lugubrious and punctual and facetious, all at once, a combination I would have found tiresome in another person, if I had known one.

Louise and I went to her *casita* and listened to the tape. It was just Rudy going on and on with his descriptions and measurements at Ektún. I thought it would never end. The murdering tape thief would have been annoyed when he got back to the quiet of his room and heard this stuff and looked at the blood on his hands. I fast-forwarded some of it. Rudy made no mention of his plans. I left the Checker car with Louise and suggested she move in with Beth, who had a telephone. "Stay close and I'll let you know as soon as I find out anything."

The night had turned off cool. A *norte* must have blown in. I walked over to the Posada and got my truck. Refugio would be waiting for me at Doc's place. On the way back across town I caught a glimpse of the night dog. I checked the moon. It seemed to be in about the third quarter.

A word here about the night dog and *El Obispo*. It took me almost two years to figure out what the old man was muttering. I picked up a word here and a word there and finally pieced them all together. Then one day Jerry asked me what he was saying. I told him and he wrote it down in his anthropology notebook. I felt cheated of my time and labor.

The common belief was that The Bishop was simply going through his rosary, but no, I knew the sounds of that litany all too well, from mountain bus rides on rainy nights, with terrified passengers all around me telling their beads. No, it was a text from Mark he was reciting. I looked it up.

"¿Ves estos grandes edificios? No quedará piedra sobre piedra, que no sea derribada." ("Seest thou these great buildings? There shall not be left one stone upon another, that shall not be thrown down.")

Those were El Obispo's words as he marched around Mérida with his eyes cast down. That, with variations, was what he said day in and day out. At noon he sat against the shady side of the cathedral and rested and ate squash seeds. Once I stuck an ice cream cone into his curled paw. He received it passively and may or may not have eaten it. He may have been asleep. I kept moving and didn't look back. On certain nights, in his shed behind the church, he changed himself into a small reddish dog with a fox face. The animal was about eighteen inches long, exclusive of the tail, which itself was about the same length, and stiff as a new rope. It curled up and around to form a near-circle, with the tip touching his back.

At least there was such a dog, I had seen him myself many times, and Fausto and others claimed that you could never catch the two of them together, The Bishop and the night dog. He moved at a trot, a dog on pressing business, and was always just going around a corner, it seemed, out of view. He was too healthy and sleek for a scavenger.

But on what business? No one could say. As it happened, I caught a glimpse of him on this night. He was jogging into an alley. The looped tail was unmistakable. I parked the truck and got out with my flashlight.

I knew this street slightly. This was the Naroody block. The Hotel Naroody was on the corner, and next to it was Foto Naroody, a photography *estudio*, with framed pictures in the window, portraits of brides and fat babies tinted with gruesome colors. Along the way there were shops with such names as Importaciones Naroody and Curiosidades Naroody. I had never seen Naroody taking any *fotos*. The display pictures gathered dust and were never changed. Some of those falsely colored babies may have been brides themselves by now. I wasn't even sure I had seen Naroody. Whenever I spotted some likely Levantine candidate I would be told, "Him? No, that's not Naroody."

I played the light about in the alley and kicked at boxes and piles of trash. The dog was gone. I doubled back and found a chubby man waiting for me at the entrance. He too had a flashlight. His eyelids drooped. One hand was resting in the pocket of a loose smock, such as a photographer might wear in his darkroom. I asked him if he had seen the jaunty dog.

"Ah, the dog. I thought you were a burglar. Yes, I know this dog. You will never capture him."

"I'm not trying to capture him. I just thought I had found his sleeping place."

"He passes this way on his rounds but he doesn't sleep here. He never stops. Why do you wish to capture him? The little dog is not harming anyone."

"I don't wish to capture him. I don't wish to bother him in any way but I would like to get a closer look at him."

"Why?"

"I hear these stories. I'm curious."

"The stories are nonsense."

"They say he comes out at certain phases of the moon."

"I don't listen to such talk."

"You're not Naroody, are you?"

He was startled. "What? Naroody? No. I only work for him."

"I hear he's a good man to work for."

"Where do you hear this?"

"You must be the watchman."

"I keep an eye on things, yes, but I have other duties too." He looked around and drew close and his voice fell to a whisper. "May I tell you something in confidence? All his methods are out of date."

"Naroody's methods?"

"His business methods. He won't listen to anyone."

"Do you know where the dog goes from here?"

He hesitated. I gave him some money. He thanked me and apologized, saying he was not moving up as fast in the Naroody organization as he had hoped. Naroody kept him short of pocket money. He got his keep and little more. He pointed to a window above one of the shops. That was his room. He had a room of his own up there with running water, or trickling water anyway, and he ate well enough at Naroody's second table, but he saw very little cash, not nearly enough to buy fashionable clothes and take women out at night. His life was not fulfilled. There were men his age, much less deserving, who drove cars and had as many as ten pairs of pointed shoes in their closets.

"But the dog."

"They say he goes to the rail yard and later comes out of the big drain pipe behind the feed mill. After that I don't know. Who has time to listen to such foolishness? These are not good questions. You drive a fine white truck that will take you anywhere you wish to go. Do you tell me that you believe in ghost animals?"

"I believe he's a strange dog. You say yourself that I could never capture him."

"Let me say too that I am disappointed with this talk about the phases of the moon. I took you for a modern man like me."

His name was Hakim. He wanted to chat some more, but about California and career opportunities there in real estate management. I knew nothing about it. Yucatán is off the California flyway, and we didn't see many of those birds around here. There was a heavy squarish lump in his pocket. Hakim, I think, was holding a little .22 or .25 automatic in that smock pocket. He was ready to defend Naroody's property with force.

I went to the rail yard and the feed mill and even watched the round black hole of the drain pipe for a while. I crouched in the weeds like a stalking cat. It was downright cold there, though the wind had fallen off. The dog didn't show.

What we had here, according to Jerry, another modern man, was a case of conflation or confabulation. *El Obispo* and the dog, taking similar steps, made regular circuits around town. Someone had noticed this and with an imaginative leap had spun a tale combining the two elements. It was a good enough explanation except that the two gaits were not alike. The old man and the dog just didn't walk in the same way, and as far as I could see there were no points of physical resemblance whatever.

Jerry then was not above a little confabulating himself. He too dealt in fables, and this was a good name for his science, I thought, confabulation, not that Jerry ever defended his science, not with the tiniest of pistols, being trained as he was to believe in nothing. In the Anthropology Club, as I understood it, you were permitted, if not required, to despise only one thing, and that was your own culture, that of the West. Otherwise you couldn't prefer one thing over another. Of course Jerry's curiosity was no more damnable than mine, a poking, pointless, infantile curiosity, but then he got paid for his.

After cruising around the cathedral a couple of times, I gave up on the night dog and went to Doc's house to pick up Refugio. He wasn't ready to go. They were upstairs in the bedroom looking at old photographs. A little tepee of sticks was blazing away in the fireplace, so seldom used. The fat *ocote* wood was popping and there were some cedar sticks, too, some *kuche*, for the pleasant scent. How long had it been since the three of us had sat around a fire at night?

Doc said, "Look, Jimmy. See what Cuco brought me. It's by far the finest jade I ever held in my hands. This is the work of a master."

Refugio had given him the little Olmec man. Quite a gift. Quite an exchange. A $7,500 jade for a $200 pistol. Doc asked me if I would place the little *idolo* in his mouth when he died and see that he was buried with it. I refused. Then would I just clasp his dead fingers around it? A simple grave offering. No! I wouldn't put that snarling little demon into the grave of my worst enemy and I told him so. He tried to pass it off as a joke. Refugio, looking troubled, must have turned him down, too, or more likely had hedged. It took an effort to cross the great Doctor. Or he may have been having second thoughts about his generosity—if in fact he had made a gift of the thing. Doc may have misunderstood him.

The moment passed, and we went on to other things. Doc offered advice on how to conduct the search for the missing boy in the *selva*. "Chombo is the man you want for that work." Soon it was like the old days around the campfire, with Doc toasting the soles of his big white feet and Refugio spitting at the coals. We laughed and talked foolishly for hours. We must have burned up a donkey-load of pine knots, or *ocote* wood.

But then we pushed it too far, tried to make the happy occasion last, and along toward daylight our talk trailed off. Doc let his pipe go out and began heaving mighty sighs. He said, "Well, what does it matter in the long run? When you get right down to it everything is a cube." One by one we went numb. The fire died. No one stoked it. We were grainy-eyed and lost within our own heads again.

No use turning in now. Refugio and I had breakfast at the little café on the *zócalo* called the Louvre. The crazy black ants of Yucatán were at play on the tabletop. They never let up. From birth to death they went full out, racing about to no purpose on the oilcloth and crashing into one another like hockey players. The Louvre would do in a pinch. A cook was on duty all night and the onion soup was good, but they wouldn't give you enough crackers. They begrudged you every last *galleta*. The biggest and most modern cracker factory in Mexico was right here in Mérida, but you would have never guessed it at the Louvre, where they doled them out two at a time.

Refugio tried to sell some of his plastic pipe to a Dutch farmer, a Mennonite, who was sitting there in overalls spooning up corn flakes from a huge white bowl. He could have washed his hands in that basin. *Give them all the corn flakes and milk they want but make them beg for crackers.* What kind of policy was that? The Mennonite said nothing and missed not a beat with his spoon and yet he managed to show a kind of crafty interest in the pipe deal.

I was watching the jailbirds, the *degradados*, who were out early sweeping the plaza. One was a very tall American with a black goatee. It was Eli Withering. I picked up an orange from the table and walked across the street. I gave the guard a cigarette, and he allowed me to have a word with my *cuate*. My pal, that is, which was stretching it a bit.

Eli said, "They got me cold, Budro. Can you let me have $500? They got old Nordstrom too. That amber was bad news. You knew it and I didn't. I never had any luck with that stuff. Now look at me. These flat Popsicle sticks are hard to sweep up."

Yes, there was Mr. Nordstrom in the line of sweepers, working hard with a pushbroom to cover his shame, poking away, trying to get a purchase on the *paleta* sticks. He would be a model social-democratic Scandinavian prisoner. Mr. Nordstrom wouldn't bang his cup against the bars or otherwise give trouble. It was too bad, but I had told the old man not to meddle in this business.

Eli was disgusted with himself. "It was really dumb. Sauceda was tailing me and I didn't spot him."

"He would have gotten you anyway. It wasn't the amber."

I saw a third gringo in the work gang. It was Louise's friend, Wade Watson, the young man from Missouri. He was dragging a trash box along and he still seemed to be taking a dazed delight in everything. First he couldn't believe he was in Yucatán and now he couldn't believe he was a prisoner.

"That boy there," I said. "What's he in for?"

"I don't know. Sauceda grabbed him too. He was just standing there with us, asking a lot of questions. I thought he was with Nordstrom. Do you know him?"

"I've met him."

"There's something wrong with him. He won't shut up. He talked all night in the tank. Here, let me have that."

Eli grabbed my orange and ripped it apart and sucked the pulp to shreds. "I need that money today. I'm counting on you, Budro. I need to get this settled before it goes up to the Director of Investigations."

"Do you want Nardo to handle it?"

"Hell no. Bring the money to me in dollars. I'll cut my own deal. Sauceda is a man you can talk to. You know I'm good for it. I'll put my car up against it. Bring me a blanket, too, and get me a hat of some kind. Somebody stole my hat while I was sleeping."

I told him I would see what I could do. And there was poor Wade, caught hanging around the wrong people, on his first night here too. He must have been hoping to catch some sparks off the conversation of two old Maya hands. I went over to him and asked if he had any money.

"A little. Who are you? I have my credit card."

"That's no good. Here. You'll need a few pesos if you're going to eat. I may be able to get you out of this jam."

"How? I don't even know what I'm doing here."

"It's a tradeoff. I may be able to pull some strings, but first, you see, I'll have to know where the City of Dawn is."

"Oh yes, you're the curious guy from the bar. Why do you want to know?"

"I'm to meet a friend there, but she forgot to tell me where it is."

"Oh? Then she must have had her reasons for not telling you. Just as I have mine. There are good and sufficient reasons why certain people know things and others don't."

"Well, you think it over. They've got you on a pretty serious offense. Encroaching on the national patrimony. I won't be able to do anything after you're formally charged."

The guard shooed me away. I didn't want Eli's car. I didn't need a Dodge Dart with burnt valves and major oil leaks and an electrical system that shorted out every time you hit a puddle. The distributor was mounted low on the block and was readily swamped. Eli kept saying he was going to trade the Dart for a heavy car with a long trunk lid. But I did owe him for services rendered. Unclean bird that he was, he was always square with me. Or he wasn't always square but he was generous.

He had shown me the ropes in the antiquities business. It was Eli who had put me on to the job with Doc Flandin. They had worked together briefly and then fallen out over the First Fruits Rule. This was the rule whereby Doc, as boss, had the pick of the finds. It wasn't as bad as it sounds. He was no hog. Doc didn't always take the most valuable pieces. In his more swaggering moods he called this privilege his *quinto*, or royal fifth, though it was more like a half.

I felt too that I had let Eli down. I had sent Nordstrom to him. Nardo had warned me that he was in danger, and I had done nothing, sat on my hands.

So now I had to wait until the banks opened. Refugio took a nap in my room. I called Louise at Beth's place and told her about Wade. She was still in bed, her voice languid and nasal.

"You're not in Chiapas?" she said. "You haven't even started yet?"

"Not yet. If you want to help this Watson boy go to the police and carefully explain to them that he has a screw loose."

"Why do you say that? You think everybody's silly but you."

"Do you want to get him out of jail? They don't like to be bothered with crazy people. I'm telling you how to get him out, Chiquita."

"Don't call me that."

"And then I want you to find out from Wade Watson just where this City of Dawn is. You know how to talk to those people and I don't."

"What does this have to do with Rudy?"

"Nothing, but it's important. It's something else I'm working on."

"A city of dogs?"

"Dawn. The Inaccessible City of Dawn. It's something your New Age friends are talking about. You must have heard of it, an insider like you."

"No, I haven't."

"Rudy didn't mention it?"

"I don't think so. Does it have another name? What is it anyway?"

"That's what I don't know. A place. That's all I know."

"He was going to Tumbalá. That's the only place he mentioned to me."

"Yes, and that's where we'll find him. All right, get up and brush your hair and go to the city jail. Tell them Wade Watson is *loco, débil* in the head, and that he has no money and will give them a lot of problems. Tell them you will put him on the next bus to the border. Then I want you to get that information out of him. I need to know where this city is. Do you understand?"

"I still don't understand why Wade is in jail. What did he do again?"

"He didn't do anything. It was a mixup."

"I've been thinking. Maybe I should go to Chiapas with you."

"No, that's not a good idea. Just do what I tell you. Ask for Sergeant Sauceda at the jail. We can't keep changing our plans. I'll be in touch."

There was a crowd outside my bank. At opening time it always looked like a run on the funds. Old Suarez was there waiting in the *cambio* line, the exchange line, a revolutionary in coat and tie and black felt hat. He was all in black, watchful, on the lookout for little signs of disrespect to his person. A big American woman had sat down on him once. She hadn't seen him on the park bench. Today he was lecturing. The leathery woman in front of him was from Winnipeg. She painted big brown landscapes. Suarez didn't think much of Canadians either and he was setting her straight on a few things. Their nation was illegitimate. Their sovereignty had been handed to them on a platter, an outright gift, instead of having been properly won through force of arms. The birth throes had to be violent. There had to be blood. He told her too that no woman in Spain would dare to show herself in public in her underwear—a reference to her shorts. She listened in icy silence. Why didn't she slap him or claw his face? Draw some of that consecrating blood. Why didn't she forget all that dead brown topography and buy a bucket of black paint and do a portrait of the fierce little *anarquista*? I got the money in fifties. It was a big withdrawal for me, but I can't say it cleaned me out.

It would have been little enough, $500, a *gasto*, a modest business expense, back when I was selling those long tan coats and making money hand over fist and living at the Napoles. That was my first period of prosperity in Mexico, before I drifted into the relic business. I bought soft leather coats from the Escudero brothers and sold them to Rossky's in New Orleans.

Ramón Escudero had a tanning and softening process all his own, using alum and extract of oak galls and yolks from sea bird eggs and I don't know what else. Every woman in New Orleans wanted one of those coats. We couldn't deliver them fast enough. Then there was a family squabble. Ramón walked out of the workshop one day, accusing brother Rodolfo of making life unbearable for him. "The devil is in this business!" he said, and he went home and wouldn't come back. He wouldn't even come out of his house. Rodolfo, the younger brother, tried to carry on with the same workers, but the coats were never quite the same. They didn't feel right and they didn't drape right. I think I must have poisoned the lives of the Escuderos with my production demands. Anyway, the women in New Orleans stopped buying the coats and went on to newer things. Rodolfo and I were left high and dry.

It was lunchtime when I got back to the jail. I advised Eli to call in Nardo or some other lawyer. He said it would only jack up the price. We were standing in the courtyard with prisoners and visitors milling around us. This was the old municipal jail downtown, a very loose jail, nothing at all like the new one. You could keep your belt, and your shoelaces if you had shoes, and your necktie too. You were free to hang yourself. Wives and mothers and sweethearts were there with bowls of pozole, a Mexican version of grits, for their men. It was like a busy bus station. Fausto had more rules at his hotel. I gave Eli a blanket and a couple of paperback westerns and a few packs of Del Prado cigarettes. The money was taped inside a book. I didn't forget his hat. It was a cheap straw hat and of course too small. They didn't make them big enough for gringo skulls. He wanted it so he could whip it smartly off his head in the presence of Sergeant Sauceda.

I didn't see Wade Watson. Louise must have sprung him already. Say what you will, you could rely on that girl to do her job and do it right the first time. When I left Eli he was writing something in a tablet, working *zurdo*, left-handed, with his fist twisted around. A journal? Prison literature? Yes, of course, I knew about that, an old tradition, but I had no idea they started in on it so soon. Jail was a place for reflection, no doubt. Time would hang heavy. But Eli with pen in hand? Well, why not? It would make for some good reading, the confessions of *El Zopilote*. Pancho Villa himself had gone a little soft in his prison cell. He applied to a business school for a correspondence course. He would learn to use a typewriter and begin a new life, a clerical life. He would live in town and wear a clean shirt and write business letters all day. *Most Respectfully Yours, Francisco Villa, Who Kisses Your Hand*. But then after a day or two with the study materials he became annoyed, saying it was *tedioso* and all a lot of *mierda seca*, and he broke out of jail and went back to his old bloody ways on horseback.

# X

REFUGIO WAS a good salesman, a natural closer, and he had the Dutchman right where he wanted him. They were sitting on the curb in front of my hotel. Refugio was going for the No. 3 close. This is where you feign indifference to the sale, while at the same time you put across that your patience is at an end, that you are just about to withdraw the offer. On that point you mustn't bluff. You can't run a stupid amateur bluff.

It was a little trick I had picked up in a salesmanship school at a Shreveport motel. The League of Leaders, we were called, those of us who completed the three-day course and won our League of Leaders certificates and our speckled yellow neckties. I had to learn such things, but Refugio knew them in his bones. He spit in his hand and rubbed away the figures that were written there. He was washing his hands of any further bargaining. "*Dígame*," he said to the man. Say something. Speak to me.

The farmer saw that the moment had come. The polyvinyl chloride pipe was as cheap as it was ever going to get. He gave in, with conditions. He would have to inspect the bargain PVC pipe and he wanted the slip couplings and elbow couplings thrown in and he wanted it all delivered. Agreed, said Refugio, but no cattle and no checks. *En efectivo*—strictly cash. A rare Mexican, Refugio had no interest whatever in owning livestock, unless you count fighting poultry and short-haired dogs with pointed ears.

The Mennonite would go with us then to Chiapas, this big fellow in bib overalls, with his gray flannel shirt buttoned right up to his chin. He would take a 300-mile ride in a truck with complete strangers in order to save, maybe, a few dollars on some irrigation pipe.

Refugio jumped up and clapped his hands together. "*¡Listo!* Done then! Let us get out of this terrible place!" Mérida made him uncomfortable, as did all cities, with their busybody policemen and parking restrictions. I had my eye on all the street approaches, expecting Louise to appear any minute with news of Wade Watson, and perhaps with Beth, the two of them marching arm in arm, the league of women voters. But it was Gail who came instead, in a taxi, with her suitcase. Word of our trip had somehow reached her at the Holiday Inn, and here she was with her pink plump hands, wearing her field gear.

Would I take her back to Ektún? She had thought it over and decided that desertion in the field, no matter what the circumstances, would damage her career. It was particularly bad for a woman. She might never get another fellowship or grant unless she returned at once to her colleagues and made amends. She wouldn't have made such a rash move in the first place, she said, if I hadn't been there at the dig with my truck, offering an easy way out. "I know you were only trying to help, in your way."

Yes, all my fault, naturally, but what about Denise?

"She wanted to go back, too, but she lost her contact lenses at the motel. She flew home last night."

Then here came Doc Flandin, breathless, walking as fast as he could. "Wait up," he said, "Wait up, Jimmy." He was wearing his surgeon's cap and there was a machete in a canvas scabbard swinging from his belt. It was an old one and a good one that kept its edge, forged by the Aragon family in Oaxaca. All the other swords in the world were now dead ceremonial objects, or theatrical props, but the machete was still whacking about and smiting every day. Doc had his gourd canteen, and his pockets were bulging with what I took to be a change of underwear and socks. The machete pulled him over to the left. He missed the weight of the .45 on the other side, which would have put him back in trim.

"I'm going with you," he said. "I'll ride up front by the window."

"Going where?"

"To the *selva*. With you and Cuco. I want to see it all one more time, Jimmy. You can't refuse me that."

"It's a long run. Do you feel up to it?"

"I'm fine. Never better."

"What does Dr. Solís say?"

"He says onward. *Adelante.* St. James and at them! That's what he says. I'm not an invalid yet. Do you think I'm going to collapse?"

"Mrs. Blaney approves?"

"She knows."

"I don't want that woman coming back at me."

"I'm still responsible for my own actions, thank you."

"What about your book?"

"What about it? The book will keep. The unleavened lump. A few more days won't matter. It's not as though anyone was waiting for it."

"A lot of people are waiting for it."

"So you say. Well, perhaps. My loyal Jimmy. But you mustn't expect too much. I'll ride up front by the window. We'll stop at Salsipuedes on the way and pick up Chombo. He's just the man for our search."

It wasn't a bad idea at that except that Chombo had been dead two or three years. He was an old hunting guide who knew the rivers.

Rudy had it right all along—never reveal your travel plans. I didn't mind about the farmer or Gail—I would see that she paid for some gasoline this time—but I knew Doc could only be a burden.

I went into the Posada and called for Agustín, the boy, and sent him down the street to fetch Soledad Bravo. "Tell her it won't take long. A brief *consulta*, that's all."

We waited. "Just call me Dicky," Doc said, to one and all, and Gail took him at his word. I didn't like it much but then I thought, well, she doesn't know who he is. Over the years he had invited me to do the same. "Why don't you call me Dicky?" But I knew my place and I could no more have called him Dicky to his face than I could have called my regimental commander Shorty.

Soledad came in some haste with her heavy *curandera* bag. She was in her slippers and house dress, a loose *huipil* dress, and she was peeved a little when she saw that this was no real emergency.

I said, "Here's what it is, Soledad. Dr. Flandin wants to ride down to Palenque with me. Is he fit to travel? That's all I want to know."

"He is sick?"

Doc refused to answer. I said, "He is not well."

"He is in discomfort?"

"He says not."

"Can he button his clothes without help?"

"I think so."

Passing blood? No. Appetite? Good. Chest pains? No. Does he catch his feet in things and fall to the ground?

No, I had to admit that Doc was no stumbler. He wasn't easily tipped over.

She worked fast and Doc might have been a sick cat the way she went at it. She took him by the ears and blew into his nostrils to give him a start, then looked into his eyes to see what she had surprised there. She examined his fingernails. She ran her fingers around under his jaw. Then she pronounced.

"He can travel on the road for three days in a motorcar, God willing, *si Dios quiere*. Don't overfeed him. After three days he will need some rest in the shade." She held up three fingers.

That was good enough for me. She knew her business. It was all over before Doc could protest much, and Soledad was gone before I could pay her.

Here we were, all mustered and ready to go, but who got the third seat, up front? Doc had already staked out his place by the window. Who took precedence these days, a Mexican *patrón* or an American female anthropologist or a Dutch Mennonite deacon? I couldn't work it out and so left them to decide among themselves. Gail and Refugio deferred to the big solemn farmer. His name was Winkel and he was a senior deacon in his church, with authority to make major purchases. That was about all we could get out of him.

He sat between Doc and me and said nothing, staring straight ahead, when he wasn't sneaking looks at the speedometer. I mumbled and Doc fiddled with the radio. What a crew. Taken as individuals we were, I think, solid enough men, but there was something clownish about the three of us sitting there side by side, upright, frozen, rolling down the road. We were the Three Stooges on our way to paint some lady's house. It may have been our headgear.

Refugio and Gail had to rough it in the back of the truck, scooping out what seats they could amid all the luggage and junk. Refugio had bought an old oily Tecumseh engine in Mérida, and some other hardware. There was a heavy iron cylinder of welding gas and some used milk cans—he couldn't resist empty containers—and a little sandblasting chamber

for cleaning the electrodes of spark plugs. It was no longer
the custom to clean plugs in the States, the new ones were so
cheap, but down here we still practiced these little economies.
We still put hot patches on inner tubes and we still filed down
the ridges and pits on burnt contact points. We would set the
gap with a matchbook cover.

I drove fast. This racing about at my age was unseemly, but
I was still impatient. Refugio and I were both forty-one years
old at the time of these events. Few Mexicans passed us and no
gringos. The cargo shifted about as we pulled some hard G's
on the curves. The least bit of lateral tire slippage made Winkel
go stiff. He said, "You must think the devil is after you."

"The devil will never catch this truck, Mr. Winkel."

Gail was thrown from side to side. Refugio kept her amused
with his high jinks. He stood on his *dignidad* with Mexican
women, but it was all right to be a little silly before young
*gringas*. They were shallow vessels in his estimation and didn't
count for much. He popped a burning cigarette in and out of
his mouth with his tongue. He raised the lift-gate and fired
at road signs with his .45, including the ones that said DON'T
MISTREAT THE SIGNS (NO MALTRATE LAS SEÑALES). I had done
the same thing as a kid. I was an old mailbox shooter from the
Arklatex, no use lying, but I no longer approved of such behavior and I rapped on the window glass and made him stop.

Doc grumbled and sulked when I wouldn't turn off at the
Labná ruins. He said he only wanted to take a quick look at
some of the restoration work. I knew he would start pointing
out architectural errors and correcting the hapless guides, and
we would never get away. Farther along, I did pull over and let
him buy some cut flowers from a girl at a roadside stand. He
wanted a bouquet for Sula.

Winkel became more and more uneasy after the sun went
down. I felt bad about frightening the man and I told him to
relax, he was safe enough, that I was an old hand at these night
runs. I told him about the night I had driven an FBI agent
named Vance up to San Cristóbal de las Casas in the fog. These
agents, who worked out of the embassy in Mexico City, were
not permitted by their superiors to drive at night on Mexican
roads. Strange rule, for cops. They didn't call themselves FBI
agents either—their cards simply said Department of Justice.

I had found a soldier they were looking for, a warrant officer who had run off with the payroll, or a good part of it, from Fort Riley, Kansas. He had dyed his hair but was still using his own name, which was McIntire. He felt safe up on top of that mountain with all his dollars tucked away in a duffel bag. He thought he was at the end of the world in that chilly Indian town high up in the clouds, but he wasn't counting on the likes of me, with my sharp eye and my Blue Sheets. I was eager in those days. Vance identified him and called on the Mexican Judicial Police to make the arrest.

Doc said, "How much did they pay you?"

"I did well enough out of it."

"Were you proud of yourself?"

"Why not? It was a clean job."

"Jimmy, Jimmy, the things you do."

Used to do. Not so much lately. Still, it was a clean job, if I do say so myself, over and done with in two weeks and none of the usual hitches. There was no trouble at all with the extradition since he didn't have a Spanish name or a Mexican wife. He was a warrant officer, neither fish nor fowl, and his name was Gene McIntire, and he let down the people who trusted him. But there was no whimpering from the old soldier. He just said, "I'm going to miss San Cristóbal. This place is cool and pleasant the year round, a fat man's dream."

Whether Winkel followed any of this, I couldn't tell. Probably it was of no interest to him. The antics of people who were all tangled up in the world. Was it worse than he thought?

I tried to get Doc to talk a little about his so-called translation of the Maya glyphs. I couldn't draw him out. "No, not now," he said. "Not before a third party." Then he apologized to the Mennonite. "No offense, sir."

But the night ride had set him musing on other things, of his early poverty and lack of staff support as a young scholar. He talked and talked and then he sighed and said, "Well, you know, what does it really matter in the long run? When you get right down to it everything is a cube."

He had taken to saying that lately. *Everything is a cube.* I don't know what he had in mind. When you get right down to it everything is not a cube. You can look around and see that. Hardly anything in nature is a cube. Some few crystals, I suppose. Art and Mike thought it might have to do with cubic increase, geometric progression, or with some mystical notion, of life raised to the third power. Had Doc really hit on something? Who knows. Maybe he just liked the ring of the words. I made a point of not asking questions.

We stopped in Palenque to check with the police, and they had a body to show us. I knew it was going to be Rudy. A fisherman had found it bobbing about in the Usumacinta. Some loggers had brought it in on a truck.

The officer in charge, who for some reason believed Rudy to be a painter of pictures, was sympathetic. He took a flashlight, and Refugio and I followed him through the back door to a toolshed. There in the wooden tray of a wheelbarrow lay the body, wrapped in a tarpaulin. It was all very sad, the officer said, a fine artist drowned young. Even at its lower stages the big river was treacherous. There would be no more beautiful pictures from the hand of this particular young artist. But there were other artists, hundreds of them, plenty of artists, and the identification would take only a moment and then we could have some coffee in his office and deal with the various forms and fees. He was looking forward to a good long session with his rubber stamps and his stapler.

"The young man was your brother?"

"No, just a friend," I said.

"He was an unfortunate *leproso*? Your brother?"

"What? A leper? No."

He held the beam of his flashlight on the wheelbarrow. "There," he said, standing well back. He wasn't going to touch the thing. No one is more fastidious than a fastidious Mexican in uniform. It was the Chicanos in the Marine Corps who had their shirts tailored for a skin-tight fit, like those of state troopers, and who had gleaming horseshoe taps nailed to the heels of their cordovan shoes.

Refugio crossed himself, and the two of us set about unrolling the tarp. The smell wasn't so bad. The corpse hadn't gone off much because it was all leather, mummified. The eyes were two dull yellow marbles, bulging out from the face like the eyes of a Chihuahua dog. It wasn't Rudy, it was King Tut, a tiny old man, long dead, with bald head and bared teeth. It was a freak-show exhibit.

Refugio said, "This is what you call a young man? Drowned three or four days ago? This is some fine young artist you show us!" He grabbed a toe and held up one of the feet for the officer to see. It was a pitiful brown lump, badly calloused, as broad as it was long. "This is what you call the foot of a gringo? You are wasting the time of important men!"

The officer turned to me. "The man is not your brother?"

"No."

"You don't identify the person? Look carefully."

"I don't know him, no."

"They told me it was the missing artist."

"Anyone can make a mistake. We are grateful for your help."

"It was nothing, sir. Our work goes on."

The others were waiting for us out front by the truck, under a dim street light. Everyone was tired. None of these people knew Rudy Kurle. My news, that the body was not his but that of an ancient little man, caused no stir. Refugio told them it was the body of a *chaneque*. There was a dead *chaneque* back there in that shed. Here was their chance to see one of those evil dwarfs in the flesh. Did anyone want to see the *chaneque*? They seemed not to understand what he was saying. Doc was drooping. I had gone without sleep for two days. I suggested that we stop here at Palenque for the night.

At that, Winkel suddenly became assertive. "No, no, I have no money to waste on a hotel. Let us go on to the pipe place."

Doc took a handful of paper money from his pocket. Those knots in his pockets were wads of money. "Don't worry, I'm paying. We'll put up at the Motel Barrios."

But Winkel wouldn't hear of it. "No, no, please, this was not our agreement."

So we drove on to Refugio's place.

# XI

THERE IS a lot of nonpoverty in Mexico that you don't hear about. Everybody is not destitute or filthy rich. Refugio, for example, had just bought a new Dodge truck, bright red, with V-8 engine, a fine truck. He paid cash for it. But he wouldn't use it for hard service until the new was off. He was waiting for a molded plastic bedliner to come in from Veracruz.

Knowing this, I should have seen the sandbag job that was coming my way. The pair of us were up at daybreak, and Sula was serving us breakfast in the little office, where I had slept. "The Doctor is still sleeping," she said. They had put him up in their own air-conditioned bedroom.

Refugio said, "Well, don't disturb him. Let the man have his rest. Where are those beautiful roses he brought you?"

"I have them in a bowl of water."

"Bring them in here so we can smell them and enjoy them with our coffee. You see how this great man is always thinking of other people? You have a saint sleeping in your feather bed (*colchón de plumo*). Jaime and I are coarse men of business (*hombres groseros*) but look here, how the Doctor has time to think of the pretty roses."

They weren't roses. They had no smell that I could smell, whatever they were. I think they were dahlias, national flower of Mexico, shaggy and orange, nothing at all like roses. Refugio knew his trees, he could tell you the names of all the bigger trees in the forest, the local names, but any flower at all was a *rosa* to him.

He sprang his proposal on me as we ate, calling my attention to two important points. His truck was new and mine was old. Mine was sagging. One more crumpled fender, one more busted headlight, one more rock flying through my radiator could hardly matter. The only thing to do was to use my truck for the pipe delivery. He could hook up his flatbed trailer to it, and Valentín could haul the pipe away while we went on to the *selva* to look for the young gringo. We would take the

Volkswagen into the woods. This was an old salvaged delivery van that still carried the yellow markings of Sabritas potato chips.

"No, you can forget that," I said. "Valentín is not driving my truck."

"Then I myself will have to take the pipe to the *evangelistas*."

"Manolo can do it."

"Sula would never let Manolo drive to Yucatán alone."

"Valentín can go with him. Or better, Valentín can go alone in your truck."

"I don't want my trailer ball scratched up just yet."

"But it's all right to scratch mine up."

"Yours is rusty and ugly. Mine is still silver."

"Then we can switch balls. Or put a rag over yours."

"I don't want my bed exposed to the sun just yet. The sun fades red paint."

"I've been hearing about this bedliner for months. When is it going to get here?"

"God alone knows. You say all these hard things. Why can't you let me eat in peace?"

Valentín was Refugio's half brother or stepbrother. I never got it straight. I never got the relatives completely straight in my head, all these Bautistas and Peñas and Osorios and Zamúdios. Valentín was a jackleg mechanic and carpenter, fairly useful to have around, when he wasn't drunk. I didn't trust him. He was sly, with the startled eyes of a chicken. Sula didn't care for him either. She said Valentín never got his full growth because he was nursed as a baby on Coca-Cola instead of milk. She thought some of those *gaseosa* bubbles had floated up to his brain.

Winkel, of course, didn't want to impose on anybody. He had slept in the back of my truck, and then he said he wasn't hungry and Refugio had to force some breakfast on him. Winkel was up early, too, working alone, loading the pipe on the flatbed trailer. There was more than he had expected. He was delighted with his daring purchase. Small animals who had nested in the pipes scurried for new cover as they were disturbed, snakes and rats and scorpions and rabbits and lizards. Refugio showed Winkel how easy it was to cut the plastic pipe with a hacksaw. Saws with coarser teeth would splinter the ends. These were special hacksaw blades, he said, and he recommended that Winkel buy a dozen of them to insure clean cuts and no wastage. That was his advice. Winkel said he had his own *arco* blades at home.

I was walking the grounds. Gail joined me, with a mug of coffee. Dogs trailed at our heels, though not Ramos, son of Chino. Ramos didn't mix much with the yard dogs. Gail said she had slept comfortably enough in a hammock, in a small room with a great heap of red fire extinguishers bearing yellow tags that were long expired. She said, "What is that I smell? Surely they don't have an oil refinery around here."

"No, that's only the stuff in those drums out there."

"What is it?"

"Various choking and blistering agents."

"What are we waiting for now? When are we going on to Ektún?"

"First they have to stack all that white pipe on the trailer and tie it down. It won't take long after Refugio gets his people stirring."

She asked me about Doc, or Dicky, as she called him, and I told her he was a great Mayanist and a rich man who had lived in Mérida for many years.

"Great Mayanist? I've never heard of him."

I let it go but I thought she should have heard of him. If she had known her business, she would have heard of Doc.

"This coffee has cinnamon in it."

"Yes."

"What kind of business is Mr. Bautista in?"

"*Salvataje*. We're both in the *salvataje* business. *Salvamento*."

"Salvation?"

"Well, salvage."

"I heard him calling this place his *ranchita*. It doesn't look much like a ranch."

"He just says that. Anybody who lives out of town has a *ranchita*. It's a junkyard."

It was an industrial age boneyard in the jungle. It was a little kingdom. Refugio's father, the old *chiclero*, he who had gathered tree sap so we could have Juicy Fruit gum, had squatted here long ago, before there was a road. Refugio had made improvements. He kept pushing his whitewashed boundary stones outward and now claimed to own twenty-two hectares. Certainly he possessed the land. He held dominion over these fifty-odd acres, and anyone disputing his claim could expect to be threatened and called a monkey-head at the very least.

Once he had suggested that we clear the tract across the road and plant onions. Someone had told him that there was a fortune to be made in sweet red onions. But neither of us was a farmer, and besides, the soil was poor, and it seemed to me there were already enough onions in Mexico to go around, and then some, sweet or not. You pull up onions one by one and then sell them by the ton. That didn't appeal to me. We had other schemes. Now and again we talked about our kennel scheme. We would breed dogs here and train them to sniff out dope and explosives at airports. The government would pay us well. The way to get rich was on government contracts. Or we would breed war dogs. Not to work singly, leashed, on sentry duty, but in snarling packs. We would form them into platoons and train them to assault fortified positions at night. Once loosed and engaged in the actual fighting, they would be led by their own officers, such as Ramos.

The loading went forward. Refugio brought out his box of Mayan pieces to show Gail. He held them up and quoted prices to her. She was amazed that such things should be in private hands. Why not buy three or four of these little *idolos*, he asked her, all of a similar style? She could smudge them up, claim she had found them here or there, then return to her comfortable home and write books about them. Why not? Other *arqueos* did this. He knew from experience. No one would know. The pieces were genuine. They were a good investment and would put her just that much ahead of her hated rivals.

She laughed. "Yes, but I am only a poor student, you see. I can't afford such things."

"Ah, *pobrecita*. Well then, I make you a gift."

He stuffed a small ceramic bird in her shirt pocket. She protested, he insisted, and they went back and forth until she gave in. Now then, he said, shaking his finger, I will speak to you as a father. She had her Indian toy and could return home.

She had no business messing around out here in the dirt far from her comfortable home. She should be with her family at Christmas time. This filthy *arqueo* work was not suitable for young ladies.

Gail went red in the face. "I am not ready to go home yet, Señor Bautista."

At last we came to an agreement about the delivery. Manolo, sitting on a pillow, was to drive my truck and tow the load of pipe to the Mennonite farm. Valentín would go along but was not at any time to be allowed behind the wheel.

"Do you understand that, Manolo?"

"Papa knows I can do this job. How many times have I driven him to Villahermosa?"

He was swaggering and dancing about so that I had to grab his shoulder to get his attention. He had the same quick moves as his father. With a swipe of his hand he could catch a fly in midair.

"I know you can do the job, but this time you're answering to me, not your Papa. This is my truck. Do you remember when those loggers in Ocosingo jumped Flaco Peralta and me and your Papa? Do you remember what Flaco did to that Tzeltzal who called himself the Captain? Well, that's just what I'll do to you if you wreck my truck."

Manolo laughed and dropped to a crouch and began weaving about and making passes with an imaginary knife.

"No, I'm not joking now. Listen to me. I want you to show proper respect for your Uncle Valentín, but you're the one in charge. If he starts drinking, just leave him behind. Don't fool with him for one minute. Keep the tanks topped up so you won't get a lot of bad gas all at once. Don't pop the clutch and don't ride the brakes, use the gears. Keep it under sixty *millas*. Watch the heat needle. If it gets much past the halfway mark, pull over and let the engine cool down. But don't try to back up on the shoulder of the road or you'll jackknife the trailer. You'll need to add a liter of oil when you get to the Escárcega junction. Thirty-weight Ebano is good enough. Check it again in Mérida and once more on the way back. Keep your mind on your business, and remember, that trailer has no brakes and no lights. Now what did I say? Tell me what you're going to do."

You couldn't trust a sixteen-year-old kid in the States these days to look after a goldfish, and not many kids here, but I had confidence in Manolo. I wasn't really worried, for all my lecturing. He had a better feel for machinery and the flow of the road than I did, a finer touch. Still, it's just as well to have things understood.

Sula wept. Her only baby was going off into the world. "But so many leagues to Mérida!" she wailed. Valentín, in a clean white shirt, was glad of the trip, happy to be going anywhere. He appeared to take no offense at the slight—having a boy put over him. Maybe I had misjudged him. He held the truck door open for Winkel, poor man, who would have to ride in the middle again. No matter, he was taking home enough irrigation pipe to build a new Zion in the thorny scrubland of Yucatán.

At the last minute Doc came up, cap in hand, and pressed some money on him. "For your mission work, sir. Remember me in your prayers. Richard Flandin. I have always tried to do right by my fellow man. And I have gone beyond personal ambition (*aspiración*). All that is behind me now (*atrás de mé*)."

Winkel didn't understand. He couldn't follow Doc's peculiar Spanish. He held the money away from him as though a subpoena had been slapped into his hand. The Mennonites were always the first ones on the scene after a hurricane or earthquake or other disaster. They were much admired for their practical works of charity but they carried on no mission work as such around here, that I knew of. "An offering for your church," I explained to him. "Keep it."

Doc, backing away, said, "That man is much closer to God than we are."

Manolo popped the clutch and they were off with a lurch. Refugio, with Ramos at his side, was very much the *patrón* this morning. He stood apart from the rest of us, his head thrown back and his fists jammed down into the pockets of his long rubberized apron. He hadn't lifted a finger to help, as it wouldn't do to be seen performing menial labor before his people. He was proud of his son and pleased with the big sale. That PVC pipe had been a slow-moving line of goods. Saplings had sprung up around the pile. We had both known the despair of trying to sell things that nobody wanted.

# XII

O N TO Ektún in the potato chip van. The plan was that Refugio and I would drop Gail off there and then make our way down to Tumbalá along the rivers. We would catch a boat ride on the Usumacinta, as Rudy must have done. The van stood high off the ground and did well enough in the water. The hydraulic brake system was out, and Refugio had to work the hand brake and hold the wheel and shift gears, all three things, with his two hands.

Doc was glowing. "What shall we find today?" he said. He seemed to think we were off on a dig. I had tried to persuade him to stay behind at the salvage yard. He could do Refugio a real service there, sorting out his relics and appraising them, but no, he was determined to make one last venture into the forest. "My last *entrada*," as he put it. He sat up front beside Refugio, holding Ramos between his knees and calling him Chino.

Dry season or not, a shower of rain was falling when we reached the ruins. The place was deserted. Refugio fired two shots in the air. We went from tent to tent and found no one. The motorcycle was gone. Ramos barked at a wooden box in the mess tent. Refugio kicked it over and a big diamond-back *palanca* came tumbling out, or what they called a *nauyaca* around here. In any case, a fer-de-lance, who righted himself in no time. He stood his ground, with his head rolling about and his jaws flung open about 160 degrees. Don't tread on me! Ramos, still yapping, shied back, as did we all, except for Refugio. With one hand he tossed a rag over the snake's head and with the other he grabbed the tail and popped him like a whip, cracking his neck. Snakes take a good deal of killing as a rule, it's a long business, but this one was stone dead, and all at once.

Doc and Gail waited inside out of the drizzle while I went down to search along the river bank. At least the mosquitoes were grounded. I took my shotgun, slung muzzle-down from my shoulder. Soaked or dirty, the old L. C. Smith had never failed me, with its exposed hammers and double triggers. It

798

was simple and sure. The only firing mechanism I knew of with fewer moving parts was that of a mortar, with none. Refugio looked around in the woods behind the camp. I turned up nothing. He found two Lacondón Indians hunkered down in the old steam-bath chamber. They were drinking cans of beer and smoking long cigars they had rolled themselves.

He marched them back to the mess tent and questioned them sharply in their own lingo. Why had they not shown themselves? Did they not hear us calling out? The gunshots? The dog barking?

*It was raining. They were waiting out the rain.*

Where was everybody? Where were all the *arqueos*?

*Gone away for a time. To Palenque or some other town. It was the rain. They couldn't work in the mud.*

Refugio was a little rough with them. I could see they were frightened of him, with that big pistol at his side. It was Cortez grilling the baffled *Indios* again. The thin one, the one called Bol, had some Spanish, and I got it out of him that they were here to keep an eye on things. The bearded Lund had hired them. They were to sleep here and watch things and take what food they pleased from the stores—though Bol wasn't sure about the beer. He thought we might be angry at them for drinking the beer.

"No, it's all right," I said. "The beer is yours too. Don't worry about it."

But they knew nothing about any missing gringo. Everybody had gone away to Palenque. That was about all I could get because Refugio kept breaking in with accusations and Doc was roaring around the tent, having a fit.

"Look at all this equipment! I can't believe it! Cases of canned milk and a professional drawing board and electricity to boot! Look at all the logistical support these people have! They even bring their own little secretary along! And for what! When it's all over they'll turn in some piffling report that nobody will read! That nobody *can* read! Well, these are your modern road-bound explorers! They hear the patter of rain on the leaves and what do our brave boys do? I'll tell you what they do! They down tools and head for the nearest motel!"

Bol and his friend thought this tirade was directed at them, and it took me a while to straighten things out. Doc apologized and gave them hearty handshakes. He gave them some money. He had always been a true friend of the Lacondones, he told them, even though he could not accept the claim that their cultural line went unbroken all the way back to the classic Maya. No, he was sorry, but he rather thought they were a hybrid, pariah people, descendants of runaways, drifters, outcasts, and renegades, who had come together here in the forest in the not too distant past, to form a kind of tribe, and what was more, he believed he could prove it to their satisfaction. But he didn't think any the worse of them for being pariahs—he was one himself, a real outcast—and had he not always been their true friend, in thought, word, and deed? Here was some more money, take it. The whole wad was theirs if they could direct him to the Lost Books. They must understand this was his last *entrada*. He would pay well for books of the *antiguos* or any fragments thereof . . .

There was a lot more of this, and they didn't take in a word of it. I explained to them that the old man was offering a reward to anyone who found the missing young man. He had yellow hair and wore army clothes. He was last seen walking down the river a few days back. Refugio went over it again in their own *idioma*, adding for good measure that the boy was rich and would buy them new motorbikes if they brought him out safely. Then, with some gifts, we sent Bol off to spread the word among his people. The other one stayed behind.

Gail didn't know which way to turn. Her boss was dead and her friend Denise had flown home and now her entire crew was gone. She had fallen in with a pair of pyramid looters, most vicious of all criminals in the anthropology book, and a loud old man who, if she could believe her ears, had just called her a little secretary. We could hardly leave her here and she couldn't drive the brakeless van out alone. Or could she? I knew so little about her. She didn't talk enough for me to get a good reading on her. Later I got a pretty good reading.

Refugio saw a good chance to jump ship. His heart had never been in this job, a lot of gringo nonsense, bound in the end to be abortive and unprofitable.

"So. I will drive the young lady back to my *ranchita*, or Palenque, wherever she likes. That is all we can do, no?"

Gail said, "You don't have to cart me around like some old lady."

Doc said, "Palenque? What are we discussing here? Weren't we just in Palenque last night?"

Refugio couldn't get the Volkswagen going again. He ground away on the starter, but the little pancake engine wouldn't catch. Gail said that was all right. She would go on with us to Tumbalá. She would like to see the big river. Refugio told her it would be a hard and dirty trip. Doc said anybody who thought he could go to Palenque in a boat was crazy as hell. More delay and confusion. It was like those last frantic days in the coat factory. Scenes such as this had driven me to working alone. It was the old Rudy situation, where I had responsibility without authority. I couldn't tell these people what to do, but if they went wrong, got hurt, I would have to answer for it.

But then I no longer cared and I said I was going off on foot, now, down the Tabí to the Usumacinta. There I would hitch a boat ride to Tumbalá, pick up Rudy Kurle and continue on down the river by way of Yoro to the rail crossing at Teno-sique. It was the easiest way out. They could come along or stay here, just as they wished.

Doc began giving orders, left and right. I had to tell him again that this was not a dig, that he was not in charge this time, and that we would go and stop as I directed. He threw up his hands. "Fine, fine. Don't mind me. I don't know any-thing. Just tell me what to do. I'm not anybody. I'm only the man who found the big eccentric flint at Cobá."

Sula had packed some food for us, and we took some more out of the camp stores. Refugio found a square packet of del-icatessen ham in an ice chest. He held up a piece and flopped it about and laughed at how thin it was sliced. Look, he said, here was this gray and sickly meat, cut to about the thinness of a cat's ear, that you can see light through, and this was what they called a piece of ham in the great land of America! No wonder the gringos couldn't win their wars anymore!

I was glad to have him along, willing or not, and I was glad to have Ramos, too, who quickly sensed the plan and led the way, jogging ahead of us down the river bank. He knew his job, which was to give notice of any trouble down the way, to scatter varmints from our path. We walked in single file and spoke little. The brush was so thick in places that we had to walk out into the water.

We came to the opening in an hour or so, a big sandbar, where the Tabí, running deep brown, flowed into the muddy and lighter stream of the Usumacinta. The water was *café con leche*. We stopped there to rest and eat.

The rain had let up. There was a light breeze. Doc stood at the point of the sandbar with his white pantaloons fluttering. "The mingling of the waters," he said, looking across the way to the Guatemala side. Nothing was stirring over there. An unbroken line of trees, all even at the top, as though clipped with shears. "A rare day," he went on. "This is truly the Garden of the Kings. *La Huerta de los Reyes*." He drew his machete and nicked an earlobe to get some blood, then flung it from his fingertips in what he called "the four world directions." Some more of his cubo-mystico business, I thought. Gail said it was an ancient rite of the lowland Maya. An act of reverence then, in its way, which was fine with me. A blood offering, the only kind of any value, according to the Suarez. Big Dan was strong on blood, too. There had to be blood.

Doc called me out on the sandbar. "A word with you in private, Jimmy, if you don't mind." I joined him, and he asked me in a confidential way if I had heard him say that this was his last *entrada*.

"Yes, I have." I had heard him say it about four times.

"Well, that's just what I mean. I mean to lie down out here and die where I was happiest. Please don't interfere. I will just lie down under the canopy of the trees. With my old empty heart. I will die and melt away and be with all the other forgotten things in the earth."

"Where? Where will you do this?"

"Anywhere. Tumbalá will do."

"What's that in your hand?"

It was the little jade man. He was going to lie down and die with that thing in his mouth. I told him there was something heathenish about this that I didn't like, and he said no, don't worry, he had already paid Father Mateo to say seventy-eight masses for him, one for each year of his life, and none too many, he thought.

"I don't know. I'll have to think it over."

"The signal will be when I give you my machete. I want you to have it. At that point you will take the others and walk away. Don't look back and don't say anything. I couldn't bear any words. This is how I want it. You can't refuse my last wish, Jimmy. And don't let Cuco interfere."

I left it at that. He was determined, and I saw no hope of reasoning with him. But I had already thought it over and I had no intention of leaving him out here. Melt away? A nice way of putting it. Doc wasn't dying. Soledad Bravo would have seen it in his eyes. It was one thing to help along an old man on his deathbed, to dispatch him with a razor blade, but this business, no. I would tie him in the boat if it came to that, and Refugio would help me.

Gail offered to make him a sandwich. "You haven't eaten anything, Dicky."

"I got a boiled egg down."

It sounded like he had poked it down his throat whole.

Refugio shaded his eyes and made a show of looking up and down the river. "I don't see no *cayucas*." He cupped his ear. "I don't hear no boats." He was going to dwell on every difficulty.

"One will be along," I said. "Let's go. It's not far to Tumbalá. A little more walking won't hurt us."

We set off downstream and the going was easier now, though we were out of the jungle twilight, into the full blaze of the sun. The river cut its way through rounded hills, with steep wooded slopes that came right down to the edge of the water, or almost to the edge. At this season there was a sandy shelf to walk on. The big river, we called it, and so it was for Mexico, but this upper middle stretch I would put at no more than a hundred yards wide. The water had not yet taken on a dark tropical look. It was just pale and lifeless ditch water coursing along.

No boat came, up or down. Gail had some good mosquito dope, the best I had ever used. The trick is to keep them out of your face, from swarming in your face, which can't be endured. We drank from springs and small feeder streams, after I had poured the water through a paper cone, a coffee filter. It trapped all the bigger parasites, or so I told myself.

Refugio stopped to look at a hairy object washing about in an eddy. Then he jumped back and cried out, "Mother of

God! Another *chaneque*!" Another little brown man, that is, of the kind we had been shown at the Palenque police station. These small woodland creatures took sick and died, just as we did, and their bodies were always committed to flowing waters, according to Sula. Fair enough, but I didn't expect to see two of them in two days. They were washing up like sick whales.

This thing was vaguely childlike, a torso with something like a tiny arm flung out. It was just hide and bones, a headless, decaying mess of no very definite shape. Doc said it was a dog. Gail thought it might be a howler monkey. Ramos showed no interest. Much too hairy for a humanoid, I said, knowing nothing about humanoids.

Refugio snapped back at me. "Do you say I don't know a *chaneque* when I see one?"

"It's not like the one at Palenque."

Later, farther down the trail, he said, "Some *chaneques* are hairy. The older males have much body hair."

I might have believed that, coming from Sula, but Refugio knew no more about *chaneques* than I did.

He stopped us again when we reached Tumbalá. He raised his hand. "*¡Escuche!* Listen up!" Ramos was doing some furious barking around the bend. I was certain he had found Rudy. Refugio and I ran on ahead, across the ruins and up into a ravine, where Ramos had cornered something in a hole. It was a small cave in the hillside. I called out to Rudy. No answer. Then I thought it might be a jaguar. Yes, a *tigre*, I was sure of it, though real *tigrero* dogs are stalkers and don't bark at all. After all these years of going up and down in the woods, I was at last going to behold a jaguar at bay, in whose wonderful coat the Mayas saw a map of the starry heavens. Refugio said no, it was no *gato*, more likely a pig. This was pig madness. Ramos hated pigs.

Chino would have charged the hole. Ramos was content to race about in a frenzy before the entrance. Nor would Refugio, brave man that he was, enter a cave. Close places didn't bother him, or man-made holes. You could grab his ankles and hold him head down in a *chultún*, a kind of bottle-shaped underground Mayan cistern, and he would work calmly away with a flashlight in his mouth, scratching about for artifacts with one hand while swatting at snakes and scorpions with the other.

But he wouldn't go into a natural cave. Unquiet spirits still lingered there from the old days, far back in the darkness where virgin water dripped. You could go in and never come out. I was no spelunker myself. It was Doc who liked to prowl caverns, where one day the cache of lost books would be found. That was his firm belief.

Refugio fired a shot into the cave. I set fire to a dried palm frond and tossed it inside, more for illumination than with any hope of driving the animal out. There was movement. Then we heard voices.

"*¡Vale! ¡Vale! ¡No te alteres!* Okay, hold it! Take it easy!"

Two scraggly young men came out with a small chain saw and a .22 rifle. They were laughing, their eyes smarting from the smoke. I went inside with another blazing frond to make sure there were no others. There was a nest of bedding where they slept, and some scanty baggage. I poked around in it. If these two *chamacos* had done away with Rudy, they would have kept some of his fine equipment and his fine army clothes. I found nothing in that line, only three lumpy sacks hidden under a pile of brush. They were sisal sacks filled with sawed-off fragments of inscribed stone. I dragged them out into the light.

These boys were commercial pot hunters, and they had hidden here, they said, when they heard us coming, thinking we might be an army patrol. One of them had a bad arm wound, a ragged *cuchillazo*, gone purple along the edges. The chain saw had kicked back on him and ripped a long gash in his forearm. They had packed the wound with sugar and poured gasoline over it and tied it up with two pieces of rope. I got some antibiotic capsules from my shoulder bag and told him to take one every few hours. Leave it to me to have some antilife pills tucked away somewhere. He swallowed the lot, which hardly mattered, as the stuff was old and probably inert anyway. Doc and Gail came up. She gave the boy some aspirins, and he gobbled those down too.

I questioned them. They laughed and jabbered. The long and the short of it was that they hadn't seen Rudy. They had seen no one for four days.

Doc looked over the cave. He had a good eye and a good feel for these places. He pronounced this one a dud. It was barren, sterile, he said. And yet all around us were the tiny temples of Tumbalá, doll houses of stone and scaled-down shrines that stood no higher than your waist, a wonderland for flying saucer theorists. I don't know how Doc could tell so quickly, but he was always decisive. He kicked at the sacks of carved stone and asked the boys if they had come across any *libros*. He made a show with his hands, as of someone unfolding a road map, not an easy idea to put across. He gave them some money.

But of course they had found no books. Were there any left to find? There were only three Maya manuscripts or codices extant, and none dating back to the classic period. All three had turned up in Europe many years ago, with no back trail, no provenance, as they say. No one knew where they were written or where they were originally found.

Not around here, I would bet. Somewhere up in dry Yucatán perhaps, or in the high mountains of Guatemala. Not even bones survived in this sour soil. They were soon leached away to nothing. I had heard a lot about bones, too much about bones, from people who called us ghouls and grave-robbers and other hard names. Their idea was that we trampled about ankle-deep in old bones, crunching skulls and femurs heedlessly underfoot and raising great clouds of unhealthy bone dust in our bone-mad search for treasure. In fact, there were no bones. We came across a tooth now and then but never a human bone, not one. I had never disturbed anyone's bones, that I knew of, which was more than the *arqueos* could say.

I told the boys we wanted to hire their boat.

"*No barca.*"

They had no boat and had seen no boat for days. They had not heard motors on the river since yesterday morning. But those sacks of stone would collapse a mule, I pointed out, let alone a man. How did they propose to carry them out of here if not by boat? They laughed some more. No, no, I didn't understand. A friend was coming up from Yoro tomorrow to pick them up in his dugout. A couple of nuts, Refugio called them, a pair of *chiflados*. He didn't trust them, didn't like them. They were poaching in his private valley. Their mindless laughter annoyed him. He refused to answer when they asked if he would sell his .45. Instead, he climbed a tree and came down with a yellow orchid for Gail. "A pretty rose for your hair." She stuck it in her khaki hat. It would go on living up there, disembodied. These strange flowers lived off the air, if my information was correct, in the way of Dan and his people. Again the two *chiflados* asked about the pistol. Refugio said they would never have enough money to buy this gun. "This is a man's gun!" What business did a pair of monkeys have with a man's gun? They couldn't even handle a baby chain saw with a short bar!

Then he turned on me. "You say the boy will be in Tumbalá and then our work is done. Well, where is he?"

I had no idea. Rudy had left no camping evidence here. It was all a bust. I knew the smell of failure. I was chasing after a shadow. In any case, the thing now was to get Doc away from this place, keep him moving. He hadn't gone for his machete belt yet but I was worried. I was afraid to meet his eyes. The time has come, they would say to me. Without a boat we would have to take him by the heels and drag him out of the forest against his will, with his arms folded across his chest and his head scraping a little furrow across Chiapas.

"The boy is dead," said Refugio. "That is what I think. Now we can go back to our homes."

"Not yet. Somebody must have seen him. And we may as well go on down to Yoro now. There are bound to be boats at Yoro."

The gloomy Refugio said Yoro was far, far away and that we could not possibly walk there before dark.

"It's still the easiest way out. It's better than going back. A night on the river won't kill us. And a boat may come along yet."

Gail was naturally curious about Yoro. "What is it, a town? A ruin?"

"It's a river terminal where you can buy gasoline. Just a little village with some hens pecking around in the mud. Or it used to be. I don't know. They may have a yacht club there now."

I hadn't been to Yoro in years. The first time there I nearly starved to death on a 500-peso note. Nobody could change it. The widow woman who served meals wouldn't accept my *tortuga* note and she wouldn't feed me on credit. They used to call that note a turtle because it moved so slowly. Now you could just about buy a pack of cigarettes with 500 pesos.

Doc, to my surprise, said, "Yes, Yoro is a wonderful idea, Jimmy. Why didn't I think of that? Yes, Yoro and Yorito. We can go up on the bluff and see the great old city of Likín again. We can drink from the hidden spring of water. Is it still flowing, I wonder? What's wrong with me? I had forgotten all about Likín."

So had I. It was a sprawling hilltop ruin across the river in Guatemala. I had also forgotten, if I had ever known, that "Likín" was the Yucatec Maya word for "east" and "sunrise." An important word, as it turned out, though it wasn't until the next day that I made the connection, what with so many things on my mind. Had Doc then decided against lying down and giving up the spirit, or was he only putting it off? Best not to ask. He may have feared that the two *chiflados* would disturb him after he had arranged himself on the ground here. They might stand over him and look down on him with disgust and talk over his condition, in the way of medical students.

I got the party moving again and picked up the pace a little. At least our way was downhill. A night on the river wouldn't be so bad, if it didn't rain, and if Gail's mosquito dope held out. Strong stuff, though I believe my powder bag—a knotted sock filled with sulfur—was more effective against the ticks. Where were all the boats? Doc was holding up well, his little cap now dark with sweat. He wanted to keep those vapors in his head. Everybody else in Mexico was trying to keep them out. Straggling behind a bit, he and Gail were lost in a lively chat. He told her about the panoramic view from atop the great *Castillo* at Likín.

Refugio glanced back at them over his shoulder. "This Gail," he said to me. "She will make you a good enough wife, Jaime." *Esposa regular.*

"You think so?"

"Look how round and fat her arms are. She is quiet, too, and dedicated to bennee."

"Yes, well, Gail is all right."

But I wasn't interested in her in that way, nor she in me.

Around each bend we foolishly expected to see something new, and it was always the same line of trees and another stretch of brown water leading to another bend. A thousand years ago this valley was inhabited with stone cities every few miles. Now it was an empty quarter. No one lived here now except for a sprinkling of drifters and outpost people. We saw none of them, a shifty lot on the whole, not much given to the planning or building of cities. We saw no animals other than bugs and snakes and circling eagles.

The low-water trail was too good to last. At a gap where the river cut between two hills, we came up against a thick and impassable stand of bamboo. Not even Ramos could penetrate that canebrake. I went to borrow Doc's machete, only to find that he had given it to Gail. What was this? She had taken up the web belt a notch or two and strapped on the whole business. Something significant here? The passing on of the Aragon machete? Or had she only relieved him of the weight? Neither of them offered an explanation, and I asked no questions.

Refugio and I hacked away and cleared a narrow path along the edge of the water. It was hot work. Colonies of ticks showered down on us. They swarmed all down Ramos' haunches. He made for the river and took a quick dip and then well and truly shook himself off. When everyone had passed around the thicket, we stopped to beat each other with branches, trying to brush off the teeming *garrapatas*. I pounded at them with my sulfur bomb. Then, right in the middle of this whipping and dusting dance, and very much startled, we were hailed from across the river by three Guatemalan soldiers.

One was a young officer, a military policeman, with a red PM brassard on his sleeve. The other two were even younger, mere boys, carrying old American carbines with long banana clips, which made me suspect they were the fully automatic models. You can't really tell at any distance. The officer had drawn his pistol, and all three weapons were at the ready, if not quite pointed at us.

The water was turbulent at this narrow cut, and the officer had to shout. "What is your business here? I want to know your business!"

"*¡Pescadores!*" Refugio called out to him. "We are fishermen who lost our boat! Do you have a boat? We need a ride to Yoro! We lost our boat and one of our people! A gringo! Have you found a young gringo?"

The soldiers consulted among themselves. Then the PM came back to us. "What, will you shoot the fish? No, I don't believe you are fishermen!"

"Yes, can't you see? Look for yourself! A party of gringos! Their *equipaje* went down with the boat! They come to catch the fish and shoot the birds! You are brave soldiers serving on the *frontera*! We are nothing but fishermen and gentlemen shooters! ¡*Escopetas blancas*! Don't you have a power boat?"

Another consultation. The young PM pointed downstream with his revolver and fired off a round, for the joy of it, I think. "¡*Mas abajo*! On down! At the *ruinas*! The *arqueos* have a boat! At Chupá!"

"How far?" I shouted.

"Not far!"

"Have you seen a young gringo?"

No answer.

"The young man is lost! He may be in your country! Will you make a report to your *comandante*?"

No answer. Policemen, lawyers, soldiers, doctors—they hate to tell you anything.

"Then with your permission we will be on our way!"

Again they said nothing. The parley was over. We moved off warily, unlikely communists, and they watched us, not altogether satisfied with our story. We were in Mexico, the Colossus of the North, and didn't need their permission. They would have been lucky to hit us at that range with those pieces. Still, it's just as well to step lightly around teenage boys in uniform carrying automatic weapons. I had been one myself and I had known, too, with my heart knocking against my ribs and my finger on the trigger of that BAR, that there was nothing sweeter than cutting down the enemies of your country.

Doc said, "An important lesson back there for all of us."

We waited. What lesson? It pays to be courteous to the army? Something to do with the ticks? What? No, the lesson was to be careful with chain saws. Doc's thoughts had drifted back to the cave of the two laughing *chiflados*.

"That poor boy could very easily have lost his arm. A chain saw is a very tricky customer, and if you don't know what you're doing, leave it alone. You must always grasp it firmly with both hands and never, never raise it above your head."

Refugio didn't know Chupá. Doc, calling it Shupá, claimed he had been there once, around 1946, and knew it like the back of his hand. Gail was familiar with the name. The ruin was on the Guatemala side, she said, and some Mormons were reported to be digging there. I had never heard of it, though it was situated on the river. You can float right by some of those old cities, walk right through them in the jungle and never notice a thing. The trees and roots strangle them, the humus accumulates and the temples lose their sharp edges, become rounded hills, little wooded *cerritos* that appear natural.

"We're coming up on it now," Doc said, time and again. "Over there . . . in the shade of that headland. . . . No, that can't be it . . ."

Probably he had been to Chupá, just as he had been to hundreds of these sites, but now they all ran together in his head. Not far, the officer had said, which could mean anything. If the *arqueos* had hidden their boat and set up their camp back from the river, we might well miss the place. We might already have missed it. The red sun was almost down. I was looking for a good place to hole up for the night, some hillside depression with a nice overhang.

"Two boats! There!" Refugio saw them first. We could just make them out in the shadows, a *cayuca* and a green plastic boat on the far shore, tied up in the mouth of a creek. A thin line of white smoke rose from the forest. It was a camp, all right. We shouted across the river in Spanish and English. Out of the trees came a tall bearded man in a baseball cap. He looked us over with his binoculars in the failing light.

Here is how fast night fell. We watched the man climbing into the green boat and starting the engine, and then as he came to us across the river we lost sight of him. We could see the boat and then we couldn't see it. He pulled up short of the bank and turned a spotlight on us, still not sure of us.

"We're looking for someone," I said. "We're making our way down the river. Can you put us up for the night?"

"Do you have papers for Guatemala?"

"No, but we'll be off in the morning. We'd like to hire your boat. Can you run us down to Yoro?"

"There is a sweet young lady here with us," said Doc. "Otherwise we wouldn't bother you. I appeal to your gallantry."

The man laughed in the darkness behind his bright light. "Okay."

Roland was his name, and he ferried us across and took us up the hill to a green tent and fed us well. Mashed potatoes are all the better for a few lumps, in my opinion, and gravy too for that matter. Roland was our solitary host. There were three other gringos in this Chupá crew that we didn't see, all laid up sick in their cots. Roland himself was healthy enough, a big strapping fellow with a clean beard and clear eyes, a walking tribute to the Mormon dietary laws. So many *arqueos* are sallow, bony little men with leg ulcers and bad skin rashes on their hands and arms.

It was a fine supper, with fresh peaches for dessert, out here where no peaches grew. "Might as well finish them off," he said, and so we did, piggishly, downy skins and all. We ate everything but the pits. It didn't occur to this decent man to hide the peaches until the plague of guests had blown over. After the meal, with a playful wink, he said he was sorry but he had no "highballs" to offer us. "Gentiles" of our type, he knew, just barely made it from one drink to the next.

I had served with some Mormons in Korea and they were good Marines to a man, if untypical ones. They didn't smoke, drink, swear, malinger, or complain, except occasionally, about the P for Protestant that was stamped on their dog tags. They claimed to be some third thing in Christendom, neither Protestant nor Catholic, or rather some unique thing, but the point was too fine for the Marine Corps to grasp.

What they called themselves down here, in this work, was the New World Archaeological Foundation, their aim being to find evidence of early settlement by the "Jaredites" and Hebrews. All the Indian civilizations, they believed, were founded by these people, who came here by boat from the Middle East in two separate waves, the "Jaredites" or Sumerians in 2800 B.C., and the Hebrews around 600 B.C. It was a variation on the Lost Tribes of Israel theme, with certain strange Mormon wrinkles—strange to me—such as that Quetzalcoatl, the Toltec man-god from Tula, known to the Maya as Kukulcán, was the same person as Jesus. There was a tradition, they said, that Quetzalcoatl, the crested serpent, was crucified.

Not that they pushed the belief on anyone, far from it, for all their missionary work elsewhere. They were reluctant to discuss it with outsiders, or with me anyway, no doubt fearing that it would be hopelessly misunderstood, a religious quest mixed up with practical field work. It was all I could do to drag it out of Dr. Norbee, bit by bit, when I was hauling freight for him at a New World dig in Belize. Once I asked him outright—had they found any evidence to support the theory? Dr. Norbee, leery of casting pearls, put me off with a nonarchaeological example. There was a town in Honduras called Lamana, he told me, and Laman was one of the early Israelite chiefs here, chief of the Lamanites in fact. Laman of the Lamanites. Lamana. He left me to think that over. Pretty thin soup, but then the secular *arqueos*, always going on about the scientific purity of their motives, were usually out to prove some case or other themselves. From all I heard, the Mormon diggers were honest men who refused to fake or stretch the evidence. No more than anyone else, that is.

Roland knew Dr. Norbee and gave me news of him in Utah. He had heard nothing of any American boy being lost or found in these parts. Still no sighting. But he had seen a lot of gringos coming downstream in powered dugouts. Some had stopped here to stretch their legs. Hippies, they were, who had put in, most of them, at a place called Sayache, on the Pasión River, which is the upper Usumacinta. They were on their way to Yorito, or actually to the ancient city of Likín, for some sort of hippie jamboree. This accounted for the absence of boats. The boatmen were all lingering down at Yoro and Yorito, ferrying the hippies back and forth across the river and making a killing.

Yes, if you're going to Likín, Sayache would be the place to put in. It was one of the few towns on the upper part of this river system that you could reach by car or bus. You drove to Belize, then over to Flores in Guatemala, then down to Sayache, end of the road. Rudy, of course, wouldn't want to do it that way, the easy way, but why would he do it at all? Could he be part of this? Rudy was no hippie.

I asked Roland what the occasion was. "What are these people gathering for?"

"The annihilation of the world. Tomorrow, on the stroke of midnight."

"They're celebrating that?"

"Well, they say they're trying to stop it, with a blood sacrifice. There's supposed to be another group doing the same thing down at Machu Picchu in Peru. They seem to think this is the end of the thirteenth *baktun*. The end of time. Unless their sacrifice proves acceptable. They're expecting to meet someone there called *El Mago*."

Doc had gone all heavy and slumped from the big feeding, which Soledad Bravo had advised against. Now he was roused. "What's that? *Baktuns?* The completion of the *baktuns* doesn't come around until the year 2011."

"Yes sir, but they don't go by the Thompson correlation. They have some reckoning of their own. I couldn't follow it. They've tied it all in somehow with New Year's Day."

"What nonsense. Our January one, Gregorian, is in no way related to the beginning of the Mayan year."

"Unless by chance."

"No, not even then, if you mean the approximate year. It was in summer that the Mayan year began, and certainly not at midnight. They must be thinking of the Aztecs."

Gail said she didn't see how the Incas could be involved. "What does Machu Picchu have to do with it?"

Roland said he didn't know. "I couldn't follow that either."

"And the Spinden correlation is out." She took a small calculator from her shoulder bag and punched around on the keys. "It's not the Weitzal correlation . . . or the Escalona Ramos correlation . . . I can't imagine what system they're using . . . wait . . . let me try the day itself against the heliacal rising of Venus . . ."

"Try it against all four phases."

She and Roland and Doc continued to wrestle with the problem, surely knowing it to be an empty exercise. The hippies knew nothing about the Mayas and their *baktuns*—400-year periods—or the Incas, or the planetary movements, much less the end of the world, certainly nothing that could be worked out on a calculator. Rudy carried one, too, in his shirt pocket. He was fond of decimal points. He would add up his guesses and rough estimates in an exact way on the thing and come out with falsely precise figures, which looked like hard-won data, very pleasing to the eye. Still—Doomsday at hand. The prophecy never fails to pull you up short. You stop a bit, before going on. No one knows and so anyone might hit on it.

It got worse, embarrassing. Doc went on to repay Roland's hospitality by trying to provoke a quarrel, telling him bluntly that he was all wrong with his Hebrews wading ashore at Veracruz. It was the Chinese who had settled this country. The Meso-Americans could not possibly have come from the Mediterranean, because there, as in Europe, the snake was a symbol of evil. No, it was in the Far East, in China, where you found benign reptiles, holy lizards, celestial dragons, and such, as you also found here with the iguana god and the cult of the mighty plumed serpent. The same lotus theme too. Just as it was here, as in China, that jade was believed to have divine properties. And was not every Indian baby born with the Mongolian Spot at the base of his spine?

Roland took all this in a good-natured way, deferring to the old man, calling him Sir, saying he made some good points, that the jury was still out on so many things down here.

Gail was drowsy, and I was nodding too. Ramos moved about impatiently under the table, nudging my leg for more scraps. Doc tried again. He asked Roland where he stood on carbon-14 dating. Roland said it was a useful tool, but he said it with no confidence, sensing he was going to be on the wrong end of this argument too. Doc informed him that carbon dating was a colossal hoax, perhaps the greatest scientific scandal of the twentieth century. "You can get any date you like. If you don't like the reading, you just say the sample was too small or it was contaminated. You keep running the stuff through the lab till you get a reading you do like. Look at what they did to Spinden. First they said he was right, and then they said he was wrong. Off by 260 years. Of course he *was* wrong, but they had to keep cooking their numbers to show it. You boys are easily taken in, if I may say so."

We put up for the night in a temple chamber with thick walls of glittering crystalline limestone. It was the camp storeroom. The ceiling was high and at least fifteen feet across, about as wide a free span as you will see in this land of the false arch. Most of the chambers in these great structures were no bigger than closets, and Art and Mike maintained that the Maya were not really architects at all but essentially sculptors. Their purpose was to throw up solid white platforms against the sky, and only incidentally to enclose space. There was a single doorway. Roland took pains to close it off with a double thickness of mosquito netting. He wished us goodnight.

"Nice boy but a mere technician," said Doc. "He has no comprehensive vision." We settled in against boxes and lumpy sacks. Ramos did two or three tight little dog turns in place before dropping down at Refugio's feet. Doc prowled around with a citronella candle. He looked in corners and ran his hands over niches in the wall. "The ceremonial vesting room, I think. Yes, it seems we have been assigned to the vesting room." He was never at a loss to explain the function of ancient things. Show him a rough, wedge-shaped rock, and he would identify it as a *coup-de-poing*, or hand axe. Show him a smooth one and he would say, "Ah yes, a nice votive axe." Sometimes it *was* a votive axe, and for all I knew this was an old vesting room. These dead cities still lived and sparkled for him in the distance as they did not for me. This room had no message for me.

We slept. Doc woke us in the night. He came to us with his yellow candle and a scrap of paper. It was headed "Xupáh [as he spelled it] Guatemala," and dated. Underneath that he had written, "I swear or affirm that I accept without reservation Dr. Richard Flandin's theory of direct trans-Pacific Chinese settlement of Meso-America."

"Would you look this over and then sign it, please? Take your time. I don't like to disturb you but I might forget this in the morning. I'm not a hard man to work for. I do however insist on staff loyalty. If we're not all pulling together then how in the world can we ever hope to accomplish anything?"

Refugio and I signed, he, writing with a flourish, "Refugio Bautista O." We had done it before, though these chits usually ran to vows of silence about particular finds.

"I can't sign this," Gail whispered to me.

"Why not? Just put something down."

She signed Denise's name by the light of the candle.

"And I thank you very much," said Doc, simpering over the paper, all but rubbing his hands together. He was a salesman closing out on a big and unexpected order. "A formal gesture like that gives the pledge more weight, I think. I say 'theory' and that will do for our purposes here, but it's much more than that. It's more than a theoretical construct, it's a hard fact."

Later he woke us again. "Excuse me, but I forgot to mention that this loyalty business goes both ways. It must come down from the top too. I'm fully aware of that. Here is a token of my trust in you."

He set fire to the scrap of paper, watched it burn, and then left us alone. No word about lying down here and not getting up again.

# XIII

O N TO Yoro. It was still dark when Roland came and said the boat was ready. I couldn't blame him for speeding us on our way. He stood to lose his digging permit, so hard to come by these days, if Guatemalan soldiers found us here with no papers. I offered to pay him for his trouble, and he said no, just tip the boatman when we reached Yoro.

He, the skipper, was a shirtless little river rat, proud of his *cayuca*, this being a dugout canoe fashioned from a mahogany log. It was a good sturdy hull about thirty feet long, well shaped and finished. The hacking marks of the axe and the adze were sanded down. The sides were damp and had a nappy, velvet feel from long use. He pushed off from shore with his sounding pole and started the engine, and we slipped away into a fog bank. Roland trudged back up the hill to search for traces of Lamanites in the rubble of Chupá. A comprehensive vision, it seemed to me, was the very thing he did have.

Our man knew the channel well. There were no lights on the boat, but he ran his engine full out. He couldn't even see the front of the *cayuca*. A heavy night bird swooped, came flapping right over our heads, confused by the fog, perhaps still looking for something small and live to eat. After that we had the river to ourselves. Doc lost his little Chinaman's cap, and he looked better, more dignified, with his white hair loose and blowing. Then he lost his wristwatch trailing his hand in the water. Refugio said, "You never know what the day will bring."

The morning light came slow and the sun was well up before we could see it through the vapor, a pale disk. Surely it would rise again tomorrow. Gail passed around some cheese and tortillas and mashed cake. Soggy cake is bad but mashed cake is not so bad. Ramos clambered from one end of the boat to the other. He couldn't find a good place to settle. The river rat had nothing to say to us. He kept his hand on the tiller and held his head high and sucked on a dip of snuff. The cud was packed under his lower lip, and it appeared to be a satisfying snuff of the very finest quality. My guess was that he was silent at home, too, if he had one. Gliding up and down the river in your own boat, knowing you had plenty of snuff in reserve, was better than yapping all the time, and being yapped at.

The engine sputtered out three or four times, and we lost half the day drifting, wiping oil off the fouled spark plug, blowing through the fuel line, yanking on the starter rope. Good mechanics that they are, and for all their Latin delicacy in other matters, Mexicans are not much troubled by a firing miss in an engine. Almost every taxicab has an ignition skip or a faulty carburetor. The missed beat doesn't gnaw at them. Time enough to fix the thing when it goes out altogether.

We arrived in the afternoon. Some of the hippies had fallen sick here at Yoro and were lying about in the shade or just sitting on the riverbank hugging their knees. Others had moved on to Likín for the big event. Nothing was moving on the river. Most of the *cayucas* were beached across the way on the Yorito side. A late afternoon stillness. No women washing clothes in the shallows.

I went to pay our boatman, and Doc said, "Here, no, I'm taking care of this. Give the fellow some money, Gail." He had turned over all his money to her.

There was a new and bigger gasoline storage tank at the landing. It seemed there were more children about, and the tire swing had been introduced here since my last visit. Otherwise Yoro looked much the same. A dirt track ran up from the landing through two rows of shacks and then petered out against the forest wall. A *ranchería*, they called it, and you could take it all in at a glance. It was still a sad little outpost.

The restaurant was the same, too, known only as the widow woman's place. The woman prepared food in her house and brought it out back to a small *ramada* open on all sides. There were four tables under a palm-thatched arbor. It was this same woman, now scowling at us, somewhat fatter but not looking much older, who had refused to take my *tortuga* note years ago.

We had disturbed her nap. It was nap time in Yoro. All the food was gone, she told us, there was nothing to be had here, the young gringo beasts had eaten everything as fast as she could cook it. They had frightened her cat Emiliano away, and look how they had trampled down her morning glory vines and her tomato plants, her fine *jitomates*—in the season of the

Nativity!—bringing their social diseases and their foreign eye diseases! There was a place in Hell for them, for dirty *gorristas* like that one there!

She pointed to a hippie who was stretched out on the ground with a hat over his face. It was a touristy hat made from green palmetto blades. I thought he was asleep, but he must have been watching us through the weave cracks. "There's not a single Pepsi left in town," he said. "They're all out of bread, too, and ice."

Refugio told the woman that we were forest rangers and that she would do better to show more respect for the government. Was she blind? Couldn't she see that we were important captains from the *forestal* and not young *viciosos*? "Now go to your pots and bring us what you have." She served up some black beans and fried plantains and coffee. We had our own tortillas. Refugio said she could put on a new red dress and red shoes, do whatever she liked, crawl on her knees to the Shrine of Guadalupe, and still she would never find another husband, a scolding woman like that.

The hippie spoke up again. "My car doors are frozen shut in Chicago. All the ice you want up there." His jeans were pressed, and if anything he was cleaner and more presentable than we were. But then he really wasn't a hippie and he was quick to set us straight on that point. Right off the bat he showed me his new Visa credit card. His name was Vincent. He and his sweetheart, Tonya Barge or Burge, had flown down here to celebrate the end of his apprenticeship. He had just won his "electrician's ticket"—which I took to mean a union card or some kind of professional certification. And it was true, he had come down the big river with this wandering tribe, but he wasn't one of them.

"I thought we were going to the beach. Christmas on the beach, that was our plan, see, just the two of us, staying in bargain hotels and eating bargain food. Like bananas, you know, and tacos, and those real big Cokes? Then we ran into these interesting people, or anyway Tonya thought they were interesting, with all their talk about cosmic energy. I'm not into pyramids myself and I can't buy the mind science these people are putting out. Forget it. I like the beach. What's wrong with that? There's plenty of cosmic energy coming down on the beach."

I said, "You need to keep better company, Vincent."

"Hey, don't I know it! I mean, come on, all these potheads giving out their bum information! This big brownout they're talking about? The death of the sun? Who wants to hear that? Who needs it! And this *El Mago* that nobody knows who he is? With all his strange powers? Nobody has ever seen him here yet but oh yeah he's going to work wonders! Dark forces are gathering! Signs and wonders! Give me a break, will you! I don't like to hear stuff like that and I don't go for this sleeping dirty either and all their weird baloney about the mystery of the underground colonies! Don't get me started on that! Am I talking too loud? It's a bad habit I got to watch."

"No, don't let it get a foothold."

"Say, I been meaning to ask you. What are all the guns for?"

"Songbirds. We're hunters. Trophy kills."

"Well, hey, that's your business, not mine! I don't know one bird from another except for robin redbreast! I'm no sportsman, I'm just passing through! I'm not even supposed to be here! I mean the country is green and beautiful but all these bugs. We didn't see any alligators yet, just snakes so far and those iguanas with the ugly spines on their backs. The boat ride was fun though, I got to admit that, and last night we watched a falling star all the way down. Wait, did I dream that? No, what am I saying, everybody saw it. They were all talking about it. They said it fell out there in the water somewhere. Don't tell me you people live around here."

"I live in Mérida."

"Mérida, right, I've heard of it. And you live there! With your dog! And the old man and the girl with the machete, they're after these little birds too?"

"No, I was only playing around with you a little bit there, Vincent. We're just making our way down the river. We're looking for someone."

He put up his hands in surrender. "Hey, don't worry, I can handle that! No problem! I'm not offended! I can take a joke! You think I don't know decent people when I see them? So let me see now if I understand this. You're taking your river trip and the chunky Mexican guy, he's not a policeman or anything like that with his big pistol?"

"No, he's not a policeman."

"Then let me ask your advice on something. Should I be waiting on the other side of the river? I know this is Mexico and I don't have my Mexican papers."

"You're okay. Nobody in Yoro is going to bother you about papers."

"The last thing I want down here is trouble with my papers. Know what I mean? I don't like to break the law. That's just the way I am. I mean it's there for a purpose, right? But there's nothing to do over in Yorito, and those boat guys won't talk to you. Let me tell you what Tonya did. When we got out of the boat at Yorito. This is a great story. She went right on up the hill to that old pyramid city—in her sandals! Right off into the woods I'm telling you! With all those nuts! A long line of marching nuts and bums not saying anything! No way I'm walking into that jungle in my jogging shoes. It's so dark and shady you can't see where you're stepping and you just know the place is full of snakes and these marching ants that can bite right through canvas! Do you think I was cowardly? Tell me the truth."

"No, it makes sense to me. I wouldn't go out there without boots."

"Tonya wouldn't listen to me. I told her not to go. Are you saying I was right not to go? Just what are you saying?"

"I'm saying you were right and Tonya Barge was wrong."

"So you seem to think I can live with my decision then."

"She'll be back. I wouldn't worry about it."

"They got to her head with their mind science. She went right on up the hill in her sandals. Some of those people are barefooted. I still can't believe it. Women should be cleaner than men, right? Well, let me tell you, some of those old gals could use a bath."

"How many are up there?"

"A lot."

"Fifty? A hundred?"

"More than that. Sometimes you can hear them chanting."

I listened but couldn't hear them. Maybe the wind was wrong. You couldn't see the ruin itself from here, just the green mass of the hill downstream at the bend. Ramos came to his feet. A yellow tomcat was looking at him from a patch of weeds. They looked at each other. It was a staredown. Then the cat, who must have been Emiliano, withdrew, but in no haste. It just wasn't time to come back yet. Ramos did his dog turn and settled down again. Emiliano wasn't even worth a growl.

Doc spoke to me with his eyes shut. White stubble glittered on his face. "When are we going over to Likín, Jimmy? I want a long cool drink from the spring. Gail does too. I hope it's not silted up." She had him lying on the ground in the shade of the *ramada*, with his head on her bag. She was fanning him. One panting old man had already died before her eyes, at another dinner table.

"We'll be going soon," I said. "After we've rested a little."

"Can we stay there overnight?"

"What for?"

"I want to take Gail up to the top of the *Castillo* and show her the Temple of Dawn. How the first beams of the day strike through that little aperture. With blinding splendor."

"It's a steep climb."

"We'll take our time going up."

"Yes, well, it's okay with me. It's just that all those people are over there now. We'll see how things work out."

A white vapor trail stretched halfway across the arch of the sky, so high that we couldn't see the airplane that was spinning it out, or hear it.

Vincent said, "That's the only way to cross this jungle if you ask me. They're up there in their seats and we're down here without any Pepsis."

He had seen some young men wearing odds and ends of military garb but no one quite like Rudy. I went around to the villagers with my questions, hoping the women wouldn't snatch up their babies and run from me. In one hut I interrupted some men hanging green tobacco leaves over the roof stringer poles. They were polite but of no help. My description of Rudy meant nothing to them. Gringos were phantoms. A few more minutes and I too would be gone from their memory. Down on the river bank I woke up a pair of hippies who had fallen asleep fully clothed and all locked together in a tight embrace, like that petrified couple they found at Herculaneum. The boy was surly, not feeling well. The girl blinked at me through her hair and said she had seen a blond fellow in army clothes back at the lake town of Flores. No, not my man. I thought not. Wrong way. He wouldn't have gone upstream. I spoke to all the sick stragglers, and, I think, to every adult resident of Yoro. None of them had seen Rudy Kurle, planner of cities. I was convinced of that, unless someone was lying. Even in this flock of migrant cockatoos he would have stood out. In khaki or blaze orange Rudy would have made an impression. He would have been noticed, pointed out, discussed, and remembered.

I would have to investigate the others across the river, go through the motions at least, but not now. I was drained. All these futile questions. I went back to the *ramada* muttering a little and lay down. Doc and Gail and Vincent were talking about art. What a subject. A girl with a round belly came by. Refugio shielded his face with his hands and shouted, "*¡Ay!* Look out! God help us! She's about to pop!" The pregnant girl made a face at him and he laughed and said, "Be brave! It won't be long now! You won't regret it when you see that little wet rat!" The girl laughed too and waddled off with her plastic buckets. The women of Yoro were carriers of water.

It was Vincent's souvenir, a lacquered gourd, that had set off the art talk. Black monkeys were painted on it, under a clear coat of lacquer. Very poor workmanship, said Doc, who was drinking something from a bottle. The monkeys looked like squirrels, he said, and sick squirrels or dead squirrels at that. It was nothing, *basura*, trash. This was the only part of Mexico where the people had no gift for the graphic arts. There was no vigor or joy in their work. They lacked a sure hand. They had no more art in their bones than—he looked at me—than the people of Caddo Parish, Louisiana. Vincent defended his gourd. The monkeys looked okay to him. This art was okay. What he couldn't appreciate was diamonds and rubies and such. "I mean, why all the fuss?" What he couldn't understand was the point at which pretty stones became precious gems, worth millions of dollars, that people gloated over. Gail said she had a similar problem with the mystery that surrounded the serpent. As a child, of course, she had feared snakes and gone in awe of them, as of some fabulous beasts. Now, of course, she knew better. She knew now—they had explained it all to her in college—that snakes were neither horrible nor magnificent, but only creeping digestive tracts. And in many cases they destroyed harmful rodents and other agricultural pests. Yet the myth persisted! She and Vincent both were from Illinois but nothing was made of it. Some social gap there. Doc said that Humboldt, usually so wise, had denied that there was any art in ancient Meso-America. Carvings, paintings, sculpture, ceramic pieces, funeral masks—all very nice in their way but only proto-art. It was just something on the long road that leads to art.

I was trying to think of some Shreveport artists. We had some, I had seen their huge swirling works hanging in bank lobbies, but I could hardly be expected to know their names. Who was Humboldt anyway and how was it that the pre-Columbian stuff fell short in his eyes? No soul? Too cluttered? Too stiff? What? You wonder what people have in mind when they speak with confidence on such tricky matters. Old Suarez had his doubts about it, too, because it wasn't socialist art. Only the royalty and the soldiers were glorified. We needed him here for this seminar, and Beth and Professor Camacho Puut and Louise and Nardo and Eli and Art and Mike. Bollard too; he could give us the very latest line out of New York, or fake it plausibly enough.

The orchid on Gail's hat had gone brown along the edges. My information was wrong. Air alone wasn't enough to keep the blossom going. They didn't feed off wind after all.

"Well, Mr. Humboldt never saw anything like this," she said. "This is art. You can tell right away. Look how it jumps out at you. Look how—*strong* it is."

Ugly was the word she wanted. She was showing us the little Olmec figure with the demonic face. So now our Dicky had given that thing to her, too. What was going on here? She rubbed around on it, the way you do with jade, then buttoned it up again in her shirt pocket. No questions about the ownership, the way she patted that pocket. The ceramic bird, the jade man. Everything buttoned away there was hers.

But now Doc was off art and onto famous men he had known. Morley, Thompson, Stirling, Caso, Ruz Lhullier—they had all come to him for advice and consultation, to hear him tell it. Great Mayanists all! He too stood in that apostolic chain, nor was he the least of them! But what could he not have done with a proper staff and a little recognition now and then! From these low-life professors who controlled everything with their petty politics! These very little men! These gray mice! Who pretended not to know him while all the time they were stealing his ideas!

Purple drops ran down through the stubble on his chin. Gail had found a cold bottle of grape soda somewhere, and she was sharing it with him. The old lizard still had a way with the ladies. She hung on his every boastful word. Refugio, too, he loved the hot words and the bluster. This was the way a man should speak, out of the abundance of the heart. Vincent was poking away at embedded ticks on his legs with the burning end of a cigarette. But Refugio stopped him, grabbing his wrist and saying, "No, don't do that while the Doctor is speaking." He said to Gail, "My name is in his book. Refugio Bautista Osorio."

Doc lay back on Gail's pack and closed his eyes again. "Oh, my vindication will come, all right, but much too late for me. You will live to see it. You will hear the acclaim. You can tell your children that you were with Flandin on his last *entrada* into the Garden of the Kings. Or call it the Valley of the Kings if you like, the pharaohs be damned. Don't forget, this was a great empire, too. You can say, 'Yes, I was with the poor old fellow shortly before he died of malicious neglect.' A victim of envy, too. A man literally murdered by the envy of cunning and hateful mice."

He paused there on the *mice*, which was just as well, and I saw a chance to get a word in. I took off my boots and directed this crew of mine in perfectly clear language to wake me in an hour. That would give me time to cross the river and climb the hill and look over that pack of hippies before sundown. I dozed. The chatter went on and on under the arbor, though a bit subdued now. It didn't bother me. There was no moving about. No one seemed able to move. We were in the grip of a curious Yoro paralysis. Refugio said to me, whispering, that, seriously now and all joking aside, the mature *chaneques* could grow hair all over their bodies whenever they pleased, at will, through their sorceries. "All the world knows this to be true, Jaime." He would be telling me next that the little men had furry paws. *Chaneques* didn't interest me at the moment. Vincent's falling star was still on my mind. I was thinking of a fiery pebble blazing out of the night and striking the river with a faint hiss, then settling with the side-to-side motion of a falling leaf to the mud at the bottom, journey's end. Down there with Doc's watch and other forgotten things, and that little jade *idolo*, too, if I could get my hands on it.

# XIV

O F COURSE they didn't wake me and how could they, being asleep themselves, all sprawled together in a pile like a litter of puppies, not knowing or caring that sleeping on watch is a terrible offense. Night had come. An oil lamp was burning in the widow woman's house. There was sheet lightning to the west, far off in the mountains. It must have been the thunder that woke me. I gave Refugio a shake, and we slipped away with Ramos down to the landing.

Two boatmen were there squatting before a fire. One of them had a fighting cock tied by the leg. They were roasting river mussels in the coals. I wished them a prosperous new year. They flipped a coin to see who got our business.

"Yorito?"

"*Sí.*"

But I changed my mind when we were launched out into the river and I told the man to take us downstream, around the bend, to the foot of the bluff. We wouldn't have to walk so far. The old city of Likín would be directly above us. Yes, Rudy might well be up there observing the hippies. There seemed to be no point in taking notes on the end of the world, but he would probably feel the need to make some record of it. I was curious myself, and besides, I wanted to drink from the old spring again. I would press my face into the pool and open my eyes underwater and clarify my thoughts. It might help. For Doc everything came down to a cube. One night at Camp Pendleton I heard Colonel Raikes say that the key to it all was "frequent inspections." How right he was too. You had only to look at my unconscious crew to feel the force of that truth. But I had not yet worked out any such master principle of my own, to guide my steps. It wouldn't hurt to try the spring. I would gulp the water and clear my muddled head.

The man shut off his engine, and we could hear singing up there on the hilltop. We could see the red glow of a fire. It was an old song they were singing, something jolly like "Oh Susannah," only that wasn't it. I had expected wailing. The *cayuca*

828

slid into the sand and went aground. I knocked against a bush in getting out, and mosquitoes rose from the branches in a cloud like blackbirds. Ramos was trembling, keen. He must have thought we were on a pig hunt. One whiff from the musk gland of a peccary and he would be off like a shot. But not all dogs hunt by scent. The greyhound must catch sight of his quarry, just as I did, and the night was black here in Chiapas, or rather Guatemala. There was no moon. Monkeys were screaming back and forth at one another across the river. The lunatic monkeys knew something was up.

I led the way with my flashlight along the bank till we came to a gully that was cut by the runoff water from the spring. Then up we went, straight up the gully, grabbing at bushes and slipping on wet moss. The spring, little used now, was about halfway up the cliff, enclosed in a circular revetment of ancient masonry. I was afraid the hippies might have found it and fouled it in some way, but no, the water was clear, with a few leaves floating in it and some bugs skittering across the surface. I pushed the head of my plastic flashlight beneath the surface. At the bottom, farther away than it appeared, grains of sand tumbled about where a jet of water surged out of the earth. I couldn't fix the exact point. The source, the *ojo de agua*, the eye of water itself, was a mystery under the whirling sand. It was a small shifting turbulence, nothing more, a spirit.

We drank and then washed our faces, saying nothing. My dripping head was perhaps a little clearer than before. It was hard to say. My bad knee was a good deal worse for the climb. There was a smooth outcropping of rock here about the size and shape of a bus. We sat on the ledge and had a smoke.

Refugio said, "The boy is up there then? With the *tóxicos*?"

"I don't know. We'll see."

"I think he is dead."

"You may be right."

"The two *chiflados* killed him and threw his body into the river. All that laughing didn't fool me."

"They would have kept his equipment and his clothes."

"It was hidden. With their boat. They had a *barca* somewhere. Or a raft, a *balsa*. They won't need a motor to go back downstream to Yoro."

"No, they would have forgotten something. Some little something of Rudy's. I don't miss much when I'm looking hard."

"You will die out here, too, a fool, with no money in your pocket and no wife at home and no pretty little child of your own."

"Not me. I have my plans."

"*Qué va.* You don't have no plans."

"I have long-range plans that I never talk about."

"*Qué va. Poco probable.* . . . Do you know what I am doing, Jaime? I am praying for my baby. Sula was right. I should be with Manolo on his long drive to Yucatán and you take me out here on your foolish *paseo.*"

The *opresión* was on him. It was a terrible thought, that he might have to put up one of those little roadside crosses for his dead and mangled son.

"Your Manolito is all right. He's a better driver than you are. Manolo is in Mérida right now. He's in some game room playing a *futbolista* machine."

"I should have listened to her. Sula is never wrong. You must drag the Doctor out here, too, and he is old and sick."

"We'll have a quick look around the *ruinas.* If the boy is there we're done and if he's not there we're done. We'll go home."

He sighed. Not a word of concern about my truck. From here to the top, about 300 feet above the river, a flight of steps had been cut into the rock, still useful though overgrown and eroded. We were huffing and puffing as we came over the crest, two blowing men out of the night with guns and a dog. We appeared suddenly before a ring of hippies around a fire. There were open cans of food in the embers. A hobo jungle, you might think, if hoboes sang. They stopped singing and looked at us. Someone was always breaking in on their fun. In the heart of the Petén forest they still couldn't get away from the likes of me.

I saw other watchfires here and there in the clearing. The place was a campground. There were beach towels and little orange tents and coconut shells and a stalk of bananas and pickle jars and bread wrappers and water jugs and sleeping bags and colorful serapes and pitiful shelters made of plastic raincoats. There was a girl with lightning bugs in her hair. One brave boy had made it up here on aluminum crutches. He supported himself on those half-crutches called forearm canes.

Many others must have dropped out along the way. These were the hardy ones. There may have been a hundred people scattered about on the plateau but no more. Vincent had led me astray there. I was expecting I don't know what, a shrieking mob, the last hours of Gomorrah, a good deal of eye-rolling, but in fact the crowd was thin and listless, such as you might see at a track meet. Nothing of a ceremonial nature was going on. There was no apparent focus to the thing. No one seemed to be in charge. It was just one more herd of hippies milling around in a pasture. Had something gone wrong? Maybe the frolic was to start later.

A pasture, I call it, this long plaza or courtyard of the old city of Likín, which the people of Yorito kept cleared for their single milk cow to graze on. It was a rectangle bounded on the long sides by a series of mounds, with temples underneath the dirt and greenery. The Mayas had flattened the hilltop and built their City of Dawn here high above the jungle roof, where they could get a breeze now and then. This end of the plaza was open, overlooking the river, and at the far end there was a partially excavated pyramid, known as the *Castillo.* Most of the digging had been done there, at the pyramid complex. The grand staircase was exposed, leading to a shrine at the top, a stone box, and on top of that, capping the whole thing, was a decorative bit of stone fretwork, what they call a roof comb. No one was moving about on the *Castillo* stairway. It was odd. When travelers come upon a pyramid, they must climb it and crawl all over it and wave from the top.

I spoke a bit loud to the hippies. It was my experience that their attention wandered. "We're not here to bother you," I said. "We're not going to interfere with your—program. I'm looking for a friend. An emergency has come up at home. His wife is sick, and I know you'll want to help me. His name is Rudy. Can everybody hear me? Rudy Kurle is the name. From Pennsylvania. He's a big blond fellow in army gear. A brown army outfit and heavy boots. Does that ring a bell? You may have seen him speaking into a tape recorder. He carries a lot of stuff on his belt. How about it? If you've seen him, please tell me. You'll be doing him and his wife both a big favor."

Someone said in a very low voice, "He may have his reasons for staying away from home."

A Scandinavian girl with hairy legs said, "I am not even listening to you. Your words have no more significance to me than the buzzing of flies. I am no longer hearing all these dead words floating around in the air."

Not a bad policy on the whole. "Suit yourself," I said. "But we're not leaving here till we find him. I think he's around here somewhere. The sooner we find him the sooner we'll be gone."

The others had nothing at all to say to me. They weren't so much defiant as puzzled and annoyed. Tired too, no doubt, from their long trek. It was hopeless. I would need a bullhorn to get through to these people. I went about my old business of looking them over one by one. I put my light into the faces of those in the shadows. Some took this indignity better than others. I interrupted their feeding. I lifted the flaps of their little tents. We moved from campfire to campfire. Refugio walked behind me, grumbling. Ramos drew back and bared his teeth at those who tried to pet him. They took him for a Frisbee-catching pal, a great mistake. The girl with the lightning bugs followed me around too, saying the same thing over and over again.

"Share the wonder, bring a friend."

"I did bring one."

"Share the wonder, bring a friend."

"Most people wouldn't want bugs in their hair."

"Share the wonder, bring a friend."

The bugs were tied to her hair with thread, and they flashed on in ragged sequence with a cool green light. Refugio said we should have brought along something to sell. We could have coiled great long ropes of sausages around our necks and sold them here at monopoly prices. I agreed, we should have thought to bring sausages and a megaphone. The *arqueos* or some other looters had been here since my last visit. All the inscribed stelae had been uprooted and carried away, leaving only the blank ones. They looked like blank tombstones. They were memorials to nothing, or perhaps some daring artistic gesture.

The Yorito milk cow, of a stunted breed unknown to me, stood very still in a sunken place, a walled-in arena where the Maya once played a game with a rubber ball. She was ivory-colored with drooping ears and a pink deflated udder not much bigger than a goat udder. The weeds looked tough and wiry there in the ball court, but it was a quiet place to wait out the siege. All this vegetation and you could see her ribs. I wished I could have given her an armful of sweet alfalfa.

They weren't all young dopers at this *congreso*, as Refugio called it. A middle-aged man with bangs came up to me. He wore a baggy shirt with a dazzling floral pattern, and of course sandals. Feet are all the better for a good airing out, and I would be the last one to deny it, but I think these people had something more than ventilation in mind. They were down-right aggressive about displaying their feet to the world. The man came up to me, hesitant and polite, and asked if I might by any chance be *El Mago*.

"Who? No."

"No, I didn't think so. Excuse me. I didn't really expect *El Mago* to be armed, though they do say he is a complex and unpredictable brute. The thing is, I don't know what he looks like. He could very well be right here among us."

So, they were waiting for this *El Mago* fellow to appear. He, The Wizard, was overdue and there was growing fear that he might not show. Just who was he? What would he do? No one seemed to know. The only *El Mago* I knew was a very old man who lived in the town of Valladolid, if indeed he still lived. He was a famous *brujo*, a witch, who could read the future from the flopping throes of a decapitated turkey, and who was credited with forty-four sons out of a long series of wives and mistresses. The daughters went unnumbered. I knew of him, that is, from newspaper articles and photographs. I had never actually seen him give a reading. But that scrawny old bird could hardly be described as a complex brute, nor at his age would he be fit to make the hard journey to Likín. Unless they had lashed him to a chair and borne him in here on shoulder poles, with his old head lolling from side to side. I put nothing past them.

I wondered about their theory and what part *El Mago* would play and how they saw the end coming. Why gather at this

place? Why gather at all? Was there to be a spectacle or just
lights out? No wrath? I couldn't get a feel for the mechanics
of the thing or for the shape of it. I was curious but too proud
to show much interest. The line I took was one of indifference
—no lofty contempt, just that I couldn't be bothered. In fact
I was uneasy. These lost sheep knew nothing. I was pretty sure
of that. They simply wanted to be on stage for the dramatic
finish. It must all wind down with them and nobody else. The
thought of the world going on and on without them, much
as usual, and they forgotten, was unbearable. Nothing important was going to happen here. The burning light from heaven
might indeed fail one day, but not, I thought, tomorrow. And
yet I was uncomfortable. I didn't like meddling in such things.

Down the way from the ball court, a dead woman lay
stretched out on a striped blanket. Two girls were sitting there
fanning the body. The dead woman's name was Jan, I was relieved to hear, and not Tonya Barge. Then I saw that she was
probably too old anyway to be Vincent's sweetheart. One leg
of her shiny black slacks was cut off, exposing a black swelling
on her calf. Boots might or might not have helped. The snake
had struck her a few inches below the knee, a *palanca* I had
no doubt. By way of treatment someone had squeezed lime
juice over the wound and poked around in it with a knife—
a red-hot knife, the girls said. They didn't know the woman's
last name or where she was from. She wore a white blouse
and braided gold belt. The metallic strands gleamed under my
light. No watch, no finger rings, one silver bracelet. It was my
habit to note such things in case the description turned up on
a Blue Sheet. The girls said she had passed out at once from
the shock of the bite and never came around, never opened
her eyes again. They were fanning her with branches to keep
the flies off. The male fanners had already slipped away, if they
had ever been here. You couldn't count on men to stick with a
thankless job like that.

A gust of raindrops came and went. The lightning drew
closer. Sula had told me that you can only see a person's true
face in the glare of lightning. Refugio was disturbed by the
way these *congreso* people walked, or he pretended to be.
Youngsters should show more spirit, he said, more gaiety, *mas
alegría*. It was a shame the way they moped around. They

should stand up straight and carry themselves through life with a manly bearing—like Refugio, that is, who strode about like the Prince of Asturias. With that carriage and that air, he had no real need for elevated loafers. Now he dropped into a slouch and imitated the hippie movements. He went into a creeping shuffle and then did a kind of slow chicken walk. I was limping myself. The rain came back in a scattering of fat drops. The *congreso* people said various things to me.

"I have styes on my eyelids and ulcers on my tongue because I haven't been eating right."

"*El Mago* feeds on human hearts."

"Just what is your authority?"

"This is the landscape of my dreams."

"There are food thieves in this camp."

"*El Mago* is worth a hundred of you."

"They told me there was going to be a golden pavilion here with plenty of good food for everybody. They said you could pick grapes right off the trees."

"*El Mago* is waiting in his great house. You must know the right word before you can see him."

"It's early yet."

"Why don't you set your own house in order?"

"*El Mago* can see the hidden relation between things."

"I almost didn't come."

"I can't get anything on my radio but static."

"Touch *El Mago* and your hand will curl up and wither into a claw."

"When *El Mago* needs something he always finds it."

But there was no Rudy news and not much about the sun and nothing at all to the point. Some of these folk were pale and shaky, barely able to stand. These, the fasters, had eaten nothing for days, so as to make themselves lightheaded, the better to see visions. Only one of the entire lot had anything to say about the Maya, and he told me that they had invented soap and "wireless telegraphy."

Refugio said, "What is it they say? I can't hear. Do they speak well?"

"No, they don't. They make a poor showing there, too."

Art and Mike in one of their flights once claimed that, given some plague or holocaust, our little gang at Shep's In-Between

Club, an ordinary lot at best, was quite capable of reestablish-
ing Western civilization, over time, with the help of a Bible
and a dictionary and Simcoe's old broken set of encyclopedias.
They didn't say how much time. But could it all spring anew
from the crowd on this hilltop? I thought not. Better that a
band of guerillas out here in the woods should survive, or an
army patrol, with their camp women. Or a single lodge of the
Elks Club. An Elk culture. My knee was blazing. I vowed never
again to set foot outside Mérida.

Refugio turned up his hands. "*¿Listo?*"

"Yes, I've seen enough. Let's go."

All at once rain came sweeping across the plaza in dense curtains that quenched the campfires and raised clouds of steam.
There was a scramble for cover. In the hurrying confusion, I
thought I caught a glimpse of my hotel neighbors, Chuck and
Diane, if that was their names. In the lightning glare, I thought
I saw them running together hand in hand, and then they were
gone. Refugio and I ducked through a doorway into a narrow stone chamber. Ramos, too, and with each clap of thunder
he barked at the heavens. Chino would have tucked his tail. I
turned my light about to see if we had guests. I smelled sour
clothes. No, it was us. We reeked. On the back wall there was a
small black handprint and the words A KOBOLD FEB 1941. Old
Alma had been here, in this very room! Perhaps waiting out a
rain herself, or just getting away from Karl for a bit. She had
left her mark in the way of the Mayan architects, who sometimes signed their monumental projects with a red handprint.
*All that you see here is the work of this hand.* My flashlight filament was getting redder and weaker. I turned it off, and we
waited in darkness with the mosquitoes.

It was a black night again in the old city of Likín. Others had
found shelter across the way in cubbyholes like this one. Here
and there through the rainy blear, I could see feeble points of
candlelight. Then we did get a guest, a young man in dripping
jeans and a sailor's blue woolen jumper, who asked if we had
room for him. He had been running. We made way and he
came in breathing hard. His sleeve cuffs were folded back one
lap, and I almost ordered him to turn them down and button
them properly. When I was on gate duty at the Bremerton
Navy Yard, I made the sailors button their sleeves and square

away their caps, among other things. It was for their own good, a kindness really. We couldn't let them get jaunty. It was their great weakness in those outfits they wore. They liked to turn their cuffs back to show the golden dragons embroidered there, which meant they had served in the China Sea or some such thing. They hated us and we loved it. We cherished our power at Marine Barracks. Nobody could get to us. We even had our own bakery. I should have stayed there in the guard shack, imposing a petty bit of order on the world.

The boy wiped off his glasses, which were of the utopian communard model, with small round lenses and earpieces of the very thinnest wire. He had to raise his voice over the roar of the storm. "I got caught out there in the woods behind the big pyramid," he said. "It's really tough going out there without a machete. There must be a trail to the top, but I couldn't find it."

I said, "Why not go up the front way? The staircase is cleared."

"They won't let anybody on those steps. They'll run you off. They won't let you up there unless you know the right words."

"Who won't?"

"The two baldheaded guys. They pushed some people down earlier with their forked poles. It's like they own the place. I don't know who they are or what words they're talking about. You can take a bad fall down that thing."

"There are people up there now?"

"Yes, in that square chapel or whatever it is on top."

"How many?"

"I'm not sure. They have a goat. All I've seen is the goat and the two bald thugs, but there are some others moving around inside. *El Mago* himself could be in there."

He was a sensible kid and you could talk to him. Here was a piece of news. Yes, now I could make out a yellow light up there on top of the *Castillo*. Of course, that's where Rudy would be, at the heart of it all, at the citadel, taking useless measurements and perhaps chatting with the temple bullies. I would have to drag my inflamed knee all the way to the top, step by step. We waited. Rain this hard couldn't last. On summer afternoons we got these pounding showers in Mérida, and in five minutes the sun was shining again. And when it didn't rain, Fausto would run a hose on the sidewalk and let the water pool up in hollow places so the birds and the town dogs could get a drink.

We shared our dank closet with mosquitoes. They had done their worst to Refugio and me years ago, infecting us for life with malaria and dengue bugs, all the various fever bugs they carried. But in their numbers here and their agitated state, these big black Petén *bichos* were driving us crazy. They had only one raving thought and that was to get at our blood. They swarmed in our eyes and clogged our nostrils and our ears and finally drove us out into the rain.

Refugio thought we were making for Yorito, and I had to grab his soaked and flapping shirttail. "No! Up there! The *templo*! We'll have to check it out!"

"You say we are done! *¡Término!*"

"We've come this far! We can't get any wetter! A quick look and we're done!"

The pyramid was tilted slightly, with water coursing down one side of the staircase in a hundred little cataracts. The thing had not been designed for easy ascent, certainly not for the Maya themselves, who stood five feet high at most. The pitch was too steep, the stone risers too high, and the stone treads too narrow. You couldn't get into a comfortable stride no matter how long your legs or how sound your knees. We struck off up the higher side, away from the falling water. The incline must have been close to sixty degrees, and the wet lichen on the stone was slippery. It was like climbing a ladder without using your hands. We could have tacked, gone up in prudent zigzag fashion, but no, it was straight up to the top for us in one go, with Refugio leading the way. He was angry. I hobbled along behind using my old Smith shotgun as a support stick. Ramos followed me, advancing in awkward hops, until, just short of the crest, he stopped and froze in place, spooked, like a frightened housecat up a tree. His hair, wet and heavy though it was, stuck up in a spiky ruff around his neck from all the lightning in the air.

Let him wait there and ponder the glyphs carved on the riser faces. We could pick him up on the way down. I knew, looking at those strange symbols, that Doc could no more read them than Ramos could. Probably he would "interpret" them, not translate them. But that was all right with me, he was still a formidable man and in his own way a great man.

I knew too, suddenly, and so late, that we were dealing here with Big Dan and his people. This was the sunrise city, Likín, the City of Dawn. And now the two bald boys. But my poor head was so muddled that I didn't work it out until that moment on the pyramid steps. It came to me all at once. I stopped dead in my tracks and took off my hat in this driving rain and offered up a prayer of my own. I asked God to let me find the little girl, LaJoye Mishell Teeter, promising not to let her out of my hands this time. I promised not to take any money for her recovery. The wind was fierce up here above the forest canopy. The rain came sideways. Down there in the treetops the monkeys must have been hanging on for their lives.

The little temple was oblong rather than square, and it took up the entire summit platform, except for a narrow bit of deck space on each side. There was a single doorway, or so I thought, in the front. A male figure stood there in the opening with a faint light behind him. I could smell the burning wax of candles.

He didn't see us until we had stepped up onto the platform, and then he gave a start. "Hey, that's far enough!" He came forward holding a six-foot length of trimmed sapling that was forked at the slender end. "Hold it right there! Let's have the words! Do you know the words?"

I put my light on him. There were colored stripes painted front to back across his shaved head. He was one of Dan's Jumping Jacks.

"The password tonight is L. C. Smith," I said.

"What?"

"Put that pole down and get out of the way. I don't want to hear any more out of you."

He must have seen the shotgun leveled at him, and still he made a lunge. He came at us like a pole vaulter, with the pole held low. Refugio was a small barrel of a man standing on two stumpy and bowed legs, but he was fast on those legs. He sidestepped and grabbed the middle of the sapling and jerked the boy off his feet, and then with a kick sent him tumbling down the stairway. The boy didn't cry out. He fell on his back with a grunt and was gone, just like that. Ramos yelped down below. He came hopping up to join us, barking away, all fight again now, as though he had stopped back there only to take a leak or look at an ant. Now he was Ramos again of the 1st War Dog Platoon.

I moved fast on the others, who had crowded into the doorway to watch. "Back inside! Let's go!" I wanted to get in there out of the night so they could all see the gun. No need for any more trouble. It was a smoky, high-vaulted room. I drove them into a corner and made them sit. Their faces too were painted with vertical stripes. They looked sick and hungry. Each one held a sprig of something green. But I had bagged only five Jumping Jacks and these were the lesser, dimmer ones. Dan wasn't here, nor was LaJoye Mishell Teeter, nor the big woman, Beany Girl, nor the second skinhead. There was no goat. Rudy Kurle wasn't here either.

"Where is Dan?" I said. "Listen to me now. I don't have time to fool around with you people. Where is the little girl you call Red? Where is Dan?"

"*El Mago* is biding his time."

"His knife is keen and yet it gives life."

"He is one set apart. He is no longer Dan."

"*El Mago* is our father. You will never enjoy his favor and intimacy."

"He used to give us doughnuts sometimes when he was Dan."

They went into their group hum and said nothing more. I had given them time to recover. I should have struck faster and harder. I should have knocked one of them down right away and got in his face. But the moment had passed, and to compound my foolishness I said, "Dan is the false *El Mago*. I was sent here to tell you that Dan is a false teacher. Look at me when I'm talking to you! Can you at least understand what I'm saying?" All a waste of breath. They sat there droning away with their mandrill faces cast down. Their hymn had one disagreeable note and no words. They had tuned me out. Old Alma had a word for this. It was *urdummheit*, primitive stupidity, which she used freely with servants, and with me as well when I let the wheels of her chair drop down hard off a curb. *Urdummheit!*

"Such people!" Refugio kept saying. "What a mess! . . . *¡Qué gente! ¡Qué embrollo!*" He had his .45 out and the hammer was pulled back. Mine was cocked too. L. C. Smith was known for his "hammerless" shotguns (and for his typewriters, later to be called Smith-Corona), but this old fowling piece had two big upright S-curved hammers like they don't make anymore, and when drawn all the way back under tension, they gave you some sense of the detonation to come.

A few candles burned in wall niches. At this end of the room there was a small campfire on the floor, with the flames jumping and falling. The gusts of air should have told me there was another big opening somewhere. This was the east end, where two wall slits in the shape of a T caught the first rays of the morning sun. Those dawn rays were said to light up the shrine for an instant in some striking way. I had never taken the trouble to see this flare effect for myself, perhaps a mistake, though such sights are often disappointing. A tau-window, it was called. Now a dead toad was stuffed there at the intersection of the slits, with his belly cut open and a length of red yarn tied around his neck in a bow. I pulled the bloody slimy thing out of the crevice and flung it into the lap of a Jumping Jack. He didn't move. The girl next to him was twisting something in her hands, a greasy rag. She pressed it to her face and kissed it and moaned. It was Dan's old head covering, the knotted blue bandanna, in decayed tatters. I noticed too that she and the others had smears of blood around their lips. They were off doughnuts now and on toad blood.

"Here's our rathole," said Refugio, at the far end. "This is the way he left, all right. You can see. But why should the boy run from you?" He had found the other opening behind a partition wall. There were two walls, with a wide space between them, and a passage, and the outer wall was split from top to bottom. The crack had spread and eroded into a hole at floor level. It was a bolthole big enough even for Dan to crawl through.

"No, it's not the boy," I said. "We're not looking for the boy now. We're looking for a dangerous fat man and a little girl." I snatched the rotten bandanna from the hippie girl's hands and took Ramos by the scruff of the neck and rubbed his nose around in it and spoke soft and unusual words to him. I could always talk to dogs, certain dogs, if not to people very well. It was a gift; the words just came to me.

We made a quick circuit around the outside deck and then struck off down the backslope. This side was uncleared but not nearly as steep. There were trees and earth and tangled undergrowth and rushing water madly seeking an ever lower place. Ramos was in the lead, taking us below and off to the right. He knew what was wanted, and even with the rain there was still a good smelly trail to follow. That bandanna was strong, and Dan himself would be pretty ripe by now. There was the goat, too. Refugio said, "What a night!" I told him to be careful.

Our path was littered with yellow blossoms which the rain had beaten off the *palo blanco* trees. I lost my hat in the vines. Down to our right there was a complex of structures, still half buried, called the acropolis, though it was by no means the high point of the place. It was a maze of galleries and chambers, most of them roofless shells, set at different levels on terraces. We broke out of the woods onto the topmost terrace, and Ramos was off at a lope and into the maze. We lost sight of him. We had to follow his barking through twists and turns, up and down. Diggers had been here recently. They had cleared one corridor and put up marker ribbons along the way. Strange looters though, to leave the artworks behind. I saw a fine stucco mask of the long-nosed rain god, with the fragile nose intact, a rare find. There were wooden door lintels, untouched. That carved sapodilla wood had endured tropical heat, rain, and insects for a thousand years, and it was still in place and still bearing a load. Iron would have crumbled away centuries ago.

We passed through a small forest of derelict stone columns, supporting nothing, and then we were suddenly out in the open once more on a bare terrace. It was good to get on level ground again. I thought we would catch up with Dan somewhere in the woods, crashing through the brush, but there he was standing in the rain at the very edge of the terrace, he and three others and a dead goat. A kerosene lantern burned at their feet. Ramos was running about before them in a fury. The second baldheaded boy was keeping him at bay with a forked pole.

I didn't see the tall woman. Dan wore a white headband and a long white or tan smock over his old outfit, nothing very priestly, more like something from the early days of motoring. There were dark splotches down the front. The skinhead made a swipe at us with his sapling, and we stopped just outside his range. I had never known anyone so crazy that he couldn't understand a 12-gauge shotgun, and here we had run into two of them in one night, or three. They had courage. Raindrops sizzled on the hot lantern. I could see the dead goat, a brown and white billy goat, with a red string around his neck and the black lump beside him that had been his heart. Dan had just cut his heart out. It was still bleeding—I won't say smoking.

Big Dan was lifting one foot and then the other about an inch off the ground. He was rocking from side to side like an old bull elephant. He had a crude knife of chipped flint or obsidian in one hand. In the other he held a lead rope loosely at his side, with LaJoye Mishell Teeter and a small Mexican boy in tow. The two children were bound wrist to wrist with baling wire, and the rope was tied to the wire. The girl now wore an outsize football jersey that drooped below her knees. She was number 34, a little mite of a fullback. A bow of red yarn was tied at her throat. The Mexican boy had one too. I thought at first that his face was painted. The face paint on the others, if any, had washed away. The boy was about six years old and he was in a torn white shirt and some pathetic little blue trousers. They were dress trousers with cuffs and creases. Dan must have grabbed him on a Sunday.

I said, "What's all this about the sun, Dan?"

"Who is that? Where is Harvey? What do you want with me?"

"We came for the kids. Tell your boy to put the pole down."

"Who gave you permission to approach me? You don't belong here."

"No, we don't. So we'll just take the kids and be on our way. I want you to drop that rope and move away from them. Okay? None of your crap now. Just do what I say and we'll get this over with."

"You can't interfere with me in my own city. It wasn't easy getting here at the appointed time. You don't know the kind of people I've had to work with. Even *El Mago* let me down."

"Yes, but it's all over now, Dan. Those folks out there want their money back. I told them you were a fake."

"This is the City of Dawn. You don't have no business here."

"Our business won't take long."

"Wait. I know that stupid sharecropper voice. You're the one who broke my staff. And my car windows. How did you get here? Beany Girl had a disturbing dream about you."

"I don't want to hear about your dreams."

"A prophetic dream. 'We're not through with Curtis yet.' That's what she said. I didn't believe her. All right. A sign then. But that's all you are. You can't touch me. You don't have no power over the *Balam*. Do you know who I am? I have three yards of fine linen wrapped around my head."

"No, we're not going to talk about your wrappings. You can save that stuff for somebody else."

"Where is Harvey? Who is that with you?"

"He's a policeman from Guatemala City. He has some questions for you. Let go of the rope now and step aside. And you better get your boy here under control pretty fast. The other one is dead. Harvey is dead and you better get this loco son of a bitch out of my way before you lose him too."

Dan looked bad. There were inflamed swellings on his face and knots on the side of his head the size of hickory nuts. The bridge of his nose was bruised and puffy, perhaps broken. One ear was flopped over at the top with the cartilage crushed. All this from the police beating, I supposed, but it was more than that. I think he had been fasting. He was still a big round man, the belly undiminished, but his face had gone slack. There were sagging yellow pouches under his eyes like folds of chicken fat. The mosquitoes had been at him too. He was breathing hard through his mouth, gasping. Two or three buttons were missing from the smock, and I could see a bit of his hairy white belly and the expando waistband of his pajamas.

Refugio said, "What a fine gringo circus this is!" I touched his arm, the one holding the pistol. "Don't spook the big one," I said. "Keep your eye on the boy with the pole."

"If he strikes Ramos I will choot him."

"No, not until we have the *niños*."

There was a drop of about forty feet behind them, and I didn't know what Dan might do with that demon in him.

Would he go over the side and take the children with him? Just how crazy was he? Then there was the knife, a stubby double-edged thing. No Mayan priest had ever used it to tear open a human breast. It was a cheap souvenir letter-opener from a curio shop but no less a sharp ripper for that. I put my light on the Mexican boy and spoke to him in Spanish, with a bit of English for Dan's benefit. "Don't worry son. Dan has thought this over and he's going to let you go. It's all he can do. He's not dumb. Everything will be all right. Can you tell me your name?" He was crying and too terrified to speak. I could see now that the little fellow had *mal del pinto*, a skin disease that left pink and blue patches on his face, like the markings you see on piebald Negroes back home. The rain was letting up. I spoke to the girl. "LaJoye Mishell? I know your name and I came here to see you. I have a cold Coca-Cola here for you. Can you just step over here a minute? You and the boy. Come on, the dog won't hurt you. He does just what we say. His name is Ramos. Come on, Dan is all finished with you now." She didn't respond at all. Wet strands of hair lay stuck across her face.

Dan jerked the rope tight and pulled the two small bodies up against him. He said, "My offerings are blemished, as you see. A spotted toad and a spotted goat and a spotted boy and a speckled girl with vile red hair. It was the best I could do. You don't know how hard it's been. Finding the correct path. People like you can't never understand anything. I had to take the hard road. I could have been a famous musician. I could have cut an album and rocketed to stardom and won awards on TV if it wasn't for people like you controlling everything."

Now I was the master sharecropper in control of things. There was nothing else left to do. I put the shotgun to my shoulder. "You're all done now anyway, Dan."

"Why do you call me that? Dan died long ago. There is no more Dan. Some call me *El Mago* but my true name is *Balam Akab*. I am the Jaguar of the Night."

"No, I tell you we're not going to have any more of that. Here's how it is. We're all wet and tired and hungry. We're a long way from home. You're not thinking straight. Now listen to what I'm saying. I won't say it again. Turn loose of that rope or I'm going to send you back to the Gulf of Molo."

His voice changed a bit. He stopped being crazy for just a moment. "All right then. Take the boy and go. He's no good to me anyway. I can't let you have Red. We've come too far. She is prepared. I have my instructions. And now I have the final sign. Which is you. I have my work to finish here on this rainswept promontory. Even you can understand that, Curtis."

"No, I can't."

"I deny that you have any power over me."

*Rainswept promontory. Blemished offerings. Rocketed to stardom.* This was what came of reading a lot of books and magazines in prison. The tireless baldheaded boy irritated me with his jabbing and dancing about. Ramos had had enough, too, and he made a dash under the swinging pole and went for a leg. The boy kicked him. Dan tried to change hands for some reason, switching the knife and rope about, to get the knife into his right hand, I think, for a quick thrust at the girl. Refugio fired once at the skinhead and killed him. I let go of both barrels at Dan. There were two sheets of flame and his headband and the top of his head went away. The girl squealed. I gave Dan both barrels up high of No. 2 shot, goose shot, which scalped him and blinded him and shattered his teeth and all but severed his thick neck. He was a dead man on his feet. The knife slipped from his fingers. His knees buckled and he fell backwards over the side, still holding the rope with a feeble grip. I went for the *niños*, slipping on the wet stone, knocking the lantern over and grabbing at the wire that joined their wrists. They were both howling as I dragged them back from the edge.

Then something struck me across the back, not very hard. It was the other skinhead, the one we thought was dead. It was the faithful Harvey, all crippled up, come back from his long tumble. I couldn't believe it. He held a short stick in one hand and beat at me with it and spit blood on me. The other arm hung broken and useless. The dome of his head was bleeding. Refugio shot him twice. Harvey was just as tough as whitleather but he could take no more. He dropped the stick and broke away in a stumbling run. Ramos was right behind him, and then Refugio, who fired again. The boy had at least two .45 *balas* in him—they don't make handgun balls any bigger—and he was still on his feet when I saw him last.

"Let him go!" I called out. "That's enough! We don't have time for that! Get Ramos back here!" One time you smash a bug with no mercy. Another time you find one helpless on his back with his legs flailing the air, and you flip him over and let him go on his way. The struggle that touches the heart. Refugio rightly paid no attention to me. I broke the breech of my gun and re-loaded quickly out of habit. The girl wanted to know where her Coke was. I tore the red string from her neck and the one from the boy's neck.

The thing now was to get back across the river, out of Guatemala and into Mexico. It wasn't such a serious matter as all that, one gringo killing another in Latin America, and when the dead one needed killing to boot. Down here too you could always plead that you had acted from motives of honor. I could say that the *cabrón* had insulted me. But sorting out the mess would be a long and expensive business, and I wanted to be many miles away in another country when the military police came, if they came.

Not far off in the darkness I heard two more booming shots, the *golpes de gracia*. Ramos came back and ran around in mad circles, eager for more of this sport. Then here was Refugio shouting in my face. "You can't stop in the middle of a bloody *fregado* like this! You have to finish it off!"

"All right! It's done now!"

"You have to finish it! Ramos knows that much! In the name of God! What's wrong with you!"

"You're right. But we're wasting time! Let's go!"

"You can't just stop in the middle of a stinking business like this!"

"I said all right! Can't you hear! But now we're done!"

"So now you say it! Now you say we're done!"

"Yes, I say we're done! Does that suit you! *Término!*"

We were yelling at each other face to face, and I was never one to do that much, even when provoked.

# XV

T HE MEXICAN boy was so weak from hunger that he could barely walk. Refugio carried him down the hill on his back. Not a single light burned in Yorito. The rain came back in a soft drizzle, and I had the devil of a time rousting out two boatmen from their dry hammocks. I had to pay through the nose for this rainy night emergency service. It was no time for haggling. We would need two *cayucas* to carry this growing flock of mine downstream to the railroad bridge near Tenosique. There we could flag a train to Mérida.

All four of us made the crossing to Yoro in the lead boat. The river was up. Our skipper wore a knitted cap pulled down over his ears to keep the malignant *aires* out of his head. LaJoye Mishell told me that she had been given nothing to eat for two days. I fell to muttering and then realized that Refugio was speaking to me.

"Who was that *hipopótamo*? Who was that big lop-eared *pagano*?"

"His name was Dan. That's all I know. Some wandering *cabrón*. He tampered with my truck once at Tuxpan. A jailbird, I think. Some *preso* from the States."

"But all the same a *mago*? He could cast spells?"

"Just on certain people. Not on us."

"What was it all about?"

"I don't know. But we'll keep it to ourselves. The less said about this the better."

"His neck was bloated with poison."

"Yes."

"Did you see his breath? It was green."

"I didn't notice that."

"The two boys were drugged."

"No, I don't think so."

"Yes, a pair of *tóxicos*. Didn't you see their ugly naked heads? Like baby heads! Not a natural thing! It was dope that turned them into beasts! And not one but two! Who would expect to see two of them!"

"Harvey was the hard one. That first one who came back."

"But the dead goat. What was that for?"

"I don't know. Some *pagano* stuff about blood."

"Ay, then they get all they want, no? We show them plenty of blood! Maybe they get just a little more *sangre* than they want! We teach those animals some Mexican manners, no?"

I told the boatmen to keep their engines running, and we left them at the landing with the props churning the muddy water. The widow woman's *ramada* had collapsed into a heap of sticks and fronds. Her morning glories had been stripped clean by the storm and her fine *jitomate* plants battered down in the mud. Yoro was if anything darker than Yorito. We found our people and the stragglers huddled together in a storage shed behind the big fuel tank. Vincent was grumbling about the fleas. The dirt floor was infested with them. I had to wake Doc and Gail. She thought the little Mexican boy, Serafín, thirty-two inches high, was Rudy Kurle. "You found him!" she said.

"No, but we're leaving anyway. Where's the food sack? Let's get a move on."

Only a few tortillas were left, curled leather flaps now. The two children chewed on them greedily and ate them without salt. I assured Vincent that Tonya Barge was fine, not really knowing. "She'll be back by daylight. They'll all be back. The show was a bust. It was a complete washout." He said he wished now he had taken his chances with the storm rather than suffer here in this nest of fleas. Doc advised him to eat brewer's yeast and plenty of it. "It comes out in your sweat, don't you see, and repels them." I promised Vincent that his sweetheart would appear very soon out of the mist, and I left him there with my knotted sock sulfur bomb and my earnest good wishes.

So now there were seven of us in two *cayucas*, not counting the boatmen—Doc, Gail, Refugio, me, the two children, and Ramos, and we were off on another night ride in these mahogany dugouts. We could have used some name tags. Doc asked why we were traveling in the rain and when would we reach Likín.

"We've already been to Likín," I said. "We're going home now. We're leaving this garden."

"But I wanted to show Gail how the sun strikes the tau-cross window. The radiance."

"We'll do that another time."

"But she wants to see the House of the Consecrated Bats and the hieroglyphic stairway. She is particularly interested in that. I promised to show her how easily you can read the dynastic information with my key. How it all flows down in a connected way in columns of twos."

"Maybe another time. We're going home now."

"You won't give us time to see anything! All these boats! You're just a terrible person to travel with, Jimmy! All this mindless movement! It's a sickness with you! I think you positively enjoy driving helpless people about!"

We spoke in darkness above the engine noise, our faces unreadable. I explained that we had to get in ahead of the hippie brigade, who would be departing now and taking all the boats. Then there were the two children. They were homesick runaways who had been traveling with the hippies, and I knew that he, Doc, would want them restored to their families without delay. He said nothing more. I let it go at that.

LaJoye Mishell didn't know where she was or where she had been. Her lips were cracked and her skin was peeling and her arms and legs were criss-crossed with red scratches. She was numb. It was all the same to her whether Dan cut her heart out or she went back to Perry, Florida. The boy could tell us little more than his name, Serafín. Mostly he slept. Dan had picked him up, the girl told me, in a city with a long main street that led to a pretty little seaside park. The Mexican port town of Chetumál was my guess. She said it was later when the big woman, Beany Girl, left them, deserted the Jumping Jacks, she didn't know why, at an island town on a clear green lake. That could only have been Flores, in Lake Petén Itzá in Guatemala.

The storm had passed, but the river was still choppy. These *cayuca* boys had only one speed and that was flat out, which suited me. We were well sprayed. As the morning light came, I saw sparklets of gummy blood stuck to the hairs on my arms, from Dan's face, and from Harvey, who had spit blood on me. I sloshed my arms about in the rushing water and washed my face too for good measure. But you can't get those stains out of a cotton shirt. There was no fog on this first day of the new year. It was a day like other days. The sun came up full and warm. The greater light that rules the day. It would never scorch Dan again or dazzle his eyes. Wrong about so many things, he did get the terminal day right. Jan, too, and Harvey, and the other hairless thug. For them it was truly the end of this world.

Yes, a strange business back there on that high terrace, and over so fast too. Shotgun blast or not at close range, I was still surprised at how fast and clean Dan had gone down. It was like dropping a Cape buffalo in his tracks at one go. I wasn't used to seeing my will so little resisted, having been in sales for so long. We passed more ruins and a village here and there, but they were all on the Guatemala side.

Everyone was hungry. Doc said, "Now you won't even let us eat!" I didn't permit a stop until we came to a settlement called Punta de Arenas, or Sandy Point, on the Mexico shore. It was a smaller Yorito, a Yoritito, an old *chiclero* camp, with the shacks now occupied by a few fishermen and squatters. In the woods behind it there was a minor ruin of four or five mounds, well picked over and too small even to have a name.

The skippers nosed the boats in around a jam of floating trees, brought downstream by the high water and stuck here at the point with a lot of dirty foam. The resident fishermen were at breakfast and made a hospitable fuss over us. There is always room for unexpected guests at a Mexican feed. We sat on a log and joined them for black coffee and some rice with scraps of pork mixed in, and peppers on the side. No fish. They trafficked in fish the way I trafficked in art. It was for other people. All the talk was about the storm, the big *tronada*, so unseasonable. The trees here were still dripping. Doc asked if they had come across any writings of the old ones, but they couldn't understand a word he said. Refugio asked if any *ídolos* had been turned up lately from the mounds here. They laughed. "No, no, no. *No hay nada aquí.*" *There ain't nothing here.* They had only three coffee cups, and we passed them back and forth. An old man, too old to work, just hanging around now, showed us he could still crack nuts with his teeth.

Gail bathed the kids in the backwater and scraped up some clean clothes for them, shabby adult garments but dry enough. She found a jar of yellow salve in the camp and rubbed it on their sores. Poor little LaJoye Mishell had taken the worst of it. Her scalp was spotted with scabs where Dan had pecked her with his stick when she displeased him. She couldn't learn how to answer him properly. Whatever she said was wrong.

I could hardly keep my eyes open. This was the green and wet part of Mexico, and I liked it and this place in particular, Sandy Point. I liked the old man and the bushes covered with white blossoms like snow and the way the clearing opened up to the sky, some happy combination of things. I marked it down in my head as a good place to come back to for an extended stay. But then I liked the brown parts of Mexico, too, and I had marked down so many places, never to see them again. Refugio shook me awake and said we had best not linger here. He had just been told there was a soldier prowling about. The big *soldado* had come down the river a few days ago, a lone passenger in a *cayuca*. "They say he is a big clean fellow in fine boots with many badges on his fine uniform." An officer then. He would want to see our papers. He would be curious. What was our business here on the *frontera*? We were an odd enough party, worthy of a report, and he would remember our guns and our faces if not our names. It was indeed time to leave this sandy hook.

Refugio rounded up the crew. Doc was no longer speaking to me. We were already in the boats when the lone *soldado* appeared. It was Rudy Kurle in his military rig. I hadn't even bothered to ask about him here. He and three local boys came out of the woods with a plastic dishpan full of dark honey, all clotted up with leaves and sticks and dead bees. They had robbed a bee tree. Rudy was chewing on a sticky comb. A gleaming strand of honey hung from his chin and swayed. Something new was attached to his belt. I thought I was familiar with all his field gear, but the pedometer was new to me.

"Hey, Burns!" he said. "Is that you? What in the world are you doing here? Look! Do you know what this is? Nature's most perfect food! A field expedient! Living off the land!"

"I've been looking all over for you, Rudy."

"Yeah, why?"

"You've had everybody out beating the bushes for you."

"What for? You should see how these little guys can climb. They don't speak a word of English."

"You've put a lot of people to a lot of trouble. Did you know that? Why did you have to sneak off like that from Ektún? Can you tell me what you're doing here?"

"I'm here for an international conference if it's any of your business, which I doubt. Now I'll ask you a question. Do you have any idea of where you are?"

"Yes, I do."

He laughed. "I mean where you really are. Right back there, Burns, is the site of an ancient city that you never heard of, known in our modern language as the Inaccessible City of Dawn. I've had it all to myself. There's not much to see, you think, and then you realize that this is just the tip of an extensive conurbation. It goes back for miles in the jungle. Other people will be coming along soon, but I can't discuss that. I can't talk about our agenda. I can tell you that a compass needle does some very crazy things here. Mine won't even move. There's a powerful magnetic force field here and it's highly localized. It's an entry window. You've always underestimated me, Burns. You never dreamed that I would find an entry window all on my own. Did you know I was the first one to arrive? But I think now I may have gotten the day wrong."

"All right, get your stuff together. We're going downstream to catch a train. We're going back to Mérida."

"Oh, no. The other delegates will be along soon. I've already made a rough map of the central court, what I am calling the Promenade, and I've dug two latrines. A lot of these conference chumps won't know the first thing about field sanitation. Right now I'm trying to clear some separated areas so we can have several workshops going on at once. It's the hardest work I've ever done in my life. The brush is too wet and green to burn. We killed two snakes just this morning."

"Nobody's coming, Rudy. They called it off. This is the wrong place anyway."

He finished off the honeycomb and licked his fingers. There were bee stings on his face. "Oh? Is that a fact? And just how would you know?"

"The City of Dawn is a long way upstream on the other side of the river. You got the day right but you came down too far and you're in the wrong country on top of that."

"How would you know? Who invited you?"

"We just came from there. Ask any of these people. It's all over. Your conference got rained out."

"You're not a trained observer."

"No, but I could see that much. I was there."

"It's odd how you keep turning up. Anyway I'm not going downstream. I left my trailer and my Checker Marathon back at Ektún."

"Your car is in Mérida. There's nobody at Ektún. They're all gone. Now get your things and let's go. Louise is worried about you."

"Louise sent you out here?"

"She thought you were lost."

"Me lost?"

"Yes."

"It's funny how she keeps running to you with every little thing. You never even went to college. What's that on your head? Who are all those people with you?"

They were prisoners. I was dealing with prisoners, and here was one more. All I could think of was to keep my head count straight and get them back to the brig intact and sign them over to the turnkey and be done with them. As for my head-gear, it was one of Doc's gift handkerchiefs with the corners knotted, a skullcap, a Dan cap.

Finally I got Rudy into the boat, after telling him about the shriveled corpse at Palenque. It was a mystery. I could make nothing of the thing and the police too were baffled. My friend Refugio believed it to be a kind of woodland elf, or in any case something less than human, or more. He, Rudy, might want to investigate the matter before other writers got wind of it, or before the remains were buried. I couldn't promise anything. This might or might not be a quality contact. No wreckage was found near the body, as far as I knew, no melted fragments of an unknown alloy. But it seemed worth looking into, a little man with spindly limbs and yellow eyes and a great swelling globe of a head. I exaggerated the size of the head. Refugio confirmed my story, showing with his hands just how wide the creature's feet were. He confirmed too that the yellow car was in Mérida. He himself had driven it there.

How about it then? The body was there at Palenque to be claimed. Rudy only half believed us, and the big feet weren't a selling point, as space aliens were known to be the daintiest of steppers. And yet he couldn't take a chance. There might be something in this, and if so he would have to move fast. Other writers were pigs, to be sure, but worse, there were government agents to fear, so efficient in their neat business suits and gray Plymouths. They would spirit the body away to a hangar at some remote air base and then deny all knowledge of it with their fixed smiles.

On the way back he made a nuisance of himself in the boat with his calisthenics. He flapped his arms and shook his fingers and twisted his head about and bicycled his legs up in the air. From now on I would work alone and travel alone. Once again I made that vow. He showed me some shiny black pebbles, vitrified, he said, from exposure to extremely high temperatures, as from rocket exhaust gases. I asked him how many miles he had registered on his pedometer. He said it had stopped working, as had the drive gear in his tape recorder. Humidity and rust and dirt, I suggested, but he said no, it was the magnetic blast that had jammed so much of his equipment. And somewhere up the river he had lost his signalling mirror and his giant naval binoculars.

Rudy knew about the City of Dawn but not about the death of the sun. He thought he was coming to a high-level UFO convention at a reported landing site. He wouldn't tell me how he knew about it or who was behind it, and I suspected he really didn't know. Some of the people at Likín thought the event had to do with seed crystals or pyramid power or harmonic solar resonance, and for a few it was the end of the Mayan calendar, the end of the fifth creation, the end of time. Others were ignorant of the last-days theme and saw it as nothing more than a hippie festival in the jungle. They had come, one and all, I gathered, on the strength of rumor. Such information as they had about *El Mago* appeared to be hearsay too. It was just something going around, a buzz of magical words in the air, of big doings on the Usumacinta.

For Dan it was to be a blood ceremony to appease the sun or something along that line, but then it seemed Dan was not the principal either. There was another *El Mago* behind him, according to LaJoye Mishell. She had never seen the other man but said she had heard Dan speaking to him on the telephone,

or pretending to speak to someone. But all that came later, the
*El Mago* business. They had been knocking around in Texas
and New Mexico, these Jumping Jacks, stealing cars and running over dogs and peeping in windows at night and humming
together. Then one day Dan told them that the correct path
led through the deserts of Mexico. There they would clarify
their thoughts. He said he had received an urgent long distance telephone call from the Gulf of Molo, with orders to go
directly to Mexico and seek out a particular white goat. They
made their way south, and it was at a hippie campground near
a tropical river town (Tuxpan, perhaps) that they first heard of
*El Mago*. There was something written about him in a paper
or magazine that they were passing around, and all the hippies
were talking about him. Dan became excited and said that he
was now being directed by this *El Mago*. He had new orders.
They were to proceed without delay to a coastal town called
Progreso, where *El Mago* would meet them and lead them to a
place called the City of Dawn. So they went to Yucatán. Along
the way Dan made telephone calls, to this same *El Mago*, he
claimed. But *El Mago* didn't show on the beach at Progreso.
They waited and waited. Someone stole their belongings, their
plastic garbage bags. Dan then declared that he himself was
*El Mago*, it had come to him in a dream. He himself would
lead them to the City of Dawn with three yards of fine linen
wrapped around his head. They would live there for a time under the roots of a giant tree called Ogon or Agon, with a white
goat. It would be a time of fasting and purification. Then he
would complete his historic mission.

   Well and good, but *was* there another *El Mago*? Who?
Where? Had Dan killed him? LaJoye Mishell thought so. She
said Beany Girl had dropped hints to that effect, this being
their tiresome way of communicating. The Jumping Jacks
didn't go in much for plain talk, not even among themselves.
But LaJoye Mishell couldn't be sure and she admitted that
Big Dan may simply have broken with his master and struck
off on his own. If in fact there were a master. What was I to
make of that truly long distance call from the Gulf of Molo?
Who was at the other end? A diabolist? A joker? An insane
alcoholic mother? Anyone at all? It was hard to know how
much of the story to credit. I got it from a dazed little girl

who thought she was traveling with a rock and roll band for the first few days after the Jumping Jacks picked her up. That was what she yearned for, a life on the road with rock musicians, though she had no wish to sing herself or otherwise make music. She just wanted to live with them and do their laundry and fetch and carry for them and pick bits of trash out of their hair, and so she ran away from home and jumped into the first old car she could find that was packed to the roof with hoodlums.

# XVI

IT WAS the first time Ramos had ever ridden on a train. Emmett was dead when we got back, and Alma was in the hospital. Art and Mike and Coney and McNeese had been turned out of their rooms by Señora Limón, their landlady, who said she was tired of looking at their faces. They had stayed on too long. She wanted to paint her walls a bright new color and put down some new linoleum with new geometric patterns and get an altogether fresh set of roomers to go with the other improvements. It was a reverse revolution, with the dictator kicking the people out. Louise had seen Wade Watson off on a flight to the States, or so she said. Eli and Mr. Nordstrom had been deported. The city of Mérida had swung big new green signs across the entrance highways, with new words of welcome and a new and greater population figure. The rush of events wasn't quite over. There was another letter waiting for me from my secret enemy, and this one was shorter and sweeter than ever. "Just looking at you makes me want to vomit up all my food," the message read, and it was signed "Alvarado." A strangely feeble performance. I thought the writer must be growing bored with the game, or perhaps was simply too tired to think up any more really wounding words. A falling off in any case. Señora Limón? Was she weary of my face as well? Even sickened by it? Possibly, but I couldn't see her taking the trouble to write this stuff and mail it. I hardly knew the woman.

Nardo drove me down to Chetumál to return the boy Serafín to his family. He was pretty sure he could keep the Judicial Police out of it. Nardo knew the ropes. He was well connected. For a modest fee he could get your tourist visa renewed, saving you a trip to the border every six months. He worked it through some *coyote* in faraway Guadalajara, which I never understood—why the fixer should be there instead of in Mexico City. He told me again at some length about his football days at Bonar College, how the opposing teams would laugh and jeer at the Bonar boys when they pulled up to the stadium in two yellow school buses, with the coaches driving the buses.

"But they didn't laugh long. We went twenty-eight and two in three years."

We bought Serafín some toys. He rode in the back seat and blew bubbles into the air, nonstop, all the way to Chetumál, with his wire loop and his bottle of pink viscous stuff. Quivering pink transparent bubbles floated about inside Nardo's car and broke against our ears.

Serafín knew his city when he saw it, though he still couldn't call the name. Nor did he know the name of his street. We drove back and forth around the downtown blocks, and he knew it when he saw it. The familiar buildings made him laugh. "¡Allí! ¡Allí! There!" He pointed to the dark doorway of a home tailor shop. That was where he lived. I saw two women inside, with the older one pumping away on the treadle of an ancient sewing machine. The floor was earth. Many straight pins must have fallen there and been lost forever.

I left Nardo to handle it from there, leaving it to him, the *licenciado*, the lawyer, to cook up a convincing lie, advising him only to keep it vague and leave me and Refugio out of it. He said he would blame it on gypsies. This would be readily understood. A band of *gitanos* had taken the child away, deep into a wet forest, where, weeping bitter tears but unharmed, he was found by some kind hunters and rescued from a life of thievery and certain spiritual ruin.

I waited. I walked up and down the main street of the old smuggling port, so different with its salty maritime air from Mérida, which itself was only twenty miles from the sea and might as well have been 200. Downtown I came across a Presbyterian church, which I had not noticed on previous visits. Some kind of Anglo-Scotto cultural overlap from nearby Belize, I supposed. You never know what you'll run into in Mexico, John Knox in a guayabera shirt, or a rain of tadpoles in the desert, or a strangely empty plaza in the heart of a teeming city with not even a bird to be seen. Once in Mazatlán I rounded a corner and literally ran into an old American movie actor I would have thought long dead. He was a big man who had played the boss crook in hundreds of cheap Westerns, the only character in coat and tie, directing all his dirty work out of the back room of a saloon. His name was usually Slade or Larkin. I apologized to the old crook.

"One of these fast-walking guys, huh?" he said to me, in the old Larkin snarl. Here in Chetumál the traffic police, unlike other police in Mexico, were fitted out in U.S. Marine undress blues, but with a deep Latino swoop in the wire frames of their white hats. They were hard little *Indios* with no body fat. The air trembled with heat. I was dripping. They stood buttoned up under the sun all day in a cloud of engine fumes, and their starched cotton shirts remained crisp and dry.

Someone was haranguing a crowd behind the bus station. There were gasps and cheers and applause. Surely the revolution wasn't starting here in Chetumál. So far east? The straw catching fire at last? I shouldered my way in to get a look at this fellow who was inciting the people. What I found was a fast-talking young man in a T-shirt selling cake decorators. They were soft plastic tubes with adjustable nozzles. He squeezed pink icing onto white strips of cardboard, showing how you could make little rosettes and stars and hearts, and spell out birthday greetings. He was an artist with a sure hand, and a funny speaker, too, a fine salesman. "Add a personal touch to *all* your cakes!" he kept shouting at us, and he meant right down to our very smallest muffins.

Nardo reported that all had gone well. The boy lived in the tailor shop with his mother and two older sisters, who had fallen upon him with kisses and thanks to God. They feared that Serafín had gone wading off the municipal beach and been swept away by the undertow or taken by sharks. The sea had swallowed up so many young ones. Nardo said the women were too overcome to ask many questions but that they did offer him money, whatever they had, which he refused. He told them it was nothing, *de guagua*. The kind hunters were only too glad to oblige, as was he, a representative of the PRI, the party of all the people. He made me wish I had been there to see them hugging brave little Serafín, loved all the more for his *mal del pinto*. So often I missed things, hanging back, always expecting the worst.

Back in Mérida I did get to see the reunion of LaJoye Mishell and her father, Dorsey Teeter, a bony man of about my age in a pale blue suit made of some spongy looking cloth. He was a logging contractor. I had telephoned him in Florida, bypassing Gilbert, at the Blue Sheet office, and now here he was at the airport. I stood aside and looked away as he and his daughter came together in an embrace. He wept. "Your mama and them thought you was dead but I never did give up." LaJoye Mishell was pleased enough to see him, too, but in no way upset or remorseful. She still held her sprig of Jumping Jack greenery. It was acacia, she said, though she didn't know what acacia was. I didn't either. She wore a new orange dress and a flattop Zorro hat with little balls swinging from the brim, and some big earrings, silver-plated hoops, bought with a little money I had given her. Dorsey was uncomfortable with me. In his eyes I was guilty of something, too. "What do you do down here anyway?" He asked me that two or three times. He was eager to get the business over with, just as I was, and so I spared him the details. I simply told him, again, that his daughter had been traveling around with a pack of hippies, more or less against her will, in a spotted station wagon.

"No," she said. "Not the first one. The first car was a blue four-door Oldsmobile Regency Brougham with a moon roof and dual glass-pack mufflers and blue velour seats. But Dan rolled the Regency in Texas, totalled it out, and that's when Harvey stole the Country Squire wagon. Then we came down here to Old Mexico to clarify our thoughts. Dan kept saying he was going to put us all in white coveralls, but we never did get our white coveralls. He told us we were going to live far away from everybody under the roots of a giant tree called Ogon. Every night he said the same thing to us. He said, 'Death is lighter than a feather.'"

So, it was worse even than rockers; his daughter had run off with some nasty poet, but Dorsey had little interest in the man and his remote burrow. A little of this stuff went a long way with Dorsey. He cut down pine trees by the thousand, like weeds, and not one of them had a name of its own. He didn't want to linger in this country and he wouldn't even set foot outside the terminal. There was a general smell of flyspray, as with all Latin American airports, and long dim corridors that led nowhere, with empty offices along the way. The ones here had a quiet yellowish Mexican vacancy all their own. We went to the cafeteria. Dorsey had a Coke, not wanting to eat whatever kind of food it was they had here. He laid two book-lets of travelers' checks on the table and got out his pen to

countersign them. I explained once again that there was no
fee, that I was in the woods on other business when I found
the girl, and so was really out nothing in the way of expenses.

"But what about the Blue Sheet man?"

"I'll square it with Gilbert. You don't have to worry about
that. There won't be any bill."

"Don't I need to see the police about anything? Sign some
papers?"

"No. Unless you want to hang around here for two or three
weeks."

"LaJoye Mishell is a good girl."

"Yes, and she's had a hard time of it, too. You're not going
to whip her, are you?"

"Naw, I'm not."

"She's too old for that now."

"I never taken a switch to her in her life but two or three
times. She never did have a smart mouth."

"Just go easy on her for a while. She'll be all right."

"Well. I feel like I ought to give you something for your
trouble."

"It's all taken care of, thanks anyway. We do a free one every
now and then for tax purposes. You can pay for the Cokes."

"I'll tell everybody what a good job ya'll done for us."

"You tell them we deliver the goods."

Dorsey was still looking for the catch. He couldn't size me
up except that he was pretty sure I didn't report to work every
morning. The back of his neck, a web of cracks, was burnt to
the color and texture of red brick from much honest labor in
the sun. A badge of honor, you might think, but no, it was the
mark of the beast. The thanks Dorsey and his people got for
all their noonday sweat was to be called a contemptuous name.
Few rednecks actually had red necks these days, but Dorsey
Teeter had one that glowed. At least he had come here personally to pick up his lost child, which was more than his betters
could find the time to do. Usually I had to turn these kids over
to the protection officer at the embassy in Mexico City.

I said my goodbyes and got up from the table, and my head
went light and strange for a moment. The dengue fever was
coming on again. I thought it might go away this time without really taking hold. I gave everything a good chance to go

away before seeing a doctor, and then I saw Soledad Bravo. But what a relief, to get to the end of this mess, this custodial care. It had been a problem, keeping watch on LaJoye Mishell. She could say what she liked in Florida, but I didn't want her talking around here about Dan and how he came to a bad end, and I could hardly stuff a sock in her mouth and lead her around wired to my wrist, not here in town. She had already told Fausto that I had blown her master's head off with a bazooka.

Dorsey called out a parting word as I reached the glass doors. "I appreciate it," he said, and Little Red said, "Bye," with her hat balls in agitation and the heavy hoops swaying from her peeling red ears. She was still clutching her weeds. Was she going to press them in a book? It galled me that Dorsey seemed to think I was a hippie of some kind myself—why did I need his approval?—but no matter, I was done with all the Teeters of Teeterville, and I thought I had seen the last of the Jumping Jacks.

Neither of Emmett's sons came down from the States for the funeral. They must have written him off long ago. He said to me once, "I love my children but I don't rejoice in them." We buried him in Doc's mahogany coffin, and it was all I could do to hold up my end of it, what with the bad knee and the fever coming on. Old Suarez was a pallbearer, too, for the first time ever, he told me, in a long friendless life. He couldn't lift much weight at his age, and then there was hunchback Coney, in no shape for this work, and Professor Camacho Puut, frail and thin, flicking his head to one side, like a swimmer trying to clear an ear. The others were sturdy enough.

Huerta's coffin was a fine piece of work, though the copper fittings showed to no advantage, being the same color as the wood. Ulises' shallow carvings were hard to make out, too. More art to be buried. Doc said he wouldn't need the coffin now that he had some decent staff support and wasn't going to die. He said cancer was all in your mind. You couldn't let your body cells give way to cubic replication. Gail had moved into the big house on the Paseo Montejo and was helping him with his book. There was no more talk about lying down in the forest and melting away. But Doc wouldn't come to the service because he couldn't bear to see a person he knew let down heavily into the earth, hand over hand on the two ropes. He said Emmett had no one but himself to blame, guzzling all that pure cane alcohol day after day. Only two women came. Louise was there with her ringlets brushed out soft, and one of Emmett's former wives, an American widow he had met on a bus. It was one of the later, shorter marriages, and this woman, Geneva, who had some retirement income of her own, still lived here in town somewhere.

Father Mateo, good man that he was, came boldly to the graveside wearing his cassock, in defiance of the anti-clerical laws. He said what words he could over the remains of a non-Catholic. After the prayer, Harold Bolus sang "Let me be your salty dog," a lively bluegrass tune. He stood leaning on his canes in a cream-colored coat and sang:

> Let me be your salty dog
> Or I won't be your man at all
> Honey, let me be your salty dog . . .

I don't know whose idea that was, but it fell flat. At the proper time and place, yes, by all means, let us have a song from Bolus, give us "The Orange Blossom Special" on the harmonica, but here it didn't work at all. Supposedly it was Emmett's favorite song, which was news to me, and the idea was that we would make merry in the presence of death, take it lightly in our stride, raffish crowd that we were, in fitting remembrance of our old friend. But it was forced, we couldn't bring it off, and the appearance was that we were meanly and nervously celebrating our own survival. Bolus himself admitted as much later. And how could that be anyone's favorite song, least of all Emmett's, he who was never known to dance the two-step, or any other step? Otherwise the service went off well. Suarez addressed the *padre* as *Señor Cuervo*, Mr. Black Crow, but otherwise behaved himself. Father Mateo called Suarez a *godo* (Goth) and said he should learn to curb his evil tongue, that other unruly member.

Emmett left his money, what little remained of the family fortune, to be distributed among blind street musicians, with Shep to control the share-out. An odd choice for a steward. Emmett had some odd ideas. He left me the trailer and that was odd, too, quite a surprise. I had done him a few trifling favors over the years but nothing to justify this gesture. He meant Louise to have it, I think, and just never got around to changing his will. But I took it and gladly, and it was unseemly the way I moved into the Mobile Star so fast, ahead of the legal process and with the fill dirt still loose on his grave. I found hundreds of brown paper sacks stuffed under the bed and crammed into the cabinets and closets. "So, he saved sacks," I said aloud to myself. In a drawer I found a stack of newsletters from a foreign matrimonial agency called *Asian Gals Seeking U.S. Pals.* There were small photographs of the gals with a few lines underneath listing their hobbies and telling of their sunny natures and other good points. But it seems Emmett was only browsing here, thumbing idly through a mail order catalogue of women, window shopping, as none of the pictures had been circled or checked off in any way.

Fausto said I would soon be back downtown asking for my old room, that he knew me too well, that I would not stay long confined in a tin box on the edge of town. It was just one step up from a tent. It would be an oven and there would be no maid service and a storm would blow it away and the beds and toilet seats in those things were less than full size and trailer air was unhealthy and so on. He had already tacked up a photograph of Frau Kobold in the hotel lobby. She was still alive, barely, but there was her face, that of a younger Alma, but with the bloom off, already gone hard, up on the wall in the company of Mr. Rumpler, who had taken a heart walk every morning to no avail, and the Pedrell woman from Cuba, and other deceased guests. Fausto put up pictures of all the people who died in his hotel, or who had been residents near the time of their deaths. There was also in this gallery a newspaper clipping showing the inky, murky likeness of a young boy, not a guest, who had been struck and killed by a speeding motorcycle in front of the hotel. Fausto claimed him too.

I saw Alma once more before I collapsed into my own bed. This time I had no stale cakes for her. She was all doped up with an intravenous tube in her arm but she knew me. She was waiting for me. "Ah, *der schatzgraber.* You took your time getting here. I have an urgent commission for you." She lay in a high bed in an open hospital ward. A bowl of tomato soup had gone cold on her table. *No Fumar*, the sign said, but I lit a Faros cigarette for her, with the sweet-tasting paper, and she polished it off with three deep drags. The commission wasn't so urgent that she couldn't tell me again about the time she and Karl were filmed by the Fox Movietone newsreel crew. "They showed it in theaters all over the world. 'Bringing an Ancient Civilization to Light.' With march music in the background. Did you see it?"

"Everybody saw it."

I told her about finding her handprint at the Likín ruin. Likín? She had never heard of the place. Then she said wait, yes, she did remember it, high on a bluff, Late Classic, with the medial moldings and the high roof combs, though not the business about pressing her blackened hand to the stone. "What a goose I must have been in those days. Writing my name on walls. Well, I'm properly ashamed. Fools' names and fools' faces are often seen in public places."

"The City of Dawn," I said. "That's what some people call it."

She looked at me in an odd way and said something I didn't understand at the time. "Yes, of course they do. With the tau-cross window. My mind is going. They've got me on all this dope. Well, well, the City of Dawn. Mercy me. Hee hee. The young gringos at their foolery. Were there many fools there? Besides you?"

"A few."

Then she got down to business. Night was gathering fast and there were things to be done. Fausto was the beneficiary of her small insurance policy. What she wanted me to do was clear out her room, load all the boxes of relics and photographs into my white truck with great care, and deliver them to Terry Teremoto, the crank sculptor of Japanese descent, in Veracruz. Terry had once worked with Karl Kobold in some way and had shown Alma many kindnesses in her long widowhood. Well and good. The problem was that Terry was dead, along with all his works. I had to stop and think but I was pretty sure of it. At this point I, too, was confusing the living and the dead in the moist folds of my brain. My eyes hurt. The chills would come next.

"Take special care with the glass negatives," she said. "They will make Karl immortal if you don't break them."

She feared that the Kobold collection would fall into the hands of some university or museum, hated institutions, or that "the old chinch bug Flandin" with his influence might wangle possession. She disliked Doc because he posed as the scorned outsider while all the time he lived like a king. I was to move fast, before she died, intestate. Otherwise the vice-consul would seal her room and take inventory, and, there being no immediate kin, dispose of her things to all the wrong people, the tired old official gang of committee sitters, funded scholars, and the like, who so enjoyed clipping the wings of genuine artists like Karl Kobold.

I agreed to do it if she would sign a note spelling out these instructions. A writ of removal, or was it conveyance. It took me some little time to compose the thing, in my pitiful hand. Writing is hard—it's a form of punishment in school, and rightly so—and I stood paralyzed before all the different ways this simple message might be put. I called over a nurse to witness Alma's signature. In the note, however, I named Professor Camacho Puut as the recipient instead of Terry Teremoto. The Professor was a good old man, a retired Mérida high school teacher, certainly a poor outsider, an amateur Mayanist, something of a crank himself with his snake cult theories and his shabby pamphlets, held in thorough contempt by Mexican and American scholars alike, and so, I thought, just the man to get these goods, and all in keeping with the spirit of Alma's wishes.

That was how I handled it, taking only her Spanish typewriter for myself, and some detective books, and her oscillating fan and the heavy San Cristobal blanket and an electric Crock-Pot, like new, still in the box, for carefree bachelor cooking, and a small Mixtec piece that caught my eye, a jaguar carved from some speckled stone, sitting up on his haunches like a house cat, and one or two other items. I threw out all her magazines, including the *Gamma Bulletins*. The pasteboard boxes packed with loot fell apart, and I had to get new ones. Many of the prints and the glass negative plates were ruined, all stuck together with blue mold. Still, there was enough that hadn't gone bad. It was a treasure. The Professor couldn't believe his

good fortune. "All these amazing *retratos*!" he said. "Look at
the clarity and the force!" They were truly amazing, different
in some important way from photographs that other people
took of the same things. Sick though I was, I had to stop and
look at them, too. After you had seen Kobold's work, everything else was just Foto Naroody. "Spiritualized artifacts," the
Professor called these brownish prints, this being his definition
of art. I knew we should have had the old man at our Yoro art
clinic on the bank of the river.

My white truck. I had forgotten to tell Manolo about the
sticking gas gauge needle and how you had to thump it, and
about how the first gear, granny low, was nonsynchronized,
and about how the steering would be light and dangerous
with all that tongue weight on the back, but I needn't have
worried. What a fine capable boy Manolo was. A true-bred
Bautista. He had made his long delivery run and collected his
father's money with no other mishap than a blown tire. My
old Chevrolet came back in good shape. I parked it beside the
trailer where I could see it when I sat up in bed. When I was
able to lift my head from the pillow. You forget how heavy
your head is.

For almost two weeks I lay tangled in wet sheets. About all
you can do with breakbone fever is ride it out. Soledad Bravo
treated the symptoms with sea salt and sour red wine and tar-
water and some yellow powders. The skin peeled off the palms
of my hands. Louise sat with me. She put blankets on me and
then whipped them off again five minutes later. I kept her hopping, poor girl, peevish invalid that I was. It was in this same
scaled-down bed that Emmett had died. She had sat with him,
too. Toward the end he spoke of how the years had flown, and
at the very end, she said, he was hearing things. Someone was
inside his head shouting nautical commands. At other times
there were some children in his head singing a spirited song
with many verses. Louise thought it might have been their
school song. She sat there beside me drinking limeade from a
big glass and writing letters and reading a book called *Famous
Travelling Women*.

Beth came by with some fruit and a piece of news to cheer
the sickbay. She said Bollard was putting us all into a new novel
he was writing—without our permission, of course. He would

make lifelike puppets of us and contrive dim adventures for us with his hard-lead pencil on yellow legal pads. Alma had made it into Movietone News while the rest of us were to be buried alive in one of Bollard's books. Beth said it was going to be a modern allegory, with me representing Avarice. This was pretty good coming from a short-faced bear who ate four or five full meals each day and who talked of nothing but the fat profits he expected to reap from his Mexican telephone bonds. Beth deserved something better, but what can you do, you can't stop women from chasing after these artistic bozos. Look at LaJoye Mishell. Look at Alma. Still, I was pleased that Beth had at last broken the series of ever paler poets. Bollard had his points. She could have done worse.

Louise brought out the shoebox and unrolled Emmett's Jaina figurine from the towel. We had decided that Beth should have it for the *niños* museum. She touched her fingertips to the nose and lips of the terracotta woman. She was delighted. "Such a delicate face. It looks like the portrait of a real person. Is this genuine?"

"Yes, and extremely valuable," I said. "Don't leave it out at night."

"What do I put on the card?"

"Put down 'Royal Lady. Island of Jaina, off Campeche. A.D., say, 722.' And put down that it was a gift from Emmett."

"I believe you're feeling better."

"Much better, yes, thanks to Soledad and Louise."

It was Art and Mike who called Bollard the short-faced bear. They knew all about the book, of course, you couldn't spring anything like that on them, and besides, they had more interesting news of their own. Rudy had left town, for good, they believed. He had pulled stakes and was off on a lecture tour in his Checker Marathon, minus the camping trailer, which Refugio was still holding against the fee for his search services. I had heard not one word about this from Louise.

They showed me a clipping from a Mexico City newspaper telling about a speech Rudy had given at the big federal prison there. The report identified him as "a well-known explorer and *científico* and authority on *platillos voladores*, from Penasilvana E.U.A." He had displayed "the well preserved corpse of an unfortunate invader from the stars," and had brought to his

audience "*una relación de alegría y llenura.*" A message of joy
and fullness, that is. The landing site in Chiapas, he had told
the Mexican convicts, was marked by a spot of scorched vegetation and a circular arrangement of white pebbles and black
pebbles, which he believed to be a form of digital computer.
One or two crew members of the spacecraft had died there,
perhaps choked by toxic earth air, and all that remained of
them was "a cheese-like residue," this matter being on display
as well, in a glass jar.

Rudy then had lost no time in making a run to Palenque and
claiming the pygmoid cadaver in the police shed. Art and Mike
said the tiny old man was now wrapped in aluminum foil and
wearing a tight-fitting silvery rubber cap, something like a girl's
bathing cap, with a strap under the chin, and that Rudy was
carrying him around in something like a trombone case, with
the head nesting neatly in the bell end. They knew nothing
about the big feet and couldn't tell me how he had managed
to pack them. His first speech, his first public showing of the
invader, had gone off well before an assembly of students here
at the University in Mérida. Professor Camacho Puut had introduced him in a guarded way. Art and Mike were there and
they said Rudy had good stage presence, made a good appearance in his belted safari jacket, that the lecture was no worse
than other lectures and didn't go on too long—not too much
fullness. But they wondered at this foolish desire of his to distinguish himself in the world.

I was pleased for him myself. Erich von Däniken had never
found the least bit of extraterrestrial flesh, as far as I knew,
and here was Rudy Kurle with a complete captain all his own,
if a small and very old one, unless it was an old *Indio*, or the
king of the elves. Rudy was well launched on the career he
had dreamed of, a life at the lectern, of captive listeners in jails
and schools, of long days and nights spent hanging around the
hallways of public buildings, radio stations and television studios, a life of confabulation. But why had Louise, such a ready
talker, been mum about all this? Weren't they a team? Why had
she not gone with him?

"Because I didn't want to go," she said.

There had been a row. She refused to give details, other than
to say Rudy had gone off with all their papers and tapes. She

took up an actress-like pose at the window with her back to me, not very effective, theatrically, here in the trailer, and I thought she was going to say something like, "My marriage is on the rocks, Jimmy." But she just stood there in unusual silence. That night I told her I was deeply grateful for all the nursing care and that I knew she must have a lot of things to catch up on back at her own place, back at the Casitas Lola.

"I don't live there now," she said. "This trailer is just as much mine as it is yours. More mine really. I have a moral right to it and yours is merely legal. On three separate occasions Emmett promised me that I was to have the Mobile Star. I've already moved out of the Casitas and got my deposit back. This is where I live now."

She held up a spare key Emmett had given her, to our one and only door.

"Well, I don't see how you can do that, Louise. I mean you're welcome but I don't see how you can *live* here. A married woman."

"Rudy is not my husband, he's my brother. Everybody in town knows that now but you. Beth has known it all along. Emmett knew it. I can't believe you're so dense."

I hadn't seen this coming but I knew it to be true at once. I could see the faint but real resemblance now, something about the sunken blue eyes. She wore no ring on her finger, and I had seen no photograph of bride and groom stuffing hunks of wedding cake into each other's mouths, with their arms linked and their eyes goggling at the camera. The wedlock pretense was Rudy's idea, she said. He had important stenographic work for her to do at home, and with this arrangement she wouldn't be distracted from her duties by male callers. It would offer too a kind of flimsy protection against all those flirting Mexicans who would be inflamed by her sandy ringlets and make wet kissing noises at her on the street. I wondered how she got her deposit back from Lola. Other questions came to mind. What would become of my privacy?

"Your brother then. Well. I wouldn't have guessed that."

"No, of course not. You can't see things right under your nose. You never listen to what people are saying. You think you're so smart and you don't know what's going on half the time. You call yourself a salesman and it takes you two years to find out what anybody's name is. You won't confide in anybody. You won't tell people anything and that's why they don't tell you things."

"We'll talk about this later. When I'm feeling stronger."

"I'd rather talk about it now and get it settled."

"We'll see how it works out. We'll sit down and have a long talk about it when I'm feeling better."

"No, I'd rather not put it off. I've thought this over, and it can only work out in one of two ways. You can pack your things and go back to Fausto's place or you can stay here. But if you stay on here with me, it will have to be marriage. I'm not interested in setting up light housekeeping with you. Not with you healthy. Now there it is and you'll just have to make up your mind. You're badly mistaken if you think we're going to live here together in some common-law arrangement."

Here was another grenade, blinding white phosphorus this time. Until this moment the thought of marrying into the Kurle family had not entered my head. Rudy would be my brother-in-law, and there was another one back in Pennsylvania named Glenn Ford Kurle. Why would she pick me? What was this weakness Louise had for older men with red faces? Or was it that she saw me as going with the trailer, like the butane bottle? I had expected marriage to arrive in a different way, not so suddenly, and yet here we were together, already settled in at home with our Crock-Pot and our sectional plastic plates, trisected with little dividers to dam off the gravy from the peas, and already we were having a domestic scene of the kind I had heard about but which I thought came later. She wanted to talk about it some more. Louise enjoyed extended discussion. She had dropped out of the Textile Arts Club because they didn't have enough staff meetings to suit her, and the ones they had were too short. I told her we would see how it worked out and have a long talk about it at another time.

In a day or two I was on my feet again and able to creep about. Doc sent a boy over with a message, a command. *Bring my field notes back right away.* His dusty notebooks that I never wanted in the first place. Louise helped me get the box into the truck and we set off for Izamál. As we turned onto the Naroody block, I saw a white-haired old man unlocking the door at Foto Naroody.

"Look, there's Naroody."

Louise said, "That's not Naroody."

"Who is it then?"

"I don't know but it's not Naroody. Some cousin or employee. He's nothing at all like Naroody."

She claimed she had spoken to Naroody on several occasions and had even gotten money out of him for some charity or other. She claimed further that she was on these same familiar terms with yet another old man, *El Obispo*, who responded to no one. They had chatted. She had given him a pocket knife. His name was Arturo. This irritated me, being told of such things here on my own ground by a relative newcomer. But she knew nothing of how he changed himself into a dog at night. She thought I was making it up.

Already she had suggestions about home improvements. Would it be possible to get a telephone installed in the trailer? How about putting up a patio awning and buying some lawn chairs? Or how about putting wheels back on the trailer and going off on a trip to Costa Rica together? There was a thought. In my mind the Mobile Star was part of the landscape, a rooted object, and it hadn't occurred to me that the thing might be set rolling again. It hadn't occurred to me that Louise might have some good ideas. I had been unfair to her, unless this was the only one she was ever going to have. She had called me a bum and a vandal and an enemy of the human race. I thought she was slightly insane, and of a bone-deep lunacy not likely to be corrected by age. And yet we were comfortable enough together. We didn't get on each other's nerves in close confinement.

Doc said I could keep the twenty-two handkerchiefs but he wanted Gail to go over the notebooks and transcribe them, put them in order. "It was providential the way that girl was sent to me. She is perhaps my greatest find. Working is fun again. We have a lot of fun working together in the radio. Do you know what I'm going to do? I'm going to buy Gail a pretty red car to drive around town in. She wants an open car."

"Working in the radio?"

"In the studio, I mean." He dipped his hands into the box and stirred the notebooks about. "A lot of gold here. A good part of my life. How far did you get? Toward consolidating my notes?"

"Not very far."

He treated us to lunch, if that's the word, outdoors by the pool with Gail and Mrs. Blaney. Lorena the maid served some vegetable mess. Doc was on a new health program and so everybody else had to eat stewed weeds too. There was no meat on the table and no bread and butter and no *salsa*, red or green, and nothing to drink but mineral water. We could no longer smoke in his presence. He had thrown away his pipes. It was like eating with Hitler. Mrs. Blaney was watchful. She had her position to think of and she was still trying to take the measure of this plump Gail person who had moved into don Ricardo's house and who dared to call him Dicky. Mrs. Blaney was wary, smiling, very quick to pass the salt and pepper to Gail. She no longer had the upper hand, and I felt sorry for her.

Doc pestered me with questions. He had heard some things about Dan from Refugio, though not the part about the shooting and killing. He thought that Danny, as he called him, had grudgingly turned the two kids over to us after a bit of palaver. But who was the fellow? What was he up to? What were his teachings?

"I don't know. I have no idea."

"But what are you saying? A prophet with no teachings? Look at what you're saying. Cuco has informed me that the fellow preys on children. A corrupter of children. A man with no regard or respect for innocence. All right. Then you go on to say that he has followers of a sort. Now I don't know about you but to me that implies teachings of some kind."

"I'm not saying he didn't have any teachings, I'm just saying I don't know what his teachings were."

"Excuse me, maybe I'm stupid today, but I fail to see how he can lead people around like that without some kind of teachings. Tell me this. Does he wear magnificent robes?"

"No."

"Just what was his business at Likín? Why should he go there, of all places?"

"I don't know that either."

"Can you tell us anything about his ritual? Were there lowland Mayan elements, for instance?"

"As far as I could see, no, none."

"To the best of your limited knowledge, that is."

"Very limited."

"Yes, that's the difference between us, you see. The complacent mind and the inquiring mind. You couldn't trouble yourself to ask a few simple questions. I would have given this Danny a grilling he wouldn't soon forget. I would have held his feet to the fire and shown him up for what he is. I would have dealt with him. You couldn't be bothered."

"We were in a hurry and I really didn't care what his teachings were."

"Too lazy to get involved," said Louise. "Character flaw."

"Exactly," said Doc. "Here's what it boils down to then. You want us to believe that this fellow has no natural gifts. A brute without the least trace of nobility in his features. A man with no winning ways, no message, no teachings whatsoever. And yet somehow he manages to gain ascendancy over these people. Correct me if I'm wrong."

He couldn't get a rise out of me and so he did the next best thing. What better way to annoy all the guests than to lecture them on ancient Indian ritual, on *Hunab Ku* or *Itzam*, the great lizard god, on the *Chacs* and the *Bacabs* and the red goddess. Soon he was lost in that thicket himself, trying to describe a forgotten religion that was thought to be formless, creedless, and without moral content. It was worse than a pottery talk. Even those who professed an interest in the subject were finally stupefied by it. It was a teeming and confused throng, the Maya pantheon, and no one had ever sorted it out in a very convincing way. Doc certainly wasn't going to do it here over lunch. Art and Mike had given up on it long ago. Their current theory was that everything about pre-Columbian America was completely misunderstood.

I took Gail aside after lunch and asked her about the Olmec jade. As long as we were calling in gifts I thought I would have a go at it. The little green *idolo* was worth several thousand dollars, I told her, and it wasn't Doc's to give away. There had been a misunderstanding. It was on loan. The piece really belonged to Refugio, and I knew she would want to see it returned.

But she no longer had it, or so she said. The thing had disappeared. She had last seen it in the hands of LaJoye Mishell Teeter. Perhaps the girl had stolen it. "I've looked and I've looked. Such a beautiful work too. I'm so sorry."

I said it didn't matter. Good riddance. Let it remain in the piney woods of Florida. Art and Mike thought all the virtue had probably gone out of it anyway, the spirit fled, as with objects in museums. I said to her that Doc still had a bad gray look, for all his sparkle and new plans, and I urged her to press on with the big book and get it done *de prisa*. Time was short. Get on with it. That was my advice to Gail.

"It's going to be quite a job," she said.

*Quite a job.* This peculiar girl gave out even less information than I did. She was humoring me, almost defying me to make some comment on the new situation here. The water in the pool was still and no leaf trembled on the bushes. It was a warm day in January. She wore a loose flowery housedress to show that she was at home, that she was receiving guests at her home. She was at perfect ease. I suspected that she still had the jade. I couldn't be sure. This pool and this big house would soon be hers, too. A clean sweep for Gail. While I wound up with the handkerchiefs and the trailer. She was dedicated to bennee, all right. Well, she had her way to make in the world, too, just like the rest of us, but I thought she was lying through her teeth and still had Refugio's jade man. I was pretty sure of it, if not absolutely sure, and now I wondered too about Denise's lost contact lenses at the Holiday Inn and how they came to be lost.

"Yes, but I believe you can handle the job, Gail, if you put your mind to it."

"Do you think so?"

"I know you can. By the way, you owe me some money for gasoline."

"What? Oh, I see, you're charging me for the ride. I didn't realize. How much does it come to?"

"Let's say twenty dollars."

"So much? And you want it now? This minute?"

"If it's convenient."

"My purse is upstairs in our bedroom. But I tell you what. Maybe this will do. That should cover all expenses, don't you think?"

The loose dress had two pockets and from one of them she had taken a heavy silver coin, badly out of round and worn down smooth as a river pebble. It was an old Spanish dollar, a piece of eight. She had found the trunk in the attic. Already she had been into Doc's coin hoard with her plump little starfish hands.

"Yes, this will settle it."

"I should think so. Eight reales. It will make a nice memento for you, too, from Dicky's last *entrada*."

I was sure of it now—she still had the jade. LaJoye Mishell was no thief. Well, let Gail keep the thing and much good may it do her. Or maybe I would speak to Doc about it later. Refugio came out of it well enough anyhow, with his big pipe sale and the pop-top trailer that he claimed as a forfeit. The shooting out in the woods became a pivotal date for him, replacing another memorable occasion—*That time we changed out the ring-and-pinion gears.* It made him laugh every time he thought of it. What a filthy knuckle-busting job. I wouldn't do that again if you gave me the bus. We were repairing the differential of an old school bus. The shop manual said it was a six-hour job for one man and it took Refugio and Valentín and me three days. But now the ring-and-pinion comedy had given way to—*That time we killed the pagans.* Now Refugio would place some event by saying, "It was before that time we killed the pagans," or, "It wasn't long after that night we killed the pagans in the rain."

Louise had me stop at the In-Between Club on the way back. She wanted to check up on Shep and see what he was doing with Emmett's money, which wasn't a bad idea. The place was darker in the afternoon than it was at night. Cribbs was standing alone at the near end of the bar, away from the strangers. Louise warned him that this day drinking would kill him, just as it had killed Emmett, and not only that but he never gave blood to the Red Cross either. "You old barflies never do anything for anybody and you never do anything to promote international understanding." Cribbs told her that a bottle of beer or two in the afternoon wouldn't hurt a baby. He told Cosme to bring me one and he said let us all drink to better days. Louise went to confer with Shep in the office.

Back in the shadows the strangers were talking about UFO's. Some new blood in town. It didn't take long for arriving gringos to nose out this place. One of the voices, a high-pitched drone, overrode the others and made me think of Wade

Watson, but I knew he was gone. This fellow had the floor.
He spoke with the insistence of an expert and he kept inter-
rupting the others, who made themselves out to be sensible,
judicious men, open-minded but no fools. They deferred to
him. It wasn't enough, their good will. They were out of their
depth, and the scornful expert wanted to show up their ignorance. He had them reeling with his command of detail. They
could have used some tips from Art and Mike, who had refined
the position of having it both ways right down to a fare-thee-
well. Art and Mike conceded the existence of flying saucers as
a general proposition but refused to believe in any particular
sighting or landing.

The strangers began to drift away. A small fire erupted on
the bar back there. Cosme beat it out with a wet rag. The droning fellow came edging up toward me.

"Sir? Sir? Excuse me? Sir? May I relate a personal experience?"

I saw him in the light now. It *was* Wade, dirty and smelly and
rumpled. The police had let him go, poor Wade, into Louise's
care, on the condition that she get him out of the country. She
thought she had done so, having taken him to the airport and
put him on his honor, if not actually on a plane. He missed the
flight and had been hanging about town ever since.

He recognized me. "Oh yes, you. Burns, isn't it? The nosey
one with all the questions. Are you very busy right now? May
I relate an interesting personal experience?"

I couldn't get anything out of him before. Now there was
no shutting him up. Cribbs knocked back the rest of his beer
and stumbled away in haste, but it seems to me you must let a
haunted man make his report.

"All right. Sure."

"Thank you. First, who am I? I am a payroll programmer
for the state of Missouri and I wear nice shirts and nice suits
when I'm at home. I live in a garage apartment, which suits
me, though I could afford something much, much nicer. It's
comfortable enough and very private. I sleep upstairs, alone,
needless to say, and my bedroom window faces southwest. At
a little after 11 o'clock on the night of August third I was awakened by an expiring rush of air. Then there came a pulsing
light and a low-frequency hum, or a sort of throbbing. There
really is no name for this disturbance I heard, and felt more

than heard. Now it is important for you to understand, Mr. Burns, that I am not a repeater. Get that through your head. This was my first and only contact. I am a professional man with a peptic ulcer and chronic scalp problems. Otherwise I enjoy normal good health. In my spare time I write stories of a speculative nature, if you want to hold that against me. People like you would call them fantasy or science fiction. Other hobbies? Well, I enjoy certain light operas. I play polka tunes on the concertina for my own amusement and for the entertainment of my friends. And yes, I am a student of the great Maya civilization, but that is not invariably a sign of madness. In my room the light rose and fell, in phase with the hum. There was sharp pressure on my chest. . . ."

He made a smooth story of it. Two shining androids one meter tall came through his window and stood at the foot of his bed. They wore white coveralls. They spoke a guttural, synthesized English and put it across to him that he must go soon to the ancient home of "the old earth mutants," which was Mayaland in Mexico, there to await—"something incommunicable." Always that. I was waiting for it, the point at which things go blurred. Wade said he had written a long account of his bedroom contact and that it was published in a UFO newsletter called *Gamma Bulletin*, out of Tempe, Arizona. The October edition was given over entirely to his story, an unprecedented event. No other contributor had ever been so honored.

Then, in the November issue, there came further instructions for him, via the mail this time, in the form of a letter to the editor from the city of Mérida, in Mexico. It was dated "End of the Fifth Creation," and in this letter Wade was told that he must come to the eastern beach of a small seaside town called Progreso, in Yucatán. He must wait there "near the turn of the year" and be patient. After a brief period of observation he would be met there and led to an ancient city in the heart of the Petén forest. This was the City of Dawn. Certain things would be revealed to him there. The letter was signed "*El Mago*." Underneath it, Wade said, the editor of *Gamma Bulletin* had appended a note stating that while he personally could not vouch for the authenticity of this *El Mago*, he could say that the Petén jungle was known with certainty to be an ancient mutation center. Furthermore, it was reported to be active again, in current and quite heavy use as an entry window.

So Wade came to Mérida, but then he began to lose heart and stall around. He couldn't be sure of the appointed day. He was afraid it had passed with the coming of the new year. The day had come and gone, and he had hesitated out of fear. He couldn't bring himself to leave town. He felt safe enough in Mérida but the countryside of Mexico was an unknown place of terror to him. He feared bandits, strange hot food, stinging plants, unsanitary pillows, transport breakdown. He was afraid to get on a bus or take a taxicab to Progreso, twenty miles away on a perfectly good paved highway. Now he was broke and had lost his suitcase and his credit card.

As it happened, I said, some friends and I had visited this same City of Dawn just a few weeks back.

"What? You? Not the real city in the jungle?"

"The Likín ruin, yes."

"But you weren't there at the first of the year."

"We were, yes."

"I don't understand. Why would you be there?"

"No special reason. We were just going down the river at the time."

"This is amazing. You were actually on ground zero. What happened?"

"Nothing much. Some hippies were there."

"*El Mago?* You saw him?"

"No, I don't believe he showed."

"But I wonder if you would even recognize him. Was there a faint smell of ammonia in the air?"

"Not that I noticed."

"Muriatic acid?"

"I wouldn't know that smell."

"Any animal panic?"

"The monkeys were howling."

"Monkeys! I hadn't counted on monkeys! Did you see any-one collecting leaves or soil samples? Usually these creatures work in pairs. But only one carries the sample bag. Two busy little shining men."

"I didn't see anything like that."

"Any aerial phenomena?"

"No. Well, yes, it rained. That's about it. Some hippies were there and had a kind of party."

"Wearing white coveralls? Calling themselves the Children of the Sun?"

"Not in so many words. I don't remember hearing those exact words. They did talk some about the sun. A few of them were wearing coveralls."

"You say the monkeys were howling."

"Yes, but that's what they do. They're howler monkeys."

"Likín. I've seen it often in my dreams but the light is so poor in my dreams. It must have been a hard trip."

"Not all that hard. It takes a few days to get there, but it's accessible enough. Once you reach the river it's nothing more than a boat ride."

"I wonder. The rain. The monkeys. Not much in that. But something may have happened and you didn't recognize it for what it was. Some small thing. Something arbitrary— something—of grace. A tiny pressure surge or some slight shift in the balance of things. The significance may have escaped you."

"That's possible."

"What are people here whispering about me behind my back?"

"I don't believe I've heard anything."

"I see. You're going to be polite. I wouldn't have expected that. Most of the Americans here are of a very crude type. The kind who would fire .22 shorts at superior beings, the way those barnyard louts did in Texas last May. Never mind, let me tell you what they're saying." He stuck his thumbs in his belt, in what he took to be barroom swagger, and spoke in what he took to be our comical lingo. "'That there feller? Why I reckon he's plumb loco, Clem!' Well, you can just inform your pals that their ignorant remarks don't bother me in the least. I merely consider the source."

He had nothing to say about his jail time. I gave him my opinion that it was less dangerous in the countryside than in the cities. I asked if he had ever heard of a place called the Gulf of Molo, but he was no longer listening to me or talking to me. Cosme told me that Wade had been here most of the day and had set little fires here and there, on the tables and the bar. He

would tear paper napkins into strips and make mounds of them
and set fire to them.

"We can't have that, *Señor Jaime. No se hace así.* It won't
do."

"No, it won't."

I sent over to the Bugambilia Café for a chicken sandwich on
toast, always good. Wade ate it in silence, and then Louise and
I took him back to the airport. She told him that he had let her
down and that he really must go home this time.

"I can't get you out of jail again. If the police find you here
they're going to lock you up. You don't want that, do you?"

"No."

"This will all blow over. You can come back another time
when you're feeling better and go to the Forbidden City."

"The City of Dawn."

"That's what I meant to say."

"Too late for me now. I had my chance. I didn't measure
up."

Wade was agreeable enough in his distracted way. He went
where we pointed him and stopped when we stopped. He
stood perfectly still, but rigid, like a dog being washed, as I
turned out his pockets and removed all matches. There was no
luggage—he had lost that on the first go-round. The woman
at the Mexicana counter rolled her eyes and groaned and in
the end agreed to honor his expired ticket. Louise thought
we should take our leave of him in the departure lounge. To
linger on and hover would be insulting. We had his word. But
that wasn't my idea of seeing Wade off. I said no, we would
wait here until he was boarded and the hatch dogged down
behind him and the plane airborne, until wheels up at the very
earliest. We waited, behind tinted glass. We watched from a
distance as the passengers straggled across the hot concrete,
and I thought I saw Chip and Diane in identical red knit shirts
going up the boarding stairway, if that was their names. They
carried matching green duffel bags and disappeared into the
belly of the plane before I could be certain. Then Wade Watson
taking his mechanical man steps. He was embarked. We didn't
see him again.

It was now late afternoon and Louise had another errand,
which was to give *El Obispo* his $50. She had talked Shep out of

it, though strictly speaking the old man didn't meet the conditions of Emmett's will, being neither blind, nor, as far as anyone knew, musical. It couldn't have been easy, getting money out of Shep. She had kept after him. "He knew somewhere in his false heart that I was right."

I dropped her off downtown and then went to the zoo for a quick look at the fine new jaguar. It was embarrassing. I had traveled all up and down the south and east of Mexico, and over into Belize and Guatemala, much of it on foot, and still I had to go to the zoo like everybody else to see this wonderful beast. He was a big fellow, built low to the ground, all rounded muscle, a heavy cat, nothing at all like the bony puma with his long legs and lank folds of skin. He paced about behind the bars taking no notice of us. Some children stood there with me and spoke in whispers. His coat was a light orange. The spots were black rosettes and broken black rings, and in the center of the rings there were black dots. It was a map of the starry night sky, but I couldn't read it. People here were right to call him *the* tiger.

A quick look and out for me. The place was fairly well kept, but I could never stay long. My mother didn't approve of zoos. She took things as they came, and it was always startling when she expressed some strong opinion like that. We would stop and look at each other, startled members of the Burns family, when she came out with something like that. She didn't approve of circus clowns. They were only making fun of tramps, she said, and poor fun it was. I wondered if in fact I had missed something back there at Likín. I couldn't read that pattern either. The surge, the slippage, the convergence, the vibrations, the whiff of ammonia, the design—all was lost on me. Rudy had said, correctly, that I was an untrained observer, and Wade thought I was incapable of recognizing any sign or portent short of a crack in the earth. Wade, of course, may have gotten his instructions wrong, or the androids may have lied to him, though you don't expect such radiant creatures to be jokers, swooping down on Jefferson City with their light show to have some fun with Wade Watson. You don't raise the point. You never question the veracity of the invaders.

Louise was talking to *El Obispo*, or Arturo, as she called him, on the shady side of the cathedral. Always he came back to this sanctuary. He was slumped against the wall. Did he ever go inside? Take communion? I waited by the truck, eating popcorn from a sack, thinking she should leave him alone. *Born to Meddle.* She should have had that tattooed across her forehead, to give people notice. It was a one-way chat. She had lied to me about getting a response out of the ragged old man. I was learning more about her day by day. She had a heavy tread for such a small person, coming down harder on her heels than I would have liked. Floor joists creaked under her step. I would come to recognize it at a distance, that smart little step, if I went blind, and take comfort in it, knowing my soup was on the way. Here was another thing. Where I spoke to myself, properly, in the second person, she used the third. If she dropped a coin, for instance, she would put her fists on her hips and say, "Well! Look at Louise! Just throwing her money away!" She wanted me to buy some new shirts and stop wearing boxer shorts and rearrange my hair, let it grow out into a bush and fluff it up in some way. She wanted me to confide in her and tell her my long-range plans that I couldn't bear to disclose. She wanted me to start reading nature books. We were both early risers. That had worked out well enough. She made a good meatloaf, with a nice crust, the way I like it. She knew how to make deviled eggs. She wasn't a bad cook and she didn't mind cooking.

But no, she hadn't lied. Here was *El Obispo* on his feet all of a sudden, chattering away at her, and this time about something other than the doomed towers of man. "*¡Izquierda!*" he said, flinging one hand around and around. "*¡Siempre a la izquierda!* Always to the left!"

What had roused him was her mention of the night dog. He held the dollars she had given him in one claw and made wild gestures with the other. Still he spoke with his head down. The people of Mérida, he said, were wrong to associate him with the dog, just as they were wrong and profane to call him The Bishop. He had nothing to do with the animal. He, Arturo, went one way and the dog went another. The courses they took around town were entirely different. The little dog was far too proud, like his master, a sly man, but there was no mystery about him. He was a *pelón*, a hairless *xolo* or *sholo* dog, with cropped ears, owned by a rich man, proud and sly, who turned him out every night, as with a cat. The dog made a patrol around town, stopping for nothing, going always at a trot to the left, in a diminishing spiral, until he fetched up back home in the early hours. That was his way. That was his habit, his daily exercise. Nothing more. This was the true story of the night dog, and the ignorant people of Mérida were wrong to say otherwise, to say that he, Arturo, was possessed and in demonic league with the proud little dog. They told other lies about him, too! They said that he, Arturo, stole milk! And lapped it up like a dog! That he ate no more than a snake! Just gobbled down a rat or a frog every two or three weeks! One day they would answer for their lies! And for every idle word they spoke!

He was worried that Louise might go away with the wrong idea. She might go away foolishly thinking that the dog sometimes turned to the right on his circuit. "*¡Izquierda!*" he shouted at her, making a loop with his gnarled hand. "*¡A la izquierda!*"

What a word. A truly sinister mouthful for so simple an idea as *left*. Louise found it all convincing enough. The mystery was dispelled. So much for me and my unnatural dog. I let it go without argument but I didn't believe a word of it. The night dog had a sleek red coat and a curling tail with a bit of fringe. His tail was a kind of plume. His ears were uncropped. A *sholo*, on the other hand, is naked as a jaybird, with shiny black skin, and with sweat glands, too, unlike other dogs, and with the tail of a rat. I knew my *sholo* dogs. *El Obispo* had cooked up the story. He was sly, like his invented rich man, and proud too in his rags. I offered him what was left of my popcorn, my *palomitas de maíz*, my little doves of corn, but he had already dropped down to his resting place against the thick yellow masonry and was safely back inside his own head again.

A few hippies were passing through town, not so many as before. I looked them over, half expecting to see some of the Jumping Jack stragglers. Sometimes I thought I saw one. There were days, certain hot afternoons, when the sightings were frequent. It was like watching a wave of alarm running through a prairie dog village, the way I saw their Jumping Jack heads jumping up here and there before me. But it was always someone else. Louise wanted me to stop looking these people over. She thought I should put away my Blue Sheets and my flashlight and stop working for Gilbert. I said I would have to think about it. We had to have some money from somewhere. There were no remittances coming in. I knew I would miss going out at night and putting my light in their faces.

# XVII

LOUISE WAS addicted to dramatic gestures, and I had the feeling she would wake up some morning and announce that she was going to law school, or that she had decided to open up a metaphysical bookshop, some such bolt from the blue as that. She knew that my conversation, no bargain now, must soon be that of an old coot, all complaint and gloomy prophecy. We went ahead with the marriage all the same. Soledad Bravo said the auspices were fair, good enough, *bastante*, if not entirely favorable. She had seen a spider laying eggs in a dark closet. But then she had seen worse omens in January. It was surprising how fast I moved on the thing, at my age, with so few reservations, how quickly I became a husband, and an indulgent one at that.

We were married at Doc's house. Louise had a friend, Aurélio, who came by and sang, with an accompanist. It was the first time I had ever heard that grand piano played. I didn't know Aurélio and I was expecting some fat little man in frilly white shirt and tiny black plastic shoes with a Mexican night club *quiverando* delivery, some fellow sobbing out that Granada would live again. Not at all. I couldn't have been more wrong. Aurélio was a young college student with a crystal-pure tenor voice and no tricks. He sang "Because God Made Me Thine," first in Spanish and then in English.

*Because—you come to me with naught save love . . .*

Aurélio brought tears to my eyes, and to everybody's eyes. We took the Mobile Star down to Costa Rica, stopping uneasily in Guatemala only for gasoline, where they sell it not by the liter but by the gringo gallon. We were getting the hang of trailer life. It was like towing a barge. It was like living on a small boat, or in a bank vault. We went to the Pacific side of Costa Rica, to the Nicoya Gulf, and set up camp near a village called Lepanto. Here in the bay water Louise went fishing for the first time in her life. She took up fishing with my little freshwater rod and spinning reel, and I couldn't get her to stop. We had the place pretty much to ourselves. Some kids came over from the village now and then to look at us. At night the crabs dragged themselves about over the sand and fought over our potato peelings. One afternoon a motorcycle came roaring in through the palm grove. A young American couple dismounted and took off their helmets and set up a tent on the sand. They wanted to know where they were. They borrowed a funnel and then a bar of soap. Then a towel. Then a crescent wrench.

We had them over for supper. They had been to Panama, to the end of the road in the Darién jungle, and were now making their way back to Denver. Louise asked if they meant to stay on for a while.

The girl, offended, said, "What? Here? No, we're not beach people."

Snubbed on our honeymoon by a female biker. We fed them anyway and fed them well on boiled lobster tails and melted butter. Their plan, when they left home, was to go to a place called the City of Dawn—in Mexico, they thought it was—but they had no map and couldn't figure out how to get there. They had asked questions along the way, but that was unsatisfactory too, as most of the answers they got were in a foreign tongue. Once started, though, rolling on was the thing, inertial forces at play, and so they had continued south down the isthmus until they came up against a forest wall deep in Panama, where the road stopped dead in their faces, at the Darién gap. Their pilgrimage had turned into a brainless endurance run. The boy, who had some name like Rusty or Lucky, said he had learned about the City of Dawn from a very interesting report in a magazine I would never have heard of, called *Gamma Bulletin*. I asked if he had a copy.

"No, I don't keep things."

Not even a map. Too programmed and stifling for their taste. He still wasn't quite sure where he was. He was much surprised that we had heard of the City and the UFO magazine, and a little doubtful that we actually knew the writer of the article.

"The same Wade Watson?" he said. "There are probably a lot of people going around claiming to be him. I sure would like to talk to that guy sometime, the real Wade Watson, just me and him rapping together. That contact of his is already one of the most famous in all the literature."

The girl said she no longer believed there was such a place as the City of Dawn, or that there was a real person named Wade Watson. She said she had learned how to sleep on a moving motorcycle, with her heels hooked on the foot pegs, or how to go into a restful trance anyhow. She was homesick and weary of straddling the noisy bike day after day. Their appetite was good. They made short work of our tasty *langostinos* and said goodnight. In the morning they were gone. One of them—Louise suspected the girl—stole a jar of grape jelly from us. But there it was, independent confirmation from this Randy or Rocky, or at least evidence enough for me, that Wade Watson and *Gamma Bulletin* were behind the whole business. It was good enough to settle the point for me and put my mind at rest. A kind of rest. Wade had started the thing rolling with his curious pulsing dream, but he wasn't *El Mago*.

We got back to Mérida in March. There were no nasty letters for me. The hate mail had stopped for good, and I rather missed it. Doc and Gail were working away. Mrs. Blaney was still in place, hanging on. Alma was dead and buried in the warm sand of Yucatán. They had put her in on top of Karl's bones, to save the cost of a separate plot, about seven dollars. The Posada Fausto was still for sale. McNeese was living there now, in Alma's old room, and Art and Mike had taken a double room upstairs. They said the rush of events was over. Nothing at all was going on. The sea gathers force and breaks at last on the ninth and greatest wave. Then the ebb. Fausto said there were no such neat cycles in his life. Things never let up, no matter what he did. He said a man would make any bargain, however degrading, to have peace at home, and that the radio people in Mexico City should put the story of his life on the radio for all to hear and call it "Female Complaints."

It was odd seeing Art and Mike without their soft white straw hats. They had taken to sitting around all day like convalescents in their bathrobes and socks. Louise got the impression that they meant to sit there in the lobby like that from now on, not venturing out much anymore. She had a premonition that they would end up there with their pictures on the wall, in Fausto's gallery of the fallen, perhaps dead in a suicide pact. Art and Mike had a dark side, she said, that I was unwilling to see or too dense to see. "You and Fausto don't know what's going on half the time." There was something about them, my friends the Munn brothers, that she didn't care for. "Two smart guys living in smug obscurity," she said of them.

She found us a shady spot under a tree at an older and cheaper trailer park. On the first day there I killed a *cascabel* at our doorstep, a rattlesnake, what Alma called a *Klapperschlange*. Try to save a few pesos on the rent and you end up beating off pit vipers.

She was the one, old Alma, it turned out, who had sent me the poison pen letters. You never really know where you stand with anyone. There I was secretly preening myself over my good deeds and all the time she despised me. My clumsy gestures of help must have been intolerable for her. It was Louise who caught it, not me. She had a good eye and she showed me how the typing from Alma's *máquina* matched that of the letters. She said the spiteful old woman had too much time on her hands and had probably sent many such letters to any number of people, an old mama spider dropping her venomous eggs here and there in secret places. Alma was Ah Kin and Alvarado and Mr. Rose. She was *El Mago* too. I wasn't too dense to see that. She had written the City of Dawn letter.

Louise said a plastic owl would have frightened the snake away. Why had I not set out a dummy owl, a great horned owl made of plastic? I told her it would have taken a plastic owl nine feet tall to get the attention of that *cascabel*, and I pointed out further that it was an eagle, not an owl, with a writhing snake in his beak, that the Mexicans had adopted as their national symbol. She said I should have picked the snake up on a pole and flung him over into someone else's space. Let someone else deal with him, with his horny tail plates klappering away. Keep the blood off our hands. I had no pole. With anyone else's difficulty Louise always assumed a plastic owl or a handy pole of just the right length. I didn't go out of my way to kill snakes, she knew that, but neither would I have these big fellows gliding around underfoot in my yard.

It was called The Five of May Trailer Park. On the third day Eli Withering showed up in an old Cadillac. Plenty of room in that cruiser to stretch out his long legs. Or rather it was the middle of the third night. He came tapping on the window glass with his thick yellow fingernails, of some layered, hoof-like material, which he could have used for screwdrivers. He made quite a racket. "Hey! In there!" he called out. "About time to warsh this old wore-out truck out here, ain't it?" I turned on the floodlight and went outside shirtless to greet him. He was clean-shaven and his hair was trimmed. He stood beside a pale green Coupe de Ville with a white vinyl top.

"Put out the light," he said. "I don't want anybody to see me. They told me you got Emmett's trailer. Not a bad deal for you. I didn't know it would roll. Here's something else you won't mind."

He switched on a flashlight and counted out my $500 on the hood of the car.

"What, it wasn't enough?"

"A thousand wouldn't have been enough. Sauceda took it, all right, for all the good it done me. What he didn't tell me was that the federal *acusador* already had me lined up for an Article Thirty-three."

"I told you to get Nardo."

"He might have put it off a day or two, that's all. Naw, they wanted me out bad. I was gone the next morning for moral turpitude on top of abusing the hospitality of the Republic and disturbing the national patrimony."

He paused and then counted off two more twenties. Interest, he called it. "There. Past due but there it is."

"I wasn't worried about it."

"Then you should have been, Budro. I wouldn't be here except I need to talk some business."

A sleeping woman lay sprawled across the back seat. "That's Freda." He said he was living with her in Belize now, it made for a change of air. He was scouting around and working some ruins, mostly picked over. Lately he had found one in the hills up from the Sarstún River. It was small but untouched and he wanted me to help with the excavation. The fever was on him.

"People down there don't know what they're doing. They missed the causeway. It's just like the ones at Tikál, and I saw what it was right off. At least three temple mounds. They look like spurs off a hill and that's why nobody can see them. We'll have it all to ourselves. We'll cut three quick trenches and see what we've got. Then a month's hard work and we'll skim the cream and be out. I'll split right down the middle with you. One month and we're out clean with a nice haul. I guarantee it. Or two months at the most. We'll move a hundred cubic yards of dirt, just you and me. Look at this. I turned this up in the first hour, just poking around with a machete."

It was a small alabaster figure of a seated fat man. His arms were folded across his belly and his cheeks were puffed out. One hand was missing. He looked like the pink plastic pig on Louise's key chain.

"Not bad. It's old."

"Old? It's pre-classic white goods. How much of that stuff do you see? And that's a surface find. Keep it. Go ahead. You just keep that little booger. For me that's a cull."

No one was better at this work than Eli, snuffling around in the woods like a pine rooter hog. A steady and silent digger, too, from daylight to dark, stopping only now and then to gulp warmish water from a jug, or to eat two or three strips of raw bacon, with his head thrown back in the way of a sword swallower.

"The thing is, I'm out of the business, Eli."

"Yeah, I know you say that. Once you see this place you'll change your mind. It won't hurt you to take a look at it. I'm telling you, man, I'm on to something here. Valuable early stuff. We won't even mess with the pots. My luck is turning. I got me a good car now. The niggers are right. Buy old Cadillacs and expensive shoes and white corn meal. I found me a good woman, too. If you're real lucky you might find you a woman like Freda one of these days, but I doubt it. What do you say?"

"I'll think it over."

"Don't think too long."

"Why don't you get Rex Tully? He's down there somewhere, isn't he?"

"Him? Whining all the time? In his two-tone shoes? You can't get that guy to do any work. Always down with his risons or his hernia or the pink-eye or something. He wouldn't last two days." "Risons" (risings) was Eli's word for boils.

"He's not all that bad. Tyrannosaurus Rex. He's good company anyway."

"He's bad enough. You can have him. I don't want no part of him myself. Let me tell you what he's doing. Him and his pal Fisher, this deserter from the British Navy, have got this old rotten wooden boat anchored out there behind the breakwater. Rex says they're going to load it up with live birds and go to Florida, him and this English wino that you couldn't trust for one minute out of your sight. Little silky green birds that sing. Rex says the Cubans in Miami will pay big money for these birds. But just this certain kind of bird. They all want one of these birds at home. They miss their birds. They can't get the kind of birds they want in Florida."

Louise was stirring inside. She said, "Who is it, Jimmy?"

"An art student."

"Well. Why are you standing around out there in the dark? Bring him in and I'll make some coffee."

"All right."

I passed on the invitation. "Come on. Wake up your friend. We'll have something to eat."

"Who is that you got in there?"

"I don't think you know her. It's a girl I married. Louise Kurle."

"Married. God almighty. They didn't tell me that."

He was hesitant to wake his woman, and then did so in a gentle way, leaning through the car window. He touched her. They spoke. He popped back out and said, "Naw. Freda's not hungry. She's been eating soft cheese all night. We can't stay long. I didn't even stop at Shep's. I ain't got paper one and I got to be back across the Hondo River before sunup. I'm in with a couple of guys there at the border. They work out of the fumigation shack. Here, let me show you something else."

He threw up the big trunk lid and dragged out a wooden box with an open end. Inside the box there was a ramp with riffle bars—narrow wooden strips nailed down in a pattern of broken V's—and at the bottom a swatch of carpeting to trap particles of gold. It was a homemade sluice box.

"See? We can work the fast streams, too, while we're at it. How about it? I found the place and got everything lined out and still I'm giving you half. You won't never get a better deal than that and you know it."

The woman was fully awake now. She got out of the car and stretched her long arms, then got back in—the front seat this time.

I said, "You might take her with you."

"Who? Freda? What makes you think I would take a nice lady out in them stinking woods?"

"She could help around the camp while you dig."

"I wouldn't never let her live like that. We got us a nice little apartment in Belize City with a balcony and a kitchenette and a propane cookstove. Up in the front room is where we have our couch and our record player and our magazines. That's where we sit at night when we want to listen to our music or look through our magazines. That's our place on Euphrates Avenue that I got fixed up real nice for her. The mattress on the bed is all hogged down and wallered out in the middle but we're going to get a new one. What makes you think I would let her live like a pig out in them woods? Freda don't even drink. She knows how to keep books and that's a good trade to know. Bookkeepers can go anywhere and get work any time they want it, like sign painters."

He gave me his address on Euphrates Avenue and said he would wait two weeks for me and no longer. I was to bring all my tools and a roll of coarse-mesh screen wire for sifting boxes and my three-burner Coleman stove and a can of white gasoline.

"But you ain't coming, are you, Budro?"

"No, I'm not."

I said I probably wouldn't be venturing out much anymore, into the *selva*. He opened the car door, and a pomegranate rolled out. Neither of us made a move to pick it up. A sour and messy fruit. Somebody gives you one and you haul it around until it turns black or rolls away out of your life. He introduced me to Freda. In the light of the dome lamp, I saw her face for the first time tonight. It was Beany Girl, all cleaned up and looking pretty good in a white shirt with faint blue stripes. Her hair was tied up with a blue ribbon, and there was some more blue on her eyelids. She was coordinating her colors these days. She was brushing her hair and washing her face and even painting it. But still jumping into cars, it seemed, like LaJoye Mishell Teeter. She had put on a pound or two. Beany Girl was getting regular meals now out of the kitchenette, and perhaps snacking a bit on that couch. Eli and Beany Girl at home with their magazines. An evening at home with the Witherings.

"Glad to meet you, Freda."

"Hi."

"You doing all right tonight?"

"Yeah, I'm okay."

A spark there of the old defiance. She recognized me, all right. I had some questions for her but I couldn't think of how to put them, with Eli standing there. He showed me some of the advanced features of the Cadillac radio, how in the scanning mode the needle would glide across the dial and stop for a bit on the stronger signals. I told him I wouldn't be needing my three-burner stove and he could take the thing along if he wanted it. He went to get it out of the back of my truck.

Beany Girl spoke to me without looking at me. "All right, it's me. So what? What have you got to say to that? I knew I would run into you again somewhere. I told Dan we weren't through with you."

"I heard you left him at Flores."

"You heard right, Curtis."

"Good move. What happened there?"

"That's my business. I suppose now you'll go running off to tell him where I am."

"No, we won't be seeing Dan anymore. Dan is right where he ought to be."

"That's how much you know."

"I know he's gone."

"That's what you think. You don't know him. There was a girl in Seattle who refused to dance with him. It stayed on his mind real bad and he came back two years later and smothered her with a pillow. You don't know his powers. He'll find me if he takes a notion to."

"Not this time. He's dead."

"Where? What happened? I don't believe it. How do you know? He hasn't completed his mission yet. Dan has a glorious destiny."

"He's gone, don't worry. The mission didn't work out."

"Who told you about Flores?"

"That's my business."

"Do you know for a fact that he's dead?"

"Wild pigs are feeding on Dan. You can take my word for it, Beany Girl."

"I still don't believe it. Are you going to tell Eli about me? Well, go ahead and see if I care."

"Why would I do that?"

"Do you know what happened to Little Red? I keep thinking about her. Do you remember that little skinny girl?"

"She's okay. The Mexican boy, too, if you're interested. It's a little late in the day for you to be worrying about them, isn't it?"

If there had been a hatchet on the seat, she would have split my skull with it. "I wish Eli would tear your head off. He could do it too."

"You think so? He's certainly got the reach on me. I think he might want to quit before I did. Hard to say. But you may be right. I better not start anything."

"All right, I should have taken those kids with me but I was afraid of Dan. You don't know how it was. I had to slip away in the night. You don't know anything at all about his powers. He was a beautiful man five years ago. You don't know anything about me either. You think I'm just some old trashy bag but you don't know the first thing about me. I don't suppose you ever made any bad mistakes in your life, Curtis. You think you're a just man too, just like Dan does."

I asked her about the Gulf of Molo. Where was it? What was it? She was going to give me some kind of answer, too, but then the trunk lid came down with a thud and here was Eli again. Anything in the way of a door *El Zopilote* shut with decisive force. The stove was packed away in the trunk—and so was my Coleman lantern, I learned later, with a box of spare mantles. He gave me his hand.

"We got to get on the road. You give it some hard thought now. If I don't see you in two weeks, I'll catch you sometime on the go-around. I'll holler at you one of these days. Tell everybody at Shep's to kiss my ass. Don't let your plow get caught in a root, Budro."

He drove away at a creep, lights out, down the lane of darkened trailers, and when he reached the highway his headlights blazed up and he honked once.

The only lighted box in the park was our Mobile Star. The coffee was made and so Louise and I sat up in our own kitchenette and had coffee and broken cookies from the Hoolywood bakery. She wanted the names of my visitors for her diary, to get it up to date, right up to the minute, the last event of the day duly recorded. *Some people named Eli and Beany Girl came to call from Belize in an old Cadillac.* Rudy sometimes made false entries in his diary, she said, and he saw nothing wrong in the practice. We talked some about going home, or I talked about it, going back to Shreveport. Louise thought we should stay on here for a while.

"It's early in the year. Let's give Mérida another year."

She knew she could count on me to put things off. She had a plan, too, and nothing to do with sitting on a rock and watching milk goats this time. If we could get loans from Beth and Dr. Flandin, she said, we could make a down payment on Fausto's hotel. My good friend Refugio Bautista could be a partner and serve as the owner of record. Fausto himself might be persuaded to carry the note. We could have our own hotel on Calle 55. Neither of us had ever learned a useful trade, but we weren't dumb. We were quite capable of managing a narrow hotel. After all, we weren't genuine drifters, not by nature. We weren't really beach people. You had to commit to something. You finally had to plant a tree somewhere.

"What do you think?"

It wasn't a bad idea, if we could put together the down money and get some long-term credit. She had thought it all out. A mom-and-pop hotel, with mom no doubt perched behind the cash register all day. There was no telling what innovations she had in mind for the old Posada. I feared debt and already I missed going out at night and putting my light in people's faces but it was a better plan than any plan of mine and I said we would see. I said we would talk some more about it. It comes to me now, late, as I wind this up, what it was those hippies were singing on the hilltop above the river. It was "My Darling Clementine," a good song.

COLLECTED STORIES

# *Your Action Line*

(YOUR ACTION LINE SOLVES PROBLEMS, ANSWERS
QUESTIONS, CUTS RED TAPE, STANDS UP FOR
RIGHTS. YOUR ACTION LINE WANTS TO HELP!)

Q—I have a 1966 Roosevelt dime that has turned brown. A guy in the office told me it was worth $750 and I now have it hidden in a pretty good place. Where can I sell it?

A—Benny Mann of Benny's Stamp and Coin Nook informs Action Line that the "1966 Brown" is not as valuable as many people seem to think. In fact, he tells us that some shops and restaurants will not even accept it at face value. But if you take your dime by the Coin Nook, in the Lark Avenue Arcade, Benny will be glad to examine it under his Numismascope and give you a free appraisal.

Q—Last May I ordered a four-record album called "Boogie Hits of the Sixties" from Birtco Sales in Nome, N.J. They cashed my check fast enough, but I got no records. I tried to call the place and the operator said the phone had been disconnected. I wrote and threatened legal action and they finally sent me a one-record album of Hawaiian music. Now they won't even answer my letters.

A—Your boogie tunes are on the way. Action Line tracked down the president of Birtco, Al Birt, to Grand Bahama Island, where he moved after the settlement of the Birtco bankruptcy case (the company's inventory and good will are going to Zodiac Studios, of Nash, N.J.), and Mr. Birt explained that your misorder was probably attributable to an "anarchy" condition in the shipping room. Zodiac has knocked the bugs out of the system, he assures Action Line, and all orders will be processed within seven months or he'll "know the reason why!"

Q—We have just moved into the Scales Estates. The house is O.K., but we can't get a television picture at all, and we can't pick up anything on our radio except for American Legion baseball games and rodeo news. We can't even tell where these broadcasts are coming from, what town or what state, because the announcers never say.

A—Developer Zane Scales tells Action Line that part of the Scales Estates lies on top of the old Gumbo No. 2 mercury mine. This cinnabar deposit, in combination with the 30-story, all-aluminum Zane Scales Building, makes for a "bimetallic wave-inversion squeeze," he says, and that sometimes causes freakish reception. Scales hastens to add that the condition is nothing to worry about, and that only about 400 houses are affected.

Q—There is a beer joint called Hester's Red Door Lounge in the 9300 block of Lark Avenue. It doesn't look like much from the outside, but I have heard some very curious and interesting discussions there at the bar. I am told that you can send off somewhere and get transcripts of what is said there and who said it. I can't stop at the lounge every day, you see, and even when I do I forget most of the stuff as soon as I leave.

A—Only weekly summaries of the conversation at the Red Door Lounge are available at this time. Send one dollar and a stamped, self-addressed envelope to Box 202, Five Points Station, and ask for Hester's White Letter. Hester Willis tells Action Line that complete daily transcripts (Hester's Red Letter) have been discontinued because of soaring stenographic and printing costs. Many subscribers actually prefer the summary, she says, particularly during football season, when there is necessarily a lot of repetitive matter. Hester hastened to assure Action Line that all the major points of all the discussions are included in the White Letter, as well as many of the humorous sallies. Sorry, no names. The speaking parties cannot be identified beyond such tags as "fat lawyer," "the old guy from Texarkana," and "retired nurse."

Q—Can you put me in touch with a Japanese napkin-folding club?

A—Not with a club as such, but you might try calling Meg Sparks at 696-2440. Meg holds a brown belt in the sushi school of folding, and she takes a few students along as her time permits. Beginner napkin kits ($15.95) are available at the International House of Napkins, on Victory Street, across from Barling Park.

Q—What happened with the Salute to Youth thing this year? We drove out there Saturday night and the place was dark. If they are going to cancel these things at the last minute, the least they can do is let somebody know about it. We had a busload of very disappointed kids, some of them crying.

A—Drove out where? The Salute to Youth rally was held Saturday night at Five Points Stadium, where it has always been held. The program lasted seven hours and the stadium lights could be seen for thirteen miles. There were eighty-one marching bands in attendance, and when they played the finale the ground shook and windows were broken almost a mile away in the Town and Country Shopping Center.

Q—I joined the Apollo Health Spa on June 21st, signing a thirty-year contract. It was their "Let's Get Acquainted" deal. I have attended four sessions at the place and I am not satisfied with either their beef-up program or their weight-loss program, which seem to be identical, by the way. The equipment is mostly just elastic straps that you pull. No matter how early you get there, the lead shoes are always in use. I want out, but they say they will have to "spank" me if I don't meet all the terms of the contract. Those people are not from around here and I don't know what they mean exactly, whether it is just their way of talking or what. That's all they will say.

A—Action Line will say it once again: Never sign any document until you have read it carefully! Don't be pushed! So much for the scolding. You will be interested to learn that the Attorney General's office is currently investigating a number of spanking threats alleged to have been made by the sales staff at Apollo. Ron Rambo, the Apollo Spa's prexy and a former Mr. Arizona, tells Action Line that he, too, is looking into the matter and that he has his eye on "one or two bad apples." As for the equipment, he says your cut-rate membership plan does not entitle you to the use of the Hell Boots, the Rambo Bars, the Olympic Tubs, or the Squirrel Cage except by appointment.

Q—Help! I live on Railroad Street and I have been driving to work for many years by way of Lark Avenue. Now they have put up a "NO LEFT TURN" sign at the intersection of Railroad and Lark and I have to turn right and go all the way to the airport before I can make a U-turn and double back. This means I have to get up in the dark every morning to allow for the long drive.

A—You don't say where you work. If it's downtown, then why not forget Lark and stay on Railroad until you reach Gully, which has a protected left turn. You may not know it, but Gully is now one-way going east all the way to Five Points, where you can take the dogleg around Barling Park (watch for slowpokes in the old people's crossing) and onto Victory. Bear right over the viaduct to twenty-seventh and then hang a left at the second stoplight and go four blocks to the dead end at La-grange. Take Lagrange as far as the zoo (stay in the right lane), and from there it's a straight shot to the Hopper Expressway and the Rotifer Bridge.

Q—My science teacher told me to write a paper on the "de-tective ants" of Ceylon, and I can't find out anything about these ants. Don't tell me to go to the library, because I've al-ready been there.

A—There are no ants in Ceylon. Your teacher may be think-ing of the "journalist ants" of central Burma. These bright-red insects grow to a maximum length of one-quarter inch, and they are tireless workers, scurrying about on the forest floor and gathering tiny facts, which they store in their abdominal sacs. When the sacs are filled, they coat these facts with a kind of nacreous glaze and exchange them for bits of yellow wax manufactured by the smaller and slower "wax ants." The jour-nalist ants burrow extensive tunnels and galleries beneath Bur-mese villages, and the villagers, reclining at night on their straw mats, can often hear a steady hum from the earth. This hum is believed to be the ants sifting fine particles of information with their feelers in the dark. Diminutive grunts can sometimes be heard, too, but these are thought to come not from the journalist ants but from their albino slaves, the "butting dwarf ants," who spend their entire lives tamping wax into tiny stor-age chambers with their heads.

*1977*

# Nights Can Turn Cool in Viborra

"WHAT WERE those dull bonks I heard this morning?" Jason and Mopsy had just come down to breakfast, and I threw up my hands in mock dismay as she put that old, old question to me.

"Why, Mopsy, don't tell me you haven't read my travel articles! Shame on you! Those were the famous thudding church bells of Viborra! '*Thunk, thunk, thunk,*' they say. 'Welcome, Mopsy! Welcome to Viborra!'"

The poor girl went pink and the dining hall of the Pan-Lupus Hotel erupted into good-natured laughter. The diners laughed and the waiters laughed and so did Ugo, the jolly old elf at the buffet table, who was sprinkling a bit of this and a bit of that into his tangy and oh so scrumptious herring paste— a Viborran delight called *huegma*.

Nonresonant church bells? Freshly pounded *huegma* smeared on warm buns straight from the oven? Romantic moonlight rides in circular boats not much bigger than tubs. The gaiety of an open-air market with unfamiliar vegetables on display—so knobby and streaky? Narrow cobbled streets? Bargain belts— and purses too? Great fun at breakfast?

Well, yes, and these are just a few of the joys awaiting the traveler who finds his way to this lovely old colonial city nestled in a sapphire cove under a cerulean sky on the Sea of Tessa— known locally as Da Magro, or "the Burning Sea."

We had arrived the night before on a high-wing Tessair Fokker—I and my new chums, Jason and Mopsy Crimm. With my port-of-entry know-how I soon had us cleared through customs—a painless business on the whole. The Crimms were dazzled by my moves as I pushed in ahead of others, jumping this line and that one. With a wave and a knowing wink I steered them quickly through all the control points. There was one awkward moment, when the Propriety Officer caught sight of Jason's hideous jogging shoes. But then the officer— doing a priceless double-take—recognized my distinctive turquoise velveteen smoking jacket (so loose and comfy on long flights), and the poor man was all but speechless.

905

"Chick Jardine!" he sputtered. "Winner of five gold Doobie Awards for travel writing! How I envy your powers of description, sir!"

After that, as you can imagine, the city was ours.

This brings me, however, to my one teeny caveat for you folks planning your first trip to Viborra. Be advised that the Ministry of Fitness and Propriety maintains a Vigilance Desk at the airport. If the duty officer there perceives you to be a lout, rich or poor, he will assign you to the Morono Palace, a magnificent hotel for louts on the eastern beach, or mud flats, just across the Bal River from Viborra proper, regardless of any previous arrangement you have made. As a registered lout (stamped thus on your visa in luminescent orange ink— LOUT), you will be somewhat restricted in your movements, to the eastern beach and to the markets, bars, and shops around the Arch of Nimmo, or the Plaza of Louts. You will also be fitted with and made to wear an orange plastic wristband for ready identification.

But not to worry. The guests at the Morono Palace have loads of fun in their own way, and prices are considerably cheaper in that district—particularly on belts, yo-yos, fishnet tank tops, heavy woolen shower curtains, and tortoise-shell flashlights. You can even watch these unique torches being made in ancient workshops, where the delicate craft of shell-routing is jealously guarded and passed on from father to son. And the central dining hall at the Morono is a show in itself, with its famous rude waiters cavorting comically about in striped jerseys as they insult the guests, and with its Morono Mega-Spread, a free-for-all salad bar 188 feet long. Then, blazing and blaring atop the Palace, there is the legendary Club Nimmo, reputed to be the world's loudest nightclub, with music and hilarity and flashing lights twenty-four hours a day.

"No, no," I said to Mopsy, as I caught her making a move toward the bud vase on our breakfast table. "Smell, but don't touch. That delicate white blossom is not so innocent as it appears. That, my dear, is an *artu* flower from the volcanic highlands, and it exudes a toxic alkaline resin that can blister the fingers. A defense mechanism, you see."

It was all coming back to me, remarkably enough—a torrent of Viborran memories and lore, on this, my first visit to the old city in many years. I thought how lucky the Crimms were to have scraped acquaintance with me, for I seldom reveal my identity to ordinary people on my jaunts around the world, knowing and hating the fuss that always follows. My helpful tips to less experienced travelers are strictly confined to my prizewinning magazine articles and my widely syndicated newspaper column, and when I hear star-struck people murmuring around me (they having spotted my trademark turquoise jacket), I go all deaf and ignorant.

But then, how natural it is that celebrities should gravitate to one another. In our chat on the Fokker it came out that Jason and Mopsy, far from being ordinary, had appeared on the covers of nine popular financial magazines in the past year, posed in front of their restored Victorian house, with expensive new silvery cars parked in the driveway. Mopsy showed me the most recent cover, and an amusing photo it was, too. Jason, his arms straining under the load, is standing behind a red wheelbarrow that is filled and indeed spilling over with documents representing his sensible budgets, wise investments, and long-range tax-planning strategies. At his side is our little gamine, Mopsy, with a sheaf of CDs and tax-free municipal bonds spread fanwise and peeping out ever so coyly from her bodice. She confided to me, with pardonable pride, that of all the grinning young couples ever to appear on the covers of these magazines in front of their restored Victorian houses, she and Jason were judged to have the least-blemished shutters and the most beautifully complacent grins.

People who matter, then, people worth knowing, and the feeling was mutual, to put it mildly. Can you picture the scene at the airport when the officer spilled the beans—that I was award-winning syndicated columnist Chick Jardine? The Crimms were addled with delight!

It also turned out that none of us was paying for anything. Plane fare, hotel rooms, meals—all free. I never pay, on principle, as a guest of the world, and the ever-calculating Crimms, who read forty-one financial newsletters each month, had managed to get in on the ground floor of something called the Ponzi Travelbirds, through which society, as Early Birds, they will enjoy free travel for life, at the expense of all Late Birds joining the club. Need I say it? My kind of folks!

*

After breakfast we were off for a day of adventure under the azure vault of the sky, with yours truly acting as cicerone. We clambered up the winding stone staircase to the topmost battlement of the old fortress known as the Castle of Abomination. We made our way down narrow cobbled streets to the Thieves' Market, and we took a bus ride to the Crispo Lupus Windmill Plantation. There is little to see on that barren hilltop—a tangle of copper wire and seven or eight rusting steel towers with broken windmill sails. Not one watt of electricity was ever generated by the project. But I knew this little excursion would be a treat for the Crimms. Back home they could entertain their friends with the story of how they had ridden on a ramshackle bus in a tropical country—*with pigs and chickens aboard*!

We inspected the bushes at the National Arboretum, running mostly to prickly, grayish xerophytic scrub. We toured the Arses Lupus Mask and Wig Factory downtown. We admired the slavering ferocity of the women gnawing on leather (to soften it) at the Arses Lupus Belt and Purse Co-op. We descended (watch your head!) into the dark, dripping dungeons of Melanoma Prison, now a horror museum complete with shackled skeletons artfully laid out on straw. In the lower, blacker depths of that infamous hole you will need a candle, on sale at the reception desk for fifty pilmiras. Luckily, I had my own penlight, and the alert Crimms neatly got around the fee by exchanging some little foil-wrapped bricklets of butter (lifted from the hotel buffet) for their candles.

Then once again out into the shimmering light of day, and under a sky of that heartbreaking shade of delft blue you will find nowhere else in the world, we took a pleasant stroll along the bayfront promenade. We ate flavored ices and watched the children clubbing rat fish in the shallows.

Jason was fascinated by the Viborran coins, light as fine pastry. (Even the money is fun in Viborra!) I explained that they are minted from a curious alloy of chalk and aluminum, or actually baked, on greased sheets, in government kilns, and that, unlike all other coins in the world, they float. The 500-pilmira pieces are particularly buoyant, and these huge gray discs are used to stuff life jackets.

Pilmira coins have a dusty surface somewhat like that of a butterfly's wing. This creepy feeling or quality of dry slipperiness is held in great esteem by Viborrans, and they have a word for it—*rhampa*, which translates not only as "free of asperities" but also as "charm," "magic," "felicity," "a leap of the heart," "brutal cunning," "inner certitude," or "a sudden white spikiness, as of a yawning cat's mouth," according to context. If you wish to say "Thank you" or "Is it not so?" or "Beat it!" or "The bill, please," you can never go far wrong with the all-purpose phrase *"Ar rhampa palayot,"* delivered with a servile bob of the head.

"Our free tub ride!" Mopsy cried out, as she looked at her watch. "It's almost noon! Are we far from the tub docks?"

Not far, I assured her, and cautioned her against using such derisory terms as "tub" and "bucket" around the fishermen. These proud fellows do not laugh at jokes about their small leather coracles—called *moas*. Mopsy had her coupon ready. Through clever booking—all their trips are planned in detail a year in advance—the Crimms had received from Tessair a free bottle of skin lotion and a book of valuable coupons, one of which entitled them to a free *moa* ride in Viborra Bay on any weekday before noon, between April 20 and December 5.

Hearty singing told us that the fishing fleet was coming in —and with a good catch! The little round vessels, painted in soft pastel colors and decorated with painted human eyes, gyrated and jostled against one another like bumper cars at the fair as the men struggled to bring them in against the current. Steering a *moa*, or indeed making it go at all, in a particular direction is a difficult art to master.

And noon is not, perhaps, the best time of day to take a *moa* out into the Burning Sea. The sun at meridian is a fearful thing in Viborra. We paddled frantically and our goatskin craft kept spinning around and around in place. There was no breeze. Stinging sweat blurred our vision. (But nights can turn cool in Viborra, so be sure to pack a sweater or light wrap.) Still, you must make the effort, because the only proper way to see the Melanoma Memorial is from the sea.

This is a colossal equestrian statue of the late President Eutropio Melanoma, rising up against a cobalt sky at the end of a long mole, or breakwater. Fabricated of ferro-concrete on site,

and standing as high as a nine-story building, it commemo-
rates the long rule (more than forty years) of the beloved old
President. It is a robust, lumpy work (what one art critic has
called "the apotheosis of portland cement"), and a grand tribute to the man's political genius and "The Year of the Edict"
—1949—which is sometimes called "The Year of Decision."
The horse is rearing up in a fine capriole, and the presidential
sword (giver of victory) is pointed out to sea. A black rubber
raven (bird of prophecy) is perched on his shoulder.

The old President was elected over and over again by ac-
clamation and is still fondly remembered here for his dishev-
eled hair and clothing, for his dramatic and alternating acts
of mercy and cruelty, and for the mischievous teasing of his
ministers, some of whom he made give their reports while
running alongside his moving Packard, with the window glass
only partly rolled down. He also undertook to teach lawyers
humility, giving his Supreme Court justices the choice of
working for three months of the year in the nitrate mines or
serving for three months on road-repair crews, wearing red
vests and flagging traffic.

At the Café Tessa, a waterfront bar where dissident jugglers
and poets meet to grumble and conspire, you will hear that it
was the old man's simple tastes in food and his modest pleasures that most endeared him to his people. One of his favorite
amusements was to prowl stealthily about the grounds of the
presidential mansion with a garden hose, squirting water on
cats and servants, and taking gopher colonies by surprise with
sudden inundations of their little underground apartments. At
night, after a light supper of a single warmed-over bean cake,
he liked to retire to the ballroom for an hour or so of running
his fist up and down the white keys of a piano.

Something of a prodigy, Melanoma consolidated his power
early on, as quite a young man, by disposing of all likely claim-
ants to the office of chief executive. His father and his infant
sons he garroted personally. With his brothers, uncles, and
nephews, for whom he felt less natural affection, he was more
severe, condemning each of them to a protracted, popeyed
death in leather harness, dragging ore carts out of the nitrate
pits. But he had overlooked someone in his planning, and so
the Melanoma era came to an appalling, not to say sizzling,

end in 1979, when his only legitimate daughter, Arses Melanoma Lupus, plunged a white-hot poker into the sunken belly
of the ascetic old man. The puncture was mortal. Arses's husband, Crispo Lupus, then succeeded to the presidency, after a
brief scuffle with guards on the veranda of the mansion.

Elderly firebrand poets at the Café Tessa, whose subsidies
were sharply cut back by the new administration, will tell you
that Crispo Lupus lacks *rhampa* and a masterly hand; that he
neglects his duties; that he is not a man of bold strokes, of
deeds you could sing. They say he does nothing but fool about
with his hunting birds, leaving the much feared Arses in full
and very active command at the mansion. Under the Lupus re-
gime, the poets say, the people of Viborra have actually become
shorter and uglier, and everybody's hair has gone all gummy.
Whatever the truth of the matter, it is certain that Lupus has
never captured the hearts of his countrymen in the way that
Melanoma did with his Edict of 1949, by which decree the
listings in the telephone directory were alphabetized.

Anyone can direct you to the Café Tessa, which is situated
near the base of the natural rock pinnacle known as the Needle of Desolation, and just around the corner from another
downtown landmark, the Arses Lupus Black Pavilion, or the
Dark Hall of the People. This very modern structure, with lots
and lots of darkish glass, is something of a barren shaft itself,
rising up in bleak splendor under the gentian bowl of the sky.
The thing fairly takes your breath away, and in Chick Jardine's
humble opinion there is nothing in New York to touch it for
sharp angularity of line and blankness of aspect.

It is here, in the spacious atrium of the Hall, that Carnival
season begins each year with the auction of public offices and
preferments. Nimmo Lupus, the playboy son of Crispo and the
imperious Arses, presides over the bidding in the red silk robes
of Grand Chamberlain, to which is affixed the golden sunburst
badge of Inspector of Libraries. He is usually accompanied on
these state occasions by his youngest son, Bungo Lupus, a cute
toddler, who, all decked out in a little policeman's uniform, sits
dozing on his father's knee. One frequent bidder told me that
he took the limp Bungo at first for a dummy! The poets say
that Bungo has the same weak eyes as Nimmo.

So—Carnival in Viborra. Should you go? Yes, but be prepared for something a little different. The revels in Viborra proper are nothing at all like those in Rio and New Orleans. There are no gala parades or balls. The people simply go out at night wearing dog masks or dog helmets and mill about in darkness and eerie silence. They take measured steps and move in slow tidal fashion up and down the narrow cobbled streets. Now and then they stop and look at one another, nose to nose, without speaking, rather like dogs, for some little time. And when the shuffling stops—such stillness! The ceremony, it seems, is not an ancient one, but I have been unable to find out when or how it started, or just what the point of it is. The Long March of the Dogs, they call it, though there is no canine friskiness about the thing; it is really more like a shambling procession of cattle. Bring comfortable walking shoes. Leave your dog helmets and dog masks at home, as they will only be confiscated at the airport. Only those made in Viborra (with longish snouts) and certified by the Central Committee can be worn in the March.

Things are livelier, of course, across the Bal in transpontine Viborra, where, every night at midnight, there is the celebrated Stampede of the Drunks, around and around the Plaza of Louts. It is not for everyone, this stumbling, boisterous race, but to say you have run with the international drunks on the River Bal—well, take it straight from Chick Jardine, few travel claims confer more prestige these days. Your application for the Stampede of the Drunks, with passport-grade photo and $200 entry fee, must be made to the Central Committee six months in advance.

All other events are open to the public. Everyone (with orange bracelet) can join in the frolic around the fountain and in the reflecting pool and along the narrow cobbled streets radiating out from the Nimmo Arch. Wear casual clothes. Beware the melon ambush. Take care when rounding corners or you are likely to have a watermelon or some rotten and unfamiliar vegetable smashed down on your head—with what seems to me unnecessary force. Stay well clear of those roving gangs of hooded urchins who call themselves the Red Ants; they will seize you and gag you and truss you up and scrawl Red Ant slogans across your belly and then toss you about on a stretched bull hide. Keep a sharp lookout for boulders and burning tires rolling down the hillside streets. There is a certain amount of capering around bonfires. After the first night the streets are littered with putrefying vegetable fragments. There are one or two deaths each night and a good deal of broken glass.

In recent years the season has been spoiled a bit by nightly typhoons, which are sometimes followed by predawn tsunamis. The poets claim that something has gone wrong with the prevailing winds, and they blame the unholy Arses and her practices in necromancy. Despite this, the merrymakers still come in swarms, and I must caution you that there is a lot of shameless overbooking in Viborra during Carnival. You may be forced to double up in your hotel room with unsavory strangers, and sleep in shifts. "Hot bunking," as we call it in the trade. Three years ago, I am informed, the Morono Palace was so jam-packed with louts that the hotel itself subsided eight and a half inches into the mud.

Poor Mopsy was ready to drop. It was just after one in the morning and we were weary and stuffed. We were fairly water-logged with oysters. But we still had a gratis supper coming, and the dining hall at the Pan-Lupus didn't open until 2:00 A.M. (Note well: It is not fashionable to sup in Viborra before about 2:30 A.M. This by way of showing you do not have to rise early.)

What to do? Fighting off sleep, and determined not to be done out of any meal that was due us, we gave each other playful slaps and dashed cold water in our faces. We went to the bar to kill some time and found it filled with English travel writers in suede shoes and speckled green suits. What a scene! They were laughing and scribbling and asking how to spell "ogive" and brazenly cribbing long passages of architectural arcana from their John Ruskin handbooks, which are issued with their union cards.

"Look, that sod Jardine is here too!" one of them shouted. Then he and the others came crowding around, seething with bitter envy of me and my *Chick's Wheel of Adjectives*, a handy rotating cardboard device, which, at $24.95, was such a super hit with the travel journalists at our winter conference in Macao. Mopsy feared for my safety as the chaps bumped up against me and heaped childish ridicule on my cluster of lapel pins, tokens of numerous professional honors. A serene and scornful smile soon sent them reeling back in confusion.

We left them there, stewing in resentment and muttering over their pink gins, and at two on the dot we were standing first in line outside the dining-hall doors. From campaniles all over town the bells of Viborra were striking the hour, with paired thuds and thumps of slightly different pitch. I was explaining how these strange dead bells are cast from a curious alloy of pumice and zinc when Mopsy silenced me with a raised hand.

"No—listen," she said. "Those—bells. They seem somehow to know we're off tomorrow on the morning Fokker. They seem to be—saying something."

"But I don't understand," said Jason. "How do you mean, Mopsy? Just what is it they—seem to say?"

"Those—sounds on the wind. Can't you hear? 'Come back!' they seem to say. 'Come back, Mopsy! Come back, Jason! Come back, Chick! Come back to the sparkling shores of the Burning Sea! Come back in time to a more gracious and all but forgotten way of life in the enchanting old city of Viborra nestled snugly in a sapphire cove 'neath the vast rotunda of an indigo sky!'"

*1992*

# I Don't Talk Service No More

O NCE YOU slip past that nurses' station in the east wing of
D-3, you can get into the library at night easy enough if
you have the keys. They keep the phone locked up in a desk
drawer there but if you have the keys you can get it out and
make all the long-distance calls you want to for free, and smoke
all the cigarettes you want to, as long as you open a window
and don't let the smoke pile up so thick inside that it sets off
the smoke alarm. You don't want to set that thing to chirping.
The library is a small room. There are three walls of paperback
westerns and one wall of windows and one desk.

I called up Neap down in Orange, Texas, and he said, "I
live in a bog now." I hadn't seen him in forty-odd years and I
woke him up in the middle of the night and that was the first
thing out of his mouth. "My house is sinking. I live in a bog
now." I told him I had been thinking about the Fox Company
Raid and thought I would give him a ring. We called it the Fox
Company Raid, but it wasn't a company raid or even a platoon
raid, it was just a squad of us, with three or four extra guys
carrying pump shotguns for trench work. Neap said he didn't
remember me. Then he said he did remember me, but not very
well. He said, "I don't talk service no more."

We had been in reserve and had gone back up on the line
to relieve some kind of pacifist division. Those boys had something like "Live and Let Live" on their shoulder patches. When
they went out on patrol at night, they faked it. They would go
out about a hundred yards and lie down in the paddies, and
doze off, too, like some of the night nurses on D-3. When they
came back, they would say they had been all the way over to
the Chinese outposts but had failed to engage the enemy. They
failed night after night. Right behind the line the mortar guys
sat around in their mortar pits and played cards all day. I don't
believe they even had aiming stakes set up around their pits.
They hated to fire those tubes because the Chinese would fire
right back.

It was a different story when we took over. The first thing
we did was go all the way over to the Chinese main line. On

the first dark night we left our trenches and crossed the paddies and slipped past their outposts and went up the mountainside and crawled into their trench line before they knew what was up. We shot up the place pretty good and blew two bunkers, or tried to, and got out of there fast with three live prisoners. One was a young officer. Those trenches had a sour smell. There was a lot of noise. The Chinese fired off yellow flares and red flares, and they hollered and sprayed pistol bullets with their burp guns and threw those wooden potato-masher grenades with the cast-iron heads. The air was damp and some of them didn't go off. Their fuses weren't very good. Their grenade fuses would sputter and go out. We were in and out of there before they knew what had hit them. It could happen to anybody. They were good soldiers and just happened to get caught by surprise, by sixteen boys from Fox Company. You think of Chinese soldiers as boiling all around you like fire ants, but once you get into their trench line, not even the Chinese army can put up a front wider than one man.

Neap said, "I don't talk service no more," but he didn't hang up on me. Sometimes they do, it being so late at night when I call. Mostly they're glad to hear from me and we'll sit in the dark and talk service for a long time. I sit here in the dark at the library desk smoking my Camels and I think they sit in the dark too, on the edges of their beds with their bare feet on the floor.

I told Neap service was the only thing I did talk, and that I had the keys now and was talking service coast to coast every night. He said his house was in bad shape. His wife had something wrong with her too. I didn't care about that stuff. His wife wasn't on the Fox Company Raid. I didn't care whether his house was level or not but you like to be polite and I asked him if his house was sinking even all around. He said no, it was settling bad at the back, to where they couldn't get through the back door, and the front was all lifted up in the air, to where they had to use a little stepladder to get up on their front porch.

You were supposed to get a week of meritorious R and R in Hong Kong if you brought in a live prisoner. We dragged three live prisoners all the way back from the Chinese main line of resistance and one was an officer and I never got one day of R and R in Hong Kong. Sergeant Zim was the only one who ever did get it that I know of. On the regular kind of R and R you went to Kyoto, which was all right, but it wasn't meritorious R and R. I asked Neap if he knew of anyone besides Zim who got meritorious R and R in Hong Kong. He said he didn't even know Zim got it.

He asked me if I was in a nut ward. I asked him how many guys he could name who went on the Fox Company Raid, not counting him and me and Zim. All he could come up with was Dill, Vick, Bogue, Ball, and Sipe. I gave him eight more names real fast, and the towns and states they came from. "Now who's the nut? Who's soft in the head now, Neap? Who knows more about the Fox Company Raid, you or me?" I didn't say that to him because you try to be polite when you can. I didn't have to say it. You could tell I had rattled him pretty good, the way I whipped off all those names.

He asked me how much disability money I was drawing down. I told him and he said it was a hell of a note that guys in the nut ward were drawing down more money than he was on Social Security. I told him Dill was dead, and Gott. He said yeah, but Dill was on Okinawa in 1945, in the other war, and was older than us. He told me a little story about Dill. I had heard it before. Dill was talking to the captain outside the command-post bunker, telling him about the time on Okinawa he had guided a flamethrower tank across open ground, to burn a Jap field gun out of a cave. Dill said, "They was a whole bunch of far come out of that thang in a hurry, Skipper." Neap laughed over the phone. He said, "I still laugh every time I think about that. 'They was a whoooole bunch of far come out of that thang in a hurry, Skipper.' The way he said it, you know, Dill."

Neap thought I must be having a lot of trouble tracking people down. I haven't had any trouble to speak of. Except for me and Foy and Rust, who are far from home, and Sipe, who is a fugitive from justice, everybody else went back home and stayed there. They left home just that one time. Neap was surprised to hear that Sipe was on the lam, at his age. How fast could Sipe be moving these days, at his age? Neap said it was Dill and Sipe who grabbed those prisoners and that Zim had nothing to do with it. I told him Zim had something to do with getting us over there and back. He said yeah, Zim was all right, but he didn't do no more in that stinking trench line than we did, and so how come he got meritorious R and R in Hong Kong and we didn't? I couldn't answer that question. I can't find anyone who knows the answer to that. I told him I hadn't called up Zim yet, over in Niles, Michigan. I wanted to have the squad pretty much accounted for before I made my report to him. Neap said, "Tell Zim I'm living on a mud flat." I told him he was the last one I had to call up before Zim. I put Neap at the bottom of my list because I couldn't remember much about him.

I can still see the faces of those boys who went on the Fox Company Raid, except that Neap's face is not very clear to me. It drifts just out of range. He said he could feel his house going down while we were talking there on the phone. He said his house was going down fast now, and with him and his wife in it. It sounded to me like the Neaps were going all the way down.

He asked me how it was here. He wanted to know how it was in this place and I told him it wasn't so bad. It's not so bad here if you have the keys. For a long time I didn't have the keys.

*1996*

# The Wind Bloweth Where It Listeth

THE EDITORS are spiking most of my copy now, unread. One has described it as "hopeless crap." My master's degree means nothing to this pack of half-wits at the *Blade*. My job is hanging by a thread. But Frankie, an assistant city editor, is not such a bad boss and it was she who, out of the blue, gave me this choice assignment. I was startled. A last chance to make good?

Frankie said, "Get some bright quotes for a change, okay? Or make some up. Not so much of your dreary exposition. Not so many clauses. Get to the point at once. And keep it short for a change, okay? Now, buzz on out to the new Pecking Center on Warehouse Road, near the Loopdale Cutoff. Scoot. Take the brown Gremlin. But check the water in the radiator!"

An introductory word or two on the subject at hand will not be out of place before we come to the exciting work now going forward inside the new Hazel Perkins Jenkins Pecking Center at 75002 Warehouse Road, near the Loopdale Cutoff.

Readers of the *Blade* will recall an old theory/prophecy that went as follows: a hundred monkeys pecking away at random on a hundred typewriters will eventually reproduce the complete works of William Shakespeare. The terms may be a little dated, what with the typewriters, and that modest round number, meant to suggest something like "many," or even "infinite." And one monkey, of course, would suffice, given enough time and an immortal monkey. In any case, the chance duplication would require the monkeys—let us say a brigade of monkeys—to peck out 38 excellent plays and some 160 poems of one metrical beat or another.

Is the musty old prophecy at last being fulfilled? We now have millions of monkeys pecking away more or less at random, day and night, on millions of personal computer keyboards. We have "word processors," the Internet, e-mail, and "the information explosion." Futurists at our leading universities tell us the day is at hand when, out of this maelstrom of words, a glorious literature must emerge, and indeed flourish.

So far, however, as of today, Tuesday, September 14, late afternoon, the tally still seems to be fixed at:

Shakespeare: 198, Monkeys: 0

They plead for more time, for just one more extension. And then another. We are all familiar with their public-service announcements on television in which they make these irritating appeals.

Perhaps the goal has been set too high. Let us then leave the Bard for a moment and look at some even more disturbing numbers, from UNESCO's ten-year world survey (1994–2004) of not very good plays written in blank verse, and not very good sonnets, villanelles, sestinas, elegies, and odes. The result:

Not very good blank verse plays, sonnets, etc.: 219,656

That figure was widely reported and has not been seriously disputed. Less well known—hardly known at all—is this tidbit, which was buried deep in the appendix of the thick UNESCO volume:

Not very good odes, blank verse plays,
etc., composed by monkeys: 0

So again, nothing, no blip of art from random pecking, good or bad, nor even of proto-art, unless one counts the humming, haunting, and hypnotic page of $z$'s which turned up last year in Paris. Never much taken with Shakespeare themselves, the French await the appearance and reappearance of their own Francophone glories. They wait for art to happen. Their central clearing house has been established in Marseilles, at the international headquarters of Peckers Without Borders.

As for the recent American commotion over the DeWitt Sheets affair, it has largely and mercifully subsided. Young Sheets, the *Blade* reader will recall, is the Memphis tyke, four years of age and illiterate, who was said to have pecked out with his tiny tapered fingers, uncoached, on a personal computer, this complete line from one of the three weird sisters in the tragedy of *Macbeth*: "And, like a rat without a tail, I'll do, I'll do, and I'll do."

It was complete even to Shakespeare's rather excessive punctuation. The Sheets woman, mother of DeWitt, later made a full, weeping confession to the fraud. Later still, alleging coercion, she recanted. She insists once again that DeWitt alone hit on the rat line. The woman is currently reported to be traveling about the country in a small car with young Sheets. She presents him on stage in his little professor's rig—gown, mortarboard—at state fairs and rock concerts, where he recites selected passages from time-honored soliloquies.

Now, without more ado, we come to the amazing new enterprise out on Warehouse Road, near the Loopdale Cutoff, where organized ape-pecking has finally arrived in our town —with bells on! In a *Blade* exclusive, I can take *Blade* readers inside the strange writing factory, to which I gained immediate entry with a flourish of my *Blade* press card. The "line chief," a sort of superintendent, was favorably impressed by the card, stupefied even, by the legal-looking scrollwork and the sunburst seal, which seems to radiate some terrifying powers of the state. He granted me full floor privileges.

I spoke there on Tuesday with some of the monkeys. Row upon row, they were ranged about at their pecking stands, in a high, open, oblong room, something like a gymnasium. The first one I approached, actually a surly mandrill, said, "Beat it. Can't you see I'm pecking?" The line chief came scuttling over to suggest that I put off all interviews until the mid-morning break.

I wandered around in my socks. This shoeless, paddingabout policy had to do with preserving quiet, rather than from any Oriental sense of delicacy. Eavesdropping is a big part of my trade (I hold a master's degree in tale-bearing from one of the better Ivy League schools), but I saw no opportunities here. All was pecking with this crew, or a furious clicking.

White placards were posted along the walls exhorting the monkeys to STAY IN YOUR SEATS! PLEASE! At the upper end of the long room, on a dais, a string quartet was playing, softly, a medley of Sousa marches. Above the musicians, high on the wall, there was an oil portrait of the poet and billionaire widow herself, Mrs. Hazel Perkins Jenkins, in her signature white turban. She smiles down on her workshop monkeys.

Mrs. Perkins Jenkins is, of course, their patroness. All of these Pecking Centers—thirty-seven, to date, nationwide —are lavishly funded by the Hazel Perkins Jenkins Foundation for the Arts, in Seattle. She is a widow many times over. Of her five husbands, all rich and all now dead, only one, Jenkins, professed any love for—or even the slightest interest in—poetry. After his death she was saddened to learn, on flipping through his diaries, that Jenkins himself had been faking the passion all along. "I don't get it," he had confessed, in a number of entries. "But then men were deceivers ever," she said, taking the disappointment in stride. "Poor Jenkins, yes, it now seems that he too had a tin ear, but he was only trying to please me. He had his quirks, as we all know." This was a vague reference to the declining days of Jenkins, when he annoyed ladies on city buses as he roamed aimlessly around Seattle.

There, in the drizzle of Puget Sound, atop the Foundation's south tower, is the famous Shakespeare Countdown Clock, some thirty feet in diameter. The minute hand stands, or appears to be standing, at eight minutes before midnight—and The New Day. A few veteran observers say they can perceive constant, unbroken movement of the hand, though conceding it to be slight.

As it happened, I was looking at my own watch when, at 10:15 sharp, the musicians stopped their scraping abruptly in mid-passage, and there came two blasts from a Klaxon horn. I gave a start and an involuntary and embarrassing little chirp of alarm. It was the morning break. The peckers rose as one and stepped away from their stations. Heads thrown back, mouths agape, they squirted soothing drops of balm into their eyes. They flexed their simian fingers and twisted their necks about. They performed a few side-straddle hops in unison.

Trolley carts appeared, laden with bananas, grapes, and assorted nuts, less than fifty percent peanuts. There were small club sandwiches, crustless and elegant, and pitchers of organic fruit juices.

These monkeys were, for the most part, good-natured little fellows, proud of their work and eager to talk about it. They are paid, I learned, by the "swatch," this being a standard printout sheet densely spattered with letters of the alphabet, numerals, and the various punctuation symbols. The peckers are penalized (token fine) for leaving spaces between the characters, and rewarded (token bonus) when one of their swatches, seen from a little distance, gives the appearance of a near-solid block of ink, similar to *The Congressional Record*.

Their work is transmitted instantly to Seattle, where it is given intense scrutiny, line by line. And there is a redundancy arrangement to insure that nothing pecked is ever quite lost, into the void. For backup swatches are also printed out in the local Pecking Centers, then gathered, compressed, and bound into bales, like cotton. These monstrous, cubic haikus are shipped out weekly, air freight, to the Foundation's 2A Clearing House, which is a hangar leased from the Boeing company.

It is there that the American pecking harvest undergoes a final scanning, in the search for words and coherent snatches of language. A long white banner hangs across the cavernous work bay, reading, THE WIND BLOWETH WHERE IT LISTETH. The scanners, known as "swatch auditors," are 720 elderly men in baseball caps. They work in three shifts around the clock. They are paid well and seated comfortably on inflated doughnut cushions.

During breaks the auditors play harmless pranks on one another. These antics once caught the indulgent eye of Mrs. Perkins Jenkins, who was looking on from an observation gallery, and thereby hangs the tale of how her most celebrated poem, and by far her shortest one, "just popped into my head." It was not, that is, fabricated. The two stanzas simply came to her, suddenly and all of a piece, complete with title, "The Levity of Old Men." She dictated the words to her secretary at once, before they could evaporate. Such was the origin of this gem of the modern anthologies, and thus the grand old lady's unwavering trust in her muse.

My interviews went well enough until I came upon another touchy mandrill, Red Kilgore by name, as I could see by the prism nameplate on his pecking stand. He had been watching me, glowering.

"So," he said. "What is this thing you have about monkeys?"

"Well, I do, you know, associate monkeys with chattering and gibbering and shrieking."

"You don't approve of chattering?"

"I approve of chatting."

"Cute distinction. Do you find me gibbering now?"

"Not at all, no. But there on your screen, just a minute ago, I did see something that appeared to be, excuse me, gibberish."

"How many of our swatches have you actually read?"

"Some. A few. I extrapolate freely, of course. Like poll takers. It's an accepted practice."

"I suppose you think all that stuff you churn out at your paper is a lot better than the stuff we churn out here."

"Well, it is better, yes. But then we still use typewriters at the *Blade*."

"Say what?"

"Manual typewriters. They don't hum at you like the electric ones. And the ribbons are cheaper."

"But *typewriters*."

"They give you black words fixed hard on white paper."

"And that's good in some way?"

"Good enough. There are critics who say that things written with quivering cathode rays on greenish luminescent tubes have a different tone altogether. A loose, thin, garrulous feel."

"Tone. Feel. You seem to be saying to me that all those old Smith-Coronas in your office are so many Stradivaris."

"We use Underwoods and Royals."

"When will this report of yours be in the paper?"

"Tomorrow, with any luck."

"Will my name be in it?"

"Yes."

"On what page?"

"I don't know."

"What will the headline say? So I don't have to wade through all the other junk."

"Again, not my department. Probably something like 'Monkey Business.'"

"Look here, I know I'm wasting my breath, but let me try to explain something. Are you familiar with the law of large numbers?"

"That law, no, it doesn't ring a bell."

"Well, the idea is that a great many little uncertainties—a long series of coin-flippings, say—will miraculously add up to one big certainty. You will get half heads and half tails."

"How does that apply?"

"Order from disorder, you see. The moving finger of grace, unseen."

"Then you are in the disorder business here."

"We are in the volume business, sir. Moving product. And allow me to tell you this, that a certain brute quantity can attain a special quality all its own. We are not the least bit interested in your old elitist notion of writing as some sort of algebra."

"But Red, listen to yourself. Here you are speaking to me in that algebra."

"Not for long. Vamoose."

My article—this article—was much longer. Two editors slashed away on it, turn and turn about. But it was not spiked. What remained, now somewhat garbled, was actually set in type and scheduled to appear in the Sunday feature section. I was delighted. On Friday, however, the *Blade* went broke and out of business. There was no Sunday edition. Neither was there any money left for our final salary checks, let alone severance pay.

The closing out was poorly managed, overall. A scrap-iron dealer hauled away our typewriters. They were flung into his dump truck from a third-floor window of the city room. Even some of our clothes were seized, with the lawyers for the bank declaring them to be "workplace specific apparel, i.e., company uniforms, and as such, *Blade* assets." Can you imagine —making off with the old coats and ties and *shoes* of newspaper people? Frankie retaliated by stealing the blue Gremlin and keeping it hidden under a tarpaulin in some woods until the legal dust had settled. It was the pick of the litter. The blue one still had two or three hubcaps. It had come to this pass then, with the *Blade*'s ancient flotilla of Gremlins, once so jaunty, and always great favorites of the crowd when they cruised down Main Street in attack formation with the floats and fire trucks of city parades. Frankie picks me up every weekday morning at 7:40 in that blue car. She gives five or six impatient toots of the horn, when one light toot would do. We are both working now as peckers, level three, at the Pecking Center on Warehouse Road, not far from the Loopdale Cutoff, and happily so, I may say. The sheer abandon of it all. A revelation. I had no idea. The joy of writing in torrents. In swatches! By the bale! My master of arts degree means nothing at all to these monkeys and I have come to share their indifference. Red Kilgore was on to something. There is much to be said as well for the largesse of Mrs. Hazel Perkins Jenkins.

At odd moments, Frankie and I will pause in our work and look each other full in the face, then break out laughing again, over our old nonsense of writing by design. All that misplaced striving. We laugh till our eyes water up. Ever bold, Frankie said her formal goodbye to artifice some weeks ago, and this, today, is mine. We may have another little announcement quite soon.

*2005*

# REPORTAGE, ESSAYS,
# & MEMOIR

# CIVIL RIGHTS REPORTING

*How the Night Exploded into Terror*

BIRMINGHAM.
It was a hot night and down in the Negro section of town, around the A. G. Gaston Motel, the beer joints and barbecue stands were doing a good, loud Saturday night business. In a three-block area more than 1,000 Negroes were milling about.

Over at Bessemer, 12 miles away, the Ku Klux Klan was having an outdoor rally in the flickering light of two flaming 25-foot crosses. On hand were 200 hooded men, including the imperial wizard himself and a couple grand dragons and about 900 Klan supporters in mufti. There were a lot of bugs in the air, too, knocking against the crosses and falling into open collars.

For a month, through all the Negro demonstrations here, little was heard from the tough white element in the Birmingham area—very likely, the toughest in the South. Everyone wondered why, and then, Saturday night, the explosion came, literally.

Earlier in the day, the Rev. Wyatt Walker, Dr. Martin Luther King Jr.'s executive secretary, asked the police to place a watch on the Gaston Motel because some white men had been observed "casing it." At 7:30 P.M. a call came through the motel switchboard, warning that the motel would be bombed that night. It was a straight tip.

At 11:32 P.M. some night riders tossed two bombs from a car onto the front porch of the Rev. A. D. King's home in the suburb of Ensley. The front half of the house was ripped apart, but no one was injured. Mr. King is Martin Luther King's brother.

The night riders then sped four miles across town to the motel, headquarters for the Negro leaders, and threw another bomb. It blasted a four-foot hole through the brick wall of one of the bedroom units. Three Negro women were sent tumbling—including one about 80 years old—but they were not seriously injured.

That did it. The Negroes in the area, many of them just leaving the beer joints at midnight closing, went into a frenzy of brick-throwing, knifing, burning and rioting that took four hours to stop, and then just short of gunfire. It was the worst night of terror in the South since the battle of Ole Miss. More than 25 people were injured and property damage was estimated at many thousands of dollars.

A few of us at the Tutwiler Hotel, four blocks away from the Negro motel, heard the midnight explosion—a dull whoomp —and got there a few minutes later. Only about 35 city policemen were on the scene, and they were standing in a small perimeter, arms over their heads, under a barrage of rocks and bottles from a mob of cursing and shouting Negroes closing in on them.

Mr. Walker—a Negro—was catching it from them, too, as he moved about with a bull horn pleading for calm.

"Please, please. Move back, move back. Throwing rocks won't help," he said. "This is no good. Please go home. It does no good to lose your heads."

"Tell it to Bull Connor," they shouted back to him. "This is what non-violence gets you."

Some of the rioters were attacking the police cars, smashing the windows with chunks of cinder blocks and cutting the tires with knives. One group kicked over a motorcycle and set it afire. Some others got around a paddy wagon and tried to upset it, but it was too heavy, so they battered the windows in.

Patrolman J. N. Spivey, alone and encircled in the mob, was stabbed in the shoulder and back. Capt. Glenn Evans and a deputy sheriff were kicked and punched pulling him free.

Help arrived soon in the form of a Negro civil defense unit with helmets and billy clubs, and more white police. These emergency Negro officers took just as much abuse and pummelling as the whites.

The city's armored car arrived shortly before 1 A.M. and its appearance provoked the mob anew.

"Let's get the tank," they yelled. "Bull, you — —, come on out of there." Public Safety Commissioner Bull Connor was not in the "tank" though this idea persisted throughout the night. (No one seemed to know where he was.)

The little white riot vehicle roared back and forth under a hail of rocks to scatter the crowd, and it mounted the sidewalk once and made a headlong pass down it, sending about 50 of us spectators diving for the dirt.

Some of the newsmen were hit with rocks and beer cans, but most of them quickly learned to stay away from such targets as the armored car and any large group of police.

Two blocks away, in a quiet zone, a gang of white boys were gathered on a corner throwing rocks and smashing the windows of Negro ambulances on their way to the motel. Police removed boys from the scene early, though, and no other whites appeared in the melee.

There came a frightening development at 1:10 A.M. That was when Col. Al Lingo, director of the Alabama Highway Patrol, arrived, itching for action. He and a lieutenant sprang from their car with 12-gauge pump shotguns at the ready, and moved toward the crowd.

"I'll stop those — —," he said.

"Wait, wait a minute now," said Birmingham Police Chief Jamie Moore, intercepting him. "You're just going to get somebody killed with those guns."

"I damn sure will if I have to," said Col. Lingo.

"I wish you'd get back in the car. I'd appreciate it."

"I'm not about to leave. Gov. Wallace sent me here."

In the end, he did go back to the car, jabbing a couple of Negroes with his gun on the way. But Col. Lingo would be heard from again before the night was over.

Chief Moore and his chief inspector, William J. Haley, used little rough stuff in trying to disperse the mob. The dogs and fire trucks were on hand but were never used.

Inspector Haley, his head protected only by a soft hat, moved fearlessly from one hot spot to another, taking punches and kicks and rocks, yet never losing his head.

The action took place on all four sides of the city block, bounded by 15th and 16th Sts., and Fifth and Sixth Aves. The motel is on Fifth Ave., between the two streets. It is a neighborhood of small grocery stores, taverns, frame shanties and churches.

The 16th St. Baptist Church, the starting point of all the recent demonstrations, is a block diagonally away from the motel at the corner of Sixth Ave. and 16th St. For a while it was thought the church was burning, but it turned out to be a taxicab that had been turned over and set afire in front of the church.

The Rev. A. D. King arrived at 1:45 A.M. and joined Mr. Walker and a number of other Negro leaders in trying to quell the riot with bull-horn pleas. Around 2 o'clock he climbed atop a parked car in the motel courtyard and gathered an audience of about 300 Negroes.

"We have been taught by our religion that we do not have to return evil for evil," he told them. "I must appeal to you to refuse any acts of retaliation for any acts of violence . . . We're not mad with a soul . . . my wife and five children are all right. Thank God we're all well and safe."

As he spoke and prayed, and as the gathering sang, "We Shall Overcome," a white grocery store was burning on the corner of 15th St. and Sixth Ave. Firemen trying to put it out were stoned by the mob. After a few minutes they retreated and the fire burned unchecked. The firemen pulled out so fast that they left a hose in the street, and it lay there burning in the no-man's land.

At 2:30, another grocery store directly across the street blazed up. Two frame houses on either side of the store caught fire, then a third, a two-story house. The rocks kept the firemen out, and it appeared the whole block would go.

"Let the whole — city burn, I don't give a God damn," said one of the rioters. "This'll show those white — —s."

"We have just spoken with the President's press secretary, Andrew Hatcher, and he asked you to return to your homes," announced one of the Negro leaders. "Please go to your homes. This is no answer."

At 3:05, with a police guard of about 75 men, the firemen returned to the blazing houses with two trucks and went to work again. The rocks and bricks were still flying, but a skirmish line of Negro leaders kept the rioters out of throwing range of the fire fighters.

In this scrap, Inspector Haley caught a brick on the forehead. With blood running down his face into his eyes, he stayed on the skirmish line calling, "Get back . . . get back, you must get back." He became so weak he had to be carried away.

An infuriated city policeman started toward the Negroes with a shotgun. When Mr. King tried to stop him, he knocked the minister out of the way with his gun. But a police lieu-tenant grabbed the angry patrolman and ordered him back. A few minutes later another policeman advanced on the mob and sighted his pistol across his left arm. Again the lieutenant stepped in and stopped him.

Soon there was left only a small pocket of rioters, young men in their teens and twenties, confined to 15th St. between Sixth and Seventh Aves. This group set fire to yet another grocery store at 15th St. and Seventh Ave. The blaze was nipped by Negro Civil Defense men.

It was pretty much all over at 3:40, when the state troopers began clubbing Negroes sitting on their porches. They had been sitting there watching all along, taking no part in the fight.

"Get in the house, God damn it, get, get," shouted the troopers, punching and pounding them with their nightsticks. And so the battle ended with the state policemen, who had played only a very minor role in the actual quelling of the riot, rapping old Negro men in rocking chairs.

Col. Lingo and his men had been chafing all week at the moderation and restraint of Chief Moore and his city police. "Moore is a Boy Scout," said Col. Lingo.

When daylight began to break at 4 o'clock, there were no Negroes in sight. The only sound to be heard was the scream-ing of sirens as more and more state troopers poured into the city, with their shotguns at ready and carbines with bayonets fixed.

The police, about 1,000 of them, cordoned off the troubled area around the motel from 14th to 17th Sts. and from First to Eighth Aves., allowing no one to leave or enter the area.

Shortly before 6 A.M. a state police sound vehicle cruised about downtown warning individual Negroes to "get off the God damn streets, get."

But someone put a stop to that, evidently because it was Sunday and Mother's Day.

After that the city was deathly silent, and no one was to be seen on the streets for several hours—until church time. It was a sparkling morning, and around the post office the air was fragrant with the scent of magnolia blossoms.

*May 13, 1963*

## Klan Rally—Just Talk

BIRMINGHAM.
A Ku Klux Klan meeting, for all its cross-burning and hooded panoply, is a much duller affair than one might expect. The masked Klan rally in Bessemer Saturday night—just before the bombings in Birmingham—limped along for three hours of nothing but Kennedy jokes and invocations of Divine guidance.

It's hardly worth driving 12 miles and risking a clout on the head to hear President Kennedy and his brothers slandered, when you can get that on any street corner in Birmingham.

The rally was held in a well-kept little roadside park, a gift to the City of Bessemer from the Loyal Order of Moose. Moose Park, they call it. Two huge crosses were burned, one with an effigy of Martin Luther King on it. The crosses were some 25 feet high and about the heft of telephone poles.

There were 200 hooded and gowned men on hand and about 1,000 spectators in street dress. Entire families came, some with tow-headed kids that couldn't have been much more than 4 years old.

About 25 of the gowned Klansmen were in fancy red regalia —they were the dragons and kleagles. The others wore white. Their outfits are in three pieces—blouse, gown and pointed hood.

Some wore badly tailored cotton sheeting, but others had costumes of well-cut shiny nylon. Only a few concealed their faces. Most of them had their face flaps tied back.

"Klansmanship . . . Kennedy . . . niggers . . . Jews . . . the white man . . . Our Heavenly Father," these were the recurring words in all the speeches. One or two spoke vaguely of bloodshed to come, but only in the sense of some unscheduled Armageddon.

A few references were made to the Birmingham situation. All were advised to cancel their charge plates and stop shopping at downtown stores there.

"We know who the men are who are selling out our country," said one dragon. "The K.B.I. (Klan Bureau of Investigation) has learned their names."

The imperial wizard of the Klan, Robert M. Shelton, presided and introduced the speakers as they appeared, one by one, on a big flat truck trailer bed.

Honored guests were the grand dragons of Georgia and Mississippi.

By 10:30 P.M. one of the crosses had collapsed and the other was just smoldering. Everyone drifted away and the grand dragon of Mississippi disappeared grandly into the Southern night, his car engine hitting on about three cylinders.

*May 13, 1963*


## A Long Day of Defiance

TUSCALOOSA, Ala.
Down a path lined by steel-helmeted troopers and cleared by soldiers in battle dress, James A. Hood and Vivian Juanita Malone went to college yesterday.

They are both 20, they are both Negroes. They were both, for a day, in the center of the national stage as the President of the U.S. issued first a proclamation to "cease and desist" and then an order Federalizing the National Guard to stop the Governor of Alabama from keeping them out.

Together, they represent integration for an all-white state school system that has resisted integration longer than any other state in the union.

But as they walked into the red-brick registration building on the university campus, Gov. George C. Wallace—who backed down under the threat of a force greater than any he could muster—breathed defiance and told the world:

"We are winning this fight because we are awakening the people of the nation to the trend toward military dictatorship."

And then he quickly added, "We must have no violence today or any day."

That was the pattern of the hot, airless day: like a strange ballet, the forces on each side slowly took up their positions and slowly changed as strategy called forth counter-strategy. Seemingly, the only non-determined item was the fact that Miss Malone came to the campus yesterday morning in a black dress and yesterday afternoon went in to pay her $175 summer-term fee wearing a bright pink dress.

In a suddenly called national television and radio address last night, President Kennedy praised the students of the university —conspicuous by their silence, their restraint—and pointed out the lessons for every state made clear by posing the moral issue in Alabama as to "whether all Americans are going to be treated equally."

It was an epilogue to a moral drama.

The final act was set in motion at 1:34 P.M. when President Kennedy signed the executive order that brought the 15,000 troops and 2,000 air personnel of the Alabama National Guard under Federal jurisdiction.

The last time Alabama's crack 31st Infantry Division had been called up to national duty was in 1961—when Berlin was the crisis that called forth the headlines.

The President's order was transmitted immediately to Secretary of Defense Robert S. McNamara, and down the chain of command it went until Brig. Gen. Henry Graham, assistant commander of the 31st, marched to the doorway where Gov. Wallace stood—just as he had pledged in his last campaign—in the final effort to keep the Negro students out.

Dressed in fatigues, a Rebel flag patch on his shoulder, four tough special guardsmen flanking him, Gen. Graham said:

"I am Gen. Graham, and it is my sad duty to ask you to step aside, on order of the President of the U.S."

"General," the Governor said, reading from a crumpled piece of paper at a lectern set up just for the occasion, "I wish to make a statement first.

"But for the unwarranted Federalization of the National Guard, I would be your commander-in-chief. In fact, I am your commander-in-chief. I know this is a bitter pill to swallow for the National Guard of Alabama. . . .

"We must have no violence . . . the Guardsmen are our brothers . . . God bless all the people of this state, white and black."

After a final vow to "continue this fight on the legal questions involved," the Governor got into his car and drove off in a roar of motorcycle police. Several students cheered.

And that was it.

Mr. Hood, who wants to study psychology, and Miss Malone, a business administration student, walked in minutes later with several Federal marshals and registered. A group of white students watched with no comment.

"This is our first and final news conference," Mr. Hood said afterward to part of the 400-man press corps that almost out-manned the 500-man state trooper contingent called up by the Governor. "We are very happy our registration has taken place without incident. We hope to get down to our purpose —study."

Both obviously looked forward to a procession before caps and gowns, not helmets and rifles.

So, too, did Deputy Attorney General Nicholas de B. Katz-enbach, who directed the desegregation moves on the scene for the government, faced up to Gov. Wallace and his troopers in the morning and wore a broad grin and a ringlet of sweat beads as he came back at 5:17 P.M. for the final moves of the game. It was when Mr. Wallace saw 100 Federalized guardsmen —first of a contingent waiting a few blocks away on University Ave.—that he gave in.

Even when the day started, Mr. Wallace was under court order "not to interfere in any way" with the enrollment of the two Negroes. Under a carefully contrived technicality, he may not have done so, since he never actually confronted them.

In the early morning, before the two Negroes first came to the doorway of Foster Hall to register, President Kennedy is-sued a proclamation ordering the Governor to stop impeding the course decreed by the courts.

Ironically, it was countersigned by Secretary of State Dean Rusk, who must put the seal on all such proclamations, but who is particularly concerned at the propaganda picture the situation presents abroad.

The dramatic morning confrontation between state's rights and the Federal government took only 13 minutes.

It was 12:45 and the would-be students arrived in a three-car convoy. They had driven over earlier from Birmingham. Each had a $500 scholarship check from Negro organizations. Mr. Hood was prepared to pay his $280 to register in the college of arts and sciences, Miss Malone $205.20 to register for courses in the business school.

Around the building where the registration was to take place, a ring of state troopers stood in tight formation. Newsmen were clustered at the entrance, many of them wearing newspaper hats to ward off the sun. It was deadly hot.

A few students had been drifting in and out of the building all morning, but now none were to be seen.

Gov. Wallace was just inside the doorway, waiting, with a phalanx of state troopers behind him.

Deputy Attorney General Katzenbach, accompanied by U.S. Attorney Macon L. Weaver and U.S. Marshal Peyton Norville, both Southerners and graduates of the university here, got out of the lead car and walked the 20 or 30 steps to the entrance. Miss Malone and Mr. Hood remained in their car.

Gov. Wallace stepped forward to the lectern that had been set up and raised his hand to stop Mr. Katzenbach, actually touching Mr. Katzenbach's chest with his fingertips.

"I am here for the Attorney General of the U.S. and I have a proclamation here signed by the President of the U.S.," said Mr. Katzenbach. He then introduced Mr. Weaver and Mr. Norville, read the proclamation, explained that he was there to enforce a court order and asked the Governor to step aside and allow the Negro students to register.

Mr. Katzenbach said, "All they want is an education . . ."

"We don't need you here to make a speech," the Governor broke in. "Just make your statement."

Mr. Wallace then launched into his remarks, a five-page speech.

He used as his text the State's Rights Amendment of the Constitution—the 10th Amendment—and he spoke of "unwelcomed, unwanted, unwarranted and forced, indeed intrusion, upon the campus . . . by the might of the central government."

He concluded with a "solemn proclamation" saying: "Now, therefore I, George C. Wallace, Governor of the State of Alabama, have by my action raised issue between the central government and the sovereign State of Alabama . . . and do hereby denounce and forbid this illegal and unwarranted action by the central government."

"I take it from that statement that you are going to stand in the doorway," said Mr. Katzenbach.

The Governor, who had stepped back to block the double doorway with two troopers on either side, said simply, "I stand on my statement."

"Governor, I'm not interested in a show," said Mr. Katzenbach. "I don't know what the purpose of the show is. I'm here to enforce an order of the courts. . . . These students have a right to be here. . . . It is a simple problem. I ask you once more to step aside. It is your choice."

But the Governor had nothing more to say. Mr. Katzenbach asked him twice more to "step aside," and then said of the Negro students in his charge, "They will register today, they will go to school tomorrow and they will attend this summer session. They will remain on the campus."

And with that he, Mr. Weaver and Mr. Norville turned and went back to the car. The Governor had made his stand, and now the only thing to do was to bring in troops.

Miss Malone got out of the car, and three marshals escorted her to Mary Burke Hall, her dormitory, directly behind the auditorium. Mr. Hood was driven to his dorm, Palmer Hall, on the other side of the campus, a half-mile away. No troops were posted at the dorm entrances, and they had no trouble getting in.

The word "show" used by Mr. Katzenbach was a good choice. It was a well-staged pageant from start to finish.

Asked afterward if there was any plan to arrest the Governor, Edwin Guthman, Justice Department spokesman, said, "None whatsoever."

The troops will remain on the campus indefinitely, he said, but the Justice Department considers the campus under civil patrol. State troopers and Tuscaloosa police remained on duty at the university after the Governor left, and apparently will stay, with security under the dual control of Gen. Graham and Col. Al Lingo, head of the State Highway Patrol.

Personal guardians for Miss Malone and Mr. Hood will be the 30 U.S. marshals and border patrolmen brought in for the enrollment yesterday.

The president of the university, Dr. Frank A. Rose, was delighted with the way things turned out. "We could not have hoped for more exemplary conduct than that displayed by all those present for the crucial hours this morning and afternoon," he said. "We confidently expect that the University of Alabama soon will be able to return to normalcy, and we look forward to resuming fully our dedicated mission."

*June 12, 1963*

## Murder in Mississippi

JACKSON, Miss.
Medgar W. Evers, the respected 37-year-old field director of the National Association for the Advancement of Colored People, was driving home.

He had been at one of those countless NAACP rallies he had attended during the nine years he led the crusade for civil rights in Mississippi.

It was shortly after midnight yesterday (about 2:30 A.M. New York time) when he got out of the station wagon in front of the house. He picked up a pile of NAACP sweatshirts, emblazoned "Jim Crow Must Go," and started into the house where his wife and three small children were waiting up for him.

He never made it. Lying in ambush, apparently in the fragrant honeysuckle bushes about 155 feet away, an assassin squeezed the trigger of a high-powered 30-30 rifle.

Mr. Evers, his white shirt forming an easy target in the porch light, was shot in the back. He died 50 minutes later in a hospital.

The rifle blast touched off a wave of shock across the nation. President Kennedy, who had made an appeal to the nation for an end to racial discrimination only a few hours before, was described as "appalled by the barbarity of this act."

Mississippi Gov. Ross Barnett, a staunch segregationist, called the killing of the Negro leader "a dastardly act."

Jackson Mayor Allen Thompson said the citizens were "dreadfully shocked, humiliated and sick at heart" and announced that the city was putting up a $5,000 reward for information leading to the arrest and conviction of those responsible.

The killing seemed to be the main conversational topic of everyone, from groups of idlers on Capitol Ave., the city's main street, to Southern belles in big white hats drinking iced tea in the dining room of the Heidelberg Hotel. Many feared it would trigger further violence.

A man in a beer joint at the edge of town seemed to represent the tougher elements of the city when he commented: "Maybe this will slow the niggers down."

In all, rewards totaling $21,000 were posted, including $10,000 from the NAACP, $5,000 from the city of Jackson, $50 from Jackson District Attorney Bill Waller, $1,000 from The Clarion Ledger and Jackson Daily News, and $5,000 from the United Steelworkers.

Shock and anger spread through Jackson's Negro district. At midday, 13 Negro ministers and a church layman staged a "mourning march" to the downtown area. They were arrested. A short time later Negro youths started a march to protest the slaying and 146 were arrested immediately by no less than 200 officers of the law.

Attorney General Robert F. Kennedy offered the full services of the FBI to track down the killer, but by nightfall about the only solid clue was the murder rifle, which was found in the bushes not far from Mr. Evers' house. A friend of the NAACP leader said he saw a "tall white man" running through a lot near the scene of the killing. Investigators also had a report that three men ran from the scene immediately after the shooting.

Threats and violence were not new to Mr. Evers, who has been in the forefront of the long drive for integration in Mississippi—a drive that has resulted in 804 arrests, including yesterday's, since May 28.

Only two weeks ago, a soft-drink bottle filled with gasoline was tossed into the carport next to Mr. Evers' house. It did not explode.

In an interview last summer with a CBS television reporter, Mr. Evers was asked about threats. This was his answer:

"I've had a number of threatening calls—people calling me saying they were going to kill me, saying they were going to blow my home up and saying that I only had a few hours to live.

"I remember distinctly one individual calling with a pistol on the other end, and he hit the cylinder and, of course you could hear that it was a revolver. He said, 'This is for you.' And I said, 'Well, whenever my time comes, I'm ready.'

"And, well, we get such pranks pretty frequently. But that does not deter us from our goal of first-class citizenship and getting more people registered to vote and doing the things here that a democracy certainly is supposed to espouse and provide for its citizenry."

Early yesterday the bullet which fatally wounded Mr. Evers smashed through a window pane, pierced a wall and hit the refrigerator in the kitchen. It bounced off the refrigerator onto a counter near the sink and rolled under a watermelon.

A trail of blood in the driveway showed that Mr. Evers staggered 30 feet through a carport and alongside a bed of red petunias before he fell by the back steps.

His wife, Myrlie, and the three children, aged three to nine, rushed out to him. Mrs. Evers became hysterical. The children were crying and pleading with their father to "get up."

Neighbors quickly picked up Mr. Evers, put him in his own station wagon, and raced off to the hospital. Houston Wells, one of the neighbors, said:

"On the way to the hospital he said, 'turn me loose.' He said that a number of times. That's all he said."

At last night's rally, several ministers called upon the Negro community of Jackson to boycott downtown stores for 30 days and to wear black for 30 days in mourning for Mr. Evers.

And another mass meeting was called for 10 this morning at the church—meaning more demonstrations.

Mrs. Evers, the Negro leader's widow, addressed the meeting briefly and tearfully. "I come to you tonight with a broken heart," she said. "But I come to make a plea that all of you here will be able to draw some of his strength, some of his courage. Nothing can bring him back, but this cause can live on."

*June 13, 1963*

# ESSAYS

# *That New Sound from Nashville*

NASHVILLE, THE Athens of the South, is home to Vanderbilt University, Fisk University and at least half a dozen other colleges, as well as a symphony orchestra, a concrete replica of the Parthenon and a downtown beer joint called Tootsie's Orchid Lounge. Tootsie's is where the country-music people hang out—those who don't object to beer joints. It has a very active jukebox and shaky tables, and there are 8-by-10 glossies all over the wall and a clutter of small-bore merchandise behind the counter—stuff like gum, beef sticks and headache powder. The hostess is Tootsie Bess, a motherly, aproned woman who doesn't mind noise or a certain amount of rowdiness, but whose good nature has its limits. One night a drunk songwriter addressed Maggie, the cook, as "nigger," and Tootsie threw him out and banned him. She has three cigar boxes full of I.O.U.'s.

On Saturday nights, performers on the Grand Ole Opry step out the stage door and cross an alley and go in the back door of Tootsie's to get aholt of themselves between sets with some refreshing suds. Songwriters—"cleffers," as the trade mags say —sit around and chat and wait for artistic revelations. Deals are closed there. New, strange guitar licks are conceived.

Roger Miller (*King of the Road*), the antic poet who was too far out to have any success on the Opry itself, was singing and clowning in Tootsie's back room years ago, for free. "He wrote *Dang Me* right here in this booth," says Tootsie. But his rates are stiffer now. He just did a special for NBC-TV and is talking with them about starring in a series next year. "Yeah, Roger's doing all right," says a Nashville business associate. "He was in here the other day with a quarter of a million dollars in his pocket. It was two checks."

Tootsie's is like a thousand other beer joints in the South with such names as Junior's Dew Drop Inn and Pearl's Howdy Club, and a certain type of country boy feels right at home there, whether he has $250,000 in his pocket or just came in on the bus from Plain Dealing, La., with a guitar across his back and white cotton socks rolled down in little cylinders atop his grease-resistant work shoes. And a song in his heart about teardrops, adultery, diesel trucks.

This is the *milieu* of commercial country music, the Southern honky-tonk. Sometimes it's called "hillbilly music," which is only half accurate, because the southern lowlanders have contributed just as much as the hill folks, perhaps more; and sometimes "country and western," which is misleading because such of it as reflects the culture west of Abilene, Tex., tends to be pretty thin stuff. "Southern white working-class music" would never do as a tag, but that's what it is.

By any name, country music is prospering, and so is Nashville's recording industry, which now does a brisk non-country trade. Perry Como, hitless for almost two years, packed a carpetbag recently and went to Nashville and came back with a hit single, *Dream On, Little Dreamer*, by two country-music writers, and a hit album, *The Scene Changes*. The golf was good too, he says. Both RCA Victor and Columbia have built big new studios there in the past year, and all sorts of unlikely people—Al Hirt, Ann-Margret—are going there to record. Elvis Presley always has.

It is odd in a way that the country-music business should have settled in Nashville, instead of in a rougher, rawer town like, say, Shreveport. (Shreveport does have a lesser version of the Opry called "The Louisiana Hayride.") Nashville is an old town (1780), a state capital, a college town, and a headquarters town for southern churches.

There are some 200,000 people in the city proper. It is a pleasant, green, genteel, residential place on the banks of the Cumberland River in the rolling hills of middle Tennessee. Nashville once had poets like Sidney Lanier and Allen Tate, and now it has Ernest Tubb and doesn't quite know what to do with him, except ignore him. Few country singers manage to get themselves taken seriously in Nashville. Eddy Arnold is a big community man, and he is being discussed as a Democratic nominee for governor next year. Roy Acuff ran for governor as a Republican, unsuccessfully. But generally, the

Athenians of the South go one way, and the country-music people another. Less than 10 percent of the Opry audiences come from the Nashville area. Middle-class Nashvillians, anxious lest they be mistaken for rubes, are quick to inform the visitor that they have never attended the show. It is not for them, this hoedown. They long for road-company presentations of socko Broadway comedies. Even radio station WSM, which carries the Opry, is not really a country-music station. "Oh, no," says Ott Devine, WSM's Opry manager. "Except for the Opry and a few record shows we're a *good* music station."

But settle there the business has, and it now brings in some $60 million a year to the town. From the Opry it has grown into a complex of 10 recording studios, 26 record companies, and a colony of 700 cleffers, 265 music publishers, and 1,000 union musicians, about half of whom can read music with some facility. Nashville has replaced Chicago as the country's third-busiest recording center, after New York and Hollywood, and is probably ahead of Hollywood, says RCA Victor vice president Steve Sholes, "in the production of successful single records." The main reason is that it has developed its own style, what outsiders call "The Nashville Sound." Nobody wants to define it, but it amounts to country music with a dash of Tin Pan Alley, in the form of noncountry instruments like drums and trombones.

The music, in its present form, is not really very old. It is a blend of British balladry, American folk songs, 19th-century Protestant hymns, Negro blues and gospel songs, southern-white themes and, now, a touch of northern pop. There were important pioneers in the early 1920's such as Vernon Dalhart ("If I had the wings of an angel . . .") but for most practical purposes the music dates from 1927 when Jimmie Rodgers made his first record (Victor) for a goldback $20 bill.

Rodgers was The Blue Yodeler, The Singing Brakeman. He was a consumptive drifter from Meridian, Miss., who, in a span of six years, established commercial country music as a distinct new form. He was not quite 36 years old when he coughed himself to death in a New York hotel room in 1933. At the end he was so wasted and weakened with tuberculosis that he had to lie on a cot while recording at Victor's 24th Street studio in New York. He left a legacy of 112 songs, many of them classics like *My Carolina Sunshine Gal, I'm in the Jailhouse Now,* and

> *I'm goin' to town, honey,*
> *What you want me to bring you back?*
> *Bring me a pint of booze*
> *And a John B. Stetson hat. . . .*

With a strong assist from The Carter Family (*Wildwood Flower, Wabash Cannon Ball*) Rodgers set the pattern for the music, and the Grand Ole Opry formalized it and gave it a home. The Opry is the mother church. Actually this show pre-dates Rodgers's recording career by two years, but in the beginning it was only a fiddler's show, and it wasn't until later that it took on its present form as a singin' and pickin' jamboree.

In the 1930's the music remained pretty well localized in the South and Midwest, except for the hemispheric exposure it was given by the Mexican-border radio stations, beaming it out at 200,000 tube-shattering watts, the hillbilly songs sandwiched in between harangues from jackleg preachers and pitches for towels and chickens. ("Send your card or letter to *Baby Chicks*! That's *Baby Chicks*! Sorry, no guarantee of sex, breed or color.")

But it didn't get off the ground nationally until World War II, when the northern boys and city boys got strong doses of it in barracks and on decks and in southern camp towns. For those in uniform there was no escape from *Smoke on the Water* and *Pistol Packin' Mama* and *Detour* and *There's a Star-Spangled Banner Wavin' Somewhere*. Some of the city boys developed a tolerance for it, a few even came to like it. In 1944 the USO polled GI's in Europe to determine the most popular singer and, lo, Roy Acuff's name led all the rest. It was much the same in Korea. There were few rifle companies in that war without a wind-up record player and a well-worn 78 rpm record of Hank Williams's *Lovesick Blues*. The Chinese even used the music in an attempt to make the American troops homesick, or maybe it was their idea of torture. For whatever reason, they set up giant speakers and boomed ditties like *You Are My Sunshine* across the valleys in the long watches of the night.

The music soon went into eclipse again, as it had done after World War II, and it wasn't until the late 1950's that it began making its present comeback—this time with The Nashville Sound.

> *A White Sport Coat and Pink Carnation*
> *I'm all dressed up for the dance. . . .*

The boom started just a few years after country music was laid low by rock 'n' roll. "Elvis made *Heartbreak Hotel* in whenever it was, 'Fifty-something, and all those rock songs came along and country music took a nose dive like nobody's business," says Buddy Killen, executive vice president of a Nashville publishing house called Tree Music. "Things began to look up when Ferlin Husky made one called *Gone*. I think that was the first big one with the new sound. It had the beat and the piano and Jourdanaires. That's the thing now, the beat. It used to be the song."

Others cite Marty Robbins's *A White Sport Coat* or Sonny James's *Young Love* as the breakthrough tunes. All three records had a country flavor, but they weren't *too* country; they were country-pop hybrids that sold well in both markets. They had The Nashville Sound.

They don't call it that in Nashville, of course. They call it "uptown country," as opposed to "hard country," which is the traditional hillbilly music that is still big on the Opry and on five A.M. snuff shows. Hillbilly is characterized by a squonking fiddle introduction, a funereal steel guitar and an overall whiney, draggy sound that has never set well with urban ears.

The masterminds of The Nashville Sound have abandoned all that. They have smoothed out many of the rough edges likely to offend. They use sophisticated new chord progressions and, while the guitar remains the primary accompaniment—lead, rhythm, steel, 12-string—they have added piano, drums and choral voices, and anything that strikes their fancy—vibes, tenor sax, harpsichord, trombone. The prejudice against non-string instruments has largely gone by the way. Even the Opry now permits drums on the stage, though it is still holding the line against brass and woodwinds.

So popular is the new sound that the number of country-music radio stations has increased from 81 to 200-plus in the past four years, and that includes several 50,000-watt heavy-weights in places like Los Angeles (KGBS) and Chicago (WJJD). Even New York City—where there are restaurants for Polynesians, northern *and* southern Italians, northern *and* southern Chinese, Moors, Scandinavians, Lithuanians and Romanians, but where you can't buy a decent plate of turnip greens, purple-hull peas and fried okra—even that market has been opened up. Since last September, WJRZ in Newark, a former pop station, has been beaming Lefty Frizzell and Ferlin Husky across the Hudson all day and all night, and it has increased its audience 1,000 percent.

"This music has a new acceptance and a new dignity," says Harry Reith, the general manager of WJRZ. "It's not, you know, the old hillbilly stuff, the nasal voices, those guitars thumping and all. Our mail response has been fantastic."

Few people can agree on precisely what The Nashville Sound is, but there is pretty general agreement as to who the masterminds are—namely, Chet Atkins, Victor's Artist and Repertoire man in Nashville; Owen Bradley, A-and-R man there for Decca; and Don Law, A-and-R man for Columbia. The A-and-R man is the guiding hand in record production. He matches the song with the singer and directs recording sessions—so far as anyone can be said to "direct" a session in Nashville. He picks the recordings to be released and the ones to be shelved. He puts albums together.

Chet Atkins, who may be the best guitarist in the country, is a quiet, introspective man who sits tieless in a plush executive office on Nashville's Music Row and reflects on such things as posture as a key to character. "Look at me," he says, as though trying to puzzle out how he got the job. "All I really am is a hunched-over guitar player."

Questions about The Nashville Sound seem to bore him. He shrugs and says it is not much more than a gimmicky tag. "You can get the same sound with country records made in Hollywood," he says. "You can get it anywhere with these same musicians, boys from this part of the country. They're country boys, poor boys from the farm. The music they play has honesty. It has the same quality as Ray Charles. Soul. If you have it, it comes out in your music. That's all it is."

A few years back Atkins was playing in an after-hours club in Nashville called the Carousel, and some say this was the origin of the sound. The band was made up of Atkins, Grady Martin and Hank Garland on guitars, Floyd Cramer on piano, Buddy Harman on drums and Bob Moore on upright bass. These are the musicians seen over and over again at the recording sessions.

The tinkly, gospel-rock piano work of Cramer is one of the most distinctive things about the new sound, that and the smooth choral backing of the Anita Kerr Singers and the Jourdanaires. Nashville A-and-R men are not as much inclined to electronic trickery (echo chambers, etc.) as their rocker counterparts in Detroit and Hollywood, but in the current spirit of *anything goes,* they are moving in that direction. Already they do quite a bit of overdubbing, and if a sideman gets carried away and hits a crazy lick or makes a weird noise, it's usually left in. A lot of the unidentifiable noises are produced by Pete Drake on his steel guitar. He can make it *gronk* like a tuba if gronks are called for, and he can make it sound like someone talking underwater if this need arises.

Atkins, of course, is a soloist, but he occasionally does some personal overdubbing. That is, he will take a taped song and superimpose his own guitar runs on it to beef up the thin spots. Cramer and Drake are soloists too, but they are also among the busiest sidemen in town. The money is good, $61 for a three-hour session, double that for the leader, and they have no objection to playing nameless on someone else's record. There are about 100 sidemen in Nashville who work with some regularity at the studios, says Musicians' Local 257, and about 35 of them make from $20,000 to $80,000 a year.

Decca's Owen Bradley, another guitarist-executive, also flounders a bit in trying to define the Sound. "I've been asked what it is a thousand times and I've given a thousand different answers. And I think I've been right every time." He peers over his glasses at a clock that tells him what time it is in Hollywood and New York and smokes a cigarette in a holder and carries on a long-distance phone conversation and a personal chat, all at once. "A few years ago we were forced to take a second look at some of these songs. They were better than we thought. This *Sound* business, all it boils down to is an approach. It's the spontaneity of certain musicians here getting together and making up an arrangement on the spot. The A-and-R men are just some kind of referees."

Music Row, where the business is concentrated, runs for three or four parallel blocks on 16th and 17th avenues in a going-to-seed residential section about five minutes from downtown Nashville. A Nashville recording session is a very casual affair. There are no arrangers, no producers and no written music, except once in a while a lead sheet, and the singer has probably brought that along for the words, not the music. Usually no one has rehearsed except the singer. At the start of the session he goes through the song once, or just plays a demo (demonstration record) for the sidemen. If the A-and-R man is an accomplished musician like Atkins, he may have some definite ideas about how it should be done. If not, he, the singer and the sidemen simply work it out as they go along, and stop when everybody is more or less pleased. They know one another well and they anticipate one another's moves. Everybody is free to offer suggestions and there is a lot of fast infield chatter.

"Hey, Pig, why don't you do that twice?"

"Brighten it just a hair, Jerry."

"And right there, more ching-ching-ching."

"We're all lollygagging, come on, punch it up."

"You got any squirrels out at your place?"

"I ain't seen a squirrel this year. Plenty of hicker nuts but no squirrels."

"Bear with me, chillun, I'm 'on sing this lover if it takes all night."

There is not much written music to be seen in Nashville, except for what is embroidered on clothes, but pianists and bass players are frequently seen reading from scraps of paper on which series of numbers have been scribbled. The numbers are code—each of them represents the bass note of the chord in one bar of music. Some musicians are so deft at it that they can jot the note numbers down after listening to a demo once.

"If we gave even the most mediocre written musical test, I doubt very much if half our members could pass it," says George W. Cooper, president of Local 257. "But that's not to say they aren't good musicians. We've got some of the best." "Oh, they read music all right," Atkins says. "But they read it with their ears instead of their eyes."

Atkins is an artist and he naturally takes his own guitar work seriously. The same goes for Bill Monroe, the father of bluegrass picking, and his protégés, Flatt and Scruggs. For the most part though, to ask serious questions about country music—apart from what it's doing in the charts—is to draw blank looks. The songs have been scorned and ridiculed so long by outsiders that the performers themselves have come to place little value on them. A good many of the singers, one gathers, would turn to pop music tomorrow morning if they could change their accents and get booked in Las Vegas. They yearn to see their records in the pop charts, where the money is. At the same time they must not *seem* to be wanting this; they must be careful not to alienate their country fans, who are a jealous lot.

The situation makes for curious ideas of loyalty.

Wesley Rose, who runs the town's largest publishing house, Acuff-Rose, is known as a passionate advocate of pure country music. "I've been fighting this battle for years," he says. "I tell my boys to keep their eyes off the pop market and concentrate on making good country songs. If they're good enough they'll make their way anywhere." A few days later one finds Rose directing Roy Orbison, a rock-pop singer, in a recording session. Orbison was one of the rockers with Sun Records in Memphis in the 1950's who dealt country music such a terrible blow.

Or take Audrey Williams, who is the handsome platinum-blonde widow of Hank Williams, probably the most legendary figure country music has produced. Audrey Williams is something of a celebrity herself, having been the provocation for so many of Hank's famous laments. She now directs an operation called Audrey Williams Enterprises, which involves a small movie company, a record label and the management of her singer-son, Hank Jr. She is not without sentiment. She keeps in her garage the 1952 blue Cadillac convertible that Hank died in on New Year's Day, 1953. But when Sam Katzman made a movie based on Hank's life (*Your Cheatin' Heart*), she agreed with the boys from the Coast that Hank's twangy, countrified singing should not be used on the sound track. The much blander voice of Hank Jr., then 15, was used instead, along with new arrangements and instrumentation. Of course it was Hank, not Hank Jr., who sold all those records, but Mrs. Williams does not see the point of the objection. "We thought it would reach more people this way," she says. "A lot of people don't like that old fiddle-and-steel-guitar sound. I believe in progress."

Then there's Buck Owens (*I've Got a Tiger by the Tail*) who has the Buck Owens Pledge to Country Music. It's in scroll form, and free copies are available, suitable for framing. "I shall sing no song that is not a country song," it goes, and "I shall make no record that is not a country record," and so on. Fair enough, except that one of Buck's latest releases, a big seller, is an instrumental called *Buckaroo* that you can do the Watusi to.

It is probably foolish to pursue this sort of thing, and it is certainly unrewarding—like trying to get a triangulation fix on Roger Miller, the biggest thing out of Nashville since Hank Williams. "Oh yeah, we still think of Roger as a country singer," says Buddy Killen, Miller's publisher in Nashville. "No, no, Roger's not a country singer, not anymore," says Don Williams, Miller's agent. "I don't know just what I am," says Miller, rehearsing for a television show in New York. "I like to entertain everybody. Scooby doo."

> *I see you going down the street in your big Cadillac,*
> *You got girls in the front and got girls in the back,*
> *Yeah, and way in the back you got money in a sack,*
> *Both hands on the wheel and your shoulders rared back,*
> *. . . I wish I had your good luck charm and you had a*
> *do-wacka-do wacka-do.*

To many people the most interesting thing, the *only* interesting thing about the business is the money—the idea of all them old country boys being in the chips, driving Cadillacs with six-shooter door handles and wearing outrageous, glittering

Western suits, designed by Nudie of Hollywood. Country singers are growing weary of this image, if not weary enough to stop making money.

"I guess you're going to write another one of those articles about how we're all a bunch of rich idiots," said Faron Young, the Singing Sheriff. "Rhinestones on our clothes and all that." "Well, a lot of you are idiots, Faron, remember that," said Jan Crutchfield, an irreverent cleffer. The former movie lawman was not amused. "Not all of us, neighbor. Not by a long shot."

The big money is in personal performances—state fairs, coliseum shows, one-night stands in tank towns. Young Johnny Cash grosses around $500,000 a year on personals alone. He, Roger Miller and Buck Owens are the superstars, and they get $2,500 and up for a single show, against a percentage of the gate, usually half. Porter Wagoner, The Thin Man from West Plains, gets $1,400 and up for a show, and Ernest Tubb (*I'm Walking the Floor Over You*) gets upwards of $1,000. Tubb and his Texas Troubadours are on the road some 200 days a year, traveling as much as 500 miles a day. Tubb has been at this grind since 1933, and you can see it in his seamed, exhausted face. "Just to look at him you wouldn't think Ernie was only twenty-eight years old, would you?" says Miller, with a straight face. "That's what the road'll do for you." But Tubb's schedule is not unusually rigorous. Some of them are on the road 300 days a year.

A lot of them also have to rush back from the man-wrecker road to meet their Opry commitments, or to tape their syndicated television shows. This is the new mark of prestige, the syndicated television show. Flatt and Scruggs have one, and so have the Wilburn Brothers and Leroy Van Dyke. Carl Smith has a network show on Canadian television. Porter Wagoner's show, sponsored by a purgative called Black-Draught, is probably the most successful. It is shown in 80 "markets," and claims an audience of 20 million people. This is about the same size as Jimmy Dean's ABC network audience.

For most country singers there is not much money in records. "Country records are like salt and pepper in the grocery store," says Owen Bradley. "The turnover is not big but it's steady." This reassuring salt metaphor (sometimes flour) is often heard in Nashville.

Eddy Arnold (*Bouquet of Roses*), most durable of the country crooners, has had 56 top-10 records since 1948, which makes him far and away the leader over a period of years. He, Miller, Cash or Owens could make a handsome living on record sales alone, but not many could.

In fact, a record can make the top five in the country charts and not sell more than 15,000 copies. At a wholesale price of 50 cents per record the company gross on a 15,000 seller would be $7,500. Take at least $700 off the top for the cost of the recording session ($850 if choral voices are used, $1,200 with strings) and that leaves $6,800. The singer would then get about four percent of that or a $272 check for his "hit."

And that's all he'd get. Jukebox operators, who buy most of the country singles, pay no royalties to anybody because of a curious interpretation of the copyright law, and radio stations pay no royalties to the "artist" or singer. The stations do, however, pay royalties to the publisher and composer. So almost every singer and picker in Nashville seems to be a music "publisher" these days. The word actually is a misnomer, a holdover from the days when sheet music was a substantial part of the business. Acuff-Rose still prints sale copies of its songs, and Tree Music contracts out the printing of Roger Miller's songs, but few others print anything. If you went to a small "publisher" and tried to buy a sheet copy of something like *You Broke My Heart, So Now I'm Going to Break Your Jaw*, the chances of getting it would be slim, unless you had a subpoena.

These days the "publisher" is really a talent scout and a copyright agent. He seeks out songs, copyrights them and peddles them, usually on demo tapes, to the singers and the record companies. For this service B.M.I. (Broadcast Music, Inc.) pays him four cents per radio play (the composer gets 2.5 cents). The composer and publisher get a penny apiece for each record sold.

At one time, in true folk tradition, just about every country singer wrote his own songs. Most of the classics are productions of the singer-writer: Jimmie Rodgers's Blue Yodel series, Roy Acuff's *Great Speckled Bird*, Jimmie Davis's *You Are My Sunshine*, Hank Williams's *Cold, Cold Heart*. The singer-writer is still very much around—Roger Miller sings only his own material—but in recent years there has been a proliferation of nonperforming writers. It is a precarious trade.

Miller himself first made his reputation as a writer. "The Opry never figured me for much of a singer," he says. In 1958 he wrote a string of country hits such as *Half a Mind* (Ernest Tubb), *Invitation to the Blues* (Ray Price) and *Billy Bayou* (Jim Reeves). "I was a great big success; the only thing was, I wasn't making any money."

Writer Jan Crutchfield explains about that kind of success: "I wrote one in 1961 with two other guys that was in the charts 26 weeks. It was called *The Outsider*. Bill Phillips cut it. You know what my royalty check was? Thirty-three dollars. Yeah. I looked at that check and I thought, 'Yeah, a few more hits like this and I'm going back to gospel singing.'" Crutchfield's third of the royalty represented a sale of about 10,000 copies. Nevertheless, with a few really big sellers and a small catalog of standards, a writer can retire young.

Crutchfield and collaborator Fred Burch, both thirtyish and Kentuckians, are two comers, part of Nashville's new wave. They wrote *Dream On, Little Dreamer*, which Perry Como recorded and which shows signs of becoming a standard, and they have had a number of moderate successes. Crutchfield is a tall, thin, moustachioed country hipster who used to share a boardinghouse room with Roger Miller. Burch is an admirer of author Terry Southern, and he has an upper-middle-class, tousled, campusy air. He once planned to attend the New School for Social Research in New York, and is writing a novel about the Nashville scene. Together he and Crutchfield write rock songs, pop songs, uptown country and hard country. At taping sessions, Crutchfield does the singing—now he's Fats Domino, now T. Texas Tyler—and Burch sits in the control room and makes suggestions and laughs at the songs and Crutchfield's antics. In two hours, with four pickup sidemen, they get eight songs on tape.

Afterward they sit in an office at Cedarwood Publishing and decide on the disposition of their newly minted tunes. One is called *Push My Love Button*. It breaks Crutchfield up. "That is one more raunchy song, ain't it? Yessir, that goes to Ann-Margret." Ann-Margret? Does she sing? "Hell, naw," says somebody, "but she makes records." Other people have drifted in, bookers and secretaries, to listen and offer advice. "Do me a favor, Crutch, and pitch that one to Lefty Frizzell. . . . Now that's a George Morgan song if I ever heard one. Or Buck Owens. Buck's would sell more, but I kinda like to hear George do it. . . ."

> *Detour, there's a muddy road ahead.*
> *Detour, paid no mind to what it said,*
> *Detour, all these bitter things I find,*
> *Should have read*
> *That Detour sign.*

Nashville is not a closed shop anymore, but, say Burch and Crutchfield, it's still much safer not to stray too far from the mainstream of traditional country music. "Look at Roger Miller," says Crutchfield. "He's a genius and he was knocking around here for years and couldn't get anywhere. They didn't even know what he was trying to do."

Miller's career is a good measure of what the Grand Ole Opry is all about. In the bad old rock-'n'-roll days, the Opry stood firm when other hillbilly shows around the South were giving way. The Opry came through it and the others only managed to lose both audiences. But this same conservatism led it to overlook Miller.

The pay is bad on this show and the working conditions are primitive, but a country singer will do anything—lose money, drive a log truck up from Moultrie, Ga.—to get on it. A few years ago a singer named Stonewall Jackson did that—parked his log truck outside the WSM building, went in, sang a song and won a spot on the show. The Opry's pay scale starts at 10 dollars, and nobody, big star or jug blower, is paid much more than $60 for a Saturday night's performance.

Many singers have a deep loyalty to the Opry. Roy Acuff, the King of Country Music (Dizzy Dean gave him the title), has been a regular since 1938. He certainly doesn't need the billing or the money, and he couldn't be dragged off the show. "I never thought the Opry needed me," he says. "I need the Opry. I still get a little shaky every time I go out on that stage."

Every Saturday night in the cold and heat, people line up for blocks outside the ratty old Opry auditorium and wait patiently for three hours to get inside, where they will sit on hard church pews for five more hours of Hank Snow and Stringbean and Wilma Lee and Stony. Surprisingly, most of the people who come are not from the South but from Indiana, Illinois and Ohio. Family groups prevail—grim, watchful guys who you know are not going to clap, their subdued wives and small kids, who will be asleep on the pews, mouths open, before it's all over. Along the waiting route there are souvenir shops that sell Kitty Wells cookbooks. A man out front with a big card in his hat sells chicken cacklers, little oral noisemakers. People are afraid it's a trick, that the cackler won't work when they get it home, but they are even more afraid to try it out there on the sidewalk and have 3,000 people watch them make hen noises. "I sell more than you would think," says the cackler salesman.

Backstage, there is a lot of socializing and a lot of coming and going to Tootsie's. There are two bare dressing rooms, but nobody seems to dress in them, because they are always open. Jim and Jesse, a new bluegrass team, are in one of them, jamming. Over there is Porter Wagoner, resplendent in a purple brocade creation, signing a popcorn box for an autograph hunter who got past the guard. Pretty Loretta Lynn (*Blue Kentucky Girl*) is sitting on a bench telling a stranger about her recent European trip. "Put in your article about how bad the toilet paper is over there," she says. "I wish you could see it, hun, you wouldn't believe it." A chubby woman comes by and says, "Loretta, have y'all eat up all them butter beans?" Loretta says, "Girl, what are you talking about? I put up fifteen quarts last Saturday. Come on out to the house and get you some." Married at 14, now a 31-year-old grandmother, Loretta can sing like nobody's business.

While the show is going on, wives, girl friends, children wander idly back and forth across the stage. The announcer, Grant Turner, looks around to see if the singer he is announcing is actually there. If not, he brings on another one. The show runs in 30-minute segments and for radio purposes it must run on time. Somehow it does. No one is even sure who is going to be on the show until Thursday or Friday. "But that's the Opry," says manager Devine. "If we produced it we'd kill it."

Hank Williams, who couldn't stay sober, was dropped by the Opry in August 1952, for missing shows, and banished to The Louisiana Hayride in Shreveport, whence he came. He was making $200,000 a year, and people like Tony Bennett had begun to record his songs. If ever a country singer didn't need the Opry, it was Hank Williams. And yet for the next five months, the last five months of his life, he was on the phone to Nashville almost every day trying to get back on the show.

"If you were an opera singer, you'd want to sing at the Met, wouldn't you?" said Carleton Haney, a promoter who books Coliseum shows. "Look, there's what?—four billion people on earth, and only forty-eight of them can be on the Opry. Think about that."

> *Cigareetes and whusky*
> *And wild, wild women,*
> *They'll drive you crazy,*
> *They'll drive you insane. . . .*

The legend is that the country singer is a hell of a fellow. Big spender, big drinker, a poolroom fantasy come true. It is based largely on the life of Hank Williams and, to a lesser extent, that of Jimmie Rodgers. Rodgers set the style—sudden fame and riches, a short, tragic life—and Williams fulfilled it.

Rodgers's influence on the music was all-pervasive in the 1930's. Young Clarence (Hank) Snow heard his records in remote Nova Scotia and marveled, and left the farm to sing and yodel like Jimmie, so far as he could. Down in Texas and Oklahoma, Ernest Tubb and Gene Autry were doing it. Of this lot the widow Rodgers pronounced Tubb the champ, and she presented him with one of Jimmie's fancy guitars, one that said THANKS on the back in mother-of-pearl. It remains an object of veneration in the country-music world, and Tubb plays it only on special occasions.

Rodgers was known to take a drink, and because of his tuberculosis he came to rely on drugs, but his excesses were as nothing compared to those of Hank Williams. Hank had troubles. Thin and sickly, he too had a legitimate need for drugs. He suffered chronic bouts of pain from a spinal injury. He was an alcoholic, the kind who can get drunk in 20 minutes; and, beset by chippies, his home life was often rancorous and stormy.

No one since Rodgers had shown more talent in the field. If it took him longer than a half hour to write a song, he said, he threw it away. He was known for his generosity, and for his black, bitter moods. "Y'all don't worry," he would tell his audiences, "cause it ain't gonna be all right nohow."

In 1952, as his drinking grew worse, he was fired by the Opry and divorced by his beloved Audrey. He went to Louisiana and married a pretty young divorcée ("To spite Audrey," he said) named Billie Jean Jones Eshliman, who, as it turned out, wasn't quite divorced. He married her once in a more or less private ceremony, again on the stage at a matinee show in New Orleans, and yet again on the night show, for those who had missed the matinee. He picked up a paroled forger who treated him for his alcoholism at $300 a week. This was H. R. (Toby) Marshall, "B.A., M.A., D.S.C., Doctor of Science and Psychology and Alcoholic Therapist"—who later admitted he had never got beyond high school. "Doctor" Marshall administered, among other things, chloral hydrate, a knockout potion he was fond of.

Hank was desperately trying to get hold of himself, and, right at the end, on Jan. 1, 1953, he got a bit of hope. The Opry finally gave in to his pleading and agreed to give him another try, in February. That day, with this happy news, he left Knoxville, Tenn., in the Cadillac with an 18-year-old chauffeur, Charles Carr, for a show in Canton, Ohio. Before leaving Knoxville he managed to get two shots of chloral hydrate. He stretched out on the back seat and Carr drove.

At Rutledge, Tenn., a policeman stopped the car for speeding. He wrote out a ticket and peered through the window at the form in the back. "That guy looks dead," he said. Carr explained about the sedation, paid a $25 fine and drove on. But by the time he got to Oak Hill, W. Va., he sensed something was wrong. He touched Hank, found him cold and drove him to a local hospital, where he was pronounced dead. Hank was 29. A coroner's jury declared he had died of "a severe heart condition and hemorrhage."

More than 20,000 people came to the funeral in Montgomery, Ala., including all the Opry luminaries. Red Foley sang *Peace in the Valley*, and "Doctor" Marshall presented the widow Billie Jean with a bill for $736.39 for his therapy services, possibly on the basis that he had stopped Hank's drinking. Billie Jean suggested there was more to Hank's death than met the eye. "I will never accept the report that my husband died of a heart attack," she said. Later she and Marshall both testified at a legislative committee hearing in Oklahoma on narcotics traffic, but nothing came of it as far as shedding light on Hank's death was concerned. Probably he did die of a heart attack. This was a clinical detail. He knew and his friends knew that he was running out of time. "I just don't like this way of living," he sang, and, "I'll never get out of this world alive. . . ."

Disaster and sudden death have come to be a part of the country-music scene. In 1960 the unlucky Billie Jean was widowed once again by a country singer when her third husband, Johnny Horton (*Battle of New Orleans*), was killed in a car wreck. In March, 1963, Opry stars Patsy Cline, Hawkshaw Hawkins and Cowboy Copas were killed in a plane crash near Camden, Tenn.

Two days after that accident, singer Jack Anglin (of the Johnny and Jack team) was killed in a smash-up while driving to Patsy Cline's funeral. The venerable Texas Ruby was next; she died in a house-trailer fire. In August, 1964, Gentleman Jim Reeves, a crooner whose posthumous releases still appear in the charts, was killed in a plane crash just outside Nashville, along with his accompanist.

"We were burying 'em around here like animals for a while," Roy Acuff recalls. "I don't even like to talk about it." Last July Acuff, who wrote *The Wreck on the Highway*, and guitarist Shot Jackson were badly injured in a wreck on the highway near Sparta, Tenn. Acuff, who is back on his feet now, had every sizable bone in the right side of his body broken. He thinks he and all the other singers who haven't been killed yet are lucky and ahead of the odds, when their mileage, often mileage under pressure, is considered. Since the late 1930's he has traveled about 100,000 miles a year. "But I'm thinking about cutting down."

It's not an easy life at all. There's fame in it, of a sort, and money, and that keeps a lot of them going. But there's some deeper feeling too that keeps them out on the road, with a night here and a night there and a long drive in between, singing their songs, some trash, some gold, about hearts and wrecks and teardrops. They can't talk about those things, so they sing them.

*1966*

# An Auto Odyssey through Darkest Baja

THE IDEA was to get something sturdy and fairly reliable for a drive down the Baja California peninsula. Something cheap, too, expendable. Something you wouldn't mind banging up, or even abandoning if it came to that. The best thing is a jeep or a Scout or some other four-wheel-drive vehicle but for a one-shot trip a standard pickup truck is good enough.

I found what I was looking for on a Santa Monica car lot. It was a rat-colored 1952 half-ton Studebaker pickup. Just the thing. It had character and looked eager to please. It had big tires too, snappy 9.00/15 Cadillac whitewalls, a bonus in appearance, traction and height. There was a black diamond painted on the tailgate.

A crew-cut salesman spotted me and came over and said a man and his wife from Big Bear sure were interested in that truck and they were expected in momentarily. He looked at his watch. I got in the cab and turned the wheel and messed around with the pedals.

"It's got overdrive and 40 pounds of oil pressure," he said. "I didn't believe that oil pressure myself at first. Both those spotlights work."

I couldn't find the starter.

"It's under the clutch," he said.

It wouldn't start.

"We'll have to get that battery charged up for you," he said. "Kids come around at night and turn those spotlights on." He called for a boy to bring over a booster battery. "I believe if you drive this little truck you'll buy it. And I'll tell you something else. You're going to be happy with your gas mileage. Surprised. You've got your little Champion Six going for you and then your overdrive cutting in at about 35."

We got it started and I drove it around town. The clutch chattered a little and the shock absorbers were busted but there seemed to be no serious organic ailments. He had $495 on the windshield and we closed out at $375. That still sounds like too much but even now, after what happened, I'm not kicking about the price. It was in the back of my mind that I could sell that piece of iron for about $600 in Mexico. Pay for the trip. I did feel bad about getting in ahead of the Big Bear folks. They must have had an accident or a death in the family as they did not show.

I bought two new tires and put shocks on the truck and had it serviced and tuned up, new plugs and everything, and altogether sank another $50 in it. Then for $20 more I joined the Automobile Club of Southern California so I could get a big map of Baja and a detailed driver's log. This is a fine map (although it doesn't show elevation), and the log is good too, but I believe the best mile-by-mile guide for the Baja run is the *Lower California Guidebook* by Peter Gerhard and Howard E. Gulick (the Arthur H. Clark Co., Glendale, California).

I didn't know this fact at the time because it's hard to get any straight, first-hand dope about Baja in Los Angeles. A woman at the Mexican Government Tourist Office gave me a *turista* card, said the road was very bad and sent me to the Auto Club for any further information. A girl there gave me the map and log and her best wishes, but no, she didn't know how I could get in touch with anybody who had made the drive. People I knew said, "Why don't you fly down like Eisenhower?" and "Did they ever find those people that were lost down there?"

At the Mayan temple that is the Los Angeles Public Library I read the works of such veteran Baja desert rats as Erle Stanley Gardner and Joseph Wood Krutch. I pored over the Auto Club map and log, which carries a list of exactly 100 items of equipment to be taken on the drive—things like spare axles and leaf springs and a short-wave radio. And a calendar. Probably so you can note the passing seasons while you're trying to change an axle down there on the Vizcaino Desert. "Confound this list!" I exclaimed, after calculating the expense, and went out and bought a few things you would take on an ordinary camping trip, plus some gasoline cans and water cans. (A small roll of baling wire was the lifesaver.)

I am not a hunter or a fisherman or an adventurer, nor do I have any particular affection for Mexico or the beauties of the desert, but I do like maps and I had long been curious about that empty brown peninsula. It snakes down through almost

10 degrees of latitude from Tijuana to the Tropic of Cancer. It is 800 miles long (more than 1,000 by road) and ranges in width from 150 miles at its bulging midriff to about 30 miles at the Bay of La Paz.

People live there of course, and by choice, but then people will live anywhere, even in New York City and Presidio County, Texas. The 800,000 inhabitants of Baja are not enough to clutter up the landscape. Most of them are concentrated in and around the northern border towns of Mexicali, the capital (200,000), and Tijuana (250,000), with a sprinkling of farmers and fishermen and billy goat ranchers and cattlemen scattered all down the line.

The Spaniards first saw Baja in 1533 when an expedition sent out by Cortez sailed into the Bay of La Paz. A number of abortive attempts were made to colonize the place but no Europeans were hardy enough to stick it out until the Jesuits came in 1697. The Indians then living there (estimates of their number range from 12,000 to 70,000) were possibly the most primitive of any in the New World. They slept naked on the ground and wandered aimlessly about eating worms and roots and the lice from one another's hair. When the Jesuits came they found "not a hut, nor an earthen jar, nor an instrument of metal, nor a piece of cloth."

In 1768 Fra Junipero Serra and his Franciscans replaced the Jesuits, who had fallen from favor in Madrid, and the Franciscans in turn were replaced by the Dominicans in 1773, with Serra going on to bigger things as a missionary to the upper desert of Alta California, now a fruited plain governed by Ronald Reagan.

American forces seized Baja and held it throughout the Mexican War, but the treaty negotiators at Guadalupe Hidalgo gave it back to Mexico in a fit of indifference. Five years later, in 1853, a 29-year-old Tennessee *filibustero* named William Walker sailed into La Paz with 45 men, captured the town and the governor without firing a shot and proclaimed "the Republic of Lower California." The central government of Mexico did not offer much resistance, but the United States, then trying to swing the Gadsden Purchase, disapproved of Walker's adventure and forced him to abandon his new republic after seven months by blocking shipments of men and supplies. (Walker later became president of Nicaragua. In 1860 he was executed by a firing squad in Honduras.)

This then was the place that Andy Davis and I set out for last July 15 in the gray truck that we had come to call, in our humorous way, "the Diamondback Rattler." Andy is a friend from college days at State U., a fellow Arkie exiled in California and a pretty fair hand with a crescent wrench. He got clear to go right at the last minute, and a good thing too.

We entered the freeway off Sunset in Los Angeles at 6:30 A.M. hoping to beat the rush-hour traffic, since I had no U.S. insurance on the truck. (I did have Mexican liability insurance. Not having it can lead to trouble, like jail.) The freeway was busy even at that hour but we were aggressive, if slow, and held our own. We hadn't quite got to City Hall when the front wheels started shimmying. A sudden, terrible vision appeared of Andy's wife driving out to pick us up at about the Disneyland exit. Then we found that the shimmy started at 48 m.p.h. and went away at 56 m.p.h., so we were okay as long as we kept the speed above the critical point.

We had about 600 pounds of gear in the back, the heavy stuff being four 5-gallon cans of gasoline, three 5-gallon cans of water, three 1-gallon water bags, one 2-gallon can of motor oil and a sack of spuds. The tires were aired up hard and tight and there was not much sag. At San Diego we bought some ice and piddled around, then crossed the border at Tijuana and drove through town resisting shouts on all sides from auto upholsterers and hawkers of religious statuary.

The road is paved for about 140 miles south of Tijuana and it is a pretty drive in the mountains and coastal stretches around Ensenada. This is a port city of about 35,000 people and the last town of any size before jumping off into the interior. We had a mechanic there check the shimmy and he said the trouble was a warped wheel. If we drove 3,000 kilometers at 50 m.p.h. the vibration would cause the front end utterly to collapse. He seemed sure of those exact figures. We could have put the spare on but for some reason we didn't do anything.

A few miles south of Ensenada there is a roadside stop where a uniformed officer checks tourist cards. The card is all that is necessary for driving in Baja. In mainland Mexico a *turista* windshield sticker is required, and a much closer check is kept on vehicles. Some idlers were hanging around the guard shack and when it became known that our destination was La Paz, one of them divined my plan and said the truck ought to bring about $750 down there. Wasn't that illegal, bringing a vehicle into Mexico and selling it? This got a big laugh from everyone except the officer.

We stopped for the day not far from Ensenada on a high bluff called Punta Banda overlooking the sea. Beautiful prospect. The two-burner gasoline stove worked okay and we had bacon and eggs and potatoes cut up with the peelings left on and fried with onions. The bargain Japanese canteen cups were a mistake. The metal was some Oriental alloy that had the property of staying 38 degrees hotter than the coffee therein. Fried your lips.

July 16. Odometer read 247 miles from Los Angeles. A cold white fog blew in during the night. Hated to get out of those sleeping bags. We couldn't see the sea. We had a leisurely breakfast of eggs and corned beef hash and were on the road at 8 A.M. This pace didn't last long. We told ourselves we were not going to rush, but before the day was out we were leaning forward on the seat just trying to get miles behind us. At a store called El Palomar we gassed up. The Rattler was getting 17 miles per gallon. Also bought some 2-inch Rocket Boy firecrackers from Macao. ("Light Fuse. Retire Quickly.") Some surfers from San Diego stopped by in a Volkswagen truck and asked if we had a firing pin for a .22 pistol. Sorry.

We left the pavement at Arroyo Seco and the gravel surface wasn't too bad for the first 15 miles or so, then it got murderous. The road was built up about 3 feet above the desert floor and drainage had made corduroy of it. We drove the ditches mostly where it was not so rough, although much dustier. Red dust. Several times we had to stop when it enveloped us. We picked up a hitch-hiker named Miguel. He refused to understand my Spanish even after I had treated him to a pack of Dentyne. A lug nut worked loose and rattled like crazy in the hub cap. Put it back on and discovered five others loose.

It was siesta time at San Quintin Bay but we woke up the owner of a little resort there and bought two cans of beer. We drove around the bay and ran into some more surfers. They were in a Volkswagen car and a Nissan Patrol, a kind of Japanese jeep, and had driven down from La Jolla. The Nissan owner, a four-wheel-drive snob, said they were turning back here, and intimated that we would be wise to do the same with our clunker. We showed them our tailgate.

We had hoped to make El Rosario that day but at 7 P.M. we gave up and pulled over near a rocky beach for the night. The desert—sand, cactus—runs to the very edge of the sea here. You expect a fall line and a marginal strip of something or other, but the desert simply stops and the water begins. For miles up and down the coast big breakers were crashing. There was nothing else to see. We built a fire of driftwood and had a big feed—bacon, potatoes and two cans of black-eyed peas. We had passed up lunch, and continued to do so. It would waste valuable driving time. The surf here was violent and as it retreated through the rocks it made a weird grinding noise that kept us awake for some time.

July 17. Mile 401. Off at 7 A.M. in a mighty burst of Studebaker power. Too much; the vacuum hose to the windshield wiper popped loose. Got it back on, then saw that one of the arms from the little motor had fallen off. Could have fixed it easily with a piece of wire but kept putting it off. *Mañana.* We had used the wipers to clear dust away.

El Rosario has 400 people and a green jail, and the weekly bus going south turns around here. Ditto the telephone line and mail service. We stopped for gasoline and children stood in doorways to watch us. South of town we saw our first Auto Club road sign. The American club posted the entire route with metal signs a few years ago, but few are left and most of those have been shot up so as to be unreadable. Probably by Americans as it does not seem likely that Mexicans would waste expensive .38 and .45 cartridges on such mean foolishness. Mean because it's so easy to get off the main road—Mexico 1—even with a good map and a compass and a close mileage check.

We met two big trucks hauling slabs of marble or onyx and pulled over out of the ruts to let them by. They stopped to pass the time of day, as is the custom, and we had our question ready.

"*El camino a San Agustin es malo?*"

A gringo-sounding Mexican at the wheel said, "Yeah, it's *malo* as far as you're going."

We kept foolishly asking that question, hoping someone, even if he was lying, would say the road got a little better. It got very hot that day but we had no way of knowing the temperature since our thermometer was no good. It would register 50 degrees one minute and 130 the next. At mid-afternoon the needle in the amp meter stopped moving. We pulled up short thinking the fan belt had broken. It was okay but the distributor wires were loose and the screws that held the top on the voltage regulator had shaken out. The top was just hanging on. Andy messed around with things and eventually got some movement out of the needle and wired the top back on.

We started climbing a range of burnt red mountains on a roadbed of sharp rocks. On the harder pulls—some stretches appeared to be 45 degrees—the engine began to miss and sputter. Too hot? Water in the gasoline? Bad points? The spark plugs were new. By getting running starts we rammed that poor old truck up and over each crest. The Cadillac tires never bargained for this but they held up.

On the downgrade the engine smoothed out and it was running like a sewing machine when we reached San Agustin. This was a forlorn hut right out on the desert with a windmill, not moving, and seven or eight guys sitting around drinking tepid Modelo beer from a kerosene refrigerator. One played a guitar and sang. We got some water for the radiator out of their storage tank. The water is no good to drink, they said.

A cloud of dust in the distance drew closer and soon an air-conditioned Jeep Wagoneer pulled in bearing a San Diego dentist, his wife and eight-year-old son. "La Paz or Bust," said a little sign on the window. "We're going all the way to Cabo San Lucas," said the boy, which news the Mexicans received with equanimity. The dentist said he too had had trouble with things shaking loose, and had had one flat. When driving in sand, he said, he let some air out of his tires for better flotation. He had a spark plug device that used engine compression to pump them back up. Nifty.

A few miles below San Agustin we saw our first palm tree, in a low wash where there was some underground water near the surface. There was a house nearby in some shade, and a very hospitable woman who let us draw some water from her well. "*Es muy bueno*," she said, and she was right, it was sweet, cool water. Such ground water as exists in Baja is often brackish or alkaline to the taste. We drove on and began to look for a place to stop but this was flat desert with no natural features that would make one place better than another so we finally just stopped. In 11 hours driving we had made 98 miles.

After supper we broke the code of the desert by needlessly hacking open a barrel cactus. The hide was thick and bristly and it took about five minutes with a sharp machete to get to the middle. Bulletin: There's no water in those things. Not in this one anyway, just a damp core that could have done little more than infuriate a thirsty man. It was too hot that night to get inside the sleeping bags so we lay on top of them under the wide and starry sky. Then some bats came around and I zipped up and sweated. Andy's concern was for snakes. We never saw one.

July 18. Mile 499. Corned beef hash with Tabasco for breakfast. We had other things but Andy kept wanting to eat that stuff, going on about what a hearty dish it was. The next settlement down the line was Punta Prieta, once a gold mining center, now a handful of huts on either side of a dry wash. The gasoline man was David Ramirez. He siphoned it out of a 55-gallon drum and we filtered it through a chamois skin. We told him about the sputtering and he removed the points from the distributor and filed them with an emery cloth. Still no good. He took off the carburetor and cleaned it. Not much better but we decided to press on for Santa Rosalillita, of the three L's, a fishing camp on the coast. You don't have that trapped feeling on blue water. Ramirez had worked on the truck for about two hours but said there was no charge. Maybe a pack of cigarettes. We gave him some smokes and had to force money on him.

On the way to the coast we saw a lot of ground squirrels, or anyway some kind of speedy rodents with tucked-up white tails, and hundreds of quail, the gray kind with crested heads. And a sand-colored bobcat, who stopped in the road for a moment to see what was coming, then fled. The Rattler choked and popped on the hills but made it in.

There was rejoicing in the fishing camp. The supply truck from Tijuana had arrived just ahead of us. It was a week late and the fishermen—there were some 30 or 40—were out of gasoline and cigarettes and down to short rations. Now the smoking lamp was lit and a blue haze hung about. A young abalone diver named Chito was the mechanic of this lash-up and he was under our hood in a flash filing the points, resetting the timing and blowing through the gas line. A solemn little shirtless boy held Chito's cigarette while he worked, between drags. He held it still and was careful not to get his thumb and finger on the mouth part. Chito declared that the spring was bad in the spark advance. He found a similar one, cut it for length and put it in. That didn't do it either. Chito gave up. Must be the *puntas*, he said.

What to do? There was an old 1-ton Studebaker truck in camp that might have some usable points in it but the owner was gone and would not be back for a day or two. Pete, the skipper of a launch, said he would be going to Ensenada in about a week and we could ride up on the boat with him, get the points and come back with him. Thanksgiving in La Paz. Or we could try to make it down the coast to Guerrero Negro where there was a big salt works and probably some repair facilities. Scammon's Lagoon was down that way too, where the California gray whale breeds and calves. We didn't want to miss that. This seemed the best course.

We had to cross a deep gully getting out of the camp and it took about 20 running starts before we finally got up the other side, to loud cheers from the *pescadores*. (Let me say emphatically that the Champion Six, power-wise, was equal to any grade we met with; it was just that the firing system was on the blink.) Another young diver named Adam Garcia hitched a ride with us. His family lived down the coast.

About two miles from camp we hit some deep sand and in getting out of it we let the engine stall and die. Now it wouldn't even start. Well, that was it. Garcia asked if we wanted to sell the truck. No, not quite yet. He continued on by foot. It was growing dark. After some cussing and some recriminations we decided we would walk back to the camp in the morning and see about the points in the derelict truck. Sufficient unto the day was the evil thereof. But was it the points? So many hands, including our own, had been in that distributor. Maybe the coil. A cold wind was blowing from the sea and we took all the gear out of the back of the truck and slept in there under the tarp.

July 18. Mile 597. Just before setting off on the hike we had a last-minute go at the starter. The engine caught the first time. Hurrah for the bonnie blue flag! We loaded quickly and took off once more for Guerrero Negro. In about a half-hour we came to the Garcia fishing camp on a wide sandy beach. The main business here was catching *cahuamas*, big sea turtles, for canning. Garcia was surprised to see us. He rounded up a brother or a cousin who was something of a *mecanico*.

They found an old, rusty, six-volt coil in a shed and Andy went to work with them on the Rattler while I had coffee with Garcia's mother, who spoke very good English. "You'll be okay when you get to Guerrero," she said. "They have everything there." We sat at a table in her dark kitchen, earth floor. A timid teenage girl poured the coffee and two men stood in the door- way blocking the light. I sat there like a boob for some time smoking and drinking their coffee before it occurred to me to offer the cigarettes. Nobody asked for one, and they had been out of smokes for 10 days, I learned.

Señora Garcia said the market for canned turtle meat was not so good. Did I think the people in the States would like it? It added a nice touch to many different dishes. I said it might go over in Southern California, which came out like—those nuts will buy anything—although I don't think she took it that way. I hope not.

The change of coils was an improvement, temporary at least, and Andy got the voltage regulator perking again. The points in it had been sticking too. We left the Garcias some stuff and struck out once more for Guerrero.

Almost immediately we got lost trying to thread our way through a maze of ruts down the coast. We kept bearing right, seaward, which was a good plan except that it didn't work. Twice we had to double back; one road led to a deserted beach and stopped, and another took us into some impassably deep sand. The spare tire fell off but we didn't know it for a while, with all the other noise, until the spare carrier started dragging and making a terrific racket. We wired the carrier back up under the bed and backtracked again until, very luckily, we found the tire.

Soon we were traveling inland, southeast, you couldn't fool the compass, but there was no way to get off that road. At Rancho Mezquital a couple of cowboys in leather chaps told us we had left the coastal road far behind but that we could still reach Guerrero by taking a certain right turn down the way. Good. Now we were out on the Vizcaino Desert, driving and driving and not getting anywhere. The road was not so bad here, smooth sand ruts. We rode up high on the sides to keep from dragging center.

This was no open desert but a thickly growing forest of cardon and cirio. The cardon cactus, with its right-angle traffic cop limbs, is like the giant saguaro of Arizona, although there is said to be some small difference. The cirio (candle) looks like a big, gray, bristly carrot growing upside down, with a yellow flower on top. It grows in Baja and in one spot in Sonora and no place else on earth. Naturalist Joseph Wood Krutch calls it the boojum tree.

We came to a village and an old man there said it was El Arco. This could not be because El Arco was way below Guerrero, almost 50 miles, and we got out the map and showed the old timer how he was wrong. He insisted that he knew the name of his home town. Again we had missed the cutoff. It was not in the cards for us to see the fabled Guerrero or Scammon's Lagoon.

The store in El Arco was out of gasoline. This village, too, was once a gold mining center, with more than a thousand workers, but the mines closed after a long strike and perhaps 100 people live there now. All of them were indoors on this day except for two little girls who were wiping the dust off the storekeeper's Chevrolet pickup. He gave us a pan of water to wash up with, and offered $10 for the radio that was slung under the dash in the Rattler. I said okay and he and a pal went to work. Those two should enter a Motorola removal derby. They had it out in about a minute, antenna and all. Parked beside the store was the dustiest 1965 Ford Mustang in the world. The foolhardy owner was taking it to La Paz and got this far before busting up the radiator. He had hitched a ride back to Tijuana to get a new radiator, the store-keeper said, and was now gone two weeks.

We camped that night south of El Arco beside the biggest cactus we had ever seen, a cardon with 12 spires, nine of them 30 to 40 feet high.

July 20. Mile 792. Up at 5:15, before sunrise, some quick hash and coffee, then onward across the Vizcaino. The road was rocky, something like a dry creek bed, and we soon lost high gear—that is, we couldn't shift into high. We drove in second much of the time anyway but this was a nuisance. At 11:30 A.M. we reached San Ignacio, which is a true, classic oasis. You come over a hill after hours of desert driving and there it is below, two limpid ponds fed by springs, a large grove of date palms and a shady little town square. Some 900 people live there. On the square is a whitewashed stone church that has walls 4-feet thick. It was built by the Dominicans in 1786.

We asked around and located a garage. It was run by one Frank Fischer, an elderly gent who said he had been in Baja since 1910, when, as an engineer on a German freighter, he had jumped ship in Santa Rosalia. "It was the second mate," he said. "I didn't like the S.B."

He called in the house for his son, a man about 40, and set him to work on the Rattler while he, the elder Fischer, told us a few things. He had been to the United States once, in San Diego, in 1917, but had found no reason since to return. American and Mexican beer did not compare with European beer because the water in the Western Hemisphere has saltpeter in it. Mexicans did not know how to fix roads. He looked over our 9mm. pistol. "German?" No, Spanish. He handed it back. "Then it's no good." The United States had been wrong everywhere since 1945 and was decidedly wrong in Vietnam.

"The U.S.A. is no good splitting these countries up," he said. "Germany, Korea, Vietnam. All those boys getting killed are poor boys, they are not rich men's boys."

We agreed that the draft was not fair.

"Look at goddam L.B.J. Johnson," he said. "His sons are not over there."

We said we didn't know the President had any sons.

"He has two sons hidden there on the ranch. He's keeping them out of the war."

He said he kept abreast of these things from a German newspaper he subscribed to. We argued with him a little about Vietnam, then decided to let it ride, remembering the Mojo proverb—*man with faltering '52 Studebaker not wise to antagonize mecanico in middle of Baja.* (And yet the Mojos—squat, hairless, loyal—were foolish in many ways and the tribe was no more.) The young Fischer said a small flange had fallen off the gearshift column. He fixed it and put a new spring in the voltage regulator. That, he said, would correct our electrical trouble. Could be, but Mexican mechanics seemed to be spring happy. The charge was only $4. Did they want pesos or dollars? "Dollars," said the old man.

At a roadside stop called the Oasis we bought all the gasoline in stock, about 12 gallons, and had a shower and a change of clothes. We were filthy. The owner of the place had magazine pictures of John F. Kennedy and Lopez Mateos tacked up all over the walls. As I was shaking the dust out of a shirt he said, "*Mucha tierra,*" then asked what *tierra* was in *Ingles.* He had a tablet in which he entered English words that came in handy with the gringos passing through.

"Tierra es dirt."

"Dort?"

"No, *dirt.*"

"Si, dort."

"Dirt!"

"Dort!"

"Okay."

On the road again, high gear working, amp meter showing charge. Below an extinct volcano called Las Tres Virgenes we ran into a roadblock. A 2-ton grocery truck coming north on the one-way shelf road had a flat, right rear, and the driver and his partner were repairing it there with a cold patch. They had no spare. The truck was built for dual wheels but like most big trucks in Baja this one was running with single wheels because of the narrow ruts.

A '58 Ford car going South had tried to drive around the truck but had slipped sideways down the hill and bogged in the sand. So now everything was blocked. Another car, a '58 Mercury and two pickups were also ahead of us. The cars and pickups were all together, a convoy from Tijuana to La Paz. When Mexicans deliver cars down the peninsula they usually travel in a pack, with a truck or two along to carry gasoline and other gear. It would be hard to make it with a loaded car, the clearance would be so low.

The repair took about two hours and a good part of the time was spent pumping up that big 9.00/20 12-ply tire. The driver had the stamina of a horse. He wore an Afrika Korps cap and had a bandanna tied around his forehead. Andy pitched in and helped pump while the convoy drivers and I sat in the skimpy shade of mesquite bush and passed around a water bag and smoked Domino cigarettes. It must have been 120 out in the sun.

Late that afternoon we reached the Sea of Cortes, or, as current maps insist on calling it, the Gulf of California. No cold blue Pacific breakers crashing here. The water was green and very salty and warm, almost 80 degrees, and still as a lake. A slight lapping along the black gravel beach was the only movement. It is not always like that, we were told. Treacherous winds come up often on the Gulf, and from time to time a big blow called a *chubasco*.

We breezed into Santa Rosalia (pop. 5,361) on a strip of blacktop at 40 and 50 m.p.h., just flying. The shimmy was gone. This is the first real town you hit after leaving Ensenada and we cruised around a while taking in the sights—the new police building, a pastel blue church made of galvanized iron. Santa Rosalia is a copper town; the mines are nearby and the smelting and shipping is done here. A French company used to run it (they brought that odd church over in sections) but it has been a Mexican operation since the early 1950s.

At the Hotel Central we had fried shrimps, caught that afternoon, and a salad, paying no heed to guidebooks warnings against eating fresh vegetables in Baja. A truck driver from Tijuana who was a little tight on beer joined us. He was on his way home from La Paz. We struck him as a couple of good sports, he said, and he believed he would turn his truck around and go to La Paz with us.

"I know many beautiful ladies in La Paz," he said. "Many." He elaborated. Two pals came and dragged him back to the truck. You can take the boy out of Tijuana but can you take the Tijuana out of the boy?

A young married couple from Santa Monica named Bob and Judy (Dick and Jane had just left) were also stopping at the Central. They had sailed down the Gulf in an 18-foot catamaran. Or rather they had sailed as far as the Bay of Luis Gonzaga, about 300 miles up the coast, where the fiber-glass cat had cracked up on some rocks. They hitched a ride in the rest of the way with their cat loaded on top of a truck carrying 1,000 gallons of lard. It took five days; the truck had six flats and broke an axle. But they made it. Things have a way of working out in Baja. Santa Rosalia was the nearest place they could get fiber-glass repairs.

Crime fans will remember Billy Cook, the desperado with the bad eye and the tattoo "Hard Luck" on his knuckles who murdered six people in 1951, including an entire family, and movie fans will remember the Edmund O'Brien film, "The Hitch-hiker," about Billy's auto flight down the desert with two hostages, but who remembers that right here near the Central was where Billy was tracked down and nailed by Tijuana Police Chief Kraus Morales? That evening we sat outside and listened to the local mariachi band. Bob and Judy had been planning to sail around the tip of the peninsula and back up the Pacific coast. They were making a film of the journey. But now maybe they would sell the cat in La Paz if they could get a good price. Bob said I might get as much as $1,000 for the truck there. The band played until well after midnight.

July 21. Mile 919. Up early and down the street to the Tokio Cafe for Spam and eggs. A big gringo in a cowboy hat who looked and sounded like Lee Marvin, the actor, flagged us over to his table. He said his name was Jim Smith and he lived in San Ignacio.

"I saw you guys there yesterday at Fischer's," he said. "I didn't stop because I don't get along with the old man. I guess he told you all that crap about jumping ship."

We said he had, whereupon Smith gave us his version of the Mexican advent of Frank Fischer. Without prejudice, it was even harder to believe. I won't repeat it, just as Sherlock Holmes would not tell about his case concerning the Giant Rat of Sumatra. (He said the world was not ready for it.)

Smith said he had been in Baja on and off since 1953. He had been a cop in Lubbock, Texas where he missed capturing Billy Cook by minutes, and in Los Angeles, where a motorcycle accident had banged him up and provided him with a pension, which he didn't think was big enough. Now at 35 he was "guide, hunter, pilot, boat skipper, writer and freeloader." He had ridden the length of Baja on muleback, a five-month trip, and it had once taken him six weeks to deliver a truck to La Paz; he had to replace the engine and differential on the way.

He said he was related to President Johnson ("I'm kin to half the folks in Texas") and then went on to attack him with great passion, exceeding even Frank Fischer on this score. But from a different angle.

"That's why I'm down here, to get away from that crap. I'm making my last stand here. You know what they're trying to do now? Boy, the Great Society. They're trying to send some of those Peace Corps punks down to Ignacio for training. Well, you can take the word back, Shriver better not send any of those ———— beatnik ————s around my place or somebody is liable to get his head blown off."

Song: *I Left My Head in San Ignacio.* Smith said his first wife had remarried, a man named John Smith, and that he, Jim Smith, was now engaged to a wealthy, 31-year-old Mexican widow. ("They got this priest checking up on me.") He expressed contempt for most writers about Baja (he likes Antonio de Fierro Blanco's novel, *The Journey of the Flame*) and for all dudes and tourists, but he likes to talk, too, so he has to make do with what comes along.

We all went down to the waterfront (where there was a rusty, half-sunken ship) and watched Bob work on his catamaran. It was blue and looked sturdy enough. There was no shelter on it except for what shade the sail provided. Judy, a pretty blonde, was a game girl. We got a mechanic there to check out the Rattler. He wore his cap sideways like Cantinflas, not for any antic effect, as he was very gloomy, but for some practical reason of his own. He put on a new voltage regulator. It didn't do much good but, like hypochondriacs, we no longer expected results, we just wanted attention.

Smith said Mexican mechanics were ingenious. He said one down below La Paz had managed to break an anvil. How much did he think the truck would bring? "You might get $500," he said. "Studebaker parts are hard to get. They like Chevys." Smith himself had a Volks camper and renovated weapons carrier with high clearance. "You could sling a cat under that baby," he said.

The guidebooks dismiss Santa Rosalia as a boring mill town but we hated to leave. Down the line we ran into some long stretches of deep sand and drove across them as fast as we could, using some principle of momentum I don't fully understand—as though you could catch the sand napping. We got stuck a couple of times but rocked free without too much trouble. With four-wheel drive these places would be a breeze.

Mulege was the next settlement and it looked like something out of Central America, with its little river, date palms and thatched roofs. There are several expensive resort hotels here to accommodate American fishermen who fly down in their own planes. The place also seemed to mark the end of the hospitality belt. Behind us we had met with nothing but a ready generosity; now when we asked directions we got grudging, mumbled answers. The same with the Yanks, no more wilderness camaraderie. We had supper that night at one of the hotels, *La Serenidad*, and our table was next to one at which two American couples were sitting. An uncomfortable hush prevailed. Nobody spoke to anybody. Maybe we just wanted them to ask about our trip.

It was the off-season and there were no other guests. The manager said 42 planes had come in on Memorial Day. His big problem, he said, was getting good help and supplies. "For days now I have been out of Cointreau." Roughing it at *La*

*Serenidad.* We left and did some night driving for the first time, and played around with the spotlights. But we couldn't distinguish the little potholes from the big ones, the axle busters, because of headlight shadows, and we gave it up after a while. My air mat had blown away and I folded up the tarp and used it for a pad. We heard a coyote yipping and howling that night but he was not close by.

July 22. Mile 985. Up at 5:30 anticipating the drive on the ledge of terror above the Bay of Conception. An American in Santa Rosalia had described it in fearful terms. "All I can say is, don't look down," he said. This was misleading. It was a one-way shelf road above the water and if we had met another vehicle it would have been inconvenient, but there was plenty of room for anything short of a Greyhound bus. The water in the bay was so clear that we could see big fish lolling around from 200 feet up on the cliff. There were good white beaches along here too, and lots of pelicans.

We stopped for a swim with the mask and snorkel and tried out our Hawaiian sling. This was a fish spear (really a frog gig) with a loop of rubber wired to the end of the handle. When you grasp the handle up near the business end you have a cocked missile. Catamaran Bob told us how to make it. We got two gray fish about as big as your hand and grazed some bigger ones, fat groupers, but before we had mastered the use of the thing we had broken three of the four tines on rocks. The fish were plentiful and multi-colored. It was like swimming in an aquarium. The pelicans had better luck. They dive-bombed all around us with heavy splashes and scored almost every time.

After leaving the bay the road got worse and worse and the terrain took on a sinister aspect. Big volcanic slabs of rusty brown rock we had not seen before. It was the hottest day so far. Andy started belching, more than seemed necessary, and blamed it on the heat. I said that didn't make any sense. He said it made as much sense as my wearing that stupid cow-boy hat all the time. Then there was a dispute about who was responsible for the chocolate mess in the glove compartment. Leaving those Hydrox cookies loose in there. Over the door there was a strip of metal that pulled out about four hairs every time you put your head against it. It had been a small joke; now we beat on it with fists and wrenches. We were having trouble again shifting into high gear and we argued about whose was the better shifting action—his double-clutching maneuver with a brief pause in neutral, or my fast jamming move.

He must have been right because I was driving when it went completely out of whack, just limp. It wouldn't shift into anything. We stopped and investigated. There were four empty bolt holes on the shift column. We walked back down the road almost a mile looking for we didn't know what, found nothing and came back.

The silence there—after the hot engine had stopped contracting and popping—was total. No birds, no insect noises, no wind, nothing. All you could hear was the blood humming in your ears. Andy checked the column closer and decided there was no piece missing, only the bolts. He ran wire through the four holes joining whatever parts they were together, then crawled underneath with a 10-inch Crescent wrench and tightened up some boss nut that held the entire truck together. He knew his stuff; we had gears again.

Not far from there in a dry wash we came upon the carcass of a pony, dried, perfectly preserved, as in a museum. It was standing upright, or rather hanging. Someone had taken thick strands of hair from his mane and tail and tied them to the branches of a mesquite tree. Whether before or after death we could not tell.

Soon we were climbing a range called Sierra de la Giganta. The road goes right over the top and on the steep switchbacks the engine started missing again. At each new level we stopped to regroup and plan the running start for the next stretch. Sometimes there was a choice of roads, a short steep one or a long, not-so-steep one. The way we were gunning the truck in low it's a wonder we didn't throw a rod. On one long grade near the very top going about 3 m.p.h. in low, engine shrieking, the Rattler coughed and misfired completely and we were almost in a dead stall when Andy bailed out and began to push. If he hadn't I believe the truck would still be there. The reduced load and added thrust of one manpower just got us over.

That afternoon we descended into a deep canyon and entered Comondu, a strange place indeed. It is an oasis of springs and date palms on a narrow canyon floor, bounded by towering cliffs. Hidden, isolated, it is the Shangri-La of Baja. About 700 people live there and they have the power to cloud men's minds. At least I find no entry for the place in our notebook, except for arrival and departure times. Of course we were already loopy from the heat.

Just before sundown we hit gravel. It was a head-rattling washboard road but nonetheless gravel, two lanes wide, the work of some official road gang up from La Paz. Andy scented victory. He took the wheel and drove like a madman, jaw set, eyes hooded. We bounced and skittered all over the road at speeds approaching 35 m.p.h. and such was the racket that we didn't talk again—we couldn't—until 11 P.M. when we reached the pavement and I finally got him to stop. I was glad I didn't have to use the pistol. We flaked out in the ditch, spent.

July 23. Mile 1,170. A long pull at the water bag, no hash, and off at 7 A.M. The pavement was good and a little after 9:00, at mile 1,268, we rolled into La Paz. We were very proud of the Rattler.

La Paz (Pop. 34,000) is situated on a pale green bay, and oddly, for a Gulf-side town, faces west. For 400 years it was one of the world's great pearl fisheries but there has not been much pearling in recent years. The locals say their Japanese competitors put "something" in their water before World War II and ruined the oyster beds. The town now caters largely to Americans who fly down to catch marlin and sailfish and such. (The richer anglers go to Punta Palmilla, down on the Cape, where there is an exclusive luxury hotel suitable for high-level, right-wing plotting.) In La Paz there is a pretty drive along the bay called El Malecon. The bay is shallow but there is a channel that permits sizeable ships to come in and tie up at a T-head pier. A big new ferry shuttles back and forth to Mazatlan on the mainland.

We checked in at the Perla Hotel and had breakfast in the outdoor café. Our hands were swollen from gripping the wheel. Fat fingers. Nobody from the local paper came around to interview us, but we were joined for coffee by a thin American lad from San Francisco named Gregory. He wore a Bob

Dylan cap and sported a ban-the-bomb button and one with
*Huelga!* (Strike!) on it.

He said he had been there two months working at the John
F. Kennedy Bi-lingual Library. But the library business was a
drag and the fish cannery workers were afraid to organize and
he was anxious to go home and get back in the vineyards with
the National Farm Workers' Association. He said he didn't
know Jim Smith.

"The thing is, nobody reads books here," he said. "You just
sit there all day. All they read is schlock stuff like the Police
Gazette and Bugs Bunny and those photo-novels."

Andy and I discussed going fishing. Or skin-diving. Or
maybe driving down to the Cape, to the very tip of Baja. We
still had half a roll of wire left. But a tropical lassitude had set
in and we didn't want to do anything.

That night we ate at one of the fancier hotels, Los Cocos, in
a grove of coconut palms on the bay. The dining area was outdoors, paper lanterns and all. Aeronaves pilots frolicked in the
pool with stewardesses. A good many Americans were there, all
of whom seemed to be talking fishing except us and two men
in the bar who were still mad about Truman firing MacArthur.
One said, "You can have Nimitz. MacArthur won that war. He
was the finest soldier that ever put a foot in a boot."

Later we went to a nitery outside town called *Ranchita*,
sharing a cab with a talkative sport from Las Vegas and his silent, unhappy girlfriend. They had flown down that afternoon.
"I didn't realize it was so *far*," he said. "I thought we'd *never*
get here." We let that one slide, with difficulty.

The *Ranchita* had colored lights and a cornet player with a
sharp Latin attack but everybody seemed to be down in the
dumps. Surely they weren't all worrying about Mac. Then a
tall drunk fell on the dance floor, right on his chin, and this
brought what Franklin W. Dixon, author of the Hardy Boys
books, would have called whoops of laughter. Jim Smith had
told us he once had a difference of opinion in the *Ranchita*
with "Duke Morrison." Who? "Duke Morrison. You know
him as John Wayne." He said he didn't come off badly either.

July 24. Andy had to get back to Los Angeles and he caught
the morning plane. I stuck around to see about the Rattler. A

customs agent said yes, he understood I wasn't trying to prof-
iteer, and yes, vehicles were needed there, but the law was the
law. It would not be possible to sell the truck. Then I would
give it away, perhaps to an orphanage. Was there one in town?
Yes, but that too was prohibited, unless the arrangement was
handled through customs.

Word got around that the truck was for sale. For the next
two days prospective buyers came to my table at the *Perla*
where I sat drinking coffee and reading the Warren Report
amidst a swarm of small, barefooted Chiclets salesmen. But I
couldn't close a deal the way I had worked it out. On the third
day a cab driver came over. His card identified him as Abrahan
Wong V., Taxi No. 17 (English Spoken). I couldn't figure out
the name; was there a country club anywhere in the world that
would accept this man? I told him the truck had overdrive and
40 pounds of oil pressure. Both spotlights worked. It had used
only one quart of oil on the drive from L.A., which was true.

Yes, yes, he could see, the truck was *bonita*. He had once
owned a Studebaker Commander himself. Very good car. He
had broken his arm and nose in it. He showed me the place on
his nose. How much was I asking?

How much would he give? He thought for a minute and
said $300. I said okay. Like a fool, too fast. He smelled a rat
and started backing off.

"Have you got tlikslik?"

"What?"

"Tlikslik. Tlikslik." He mimed a piece of paper.

The pink slip, the title. I said "no" because I had only recently bought the truck myself but I had the temporary thing
and the bill of sale. It was clear.

"Must have tlikslik," said Abrahan Wong V.

That afternoon I made a deal with the owner of a sport fishing boat. I would sell him everything on the truck—gas cans,
water cans, a 3-ton jack, crowder peas, Mazola, two spare tires
—the lot—for $200, and give him the truck free, if he could
get an okay from customs. Done, he said. Except. Wait a minute. He was a little strapped right now. He would give me $100
now and mail the other $100 later. Oh, but he would send it
very soon. All but weeping, I let the Rattler go for five $20
bills.

On the $51.25 flight back to Los Angeles they served a good baked chicken lunch. A man across the aisle asked if I had been down on the Cape and I said no. "You missed the best part," he said. The peninsula looked more barren and forbidding from the air than at truck level, and if I had flown it first I'm not sure I would have gone overland. Jim Smith said a woman in San Francisco once told him she was planning to make the Baja run, and what should she do for preparation? He told her to pack a lunch.

*1967*

# The Forgotten River

THE FOREST rangers at Mena were all very nice but they could tell me only approximately where the Ouachita River began. It rose somewhere out there in the woods, they said, above the little bridge at Eagleton, where I would find the first Ouachita River road sign. I wanted to see the very origin and so I floundered about between Rich Mountain and Black Fork Mountain with further inquiries.

Through that forested valley runs Highway 270, as well as the Kansas City Southern Railway, and the headwaters of the Ouachita, at an elevation of 1,600 feet above sea level. The two mountains rise another thousand feet or so from the valley floor. A sign warns hikers about the presence of black bears.

Nearby, right on the Oklahoma line, there is a log cabin beer joint, which might have once served the Dalton Brothers; Bill, Grat, Emmett, and Bob. It was dark inside, like a cave, with a very low ceiling. The girl behind the bar knew nothing, which was all right. You don't expect young people to know river lore.

Then a young man sitting far back in the gloom—the only customer—told me just how I should go. I was to enter the woods at the start of the Black Fork Mountain hiking trail. When I reached the river, here a small watercourse—"so narrow you can straddle it"—I was to walk upstream for about a mile, and there I would find three or four trickling threads of water coming together to form the Ouachita River.

This would have to do, though I had hoped for a spring, a well-defined source. Probably I didn't walk the full mile. I followed the diminishing rivulet up to the point where it was no wider than my three fingers, and declared victory. After all, it was much the same as spring water, cold and clear. I drank some of it. From here it flows 610 miles, generally southeast, to Jonesville, La., where it joins other streams to form the Black River.

I grew up in south Arkansas and thought of the Ouachita only in local terms, certainly not as an outlet to the sea. It was a place to swim and fish. I knew you could take a boat down it from the Highway 82 bridge near Crossett to Monroe, La., because I had done it once with a friend, Johnny Titus. It was shady a good bit of the way and we had the river pretty much to ourselves. The keeper at the old Felsenthal lock was annoyed at having to get up from his dinner table to lock through two boys in a small outboard rig.

But I knew no river lore, less than the Oklahoma barmaid, and it came as a great surprise to me lately when I learned that there was regular steamboat service on this modest green river, as late as the 1930s, and as far up as Camden. I am not speaking of modern replicas or party barges, rented out for brief excursions, but of genuine working steamboats, with big paddle wheels at the rear, carrying bales of cotton down to New Orleans and bringing bananas and sacks of sugar back upstream, along with paying passengers.

There were two vessels, the *Ouachita* and the *City of Camden*, and they ran on about a two-week cycle—New Orleans-Camden-New Orleans, with stops along the way. The round-trip fare, including a bed and all meals, was $50. Traditional steamboat decorum was imposed, with the men required to wear coats in the dining room. At night, after supper was cleared, the waiters doubled as musicians for a dance.

It was Dee Brown of Little Rock, the author of *Bury My Heart at Wounded Knee*, who told me about this, and how as a teen-aged boy in the late 1920s he took the *Ouachita* from New Orleans to Camden. He had a summer job at a filling station between Stephens and Camden, and had often watched the steamer tie up and unload. "'I've got to ride that boat,' I kept telling myself." He saved up a bit more than $50 for the adventure—"an enormous sum in those days"—but then thought better of this extravagance. He would keep half of it back. "So I made a reservation for the other end and hitch-hiked down to New Orleans. Hitch-hiking was easy and safe then, and faster than the boat."

His timing was good, which kept expenses down. He paid a dollar for a night's lodging at a boarding house near the French Quarter. The trip back was a delight, as Mr. Brown remembers, a leisurely voyage of five or six days. He got full value for his $25. The big splashing wheel pushed the steamer up the

Mississippi, the Red, the Black, and at last into the Ouachita at Jonesville, with the two walls of the forest closing in a bit more day by day.

There were fine breakfasts of ham and eggs, when ham was real ham, with grits and hot biscuits. At lunch one day he found a split avocado on his plate, or "alligator pear," as it was called on the menu. "I had never seen one before. I wouldn't eat it." Young Mr. Brown was traveling light and so had to borrow a coat from a waiter at each meal before he could be seated. He had a tiny sleeping cabin to himself with a bunk bed and a single hook on the wall for his wardrobe.

He enjoyed the nightly dances, though he had to sit them out as a wallflower because he didn't know how to dance. Townsfolk along the way came on board just for the dance, and among them were young Delta sports sneaking drinks of corn whiskey and ginger jake. These were Prohibition days. A young girl from New Orleans, traveling with her family, offered to teach Dee Brown how to dance. "I wanted to dance with her, too, sure, but I just couldn't bring myself to do it." This family, he recalls, who had never seen any high ground, marveled over the puny hillocks of the upper river. He remembers an Arkansas woman vowing never again to eat sugar, after seeing the deckhands, dripping with sweat, taking naps on the deck-loaded sacks of sugar.

Dee Brown, then, got me interested, and so in late May and early June I drove down the Ouachita valley to take a look at things.

The Ouachita National Forest, where the river rises, is still a dark green wilderness, if not quite the forest primeval that DeSoto saw when he came crashing through these woods 450 years ago, with some 600 soldiers, 223 horses, a herd of hogs, and a pack of bloodhounds. He was looking for another Peru, out of which he had taken a fortune in gold, more than enough to pay, from his own pocket, for this very costly expedition. As it turned out, there was no gold or silver here in "Florida." What he found was catfish.

"There was a fish which they called Bagres: the third part of it was head, and it had on both sides the gilles, and along the sides great pricks like very sharp aules; those of this kind that were in lakes were as big as pikes: and in the River, there were some of an hundred, and of an hundred and fiftie pounds weight, and many of them were taken with the hooke . . ."

This comes from a report written by one of DeSoto's Portuguese officers, who identifies himself only as "A Gentleman of Elvas" (the town of Elvas, in Portugal). The Portuguese version was published in 1557, and was rendered into this King James English by Richard Hakluyt, and published in London in 1609, under the misleading title of "Virginia Richly Valued." Hakluyt was promoting English exploration and settlement in the New World, and any news at all from that quarter was grist for his mill. There is not one word about Virginia in the text, and a more accurate title would be "Florida Poorly Valued." By Spanish reckoning, the continent belonged to Spain, being a gift from Pope Alexander VI, himself a Spaniard, and all that country lying east and north of New Spain (Mexico) was regarded more or less as Florida.

Elvas tells of seeing ". . . many Beares, and Lyons, Wolves, Deere, Dogges, Cattes, Martens and Conies. There be many wild Hennes as big as Turkies, Partridges small like those of Africa, Cranee, Duckes, Pigeons, Thrushes and Sparrows . . . There are Gosse Hawks, Falcons . . . and all Fowles of prey that are in Spaine . . ."

He spoke too of "small chestnuts" and of "many Walnut trees bearing soft shelled Walnuts in fashion like bullets," which could only have been pecans. Some of his "Plummes and Prunes" were very likely muscadines and persimmons. There is no mention in his bestiary of buffalo, or bison, then roaming the country from coast to coast. DeSoto's men knew about these "hunch-backed cattle," as they had traded with the Indians for their hides, which made good bedding, but they had no luck in hunting them and there is some question whether they ever saw one on the hoof. There is only one passing, inconclusive mention of a hunt. It is a wonder, perhaps, that they saw any wild creatures, who must have heard this band approaching from some distance away, clanking, snorting, grunting, barking.

The forest has changed; it is no longer a virgin stand of timber with a high canopy and an uncluttered, parklike floor, on which horses could move about. The Beares and Deere still thrive, but the Lyons are gone, or so believes Larry Hedrick, of the National Forest's Game and Wildlife Division. "We do get occasional 'sightings,' but there is just no good evidence of free-living, free-ranging cougars out there. Of course, they are reclusive, like bobcats. We're overrun with bobcats, but you don't see them." As for the native red wolves, they have mated with intruding, wily, trickster coyotes to form a curious hybrid pack. The chinquapin, sweetest of nuts, has disappeared too, in my lifetime, or it is almost gone, a victim of the chestnut blight.

Yet even with change the forest remains an impressive tract of mountain greenery, bigger, at 2,500 square miles, than the state of Delaware, and the river that flows out of it is one of the prettiest in the country.

Early trappers and market hunters paddled their canoes up it, far past Camden, the present head of navigation, past the bluff where the Caddo enters at Arkadelphia, past "the hot springs," and on to the hills not far from the present town of Mena. This upper stretch is still navigable by canoe, in season, in the familiar pattern of a fast-flowing stream: shoal water followed by a pool followed by a shoal. For some reason, however, it has not caught on well with recreational floaters, slaves of fashion that they are. On a warm day in late spring, with plenty of water running, when there must have been war parties of canoes colliding at every bend of the Buffalo River, I saw not a single floater on the Ouachita between Ink and Oden, nor a bank fisherman nor a swimmer.

The parks and campgrounds were spruced up for the summer season. The state roadways were clean, too. Where was all the litter that people complain about in letters to newspapers? Also, where was the old rural shabbiness?

The farmhouses on Highways 270 and 88 were well-kept, in fine trim, the mobile homes neatly skirted. Around them were shade trees, ornamental shrubs, flower beds and well-tended lawns. Not what we used to call landscaping in the Arkansas countryside, when the custom was to level every living thing around your house for about a 50-yard radius. We were the original clear-cutters, and this dead-zone tradition lives on in east Arkansas, where you can see a new brick house plopped down in the middle of a muddy soybean field, without so much as a crabapple tree or a petunia out front—as though people who farm in a big way couldn't be bothered with mere horticulture.

The new attention to lawn care can be attributed, I think, to the invention and spread of the riding mower. Cutting the grass is no longer seen as a chore, as men don't outgrow their boyhood love for dodging about in midget cars with tiny steering wheels. I believe this also accounts for the popularity of golf. Take away the little motorized carts and the links would be largely deserted.

It may be that outlanders have brought in new ideas about some of these things, along with their comfortable retirement incomes. You hear a lot of non-Arkansas voices these days in the Ouachitas. At Lum and Abner's Jot-em-Down Store in Pine Ridge, I was greeted by a nice lady from some northern clime who never in her life said, "Well, I swan!" much less, "Ay grannies!" At another store, in neighboring Polk County, there were flat white wicks for sale, for kerosene lamps, but I found no country store so humble or remote that it didn't offer a selection of video cassettes. In the towns there are signs of a modest prosperity, such as new police cars (big Chevrolet Caprices, mostly) and new Masonic halls, Moose lodges, and American Legion huts. All these brotherhoods seem to have hired the same architect, a grim man, who likes to build on defensive, bunker principles. His signature is the blank wall. The new clubhouses, with few exceptions, are long, low buff-brick structures with no windows.

There is no longer much agriculture in this country, in the strict sense of field crops. The old straggling hillside corn patches are now pastures where polled Hereford and Angus cattle graze. A lot of fat healthy saddle horses are running about too. The long metal chicken sheds appear to be mostly abandoned, or in use for storage of those big cylindrical rolls of hay. The vegetable gardens are still deadly serious, with rows of pole beans and squash 90 feet long.

Mount Ida is where the hexagonal quartz crystals are found, with their radiant powers. Just north of town the mountain stream loses its "rolling impetuosity" as Dunbar would put it, and begins to spread and go still and blue as it is penned up by the hand of man. Here, for some 50 miles, the river loses its identity in a chain of dams and lakes—Ouachita, with a shoreline of almost a thousand miles, and the older and smaller Hamilton and Catherine. All are associated with Hot Springs, though the city itself is not on the river.

For William Dunbar and his expedition up the Ouachita, from October, 1804, to January, 1805, it was a nine-mile hike from the river bank to the valley of "the boiling springs," which is now Central Avenue downtown. Dunbar was an immigrant from Scotland who had done well in America. He owned a plantation near Natchez and had a good education. He knew how to do things, which made him a man after President Thomas Jefferson's heart. Jefferson and the U.S. Congress had just paid Napoleon $15 million for the entire western drainage of the Mississippi River—the Louisiana Purchase—and exploring parties were being organized to look over the new territory. Dunbar was sent up the Ouachita. He went in an unwieldy barge 50 feet long, with a Dr. George Hunter of Philadelphia, a guide, three of Dunbar's slaves, and a rowing party of 14 soldiers from the New Orleans garrison. It was a small, regional version of the Lewis and Clark expedition up the Missouri, and on to the Pacific.

Surprisingly little was known at that late date of the country between the Mississippi and the Shining Mountains, or the Stony Mountains, as the Rockies were then called. Jefferson, perhaps the best-informed man of the country, thought there still might be mastodons or mammoths grazing to the west. They would be much bigger than the tropical elephants. Jefferson wanted our New World animals to be the biggest. In the same spirit, Robert Livingston, negotiating in Paris for the purchase of *La Louisiane*, told the treasury minister that, anyway, the French would never be able to sell their goods here, such as Cognac, because Americans preferred Kentucky peach brandy, "which, with age, is superior to the best brandy of France." It was truly morning in America.

The cynical Napoleon, 33-year-old First Consul, may or may not have believed it. On first meeting Livingston, at a reception, he took a playful line with the presumptions of the new nation.

"You have been in Europe before, Monsieur Livingston?"

"No, my General."

"You have come to a very corrupt world." Then, to Talleyrand, "Explain to Monsieur Livingston that the old world
is very corrupt. You know something about that, don't you,
Monsieur Talleyrand?"

The Anglo-Americans were slow to learn from the Indians
and the French that canoes were the thing. Dunbar's monster
barge, designed by Dr. Hunter, drew two feet of water and had
an external keel. Over and over again the soldiers had to jump
into the cold water with a rope and drag the thing off snags
and over sandbars and shoals. At Fort Miro, or the Washita
Post (Monroe, La.), they changed to a lighter boat and the
going was faster, but they still had to manhandle it over the
rougher shoals. One, north of the Caddo, had a straight vertical drop of four-and-a-half feet.

Dunbar remarks on the beauty of the river and how it was
clear and drinkable along the entire course, unlike the Red and
the "Arcansa," which were always muddy, "being charged with
red terrene matter." The trees on the banks—willow, black
oak, packawn, hickory, and elm—were not so grand or lofty
as those along the Mississippi, but had their own charm and
"appear to bear a kind of proportion to the magnitude of their
own river."

The Ouachita wasn't completely unknown. It was late fall
and the bears were fat with oil and their furs were prime. Dunbar met hunters along the way "who count much of their
profits from the oil drawn from the Bear's fat, which at New
Orleans is always of ready sale, and is much esteemed for its
wholesomeness in cooking, being preferred to butter or hog's
lard; it is found to keep longer than any other oil of the same
nature, without turning rancid . . ."

He comments on the indolence of the white settlers—
"always a consequence of the Indian mode of life"—and tells
us that the young army officer in command at Fort Miro, a
Lieutenant Bowmar, while capable enough, lacked "the polite
manners of a gentleman." At another point he suddenly seems
to remember that he is writing this report for Jefferson, the
great democrat, and he praises the industry and sturdy independence of a man and his wife who had cleared a little two-
acre farmstead in the woods. They had corn for bread, plenty
of venison, bear oil, fish and fowl for the taking, and there were

hides and wild honey to sell for cash. Their prospects were indeed bright, and he stops just short of having them reading a bit of John Locke or Rousseau by firelight, before turning in.

"How happy the contrast, when we compare the fortune of the new settler in the U.S. with the misery of the half-starving, oppressed, and degraded Peasant of Europe!!" Dunbar is not a man for exclamation marks, and when he gives us two of them here, we feel his discomfort with this kind of talk—however genuine the sentiment.

They found two abandoned log huts at the base of Hot Springs Mountain, where the smoking waters poured forth to form a creek. The sick from Natchez were already coming here to soak their bones. Dunbar examined the rocks and vegetation. Dr. Hunter, of whom Dunbar speaks in a guarded way as "a professed chemist," conducted experiments with his pans and beakers. Dunbar determined the latitude with his sextant. (Is there anyone today living between Natchez and Hot Springs who could do that—go off into the forest and calculate the angular distance of his position in degrees and minutes from the equator?) He measured the temperature of the springs and pools, and his readings of 132 to 150 degrees F. tally pretty well with the current reading at the source of 145.8 degrees. So we can't blame a badly defective thermometer when he tells us that the air temperature fell to 6 degrees on January 2, 1805, as they were camped on the river bank in 13 inches of snow. They ate well, bagging turkeys and deer at will. They shot one young bear. But, as with DeSoto's men, they had no luck with the buffalo. On two occasions in south Arkansas these beasts were "shot at and grievously wounded, with blood streaming from their sides." The soldiers couldn't bring them down, however, and couldn't or wouldn't track them down. Soldiers perhaps lack the patience to be good hunters.

Elvas puts it this way: "The Indians want no fleshmeat; for they kill with their arrowes many deere, hennes, conies and other wild fowle: for they are very cunning at it: which skills the Christians had not: and though they had it, they had no leasure to use it: for most of the time they spent in travel, and durst not presume to straggle aside . . ."

Dunbar doesn't identify his weapons, other than to call them "rifles," which suggests they weren't smoothbore muskets. It is possible his party was fitted out, as were Lewis and Clark, with the army's new 1803 model rifle, a flintlock of .54 caliber. DeSoto's troops had a few firearms, of a kind known as the arquebus, a primitive matchlock shoulder weapon firing a .65 to .75 caliber ball, and using a smoldering wick called a match or matchcord to ignite the powder charge. These pieces were cumbersome, inaccurate, with a much shorter range than the crossbow, which was DeSoto's primary weapon, together with swords and lances. The thundersticks weren't even of much help in terrifying the natives, who, as one account has it, "not only had held no fear of the arquebuses but had scorned and ridiculed them . . ." In the end the survivors of the expedition melted down the useless guns to make nails for their escape boats.

Was DeSoto at Hot Springs? Here is the brief passage, again from Elvas, that is the basis of this belief: "The Governor rested a moneth more in the Province of Cayas. In which time the horses fattened more than in other places in a longer time, with the great plentie of Maiz and the leaves thereof, which I think the best that hath been seene, and they drank of a lake of very hot water, and somewhat brackish, and they drank so much, that it swelled in their bellies when they brought them from the watering."

There are three accounts of the expedition written by participants. The one from Elvas is the longest, at 179 pages, and there are short, brisk, official reports from Hernandez de Biedma, the king's factor, and Rodrigo Ranjel, DeSoto's private secretary. Some 50 years after the event, one Garcilaso de la Vega completed a fourth account, a long, literary book, which he claimed was based on interviews with a knight and two soldiers who accompanied DeSoto. This work is held to be the least reliable.

In only one of the four—Elvas—can I find mention of geothermal water, warm or hot, and his water is somewhat brackish. The Hot Springs water is not at all brackish, and contains no particular belly-swelling agents. The "lake" comes from the Portuguese word "lagoa," which can mean anything from a small lake to a puddle.

The U.S. DeSoto Expedition Commission cites a mention of "hot streams" from Ranjel—"from the missing parts of his diary." It is still missing from the only published Ranjel account I could find. This commission, a blue ribbon government panel, of which Col. John R. Fordyce of Arkansas was vice chairman, delivered its report in 1939, on the 400th anniversary of DeSoto's landing at Tampa Bay. Colonel Fordyce and his colleagues made an exhaustive effort to map out DeSoto's wanderings, from vague topographical clues and the rough estimates of distances and directions given by Elvas and the others. (Coronado, then exploring to the west, was better organized; he had a man designated to count off the paces of each day's march.)

The DeSoto distances are given as so many days' journey, or so many leagues, when given at all. But what was a day's march? What league were they using? With eight to choose from, the commission members finally settled on the Spanish judicial league of 2.634 miles, not to be confused with the ordinary Spanish league of 4.214 miles or the Portuguese league of 3.84 miles. The report is an impressive work of scholarship, conjecture, and divination.

But if not Hot Springs, where was this Province of Cayas? It is pretty well established that the Spaniards were in the central part of the country at that time, and nowhere else in the region (except at nearby Caddo Gap) are there springs of warm water coming from the earth, fresh or brackish. Anyhow, I like to think that DeSoto was here in 1541, and I like to think that Shakespeare, still working in London in 1609, picked up the little Elvas-Hakluyt book and read about the hot lake, and about Camden and Calion, and the earlier crossing of the Great River near Helena. It is just the kind of chronicle he quarried for his plots and characters, and DeSoto, a brutal, devout, heroic man brought low, is certainly of Shakespearean stature. But, bad luck, there is no play, with a scene at the Camden winter quarters, and, in another part of the forest, at Smackover Creek, where willows still grow aslant the brook.

(A note here on Hakluyt's English: Those earnest enunciators who say "bean" for "been" should know that Hakluyt, the Oxford scholar, spelled it "bin," as did, off and on, the poet John Donne.)

Below Lake Catherine the Ouachita runs free again, for a while. The momentum is less, the river having already dropped

from 1,600 feet to 315 feet at Malvern, and the rate of fall is lev-
eling off fast. But there is still shoaling, as you can see from the
Interstate 30 bridge near the Malvern exit. Above and below
the bridge the water breaks on shelving rock, and we can imagine the trouble Dunbar had in dragging a heavy boat over it.

Sturdy bricks are made at Malvern, 200 million of them each
year, and in the adjoining and older community of Rockport,
there is a white frame church, the Rockport United Methodist
Church, with a sign proclaiming it to be the "Oldest Church
West of the Mississippi/Est. 1809/Elmo A. Thomason, Pastor." Oldest Protestant church, I gather, is the meaning, but on
the day I stopped, the Rev. Mr. Thomason was not around to
clarify the point. Yellow ribbons girdled the shade trees around
the church—none of your latter-day Wesleyan revisionists at
Rockport. Little Rock did well enough in welcoming home
the troops from Desert Storm, but I noticed that the small
towns in Arkansas and Louisiana, more directly affected by the
call-up of Reserve and National Guard units, did much better.
They were more exuberant, more lavish with their ribbons and
banners.

At Arkadelphia (Blakleytown, until 1838) we know we are
out of the hills when we see the statue of a Confederate soldier
on the courthouse lawn, and an African Methodist Episcopal
Church, and a snarling yellow Ag-Cat cropduster dipping low
over a rice field—irrigated from the Ouachita. The Ag-Cat is
an excellent workhorse, but the bulging cockpit canopy is ugly
and the plane just doesn't have the pleasing lines of the old
Stearman.

The Caddo enters the Ouachita here, and at one time you
could freely drive to a bluff overlooking the confluence. No
more; you are now confronted by a locked gate. Arkadelphia
had irregular steamboat service from 1825 until the 1870s,
when the Iron Mountain Railroad came through, and even
after that a few boats came up from time to time. One, in 1912,
reportedly took on a load of 2,000 bales of cotton. But commercial navigation this high on the river was always seasonal
and chancy.

Highway 7 south of town becomes a shady corridor of tall,
skinny pines. Below Sparkman ("Welcome to Sparkman/
A Good Town/Raiders are Winners") there is a turn-off to

Tate's Bluff, where the Little Missouri joins the Ouachita. A low concrete bridge, which washes out now and then, spans the river. I ran into my first floaters here, two young men in a canoe, who had made their way some 30 miles down the Little Missouri. "We only had to drag once." Did they ever float the Ouachita? "Not this far down. There's just not enough current. Too much paddling." Did they know of any songs about the Ouachita? Well, no. They tried hard, too, to think of a song. Everybody was very obliging.

Camden, head of navigation, has the feel of a river town, though you can no longer get a catfish lunch downtown, or any kind of plate lunch. Along the bar pits middle-aged black women are fishing with cane poles. They stand very still watching their corks. They are all bundled up against the heat and the mosquitoes, and their broad-brimmed straw hats are well cinched down with colorful sashes.

Between the railroad track and the river there is a big metal building with the hopeful words, "Port of Camden," painted on it. But where are the tugs and barges? It seems there are none. According to Mrs. Eunice Platt, there hasn't been a commercial run up this far since December 1989, when four barges, pushed two at a time, came from Monroe to get a load of gravel for rockless Louisiana. Mrs. Platt, of Camden, is the executive director of the Ouachita River Valley Association, and a tireless worker in promoting navigation improvements on the upper Ouachita.

The situation, as I understand it, is this: The old dams and locks, completed in 1926, provided a six-and-a-half-foot channel from the Black River to Camden. The new system was finished in 1985 and provides a nine-foot channel with new dams and locks at Calion and Felsenthal in Arkansas, and Columbia and Jonesville in Louisiana. The locks will accommodate four standard barges tied two abreast ahead of a tugboat. Some of the bends in the river, however, are so tight that these four-barge units can't negotiate them. The shorter, two-barge units, are said not to be commercially feasible. To remedy this, Mrs. Platt and the Corps of Engineers want to lop off some of the meanders, most of them in Arkansas.

"They say we're trying to make a muddy ditch out of the river," she said. "Well, that's just not true. We're talking about a total of 14 bend widenings and eight cutoffs, out of what, more than 300 bends in the river? We're talking about a total of 341 acres of land. That's all that will be used. I'm trying to help the river, not hurt it. I'm an environmentalist too. I'm just as much an environmentalist as Richard Mason is."

Mr. Mason, of El Dorado, co-chairman of the Businessmen's Coalition to Save the Ouachita, agrees with the numbers but thinks they are misleading. He said, "Some of those cutoffs are huge and will really take in as many as seven smaller bends. Look, every conservation and wildlife group in the state is against this thing—every single one." He also thinks it's a waste of money. "An obvious pork barrel proposition, nothing else. You could make that river as straight as an arrow and nobody would use it." It is much cheaper, he claims, to haul goods by truck from Crossett to Greenville, Miss., or from Camden to Pine Bluff, on the Arkansas, and offload on barges there, than to ship down the Ouachita. As for the El Dorado petroleum products, there are existing pipelines. "You can't ship cheaper than a pipeline."

The cutoff project is now hanging fire, pending acquisition of the 341 acres, which the five affected counties in Arkansas must pay for. In Louisiana, the state government must pay. I came away with the impression that Mrs. Platt is right about the predicted damage to the river being exaggerated, and that Mr. Mason is right when he says that the prospects for high-volume barge traffic are not very good.

When Dunbar came through here in 1804 he noted the presence of a trail through the woods: ". . . the road of the Cadadoquis Indian Nation leading to the Arcansa Nation; a little beyond this is the Ecor a Fabri 80 to 100 feet high: it is reported that a line of demarkation run between the french and spanish provinces, when the former possessed Louisiana, crossed the river at this place; and it is said that Fabri, a french-man and perhaps the supposed Engineer deposited lead near the cliff in the direction of the line . . . The additional rapid-ity of the current indicates that we are ascending into a higher country. The water of the river now becomes extremely clear and is equal to any in its very agreeable taste as to drinking water . . . The general breadth of the river today has been about 80 yards."

The Ouachita remains about the same width but the bluff is not half that high today, having been trimmed down over the years by railroads and other developers.

Again, the question arises: Was DeSoto here? The DeSoto Commission thought so, tracking the expedition south along the Little Missouri and the Ouachita, as the Spaniards made their way back toward the Great River in late 1541. Camden, or perhaps Calion, says the report, was very probably the Autiamque of Elvas, or Utiangue, as Garcilaso has it. Here is Elvas:

"The next day they came to Autiamque. They found much Maiz laid up in store, and French beanes and walnuts, and prunes, great store of all sorts. They took some Indians which were gathering together the stuffe which their wives had hidden. This was a Champion countrie, and well inhabited. The Governor lodged in the best part of the towne, and commanded presently to make a fense of timber round about the Campe distant from the houses, that the Indians might not hurt them without by fire . . . hard by this town passed a River, that came out of the Province of Cayas . . ."

So far, so good. The puzzling part comes next. Elvas tells us that they spent the winter at Autiamque, three months in all, with plenty of food. The Indians showed them how to snare rabbits, both cottontails and another breed which were "as big as great Hares, longer, and having greater loines." These may have been swamp rabbits, whose loines are great indeed.

They passed the winter there resting and trapping rabbits "which until that time they knew not how to catch . . . The Indians taught them how to take them: which was, with great springes, which lifted their feete from the ground: and the snare was made with a strong string, whereunto was fastened a knot of cane, which ran close about the neck of the conie, because they should not gnaw the string. They took many in the fields of Maiz, especiallie when it freezed or snowed. The Christians staied there one whole moneth so inclosed with snow, that they went not out of towne . . ."

Snowbound in Camden for a month? Or Calion? Garcilaso puts it at six months:

"There was much snow that year in this province, and for a month and a half they were unable to venture into the country-side because of the extensive amount that had fallen. Never-theless, with the great luxury of firewood and provisions, they passed the best of all winters they experienced in Florida, and they themselves confessed that they could not have been more comfortable in the dwellings of their families in Spain . . ."

DeSoto left Autiamque-Camden in March of 1542, moving down the Ouachita, and after 10 days' journey, which would put him somewhere in Louisiana, "there fell out such weather, that foure daies he could not travell for snow . . ." Snow-bound in Louisiana in March?

An exceptionally severe winter. Either the geography is all wrong or the weather, over 450 years, has changed. Knowing nothing about changing weather patterns, but, being a jour-nalist and thus having no scruples about commenting on the matter, I think they may well have changed. It was, after all, not quite 200 years ago when Dunbar and his men were be-sieged with snow and ice near Hot Springs, with temperatures in the single digits.

Two months after leaving Camden, somewhere on the Great River in the Ferriday-Natchez area, Hernando DeSoto died on May 21, 1542, of malaria or fatigue or despair. The soldiers hid the body so the Indians couldn't see that this Childe of the Sunne (as he had introduced himself) was mortal, and then they placed it in a hollow live-oak log, or in a shroud weighted with sand (the accounts differ), and by night rowed it out into the Mississippi, at a place where it was 19 fathoms or 114 feet deep. ". . . They lowered him in the center of the river, and commending his soul to God, watched him sink at once to its depths."

I asked about local historians and was directed to a lawyer, Col. John Norman Warnock, U.S. Army, Retired, who is al-most 80 years old. He lives south of Camden in the community of Elliott and kindly agreed to see me. His house had recently burned, he told me over the telephone, and he was now living and working in a trailer.

I took this to mean a mobile home, but it was in fact a trailer, a blue and white 28-footer that you could hook up to your stretched black Cadillac limousine, if you had one, and be off with in short order, with a good laugh for everybody left behind. The Colonel has two of these extra long Cadillacs, a 1974 and a 1979 model. The battery and the alternator—"that big, $180 alternator"—had been stolen from the '74, and one tire was flat, but the '79 was running fine.

"I buy them from a man in Dallas," he said. "I like the protection and comfort of a big car."

The trailer was parked in the shade of big pinoak trees. Two shaggy little Pomeranian dogs yapped at me. There were eight Rhode Island Red hens in the yard. They were older chickens, laying hens who no longer laid eggs, but who were still proving useful in their retirement years. "Look. See how they peck at everything that moves? They keep this yard completely free of ticks."

The Colonel, who retired from the army in 1965, is a small, dapper man with soft white hair. He reminded me of Lew Ayres, the actor. He wore a tan cord suit, tan shirt, and tan bow tie. His manner was quiet, polite, very Southern. The trailer was packed to the roof with boxes, files, books, clothes, leaving only a tiny space at one end for his office. His secretary, a young lady, was typing away at something. She sat at a little shelf-like table similar to the ones used by flight engineers on the smaller Boeings. The Colonel graciously gave me the only other seat, a stool, and he stood as we talked about the Ouachita. I believe there would have been more room in one of the Cadillacs, as there was no more than 18 inches of space between us.

His family, he said, both the Warnocks and the Moons, had been in Ouachita County since the 1830s, and an enormous amount of valuable documents and memorabilia had been lost in the house fire. Did he plan to rebuild? He said he didn't know, hinting at certain dark obstacles, "You lend people money, and they won't pay you back."

He, too, like Dee Brown, rode the steamboat *Ouachita* in the 1920s, and he remembers how it would stop to pick up driftwood for the boiler furnace. It got stuck on a sandbar once, and by the time it reached Camden all the bananas had turned brown. "They sold them for 25 cents—a stalk! The boys around here got sick stuffing themselves with soft bananas."

As he recalls, this last gasp of steamboat service came in right after the locks and dams were built in 1926. "That was old Captain Cooley who started it, and I believe it all died with him too, around 1934 or '35. It was quite a thing, the band playing, the dancing at night on the river. All this was cotton country then. Gins everywhere. A lot of cotton was shipped out of here. Now it's all in pine trees."

Colonel Warnock himself brought a boat up to Camden from New Orleans at the end of World War II. He bought it in Germany, a 40-foot cruiser with a steel hull, and had it shipped to New Orleans on the deck of a merchant vessel. "It drew three feet of water, about the same as the steamboats. I came up in June and had no trouble at all." The "liquor" discharge from the local paper mill damaged the hull, he claims, and some years back he sent it to Louisiana for repairs. It remains there, beached, in some sort of legal limbo "at a Lebanese-Italian boat-yard in Morgan City."

I asked him why Camden did not make more of its history. There is, for example, no DeSoto Street.

"No, they don't make much of anything around here. You try to put on some Civil War thing and nobody's interested. Why, there were more Civil War battles fought around here than around Natchez. Small ones, yes, but still."

The oil country begins a few miles south at Louann. There are stripper wells along the highway. The horsehead pumping units bow and rise ever so slowly as they pull up four or five barrels of crude a day. "The strippers have become drippers," I was told in Smackover. Here in a downtown park, a metal plaque states that ". . . the French settlers called this area 'Sumac Couvert.' This was anglicized to 'Smackover' by later English settlers . . ." Covered with sumac? Sumac bower? Sumac shelter?

Perhaps, but I suspect Dunbar is more likely correct. He made this entry for November 20, 1804: "At 7½ A.M. passed a creek which forms a deep ravine in the high lands and has been called 'Chemin Couvert.'" This was Smackover Creek, where it enters the Ouachita from a deep cut. Dunbar was dealing with hunters, guides, settlers, soldiers, and such maps as there were, and he very probably got the name right, "Chemin Couvert," covered way, which was soon corrupted into Smackover. Upstream from the creek he tells of seeing an alligator "which surprised us much at this late season and so far north."

I paid $1.23 a gallon for regular gasoline at El Dorado, the oil city, more than at any other place along the way. On the other hand, my motel room cost only $21, and, a bonus, a man was practicing law in the next room. Two strange law offices in one day. This one, an ordinary motel room, had the lawyer's shingle fastened to the door, just above the number, with a single screw in the middle. There were bits of Scotch tape on the ends to keep it from tilting, perhaps demoralizing his customers. I was all set if I woke up in the night with a start and the urgent feeling that I should dictate a codicil to my will. Against that piece of luck, however, I had to weigh this: The cafe I like in El Dorado was no longer serving an evening meal. The new, shorter serving hours were explained to me this way: "That woman that runs it, that was her sister that run it at night, and she got married and moved to Shreesport."

El Dorado, of course, is not on the river, but is close enough, and the town had steamboat service in the 19th century by way of the Champagnolle Landing. At Calion I looked over the first of the four new dams on the river, this one named for the late H. K. Thatcher, who worked for many years as a lobbyist and gadfly for the project. It is a mighty work of concrete and steel. On the far side, the Calhoun County side, high water was streaming unchecked over the low part of the dam. No one was about. No boats were in view. The lock water appeared stagnant, as though it had been standing undisturbed for some time. A dead and bloated buffalo fish with a cloudy eye lay washing about in the debris. The river looked almost as wide as the Arkansas at Little Rock.

Because of the high water, the ferry at Moro Bay wasn't running. I was to be denied another ferry ride south of Columbia, La., for the same reason. The Arkansas Highway Department has only two other ferries left in operation, at Spring Bank on the Red, and at Bull Shoals Lake. Here in the backwater at Moro Bay, I saw a moccasin about two feet long. He was swimming toward me and then stopped when he saw me, undulating in place, but not showing much fear.

The Saline River now comes in from the east to meet the Ouachita and form a kind of overflow swamp known locally as the Marie Saline. It is not named for a lady, as we used to think. Dunbar explains: "Between 11 and 12 o'clock passed on the right the 'marais de la Saline' (Salt-lick marsh). There is here a small marshy lake, but it is not intended by its name to convey any idea of a property of brackishness in the lake or marsh, but merely that it is contiguous to some of the licks." It was the same for the Saline River, then going by the name of "the grand bayou de la Saline (Salt-lick Creek) . . ." Hunters, Dunbar says, took their boats some 300 river miles up the Saline, and "all agree that none of the springs which feed this Creek are salt; it has obtained its name from many buffalo salt licks which have been discovered near to the Creek."

Here, where the river crosses into Louisiana, is the lowest point in Arkansas, with the state Geology Commission giving it as 55 feet above sea level and the Corps of Engineers at 43.8 feet. This water has fallen 1,550 feet since it left Polk County, and it still has a long way to go before reaching the Gulf of Mexico, and only another 50 feet to fall. All this low country is now the Felsenthal National Wildlife Refuge, a swampy wilderness much like that of the White River Refuge, but with not quite so much hardwood timber.

West of Crossett near the Highway 82 bridge there is a new slack-water harbor, ready for business, with a wharf on concrete pilings and a new and empty warehouse. Again, no one was about. There were no boats. I drove the back roads above the Felsenthal Dam. Always at some point I would run into a body of water and have to turn around. These are deep woods. I saw a house on stilts near the river, not a hunting lodge but a home, with clothes on a line and broken toys in the yard. There was no power line, and no telephone line, television antenna, satellite dish, or mail box. Getting your news by barge might not be so bad.

I detected no immediate cultural change as I entered Louisiana, perhaps a bit more clear-cutting of timber, but not much more than I saw in the Huttig area. At Sterlington I did find an industry that uses the river for shipping, the Angus Chemical

Co., which has little docks and terminal pipes projecting out from the river bank. But much of this plant was destroyed by an explosion and fire in May, in which nine workers were killed and more than a hundred injured.

All along the lower river I stopped in towns and asked about the tonnage shipped on the river. The current tonnage, I thought, when compared to the tonnage of bygone years and the projected tonnage of the future, would give us all something to mull over. At city halls and chambers of commerce I would be shown into the office of a very courteous if puzzled man. He would tap a pencil on the desk. "Yes. Let's see now. The tonnage. Brenda, why don't you get Charles some coffee." Brenda would later be sent here and there in search of an elusive folder that just might contain some river matter. Long after it became clear that no one knew or cared about the tonnage, I asked about the tonnage. I didn't care either, but I felt a nagging dreary duty to come up with some figures.

Monroe is the biggest city on the Ouachita, with a population, including West Monroe, of 65,000. The river splits the two towns. There is a high bridge on Interstate 20, and three older bridges that can be raised or pivoted on turntables to allow river traffic to pass. But days go by at a time with no call to raise or swing the bridges, I was told by Bruce Fleming, planning director for Monroe, and there is no "Port of Monroe," as such, though the city does own an excursion boat, the *Twin City Queen*, which it rents out to clubs.

It was getting through to me that people living on the Ouachita no longer see their river as a highway, in any important commercial sense. It is just there, every day, a pretty stream of water, handy for recreation, useful in dry years for irrigation, inconveniently overflowing every spring.

Somewhere along here in the pecan groves on Bayou De-Siard I stopped talking about tonnage and started asking people how they pronounced "bayou." It came out "by-yoo" and "by-oo," about half and half, with an occasional "bya." We said "byo" in southeast Arkansas, or "bya." In defending this usage, I pointed out to a woman in Monroe that Hank Williams says "byo" in his song "Jambalaya." Yes, she said, but Hank was forcing a cheap rhyme with "me-o-my-o." I countered by informing her that Arkansas Post (1686, Tonti) is older than New Orleans (1718, Bienville). She didn't believe me. Nor did she believe me when I informed her that "bayou" is not a French word.

It is a Choctaw word, "bayuk," which the French explorers adopted for use in the Mississippi valley, calling any sizeable stream entering one of the bigger rivers a "bayou." But then it seems they left it behind when they returned home. The word is not listed in Cassell's or Heath's French dictionaries, so I suppose it is actually Choctaw-French-American. The Corps of Engineers could not give me an official definition of a bayou, or of a creek or a river. I would have expected these officers —soldiers, engineers, bureaucrats, all tidy men—to have had some strict system of classification and nomenclature, but not so. In this matter they defer to local tradition. If the people of north Arkansas want to call their fast-flowing, whitewater, mountain stream a bayou, the Illinois Bayou, say, then a bayou it is, and there is no objection from the Corps.

South of Monroe the river was out of its banks, lapping at the highway in places and pushing into the cotton and soybean fields. As it draws closer to the Mississippi, it joins a tangle of rivers and bayous that are flowing more or less parallel here on the alluvial plain, and sprawling in wide meanders. Roads and ferries were closed and I had to make detours. Highway builders in Louisiana work on the Jeffersonian assumption that west (and east) is the proper direction of travel. There are fine east-west interstate highways, but traveling north and south is slow going. But then road building is an expensive business here, with so much fill dirt being required for the elevated and literal high ways.

I stopped at Columbia to pay a call on former Governor John McKeithen of Louisiana. He lives on a farm here and keeps an office downtown. Something of the squire in these parts, he is perhaps the most notable figure living on the bank of the Ouachita. But he was out of town.

More failures: I couldn't track down a commercial fisherman, and there are a few left, from Calion on down, netting catfish, buffalo and drum, in descending order of value. I turned up no song about the Ouachita, and it is certainly as deserving as the Wabash or the Swanee or the Red. I did find two poems celebrating it, both written in the 19th century, by Albert Pike and a George P. Smoote. I showed them to a woman who is a judge of such things, and she read them unmoved.

"Welcome to Jonesville/Where the Four Rivers Meet." It is the end of the line, Jonesville, population 2,620, some 30 miles by road and bridge from Natchez. Jonesville makes the further claim of being DeSoto's ancient Indian town of Anilco, at the mouth of the Anilco or Ouachita River. No one knows if these Indians were the same as the "Ouasitas," a small Caddoan tribe first mentioned by Tonti in 1690. They moved west in the 18th century and were absorbed by the Natchitoch Indians.

I stood behind the grain elevators of the Bunge Corporation and watched the Ouachita, still greenish, for all the flooding as it poured into the Tensas (pronounced Tensaw), and where they both suddenly became the Black River. The fourth river, called the Little River, enters the flow a bit farther down. A half-mile upstream from the mouth of the Ouachita the Bunge Corp. has a dock and a big blower pipe, where barges are loaded with soybeans and other grain. Here at last was a volume shipper.

"Oh, yes, we use the Ouachita all the time," the manager told me. "That last half-mile of it, anyway."

*1991*

# Motel Life, Lower Reaches

## MOTEL #1

BACK WHEN Roger Miller was King of the Road, in the 1960s, he sang of rooms to let ("no phone, no pool, no pets") for four bits, or fifty cents. I can't beat that price, but I did once in those days come across a cabin that went for three dollars. It was in the long, slender highway town of Truth or Consequences, New Mexico.

That cute and unwieldy name, by the way, was taken in 1950 from the name of a quiz/comedy radio show, and has stuck, against long odds. The show was okay, as I recall, a cut or two above the general run of broadcast ephemera, with some funny 1949 moments. But why re-name your town for it? And by now, a half-century later, you would think the townsfolk must surely have repented their whim and gone back to the old name, solid and descriptive, of Hot Springs. But no, and worse, the current New Mexico highway maps no longer offer both names, with the old one in parentheses, as an option, for the comfort of those travelers who wince and hesitate over saying, "Truth or Consequences." Everyone must now say the whole awkward business.

I was driving across the state at the time, very fast. There were signs along the approaches to town advertising cheaper and cheaper motel rooms. The tone was shrill, desperate, that of an off-season price war. It was a buyer's market. I began to note the rates and the little extras I could expect for my money. Always in a hurry then, once committed to a road, I stopped only for fuel, snake exhibits, and automobile museums, but I had to pause here, track down the cheapest of these cheap motels, and see it. I would confront the owner and call his bluff.

There were boasts of being AIR COOLED (not quite the same as being air-conditioned) and of PHONE IN EVERY ROOM, KITCHENETTES, LOW WEEKLY RATES, CHILDREN FREE, PETS OK, VIBRO BEDS, PLENTY OF HOT WATER, MINIATURE GOLF, KIDDIE POOL, FREE COFFEE, FREE TV, FREE SOUVNIERS. (Along Arkansas roads there are five or six ways of spelling *souvenirs*, and every single one of them is wrong. The sign painters in New Mexico do a little better with that tricky word, but not much better.) The signs said SALESMEN WELCOME and SNOWBIRDS WELCOME and TRUCKS WELCOME/BOBTAILS ONLY—meaning just the tractors themselves; their long semi-trailers would not be welcome. And there were the usual claims, often exaggerated, of having CLEAN ROOMS or NEW ROOMS or CLEAN NEW ROOMS or ALL NEW CLEAN MODERN ROOMS.

I decided not to consider the frills. How could you reckon in cash the delight value of a miniature golf course with its little plaster windmills, tiny waterfalls, and bearded elves perched impudently on plaster toadstools? I would go for price alone, the very lowest advertised price, which turned out to be three dollars. It was a come-on, I knew, a low-ball offer. Sorry, I would be told, but the last of those special rooms had just been taken; the only ones left would be the much nicer $6.50 suites. I would let the owner know what I thought of his sharp prac-tice, but not really expecting him to writhe in shame.

The three-dollar place was an old "tourist court," a horse-shoe arrangement of ramshackle cabins, all joined together by narrow carports. The ports were designed to harbor, snugly, small Ford sedans of 1930s Clyde Barrow vintage, each one with a canvas water bag ("SATURATE BEFORE USING") hanging from the front bumper, for the crossing of the Great American Desert.

But there were no cars here at all, and no one in the office. I gave the desk bell my customary one ding, not a loutish three or four. An old lady, clearly the owner, perhaps a widow, came up through parted curtains from her cluttered female nest in the rear. She was happy to see me. I asked about a three-dollar room, for one person, one night. She said yes, certainly, all her cabins went for three dollars, and there were *vacancies*. This, without bothering to crane her neck about and peer over my shoulder, by way of giving my car out there the once-over. Desk clerks do that when I ask for a single, to see if I am trying to conceal a family. These clerks are trained in their motel acad-emies to watch for furtive movement in the back seats of cars, for the hairy domes of human heads, those of wives, tykes, and grannies left crouching low in idling Plymouths.

This old lady had come up in a gentler school. She was honest and her signs were honest and her lodgers were presumed to be more or less honest. She had caught me up short and rattled me. Who was bluffing now? I couldn't just leave, nor, worse, give her three dollars and *then* leave, compounding the insult to her and her yellowish cabins. I paid up and stayed the night, her only guest.

My cabin had a swamp cooler, an evaporative cooling machine that is usually quite effective in that arid country. A true air conditioner (brutal compressor) uses much more electricity than a swamp cooler (small water pump, small fan). But then the cooler does consume water, and the economy of nature is such—no free lunch—that the thing works well only in a region where the humidity is low—under forty per cent, say. Where water is scarce, that is, and thus expensive.

It was dry enough here, but my cooler was defective and did nothing more than stir the hot air a bit.

I looked the room over for redeeming touches. It wasn't so bad, beaten down with use and everything gone brown with age, but honorably so, not disgusting, shabby but clean, a dry decay.

The bedding may have been original stock. That central crater in the mattress hadn't been wallowed out overnight, but rather by a long series of jumbo salesmen, snorting and thrashing about in troubled sleep. A feeble guest would have trouble getting out of the mattress. He would cry out, feebly, for a helping hand, and nobody in earshot. The small lamp on the bedside table was good, much better for reading than the lighting systems in expensive motels, with their diffused gloom. Motel decorators, who obviously don't read in bed, are all too fond of giant lampshades, a prevailing murk, and lamp switches that are hard to find and reach. The bath towels were clean but threadbare, and much too short to use as wraparound sarongs while shaving. The few visible insects were dead or torpid. There were no bathroom accretions of soft green or black matter. The lavatory mirror was freckled and had taken on a soft sepia tint. Mineral deposits clogged the shower head, making for a lopsided spraying pattern, but the H and C knobs had not been playfully reversed, nor did they turn the wrong way. There were sash windows you could actually raise, after giving them a few sharp blows with the heels of your hands, to break loose the ancient paint. Here again the feeble guest, seeking a breath of air, would struggle and whimper.

I had paid more and seen worse—murkier and more oppressive rooms, certainly, with that dense black motel murk hanging about in all the corners, impossible to dispel and conducive to so many suicides along our highways, I had seen worse rooms, if not thinner and shorter towels. There was plenty of hot water. I had the privacy of a cabin, and indeed not a single neighbor. What I had was a cottage, and a steal at three dollars.

Early the next morning the lady came tapping at my door. She had a pot of coffee for me on a tray with some buttered toast and a little china jug of honey. It was that unprecedented gesture, I think, and the grace note of the honey—no sealed packet of "Mixed Fruit" generic jelly—that made the place stick in my head so, and not the price at all. I like to think the old cabins lasted out the good old lady's widowhood. It must have been a close-run finish. And it comes to me now, late, a faint voice, saying the price was really two dollars.


MOTEL #2

A FEW years later. This one was in the Texas border town of Laredo, across the Rio Grande from Nuevo Laredo, in Mexico. You expect it to be the other way around, with the older, primary Laredo on the Mexico side, and so it was in origin (1755) when the north bank of the river *was* Mexico—or, actually, New Spain then. You might also expect the Rio Grande here to be a mighty stream, so far down on its 1,900-mile run to the Gulf, but it's more like a weed-strangled municipal drainage ditch than a Great River.

I was driving up out of deeper Mexico. On the U.S. side of the bridge I was greeted, if that's the word, by a suspicious INS agent in a glass sentry booth. He asked me a few questions and directed me at once to the customs inspection shed. No doubt I made a good fit for one of his Detain profiles. *Lone white dishevelled Arkansas male in four-wheel-drive pickup with winch. Subject admits to extensive travel in rural interior of Mexico. Tells lame story re purpose of trip.*

The big shed was open along the sides but still very hot. I had to unload all my baggage from the truck, everything moveable, and spread it out on an extended table. A customs agent went first to the opened suitcase, so inviting, the bared intimacy of it. He made a long business of inspecting my paltry wardrobe, lifting articles of clothing one by one with the deliberation of a shopper. Then he moved leisurely along to the loose gear— fuel cans, water jugs, cans of oil, cans of quack chemical engine remedies, tools, books. These things, too, he picked up one by one, and as he turned them over in his hands he appeared to be muttering words of inventory, thus—*lantern, bottle jack, scissors jack, some sort of dried gourd here.* . . . He lifted the books and read the titles to catch their heft and flavor, but made no critical comment.

Another agent was going over the truck itself with a flash-light, a small hammer, and a dental inspection mirror, with the little angled head. He rolled himself underneath, belly up, on a mechanic's creeper, and peered into crevices and felt about in them. He made delicate, cache-detecting taps on body panels with the toy hammer. The searches are necessary, granted. I knew I had no contraband but the agents didn't know. Still, the innocent—blameless in this matter, at least—grow impatient. At last, after a whispered conference, the two men gave up and said I could go. I had looked so promising, then let them down. Not that I was cleared, exactly, just sullenly dismissed for lack of evidence, and left to load everything up again.

I drove into Laredo for a bit and stopped at what, in my road stupor, I took to be a chain motel in the middling price range. I was wrong. The national chain had depreciated this one out and dumped it on the local market. An older couple I will call Mom and Dad had picked it up.

In the office lobby there were two women seated at a low table, drinking iced tea and having a chat. One was Mom. I asked about a room. The women looked me over. I was a mess, dead on my feet. For a night and the best part of a day I had been driving hard, without sleeping, bathing, or shaving. My khakis, heavy with sweat, were clinging to my flesh here and there.

Mom said, "We don't take no show people here."

"Show people?"

The other woman explained the situation. "It's a carnival come to town down there. We were just now talking about it."

So, this was just more of the Welcome Home party. First the fun in the customs shed and now I was accused of being in show business. I told Mom that I was no such romantic figure as a carnival worker, but only a road-weary traveler. Did she have a room or not?

She relented, though still perhaps suspecting me of running a Ferris wheel or a rat stall. This being the one where you put your money down, gaping rube that you are, and watch a white rat race about on an enclosed table top. The rat eventually darts into one of several numbered holes, but not your numbered hole. Or maybe she really didn't care and was only showing off a little before her friend, who could now spread the word about Mom's high social standards as an innkeeper.

She had given way pretty fast. It might well be that Mom enjoyed nothing more in life than filling her rooms with jolly roustabouts ("My boys") and the more tattoos the better.

The room was okay, which is to say it was pretty far along on the way down but not yet squalid, just acceptable. A sharp distinction for those of us in the know. We can tell at a glance, from the doorway. The swimming pool was nearby, too. Just the thing in this heat. I took a shower and put on some trunks.

It was a big pool from a more expansive motel era, with a deep end that was deep, but with a derelict look overall. No one was about. The chain-link fencing sagged, and there were rips and gashes in the wire. The non-sparkling water was of a cloudy green hue and perfectly still. Floating leaves and styrofoam cups bobbed not at all. A Sargasso calm. Perhaps the pump was broken. No diving board, of course, the diving board lawyers having seen to that, even then. Only the stanchions remained, the chrome-steel pipes rooted in concrete.

I made a ground-level entry dive and swam one lap. The water had a prickly, tingling feel. It stung my eyes. The pool chemicals gone bad, I thought.

Now here came Dad at a limping trot, shouting at me, "Hey, get out of there! Can't you read?" I was already climbing out when he started this, and he was still telling me to get out of the pool when I was standing there safe ashore, upright and dripping, before his eyes. Once a tape got rolling in Dad's head, it wasn't going to be cut short by any external event.

He looked around, baffled, then saw that his DANGER/KEEP OUT/NO SWIMMING sign had fallen from the wire fence. He picked it up and showed it to me. Electricity, it seems, was leaking into the pool water from corroded wires and terminals near the underwater lamps. I asked Dad why he didn't drain the dangerous electrified pool. Because, he said, it was only the great lateral pressure of all that water that kept the thing from collapsing in on itself, and he didn't want to lose his pool. He pointed out cracks and bulges in the retaining walls.

I said I had suspected toxic chemicals and wouldn't have thought of electricity coursing through a swimming pool. As for that, Dad said, his chemicals had gone sour, too, under the beating sun, and what with the stagnation . . . but they didn't account for the prickle, only for the sting and the unnatural greenness and the sharp metallic taste of the water.

Wasn't there a lawsuit here? I could hire one of the diving-board lawyers, preferably one in cowboy boots. Into the mixed bag of damages we could throw the pain I had suffered from Mom's suggestion, before a witness, that I was in show business. We would pick Mom and Dad clean, seize everything, and kick them out of the motel, destitute, into the streets of Laredo. Then it occurred to me that Mom's lawyer might have some boots of his own, made of animal skins even more exotic, costly, and menacing than those sported by my man. What if he put me in a line-up parade before the jury, full face and profile views, with some carnival guys trucked in from the midway? How would I fare? I saw, too, that on the witness stand, under oath, I would have to admit that I had actually felt better, perked up a little, after my dip in Dad's electro-chemical vat. Best maybe just to let this slide.

That evening after a nap, I tried to make a long-distance call from my room. I was expecting a check in the mail. Like a carnival guy, I had no fixed abode then (had Mom sensed this?) and was using the home of my father and mother in Little Rock as a mail drop. The bedside telephone had the full array of buttons. Some, however, were dummies. Pressing 8, the long-distance one, got me nowhere. I couldn't even get the desk.

I walked up to the office, where Mom informed me with relish that she and Dad were no longer set up for long-distance service. It was nothing but trouble. People were always using it. Local calls only. But couldn't I make the call here, now, on that office phone, under her gaze and supervision? A brief one? My credit-card billing for the room was still open, and she could add to it whatever she liked in the way of fees, for the call and her inconvenience. I wouldn't be calling Shanghai, only Little Rock.

"We're not set up for that. There's a pay phone out there."

I had no American money in my pockets. Mom, living here in a border town where the banks readily exchanged pesos and dollars, didn't see how she could possibly give me a handful of quarters and dimes for my Mexican currency. She shrank from handling the alien notes. The republic of Mexico was a half-hour stroll from here and for Mom it was *terra incognita* and would on principle remain so.

Back to my room where I rooted about in luggage and found a few coins, enough to spring open a circuit at the pay phone and gain the ear of an operator. She dialed the number in Little Rock. Home is the place where, when you have to call it collect, they have to accept the charges. My mother answered. The operator told her that this was a collect call from her first-born son Charles, in Laredo, Texas. Would she accept the charges? My mother, not always attentive, said, "I'm sorry, he's not here, he's down in Mexico somewhere," and hung up, before I could gather my wits and shout to her.

The close of a long day. I meant to ask Dad about the curious slashes in his pool fence. Berserk vandals with chain saws? Environmental zealots with axes? In Laredo? But I kept forgetting, and at dawn, still ignorant on that point, and not much worse for the wear, I was off and away again in my white Chevrolet truck. And I saw on further reflection that Mom had been right to place me in a pariah caste. It was just one she didn't know about, that of the untouchable wretches called freelance writers.

## MOTEL #3

NOW TO the more recent past and a place in southern New Mexico, bright land of bargain motels and fair dealing, where I was doing some research on Pancho Villa's 1916 raid across the border. My room was in a motel I will call the Ominato Inn, not quite a dump, with a *weekly rate* of $130 flat, no surcharges. The price quoted was what you paid, with no tourist penalties, bed taxes, bathroom duties, or other shakedown fees piled on, such as to make a joke of the nominal price. There should have been a pair of signs out front, flashing back and forth:

NOT QUITE A DUMP      AT DUMP PRICES

Or no, they weren't needed. By late afternoon, almost every day, the parking lot was filled with a motley fleet of cars, vans, trucks, and motorcycles, giving the appearance of a police impound yard. Far too many of these vehicles had weak batteries.

It was in the Ominato that I came to know celebrity, two onerous weeks of it, as "that guy in number twelve with the great jumper cables." The first to seek my help was an old man I will call Mr. Sherman Lee Purifoy. He was a retired policeman, a widower, from southern Illinois, of that region near the confluence of the Ohio and the Mississippi. Year after year he came here to stay the winter months, in the Ominato, and in the same, much-prized room, number three, the only one with a kitchenette. The Purifoy Room, but without a plaque.

I had just checked in when he accosted me in the sandy courtyard, which was the desert floor itself, unpaved. His battery was dead. Could I give him a jump? His car looked like other cars, but it was one I had never heard of, a Mercury Topaz. When I mentioned this, intending no slight, that the Topaz was a new one on me, he took offense. He took me to be suggesting that he was the kind of man who would drive a freakish, not to say ludicrous car. As though I had accused him, say, of wearing sandals. The Topaz happened to be a very good ottamobile, he said, and for my information there were plenty of Topazes out there on the highways, giving good service every day. And any car at all could have a bad battery.

Except mine. With my hot battery and my two-gauge, all-copper cables I soon had his Topaz humming away again.

Santiago—let us call him that—had come by to watch. He was the assistant motel manager, electrician, and handyman. He admired the heaviness of my cables, their professional girth. And those fierce, spring-loaded clamps! Such teeth! People who needed cables usually didn't have them, he said, or they had the cheap, skinny kind that couldn't carry enough amps to do the job. Mine were the best he had ever seen, and he had seen a few. Already I was basking.

From there the word went around, down the road, even, into a motor home park, to which I felt no ties of loyalty. I was on call night and day with my cables. I feared the knock on the door. I found myself lingering, to the point of loitering, in places away from the Ominato and the room I had paid for. Celebrity turned out to be disappointing, but it was hard to say no when you had been given the power to raise the dead.

And Mr. Purifoy was okay, if a little too much underfoot, a great accoster, and something of a tar baby, with time on his hands. He caught me going out and coming in, and, on occasion, he would catch me in an ambush at some unlikely place miles away—once, in the lobby of a county courthouse.

One afternoon he stopped me cold in my tracks and said, "Just look around. Half the people in this motel are criminals."

"That's a lot of criminals, Mr. Purifoy."

"At least half. I'm not even counting some of the dopers in that."

I looked around. Mr. Purifoy, I thought, must have lumped in with his bad boys, willy-nilly, all the scruffier transients who stopped here, and so had arrived at his high estimate of the criminal density. Drifters as such were guilty, of drifting. My guess was that on a given night at the Ominato no more than ten per cent of the lodgers were genuine felons on the lam, some with their molls. Of the rest, only about two per cent would be British journalists named Clive, Colin, or Fiona, scribbling notes and getting things wrong for their journey books about the real America, that old and elusive theme.

Another time he asked me what my business was here in New Mexico. Against my better judgement I told him. He didn't think much of the Pancho Villa project, taking it to be one of glamorizing a thug and serial rapist. He said I could expect no help from him in working this thing up, whatever it was, nor, when it was done, would there be any use asking him to look it over, as he had better things to do.

Another time he told me that he never bothered to turn off his television at night, his sleep being fitful. He would doze for an hour or so, wake, and watch "the TV" for an hour or so. It didn't matter what—golf highlights of 1971, the giant termite mounds on the African *veld*. There was no roaming about through the channels. But what a lot of people didn't know was this: *You can do other things while watching the TV.* Little mindless chores. Sometimes he polished his shoes. And so he drowsed and woke through the long night, drifting in and out of alternating dreams.

Then daybreak at last, always a joy, when he could pop out of his box and go into the world again. A third hallucination, perhaps, though with its sunny radiance much brighter than the others. Better still, in this one was a blue Mercury Topaz.

He rose early and drove to a McDonald's restaurant for a breakfast of biscuits and gravy, many free refills of coffee, and for a long visit with his retirement cronies. It was a gathering place. Some weeks back he had taken the trouble to write down a good recipe for "thickening gravy"—milk gravy. He gave it to one of the girls at McDonald's but suspected that she and her bosses had never even so much as tried it. They were still dishing out the same old stuff.

There were other cronies who preferred Wendy's restaurant, but Mr. Purifoy said he wouldn't be going back to that place any time soon. Some woman was always there in the mornings, reading things out loud from a newspaper to her husband, who was neither blind nor illiterate. Humorous snippets mostly, but longer pieces, too. How could you think straight or talk to your friends with this woman droning on like that? Well, you couldn't, and she never let up. She kept finding nuggets, as she thought, here and there in the low-grade ore of the newspapers.

As a gentleman, in his way, Mr. Purifoy could hardly scold the woman herself, directly, but neither was he one to shirk a clear social duty. He said he took the husband aside and spoke firmly to him about this nuisance. With no effect. The poor man was henpecked, his spirit broken years ago. He had shamefully admitted he could do nothing to stop his wife from reading things out loud to him, in private or public. Mr. Purifoy said one day that quiet bird would club her to death. One AP snippet too many.

The least of our criminals was probably Lash LaRue. With his black boots, jeans, shirt, and hat, he reminded me of the old black-clad movie cowboy of that name, who popped revolvers out of the hands of saloon louts with his bullwhip. But this younger Lash had no whip, and the sinister outfit was only a costume.

Santiago brought him to my door one morning. Lash said he had left the headlights of his truck burning all night, and his "battery"—singular—was down. It was a big Ford pickup a year or two old, with a diesel V-8 engine and a Louisiana license plate. Lash spoke of it as "my truck," and he did possess the truck but I don't believe he owned the truck. First, he couldn't find the hood-latch release, then he had trouble working it. With the hood up at last, he was struck dumb by what must have been his first sight of the monster engine. He was a calf looking at a new gate. I, too, was impressed. It was a beautifully organized work of industrial art, filling and overflowing the engine bay.

His plump young female companion (Brandi? Autumn?) lurked and pouted in the doorway of their room. They were running away to California, that must be it. They had stolen her Daddy's newish truck, his treasure, and left him back in Opelousas, to putt around in Lash's little Dodge Omni.

I pointed out the two big batteries up front, wired in series, one on either side of the radiator. More amazement from Lash. "*Two* batteries!"

Diesels with their high compression are by nature hard to crank, thus the booster. I wanted to walk away. These peculiar engines make me uneasy. Hard to start when cold, and then, once going, they sound like machines trying to rip themselves apart in a furious suicidal clatter. So much for my ignorance. They manage to clatter away like that for years on end.

No matter, I still don't like them, and already I had lost face with Mr. Purifoy in failing to jump-start a diesel motor home owned by one of his cronies, in the nearby park. My excuse, plausible enough, was that the man's battery cells were so absolutely stone dead as to be no longer conductive.

I told Lash it wasn't going to work, that I couldn't pump enough amps through all the batteries and circuitry to turn over that diesel crankshaft. He said maybe then we could push-start the truck, and he must have known better, the transmission was automatic. But he was going into a panic. Brandi said maybe we could tie a rope from my bumper to theirs and pull-start the truck. She had not moved from the shadowy doorway. Preserving her lily pallor? Those white cheeks would pink up pretty fast in the desert sun.

Lash ignored her and was now begging. Please, couldn't we at least try a jump-start? With those deluxe cables he had heard so much about?

A shrewd appeal to my pride. Well, why not humor him? It wouldn't take long to go through the motions. I broke out the cables yet again and hooked them up. I started my engine, leaving it to run for a bit and do some charging. Then I climbed up into the truck cab and turned the starter key one notch over to light the glow-plug. This is a little Zoroastrian fire prayer ritual, which must be observed. After what I judged to be the proper interval, I turned the key all the way over to engage the starter motor, expecting to hear nothing, or at most a click. But the starter *did* spin, and then we had compression-ignition. The infernal oil-burning machine had come alive and was clanging away on its own.

Lash was so crazed with relief that he offered to pay me. He and Brandi lost no time in fleeing the Ominato. She waved bye-bye from the cab and told me not to worry, that they would take care to park the truck on the slope tonight when they stopped. She still thought you could roll-start the thing. I noticed some stenciled words in white on the tailgate: LI-CENSED AND BONDED. Licensed as what? Who would license Lash and what body of underwriters would stand good for his handiwork? California can always use one more Lash and one more Brandi, and I wished the young lovebirds well, but no, that big fine work truck didn't belong to Lash LaRue.

My Saturday afternoon loitering place was a small bar in a small American Legion post. It was like some forgotten

outpost where the soldiers had grown old waiting for the relief column. Here I drank and brooded with others of this
lost platoon, who had their own reasons for not going home.
There was a pool table, always in use, and a juke box, not
much played, though it had a good repertoire of older stuff.
No din, that was what we wanted, but now and then out of the
blue we would hear "You Win Again" from Hank Williams, or
Fats Domino singing,

> *You broke*
> *My hort,*
> *When you said*
> *We'll port*
> *Ain't that a shame.*

One Saturday Mr. Purifoy appeared there, to my surprise.
He was AA, or as he liked to call it, ND. The letters stood
for Nameless Drunks, his jocular cacophemism for Alcoholics
Anonymous. Saying the words always made him laugh.

He said he had seen my car out front and just thought he
would drop in for a minute. He had some news. But I wasn't
to hear it until he had gone through a long and disruptive
business of settling in. It took him some little time to get
seated properly, then clear away his bar space and give his order: "JUST A GLASS OF ICE TEA FOR ME, PLEASE." A general
rebuke but no one was put to shame or flight. He went on to
tell the bartender, who hadn't asked, that his health, on the
whole, overall, for his age, was pretty good, "except for all
these blood sores on my arms." They weren't as bad as their
name. He pushed back his sleeves to show us some subcutane-
ous splotches, like red bruises.

The news was that he had bought a new battery—but we
could look at it later. He could show me the expensive new 72-
month battery later, in the Topaz. Then, by way of throwing
out a conversational tidbit for the bar at large, he said that over
in neighboring Arizona there happened to be certain chapters
of Alcoholics Anonymous which allowed you to drink two cans
of beer every day. What they called a maintenance dose.

Our fellow Legionnaires scoffed. Baloney, they said, and
worse, but wanting to hear a little more. I was sitting between

Mr. Purifoy and a hard, sun-dried little man called Vic, a pygmy sea lawyer, bald, yet still with scarcely any forehead at all. Possibly an old brig rat. Vic, like so many others, had come to the desert to make a clean end to his life, to shrink further here and indeed to waste away by degrees from evaporation until he vanished. He said he was from Montana—we were all carpetbaggers—but he told anecdotes in the dramatic New York City manner. With the injured tone, that is, and exuberant gestures and that fast delivery in the historic present tense ("So then this creep, can you believe it, he turns around and says to me . . .").

Vic wondered if it might not be possible under the Arizona indulgence to count malt liquor, a stronger brew, as a kind of beer. And if the ration were stated simply as "two cans of beer," not further qualified, then why couldn't you just buy the bigger cans, huge ones, even, which would require the use of both hands to lift from the bar?

He and some others challenged Mr. Purifoy and pressed him hard to give the precise locations of the renegade AA groups. Mr. Purifoy couldn't remember offhand. Globe, maybe, was one of the places. You can't remember everything. Some fellow from Arizona was telling him about this, and he would know, wouldn't he? The man was from Arizona and an honorable lodge brother in good standing who drove a good car and made a pretty good living as a professional square-dance caller and who stood to gain nothing at all by telling a gratuitous lie about the two cans of beer. Could any one here dispute that? No? Then maybe some people should just shut up for a change and then maybe talk about something they did know something about for a change. How would that do? He finished his tea and left.

Later, there was a commotion, a diversion, at the pool table. One of the players fell unconscious to the floor—of a diabetic fit, it was said. He was a fairly young man, the very last one of our crew you would expect to keel over. Someone called for an ambulance. Everyone, Vic included, jumped up to offer help, with an alacrity that wouldn't be seen in a public bar. But how to help, exactly? Some said it was the head that must be elevated in these cases, and others the feet. The feet, I thought, but wasn't sure. The poor fellow was tilted first one way and then the other.

He soon came around, despite our efforts, and was shooting pool again when the ambulance arrived, flashing, shrieking, and setting all the neighborhood dogs barking. A welcome diversion for them, too. But the young man refused to be examined or wired up to any diagnostic machine or hauled away to a hospital—and he certainly wasn't going to sign his name to no paper on no clipboard. Forget it, he said, a false alarm.

There were angry words with the two paramedics. The senior one, the driver, was a heavy and hairy young man (Bull?) with nothing much of the nurse about him. He looked like the senior bouncer in a very big highway honky tonk, the bouncer of last resort. He dug in. Someone here, he said, and make no mistake, was going to sign this trip log and take responsibility for this deadhead run. It was a hard job he had, one demanding a healing touch of sorts and the driving skill of a stock-car racer, along with the brass and belligerence of a debt collector. The row was still going on when I left for the day, with the yard dogs still raving and foaming. I don't know how it came out, but I would have bet on the big medico-bouncer.

MOTEL #4

I LEFT the Ominato for good the next morning, rising earlier than Mr. Purifoy himself, our early bird. The Topaz was in place. No one at all was stirring. Criminals become criminals so they can sleep late. All their cars here would be at least a quart low on oil. I virtuously checked mine, then slammed the hood down with no consideration for their rest. And in motel life at the low end, you don't bother to say good-bye. It isn't done, you must keep a certain churlish distance, unless you're young and still human like Brandi and haven't yet learned the ropes. One day you just steal away and your disappearance is little noted if at all.

I drove up to Truth or Consequences on a whim, going out of my way, for a look around. I could find no trace of the old yellow cabins, nor even locate the site. Things disappear, too, utterly. The hot springs downtown were still flowing hot, or warm. The name of the place still grated, but less so now, burnished as it was a little by time and the friction of use. Some of the locals had taken to calling it "T or C." No improvement there, the cute made cuter.

That evening I stopped at a small motel called the Desert View—the real name this time. My room was a bit small but clean, new, modern, all those things, with a gleaming white bathroom. The bed was flat and firm. Over the headboard there were two good reading lamps mounted on pivots. I had air conditioning, cable television, a refrigerator, and a microwave oven. It was a quiet place with few guests, none of sly or ratlike appearance. I could park directly in front of my door. The nightly rate was twenty-five dollars flat, no surcharges. Allowing for inflation, this was little more than I had paid for the old cabin.

The Desert View was, in short, something pretty close to that ideal in my head of the cheap and shipshape roadside dormitory, what I kept looking for all those years. Now, after finding it, I was confused. This place was too good to be true. I sat on the firm edge of the firm bed, very still, wary, taking stock. Something felt wrong. Everything, more or less, but something bizarre in particular that I couldn't put my finger on. Then it came to me—the very *carpet* was clean. *Motel carpet!* What was going on here? I didn't get it. Who were these Desert View people? Where was the catch? I cleared out of there at dawn and still don't know.

*2003*

# MEMOIR

## *Combinations of Jacksons*

I MADE my first experiments in breathing underwater at the age of nine, in 1943. It was something I needed to learn in life so as to be ready to give my pursuing enemies the slip. At that time they were Nazi spies and Japanese saboteurs.

The trick looked simple enough in the movie serials, which pulled me along from one Saturday to the next with such chapter titles as "Fangs of Doom!" and "In the Scorpion's Lair!" First you cut a reed. You put one end of the reed in your mouth and lay face up, very still, on the bottom of a shallow stream. The other end was projected above the surface of the stream, and through this hollow shaft, as you lay buried alive in water, you *breathed*.

Agents of the Axis Powers were never far behind me. I could slow them a little with pinecone grenades, but I couldn't stop them. They came crashing through the woods firing their Lugers at me as I raced barefooted for the reed beds of Beech Creek, a last hope. If I could get there in time to make my arrangements, then the agents in their stupid fury would overlook the life-giving reed, one among so many, and, with their boots splashing down eight inches away from my rigid underwater body, go stupidly on their way downstream.

My attempts to bring this off took place in Cypress Creek and Smackover Creek, too—"smackover" being an Arkansas rendering of "chemin couvert," covered path, or road. These and Beech Creek were the swimming streams nearest to my home town, at the time, of Mount Holly, in Union County, Arkansas, which adjoins Union Parish, Louisiana. The name dates from the territorial days of the 1820s, when "Union" had a pleasing ring to it in the Jacksonian South, where the many sons of Jack came to settle and multiply.

Reeds grew here in abundance, in ponds and swamps and along creek banks, or what I took to be reeds, but they were the wrong kind of reeds, if in fact they were reeds. The green ones weren't hollow. The brown ones, the dead and withered stalks, were somewhat hollow but too thin to carry much air, not even enough to sustain a gasping kind of life in a skinny little boy. They also tended to collapse, like wet paper drinking straws, with the first sharp intake of breath. In or out of the water, you couldn't breathe through our reeds.

Our quicksand was a bust too, or I would have lured those running men to their deaths in the slough near Cypress Creek. Not Cypress Slough or the Slough of Despond or of anything else. That dark marsh wasn't big enough or distinctive enough to have a proper name; it was just "the slew." When I had led the men there and they were stuck fast in the gray mud, I would have looked on from a hump of firm ground, deaf to their pleas, refusing to hold out a pole to them, waiting—will these spies never sink?—until the earth had swallowed them whole. It couldn't have worked out that way though, because our quicksand, or quickmud, while quivering nicely underfoot, had no lethal depth, and may even have been slightly buoyant, and therapeutic to boot. I could never manage to sink more than about knee-deep in it.

Bamboo ("cane," we called it) was more promising than reeds, and we had plenty of that in the canebrakes. These woody shafts were thicker and stronger than reeds, and almost hollow, if not quite. Inside, at each circular joint, there was a partial blockage of some white pithy matter. With a long rattail file and a good deal of poking and blowing, it took me about five minutes to clear the pith. This was more like it. Now I had a sturdy and serious breathing tube, made on the spot from the materials at hand. I was man, the toolmaker.

Still, questions remained. My knife would be there, ready, in my pocket (or one of a series of knives, two-blade Barlows mostly, which I kept losing)—ready for cutting reeds and cane, for carving crude, non-returning boomerangs, for slicing two neat little drainage Xs across snake-bite punctures, for cutting off the sputtering ends of fuses leading to well-marked kegs of BLASTING POWDER planted in the bowels of hydroelectric dams, for cutting loose the ropes from any female reporters I might come across who had been left bound and gagged in remote cabins—ready for any wartime emergency. My Barlow was at the service of the nation. So much for the knife.

But was it likely that I would have a rattail file handy? Or —with a pack of killers at my heels, led by a tall man who ran with his monocle in place—the necessary five minutes, undisturbed, for all that reaming and poking of pith? Making every allowance for that, would my bamboo breathing tube, standing stark upright in the shallows of Smackover Creek, really fool anyone? It looked just like a breathing tube.

The war was much on my mind in those days, and it was almost entirely the one being fought on movie screens and in the pulp pages of "funny books," known as comic books in other parts of the country. Both names were misleading for the kind I liked, the ones featuring costumed vigilantes who made violent swoops on spy rings and gang hideouts, with no Miranda palaver. Along with Superman and Batman, there were many others, now largely forgotten, such as Bulletman, Plastic Man, The Sandman, Doll Man (a fighting homunculus about six inches tall, in a red cape), The Human Torch, Daredevil, Blue Beetle, Captain Marvel, Captain Midnight, and Captain America. Under any name the books were quite a bargain early on, at sixty-four pages in color for a dime. Or a kind of color. The palette was limited; Superman had blue hair. I never tired of the repetitive stories or the familiar scenes that were enacted over and over again.

> LOIS: But wait, Superman! What about my scoop?
> SUPERMAN: (Bounding skyward) No time for that now, Lois! I'm off to scramble some—YEGGS!!
> LOIS: (Tiny fists on hips) Well, of all th—!!??

The course of events in the early part of the war, the real war, was much too confusing for me to follow. My picture of the fighting in Europe, vivid if false, was of two great armies, and only two, facing each other at some one fixed place. Like many generals, I was fighting the last war. The armies were locked in constant battle, night and day, winter and summer. The din never ceased, and there was a lot of smoke. I may have picked up the smoke from a popular country song of the time, which still chimes out in my head every two or three years, as though from a long tape loop.

> *There'll be smoke on the water*
> *On the land and the sea*
> *When our armee and navee*
> *Overtake the enemee.*

The only movement was a certain ponderous wavering of the battle line. One side would at last falter and give way altogether, and that would be the end. I knew we would win. A great-uncle by the name of Satterfield Fielding had assured me of that.

I was only eight years old but I remember the day well, early in 1942, when he told me the war would be over in ninety days—that we would sink the Japanese fleet in no time, just as we had taken care of the Spanish fleet at Manila Bay in 1898, the work of a few hours. He also told me that if I would dip a brand of snuff called Garrett Scotch, I would never get TB, but that Garrett Sweet was no good and I would do well to leave it alone.

Uncle Sat shot deer the year round, like Robin Hood, in season and out, as the whim or the need moved him, and he may well have been the last man in America who without being facetious called food "vittles" ("victuals," a perfectly good word, and correctly pronounced "vittles," but for some reason thought to be countrified and comical). He was a strong and fluent talker with far-ranging opinions. Attention wandered in the family as he ran on, except when he spoke from experience. There would be bits of hunting lore ("A real turkey could never win a turkey-calling contest") and tips on growing unfashionable corn (nonhybrid) and bumblebee cotton (hill cotton—stunted, unfluffy bolls) and on the best ways of dynamiting fish ("dinnamite," he called it) in the Saline River and Hurricane Creek.

There was some sort of family gathering on that day at his farm, small but his own, in the backwoods of Grant County, Arkansas, and everyone was scoffing and laughing at his notions about the war. Always impatient with him, groaning and rolling her eyes, his sister Emma (my grandmother) could be counted on to check him in his longer flights with "Oh, why don't you just hush, Sat. All you know is what you read in *The Sheridan Headlight*." Wounding indeed, if true.

He came out onto the back porch alone, already angry, and caught me dropping feathers into his water well. I was hanging over the upper framework of the well, dropping chicken feathers and guinea feathers one by one, to watch how they floated about on the surface of the still round pool down there. He gave me a shaking for feathering his drinking water, and then took me into his kitchen and showed me some blurred newspaper maps, perhaps from the *Headlight*.

They were scale maps of Japan and the United States, comparison maps, side by side. Here were the Japanese home islands, a little ragged chain of fragments, mere bits of flotsam. Over here, all of a piece, was the great continental mass that was the United States of America. A revelation. No one had told me about this. Uncle Sat watched me closely to see if I alone out of all these dense Fieldings, Waddells, and Portises could grasp his strategic point. It was clear enough to me: a small country had foolishly attacked a big one. It was fangs of doom. There was nothing more to worry about.

And yet I did worry. The war went on and on. Enemy agents with the faces of rats and hogs appeared to be gaining the upper hand in the funny books I read so greedily. These busy men were all around us, wrecking trains, scattering tacks on our highways, stealing the plans for our Boeing P-26 and our Brewster Buffalo, pouring deadly poisons into our city reservoirs, always from a "vial" or some curiously small bottle. They tempted us to waste gasoline and whispered that we need not save cooking fats for the munitions industry if we didn't feel like it. They changed some of our most brilliant scientists into morons with a colorless and odorless moron gas, pumped into the scientists' laboratories by way of a hand-bellows rig and a piece of rubber tubing.

It was possible to lose, as I was reminded whenever I saw my great-grandfather, Alexander Waddell, usually at family reunions, where he would be seated on display in the parlor of a great-aunt in Pine Bluff, holding a walking stick between his knees with his purplish hands. "Uncle Alec," as he was known generally, in and out of the family, was born in 1847, the same year as Jesse James, and, like Jesse, had fought for the Confederate States of America as a boy soldier, though not as a regular.

I don't know how zealous he was for the cause—enough, at least, to take up arms in defense of Jefferson County and the rest of southern Arkansas. The blood was up, at varying degrees of heat, out of a vast agricultural tedium from East Texas to Virginia, and the (white) boys walking behind mules and middlebuster ploughs rallied to repel what they saw as the invader of their new sovereign nation. President Lincoln had called out his troops to put down what he saw as an insurrection, "by combinations of Jacksons too powerful to be suppressed by the ordinary course of judicial proceedings." I think he wrote "combinations of Jacksons" in that momentous proclamation, but I quote from memory.

The southern boys responded to such recruiting notices as this one, placed in a Memphis newspaper, *The Appeal*, by Nathan Bedford Forrest, the rich slave trader and legendary cavalry commander, who was to have twenty-nine horses shot from under him:

> 200 Recruits Wanted!
>
> I will receive 200 able-bodied men if they will present themselves at my headquarters by the first of June with good horse and gun. I wish none but those who desire to be actively engaged. My headquarters for the present is at Corinth, Miss. Come on, boys, if you want a heap of fun and to kill some Yankees.
>
> N. B. Forrest
> Colonel, Commanding
> Forrest's Regiment

I suspect that the first part of that was written or edited by a meddlesome young staff officer, chewing on a pencil. ("Can't have *wish* here twice in a row, so I'll make it, what—*desire*, yes—the second time around.") The last sentence, shifting into the imperative mood, is Forrest himself, forthright as a pirate.

Uncle Alec had been a county and probate judge, and he still had his wits about him in 1943—no mismated shoes, no long hesitations in speech, groping for a name or some common noun. But his memories of the Civil War, or the ones he saw fit to recall in mixed company, ran mostly to jocular anecdotes, at least in my hearing. I didn't have sense enough or interest enough to ask him questions, and I was further impaired by lockjaw in the presence of very old people. Apart from the comic stories, three things that he said about the war have stuck in my head.

1. That his duties as a young private, and a small one at that, were, for the most part, watering and saddling the horses, and riding off here and there at a gallop on a partly blooded horse, a fast horse, with messages. (A great drama must have a young messenger appearing briefly onstage, to bring some piece of devastating news and move the story along.)

2. How a heavy bank of fog settled low over the battleground at Jenkins' Ferry on April 30, 1864, and how the steady Yankees from Wisconsin and Iowa, backed up there against the flooding Saline River but not lacking for ammunition, stopped one frontal assault after another by firing blindly but effectively in volleys, through the fog and under it. The Arkansas troops made a try, and then the Missouri and Texas troops, 6,000 men all told. All were cut down or sent reeling back. In a matter of hours they took a thousand casualties. (Missouri, a slave state, didn't secede, despite the efforts of the governor, a Democrat named Claiborne Jackson. Nor did Kentucky, another slave state. But they did provide the southern armies with many fine soldiers—many more wore blue—and the eleven-state Confederacy did claim them as part of the new federation. Thus the auspicious—it was vainly hoped—thirteen stars on the battle flag, in this "second war for independence.")

3. How, after that fight, and after the Union soldiers had made their escape across the river on a shaky "India-rubber" pontoon bridge, hundreds of abandoned mules were running loose in the canebrakes, big 1,200-pound U.S. Army mules—which is to say free tractors for the destitute local farmers, or such few as were left, and them mostly old men, women, and children.

That Federal army of 12,000 men, commanded by Major General Frederick Steele, had set out from occupied Little Rock on March 23 for Shreveport, where it was to meet another Union Army column, escorted by a naval armada of sixty-two gunboats and transports with a brigade of U.S. Marines aboard, coming up the Red River in Louisiana. Neither force made it to Shreveport. The trans-Mississippi South, much neglected by Richmond, still had a few kicks left.

Steele was stopped in southern Arkansas at Camden, eighteen miles from Mount Holly. In a series of battles, culminating with the one at Jenkins' Ferry, the Federals were driven all the way back to Little Rock, on short rations and in cold rain and mud. Steele lost 2,750 men on the expedition, along with 635 wagons, 2,500 mules, and "enough horses to mount a brigade of cavalry," and counted himself fortunate. A fast-moving Stonewall Jackson, had one been present, would have cut him off in the rear and bagged the entire lot.

Steele almost had one more casualty in Wild Bill Hickok, a Union scout, who rode into Camden ahead of the army, put on a gray uniform, and did some spying. Something of a regional celebrity even then, he was soon recognized and had to make a run for it, "a bold dash" across the battle lines at Prairie d'Ane, on his horse, Black Nell. One account has him shooting two pursuing Confederate officers as Nell made "a mighty leap" over "an obstruction" (log? rail fence? ditch?). That is, Hickok twisted about in the saddle or stood in the stirrups and turned, cocked and fired his single-action revolver at least twice, and picked off two closing riders on the fly, all this while Nell was airborne. Well, maybe. In any case, it was a bold escape, and "a shout of triumph from the ten thousand troops in line greeted him, and he was the hero of the day."

In the fight at Poison Spring there were some scalpings, when a C.S.A. brigade of Choctaw cavalry clashed with a Federal regiment of black troops, the 1st Kansas (Colored), which had been operating, and plundering, on Choctaw lands in the Indian Territory, later to become Oklahoma. (The "poison spring," now in a state park, was misnamed through a misunderstanding. It still flows and still bears that name, but the unremarkable water isn't toxic or even bad-tasting.)

A white cavalry regiment, the 29th Texas, also carried a grudge against the 1st Kansas troops, who had driven it from the field in an earlier fight at Honey Springs, in the Territory. When the two met again, here at Poison Spring, in Arkansas, the Texans shouted across the lines that they would give no quarter. This time they won, and they gave no quarter. The Texans, the Arkansans, the Choctaws, and the Missourians shot some prisoners and finished off some of the wounded with bayonets and scalping knives. Not for the faint of heart, these late, bitter engagements. Murder and brutalities on both sides were common enough in this remote corner of the war, where it was waged, as the military historian Edwin C. Bearss writes, "with a savagery unheard of in the East." Little was made of it. To those eastern gentlemen in Richmond and Washington, the trans-Mississippi theater of operations wasn't so much a theater as some dim thunder offstage.

It may be that by 1943 Uncle Alec was just bored with all that, as with many other things, all cold potatoes now, but the memories hadn't evaporated. Long after his death I heard a few things he had told the men in the family, now a little garbled in the retelling by second and third parties. One said that he had joined a Jefferson County militia unit at the age of sixteen or seventeen, after his brother Joseph was killed fighting in Georgia, and that he remained with that unit until the war ended. Another one said no, that was only partly true, that he and another boy had later left the militia to ride with what Uncle Alec called "a company" (troop) of partisan cavalry, raised and commanded by a shadowy Captain Jonas (or Jonus) Webb, from Pine Bluff (Jefferson County).

This Webb, all business, not much in the chivalry line, carried on a rough and semi-private little campaign of his own across southern Arkansas. He did on occasion, at his own convenience, work with the official C.S.A. command, as at Jenkins' Ferry. A Confederate soldier named Fine Gordon, in a reminiscence after the war, mentioned Webb in passing, and darkly enough, as "a mean captain of the Southern Army at Camden."

Webb's troop and similar bands roamed freely in that last, lawless year of the war, and were something of a nuisance to both armies, to say nothing of the local farmers, who were being bled white by foraging parties demanding food, fodder, livestock, and whatever else they fancied, at gunpoint. Brigadier General Joseph O. (Jo) Shelby, commanding a C.S.A. brigade (and sometimes a division) of Missouri cavalry in

Arkansas, regarded the guerrillas as little better than slackers and highwaymen, and became so furious with them as to publish a general warning: "I will enlist you in the Confederate army; or I will drive you into the Federal ranks. You shall not remain idle spectators of a drama enacted before your eyes." Here again, I think, we see the hand of a literary adjutant.

The general did, however, have a soft spot for Quantrill's bushwhackers, and for one in particular, Frank James, who had saved Shelby from capture earlier in the war at the Battle of Prairie Grove, Arkansas. Some twenty years later, in August of 1883, Jo Shelby appeared as a defense witness for Frank, at his murder trial in Gallatin, Missouri. The charge was that in July of 1881, while robbing a Chicago, Rock Island and Pacific train with four other men, Alexander Franklin James had shot and killed a passenger named Frank McMillan. One of the bandits, Dick Liddil, characterized by the prosecutor as "the least depraved" member of the James Gang, identified Frank in court as the killer. Perhaps he was, or it may have been his brother Jesse who did the deed; it was almost certainly Jesse who shot and killed the conductor of the train, one William Westfall. But in 1883 Jesse James was beyond the grasp of the court, having been murdered himself the year before—shot in the back of the head by Bob Ford, of ballad infamy.

> *It was Robert Ford, that dirty little coward,*
> *I wonder how he does feel,*
> *For he ate of Jesse's bread and he slept in Jesse's bed,*
> *Then he laid Jesse James in the grave.*

Frank was found not guilty, and there followed an uproar in Republican newspapers over what was seen as a scandalous verdict. It isn't clear how much influence General Shelby had on the jury, if any. Not that it mattered. The defense attorneys, in connivance with the sheriff, had packed the jury with twelve Democrats. And Jo Shelby wasn't at his best on that day. He —who had refused to surrender in 1865 and rode to Mexico City on horseback with his brigade, fighting his way through bandits and Juaristas, to offer his saber, in the service of another lost cause, to Maximilian, the young Hapsburg Emperor of Mexico—came to the Missouri courtroom a little drunk and unsteady on his feet.

He had to be guided to the witness chair, and, once seated, had some trouble locating the judge and jury. Twisting about in his seat, he tried to address first one and then the other. He argued with the lawyers and abused Dick Liddil. "God bless you, old fellow," he said to Frank, catching sight of him at the defense table. The judge wasn't amused. He found the general in contempt for coming to court "in a condition unfit to testify" and fined him $10.

That was more punishment than Frank got, or was to get the next year, when he was tried in Huntsville, Alabama, for the 1881 robbery of a Federal paymaster. Once again, a jury with Confederate sympathies found him not guilty.

Other charges against him here and there, such as the one in Hot Springs, Arkansas, near which he and Jesse and the Younger brothers had robbed a stagecoach in January of 1874, were dropped or simply not pressed. (All the coach passengers were robbed. One, a G. R. Crump, of Memphis, got his watch and money back when Cole Younger learned that he had been a Confederate soldier—or so one story has it.) The State of Minnesota might also have made a claim on him, for the Northfield bank raid in September of 1876, but didn't bother to pursue it.

The law, for all practical purposes, was now finished with Frank. An old friend advised him to go back home to the farm in Missouri, to keep his head down and stay away from low company and fast horses. He had already surrendered his cartridge belt and his Remington .44 revolver. That was the end of the James Gang, and in a sense, in a kind of inglorious coda, the end of the end of the war, too, at long last. Or, no, that sounds pretty good, "coda," almost convincing, but it's wrong. The real end of the war came twenty years later, in 1904, in the very heart of the country, far from Fort Sumter, at a reunion of Quantrill's guerrillas in Independence, Missouri. There, in that election year, Frank brazenly announced that his choice for President was the sitting one, Theodore Roosevelt—*the New York Republican*. This didn't go down well, and he almost came to blows with his old hard-riding comrades. Unseemly spectacle, coots flailing away.

Unless there was another, better ending still later. For more than a century now, at intervals of about five years, southern editorial writers have been seeing portents in the night skies and proclaiming The End of the War, at Long Last, and the blessed if somewhat tardy arrival of The New South. By that they seem to mean something the same as, culturally identical with, at one with, the rest of the country, and this time they may be on to something, what with our declining numbers of Gaylons, Coys, and Virgils, and the disappearance of Clabber Girl Baking Powder signs from our highways, and of mules, standing alone in pastures. Then there is the new and alien splendor to be seen all about us, in cities with tall, dark, and featureless glass towers, though I'm told that deep currents are flowing here, far beyond the ken of editorial wretches in their cluttered cubicles. A little underground newsletter informs me that these peculiar glass structures are designed with care, by sociologists and architects working hand in glove with the CIA, as dark and forbidding boxes, in which combinations of Jacksons are thought least likely to gather, combine further, smoke cigarettes, brood, conspire, and break loose again out of a long lull.

Unlike the border ruffians Jesse (who sometimes called himself J. T. Jackson) and his brother Frank, Uncle Alec taught school for a while after the war, in cahoots with a carpetbagger from Indiana, one of the dumber ones, come south with his roomy bag to get in on the political plunder, to make his fortune in impoverished and all but depopulated Grant County, Arkansas. They were a pair of unlikely pedagogues. Uncle Alec could read and write and do his sums, which is all you need to know, but he was a very young man. The carpetbagger was older but illiterate. Uncle Alec, then, did the teaching, probably of a more basic and effective nature than is common today in public schools, and the carpetbagger did nothing except collect the monthly salary, of something like $20, which they split down the middle. The victor's spoils came to around thirty cents a day.

It was the carpetbaggers, of course, who named the county —a new one, formed largely from the western end of Jefferson County—for General Grant. Rubbing a little more salt in the open wound, they called the county seat Sheridan. That postbellum movement into the South of all the pale cranks in the Midwest, similar to one of those sudden squirrel migrations in the woods, has been overlooked, I think, as a source of some of the weirdness to be met with in our region.

I never knew my paternal great-grandfather, Colonel John W. Portis, who was a much older man (1818–1902) than Uncle Alec. He commanded an infantry regiment, the 42nd Alabama, was wounded in the Battle of Corinth, and was starved out in the siege of Vicksburg. I have the surrender parole he signed there on July 10, 1863 (the garrison had actually surrendered on the fourth), in which he gave his "solemn parole under oath that I will not take up arms again against the United States . . . until duly exchanged."

Some Uncle Sat of the day, looking up from his maps, could have told him and President Davis (shouted it, more likely) that with the fall of this city fortress on the bluffs of the Mississippi, and the simultaneous disaster at Gettysburg, in distant Pennsylvania, President Lincoln's re-election was pretty well assured, and the war lost. They wouldn't have listened. One more good push or two and the weary Yankees—"Those people," General Lee called them (graceless humanoids?)—must lose heart, flinch, and cut their losses. *Enough of these Jacksons! Great God almighty! Let them go and be done with them!* Such were the hopes. The next summer, duly exchanged, Colonel Portis was back in the field, at the Battle of Atlanta, and he didn't sign his final surrender parole until June 2, 1865, at Citronelle, Alabama, some two months after General Lee's surrender at Appomattox. This parole document gives a physical description: six feet tall, gray eyes, white hair. In three years of war he had gone white.

My Alabama grandmother wasn't pleased when her youngest son (a seventh son, my father) told her of his plans to marry an Arkansas girl. She kindly explained to him that the unfortunate women living west of the Mississippi River had, among other defects, feet at least one size bigger than those of their dainty little sisters to the east. No Cinderella to be found in the Bear State. Any mention of that old slander, even a teasing one fifty years later, could still make my placid mother bristle and blaze up a little. In any kind of refined-foot contest, she said, she

would pit her Waddell-Fielding-Arkansas feet against all comers with Portis-Poole-Alabama feet.

My father was a dutiful son, but he defied his mother in this
matter and married Alice, the Arkansas girl. So, a new family, a
mingling of blood, a new combination of Jacksons, so to speak.
We fetched up in southern Arkansas, at Mount Holly, where at
dusk ("dusk-dark," it was called there) flying squirrels glided
across our front yard, from oak to oak. I haven't seen one since.

Now a not quite deserted village, Mount Holly then had
two cotton gins, a sawmill, two schools (white and black), a
bank, a post office, a café, a barbershop, an ice house, three
general stores and a sawmill commissary, a few moonshiners
and bootleggers, one auto mechanic, one blacksmith, who was
also the constable, and one known white Republican. My father pointed him out to me. (Now in much of the South it
is the white Democrat to be pointed out with a whisper, as
for a sighting of the ivory-billed woodpecker.) Some blacks
still voted, when not deterred by the poll tax or some courthouse chicanery, for the Grand Old Party of Lincoln and Theodore Roosevelt, but by that time, the early 1940s, most had
switched their allegiance to Franklin Roosevelt if not to the local "lily white" Democratic Party groups. They had also begun
to christen their baby boys with his Dutch surname.

What was a bit odd, on two counts, Mount Holly proper had
only one church, and that the true church of the elect, Presbyterian. The normal ratio at that time and place was about two
Baptist churches or one Methodist church per gin. It usually
took about three gins to support a Presbyterian church, and
a community with, say, four before you found enough tepid
idolaters to form an Episcopal congregation. There was always
difficulty in getting a minister who pleased everyone. What the
elders of the church kept looking for, my father said, and what
was hard to find in the 1940s, was a wise, saintly, hearty, scholarly, eloquent thirty-five-year-old Confederate veteran, who
would be content to live on a small salary, in something pretty
close to apostolic poverty.

On Saturdays we usually drove to El Dorado, the county
seat and a flourishing oil town then, with two refineries. One
was owned by Lion Oil, a palindrome. Black-market gasoline
was readily available, outside the rationing system, but my

father, scrupulous in such things, refused to buy it, and we made do on the four or five gallons a week he was allotted by the B sticker on his windshield. (B was better than A; an A got less.) There was little chocolate to be had. The schoolyard rumor was that all the Clark bars were going to the Japanese-American internment camps over at Rohwer and Jerome, in the Delta, and to the German prisoners of war (most of them from Rommel's Afrika Korps) up at Camp Chaffee, in the hills. A patriot like me had to do without. (We schoolboys would have been hard pressed to explain the difference between the two classes of prisoners. I can't remember hearing anyone, adults included, question or even discuss the need for "relocating" the Japanese-Americans from California. President Roosevelt had sent them here, so it must be all right.) We lived in a place where they sent prisoners; what to make of that?

Gasoline and candy bars were much less important to me than movie theaters, or, as we called them, picture shows. The tale unfolding on the screen was a picture show, and the theater building itself was also a picture show. El Dorado had four. The Majestic was fairly noisy, and the Ritz a little noisier. The shabby and disreputable old Star was very noisy indeed, with the hubbub of a pack of unruly boys, much on the move. At the Star you sometimes had to try two or three of the folding seats before finding one that didn't pinch your leg, or tip you forward and dump you. There were frequent delays, as the celluloid film itself, or an image of it, turned brown, writhed, curled, and caught fire before our eyes. The breakdown would be followed at once by piercing whistles and animal howls of outrage, a performance in itself by little shriekers who had been eagerly awaiting the cue to show their stuff. No rats, though, in disgusting numbers, pattering about underfoot at the Star, as was widely believed. The story was kept alive by my fastidious older sister (Star = rats at play) and others like her who had never set foot in the place. This isn't to say that an occasional rogue rat never darted down an aisle there.

I made a round of these three picture shows (and how well I knew that circuit, starting from the courthouse square), seeking out the best program. Decisions came hard. A very good bill would have been a chapter of the Captain Marvel or Dick Tracy serial, a Spike Jones comedy short, a Boston Blackie feature, and a Western with Tim McCoy, George O'Brien, or Johnny Mack Brown, my favorite cowboys. And yet there were so many things to consider before I committed myself irreversibly to a twelve-cent ticket. For example, Bob Steele was better with his fists than any of my favorites. Ken Maynard was a better rider. Ken—and even I could sense that he wasn't much of an actor, perhaps to his credit—vaulted over the rump of his horse in the fast-getaway mount with a light swagger that always pleased me.

When I was younger and in her keeping, my sister sometimes took me against my will to the fourth picture show, the quiet Rialto, where an attentive and well-mannered audience remained seated, and where the more ambitious pictures played. Even very fat people could settle in at the Rialto without fear of being dumped and laughed at, or of having their tender and spreading flanks nipped at by the seats. I didn't object to the decorum or the comfort, just the pictures. The posters outside, which I always carefully read ("Theirs was a passion not to be denied!"), were enough to sink the hopes of a small boy. In these stories there would be some strange men scheming against each other and beating each other's brains out to see who got to marry Bette Davis, or it might be Joan Crawford. The winning suitor would get to spend every minute of the rest of his life in the company of a harridan. I was soon asleep.

Mount Holly had its own summer pleasures. We, the village boys, swam like seals by day in the creeks and ponds, and at night, with our carbide lamps, we ran trotlines—a series of fishing lines hanging from a central support line that was strung across a stream. We swung from vines in the bottomlands, trying to reproduce, and never bringing off anything remotely like, Tarzan's aerial glide across the jungle, leaping from one opportune vine to the next. That, I've since learned, was even more of a cheat than I suspected: it was all done with ropes. Ignorant of the laws of physics, I did know from experience that when you jumped from a swinging vine to one that was hanging dead still and vertical, you weren't going any farther, and could only be left looking foolish, dangling there at rest. I was also uneasy, not knowing exactly why, with Batman's practice of shooting a rope line from atop a tall building across to a lower building, and then swinging *down* to the lower building on that line, which somehow remained taut.

We made model airplanes, little replicas of warplanes built far away from Mount Holly in huge factories with such satisfying corporate names as Chance Vought and Consolidated Vultee. First, with the models, there was the fragile skeleton to be assembled, of balsa ribs and stringers, and droplets of glue; this was then covered with a thin skin of paper, and painted with a dope sealant that smelled of bananas. The delicate work tried my patience, and gave me an early appreciation of how it is that real aircraft, no matter how fierce in appearance, must be the tinny and flimsy shells that they are, in order to leave the ground. In my haste, and with twinges of guilt, I sometimes cut corners, leaving out a troublesome strut or spar, like some crooked defense contractor.

We rigged up our own fireworks, with carbide (granular calcium carbide, bought in cans; it fizzes and gives off a combustible gas when mixed with water) and with black powder we compounded ourselves. We burned our own charcoal, and bought the other ingredients, sulfur and saltpeter, in little paper cartons at Bailey's store, arrayed there on the patent-medicine shelf with the big bottles of liniments, violent purgatives, female tonics, chill tonics, croup tonics, cramp tonics, catarrh tonics, and nerve tonics. No need in those days of tonics to be put through the indignities of "a full battery of tests," at great expense, for every little sinking spell. I no longer see tonics on the shelves of country stores, that space now being given over to videocassettes. Catarrh, with its fine pair of purring *r*s, seems to have gone away too, whatever it was.

Our watermelons (not always lifted from a melon patch; you could buy one, preferably a long green Tom Watson, for about fifteen cents) we left floating in the creeks to cool as we swam, mostly in Swift Hole, on Beech Creek. The water in Swift Hole wasn't swift; moccasins swam calmly about on the surface, untroubled by the slight current. We—David Bailey, Max Lewis, Gerald Lewis, Francis Crumpler, Richie Bidwell, Buddy Portis —paid little heed to the snakes and soon scattered them with our noise and splashing and, low comedians all, with our strutting antics along the banks. No one, that I recall, was bitten there. But Swift Hole was a hole, deep enough that we could dive into it from a height of eight or nine feet and not crack our necks on the bottom.

A leaning tree shaded the pool, and from a high limb there hung a rope with a stick tied at the end. You grabbed the stick with both hands, ran down the sloping bank, took flight, and at the peak of the upswing let go, doing a back flip or a half gainer on the way down. Some unknown person had patiently spliced the long rope together from the separated strands of a thick oil-field hawser, and hung it there for our delight. One day it was just there. With the ingratitude of children we accepted it as part of the natural order of things, as no more than our due, and asked few questions.

Mount Holly was just outside the oil fields, but we did have one lone gas well, on Cypress Creek. A man would drive up a dirt lane to the unattended wellhead in his 1928 Ford Model A roadster, or his 1939 Chevrolet Master Deluxe sedan, and look furtively about. He would see us, some boys with purple stripes on our faces (pokeberry juice), pulling a ragged seine through the creek. Unterrified by the war paint, he would dismiss us as a threat and proceed to drain off something called "casing head" from the well, which he then poured into his gasoline tank.

This was a liquid condensate that formed in gas lines, and although it burned a little rough in car engines, it did burn, and was unrationed and free for the taking. There must have been some kind of bleeder valve in that tangle of high-pressure gas pipes, but I've forgotten how it worked, if I ever knew. I do seem to remember a Stillson wrench, an adjustable pipe wrench, in the hands of one of those furtive casing-head thieves. I remember, too, that we once dredged up a curious snake in our seine, along that same stretch of Cypress Creek. It was a rusty-orange color with a thick body and what appeared to be a barbed stinger protruding from its tail. Zoologists, who should venture outdoors more often, say the stinging snake exists only in folklore, but we were there and saw that beast. We all agreed it was a stinging snake.

It was in Beech Creek, in the shoal water below Swift Hole, that I carried on most of my underwater contortions with breathing tubes. Reeds were out, and among other rejects was a copper pipe, which left a sharp taste in the mouth. Another one, tasting worse, was a black and smelly rubber hose, a piece of old fuel line from a car, with a spiral curl to it like that of a pig's tail. I had to expose a small but conspicuous hand above the surface of the water to keep this one upright.

I kept coming back to bamboo, the best of a poor lot, and soldiered on. There was always another obstacle. When I was underwater, clutching a tree root, lying more or less supine, and took a deep draft of air through my mouth tube, an equal volume of water would come rushing in through my nose, with a strangling effect. The nose clip existed then and might have solved the problem, but I couldn't be seen with a nose clip. Only girls used nose clips. Far better to strangle. Couldn't I simply have pinched my nostrils shut with thumb and finger? Yes, nothing easier, except that both hands were already occupied, with the tube and the root. And as I lay there more or less supine on the creekbed, struggling to breathe and to hold my upper body down, then my telltale feet would rise. Feet unfettered float, for all their bones, and when toes break the surface and bob about, they will catch the eye of the dullest observer.

I never did get it all worked out to suit me, and when the war ended, in 1945, I lost interest in breathing tubes and model airplanes and black-powder bombs and cigarettes rolled with rabbit tobacco or corn silk. A spell was broken. The world had changed. I put all that juvenile dementia behind me. It was time to take on some serious responsibilities in life. I cut a coupon from the back of a funny book and bought a $1.98 money order at the Mount Holly post office and sent them off to a place in New Jersey for a home-study course in ventriloquism.

Uncle Alec didn't quite make it to a hundred, dying a year short, in 1946. He had lived to see the U.S. Army, still with plenty of ammunition, if not mules, on the winning end of another great war, and he was probably the last man who could remember seeing Jo Shelby riding at the head of his mounted column along the Ouachita River near Camden, or hearing another general, the portly Sterling Price, calling out for one more charge into the fog and powdersmoke at Jenkins' Ferry.

No peevish coot, he made a good showing toward the end, still jaunty, laughing quietly in his chair, and with no bits of food on his chin that I can remember. A better showing, in his dark suit, vest, watch chain, and polished leather shoes, than many of the old-timers I see today, men who went ashore at Tarawa and Anzio, now much reduced in their retirement costume of grotesque white athletic shoes, pastel resort rompers, and white baseball cap crammed down hard on the head, bending the ears. Their model seems to be The Golfer.

A coot now myself, slightly peevish, of three score and five, I recently saw a vision in broad daylight of The Ghost of Christmas Yet to Come. The apparition was an old man at the wheel of an old tan Pontiac station wagon. He had stopped next to my car at a traffic light here in Little Rock. The wagon was a long, sagging barge, packed inside to the roof with lumpy objects bundled in green-plastic tarpaulins and tied up with what looked like clothesline. But what objects? At a guess, all his goods, his assets, now luggage: bits of chain, rolls of duct tape, forgotten cans of soup, jumper cables tangled around a jack frozen with rust, encrusted bottles of Tabasco sauce, sacks of Indian arrowheads, sacks of silver dimes, sacks of cat food, an old owlhead .32 revolver with a wobbly cylinder and a pitted barrel, corroded flashlights, ivory, apes, peacocks, and bottles of saw-palmetto capsules to treat the sinister prostate gland. The old man was smirking. It was the gloat of a miser. Stiff gray hairs straggled out of the little relief hole at the back of his cap, above the adjustment strap. In short, another Jackson, and while not an ornament of our race, neither was he, I thought, the most depraved member of the gang. He might even have made some claim to being a gentleman, as defined by my *Concise Oxford Dictionary*: "n. Man entitled to bear arms but not included in the nobility . . ."

There I was in the flesh, a little more weathered, just a few years from now. The resemblance was close. I saw myself sunk low there under the wheel, even to the string bolo tie with its turquoise slide, and even to that complacent smirk, knowing that all my flashlights and other treasures were right behind me, safely stowed and well hidden from the defiling gaze of others. I could see myself all too clearly in that old butterscotch Pontiac, roaring flat out across the Mexican desert and laying down a streamer of smoke like a crop duster, with a goatherd to note my passing and (I flatter myself) to watch me until I was utterly gone, over a distant hill, and only then would he turn again with his stick to the straying flock. So be it.

Uncle Sat, who never got TB and who wouldn't let young government agents tell him how to prune his peach trees and cure his hams and who ate better food than a rich man can buy today and who never lost so much as a finger while fooling around with his detonator caps and his sticks of dinnamite, was eighty-eight when he died, in 1964. I saw him now and then over the years, talking away, as ever, but I can call up his face more clearly, his red farmer's face, from an earlier time, at that kitchen table, over the newspaper maps. I can see the winter stubble in his fields, too, on that dreary January day in 1942. Broken stalks and a few dirty white shreds of bumble-bee cotton. Everyone who was there is dead and buried now except me.

*1999*

CHRONOLOGY

NOTE ON THE TEXTS

NOTES

# Chronology

| | |
|---|---|
| 1933 | Born Charles McColl Portis on December 28 in El Dorado, Arkansas, the second child of Alice Waddell and Samuel Palmer Portis. (Mother Alice Waddell Portis [1903–1987] was a writer and columnist, under the heading "Gal Thursday," for newspapers in south Arkansas and a poet and officer in the Poets' Roundtable of Arkansas. Charles, whose family and friends called him Buddy or Charlie, once said in an interview, that she was "a good poet with a good ear." Her grandfather Alexander Waddell was born in 1847, fought for the Confederacy in the Civil War ["I don't know how zealous he was for the cause," Charles later wrote], and died in 1946, long enough for his great-grandson to hear stories of his service. Father Samuel Palmer Portis [1905–1984], born in Clarke County, Alabama, was a school superintendent, primarily in Hamburg, Arkansas, from 1948 to 1970. His grandfather was Colonel John W. Portis, who commanded the Forty-second Alabama Infantry Regiment in the Civil War. Of his father's side of the family, Charles later said, "A lot of cigar smoke and laughing when my father and his brothers got together. Long anecdotes. The spoken word." A sister, Alice [her preferred spelling was Aliece] Kate, had been born in 1931. The family lives in Norphlet, just north of El Dorado.) |
| 1939–41 | Attends Hugh Goodwin School in El Dorado for first and second grades, after family moves from Norphlet. |
| 1942–46 | Spends grades three through seven in Mount Holly, the location of his 1999 autobiographical essay "Combinations of Jacksons," after the family moves. Brother Richard is born there in 1944. |
| 1947–51 | Attends high school in Hamburg after his family moves when his father becomes school superintendent. Brother Jonathan is born in 1949. Charles works as an apprentice mechanic at a Chevrolet dealership. Graduates from Hamburg High School. Goes to work in Hamburg as an auto parts salesman. |

1952–55    With the Korean War in progress, enlists in May in Little
           Rock as a private in the U.S. Marine Corps. Parents had
           written letters to Arkansas congressmen trying to get him
           assigned to officer training but he is determined to serve
           in combat. Denied admission to the navy's officer training
           program because he "has no natural molars on the lower
           right side." Sees combat in Korea. Earns several service
           medals and a Good Conduct ribbon. Promoted to sergeant
           in March 1955. While at Camp Lejeune, North Carolina, a
           fellow Marine gives him a copy of Thomas Wolfe's *Look
           Homeward, Angel*, which he had never heard of and later
           said was "a revelation." Discharged May 28, 1955, at Camp
           Lejeune. Returns to Hamburg. With a friend from home,
           decides to enroll at the University of Arkansas for the sum-
           mer session, and they drive to Fayetteville together.

1956       Chooses a journalism major and begins writing for the
           student newspaper, the *Arkansas Traveler*, where he even-
           tually becomes feature editor. Enlists in Marine Corps Re-
           serve while a student and serves at Fort Chaffee in nearby
           Fort Smith.

1957       In October, publishes his first national short story,
           "Damn!," a comic piece about a patent medicine scam
           artist, in *Nugget*, a mildly provocative "gentleman's mag-
           azine" with literary pretentions in the *Playboy* mode. (A
           Grace Paley short story also appeared in the issue.) During
           his last year as a student, works as a reporter and editor
           for the regional daily *Northwest Arkansas Times*, on the
           courthouse beat in Fayetteville and editing copy from
           small-town stringers. Column for the student newspaper
           about Henry Luce and *Time* magazine (in response to a
           cover story on Arkansas governor Orval Faubus) is picked
           up by national newspapers. Takes a creative writing course
           from science fiction writer Wesley Ford Davis.

1958       Graduates from the University of Arkansas in May with
           a B.A. in liberal arts and major in journalism. Moves to
           Memphis to take a job with the *Commercial Appeal* as
           general assignment and police beat reporter. While check-
           ing the hospital for news one night, spots and interviews
           Elvis Presley, home from army duty because of the singer's
           mother's illness. Two days later, when she dies, Portis cov-
           ers the funeral. In December, sister Aliece dies unexpect-
           edly at age twenty-seven of a cerebral hemorrhage.

1959        Early in the year, moves to Little Rock to take a job with
            the *Arkansas Gazette*, first on the police beat and then as a
            general assignment reporter. (The paper had won two Pu-
            litzer Prizes in 1958 for its coverage and editorials during
            the previous year's Central High integration conflict.) At
            the newspaper, meets and works with William Whitworth,
            who will later write and edit at *The New Yorker* and, as
            editor of *The Atlantic*, publish three pieces and a novel
            excerpt by him. In summer, Portis takes over the *Gazette*'s
            "Our Town" column, a coveted spot allowing the writer
            to riff on local happenings, but later admits he could never
            "get into a stride" with it.

1960–61     Writes to Dick West, the city editor at the *New York Her-
            ald Tribune*, who after reading his clips and meeting with
            him in New York City, hires him as a general assignment
            reporter. Sits in the office "in a clump," as he later recalls,
            with others on the general assignment beat, among them
            Lewis Lapham and Tom Wolfe. (In addition, a number of
            editors and reporters from the *Gazette* will end up at the
            *Herald Tribune*, including Bob Poteete, Inky Blackmon,
            William Whitworth, and Pat Crow.) Files stories on a man
            who keeps a lion as a pet in his Brooklyn home, the city's
            attempts to curb jaywalking, and the National Barber
            Show convention.

1962        In June, files a four-part series published on consecutive
            days of his ultimately futile attempt to stop smoking un-
            der the aegis of a program run by the Bates Memorial
            Medical Center in Yonkers, New York. The articles con-
            tain narrative hallmarks of his later wry style, including
            his description of beating a "kid" at Ping-Pong because
            "he had little short arms and all I had to do was tip the
            ball over the net out of his reach." Breaking news stories
            includes reporting from the scene of a boiler explosion
            in October in uptown Manhattan that kills twenty-three
            and injures ninety-four: "A disembodied desk phone
            was on the floor ringing, its little red extension light
            winking." In December, during a printers' lockout that
            lasts 114 days and shuts down all of New York's major
            newspapers, starts working at *Newsweek* as a national
            affairs correspondent. There, meets and dates Nora
            Ephron, who is working as a fact checker. (They con-
            tinue to correspond with each other throughout their
            lives.)

1963    Returns to the *Herald Tribune* after the lockout ends on
        March 8. During the tumultuous civil rights struggles
        in the summer, covers the movement across the South:
        the jailing of Dr. Martin Luther King, Jr., in Albany,
        Georgia; an all-night battle among night riders, police,
        and protestors after racially motivated bombings destroy
        Black businesses and homes in Birmingham, Alabama;
        a Ku Klux Klan rally in Bessemer, Alabama; Governor
        George Wallace's segregationist stand to prevent two
        Black students from registering at the University of
        Alabama in Tuscaloosa; the murder of NAACP repre-
        sentative Medgar Evers in Jackson, Mississippi; and the
        March on Washington. In a letter to his parents, writes
        that he's working on his first novel. In November, moves
        to England to head the *Herald Tribune*'s London bu-
        reau, covering events on the continent as well. Lives at
        39 Tite Street, a block from the Thames and near Os-
        car Wilde's house. Reports on the new prime minister,
        Sir Alec Douglas-Home, reaction to the assassination
        of President John F. Kennedy, and Winston Churchill's
        eighty-ninth birthday.

1964    Files stories from Cyprus on the outbreak of fighting be-
        tween Greek and Turkish Cypriots on the island. Also re-
        ports on the victory of American Tony Lema in the British
        Open golf championship and the trial of a modern-day
        witch who carries a jackdaw named Hotfoot Jackson on
        her shoulder. Traveling to Ireland, visits "James Joyce's
        Martello Tower" and reports that "there were no pilgrims,
        no Americans, no one," an early sign of his growing inter-
        est in a literary as opposed to a journalism career. Quits
        the paper in November after the British elections and sails
        for New York on the RMS *Mauritania*, about which trip
        he writes to a friend, "Rough crossing. Many sickly faces.
        Had to heave some myself. The old Technicolor yawn."
        Watches a burial at sea.

1965    Rents a cabin at Hickory Hills resort in Gamaliel, Ar-
        kansas, near the Missouri border and Lake Norfork and
        in some five or six months completes the novel that will
        become *Norwood*. Visits New York occasionally during
        the year, staying sometimes with his friend William Whit-
        worth, who is now writing at *The New Yorker*, or at the
        Chelsea Hotel. Agent Lynn Nesbit, then with Sterling
        Lord's agency, sells *Norwood* to editor Robert Gottlieb

at Simon & Schuster. In the fall, begins reporting for *The Saturday Evening Post* on Nashville's music scene.

1966 In January, fills out the marketing form for *Norwood*, listing his residence as "New York and Hamburg, Ark., alternately." Asked on the form to briefly describe his novel in two hundred words, types only "It defies brief summary," a reply that presages his lifelong resistance to the industry's need to publicize and market authors. (None of the first editions of his books contain an author photo.) Early in the year, undertakes reporting on Arkansas senator William Fulbright for *The Saturday Evening Post* but never completes the story. The Nashville music piece, entitled "That New Sound from Nashville," appears February 12. Excerpts from *Norwood*, under the title "Traveling Light," are published in the *Post* in consecutive issues on June 18 and July 2. Moves to the Beverly Grove neighborhood of Los Angeles, staying with fellow writer William Price Fox, who has earned good film-option prices for his books. In July, plans a ten-day trip with college friend Andy Davis, an actor, to drive the length of Baja California and write about it. Returns to Los Angeles July 26, three days before *Norwood* is published. Reviews are favorable. In the *Washington Post Book Week*, Ross Wetzsteon calls it "a comedy of perception: truth comes as a surprise and laughter comes from joy." Already working on next novel, *True Grit*.

1967 In January, turns in a portion of the manuscript of *True Grit* to agent Lynn Nesbit, now working for Marvin Josephson Associates, who secures a contract, again with Robert Gottlieb at Simon & Schuster, for a $6,000 advance. In February, "An Auto Odyssey through Darkest Baja," documenting the Mexico road trip with his friend Andy Davis, is published in *West* magazine, a Sunday supplement to the *Los Angeles Times*. (An excerpt from Hunter S. Thompson's book about the Hells Angels also appears in this issue.) Drives to Mexico from Hamburg at the end of May, this time to San Miguel de Allende, where he rents an apartment at Terraplén 41, and works on *True Grit*. In July, he returns to Little Rock, renting an apartment on 18th Street near the Governor's Mansion downtown. In September, turns in manuscript for *True Grit* to Gottlieb. At the end of November, receives galleys and Gottlieb asks for them to be returned with changes and corrections within two weeks. Gottlieb later writes in his autobiography, *Avid Reader*, "If we ever did any editorial work on it I can't imagine what it could have been. . . . Talk about pitch-perfect voice!"

1968    Moves to Regency Apartments on Cantrell Road in Little Rock. Advance readers' copies of *True Grit* go out to Hollywood, and there is avid film interest in the book, which is to be published June 10. By the end of January, three competing producers offer $300,000. Chooses Hal Wallis—who partners with director Henry Hathaway, with John Wayne eventually attached—when Wallis also purchases the rights to *Norwood*. (Admires Wayne but envisioned George C. Scott as Rooster Cogburn.) Prepublication enthusiasm is high. The Literary Guild makes it one of its dual selections for June. *The Saturday Evening Post* excerpts the novel over three consecutive issues: May 18, June 1, and June 15. Full-page ads in newspaper book sections feature blurbs from Walker Percy, Roald Dahl, and Robert Crichton. Early reviews are positive and sometimes rapturous, most often drawing comparisons to Mark Twain. Published June 10, the book is soon on *The New York Times* best sellers list and will spend twenty-two weeks there overall. In August, travels to Mexico. In September, the *True Grit* film begins shooting in Colorado, with a script by Marguerite Roberts. Joining Wayne in the cast are singer Glen Campbell, a native of Arkansas, as the Texas Ranger LaBoeuf (a part originally offered to Elvis Presley) and the relatively unknown Kim Darby as Mattie Ross. (Mia Farrow is originally cast as Mattie Ross but backs out when Robert Mitchum tells her to avoid working with Hathaway.) Portis spends some time on location in Montrose, Colorado, and tinkers with the screenplay, including writing the final scene with Rooster and Mattie in her family's graveyard, a scene that didn't appear in the book.

1969    Early in the year, Hal Wallis announces that Glen Campbell will star in a film version of *Norwood*. In the spring, Portis buys a house for his parents in Little Rock's Kingwood neighborhood, anticipating his father's retirement in 1970 as Hamburg school superintendent and his parents' subsequent move. Drives to Key West and rents an apartment at 1425 Alberta Avenue. As the release of the film of *True Grit* nears in June, a controversy over the premiere erupts. The Democratic Party of Arkansas organizes a world premiere in Little Rock for June 12 with the participation of Glen Campbell. Objecting to the use of the film as a $50-per-head fundraiser for the party, holds alternate premiere in Hot Springs on the general release date of the film the next day with tickets at $10 and all proceeds going to the Arkansas Children's Colony. Reviews of the film are largely positive, with John Wayne receiving Oscar acting mentions. Returns to San Miguel, renting an apartment at Sollano 80 and frequenting the American Legion post and a bar called the Cucaracha (a similar bar with the same name appears in *The Dog of the South*).

1970    John Wayne wins an Oscar for Best Actor for *True Grit*. Receives letter from agent Lynn Nesbit encouraging him to finish his next novel to capitalize on current popular attention. In May, the film of *Norwood* opens in theaters nationwide.

1973    Settles in Little Rock, where his brothers Richard and Jonathan as well as his parents live, and continues to travel to Mexico and Central America. Works on an original script treatment for a Western for Hal Wallis.

1974    During the first half of the year, writes and revises drafts of a script for a *True Grit* sequel, which Hal Wallis will produce. Wayne reups and is joined by Katharine Hepburn. The final script for *Rooster Cogburn*, for which shooting begins in Oregon in September, is credited to Martin Julien, a nom de plume for Martha Hyer (an actor and Hal Wallis's wife), with contributions from Wallis and Portis.

1975    Contracts with Wallis to write another sequel with Wayne and Hepburn called *Someday*. Turns in a draft in July and makes changes in October. *Rooster Cogburn* opens in October. Reviews are mixed, from "plodding" to "a breezy delight."

1976    In June, Wallis announces that *Someday* is in development for Wayne and Hepburn, but production never begins, perhaps because both Wayne and Hepburn have health problems.

1977    Makes first and only appearance in *The New Yorker* with the short comic piece "Your Action Line."

1979    Alfred A. Knopf, where his editor Robert Gottlieb has moved from Simon & Schuster shortly after acquiring *True Grit*, publishes *The Dog of the South*. Reviews range from the dismissive "flawed" to "as colorful a collection of characters as has been in print since Charles Dickens." As with his two previous novels, refuses to include a photograph or a biographical note on the jacket.

1984    Owners and employees of the Madison Avenue Bookshop in New York become so enamored of *The Dog of the South* five years after its publication that the store orders all 183 hardcover copies remaining in print (the book had never been published in paperback) and constructs a window display composed solely of these copies. A story about the store's enthusiasm for the book appears in *The New York Times*. Reached at home in Little Rock, tells the *Times* reporter he is "surprised and pleased" with the attention and that he works in "a little office without a phone, behind a beer joint called Cash McCool's," and pays $85 per month for it. The publicity leads to a small revival and a paperback sale. Father dies. Moves mother into an apartment in his complex in Little Rock's Riverdale neighborhood. Resides in this area for the next three decades, while traveling for extended stays in Mexico (primarily Tampico, Mazatlán, and San Miguel de Allende), Texas (Port Aransas and South Padre Island), and New Mexico (Deming).

1985    Knopf publishes *Masters of Atlantis*. The book is largely reviewed warmly as his most ambitious and comically trenchant on the American character. Again, the jacket contains no information or photo about the author. Consents to a rare in-person interview with the *Commercial Appeal* of Memphis, his first employer, and tells the reporter, "I'm not anti-social. I object to being put on view. It would make me uncomfortable, so I don't do it." Also speaks with Gene Lyons of *Newsweek*, telling him: "Anything I set out to do degenerates pretty quickly into farce. I can't seem to control that."

1987    Mother dies.

1991    Simon & Schuster publishes *Gringos*; works not with Gottlieb as with his prior four novels but with editor Michael Korda. Critics begin to reckon with the unusual oeuvre: Roy Blount, Jr., concludes in the *Los Angeles Times*, "What do you think this book ought to win Portis? Nothing, probably. He's better than prizes," and the *Atlanta Constitution* calls him "America's infernal comic genius." Also for the first time, a first edition of a novel of his includes a short bio on the dust jacket. Publishes long travelogue about following Arkansas's Ouachita River from source to mouth, "The Forgotten River," in the *Arkansas Times*. Inspired to undertake the trip by Dee Brown, a friend, fellow Little Rock resident, and south Arkansas native, and author of *Bury My Heart at Wounded Knee* and many novels.

1992    Publishes "Nights Can Turn Cool in Viborra," a spoof of travel journalists, in *The Atlantic*, now edited by William Whitworth.

1996    Writes only play, *Delray's New Moon*, performed in April at Arkansas Repertory Theatre in Little Rock, directed by Cliff Baker. Attends a talk-back after one performance. Publishes short story "I Don't Talk Service No More" in *The Atlantic*.

1998    In an essay in *Esquire* entitled "Our Least-Known Great Novelist," Ron Rosenbaum describes Portis as the "most original, indescribable *sui generis* talent overlooked by literary culture in America," spurring Overlook Press to bring out three novels in paperback editions (and eventually to republish all his novels).

1999    Publishes autobiographical essay "Combinations of Jacksons" in *The Atlantic*.

2001    Grants rare long interview to his old *Arkansas Gazette* colleague and *New York Times* writer Roy Reed for the David and Barbara Pryor Center for Arkansas Oral and Visual History at the University of Arkansas. (David Pryor was a former governor and U.S. representative and senator from Arkansas who attended the university at the same time as Portis; upon publication of *True Grit* in 1968, Pryor, then a U.S. congressman, entered into the House record remarks praising the book.)

2003    Publishes essay "Motel Life, Lower Reaches" in the *Oxford American* magazine, based in Little Rock and edited by Marc Smirnoff.

2005    Publishes story "The Wind Bloweth Where It Listeth" in the *Oxford American*.

2010    Accepts an award for Lifetime Achievement in Southern Literature from the *Oxford American*. (Morgan Freeman is a co–headline awardee for Outstanding Contributions to Southern Culture.) Dons suit for the black-tie event at Little Rock's Capital Hotel, but leaves and returns home before the ceremony, before being located and lured back, dressed in khakis and a zipper jacket. Presented with a rooster statue (based on the magazine's colophon) and a $10,000 check. The Coen Brothers' new adaptation of *True Grit* opens over Christmas, bringing renewed attention to the novel and the author.

2011    Filmmaker Katrina Whalen produces and directs a short film based on "I Don't Talk Service No More."

2012    The Butler Center for Arkansas Studies' book division, headed by Rod Lorenzen, a former Little Rock journalist and bookseller and Portis friend, publishes *Escape Velocity: A Charles Portis Miscellany*, a collection of newspaper and magazine work, short stories, humor, and his one play, along with appreciation essays and the interview by Roy Reed. Reviews, from John Powers on National Public Radio's *Fresh Air* ("deadpan brilliance") to *Publishers Weekly* ("No other writer can so accurately be compared to greats as diverse as Twain, García Márquez, Chaucer and McCarthy"), praise the uniqueness of Portis's style and vision. Begins to show increasing signs of cognitive difficulties and is diagnosed with Alzheimer's. Enters care facility in Little Rock.

2014    Awarded in absentia the Porter Prize lifetime achievement award, presented every five years to an "Arkansas writer who has accomplished a substantial and impressive body of work," during a ceremony at the Arkansas Governor's Mansion headlined by Roy Blount, Jr., long a champion of Portis's work.

2018    The *Oxford American* sponsors a celebration of the fiftieth anniversary of the publication of *True Grit*, including a bus tour from Little Rock to Fort Smith with readings and a visit to the Fort Smith National Historic Site, screenings of both films with discussions afterward, and a variety show featuring humorists Calvin Trillin, Roy Blount, Jr., and Harrison Scott Key, and music by Arkansas native Iris DeMent.

2020    Dies in hospice care on February 17, 2020. Buried in Hamburg.

# Note on the Texts

This volume contains each of Charles Portis's five novels, published from 1966 to 1991: *Norwood* (1966), *True Grit* (1968), *Dog of the South* (1979), *Masters of Atlantis* (1985), and *Gringos* (1991). Also included here are four short stories published in magazines from 1977 to 2005, a selection of Portis's civil rights journalism, four essays, and a short memoir.

Portis's first novel, *Norwood*, was written over a period of several months in 1965 while Portis was living in a cabin at the Hickory Hills resort in northeast Arkansas. Later that year his agent at Sterling Lord, Lynn Nesbit (who would go on to represent him for the duration of his career, later at Marvin Josephson Associates, International Creative Management, and ultimately Janklow & Nesbit), sold the manuscript of *Norwood* to Robert Gottlieb at Simon & Schuster. An abridged version published in *The Saturday Evening Post*, entitled by the magazine's editors "Traveling Light," was featured in two installments, June 18 and July 2, 1966, shortly before the novel was published by Simon & Schuster on July 29. In lieu of an author photograph on the back cover there appeared a "Note from the publishers," praising Portis for "giv[ing] the reader a fresh way of perceiving, a sense of moving easily through life":

> Every once in a while a first novel comes along whose special tone of voice, unlike any other, at once opens up for the reader a new frame of reference, an additional window on the world. To discover such a voice [. . .] is one of the most intense pleasures of reading and of publishing fiction. We believe Charles Portis' first novel, *Norwood*, is such a discovery. Its tone of voice—funny, open, straightforward—is totally individual.

The movie producer Hal Wallis acquired film rights to *Norwood* in 1968, and a film version directed by Jack Haley, Jr., was released in 1970. Using the same typesetting for the text as the Simon & Schuster edition, Random House included *Norwood* in its Vintage Contemporaries series of paperbacks in 1985. As with his other four novels, *Norwood* was brought out in paperback by the Overlook Press (in this case, in 1999); Portis did not revise any of these novels for the Overlook editions. The text printed here is taken from the 1966 Simon & Schuster edition of *Norwood*.

*True Grit* was composed in 1966–67. A portion of the manuscript was sufficient to garner a contract and a $6,000 advance from Simon & Schuster early in 1967, once again under the aegis of Robert Gottlieb. Portis completed the novel by September, when he submitted his typescript to Simon & Schuster. Gottlieb, who would soon leave the publishing house, later recalled that the text of *True Grit* required scarcely any editing. As for Portis, his hopes for the novel were modest. "I thought Bob and a few people would like it," he said around the time the book was published in 1968. "But I was apprehensive about general acceptance." Response to the advance reader's copies sent out in the first half of 1968 were exceedingly favorable: the novel was named a selection of the Literary Guild and attracted favorable jacket blurbs from the likes of Roald Dahl and Walker Percy. Film rights were sold to Hal Wallis, with shooting beginning in September for a 1969 movie that was directed by Henry Hathaway and starred John Wayne and Kim Darby. (A second film adaptation, directed by Ethan Coen and Joel Coen and starring Jeff Bridges and Hailee Steinfeld, premiered in 2010.) An abbreviated version of *True Grit* was published in *The Saturday Evening Post* in 1968, spread out over the magazine's May 18, June 1, and June 15 issues. The novel was published on June 10, 1968, by Simon & Schuster in New York and by Jonathan Cape in London the following year. It soon became a best seller and has been reprinted in several paperback editions over the years, including in a mass-market 1969 Signet paperback edition and a 2012 Overlook Press edition. This volume prints the text of the 1968 Simon & Schuster edition of *True Grit*.

Portis's three subsequent novels were written while Portis was living in Little Rock, for the most part graciously refusing to grant interviews and opting not to publicize himself or his work as a writer. As noted by Jay Jennings in *Escape Velocity: A Charles Portis Miscellany* (2012), Portis "usually politely declines to speak to the press, but otherwise he seems to lead a fairly ordinary life, which includes having a beer at a local bar and visiting family and watching the Super Bowl and enjoying conversation with friends and going to the library and, the one extraordinary thing, laboring over his writing until he gets it perfect." The writing of these novels was also informed by Portis's travels, including several trips to Mexico. In June 1979 *The Dog of the South* was published by Alfred A. Knopf, with Robert Gottlieb once again his in-house editor (as he was for all of Portis's novels except *Gringos*). It was first published in paperback six years later, by Bantam in 1985; the Overlook Press published a paperback edition in 1999. The 1979 Knopf edition of *The Dog of the South* contains the text printed here. *Masters of Atlantis* was published in October 1985 by Knopf in the edition that contains the text printed here; it was first brought out in paperback by the Overlook Press in 2000. For *Gringos*, Portis returned to Simon & Schuster as his publisher, with Michael Korda as his editor; the Simon & Schuster edition, the source of the text printed here, was published in January 1991. Overlook Press published a paperback edition in 2000.

The texts of the short stories and the nonfiction writings gathered in this volume are taken from the collection *Escape Velocity: A Charles Portis Miscellany*, ed. Jay Jennings (Little Rock: Butler Center for Arkansas Studies, 2012). Listed below are the original periodical publications of these writings:

## STORIES

"Your Action Line." *The New Yorker*, December 12, 1977.
"Nights Can Turn Cool in Viborra." *The Atlantic*, December 1992.
"I Don't Talk Service No More." *The Atlantic*, May 1996.
"The Wind Bloweth Where It Listeth." *Oxford American*, Winter 2005.

## REPORTAGE

"How the Night Exploded into Terror." *New York Herald Tribune*, May 13, 1963.
"Klan Rally—Just Talk." *New York Herald Tribune*, May 13, 1963.
"A Long Day of Defiance." *New York Herald Tribune*, June 12, 1963.
"Murder in Mississippi." *New York Herald Tribune*, June 13, 1963.

## ESSAYS

"That New Sound from Nashville." *Saturday Evening Post*, February 12, 1966.
"An Auto Odyssey through Darkest Baja." *West*, February 26, 1967.
"The Forgotten River." *Arkansas Times*, September 1991.
"Motel Life, Lower Reaches." *Oxford American*, Jan.–Feb. 2003.

## MEMOIR

"Combinations of Jacksons." *The Atlantic*, May 1999.

This volume presents the texts of the original printings chosen for inclusion here, but it does not attempt to reproduce nontextual features of their typographic design. The texts are presented without change, except for the correction of typographical errors. Spelling, punctuation, and capitalization are often expressive features and are not altered, even when inconsistent or irregular. The following is a list of typographical errors corrected, cited by page and line number: 5.25, Vernel; 46.11, Cardinal's; 51.1, Norwoood, 61.1, way; 72.25–26 and .28, Lewisville; 74.15, at this; 89.17, Yeah?" How; 103.12, and them; 103.14, pocket.; 104.39, staton; 154.22, borders; 272.30, no ¶; 459.15, she'd; 549.17, belive; 841.19, and length; 934.22, other; 935.3, on big; 956.38, me."; 971.8, Garica's; 981.2, Shangrai-La.

# *Notes*

In the notes below, the reference numbers denote page and line of this volume (line counts include headings but not section breaks). No note is made for material clear from context or included in standard desk-reference books or comparable internet resources such as Merriam-Webster's online dictionary. Foreign words and phrases are translated only if not translated in the text, not evident from context, or if words are not English cognates. Quotations from Shakespeare are keyed to *The Riverside Shakespeare*, edited by G. Blakemore Evans (Boston: Houghton Mifflin, 1974). Biblical quotations are keyed to the King James Version.

## NORWOOD

3.11–12   Camp Pendleton] U.S. Marine Corps training base in San Diego County, California.

4.35   boomers] Slang for itinerant workers.

4.38–39   16-gauge Ithaca Featherweight] Pump shotgun manufactured by the Ithaca Gun Company.

5.14   ROYAL AMERICAN] Large and successful traveling carnival show performing throughout North America from the 1920s through the 1990s.

5.17   ACTS 2:38] "Then Peter said unto them, Repent, and be baptized every one of you in the name of Jesus Christ for the remission of sins, and ye shall receive the gift of the Holy Ghost."

5.22   pankled] Portis's neologism.

6.24   Porky Pig] Animated figure in Warner Bros. cartoons, whose catch-line at their conclusion is "That's all Folks."

7.3–4   hat with a Fort Worth crease] Creased in the front of the hat.

7.5   "Always Late—With Your Kisses,"] Hit country song (1951) for the singer Lefty Frizzell (1928–1975), who also wrote it.

7.6   "China Doll" . . . Slim Whitman] Song (1952) written by Gerald Cannan and Kenny Cannan, recorded in 1952 by the country singer Slim Whitman (1923–2013), known for his yodeling.

9.38–39   B & PW Club] Business and Professional Women's Club.

11.21–22  *Pageant*] Pocket-sized magazine featuring general-interest stories published from 1944 to 1977.

11.22  *Grit*] Publication founded in 1882 aimed at a rural audience, often sold by youngsters and teenagers.

11.37  "Springtime in the Rockies"] "When It's Springtime in the Rockies" (1929), song with lyrics by Mary Hale Woolsey (1899–1969) and music by Robert Sauer (1873–1944).

12.38–39  Dick Tracy] Detective hero of the eponymous comic strip created in 1931 by Chester Gould (1900–1985).

13.36–38  the Marines' talk of the Halls of Montezuma . . . siege of Chapultepec.] "From the halls of Montezuma" is the first line of the U.S. Marine Corps hymn, officially adopted in 1929; it makes reference to the Marines' involvement in the Battle of Chapultepec fought outside Mexico City, September 12–13, 1847, an American victory led by General Winfield Scott (1786–1866) in the Mexican-American War.

14.12  clear channel station] A radio station intended to serve a wide geographic area, allotted a frequency by the Federal Communications Commission protected from possible interference by stations on adjacent frequencies.

16.14  Alvin Karpis] Canadian-born American gangster (1908–1979) also known as "Old Creepy," a leader of the Barker-Kipnis gang active in the 1930s.

16.25  "Under the Double Eagle."] March (1893) by the Austrian composer Josef Franz Wagner (1856–1908).

16.38–39  Future Farmers of America] Youth organization founded in 1928, now known as the National FFA Organization.

20.9–10  like Stonewall Jackson took Nathaniel P. Banks . . . Shenandoah] The spring 1862 Valley Campaign led by the Confederate general Stonewall Jackson (1824–1863) in the Shenandoah Valley included victories against Union forces under Major General Nathaniel P. Banks (1816–1894) at the Battle of Front Royal and in and around Banks's headquarters in Winchester, Virginia, causing Banks's troops to retreat into Maryland.

26.26–27  the Durango kid . . . Charles Starrett.] From *The Durango Kid* (1940) through *The Kid from Broken Arm* (1952), Charles Starrett (1903–1986) portrayed the masked hero the Durango Kid in a prolific series of movie Westerns.

33.3  Nugrape] Brand of grape soda.

36.1–2  *Moonglow with Martin.*] Late-night jazz radio program hosted by disc jockey Dick Martin on WWL, New Orleans radio station that reached much of the United States.

36.7–8  they don't have any pianos in the Church of Christ.] Church of Christ, a Protestant denomination, forbids instrumental music during its worship services.

36.24 "Hank Snow's son is a preacher,"] After starting a career in country music in the footsteps of his father, Canadian-born singer Hank Snow (1914–1999), Jimmie Rodgers Snow (b. 1936) became a minister and led the Evangel Temple in Nashville.

41.4 Noveltoons] Series of animated theatrical shorts debuting in 1943 from Paramount Studio's Famous Pictures division.

43.21 Vita-White] Referring to fortified white bread.

43.38–39 Junior Tracy haircut] The adopted son of comic-strip hero Dick Tracy (see note 12.38–39) had his hair thickly piled on the top of his head and the sides shaved.

44.16 L & N] Louisville & Nashville Railroad.

47.38 Granger] Brand of pipe tobacco.

48.17 Tojo] The Japanese general Hideki Tojo (1884–1948), prime minister of Japan, 1941–44.

51.12 *Tarzan's New York Adventure*] Film (1942) in the Tarzan series based on the character created by the fiction writer Edgar Rice Burroughs (1875–1950).

52.14 BMT] One of several New York City subway lines operated by private companies prior to the unification of the system under the Metropolitan Transit Authority.

53.10 Mayor Wagner,"] Robert F. Wagner (1910–1991), mayor of New York City from 1954 to 1965.

59.1 *Trib*] The newspaper *New York Herald Tribune*.

59.23 Congress gaiters."] Ankle-high boots designed for comfort, with elastic inserts in the sides for flexibility.

62.15 The Cloisters] Museum located on a large campus in Upper Manhattan exhibiting art of the Middle Ages from the Metropolitan Museum's collection in reconstructed buildings from medieval Europe.

62.30 *The Prophet*] Best-selling book (1923) comprising a sequence of lyrical parables by the Lebanese-born American author Kahlil Gibran (1883–1931).

65.25–27 *Gabby . . . Dale and the Sons of the Pioneers . . . Leonard Slye*] The singer and actor Roy Rogers (b. Leonard Slye, 1911–1998) starred in many Western films released by Republic Pictures and on *The Roy Rogers Show* on NBC television, 1951–57. He was also a founding member of the country-and-western vocal ensemble Sons of the Pioneers. The singer Dale Evans (1912–2001), Rogers's third wife, performed with Rogers and with the group, including on television. Gabby Hayes (1885–1969) played one of Rogers's sidekicks.

66.26–27 Camp Lejeune] U.S. Marine Corps training base in Jacksonville, North Carolina.

67.8    Silver Star] U.S. military combat decoration.

68.7    FHA] Future Homemakers of America.

68.10–11    Webb Pierce] Honky-tonk country star (1921–1991).

68.37    Rory Calhoun] Actor (1922–1999) whose film work included roles in *How to Marry a Millionaire* (1953) and numerous Westerns.

69.30–32    Kitty Wells . . . 'Makin' Believe.'"] "Making Believe" (1955), written by Jimmy Work (1924–2018), was a hit in 1955 for the country singer Kitty Wells (1919–2012), often called "the Queen of Country."

70.6–7    Lefty Frizzell sing 'I Love You a Thousand Ways'] Hit single (1950) for Frizzell (see note 7.5) early in his career.

76.11–12    get that wall Kem-Toned] Kem-Tone interior wall paint was developed and introduced to consumers by the Sherwin-Williams Company in 1941.

76.16–17    Sydney Greenstreet] Character actor (1879–1954) whose films included *The Maltese Falcon* (1941) and *Flamingo Road* (1949).

76.35    GCT] General Classification Test, an intelligence test used by the U.S. military.

76.36    OCS] Officers' Candidate School.

77.31–35    Hank Williams? . . . Hank Thompson? . . . Hank Locklin?] Popular and influential country singer-songwriter (1923–1953); Hank Thompson (1925–2007) and Hank Locklin (1918–2009) were also country singer-songwriters.

77.37–39    "Hank Snow?" . . . *soon be gone*] From "I'm Moving On" (1950), hit song by Hank Snow (see note 36.24), also known as "The Singing Ranger" (78.6).

79.29    U.S.O.] United Service Organizations, privately funded organization providing entertainment and support for soldiers.

86.10    Dominecker] Dominique, an American breed of chicken.

86.36    Nabs crackers] Peanut butter cracker sandwiches, so called after their manufacturer, National Biscuit Company (renamed Nabisco in 1971).

87.17–18    Erskine Caldwell] Prolific writer (1903–1987) best known for *Tobacco Road* (1932), a novel about Georgia tenant farmers adapted as a film in 1941.

93.33–34    like the one of Popeye in the Texas spinach capital.] In Crystal City, Texas; the Popeye statue was erected in 1937.

94.6    "Dick Powell is from Arkansas."] Powell (1904–1963) starred in musicals before turning to film noir roles with *Murder, My Sweet* (1944), *Pitfall* (1948), and other films. Born in Mountain View, Arkansas, he moved with his family to Little Rock at the age of nine.

94.18–19  1912 . . . the tariff] In the 1912 presidential campaign issue, Republicans defended a protectionist high tariff on imported goods, whereas the Democrats advocated for a free-trade policy and the repeal of the 1909 Payne-Aldrich Tariff Act.

94.29  Snopesian] Referring to the fictional Snopes family of poor whites whose unscrupulous seizure of wealth and power is recounted in a series of short stories and novels by William Faulkner (1897–1962).

94.39  gentle Lew Ayres doctor] Ayres (1908–1996) played Dr. James Kildare, an idealistic young doctor created in 1936 by author Max Brand (pseud. Frederick Schiller Faust, 1892–1944), in a nine-film MGM series, 1938–42.

95.1  usurper Cromwell] Oliver Cromwell (1599–1658) led parliamentary forces in the English Civil War and was Lord Protector of the Commonwealth, 1653–58.

95.7  General Pat Cleburne] Irish-born Confederate officer (1828–1864) from Arkansas who commanded a brigade and later a division in the Army of Tennessee. Arkansas's Cleburne County is named for him.

98.25  *ChipOutOfTheWhiteOak*] "Chip-fell-out-a-white-oak" and similar variants have been used to describe the call of the chuck-will's-widow, a bird related to the whippoorwill.

98.25  *TedFioRito*] Birdcall transcription matching the name of Ted Fiorito (1900–1971), a touring pianist and bandleader for top radio shows in the 1930s and '40s.

99.20  "My Filipino Baby."] Song (1899) with lyrics and music by James G. Dewey.

100.19–20  Dr. Vannevar Bush] Scientist, engineer, and polymath (1890–1974), head of the wartime Office of Scientific Research and Development, which oversaw military-scientific cooperation on many new technologies, including the atomic bomb.

109.26  Canal Zone] Territory surrounding the Panama Canal administered by the United States, 1904–79.

# TRUE GRIT

113.20  Henry rifle] A lever-action repeating rifle patented in 1860 and manufactured 1862–66 by the New Haven Arms Company; the forerunner of the Winchester rifle.

114.12–13  Cumberland Presbyterian] Member of a revivalist Presbyterian sect that emerged in western Kentucky and Tennessee out of the early nineteenth-century Second Great Awakening. By the end of the nineteenth century it numbered nearly three thousand congregations nationwide. See also note 184.10.

114.14   battle of Elkhorn Tavern] Civil War battle (also known as Pea Ridge) fought in northwestern Arkansas, March 7–8, 1862, a Confederate defeat.

114.15   Lucille Biggers Langford . . . *Yell County Yesterdays.*] Fictional work and author.

114.17   Chickamauga] Civil War battle fought near Chickamauga Creek in northwestern Georgia, September 19–20, 1863, a Confederate victory, though they failed to capture nearby Chattanooga.

115.14   dragoon pistol] Small firearm developed in the eighteenth century.

115.30–33   Like Martha . . . like Mary . . . "that good part."] See Luke 10:38–42, where Jesus visits the sisters Martha and Mary, the former attending to domestic matters of hospitality and the latter listening to his teaching. The episode ends with Jesus addressing the sisters: "Martha, Martha, thou art careful and troubled about many things: But one thing is needful: and Mary hath chosen that good part, which shall not be taken away from her."

117.6   "The wicked flee when none pursueth."] See Proverbs 28:1: "The wicked flee when no man pursueth: but the righteous are bold as a lion."

118.25–26   not Oklahoma across the river then] Formed from what had been the Oklahoma and Indian Territories, Oklahoma became the forty-sixth U.S. state on November 16, 1907.

119.29   the G.A.R.] Grand Army of the Republic.

119.33–34   "Amazing Grace, How Sweet the Sound"] First line of the hymn (1779), with lyrics by the Anglican clergyman John Newton (1725–1807), usually sung to the tune "New Britain" in an arrangement (1835) by American composer William Walker (1809–1875).

120.9–11   the thief on the cross . . . place in heaven.] Jesus told one of the two thieves crucified with him that "today shalt thou be with me in paradise" (Luke 23:43).

121.4   Judge Isaac Parker watched all his hangings] Isaac C. Parker (1838–1896), federal judge for the Western District of Arkansas and Indian Territory, 1875–96, was notorious for the death sentences he handed down.

126.36   read Luke 8:26–33] The story told in this passage recounts how Jesus heals a man long possessed by demons, who then inhabit the bodies of a herd of pigs. Driven mad by the demons, the pigs drown themselves.

128.16–17   popular steamer *Alice Waddell*] A tribute to Portis's mother, whose maiden name was Waddell.

132.32–33   ridden the "hoot-owl trail"] Western slang for the actions and lifestyle of fugitives and outlaws, a variant form of "owl hoot trail."

133.24–25   when the Supreme Court started reversing him] An 1889 act of Congress permitted the U.S. Supreme Court to review capital crime cases in Parker's Western District.

133.28   Solicitor-General Whitney] Edward B. Whitney (1857–1911) served as assistant attorney general of the United States during the second Grover Cleveland administration.

135.13   Panic of '93] Economic depression beginning with debt defaults and bankruptcies in the overbuilt and overexpanded railroad sector, soon leading to hundreds of bank failures, millions of unemployed workers, and widespread social unrest.

135.16–17   Governor Alfred Smith . . . Robinson.] Al Smith (1873–1944) was four times elected governor of New York from 1918 to 1926 and was the Democratic candidate for president in 1928; his vice-presidential running mate was Joseph Taylor Robinson (1872–1937), U.S. congressman, 1903–13, and U.S. senator from Arkansas, 1913–37.

147.9   General Sterling Price] Politician and soldier (1805–1867) who was governor of Missouri, 1853–57, and as a Confederate officer led an invasion of southern Missouri in September 1864; after the defeat of his forces he fled to Indian Territory. After the war he and other former Confederates founded a short-lived colony in Mexico.

152.16   Harrison Narcotics Law] Named for its sponsor Francis Burton Harrison (1873–1957), Democratic U.S. congressman from New Jersey, the Harrison Narcotics Tax Act (1914) regulated the use of opiates and cocaine.

152.16–17   the Volstead Act] Common name for the National Prohibition Act, after its sponsor, Minnesota Republican congressman Andrew J. Volstead (1860–1947). Passed over President Wilson's veto on October 28, 1919, the act enforced the Eighteenth Amendment by making illegal the manufacture, transport, and sale (but not the possession) of intoxicating liquor.

152.17–19   Governor Smith . . . first loyalty is to his country] Smith (see note 135.16–17) was the first Roman Catholic to run for president on a major party ticket, and during the campaign some of his opponents smeared him with the accusation that his primary loyalty was to the Pope and the Church in Rome. "Wet" refers to Smith's support for the repeal of Prohibition.

153.30–31   "Wild West" show.] Any of a number of traveling Western-themed shows, such as Buffalo Bill's Wild West Show, which, managed by William F. Cody (1846–1917), successfully toured the United States and Europe from 1883 to 1916.

156.38   a mark on his face like banished Cain] The biblical Cain, oldest son of Adam and Eve, bears a mark ("lest any finding him should kill him") after he murders Abel, his brother, and is condemned by God to wander as a fugitive; see Genesis 4:1–16.

159.20   even a Campbellite] The Campbellites were an American Protestant movement named for two of its founders in 1830, the Irish-born minister Thomas Campbell (1763–1854) and his son Alexander Campbell (1788–1866); they sought a return to primitive Christianity.

161.7 the 'Bear State.'] Nickname for Arkansas.

164.7–8 R. B. Hayes is the U.S. President . . . Tilden] The contested 1876 presidential election between Democrat Samuel Tilden (1814–1886) and Republican Rutherford B. Hayes (1822–1893) was resolved via a compromise that awarded twenty disputed electoral votes to Hayes in exchange for the withdrawal of federal support for Republican state governments in the South, effectively ending Reconstruction.

167.30 Drowned like the fair Ophelia.] See Shakespeare, *Hamlet*, act IV. Her death by drowning is announced in scene vii.

168.18 Quantrill and Bloody Bill Anderson] Confederate guerilla leaders active in Missouri: William Quantrill (1837–1865) and William "Bloody Bill" Anderson (1840–1864). In 1862 Quantrill became the leader of a paramilitary group based in Jackson County, Missouri, and later as a Confederate officer led a unit of Partisan Rangers.

168.19 *particeps criminis*] Latin: party to the crime; an accomplice.

170.22–23 Sharps carbine . . . buffaloes or elephants] Sharps carbines were frequently used by cavalry in the Civil War and were popular in the nineteenth-century West, including for hunting buffalo and other large animals; they were named for Christian Sharps (1810–1874), inventor of its breech-loading mechanism and affiliated with three manufacturers bearing his name.

173.25 the Alamo with Travis."] During the Texas Revolution William Barret Travis (1809–1836) died commanding the defenders of the Alamo, a fort in what is now San Antonio that was captured on March 6, 1836, by Mexican forces under General Antonio López de Santa Anna (1794–1876).

175.10 *Beulah Land*] Hymn (1876) with lyrics by the American Methodist Edgar Page Stites (1836–1912), music by John R. Sweney (1837–1899).

182.9 brush-popper."] Cowboy who worked in brush country, also known as "brush-whacker" or "brush-thumper."

184.4 "the highways and hedges."] See Luke 14:23 in the Parable of the Banquet: "And the lord said unto the servant, Go out into the highways and hedges, and compel them to come in, that my house may be filled."

184.5 Cumberland Presbyterian."] See note 114.12–13.

184.10 not sound on Election.] The Cumberland Presbyterians accepted certain tenets of the Calvinist doctrines of predestination and divine election but broke with Presbyterian orthodoxy on several matters, for example believing that all infants who die in infancy (and not only those among the elect chosen by God) would be granted eternal salvation. More broadly they adopted a view of greater human agency in conduct and action.

184.15 Silas] Companion of St. Paul and an early Christian missionary.

185.8 Admiral Semmes] Reference to the Confederate navy officer Raphael Semmes (1809–1877), an admiral who commanded the CSS *Alabama*.

186.30 Texas waddies] At the time, derogatory slang for cowboys.

189.26 M.K. & T. Railroad] Missouri, Kansas & Texas Railway.

193.2 sofky] Sofkee, a boiled corn mixture of varying consistency from liquid to porridge.

194.15 as Dick's hatband] Vernacular southern phrase used in comparatives, not only as here with "tight" but also with "odd," "queer," etc.

197.38 Katy Flyer] The Missouri, Kansas & Texas Railway's luxury train for passenger travel.

198.13 circuit rider] Itinerant preacher.

202.28–29 Elkhorn Tavern . . . Chickamauga] See notes 114.14 and 114.17.

202.31 General Churchill's brigade."] Thomas James Churchill (1824–1905), officer in the Confederate army and later governor of Arkansas, 1881–83.

202.34 fight at Lone Jack] Civil War battle in Missouri, August 15–16, 1862, a Confederate victory.

202.35 Cole Younger] Before becoming a member of the James-Younger gang, Cole Younger (1844–1916) fought with William Quantrill's Confederate guerillas in the Civil War, including at Lone Jack.

202.36–39 Poor Cole . . . Jesse W. James . . . cashier in Northfield.] On September 7, 1876, the James-Younger gang attempted to rob First National Bank in Northfield, Minnesota. The bank's cashier, Joseph L. Heywood (1827–1876), was murdered when he refused to open the bank safe; the gang also killed an unarmed Swedish immigrant youth outside the bank. Two of the gang's members were killed in an ensuing gun battle with townspeople, and a third was slain by a posse in pursuit of the outlaws. Cole Younger and his brothers Bob (1853–1889) and Jim (1848–1902) were seriously wounded by their pursuers and were captured; they were each sentenced to life imprisonment at the Stillwell state penitentiary after pleading guilty to robbery and murder charges. Bob Younger died in prison; Cole and Jim were paroled in 1901. The outlaws Jesse James (1847–1882) and his brother Frank James (1843–1915) evaded capture.

203.8 The Red Legs] Paramilitary organization of about fifty to one hundred abolitionists who engaged in scouting and espionage operations for the Union and conducted raids in Kansas and Missouri during the Civil War.

203.21 bushwhackers."] Pro-Confederate guerilla fighters in Missouri during the Civil War.

203.25–26 Bill Anderson and Captain Quantrill] See note 168.18.

203.28   jayhawker] Originally a name for a member of antislavery Missouri militia groups in Kansas Territory during the 1850s, the term was applied during the Civil War to Union troops in Kansas and ultimately to soldiers engaged in looting and plunder.

204.7   *Daniels on Negotiable Instruments*] *A Treatise on the Law of Negotiable Instruments* (1876), legal treatise by the lawyer and politician John W. Daniel (1842–1910).

205.18   navy sixes] Pistols.

206.38–39   Jo Shelby had vouched for him to the chief marshal] The Confederate cavalry commander Joseph Orville Shelby (1830–1897) led his "Iron Brigade" in several western Civil War battles and conducted raids in Missouri and Arkansas; after the war he served as a U.S. marshal.

213.14–16   "Soldier's Joy," . . . "The Eighth of January,"] Fiddle tunes of Scottish or Irish origins.

213.34   General Kirby-Smith] Confederate Lieutenant General Edmund Kirby Smith (1824–1893).

213.40–214.1   Five Forks and Petersburg] Confederate defeats in Virginia, April 1–2, 1865.

214.3–4   Stuart or Forrest . . . Shelby and Early] Prominent Confederate generals: J.E.B. Stuart (1833–1864), cavalry commander of the Army of Northern Virginia; Nathan Bedford Forrest (1821–1877), cavalry division commander in the Army of Tennessee; Shelby, see note 206.38–39 as well as pp. 1034–35; Jubal A. Early (1816–1894), commander in the Army of Northern Virginia.

214.25–26   at Lawrence, Kansas."] On August 21, 1863, Quantrill (see note 168.18) and his Partisan Rangers attacked Lawrence, Kansas, killing more than 180 men and teenage boys.

214.34   missed Jim Lane."] James H. Lane (1814–1866), a Republican U.S. senator from Kansas, 1861–66, had commanded an irregular Kansas brigade that looted and burned the town of Osceola, Missouri, on September 23, 1861; it has been claimed that Quantrill's raid on Lawrence was taken in revenge for the Osceola raid. Lane fled the scene of the massacre in Lawrence though his property, except for a horse stable, was burned to the ground.

216.13–14   Order of the Rainbow for Girls.] Masonic youth service organization founded in 1922 by the Christian minister William Mark Sexson (1877–1953).

226.21   the "land of Nod."] Expression for sleep, based on a territory mentioned in Genesis 4:16.

232.37   Henry Starr] Prolific part-Cherokee bank robber (1873–1921), whose exploits as an outlaw and criminal were dramatized in the film *A Debtor to the Law* (1919), in which he starred, and were recounted in his autobiography *Thrilling Events* (1914), written while he was serving a prison sentence.

232.37   the Dalton brothers] Outlaws who with Bill Doolin (1858–1896) and others committed bank and train robberies and other crimes as members of the Dalton Brothers and Wild Bunch gangs. The Dalton brothers were Bob (1869–1892), Bill (1863–1894), Emmett (1871–1937), Grat (1861–1892), and Frank (1859–1887).

238.22   Barlow knife] A folding pocketknife, often with two blades.

239.6–7   Marshall Purvis] The name of one of Portis's good friends.

240.40   "brown study."] Phrase to describe someone in deep concentration, frequently immersed in sad or melancholy thoughts.

247.14   "Hydrophobia,"] Former term for rabies, so called because in its advanced stages the afflicted person can exhibit a fear of water.

253.29–31   *The stone which the builders . . . the corner.*] Luke 20:17, a quotation by Jesus of Psalms 118:22.

257.25   nesters and grangers] Homesteaders, the former term often applied to squatters.

257.27   the "Johnson County War."] Armed conflict between large ranchers and homesteaders in Wyoming, 1892.

258.14   Rock Island] Extensive rail network in Arkansas owned by the Chicago, Rock Island and Pacific Railroad.

## THE DOG OF THE SOUTH

263.8–9   .410—a boy's first gun] The .410 shotgun, or .410 bore, is one of the smallest caliber shotguns.

263.30   Hernando De Soto] Spanish conquistador (1496/97–1542) involved in the conquests of Peru and Central America. From 1539 until his death, he led an expedition through what is today the southeastern United States and encountered the Mississippi River.

264.30–31   "Around the World in 80 Days."] Title of the English translation of *Le tour du monde en quatre-vingts jours* (1874), adventure novel by the French writer Jules Verne (1828–1905).

265.14   "Wallace Fard."] Wallace D. Fard Muhammad founded the Nation of Islam, a Black separatist religious movement, in Detroit in 1931. He disappeared under mysterious circumstances in 1934. The movement was led thereafter by Elijah Muhammad (born Elijah Poole, 1897–1975) from 1934 until his death.

266.12–13   Ole Miss] The University of Mississippi.

266.15   Forrest!] See note 214.3–4.

266.17   Siege of Vicksburg] Union siege of the Confederate stronghold of Vicksburg on the Mississippi River, May 18–July 4, 1863. Under General

Ulysses S. Grant (1822–1885) the Union forces gained control of the river, a critical supply line.

266.31–32    Pemberton] Confederate General John C. Pemberton (1814–1881).

268.16–17    carbide cannon!] Or the Big-Bang Cannon: an American toy cannon that fired off carbide-produced acetylene gas.

270.12    Leavenworth] U.S. federal maximum-security penitentiary in Leavenworth, Kansas.

270.18–19    "Don Winslow of the Navy,"] Eponymous hero of syndicated comic strip, 1934–55, the basis for radio and film serials.

272.12    Hope Diamond] Renowned 45.52-carat diamond known for its distinctive deep blue color, sourced in the seventeenth century from a mine in India.

272.19    E bonds] Series E Bonds were war bonds issued by the U.S. government during World War II.

273.5    Blackstone's *Commentaries*] The four-volume *Commentaries on the Laws of England* (1765–69) by William Blackstone (1723–1780).

275.9    Hallicrafters] Chicago-based manufacturer of radio equipment, 1932–66.

275.16    Raphael Semmes] See note 185.8.

277.11    Larks] The Studebaker Lark was a compact car manufactured from 1959 to 1966.

279.19    Gator Bowl] Football stadium in Jacksonville, Florida, 1928–94, the site from 1949 to 1993 of the annual college football bowl game of the same name.

283.19    Old Charter] A brand of bourbon whiskey.

283.20–21    boot camp with Tyrone Power.] A first lieutenant in the Marine Corps, Power (1914–1958), famous as a screen actor, flew twin-engine transport aircraft in the Pacific during World War II.

287.16    Lions Club] Lions International, also known as the Lions Club, a large community-service organization founded in Chicago in 1917.

290.9    Cortez . . . burned his ships at Veracruz] Spanish conquistador Hernán Cortés (1485–1587), who led the conquest of the Aztec Empire, arrived in Mexico in 1519 with some five hundred men and burned his ships to signal there was no turning back.

290.37–38    *The Life and Glorious Times of Zach Taylor*, by Binder.] Invented biography of Zachary Taylor (1784–1850), who became a war hero among the American public for his actions during the Mexican-American War and as a Whig was elected U.S. president in 1848.

292.5  Archibald Yell] Politician (1797–1847) killed at the Battle of Buena Vista, an American victory at Buena Vista, Mexico, February 22–23, 1847. A Democrat, he had served as a U.S. representative, 1836–39 and 1845–46, and as governor of Arkansas, 1840–44. Yell County, Arkansas is named for him.

292.7–8  "A little more grape, Captain Bragg."] This remark attributed to Taylor during the Battle of Buena Vista was used as a slogan in Taylor's 1848 presidential campaign.

293.27  Airstream] Travel trailer introduced in the 1920s, known for its polished round aluminum exterior.

295.22–23  watch factories . . . Little Rock] Referring to the large Timex plants in the city, the last of which closed in 2001. At one time the company was the largest employer in Arkansas.

296.19  Simca] French automobile manufactured from 1934 to 1981.

297.35  British Honduras] Known since 1973 as Belize; it was a self-governing British colony until 1981, when it became independent.

299.1  the Flying Tigers] China-based combat force during World War II established as the American Volunteer Group in December 1941. Later known as the "Flying Tigers," it became part of the U.S. Army Air Forces in the summer of 1942.

300.2–3  "It's Magic" by Doris Day] In the film *Romance on the High Seas* (1948) Doris Day (1922–2019) sang "It's Magic," music by Jule Styne (1905–1994), lyrics by Sammy Cahn (1913–1993).

301.2  Audie Murphy] Highly decorated U.S. combat veteran (1925–1971) who later appeared in films, including *To Hell and Back* (1955) and *The Quiet American* (1957).

301.3  St. Vincent's Infirmary] Hospital in Little Rock founded in 1888.

305.9–17  Celaya . . . big battle here in 1915] The Battle of Celaya (April 6–15, 1915), fought in Celaya, Guanajuato, between the revolutionary factions of Álvaro Obregón (1880–1928) and Pancho Villa (Doroteo Arango Arámbula, 1878–1923) during the Mexican Revolution of 1910–20.

306.2  Pemex] The government-owned Mexican petroleum company.

308.17  Billy Cook] Billy Cook (1928–1952) was executed in California for the murder of Robert Dewey, one of six victims in Cook's eighteen-day crime spree in the Southwest and Mexico in 1950–51.

310.4  Albert Sidney Johnston] Confederate general (1803–1862) fatally wounded during the first day of fighting at Shiloh.

310.6  Braxton Bragg] Confederate general (1817–1876), commander of the Army of Tennessee, November 1862–December 1863.

310.6 Joseph E. Johnston] Confederate general (1807–1891), who commanded forces in Virginia, 1861–62, and the Carolinas, 1865.

310.12–13 Sugar Bowl] College football bowl game played in New Orleans.

310.36 he lost at Chickamauga."] See note 114.17.

310.38–39 Joseph E. Johnston's excuses either for not going to help Pemberton] Johnston did not send troops to aid the Confederates commanded by General John C. Pemberton (see note 266.31) in besieged Vicksburg, as Pemberton had hoped.

311.2–3 Pollard . . . account of the thing."] *The Lost Cause: A New Southern History of the War of the Confederates* (1866) by Edward A. Pollard (1832–1872).

316.3–4 Winfield Scott and the heights of Chapultepec.] See note 13.36–38.

317.4–5 asthma . . . Chihuahua dogs] In American southern lore, keeping a Chihuahua in the house was said to cure one's asthma.

318.10 "My Happiness"] Pop music standard, music (1933) by Borney Bergantine (1909–1952), with lyrics added in 1947 by Betty Peterson Blasco (1918–2006). It was first a hit for Jon and Sondra Steele in 1948 and was revived in 1959 by Connie Francis.

318.11–12 "He's the Lily of the Valley, the bright and morning star."] From the 1881 hymn "He's the Lily of the Valley" (or "I've Found a Friend in Jesus") by William Charles Fry (1837–1882).

321.11 Sells-Floto] Early twentieth-century traveling circus.

332.35 Sam Browne belt] A belt invented by the British general Samuel Browne (1824–1901) and worn by U.S. Army officers; it has a supporting strap over the right shoulder.

333.20 'Sweet Lorraine'] Jazz standard (1928), music by Cliff Burwell (1898–1976), lyrics by Mitchell Parish (1900–1993).

333.22 'Twilight Time'] Song (1944) with lyrics by Buck Ram (1907–1991) and music by the trio the Three Suns, a hit for the group in 1946 and for the Platters in 1958.

333.35 T-head pier] A pier with a perpendicular cross section at its head.

343.15–19 Emanuel Swedenborg . . . book about his experiences.] *Heaven and its Wonders and Hell from Things Heard and Seen* (1758), commonly known as *Heaven and Hell*, by the Swedish theologian, philosopher, and mystic Emanuel Swedenborg (1688–1772).

343.22 Mrs. Eddy's books?"] Mary Baker Eddy (1821–1910), founder of the Christian Science movement, wrote books including *Science and Health with Key to the Scriptures* (1875) and *Retrospection and Introspection* (1891).

346.10   Florence Nightingale] English nurse, social reformer, and public-health advocate (1820–1910).

346.13   "I'm the Light of the World."] Cf. Jesus' self-description in John 8:12.

350.17   The great Humboldt] The German naturalist and explorer Alexander von Humboldt (1769–1859).

354.2   Heckle and Jeckle cartoons] Pair of magpies created by the American animator Paul Terry (1887–1971) and featured in the "Terrytoons" film shorts (1929–68) accompanying films released by 20th Century Fox.

354.29–32   George Sanders movie . . . a Falcon picture.] George Sanders (1906–1972) was a British actor often cast in villain roles. He played a detective nicknamed "The Falcon" in *The Gay Falcon*, a 1941 B-movie, and in three of its sequels.

356.33–34   'Hawking and spitting, we lay waste our powers.'] Cf. "Getting and spending, we lay waste our powers," from the sonnet beginning "The world is too much with us" (1802–4) by the English poet William Wordsworth (1770–1850).

358.7–8   Hill-Burton funds] The Hill-Burton Act (1946), federal law authorizing funding for the building of hospitals.

358.8   Act 9 industrial bonds] Industrial revenue bonds issued in Arkansas to private companies that can be used for property, plant, and equipment costs.

360.23   Felix the Cat] A cartoon character from the silent film era, whose creation in 1919 has been credited to Pat Sullivan (1885–1933) and Otto Messmer (1892–1983).

360.25   Edgar Kennedy] American comedy actor (1890–1948) nicknamed "Slow Burn" for his portrayal of characters who slowly angered then blew up.

360.25–26   Ted Fiorito with his dance band.] See note 98.25.

365.2–3   "My Carolina Sunshine Girl"] Song by the American country singer-songwriter Jimmie Rodgers (1897–1933) recorded in 1928.

365.10   Mount of Olives?"] Where Jesus preached, stood when he wept over Jerusalem, and returned to on the night of his betrayal (Matthew 26:30).

370.5   Black Hand Society] Name used for Italian-American criminals who ran extortion rackets in the late nineteenth and early twentieth centuries.

372.19–22   the ancient Egyptians . . . and yet they worshipped a tumble-bug!"] Scarab beetles, also called dung beetles or tumblebugs, were sacred to the ancient Egyptians.

374.15   Scipio Africanus] Roman general (236/235–183 B.C.E.) who defeated Hannibal at the Battle of Zama in 202 B.C.E. during the Second Punic War.

375.19 Bland's *Exercises* and Sime's *Military Guide*] *A Treatise of Military Discipline* (1727), military drill book by Humphrey Bland (1686–1763), an Irish officer in the British army; Thomas Simes, *The Military Guide for Young Officers, containing a system of the art of war* (1772), British military manual. The claim about Washington's purported reading on war is given in Paul Leicester Ford, *The True George Washington* (1896).

379.1 pump gun, an old Model 42] The Winchester Model 42, a .410 pump-action shotgun introduced in 1933 and discontinued in 1963.

397.13 "Mockingbird Hill."] "Mockin' Bird Hill" is a song composed by the Swedish accordionist Carl Jularbo (1893–1966), with lyrics by George Vaughn Horton (1911–1988); it was covered in 1951 by both the American singer and actor Patti Page (1927–2013) and the duo Les Paul (1915–2009) and Mary Ford (1924–1977).

400.35–36 Little Lulu comic book] *Little Lulu* was an American comic strip created by Marjorie Henderson Buell (1904–1993) that ran in *The Saturday Evening Post*, 1935–44.

402.29 We were just like David and Jonathan.] David and Jonathan form a covenant in the book of Samuel. "Jonathan made a covenant with David because he loved him as himself" (1 Samuel 18:3).

403.6–8 'Tis so sweet to be remembered . . . Bill Monroe himself.] Lyrics from the 1951 solo single "'Tis sweet to be remembered" by Mac Wiseman (1925–2019). Wiseman later played in the Bluegrass Boys, the band of Bill Monroe (1911–1996), an American singer, songwriter, and mandolinist considered the father of bluegrass.

411.37 Jack Dempsey] American boxer (1895–1983), world heavyweight champion, 1919–26.

412.29 Buster Crabbe] Olympic swimmer (1908–1983) and later an actor who played roles in the *Tarzan* and *Flash Gordon* serials starting in the 1930s.

412.33 Johnny Weissmuller] Actor (1904–1984) who portrayed the title character in the Tarzan movies of the 1930s and 1940s; as a competitive athlete he had won five Olympic gold medals for swimming in the 1920s. The film referred to at 413.12–13 is *Swamp Fire* (1946).

417.10–11 the Clouds of Magellan] Or the Magellanic Clouds, two satellite galaxies of the Milky Way.

423.10 Pancho Villa] See note 305.9–17. "Dorados" ("the golden ones") at 423.16 refers to the cavalry that fought with him.

425.3–4 von Guericke's vacuum] Otto von Guericke (1602–1686) was a German physicist, engineer, and natural philosopher who invented an air pump and performed pioneering experiments with vacuums.

428.28 The three little kintons they lost their mintons . . .] From the nursery rhyme beginning "The three little kittens, they lost their mittens."

438.15 Webley revolver] Standard-issue British service revolver.

439.34 Comstock Lode] Large silver deposit discovered in 1859 on the property of Henry Comstock (1820–1870) in present-day Nevada.

459.28–29 "Goodnight, Irene"] Waltz-time love song (1933) by the blues singer, songwriter, and guitar virtuoso known as Leadbelly (Huddie William Ledbetter, 1888–1949).

460.35 Southey's *Life of Nelson*] Robert Southey (1774–1843) was an English Romantic poet whose biography of the British admiral Horatio Nelson (1758–1805) was published in 1813.

## MASTERS OF ATLANTIS

465.3 American Expeditionary Forces] The U.S. Army sent to France in World War I.

465.4 Balloon Section] During World War I there were thirty-five American balloon companies in France, used primarily for reconnaissance missions.

466.5 Hermes Trismegistus] A series of Greek writings on astrology, alchemy, and magic from the first three centuries C.E., attributed to the god Hermes Trismegistus ("thrice greatest").

466.11 Cornelius Agrippa] Heinrich Cornelius Agrippa von Nettesheim (1486–1535), German philosopher, occultist, and alchemist.

466.12 Cagliostro] Count Alessandro di Cagliostro, pseudonym of Giuseppe Balsamo (1743–1795), Italian adventurer posing as a freemason, physician, and alchemist. He engaged in many intrigues and sold amulets and purported elixirs of youth throughout Europe before being arrested by the Inquisition in 1789. He died in prison.

468.3–4 the Knights of St. John of Jerusalem] The Hospital of Saint John of Jerusalem, or Knights Hospitaller, was a Catholic military order based in Malta from 1530 to 1798. They are also called the Order of Malta and the Knights of Malta.

469.13 so-called Rosicrucians] Secretive organization dedicated to alchemy, gnosticism, and occult thought whose founding was attributed to Christian Rosenkreutz (most likely a fictional figure) in fifteenth-century Germany.

473.2 "Beautiful Dreamer."] Popular song by the American songwriter Stephen Foster (1826–1864) published posthumously in 1864.

473.26–27 like Napoleon crowned himself with it.] On December 2, 1804, Napoleon Bonaparte crowned himself Emperor of France at Notre-Dame.

477.13–14 Cicero . . . blazing machine guns?] During the 1920s Cicero, Illinois, was the home and the center of operations for the American gangster Al Capone (1899–1947) and his organized crime activities.

486.3 the bird's name, Squanto] Patuxet man also known as Tisquantum (c. 1580–c. 1622), a guide and interpreter for the Pilgrims at Plymouth.

489.18–19 Donation of Constantine] Forged document from around 750, allegedly by Emperor Constantine the Great (c. 272–337), granting possessions and privileges to the pope.

492.23 General Marshall] George C. Marshall (1880–1959), American general and U.S. Army chief of staff during World War II under Presidents Roosevelt and Truman; secretary of state, 1947–49; and secretary of defense, 1950–51.

492.31 the Blue Network] NBC Blue Network, one of two radio networks operated by the National Broadcasting Company until they were broken up into separate entities in the mid-1940s, the NBC Blue Network becoming the current American Broadcasting Network, and the NBC Red Network becoming the current NBC.

493.11–13 "Archimedes. . . . Syracuse . . . Tamerlane] The Greek philosopher and mathematician Archimedes (c. 287–c. 212 B.C.E.) was killed during the Roman soldiers' siege of Syracuse in 214–212 B.C.E. Timur, or Tamerlane (c. 1336–c. 1405), was a Turkic conqueror of India, Russia, and the Mediterranean.

493.16 "Didn't he ask Tamerlane to get out of his light?"] A faulty memory of a well-known anecdote: the Greek Cynic philosopher Diogenes (412?–323 B.C.E.), reputed to have lived in a tub, was said to have asked Alexander the Great to move out of his light while they were conversing.

494.3 stamp his feet like Rumpelstiltskin] The gnomelike man in a German fairy tale who spins straw into gold for a poor miller's daughter, in exchange for her promise to give him her firstborn when she becomes queen. After she marries the king and gives birth, Rumpelstiltskin threatens to take her child unless she can guess his name in three days. On the eve of the third day, a messenger comes across the little man preemptively celebrating around a fire and singing his name. The messenger tells the queen, and when on the third day she guesses correctly, Rumpelstiltskin stamps his leg so hard he sinks into the ground and tears his body in two.

498.20 Battle of Midway] Naval battle in the Pacific, June 3–6, 1942, a decisive U.S. victory against the Japanese.

498.30 the Naval Observatory] The U.S. Naval Observatory, scientific facility in Washington, D.C., that provides timekeeping and navigational data to the U.S. Navy.

500.14 a Brother of Luxor] Member of the Hermetic Brotherhood of Luxor, a British occult society founded in 1884.

501.3   the breadbasket of Europe?] A description customarily applied to both Ukraine and Romania.

501.29–30   the Third Murderer in *Macbeth*] A character in Shakespeare's *Macbeth* (1606) who appears in one scene (III.iii) with the First and Second Murderers, to plot the assassination of Banquo and Fleance for Macbeth.

501.30–31   the Fourth Man in Nebuchadnezzar's fiery furnace.] In Daniel 3:24–26 King Nebuchadnezzar II orders three Hebrew men, Shadrach, Meshach, and Abednego, to be burned in a furnace for refusing to bow to him. After doing so, he sees four men alive and walking in the fire, the fourth a divine being.

501.31–32   the Lost Word of Freemasonry] In Freemasonry, the yet unknown sacred key word that will unlock the mysteries of creation.

501.33   Incommunicable Word of the Cabalists, the *Verbum Ineffabile.*] The Tetragrammaton, or sacred name of four letters, is a symbol of the proper name of God (transliterated as YHWH or JHVH).

501.35–36   what the Oracle of Ammon had told Alexander.] Alexander the Great (356–323 B.C.E.) met with the Oracle of Ammon in the Libyan desert in 332 B.C.E.; what the Oracle told him has been a matter of speculation and debate.

501.40–502.1   Colonel James Churchward's *The Lost Continent of Mu* . . . *The Sacred Symbols of Mu*] In five books published from 1926 to 1935 Churchward (1851–1936), a British writer, popularized the idea of a lost continent Mu somewhere in the Pacific Ocean.

502.2   Ignatius Donnelly's *Atlantis: The Antediluvian World*] Donnelly (1831–1901) was a farmer, editor, populist author, orator, and politician who served as lieutenant governor of Minnesota, 1860–63, and as U.S. congressman, 1863–69; his book *Atlantis: The Antediluvian World* (1882) argued for the existence of the legendary island of Atlantis cited in Plato's Dialogues.

503.4–5   "the Motherland of Man"] "The Motherland of Men" was the subtitle of Churchward's *The Lost Continent of Mu* (1926).

506.4   Central Powers] The alliance that fought the Allies in World War I: Germany, Austria-Hungary, Bulgaria, and the Ottoman Empire.

506.8   Lewis guns] Light machine guns used by British and American forces in World War I.

509.20–21   motto of California . . . *Eureka. I have found it.*] Archimedes (see note 493.11–13) is said to have exclaimed "Eureka" (Greek, "I have found it") when he discovered a buoyancy principle while in a bathtub, which he applied to test the gold purity of King Hiero's (308–215 B.C.E.) crown. "Eureka" was later taken up by miners during the California gold rush and became the state motto.

509.29   a picture of Mount Whitney.] A mountain in the Sierra Nevada range, in present-day California, and the tallest mountain in the contiguous United States.

513.23   Theophilus the Monk and Dr. John Dee] Theophilus (c. 1075–1174), German monk and medieval craftsman; John Dee (1527–c. 1608), English alchemist and scholar.

534.35   came to Dacia under Trajan's Roman Eagle.] Trajan (53–117 C.E.) was a Roman emperor (98–117 C.E.) known for his expansion of the empire via campaigns into Dacia in 101–2 and 105–6 C.E.

534.38–39   if Remus had killed Romulus] Romulus and Remus are the brothers who, according to legend, were the founders of Rome. After being abandoned to die as newborn infants they were found and suckled by a she-wolf. Romulus or his followers later murdered Remus.

536.12   Colonel Churchward's book] See note 501.40–502.1.

538.18–19   The Führer at his map table.] Adolf Hitler (1889–1945) was often photographed standing over spread maps alongside his aides.

538.27–28   King Zog." . . . Zog of Albania?] Ahmed Bey Zogu (1895–1961) was the president, 1925–28, and self-proclaimed king, 1928–39, of Albania. Italy's Benito Mussolini (1883–1945) ousted him before World War II, ending their alliance.

539.14–16   Poe's tale "The Purloined Letter," . . . best hiding place] A short story by Edgar Allan Poe, first published in 1844, about a stolen letter that evades discovery despite being hidden in plain sight.

539.31   Brothers of Luxor] See note 500.14.

545.9   Pythagorean harmony] Greek philosopher Pythagoras (569–475 B.C.E.) is credited for first articulating the mathematical ratios that produce musical harmonies.

549.23   Madame Blavatsky's people] Helena Petrovna Blavatsky (1831–1891), spiritualist mystic born in Russia, came to the U.S. in 1873 and founded the Theosophical Society.

549.23–24   Aleister Crowley's grisly gang] English writer and occultist (1875–1947) who died in poverty and obscurity but became a cult figure after his death.

549.30–31   sons of Hiram] Name of a Masonic lodge.

559.7–8   the GI Bill] Officially called the Servicemen's Readjustment Act (1944), the law guaranteed veterans access to higher education and provided tuition funding.

563.6   Joplin tourist court] A motel in Joplin, Missouri.

567.20   WPA] The Works Progress Administration, a federal agency created under the Emergency Relief Appropriation Act of 1935 to provide public jobs for the unemployed; it was severely cut back in 1937 and 1939 and dissolved in 1943.

570.22   Robert Fludd, the great Rosicrucian] Robert Fludd (1574–1637) was a British physician and occultist. For Rosicrucian, see note 469.13.

572.11   Dresden doll] Also known as a Parian doll, a porcelain doll manufactured in Dresden, Germany, in the mid-1800s.

576.1–2   Hermes Trismegistus] See note 466.5.

595.24   Cunard liner] Cunard Line is a British cruise line dating back to 1840.

598.5   the Continental Triangle] The triangle formed by Burnett, IN, La Loma, TX, and Naples, FL.

608.22   Zeno tells us that motion is impossible] Zeno of Elea (c. 495–c. 430 B.C.E.) was a Greek philosopher known for his paradoxes, including his paradoxes of motion, which logically argue against the possibility of motion.

610.33–34   more uniforms than Hermann Göring] Hermann Göring (1893–1946), Nazi Party leader, was known for his flamboyant attire.

612.18   Chang and Eng] Siam-born Chinese twins (1811–1874) joined at the waist who were exhibited as curiosities in America and later became naturalized American citizens.

628.37   Golden Gloves] Annual amateur boxing competition.

650.6   Devil's Island] Penal colony in French Guiana.

652.5–6   the Andrews Sisters] A famed musical trio composed of three sisters, Patty Andrews (1918–2013), Maxene Andrews (1916–1995), and Laverne Andrews (1911–1967).

678.17   indestructible Herculon] Olefin, a kind of textile material known by its brand name Herculon.

## GRINGOS

683.25   *anticipo*] advance.

683.36   "Ah Kin"] Mayan: He of the Sun. Name of Mayan sun god and religious order.

684.19   old President Díaz] Porfirio Díaz (1830–1915) was a Mexican general and dictator who served as Mexico's president, 1877–80 and 1884–1911.

684.39   Houdini] Harry Houdini (1874–1926), magician and escape artist.

686.6–8  Lord's Prayer, the King James Version . . . trespasses.] The translators of the King James Version rendered the Greek work "ὀφειλήματα" in the Lord's Prayer at Matthew 6:12 as "debts"; the 1526 Tyndale Bible reads "trespasses," as do all editions of the Book of Common Prayer (1549), used in the Anglican Church.

687.9  Dionne quintuplets] Annette, Cécile, Yvonne, Marie, and Émilie were born on May 28, 1934, in Callander, Ontario, and were the subject of intense public interest. All survived to adulthood.

688.28  *copita*] Small glass.

689.11  *Yamato*] The *Yamato*-class battleships were two battleships, *Yamato* and *Musashi*, built for the Imperial Japanese Navy during World War II.

691.7  *zopilote*] Vulture.

693.19  *chismosa*] Gossip, bigmouth.

694.17–18  *chaneques* (chanekkies)] Small, spritelike creatures of Mexican folklore.

695.19  Dust Bowl] Term first used in 1935 for drought-stricken regions of Texas, Oklahoma, Kansas, and Colorado that were suffering from severe soil erosion.

696.7  *El Mago*] The Magician.

701.37  Ocosingo cheese] Cow's milk cheese from Chiapas.

702.17  Palenque] Ancient Mayan city in the state of Chiapas, now an archaeological site and national park.

703.1  von Däniken] Erich Anton Paul von Däniken (b. 1935), Swiss author and forefather of the theory of "ancient astronauts," which posits that extraterrestrials were involved in early human civilization.

705.18  *Las mil y una.*"] A thousand and one.

708.20  *selva*] Woods.

709.1  Copán ruin] Ancient Mayan ruin located in present-day western Honduras.

710.20  *finca*] country house or estate.

710.22–23  Bonampák, of the famous wall paintings] Bonampák, the modern Mayan word for "painted walls," is also the name of the site in Chiapas, Mexico, where ancient murals can be found inside one of the structures, known as Temple of the Murals.

717.1–2  Schliemann at Hissarlik, or Lord Carnarvon at King Tut's tomb.] Johann Ludwig Heinrich Julius Schliemann (1822–1890) was a German archaeologist who claimed in the 1870s to have found the site of Troy in the ancient city of Hissarlik, in present-day Turkey. George Edward Stanhope Molyneux Herbert (1866–1923), 5th Earl of Carnarvon, was a British Egyptologist and patron of the archaeologist Howard Carter (1874–1939), who discovered the tomb of the fourteenth-century B.C.E. Egyptian ruler Tutankhamen in 1922.

721.11   *chiclero*] A harvester of natural gum in the ancient Mayan tradition.

723.8   *puros*] "Pure," the term for a cigar whose tobacco is made entirely in one country.

725.39   Chichén Itzá."] An ancient Mayan city in the Yucatán Peninsula of Mexico.

726.37   *pagano*] Pagan, heathen.

731.18   *pastelitos*] Little pastries.

731.22   *pan dulce*] Sweet bread, pastry.

732.1   M-16] American assault rifle used by the U.S. military.

735.26   like Harry Truman at the piano] Harry S. Truman (1884–1972) was known to play the piano, and sometimes did so publicly, during his presidency.

737.1–2   the kind James Cagney used to wear in prison.] James Cagney (1899–1986) was cast in criminal roles; in *White Heat* (1949) he played an imprisoned gangster.

737.4   Pork Chop Hill?] A hill that, though lacking strategic utility, was the site of fighting between American and Chinese forces in April and July 1953 during the Korean War.

737.4–5   Leyte Gulf?] A series of air, submarine, and night and day surface engagements fought around northern and central Philippine islands, October 23–27, 1944, an American victory against the Japanese.

737.5   Chesty Puller?] Colonel Lewis B. "Chesty" Puller (1898–1971), highly decorated U.S. Marine Corps officer who fought in the Pacific theater during World War II as well as in the Korean War.

737.5–6   Fort Benning?] U.S. Army post near Columbia, Georgia.

738.29–30   Quetzalcoatl or Kukulcán] Names for a feathered serpent god in Mexican mythology. In Toltec and Aztec mythology, Quetzalcoatl is the feathered serpent god. In Yucatec Mayan mythology, the feathered serpent god is Kukulcán. Both recognize the feathered serpent god as the bringer of rain and wind.

738.38   Fernando Valenzuela of the Los Angeles Dodgers.] Fernando Valenzuela Anguamea (b. 1960), Mexican baseball pitcher who spent most of his Major League career with the Los Angeles Dodgers.

739.2   "the dancing men" at Monte Alban] "Los Danzantes" is a collection of more than three hundred stone glyphs at Monte Albán, an archaeological site in the Valley of Oaxaca, Mexico. The reliefs depict men with loose, fluid figures.

739.3–4   "elephant" carving at Copán.] A stone carving called "Stela B" in the ancient Mayan city of Copán (see note 709.1) features what some have described as two elephants.

742.24–25   Eric Thompson, the great Mayanist] J. Eric S. Thompson (1898–1975), British ethnographer of Mayan culture whose study of early Mayan glyphs revealed that they contained both historical and religious records.

742.32   Al Jolson singing "April Showers."] "April Showers" is a 1921 song with music by American composer Louis "Lou" Silvers (1889–1954) and lyrics by American songwriter George Gard "Buddy" DeSylva (1895–1950). It was performed and popularized in the 1921 Broadway musical *Bombo* by American singer and actor Al Jolson (1886–1950).

742.35   Uxmal style] Uxmal is an ancient Mayan city in Yucatán, Mexico.

745.11   Gem blades] Best-selling shaving razor during the early 1900s.

746.4–5   glyph writing and the bar-and-dot numeral system and the Long Count calendar] The Mayans developed two number systems: the system used by common people, consisting of combinations of three symbols, a dot representing the quantity 1, a horizontal line representing 5, and a shell-like symbol representing 0; and the system used by priests, known as the Long Count calendar, wherein days of the year were represented by the heads of corresponding gods.

747.6   those travel books of John Stephens."] American explorer John Lloyd Stephens (1805–1852) wrote popular accounts of his travels in Central America, Chiapas, and Yucatán, including *Incidents of Travel in Yucatán* (1843).

747.8   Mauser] Mauser rifles were German bolt-action rifles designed by Peter Paul Mauser (1838–1914) in the late nineteenth and early twentieth centuries.

749.17   Carnegie Medal for heroism] The Carnegie Hero Fund awards the Carnegie Medal to Americans or Canadians who risk their lives saving or attempting to save others.

754.31   the old *gachupín*] A Spaniard living in the Americas.

754.32   Ron Castillo] Bacardi's low-cost rum brand.

755.14   *tontería*] nuisance, foolishness, silly joke.

755.32   The *Alzamiento*."] The Rising.

755.34   "*Habladores*,"] Talkers, chatty people.

755.35   *Cruzanos*] Short for Veracruzanos, people from Veracruz.

761.3–6   Harry James . . . "Ciribiribin," . . . Betty Grable] Harry Haag James (1916–1983) was an American jazz trumpet player and bandleader. "Ciribiribin" is a ballad from the Italian Piedmont region composed by

Alberto Pestalozza (1851–1934) with lyrics by Carlo Tiochet (1863–1912). Betty Grable (1916–1973), American actor, dancer, and singer, most active in the 1940s.

763.11–12  Samson in the Bible? . . . his long hair."] Samson was a biblical Israelite judge and warrior. In Judges 16 he tells Delilah that shaving his head will diminish his great strength. One night, while he is sleeping on her lap, Delilah, in exchange for payment from the Philistines, orders her servant to cut off his hair, which enables the Philistines to capture and blind him.

763.13–15  Absalom . . . a great oak."] The biblical Absalom, son of David, rebelled against his father and was killed in battle when his hair caught in an oak under which he was riding his mule, leaving him suspended in the air (2 Samuel 18:9–33).

763.16  Samuel?] "And the child Samuel grew on, and was in favor both with the LORD, and also with men" (1 Samuel 2:26).

763.19  "Nebuchadnezzar] King Nebuchadnezzar II. See note 501.30–31.

768.39  a gringo *bulla*] A noisy gringo.

770.3–4  L. Ron Hubbard] Writer and founder of the Church of Scientology (1911–1986).

778.10  *galleta*] Cookie.

778.35  *paleta* sticks] Popsicle sticks.

783.29  *mierda seca*] Dry shit.

787.33  the Three Stooges] Vaudeville and film comedy troupe known for their slapstick humor.

788.24–26  the Labná ruins] Labná is a Mayan archaeological site in Yucatán, Mexico, linked to the city of Uxmal by the Puuc Trail.

794.5  *arco*] Bow.

805.17  *chamacos*] Kids.

810.5  *equipaje*] Baggage, equipment.

810.8  *¡Escopetas blancas!*] "White shotguns!" literally; idiomatically, amateur hunters.

810.24–25  the Colossus of the North] Epithet for the United States registering criticism of its imperial ambitions and projection of its power, particularly in the Western Hemisphere. Here applied to Mexico itself.

810.30  BAR] The American-made Browning automatic rifle, fed from a twenty-round magazine and weighing nineteen pounds.

812.24  P for Protestant that was stamped on their dog tags.] U.S. military dog tags were marked "C" for Roman Catholics, "J" for Jews, and "P" for Protestants, with the latter designation also applied to Mormons.

812.35   Lost Tribes of Israel theme] In ancient Jewish history, the Lost Tribes of Israel were the ten (of twelve) tribes of northern Israel that fell to Assyria in 722 B.C.E.

813.12   Laman of the Lamanites] In the Book of Mormon, the Lamanites are descendants and/or followers of Laman, the firstborn son of the prophet Lehi, who migrated from Jerusalem to America around 600 B.C.E.

814.12   Thompson correlation] In his 1927 paper "A Correlation of the Mayan and European Calendars," J. Eric S. Thompson (see note 742.25) proposed a new method of correlating dates between the Mayan and Gregorian calendars that aimed to reconcile existing sets of historical and astronomical evidence. A correlation attempts to identify the exact number of days by which the two calendars are offset.

814.24–27   Spinden   correlation . . . Wietzal   correlation . . . Escalona Ramos correlation] American anthropologist Herbert Spinden's (1879–1967) 1924 correlation, as well as those made in 1947 by Robert Boland Weitzel and by the Mexican archaeologist Alberto Escalona Ramos (1908–1960) in 1940.

815.14–15   the Mongolian Spot at the base of his spine?] A Mongolian spot is a bluish gray birthmark, typically found at the base of the spine in Asian and Indigenous American infants.

819.30   *ramada*] Shelter made of branches.

819.40   *jitomates*—] Red tomatoes.

820.2   *gorristas*] Deadbeats.

820.13   *forestal* and not young *viciosos*?] *Forestal*: forestry. *Viciosos*: brutes.

824.1   that petrified couple they found at Herculaneum.] Herculaneum was an ancient city buried with the nearby city of Pompeii by the eruption of Mount Vesuvius in Italy in 79 C.E. Among the petrified remains of bodies unearthed in archaeological excavations are those of a couple that appear to be embracing.

825.40   Morley, Thompson, Stirling, Caso, Ruz Lhullier] Sylvanus Griswold Morley (1883–1948), American archaeologist and scholar of Mayan hiero-glyphs. Thompson, see note 742.24–25. Alfonso Caso y Andrade (1896–1970), Mexican archaeologist who excavated a tomb at Monte Alban (see 739.1). Alberto Ruz Lhuillier (1906–1979), Mexican archaeologist who led excavations at Palenque (see 702.17).

826.24–25   Valley of the Kings . . . the pharaohs be damned.] Archaeolog-ical site in Egypt along the Nile River where there are sixty-two known pha-raohs' tombs.

828.26–27   Camp Pendleton] See note 3.11–12.

828.35–36   "Oh Susannah,"] "Oh! Susanna" (1848), song by Stephen Foster (1826–1864).

830.8–10 *"Qué va. . . . Poco probable.*] No way. . . . Unlikely.

830.13 *paseo."*] Walk.

831.9 the last hours of Gomorrah] God destroyed the wicked cities of Sodom and Gomorrah in Genesis 19.

835.3 the Prince of Asturias] Title given to the male heir to the throne of Spain.

836.39–40 Bremerton Navy Yard] U.S. naval base in Bremerton, Washington, across Puget Sound from Seattle.

842.14 *palo blanco* trees.] "White stick" trees: common name of an evergreen tree species native to Mexico that have white bark.

842.25 the long-nosed rain god] Chaac, or Chac, is the Mayan rain deity, depicted with fangs and a long nose.

844.12 the *Balam*] Mayan word for jaguar, which can also be used to refer to a priest or shaman.

845.34–35 *Balam Akab*] Or Balam Acab, Mayan demigod.

847.15 *cabrón*] Idiot.

847.20 *golpes de gracia*] Fatal blows.

847.23 *fregado*] Colloquial: mess.

848.18 *pagano?"*] Heathen, pagan.

859.21 *gitanos*] Roma.

859.32 John Knox] Scottish religious reformer (c. 1514–1572), founder of the Presbyterian Church of Scotland.

864.20 "The Orange Blossom Special"] Classic fiddle tune (1938) by Ervin T. Rouse (1917–1981) whose title refers to a deluxe train running from New York City to Miami.

865.38 *der schatzgraber*] German, *der Schatzgräber:* treasure hunter.

869.38 *platillos voladores*] UFOs.

875.18–20 ancient Indian ritual, on *Hanub Ku* or *Itzam*, the great lizard god, on the *Chacs* and the *bacabs* and the red goddess.] Hanub Ku ("One-God") is a Mayan creator deity. Itzamná ("Iguana House"), the ruler of heaven, day, and night, was his son. For Chacs, see note 842.25. Bacab, or the Bacabs, are any of four gods who are thought to be brothers, each corresponding to a cardinal point from which, according to a creation myth, they held up the sky; each cardinal point also corresponds to a color (east, red; north, white; west, black; south, yellow) that was important to Mayan rituals and the calendar. Ixchel, Ix Chel, or sometimes Chak Chel, the latter meaning "Great Rainbow" or "Red Rainbow," is the Mayan moon goddess and patron deity of fertility, childbirth, and weaving; she is also the wife of Itzamná and the Bacabs are believed to be their sons.

876.6 *de prisa*] Fast; quickly.

887.23 "Because God Made Me Thine,"] "Because" (1902), music by Guy d'Hardelot (1858–1936), lyrics in English by Edward Teschemacher (1876–1940). The song originally had different French lyrics. "Because God made thee mine" is the first line of the Teschemacher third verse.

890.18 *máquina*] Machine.

897.38–39 "My Darling Clementine,"] Western folk ballad often attributed to Percy Montross.

## COLLECTED STORIES

905.27 Fokker] Dutch-based airplane manufacturer.

913.32 John Ruskin handbooks] The English art and architecture critic John Ruskin (1819–1900) elaborated on design and building principles in *The Seven Lamps of Architecture* (1849) and other works.

917.20 Okinawa in 1945] American invasion of the Pacific island of Okinawa, April–June 1945.

919.1 *The Wind Bloweth Where It Listeth*] From John 3:8: "The wind bloweth where it listeth, and thou hearest the sound thereof, but canst not tell whence it cometh, and whither it goeth: so is every one that is born of the Spirit."

921.3–4 *Macbeth:* "And, like a rat without a tail, I'll do, I'll do, and I'll do."] Macbeth, I.iii.9–10.

922.1 Sousa marches] The American bandmaster and composer John Philip Sousa (1854–1932), whose compositions include the march "Stars and Stripes Forever" (1896), was known as "The March King."

## REPORTAGE, ESSAYS, & MEMOIR

932.13–14 "We Shall Overcome,"] Protest folk song often sung at civil rights demonstrations.

936.15–16 in 1961—when Berlin was the crisis] The Cold War conflict over West Berlin between the Soviet Union on one side and the United States and its Western allies on the other, along with the steady migration of East Germans to the West via West Berlin, led to the construction of the Berlin Wall by the German Democratic Republic in August 1961.

942.32 live on."] Byron de la Beckwith (1920–2001), an avowed white supremacist, was arrested in Greenwood, Mississippi, on June 22, 1963, and charged with the murder of Medgar Evers. Two trials in 1964 ended in mistrials when all-white juries voted 7–5 and 8–4 for his acquittal. The case was reopened in 1990, and a third trial before a racially mixed jury in 1994 resulted in his conviction. Beckwith died in prison.

944.21–22  unlikely people—Al Hirt, Ann-Margret]  Trumpeter Al Hirt (1922–1999), nicknamed "Jumbo," a popular recording artist and host of the CBS television variety show *Fanfare* (1965); Swedish-born actor, singer, dancer, and sex symbol Ann-Margret (Ann-Margret Olssen, b. 1941).

944.33–34  poets like . . . Ernest Tubb]  Tubb (1914–1984) was a country singer-songwriter.

944.36–38  Eddy Arnold . . . Democratic nominee]  Arnold (1918–2008), an enormously successful country singer and pioneer of the Nashville sound, ultimately declined to run for political office in Tennessee.

945.31  "If I had the wings of an angel . . ."]  From "The Prisoner's Song" (1924) by the country singer Vernon Dalhart (pseud. Marion Try Slaughter, 1883–1948).

946.4–7  *I'm goin' to town, honey . . . John B. Stetson hat. . . .*]  From Rodgers's "Mule Skinner Blues" (1930), the eighth in Rodgers's "Blue Yodel" series of songs.

946.25–27  *Smoke on the Water* and *Pistol Packin' Mama* and *Detour* and *There's a Star-Spangled Banner Wavin' Somewhere.*]  "Smoke on the Water" (1943), song written by Zeke Clements (1911–1994) and Earl Nunn (1908–1990), a hit for Red Foley (1944) and Bob Wills and His Texas Playboys (1945); "Pistol Packin' Mama" (1942), song written by Al Dexter (1905–1984) and recorded in 1943 by Bing Crosby and the Andrews Sisters; "Detour (There's a Muddy Road Ahead)" (1945), song written by Paul Westmoreland (1916–2005), a hit for Patti Page among others; "There's a Star-Spangled Banner Waving Somewhere" (1942), song written by Paul Roberts (pseud. Paul Metivier, 1915–2007) and Shelby Darnell (pseud. Bob Miller, 1895–1955), first a hit for Elton Britt, among other popular recordings.

951.9  his protégés, Flatt and Scruggs]  The bluegrass musicians Lester Flatt (1949–1979) and Earl Scruggs (1924–2012), who were members of Bill Monroe's band and later frequently collaborated with each other; Flatt played guitar and mandolin, Scruggs banjo. They starred in the half-hour syndicated television variety show *Flatt and Scruggs Grand Ole Opry*, 1955–69.

952.29–34  *I see you going down the street in your big Cadillac . . . wacka-do.*]  From Miller's "Do-Whacka-Do" (1965).

953.1  Western suits, designed by Nudie of Hollywood]  The tailor and designer Nudie Cohn (1902–1984) created rhinestone-studded suits and other flashy western-themed clothes for celebrities including Roy Rogers and Elvis Presley.

953.5–8  Faron Young . . . former movie lawman]  Young (1932–1996), a country singer and songwriter, also had an acting career whose roles included that of the sheriff's deputy in *Hidden Guns* (1955).

953.29–30   so have the Wilburn Brothers and Leroy Van Dyke] The half-hour syndicated television variety show *The Wilburn Brothers Show* was hosted by the singers Doyle Wilburn (1930–1982) and Teddy Wilburn (1931–2003); the singer and guitarist Leroy Van Dyke (b. 1929) was a cast member on the hour-long ABC variety show first called *Ozark Jubilee*, 1953–63.

953.30–31   Carl Smith has a network show on Canadian television.] *Carl Smith's Country Music Hall*, a program also broadcast in syndication in the United States, hosted by the country singer Carl Smith (1927–2010).

953.31–32   Porter Wagoner's show] *The Porter Wagoner Show*, long-running half-hour syndicated television musical variety show, 1961–81, hosted by the singer Porter Wagoner (1927–2007).

953.35   Jimmy Dean's ABC network audience.] The variety show *The Jimmy Dean Show*, 1963–66, was hosted by the country singer and musician Jimmy Dean (1928–2010) and his sidekick puppet Rowlf the Dog, one of the Muppets created and performed by Jim Henson (1936–1990).

955.26   author Terry Southern] Satirical novelist, screenwriter, and essayist (1924–1995) whose novels include *Candy* (1958) and *The Magic Christian* (1959).

955.31–32   now he's Fats Domino, now T. Texas Tyler—] Pioneering rock-and-roll singer, songwriter, and pianist Fats Domino (1928–2017); Arkansas-born country singer T. Texas Tyler (1916–1972).

955.38   *Push My Love Button*] The song (1966) was recorded not by Ann-Margret but by the singer Sandy Layne.

956.33   Dizzy Dean] Hall of Fame baseball pitcher (1910–1974) for the St. Louis Cardinals, 1932–37, and the Chicago Cubs, 1938–41.

957.4–5   Hank Snow and Stringbean and Wilma Lee and Stony.] Snow, see note 36.24. Stringbean, stage name of David Akeman (1915–1975). The country and bluegrass singer Wilma Lee Cooper (1921–2011) and her husband Stoney Cooper (1918–1977) were members of the Grand Ole Opry and a popular act for several decades.

957.11   Kitty Wells cookbooks] Starting with the *Kitty Wells Country Cook Book* (1964), Wells (see note 69.30–32) wrote a series of popular cookbooks.

958.14–17   *Cigareetes and whusky . . . They'll drive you insane. . . .*] From "Cigarettes, Whiskey, and Wild, Wild Women" (1947), written by Tim Spencer (1908–1974) and first recorded by his group Sons of the Pioneers.

963.22–23   "Why don't you fly down like Eisenhower?" . . . people lost down there] In the years after his presidency Dwight D. Eisenhower (1890–1969) visited Baja California and stayed at Rancho Las Cruces, a private hunting and fishing resort on the gulf side. Two teenagers from Southern California, the eighteen-year-old Steven Bunch and the nineteen-year-old

Harold Dean Slaght, disappeared on a trip to Baja California in July 1964; their abandoned pickup truck was found eight months later but their bodies were never found.

963.25–26 works of such veteran Baja rats as Erle Stanley Gardner and Joseph Wood Krutch.] The creator of the popular Perry Mason crime novels, Erle Stanley Gardner (1889–1970), wrote seven books about Baja California. The works of American naturalist Joseph Wood Krutch include *The Forgotten Peninsula: A Naturalist in Baja California* (1961) and *Baja California and the Geography of Hope* (1967).

964.38 Gadsden Purchase] Territory purchased from Mexico by the United States in 1853, comprising parts of Arizona and New Mexico.

968.3 *"El camino a San Agustin es malo?"*] "The road to San Agustin is bad?"

970.16 *puntas*] Points.

970.30 *pescadores*] Fishermen.

974.21 Lopez Mateos] Adolfo López Mateos (1910–1969), president of Mexico, 1958–64.

975.14 Afrika Korps cap] Long-visored cap worn by German soldiers in North Africa under the command of Field Marshal Erwin Rommel (1891–1944) during World War II.

977.6–8 Sherlock Holmes . . . the Giant Rat of Sumatra . . . not ready for it.)] In "The Adventure of the Sussex Vampire" (1924), a story by Arthur Conan Doyle (1859–1930), the detective Holmes mentions in passing a case involving an enormous rat, "a story for which the world is not yet prepared."

977.29 *I Left My Head in San Ignacio.*] Cf. the title of the popular song "I Left My Heart in San Francisco" (1953), music by George Cory (1920–1978), lyrics by Douglass Cross (1920–1975), and associated with the singer Tony Bennett (b. 1925), who recorded the song in 1962.

981.2 Shangri-La] In *Lost Horizon* (1933), novel by the English writer James Hilton (1900–1954), Shangri-La is an earthly paradise deep in the Himalayas.

982.21 Truman firing MacArthur.] On April 11, 1951, President Truman relieved General Douglas MacArthur (1880–1964) of his command of U.S. forces in Korea for repeated insubordination. MacArthur had called for the bombing of China and had ordered U.S. troops past the thirty-eighth parallel, the rough boundary separating North from South Korea, thus interfering with attempts to negotiate a cease-fire in the conflict.

982.22 Nimitz] Chester W. Nimitz (1885–1966), commander of the Pacific Fleet during World War II.

983.9   Warren Report] The 888-page report investigating the assassination of President John F. Kennedy, the work of a seven-member commission headed by the Supreme Court's chief justice Earl Warren (1891–1974).

985.15   the Dalton Brothers] See note 232.37.

990.38   "rolling impetuosity" as Dunbar would put it] In the journal of the 1804–5 Ouachita expedition by the Scottish-born explorer William Dunbar (1749–1810), from which the subsequent citations by Dunbar are also taken.

1001.19–20   Lew Ayres, the actor.] See note 94.39.

1006.40–1007.2   two poems . . . Pike and a George P. Smoote.] "Annie" (1844), by the writer, lawyer, and Confederate general Albert Pike (1809–1891); "The Ouachita," collected in *The Mississippi, and Other Songs* (1890) by the lawyer George Parker Smoote (1828–1891).

1007.10   Tonti in 1690] Henri de Tonti (c. 1649–1702), Italian explorer in the service of the French, who founded a trading post in Arkansas.

1009.23   Clyde Barrow] Bank robber and murderer (1909–1934) who with his partner Bonnie Parker (1910–1934) terrorized the Midwest during the Depression. They were gunned down in a police ambush in 1934.

1016.4   Pancho Villa's 1916 raid across the border.] A raid by the Mexican revolutionary Pancho Villa in Columbus, New Mexico, on March 9, 1916.

1021.8–13   Fats Domino singing . . . shame.] From Fats Domino's 1955 hit "Ain't That a Shame," which he cowrote with Dave Bartholomew (1918–2019).

1025.20   Lugers] German semiautomatic pistols.

1026.10   Slough of Despond] Bog in which Christian, the protagonist of John Bunyan's *The Pilgrim's Progress* (1678), sinks under the weight of his sins.

1027.16–17   Miranda] The U.S. Supreme Court decision *Miranda v. Arizona* (1966), which determined constitutional standards for police conduct toward suspects, including the right to an attorney and the right not to incriminate themselves.

1028.3–6   *There'll be smoke on the water . . . the sea*] From "Smoke on the Water" (see note 946.25–27).

1028.14–15   just as we had taken care of the Spanish fleet at Manila Bay in 1898] The Battle of Manila Bay (May 1, 1898) was fought in the Philippines during the Spanish-American War. Commodore George Dewey (1837–1917) methodically bombarded the Spanish line of ten vessels, destroying all of them by twelve noon; no American ships were damaged.

1029.26–27   Boeing P-26 and our Brewster Buffalo] Boeing's P-26 Peashooters, monoplane fighters with an open cockpit, in service 1934–41; F2A Buffalo, monoplane manufactured 1938–41 by the Brewster Aeronautical Corporation for the U.S. Navy and several other countries' militaries.

1030.14–15    I think he wrote] Portis has knowingly added "of Jacksons" to his citation of this passage from Lincoln's proclamation of April 15, 1861.

1031.31    "India-rubber"] The milky white latex of the *Ficus elastica*, an ornamental houseplant also known as the India rubber tree, was once used to make rubber.

1032.14–15    Wild Bill Hickok, a Union scout] James Butler Hickok (1837–1876), frontier gunfighter, scout, soldier, and marshal whose exploits became legendary and were popularized in dime novels and comic books.

1033.7–8    military historian Edwin C. Bearss writes, "with a savagery unheard of in the East."] In his *Steele's Retreat from Camden and the Battle of Jenkins' Ferry* (1995).

1034.8–9    Quantrill's bushwhackers] See note 168.18.

1034.9    Frank James] See note 202.36–39.

1034.10–11    the Battle of Prairie Grove, Arkansas.] Battle in northwest Arkansas on December 7–8, 1862, an unsuccessful Confederate attack on Union forces.

1034.37–1035.1    another lost cause . . . Hapsburg Emperor of Mexico—] In April 1862 a French invasion force landed in Mexico. Despite a major defeat at Puebla on May 5, 1862, the French were able, with the help of reinforcements, to occupy Mexico City on June 10, 1863, and installed the Habsburg archduke Ferdinand Maximilian (1832–1867) as Emperor Maximilian I the following year. After Mexican partisans led by Benito Juárez (1806–1872) took back the country, Maximilian was executed by firing squad on June 19, 1867.

1035.23    Northfield bank raid] See note 202.36–39.

1036.22    border ruffians] Term for proslavery Missouri bushwhackers and outlaws.

1037.8    Battle of Corinth] Civil War battle in Mississippi, October 3–4, 1862, a Union victory.

1037.25    the Battle of Atlanta] Civil War battle, July 22, 1864, a Union victory.

1038.18    poll tax] A fixed tax levied on every person within a jurisdiction. In the South after Reconstruction, the payment of a poll tax was often made a requirement for voting as a means of disfranchising African Americans and, in some cases, poor whites.

1039.40–1040.1    a Spike Jones comedy short, a Boston Blackie feature] Spike Jones (1911–1965), musician known for the comic and musically adventurous recordings he made with his group The City Slickers as well as appearances in movies; Boston Blackie was a fictional detective played by Chester Morris (1901–1970) in numerous films of the 1940s.

1044.2–3   who went ashore at Tarawa and Anzio] World War II troop landings. Tarawa, an atoll in the Gilbert Islands in the Pacific, was the site of a battle, November 20–23, 1943. Anglo-American and German forces fought each other on the beachhead between the towns of Anzio and Nettuno, thirty miles southwest of Rome, January 22–May 23, 1944.

1044.8–9   The Ghost of Christmas Yet to Come] Fictional character in Charles Dickens's novella *A Christmas Carol in Prose, Being a Ghost-Story of Christmas* (1843).

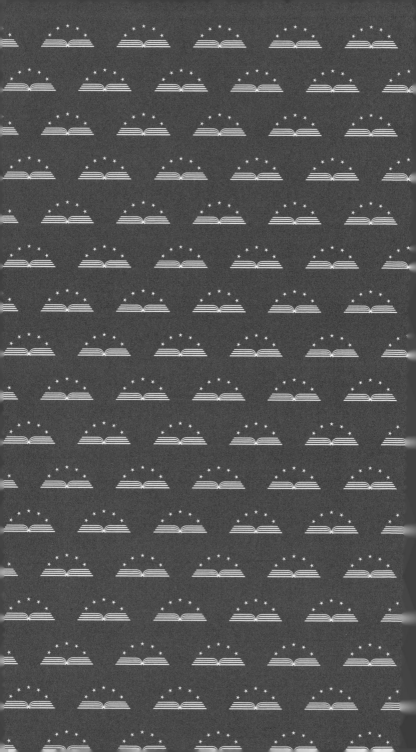